THE SKY REMEMBERS

The Battle of Britain was going badly and the young, inexperienced fighter pilots needed an inspired leader. Group Captain Allard thought that Wing Commander Jimmy Butler was the man for the job and fit for duty again, but Butler was not so sure. Butler's struggle to regain his nerve is long and hard, but it is a struggle he knows he must win as the tired Spitfire pilots take on the deadly new Messerschmitts in the battle which will decide the outcome of the war.

THE SKY REMEMBERS

THE SKY REMEMBERS

by
Dan Brennan

Magna Large Print Books
Long Preston, North Yorkshire,
England.

British Library Cataloguing in Publication Data.

_____

Brennan, Dan
  The sky remembers.

  A catalogue record for this book is
  available from the British Library

  ISBN 0-7505-1351-9

First published in Great Britain by NEL, 1978

Copyright © 1977 by Nordon Publications, Inc

Cover illustration © Len Thurston by arrangement with PWA
International Ltd.

The moral right of the author has been asserted

Published in Large Print 1999 by arrangement with Laurence
Pollinger Ltd.

Magna Large Print is an imprint of
Library Magna Books Ltd.
Printed and bound in Great Britain by
T.J. International Ltd., Cornwall, PL28 8RW.

Always the sky remembers what the
land does not forget:
The roses' fragrance in the tarnished wind:
the bloody glen
Where oaks still grow; the shallowed faces
which black in silhouette
The evening sun; the random dust
and lonesome words of men.

Earl Guy

For
GERALD BARRETT
Squadron Leader
No. 10 Squadron
Royal Air Force

and

PILOT OFFICER—*Harry MacDaniels*
PILOT OFFICER—*Redge Folkes*
SQUADRON LEADER—*Harry Ratcliffe*
FLIGHT/SGT.—*Bus Hill*
FLIGHT/SGT.—*Mac Mullaney*

INTRODUCTION

Those who saw her riding up Piccadilly in a taxi in the spring sunlight ten years after the war saw a small woman with a white round face and tiny bright eyes and a trick spring hat on the back of her head. 'An American,' they said, seeing the cut of her clothes. The taxi stopped in front of the Savoy. Her glance right and left as she descended from the cab was at once bold, curious, cheerful and with something in it like amusement. But few people looked at her. They had all seen American tourists in London since the war. Later when she came out of the hotel and hired a taxi to drive her around London her eyes still glittered brightly with amusement and interest. She drove around London in a taxi for five days. Always the same driver. 'Well,' she said to him on her last day. 'I have seen everything. Tomorrow I will go to Paris.' She reached for her purse. The driver turned his head, looking back into the cab where she sat in the corner

11

of the rear seat. 'Pardon, madame,' he said, smiling. His voice was affable yet insistent: ''aven't shown you the war yet.' She did not answer immediately nor look up. She was busy looking in her handbag for a cigarette and when she spoke her voice was abstracted. 'The war? Oh, yes ... here it is ...' The silver lighter gleamed in her hand. 'What ... oh, yes ... the war. Yes, of course, St Paul's ... I must see it.' She lit the cigarette. Then she said: 'I thought we saw St Paul's.' She slanted her head thoughtfully, blowing a plume of smoke against the roof of the taxi. The driver shook his head. 'Not St Paul's,' he said. 'The war.' He drove fast. She did not speak, sitting there smoking, watching the mean streets. Suddenly they passed a gutted wall rising in the sunlight. The cab stopped. The driver got out, opened the door. ''ere,' he said. 'Right 'ere.' She got out, followed the driver across a sidewalk veined with weedchoked cracks.

Three buildings with gutted walls stood on the corner. The doors and windows were empty. 'Jerry dropped one right 'ere,' said the driver. 'Remember it ... Was on me way to work and ...' His voice and face seemed to change as if he were speaking of some strange lost excitement. 'I 'eard the siren goin' and me sister says ... I was drivin' 'er ... 'eard it comin' like a tube train and I stopped up there.' He pointed up the street. But the woman did not appear to hear him. The woman stared down into the gutted and ruined basement. A wall had toppled down inside making a pile of bricks and masonry upon which willow-herb sprouted pale and pink. She looked at it a long moment, then again at the building, the sky, the mute and ruined atmosphere of the street. The sky was ineffably blue through the unwindowed rectangle in the jagged shard of a wall. White clouds were motionless on the horizon. Over it all the sky, the ruined house seemed to brood, as if there were something secret, lost in the weeds and masonry. A cool breeze drew suddenly through the sunny silence. The woman's arms were suddenly cold. 'Come on,' she said sharply. 'I have an appointment at the hairdresser.' She touched her arms, glanced briefly at the house again. 'I shouldn't have come here,' she thought. 'I don't like it. This was never any of my business.'

CHAPTER ONE

A long time ago on one of those August afternoons the high blue sky was shimmering. It was sun-filled, vivid, shining like glass. Fat white clouds like gobs of whipped cream hung motionless in that unbelievable soft radiance of English summer.

There was no sound anywhere. From the roofs of buildings across London and beyond to the green fields of Kent and Surrey, the sirens had ceased. The noon sun stood overhead; almost soundless the air seemed to quiver in the sunlight as though the atmosphere still held the last thin, invisible vibration of sirens mounting to a crescendo a few hours ago.

The greenish building loomed, square, block-like, of artificial stone. It stood among the trees away from the village-like group of Nissen huts and rows of greenish concrete buildings. This was the aerodrome of Hawksham. The concrete wall above the door in the square building bore the words

GROUP HEADQUARTERS.

Inside, all that August morning, the tall man with a bronze face and cavalry moustache and black hair and the two rows of good ribbons below the down-swept tips of the pilot's wings on his blue tunic had sat on the dais where he looked down at the women's figures in blue tunics and skirts moving carefully around the huge map table in the centre of the room. His eyes looked strained but there remained a gaunt assured, strong air about him.

Group Captain Kenneth Allard sat there every day. He knew what he must do but he was no longer sure now after two months of attack that he could fulfil his responsibilities.

He had been a Regular before the war with the usual service record, home, middle east, India. He was no longer young for a fighter pilot. He was thirty-seven. He had fought in France, flying Hurricanes. He had gone out with the AFC ribbon and come back with the DFC and Bar and the DSO. He wanted only to hold here in England the line he had been given to hold, and he saw it now in his mind, looking down at the legend of England on the map, Margate to Dungeness. It seemed to him now he could actually see the cliffs, the mist rising over the channel, burning away in the morning sunlight, and all out before him, as though ribboned to his fingers, as if his hand lay spread upon the map, the Spitfires standing ready on the fields he controlled.

A vague stirring of fright passed through him. It was too quiet this morning, he thought, they're getting ready. They're coming again. Next time we may buy it. They've been too quiet all week.

Again his mind filled with the image of a figure, and again, as he had done all morning, he pushed the image away, thinking, 'We're not ready ... if I could get Butler ... we might ...' But I can't get him, he told himself, while another part of his mind seemed to say, 'If you can't, Allard, you've had it. You better get him. You better try to get him. He's the only one who can do it. He's the only one who will make the others do it now.'

He picked up his hat and put it on. He came down off the dais and went out through the door behind his desk and along the hall. The Morris was waiting outside and the sergeant behind the wheel got out and opened the door.

It was a dry, hot day, dusty, and as the Morris rolled smoothly along the road to the other gate of the aerodrome Allard saw the Spitfires, sharp-nosed, fish-like, rising on their fragile-looking undercarts, standing at readiness in a line, the dust blowing in clouds across the bright, green field.

They're good, he thought, but not good enough, not good enough without somebody to lead them. They can't go on this way. Then he thought, I wonder if Butler will fly again. I wonder if he'll do what I want him to do. They're coming again. First, the ports. They've clobbered those. Then the airfields. We've beaten them there. But they're too quiet now. They're thinking of something else. Can we stop them? It's here we stop them. We stop them here or we never really stop them. Margate to Dungeness. And they're cutting us down. He thought of the key wing, thirty-one pilots shot down in a month. I wish I could fly as well as half of them. I wish I could fly with them. Anybody can run my job. I should fly. There must be something I can do. Nobody can expect the Wing to keep taking it. Three officers and two sergeants left out of the entire wing in a month of fighting. We're going to have to hold, though. But how? Who can lead those sprog pilots? They've had it without a good Wing Commander. But who can do it except Butler?

I wish I had him here, he thought, I wish I knew he were going to be here.

The car sped up the road to London. At two o'clock Allard walked into Hatchett's American Bar.

Major Thomas Barton and Colonel Fred Carlson saw him come in. They were standing at the bar and they asked him over to a table. Allard looked at them, unwinking, smiled, nodded his head.

'Good to see you, Pete,' said Carlson. He was tall, sandy-haired, with red cheeks, maybe forty or forty-five. He wore what Allard had learned were command pilot's wings in the American air force. There was a small star mounted above the shield in the centre of the wings.

The second American, Major Barton spoke: 'How've you been, Pete? That was quite a shindig you boys threw.' Barton was also a pilot. But he was younger than Carlson, perhaps thirty-five.

He wore the pink trousers, and the olive-brown American tunic.

Pete, thought Allard. He gave them a single glance, brief, still, feeling his back stiffen, something deep inside of him became deliberate. He did not speak for a moment.

Pete, he thought again, feeling his breath tighten faintly, thinking, all right, all right, easy, don't show it. That's the way they are. Meet them one day at a party, and the next they're calling you Pete. Never been called that before. Peter. Why don't they use Peter? That's my name. They're Americans. Yes, that's it.

Our allies, he thought, but not yet. Don't rush it. Maybe next year. Give them time. They like to rush things but they don't like the English rushing them. Decent chaps, though. He thought of the first time he had met them at Fighter Command Headquarters. They were over from America, attached to the American embassy, observers. Well, with luck, they might even be in it a year from now. I hope they will, Allard told himself. But I hope they have the right kind of planes. Their own aren't any use here now.

'Peter,' Allard heard himself say aloud.

Colonel Carlson was saying something to the waiter.

'Sure,' Barton was saying. Allard felt Barton's hand resting on his shoulder without remembering when Barton had put it there. He looked at Barton and Barton was grinning.

'That was a hell of a swell party you boys tossed,' Barton said. He held out a package of Luckies. 'Cigarette?'

Allard took one. He did not like American cigarettes. They were too strong. Players. Give him Players any day. The trouble was the Americans always looked offended if you turned down their cigarettes. Yes, he thought, they're a funny people, always wanting to be generous. Maybe they don't know how much they enjoy having people grateful to them. I hope their aircraft are better than their cigarettes if they ever get into this.

'I ordered you a Martini,' Colonel Carlson said, the waiter walking away. 'O.K.?'

'Fine. Thank you,' said Allard. He wanted a whisky. It was too late to say anything about it. Allard laughed quietly to himself. It's like our cooking, he thought, it

21

takes the American or French to mix good Martini.

The waiter brought the drinks.

'Well, here's luck,' said Carlson raising his glass. 'You boys are going to need it.'

All three touched glasses, cold and beaded.

'We were just thinking about you,' said Barton.

Allard smiled quietly. He did not say anything. Yes, they're good chaps at a party, he thought remembering the weekend several days ago in the mess when they had debagged the Americans and tossed their trousers out of the window. The big one, Carlson, Allard thought, he might have been good at rugger if he had ever played it when he was young.

'How long are you going to be in England?' Allard asked.

'Until we see what's going to happen,' said Carlson.

'Quite a show, isn't it?' said Allard.

'It's only the second act,' said Barton.

'What?' Allard looked at him thinking, did I hear him, second act? He stared at Barton.

Barton smiled.

'You haven't looked under the curtain yet, have you?'

Allard shrugged, then he thought suddenly, oh, God, they must think I'm slow.

'Second act,' he laughed. 'I say, yes.' He shook his head, sipped his Martini, put the glass down.

'Who do you people figure is doing the script?' Barton said. 'Goering or Hitler himself?'

'Spot of collaboration, I imagine,' said Allard.

'How do you people plan to handle it?' asked Carlson. 'I'd say the Jerries've got you in a corner.'

'You mean another Dunkirk?' Allard asked slowly, with something deliberate in his voice.

'Where are you going to evacuate to this time?' said Barton.

Allard looked at them for a long moment, the cigarette weaving a plume of smoke across his face. Again his eyes were harried yet purposeful.

When Allard spoke his voice was careful, quite deliberate, almost grave: 'I assure you, it won't be America.'

Carlson and Barton looked at each other

and laughed. Barton slapped Allard on the back.

'Listen pal, we were only kidding. I didn't mean to needle you. You know, we've been over here almost six months and we've learned a lot from you people. I'd like to tell some people back in Washington a few things about some ideas they think are hot stuff in air combat. Hot stuff for the civil war.'

'Seriously,' said Carlson. 'How're you people going to handle it? You know what's coming. London's next. You know that.'

'It is very difficult,' said Allard. He looked up for the waiter, caught his eye.

'Another, gentlemen?'

The Americans nodded. Allard lifted three fingers to the bartender.

He did not say anything more about the problem. The Americans chatted on about the weather, how after the spring with the rain and wind, they couldn't believe England could have so much sunshine. The second Martini tasted better to Allard. He did not feel so tired now.

'A good man might turn the trick,' he said suddenly.

'Man?' Carlson looked at him. 'What do you mean?'

He never knew Butler, Allard thought, he never saw Butler take the squadron in through the flak at Maestricht Bridge. They never saw flak like that in their lives. I sometimes wonder if we have enough guns in England to put up as much flak as they had on that bridge that day.

'We have a plan,' Carlson said. He glanced at Barton who winked. 'It is only our plan.'

Is this a joke, Allard thought. Do they think because we debagged them in the mess the English are interested only in school-boy jokes?

'What do you suggest?' Allard asked.

Carlson leaned forward.

'Have you thought of a counter-invasion? How about attacking their airfields? Send over bombers, bring their fighters up and knock them down over France?'

Allard's eyes were unwinking, rigid.

'Do you mind if I ask, how do you propose to defend our cities after that? We have only so many aircraft. Do you actually believe it is possible to spare that many aircraft from our inner defences?

They would have to come from there.'

Allard could feel himself getting angry. Are they complete fools, he asked himself. Do they actually believe it is possible for us to throw away our reserve aircraft? He thought of Langton aerodrome where the last week of July only three aircraft were serviceable on the field. And that's only a month ago, he thought. These Americans talk as if they've only been over here six days, not six months.

'Sir.' Barton looked at Carlson. 'Perhaps we're thinking too much in terms of using our own aircraft. Our plan would require the use of four-engine bombers. Pardon us,' he smiled at Allard. 'It's one of our happier obsessions. The four-engine bomber. Perhaps we will have the opportunity someday to prove its worth to you. How else can you expect to raid German airfields? And that is the only way to defeat their air force. Get 'em in the air and knock them down.'

'Oh, we're getting them up in the air,' all right,' Allard said. His voice was faintly sarcastic.

Barton smiled, shook his head at himself.

'Well, if anything can do it, the Spit will do it,' he said. 'There's no getting around it, you've got the best fighter plane in the world.'

Allard's eyes were still unwinking.

'I hope you're right. However, the new Messerschmitt appears to dispute this. In force, they are too much for the Mark One Spitfire.'

'Who's leading the Wing out of the Dover area?' Carlson asked. He stared at Allard.

All right, all right, Allard thought, feeling the worry rising in him, thinking how he had stopped in here for a relaxing drink. All right, you've touched the quick, he thought, you have your finger on it.

He felt them watching like a bug under glass. The worry in his mind made him feel physically smaller for an instant. He thought he had put the problem away briefly on his ride up to London. He could solve it tomorrow. Oh, very easily, he told himself, you can't bloody well solve it and you know it. He could feel Carlson and Barton watching him now.

'We have several good types in mind,' Allard said. He did not look at them. He looked at the rim of his glass.

'Williams is dead, isn't he?' Carlson asked.

So they have been studying our combat reports, Allard thought, they have not just been going to parties for six months. Why is it the Americans always look and sound so incompetent as compared to us? Yet they have their nose in everything. Yes, he thought, Williams is dead, rotting someplace in the channel. He remembered Williams at Cranwell before the war. Good type. A little crackers perhaps, but it had helped when he had led the Wing before Butler. And before Wiljams? July seemed a century ago. Too many had gone for a Burton since then to keep track.

'Yes,' Allard said. 'Promotions come fast these days.'

He thought of the New Zealand Pilot Officer who had risen to Squadron Leader in a week during the first week of July because all the officers ranking him had been shot down.

'Why don't you lead them?' said Carlson.

'Staff has the peculiar idea that men over thirty-five should sit behind desks,' Allard said.

Barton looked at Carlson and grinned.

'Sounds like the Pentagon.'

Carlson did not move.

'Who then?' he asked.

28

There wasn't a chance, yet it must be Butler. Butler is the only one who can do it, Allard thought, but with his arm bad now ... Bloody hell, it was more than his arm. It was three times in the drink and five times bailing out in two weeks. Every man had his breaking point. There's only so much you can expect of the best but he felt his lips moving as though of their own volition.

'Butler,' he said. 'I think Butler will be ready.'

'Brother, he's terrific. I saw him—' Barton paused. Then: 'Isn't he in the hospital?'

They check everything, Allard thought. I would like to see their reports before they go back to the States. They will probably write what I was thinking at three o'clock today.

'He's getting better,' Allard lied, knowing Butler still had dry bandages on his arm.

'You're going to need him or somebody like him to take those green kids you've got left down among 'em. I never thought those Krauts would be much good against competition,' said Barton. 'I saw them in France. Strictly pushover for them. But don't let anybody ever tell you they can't

29

fly. Well, you've seen them—'

Allard nodded slowly.

'You're going to need more than Mark One Spits, though, in that Wing,' said Carlson. 'Can you get them? Are they ready?'

'Maybe,' he said. He was lying. He knew he was lying. He knew that perhaps the new Spitfire might be ready but would there be enough of them for the Wing? With the new Spit the key Wing could maul the Messerschmitt high cover so badly the Mark One Spits and Hurricanes further back could go in and finish them off. Sure, they would be ready, but would there be enough?

'Whoever's gonna jump those new ME's first deserves the best aircraft you've got,' said Carlson. There was something harsh, assertive in his voice.

Allard looked away, thinking, why do they have to sound so aggressive, so challenging, as though it were going to be my fault if the chaps don't get the new Spits in time. What is the matter with these people, Allard asked himself. They are on our side. They are friendly and yet they are always so bloody assertive somehow. Sometimes they even sound a little glad

30

when we take a drubbing now and then just so we win in the long run. Can they still have their back up because we burned their White House down once?

Barton glanced at Carlson.

'We saw Butler the day he took on ten Jerries over Manston. Christ, can that guy fly!'

'Good chap,' Allard said. Then he looked briefly at Carlson and then at Barton. 'Hope you chaps don't mind me saying this,' Allard went on chattily, pleasantly. 'But he was flying for you chaps, too. You'll be in this sooner or later, you know.'

Barton grinned and put his hand on Allard's shoulder.

'Brother, you aren't kidding. I wish we were in it now!' There was something hard-bitten yet boyish in his white smile. 'Let's have a drink on that.'

Allard held up one hand.

'None for me, thanks. I must be going.' He rose, put on his hat. 'Nice seeing you chaps again.'

He put a ten shilling note on the table and Carlson insisted they had invited him for drinks. Carlson picked up the bill and stuffed it in Allard's tunic pocket.

'Listen,' he said. 'We drank enough free

31

scotch at your squadron shindig.'

They strangle one with generosity, Allard thought, but what can one do? By paying now I would only insult them. He thanked them for the drinks and walked outside. The sun was shining on Piccadilly. Several people were lined up waiting on the corner for a bus. It was a lovely, sunny day. He passed the Green Park tube station and went on and turned down Half-Moon Street and along Curzon Street to his flat in Charles Street.

He opened the door of the yellow stone building. It was cool and dark in the narrow stairway and he walked slowly up the steep steps and opened the door of his flat. It was dark inside. He crossed the sitting room and opened the black-out curtains. A bar of sunlight fell into the room. It shone on the photographs along the wall. The portraits of the living and dead, pilots of squadrons out in India and Malta before the war, leaning against the rudders and wings of Gladiator fighters.

Allard went into his bedroom and picked up the telephone on the desk beside his bed. He called a number and waited while it rang.

He heard the wire pop open: 'Squadron

Leader Dunham,' he said. 'Hello, Dunham, ... Allard ... Listen, we need oleo
legs, tyres. I am asking you because I
know you can get them for me ... Yes,
I know, it's all rationed ... I sent in a
request a week ago. Has it come across
your desk?'

'Yes.'

'I've never had so many blown tyres
and damaged undercarts in a week's time.
You know how they are landing now. Very
ropey. Anyway, see what you can do for
me, will you?'

'Everything I can,' said Squadron Leader
Dunham, supply officer at Uxbridge. They
had known each other on a Hurricane
Squadron before the war. Allard hung
up.

Group Captain Allard lay down on his
bed and closed his eyes. Yet as he lay there
for a few minutes, he seemed to see now
in his mind the photograph on the wall
of his bedroom of a young man's pink
and white face and blue eyes, and upon
his blond head the helmet and goggles of
a flier. 'I should put it in the drawer,'
Allard thought. 'I should put it away.'
He blinked and tried to focus his eyes
in the dim light. It was the face of a

33

twenty-one year old boy, now Major Paul Wernick, who in '36 had raced a civilian model of the Messerschmitt against Allard in Berlin. Allard sat up and squinted at the photograph. He wondered if they would ever meet again. Probably, Allard thought, and then with regret. 'God, I wish I were young enough to lead that wing myself. Paul, you bastard, I'd like to take you on now. I'd like to get you up there alone for five minutes!' Go on, Allard, he said to himself, you sound bloody brave. He'd probably shoot you down. Well, Butler could take care of him. He might get the chance yet. Intelligence said Wernick was leading the yellow nose gang out of Abbeville. They would be over in the first wave, the high cover. They always sent the best in there. Damn, he said, Allard, why did you have to get old so fast?

The phone was ringing. Allard picked it up.

'Hello ... Yes, Scott ... Quiet? Well, good ... Yes, keep Tudor at readiness ... Fine ... I'll call you in the morning.'

Yes, they're coming, thought Allard, they're lying over there sharpening their teeth. They're too quiet to be doing anything else. They're getting ready.

He got out of bed and went into the kitchen. He opened a lower cabinet drawer and took out a bottle of whisky and mixed a drink. He went into the sitting room and lay down on the davenport and stared up at the ceiling.

Whoever said there was always somebody to fit anybody else's shoes was quite a liar, Allard thought. Whoever it was never met Butler, never had my job. If only to show those Americans—come on, Allard, he told himself, thinking of Carlson's harsh, assertive voice, you're getting jumpy. That's just the way Americans talk sometimes. They weren't challenging the entire RAF to prove the war is merely to show America how good the RAF is.

We've got to do it anyway, he thought. We better do it.

The time Butler took B Flight out against those ME 110s. He knows how to stage an attack. He knows how and where to strike. But with that bad arm. No, he'll never be as good again.

He drank the whisky and water slowly, wondering if he put it on a personal level with Butler if Butler would lead the Wing. Of course, the doctor could be wrong. The doctor said Butler ought to have at least

35

another month's rest. But could the doctor hold him down if he wanted to go? But wouldn't it be like asking a man to kill himself for one last show? That was the trouble, unless everybody went all out this was going to be the last show. Oh, hell, he thought, there's no way. He's been trained and paid to die, if ever he's asked. We've all been. It's my job to ask him. Allard got up, went straight into the bedroom, paused in front of the phone a long moment. Then he picked it up.

'Get me Whitehall one-nine-six-two, please.'

CHAPTER TWO

From the lawn in front of the big square stone house Wing Commander Jimmy Butler could see the hills across the Buckinghamshire valley. They were clear and green and beautiful. In the morning light he could see the shadow of the trees in the woods, and the smooth grass between the trees. He liked looking at the trees, sitting out here in the morning light. They

36

filled him with a feeling of peacefulness. It was hot and the sun felt good on his arm. There was a soft, hazy summer light in the sky, and everywhere in the valley there was a somnolent, tranquil air. He moved his right arm on the wooden rest of the canvas deck chair and felt the muscle twitch and burn faintly through the bandages. His shirt sleeves were rolled up above his elbows and he could feel the warm sunlight passing through the dry bandages into the wound. 'Well, it's stopped draining anyway,' he thought. 'That's something.' He seemed almost to feel the sunlight drying the wound inside his forearm.

He closed his eyes and put his head back on the slope of the canvas chair and let the sun beat through his eyelids.

He could feel a cool morning wind blowing in the valley. As it touched his face he felt a strange child-like sensation of happiness. 'I never thought I'd be this way,' he told himself. He felt rotten thinking about it because there was a small pool of fear far down inside him that he did not want anything to touch. And the thought and feeling he had just experienced had touched it. More than anything in the world he feared stirring it up again. It filled all his thoughts but here in the sunlight, without moving, he had felt how he could keep it quiet. 'I mustn't let it rise,' he thought now. 'I mustn't let it get me.' He felt it quieting inside again and was sure that if he moved his body, or even his arm, made the most infinitesimal physical motion, the pool of fear far down inside him in some secret place would stir again, frightening him. Ever since he had been here he had felt better. The wound was a relief. He hated to think this because it made him feel ashamed. 'I'm not afraid,' he thought at once, immediately, as the fear rushed abruptly, whirling inside him. 'I'm not afraid. I'm not! I'm not!'

'Goddamn it,' he cursed aloud, sitting up. There was nothing that would let him rest. If only his mind were numb and dead now as it had been when first he came here out of the hospital. At least, there had been peace in that, he thought. Now, poised on the edge of the chair, about to rise, he thought, no, there's no point of getting up, moving around. That will only make it worse. Better I lie down again, better I let the sunlight hold me here.

Slowly he lay back, slowly he tried to recollect the peacefulness of the moments before his mind had disturbed him. Slowly, slowly, he felt himself slip back under the warm, soft touch of summer air and sunlight. 'I must not think,' he told himself. 'I must not think at all. I must lie perfectly still and then I won't think at all. I won't remember anything. I won't remember a thing.'

The sun grew hotter. The skin on his face felt red and warm. 'To lie here,' he thought, worry and regret and fear pushed far down, forgotten, 'to lie here forever.'

But even as he lay there happy, the feeling started inside him again of everything moving too fast, racing. He felt himself in the cockpit again, adjusting the rudder trim too quickly for take-off, both his hands moving too fast, sweat on his face, and he wasn't even in the air yet, but here he was taxiing out already, taxiing too fast, working the brakes too fast. Oh, Christ, had he forgotten to check his flaps? He was going up, always going up, always coming back, always going up again, always coming back. How many times today? He could not remember. Janson and Hollister had been shot down in the morning. Let's see. Was this the third or fourth alert? He could not remember. Damn, he'd forgotten to turn on his radio. His fingers scrabbled at the switch, then he had it open:

'Hullo, Falcon, Falcon, Amber leader calling. May I ...'

God, he thought, opening his eyes now, blind against the sunlight. I've got to find something to turn this off. I've got to stop thinking about flying. Jesus, I don't want to fly again. I never want to fly again. Never. Desire soared in him, swelling. To escape, he thought. If I could only escape, get out of the country. Maybe I could get a job instructing, he thought, and almost at once his whole being was filled with shame. I mustn't, he told himself. I mustn't think like this. I will lose everything. I will lose all myself. I mustn't think like that. God, why do I have to keep turning it over in my mind? Over and over again. Can't I ever forget it? Do I have to keep hurting myself to feel better? But he knew he did not really feel better, either, no matter how he answered himself. He would never feel better.

The Huns have a new fighter, he started saying to himself. They'll knock hell out of the old Spit One. They'll kill all of us if they get enough of them. He felt a kind of ease as suddenly he thought of himself flying a new Spitfire, taking it into the sky against an old Messerschmitt.

I'm a coward and scared, he told himself. Even with a new-type Spitfire I'm scared of the new Messerschmitt. Even with a new-type Spitfire I'm afraid of the old Messerschmitt.

But suddenly a part of him seemed very brave, his body mostly seemed to feel this way, and he felt as if he could go right now to his Spitfire and fight without fear. But this won't happen, he thought. In a second, or maybe longer, it will come again, the fear. I will be afraid again. How did I get here all of a sudden? How did I get here—brave all of a sudden?

Because I'm all through, washed up. The longer I stay here getting well, maybe the worse it gets. I don't get any better, really. Just my arm. No, he did not want his arm to get well too quickly. He knew this was true. He did not ever want it well, and yet there was a part of him that kept making it well, and yet there was a part of him he knew, too, his whole being longed for this part of him to grow stronger. But he could not stop thinking:

That morning we lost an entire squadron and a half from the Wing and then

41

MacCumber going slap into the drink and the air-sea rescue never found him. This bloody arm. If I had moved it an inch. It wouldn't have happened. Next time your head or your guts. And Fletcher's nephew. There were too many things to think about. I can't watch out for all of them all of the time, everybody's son or brother or husband. I wish I could. I wish I could bring them all back every time. But MacCumber. That was very bad luck. He was the best Squadron Leader I ever had.

He felt the wound twitch again in the sunlight and he moved his arm into the shade on his lap. The damn Hun is better than all the stories the press has told about the Hun not knowing what to do when a set plan of attack is broken up. How the hell did the bugger get me? We had that Hun squadron scattered all over the sky. Maybe they've got a set plan for that, too, one the papers haven't heard about. But what can you expect? The papers never really know anything, or if they do they're scared to print it. I wish I never had to fly again. Maybe I won't have to. Maybe I'll get a cushy job up at Air Ministry. Hell, I never could do that. Butler, the ground pounder. That would do it. That would really do it.

He thought of before the war and he longed again for those days, the squadron mess, the long training exercises, the thrill born out of death being always a possibility but never as certain as it was now. I remember when I believed I could die, that I would never die in any bloody aircraft, that I was better than any aircraft in the world, he thought, blinking into the sunlight.

He heard someone whistling, coming down the long green slope of the terrace. He turned and sat up and looked over the back of his chair. It was Bob Fletcher. He still limped a little but the cane was gone. For a moment he made Butler feel ashamed. Fletcher was always talking about getting back to the Squadron. Butler wondered if all this talk wasn't only whistling in the dark. He remembered Fletcher sick and pale looking in the dawn light one morning after his squadron lost four pilots in half an hour, the second week Fletcher had been on ops. Well, maybe he isn't scared, Butler thought, you know, they're not all like you.

'Getting a little sun?' Butler called. Fletcher was still only half way down the terrace.

Fletcher did not answer. He nodded and smiled and came on.

He walks too well, Butler thought, if the doctor sees that he'll have him back in the air in a week.

'Air Ministry,' Fletcher said coming up, talking before he stopped beside Butler's chair. 'They're on the wire.'

'Who?'

Fletcher shrugged.

'Don't know. Girl in the office merely said air ministry. I was walking by, said I'd get you.'

'Air Ministry?' Butler shook his head. 'What do they want? Don't they ever let a body rest?'

'I say, if you have any influence, see if you can get me promoted.'

Butler rose.

'Sure, boy, I'll get you a Variety contract, too.'

Butler picked up his tunic where it lay on the lawn. He put it on carefully, drawing the right sleeve slowly over his arm where the dry bandages bulged. The stitches hurt when the bandage shifted.

They ought to take those out soon, he thought. He put on his cap, raked with the unmistakable swagger-like slant seen nowhere save in the air force. He went up on the lawn, under the trees, seeing the stone house looming old and big and high against the blue summer sky. In the field to the right of the house he saw rooks flying, disappearing down among the high weeds.

He went on up the stone steps and across the stone floored porch inside to the cool hall.

'How're you feeling this morning?' said the Nursing Sister, passing him in the hall. She was in charge of the younger nurses. She was older and she smiled and nodded.

'Much better, thank you,' he said, regretting almost at once he had told the truth.

He went on to the table at the end of the hall. Behind it sat the WAAF Corporal facing the switchboard.

'Call for Butler?' he asked. There was a phone on the table.

'Yes, sir,' the girl smiled. Her eyes watched his face. 'Do you want to take it here, sir, or in the lounge?'

Butler nodded towards the door at the

end of the hall running at right angles to the hall in which he now stood.

Sitting on the davenport, Butler picked up the receiver: 'Butler speaking.'

'Hello, Butler?' said a man's voice he did not recognize at first. The wire popped and clicked a little as though it were a bad connection.

'Butler speaking,' he repeated, waiting.

'That you, old chap? This is Fletcher. You know my nephew, of course.'

Oh no, thought Butler, feeling his stomach tighten faintly, what can he want? Why is he calling me?

'How's it going, old chap?'

'Fair.'

No, that sounds too depressing, Butler thought.

'Pretty good,' Butler said almost at once, immediately, making his voice sound brighter, yet at once almost more detached.

'Fine. Listen, Butler, how soon will you be well?'

Christ here it comes, Butler thought. Here it comes, over the top again. Why doesn't he ask the doctor? Why does he have to ask me? He's an Air Vice Commodore, the doctor'll have to tell him the truth.

'I can't say, really. I've got dry bandages on now. Shouldn't be too long.'

No, no, he thought, something frantic— was it fear? clawing at his insides, while thinking went quickly, I mustn't tell them the truth. I mustn't tell them how well I am. But you're not, he longed to tell himself, while a part of his mind stopped the lie before he could tell himself he was not well. He knew he could fly now if he had to. Yes, even with the bad arm. Hell, even with a bad leg.

'Butler, could you lead the Wing again in about two weeks?'

'Two weeks? What?'

'The Hun's lying doggo. It's only a matter of days, perhaps hours, we're not sure, before they're going to have a real go at London.'

'Gen?'

'Everything points to it. Intelligence has it, the squadrons in Flanders are all being brought up to full strength again.'

'Bloody hell, don't they ever run out of kites?'

'We need you, Butler. Unless your Wing is ready, believe me, I'm afraid we might all buy it this time. Some of your old boys are back on the Wing. But we need somebody who can hold them all together, the old and the new, and take them up there the right way and break up that first wave of fighter cover as it hits shore. Can you make it?'

Butler did not say anything for a second, but in that second everything changed inside him. He could not say why. There did not seem to be time to think, to feel anything, nor to put the fear and doubt into words inside himself. He saw later that he actually had had a flashing picture in his mind on the instant he had been asked. It had lasted only a second then, the faces there, fleeting, gone almost as soon as he held them in his mind, the old faces. They had only been gone a few weeks. They seemed to stare at him out of death. But they were old now, burned and dying only a few weeks ago, the smoke ribboning black across the sky, Kilgore, Loftus, Whitfield, Smith, Watson, down over the North Sea, falling in flames across the May sky in Flanders, smashed on the beaches of Dover, rotting far down in the channel water, tumbling with a wing shot off over Kent. Butler's whole body felt cold, but he could hear his voice almost as though of its own volition:

48

'All right, sir,' Then quickly, for the fear touched him again: 'How about kites? Can you get us some decent kites?'

'They're not ready. They're up at the factory. But they're not finished. I have some pictures, though, to show you.'

'Of what?'

'The Hun. New Kites.'

'Wonderful. You're going to show me their new kites. My God, sir, what do you think we—?'

'How's the arm, really old chap? Can you make it?'

'I said so, didn't I? How's Adams doing with the Wing?'

'Not too well. Lost six kites last week. Squadron was jumped over Southend last week by about thirty Jerries and Adams got rattled and called to them to dive instead of telling them to climb into the attack. You can imagine what happened. Wing's too big for Adams to handle.'

'He's still a good type,' said Butler.

'Yes, oh, yes. No mistake, old chap. Adams grand chap. None better. Leading a squadron, perhaps. Wing, no.'

'That's right.'

'Incidentally, old chap, you know. This is embarrassing. Spoke to you before.

Fletcher. My nephew, whom you know. Rather decent pilot. Said so yourself. Well my sister, uh, well, uh, I wonder ... he'll be back on ops soon. Like to have him in your flight. Your decision, you know. Don't interfere squadron level, you know. Never have. Bad show, I always say. Wonder if you could keep an eye open, you know. Sister deuced nuisance, calling me all the time. Wants a cushy job for him. Can't do that, old chap, you know that. Chap wouldn't take it. Keep an eye on him though, if you chaps go back together.'

'Don't worry about your nephew. He can take care of himself. But—'

'Yes. Yes. Wizard pilot. Said so yourself. We're all counting on you, Butler. Allard asked for you, you know.'

'No, I didn't,' said Butler.

'As I said, old chap, would appreciate it ... sister keeps calling. You know how it is. I could tell her he was with you. Make it better for her, you know.'

'Sure, but tell her we'll all be dead in a couple of weeks if we're going to take on those new Jerry kites with those pieces of piano wire and chewing gum we have now. How many does intelligence say Jerry can put up?'

'Estimate one wing. Blitzkrieg us, you know. That's their plan. Break through our outer defences first and then pour in with the older type Messerschmitt and let the new ones through to take on the Hurricanes. Massacre if they ever reach the Hurricanes.'

'I'll go, but if those kites aren't ready, we haven't a chance. You tell Allard that. He knows that. I'd like to tell him. I'm tired of going up in a patch work quilt. I'll be frank. You know it and I know it, so I can say it here, those patched-up kites are falling apart. Those kids'll get slaughtered.'

Butler was surprised at his own audacity. He had known Air Vice Commodore Fletcher for several years, worked closely with him, drunk with him. He had never challenged him before, but as he thought of it now he was not too surprised Fletcher did not resist or react to his challenge. They're letting me work off steam, Butler thought. Fletcher was in the last war and he knows how these things work, so he's going to make it work my way.

But suddenly Fletcher's voice was changed. It was sharp, cold, almost remote.

'Are you implying you won't go back on ops if the kites aren't new?'

I fell into that one, both feet, thought Butler, I'll learn. I've been in service long enough to know better. Guess I've been here at this home too long.

'Did I say that?' Butler asked. He wasn't going to be trapped.

'You might as well have said it.' Fletcher's voice was hard.

'All right, I'll say it. I've a wound here. It isn't well yet. I don't know when it will be well. I've been flying and fighting since last April. I've done everything I can. I haven't taken any leave. Call this talk what you want, lack of moral fibre or anything else. I'm not leading a bunch of kids out to die in kites held together by bailing wire.'

No, no, his mind told him to stop talking, it's not them you're protecting, it's yourself. You don't want to go. You are using any excuse now. You are afraid to die. Yes, I'm afraid. All right, I'm afraid. All right, I'm using those old kites and kids as an excuse. But I'm not going. I'm not going. Those kids aren't going. Christ, I don't want to die. I wish I were in London with Helen. It would all be better in London with Helen.

Fletcher said: 'All right. I'll see what I can do. No promises.' His voice was changed. They were friends again.

'I'll go to the factory with you first.'

'Easy, old boy. Come up tomorrow. Meet me in the office.'

'All right. Cheer oh.'

'Cheer oh, Jimmy.'

He put the receiver back on the cradle. He looked up at the wall a moment. I shouldn't have blown up like that, he thought. I am getting washed up. One more steam letting like that and they'll want to put a jacket on me.

He walked out past the switchboard.

'Was the connection all right?' asked the telephonist.

Butler nodded and smiled. He went along the hall and upstairs to his room and shut the door and lay down on the bed. It was a front room. The furniture was very old. The house was old. The head nursing sister said it belonged to the Dewars long before they made their money in whisky, even before they made their money in mining. Well, they knew how to select a nice view. He looked out the bedroom window at the lawn, the sunlight shining on the grass and trees.

It was impossible to believe here there was war. Butler rolled over on his bed and saw a letter addressed to him on the night stand beside his bed. He picked up the envelope and pulled out the sheets of stationary. There were four sheets. They were all written in the small girl's school script of his sister. She was fourteen. If the war went on. Well, it would. They would have her in service before long. He read the first page without realizing until he had finished what it really said. My God, they had been bombed out. Jerry had dropped one two houses away, and all the windows had been blown out. She and mother were staying in the cottage in Dorset. They were all right, not hurt but 'mother is quite foolish, she talks about going home again, and she doesn't sleep at night. I wish you would come up and see us. I don't know what to do with mother. We read about you in the papers. Darling, I hope you are getting well. I told all the girls at school you will probably get the VC. Do you think you might? Mother is really upset, so if you can get away some weekend, give us a ring and come up. Love, Barbara.'

He folded the letter and put it in his tunic

pocket and buttoned the pocket. Then he rose and with both hands smoothed the creases out of his uniform that had come from lying down. He wished he hadn't received the letter from his sister. He couldn't see them. There wasn't time.

There wasn't time anymore for anything. Barbara was almost fifteen. Well, she would have to cope with mother. Why couldn't the woman get hold of herself? Sure, and why don't you get hold of yourself, he thought, go on now, you know where you're going but you don't want to.

He walked quickly out of the room before he changed his mind. He knew if he stayed longer he would change his mind and he would never go to London.

The doctor's office was in the ballroom upstairs, and Butler quickly mounted the stairs. The nurse behind the desk with the screen behind her, making the office in the rear of the room, said the doctor would see him in a few minutes.

It was hot up here. Butler looked at the nurse. She was pretty. There was something about her that made him think of Helen, the straight nose, high cheekbones; they weren't quite the same. Helen was better looking. He wished she had been able to come down to see him more often.

'Well, my boy,' the doctor said when he sat with him at the rear of the room, 'how're you feeling?'

'I'm about ready, Doc.'

The doctor smiled.

'I don't think a couple of weeks more will hurt you.'

'No.' He stared at the doctor, thinking, don't try to talk me out of it, doctor, it will be too easy, don't start, please, don't say anything, just say, all right, if you must say something.

'Why don't you come up the end of the week?' The doctor was still smiling. He had a round, red face. He looked about forty, as if he led a good, comfortable life before and since the war. 'We'll see how that wound is the first of the week.'

Butler shook his head.

'I had a call this afternoon. They want me back on ops.'

'You're not ready.'

'I'm ready. They asked me.'

'I'll call. Who called?' The doctor looked angry for an instant. 'I heard nothing from anyone.'

'They called me.' Butler's voice was quite flat, while he thought, come on,

56

come on, Doc, don't push me, please, God, don't let him push. He sat there feeling cracks opening inside himself, the old dread, the fear, shifting in like fine dust, a little bit at a time as the seconds passed.

There was a bar on the ground floor of the house. It was connected with the kitchen, an opening in the wall with a serving shelf. At five that afternoon, Butler was standing there with Fletcher. They were drinking glasses of Burton's dark ale. Butler felt better. He felt that somehow in his decision to go back on ops he had closed the cracks. He could feel nothing of fear now. It was there, but he had put it away. Maybe it will stay there wherever it has gone, he thought. I'm getting tired of it. It's a rotten companion. The beer made him feel good. He had had two glasses. The doctor had not called anyone. The doctor had seen he could not keep him here. Dry bandages could be taken care of by any station doctor.

'I'll be with you before you know it,' Fletcher said. 'A few days in London and you'll be seeing me.'

'When do you think you'll be going?'

'Soon as the doctor checks me out.'

'How's the leg?'

'It'll work. Don't you worry about that. Perhaps not rugger. It'll work. I know.'

'Do you really think you can fly with it?'

'Piece of cake,' said Fletcher.

'Yes, only—'

'Let's discuss your arm,' said Fletcher.

Butler smiled and put his hand on Fletcher's shoulder. 'Take it easy, old boy.'

'Think I'll just go down to the squadron a few days first without doing any flying,' said Fletcher.

'Skip London?'

Fletcher laughed. 'It might become dangerous. Going up to the Ministry?'

'Maybe,' Butler said.

'Say hello to Uncle Dick if you run into him. Not a bad type, even if he is a Commodore.'

'Sure. Incidentally, I'll try to have a spot for you in my section.'

'Good show,' said Fletcher. 'It'll feel like another war. Haven't flown, you know, for more than a month.'

'Few circuits and bumps and you'll be set again. Don't worry about it. You better watch yourself though if we get mixed up with any of those new ME's. They'll climb and dive the hell out of us and do it over again. I know you know the ropes, but if they get those kites on us, you better just keep turning. Don't do anything else—famous last words by Butler as he forgot to turn himself.' He smiled and picked up his glass.

When Butler went outside to get in the Morris for a ride to the station there were three young nursing sisters there on the steps waiting to say goodbye to him. They were shy and pink-cheeked and laughed embarrassedly when he spoke to them.

'I'll ride down to the station with you,' Fletcher said and got in the back seat beside Butler.

They rolled down the driveway and then straight out between the long rows of green trees on each side of the dusty road.

'Did you ever hear anything about Al?' said Fletcher. 'You remember he was just nabbing that Jerry coming out of a slow climb and then he went down after him.'

Butler smiled. 'Let that be a lesson to us.'

'Certainly hope you can work me into your section.'

Butler grinned. 'I want somebody watching my tail.'

Fletcher laughed. Butler was thinking of the new Messerschmitt. He felt sweat forming faintly on his hands. He wondered if their armament would be heavier.

The Morris turned and stopped in front of the station. The train was in and Butler got out hurriedly and Fletcher handed him his bag.

'See you soon,' Fletcher said.

'Cheer oh,' said Butler and turned and walked into the station.

CHAPTER THREE

Two days later, Flight Lieutenant Ian Fletcher was standing in the middle of a country road listening to a bus grind into gear. Picking up his kit bag, he turned, saw the bus going along the road, the golden summer dust rising behind it. He started walking down the road to the aerodrome. Ahead the hangars rose curving in the sunlight. He felt this should have been a kind of homecoming. Back to the squadron. But it did not feel like a homecoming. He did not know why but he felt alone, older. It felt uncomfortable to think about it. He walked along the dusty road, seeing the immense fat white clouds ringing the empty world around the horizon and somewhere, invisible, seemingly sourceless, the high far-faint whine of a Spitfire above the clouds. He began to feel low again but he did not want to think about the feeling. 'I should feel pretty good,' he told himself, trying to feel better, telling himself how glad he was to get out of the hospital. The leg didn't bother him too much if he didn't walk on it too long. If he did that, the dry scab covering the wound was painful until he stopped. Well, it would be better, he thought, by the time Butler came down to lead the Wing. Butler would be surprised to find him here already. Well, he couldn't stand it there anymore, alone at the rest home. He had been lonely there, nobody from the Squadron, a lot of light bomber types off Blenheims, but they were really quite different people. He couldn't explain why. It was like knowing somebody from another club or family, nice, pleasant all right, but after a few words there wasn't the feeling of any common bond. He guessed that was it, though it embarrassed him to think about it that way. You're getting maudlin, Fletcher, he said to himself. The sun was hammering down the heat. He shifted the kit bag to his left hand. His right thigh began to ache. He stopped and sat down and lit a cigarette, watching the plume of smoke drift and dissolve in the hazy blue summer air. The high sky shimmered. He looked up, thinking of flying again, not wanting to, not because he was afraid. He was afraid, too, but he did not think of that now as much as he thought of flying again as Butler's wing man. It was nice knowing you were protecting a good man like Butler, but it would be more satisfying if he could find somebody to fly wing for him. Bloody hell, he'd like a crack at a few Huns himself. Without a good wing man, you were a dead duck sometimes, especially in a dive and climb game with the Huns. Of course, it was different if you could get them to play merry-go-round with you. Then you could tighten up that circle yourself and clobber the bastard about the third time around if the Hun were stupid enough to think he could turn inside a Spitfire, but there weren't enough stupid ones, anymore. The stupid ones were dead, and the wise boys were around, and if you were going down among them you needed a good wing man. 'All right, all right,' Fletcher told himself, stop thinking about being a bloody hero. You've a couple good medals now. You know Butler is a better flier. You know he needs a wing man more than you. You know if he were flying wing for you that you couldn't take advantage of situations as Butler can. You know, and if you don't know it, it's time you do. All right, you know it. You know it comes down to only one thing, Fletcher, Butler can fly better than you. Bloody hell, Fletcher said aloud, ditched the coal of his cigarette on his thumb, tossed the butt into the grass and rose.

But walking along he could not seem to stop day dreaming of himself as an ace, a bigger ace than Butler, the sky filled with wasps, whirling. He saw himself alone among them, the oil dropping in his eyes as he rolled over on his back, the Spitfire wing tip flickering silver in the sunlight, the sudden ball of fire falling across the sky. He felt his hand suddenly sweaty on the control stick grip. He could feel the engine pulling. He was climbing now, myriad eyes of a million invisible figures far down searching the sky. He felt the blood pumping in his throat. For a flashing second his body was rigid. The sun seemed to stand overhead, filling the world, the sky with dazzling light. His eyes were watering. Then he realized without remembering he had seen it only a second before, the blue under-surface of a fish, just above his eyes. It appeared to float, finless, headless. He stared at it for a second. He seemed to sit in an attitude at once detached and quietly astonished. Then almost like an explosion knowing and understanding connected in his mind with his line of vision. 'Christ,' he thought, as though waking in a dream, 'a 109,' seeing the one wing, the big black cross. Then like a skylark slanting motionless on the summer sky, he held the Spitfire climbing up, up, up, feeling the engine pulling without an inch of gain. The fish was there again. His trained fingers pressed the firing button. He heard the guns hammering above the sound of his engine. He felt the distinct shock of the whole aircraft shuddering under the recoil. He fired again. The empty bowl of the summer sky suddenly belched flame back upon his eyes. Jesus, he thought, I'm going fly right through him. He shut his eyes, flung his right hand in front of his face.

The road turned. He walked up to the Mess building, rising green and mottled, ugly in the lazy summer sunlight. Gerald Harper and Stuart Dunlop sat in cane chairs. Their legs stretched straight out in front of them, their heads lolled over the backs of the chairs. Their eyes were closed. They were Fletcher's friends. Both were Pilot Officers. They had all flown together in France and here in England. Fletcher kicked the soles of their shoes and stood there looking down at them. They woke up, grunting and grinning. Fletcher remembered saving Harper's life once over Calais. He felt no pride or pleasure in it now, though he remembered once feeling this just after it was over. Now he felt only that life was simple and wonderful. He felt beyond all pride and pleasure. He was back among friends. He felt as though he were home again. He was filled with joy for a second. 'All right, all right,' he told himself. 'This is wonderful. Don't get carried away. You feel this way only because you've been cooped up in that hospital. Wait until you're flying again. It won't be so grand then. You'll wish you were back in the hospital. Sure, sure, sure, turn it off, Fletcher.'

'I'm going up to Dishforth,' he said. 'Refresher course. Chaps care to go along?'

Harper jumped up grinning and hit Fletcher on the arm. 'We were beginning to think you were shot down. Nurses, old boy? How are you, Fletch?'

'Fine. What's new?'

'Chapman and Hendrix bought it last week. Where's Butler? Is he coming back?'

Fletcher smiled and nodded.

Stuart looked up. He had not moved. He still lay in his chair. He eyed Fletcher with one open eye.

'What's the gen? When's Jerry going to show his nose again?'

'Don't worry. He'll give you a chance to be an ace. How about going to Dishforth?'

He did not really want to go to Dishforth. I should stay here and fly again right away, he thought. Well, no, it would really be better to work slowly into the game again. At Dishforth you could arrange for a local bombing squadron to give you a little practice, simulating attacks on Whitleys. Good to get a chap's hand in again. Still, it would be lonely up there. Types in the mess he might not know. Better with a few squadron types from here. Harper and Stuart.

'Take our own kites?' Stuart asked.

Fletcher did not know what to say. He did not even know for certain who was commanding the Wing. He had called Group to be released from the hospital, gained permission there for short posting to refresher course at Dishforth. Chaps here might not be able to go, he thought, well, worth a try.

'Up to Adams,' said Harper. 'Doubt it.'

'Adams running the show here now?' Fletcher asked.

Harper and Stuart smiled slowly together, fixing their eyes on Fletcher. Then, as though on a signal, they nodded.

'We haven't had the same aircraft serviceable more than two days running,' said Stuart.

Harper glanced at him.

'That's because the way you fly, chum. The Hun will win yet. Keep Stuart in the air. He'll wear out all our kites.'

'Ace Harper,' said Stuart. 'Scourge of the Luftwaffe.'

'Listen, scourge,' said Fletcher. 'Do you

want me to ask Adams? What do you think? Can he spare you experienced types at this point?'

Harper put his hands together in an exaggerated pose of a choirboy-like figure engaged in prayer and rolled his eyes.

'I want to lie on the Yorkshire moors, sir. I don't want to set Berlin on fire. I want a little camera gun exercise with our dear and deep friend, the intrepid Stuart. Shoot him down for a change.'

'Asked right, the old man might let us all go,' said Stuart.

'Quiet now and everything,' Fletcher said. 'What about A flight. Let them go?' Where's Butler, he thought.

'Might,' said Harper. Then quickly: 'I say, Stevens copped it last week. Stanhope and Corning still around. And Fairbanks. Good types.' His voice was bright, with something in it that was almost amusement.

'What about Gale?' asked Fletcher. Now, in his mind, he saw Gale suddenly again, the blue Spitfire, the flash of the Messerschmitt cannon, the explosion in his ears, Gale shouting, 'Break, Fletcher! Break!'

If it weren't for Gale, Fletcher thought, I

68

might not be here, or I might have lost my whole leg. He remembered now coming into Manston afterwards, following Gale into the landing pattern. He seemed to feel even now the hot, shocking, burning sensation of the shell fragment in his leg that afternoon, his stomach twisted with pain while he fought to keep pressure on the rudder.

'Gale's still around,' said Harper. 'Inside. Easing his nerves over a little mild and bitter. Pranged a kite landing yesterday.'

They walked into the Mess building and along the hall with mail racks on the wall and passed the empty dining room with all the tables lined up, row after row, all the table cloths white, and into the lounge where all the chairs were empty.

Just beyond the window they heard the diving whine of a Spitfire and they moved forward quickly and looking out through the trees, saw high in the sky, the Spitfire standing on its nose, fierce in relief against the sunlight, the engine pulling, the Spitfire gradually diminishing, becoming smaller and smaller, rolling over on its back, gnat-like, snarling and whining. Another aeroplane, another Spitfire, came down out of the sun. Fletcher watched him roll onto his back, diving. Then he heard the twin engine whine, saw the two Spitfires diving, increasing in size—the blue one in front, the silver and grey still some distance back, gaining.

'Jesus,' Harper said. 'Why don't they try to pull the wings off?'

'Who is it?' asked Fletcher.

'Looks like Corning and Fairbanks. They're always working out on each other.'

Then the room, the windows trembled in the road, the savage snarl, as the Spitfires pulled out over the field shot skyward again, diminishing tiny, like two bugs chasing each other. Fletcher watched the blue aeroplane half roll, climb upside down for a second, skid off on one wing, appear to tumble against the ineffable blue sky doming the slumbrous afternoon air. Sun glinted on the wings.

'He's right on him,' Harper cried. 'Jesus, can he fly!'

'Which?' Fletcher asked. He had forgotten who flew which plane. All the aircraft had changed since he had been in hospital.

'Fairbanks,' said Stuart. 'Bloody good lately. There, he got him. Corning can't get out of that one.'

The two aeroplanes slanted downward, the droning roar of their diving engines seemed to explode abruptly ahead of them, entering the room, the building, before the two aeroplanes, one behind the other, looking almost inextricable, shot over the building and up into the sky again.

'Fletcher's going to ask the old man about sending us all up to Dishforth for a little refresher course,' Harper said a few minutes later, standing at the Mess bar with Fairbanks and Corning.

'I'll ask,' said Fletcher. 'But you know the old man. Probably a big no for all you experienced types.'

They were passing out the glasses of beer through the bar which was no more than a doorway with the top half of the door cut away and a shelf nailed atop the bottom half. There was room for only one man to stand at the bar and receive drinks from the barman.

'Where's Gale?' asked Fletcher.

'Flap. He loves flaps. A bloody volunteer today for extra duty. Special recco.'

'No eager types, please,' said Stuart. Fairbanks laughed, wishing he had been around this afternoon when Adams, the acting Wing Commander, was looking for a volunteer for special recco on the barges in Cherbourg harbour.

'How about some of these sprogs around here?' Corning asked. 'They're sending kids to us now. No real combat training until they see their first Hun.'

'How did you get it?' Fletcher asked.

'Right. Right. Right,' said Corning, drinking his beer fast. He was always patronizing the new pilots on the squadron. Fletcher couldn't understand it. 'Maybe he thinks it's all luck, he's shot down nine Jerries,' Fletcher thought. Maybe it is.

It was twilight before Fletcher had straightened out everything, sitting in the office with Adams, seeing the look of discomfort in Adams' face when he asked him for permission to take a flight to Dishforth for a little rest and training. Poor Adams, Fletcher thought, he doesn't know whether he's coming or going. He looked at the pile of paper on the desk, the photograph on the wall of the Squadron standing in front of the Mess in France. What a piece of cake, what a vacation, Fletcher thought, remembering the time. It seemed years ago. Yet it was only a few weeks. He felt odd thinking of that time such a short time ago. He looked at himself in the photo, feeling it was another person, while Adams tinkered with his pencil and looked thoughtfully at the wall.

'You can spare them,' Fletcher said. 'It's quiet now. It's going to be worse later. A little rest and they'll be better.'

'I don't know.'

'They're worn out. You're worn out. You can't even see it yourself.'

Adams looked up, drumming the pencil against the top of his desk, and gave Fletcher a single pale, nervous look, saying quickly:

'All right. Off with you. Tomorrow.'

Walking back to the Mess, Fletcher started thinking about his mother, wishing he had gone home on leave. He should have seen her for a few days, but it was bloody awful being with her. The way she kept making him feel as if he were two years old, always picking pieces of dust off his tunic and asking him if he wasn't tired and wouldn't he like to go to bed and get a good night's rest. Of course, she was trying to be nice, but it was too much. No, he could have had sick leave for some time home from the hospital, but it was too bloody thick seeing her, having to listen to her telling him to be careful, to watch out for himself. God, she acted as if he was still wearing shorts. He hated to think how little pieces of his boyhood still clung to him, how she could make him feel helpless with her chatter. The worst part, of course, was when she got started on why he didn't get a good job at staff level as her brother had, or at least get into a good regiment as his father had. She was always asking why he had turned down a commission in the Hussars, why he hadn't married the nice Thompson girl, everybody thought they would make a wonderful match. God, why did parents always object to their children trying to be themselves? How could he ever explain his love of flying to her? How could he ever explain it to anyone? How could he tell anyone of feeling free in the clear empty blue tranquility far above the earth in the warm sunny silence of morning sky doming the world? He could never tell her or make her feel why or how he loved the air, the sky, flying, the tremendous exhilaration of learning to fly; or the beautiful green light of twilight flowing up from the earth, darkness rising like water and the western sky pink and gold and indigo while you hung motionless under the first stars, watching the rivers far

74

below like monstrous silver veins evolve slowly out of the darkness of the earth; or the pure loneliness of flight in moments of peaceful beauty with great jagged walls of pure white cumulus sticking up like snow-covered mountains across the sky to form an even snow-like coating, blotting out the earth; or your life quickened by fear when your mouth was dry and your guts were cold and empty, filled with fright and fury, while the controls grew stiff with speed, down, down, down, and then at the critical instant the fear and fury a hard, cold ball in your stomach as the guns hammered fear out and elation and something almost akin to ecstasy filled you as fragments broke off in black pieces from the cowling of the Messerschmitt and drifted down like torn tissue paper.

'You bastard, you bastard,' he remembered shouting, watching the black-crossed wing fall sideways, slamming on fifty degrees bank as the wingless fuselage shot past rearward. Then the old sensation in him again, of being in a dream, with his teeth chattering, and the domed blue sky above with the engine pulling straight up.

He opened the Mess door and the faces

at the bar turned and looked at him and smiled.

Fletcher's right hand rose and his thumb and forefinger came together in an O-sign. He stood there, grinning.

'All set,' he said. 'But we can't get transport out until morning. Anybody for town?'

'Good show,' said Harper. 'Let's go.'

Outside the cars were parked beside the Mess, an old Bentley roadster and a red MG, squatting on the shadow of the building. The sky was softening now. It looked bluely remote, sea-like, immeasurably in the evening light. The cars shot out from the building, sped down the dusty road under the trees. To the left, through the trees, Fletcher saw aeroplanes, the Spitfires, motionless, ranked in readiness, rising on their stork-like undercarts. the shark-tipped line of cowling, wing-tip and fuselage blurring faintly in the evening shadows. The cars raced down the road.

The sign bore the words THE BULL. The cars stopped in front of the brick building, five miles from the aerodrome. The moon was coming up white and round through the trees behind the pub.

76

Inside the lights were on and the black-out curtains were drawn. The dark, wooden walls gleamed in the light. Harry Dawson, chewing a cheese sandwich with one side of his face, his left hand resting on the middle beer handle, greeted the fliers from behind the bar.

'Oi! Chum, 'eard Winnie talkin' on the wireless about your tabs 'ere. Never 'ave so many owed so much to—'

Fletcher laughed.

'How're you, Harry? Let's have some pints.'

Harry looked at the small overnight kit bag slung on a strap over Fletcher's shoulder.

'Where you goin'?'

'A slight sojourn in the provinces,' said Harper.

'York,' said Fletcher.

Dawson pulled the beer taps, set the full glasses, round and cold, on the bar. He watched them drink.

'Scotch,' he said. 'Scotch tomorrow.'

'Watered or pure?' Stuart asked.

Dawson blushed and leaned down under the bar, pretending he was busy.

The pilots carried their glasses to the door, and pushing it open went outside.

The darkness was summery, warm and soft. They lay on the grass, hearing guns firing down the coast, seeing searchlights bisecting the sky. But the whole dark rich earth seemed to be asleep. Stars glittered remote, motionless, in the high round of blackness of night. The air felt light on Fletcher's face. He could feel something in the summer night troubling him vaguely. There was something in the soft sound of the summer wind in the trees that disturbed him. 'It's peace,' he thought. 'Summer nights like this remind me of before the war. I should forget it. School. I'll never go back after this is over. I'll never be able to go anywhere again. I'll stay on if I live.' He did not want to think about dying. I'll get through, his mind started to say to him over and over again as it always said to him when he thought of dying.

He heard a car coming up the road. He saw flattened shafts of light cast downward through the slotted black-out shields covering the headlights. It stopped in front. Flight Lieutenant Gale walked across the lawn towards the pub.

'My hero,' Harper shouted. 'He's been scaring the German navy all afternoon.'

'Hello, sods,' said Gale.

'Smiling, the boy took the VC!'

'He's wearing a new medal.'

'How many today, Lancelot?'

'Volunteered again for tomorrow?'

'Sweep in the morning. Low level attack on Berlin at noon. Still brave at tea. No, girls, it was nothing. If I had to do it all over again—'

'Fug you sods,' said Gale. 'Ground pounders.'

'Come on in, old boy. I'll buy you a drink,' Stuart said. 'You've been working too hard. Bloody awful precedent you set for us cowards.' He put one hand on Gale's shoulder, said in a different voice: 'How'd it go? Look as if Jerry's coming over?'

'Quite a decent little fishing fleet.'

'Wish you'd been around. Fletcher's fixed us up with a nice do. Dishforth. Refresher course.'

They went inside. The figures on the lawn rose. For a moment, slapping the grass from their trousers, they stood in silhouette against the moonlight. Then they went slowly inside.

'Any whisky?' Gale asked, creasing his flat stomach against the bar.

'Come on, Harry, you've been drinking the ration for a week yourself,' said Stuart. 'One double.'

'I—' Harry began. 'Oh, all right.' He stooped down under the bar, came up with a bottle of White Horse and poured Gale a double shot.

Two Royal Artillery Sergeants who were regular patrons of the Bull had just come in and they looked at Harry serving whisky and remembered how they were told the night before that Harry was out of whisky.

The tall sergeant, a gunner, said to the other sergeant: 'You'd think the bloody air force was winning the war. I remember wondering where they were when I was lying in the water watching all those Jerry kites over Dunkirk.'

Corning grasped Fairbanks as he started towards the gunner.

'Wait a minute,' said Corning. 'Hold it, old boy.'

Maybe it was what they were all waiting for, Fletcher thought later, remembering all the terrible tension in the sky, remembering how the only time it ever left you was during a real scrap, and then when it was over, it filled you again. Maybe, he thought later, if you could board their planes and fight them hand to hand you'd feel more relaxed after you land. But it was almost unbearable at times, he knew, and all could feel it, though it was never mentioned. So here was a way out for a while, and they had been submerged in it so long, there was not even shame in any of them now for wanting to happen what they knew was wrong.

Fletcher saw Fairbanks spring at the gunner. The gunner whirled, seeing Fairbanks in midstride, his right arm lifted. The gunner hit Fairbanks in the chest and Fairbanks did not stop. Fletcher saw Fairbanks hit the other sergeant on the point of the jaw and while the sergeant was falling, Fairbanks grasped the top of the gunner's head with his left hand. He pushed the head down and as the gunner began to fall forward, Fairbanks slammed his right knee into the gunner's stomach and struck him twice with a short, chopping right hand blow on his kidneys. The gunner's face looked sick and he fell down on his face.

The sergeant started to get up and Fletcher put his hands under the sergeant's shoulders and held him.

'I'll kill you,' the sergeant said. 'I'll take

you all over the bloody grass outside.' There was blood on his lip.

Fletcher pushed him towards the door. Stuart and Harper were pouring water over the gunner's face, asking him to have a drink. The gunner shook his head, pushed them away staggered towards the door and went outside.

'What the bloody hell!' Fletcher turned towards Fairbanks. 'What's the matter with you, old boy?'

Fletcher could see in Fairbanks' eyes that he had been suffering from combat flying nerves.

'I didn't like his face,' Fairbanks said.

'Come on now. Can't blame him actually. Can't get any whisky. Ruddy poor justice.'

Fletcher could see Fairbanks was suffering now from embarrassment.

'Guess I've heard too many of them lately,' Fairbanks said. 'What's their trouble? They've had their war. Harry, how about a whisky?'

'How long since you had leave?' Fletcher asked.

Fairbanks was tall, with a gaunt face. His eyes were motionless, rigid. He stared at Fletcher.

'Stow it,' he said. 'I just don't like people,' he broke off. Then: 'Couldn't he keep his ruddy mouth shut? He's probably had whisky on the sly when somebody else couldn't get it and now he's bleating.'

'Take it easy.'

Corning slapped Fairbanks on the back. 'He's going to buy a round to quiet our nerves,' Corning said in a light, innocent voice, his American accent, as though wanting to take the tension out of the atmosphere. 'Aren't you?' He put one arm around Fairbanks' shoulder. 'Oi, Harry! Let's have a couple of pints here. Fairbanks is buying.'

The sound of night bombers going out high came to them, now, remote, droning down through the soft summer air. They drank more. There was something gay, yet forlorn in their voices, their glasses resting on the bar in a pool of spilt liquor, where they leaned against the bar, singing. Their voices floated out upon the night air, the land dark and empty beyond. In alcohol they were all beyond the world where they had lived for four months, the world of their personal fears. They were isolated out of all time in these moments, reft of all worry and fatigue, beyond all tomorrows, even beyond the guilty fear and hatred that kept them flying. They drank again, glass after glass.

'By God, you bloody Empire Builders,' Corning was saying in his American accent. 'I'm a Yank, see.' His nostrils were white against his face.

'So what, you bloody barbarian?' said Fairbanks. 'We licked you once in eighteen-twelve. We'll do it again.'

The voice sounded far away to Fletcher. He was thinking of Fairbanks. His sister had been killed in an air raid on Southampton in June. Ever since then Fairbanks had been volunteering for special flights, strafing and low level jobs. He would get himself killed yet.

'You've forgotten something,' said Corning. 'Seventeen-seventy-five. Barbarians against gentlemen. We beat hell out of you. Are there any Howes or Cornwallises present? Advance and be recognized. The barbarians, the natives, the bloody colonials are here to bail you out this time.' He raised his glass, banged it down hard on the bar.

'Lost,' Corning said. 'Too many bloody gentlemen in the room. Wouldn't be polite. Gentlemen's code. Die well but no fighting in bars.'

'Do you want to go outside?' said Harper. 'You bloody Yank.'

'You bet I'm a bloody Yank,' Corning said. 'Don'tcha ever forget it. I'm worse than that. My mother and dad came from Wales. I know that. Porthcawl. Stormy Downs. I've been flying for you bloody Empire Builders for six months. I'm not a crusader.'

'Are you bragging about it?' Harper said.

'I never was a crusader. Bloody crusaders, how'd I ever get here—' He looked at Harper. 'What'd you say?'

'Say, chum,' said Harry, leaning across the bar. 'That's about enough for you tonight.'

'Easy, chum,' said Corning, grabbing his glass as Harry reached for it. Corning stared at Harper. 'Who says I can't drink you bloody English under the bar?'

'Are you bragging again?' Harry said.

'Yes,' said Corning. 'Did I ever tell you about the time I got my tenth Hun. Did anybody ever tell you the King's costing you guys too much?'

'Leave the King out of this,' said Harper, an unlit cigarette bobbling from the corner of his mouth.

'Listen,' said Corning, 'I'm working for him. I got a right to criticize. Six months I've been taking his shilling, shooting down Huns for him. I got a right to ask. Where's he spending all that salary? How'd I ever get in this? Don't give me that crusader stuff. I like to fly. I'd still be back in Minnesota flying whisky over the border for the Indians if that damn government man hadn't double-crossed me. I wasn't paying him enough dues. Then it's too late, so I got out fast, across the border. Went to Toronto, peddled my crate. I'm going to get me a couple of Huns I decided.'

Harper looked at him calmly.

'We'll take your shilling back now and you can go home.'

Corning stared at him, his eyes blood-shot, furious. He waggled a finger in Harper's face. 'Five more Huns and I'm going home. I promised myself fifteen.' He drank.

'Come on, lads,' Harry Dawson shouted. 'Time! Time, please!' He flicked the lights off. The dark room filled with shouts.

'Hold it, Harry!'

'Half a mo!'

'Wait'll I finish this water!'

86

'Come on, lads,' Harry said, turning on the lights. He walked to the door, stood there while they finished, then watched them leave.

Outside the sky arched empty, silent. They stood there in the darkness, muttering, lighting cigarettes. The moon and stars glowed high, remote, cold. Fletcher started towards the cars.

Fairbanks said, 'It's this liquor rationing'll lose the war.' He put one hand on Corning's shoulder. 'Got anything in your room?'

'Nope.'

'Bloody Yank.'

Corning hiccupped.

'Gentlemen. Bad language.'

'Bloody Yank,' said Fairbanks.

Then they were in the car, driving back to the aerodrome. Somebody in the car had a bottle of beer. They stopped in the middle of the road and drank. Harper began singing. They drove on in the dark, singing:

'Is it one?'

'No-o-o-o-o-o-oh!'

'Is it two-o-o-o?'

'No-o-o-o-o-o!'

'Is it two-one-o-o-o-o-o-oh?'

Their voices seemed to linger upon the mooned silent land like the dying fall of chords imminent with despair and death. They sped on faster towards the aerodrome. Mist hung slumbrous in ditches on each side of the road.

CHAPTER FOUR

In the morning sky, climbing steadily into the sunlight over Middlesex, Wing Commander Butler held the wheel steady in the cockpit of the Proctor. It felt strange flying again after not having been in the air for several weeks and it felt even stranger flying a Proctor. He had borrowed it from Allard at Group. It felt like a training aircraft after all the hours he had flown Spitfires. I'll probably hold off too long on landing and boob for sure, Butler thought, seeing himself bringing the kite in too high. The sunlit air against the blue empty sky was blinding, filled with dazzling golden motes as he stared straight up for a second. Then he looked out from side to side. He was flying low, and it was quiet. Still he was not taking any chances. It was the Hun you didn't see that killed you.

Just my bloody luck, he thought, to be shot down in a Proctor on a business trip. But if you're lucky, Butler, he said to himself, you'll be flying a new Spit soon.

He wished he had gone directly back to the Squadron. It would have been better that way. Somehow—though he had been away only three weeks—he knew he would still feel like an outsider his first few minutes on the aerodrome. He did not want anybody on the Squadron to see him take a Spit around for the first time after the lay off. It was better this way, borrowing this sahib kite from Allard to lob down at home instead of going up on the train.

He remembered the first time he had flown a Proctor. It seemed like a century ago, yet it was only two years. With Hendrix, he thought, remembering his face. There was an old type. In 1939 Hendrix had gone off on Whitley bombers with 10 Squadron, bombed Poland already with leaflets.

Probably be around one of these days telling how he shot a good arrow at Crecy. What a line shooter that Hendrix will be

89

if he lives through it.

You're not a bad line shooter yourself, Butler. Remember that American nurse from the Embassy at the party up in Chesterfield House. What was her name? You didn't do so badly, Butler, after six drinks, telling her how you flew a Tiger Moth up the street in Paris and pulled back the hood so you could hear yourself setting off the air raid sirens. But what the hell were you so worried about as a flyer that you had to brag like that? Sure, you weren't kidding. Sure, some of it. But not all. Sure, you were bragging more than were kidding.

The hell with it. Everybody has to have something. You can't have everything perfect. Everybody needs something, love or bragging or booze or God or government or Toryism or Communism or flying or war. Sure, war. That's it, Butler. Climb on my knee, son, I'll tell you about the Huns daddy shot down. Christ, Butler, he said to himself, you don't even sound like a patriot to yourself anymore. What are you in this for? Glory or ribbons or patriotism or hate. That's right, tell yourself all that. Forget the fear. You know mostly you're afraid. You're scared. You don't want to go up there among them again. Tell yourself why you're in the war until you don't believe in it maybe, and maybe—no, you'll never fool yourself. You'll never be able to talk yourself into one of those desk jobs. Go on, tell yourself more. Go on, you bore. Butler, stop hating yourself and fly.

'Hello, Durban Leader,' Butler heard a ground controller calling suddenly. 'Ten Huns approaching Rye. Fifteen thousand feet. Climbing. Keep your eyes open.'

He smiled as he pushed the stick forward, felt his heart pound. Just his bloody luck. Shot down out here in a Proctor. The trees rose, increasing in size. He saw a cow, a man working in a field. Butler flew on, seeing water, swans white in the sunlight on the Thames, more trees, a great beautiful, shining white house, the hills of Kent. The hills, rising smooth and high and round, made him think of Helen. He held her in his arms in the dark room of her London apartment. A shiver passed through him. He wanted her now. 'To hell with the war,' he thought. 'This is the world that's real.' He felt for an instant the war was all a child's dream. Is it all twaddle, he asked himself. This thought frightened him until he felt pain inside himself. He cried out to himself he was saying this only so he would never have to fly again. 'I'm trying to destroy the world I know,' he thought, and it scared him for an instant to think the world of words in his mind could do this, that all those words would create images of right inside his mind until he believed he was right. 'I'm only scared,' he thought, and that's why I'm doing it, and thinking of Helen again, seeing her body in his mind, the earth and sky seemed to rush wonderfully together for an instant. But a part of him said it was not Helen he longed for but courage and the deep fear inside him was keeping out the courage so strongly his mind was making him believe the world of his desire was Helen. 'God,' he thought, 'Butler, your oxygen is thin. You're protecting yourself behind her skirts!' But he wished he were with her in London. There, in her room, the world would be immense, wonderful, beyond the sky, higher than he had ever flown, going up and up, but never right out through the sky. That was the trouble. You never could go straight through the sky to where? with any woman. Never straight through the blue dome. Never, out and out until there was nothingness or a whole limitless world. Never. There was the world again. Butler, he thought, you're wounded. You don't know what you're talking about. You're only looking for a way to talk to yourself. You're scared, terribly scared.

He looked at his compass, glanced at his watch, began to descend. The sun hung high overhead, glaring in the sky, shining on the wings. Ahead the hangars rose out of a flat green field with the sand sea beyond. The grass was more vivid in the sunlight than he had ever seen before. The beach looked white and hot. The field looked like a circus, the hangars tent-like. Jordan's dead, Butler thought, remembering flying in here with Jordan. There were Defiants on the field that day. That whole squadron was dead now.

Now in his mind Butler saw the sky over Dunkirk again, the monstrous gout of smoke rising out of the sea, the wind blowing the smoke over the beaches, and Jordan going in among the Stukas just before they peeled off. Butler remembered looking up into the sun for a second. He could still remember telling Jordan to break, the blood pounding in his head just before Jordan went down in flames and the twelve Messerschmitts flashed past in the sun.

He felt excited now for an instant like a child as he turned in to make an approach. He remembered how he had come here as a sprog pilot officer long ago. All right, all right, he told himself, what's so great now about making Wing Commander? He did not want the people here to feel he had changed. But you have, Butler, he thought, you've changed. You're scared and you're too damn proud of your rank all of a sudden. So now you need it and it's embarrassing you because you're scared. You mustn't think much of yourself today, feeling like this. Better you were with Jordan than feel this way. Well, you'll fight again, feel you're right in being called Wing Commander again. When he held off to land, he hit and bounced and almost had to put on throttle and go around again. He cursed himself, slammed the wheel back into his stomach. He waited, feeling cold, felt the shock of wheels striking, then he was rolling.

The control tower told him he could park in front and he taxied over and got out. Flight Lieutenant Baxter with black hair and blue eyes came out to meet

94

him. The Flight Lieutenant was reading Butler's ribbons almost as he saluted. He looked new too and Butler smiled, remarking the DFC. Replacement but a veteran, thought Butler, he must be all of nineteen. He wondered how long it would be before he could be with Helen in London.

'Hello, sir,' said the Flight Lieutenant. 'Good trip?'

Butler smiled, nodded.

They shook hands. It wasn't until then Butler recognized him. A 602 Squadron type.

'I say, weren't you in—?' Butler smiled, pausing, pointing a finger at the young man.

'Boyer, sir.'

'Well, hello. Thought I knew you.' They shook hands again and walked along past the control tower.

In the office building beyond, Butler went in through the side door. Adams who was now Acting Wing Commander was upstairs. He was sitting behind a desk wearing the good ribbons he had won in France flying a Hurricane.

'Hello!'

'Well!' said Adams, smiling. 'Sit down.

I was beginning to think you were never coming back.'

'No such luck.'

A WAAF came into the room. She passed Butler, and gave him a brief glance, then seemed almost to pause, and then while still moving, she stared at him. After she was gone, Adams grinned: 'That's the trouble. No heroes around here lately. Bloody heroes come. Take all our women.'

Butler looked at him, smiled.

'Get some tips in, old boy,' he said.

'You can have this desk any time you want it,' Adams smiled. Then: 'Allard said you were coming down. Flying ops yet?'

Butler shook his head.

'Will. Later. How's the new kite?'

'Not here. But we might win this war yet. Still plenty of Highland Cream in the mess.'

A bar of sunlight lay across the top of the desk. Another WAAF entered, laid papers on Adams' desk. At the door she glanced over her shoulder at Butler.

'All right, sergeant, that's all, thank you,' said Adams. The girl's face reddened. She went out.

'How about lunch?' Butler asked.

'Haven't you eaten yet?'

Butler shook his head.

'Come on,' Adams said.

He glanced briefly at a letter on his desk.

'I say, it's Monday, isn't it?' asked Butler.

Adams nodded. He did not look up.

'Bomb Berlin pudding today?' Butler asked.

Adams looked at him. 'You're just in time.' He smiled, rose.

The Mess looked about the same inside but there was something strange about it he could not understand. He had the feeling when he looked around the room that he had been away several years but here he had been gone only a few weeks. Somehow the room looked smaller and he felt a kind of emptiness in the room he had never felt before. Somehow it no longer felt like the place he had been that noon at luncheon before he had been shot down. He felt years older since that afternoon.

He went into the bar with Adams and they ordered two glasses of beer and leaned against the bar, drinking. Butler could feel his mind jumping around. He had never been like this before, as if a part of him did not want to be in the room and his mind refused to think about anybody in the room. He did not feel at home here again. I hate it, he thought. I hate it and wish I were in London with Helen. Then, he thought, they're crazy to be flying, they're crazy. What the hell is this war all about except one country wanting to take over another and they're asking me to die for England. To hell with England. The city's full of people who won't do a damn thing about fighting. To hell with bloody England. It's coal against steel mills, that's all this war is about. But there was shame and guilt in his heart as these thoughts filled his mind and he knew he must admit to himself that it was better to be a man than to be scared, even if what he thought about the reasons for the war were true. Christ, Butler, your head is a bloody ruckus.

'We're short in A flight tomorrow morning,' Adams said. 'Just a sweep along the coast to see if the Hun is sleeping or lying in wait. MacCumber bought it yesterday and there's no replacement yet. I thought perhaps—'

Adams waited. He did not look at Butler but he could feel him silent, numb inside himself. All Butler could feel was a terrible, unreasonable numbness inside himself.

Butler was silent, drinking slowly, looking over the rim of his glass across the room.

'Well, I think I'll wait a few days,' he said, finally, slowly, lowering his glass without looking at Adams. Then something warm seemed to burst inside him. He had that feeling before, going in, across the sky, his head forward, diving down on a long slant, pulling the stick back slowly, getting the gun sight ahead of the Messerschmitt, filled with fear just before it might be time to die. He put his glass down, turning his back for an instant, his head lowered, then he looked up quickly, still not putting his eyes on Adams.

His eyes gazed on some point beyond Adams' head when he spoke fast: 'Put me on if nobody turns up in MacCumber's place before tomorrow. Might as well try the old tram line again. How's Whitman? Still around?'

'He's in hospital. Lost the Battle of Piccadilly. Went up to town with some Yank pilot of 601 squadron. They rented a room in Berkeley and the Yank proceeded to throw a party that somehow wound up including taking the phone off the wall, rolling up all the carpets, and tossing the whole lot out of the window with four empty magnums of champagne.'

'Fall out of the window in the carpet?'

'They forgot to pay the bill and had to fight their way out of the lobby through almost a police cordon. Whitman claims he started to swing and some woman hit him in the eye with her shoe.'

'Rum. Where'd he get hit?'

'Head. Nasty crack. Bottle,' said Adams.

'Well, Huns'll live a few more days till he's out.'

'That Allard's crackers,' said Adams. 'Bringing Americans down here, asking us to take-off, even though there aren't any Huns in the air.'

'Maybe they're working on the Americans. Get them in. Good show. We could use some help. Too far, though. Bloody terrible kites, too. Won't come near doing what they tell the papers. Really haven't a decent fighter. Still we use their pilots.'

'Allard said there were some high level negotiations going on and if things are desperate later we may need immediate help. So we can look as if we're loafing too much now.'

They finished their drinks and walked

slowly into the dining room. The beer made Butler feel better, and the feeling of home was coming into him again. I'll fly tomorrow, he thought, and for an instant he was without fear, and then suddenly there it was inside him again, numbing his mind.

'Saw your girl in London the other day,' Adams said.

'Helen?'

Adams nodded.

'How was she?' asked Butler.

'Bloody marvellous. Never saw her before.'

'Street?'

'No, no, no, old man. Show. Damn good-looking girl. Good actress.'

'I must get up to see her. You saw her in the show?'

'That's right,' said Adams, pulling out a chair, sitting down.

He's lying thought Butler. He's lying. Saw her on the street with some chap. Lying, trying to be nice. To hell with her. Well, what can I expect? Wonderful looking girl, can't very well sit in her dressing room thinking of a bloody fighter pilot who never gets to London in four weeks.

Butler looked across the tables and saw a face that looked familiar—a stocky, blond-haired pilot, sitting alone at a table near the window. Butler saw the Squadron Leader rings on the tunic cuffs and read the ribbons under the downswept wings, the good bars to the DSC. I should know him, Butler thought. I know I've seen him before.

'Who—?' he began, turning his head towards Adams, and then looking at him, he saw Adams looking at him and smiling, their faces a few inches apart.

'Good type, eh?' said Adams, remarking Butler's glance. 'We're bloody lucky to have him. Came over from Group to help us pick up our tails after you left us.'

Butler shook his head. Now in his mind he saw the face across the room in Shepherd's Bar in London. Oh, my God, he thought, I certainly should know him. Brown. Peter Brown. Sure, about twelve Huns. Well, well, so that's Brown.

He looked at Brown, with his flat, high cheek-boned face, the blond curly hair, the heavy shoulders and chest, stolid, short. Wager he's a bloody good rugger player, Butler thought.

'Rather rough on wing men, isn't he?'

Butler said. He could feel envy inside himself, and even though he knew that what he had said was true, he felt ashamed he had said it because he knew he never would have said it if he weren't afraid he would never be a man again in the air.

'Who isn't, with twelve Huns in his belt?' said Adams. 'He'll be flying with you. Fletcher and your old flight are up at Dishforth. Wish they were here for your first show.'

'Well, Brown can take care of an old man like me,' Butler said, embarrassedly.

'Fletcher still all right?' Adams asked. 'Shaky do there, you know.'

'He'll be flying with me.'

'Wish I had your experience, Jimmy. Some of those Huns are getting too bloody good.'

'Experience?' Butler laughed. 'Luck.'

Hell, he thought, stop running yourself down, you'll feel better when you get in there among them again.

Adams shook his head.

'Luck? No,' he said. 'There's a time, that's all. You either buy it or don't. Maybe you get back from a shaky do and fall downstairs and die. That's all.' He shrugged. 'There's a time. The armour

103

plating isn't going to help if they're got your name down in the book for the old chop. Certain day. Certain hour. All down in the old chopper's book.'

'How's Harper?'

'Bloody good now. Knows the Hun. Never going to fool him and Fairchild.'

'Many sprogs?' asked Butler.

'Terrible.' Adams shook his head. 'Two new sections. Fly like they came straight out of ground school. Never should put them on a squadron yet. I'm scared they're all going to run into each other the first time the Hun jumps them.'

'If they live through five, the government'll start getting its money back,' Butler said.

'Never have time to learn. Still too many well trained Huns alive.'

'How are those bloody instrument bashers of mine? Still keeping the kites glued together?'

Half an hour later, Adams and Butler walked up the dark tarred street between the administrative buildings. The hot, cloud-filled afternoon sky was empty. The hangars loomed, big, round-topped, motionless, bulking up on the green flat field. There was the smell of oil in the hot air. The whole world seemed to lie prone, waiting under the dry September afternoon. As they turned into the first hangar the blasting roar of a Spitfire revving up shattered the peaceful silence, and looking across the field Butler saw dust rising under the trees. They entered the hangar.

'Here's your kite,' said Adams.

The fitter, a fat Yorkshire man bobbed out from under the wing of an aeroplane.

'Well, ye came back!' From other places around the aeroplane the rest of the maintenance crew appeared, wiping their hands on their trousers. Then they were all shaking hands. Butler experienced a sudden twinge of happiness he did not feel he deserved. They still think I'm the person who went away, he thought, smiling, glad to see them, feeling more at home now.

He walked over to the aeroplane, ran his hand along the leading edge of the wing. He felt good looking at the machine. It seemed very beautiful to him in this moment. All he needed in the world he felt was to be back in it, to be part of it. He stood there, looking at it carefully, studying the beautifully vicious lines.

'How is the old girl?' Butler asked.

They smiled and laughed quietly, making indistinguishable noises, muttering faintly, glancing at the ground quickly or at each other with passing faintly embarrassed looks as if all felt individually responsible and proud of having the aeroplane ready to fly again for Butler. But all were afraid to claim sole responsibility. Their lives and meaning of the war for each of them individually came to them through work on Butler's aeroplane. They looked on Butler both as a kind of son and father, worrying about him in the air, treating him with a friendly deference on the ground. They were watching him now, all their eyes, to see if there was any change in his face or eyes since the day he had been carried out of this cockpit.

'How're you feeling, sir?' asked Bascome, the rigger.

'Fine,' said Butler. 'Fine,' looking carefully along the fuselage to see the patch covering the fabric torn away by the cannon shell explosion. 'Jerry been over much since I was away?' he asked.

'Aye,' said Shearer, the Scots fitter. 'That he is, you know. Keeping Boscome short on his love life. Putting him down the bloody shelter all the time at night.'

106

Boscome grinned. He had a face like a monkey and a skinny neck.

'Cor,' he said. 'You're daft.'

'I hear you're the heartbreaker,' said Butler, winking at the others. 'Right?'

'He's England's secret weapon,' said Nelson, the armourer. 'One look at him and Jerry'll pack up.'

'Come on lads,' said Nelson, the Yorkshire fitter. 'There's other kites you've got to service.'

'Mr Fletcher back with you?' asked Boscome.

'He's gone to Dishforth. He'll be back in my flight.'

'Good luck, sir.'

'Cheer oh,' said Butler. 'Depending soon on you lads.'

He watched them walk away, across the field towards the row of Spitfires parked under the trees.

'I say,' said Adams, glancing at his watch. 'I have to post orders for tomorrow. Do you want to stay here or walk back? See you in the Mess tonight and tomorrow we can go over things in the office.'

'Righto. Think I'll hang around. Look the old buggy over.'

Butler stood alone in the hangar after

Adams was gone. He stood back from the Spitfire. It seemed empty and dead to him. He had the feeling of being almost a ghost when he saw the patch and paint where the explosion had made a jagged hole. The machine reared on its wheels, the propeller motionless, the fuselage silver and blue with a quality fierce and savage as a shark.

After a while he walked back to Mess. It was late afternoon. The lounge was empty. He wished somebody were there he knew. He wished he were in London with Helen. He wished he were flying and that now it was tomorrow and it was all over.

It wouldn't be any good being with her now, he thought. He felt rotten. Ah, hell, he thought, and there was no pity in it for himself, only disappointment and faint bitterness at life for making him aware of his fear. Ah, hell, he repeated to himself, what does it matter what happens to me, we are all nothing in this world anyway, ink spots on the blotter of history. Sure, but there was no point in thinking this. That was for the dead. For the first time in his life he wished he were dead. He did not go into the Mess that night. He lay in his room in the dark, waiting for morning, his insides cold and hollow, all the tightness gone, and then later in a dream he stared down into his own eyes staring up at him out of his dead face.

CHAPTER FIVE

Helen Collins sat in her dressing room, filing her nails, looking out of the window into the alley beyond the Savoy Hotel. The door of her room opened. It was the maid.

'Ready for tea, Miss?'

Helen nodded without looking up. She felt irritable, cross. Why did it have to be Friday and there was nothing for her in London over the weekend? Why didn't she ever hear from Jimmy any longer? She had written and they had told her at the post office her letters had been handled properly but no one would ever tell her. Why were men such frightful letter writers? Lord, how had she ever let herself get mixed up with Jimmy Butler? She wished she had never met him, lying awake the past weeks thinking, worrying, wondering where he was, when she could be at the Coconut Grove having a marvellous time with that Colonel Winders. He was really an awful bore but he took one all over London, and he was quite gay and amusing. She put down her nail file and with it thoughts about Jimmy, the war, the future. Here in the dressing room she felt secure and safe beyond the war, and now in her mind she felt the world of her own upstairs on the stage, remote and wonderful from all worry and care. I wish it were time, she thought, I wish it were time. It always took her out of herself.

The maid came in with the tea.

'Look out, Miss,' she said. 'It's hot.'

It was always hot. That was the trouble. Now for three weeks her life had been the same, longing to break the monotony of her work in her play, yet content to accept the sense of fatigue after each show, content enough to go home alone. She looked at herself in the mirror, the photograph of Jimmy on the dressing table. The broad, square face and jaw, even the smile seemed to touch her eyes with an invitation to joy and delight. Her hair was a soft chestnut cloud in the mirror. She smiled slowly to herself, remarking her face in the glass, the slow, studied smile, watching the smile spread, the green wide eyes, the blonde hair. She shook a cigarette out of the pack on her dresser, lit a match.

Now, in her mind, she was in the Cafe De Paree again the night the lights went out for the first time during a raid. She was down on the floor under a table. It was all unreal. She was laughing. People were never killed laughing in the dark. Everybody was drunk on champagne. The band was still playing, even in the dark, and beyond you could hear the rise and fall of an air raid siren.

'This is a bloody nuisance,' a voice said from beneath the table across the way. In the dark a cigarette glowed, a red eye, faded, and again the voice, a man's voice, indistinguishable. The red eye died.

'Light?' she heard her voice saying.

'Can't. Air raid wardens get you.' The lighter had been in her hand just before the lights had gone out.

She flicked the flame on, the face shadowed suddenly in the quivering feather -shaped match flare. Then just as suddenly the darkness swallowed it again. She began to pray, thinking, God, I hope this one won't hit us. She hated prayer. It always made her feel guilty. She had not been to church for five years, and every time she heard the sirens she thought of dying. God, what if I died, she thought, and for an instant she was panic-stricken, thinking of Hell. She no longer believed in God. She'd never been able to believe in him since her mother, a hard-working woman, had been hit on the street by a taxi going through a stop light. She'd never been able to understand why God thought it was necessary to kill nice people off that way. It didn't help any at the funeral when the minister told her it was one of 'God's acts we must all bear'. Still, she could not rid herself of the fear that there might be a God and she would reach heaven, finding herself being questioned at the Gate, whether she believed or not. But these thoughts scared her almost as much as the siren so she forced herself to stop thinking about them and to concentrate on controlling her fear. She could feel sweat on her hands and neck. God, she thought waiting, why don't they drop them, if only they would drop the bombs. If only they would get it over.

'Come here,' a voice said. It was dark

under the table now. The hand on her shoulder felt warm. She could still feel the trembling going on inside her, but she felt better, not quite so scared. Then she heard the first stick of bombs dropping away far in the night. It sounded, as the thudding came to her through the floor, as if the raid were up Kensington way, and then the floor reverberated, and again the arm on her shoulder held her tight. After the all clear and when the lights were on, she looked at the young man, the blue tunic, the good ribbons, the ruddy face, the blue eyes.

'Well,' he said, looking at her, smiling, surprised and pleased. 'The luck of a man in a black out.'

'Thank you very much.'

'Not at all. Where are you sitting?'

She had looked across the room. Where was Richard? How did she ever get mixed up with these young navy types? They were dancing with you one minute, very brave on ships, but get them on a dance floor in the middle of an air raid, and what happened—they left you. Then she saw him. He was young and blond and down from Lowestoft off torpedo boats, the brother of a girl in the show. He was waving from their table across the room.

She walked back across the floor with a pilot, wondering who he was, what his name was. He gave her a feeling few men had ever given her before. She could not say exactly what it was but it had something to do with making her feel he liked her for being a woman without wanting only to jump into bed with her. She shuddered. All the young men seemed to make her feel that way. It was all they really wanted to do.

He had been careful with her, though. That first time he hadn't rushed anything. He hadn't even asked her name as he took her back to her table. Usually, every man she knew either knew her from her picture in the papers or they asked her name if they had a chance to meet her. It irritated her for an instant. All right, she thought, so he was nice to me under the table, but he doesn't have to patronize me as if I'm a little girl he's been taking care of.

'Thank you,' she said coolly, but he was still standing there smiling, pulling the chair out at her table, reaching behind her to shake hands with Richard, introducing himself. She looked straight ahead, hearing Richard and this new man speaking to each other as if they were old friends. But then suddenly she realized that with their manners they were competing for her and she sat there smiling, thinking, he really wants to meet me, but he won't admit it. She was grateful to Richard when he heard his voice saying: 'Oh, sorry, I thought you knew Helen.'

She turned her head, looked up, smiled.

'Jimmy Butler?' Richard said, and the man in the blue tunic with the nice black hair and steady black eyes looked down at her and nodded and smiled and said: 'Helen Collins. This is a pleasure. Of course, I should have recognized you. I enjoyed your last show.'

She felt grateful and pleased as a child and she could feel herself going out towards him, the child part of herself, and she told herself not to be silly, to stop responding this way to people when they complimented her about her show.

'Thank you.'

'You're at the Savoy now, aren't you?'

She felt delighted he was asking, and she tried to curb her delight. She did not want him to see it. This is silly, she thought, I just met the man. There must be at least five thousand British squadron leaders who look just exactly like him. Come on, Helen, you're not a child. But she could feel her heart beating fast. This is silly, she said to herself over and over again.

But she wondered about him that night, and she thought about him. She had met hundreds of men but none of them had given her this sudden tightness in her throat and she thought of his face and there was nothing there she had not seen before in other men's faces. The nose was long and straight, almost wedge-like, and his lips were full and his jaw reminded her of her brother's, faintly cleft, with the beard dark on both sides and the thin white scar down his cheek. When she thought of the scar, seeing it in her mind, she could feel the thickness in her throat again, the tightness in her breasts and stomach.

She thought of him off and on for a week, and perhaps too much. She forgot her lines twice in a week, and had to be criticized finally by the stage manager. Remembering it now, she saw how she had refused to think about it. She saw how she had actually feared he would not call, how she had told herself it was nothing, just another face, and how she was bored it had stuck in her mind because it was a new face, but soon it would just be another face, another blue tunic with good ribbons on it, but it wasn't the tunic or the ribbons she cared about. Well, call him yourself, find him, she finally told herself, but she could not. She could never do it, and she felt weak and unhappy thinking about it, trying to find reasons in her mind to give herself so she wouldn't feel so humiliated calling him. But she didn't know where to call. No, she wouldn't. She had never called any man in her life. She promised herself she wasn't going to start now. To hell with him, if he didn't think enough of her, she certainly wasn't going to bother calling him. London was filled with good looking men. The day she would have to call him she knew she was finished as an actress. No, she'd never call him. Why should she want to? Who was he? Probably some young boy who thought he was something now as a lot of them did merely because the government had made officers out of them. He was probably some terrible little runny-nosed youngster from Paddington a few years before the war. Well, she thought almost at once, but who were you, Helen, before that agent saw you in Harrow, playing Ophelia? How ghastly you were then! How had he ever seen any potential in you? She picked up the telephone, called a Whitehall number.

'Hello ... may I speak to Group Captain Hedges?'

He was a nice old boy. She'd met him at a cocktail party, and he'd tried to hold her hand and tell her about flying SE 5s in the first show in France, '18, and she'd let him touch knees under the table. He was terribly unhappy he wasn't flying in this show, and maybe some kneesies under the table would pep up the old boy's morale. It certainly didn't trouble her, and she felt sorry for him, and towards the end of the party he asked to take her home but that was too much. Well, one thing he was a gentleman, he had bowed out gracefully and told her to call him if ever he could be a help, whatever he meant by that because it was certain she wasn't interested in going into the service. She felt guilty when these thoughts came to mind, but then she told herself, well, how many people have as much talent as I have. I can do more giving shows to the troops than working in an army canteen or office, and then she would feel all right again.

'I'm sorry,' the voice came over the wire. 'Captain Hedges has left for the day.'

She didn't say anything for a moment. What kind of a war were they running? Here it was only noon and Hedges was gone.

She hung up and looked at her watch. The whole day seemed to stretch ahead in an unending sameness. She knew exactly what she would do. She could go to the Ivy for lunch. She would know everybody there and they would all say the same things they said yesterday. Damn, why had she ever met that Butler? Where was he? She went into her bedroom and dressed, looking out the window down Curzon Street. The sky was high and clear. She wished she were down in Cornwall. It would be lovely on the beach, just to lie there and forget this smokey, dusty old city, forget everything, and soak up a little sunlight.

It was almost twelve-thirty when she stepped out into the sunlight on Curzon Street and walked slowly down the street. She was wearing a brown plaid suit and she felt very country in it, as if she were faintly an impostor, but she felt beautiful most of all, so she did not care what the ugly woman was thinking of, passed and gave her a brief, single glance of criticism as if to say, you are not fooling anybody in that tweed suit, my dear, I know an actress when I see one.

She turned into Shepherd's Market, and she began to think of a long lunch. She saw the taxi coming up the street. She went on staring at it, her mind blank, deciding in some far recess that she had slept too long this morning. She still felt tired. She saw the man get out of the taxi, turn to pay the driver and she walked on steadily, still seeing the man, thinking she would come straight home after tonight's show. No, she hadn't slept too long. That wasn't it at all. That wasn't why she felt so tired. The trouble was she had been out too late. And what a bore, just going out because somebody asked you to go out and one didn't want to come straight home alone after the show at night.

'Hello,' a man's face said.

'Hello,' she said, not really looking at him, thinking, it must be somebody I met at a party.

'Hello.' The voice was behind her now, and she turned and stared at it. 'You look like a girl I'd like to take to lunch.'

The face was smiling. She looked for an instant, and just before she spoke suddenly she thought, God's teeth, I do need some more sleep, some more something.

'Jimmy!' she said. 'Good heavens.'

She felt nervous as though she were acting like a little girl on her first date.

'Jimmy Butler,' she said, and she wondered what her hands were doing. Her mouth felt dry and she wished she were smoking a cigarette.

'Helen.' He looked up in the air with an expression of exaggerated loss of memory. 'Helen. Mmm.' He was laughing at her, but she did not have the feeling he was being mean or that he was trying to dominate her the way some men did when they joshed her good naturedly, acting almost as if they were a little afraid of her. He was laughing just as her brother used to laugh and he gave her a comfortable feeling she had never known before so quickly with a stranger.

'Helen Collins,' she said, putting on a mock air of irritation as if she felt he hadn't remembered her full name.

'West End actress?'

She stepped back and bowed as she did at the end of the show every night,

121

standing out in front of the curtain. Then she stepped back toward him.

'Jimmy Butler.' She said it as if quoting a press release. 'Gallant airman.' But she could feel almost at once she had said the wrong thing. What's worrying him, she thought.

'All right. All right,' he said, and then looking at her he began to smile. That had been three months ago, three months of waiting after lunch that day for him to come up to London every weekend, three months of lying awake at night, thinking, he's dead, he died today, seeing his body burned, staring at her out of death, three months of waking up cold and trembling, crying, thinking, he's dead someplace, he's dead, her whole body cringing in upon itself, writhing out of loss. But almost every week he came to see her. Until, well, she hated that memory now. She would not think of it. She could feel her mind fighting against it. She should not, could not go through those days again when he had been reported missing. She had never known her body could be in such agony before; she had never known grief and longing and worry could make her feel so terrible. Her whole body had become heavy, lost, and she felt as though only her mind was forcing her to lift her arms and legs. She had dropped out of the show for a week. She had seen him twice in hospital, and that had helped some because he was always laughing at her and smiling and telling her she ought to join up and get a few trips in, what did she think the government could do, win the war with stage shows for the troops. He made her angry, but after seeing him her whole body felt light and airy and her whole being was filled with joy again. He was coming up to town again tonight. This would be the first time she had seen him in London since he had left the rest home.

She sat in front of the mirror of her dressing table in her apartment. Sunday night was a heavenly night, she decided. It couldn't be better. This was the most heavenly night in weeks. No show, and Jimmy was coming up, and they would go out. He hated the Bagatelle, but she felt in the mood for something grand and slightly royal and the Bagatelle always made her feel that way at dinner. It was going to be the Bagatelle. She had made him promise on the phone. God's teeth, she didn't care where it was. Better it was here in his arms. Better that than all the Bagatelles in the world.

She dressed slowly and when he arrived, they had two drinks in her apartment. Outside in the dark they rode down Piccadilly in a taxi, seeing the searchlights coming on, the figures in the dark disappearing under the arched walk in front of the Ritz. She felt peaceful and she sat beside him silently, feeling his hand over hers, both their hands resting on her silken thigh. I love him, she thought and suddenly the impossibility of ever being able to express all of it that was in her at this moment touched her and she pressed his hand hard. He seemed to be thinking of something, and in the dark she looked at his face. He felt remote. Somehow suddenly he had gone away from her.

'Perhaps you'll be able to get up to town more often,' she said. 'Everything seems to have quieted down.'

'It would be nice if Jerry stayed home for a few weeks.'

'Flying?'

'Not yet.'

'I'd love to see you fly.'

'Can't see much.'

'I mean I'd like to see you in the air. In, uh, oh, I know this sounds silly, in a battle.'

Butler laughed.

'Wish a chap some extra leave? Much nicer, you know.'

'But why not? If you're in the air, I'd like to see it.'

'Have you ever seen dog fights?'

'Very little. You know, they haven't really touched us here too much. I can hear them firing but it's far away. Darling are you really as good as those ribbons say?'

'Much better,' he said, with exaggerated seriousness.

'Darling, did you ever know a Group Captain Allard?'

She felt his hand tighten. But he did not move.

'Yes.' His voice was quite flat. 'Do you know him?'

She wondered suddenly if she had said something wrong. Heavens, she thought, all I was trying to do was make a little conversation.

'Know him? I don't know him. I've only met him. He was with some Americans one night when they came back stage.'

'Allard back stage?' Butler laughed.

'He didn't look too happy.'

'He's a grand chap. Not exactly the stage door type.'

'He was very nice. Does he fly? Do Group Captains fly?'

Butler made a noise, put his hand to his mouth.

'What's the matter?'

'Wish a few Groupies could hear you.'

'Well, darling, I don't know. You're the nearest thing to Group Captain that I've ever known—the nearest to flight. Honestly, all the Group Captains I've met have been nice but they all worked in offices.'

'Allard's a pilot. Damn good pilot but he's better behind a desk now.'

'You do know him?'

'My commanding officer.'

Helen smiled. 'I should have been nicer to him. Perhaps he would have promoted you to a desk.'

'I'll let you know when, darling.'

'Jimmy,' she said, suddenly. 'Why not—now? You've done enough.'

He ignored her, leaned forward, spoke to the driver.

'Here we are.' He was still leaning forward, reaching in his pocket for his wallet. The taxi stopped. He seemed to evade her all the way across the pavement, with his silence until she wondered if he had heard her. All right, she thought, get yourself killed. And for an instant, she was bitterly angry with him.

Then the head waiter and the lights inside were shining on them, the head waiter's smile and face flashing and blending in the lights. 'Helen,' he said, smiling, bowing them in.

'What's the charge for this opening curtain?' Jimmy smiled and pinched her arm. And again she was happy and the anger and bitterness was gone and she felt as she always felt with Jimmy, almost lifted out of herself.

'I pay him myself, darling,' she whispered. 'Five pounds a week to call my name out.' They followed the head waiter across the dance floor.

She was glad the table was in the corner. Jimmy never liked to sit next to the door. He said he enjoyed her popularity but when he took her out, he didn't want to feel as if half the room were dining with them, and he was right because somebody was always staring at her, she could see and feel the glances, hear their voices saying, 'Isn't that Helen Collins?' It never bothered her anymore but she remembered how it had annoyed her at one time after she grew tired of the first pleasure of it happening to her.

She liked having him order. She liked what he ordered. It amused her thinking how she enjoyed having him order. All her life men had been telling her what to do. But with Jimmy—oh, she couldn't explain it to herself, and it didn't matter. It felt peaceful and comfortable sitting close to him, feeling his arm against her side, hearing his voice, the music beating in the room, the lights. The Tokay wine was clear and cold. Somehow it was just right without being too sweet. She felt her whole being blooming softly inside her heart, and she turned towards Jimmy and pressed his hand under the table.

'Dance?' he asked. They looked across the floor in the darkness, sipping the cool wine, hearing the steady, soft sound of music.

'Do you want to?' she asked. She did not want to move now. It was wonderful here, just sitting in the darkness, the wine blending her into the music and the darkness.

He lifted his glass, touched hers, drank.

'Let's wait,' he said. He did not want to move. He could feel her whole being against him, the soft curve of her thigh, the softness of her arm, the soft, sweet odour of her hair. He felt as if he would never die, as if he had never been afraid.

'Cut,' she said and smiled.

'What?'

'Cut, darling.' She tried to sound light and gay and casual. But it was all too much like a movie. She felt frightened that something more real could lie beyond this room, the world, waiting patiently, like a monster.

'Have some more wine,' Jimmy smiled. He had the wonderful feeling tomorrow was inconsequential. He knew it was a silly idea, but he knew he was not going to think about it. He was only going to enjoy the wonderful elation now of the wine inside himself.

'Darling, I love being here with you.'

'Cut.' He grinned. He felt her hand change in his hand under the table, some of the warmth and life go out of it.

'You started it,' he said, smiling. 'Come on. Some more wine.'

She looked at her glass as he poured. 'I'm sorry,' she said.

He could see she felt different suddenly. He could see he had destroyed something quite fragile between them, some blend of the wine and music, their hands touching. 'But it had to,' he thought. 'Nothing could ever go on that perfectly any longer than we have just known.'

'Who was there before?' she asked.

'Before?'

'Darling, don't tell me I was your first date.'

Jimmy laughed.

'Yes, Mummy warned me about girls.'

'What did she say?'

'They're very expensive.'

'You took her advice?'

'I'll never know until I see the cheque.'

'Butler, I hate you.'

She hit him on the shoulder and he laughed and drew back. Then he smiled and said suddenly: 'Before yourself. How about you?'

Suddenly she smiled brightly, too brightly.

'I'd love a drink, Jimmy.'

'Who?'

130

'Chap. Nice chap. Please a nice, big drink, Jimmy.'

'What happened?'

'What happens?' she asked. She held up her hands, palm out. 'What happens to everybody nice now? They get killed.'

'I'm sorry.'

'It's all right. Nice big drink, Jimmy, please.'

It scared him because he saw a face, leaning forward, the flames coming back from the cowl, the blue sea far down, the burned face staring down in death. Christ, Christ, it was himself, going down. He would have a damn big drink. That would keep it out. Whisky. Tokay was all right to start out but it wouldn't pull all the way. Not enough boost in Tokay. Chap needs whisky for the long haul. All right, he thought, all right, Butler, you've had too much Tokay.

'I don't know too much about you,' he said suddenly. I shouldn't have said that, he thought, knowing he had been rude, feeling his face hot and bright. I must stop drinking, he thought.

'I have a sister and brother.' She smiled at him as if he were a child. 'Both of them are in school. Father's in the army.

Mummy's dead. I've always wanted to be an actress. See.' She faced him smiling, holding hands palm up in a simple gesture as if she were saying she revealed all.

'Let's dance.' He started to rise. She caught his arm.

'Oh no. Now it's your turn. What about you?'

He turned his head, looking at her over his shoulder.

'The Butlers are people who are trying to live up to a game outmoded. We keep telling ourselves certain things are expected of us. Who expects it anymore?'

She felt he was all confused and miserable but there did not seem to be any way she could reach him with sympathy or understanding, and she was certain he wanted neither now. But she could not stop saying what she knew he did not want to hear.

'Jimmy, do you have to go back on flying?'

'I'd look good behind a desk.'

'Couldn't you work at headquarters or teach or—?'

'Or give lectures to the war workers. No.' He shook his head. 'It would be a waste, all I know now. It would be a waste on the ground.'

She sat there wondering what he must feel in the air, feeling as she had felt as a little girl looking far out to sea, the immeasurable blue blending into the hazy summer horizon, wondering where people went when ships vanished across the afternoon air.

'Is there something that won't let you quit?' she asked. 'Is there something you have to do? Don't tell me the RAF couldn't spare one pilot?'

'I can't explain it. It's a lot of things. It started a long time ago, in school, when I first learned to fly. It doesn't have anything do with patriotism. Perhaps it has, but I don't feel that. It's an act of individuality, that's all I can feel. It has nothing to do with ideologies, hatred or frontiers. There must be others on the other side that feel the same thing.'

You're scared, he thought, stop it. You never needed reasons until you were scared. You never even thought this much about it before.

'But you've done enough,' she said.

He shook his head furiously. Why couldn't she stop talking about it?

'No. No. You can't know,' he said. 'If

133

you've never flown, I couldn't make you understand.'

'I wish I could understand.'

'Perhaps we weren't meant to. Come on,' he laughed. 'I'm a rotten philosopher. Let's dance.'

They danced and, without speaking, she held him tight. The music sounded sad under the lights and he could feel the Tokay slipping away, the warm, light feeling inside him going. And on the floor, in the crowd, he could feel death moving, invisible, in all the faces. It had a shape. He could feel it following him around the floor.

'Let's go,' he said.

'You're tired,' she said. 'Come on, darling.'

Outside under the stars she looked up at the night. Searchlights sabred the darkness over Green Park. It was a lovely, soft summer night.

'Let's walk,' she said. They turned into Piccadilly and went on past the Ritz looming big and black and turned into Half-Moon Street.

She lived in Chesterfield House and they went up in the lift.

'You should get some sleep,' she said.

'Are you flying tomorrow?'

'No.' Why couldn't she shut up? He wished he were in the air now. He wished it were tomorrow. He hated putting it off. Christ, I've got to wind up, he thought.

'Jim, I think I'll go down to Folkestone. I could see it all from there. I want to be near you.'

'Don't hurry. They'll be over here soon.'

'When?'

'I don't know.'

The lift stopped and they got out and went along the hall. She opened the door. Inside it was cool and dark. She turned on one table lamp. The walls were white and the carpet on the floor was white. He did not like the room. It reminded him of the hospital.

'Do we have to sit in here?' he asked.

No, that was the wrong thing. He had never hurried her before. It would sound as if he were hurrying her. God, to lie down, to rest. Damn it, I drank too much, he thought. He could feel his arm throbbing.

'You're worse than the Americans, darling. Rush. Rush. Do you mind if I catch my breath for a moment?'

He heard her leave the room. He sat

staring at the wall. Where was she? She seemed to have left a century ago.

He got up and went out of the room and along the hall. The light was shining in her bedroom. She was brushing her hair. He put his arms around her. He could feel her whole body trembling, swollen with love. She turned and her lips were hot and trembling and later in the darkness when their naked bodies filled each other with love he felt again as he had felt with her the first time, that he had never known such delight and wonder before.

He had lunch with her the next noon in Shepherd's Bar. But later in the hot afternoon light, watching the fields of Kent beyond the train window, he was glad to be going back to the squadron. He stooped his head and looked out at the high white cloud motionless in the windless summer air. It was a beautiful day for flying.

But even as he thought this, his stomach fluttered. I don't want to fly combat again, he thought, I don't really want to. He had the sensation after a while that if he rose his legs would not move him. He sat there, staring out of the window.

CHAPTER SIX

Group Captain Allard looked at his watch. He should have flown up from Fighter Command headquarters instead of taking the train. The bloody train out of London to Oxford always was slow, too many stops. He should have bought another paper. He'd read the *Mail* twice now. Another hour to Richfield.

He wondered if it were going to be any use. One couldn't make an assembly line work faster simply by paying a visit to a factory and talking things over with the management. But the kites were ready. Perhaps it would be best not to go near the factory, just stay with the air force test chaps and pep them up and get them to give a quick release on the new kites available even if all the kinks had not been ironed out.

He felt oppressed. Why didn't air ministry give a release on the kites even if they weren't perfect yet? Didn't they realize the group couldn't face those new Hun kites in the old Spits? Better to take a crack at them in a none-too-perfect new kite than get killed for sure in an old Mark Four. But what if he flew one himself and got Air Vice Commander Wilder, in charge of the test field, to release the kites and send them down to group without an okay from ministry. Somebody had to act soon. There wasn't much time left. It was only a matter of days perhaps. He glanced at the *Daily Mail* again, turning the pages without seeing the print.

He looked out at the country. It was truly England here. He loved this time of day, the hour, just before dusk, with the green light in the trees rising out of the meadows, sky and earth blending, the green light rising like water slowly, steadily, trees and hills blurring greenly. But he could still see the Buckinghamshire hills now, long, low, forests of oaks on the slopes, with the last dying shafts of sunlight shining down through the leaves. The train sped along between green meadows and crossed a bridge with a clear stream shining underneath and passed through a little village with small white-walled houses. A captain in the King's Royal Rifles slept in the corner of the seat across the aisle.

He hoped they wouldn't want to talk about the Spits tonight at Richfield. He was tired. Tomorrow would be soon enough. He'd been up to headquarters all day. Nobody was certain when the Hun was coming in full strength again. It was all rule of the thumb, and be ready, and though all the plans looked good, one was never certain they would still work even though they'd worked so far. But one couldn't go on losing kites right and left, day after day, old kites, too, and if the Hun kept throwing in more and more squadrons he was going to get through eventually. His mind darted and flicked over information and plans projected at the headquarters staff meeting. On paper everything looked fine. But nothing ever worked out in the air as it did on paper. He watched the people getting on the train at Henley and then he sat back, closed his eyes, felt the train jerk. He woke in the dark upon the sound of people moving in the compartment. The compartment door was open. He looked out into the darkness, smelling cool air.

'Oxford,' the conductor was calling in the aisle beyond the compartment.

Allard rose, blinking his eyes, drew his hat and briefcase and leather overnight bag off the rack above his head and stepped out into the darkness upon the cement station platform.

He went on through the station, out under the dim light on the side facing the street. A soft breeze blew up the street, and he stood there thinking of his youth for an instant, feeling sad, seeing in his mind the buildings of Christ Church College across the town, with a sense somehow of the wartime shabbiness of a town that had had a certain magic for him in a time that was dead. He shook his head, lit a cigarette. A man came towards him out of the darkness. Under the station light Allard remarked the three chevrons on the sleeve of the man's blue tunic. He looked at Allard.

'Group Captain Allard?'

'Car here, sergeant?'

'Yes, sir. I'll drive up. We weren't—'

'I'll walk down, sergeant.'

They went down the street. The car was parked on the cobblestones towards the end of the station.

They got in, Allard in the rear, with the window open beside his face. As the engine started, a Whitley bomber passed low, blinking red and green running lights, the engines hammering sound down upon the street.

They drove on out of town, passing through almost empty streets. They passed Christ Church College, the building big and white and square in the moonlight. Then they were out on the highway, driving fast, with the fields white and silvery on each side of the road. Allard began to wish he had eaten before he left London. He felt hungry and tired. The mess would be closed. Perhaps he should stop at the Randolph Hotel and catch a drink and quick meal. No, better he had a drink in the mess and early to bed if he were going to fly tomorrow.

The road went on in the moonlight, ribboning black and shining between the fields with an even patina of silver on them as the moonlight glowed up random, thin wisps of fog rising from the wet grass.

The even speed of the car made Allard feel drowsy and he put his head back, but he could not sleep. He kept thinking over and over again what he had not wanted to think about all the way down on the train: why didn't they release the kites if they were ready? Why hadn't somebody told him they were ready? He'd only found it out this afternoon at headquarters when that young Flight Lieutenant at Fighter Headquarters had let it drop apparently. But why should Command keep it a secret from me? Why had they told me before when I asked for the new kites that they might be ready but weren't yet? Had they meant they weren't manufactured yet? Or they were and something was wrong with them or there weren't enough? But enough for what? Enough for Butler's Wing. Bloody hell, that was enough, why couldn't ministry see that and give me the gen? The Old Man himself had said at staff meeting it was going to be up to Butler's Wing to break up the attack. Why has everybody been hiding something from me? He'd been under the impression from Air Commodore Fletcher, that the kites weren't off the assembly line but this Flight Lieutenant had let the cat out of the bag when he'd said this afternoon the new 'kite was ruddy marvellous'. Well, I'll find out myself, he thought, wondering if Command Headquarters would squawk if they knew he had come up to Richfield on his own. Let them squawk, he thought, and we'll win the war.

He felt the car slowing. He opened his

eyes, looked out at the aerodrome gate, the sentry box, the sentry's flashlight shining down on the driver's identity card. Then in through the gate and along the white pavement between the administration buildings to turn and stop in front of the Richfield Mess, a big, dark, square building. Trees along one side screened the hangars beyond across a field of darkness.

The driver opened the door, reached in, took the briefcase and overnight bag. Allard followed him into the Mess.

The hall was empty, but down at the end a light shone.

'You're in room ten, sir,' said the sergeant. 'I'll put your bags in there.'

'Righto. Thank you, sergeant.'

'Good night, sir.'

'Good night, sergeant.'

Voices came out of the light that became a rectangle of light as he approached it. Inside, around a table, sat four RAF officers playing bridge. Allard paused in the doorway, saw the empty chairs by the fireplace, the long leather davenports, the big empty chairs beside the windows at the far end of the room. The bridge players did not look up. To the right, just inside the door, a corporal stood behind the bar. From the wall above the bar hung black plastic models of German fighters and bombers. Allard glanced at them briefly as he walked towards the bar. We better be ready, he thought. Dungeness. They'll be over like flies. They'll clobber us.

CHAPTER SEVEN

Allard could not sleep. He woke twice in the night, hearing planes passing low overhead, twin engines, lying there identifying the planes to pass the time. Blenheims, he kept thinking, seeing the shape in his mind until he slept.

When he woke, he felt the smallness of his room, and he got up and pulled aside the blackout curtain. Dawn light, grey, as of the colour of water, filled the air. He opened the window, taking a deep breath, smelling sweet wet morning grass.

Dressed, he walked outside, and standing on the flat low apron of cement in front of the Mess doorway, looked up at the sky glazed in the first light. From far away, he heard the thunder of bombers returning from across the channel.

He looked through the trees beside the Mess building, wishing he could see the planes beyond, but a faint mist covered the field. Soon the sun would burn it away and he would see the Spits ranked beside the hangars. He smoked a cigarette but it tasted flat and stale. He threw it away before it was half finished and went back into the Mess.

The hall was empty, silent, and he went on into the dining room. The rows of tables with white tablecloths were empty. He felt tired and longed for a cup of tea. He walked towards the kitchen and pushed open one of the swinging doors.

A tall young WAAF with a dark Cornish face and her hair pulled back flat over her head to a pug on the back of her skull stood in front of the stove with steam rising across her face. She was stirring something in a large black pot over the stove. She did not look up when she spoke:

'Yes, sir?'

'Sorry,' said Allard. 'Afraid I'm up a little early. Just stopping here. Wonder if I could—'

The girl had a long, straight beautiful face and when she smiled, he saw all her white teeth even against her faintly olive skin.

'Cup of tea, sir?'

'Grand.'

'I'll bring it in, sir.'

'Thank you. I say, does Wilder—'

'About eight, sir.'

'Thank you.'

He walked back into the dining room, sat down at a table beside the windows, smoked another cigarette. He looked out at the faint fog, the sun burning through, the branches of trees shining wet in the morning light. The tea was just what he wanted, hot and thick, strong, and he drank it fast, smoking another cigarette, feeling his body glow.

It was seven-thirty when he walked out into the hall. Pilots passed quickly, carrying shaving kits and towels. Allard walked outside.

What a day to die, he thought, looking up at the sky. It was going to be a lovely day, hot and bright, the sky empty and blue.

He looked across the road beside the Mess and through the trees saw the aerodrome beyond with the hangars looking big and curve-domed in the pale-blue morning light. Then he saw the Spits, ranked, trim, vicious as wasps, yet standing delicately on their stork-like undercarts in three rows.

He stepped down off the cement apron in front of the Mess and crossed the road. He was walking between two Spitfires when he heard the voices, and then he saw the three men. He recognized Air Commodore Calder. He began to smile. He hadn't seen Calder since middle east days when Calder had been his Wing Commander. Almost ten years.

Then Calder was smiling—coming towards him—tall, dark, with a big black moustache now, older looking but still swaggering, a little round shouldered but somehow youthful with an MC ribbon from the first war.

'Allard, old chap, how are you?'

'Hello, Bert.'

They shook hands and smiled, looking at each other, as if thinking for a brief instant of all the years in between.

'What time did you get in?' Calder asked.

'Late.'

147

'I say, this is a surprise. Didn't expect you.'

He glanced at the man on his right, short, stocky with blue eyes and brown hair, and a metal hook sticking out of his right sleeve.

'Squadron Leader Calhoun, Group Captain Allard. Calhoun's my adjutant.'

'Wish we'd known you were coming,' said Calhoun, shaking hands, watching Allard closely.

'This is Stevens,' said Calder quickly, and smiling as he looked at the Flight Lieutenant on his left with the DFC and Bar, and AFC ribbons above his wings. 'He tells us if they're going to work. If they work, Stevens still has a job. If not—' he laughed, 'eh, Stevens?' Calder's laugh sounded bright, innocent.

Stevens, was small, slight, almost frail looking, with sandy, reddish hair, and small intelligent eyes that were at once almost expressionless.

'How do you do, sir?' he said to Allard and shook hands almost shyly.

'Eaten yet?' Calder asked. Then: 'I say, this is a surprise. Last time I saw you the fuzzy wallahs were chasing you in the bazaar and—'

Allard shook his head, grinned.

'I say, Allard, this is astonishing. Never thought—'

Bloody hell, thought Allard, are we going to fight the battle of our extreme youth over again?

'Let's eat, chaps,' said Calder. They went on to the Mess. They had cold steamed fish and toast and hot tea.

'Eat too much,' said Calder. 'All of us. War will make us all healthy. I can't stand this bloody Mess food anymore.'

Allard looked across the field at the Spitfires with the sun shining on their unpainted wings.

'I haven't any flying equipment with me,' he said.

'No matter,' said Calder. 'Calhoun'll take care of you—if you need it.'

'I thought I might,' said Allard. 'I want to see what your new kites'll do.'

If I need it he thought. Does he mean all the kites are wonky here, even the new ones?

'Finished?' said Calder. 'More tea? Where are those girls?' He half turned, glanced around the room. 'Fakirs, all of them. Gone the minute one wants them.'

They drank more tea and then went

outside. They drove across the field in a Morris and parked outside an open hangar.

'Kane was down yesterday for a new kite,' said Calder. 'I couldn't let him have one, though.'

'What's the trouble?' Allard asked.

'Don't want to kill our own air force, do we?' said Calder, glancing at Calhoun.

'Structural?' Allard asked.

Calder shrugged.

'We don't know.'

Allard looked at the three Spitfires standing in the hangar. Fitters and riggers were working on them, and the wings of one were stripped, with the skeleton of ribs showing like a scaled fish.

'There isn't time to know,' said Allard, looking up at the sky.

Calder did not say anything. A slim pencil-like twin engine aircraft slow rolled over the field. Allard had never seen one before. Something experimental, he thought.

'Nice?' asked Calder. 'You'll be operating them in two years.'

'If we're lucky,' said Allard, his voice quiet.

He stared across the field at the row of Spitfires with a respectful and longing air. The Spits reared on shining wheels, newly painted, the propellers motionless, taking sunlight in rigid glints. The wings looked taut, new, the noses shark-like, the fuselages clean and bright. Allard walked along with Calder as they strolled among the machines.

Mid-morning drew on. The light in the air was beginning to turn golden.

'I say, what about some tea in my office?' Calder asked. The tone of his voice did not include the other two officers. 'Almost time, you know.'

The two officers stood a little behind Calder, erect, quite still.

'Calhoun,' said Calder. 'Ring up Mifford over at Thirty-One, tell him we'll send oleo legs down this afternoon.'

'Short supply sir.'

'I know, I know. Give him half a dozen.'

Calder turned.

'Come along,' he said to Allard.

From the square desk in the middle of the room, Calder produced two glasses, a bottle of whisky.

'*Glenlivet,*' Calder said. 'Twelve years old.'

'Oh,' said Allard.

151

'Topping for old birds like me. Gad, morning. Chap can't do it in front of his junior officer, eh?'

Allard smiled, picked up his glass. The whisky was pleasant, yet almost unbearable as it hit his stomach. He saw Calder jerk his head back, the glass empty as if by magic in his hand.

Allard sat down in the chair in front of the desk. In a moment the whisky was more pleasant inside him. He looked at the framed photographs on the wall, some of then yellow, the faces in them lean, strained, above long leather jackets or infantry regimental tunics. They looked unreal, completely out of place, standing against the canvas-covered rudders and cockpits of SE 5s, Sopwith Camels, Dolphin Fighters. All the old pilots, all the dead pilots. He could see some of their names on the faded photographs: Mannock, Ball, Barker, Bishop, Brabazon, Rees, McCudden, Hawker.

Better they all died then, he thought, seeing them thick-stomached or too swaggering now like Calder, not good enough to fly in this one, having to sit behind desks, looking with longing and regret baffled by time.

Calder was saying, 'Did my turn last time. Damn good show. Went out in 'sixteen on Pups. Caught a packet. Hip. Nothing bad. Few tracers. Chap keeps his eyes open he can get through. Good bunch of chaps today. Still have the stuff. Ruddy wonderful the way they toss these masses of gadgets around. Couldn't do it myself. Lot different than the old buses we had.'

'Suppose so,' said Allard.

'Have to laugh. We just used to ride them, you know. Ruddy Camels. Set the air valve. That's all you had to know to fly one properly. Landed in a meadow once up in Cambrai. They were shelling Amiens. I was lost. Four chaps came out of a shellhole, told me where I was.'

'About the Spits,' Allard said. He looked at the empty glasses on the table.

'Kill you chaps.'

'Chance we have to take,' Allard leaned forward. 'Listen, we have to have them. Don't care who says no.'

'Ministry would—'

'Maybe I came down here with the order.'

'Wait,' said Calder. He twisted in the chair and bent over. Allard heard the desk drawer opening. Then he saw the bottle

153

tilted abruptly above the glass across the table and then the glass lifted and Calder's throat working.

'Ah-ah,' said Calder, setting the empty glass down.

'Court martial both of us,' Calder said.

'I showed you the order releasing the kites. Remember?'

Calder smiled. He shook his head.

'Kill the lot of you.'

'What's the trouble?'

'Main spar. Something wrong. Don't really know.'

'How many have you tested?'

'Five. All ropey.'

'I'll fly one.'

'I won't even let Stevens up. Not anymore. Bloody ace. Our kites. Wings came off five. Six turns in a spin. Almost didn't get out last time.'

'You've got to.'

'I can't.'

'What difference will it make? Huns'll kill us anyway in that first wave in the ruddy old kites we're using.'

'I know. I know. Just how you chaps feel. Like 'seventeen. Couldn't fly the Dophins. Ruddy Albatross scouts murdered us.'

'But if we win?'

154

'What?'

'If we win?'

'What do you mean, Allard?'

For an instant there seemed something gaunt and tragic in Calder's face, as if he felt something might happen to make up for all the lost years since the war. He's been dead all those years, Allard thought, since the night in November 1918, when they called it off.

Yes, a voice said inside Allard, and when this is over, and ten years afterwards, if you live through it, you'll be taking the morning train to the desk job at Ministry in London, still wishing for those extra years in the war that would have made you young enough now to fly. Thoughts of a time when he flew regularly enveloped his consciousness again, and he felt, as if in an old dream, that once he was in a Spitfire it would all feel as if he had never been away.

'If we win you'll be in the clear,' said Allard. 'It's funny. Perhaps even a medal.'

Yes, Allard thought, perhaps that will do it, that will sell him.

'Really,' said Calder, as if faintly shocked, but there was interest in his eyes.

'Look. I brought the release from the ministry. That's all you know. However, when and if they ask, you can also say that despite the release, you were quite uneasy about letting the machines go so—' He paused. 'There's nothing to worry about.'

'I'm not worried,' said Calder.

'Were the five wonky ones all of a consecutive series?'

Calder nodded.

'All right. I'll test one. Like I said. That should ease your mind.'

'You'll kill yourself.'

'How do you know they're all wonky?'

'We don't.'

'There you are,' Allard smiled. 'Can't you see yourself at the board of inquiry. "Sir, Allard had the release form, and he tested the next in the series and it worked, so I released them."'

Calder did not smile, his face motionless, quite grave.

'We won't know until all the wing spars are checked.'

'But it could be?'

'What?'

'That they're not all wonky. Besides, what difference does it make?' Allard's voice and eyes changed. His voice became intense, urgent. 'Can't you see it? We're damned if we don't use these kites and we're damned if we do. But it's worth a chance to find out.'

Calder did not move. He looked at his empty glass.

'All right?' Allard asked.

After a long moment, Calder looked up.

'I don't know. I can't say now,' he said. He picked up the whisky bottle. 'Ruddy awful, isn't it? Price a chap has to pay for good whisky in a bar.'

That night, Allard dreamed of the morning sky and in the dream he saw himself falling with the blood drained from his head and his eyes blind while his hands scrambled at the cockpit hood release ... I don't have to do this ... he kept saying over and over again in the dream ... Calder will release them without a test ... I don't have to test one ... I don't have to spin it ...

But in the morning he knew why he was going to spin one. He must. The time had come when he must risk himself again, not for the planes so much but because it had been too long, too long behind the desk, too long glorifying incidents of peace time flying when he had never flown combat in the war, too long since the fear of death had glowed in his mind.

CHAPTER EIGHT

Two hours after daylight, Allard sat high in the cockpit, feeling the parachute straps pressing hard against the inside of his thighs. His stomach felt tight and his mouth dry. He manipulated the hand pumps and pushed the starter button, watching the propeller turn slowly. Suddenly he felt the engine fire and the whole machine shuddering under him. He raised his hand for the chocks to be pulled.

In a silent group, the mechanics strolled over to Calder and two pilots who stood watching a few feet away. Allard smiled and waved but he could not keep from thinking, 'Whatever made me volunteer for this? What if the bloody wing does pull off?' He felt for the rip-cord ring, making sure he knew where it was. Then he smelled carbon-dioxide from the exhaust fumes seeping into the cockpit and he hurriedly put on his oxygen mask and turned on the intake valve. It was always like this on take-off, and everything was all right as long as one stayed on oxygen.

He looked around the cockpit, everything in its ordered place, petrol cock, magneto switches, the myriad of dials of instruments. He touched the undercarriage retraction button, the trim tab lever. Everything was set. He saw all the instruments and levers in his mind, even himself sitting in the cockpit.

Why am I here, why am I doing this? he asked himself again, knowing it was not truly necessary, but even as he was thinking his hands were moving, the stick hand back in his stomach, holding the brakes on, his eyes darting over the instruments, checking revolutions, oil pressure. Slowly he shoved the throttle forward. He began to feel the machine trembling deeper and deeper in the fuselage. Blasting waves of roaring sound crashed against the cockpit canopy. He found he was holding his breath, a faint worm of fear moving minutely in his stomach. He throttled down, checked to see if the radiator was open wide. Damn. It was closed. That's what came from sitting behind a desk too much.

Then he turned his head and smiled and saw Calder's lifted hand. With it, Calder made a short, cheery thumbs-up salute. Then Allard was taxiing out. At the mouth of the runway, he looked up at the sky, high, clear, quite empty.

Holding his breath, he pushed the throttle wide open and held the stick hard back. Abruptly, the engine snarled at full speed, and he felt himself filled again with an old sensation of childlike interest and delight at the thought of flying. He could feel the noise of the engine outside, the deafening, snarling roar. He pushed the stick forward. He did not feel as if he were moving fast, but almost at once he saw hangars and trees and parked aeroplanes fleeing backwards at a dizzy speed from the corner of his right eye. He saw the end of the field coming nearer, the jagged crest of a row of trees. He pulled up the undercarriage, hauled back on the stick, felt himself tilt suddenly and rush skyward, as if the machine had been freed of a weight. He felt himself zooming in a long upward climbing turn. He pushed the stick forward, throttled back. Then he looked back and down. Far away a black ribbon bisecting a green field marked the runway.

A few minutes later the trees, the field of open country were far beneath him. He looked at the altimeter. Fifteen thousand feet. He hauled the stick back hard, felt the machine mush, watched the air speed drop. He eased the stick forward, watched the ground hurtle upward, feeling sweat on the back of his hands. He watched the revolutions needle rise, with a hard, hot ball in his stomach, thinking, now, now, while he looked out at the wings. He checked his air speed. Three fifty, and scared, he moved the stick back. His forehead was damp. He held the stick back, grunting, feeling his eyes growing darker and darker, lifting into his skull. He said Ah-ah-ah, as if it might bring back vision. Then his eyes were open, and looking out, he saw he was flying straight and level, and he eased back the throttle.

He checked the controls carefully, all the instruments, tried a flick roll, came out too fast and almost fell off in a spin. He closed the throttle, stroked the stick back, flew level, checked the controls and instruments again. He did not want to spin it. He did not want to try even two turns. He was scared and ashamed. Maybe Calder was right. Maybe the wing spar was weak on this one, but if I don't he thought, if I don't. Thinking stopped for an instant in his head. Then he thought, I must, I must. Chap never knows himself until he's scared. Then he thought firmly, with a kind of triumph, all right, Allard, go on, kick it over, kick it over.

He closed the throttle, eased the nose up, watched the air speed drop, feeling the hard, hot ball of fear growing bigger and bigger in his stomach. The stick felt sloppy in his hands. He kicked right rudder, saw the sky tilt. He hauled the stick back hard.

The nose dropped as if it were something human suddenly bitten by a snake. With his face to the sky, he felt the machine going into the first turn of a spin. He felt himself banged against the back of the seat, pressed down.

The earth and horizon whirled and he seemed to be plunging through an immense water-like pool of sunlight. He saw a clotting of black dots swooping up, the sky empty. The earth rolled upward. He counted five turns, looked out at the wings, mirror-like, glinting in the sunlight, cold and smooth. Thank God, they're holding. Yet fear sucked his guts.

He kicked top rudder, pushed the stick central, waited for the machine to come out. It bucked and spun again and he cursed it and held the stick forward, putting on the opposite rudder. He worked the throttle furiously. He could feel the blood pounding in his ears. He started to think about bailing out. Over the left side, he could hear his mind saying, over the left side, and felt for the locking web in his Sutton harness. He hoped he would be able to get out. His legs felt weak, and for a fraction of an instant, he felt panicked, unable to move.

Abruptly, the machine stopped spinning, and rushed downward. He felt a trickle of saliva running down his chin. Everything seemed to happen in a second. He stroked the stick back slowly. Thank God, he'd never do this again without keeping his hand in more at flying. Bloody fool ... showing off ... still it proved something ... wings still on ... has to give us at least this kite now ... at least this one.

He approached the field uncertainly, feeling tired, wondering if he would have trouble landing. Then he was down. He almost wasn't aware of it until he found himself at a standstill. Calder was suddenly there, jumping up on the wing, helping Allard off with his parachute. Allard's face was pale, drawn, with two white lines at the base of his nostrils and sweat on his forehead.

He jumped down, felt himself stagger, put one hand against the fuselage.

'Good show!' said Calder.

Allard looked at the ground, feeling happy, thinking how he had stayed instead of bailing out. But this fright was almost new to him. He'd forgotten the sensation. He hadn't felt anything like this since his early training days. A feeling of elation came over him suddenly.

'She's all right,' he said, staring at Calder.

'Come on,' Calder said. His face was different now. His eyeballs looked different, his whole face quite grave, serious.

'They're everywhere,' he said.

'Who?'

'Huns.'

My God Allard thought, it's started and I'm standing here.

'How many?'

'Don't know. Attacks all along the coast.'

'Come on,' said Allard. He caught

164

Calder's arm. They went on towards the control tower.

'Are you all right?' Calder asked.

'Yes,' Allard said. 'I'm all right. Bloody kite didn't want to come out. Thought I'd had it.' He began to feel tired.

Calder looked at him and smiled. Together they entered the control tower.

'Hallo, hallo,' they heard over the radio loudspeaker on the wall. 'This is Tudor Red Leader, Red Two calling. Oil pressure packing up. Have to go home.'

When Allard spoke, his eyes were round for an instant. 'That's Butler's wing.' He went over to the desk, stood there, head down, listening.

'Tudor aircraft, reform!' said the radio, the voice clear, urgent.

'Come on! Come on! Join up! Get your fingers out!'

'That's Adams,' Allard said. Calder did not speak. They stood side by side, contemplating the wall, listening.

'Break port, Tudor!' Adams was shouting.

'Hallo, Tudor Leader. Kenwood calling,' said the radio voice of the Ground Controller. 'What's your position? Over to you.'

'Hallo, Kenwood, Tudor Leader answering. Approximate position is ten miles south of Tangmere. Out.'

'O.K. Keep your eyes peeled. Huns around. Out.'

'Righto.' Then suddenly, a minute later. 'Look out for Huns. Coming down at three o'clock! About fifty! Join up!'

Now, in his mind, Allard could see the Messerschmitts in formation, bug-like against the high blue dome of the sky, hanging suspended, wings dropped to dive.

'Break port, Tudor!' he heard Adams shouting on the radio.

In his mind, Allard seemed to hear the roar of the engines, the snarling, wasp-whine rising across the sky, the siren wailing to a crescendo over Surrey and Kent and London.

'Climb flat out! Keep your speed up!' It was Adams' voice again.

Allard could see them all, leaning forward, turning their guns to Fire, staring up, in a kind of terrible and unbreathing suspension, all of them, Fletcher, Brown, Dunlap, Dawson, Harper, Stuart, thinking, here they come, here they come, steady now. Vaguely Allard wondered if any of them would die this afternoon.

Now the Germans will be waggling their wings, Allard thought, sitting up there high, looking down, seeing the long, graceful, pointed wings of the Spits. Again Adams' voice: 'Hallo Trainway, rats are breaking up. Two sections. Can you give us a hand?'

That will be the other formation of his squadron he's calling, Allard thought. They better get over there or Adams is trapped. Get away, he wanted to shout to Adams, get away, there aren't enough of you. Trainway, the other formation, would be perhaps twenty miles away, on a parallel course.

'Join up, Red Three. For Christ's sake!'

'Hurry up, Trainway. Steer two six zero magnetic. There is a do near Tangmere.' The controller was calling the other formation, trying to get them on track with a radar fix.

Hurry, Allard thought, hurry come on. Those Huns will be down on him on both sides.

'They've had it if Trainway doesn't get there soon,' said Calder. His voice was harsh.

'Red Three!' Adams was calling. 'Oh, hell, here they come! Red Three! Break!

167

For Christ's sake, break! Tudor, break starboard. Attack!'

It's too late, Allard thought. It's too late. They've come down on them, and Red Three is some sprog. He'll die.

The room was silent. Calder and Allard stood with their hands behind their backs. Allard closed his eyes, seeing, in his mind, the spirals of the Messerschmitt propellers hurtling down across the air, the cannons winking bluely, the line of single-seater fighters with square wing tips, another with pointed wing tips turning slowly over on its back, the green land waiting far below, then the splash of flame exploding around the cockpit into a central mass of fire and a long, thunderous plume of flame falling across the bright, sunny air.

He could see them swarming like fish up there, darting and flicking, with the sky like a vast sea; all the tiny silver machines swirling upward through long, graceful threads of tracer fire, their engines hammering a single far-faint roar like in a dream, hammering, thudding in a peaceful void.

'Keep your speed up,' Adams was shouting. Above the sound of his voice came the sound of cannon fire, heavy and muffled.

They'll be flying at full throttle, Allard thought, some of them trying to barrel roll, the sprogs, over on their backs with the big, yellow-edged black crosses sliding past just over one's head, hanging there while one throttles back only to have what looked like a sprog swing away fast.

'Turn starboard, Red Five,' Adams yelled.

Who's in a jam, thought Allard, who's horsing up the show?

He could see Adams staring out of the cockpit, looking ahead, sweating heavily now, shouting orders, with a big yellow-nosed Messerschmitt coming straight at him, swift as an arrow, the nose up, the cannon winking fire, coming faster and faster, growing bigger and bigger, red flashes in the wing blinking like little red eyes. Then Adams turning, facing the attacking machine, watching the wicked little wing-gun flashes. Pull your nose up, Adams, Allard's brain registered automatically as he visualized the fight in the air; Adams firing now, unhearing the hammering of his guns as he concentrated on correcting aim until

169

the first fragments burst from the fish-like snout of the Messerschmitt which rose; then Adams correcting his aim again, aiming carefully now to shoot with the Messerschmitt almost upon him, into the flash of fire under the Messerschmitt's belly, ducking and slamming the stick forward as a blinding flash of sparks exploded overhead.

'Tudor Leader,' a pilot was shouting on the radio. 'Look out. You've got a bastard on your tail.'

A long pause, then Adams' voice: 'Thanks, old boy. That was too bloody close.'

Allard sat now on the edge of the desk, filled again with the sensations which he had felt in the spin. He could feel his heart pounding and his mouth dry.

They'll be going flat out, he thought, three fifty and four hundred. He wished he were there. He could see the empty machine gun and cannon shells falling through the skies like a flock of brown lozenges.

Adams' voice broke the silence: 'Tudor, Red Five,' the voice was screaming, 'don't go down! Look out! Brown ... you fool! ... Break!'

170

Brown can't be stupid, Allard thought. Why should he have to be told? Stupid chap doesn't live as long as Brown. Doesn't have gongs Brown has. Can't be a fool.

But again Adams was yelling: 'Brown, are you crazy! Break ... Brown!' Adams voice began to fade. 'Brown!' The voice faded. A mute, hollow sound issued from the radio, filling the room. It drove all thought from Allard's mind. He was filled with an old sense of horror and dread.

'Brown,' he said aloud.

'Goodbye, chaps,' a voice said over the radio. 'I've had it.'

Again the radio hummed, a hollow, muted sound. Then it too ceased, and the room was silent.

Allard said quickly, 'I must go down to Wing tonight.'

Calder did not appear to hear.

'Brown ... Brown,' he muttered, shaking his head. He rubbed the back of his neck with one hand. 'Brown,' he repeated with an air of disbelief. Then he looked at Allard, but his gaze was abstracted.

'Certainly never thought—' he began. 'I mean, good God. Ferried kites from here several times ... certainly never thought ... actually chap like that ... well, really

171

shouldn't get killed. Much too good.'

Allard was watching him as though he had not been listening.

'What about the kites?'

Calder did not speak. He looked at the floor, contemplated.

'Well, do I get them?' Allard asked.

Calder did not appear to hear. He did not move.

'All right,' he said, after a long moment. Then his eyes blinked fast, stopped. He looked up.

'You're going to need more than these kites.'

Allard nodded.

'I know.'

Calder smiled.

'Butler?'

Allard stared at him steadily.

CHAPTER NINE

Before the funeral column reached the road it circled the aerodrome, Butler heard the bagpipes wailing again. From above the company of kilted Highland Light Infantry the thin, high notes seemed to stream back upon the still summer air like the shrill, wild screaming of dying animals. There was no sound in the work sheds on each side of the road that passed through the centre of the built-up area which housed the mechanical and administration squadron offices.

Butler marched slowly, a dead man's march, the flag-covered catafalque moved with terrific slowness behind two horses. Butler wondered why he had never thought of Brown before as a Scotsman. He looked at the sky, the back of Fletcher's head. The sky was pale, vividly blue, like glass, through which the sun glared hot and sharp.

The wailing music of the bagpipes ceased. The column did not stop. On each side of the catafalque figures in blue uniforms marched. There was no sound now save that of marching feet, sullen, muffled.

Then, for a brief moment, the rear half of the column halted as the company of bagpipers turned on to the road that circled the flying field. Butler looked across the level green field, feeling guilt and shame and regret, thinking, 'I should have gone yesterday,' saying it over and over again in his mind. 'I should have gone ... should have led the squadron ... could have saved Brown ... my fault ... might not have happened if I'd been there.' He looked on across the field, at the far end, marked by a jagged crest of trees. Far away in the sunlight, he saw six Spitfires, standing just under the trees. There was no sound in the sky. The field looked deserted, empty. In the silence Butler could hear only the single, muffled, sullen sound of marching. Then above this sound there rose again the music of the bagpipes, crying, wailing, thin and high. Flowers of the Forest, Butler thought, watching the catafalque as its wheels turned slowly onto the air strip road, poised there in profile, decorous, flag-draped, bearing a single wreath.

Then the whole column was moving again. When Butler turned onto the road, he saw three women in black, with black veils over their faces, standing, with heads bowed as the column passed. Mother, wife and sister, Butler thought, listening to their keening cries, sharp, piercing, carried away upon the sunny air into the music of the bagpipes.

Suddenly the pipes ceased and again in

the silence only the clash of marching feet, a single, muffled, sullen sound. Butler felt he could hear silence in the sound of marching. His mind started to think about Brown; his mind kept on nagging at him, blaming him for Brown's death. He tried to tell himself that perhaps he could not have saved Brown but he could not make himself believe this. He was certain that Brown would have obeyed him in the air, and he could not keep from thinking that he had been well enough to take to the air yesterday. He wanted to void this thought but it would not cease. 'I should have gone. I should have led the squadron.'

The column went on. Sunlight lay thickly over everything, and high overhead the sky was a curved dome of glass. The sound of the women mourning reached him, their sobbing mounting to a furious animal wail that seemed to pass completely out of the realm of human grief straight into the crescendo of bagpipes.

The column moved steadily across the field with the sun rising higher. The golden all-encompassing glare of the noon sun poured down. The wind in the field beyond the column was quiet, as though waiting for silence.

'I could use a drink about now,' Fletcher said in a low voice, half turning his face.

Butler did not answer. He turned his head slightly. The roofs of the little town beyond the field were visible between the thin green trees.

'Brown must be laughing,' Fletcher whispered. 'Making us pass two pubs up ahead with our tongues hanging out.'

Then the church came into view, spire first, sticking up across the flat fields, above the red tiled roofs of the square stone houses. It was an old church, an old town; a hamlet. It might have been six or seven hundred years old. The houses were of harsh grey stone.

The stone curved and the head of the column turned, vanishing slowly behind the row of trees on each side of the road. The bagpipes ceased, and from beyond the trees, filling the air, the sky, the light, and the fields, came the sound of Rolls-Royce Merlin engines being warmed up for an alert. The first explosive snarl of the engines seemed to rush out upon the pale sunny stillness like the roar of artillery fire; upon that blasting, snarling engine roar the thought of tomorrow rushed into Butler's mind with a sense of despair and old disasters, like old echoes from a far distance.

Then the sound of the engines faded, almost died, became a steady, far-faint vibration. The bagpipes wailed again. The column passed between rows of small grey stone houses. In the doors the occupants leaned, watched, their faces grave, musing, with also a curious expression that was almost suspicion. The bagpipes faded, died. The column turned into the front of the churchyard, stopped in the grassy graveyard behind the church. The pall bearers, lifting the coffin from the catafalque, stumbled. The spire, stuck up against the sunny sky, above the ranked figures surrounding the open grave.

Suddenly the air seemed soundless, windless. The group stood, watching the chaplain at the head of the grave, his face smooth, serene, above the little book now held in both his hands.

The grave yawned downward into its own cool gloom of moist earth, like a steady blank face staring up at the group of bowed figures. Butler swayed at the edge of the grave. 'God,' he thought, frightened, feeling dizzy, staring into the black earth in the bottom of the grave.

177

'Don't fall in,' Fletcher smiled, without moving his head. 'You'll get one of your own soon enough.'

Butler longed to hit him suddenly. Then the chaplain's voice rose, over the bowed heads. It went on in the sunlight, full and soft, then it began to die away, fading into the sunny noon air.

There was a clash of metal and wood. Butler raised his head. He watched the pall bearers slowly lower the coffin. Somewhere a bugle blew, slow, mounting notes, echoing in the distant hot stillness, inevitable with tomorrow and death.

Then the column was forming up again, bagpipes bobbing along the dusty road. Butler watched the people in the open doors of the small houses. Above them, seemingly beyond the town, the bagpipe music rose, soaringly into the golden light of afternoon, gay, yet sorrowful and triumphant, notes blending into sound shapes like gold-winged birds. It gave Butler ease, a sudden illusion of old strength and confidence. 'I'll fly tomorrow,' he thought. 'Hell, I was never afraid.'

The column marched quickly now. The bagpipes were gleeful. There was a sound of voices, a haze of talking in the column.

178

In the sudden illusion of an old confidence, Butler felt touched with a sense of newness. The field came into view beyond the curve in the road, and the sky seemed to open up above the hills and trees on the horizon. Butler had the sensation of looking far down from a mountain into a valley. The fields looked warm and pleasant, somehow comforting in their simplicity. As he approached the aerodrome even the lines of the buildings seemed less harsh. But as he passed the administration building, the shadow cast upon the grass looked dim and cool, almost cold out of the sunlight, and he suddenly had the feeling of the sun sinking, though when he turned and looked upward, he saw by the sun it was not even mid-afternoon yet.

'Come on,' he said to Fletcher. 'Let's get a drink. I'm parched.' He could feel sweat on his back from the sunlight.

They walked on towards the Mess.

'Those things are too bloody long,' Butler said. 'They could cut the time in half.'

'Sure.'

'Brown never should have been shot down. The Huns aren't that good. What could have happened? It doesn't add up, not with Brown, unless he simply lost his head.'

'I wish I knew. I saw him go down.'

'How did they get him?'

'One burst. Right on top of him. Three Huns came down. Stitched him right up the fuselage. He just didn't seem to see them.'

They went into the Mess. The *Daily Mirror* was on the magazine table. There was a front page story, one column, with a picture of Brown. BROWN REPORTED MISSING.

Butler sat down.

'Be a good chap,' he said. 'Get us a couple of pints.' He sat there, reading the story of Brown's death.

Fletcher returned with pints of beer.

'I should have been on that do,' Butler said. 'Maybe Brown was tired. Just didn't keep his eyes open for a second.'

'Forget it.'

'Won't be long and my arm'll be ready.'

'Sure, I know.'

'Brown was about as good a pilot as I've seen. If they can shoot him—if a blade like that—'

'Quit worrying,' Fletcher lifted his glass, drank.

'Brown had fifteen victories.'

'You could fly circles around him.'

'I know. I know. But they got him. That's what counts. He was bloody good and he's had it.'

'He shouldn't have been shot down, even if he was careless. He knew how to take chances.'

'Maybe there aren't anymore a chap can take,' Fletcher laughed.

'Calculated, yes. Chap can measure them if he's been around enough. Brown knew the score.'

'Don't worry,' Fletcher joked. 'You've got the best wing man in the business.'

Butler smiled and socked Fletcher in the arm.

'Thanks. But when the best types go for a Burton ... bloody hell.' Butler shook his head uncomprehendingly.

'Ah, forget it, Jim.'

'But just sitting there, without breaking, and Adams telling him to break. I heard Adams calling him. Was Brown asleep?'

'Ah, hell, pack it up, Jimmy. What's the good of going over it?'

'So much time. Everybody's got so much time. I never used to believe it. I believe if you know this business, one can take care of oneself straight through to the finish.'

'How do you know you won't?'

'That's it. I don't know anymore. I'm not like I used to be. For God's sake, don't tell anybody.'

'You're dreaming, Jim.'

'I only wish I were.'

'Drink up. We'll have another pint.'

The next day rain drummed against the Mess windows and the green fields blended into the grey, sombre sky.

'Good old Harry Clamp,' Fletcher said. 'Bet the Hun's even glad he doesn't have to work today. It's really pouring out there.'

After breakfast they went into the Mess lounge. The morning papers were on the tables. The rain had cooled the room and they sat in front of the fire and read the papers. Butler found himself looking through each paper for stories about Brown, feeling almost disappointed when he found none. He sat there a long time, filled with a sense of guilty pleasure that Brown and others were dead and here he was, still alive. The room began to fill up with pilots, with a haze of voices and cigarette smoke. The morning wore on; rain slashed the window. Butler sat, staring into the fire, thinking of old battles, faces dead only a few months now seemed long forgotten, almost as if they had died in another war. June, three months behind, seemed years ago. He got up and went over to Fletcher.

'I'll check the weather, see how long it'll hold. If it's going to clamp down for a few days, I'm for London. This sitting around gets me down.'

Fletcher looked up.

'Good show. I'm for it.'

Just then the Mess sergeant came in.

'Telephone, sir,' he said to Butler.

Butler went out to the phone in the hall. Air Commodore Fletcher was calling from London.

'Good to hear you're back on duty, Jim. Bad show about Brown.'

'Very bad, sir.'

'How're you feeling?'

'Arm's coming along nicely, sir.'

'Flying?'

'Haven't been on ops yet. Just getting my hand in again. Tell Allard to get us some decent kites. We're heading into the home stretch, I'm afraid.'

'Wish I could come down. I'll speak to Allard.'

'My God, sir, there's hardly any time. I've phoned him and phoned him and he hasn't had any word. Can't you get some action up above?'

'We'll do our best.'

'We've got to have them, tell ministry, tell somebody.'

'We all know it, Jim. How soon do you think you'll fly ops?'

'Soon.'

'When?'

'Tomorrow,' he blurted out angrily. Did they think he was afraid?

'Oh, good show. Keep your eyes peeled, Jim. We'll do everything we can up here. How's that nephew of mine?'

'Wizard, sir. Never better.'

Fletcher laughed.

'Fine. You chaps are doing a grand job.'

'Thank you sir,' Butler said, feeling guilty. Me, he thought, I haven't done anything. He put the phone on the hook, returned to the lounge. It was still raining, falling in grey sheets beyond the windows. He could see the trees dripping with water, the leaves shining and green. At noon he didn't feel hungry. He drank three shots of whisky, thinking it might make him feel

184

better, but there was no lift. All he could feel was a dull ball of confused thoughts in his mind. His brain felt heavy and thick, and he wished the weather would clear. If he started flying, he decided, he might feel better. He considered London, but that only made him feel guilty. Even if Adams could run the squadron, he ought to stick around. After all, he thought, it's my responsibility now that I'm back. I should be here when the weather clears. Yet he knew that he longed for some escape. No, he must not think about it. That only made it worse. If you thought about it when you couldn't do anything about it, then everything became worse. No, have a drink, do something. God, he hated this sitting around the mess, waiting and waiting.

At three o'clock he felt he ought to eat though his stomach felt numb and without desire for food. He went into the kitchen and had the cook fix him a slice of Spam and toast and a cup of tea. He sat alone eating the tasteless, flat food in the dining room, looking out through the long glass windows at the trees bending in the wind and rain. When he returned to the Mess, he played three games of skittles and lost.

185

He tried reading *Sphere* and *Tatler* but he could not concentrate on the print, and the gay quality of society events in *Tatler* depressed and embittered him though he fought against the feeling. He decided he would put on a raincoat and go for a walk. He started out of the Mess just as Adams came in, smiling.

'Hi-ho! We're in.' Adams put his hand on Butler's shoulder. 'Allard called. New kites coming down.'

'Mark Fives?'

'They're on the way. Or will be.'

'I can't believe it.'

'Pukka gen.'

Butler smiled stiffly, pretended to sound happy.

'Wonderful!'

'Mark Fives!' Adams went on. 'Allard went up to Richfield. Says he's sprung them loose. No more chewing gum and hair pins.'

'How did he do it? I heard they weren't ready.'

'He told ministry you were back. We had to have them, because you're leading the Wing.'

'When?'

'Soon as the kites get here. Day or two.

186

You'll be ready then, won't you?'

'Uh—oh, sure.'

'Good show.' Adams smiled and slapped Butler's arm, and turned and walked out of the room.

A new pilot was playing the piano against the wall.

Butler did not move. He stared dazedly at the wall for a moment, hearing the piano chords crash and fall upon the air. The music seemed to grow louder, pounding in his ears. He felt as if the sound were flowing into his head, beating painfully against his skull. His head seemed to grow tighter.

'For God's sake,' he said, turning to the pianist. 'Pack up that racket, will you?'

CHAPTER TEN

Through the dim light Butler could hear the orchestra playing. Soft and saccharine the horns and trumpets crashed and rose in the darkness beyond the dance floor. Then the horns faded and waves of music filled the room softly. Dancing figures clasped and blended. Butler stared on into the darkness as if not hearing the music. The room seemed peopled with ghosts ... Hollister ... Breckenridge ... Brown ... Butler pressed Helen's hand, feeling outmoded, as if he were gradually drawing closer to the dead. He felt wearied. He felt death in the sound of the music in the room. He sat there feeling at once heavy in body and empty inside himself. He felt he must move, do something, stop thinking.

'Dance?' he asked.

Helen did not move. She shook her head briefly. She seemed to muse upon the waves of music filling the darkness.

'I shouldn't have come up here,' he said.

'Stop whipping yourself, Jimmy.'

'It's funny. I used to sneer at chaps on the squadron when they had wind up. Couldn't happen to me. Oh, no, not Butler. Never.' He shook his head regretfully. 'No, not Butler. He doesn't dream. He never gets shot down. He never sees himself falling in flames. No, not the great Butler. Wing Commander Butler. Christ, what a laugh.'

'Go on, quit. Tell them the truth.'

'I might as well be dead.' He shook his head. He laughed harshly. 'I used to be good, Helen.'

'You still are.'

'Nobody knows.' He hated the softness of her hand suddenly. It made him feel weak, more empty inside himself. Better he was home in bed with her. One could forget there. Here, staring into the darkness, listening to treacle jazz, he felt numb and dead inside. Six whiskies, yet he could feel nothing, only a lumpy deadness in himself.

'Care to dance?' she asked.

He shook his head.

'I'm a bloody kill-joy. I should have stayed down on the squadron.'

'Let's dance.'

All right, he thought, come on, Mr Gloom, snap out of it, the girl wants to dance.

He rose, drew the table out from the wall. The floor was jammed. They danced close in the crowd.

'You'd probably be just as valuable on the ground.'

'Oh, Helen, don't talk rot.'

'It means everything to you, doesn't it?'

189

'This is a rotten evening for you. Butler, King Bore.'

'I don't mind, darling.'

'I've got to do it.'

'I know. I know. Oh, darling, I wish you could forget it. Someday I want some home life for us. Have you ever thought of that?'

'Look, when it's over, we'll have that. We'll go somewhere. Africa, Canada. Out of here. Away from everything that's worn out and tired.'

'Are you flying tomorrow?'

'I have to.'

'Can't you wait? Another week ... it won't matter that much.'

'The squadron flew seven interceptions in a day. Lost three kites. Adams is all right, but he can't lead them. It's like boxing or fencing. One chap leads. Upon the flashing second of his lead, you must counter or parry without even thinking. It's all got to be automatic. There isn't time to think. Adams thinks.'

'Did the planes come?'

'The planes?'

'The new ones. You told me.'

'Good heavens, Butler, you are daft. Chap shouldn't tell his mother. Yes ...

I mean, no. They're here, but not fully fitted yet.'

'When will they be ready?'

'Soon, I hope. Can't cope with the new ME 109.'

'Let's get out of here,' she said.

He paid the bill and they rode in a taxi to her apartment and went upstairs to her room and lay naked together in the thick darkness. He touched her and she cried out and pressed herself hard against him. He held her tight, wanting her insides to become his insides, his whole being seeking renewal, holding her tighter and closer, tighter and tighter and tighter, until in a warm, liquid rushing of joy he felt the heavy dead sensation in himself going out and out and out, completely gone, and then he felt his brain and body completely go away, high and far away, for an instant, then slowly, slowly returning.

He lay beside her, happy, yet knowing the fear still lay far down in himself. He could feel it there, faintly restive, inimical. You never escape it, he thought. Never, Neither with sex or love. Nothing is your opium, Butler. He was certain that neither religion nor some childhood belief in God were going to give him courage. He no longer was afraid of God because he no longer believed in a deity that proclaimed goodness and common sense and at the same time destroyed the innocent in their beds. No, religion was not going to do the trick for him. You're going to go this one alone, he thought. God isn't going to be your co-pilot, no matter what the squadron padre says. God hasn't been checked out on the new Spits yet.

'Please don't go back tonight,' she said. He could feel the softness of her body curving against him. She smiled and he could feel the curve of her smile upon his face in the darkness. 'You don't have to save the world tomorrow, darling.'

'Patriot, aren't you?'

'Summer soldier, darling.'

'Good.'

'Oh, darling. Now. Now,' she cried.

He said nothing for a long time, feeling all the tightness and fear and worry and tension going out of himself again, sliding far down into ineffable joy.

Then her breathing softened and he no longer could feel her heart pounding against his chest.

'I'll have to go soon,' he said quietly.

'Please.'

'I have to.'

'Why not start flying the day after?'

'I have to be there, anyway.'

'You're not going to fly tomorrow, are you?'

'Don't start that.'

'Jimmy, you don't have to.'

'I said, don't start that.'

'Come here, darling. Don't talk about anything. Please. Please. Please.'

She lay against him and in a little while he again lost himself in her but afterwards the fear was still there, waiting patiently, far down, faintly restive, like the cold waters of the North Sea. And, for an instant, he felt something like hate towards her for having shown him a measure of delight he could lose forever.

After awhile, they lay side by side, hands clasped as they stared up into the darkness.

'Darling,' she said. 'How long is a tour of duty?'

'Long enough.'

'Haven't you done one tour?'

He did not move.

'Couldn't you—'

'We've been all through that.'

'But when will you finish a tour?'

'It's never over.'

'Come now.'

'It depends. Sure, I could go to training command. Probably will in time. But when? I don't know. They need me on ops now.'

'What about after the war? Fine home life, darling, for a wife. Don't care what you think. I'm not too fond of thinking of sitting around home with you zipping around the skies until you're—how old do you have to be before they—?'

'Let's win the war first, darling.'

'But haven't you ever thought about doing something besides flying?'

'No.' He laughed. 'You see, there's something about it. Maybe it's the danger or just the sky. Being up there in the early morning or just at dawn or dusk. And keeping yourself from being afraid by being good at it. That's the thrill, too. Darling, there's all sorts of things I wish I could explain. Of course, I hate flying at times, but what else do I know? It's like the wonders of sex or good liquor. Once you become fond of them a chap doesn't want to quit.'

'Bore,' she said, smiling.

'Listen,' he turned on his side, touched

194

her shoulder. 'Someday the war will be over. Then—'

'I know. But it won't be different. There'll always be this wondering are you going to be here the next day? I hate it, Jimmy. I hate it!'

'We'll live in the country, if you don't want to leave England.'

'Who said anything about leaving England?'

'I did.' He grinned in the darkness.

'Why do you want to stay if you say the country will be worn out after the war is over?'

'I don't know. Perhaps it's the peculiar ways of the English, matching accents, and pretending certain things don't really exist, and thinking we're the superior civilization while fighting a war against a nation which claims it is. Or maybe it's fish and chips and Eros and Leicester Square or living down in Kent. Or maybe it's the tubes crammed with people. I don't know. I only know it's the only place in the world where I feel at home. Completely at home.'

'Darling, you talk a terrible lot of rubbish at times.'

'What's it to you?'

'What?'

'England.'

'I've never thought much about it,' she said.

'But if you had to.'

'I've always hated geography.'

'Really ...'

'Oh, I suppose,' she began.

'Where were you born, Helen?'

'Darling, England, my England, is not my England. Don't get rhapsodic about England to me. Do you know what England has been for me?' She paused. 'No, let me tell what it hasn't been. It wasn't living in Kent in the beginning or a table at the Ivy or Bagatelle. It wasn't the West End theatre and cocktail bars and Colonels in the Connaught. How much of that is England? Where was I born? The Midlands. Too real there for me. Too awful real. Real and dull and respectable. Lord, is there anything worse than the dull, respectable life of the average Englishman? How he keeps from going completely mad I'll never know. It makes all of them kind and honest and afraid, afraid of living and afraid of dying, afraid of their bosses, afraid of the person next to them in the train. That's the life I was brought up in. I saw my parents kicked around in that sort of life, father clerking away in a store because he had the intelligence but never the chance to go to college. Do you know what the terrible part was? He was grateful for what he had. He accepted it gratefully. And, worse, he was a kind of snob himself. Always trying to pin everybody into their exact social position after talking to them for a while, poor daddy. I had to get out. A couple of years in the province theatres. Cheap digs and frowsy cafes and pubs after shows in sad slum towns.'

'Why do you want to stay on here after the war?'

'I don't know,' she said. 'I guess it's the only place I feel at home.'

CHAPTER ELEVEN

In the next three days the squadron lost six pilots, shot down in flames. Everybody's nerves seemed in pieces. Twice Butler found himself scrambling with propeller in course pitch. The Mess was gloomy. The bar was almost empty with one pilot leaning against the wall beside the window. He held a glass of beer in one hand. To his right, three pilots sat reading letters. Another was reading the newspaper. There was no sound in the room and the barman dozed, leaning on the bar counter. It was four in the afternoon and the squadron and Wing had scrambled four times that day.

Butler sat alone and silent, drinking a glass of beer. He stared out of the window across the field. He had only come down a few minutes ago. He looked very tired, his mind busy with tomorrow, wishing there were some excuse he could give himself for not leading the squadron tomorrow. He was, above all, conscious of a great loneliness.

He had never felt this rotten before. He had never had hopeless fear still in his guts after landing. The Huns were good, but not that good. Even Adams could have done better. Even Adams would not have killed six pilots in three days. Even Adams wouldn't get the shakes so badly that when he saw the Hun coming, he waited too long to give the order that put the entire squadron at a disadvantage. Christ, why did I take so long to make up my mind, he thought. I saw them coming.

They were right above us. I should have said break port, gone into fine pitch. Now, in his mind, he saw the whole battle again, heard himself calling too late the order to turn port and dive, seeing the other Huns come down starboard and pick off Evans, Fairbanks and Dawson. I could have saved them, he thought, if I hadn't had my finger up. And even the first day out he had boobed sitting there, seeing the gnats swarming out of the sunlight, staring at them with the sweat gathering in his eyes, his whole body checked with fear. I should have checked the sky, he told himself, cursing himself for having caused their deaths. He felt sick.

He had never felt this much fear and shame before. He hated himself now. He had been afraid before, sitting in the cockpit, waiting to scramble, but never afraid like this, afraid so his mind and body felt numb when he saw the wing cannons flashing blue at him. He longed to kill the fear inside but he could feel it choking him, tightening his stomach, nauseating him. God, did the chaps in the squadron know it? Can they see it on me, he wondered, the liquor copperish, tasteless on his tongue. Oh, God, and I thought maybe I would get over it once I got up there. He detested himself. He could feel his hand shaking. His body felt weak, alone, cut off from the world, filled with lassitude. He longed to sleep but he knew he could not. His mind only went around and around and the fear ate deeper as he sat there.

Even that sprog pilot Baxter had seen the Hun to starboard. Even he had cleared the sky while he was turning port. Not Butler. No, he'd been too afraid to look anyplace except straight ahead. Maybe it was these old kites. When in God's name would all the new kites be fitted properly? No, he knew he couldn't blame his boobs on the aircraft. He sat there, feeling as if his brain were numb and weighed twenty pounds. He wasn't aware of anyone else in the room. He had never felt this sick and depressed in his life.

'How about a beer, Jimmy?' a pilot asked, standing beside him suddenly. Butler did not answer.

'I say,' the pilot touched his shoulder. 'Care for a beer?' He looked at Butler's empty glass.

'What?' Butler muttered, without moving, his eyes expressionless.

Corning came over.

'Hey, boy, how's about a brew?'

Butler did not appear to hear him. He stared on through the window, out across the field.

'Hey, pal, suck it in. Tomorrow we juggle with Jesus again.'

When Butler did not answer, Corning leaned over him and looked into his face.

'What's the matter, Jim?'

Butler blinked, smiled, handed his glass up.

'Nothing. Get me a beer, will you?'

'Hey, boy, get with it. I just asked if you wanted one. What the hell?'

An administrative sergeant came in, looked around the room crossed to Corning, stood talking with him a minute beside the bar. Corning jerked his head at the other pilot at the bar and walked over to Butler.

'Jim.' He stood looking down, holding a glass of beer in each hand. 'Jim.' His voice was grave, quite low. 'Fletcher went for a Burton.'

Butler did not move. His face and eyes and shoulder were motionless. Then he turned his head, looked up.

'Harper?'

'He's had it. Group just called. Said he went into the drink on fire just off Dungeness.'

'Harper?' He stared at Corning. 'Harper?' He turned in his chair. 'Are you sure?' His voice rose, ceased.

Corning did not move. 'Forgot to be careful, I guess,' he said. 'Some Hun came out of a cloud right onto him.' He stopped, then: 'I'm sorry about Helen.'

'What?'

'Helen.'

'Helen?' Jim stared suddenly. 'Helen! What do you mean?'

Corning stepped back.

'I,—' he began. 'Listen.' He put one hand on Butler's shoulder. 'I thought you ... Oh, my God, I'm sorry, Jimmy. I didn't know.'

'Helen?' Butler glared for an instant, then rose, caught Corning's arm.

Corning shook his head. 'Why don't I keep my mouth shut?'

Then Butler was shaking him, gripping his shoulders.

'What's the matter?' Butler's eyes rushed wild. 'What's happened to her?'

202

'Oh, God, it might as well be me. I thought you knew. It was on the wireless. She's dead.'

Butler did not move. Motionless, rigid, he stared past Corning.

'Dead?'

'Bomb. She was coming out of the flat. Just started down the street.'

'Helen?' Butler stared at Corning with dazed astonishment. 'Dead? Helen? Listen ... Oh, no.' He shook his head. 'Corn, are you sure? When did you hear it?'

'It was on the one o'clock news. I thought you—'

Butler turned, walked over to the window, leaned there, looked out. His mind felt dead, empty; his body felt numb. He turned. Corning was still there, watching him.

'Bomb.' Butler stared at Corning. 'This morning. Did she die right there?'

'I don't know. Broadcast didn't say.'

There was no sound in the room. Butler's voice came into the silence. 'Harper's gone. Lost anybody?'

'O'Connell.'

'What happened?'

'We got a bit of a mix-up. About ten Jerries.'

Butler nodded, walked straight across the room, out the door, feeling as if his insides were breaking.

He felt angry, impotent, outraged by whoever controlled events. He wanted to smash his fists against the wall. If there's a God, he thought, I hate him. I hate you, you bloody bastard. What the hell did she ever do? Giving happiness, and you have her walk out into the street to be killed.

He walked down the hall, entered his room, slammed the door. He sat down on the edge of the bed. He had never in his life felt so rotten. His body felt lifeless. He wanted to cry and nothing seemed to move inside his eyes. Only anger, cold and baffled, seemed to move far down inside him. You goddam, bloody killers, he thought. Come over tomorrow, and now in his mind he saw the Jerry kites hanging in the air, the black square tipped wings, the yellow spinners on the propellers. Then suddenly, without warning, his brain seemed to dislodge itself.

Don't tell me about God and justice and love, he thought suddenly, don't anybody ever tell me about that crap again. She wasn't doing anything, walking down the street, and they killed her. Sure, the government will have an answer, and the church will have an answer; they'll tell me how to bear it, for God and King and country. To hell with them. To hell with God and King and country. I want Helen. Helen, darling, darling, darling, they killed you. Oh, Christ, lying out there, bleeding for a while, the blood thinning down her arms. Did she suffer? Oh, God, you rotten sod, if you made her suffer. Yes, you did it. Don't tell me. If you aren't there, who in hell is handling this show? No, there can't be a God. Rotten sod. You bloody bastards, wait'll I fly tomorrow. They'll die, Helen. They'll die. And then he stopped, because he suddenly wondered for whom they would die. Because suddenly he knew he didn't give a damn any longer if the Germans died. Suddenly he seemed to see himself as a fool, somebody trapped by lust of his own desire for glory and pleasure. What the hell am I doing really in this war? he asked himself. What do I really believe in? All the cheap, petty trivial lives of England, grateful for their dull, respectable existence? Is that what I'm dying for? Or perhaps it's all the vermin sitting in the chrome-plated bars or all the stupid lives governed so simply by the latest catch phrases or the posh service Messes or the retired gentry or the mean streets and the system that keeps everybody slogging in the banal pattern of their daily lives? Is that what I'm dying for? It's England, but it's not what I want to die for, he thought. It's not what I think is worth dying for. To hell with it, he thought. It's no longer my war.

It was their war now, the British and Germans. It was no longer his. They were no longer part of his life. He was no longer part of theirs. He felt no connection with their reality. It was a lot of bloody balls, a bunch of children let out alone in the street with sharp knives. And they could tell him all they wanted about all his thoughts being based only on fear and bitterness. Go ahead, he thought, seeing myriad faces, all the tired English faces in the streets and towns, slogging through life, go ahead, you haven't got enough guts to admit this war is a lot of bloody balls, that we're suckers to fight it, that people will always be suckers to fight wars because the spoils belong only to the men who start wars. Go ahead, tell me these are all rationalizations to get out of flying, to vent my bitterness upon something for Helen's death. All right, that may be, but what I think is true anyway, and the only reason you dying snobs won't face it is that it's easier to say my thoughts are the workings of an unstable mind than to consider and weigh the truth in what I think.

Get out, Butler, he thought, this is a sucker's game, they've got it dressed up in medals for two-year-old boys like yourself. Do the fish in the North Sea care about your medals? Is there anything more foolish than connecting honour with the process of killing other people or being killed. Ah-ha, mustn't forget the political slogans, Butler. Young man, do you want to die a slave or die like a man fighting for your country? Balls. One way or the other I'll get knocked off. Why not risk safety? Let the others fight the war. They believe in it. It's their silly system. Don't be a sucker. First Brown. Now they've got Helen and Harper. You're next. Don't be foolish. Pack it up. Yes, pack it up. Only wise thing to do.

He reached under his bed, drew out a kit bag, opened it and laid it on the bed. He was putting shirts into it when Corning came in.

'Where're you going?'

Butler did not stop nor look at him. He went on carrying shirts from the bureau to the kit bag on his bed.

'Going up to London?' Corning asked. His voice was quite, quite casual.

'I'm getting the hell out of here,' he said.

'Going to her, uh—'

Butler shook his head.

'No. Out!' he said, his eyes bold, hot.

For an instant there was no change in Corning's face. Then his lips parted faintly, ceased, and his eyes rounded a little with faint surprise.

'Are you daft?' he said.

Butler did not answer. He tossed the last shirt into the kit bag, slammed it shut, and carrying it lightly, stepped past Corning and opened the door. As he stepped into the hall, Corning moved, caught his arm.

'Jimmy, you're crazy. They'll put you in jail.'

Butler turned, looked at him, gazing at him as if looking past him beyond any thought Corning might ever know.

'Better we were all dead,' he said. Then he turned again and went along the hall, walking fast.

Corning stood there for an instant. Then

he leaned out through the open door, thrusting his head around to look along the hall. He could see Butler's back, stiff, deliberate, at the end of the narrow hall where it opened onto the lobby-like entrance of the Mess.

'Jim!' he called. 'Jim!'

He ran out and down the hall. The lobby was empty. He whirled, ran into the lounge. The faces of the pilots there in the davenports and along the bar pivoted, watching Corning swiftly cross the room, the shock and consternation showing in his face. He stopped in front of the window, looked out across the field. A car, a Bentley, came into view, slowing, turned onto the road that ran straight and black along the trees away from the aerodrome. Corning turned, looked at the faces in the room.

'It's Jim,' he said. 'He's daft. Said he's all through.'

The others came to the window, looked out.

'Through?' one pilot asked.

'I just went into his room,' said Corning. 'He was packing his clothes. When I asked him where he was going, he looked at me as if I were stupid not to know. Then he said blandly it would be better if we were all dead.'

Suddenly the whole room became staccato with voices.

'Christ,' said Stuart. 'We were fooling ourselves. He didn't look right from the first day he came back. Come on, let's get him. If he's picked up in London for desertion—'

They sat in the car, looking up Half-Moon Street, watching the darkness rise between the buildings with a silver balloon hanging high against the failing sky.

Across London, down in Chelsea, the woman who had taken Butler up to his room thought his face looked familiar. I've seen his picture in the papers, she told herself, remarking his medals, his stiff, deliberate back, her eyes watchful and alert, thinking, 'There's something wrong with him. His eyes.'

Butler closed the door after she was gone, listened to her heel taps die along the hall. He sat on the bed. He rose after a long moment, turned out the light, lay down on the bed.

Stay here, he thought, stay here until I figure some way out of all of it. They'll think all I need is a few days to cool off, that I'll be back. No, I won't be back. Get a boat somewhere, get out of the country. Forget all of it. Forget everything. Start a new life someplace. Africa, India. Get a new name.

He lay on the bed a long time. Then he felt lonely after a while, outside all the world he knew, all the faces, all the friends. He felt a sudden desire for a simple relationship, a stranger in a bar, somebody he did not know, somebody who would talk to him, who would help him forget now. He would go downstairs. There was a bar in the hotel.

I'll get another woman, he thought, somebody like Helen, some woman in another country. I'll live with her. After the war, when everything quiets down, perhaps I might get work flying. They'll need fliers, live ones. The stupid war, for glory boys, medal chasers. They'll never get me in one again. It's for boy scouts. I'll get away, and they'll never find me. They can have all their stupid, petty, banal, trivial lives that they think are worth dying for. Let them save the world for their own stupid lives. I'm packing up. Let them save democracy. Now for a drink.

He went downstairs and outside and around the corner into the saloon bar where two poets and a painter wearing National Fire Service uniforms were sitting at the bar, discussing Auden's flight to America.

'I say,' one of the poets turned to Butler after his third whisky. He spoke in a soft voice with something in it of apology: 'Beg pardon. But aren't you Wing Commander Butler?' Again the apologetic tone: 'Saw your picture in the paper.'

Butler smiled, feeling suddenly like an impostor. 'No,' he said. 'No,' shaking his head. 'Don't know the chap.' He smiled again. 'Other people make the same mistake. Baker. Ostrin Baker's my name.'

'Sorry,' said the poet. He blinked his long eyelashes, smiled bashfully. 'Thought you were Butler. Look just like him.'

'No,' Butler smiled pleasantly. 'Sorry.'

The bloody newspapers, he thought, drinking fast. He did not order again. He went outside, looked up the street at Battersea Bridge rising like the black skeleton of some prehistoric monster in the hazy summer sunlight. A taxi passed. Butler whistled it over to the kerb. The driver leaned out.

Butler pulled his wallet from his pocket and produced a five pound note.

'Know where I can get a bottle of whisky?'

'Hop in, mate,' said the taxi driver.

They sped smoothly down Oak Street, turned into King's Road.

'I'm going to want more,' said Butler. 'I'll be in the Chelsea Hotel. Where can I reach you?'

'Frobisher nine-one-six-nine-eight. Missus always knows where to reach me.'

They turned up a side street, parked in front of a mews. The driver got out.

'Half a mo', mate.' He vanished up the mews.

Oh, Christ, Butler thought, oh, darling, darling, Helen. He sat there looking up the street, staring dully into the sunlight.

CHAPTER TWELVE

Corning phoned Adams and received orders to stay in London until he found Butler or until the squadron needed him desperately. It looks again as if the Huns are slacking off a few days before a big show, Adams said.

So Corning, Stuart and Fletcher sat in a hotel room in Flemmings and called every hotel in London, running through the entire list in the telephone book. No one had heard or seen anything of Wing Commander Butler. Do you have any Wing Commanders, Corning asked. Several hotels threatened to hang up when Corning asked for descriptions of Wing Commanders staying there, but the descriptions were given quickly and accurately when Corning impersonated a member of the Royal Air Force service police.

Still there were no clues. So at night they went to the bars and cafes in the West End, ranging from Hatchett's to a Knightsbridge supper club. The barmen knew them all from their furloughs in London, but none had seen Butler.

'If you wanted to get lost here, where would you go?' said Corning. 'Five bob he's swacked in some bar.'

Stuart shook his head.

'More serious than that. Not here perhaps. Took off. Old Butler never tried to solve anything with liquor.'

'Don't worry about Butler,' Corning said angrily. 'He hasn't gone AWOL. He's just reached a point, an unbearable point. Everybody reaches it sometime or other. A climax. He'll get over it. He'll come back.'

'Bad show even if he does,' said Fletcher. 'Chaps'll never trust him to lead even a flight again.'

'Well, keep your mouth shut around the squadron,' said Corning. 'The sprogs don't have to know it.'

'I still think we ought to tell the police,' said Fletcher.

'Oh, fine,' said Corning, sarcastically.

'But if he's swacked. Alone someplace. Might be in trouble.'

Corning shook his head. They drove back to the hotel. There was a message for Corning to phone Group Captain Allard at Group Headquarters.

Corning phoned. Allard spoke quietly as if he were discussing plans for new decorations in the Mess lounge:

'Corning? Allard. Any luck?'

'Can't find him, sir.'

'Any girls?'

'Not a chance. Only one is dead, you know.'

'The only one?'

'Positive. You know Butler.'

'Yes, I know. But one never knows.'

Corning did not say anything.

'Tried the cabbies in front of Shepherd's?' Allard asked.

'No luck.'

'I'll call the police.'

'Sir, uh—give us uh—'

'Chap I know at the Yard. It won't get out. Can't afford to have it out.'

'One more time around the clubs, sir. We'll find him.'

'No time. Ask for Arsdale. He'll be expecting you.'

'Yes, sir.'

They drove down to Scotland Yard. Arsdale was short and dark, with a dappling of grey hair on one side of his head. He sat behind a desk in a bare looking room and asked questions. Who, what, where, when? He left the room, returned.

'I'll call you,' he said with a brief nod of his head. 'Thank you for coming in.'

They went back to the hotel room, sat on the bed and floor, drinking, waiting.

'He must be in trouble someplace,' Fletcher said.

'Never saw him yet he couldn't handle it,' said Corning. 'Here. Drink up.'

'Suck in,' said Stuart, looking at the bottle. 'Wait'll Harper hears we've buggered off on his account. Remember the time he put that sergeant pilot on a charge for coming in the officers' Mess without a necktie on.'

Two vertical lines showed in Corning's forehead. He slanted his head thoughtfully.

'Come off it,' said Stuart. 'You remember Palmer. Flight Sergeant Palmer. Went for a Burton off Bournemouth.'

Corning shook his head.

'Butler was a bloody flight commander then,' said Fletcher. 'I remember Palmer. Bloody good pilot.'

Corning frowned as though worried; again shook his head.

'Stap me.' He shook his head. 'Palmer? Palmer?'

'He thought all Dorniers were a piece of cake,' said Stuart.

The phone rang. Corning picked up the receiver.

'Hello. Flight Lieutenant Corning please?' said a man's voice.

'Corning speaking.'

'Inspector Arsdale.'

'Any gen, sir?'

'We found him. You chaps pick him up. Best.'

'Right.'

'He's in Chelsea Arms. Bit under the weather. Room two-oh-one.'

'Good show. Many thanks.'

Corning hung up, looked at Stuart and Fletcher, and smiled.

'Upside down and hanging by his nose in Chelsea Arms.'

They sped across town, went upstairs in the Chelsea Arms to room two-oh-one, and knocked. There was no sound inside. Harper went and got the landlady. She unlocked the door but the room was empty.

They went downstairs and into the bar. Butler was sitting out in the back, in the open, alone at a table. He looked as if the liquor had all died out of him. His face was pale. He looked more alone than he had ever looked in his life. His eyes were shining but somehow he didn't look drunk. He looked as if he had once had something and lost it. The only thing that mattered. He looked as if he thought he would never find it again. He looked all gone, finished.

'Oh,' he said, moving. 'Hello.' He did not look up.

'Come on, old boy,' said Corning. 'We're going back to the squadron. Searched the bloody town for you.'

He looked up at them, smiled. His face looked strange. He winked at them and grinned.

'Ruddy fools,' he said, his head sagging a little to one side. 'Balls. It's all a lot of balls.'

Corning sat down and leaned towards him across the table. Butler winked at him, grinned again, and put his hand over the top of his glass.

'Big drink for sprogs,' said Butler. He wagged a finger under Corning's nose. 'Uh-uh. Not for you.'

Corning glanced up at Fletcher, nodded. Fletcher left.

'Drink up,' said Corning. 'Can't sit there all day. One bloody drink.'

Fletcher came back with eight whiskies.

Corning lifted his glass, looked at Butler.

'Here's to the—' he began.

'To the Kaiser,' said Butler. 'Let's drink to the Kaiser wherever he is.'

'Good show,' said Stuart, serious faced. 'Sir, I give you the Kaiser.'

'Up the Kaiser,' said Fletcher. 'Up the Kaiser's son.'

'Cheers,' said Stuart. He poised his glass at his lips, looked at Butler. 'Come on. Suck in.'

'Up the Kaiser,' said Butler.

'Shed a tear for the Hohenzollerns,' said Corning.

'Better than a bloody paper hanger,' said Butler. He drank all that was in his glass and carefully set it down. 'Let's drink to whisky. Man's best friend.'

'Good show,' said Corning. 'Sir.' He turned to Fletcher. 'I give you whisky. Get some more, old boy.'

Fletcher went to the bar.

'It's all a mistake,' Butler said. He grinned. His right eye was half-closed. 'War is for suckers.'

Fletcher came back with another tray of drinks. He set the tray down and passed the glasses around.

'Man's best friend,' said Corning, winking quickly at Fletcher. 'Bottoms up.'

They drank all that was in their glasses. They were all smiling now. They looked at Butler. His left eye was shut.

'Chap loses his guts. Chap's had it,' Butler murmured. His voice was almost indistinguishable. 'Nothing left after that. Lost mine. Finished. Seen chaps before like this.' He shook his head drunkenly.

They said nothing. Butler opened one eye blearily.

'Look at me,' Butler stared feebly. 'Shows, doesn't it? Finished, eh?'

'Drink up,' Corning handed him another glass.

Butler took the glass, did not appear to see it in his hand.

'Chaps know now. Won't get you killed now, eh?' Butler said.

'Sure,' said Corning. 'Drink up.'

They poured liquor in his glass when his other eye closed momentarily.

They lifted their glasses as he opened one eye.

'Suck in,' they said.

Butler stared at them. The terrible thing he felt faintly was they had found him drunk and alone. They would always remember him this way. He had always been brave in front of them and here he was ruined. He hated them for seeing him like this. All gone. He looked at them. His eyes were steady and glassy.

'Go on,' he said. 'Get out.'

'Let's get drunk,' said Corning.

'It won't make any difference,' Butler said.

'I'm sorry as hell, chaps,' Butler said. 'All of a sudden—hell, let's not talk about it.'

'You're all right,' said Corning. 'Drink up and stop worrying.'

Butler shut his eyes, feeling sick. He didn't want to pass out. He bit his lips once, batted his eyes fast. He could feel nausea coming over him in waves. Just as he closed his eyes again, he passed out. They carried him outside to the car. They drove along the dark streets with the air blowing on Butler's face, his head lolling against the top of the seat. At the aerodrome they took his clothes off and got him into bed.

In the morning he woke with a terrible pain in his head. Even his ears ached, and a long, hot needle seemed to turn slowly in his skull just behind his eyes. He lay there in his room looking up at the ceiling. His tongue felt thick and swollen.

Corning came into the room. Butler did not want to look at him.

'How do you feel?' Corning asked.

'Ghastly head,' Butler mumbled, feeling sick with shame.

'Sleep well?'

'I don't remember.'

Corning laughed.

'Oh, you were in lovely shape.'

'God. I have got to get out of here. I've had it.' He felt nausea again.

'Don't be a bloody fool. Nobody knows why you were gone,' Corning said.

'Oh, no?'

'Really.'

'Just the whole damn squadron.'

'Believe me, nobody.'

'I don't believe you,' said Butler.

'Come on.'

'Hell with it. I've had it.'

'Talk sense.'

'I am talking sense.'

'Balls,' said Croning.

'All right, if you all want to get killed.'

'Balls. You can get back into it again. Good to get it out of your system.'

'It never comes out,' said Butler, but he wasn't sure. It had all seemed so final. What if he tried it once more? It was an idea. The danger seemed far away now. He felt better for a second. But he had decided he didn't believe in it. He felt

223

unhappy and sick again. But do I have to believe in it, he asked himself. Can't just go without believing in it, just go so I won't be afraid? Do I have to believe in it? This frightened him for an instant because he felt guilty and ashamed just flying again for himself. It seemed selfish. There ought to be something more or it was all lost. It was all nothing without something more. But why not just for myself, he thought suddenly, why not fight them just for myself. This made him feel better, more confident for a moment. Why not fight for the privilege of feeling like a man in flying and fighting? If they win, they'll take it away. It's all that simple. They won't let you feel like a man. They'll take it all away. That's all there is to it. Declare your separate war, let the others figure out their own reasons. Let them have Democracy, Freedom and Liberty. Well, maybe they're right, freedom to fight, to feel you're a man in doing it. That's all you want. Butler, you must develop politically. No, chuck that. Let those who want to fight for the broader issues figure out the broader issues first and give them some names other than dollars and pounds and marks. He felt suddenly better. His reasons for fighting were as good as anyone's. In fact, they were better, he felt. They were at least honest. He had not lost. Maybe after the broader issues were lost again in the peace his would be even better reasons. He felt lighter suddenly. His head ached but the stabbing pain and heavy feeling in his forehead was gone. The important thing was to keep feeling alive. The important thing was to believe in his reasons for being aware of life in fighting and flying.

'Let's get some breakfast,' Corning said.

'All right,' Butler said.

Yes, the important thing was to keep feeling alive and not to think too much. If one thought too much, there was no reason for doing anything except eating and sleeping and lying in the sunlight. It was a good thing to forget thinking for a while.

He got up and began to dress. It wasn't until he was in the dining room eating breakfast that fear came to him again. He could feel it move down into his chest and stomach. It came lightly, almost as if blown there upon a wind. He sat there, longing for a drink, feeling weak.

CHAPTER THIRTEEN

In the morning, feeling worried and anxious, Group Captain Allard drove from headquarters to Butler's Wing. He had heard that Butler was back but he neither asked about him nor suggested he was interested. He was more interested now in seeing Flight Lieutenant Moore Thompson. He found Thompson sitting in his office. Before the war, Thompson had been what is known as a 'clock basher'. He was only thirty, but he was an old mechanic, a Flight Sergeant promoted to handle the technical side of the Wing. He had served in India as a rigger and fitter on a Gladiator Squadron. He thought that everybody in the RAF was a sprog who hadn't seen at least ten years of service. He had entered service at sixteen. He had, long ago, wanted to become a pilot, but now when he might have the chance he had been told he was too old for training. He supervised all repair work on aircraft of the Wing. He had known Allard in India.

'You've got to get those kites ready,' Allard said. 'Jerry's headed for a field day. How'd the pilots find out?'

'I didn't tell them.'

'Who did?'

Thompson shrugged.

'Adams doesn't even know,' he said. 'Chaps came to him and said they'd heard there was some question about the main spars on most of the new kites.'

'How much longer will it take your men to strip the wings and check the spars?'

'I don't know. We're working night and day.'

'I have to know.'

'I don't know. It isn't something—well, look, we have to keep the other kites serviced. I never know when one will be coming in shot up, so that cuts into time on checking the new ones.'

'Work all night, if necessary.'

'We are. My God, these blokes are only human.'

'All right.'

Allard went out and down to the light line. Al Craddock, a rigger, working on a Spitfire, was busy with both hands inside the ribs and skeleton interior of a wing.

'How does it look?' Allard asked.

'Fine, sir. Nothing wrong so far.'

Why couldn't we just tell the pilots they've been checked here, Allard thought, and then he saw three pilots across the hangar, standing beside a machine with the fabric stripped from the top of the wings.

Allard went on among the aeroplanes, in the sound of hammering and pounding. He crossed to an office in the front of the hangar. Thin and wiry, Flight Sergeant Hubbard, squadron fitter, smiled up from the papers on his desk.

'Dozen to go, sir,' he said. 'We're trying to work an assembly line procedure.'

'Good show.'

Hubbard pointed to a check list on the wall blackboard.

'Six finished yesterday. They'll be in the air tomorrow. Air test today.'

Allard went back to where Craddock was working and watched him for ten minutes.

'Checking the entire spar?' Allard asked.

Craddock nodded without looking up.

'Check the spar only from the wing root through the first two panels,' said Allard.

Craddock's hand ceased. He looked up, but Allard was gone. He watched Allard walking away, his back stiff.

Thinking of Butler, he drove back to Group Headquarters. He felt rotten. I should have talked to him, he thought, and then, no, it was right. Better I didn't talk to him now. He isn't ready. He won't want to see anybody yet. But will he fly? Will he be any good if he does fly or will he only fly to get himself killed and everybody else? Damn.

Who can I get in his place? Who is there who is nearly as good when he is good? There is Deere and Finucane and Malan, but take good men away where they are and—no, it would never work out. Deere, Finucane and Malan were needed at Kenley and Biggin Hill. No, it would never do. Only weaken the whole show. Why in bloody hell couldn't Butler pull himself together? Lots of chaps had had just as shaky a do. It didn't seem to make sense that a chap like Butler would let something like a wound bother him this much. Oh, yes, bloody women. That, too. Ought to ship them away during a war.

He went into his office, sat down at the desk, stared at at the wall for perhaps five minutes. Then he began to rummage through the papers on his desk. He picked up a white envelope that was addressed to him and marked personal. He couldn't imagine who would send him such a letter. He tore it open and read it.

'Sorry, old man. Have done the best I can but afraid I'm all washed up. Better you know it now while there's still time. Better I don't kill any chaps leading the Wing. Hope you understand.

Jim Butler'

Allard sat there, staring at the letter for a long time. He shook his head twice, put the letter in his desk, then sat there, resting his chin in both hands while he looked at the wall.

Then he started phoning one group commander after the other.

'Hello ... Bert ... Allard here ... Keep it under your hat, old boy ... I'm looking for a good Wing Commander or even a Squadron Leader ... yes, Butler's wounds haven't come around ... oh, righto. If you do hear ... right. Thank you ... Goodbye.'

So it went. One group after the other. He was on the verge of calling fighter command. He had the phone in his hand, then he put it down.

He got up, went into the teletype room,

and standing behind the corporal dictated a message to Butler's squadron station Butler would command and lead the Wing beginning tomorrow. He further stated that as of the same date, Adams would revert to squadron leader.

Allard returned to his office, dictated routine correspondence for an hour, then toured Group Headquarters, inspecting the airmen's quarters. While he walked around the base, he made notes on the need to clean up the grass plots in front of the Nissen Huts, oil stains on the hangar floor, and the apparent use of aircraft gasoline in some of the sports cars driven by group personnel. He returned to his office, dictated orders reprimanding certain Nissen Huts, and issued a request for facts and figures on use of gasoline during the past month by the motor pool and aircraft used for general transportation.

He was about to go into tea when he heard high overhead the far-faint snarling whine of a diving aeroplane. He went to the window, looked out as the windows seemed to quiver and a Spitfire passed low, a hundred feet away, with only ten or fifteen feet of sky and trees showing between the fuselage and the ground. He watched it zoom, the engine screaming, beating upon his ears. He saw it diminish upward, flicked bird-like against the sky, and almost immediately flash past again just beyond the window with incredible speed, one wing tipped now a few inches above the ground, to roll roaring upward, hammering sound down on the sunny air.

He did not hear the corporal open the door across the room nor his voice enveloped in the wasp-like snarl that again reached a terrific crescendo as the aeroplane shot past.

Only one person can fly like that, he thought, and smiled.

'Sir,' said a voice behind him. He turned. The corporal handed him a sheet of yellow typing paper, and went out.

As the whining crescendo died away across the sky, Allard read the message.

'Butler returning to full command per orders.

Squadron Leader Adams.'

Allard smiled and went to the phone and called Adams' squadron.

'Hello, Squadron Leader Adams' office, sir,' said a female voice.

'Group Captain Allard calling.'

'Mr Adams is out, sir. I will have him call.'

'Where is he?'

'Flying.'

'Wing Commander Butler in?'

'Yes, sir. He's in his quarters, sir. I'll transfer your call.'

'No. How long ago did Adams take off?'

'Fifteen minutes ago.'

'On an alert?'

'No, sir. Operations have him listed as routine cross-country.'

'What is your name, Miss?'

'Sergeant Evans, sir.'

'Sergeant, I have not called. Do you understand?'

'Yes, sir.'

Allard waited half an hour. He went down to the Mess, had a cup of tea, read the morning edition of *The Times*.

Back in his office he phoned Adams. There was a strange kind of tender expression on his face.

'Adams,' he said. 'Allard. Nice show Butler put on.'

'Thought you'd enjoy it.'

'Against regulations. But once ... well, knew it could only be one person. He's all set then?'

'I gave him your orders. Did the trick. Snapped him out of it.'

'Fine. I'm coming over.'

'What?'

'Want to see the new Spits in action. Spot of formation practice won't hurt the chaps. Put one squadron up.'

'Yes, sir.'

Allard hung up, sat motionless for a few seconds, opened the cigarette box on his desk, drew out one. He lit the cigarette, sat back, blew a cloud of smoke, stared at the wall. After a long moment he spoke aloud to the room: 'Adams, you liar. That's the best flying you've ever done.' Then he swore softly, sat up, dinched out his cigarette.

An hour later he stood on the balcony of a control tower watching twelve Spitfires taxiing into line for take-off. Adams stood beside him. The pale, pink skin was drawn tightly over his jaw muscles.

The engines revved full blast across the green field. The aeroplanes, with tails up, seemed to rush full speed along the grass and rise into the air as if suddenly released. Butler flew straight ahead of the aeroplanes rising behind him, then turned, climbing, and looking back,

234

saw the machines floating into formation position. Line astern, one behind the other, they climbed into the afternoon sky.

They flew back and forth across the sky, and Allard, speaking from a microphone, gave them orders. For an hour the air was filled with the diving whine of engines as Allard broke them into two sections engaging each other in combat.

He watched them land, one machine at a time appearing above the trees at the far end of the field, to vanish below the trees, and suddenly reappear, wheels down, gliding, while turning above the next machine banked downward. When the last machine touched, Adams turned to Allard.

'They look ready to me, sir.'

'Little more practice if there's time. Beautiful kites but apparently apt to flick if you turn too quickly and aren't used to them.'

'Can see Butler's got that old touch again.'

Allard looked at him carefully.

'Put on quite a show for us at group.' He kept his eyes fixed on Adams' eyes.

'Really good?' Adams asked.

Allard looked at him steadily without

speaking for a long moment. There was something like a smile in the corners of his lips.

Then he seemed for an instant to probe Adams' eyes with his expressionless gaze.

'Fair,' he said. 'I've seen Butler fly better.'

He handed Adams the microphone attached to a long cord that led back through the open balcony window into the control tower operations room.

'Take it in, will you, please?' Allard said. Then he walked down the outside balcony steps to his car parked below.

CHAPTER FOURTEEN

The fitters and riggers on the squadron were longing for a free day to go home or up to London. They had planned on it all summer, but all summer there had been only orders to be ready for duty twenty-four hours a day. Each fitter and rigger had his own Spitfire which he cared for and he was always happy to see it return, to patch and clean it as a woman cares for a home.

Now they did not like this feeling of tension in the atmosphere, this sense of waiting for the unknown which they were certain was coming, and least of all, they didn't like the way Butler had been acting.

But now in the second week of September, Butler still had not improved. They remembered him as being jolly and gay before he had been wounded and they longed for him to be that way again. But now they stayed away from him as much as possible for he constantly complained about little things, small things that he had never complained about before. They did not like the way he kept to himself either, and they watched him leaning against the rudder of his machine, looking out across the field in the early morning light as though he were thinking of something thousands of miles away. He seemed to look out towards something they could not see.

The sunlight was everywhere now, upon the smooth green grass of the aerodrome, high up in the clear, vivid blue sky, upon the trees heavy with green leaves, turning smoothly in the golden light. There was no wind, only the motionless September air, clear and hot; the gardens were bright and radiant and the Spitfires, turning at half-throttle, blew great clouds of dust upon the trees and flowers along the edge of the aerodrome.

Wing Commander Butler felt rotten. Allard, that fox, had trapped him. He knows I've got wind up, Butler thought. He's going to get me killed. Butler longed to go to him and beg to be taken off operational flying. But the longer he thought this, the worse he felt. And when the desire came to him to quit, he felt empty and dead, cheap and lonely inside. You're a gutless coward, Butler told himself, you haven't enough guts to admit it. You'll get yourself killed eventually and everybody with you.

Allard could see this. He must see it, Butler thought. Why can't he see it and take me off for the good of everybody? He's probably figuring on some utter tripe about this being good for one, and I'll snap out of it. No. You're never the same after they catch you once up there. You're never one piece again. They can't put you together right. Your hand and eye are slower, always a little more afraid each time, always too careful, always waiting too long.

His stomach felt empty and his legs weak when he thought about what must be coming. The Huns would be over soon. They were only playing cat and mouse now, sending over only a few kites each day, storing them up across the channel to slam on to London. Christ, when would it come and be over with? It was this bloody waiting and waiting and not knowing what was going to happen that killed a man even before he had a chance to fight.

He had done a little dog-fighting with Corning this morning, just to keep his hand in. Corning was better than ever, too good, and he had waited too long and Corning could have shot him down if Corning had been a Hun. He had tried to hold straight and level while he let Corning get on his tail, holding until the last instant so he could break just that split second before Corning would fire theoretically, and roll away to come back on Corning's tail. But Butler had waited too long and, breaking, Corning had followed him straight down. If Corning had been a Hun, I'd be dead, Butler thought now.

God if only the day would come. When are they coming over? I should sleep tonight. Get to bed early. Be in condition. But how to sleep, lying in bed, staring at the ceiling, thinking only of the dawn, the hand rousing him, the voice calling for the patrol. How to sleep with it all going around and around in your head. He could see the big spinners of the Messerschmitt coming at him, growing bigger and bigger, the cannons winking bluely, the terrible threads of fire coming lazily across the sky. Fire! Fire! He could feel himself holding the controls too long, waiting too long, frozen, impaled on that big spinner going straight through his machine, his body bursting into a thousand fiery fragments in a single, horrible, tearing, searing shock.

He walked over towards the hangar; it would be good flying weather up high. Yes, if they came in this, the Hun would have his hands full. He would die. Yes, that's all one could do. He felt an immense wave of calmness suddenly envelope his whole being.

'Sergeant,' he said to Craddock, the rigger. 'How long since you've had leave?'

'Just before Dunkirk, sir.'

'We'll try to get you some soon.'

'Mum's been ill. I'd like to get home.'

240

'Where are you from?'

'Northampton.'

'Bloody foreigner,' said Wilson, a gunnery sergeant. 'You want to stay here with the civilized English.'

'Listen wot's talkin!'

'How's your wound, sir?' Craddock asked suddenly.

Butler suddenly could feel their eyes on him, Craddock, the gunnery sergeant, and two clock bashers, as the mechanics were called who kept the instruments in shape. He could feel them all watching him, studying his face.

'Fine,' Butler said, trying to keep any tone of uncertainty out of his voice but knowing he was speaking unnaturally fast. 'Just fine,' he repeated.

He felt he had not impressed them with a feeling of confidence.

'How do they really stack up against us, sir?' Craddock asked.

'Who?'

'Jerry. His kites.'

'Fast,' Butler said, hoping he sounded casual. 'They can out-climb us. The new ones I don't know. Supposed to be faster than we are. Pilots? Some good. Some bad. Some absolutely wizard. Poor tactics. Just

241

keep piling them in. Only tactics they seem to know.'

A sergeant from headquarters drove up in a lorry.

'You're wanted in the office, sir. Air Commodore Winston.'

Winston, with Allard beside him, was waiting in the office and Winston, a tall, blond man of fifty, came forward and shook hands with Butler.

'Just dropped by, Butler,' said Winston. 'How are things going?'

'Fine, sir. We're ready.'

'Good show. We're counting on you, you know.'

Winston smiled.

'Do our best, sir,' said Butler. He looked at Allard, and for an instant as their eyes met, Butler thought he detected a smile, almost imperceptible, faintly curling the corners of Allard's lips, but Allard's eyes were expressionless.

'Have you had tea?' Butler asked.

'Haven't time. Thank you,' said Winston. He put his hand on Butler's shoulder.

'It won't be long,' he said.

'When do you think?'

'Few days. Can't tell. Very close.'

'Latest gen?'

'Absolutely the latest.'

'We're all set, sir, you can count on that.'

Winston looked at him. Butler could feel Allard watching him, both of them studying him closely.

'How about yourself?' Winston asked.

'Fine,' Butler said uneasily. Why do they have to keep staring at me? 'Just fine.'

'No leaves for anybody.'

'I understand.'

'Right,' said Winston. 'Goodbye.' He shook Butler's hand. 'Best of luck.'

'Patrols worked out over the field during refuelling?' Allard asked.

'All set, sir.'

'Good luck,' Allard said, but he did not look at Butler. He walked directly out behind Winston. Butler listened to them go down the hall, then the sound of their Humber going away. He sat down at his desk, stared at the wall.

Washing their tea mugs in the hangar, the fitters and riggers were discussing Butler.

'He's had it,' Craddock said. 'I've seen them with wind up before. They go along fine for a while. Even the best ones. Then

243

some young Hun on his first mission knocks them off because of some silly mistake they make. All the good ones go that way when they're scared.'

'He'll come out of it,' said one rigger. 'Remember Hollihigh on two-oh-nine squadron?'

'He was lucky, that's all,' said Craddock. 'He never should have lived so long. Four crashes after he was wounded and never hurt. Some blokes just run to luck.'

'Ten bob Butler doesn't go for a Burton,' said the rigger whose name was Jones. He had known Butler at Cranwell when Butler was training.

'Odds?'

'Even.'

Craddock shook his head.

''Ow do I know? Maybe this Butler runs to luck, too. Maybe you know that. You been 'ere longer.'

'Ten bob even.'

'He looks like he's ready to buy it to me.' Craddock scratched his head. 'But I don't know.' He looked at Jones. 'What makes you—'

'Ten bob.'

'It's a bet,' said Craddock. 'You can smell death on him.'

CHAPTER FIFTEEN

The next day was bright and clear, one of those wonderful summery English afternoons. Sunlight filled the dusty streets of London. Perspiring in their dark clothes, the people of the city looked up at the sky, seeing high overhead white ribbons like long trails of flour suspended on the empty blue air. Hurricane patrols they thought. But the planes were gone. There were no sounds of the sirens.

Group Captain Allard, seated above the plotting room board, looked down into the busy room, filled with the figures of women in blue uniforms, their heads lowered, their hands busy with long sticks moving coloured markers upon the map of Britain. They looked like croupiers. Twice Allard telephoned, talking to the maintenance officers of two squadrons, asking how many aircraft were at readiness. Then in turn he phoned the commanding officer of each squadron in his group. His voice was pleasant, light: 'Bert, how are you, how is everything?' keeping his voice low, as though he were calling for the score of a rugger match, as though there were no tension in the air, no fear, no worry of tomorrow or the days to come, talking until he was certain the confidence of his voice was communicated to each of his officers. Then he hung up and once more checked over the list of reserve squadrons standing by in the Midlands, marking the ones which had fought. He smiled as he thought of Butler. He wished Butler might meet Paul Wernick. He'll take you, Paul. He'll take you, Allard thought.

He felt happy, thinking of the hour, the day. When would it come? He knew where the happiness came from. Bloody lucky getting those kites for Butler. If only there weren't too many Jerries. Best chaps in the world in the best kites couldn't keep shooting down the world if the world kept coming. God, if intelligence were wrong. Chaps said Jerry couldn't keep coming over full strength, but he had kept coming over. Still could, just taking the breather before swarming in. For an instant Allard was filled with despair, with a sudden, terrible feeling of defeat. They might do it, he thought, they might have enough. They might break through to London.

Up in London in the Savoy Hotel suite, American newspaper correspondents sat drinking, talking of the coming German attack. They were enjoying themselves as if they were covering a Yale-Harvard football game, and they all felt themselves very much a part of the war and they all wondered if the folks back home realized how brave they were in being so close to death.

'The Krauts will land in thirty days,' said Steve Miller with United Press. Steve had worked three years in the Des Moines, Iowa bureau before going overseas. 'We will have left for home. Londoners will be reading their evening papers, unmoved, wives and husbands asking each other if the other had heard the six o'clock news report that the Germans had landed.'

'I will miss all the fair Anglo-Saxon type women,' George Nelson of the *Chicago Sun-Times* said. 'What in hell is wrong with American women that they can't have complexions like these women over here? All that gold and pink. Enough to make me join up and fight.'

'The ME will clobber that outer ring of Spits,' said Miller, cursing the lack of ice in his scotch and soda. 'Hell, I wish I were ten years younger and could fly.' He shook his head, contemplated his forefinger which was stirring his drink.

'Don't be a fool,' said George Connery of the *Chicago Tribune*. 'Wars are made for crazy old men, young men, and newspaper reporters.'

'Maybe,' said Miller, but again he shook his head. He did not look up when he spoke. 'The trouble is I was never young. I came unwittingly into the depression. Fullborn. Being broke is experiencing peril without thrill. Here in a war at least a young man has the chance to be thrilled while being in peril. We'll never have another war. After this one, not until we have another depression. Nobody in America is going to fight while they're filling their kick. You can't get them worked up. Because they aren't interested in hating, unless you scare them into this one. The fat man always has to be scared into fighting. He never hates enough to fight.'

'What do you think, Major?' Connery asked, looking at Major Barton who had been invited to the cocktail party.

'How do you mean?'

'What's the box score going to be?'

'I'm new over here. Have you ever seen any of the dog-fights?'

Connery nodded.

'The Kraut is no slouch.'

'Did you ever come across a flier named Butler?' Major Barton's voice was casual. He appeared almost disinterested. 'Some of your people get around these Limey squadrons more than we do.'

Connery smiled. 'Major, you ought to get out of the Savoy more often.'

'What for?' The Major smiled. 'The Savoy has a nice air raid shelter. I read in it each day the British air force report a nice war. Good God. Don't quote me. I like it here. Give me liberty or that wife of mine. God bless her. And keep her state side.' He picked up his empty glass and winked at it.

'Miller, who's that British female in the WAAF uniform?' Connery asked. His voice was bland. He looked at Miller with exaggerated blankness.

'What?' Miller said, looking up, surprised.

'The legs,' said Connery, his voice bright and innocent, his eyes still blank.

'What the hell are you talking about?'

'Your cousin?' asked George. 'I shall write your wife and tell her you have met some British relatives.'

Connery grinned. 'You bastard.'

'Hasn't she a sister officer?' Connery asked.

'I thought you disliked the English.'

'I've never met her sister.'

'You won't.'

'Tell me, Mr Miller, are the English women as cold as the books say?'

'What books?'

'The books about English women.'

'Here. Your drink is empty.'

'Mr Country Attorney,' said Connery. 'The witness is attempting to change the issue. Mr Miller, are the English cold?'

'The fifth amendment, your honour. I refuse to testify on the grounds—'

'Disgusting,' said Connery. 'Honour in the fourth estate at last.'

'Listen you fink,' Miller said in a different voice. 'Where did you see me with Jenny?'

'The Nut Club, that sink-hole in Regent Street.'

'My God. In a city of millions I'm found.'

'All right, Louie,' said Connery in an

exaggerated movie tough-guy voice. 'Are you gonna talk or's it gonna be rubber hoses?'

'No sister. But there's a room-mate.'

'O.K., Louie,' said Connery out of the side of his mouth. 'Take the matches out of his toe nails.'

'You will love the English,' said Miller.

'They are beautiful women. What is her room-mate's name?'

'Elizabeth Vincent Winkingham-Thorneycroft.'

'My God! I'm undone. I couldn't handle that much woman.'

Down in Kent the twilight came slowly that evening, the trees heavy with leaves, great clusters of green leaves stirring faintly like bunches of grapes in the green sea of twilight. Butler sat on the bed in his room, the smoke from a cigarette winding in a slow plume across his face. Looking at the trees beyond the window he thought of descending in fog, far down through the milky haze, like falling, falling far down in the sea, and here the clusters of green leaves seemed shaped in slowly swaying images of undersea plants, moving slowly far down in the North Sea. God, he wished it would get dark. He knew that even if he pulled the blackout curtain he could feel the light beyond the window, seeping into his eyes, waking him, and suddenly the dawn light would be in the room. Damn, it would be in the room all night. All night in his head, that grey light as of water in a muddy pool. He watched the green light die slowly across the field, the darkness rising, the roundness of the hangars dissolving into darkness. Then he drew the blackout curtain, switched on the light, undressed, and got into bed. He lay there smoking in the dark, hearing the far-faint sound of light bombers going out across the empty night sky. Then it was silent and into the silence came the sound of people moving along the hall, a door closing, the blare of the phonograph in the Mess. The door at the end of the hall opened and closed. The phonograph ceased; a piano started. He could hear voices singing ... 'this is number one ...'

He wished he felt like singing with them. But the joy in their voices annoyed him. God, why couldn't they be quiet? Bloody hell. Why didn't they sleep? Tomorrow they would be tired. For a flashing instant he hated them for being happy, while a part of him longed to be with them. He turned on his side, took a deep breath, but the piano beat on in his head. He opened his eyes in the darkness. His chest and stomach felt tight, and his mind felt numb and tired without thought, almost frozen. God, why can't I think? Think or sleep. There was nothing in his mind; the inside of his head felt numb and empty. He closed his eyes and tried to induce sleep by inhaling deeply, but he could not force sleep to come.

He lay there listening to the voices beyond the hall. He did not remember drowsing.

The day they attacked the flak boats at Antwerp. There was a long pier, lined with trucks, sticking out in the bay. There was a light flak battery firing off the end of the dock. It would never hit him. There was a flak boat anchored about three hundred yards from the end of the pier. The pier got bigger and bigger. Knowing he'd never get the squadron back when he saw the masts of the other ships beyond the pier and their guns firing almost point blank. Holding the stick hard, going in faster, faster, seeing the water breaking white against the pier. They'd all be shot down. Then, looking at the firing button. Close up, blue section. Close up. Absolutely frozen to the seat, going into the white clusters, the blue flashes, hearing a quiet voice, 'Brake left, Butler, brake left.' Then no more time to think or hear, and the next time and the next and the next and the next and no more time to think, no more time, no more time—never any more time. Never. Never time to think or feel anything. Then he was dead. They were all dead it seemed. They had all been dead since July. Ever since Dunkirk. Or was it before? How long had he been flying dead? He saw the night again. Which night? He heard the wind in the trees, the voices, the face outside in the dark. Who was it? He went to the window. There was nobody there. He had felt the face and person out in the dark how long? It frightened him when he was awake and felt the face out there, waiting for him under the trees, but there was never anybody out there when he looked. Some nights he didn't feel it. How long since he had thought of it? Am I dreaming now? It was all a dream, but not before going in frozen to the sea at Antwerp. How many had they lost there? Was Burns alive or dead? Hackett and Pettingon and Jordon? Had they been posted to another squadron or were they dead? If there hadn't been so many he could keep their faces straight. Where had Holden gone? Suddenly all the faces and names blurred and he was abruptly aware of lying in bed. His arms and legs and body were wet with sweat. He lay there frightened by all the confused dreaming.

Jesus, I'm scared! I'm scared about tomorrow! Will I go through without going into a blue funk? Will I suddenly just get frozen, maybe be unable to fly, lose control of myself? I must be as good as I used to be. I must be. I must be.

Hell, I can outfly any of those Krauts. What is there that anyone can do that I cannot? I must fly well tomorrow. I must! I must! It's only not being afraid that matters. That's all. That's the only thing that counts. Not being afraid, or going in there afraid. Going in there. Going in there fighting. Going in there fighting and afraid. Better I die out there than in bed. Oh, my God, I don't want to go tomorrow. But I must! I must. I must. I must.

CHAPTER SIXTEEN

The siren moaned low in the early morning darkness, far down the coast, and the guns crashed. Butler stirred, waking, hearing the guns, the siren, thinking, seeing in his mind the gnat-like photo-aircraft crossing the coast, the ME 109 stripped of armour, surveying the aerodrome. Butler turned over, hearing the sirens dying away across the faint light of morning. Suddenly he was aware again of the sirens, sharp, rising, and he lay wide awake. He sprang up, jerked back the blackout curtain, saw the hot, bright sun burning the faint mist off the green fields. His whole being suddenly seemed alive, urgent. His body felt tight, hard, almost trembling with haste.

He looked at his watch. Six o'clock. He should have been up an hour ago. What the hell was wrong with the bloody batman? He moved fast, dressing. His arm felt stiff.

There was a knock at the door. It opened. There was Thorpe, his batman, standing there, looking apologetic, holding a cup of tea. Butler could smell the steam rising from the hot, whitish liquid.

'Sorry—' Thorpe began.

'My God, man,' taking the cup. 'Don't you know there's a war on? You were—oh, never mind ... early chaps out all right?'

'Yes, sir. Nothing doing yet, sir.'

'There will be.'

'Big show?'

'You can bet on it.'

'Good luck, sir.'

'Thank you.'

Thorpe went out, closing the door carefully. Butler sat on the edge of his bed, staring at the wall, blowing on the hot tea to cool it, then trying it gingerly with the tip of his tongue. He felt unbelievably good, thinking of the morning flight to come. He couldn't believe for a moment that he had been afraid, but he was certain there was something artificial, thin and fragile as delicate glass, that had taken the fear away momentarily. Far down inside him he knew the dread was waiting patiently. The first smell of the wind, the first sound of aircraft would bring it back. He drank the tea slowly, looking at he floor, his stockinged feet. The warm tea in his stomach stirred fear, as though it were some small sleeping animal, slowly awakening.

When Butler was dressed, walking along the hall towards the dining room, he could feel the fear alive inside of his stomach, just his stomach tight now, the hard ball of fear forming, clenching harder and harder.

Adams was sitting behind the long white table eating toast and marmalade.

'The prisoner ate a hearty breakfast,' Butler smiled. 'Any gen?'

Adams shook his head. His face was quite grave, quiet.

Harper and a pilot named Bencher came in and sat down at the table.

'The lovely weather,' said Harper. 'The lovely, bloody weather. Just what the doctor ordered for Jerry.' He looked around for a waitress.

'Ready to juggle with Jesus?' Brown asked, grinning at Harper. 'I hate to mention this but your shoes—the new ones. I—'

'I'll wear them,' Gale said. 'You'll never get them.'

'Pass the sugar please,' said Butler.

An hour later, Butler called the squadron leaders together except the one sitting in

258

the cockpit of a Spitfire out on the field.

The pilots looked at Butler seated on the edge of the table in the operations room.

Bond, one of the new squadron leaders, studied Butler's face. 'What's the gen?'

'Usual. Nothing special.'

'No leave.' Bond smiled. 'And you call it nothing special.'

'Costin, you take your chaps down and up under,' Butler said. 'Keep in close. Gale, if they're bombers, you come down on top as you see Costin pull up.'

'Right.'

'Benson, you hold high cover on us.'

They went back to the Mess, to the morning paper, the voice of the wireless. Then even that ceased. There was no sound in the room. A WAAF corporal came in and began to clean the room, pushing the chairs around. Butler asked her if she would clean tomorrow. Somebody began to play the piano. In the morning light making a rectangle of yellow on the floor, the music sounded metallic, out of key. The piano ceased and into the silence came only the sound of a newspaper page turning, a faint whisper and rustle like the stirring of dry leaves.

Somebody entered the rear door of the

lounge. The door closed and across the floor came the tapping of high heels. It was Mrs Gordon Baker, wearing a voile dress and a wide-brimmed white hat as though she were going to a lawn fête. She was smiling. Mrs Baker was always smiling. She lived in the red brick Georgian house up the road from the aerodrome. Mrs Baker was forty and insisted that all the pilots were 'simply boys'—her 'fighter boys'. Several times she had offered to give some of the fighter boys a shower bath under her garden hose, telling them in a motherly fashion after they had finished playing tennis on her court that they could leave their clothes in the hall entrance and she would sprinkle them nude on the court. They were just her fighter boys. Mr Baker was always away on business in town.

'Hello, everybody. Surprise.' She stood there, smiling. 'I'm having some lovely girls down from London next Saturday. I want you all there.' Her voice filled with a happy lilt.

The pilots turned in their chair and smiled. Butler rose and nodded. 'Won't you have a cup of tea?'

Mrs Baker did not appear to hear.

'Group Captain Allard said all you boys

260

could come,' she called, smiling. 'I really haven't time for tea. Oh, thank you. I couldn't.'

'Two girls or one each?' somebody called.

Mrs Baker laughed. 'Oh, you boys. I do wish I were young. I dare say I'd be in the service myself.'

'Never in the field of ... has so much been owed to—' a voice far down in one of the high-backed chairs began to chant in a sing-song tone.

'Good heavens!' said Mrs Baker, glancing at her watch. 'I must go. No idea it was so late. Must do my shopping.' She went out smiling, calling over her shoulder, 'See you Saturday.' Her voice was shrill.

After she was gone and the door was closed, the room was silent for a long moment. Then from far away came the sound of sirens; they seemed to be rising everywhere, far-faint, blending, screaming across the sunny morning air. For an instant there was no sound, no motion in the room. Then the loudspeaker squawked and somebody shouted: 'Come on!' Yet for a fraction of a second nobody moved.

Butler's whole being felt suddenly dead. He could hear himself telling himself to give orders, to move, fearing the others would notice he had not given orders to move. His being seemed to hang poised at an unbearable point, a climax, in fear. His mind could not drive him forward. He felt his mouth open upon no sound, and then his body as though out of some secret reserve of almost lost and separate volition moved and Butler felt his lips move: 'Come on!' The whole room seemed to leap forward with concerted and something like orderly promptitude upon the sound of his voice.

As they rushed outside, the sirens wailed, and the crash of shell-fire came from the coast ten miles away.

They drove fast to the flight line. Inside the dispersal hut, Butler jerked open his locker. There, like some scarecrow, hung his sidcot suit, oil stained, frayed at the cuffs. The sirens died and he could hear the burst of an engine backfire with the Spits revving up across the field. Through the pounding roar of the spits he heard the loudspeaker squawking, calling the squadrons to readiness.

His helmet and goggles hung on the hook above the sidcot suit. There on the floor of the locker, limp at the ankles, his leather flying boots, black and shining, lay with the tops flopped one over the other. Parachute harness dangled from the hook on the inside wall of the locker.

Jerking the sidcot suit down, Butler thrust his legs into it, swung the silk scarf about his neck. He tossed his shoes into the locker, pulled on the fleece-lined boots, and flung the parachute harness over his shoulder. He ran outside, with the nineteen pound Irving parachute banging against the back of his knees. In one hand his flying helmet and goggles; with the other hand, while running, he pulled on dirty silk gloves and leather gauntlets.

Before one of the hangars stood the Spitfires, flaps up, propellers motionless, the new wings and shark-like bodies shining in the radiant air. Halted, Butler stooped, pulling and clipping his parachute straps.

Then he sprang up onto the wing where it joined the fuselage of his machine, swung his legs into the cockpit, slid down, and jammed the parachute pack down into the bucket seat. A mechanic, climbing upon the wing, helped him adjust his Sutton harness. He could hear the crash of engines starting down the line. He could feel his heart pounding, his mouth dry, his stomach sucked almost flat with fear. Come on, come on, he thought, it'll be all right once you're in the air. Far away the sirens screamed.

He looked out at the windsock hanging limply upon the windless morning air. The bright sun hung high overhead, glittering on the windscreen in a thousand, changing, slivers of light.

Then he started the engine and in a second felt the machine rocking gently under the steady pounding roar. He opened the throttle, switching each magneto on and off in turn. He looked back, seeing the Mess stark against the morning sky, the slip-stream from the propeller beating the grass down in a wide circle, the backs of the mechanics running, holding their hands over their ears and their overalls flattened against the backs of their legs. Butler looked down again at the instruments: his oil pressure, engine revolutions, oil temperature.

In the noise of the engine he felt completely alone, and looking up and down the line of machines, he saw the propellers flashing in the sunlight. As he sat there waiting for the sound of the controller's voice, he found himself praying:

God, give me guts today. God, don't let me funk out. Don't let me. Don't let me. He felt weak and disappointed in himself for giving in to prayer. No, it was going to be his skill against somebody else. What good did it do to pray? He felt ashamed, as though he had made a cheap bargain with a childhood dream of reality he no longer believed in. Come on, Butler, he told himself, get your pecker up, if you've had it, you've had it, let's go. But he knew he was more scared than ever before in his life.

He sat there conscious only of his feet on the rudder pedals, the stick in his right hand, his left hand on the throttle. He glanced down the line of machines, lifted his hand, thrust one thumb in the air. Hands in the cockpits gestured in return.

Christ, he hated this waiting. If only he could get off. He hated sitting here, smelling the gas fumes from the engine, the sun beating upon his face. If only the bloody controller would give them orders. He hated the smell of petrol now. The back of his neck felt damp and he could feel the silk gloves moist against the palms of his hands inside the leather gauntlets.

And, now in his mind, he saw the faces of the enemy pilots across the channel, rising into the sky, waiting for him, for Butler, the long lines of big-nosed Messerschmitts, boring down through the golden summer air. He saw them coming on, row on row, gnat-like, spinning down in long oily black trails, only more behind them, and more after that, coming on, while his mind and body grew weaker. He could hear the pounding of the wing cannons, see the flashing of their guns, hear the crash of cannon fire against the armour plating behind his back, and then the terrible hot, shocking pain in his arm and back and neck, and the strain of months of war gone forever. God, it would be a relief, just to lie down, just to relax, just to forget ever having to be here again just to drift suddenly away.

His mouth tasted copperish and he could feel sweat along the backs of his legs and on his forehead. He looked across the field. He tried to focus his whole being on the green trees and grass and hills, and though his mind told him the country had never looked more beautiful, he felt nothing save the tightness of his body, the hot, hard ball of fear heavy in his stomach. Christ, this bloody waiting. He looked at his watch, longing for the second hand to move more quickly. Never had seconds seemed so long before. He looked at the shadow of his shoulder upon the cockpit, wondering if he would be here tonight, wondering where they'd all be tonight, wondering who would be in the Mess, wondering who would be dead by noon—who will die today—Butler, will you—who will die today—who will be home tonight?

The voice of the controller abruptly filled his ears:

'Operations calling! Amber, Tartan, Baker Squadrons, scramble. Amber, Tartan, Baker. Scramble! Attack developing! Many enemy aircraft south of Folkestone. Height reported fourteen.'

'Tartan leader calling,' Butler replied. He raised his hand, looked up and down the row of machines on each side. 'Taxiing into position. Close up Amber and Baker.'

Butler felt his hand tighten over the control column handle. He leaned forward, his back stiffening, listening to his engine. Suddenly the whole world seemed to fall away, and far beyond the demonic roar of the engine he felt himself sitting inside a ball of silence. The ball seemed to grow smaller and smaller, closing around him on all sides. He shook his head, looked out across the empty field, the wide, empty sky waiting patiently beyond. The whole world seemed domed with silence and he felt himself rushing forward through the silence, trying to break out of the silence. He could taste the air, petrol on his tongue.

He glanced at the controls, checked the cylinder head temperature, the hydraulic and brake pressures. He pushed the throttle forward and the engine roared with power, beating upon his ears. From the corners of his eyes he glanced from side to side without turning his head, and saw the other machines taxiing out. He wound the tail trim forward, held the stick hard back and pushed the throttle wide open. With the tail up and the wheels still touching the ground, he pulled the undercarriage up, hauled back on the stick and went smoothly upward into the air. It suddenly seemed to him that time had no reality. And for a second he was without fear.

CHAPTER SEVENTEEN

The sky shimmered, vivid, and the formation climbed steadily towards the south. Butler saw the clouds, like monstrous white hills, motionless upon the horizon, saw the black specks, gnat-like, coming through the opening in the clouds. He heard the voice of the controller calling the enemies' position and altitude. He saw the flakbursts, black round balls of smoke, like some strange flowers, bloom against the white clouds. A voice called in his ears: 'Look out! Here they come.'

Butler's head whirled, his eyes blind against the sun. Now they were being attacked. Oh, Christ, I should have seen them. Fear swept over him in a wave. It was terrible. He could not think for an instant. The enemy machines plunged suddenly down out of the sun, single seater fighters with square wing tips.

As Butler watched them coming, rushing larger in his eyes, he estimated when to tell the squadrons to turn into the attack. Then he saw the cannons flash and the jabs of black smoke jerking from the thin leading edges of the black wings.

He shouted into the R.T: 'Twelve o'clock! Coming towards us! Line astern! Line astern! Close up!' His teeth chattered. His guts felt frozen. He cursed himself for the fright in his voice. 'Going in. Head-on attack.'

'Come on, you bastards,' somebody shouted, and an enemy fighter, hanging in the bright sunshine, rolled over on its back, smoke pouring from out its engine. The formations broke up. Butler saw the sky was filled with fighters. The crash of cannon shells banged along his wing and he kicked the rudder hard, saw a Spitfire diving ahead with a grey enemy fighter following. Two hundred yards from the Spitfire, the enemy fighter began firing, the threads of tracer lazily reaching out for the British machine. As the enemy fighter closed, lifting its nose faintly to hold the Spitfire in its sights, the Spitfire dived sharply and turned so tightly it appeared as though in a spin, and the enemy fighter shot past. The Spitfire turned back, climbing, but already the Messerschmitt had pulled around in a tight turn and was coming up under the Spitfire.

Climbing towards the enemy machine, Butler looked at the markings, the grey fuselage and bluish wings and nose and black crosses. 'Turn port,' he shouted at the Spitfire pilot who continued to climb.

Butler saw the pink flash of the Spitfire pilot's face against the sun. As the enemy fighter hung on its nose under the Spitfire, the British pilot kicked hard rudder, slipping away with the small round white balls of cannon fire smoke shooting straight up into the empty sky. The Spitfire went down diving and twisting. The enemy fighter rolled over, started down. Breathing hard, Butler pushed the stick forward. Suddenly, far down, there was a splash of flame. Jesus, the Spitfire had been hit. Butler looked over his shoulder. Tracer and fighters streamed back and forth over his head. He could hear somebody swearing in his microphone.

All right. Get him. He felt the emptiness of the sky below the circling fighters overhead as he started down after the enemy machine.

His chest felt tight as if his lungs were fighting for air and he could hear his breathing inside his oxygen mask. There it was. He felt his toes curling in his boots. Just hanging there. The greyish green back and black crosses outlined in white. He saw the pilot's head turn and the square-cut wing tip rising, the yellow belly. He was rolling over, turning. Damn! Over shot. Butler kicked hard rudder and pushed the stick over. He felt himself pressed to one side, his whole being urgent with the desire to turn tighter, seeing the enemy fighter diving away.

Pulling back on the stick, he climbed turning, searching the sky, hearing the pilots telling each other to 'break'. Then, seeing the elongated yellow belly of another enemy machine overhead, its nose faintly down, he knew he must try what was dangerous, what he would never tell any young pilot to do. He saw the air scoop under the sea-blue surface of the enemy fighter's wings; he felt his hand slowly pulling back on the stick—if the fighter sees me. He pulled hard on the stick, holding it, feeling his back jammed against the seat, getting the yellow belly in the sight now. Oh, Christ, he sees me. The nose of the Messerschmitt started down slowly. Oh, Christ, I'm trapped and a surge of something like despair swept over him.

I've got to keep climbing. I can't dive away. He'll get me. Oh, bloody Christ, why did I try climbing into him? Come on. Come on. I want to get those sights on him. Jesus, what's wrong with this kite?

The Messerschmitt dived and Butler opened fire. God, we're going to smash head on. The air scoop under the wing, the blinding flashes of the guns along the wings. Butler wanted to keep headed straight into him, firing, but at the last second, with his fingers pressed convulsively on the firing button, and his guts cold with panic, he skidded away, terrified, thinking, now, now, now, waiting for the cannon shells to tear into his flesh. The sky whirled bluely.

Then, from the corner of his eye, he saw a lone Spitfire, hurtling down in a shallow dive, followed by an enemy machine with a red nose and yellow wings. Butler stared down, opening the throttle, crouched forward, firing short bursts too far away that made the red nose fighter break off his attack on the Spitfire and skid violently and turn and head straight for Butler. Butler saw the tracers coming gracefully towards him and he lifted his nose, aiming carefully, thinking, no deflection, just hold it there and fire, feeling the guns hammering inside his head.

Suddenly a hoarse voice shouted in his earphones: 'Amber leader, break port! Butler, break port!'

Turning his head, Butler saw the big nose of the enemy fighter flashing bluely behind him. He kicked hard rudder, his body stiffening, crouching more forward, as if bracing itself for the crash of cannon shells against the back of his seat. Frightened, his machine skidded wildly, and without looking, he was conscious of the enemy fighter smoothly following him around in a diving turn. Then he saw the shell rip into his port wing and the metal fragments glint for a flashing second in the sunlight. He slammed the stick hard forward but a burst of fire struck the wing tip. He was diving now at full throttle, his mouth dry with fear. He could feel his heartbeat filling his whole being. His wrists and ankles felt heavy, almost as if weighted. His stomach contracted, frantic with excitement.

Another Spitfire came down and Butler tightened his turn. He recognized the Spitfire—his wing man. Where in bloody hell had he been? Butler saw the blinding flashes of cannon fire from the Spitfire's wing, while the enemy turned, showing now its yellow belly and black crosses, climbing to face the diving Spitfire. Butler half-rolled, trying to kill the fear in his stomach by thinking only of the enemy machine. Then he saw the tail of the enemy machine again. It seemed to hang motionless against the blue sky. When the enemy machine fired at the other Spitfire, the Spitfire turned away, showing its blue wings and rondels. A gout of heavy black smoke suddenly burst in a cloud from under the Spitfire's engine.

The enemy machine turned slowly away, headed straight for Butler who gripped the firing button, and stared out through the gun-sight. He could see the coolant tanks under the Messerschmitt wing. The Spitfire was going three hundred miles an hour across the sky and as Butler watched, the nose and wings of the Messerschmitt got bigger and bigger until he could see the dirty grey smoke trail from the engine exhaust. He was almost rigid with fear, and then he was trying to tell himself to fire only he could not seem to control his hands and feet and he felt his machine turning away, and he sat paralysed waiting to be shot down, feeling the belly of his machine exposed. Finally, he remembered to kick rudder and stick and try to roll and he heard the roar as a cannon shell bounded off the armour plating under his seat.

Then he was clear, and the enemy flashed past, and he was diving, seeing the sky filled with fighters, wondering how many of the squadron had seen him turn away. God, how many times had he told them never to turn away from a head-on attack. He was shaking now with fury and hate and disgust for himself. You gutless coward, he thought. His whole body felt dead and old.

To take one on again, to go in against a couple of them and shoot them down as he had done before without fear, with instinct, with fear controlled, suspended, though knowing it was there. That was the way. God, would he ever be able to do it again? I must, he thought, I must. He looked around the sky. He felt dizzy and his arms ached. He saw an enemy coming towards him. He could feel his body clenching, his eyes fixed on the wings, waiting to see the cannon flash.

Bluish round balls of fire. He heard a pilot calling and swearing at another pilot in his headphones. He saw the bluish round balls of fire coming towards him, getting bigger and bigger.

I must. I must. Don't turn. Go on. Go on. Don't turn.

He put one hand over the hand on the stick and pressed down, his whole being forcing him to hold his hand there, not to move the control stick. His whole being cried out to turn away, to escape.

He fired, aimed carefully, and the enemy machine came on, firing, propeller spinning a slow circular blur, smoke drifting back over the wings, the big spinner getting bigger, the pilot pushing the machine flat out, the red lights of machine guns winking along the wings. Butler, as he fired, saw fragments burst from the wing root of the fighter, and the hose jerk up slightly. He went on firing at the big spinner and saw one wing tip come up and fragments fly out from under the nose. Suddenly there was a blinding, white flash just outside Butler's cockpit.

In that instant all forced courage left him. His hands jerked the stick over. He wanted only to live, to live. No. No. Don't turn. Get that stick over. Get it back. Get it back. Shoot him down. Shoot him down. Save yourself. You'll never be able to live with yourself if you don't. Kill him. Kill him. Fly through him, into him, blow him up. Don't funk out now.

He could feel his hands weak on the controls. Shattered glass showered over his knees. Darkness and immense fatigue seemed to fill his eyes. Trying to open his eyes, he grabbed the stick hard.

A cannon shell crashed into his wing and a line of white puffs of smoke hung upon the air for an instant in front of his nose. The German machine had half-rolled over him, turned, come back in a dive, and now was behind him. He looked back, saw the red and blue lights, flashing in the wings. He chopped the throttle, tried to turn tight and slow, felt a hot shocking stab in the calf of his right leg and his whole body jerk in a spasm of terror with the air blowing in his face through the shattered windscreen. Oh, Jesus, to die, to die, this is it. Oh, God, it will be better. It will be a relief. His body and arms felt limp. Yet, far away, he heard his voice being called—'Amber Leader ... break ... Amber Leader ... break.'

He shook his head, opened his eyes. A ball of fire hurtled past with a long tail of plume-like flames. Out of it came the black figure of a man, squatting in profile, suspended for a moment against the summer sky. The flames went down in long black plumes of smoke.

Fletcher, who was his wing man, flew up beside him, waved, called over the intercom: 'Everything O.K.?'

Butler tried to smile, to speak, looking across the brief space of air that separated their machines. His face and body were soaked with sweat. Fletcher waggled his wings.

'Where've you been?' Butler asked.

'It's a mess. The air's full of them. I lost you. Got jumped first time down with you.'

'Look out, Amber Leader! Bandits!' A shout pierced Butler's eardrums. He looked over his shoulder; gnats coming out of the orange round glare of the sun.

Everything was confusion. Fletcher disappeared in a face flash.

Butler slammed the stick over and pushed hard with his left foot. He felt the machine whipping over. He thought of the squadron. In his mind he saw their

279

faces watching him from all over the sky.

They think I'm afraid. They think I've lost my nerve. I haven't. I haven't. I haven't, he shouted into his oxygen mask, his voice drumming in his head.

'Bastard!' he shouted at the Messerschmitt, seeing the square wing tips in his rear-vision mirror.

I haven't.

'Bastard!'

I'll get him. Just one.

He saw white and yellow tracers coming over his port wing. He cursed the fact that he couldn't tighten his turn. If only he could come around on this bloody bastard's tail. He kept looking around as he tightened the bank.

Then he saw the enemy opposite him, the long red nose, and squarish rudder with the round top, and the whitish blur of the pilot's face. He saw the square wing tips and the black crosses outlined in white tilted against the sky, the whole machine straining, bucking to tighten its turn and come around on his tail.

Butler kept looking across the space narrowing between the machines. He didn't see the other Messerschmitt until the tracer shot past in a long yellow thread just above his head. Butler jerked his head back. And then the machine was coming straight at him. Oh, Christ, God. His body fell away from him.

Sick with fear, he waited for the hot shocking flash that would blow him into screaming darkness. His arms and shoulders and fingers seemed to have disappeared. All he could see was the steady stream of tracer coming towards him. His whole body and mind was frozen, as if poised to rocket towards an apex filled with terrific rushing. He tried to make his hand move and then he could feel his body shaking, and all he could see was the closeness now of the guns flashing upon his eyes, the black line of the wing pricked with red flashes, coming at him, the propeller getting bigger and bigger. Oh, Christ, fire at him, fire at him, fire at him, get your hands moving. Where are your hands? Fire!

Then, as if in a sick dream, he fell forward on the stick, seeing in his mind a flash of faces overhead, watching, while he waited now for physical strain to cease, for the blackness and the explosion to envelope him. Suddenly he saw the white belly of the other machine, stained with streaks of oil, flash overhead.

It was terrible. He felt sick with shame and fear and relief. A bloody coward. That's all he was. Bloody sick coward. He cursed himself in hate and fury with his breath making a choking sound in his oxygen mask and his hands limp and free from the stick.

The machine snapped over, spun once. His eyes were filled with sweat, and the wind blew against the side of his face. He felt his hands scrabbling for the throttle and stick. He saw the sky and earth whirling and bursts of black smoke like monstrous flowers and then the earth whirling green and brown again. Butler was out of control. He was glad. He was getting out of the fight.

A quiet horror and desperation filled him. He went on spinning, staring down at the green and brown whirling fields. Then his hands, slowly, as though of their own volition, moved throttle and stick, and the jerk of the machine as it came out and roused him faintly.

He felt weak, drained, his legs and head throbbing. God, he was finished. God, he was ruined. He would never be himself again. He would never be any good again. He might as well be dead. God, why couldn't I have fired on him? Why couldn't I?

He could feel the machine swaying under his hands. His stomach ached. He closed his mouth tight. He saw the aerodrome ahead, the white ribbon of the runway forming. He felt empty and dead and filled with shame. His arms trembled.

He saw the aerodrome and came in low over the trees with plenty of flap. Then he was down, running smoothly along the runway, without remembering exactly when the wheels had touched. He let the machine roll too fast and had to slam the brakes on and for an instant thought he was going to ground loop. Then he pulled the engine switch and sat there feeling sick with everything blurred around him and an indistinguishable figure running towards him.

It was one of the riggers. He was standing on the wing, looking down at Butler in the cockpit.

'Here, sir, let me help you.'

Butler pushed him away and hoisted himself out of the cockpit, feeling dizzy as if he were going to faint.

'You better get over to the medical

officer, sir.' The rigger touched his arm, helped him down off the wing. He lurched awkwardly, then walked away with the rigger saying something he could not hear. His insides rushed hot and cold.

The intelligence officer met him in a lorry and Butler climbed in beside him and they sped across the field past the control tower to stop in front of the sick bay. They went inside.

'Where's the MO?' the intelligence officer asked the medical sergeant. He pushed Butler over to a chair. 'Sit down.' The sergeant went out.

'How did it go?' asked the intelligence officer.

Butler did not look at him. His leg felt hot, throbbing. He looked down, pulled off his right boot. Blood stained down his white leg from a purple small round hole in his calf.

The doctor who was a squadron leader came in.

'Hello,' he said in a bright, cheery voice. 'I say, Butler, they nicked you properly.'

The intelligence officer spoke in an irritable voice: 'Well, put something on it, man. He's lost a lot of blood.'

The doctor prepared a swab, inserted the

ball of cotton into a bottle of disinfectant.

'Sit still,' he said. 'Only hurt for a second.'

'Went through and out,' the doctor said, inserting the swab into the hole, twisting it to cleanse the wound.

Butler tried to remember when he had been hit. He could not remember. God, I must have blacked out completely.

He clenched his teeth, feeling the stinging, burning swab, grinding against the flesh.

From far away, a reverberation of heavy bombing came to them through the ground. First one explosion, then another, the bottles rattling faintly on the shelves. Then another explosion, now closer, another, the steady reverberant air filling the silent room; plaster fell in a faint sifting sound from the side of one wall. Butler sat there listening, his throat dry and salty. And then the sound of another bomb came dull and heavy, seeming almost to bend the window panes.

'Another piece of adhesive,' the doctor was saying to the medical sergeant. The wound burned. 'There. How's that?' The doctor squinted once at the bandage. Butler stooped to pick up his boot, draw it on.

For an instant there was no sound in the room, no sound beyond.

'Are you daft?' said the doctor, tossing the swab away.

'The leg is all right,' said Butler.

The doctor looked at Butler drawing on the boot, his lips tightly pressed.

He walked past the doctor with the doctor shouting at him and was outside walking fast along the walk to the flight line before the doctor and the intelligence officer came out and shouted at him.

The sky was filled with the sound of engines, high, quite clear. Thudding down upon the September air came the sound of bombing somewhere.

'Craddock,' Butler said. He came up, limping, to the flight line. The riggers were sitting on the grass. Craddock turned, looked up, his mouth open faintly.

Get a kite, Butler thought, anybody's. Doesn't matter. Any kite. Get in the air. You've got to go. You've got to. No matter. Get some of them before they get you. Even one. Head on. Yes, head on. That would be it.

He looked across at three Spitfires standing on the grass. They were empty, only a hundred yards away.

'Craddock,' he said. 'Come on.'

He walked past the riggers. The sun was hot. He could feel his leg bleeding again.

He looked up to see a Spitfire coming in low over the trees at the end of the field, low and fast, to zoom suddenly as if freed from a weight, and then he saw the enemy machine behind it. And as the Spitfire roared overhead, Butler saw the dice painted on the side and the flash of the white face in the cockpit and then he fell flat on the ground as an enemy machine shot overhead, firing. Fletcher, he thought, seeing the tracer going into the Spitfire.

Waiting now for the black explosion in the air, thinking, Fletcher, Jesus, Jesus, the poor bastard, he'll never make it. Then, still flat on his stomach, Butler turned his head, saw Fletcher's Spitfire go straight up in a viciously tight loop. But the Messerschmitt was hanging there, straight up on its nose, firing, and Butler saw the tracer slamming into the Spitfire. He lay there on the ground, shouting, 'Come on! Fletcher! Come around!'

He could feel the terrible sensation of suspense Fletcher must be feeling and then he saw the Spitfire whip over.

'He's had it,' a voice said.

It was Craddock. He was lying beside him. Another Messerschmitt materialized over the trees as if by magic and came flat out, a few feet above the ground, straight across the field, tearing up the ground as his machine guns and cannons crashed and rattled.

Butler rose on one knee.

'Come on,' he jerked Craddock's arm.

'They'll strafe us sure if we run for the kites.' Craddock would not move.

'Get up!' Butler shouted above the roar of engines and crash of cannons just over the field.

Butler felt drunkenly crazy, his head empty of all thought.

He bet Fletcher was either almost out of petrol or wounded or he wouldn't be trying to land with a Jerry on his tail.

'Look!' Craddock was shouting. 'Look! They got him!'

Butler did not remember hearing the crash, seeing only the wide gout of black oily smoke rushing skyward beyond the trees, the white silk flower descending slowly to vanish behind the hangar. Then he was running without feeling any progress, his mouth dry, coming around

288

the hangar. He saw the riggers catching the shroud lines and the parachute collapsed in a pile of white silk.

He knelt beside Fletcher on the grass. He saw holes like some strange smallpox along the back of Fletcher's leg. The blood stained black against the blue trousers and upon the shoulder of his tunic.

'Get the ambulance,' he shouted into a rigger's face. Already the klaxon of the crash ambulance rose across the air.

Fletcher's face was grey.

'You bastard,' he said, looking up at Butler. He went on repeating it, moaning faintly. 'You bastard, you left us ... left us ...'

Two medical sergeants lifted Fletcher, with the riggers standing there looking down at the stretcher. Butler saw them lift the stretcher into the rear of the ambulance. He stood there, watching the ambulance doors close, the klaxon wail.

Fletcher is dying. I left him. Fletcher. Left him.

He turned and Craddock was standing there, looking at him. In his life he had never felt worse. Craddock was smiling at him. Butler felt grim and furious.

Lead the squadron, lead them, die for

them, lead them again and again, outlive all of them. Yes, all right, you smiling bastard, I have to worry about you, too. I have to worry about everybody on the squadron and fight the Germans, too, and see that everybody does the same and they expect me to keep doing it over and over again. Oh, Butler never cracks, no, not Butler, old Butler, the stalwart. All right, you smiling bastard, all right, all right, I'll show you, you smiling bastard. I'll show you. I'll show all of them. I'm Butler. There is nobody else but Butler. There's nobody can fly like him. To hell with this being modest. Been modest long enough. Yes, I am the best, better than all of you. I'll show you.

'Craddock,' he said. 'Get the hell over to that kite and get it started.'

The smiling bastard, sitting safely on the ground, smiling at me. Craddock looked shocked, amazed. He stopped smiling, put one hand on Butler's arm.

'Sir,' he said awkwardly. 'You can't fly. Don't be foolish.'

'Take your hands off me, sergeant,' Butler said. 'Get the hell over there and get that kite started.'

Butler pushed his hand away. Craddock

shrugged. Butler ran towards the Spitfire.

Then he was in the cockpit, looking over the side, calling to Craddock to pull the chocks.

All right, you bastards! He wanted to curse Fletcher, all of them who had indicated to him they knew he had lost his nerve.

Butler taxied out. His head was bare. He flew towards the south, and seeing the bombing going on all along the coast, he finally saw the unbroken formation of twin-engine bombers coming in over Kent. And below, the formation of Messerschmitts. He felt at once sick and furious. He whipped over and started down. Going to go in head on, he kept saying to himself, head on, wanting to crash in among them. Then he could feel the blood in his nose and his cheeks puffing out. Then he blacked out. In the haze, he suddenly saw a flick of square-tipped single engines converging on him. It was all in a flash, the gleam of the propellers in the sun, the mass of glass-covered cockpits, fire from the wings, no undercarriages, and a voice screaming in his mind as they came at him head on and he held the stick tight. This is it. This is it. Don't quit. Don't quit. Hold it. Hold it. Kill them. Kill them. Then he saw his tracer tearing into them and black smoke and flame and his machine jolting under the crash of cannon fire. His head felt suddenly cold, clear. He wanted to laugh. He could hear his engine screaming. He aimed carefully, seeing the wireless mast disappear above the top of the enemy machine coming at him head on, seeing the machine come on as if the firing did not affect it, then the first big piece came out of it, and he could see the machine stagger in the air. Butler fired again, holding the gleaming propeller of the on-rushing machine in the centre of the optical sight's red halo. Then, abruptly, in a tremendous explosion of smoke and flame, the Messerschmitt disintegrated, ripped to pieces and, flying full throttle, Butler passed through the pieces out into a clear sky.

He looked around. The formation of Messerschmitts hung ragged against the sky; below the formation the sky was marked with black-burning streaks of the fallen.

Butler began to feel a strange kind of drunken elation. For the first time in months, he felt wholly without fear. He felt the elation rising inside his chest. It was suddenly as if all the fear had burst inside his chest. It was suddenly as if all the fear had burst out of him. Now there was only excitement and his face was shining.

CHAPTER EIGHTEEN

Butler's face was changed when he landed and inside himself he knew he was changed. He felt as if he had recaptured a lost fortune. He walked across the field feeling different, wonderfully elated. He felt the mechanics watching him, embarrassed faintly because he sensed they could see the change inside him by the change he could feel on his face. Even the skin felt different on his face, glowing soft, looser over the bones of his nose and cheeks.

'How's Fletcher?' he asked the medical officer who was standing in the ops room.

'He'll be all right.'

Butler licked his lips. He did not look at the medical officer. He was staring at the ops board, automatically checking the names in each flight to see if there had been any reports yet on the action. His lips felt dry, his mouth copperish with the dead taste of old oxygen on the back of his tongue.

The intelligence officers were sitting at the tables.

'How'd it go, sir?' one asked. Still Butler did not look at anybody. He turned now to the medical officer again.

'You're sure about Fletcher?'

The medical officer nodded.

'Lost some blood. Nerves. Shaky jump, you know. That close. Bit windy. Anybody would be. Bailing out that close.'

'I should have been up when he came in.'

'No matter. He'll be all right. Wants to fly again today.'

'Grounded. Orders,' Butler said. 'Tell him so. Put him in sick bay if he persists.'

Butler glanced once more around the room, trying to hide the change in his face from those in the room. He had the feeling of being stared at, the feeling of a man who had just returned from hospital after a serious operation to find his friends staring at him as if plastic surgery had changed his features. He glanced briefly once more at the operations boards, the list of pilots' names. Three reported down in flames.

Outside the sun stood high against the blue sky. Shadows of leaves dappled the grass. Butler went on towards the flight line, remarked the Spitfire standing motionless, the coloured rondel upon the fuselage. Far away the sirens screamed, dying across the sunny air.

He summoned a mechanic. Then strapped in, heard the engine burst to life under his hand.

He was no longer afraid. It was all gone, removed, fear gone. His mind told him he had felt it, but he no longer knew the terrible sensation. He wondered why he no longer felt it. He wondered why he had feared death. Why had the fear been almost unsurmountable, and how in a single motion of action had it disappeared? Have I been so stupid, blind, all my life as to have been impervious to pain and death? Where in pain did I fear death? He asked himself, did I fear missing life or dying or being lost in nothing. It must be all of them, he thought, all of them damn near had me shot down. But I was never brave before, he thought, just fearless because fear automatically suspended itself in me. He promised himself he would

295

never again hold in contempt as he had in the past, fliers numbed in fear and cowardice by anxiety. Still there was a barrier, like sound, they must all pierce, much buffeted against, without an inch of gain, in their numbness and deadness, until, flick, they were through. They must learn to go on and on in numbness and deadness. They must all do it or be dead in their benumbed living. There was never true bravery without cowardice first. Any fool endowed with the apparatus that automatically suspended fear could look brave without knowing the first thing about bravery. All right, he thought, turn it off, and get this kite out of here. Get the bloody hell out of here. You're a flier, not a philosopher.

Ten minutes later the enemy fighters came hurtling out of the sky over Kent. They did not see Butler. He went on over the long, low bank of clouds, looking down through lake-like blue openings, seeing the enemy fighters passing, disappearing. But high up, hanging under the sun, a single German fighter, solitary as a seagull drifting in the sea wind watched him carefully, and then it started down, the engine straining, screaming with sound, the pilot inside leaning forward, checking his fire switches, watching his air speed. The machine seemed to come down out of the very top of space, down out of white light, out of world beyond the eye that sees only the blue air, out of some vast empty, sourceless tract of space.

The clouds opened below and far down where the ground was checkered brown and grey, people in towns and fields, from backyards and streets, stared into the sky, hearing only the vicious snarl of engines, seeing only the white ribbon of vapour trailing across the sky. They sat waiting for the steady crash of guns. And, for an instant, puny, far below, they felt safe and alone, shivering a little, not out of fear now, for the bombers were past, but out of some strange compound of gladness here on earth and the lonely immensity of space, remote, cold, pitiless in the sunlight.

When the clouds opened, Butler turned and looked over his shoulder into the sun, holding up one thumb, squinting into the glaring light, seeing the dark bug hurtling down through white-orange glare. He moved none of the controls. He sat motionless, looking over his shoulder, letting the black bug come on.

The people on the ground stared into the sky at the steady horizontal white vapour trail of Butler's machine, and the unmarked sky between it and the rapidly descending vertical white trail that slanted downward towards Butler's trail.

'Why doesn't he see him?' they asked each other, wondering whether Butler was their's or the enemy.

On and on came the descending white ribbon.

Now, Butler thought.

He jammed the stick forward and felt the machine nose over and in an instant dive like a rocket. The German machine came straight down after him.

Butler watched the Messerschmitt in his rear vision mirror. It was still too far away to fire. But there it was, small, like a toy.

And as the gap closed between their machines, the people on the ground lost some of their gladness, felt some of the fear tighten their throats which they imagined the men in the cockpits must be feeling. Christ, it was high up there! Oh, God, to fall that far, to fall that far in flames!

The people stared upward without speaking.

At twelve thousand feet Butler kicked his machine up and over, and rolled over the top and came at the German machine, facing it head on. When the German machine lowered its nose to dive, Butler carefully adjusted aim, fired twice, short, sighting bursts, bang, bang, seeing the tracer just missing the German wings.

The people in the fields and streets below heard the drum beat rattle of the guns. Keeping his aim steady, seeing the gun flashes on the German wings, feeling his body blending with the speed and arc of his machine as if they were one life, he flew straight towards the gleaming arc of the German machine's propeller.

The two machines darted, wheeled and slanted upon the air like two swallows, plunging far down, rising again, plunging and circling. Circling again and again, circling, neither able to close, to tighten the circle that would kill the other.

Butler felt weightless, bodiless, legs and arms no longer seeming to fly the machine but rather filled with the sensation of being controlled, carried effortlessly through space by the machine itself, as though it had suddenly taken control of the air, space, all life itself. The sky was blinding bluish, almost water-like, slashed with flashes of orange and whitish light.

Suddenly the people on the ground gaped in shock and amazement. Out of one of the ever-tightening circles in which the machines flew one of the machines suddenly flopped, like a wounded bird, first over on one wing, then appeared to flutter down leaf-like, out of control. The machines were now at ten thousand feet and the people saw the pointed tips of the Spitfire wings as it fell, the Messerschmitt plunging after it, the roar of engine and cannon fire gearing the sky over their heads.

Butler fought the controls, feeling the rudder and elevators jammed hard, the machine mushing down in a kind of flat spin. He kicked the rudder pedals again and again. Must have put a cannon shell into the tail counter weights, Butler thought. He saw the tracer zip past the twin threads of fire. He felt there was still time. He did not feel hurried. He could hear his mind without fear telling him there was plenty of time, that he could do it, could work this machine, there was no hurry. He felt no sensation of haste and yet he could see his practised hands working with incredible speed, throttle, stick and pedals.

The German machine came closing in, firing, and when he overshot he banked, wheeling around against the sky, trailing black smoke from his exhausts.

Butler's head felt thick suddenly from spinning. He felt death just beyond now but it did not seem to frighten him. He felt confident without any basis for it, without any desire to consider complications. He felt that somehow, in a flash, in a second, he would pull the machine out. He heard the explosion of the cannon shell as the glass from the cockpit canopy splintered into his lap, shattered over his hands, an old part of him waiting patiently without fear for the next shell to blow him to pieces. He felt the machine buck and kick and slough as the violence of the next explosion tore the controls from his hands. He felt the sting of blood in his hands and his hands fighting in sudden blindness to find the controls.

But there isn't time, a voice said inside him, and his hands sought the release on his Sutton harness, and then something unbelievably solid supporting the machine and the dizzy sensation of the spin gone.

He shook the liquid blur from his eyes, saw the blood stain on his glove from the side of his face. He pushed up his goggles.

He grabbed hold of the stick, holding it tight, ramming the throttle forward, to see the jagged crest of trees expanding just ahead with the field of hops around the brown cottage getting bigger and bigger. You should have bailed out, the voice said inside him, while another part of him suddenly laughed a very hearty unbelievably natural laugh. He hauled back on the stick, watched the trees fall away.

The Messerschmitt was still behind him. Butler flew flat across the fields towards the coast. The Messerschmitt climbed up, tried to turn and come in low for a beam attack, but Butler went lower and the enemy machine dared not turn in without crashing into the trees or ground.

I'll make the coast, Butler thought, knowing if he tried to climb the German had him cold turkey, for there he still was on, behind and slightly above, patient, biding his time. Bastard, thought Butler, and grinned.

The Channel cliffs curved upward from the fields, green as leaves, marking the coast, and when Butler saw the white haze far out upon the water, he pushed the throttle fully forward. He could feel the blood running down the side of his face, but his head felt cold and clear now. As the summit of the cliffs rose in front and dropped, he saw the blue sea and the beach the colour of wheat below he felt immersed in the old unreal dream of death again, of time and motion ceased. His hands felt slow yet he could see they were doing the right thing. In the mirror he saw the Messerschmitt closing now, the bigness of the machine. Butler weaved back and forth and then, before it was too late, he did what he knew was the only thing left. He hauled back on the stick, chopped the throttle, felt the Spitfire climb, hang on its nose, beating the air, then the beginning of the sickening backslip of a whip-stall, with the trail of his machine sliding down a kind of backward diving curve, the engine still pointing towards the sky.

The sky moved down, became the sea, and the sea was suddenly the white sandy beach and black rocks tangled and there was no time. It all seemed to stop until he saw the Messerschmitt slide past underneath, just over the waves now, almost too low.

For an instant Butler had the black square-tipped tail in the red-lit ring sight, and then it was gone, and he saw the water bursting upward in splashing fragments where his cannon shells were going in too low, and then, unbelieving, he stopped firing, seeing for a lost instant the mess of tracer tearing into a great piece that fell out of the bottom of the Messerschmitt and splashed, throwing spray through which he flew.

He didn't see the Messerschmitt crash. He could feel it about to go in and he climbed suddenly and, looking back, saw only a geyser of water, a burst of flame and smoke in the air.

He banked and flew back over the water, seeing a black patch of oil. For the first time he was aware of the blast of air through the whole in this shattered cockpit cover. He began to laugh and sing and pound the time on his knee with one hand.

He landed in a blur and was glad the tail unit had held together in landing for he knew it was hit somewhere. It kept swaying as he came into land and then a hand touched him, seemed to rouse him, and he became aware somebody was helping him out of the cockpit. His head felt full and his body weak, and a voice was asking him questions ... did he have any luck ... and there was another voice laughing and pounding him on the back after he said something though he could not remember speaking. Then he was walking away from the machine.

He felt the drink they put in his hand. He heard somebody shouting his name, and, looking up, saw the oil stained nameless face, though he knew the face, and the hand below the face, holding up three fingers, and the face grinning.

The planes shot overhead, went around, one, two, three, four, five, he counted them in his head, hearing them through the roof of the room.

They're safe, he thought. Ow! The antiseptic burned the flesh at the corner of his eye. The medical officer was telling him to sit still.

The room was filling up with other fliers. They stood about him, the air filled with the hazy sound of many voices: ... 'got in a short burst ... last I saw Tom he was going down in a long slide ... rolled over on his back and went slap into the drink ...'

'Come on,' somebody was calling. 'I'll buy a drink.'

Butler did not remember walking over to the Mess. Then he was standing at the bar. Sunlight still was bright beyond the window. What time was it? There was a glass in his hand again. His head hurt. The liquor tasted wonderful, at once cold and fiery. The faces were sweaty along the bar and the voices were loud, some of them almost shouting. The room felt small and crowded. It all looked new and changed. Butler had the feeling he had never seen one of the pictures on the wall before, a strange face, and he asked somebody, a pilot whose name he could not remember. He had blond hair and a moustache and he smiled when he told Butler the pilot in the photograph was Milgrim who had been shot down in France after making himself an ace in two days. The voices went on all around him, and he could hear everybody talking a great distance away, though their faces were right in front of him. He had the strange feeling that all that had happened was a dream and that tomorrow it would be real. The

306

room, the people, all seemed like phantoms to him.

Allard came in, smiling, and caught Butler's hand and shook it heartily.

'Great show, Butler, great. The Hun will never forget it. But take care of yourself. They're still coming.' His voice had a false note of gaiety in it. He looked like a happy school boy, but his eyes still were quite grave. There was another Group Captain with him. He was from London. He insisted on congratulating everybody. He wore service ribbons from the first world war.

'Good chaps,' he kept saying. 'Good chaps,' as he was introduced around. Everybody smiled and shook his hand politely and took the drinks he offered.

The sounds in the room came clearer to Butler now. They were louder and there was a terrific celebration going on. It isn't time, he thought, it's too soon. We'll have to go up again today. Everybody looked tired and in need of sleep. Everybody was talking too loud and drinking too much as though trying to be cheerful.

Allard was asking questions. How large were the Hun formations? How many fighters did we get? Where's Collins? How did the new kites fly?

'We met them over Tunbridge Wells,' Butler said.

'Any luck?'

'Believe I got one.'

'Can they still outclimb us?'

'Not any more,' the blond pilot said. 'Their pilots are still ruddy good.'

'Collins?'

'Yes. Lost three machines.'

'Well, they haven't broken through yet,' Allard said.

Looking in the mirror behind the bar, Butler saw his face. His eyes were shining. There was a new joy and something almost akin to ecstasy in him for a second.

Far away the sirens wailed.

Butler stood there, grinning at himself. Somebody slapped him on the back. He turned. It was Fletcher. His face was pale. He was smiling. He had a cane. The sirens' dying fall filled the air beyond the room.

'Here we go again,' Fletcher said.

'Bloody hell.' It was the blond pilot, his head slanted, poised, listening. What is his name, Butler kept asking himself. The room was silent. From far away the sirens cried again, the thin high warning wail,

308

rising. The klaxon on the field whined. A bell clanged in the room.

'Come on, chaps,' Butler said. 'It's what they pay you for.'

CHAPTER NINETEEN

Messerschmitts, black-dotting the clouds, came diving. A layer of white cloud lay far below. The sky filled with enemy fighters. The golden sunlight blazed upon all the wings.

'Here comes the trade,' Butler shouted. Round black balls of flak smoke blossomed against the white cloud.

Butler's wing man fought to hold his machine steady as it bumped going down in a dive. His hands trembled. He sucked oxygen.

'Break port,' he yelled at Butler, seeing a Messerschmitt coming down, firing.

'Come on. Climb into the bastard,' Butler said in a calm voice. The other Spitfires appeared to spread and swim upward into the formation of black machines that came towards them like a school of bull fish. 'Smithton get on that Heinkel! What's the trouble?'

'Blasted Hurricanes are butting in,' Butler heard a voice call in reply. It had a Yankee accent. 'I hope the bastards dust him off. Taking sucker meat away from me.'

'Get your finger out,' a British voice called. 'Here's more trade.' Squat-nosed, with the twin rudders sticking up above the thin dark line of the wings, the formation of Dornier bombers moved ponderously towards them.

'Get going, you Limey bastards,' shouted the Yankee voice.

'Here comes the pig meat.' A plume of white smoke streaked across the sky split with blue and white flashes of tracer.

Far below, the people in the streets and farms stared up into the fields of sky. Their faces were gaunt, tired. Their upturned faces watched the plumes of white and black smoke, listened to the far-faint put-put-put sound of machine gun fire. The sun was dying across the afternoon sky, and in the Thames estuary the water gleamed in mirrored fire. The bowl of sky seemed a softer blue now, turning gold and rose, and the shimmering sunlight was turning gold and rose.

Far up in the sky, Butler's wing man sat holding the stick hard, watching Butler's wings ahead and to his left. Sweat poured down the wing man's face. His oxygen mask was wet and sticky about his nose and mouth. His arms and shoulders and hands felt tired. Another Dornier fell out of the sky, but on the Dornier squadron bore, towards the coast, towards home.

Butler heard his motor cough, looked at the petrol gauge.

'Engine packing up!' he called. 'Amber leader, take over. Going home.'

The field looked empty, deserted as Butler swung in over the trees. A faint puff of glycol rose from the cowling. He glanced at the temperature. Too hot. Then he had the wheels down, running smoothly along the ground and he was taxiing up to the flight line. He braked and climbed out, saw a Spitfire down the line with the propeller turning slowly, a figure walking towards the machine. Butler squinted against the dying sunlight. The figure was limping. For Chrissake! Butler shouted indistinguishably against the engine roar, began to run. Fletcher had one foot on the wing when Butler touched his shoulder. Fletcher turned, grinned.

'Where the hell are you going?' Butler asked.

'Juggle with Jesus.'

'You're giving the orders around here?'

'I'm one down with those buggers,' Fletcher grinned.

'Get out of there. You're not flying.'

'The hell I'm not.'

'Don't be a damn fool.'

Fletcher stepped up on the wing, raised his boot, smiled, held the boot lofted, threatening. He was holding it there when the first bomb exploded, almost knocking Fletcher from the wing. Butler heard the unmistakable sound of the German engine going away, felt the ground still shaking and the shower of stones and dirt falling all around him. But when he raised his head, Fletcher was gone and the blast of air from the Spitfire's prop wash knocked him flat. He lay on the ground with his head tucked behind his arms, not looking up until the air no longer blew upon him. He still felt the vibration of the earth.

The Spitfire was taking off. Low and flat out across the field the Messerschmitt screamed, diving, firing, tearing up the ground.

Craddock the rigger, ran towards Butler, lay flat between him. He looked up, spoke without turning his head: 'How could I stop him? He started the engine himself.'

'Yes. Yes. I know,' Butler said crossly.

They watched the Spitfire rise, vanish below the trees, come into sight again, climbing now.

The Messerschmitt banked. The Messerschmitt came roaring low across the field.

Butler saw the Spitfire suddenly fling out of a climbing turn, roll over on its back, pass upside down directly in front of the Messerschmitt. He saw the tracer lance-like striking the Spitfire; fragments came out of the rudder. Then the Spitfire fell away, and the Messerschmitt shot past and over.

Butler saw the Spitfire rear up, pull around half-stalled, try to climb, hanging on its propeller. Butler kept shouting aloud: 'Get your nose down! Get it down!' He could feel the Spitfire about to crash. One wing dipped and then the other, and then it came level and began to climb.

Butler watched the two machines approach each other.

He saw them fire, pass and pull around in a circle. Lying there, he could feel

Fletcher trying to get the last ounce of energy out of his engine, delicately holding the controls in place, just under stalling point, trying not to feel pain or strain, trying to keep cool, trying to gain a few yards on the enemy machine.

He felt all the agony of Fletcher trying to tighten the bank as the gap of sky gradually closed between the two machines. He saw the Spitfire wings dip again, first one wing tip, then the other. Christ, Butler thought, he's using everything, slots and ailerons, the works. He did not want Fletcher to lose. He felt all the old bond of their comradeship together, all their days of flying, the nights with the lights shining, the glasses, the pretty girls in the pub, everybody alive, happy, a success.

'Jesus,' Craddock groaned. 'He's gaining on him.'

Butler saw the Spitfire wobble. It was just over the trees, beyond the edge of the aerodrome. He saw himself falling in fire, the Sutton harness jammed, the cockpit filled with flames, the blood running down his arm again. Then he was on his feet, running across the field towards the trees, shouting, 'Belly in! Don't pull up! Don't pull up!' He felt if only he were in the cockpit he would know what to do. He would save Fletcher.

When the Spitfire vanished below the trees, almost in the sound of a big explosion filled with the sound of machine gunfire, a black, oily plume of smoke rose over the trees. Running, Butler felt the pain of love tear his heart. As though in a dream, he saw Fletcher's face staring at him out of death, his eyes mute, admonishing. I should have gone up, Butler thought. I should have gone up. But there wasn't time. Wasn't time, a voice called inside him.

He ran on, through the trees. Across the field he saw a plume of smoke rising in black silhouette against the pink and gold sky. The field looked all in shadow. The wreckage lay in the middle of the field, the fire roaring through the broken members, the torn remains.

Fletcher lay in the grass, thrown clear, a bloody heap, his face grotesque with blood. The skin under the blood on his face was green, and blood seeped from his broken body.

'Jesus Christ,' he said, spitting blood through his teeth. 'I've bought it this time.'

'You'll be all right,' Butler said, holding

315

him, kneeling beside him.

'My luck went, that's all.'

'Sure.'

'One more time around and I'd 've had him.'

'Sure.'

The shadows fell longer across the field. Butler held him tighter, his arm around Fletcher's back, holding him gently against his knee.

'Put me down,' Fletcher whispered. 'Jesus!' He grimaced and closed his eyes, clenching his teeth against the shock and pain.

'We've won, Fletch—'

'One more time around ...' Fletcher gasped. 'One more time and—' A light wind passed. The shadows lengthened. Dark green light was coming through the trees.

Butler knelt motionless. For a moment sunlight shimmered in the dim green tide of day. Suddenly the sun seemed to sink. There was no sound in the sky.

The publishers hope that this book has given you enjoyable reading. Large Print Books are especially designed to be as easy to see and hold as possible. If you wish a complete list of our books, please ask at your local library or write directly to Magna Large Print Books, Long Preston, North Yorkshire, BD23 4ND, England.

International Research in Sports Biomechanics

This book presents cutting-edge research material on sports biomechanics from many of the leading international academics in the field. Covering a wide range of sports, from basketball and baseball to martial arts, the book addresses key contemporary themes in the discipline, from injury prevention and rehabilitation to paediatric exercise.

The thirty-seven chapters presented are divided into nine sections:

- biomechanics of fundamental human movement
- modelling, simulation and optimization
- biomechanics of the neuro-musculo-skeletal system
- sports injuries, orthopaedics and rehabilitation
- the application of electromyography in movement studies
- biomechanical analysis of the internal load
- methods and instrumentation
- training
- paediatric and geriatric exercise.

International Research in Sports Biomechanics therefore represents an invaluable reference for sports biomechanists and sports scienc departments worldwide.

Youlian Hong is a Professor at the Department of Sports Science and Physical Education at the Chinese University of Hong Kong, and the current Vice President of the International Society of Biomechanics in Sports.

International Research in Sports Biomechanics

Edited by Youlian Hong

London and New York

First published 2002 by Routledge
11 New Fetter Lane, London EC4P 4EE

Simultaneously published in the USA and Canada
by Routledge
29 West 35th Street, New York, NY 10001

Routledge is an imprint of the Taylor & Francis Group

© 2002 Routledge

Printed and bound in Great Britain by
Antony Rowe Ltd, Chippenham, Wiltshire

Every effort has been made to ensure that the advice and information in this
book is true and accurate at the time of going to press. However neither the
publisher nor the authors can accept any legal responsibility or liability for
any errors or omissions that may be made. In the case of drug
administration, any medical procedure or the use of technical equipment
mentioned within this book, you are strongly advised to consult the
manufacturer's guidelines. **Coventry University**

Publisher's Note
This book has been prepared from camera-ready copy provided by the
authors.

British Library Cataloguing in Publication Data
A catalogue record for this book is available from the British Library

Library of Congress Cataloging in Publication Data

ISBN 0-415-26230-5

CONTENTS

FOREWORD

This outstanding volume of sports biomechanics papers represents an important milestone in the history of the International Society of Biomechanics in Sports (ISBS). While the ISBS publishes Proceedings of its annual conferences, this is the first time that the best papers from an ISBS conference have been expanded and published as a separate volume. I commend Youlian Hong and the Chinese University of Hong Kong on this timely and appropriate initiative.

Why is this initiative timely and appropriate? The ISBS 2000 Symposium in Hong Kong coincided with the eighteenth birthday of the Society. The ISBS has come of age! It is strong and independent and bristling with drive to achieve its mandate of disseminating information of high quality to sports scientists and sports practitioners. This volume supplements other recent initiatives of the ISBS to achieve its mandate. These include the establishment of a professional home website, a web based "Coaches Information Service", and a peer-reviewed coach-friendly scientific journal *Sport Biomechanics*.

ISBS 2000 was the first ISBS Symposium held in Asia. The rapid growth of the ISBS and its involvement in disseminating sports science information is paralleled by the growing application of sports science in the Asian region. It is symbolic that the eighteenth ISBS conference was held in Hong Kong and noteworthy that Youlian Hong and his team further cemented the outstanding standards established in recent ISBS conferences, while simultaneously globalising the influence of the ISBS. The membership of ISBS looks forward to returning to Asia to celebrate its twenty-first birthday at the ISBS 2003 Symposium hosted by Beijing in 2003. Coincidentally, I write this preface on the morning following the announcement that Beijing will host the 2008 Olympic Games.

I trust that you will derive great benefit from the papers in this volume. They represent "cutting-edge" research of leading sports scientists within a dynamic society, the effort and initiative of one of the ISBS' most dynamic officers Youlian Hong, and the expanding Asian contribution to sports science.

Ross Sanders, PhD
(President ISBS, June 1999 – June 2001)

ABOUT THE EDITOR

Youlian Hong, the current Vice President for Conferences and Meetings of the International Society of Biomechanics in Sports, is a Professor at the Department of Sports Science and Physical Education, the Chinese University of Hong Kong. He received an undergraduate degree in Engineering Mechanics from Qing Hua University, Beijing, a Master degree in Biomechanics from Beijing University of Physical Education, and his Ph.D. degree in Sports Science from German Sports University, Cologne in 1991. Youlian was the Chairman of XVIII International Symposium on Biomechanics in Sports, which was held 25–30 June 2000, in Hong Kong. His research interests include computer simulation of human movement, ergonomics, biomechanics of paediatric and geriatric exercise, and the scientific basis of Tai Chi.

LIST OF CONTRIBUTORS

Tim Ackland — Department of Human Movement and Exercise Science, The University of Western Australia, Perth, Australia

Takao Akatsuka — Faculty of Engineering, Yamagata University, Yonezawa, Yamagata, Japan

Kai-Nan An — Department of Orthopedic Surgery, Mayo Clinic and Mayo Foundation, Rochester, Minnesota, USA

Thomas P. Andriacchi — Stanford Biomotion Laboratory, Stanford University, Stanford, California, USA

Raul Arellano — Universidad de Granada, Granada, Spain

Takeshi Asai — Faculty of Education, Yamagata University, Japan

Moshe Ayalon — The Zinman College of Physical Education and Sport Sciences, Wingate, Israel

Rod Barrett — School of Physiotherapy and Exercise Science, Griffith University, Queensland, Australia

Roger Bartlett — Sport Science Research Institute, Sheffield Hallam University, Collegiate Hall, Sheffield, UK

Nat Benjanuvatra — Department of Human Movement and Exercise Science, The University of Western Australia, Perth, Australia

David Ben-Sira — The Zinman College of Physical Education and Sport Sciences, Wingate, Israel

Thor Besier — Department of Human Movement and Exercise Science, The University of Western Australia, Perth, Australia

Brian A. Blanksby — Department of Human Movement and Exercise Science, The University of Western Australia, Perth, Australia

Kevin A. Broughan — Department of Mathematics, University of Waikato, Hamilton, New Zealand

Eugene W. Brown — Department of Kinesiology, Michigan State University, East Lansing, Michigan, USA

Graham Caldwell Department of Exercise Science, University of Massachusetts, USA

Ajit M. Chaudhari Stanford Biomotion Laboratory, Stanford University, Stanford, California, USA

Chi-kin Cheung Department of Sports Science and Physical Education, The Chinese University of Hong Kong, Hong Kong, China

John W. Chow Department of Kinesiology, University of Illinois, Urbana, Illinois, USA

Jodie Cochrane Department of Human Movement and Exercise Science, The University of Western Australia, Perth, Australia

Blanca De La Fuente Universidad de Granada, Granada, Spain

Daniel Drouin Department of Kinesiology, University of Windsor, Windsor, Canada

Rosemary Dyson Faculty of Sciences, University College Chichester, Chichester, West Sussex, UK

Bruce Elliott Department of Human Movement and Exercise Science, The University of Western Australia, Perth, Australia

Mark A. Fadil Stanford Myofascial Institute, Palo Alto, California, USA

Rene E. D. Ferdinands Department of Physics and Electronic Engineering, University of Waikato, Hamilton, New Zealand

Tetsuo Fukunaga Graduate School of Arts and Sciences, University of Tokyo, Japan

Takeshi Furuhashi Graduate School of Engineering, Nagoya University, Japan

Francisco García CAR Sierra Nevada, Granada, Spain

Kostas Gianikellis Faculty of Sport Sciences, University of Extremadura, Spain

Albert Gollhofer Department of Sport Science, University of Stuttgart, Germany

Youlian Hong	The Chinese University of Hong Kong, Hong Kong, China
Lee Janaway	Brunel Institute for Bioengineering, Brunel University, Uxbridge, UK
Thomas Jöllenbeck	Bergische Universität–Gesamthochschule Wuppertal, Germany
Yasuo Kawakami	Graduate School of Arts and Sciences, University of Tokyo, Japan
Andreas Klee	Bergische Universität–Gesamthochschule Wuppertal, Germany
Valery Kleshnev	Australian Institute of Sport, Canberra, Australia
Klaus Knoll	Institute for Applied Training Science, Leipzig, Germany
Juergen Krug	University of Leipzig, Faculty for Sport Science, Germany
Young-Hoo Kwon	Human Performance Laboratory, Ball State University, Muncie, Indiana, USA
Mario Lamontagne	School of Human Kinetics and Department of Mechanical Engineering, University of Ottawa, Ottawa, Canada
Seok-Beom Lee	Hallym University Sacred Heart Hospital, Pyungchon, Kyunggi-do, Korea
Li Li	Department of Kinesiology, Louisiana State University, USA
Jing Xian Li	The Chinese University of Hong Kong, Hong Kong, China
Young-Tae Lim	Department of Physical Education, Yeungnam University, Kyungsan, Korea
David Lloyd	Department of Human Movement and Exercise Science, University of Western Australia, Perth, WA, Australia
Constanze Loschner	New South Wales Institute of Sport, Sydney, Australia

Andrew Lyttle	Western Australian Institute of Sport, Perth, Australia
John M. MacMahon	Stanford Biomotion Laboratory, Stanford University, Stanford, California, USA
G. Wayne Marino	Department of Kinesiology, University of Windsor, Windsor, Canada
Robert N. Marshall	Department of Sports and Exercise Science, The University of Auckland, Auckland, New Zealand
Masahiro Masubuchi	Fluent Asia Pacific Co., Ltd, Shinjyuku, Tokyo, Japan
Tsuyoshi Matsumoto	Institute of Health and Sport Sciences, University of Tsukuba, Tsukuba, Japan
Tomoyuki Matsuo	School of Health and Sport Sciences, Osaka University, Toyonaka, Osaka, Japan
Stuart Miller	School of Leisure and Sports Studies, Leeds Metropolitan University, Beckett Park, Leeds LS6 3QS, UK
Yoshiyuki Mochizuki	Laboratories of Image Information Science and Technology, Osaka, Japan
Bernard F. Morrey	Department of Orthopedic Surgery, Mayo Clinic and Mayo Foundation, Rochester, Minnesota, USA
Christie Munro	School of Physical Education, University of Otago, Dunedin, New Zealand
Falk Naundorf	University of Leipzig, Faculty for Sport Science, Germany
Rob Neal	Department of Human Movement Studies, University of Queensland, Australia
Gunnar Németh	Department of Orthopaedic Surgery, Karolinska Hospital, Stockholm, Sweden
Hiroyuki Nunome	Research Centre of Health, Physical Fitness and Sports, Nagoya University, Nagoya, Japan
Shawn W. O'Driscoll	Department of Orthopedic Surgery, Mayo Clinic and Mayo Foundation, Rochester, Minnesota, USA

Yoshiharu Ohshima   Faculty of Education, Hirosaki University, Hirosaki, Japan

Susana Pardillo   Universidad de Granada, Granada, Spain

Dan K. Ramsey   School of Human Kinetics, University of Ottawa, Ottawa, Canada

Stefan Reiss   University of Leipzig, Faculty for Sport Science, Germany

Hartmut Riehle   Sports Department, University of Konstanz, Konstanz, Germany

Paul D. Robinson   University College Worcester, Worcester, UK

Howell Round   Department of Physics and Electronic Engineering, University of Waikato, Hamilton, New Zealand

Shinji Sakurai   Research Centre of Health, Physical Fitness and Sports, Nagoya University, Nagoya, Japan

Manabu Shimoda   Graduate School of Arts and Sciences, University of Tokyo, Japan

Richard Smith   University of Sydney, Faculty of Health Sciences, Australia

Kanta Tachibana   Graduate School of Engineering, Nagoya University, Japan and Bio-Mimetic Control Research Centre, Riken, Japan

Yoshihiro Takada   Human Performance and Expression, Faculty of Human Development, Kobe University, Kobe, Japan

Manfred M. Vieten   Sports Department, University of Konstanz, Konstanz, Germany

Klaus Wiemann   Bergische Universität-Gesamthochschule Wuppertal, Germany

Per F. Wretenberg   Department of Orthopaedic Surgery, Karolinska Hospital, Stockholm, Sweden

Toshimasa Yanai   School of Physical Education, University of Otago, Dunedin, New Zealand

Part One

The Biomechanics of Fundamental Human Movement

Throwing: Fundamentals and Practical Applications

Roger Bartlett
Sport Science Research Institute, Sheffield Hallam University,
Collegiate Hall, Sheffield, UK

INTRODUCTION

This paper focuses on those sports or events in which the participant throws, passes, bowls or shoots an object from the hand. The similarities between these activities and striking skills—such as the tennis serve—make much of the research into the latter also relevant to applied work in throwing.

Throwing movements are often classified as underarm, overarm or sidearm. This paper will concentrate on overarm throws; much of the material presented can be extrapolated to underarm or sidearm throws. Overarm throws are characterized by lateral rotation of the humerus in the preparation phase and its medial rotation in the action phase (e.g. Dillman et al., 1993). This movement is one of the fastest joint rotations in the human body. The sequence of movements in the preparation phase of a baseball pitch, for example, include, for a right-handed pitcher, pelvic and trunk rotation to the right, horizontal extension and lateral rotation at the shoulder, elbow flexion and wrist hyperextension (Luttgens et al., 1992). These movements are followed, sequentially, by their anatomical opposite at each of the joints mentioned plus radio-ulnar pronation. As Bob Marshall's paper (Marshall, 2000) shows, the long-axis rotations of the arm do not fit easily into the assumed proximal-to-distal sequence of the other joint movements.

The mass (inertia) and dimensions of the thrown object—plus the size of the target area and the rules of the particular sport—are constraints on the movement pattern of any throw. Bowling in cricket differs from other similar movement patterns, as the rules do not allow the elbow to extend during the delivery stride. The interpretation of this rule is fraught with difficulty. If the umpires consider that this law has been breached, they can 'call the bowler for throwing': as David Lloyd and Bruce Elliott show in their paper (Lloyd et al., 2000), umpires can err in calling throws. One reason for this is that they only have a two-dimensional view of the three-dimensional movements of the arm.

The goal of a throwing movement will generally be distance, accuracy or some combination of the two. In throws for distance, the release speed—and, therefore, the force applied to the thrown object—is crucial. In some throws, the objective is not to achieve maximal distance; instead, it may be accuracy or minimal time in the air. In accuracy dominated skills, such as dart throwing, some passes and free throws in basketball, the release of the object needs to achieve accuracy within the distance constraints of the skill. The interaction of speed and accuracy in these skills is often expressed as the speed–accuracy trade-off. This has been investigated particularly thoroughly for basketball shooting (e.g. Brancazio, 1992). The shooter has to release the ball with speed and accuracy to pass through the basket.

Coaches of throwing events—like all coaches—are particularly interested in improving the performance of their athletes, keeping them performing well and reducing their time off through injury. The following sections are oriented to these coaching goals, which have many implications for the application of sports biomechanics research into throwing.

OPTIMIZING PERFORMANCE

In many throws, the objective is to maximize, within certain constraints, the range achieved. Any increase in release speed (v_0) or release height (y_0) is always accompanied by an increase in the range. If the objective of the throw is to maximize range, it is important to ascertain the best (optimum) release angle to achieve this. The optimum release angle (θ), ignoring air resistance, can be found from:

$$\cos 2\theta = g\, y_0\, / \, (v_0^2 + g\, y_0)$$

For a good shot putter, this would give a value around 42°. Although optimum release angles for given release speeds and heights can easily be determined mathematically, they do not always correspond to those recorded from the best performers in sporting events. This is even true for the shot put (Tsirakos *et al.*, 1995) in which the object's flight is the closest to a parabola of all sports objects. The reason is that the calculation of an optimum release angle assumes, implicitly, that release speed and release angle are independent of one another. For a shot putter, the release speed and angle are, however, not independent, because of the arrangement and mechanics of the muscles used to generate the release speed of the shot. A greater release speed, and hence range, can be achieved at an angle (about 35°) that is less than the optimum release angle for the shot's flight phase. If the shot putter seeks to increase the release angle to a value closer to the optimum angle for the shot's flight phase, the release speed decreases and so does the range.

In javelin throwing, some research has assessed the interdependence of the various release parameters. The two for which an interrelationship is known are release speed and angle. Two groups of researchers have investigated this relationship, one using a 1 kg ball (Red and Zogaib, 1977) and the other using an instrumented javelin (Viitasalo and Korjus, 1988). Surprisingly, they obtained very similar relationships over the relevant range, expressed by the equation:

release speed (m·s^{-1}) = nominal release speed (m·s^{-1})–0.13 (release angle (°)–35°)

The nominal release speed is defined as the maximum speed at which a thrower is capable of throwing for a release angle of 35°. In the javelin throw, the aerodynamic characteristics of the projectile can significantly influence its trajectory. It may travel a greater or lesser distance than it would have done if projected in a vacuum. Under such circumstances, the calculations of range and of optimal release parameters need to be modified considerably to take account of the aerodynamic forces acting on the javelin. Furthermore, more release parameters are then important. These include the angular velocities of the javelin at release—such as the pitching and yawing angular velocities—and the 'aerodynamic' angles—the angles of pitch and yaw. A unique combination of these release parameters still exists that will maximize the distance thrown (Best *et al.*, 1995). Away from this optimum, many different combinations of release parameters will produce the same distance for sub-optimal throws. The implications for coaches of this sub-optimal variability and the different 'steepnesses' of the approaches to the optimal conditions have yet to be fully established.

Another complication arises when accuracy becomes crucial to successful throwing, as in shooting skills in basketball. A relationship between release speed and release angle is then found that will satisfy the speed-accuracy trade-off. For a given height of release and distance from the basket, a unique release angle exists for the ball to pass through the centre of the basket for any realistic release speed. Margins of error for both speed and angle exist about this pair of values. The margin of error in the release speed increases with the release angle, but only slowly. However, the margin of error in the release angle reaches a sharp peak for release angles within a few degrees of the minimum-speed angle (the angle for which the release speed is the minimum to score a basket). This latter consideration dominates the former, particularly as a shot at the minimum speed requires the minimum force from the shooter. The minimum-speed angle is, therefore, the best one (Brancazio, 1992). The role of movement variability—both intra-individual and inter-individual (Hore *et al.*, 1996)—in distance—and accuracy-dominated throws has not been fully explained to date. Stuart Miller's paper (Miller, 2000) outlines his findings—and their implications for coaches—for variability in the kinematics and muscle activation patterns in the basketball free throw, a movement—as noted above—in which accuracy is crucial.

The co-ordination of joint and muscle actions is often considered to be crucial to the successful execution of throwing movements. For example, in kicking a proximal-to-distal sequence has been identified. As kicking has much in common with throwing, we might expect similar distal-to-proximal behaviour for the arm segments in throwing. This is not the case when the movement sequence includes long-axis rotations, as Bob Marshall's paper (Marshall, 2000) shows.

THROWING INJURIES

Throwers subject their bodies to loads well beyond the stresses and strains of sedentary life. The throwing techniques used, even when considered "correct", may cause injury. The use of many repetitions of these techniques in training should not therefore be undertaken lightly; the risk of injury may well override beneficial motor learning considerations. The use of an incorrect technique is usually considered to exacerbate the injury potential of sports. This has rarely been verified scientifically, although indirect evidence can often be deduced. The sport biomechanist should seek to identify incorrect techniques to prevent injury. Training to improve throwing technique and to acquire appropriate strength and flexibility is likely to help to reduce injury as well as to improve performance. However, many throwing techniques are determined by the activity, reducing possible changes to technique, particularly at high standards of performance.

Low-back pain affects, at some time, most of the world's population and has several causes. These are the weakness of the region and the loads to which it is subjected in everyday tasks, and, particularly, in sport. This involves any of three injury-related activities. These are (Rasch, 1989): weight loading, involving spinal compression; rotation-causing activities involving forceful twisting of the trunk, such as discus throwing; back-arching activities as in many overarm throws. Obviously, activities involving all three of these are more hazardous. An example is the "mixed technique" used by many fast bowlers in cricket. Here the bowler counter-rotates the shoulders with respect to the hips from a more front-on position, at back foot strike in the delivery stride, to a more side-on position at front foot strike. At front foot strike, the impact forces on the foot typically reach over six times body weight. This counter-rotation, or twisting, is also associated with hyperextension of the lumbar spine. The result is the common occurrence of spondylolysis (a stress fracture of the neural arch, usually of L5) in fast bowlers with such a technique (Elliott *et al.*, 1995). The incidence of spondylolysis and other lumbar abnormalities in fast bowlers is a good example of the association between technique and injury. Relatively few incidences of spondylolysis have been reported amongst genuine side-on or front-on bowlers. It might be hypothesized that incorrect coaching at a young age was responsible. British coaches and teachers have long been taught that the side-on technique is the correct one. However, as the less coached West Indians might be held to demonstrate, the front-on technique may be more natural. Research in both the UK and Australia has demonstrated the injury potential of the mixed technique and convinced the cricket authorities in both countries to amend their coaching texts to reflect this.

In overarm throwing movements, such as javelin throwing and baseball pitching, the joints of the shoulder region often experience large ranges of motion at high angular velocities, often with many repetitions. Overuse injuries are common and frequently involve the tendons of the rotator cuff muscles that pass between the head of the humerus and the acromion process. Examples are tendinitis of the supraspinatus, infraspinatus and subscapularis and impingement syndrome—the entrapment and inflammation of the rotator cuff muscles, the long head of biceps brachii and the subacromial bursa. Other soft tissue injuries include supraspinatus calcification, rupture of the supraspinatus tendon, triceps brachii tendinitis, and rupture or inflammation of the long head tendon of biceps brachii. Elbow injury is possible, particularly towards the end of the preparation phase, where the maximum valgus stress on the elbow occurs (e.g. Safran, 1995). We have confirmed, using diagnostic ultrasound, many of these injuries in experienced elite British male javelin throwers, with far fewer of them being present in younger top throwers. In overarm throwing for distance, it appears that to achieve the goal of the movement (maximum ball or implement speed), avoiding injury is relegated to second place.

Injuries to the lower extremity, often caused by the trunk twisting or turning while excessive traction fixes the foot, have a technique component in addition to the properties of the shoe-surface interface. The recent trend towards a side facing rather than forward-facing back foot plant in javelin throwing may explain the increasing incidence of patellar tendinitis in the right leg of right handed throwers, Achilles tendinitis and other lower extremity injuries.

CONCLUSIONS

In seeking to maximize the performance of an athlete in a throwing event, we need the correct optimal release model against which coaches can evaluate throwers' performances. In throwing activities, long-axis rotations complicate proximal-to-distal sequencing, which needs to be addressed in devising training schedules. The implications for coaches of sub-optimal variability in throwing and the different 'steepnesses' of the approaches to the optimal conditions have yet to be fully established. Injuries to throwers are mainly overuse. Eliminating injurious techniques, such as the mixed technique in cricket fast bowling, can reduce injuries. However, it appears that to achieve the goal of throws for distance (maximum ball or implement speed), avoiding injury is relegated to second place.

REFERENCES

Best, R.J., Bartlett, R.M. and Sawyer, R.A., 1995, Optimal javelin release. *Journal of Applied Biomechanics*, **11**, pp. 371-394.
Brancazio, P.J., 1992, Physics of basketball. *The Physics of Sports–Volume I*, (New York: American Institute of Physics), pp. 86-95.
Dillman, C.J., Fleisig, G.S. and Andrews, J.R., 1993, Biomechanics of pitching with emphasis upon shoulder kinematics. *Journal of Orthopaedic and Sports Physical Therapy*, **18**, pp. 402-408.
Elliott, B.C., Burnett, A.F., Stockill, N.P. and Bartlett, R.M., 1995, The fast bowler in cricket: a sports medicine perspective. *Sports Exercise and Injury,* **1**, pp. 201-206.
Hore, J., Watts, S. and Tweed, D., 1996, Errors in the control of joint rotations associated with inaccuracies in overarm throws. *Journal of Neurophysiology,* **75**, pp. 1013-1025.
Luttgens, K., Deutsch, H. and Hamilton, N., 1992, *Kinesiology: Scientific Basis of Human Motion* (Madison: Brown and Benchmark).
Lloyd, D., Alderson, J. and Elliott, B.C., 2000, Biomechanics in testing the legality of a bowling action in cricket. In *Proceedings of XVIII International Symposium on Biomechanics in Sports*, edited by Hong, Y. and Johns, D. (Hong Kong: CUHK Press), pp. 875-877.
Marshall, R.N., 2000, Applications to throwing of recent research on proximal-to-distal sequencing. In *Proceedings of XVIII International Symposium on*

Biomechanics in Sports, edited by Hong, Y. and Johns, D. (Hong Kong: CUHK Press), pp. 878-881.

Miller, S.A., 2000, Variability in basketball shooting: practical implications. In *Proceedings of XVIII International Symposium on Biomechanics in Sports*, edited by Hong, Y. and Johns, D. (Hong Kong: CUHK Press), pp. 887-891.

Rasch, P.J., 1989, *Kinesiology and Applied Anatomy*. (Philadelphia, PA: Lea and Febiger).

Red, W.E. and Zogaib, A.J., 1977, Javelin dynamics including body interaction. *Journal of Applied Mechanics*, **44**, pp. 496-497.

Safran, M.R., 1995, Elbow injuries in athletes—a review. *Clinical Orthopaedics and Related Research*, **310**, pp. 257-277.

Tsirakos, D.T., Bartlett, R.M. and Kollias, I.A., 1995, A comparative study of the release and temporal characteristics of shot put. *Journal of Human Movement Studies*, **28**, pp. 227-242.

Viitasalo, J.T. and Korjus, T., 1988, On-line measurement of kinematic characteristics in javelin throwing. In *Biomechanics XI-B*, edited by de Groot, G., Hollander, A.P., Huijing, P.A. and van Ingen Schenau, G.J. (Amsterdam: Free University Press), pp. 583-587.

movement about all the axes of rotation. An essential aspect of these skills is that the potential for rotation about each arm segment's long axis is exploited so that maximum speed may be generated at the end of the kinematic chain.

However, an inspection of the literature suggests that there are aspects of throwing and striking activities where aberrations are seen in the traditional proximal-to-distal pattern. Feltner and Dapena (1986), Sakurai *et al.* (1993) and Woo and Chapman (1994) have all shown incidences in throwing or striking motions where internal rotation velocity of the upper arm reaches a maximum after the peak speeds of the forearm and hand segments. The peak velocity of pronation has also been reported to occur immediately before impact (Woo and Chapman, 1994; Sprigings *et al.*, 1994), suggesting that this rotation also may not conform to traditional explanations of proximal-to-distal sequencing.

REVIEW OF METHODS

Two-dimensional (usually sagittal plane) studies of segmental sequencing have typically ignored independent quantification of long axis rotations. Claims for segmental sequencing evidence have been based upon data from end-point (joint) speeds, segmental speeds, joint angular velocities and resultant joint moments (see, for example, Zernicke and Roberts, 1976; Joris *et al.*, 1985; Kreighbaum and Barthels, 1985).

Several three-dimensional studies have also either ignored explicit quantification of long axis rotations or have calculated upper arm internal-external rotation from motion of the wrist relative to the long axis of the upper arm, a technique that works well until the elbow nears full extension. The closer the elbow is to full extension, the greater the error associated with this calculation (Feltner and Dapena, 1986; Vaughn, 1985; Fleisig *et al.*, 1996).

Finally, several studies have quantified long axis rotation of the upper arm and forearm in throwing and striking skills by directly monitoring upper arm internal and external rotation and forearm pronation and supination (Elliott *et al.*, 1995; Elliott *et al.*, 1996; Elliott *et al.*, 1997; Feltner and Nelson, 1996; Sakurai *et al.*, 1993; Sprigings *et al.*, 1994).

RESULTS

Results from eight studies reporting the timing and magnitude of upper arm internal rotation or pronation-supination speeds are summarized in Table 1. In all of these studies, one or both of the possible upper limb long-axis rotations reaches its peak speed at or near ball release or impact, and frequently after other shoulder and elbow rotations. These results confirm that long-axis rotations occur late in the sequencing of segmental motion in high-speed upper limb skills in contrast to a simplistic proximal-to-distal description.

Table 1 shows a range of upper arm internal rotation speeds, which appear to increase with a decrease in the mass and moment of inertia of the object held in the hand. Although a reporting of the shoulder kinetics associated with these skills is

Proximal-to-distal Sequencing Research: Application to Throwing

Robert N. Marshall
Department of Sports and Exercise Science,
The University of Auckland, Auckland, New Zealand

INTRODUCTION

Many sports demand that maximum speed be produced at the end of the distal segment in a kinematic chain. In throwing activities, for example, athletes try to generate a large hand velocity in a particular direction. Sports that use an implement to increase end point speed, such as tennis or squash, require that the racquet head develops maximum speed.

The idea that there is a 'grand plan' that would explain the multitude of different, yet similar, throwing or striking movements is appealing. Indeed, research has suggested that throwing, striking and kicking skills all exhibit aspects of proximal-to-distal sequencing. The concept upon which most others appear to have been developed is the 'summation of speed principle' (Bunn, 1972). The 'kinetic link principle' (Kreighbaum and Barthels, 1985) and Plagenhoef's (1971) 'acceleration-deceleration' concept are really variations on Bunn's definition. In essence, the principle states that, to produce the largest possible speed at the end of a linked chain of segments, the motion should start with the more proximal segments and proceed to the more distal segments. The more distal segment begins its motion at the time of the maximum speed of the proximal one, with each succeeding segment generating a larger endpoint velocity than the proximal segment.

Two- and three-dimensional kinematic analyses of throwing and striking activities are readily available in the literature (see, for example, Escamilla *et al.*, 1998; Sakurai *et al.*, 1993; Woo and Chapman, 1994). Aspects of proximal-to-distal sequencing have been confirmed, although evaluation of individual segment contributions to hand or racquet speed and the role of long-axis rotations in temporal patterning have received little quantitative consideration.

In some activities, such as kicking a ball, neither segmental long axis rotation nor movement out of the primary plane appears to contribute significantly to the speed of the foot. On the other hand, movements such as throwing a ball or a forehand drive in squash are effective only if the skill takes advantage of beyond the scope of this paper, the magnitudes involved must signal a recognition of the importance as well as the potential dangers of upper arm internal rotation to these skills.

The pronation-supination speeds reported are lower than for upper arm internal rotation, but are still substantial. The difficulty in recording this motion may be inferred from the lack of data from baseball pitching studies.

Table 1 Timing and magnitude of long-axis rotation speeds in throwing and striking.

Researchers	Activity	Upper arm internal rotation speed (IR)	Pronation-supination speed	Timing
Vaughn, 1985	Baseball pitchers	107 r/s		Elbow extension, IR, release
Feltner and Dapena, 1986	Baseball pitchers	106 r/s		Elbow extension, IR, release
Sakurai et al., 1993	Baseball pitchers		Pronation	Pronation, [IR, wrist flexion and ulnar flexion], release
Barrentine et al., 1998	Baseball pitchers		Supination: 26 r/s	[ulnar deviation and wrist flexion], supination, release
Escamilla et al., 1998	Baseball pitchers	80–105 r/s		Horizontal abduction, elbow extension, IR, release
Feltner and Nelson, 1996	Waterpolo throw	35 r/s	Pronation: 20 r/s	Pronation, IR, elbow extension, release
Elliott et al. 1995	Tennis serve	37 r/s	Pronation: 15 r/s	[pronation and wrist flexion], IR, pronation, impact
Elliott et al. 1996	Squash forehand	52 r/s	Pronation: 35 r/s	[IR, pronation and wrist flexion], impact

Table 2 Contribution of long axis rotations to hand or racquet head speed.

	% contribution to forward linear hand or racquet head speed			
	Water polo throw (Feltner and Nelson, 1996)	Tennis serve (Elliott et al., 1995)	Tennis forehands[1] (Elliott et al., 1997)	Squash forehand (Elliott et al., 1996)
Shoulder motion	29.1*	9.7	10.0–13.7	4.9
Upper arm IR	13.2	54.2	38.6–48.3	46.1
Elbow extension	26.6	−14.2	0.6–5.6	4.2
Pronation	−0.1	5.2	−0.6–4.6	12.0
Wrist flexion	4.8	30.6	1.1–15.0	18.2

[1] Ranges are from flat, topspin and lob forehands using two different grips
* Combined trunk motion (4.9% anteroposterior + 24.2% trunk twist)

Several studies have quantified the contribution of segment rotations to the speed of the hand or racquet. These are summarized in Table 2, where differences between a waterpolo throw and tennis or squash strokes can be seen. Internal rotation of the upper arm and wrist flexion are major contributors to racquet head speed; however, in a waterpolo penalty throw, trunk motion and elbow extension are the largest contributors. Presumably these differences are related to the magnitude of external forces available to the athlete as well as the mass and moment of inertia of the implement.

DISCUSSION

These studies provide quantitative information on the components of high velocity throws and racquet strokes, and confirm the importance of long-axis rotations (upper arm internal rotation and forearm pronation) in the development of speed. The concept of proximal-to-distal sequencing can now be more fully described, with the presentation of results that consistently show internal rotation of the upper arm and pronation occurring as some of the final components of the motion pattern. Data from these studies clearly show that attempts to explain proximal-to-distal segmental sequencing based upon two-dimensional information provide an incomplete description. While forearm pronation typically occurs after elbow extension and before, or simultaneous with, wrist flexion, the rotation that appears to differ from previous descriptions of proximal-to-distal sequencing is upper arm internal rotation. This movement occurs with, or after, wrist flexion in baseball pitching and racquet strokes, much later than predicted. The exception appears to be the waterpolo penalty throw where the specific and unique aspects of the skill require a modified sequencing. However, upper arm internal rotation still appears later in the sequence than would be predicted by a traditional proximal-to-distal description.

In addition, data from the studies quoted indicate the relative importance of these two long axis rotations. Upper arm internal rotation contributed between 38% and 54% of racquet head speed at impact and forearm pronation contributed between 0.6% and 12%, depending on racquet stroke. Unfortunately, data are not available on percentage contributions to ball speed for baseball pitching or football passing. In waterpolo it appears that long axis rotations are less important than might initially be expected.

This information suggests coaches and players should consider the range of motion, movement speed and timing of upper arm internal rotation in developing training regimes for strength, flexibility, speed and injury prevention.

CONCLUSIONS

It appears that most previous research examining the pattern of segmental sequencing in throwing and upper limb striking skills has simplified the movement by ignoring longitudinal axis motion. This has resulted in support for the proximal-to-distal sequence pattern as suggested by Bunn (1972) and others. Recent research indicates that, while there is a proximal-to-distal sequence in abduction-adduction and flexion-extension components of an upper limb skill, major contributions to the final speed of the hand or racquet result from longitudinal axis rotations. These results show internal rotation of the upper arm and pronation of the forearm frequently occurring as the final components of the motion pattern. Thus, this analysis also indicates traditional concepts of proximal-to-distal sequencing are inadequate to accurately describe the complexity of throwing and upper limb striking skills. It is essential to consider upper arm and forearm long axis rotations in explaining the mechanics of these movements as well as in developing coaching emphases, strength training schedules, and injury prevention programmes.

REFERENCES

Barrentine, S.W., Matsuo, T., Escamilla, R.F., Fleisig, G.S. and Andrews, J.R., 1998, Kinematic analysis of the wrist and forearm during baseball pitching. *Journal of Applied Biomechanics*, **14**, pp. 24-39.

Bunn, J., 1972, *Scientific Principles of Coaching* (Englewood Cliffs, New Jersey, Prentice-Hall, Inc).

Elliott, B., Marshall, R. and Noffal, G., 1995, Contributions of upper limb segment rotations during the power serve in tennis. *Journal of Applied Biomechanics*, **11**, pp. 433-442.

Elliott, B., Marshall, R. and Noffal, G., 1996, The role of upper limb segment rotations in the development of racquet-head speed in the squash forehand. *Journal of Sports Sciences*, **14**, pp. 159-165.

Elliott, B., Takahashi, K. and Noffal, G., 1997, The influence of grip position on upper limb contributions to racquet head velocity in a tennis forehand. *Journal of Applied Biomechanics*, **13**, pp. 182-196.

Escamilla, R.F., Fleisig, G.S., Barrentine, S.W., Zheng, N. and Andrews, J.R., 1998, Kinematic comparisons of throwing different types of baseball pitches. *Journal of Applied Biomechanics*, **14**, pp. 1-23.

Feltner, M.E. and Dapena, J., 1986, Dynamics of the shoulder and elbow joints of the throwing arm during a baseball pitch. *International Journal of Sport Biomechanics*, **2**, pp. 235-259.

Feltner, M.E. and Nelson, S.T., 1996, Three-dimensional kinematics of the throwing arm during the penalty throw in water polo. *Journal of Applied Biomechanics*, **12**, pp. 359-382.

Fleisig, G.S., Escamilla, R.F., Andrews, J.R., Matsuo, T., Satterwhite, Y. and Barrentine, S.W., 1996, Kinematic and kinetic comparison between baseball pitching and football passing. *Journal of Applied Biomechanics*, **12**, pp. 207-224.

Joris, H.J., Edwards van Muyen, A.J., van Ingen Schenau, G.J. and Kemper, H.C., 1985, Force, velocity and energy flow during the overarm throw in female handball players. *Journal of Biomechanics*, **18**, pp. 409-414.

Kreighbaum, E. and Barthels, K.M., 1985, *Biomechanics—A Qualitative Approach for Studying Human Movement* (Minneapolis: Burgess Publishing Co.).

Plagenhoef, S., 1971, *Patterns of Human Motion* (New Jersey, Prentice Hall).

Sakurai, S., Ikegami, Y., Okamoto, A., Yabe, K. and Toyoshima, S., 1993, A three-dimensional cinematographic analysis of upper limb movement during fastball and curveball baseball pitches. *Journal of Applied Biomechanics*, **9**, pp. 45-65.

Sprigings, E., Marshall, R., Elliott, B. and Jennings, L., 1994, A three-dimensional kinematic method for determining the effectiveness of arm segment rotations in producing racquet-head speed. *Journal of Biomechanics*, **27**, pp. 245-254.

Vaughn, R.E., 1985, An algorithm for determining arm action during overarm baseball pitches. In *Biomechanics IX-B*, edited by Winter, D.A., Norman, R.W., Wells, R.P. and Patla, A.E. (Champaign, IL: Human Kinetics), pp. 510-515.

Woo, H. and Chapman, A.E., 1994, The temporal co-ordination of an elite squash forehand stroke. In: *Proceedings of the Eighth Biennial Conference, Canadian Society for Biomechanics* (Calgary: University of Calgary), pp. 230-231.

Zernicke, R.F. and Roberts E.M., 1976, Human lower extremity kinetic relationships during systematic variations in resultant limb velocity. In *Biomechanics V-B*, edited by Komi, P.V. (Baltimore: University Park Press), pp. 20-25.

3

Biomechanics of Overhand Throwing Motion: Past, Present, and Future Research Trend

Shinji Sakurai
Research Centre of Health, Physical Fitness and Sports,
Nagoya University, Nagoya, Japan

INTRODUCTION

Overhand throwing has been extensively studied in Japan and the USA, with many research papers published on baseball pitching. A number of reviews summarizing these studies have been published (Atwater, 1979; Fleisig *et al.*, 1996).

In this paper, the characteristics of the overhand throwing motion will be discussed, followed by a brief review of studies published by Japanese researchers. Future research direction in this area will also be discussed.

WHAT IS "OVERHAND THROWING"?

"Overhand" does not necessarily mean the position of the throwing arm. In cricket bowling, the arm is swung through an overhead position (Figure 1). But this motion is not called overhand throwing. In baseball, there are pitchers with "overhand", "three-quarter", "sidehand", and "underhand" styles. They look initially different from each other. But if close attention is paid to the angles of upper limb joints, all are similar, with differences highlighted in trunk angle (Figure 2).

Figure 1 Cricket bowling and baseball pitching.

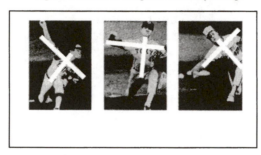

Figure 2 Overhand, sidehand, and underhand.

There are several types of throwing motion, such as bilateral or unilateral, and overhand, sidehand, or underhand. Among these unilateral overhand throwing is a motion which is acquired last from the developmental view-point (Wickstrom, 1975). In softball and cricket, the pitcher's or bowler's action is strictly regulated. However, fielders who have no restrictions on their motion usually throw a ball with an overhand motion. Overhand throwing is a motion with which we can throw fastest and most accurately.

We could define "overhand throwing" as the motion of thrusting an object into space by the use of one arm with extension of the elbow and internal rotation of the shoulder as major upper limb actions, and with which the upperarm is kept apart from the trunk.

WHY ARE WE ENCHANTED BY THE MOTION OF "OVERHAND THROWING"?

Man cannot: fly or run faster than a cheetah; jump longer than a kangaroo or swim faster than a dolphin. But we can throw farther, stronger, and better than any other animal (Figure 3). Some anthropoids such as chimpanzees and gorillas are known to throw, but their motion is mainly underhand.

We are very weak creatures, and our physical ability is very limited. But throwing is one given talent. Only human can throw. In a more accurate sense, man is the only creature who can throw with an overhand motion.

The most effective method to study how genetic and environmental factors affect development and growth is through the study of twins. In running and jumping movements, techniques of identical twins were generally similar to each other (Goya *et al.*, 1988; Fukashiro *et al.*, 1985), while Toyoshima *et al.* (1982, 1983) found that the similarity of the throwing motion between two sets of twins were low. Motions such as walking and running are often discussed as ontogenic, while throwing is regarded as a phylogenic motion. These findings suggest that the throwing motion is more highly affected by environmental factors, such as learning and practice.

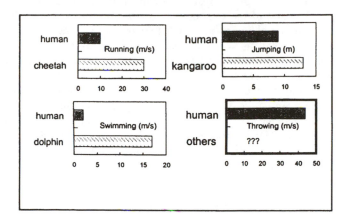

Figure 3 Comparison of the human ability with other animals.

HOW HAS THROWING MOTION BEEN STUDIED?

Throwing has attracted much researcher interest, and it has been studied with a variety of methods.

Speed changes of the body parts were reported in many papers, and the contribution of the whip-like body actions and the effect of the stretch-shortening cycle were discussed in relation to the thrown ball velocities. Miyashita *et al.* (1986) compared the horizontal velocity changes of various body parts and reported the period in which velocity change of body centre of mass exceeded that of the throwing hand. They suggested that there was every possibility of the reutilization of the stored elastic energy increasing the ball speed.

Both kinematic and kinetic aspects of throwing have also been studied. Toyoshima and Miyashita (1973) studied the relationship between ball speed and force applied to the ball during the throwing motion for balls of the same size (diameter = 7cm) and nine different weights (100g to 500g). Ishii and Nakade (1974) studied the changes in force applied on the ball during the throwing motion to the speed of male handball players with balls of six different weights ranging from 180g to 900g (diameter = 18.5cm). The force and the mechanical work exerted on the ball increased as the ball increased in weight. Almost all of the mechanical energy of the ball at release was supplied in the very short period just before release.

Toyoshima *et al.* (1974) investigated the contribution of each body segment to ball speed by restricting the motion of body segments involved in the throwing motion. They found that without stepping or trunk rotation the ball was accelerated to only 50% of that attained in a normal throwing motion. They suggested that this demonstrated the importance of muscles on lower limbs and trunk in throwing motion.

However, most of the research works were conducted in two dimensions, due to the restriction of the image analysis procedures available, although the three-dimensional (3-D) nature of the overhand throwing motion was well documented and recognized. Even in the case in which two or more cameras were used, the treatment of the data analysis was not quantitatively in 3-D space. For example, Toyoshima *et al.* (1976) filmed the throwing motions of various types of balls with two high-speed cameras set above and lateral to the subjects. Film analysis revealed the hip and shoulder rotation in the horizontal plane, however, they reported very little quantitative data on the throwing arm action.

Feltner and Dapena (1986) analysed the motion of the throwing arm of baseball pitchers using DLT procedures and 3-D cinematography. Their study included both kinematic and kinetic analyses. Their study was, as a turning point, followed by many 3-D studies on the motion of the throwing arm.

WHAT IS A "GOOD" THROWING MOTION?

It is well known that there is a remarkable difference in throwing ability between males and females. The gender difference in the throwing ability is much more obvious compared to other motions, such as running and jumping. The tendency that males are superior to females in throwing ability appears at a pre-school age and increases with age until adult status. Sakurai *et al.* (1995) used 3-D cinematography to compare the joint angle kinematics of the throwing limb in the period up to the ball release for male and female university students throwing a softball for a distance (average distance for male: 47.0m, female: 22.6m). This remarkable gender difference is considered to be primarily caused by skill differences.

The throwing arm has seven degrees of freedom of joint motion apart from the fingers; three at the shoulder, one at the elbow, one at the radio-ulnar, and two for the wrist. The following seven joint angle changes corresponding to all these degrees of freedom were obtained throughout the throwing motion.

J1 : horizontal abduction/horizontal adduction angle at the shoulder joint,
J2 : abduction/adduction angle at the shoulder joint,
J3 : internal rotation/external rotation angle at the shoulder joint,
J4 : flexion/extension angle at the elbow joint,
J5 : pronation/supination angle at the radio-ulnar joint (forearm),
J6 : radial flexion/ulnar flexion angle at the wrist joint,
J7 : palmar flexion/dorsi flexion angle at the wrist joint.

Small sticks were fixed to the hand and forearm to allow rotations of the radioulnar and wrist joints to be calculated (Figure 4).

Major differences in joint angle changes between male and female subjects were found in the shoulder motion (Figure 5). Male and female differed remarkably in the horizontal adduction/horizontal abduction angle of the shoulder. In the time period analysed, the shoulder is more abducted horizontally for male compared to female throwers. Male subjects initially abducted the shoulder horizontally beyond a line connecting both shoulders, then adducted horizontally towards ball release. In contrast to the case of male, the mean value of the horizontal adduction angle for female subjects stayed positive indicating that the elbow was always in front of the shoulder alignment.

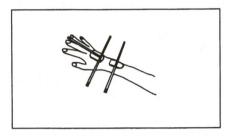

Figure 4 Small sticks for analysis of wrist motion.

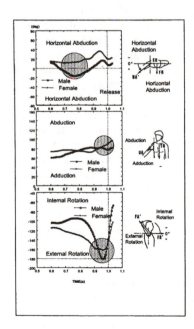

Figure 5 Comparison of shoulder joint angle changes between male and female.

Though there was no statistic difference between adduction/abduction angles of shoulder between male and female subjects in the cocking phase, the shoulder was abducted and the upperarm was elevated for females in the acceleration phase, and the abduction angle for females was significantly larger than males at the ball release.

These results show the tendency of the upperarm to be raised in front of the trunk in an unskilled throwing motion. The horizontal abduction followed by horizontal adduction in the horizontal plane is a major motion in a skilled throw.

Though the shoulder joint was rotated more externally for females than males in the cocking phase, the upperarm of the male was externally rotated rapidly and the absolute value of the external rotation of the shoulder was larger than that for females just before ball release. The extreme value of the external rotation angle for the male group was −181.3° on average, showing that the upperarm pointed almost directly posterior.

In four-footed animals, upperarm (and glenoid cavity) faces forward relative to the trunk, while it tends rather sideward in humans. Moreover human shoulder joint is considerably flexible because we do not need to support our body weight with the fore-limbs (arms). It might be said the skilful throwing motion of male subjects fully utilize the anatomical features of the arms and shoulders of human being.

Sakurai *et al.* (1998) compared the developmental trend in throwing ability and throwing skills for children from six to eleven years of age in three countries with different social conditions (Australia, Japan, and Thailand). Girls were inferior to boys at all ages and in all countries, recording throwing distances of 51–67% to those of boys. Throwing skills of girls also compared unfavourably with for boys in all groups. Thai boys and girls had inferior throwing ability and throwing skills when compared with Australian and Japanese children. The results suggested that the development of the throwing motion was highly affected by the direct and indirect involvement in sport events with throwing skills, such as baseball and cricket.

Cambell (1993) pointed out that most of the previous studies that have analysed pitching mechanics have examined adult athletes, while little data have been presented quantitatively regarding the pitching mechanics of young athletes. Considering that throwing is not an ontogenic but rather a phylogenic motion, more thorough and longitudinal approaches on skill development and training effect is expected with quantitative procedures.

HOW IS A CURVEBALL THROWN IN BASEBALL GAME? AND HOW IS IT DANGEROUS?

Curveball pitches in baseball have been thought to increase the risk of elbow injury, particularly if the athletes begin this pitch at an early age. Some researchers have claimed that overstress of the flexor and pronator muscles attached to the medial epicondyle is caused by the forearm supination required in throwing a curveball (Atwater, 1979). However, Sisto *et al.* (1987) inferred that the curveball pitch was not as harmful as had been thought because there were no major differences in forearm muscle activity between fastball and curveball pitches. Very little quantitative data concerning the forearm and wrist action during throwing had been reported because a standard analysis method was not established.

Joint angular kinematics of the throwing limb from the early-cocking phase to ball release were investigated for fastball and curveball baseball pitches using 3-D cinematography (Sakurai *et al.* 1993).

The actions were very similar for two pitches for one subject and there were no differences in the motions of the shoulder and elbow joints or in the temporal sequences between the two pitches. Though the forearm was more supinated at release in the curveball pitch than in the fastball pitch, both pitches were characterized by pronation of the forearm just before and after release (Figure 6). The results therefore did not support the notion that the curveball pitch is more likely than the fastball to cause elbow injuries.

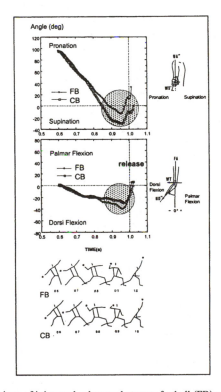

Figure 6 Comparison of joint angle changes between fastball (FB) and curveball (CB).

WHAT IS BEING DONE?

Recently many 3-D studies focused on the motion of the throwing arm from both kinematic and kinetic perspectives. Fleisig and Andrews and their colleagues have been very enthusiastic in research on overhand throwing motion from the view points of performance enhancement and injury prevention. Here I would like to introduce several recent studies from Japanese researchers.

Matsuo *et al.* (1999) investigated the relationship between shoulder abduction angle at ball release and wrist speed and injury-related kinetic parameters on baseball pitchers using computer simulation. They modified shoulder abduction angle from the values in actual pitching and were able to obtain the influence on kinematic and kinetic parameters. Though the 90° shoulder abduction angle at ball release maximized wrist velocity and decreased the elbow joint kinetics, it did not always minimize the shoulder joint kinetics (Figure 7).

Miyanishi *et al.* (1995) questioned modelling the trunk segment as one rigid body, and proposed a new model with two separate parts of a trunk, namely an upper torso and a lower torso. The angle changes of adduction/abduction of shoulder joint during baseball pitching were obtained based on the two modelling methods shown in Figure 8. They found a certain difference in angular kinematics between these two methods. Though the shoulder appeared to abduct continuously with the modelling of a trunk as one segment, adduction was found with the two segments model of the trunk. This suggested the important role of the shoulder adduction during the throwing motion.

Takahashi *et al.* (1999) recorded the hand and finger movements (Figure 9) during baseball pitch using DLT procedures with high-speed videography (1000fps), and investigated their roles in increasing ball velocity. It was revealed that the subjects who kept their fingers in a more flexed position could accelerate the ball better in the final phase before ball release.

WHAT IS NECESSARY IN THE FUTURE?

These researches suggest some of the future directions of biomechanical research on the throwing motion, namely (1) computer simulation studies, (2) improvement or modification of the modelling method especially of the shoulder and trunk region, and (3) investigation into the movement and the role of the hand.

In overhand throwing the trunk and shoulder are both taking an important role as a power generator, while the hand is also playing an important role in transmitting the momentum directly to the object. A complicated anatomical structure and fine movement skills enable us to throw skilfully. Some examples will be shown for a new modelling necessity for the trunk and shoulder region.

Each body segment such as upperarm and forearm is generally modelled as a rigid body in motion analysis studies. Each body part is represented by a stick, and sequence of the motion is drawn in stick figures by joining some certain body landmarks as shown in the upper row of Figure 10. For example, an upperarm is modelled as a stick joining imaginary centres of elbow and shoulder joint.

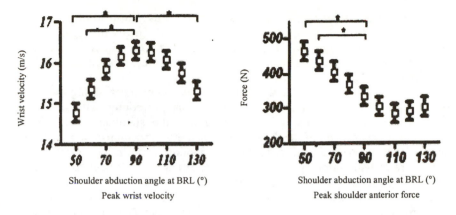

Peak wrist velocity   Peak shoulder anterior force

Figure 7 Influence of shoulder abduction angle on peak wrist velocity and shoulder joint kinetics.

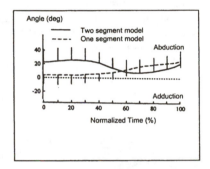

Figure 8 Comparison of shoulder abduction angle between two modelling methods of trunk.

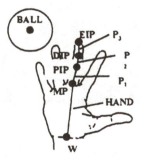

Figure 9 Model of hand.

Sometimes, a skin marker on acromion process is used instead of a shoulder joint centre. Usually, articular motion of a segment is defined with regard to the adjacent proximal segment, which is deemed fixed. In the shoulder complex, however, the scapular and clavicle are not fixed with the torso; they displace underneath the skin during the movement.

The lower row in Figure 10 shows the scapular movement during throwing motion estimated from general 3-D image analysis procedures with reflective markers which were attached on the skin around the shoulder girdle. Some correction or compensation of the data using X-ray, etc. is recommended for better estimation of the bone movements in dynamic motion. Still, these figures would provide more realistic information about the real articular movement compared to the general stick figures based on a rigid link segment model. The   ratio   of glenohumeral to scapular rotation is approximately 2:1, namely, for 180° of full arm elevation the glenohumeral rotation contributes about 120° and the scapular rotation around 60° (Zatsiorsky, 1998). Therefore, the shoulder joint angle of the throwing arm on a traditional rigid link segment model may not reflect correctly the anatomical gleno-humeral, or scapula-humerus angle. In the future, a better understanding of throwing motion, not only for performance enhancement but also for injury prevention, would require consideration of the movement of muscles and skeletons under the skin in addition to rigid link segment model analysis.

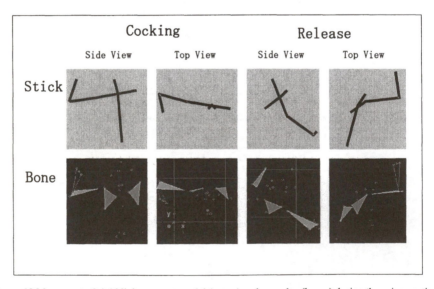

Figure 10 Movement of rigid link segment model (upper) and scapulas (lower) during throwing motion.

CONCLUSION

Past

Although throwing motion is often regarded as one of the basic motions along with walking, running, and jumping, the biomechanical studies on overhand throwing are few in number compared to other motions primarily because of the restriction of analytical procedures.

Present

Due to the progress of the techniques of three-dimensional image analysis and kinematic and kinetic motion analysis on the rigid body segment model, overhand throwing motion has been studied widely in recent years.

Future

Based on the results obtained in these analyses, research with computer simulation would be executed more frequently. Considering that throwing is not an ontogenic but rather a phylogenic motion, more thorough and longitudinal approach on the aspects of skill development and practice effect would be expected. A thorough study on the role of trunk, shoulder, and hand regions are essential, and other techniques based on a musculo-skeletal modelling may also be necessary.

REFERENCES

Atwater, A.E., 1979, Biomechanics of overhand throwing movements and throwing injuries. In *Exercise and Sport Science Reviews* (The Franklin Institute Press), 7, pp. 43-85.

Cambell, K.R., 1993, Biomechanics of pitching. In *Proceedings of the XI International Symposium on Biomechanics in Sports*, pp. 23-32.

Feltner, M. and Dapena, J., 1986, Dynamics of the shoulder and elbow joints of the throwing arm during a baseball pitch. *International Journal of Sport Biomechanics*, 2, pp. 235-259.

Fleisig, G.S., Barrentine, S.W., Escamilla, R.F. and Andrews, J.R., 1996, Biomechanics of overhand throwing with implications for injuries. *Sports Medicine*, 21, pp. 421-437.

Matsuo, T., Matsumoto, T., Takada, Y. and Mochizuki, Y., 1999, Influence of different shoulder abduction angles during baseball pitching on throwing performance and joint kinetics. In *Proceedings of the XVII International Symposium on Biomechanics in Sports*, pp. 389-392.

Sakurai, S., Ikegami, Y., Okamoto, A., Yabe, K. and Toyoshima, S., 1993, A three-dimensional cinematographic analysis of upper limb movement during fastball and curveball baseball pitches. *Journal of Applied Biomechanics*, 9, pp. 47-65.

Sakurai, S., Chentanez, T. and Elliott, B.C., 1998, International comparison of the development trend of overhand throwing ability. *Medicine and Science in Sports and Exercise* **30**(5), pp. s151.

Takahashi, K., Fujii, N. and Ae, M., 1999, A biomechanical analysis of the hand and fingers movement during baseball pitching. *Abstract of XVIIth Congress of the International Society of Biomechanics* (Calgary), pp. 917.

Toyoshima, S. and Miyashita, M., 1973, Force-velocity relation in throwing. *Research Quarterly*, **44**, pp. 86-95.

Toyoshima, S. *et al.*, 1974, Contribution of the body parts to throwing performance. *Biomechanics IV* (Baltimore: University Park Press), pp. 169-174.

Wickstrom, R.L., 1975, Developmental Kinesiology: Maturation of basic motor patterns. In *Exercise and Sports Sciences Reviews* (Academic Press), **3**, pp. 163-192.

Zatsiorsky, V.M., 1998, *Kinematics of Human Motion* (Human Kinetics).

ACKNOWLEDGEMENTS

Grateful appreciation is extended to Dr. B. C. Elliott (The University of Western Australia) for his useful suggestions. Author is also deeply grateful to Dr. T. Matsuo (Osaka University), Dr. T. Miyanishi (Sendai College), and Dr. K. Takahashi (Tsukuba University) for their provision of data.

Variability in Basketball Shooting: Practical Implications

Stuart Miller
School of Leisure and Sports Studies, Leeds Metropolitan
University, Beckett Park, Leeds LS6 3QS, UK

Basketball shooting is a dynamic, multi-segmental skill requiring considerable accuracy. The scientific and coaching literature advocate replication of movement patterns, although the extent to which this is achieved is not known. This also raises the question of whether inaccurate shots are characterized by greater variability than accurate shots. Finally, theoretical considerations suggest that long-range shots would be more variable than would short-range shots. As inaccurate free throws were characterized by greater variability in linear speed at segment endpoints than accurate shots, coaches should stress the development of a consistent movement pattern. Greater variability in the same variables for long-range shots suggest that a ball release angle close to that requiring the minimum release speed would be advantageous.

In many throwing activities, such as the shot put, the aim is to project an object as far as possible. This requires maximal effort by the athlete. It is also often the case that as the outcome (score) is determined by the best single value of a series of trials—as in the javelin throw—only one well-performed trial is necessary. Another class of activities has the objective of accuracy. Here, an object is projected towards a target, and a score is awarded on either a binary scale—hit or miss—or a sliding scale, as in archery, in which a higher score is awarded for attempts that finish nearer a specific location. These movements are characterized by sub-maximal effort, and outcome is often dependent on the sum of performances over a series of attempts. Thus, the ability to generate the same (accurate) outcome consistently is important.

Basketball shooting requires considerable accuracy. The object is to project a spherical ball of mass 0.6kg and diameter 0.25m through a horizontal circular hoop of diameter 0.45m raised 3.05m from the ground. An error in the sagittal or horizontal plane of ±0.10m from the ideal trajectory as the ball passes through the hoop will result in the ball making contact with the hoop, and possibly not passing through it. During a game, shots are normally attempted from distances up to 6.5m. A relationship between success rate and margin for error would not be unexpected, as they exhibit similar relationships with shooting distance (Figure 1). The extent to which other factors influence success, however, has not been established.

Evidence can be found in the scientific literature that inter-trial consistency of movement patterns is linked to accuracy. For example, Higgins and Spaeth (1972) stated that, to maximize accuracy, a successful movement pattern should be developed and reproduced on each trial. Similar recommendations are implicit in the basketball coaching literature, especially for free throws (e.g. Wissel, 1994). This suggests that accurate shots would be characterized by high inter-trial reproducibility. Furthermore, it may be inferred that deviation from a successful movement pattern would be a cause of inaccuracy. However, the neuromuscular system is inherently variable (Hatze, 1979), and there is little evidence that the consistent generation of identical movement patterns is possible (Newell and Corcos, 1993). A theoretical relationship between shooting accuracy and variability that would satisfy these seemingly inconsistent perspectives is shown in Figure 2. Here, the line is asymptotic to both axes such that increasingly accurate shots are characterized by decreasing (but never zero) variability, whereas increasingly inaccurate shots are associated with increasing (but never infinite) variability.

It has been established that movement variability is positively linked to the impulse generated during the movement (Schmidt *et al.*, 1979). As basketball shots from longer distances require greater impulse (all else being equal), then a positive relationship between shooting distance and inter-trial variability would be expected.

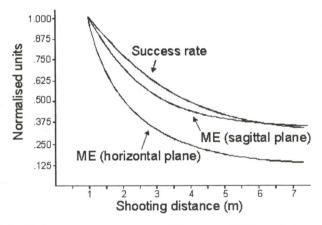

Figure 1 The relationship between success rate (adapted from Bunn, 1955), margin for error (ME) and shooting distance.

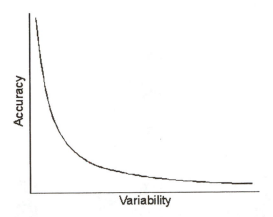

Figure 2 A theoretical relationship between shooting accuracy and variability.

The pertinent questions for basketball shooting are:

- To what extent are movement patterns for accurate shots reproducible?
- Are inaccurate shots characterized by lower reproducibility than accurate shots?
- Does reproducibility change for shots of different distances?

Twelve experienced basketball players participated in the study. Each participant contributed 5 accurate shots from short-range (2.74m), the free throw line (4.23m) and long-range (6.40m), and 5 (unintentionally) inaccurate free throws. Two-dimensional, sagittal plane, kinematic data (50Hz) were collected and digitized using the protocol recommended by BASES (Bartlett *et al.*, 1992).

Mean intra-shooter coefficients of variation for the primary ball release parameters for accurate free throws are shown in Figure 3. It is clear that intra-shooter variability exists for all parameters, and also that variability is inconsistent across the release parameters. Release height is the least variable of these, although it has the smallest effect on range. Its consistency may be due, in part, to segment lengths, which are fixed.

It is also evident from Figure 3 that there is little support for the theory that inaccurate shots are characterized by greater variability in the ball release parameters than accurate shots. Variability in ball release speed for accurate shots was not significantly different than that for inaccurate shots, and both ball release angle and release height were *more* variable for accurate shots. Figure 3 also shows the variability for short-range and long-range shots. The effect of shooting distance on the release parameters was inconsistent. The increase in variability with respect to shooting distance was greater than proportional for both release angle and release height, but less than proportional for ball release speed. The latter finding may be an artefact of the greater allowable margin for error at shorter shooting distances.

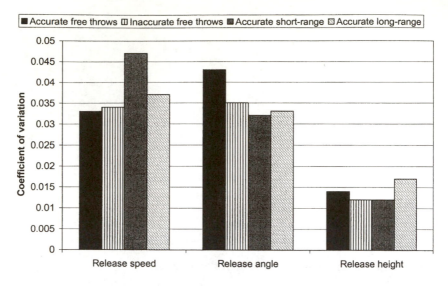

Figure 3 Coefficients of variation for the primary ball release parameters for accurate and inaccurate free throws, and accurate short-range (2.74m) and long-range (6.40m) shots.

Table 1 Standard deviations for range of motion (°) in free throws.

Parameter	Vaughn and Kozar (1993)	Miller and Bartlett (2000): accurate	Miller and Bartlett (2000): inaccurate
Wrist	11.7	7.5	7.5
Elbow	11.7	6.3	5.7
Shoulder	10.8	5.7	6.9
Hip	8.3	3.4	3.4
Knee	6.7	4.0	4.6
Ankle	7.3	5.2	4.6

Vaughn and Kozar (1993) are the only other authors to have reported intra-shooter variability data for basketball shooting, some of which are reproduced in Table 1. Their findings indicated that the reproduction of identical movement patterns during free throw shooting is not possible, and they attributed the greater variability at more distal joints to "late-stage" adjustments in movement patterns. It was not clear to what extent this phenomenon is related to outcome, however, as their data included both accurate and inaccurate shots. The data of Miller and Bartlett (2000), in which variability is presented for accurate and inaccurate shots separately, support the findings of Vaughn and Kozar (1993) that identical movement patterns cannot be generated on successive trials, although variability was consistently lower than that of Vaughn and Kozar (1993). Furthermore, the similar variability for accurate and inaccurate shots suggests that late-stage adjustments are independent of outcome.

Figure 4 plots segment endpoint speeds against their respective variabilities. The positive slope of the regression lines shows that faster moving segment endpoints tend to have greater variability. Also, there is greater variability in segment endpoints for inaccurate free throws than for accurate free throws, indicating a possible relationship between variability and outcome, although this was not apparent for ball release speed; see Figure 3. Segment endpoints in long-range shots are more variable than those in short-range shots, thereby supporting impulse variability theory. In having the steepest regression line, long-range shots are associated with greater variability (for the same endpoint speed) than both short-range shots and free throws.

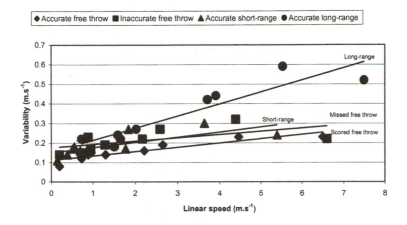

Figure 4 Plot of segment endpoint speed and variability.

Variability in linear speed also tends to be greater at endpoints further from the point of ground contact (Figure 5). These are also the faster moving segments. This suggests that variability is related to endpoint speed, as the latter also tended be greater at endpoints further from the point of ground contact. The differences in variability between accurate and inaccurate free throws are again apparent.

The increasing trend in variability along the kinematic chain was not apparent between the third metacarpophalangeal joint and ball. Indeed, variability in ball speed was less than that in the third metacarpophalangeal joint for inaccurate free throws, short-range shots and long-range shots, suggesting that some form of compensatory variability occurs during final finger-ball contact.

By contrast with absolute variability, the relative variability of all shots tends to decrease along the kinematic chain from the point of ground contact (Figure 6). This may be indicative of an organizational characteristic of the musculoskeletal system of skilled shooters, whereby variability at the endpoint of a distal segment (with respect to the point of ground contact) tends to compensate for variability at its proximal neighbour, leading to a minimization of variability in ball release speed. As this characteristic was also apparent for inaccurate free throws as well as short-range and long-range shots, this phenomenon seems to be independent of both outcome and shooting distance.

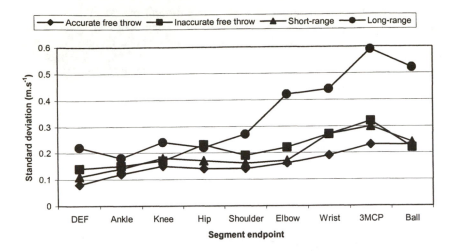

Figure 5 Absolute variability in linear speeds at ball release.

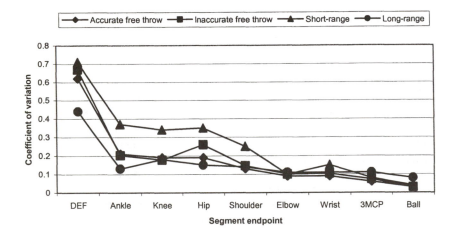

Figure 6 Relative variability in linear speeds at ball release.

For all shots analysed, relative variability tends to converge to a value of about 0.1 at the third metacarpophalangeal joint (3MCP). It is possible that this is the minimum value that can be generated during basketball shooting. The lower relative variability in ball release speed compared to that at 3MCP (Figure 4) is consistent with the principle of compensatory variability discussed above.

The finding that the lowest relative variability was found for ball release speed suggests that minimizing variability is a characteristic of basketball shooting from a range of distances. If minimizing variability is a desirable factor (although this is by no means certain, as the same characteristic was found for inaccurate free throws), then shooters would be advised to release the ball with minimum impulse.

This is achieved by releasing the ball at the angle that requires minimum release speed. For a release height of 2.4m, this corresponds to 53°, 49° and 48° for shots from 2m, 4m and 6m respectively. As margin for error when the ball passes through the basket has a positive relationship with release angle, longer shots released at the angle requiring minimum release speed have a lower margin for error.

As shown in Table 2 for both short-range and long-range shots, release angles are greater than those requiring minimum ball release speed, as indicated by positive values for RA–MRA. While it seems that shooters choose to increase margin for error at the expense of minimizing variability in release speed for short-range shots (RA–MRA = 6°), release speed becomes increasingly important for long-range shots (RA–MRA = 1°).

Table 2 Mean and standard deviation (s) of release parameters for short-range and long-range shots.

	Mean		s	
	Short-range	Long-range	Short-range	Long-range
Angle (°)	57[a]	51	1.5	1.7
Height (m)	2.16	2.13	0.02	0.11
Velocity (m·s⁻¹)	5.4	7.5[a]	0.24	0.52
RA–MRA (°)	6[b]	1	1.48	1.77

Notes: Superscripts indicate significantly larger value than the corresponding value for the other shooting distance ([a] $p < 0.001$; [b] $p < 0.01$). RA–MRA = difference between actual release angle and angle requiring minimum release speed.

CONCLUSION

Skilled basketball shooters are unable to generate identical inter-trial ball release parameters. It is possible that variability is an integral aspect of basketball shooting. However, inaccurate free throws are characterized by greater variability in segment endpoint linear speed than accurate free throws. There is evidence, therefore, that coaches should emphasize the development of a consistent movement pattern.

The lower success rate for shots from longer range is a function of both the lower margin for error in ball release speed and the greater absolute variability associated with the generation of greater impulse. By releasing the ball closer to the angle requiring the minimum ball release speed for longer shots, shooters minimise the impulse that must be generated and, by implication, reduce movement variability.

REFERENCES

Bartlett, R.M., Challis, J.H. and Yeadon, M.R., 1992, Cinematography/video analysis. In: *Biomechanical Analysis of Performance in Sport*, edited by Bartlett, R.M. (Leeds: British Association of Sport and Exercise Sciences), pp. 8-23.

Bunn, J.W., 1955, *Scientific Principles of Coaching* (New Jersey, Prentice-Hall).

Hatze, H., 1979, A teleological explanation of Weber's law and the motor unit size law. *Bulletin of Mathematical Biology*, **41**, pp. 407-425.

Higgins, J.R. and Spaeth, R.K., 1972, Relationship between consistency of movement and environmental condition. *Quest*, **17**, pp. 61-69.

Newell, K.M. and Corcos, D.M., 1993, Issues in variability and motor control. In: *Variability and Motor Control*, edited by Newell, K.M. and Corcos, D.M. (Champaign, IL: Human Kinetics), pp. 1-12.

Miller, S.A. and Bartlett, R.M., 2000, *Could you do that again? Biomechanical Characteristics of Intra-subject Variability in Basketball Shooting*, Unpublished Ph.D. thesis (The Manchester Metropolitan University).

Schmidt, R.A., Zelaznik, H., Hawkins, B., Frank, J.S. and Quinn, J.T., 1979, Motor-output variability: a theory for the accuracy of rapid motor tasks. *Psychological Reviews*, **86**, pp. 415-451.

Vaughn, R.E. and Kozar, B., 1993, Intra-individual variability for basketball free throws. In *Biomechanics in Sports XI*, edited by Hamill, J., Derrick, T.R. and Elliott, E.H. (Amherst, MA: International Society of Biomechanics in Sports), pp. 305-308.

Wissel, H., 1994, *Basketball: Steps to Success* (Champaign: Human Kinetics).

Influence of Lateral Trunk Tilt on Throwing Arm Kinetics during Baseball Pitching

Tomoyuki Matsuo, Tsuyoshi Matsumoto[1], Yoshihiro Takada[2]
and Yoshiyuki Mochizuki[3]
School of Health and Sport Sciences,
Osaka University, Osaka, Japan
[1]Institute of Health and Sport Sciences, University of Tsukuba,
Tsukuba, Japan
[2]Human Performance and Expression, Faculty of Human
Development, Kobe University, Kobe, Japan
[3]Laboratories of Image Information Science and Technology,
Osaka, Japan

INTRODUCTION

In baseball pitching, it has been established that sidearm delivery tends to cause injury to a pitcher's throwing arm. Albright *et al.* (1978) investigated the relationship between pitching style and symptom of throwing injuries. They found that pitchers employing a sidearm pitching style had a higher incidence of more severe symptoms in the elbow joint than those who were overhand and three-quarter-hand pitchers. However, the reason for this has not been elucidated.

Fleisig *et al.* (1994, 1995a, 1995b) reported several kinetic variables that had implications for throwing injuries in their series of baseball pitching studies. In their studies, it was suggested that elbow medial force and elbow varus torque were the most crucial variables for elbow injuries. In the pilot study for this research that investigated two professional sidearm pitchers, there appeared to be a tendency for them to have greater medial force, when compared with the overhand and three-quarter-hand pitchers.

There were several kinematic features of the sidearm pitchers that were investigated. These included the more erect trunk (the less lateral trunk tilt) and a greater shoulder horizontal adduction angle. For the other angular variables and any variables concerning angular velocity for throwing arm, significant differences were not found. The greater elbow force may be due to the less lateral trunk tilt and/or the greater shoulder horizontal adduction angle.

Fleisig (1994) has already investigated the relationship between elbow medial force and shoulder horizontal adduction, and found a significant correlation between increased horizontal adduction and increased maximum elbow medial force, by investigating 72 college and professional overhand and three-quarter-hand pitchers. However, to date, there has been no study investigating relationship between the lateral trunk tilt and the throwing arm kinetics during pitching, including elbow medial force and elbow varus torque. Therefore, the purpose of this study was to investigate the relationship between the lateral trunk tilt and the kinetics during pitching.

METHODS

Data Collection

Twelve overhand and three-quarter-hand professional baseball pitchers (mean height 1.84±0.05m, mean mass 81.3±7.1kg; mean age 20.9±3.0 years) served as participants. The pitchers were videotaped by two high-speed cameras (HSV-400, NAC, Tokyo, Japan) at 200Hz during pitching. Ball speed was recorded with a radar gun (PM-4A, Decatur Electronics, Inc., Decatur, IL). After the videotaping, the data set for the pitch with the fastest ball that struck the strike zone for each subject was selected for analysis. Video images were superimposed on the display of a personal computer. The third knuckle of the throwing arm, throwing wrist, throwing elbow, both shoulders, both hips, and the ball were manually digitized. In this study, data were analysed from 40 frames (0.2s) before the instant of ball release to 10 frames (0.05s) after the instant of ball release. This duration corresponded to the duration from approximately 0.05s before the lead foot contact to almost same instant of shoulder maximum internal rotation. The three-dimensional location of each point was calculated using DLT method and the data were smoothed using a fourth-order zero-lag Butterworth filter. The resultant cut-off frequency was decided for each direction in the global reference frame for each point, by residual analysis method (Winter, 1990). The range of the cut-off frequency was 6.2Hz (left hip)–13.6Hz (right wrist). Four wires with four calibration markers were suspended vertically and were positioned so that the markers formed a matrix approximately 2.0m × 2.0m × 1.5m in size. The root mean square error in calculation of the calibration markers was 0.3cm.

Simulated Motion and Kinematics

Local reference frames were calculated at the pelvis (Rp) and the upper torso (Rt). The trunk vector was a unit vector from the mid-hip to the mid-shoulder. Xp was a unit vector from the mid-hip to the right hip, Zp was the cross-product of Xp and the trunk vector. Yp was the cross-product of Zp and Xp. Xt was a unit vector from the mid-shoulder to the right shoulder, Zt was the cross-product of Xt and the trunk vector, and Yt was the cross-product of Zt and Xt. The angle of lateral trunk tilt was defined as the angle between the trunk vector and Xp in the frontal (XtYt) plane (Figure 1). To change the lateral trunk tilt angle, Rt reference frame was rotated to some target angles (every 10° from 80° to 130°) around Zt axis.

Shoulder abduction angle, shoulder horizontal adduction, shoulder external rotation angle, and elbow flexion angle, for throwing arm were calculated using basically the same methods as the previous study (Feltner and Dapena, 1986). These shoulder and elbow joint angles in the original motion remained intact, and were used in the simulated motions as well as the changed Rt reference frame and the original segments' lengths.

(a) Local reference frames (b) Original angle (c) Changed angle

Figure 1 (a) The local reference frame at the pelvis (Rp) and at the upper torso (Rt), (b) the original lateral trunk tilt angle, and (c) the changed lateral trunk tilt angle.

Joint Kinetics

Resultant forces and torques on the throwing shoulder and the throwing elbow were also calculated using the same method reported previously, which used inverse dynamics of Newton equations (Feltner and Dapena, 1986; Fleisig *et al.*, 1995a). The mass of a baseball was set equal to 0.145kg and moment of inertia of ball was assumed to be negligible. Due to the limitations in computer resolution of video image, mass of the ball and mass of the hand were assumed to be at the wrist. For the inertia properties of the body segments, Ae's regression model (Ae, Tang, and Yokoi, 1992) applying Jensen's method (1978) to Japanese athletes was used. The proximal resultant joint force and torque exerted on each link were calculated using the method reported previously (Feltner and Dapena, 1986; Fleisig *et al.*, 1995a), beginning with the ball. The resultant torques of elbow and shoulder calculated in the global reference coordinates, were then transformed into forearm reference frame, and upper torso reference frame, respectively (Fleisig *et al.*, 1995a). Although the shoulder force can be divided into three orthogonal components (anterior force, superior force, and proximal force), for the purpose of this study, it was divided into two components: shear force (resultant force of anterior force and superior force) and proximal force.

DATA REDUCTION AND STATISTICS

Selecting from data on the throwing arm kinetics, the study focused on the elbow medial force, the elbow varus torque, the shoulder shear force, and the shoulder proximal force, using only their maximum values. ANOVA was used on these kinetic parameters to assess the significant differences among the various simulated motions. Only p values <.01 were considered significant. Post hoc comparisons (Tukey-Kramer HSD test) were conducted with the p values <.05.

RESULTS AND DISCUSSION

It was concluded that the lateral trunk tilt angle over 90° indicates that trunk is tilted to the contra-lateral side of the throwing arm. On the other hand, when the angle is under 90°, this demonstrates that a pitcher tilts his trunk to the throwing arm side. The mean of the lateral trunk tilt was 120±6° and is consistent with the previous studies (Escamilla *et al.*, 1998; Fleisig *et al.*, 1995a). In following sub-sections, please note that the 120° condition can be substituted for the original.

Elbow Kinetics

Figure 2 shows the maximum elbow medial force for each condition. From 80° to 100° of the lateral trunk tilt angle, no difference was observed. Over 100° of the lateral trunk tilt, the maximum elbow medial force tended to increase as the lateral trunk tilt angle increased. Significant differences were found between 130° and 80°, 90°, 100° conditions.

   Figure 3 shows the maximum elbow varus torque for each lateral trunk tilt condition. This showed a similar pattern to the elbow medial force. Generally, it increased as a function of the lateral trunk tilt. Several significant differences were found, as shown in Figure 3.

   According to the pilot study, angle conditions from 80° to 100°, corresponded with the lateral trunk tilt angle for the sidearm pitchers. From the results of this study, it was suggested that the less lateral trunk tilt functioned to depress the elbow kinetics rather than to increase it. Using the data from Fleisig's study (1994) of the significant positive relationship between the maximum shoulder horizontal adduction and the maximum elbow medial force combined, the greater elbow force for the sidearm pitchers may be induced by the shoulder horizontal adduction movement, but not by the trunk tilt.

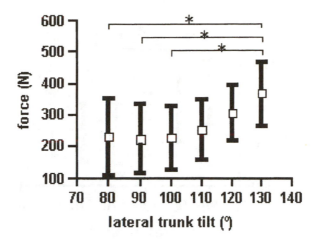

Figure 2 Maximum elbow medial force.

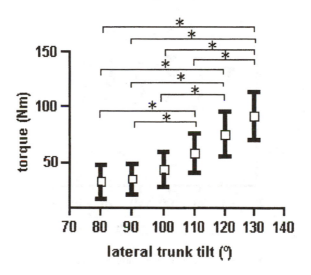

Figure 3 Maximum elbow varus torque.

Figure 5 shows the maximum shoulder proximal force. Any significant differences were not found. It seemed to be irrelevant to the lateral trunk tilt.

In the pilot study investigating two professional underhand pitchers, greater shoulder anterior forces were demonstrated. The results in the current study were in agreement with the pilot study. The lateral trunk tilt angles at the ball release for the underhand pitchers in the pilot study were 65° and 80°, respectively. The shear force of 80° condition was 35% greater than that of 120° condition. Lesser lateral trunk tilt may induce a greater shear force.

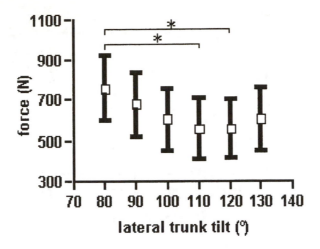

Figure 4 Maximum shoulder shear force.

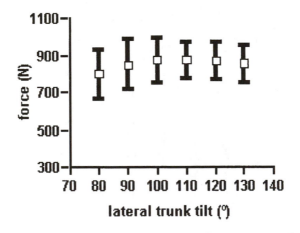

Figure 5 Maximum shoulder proximal force.

CONCLUSION

From the results of the current study on the influence of the lateral trunk tilt angles during pitching on the joint kinetics, it was suggested that the less trunk tilt did not increase the elbow joint kinetics, conversely it was decreased. On the other hand, less trunk tilt increased the shoulder shear force. Although the greater resultant force is not always consistent with the greater joint stress, careful consideration should be given to these facts. The method used in this study is not the most direct approach to elucidate the mechanism of the higher incidence of symptoms in the sidearm pitcher's elbow. However, the results of this study were useful in the elimination of one of the possible reasons.

REFERENCES

Albright, J.A., Jokl, P., Shaw, R. and Albright, J.P., 1978, Clinical study of baseball pitchers: Correlation of injury to the throwing arm with method of delivery. *American Journal of Sports Medicine*, **6**, pp. 15-21.

Ae, M., Tang, H.P. and Yokoi, T., 1992, Estimation of inertia properties of the body segments in Japanese athletes. *Biomechanism*, **11**, pp. 23-33.

Escamilla, R.F., Fleisig, G.S., Barrentine, S.W., Zheng, N. and Andrews, J.R., 1998, Kinematic comparison of throwing different types of baseball pitches. *Journal of Applied Biomechanics*, **14**, pp. 1-23.

Feltner, M. and Dapena, J., 1986, Dynamics of the shoulder and elbow joints of throwing arm during a baseball pitch. *International Journal of Sport Biomechanics*, **2**, pp. 235-259.

Fleisig, G.S., 1994, *The Biomechanics of Baseball Pitching*, Unpublished doctoral dissertation (Birmingham, AL: University of Alabama at Birmingham).

Fleisig, G.S., Andrews, J.R., Dillman, C.J. and Escamilla, R.F., 1995, Kinetics of baseball pitching with implications about injury mechanisms. *American Journal of Sports Medicine*, **23**, pp. 233-239.

Fleisig, G.S. and Barrentine, S.W., 1995, Biomechanical aspects of the elbow in sports. *Sports Medicine and Anthroscopy Review*, **3**, pp. 149-159.

Jensen, R.K., 1978, Estimation of the biomechanical properties of three body types using a photogrammetric method. *Journal of Biomechanics*, **11**, pp. 349-358.

Winter, D.A., 1990, *Biomechanics and Motor Control of Human Movement*, 2nd ed. (New York: Wiley Interscience).

Part Two

Modelling, Simulation and Optimization in Sports Biomechanics

Flexibility of the Experimental Simulation Approach to the Analysis of Human Airborne Movements: Body Segment Parameter Estimation

Young-Hoo Kwon
Human Performance Laboratory, Ball State University,
Muncie, Indiana, USA

INTRODUCTION

Simulation of torque-free movements of the human body was originally initiated by space scientists (McCrank and Seger, 1964; Kane and Scher, 1970; Passerello and Huston, 1971). The main issue in these studies was the effectiveness of the proposed reorientation movements for astronauts in space. Although the models employed and the movements studied were fairly simple, they laid a firm foundation for the simulation of more complex torque-free movements.

Later research (Miller, 1970; Huston and Passerello, 1971; Ramey, 1973; Pike, 1980; Ramey and Yang, 1981) reported on theoretical simulation studies dealing with sporting movements and Dapena (1981) introduced a new approach to simulation, the experimental simulation, in which the time history of the joint motions and the initial conditions of the airborne motion were obtained from actual trials. Yeadon *et al.* (1990a) reported an experimental simulation study of selected trampoline manoeuvres, which served as a milestone for this area of research.

Applying the simulation approach to the analysis of complex airborne movements can be beneficial to the athletes in terms of safety and performance enhancement. The probable results of new manoeuvres can be predicted through simulation before the actual trial. The cause-and-effect relationships among different biomechanical performance factors can be identified for performance enhancement. In addition, the analysis techniques employed in the simulation process, such as the non-inertial reference frames, provide researchers with tools to investigate complex human movements more effectively. For example, Yeadon and associates (Yeadon, 1989, 1993, 1994; Yeadon *et al.* 1990b) quantified the contribution of body motions to the development of twists in various sports.

In spite of its potential advantages, the experimental simulation is still not popular and only a handful of simulation studies (Yeadon, 1993, 1994; Yeadon *et al.*, 1990b; Kwon, 1993, 2000) have been reported since Yeadon *et al.* (1990a) published their work. This may be attributed to several factors, but it seems it is due mainly to the complex simulation procedures. The experimental simulation demands that investigators define and use local reference frames, perform extensive anthropometric measurements for inertial property estimation, compute the internal and external orientation angles from the transformation matrices, compute the airborne angular momentum, solve a set of differential equations for the external orientation angles, and modify the movements for further simulation.

There seem to be two main ways to improving the flexibility and applicability of the experimental simulation approach: (1) to develop a comprehensive and user-friendly experimental simulation software package which allows users to easily define the local reference frames and modify movements (Kwon and Sung, 1994); and (2) to simplify the inertial property computation procedures. It is meaningful to identify applicable body segment parameter estimation methods from the pool of readily available methods in an effort to simplify the simulation procedures and to improve the flexibility and applicability of the experimental simulation approach. In this paper, the findings of a series of papers dealing with the effects of the method of body segment parameter estimation on the angular momentum and experimental simulation accuracy were summarized.

BSP ESTIMATION METHODS

There are several indirect and direct body segment parameter (BSP) estimation methods readily available. In the direct methods, one computes the BSPs directly from the subject using either medical imaging techniques, such as MRI (Mungiole and Martin, 1990) and CT (Rodrigue and Gagnon, 1983; Ackland *et al.* 1988), or mass scanning techniques (Zatsiorsky and Seluyanov, 1983). Due to problems such as radiation, high cost, and the need for specialized equipment, however, it is difficult to apply these methods in practice. The geometric (mathematical) models (Hanavan, 1964; Huston and Passerello, 1971; Jensen, 1978; Yeadon, 1990; Hatze, 1975) may also be classified as direct methods. Yeadon *et al.* (1990a) used a geometric model that requires a total of 95 anthropometric parameters (Yeadon, 1990). Yeadon *et al.* (1990b) and Yeadon (1993) later adopted alternative anthropometric measurement strategies since anthropometric measurements were not allowed in the competition settings. The BSP ratios, regression (prediction) equations, and scaling coefficients obtained from a group of living subjects (Zatsiorsky and Seluyanov, 1983, 1985; Zatsiorsky *et al.*, 1990; Plagenhoef *et al.*, 1983) or cadaver specimens (Dempster, 1955; Barter, 1957; Clauser *et al.*, 1969; Chandler *et al.* 1975; Dapena, 1978; Hinrichs, 1985; Forwood *et al.* 1985) are commonly used in the indirect methods.

For a BSP estimation method to be used in the experimental simulation of airborne movements, it should at least fulfil the following criteria: (1) it must provide a complete set of BSPs including the three principal moments of inertia; and (2) the estimation procedures must be fairly simple, safe and inexpensive. The indirect methods based on the work of Chandler *et al.* (1975) and Zatsiorsky and associates (Zatsiorsky and Seluyanov, 1983, 1985; Zatsiorsky *et al.*, 1990), and the geometric models (Hanavan, 1964; Hatze, 1975; Jensen, 1978; Yeadon, 1990) generally suffice criterion 1. However, the Hatze model (Hatze, 1975) and the elliptical zone method (Jensen, 1978) among the geometric models do not fulfil criterion 2 since they require either an extensive anthropometric measurement (Hatze model; 242 parameters) or specialized equipment (elliptical zone method). Based on these criteria, Kwon (1996) selected a total of 10 BSP estimation methods classified into three groups: cadaver-based indirect methods, mass scanning-based indirect methods, and geometric models (Table 1). See Kwon (1996) for the details of these methods regarding the modifications and the required anthropometric parameters.

Table 1 Method of BSP estimation candidates for the experimental simulation.

Group	Method	Description
	C1	Ratios (9)[5]
Group C[1]	C2	Simple regression by mass (9)
(Cadaver-based)	C3	Stepwise regression (36)
	C4	Scaling (18)
	M1	Ratio method (8)
Group M[2]	M2	Simple regression by mass and height (9)
(Mass scanning-based)	M3	Prediction equations (38)
	M4	Scaling (24)
Group G	G1	Modified Hanavan[3] (24)
(Geometric models)	G2	Modified Yeadon[4] (67)

[1]Based on Chandler *et al.* (1975)
[2]Based on Zatsiorsky and associates (Zatsiorsky and Seluyanov, 1983, 1985; Zatsiorsky *et al.*, 1990)
[3]Modified version of Hanavan (1964)
[4]Modified version of Yeadon (1990)
[5]Number of anthropometric parameters required

BSP ESTIMATION VS. AIRBORNE ANGULAR MOMENTUM

Most experimental simulation studies (Dapena, 1981; Yeadon *et al.*, 1990a; Kwon, 2000) are based on the conservation of angular momentum. In an ideal situation, the angular momentum of a gymnast's body about its centre of mass (CM) remains constant during the airborne phase. However, the computed angular momentum fluctuates due to errors and the average value is used in the simulation as the initial condition along with the time history of the joint motions. The discrepancy in the angular momentum between the actual value and the one used in the simulation appears to be the main cause of the simulation error. Kwon (1996) investigated the effect of the method of BSP estimation on the airborne angular momentum.

SUBJECTS AND TRIALS

Nine double-somersault-with-full-twist horizontal-bar dismounts performed by three male collegiate gymnasts were analysed. Each gymnast repeated the maneuver three times with varying postures. See Kwon (1996) for details of the subject and trial data.

Body Model

A 15-segment body model based on 21 body points with at most 38° of freedom was defined. The trunk was sectioned into two segments at the navel level: thorax–abdomen and pelvis. The location of the inter-torso link (centre of the trunk cross-section at the navel level) was computed through a geometric method described in Kwon (1993).

Data Collection

The 3-D DLT method (Abdel-Aziz and Karara, 1971) was used in camera calibration and subsequent 3-D reconstruction. Four range poles (487.68cm long each) were used as the calibration frame. A digital theodolite was used to measure the horizontal angular positions of the range poles and the vertical positions of the control points marked on the pole (32 control points). The 3-D coordinates of the control points were computed from the angular position data. Four S-VHS video camcorders (Panasonic AG-450) were used for videotaping with the frame rate and the shutter speed being 60Hz and 1/250s, respectively. The Z-axis of the global (inertial) reference frame was aligned vertically with the Y-axis being in the direction of dismount. See Kwon (1996) for detailed information on equipment setup.

RESULTS

A summary of the results of the airborne angular momentum computation is presented in Table 2. All the average angular momentum components (a_x, a_y and a_z) and their respective standard deviations (SDs; s_x, s_y and s_z) were subject to normalization to facilitate comparisons among the BSP estimation methods. a_x was normalized among the methods (100% = a_x of method G2) while a_y and a_z were normalized by their corresponding a_x (a_y/a_x and a_z/a_x). s_x, s_y and s_z were all normalized by their corresponding a_x (s_x/a_x, s_y/a_x and s_z/a_x). The X component of the airborne angular momentum was the main component with a_y and a_z being approximately 5.2±1.6% and 5.2±3.3% of a_x, respectively. The minor components showed large SD-to-average ratios, 103.2% (Y) and 99.6% (Z).

The mean a_x ratios of the BSP estimation methods except G2 (100%) ranged from 88.7% to 99.1% with the maximum range being 10.4%. Significant inter-group difference (G > C) and significant inter-method differences in all groups (C3 > C1, C2 and C3; M3 and M4 > M1; G2 > G1) were observed. The overall mean a_y and a_z were 5.16±1.62% and 5.18±3.34% of a_x, respectively. The maximum ranges of the method means were 0.65% (a_y) and 0.52% (a_z), showing no inter-group or inter-method difference. All components resulted in very similar s-to-a_x ratios among the methods: 7.4–7.9% (X), 4.7–5.4% (Y), and 4.8–5.6% (Z). Based on the observation that a_x ratio revealed significant inter-method differences and a_y, a_z, s_x, s_y, and s_z showed similar ratios to a_x among the methods, Kwon (1996) concluded the method of BSP estimation significantly changed the magnitude and fluctuation of the airborne angular momentum.

Table 2 Mean angular momentum ratios (in percentages) of the BSP estimation methods (n = 9) (Kwon, 1996).

Group	Method	a_x ratio*	a_y ratio	a_z ratio
	C1	89.5±2.1	5.3±1.4	5.3±3.5
	C2	88.7±2.9	5.2±1.5	5.3±3.5
C	C3	99.1±2.0	5.4±2.2	5.3±3.5
	C4	91.3±2.3	5.3±1.6	5.3±3.5
	Mean	92.2±4.8**	5.3±1.6	5.3±3.4
	M1	91.0±2.3	5.3±1.6	5.3±3.6
	M2	93.2±3.0	5.2±1.8	5.2±3.5
M	M3	96.4±2.2	5.3±1.5	5.3±3.5
	M4	96.7±3.8	4.9±1.4	5.2±3.6
	Mean	94.3±3.6**	5.2±1.5	5.3±3.4
	G1	92.6±1.8	5.0±2.0	4.8±3.5
G	G2	100.0[1]	4.7±1.7	4.9±3.5
	Mean	96.3±4.0**	4.9±1.8	4.9±3.4

*Inter-group difference was observed (p < .05). **Inter-method difference was observed (p < .05). [1]a_x values of the BSP estimation methods were normalized by a_x of method G2.

EXPERIMENTAL SIMULATION OF AIRBORNE MOVEMENTS

Torque-free motion of a gymnast in the air is governed by the conservation of angular momentum. A set of differential equations for the rotation of the body can be obtained from this law (Ramey and Yang, 1981; Yeadon *et al.*, 1990a; Kwon, 2000):

$$\mathbf{H}^{(WB)} - \mathbf{H}^{(WB)}_{rel} = \mathbf{I}^{(WB)}_{CM} \cdot \begin{bmatrix} \cos\theta \cdot \cos\psi & \sin\psi & 0 \\ -\cos\theta \cdot \sin\psi & \cos\psi & 0 \\ \sin\theta & 0 & 1 \end{bmatrix} \begin{bmatrix} \dot{\phi} \\ \dot{\theta} \\ \dot{\psi} \end{bmatrix} \tag{1}$$

where $\mathbf{H}$ = the average airborne angular momentum, $\mathbf{H}_{rel}$ = the relative angular momentum of the body parts to the whole body reference frame (the WB-frame), $\mathbf{I}_{CM}$ = the inertia tensor of the whole body, $[\phi, \theta, \psi]$ = the somersault, inclination, and twist angles of the body with respect to the global reference frame (the external orientation angles). Note that all the vectors and matrices in equation 1 are described in the WB-frame. The translation of the body CM ($\mathbf{R}$) can be described as (Kwon, 2000):

$$R = R_0 + tV_0 + 1/2 t^2 g \tag{2}$$

where R_o and V_o = the initial position and velocity of the body CM, respectively, t = the time in flight, and g = the gravitational acceleration.

The input variables of the simulation include the airborne angular momentum (H), the initial orientation of the body (ϕ_o, θ_o, ψ_o), the initial position and velocity of the body CM (R_o and V_o), the time history of the relative orientation angles among the segments (the internal orientation angles), the BSPs, and selected anthropometric parameters. The inertia tensor (I_{CM}) of the body and the relative angular momentum of the body to the WB frame (H_{rel}) are to be computed from the time history of the internal orientation angles, the BSPs, and the anthropometric parameters. The external orientation of the body (ϕ, θ, ψ) and the position of the CM (R) are the output of the simulation. The internal and external orientation angles determine the number of degree of freedom (DOFs) of the system. See Kwon (1993) for detailed description of the simulation procedures including the local reference frame definition.

The BSPs are involved in the H, H_{rel}, and I_{CM} computation, having a potential to affect the outcome of the simulation. Different from the random experimental errors, the BSPs can introduce systematic errors to the system.

BSP ESTIMATION VS. SIMULATION ACCURACY

A summary of results of the simulations performed by Kwon (2000) on data from 9 double-somersault-with-full-twist horizontal-bar dismounts is presented in Table 3. The maximum discrepancies between the observed external orientation angles (somersault, inclination, and twist) and the simulated angles were used as the simulation errors. The simulation errors were normalized by the maximum external orientation angle ranges, respectively, to obtain the relative errors.

The overall mean somersault simulation error was 2.9±0.7% (16.1±3.7°; mean maximum somersault range = 559.8°). All estimation methods demonstrated equally accurate somersault simulations (2.7–3.1%), showing no inter-group or inter-method difference. The overall mean inclination simulation error was 42.7 ± 15.6% (8.2±2.5°; mean maximum inclination range = 20.1°). Inter-group difference (G < C) and inter-method difference in group C (C3 < C2) were observed. Methods C3, G1 and G2 generally produced smaller inclination errors than the other BSP estimation methods. The overall mean twist simulation error was 17.2±7.3% (57.4±23.9°; mean maximum twist range = 335.8°). Inter-group difference (G < C and M) and inter-method differences in groups C and M (C3 < C1, C2 and C3; M4 < M2) were observed. Methods C3, G1 and G2 scored smaller twist errors than other estimation methods. Method M4 also revealed a smaller twist error than method C2. The twist simulation error was identified as the discriminating measure of the simulation accuracy and Kwon (2000) concluded the method of BSP estimation affected the simulation accuracy.

Table 3 Mean simulation errors (in percentages) of the BSP estimation methods (n = 9) (Kwon, 2000).

Group	Method	Somersault	Inclination*	Twist*
	C1	3.0±0.5	44.8±12.8	21.1±5.0
	C2	2.7±0.7	59.2±20.6	25.9±3.2
C	C3	2.7±0.7	33.8±9.5	9.7±3.9
	C4	2.7±0.9	54.7±20.6	21.3±5.0
	Mean	2.8±0.7	48.1±18.7**	19.5±7.4**
	M1	2.9±0.7	41.5±12.9	19.4±4.8
	M2	2.8±0.7	46.0±13.6	22.9±6.7
M	M3	3.1±0.7	40.3±10.6	18.3±3.2
	M4	3.1±0.7	41.1±10.8	15.9±2.1
	Mean	3.0±0.7	42.3±11.7	19.1±5.1**
	G1	2.8±0.3	34.3±12.5	10.1±5.5
G	G2	2.7±0.6	30.7±5.9	7.1±2.5
	Mean	2.7±0.5	32.5±9.7	8.6±4.4

*Inter-group difference was observed (p < .05). **Inter-method difference was observed (p < .05).

ANGULAR MOMENTUM OPTIMIZATION

Modelling of a simple system of rigid bodies and intentional perturbation of the BSP items (mass, CM location and moments of inertia) easily reveals that the errors in the BSPs does not generate random effects on the airborne angular momentum, which implies that the average airborne angular momentum may not be the most representative measure to be used in the simulation, and that the average angular momentum may also contribute to the simulation error. This is especially probable in the case of the minor angular momentum components (a_y and a_z) since they showed large SD-to-average ratios: 103.2% (Y) and 99.6% (Z) (Kwon, 1996). In addition, the external orientation of the gymnast is to be updated in each frame based on the previous orientation and the posture. Therefore, the simulation errors are orientation and posture-dependent and the error propagation scheme involved in the experimental simulation becomes quite complex.

Based on the argument that the average airborne angular momentum may not be the most representative measure to be used in the simulation, Kwon (2000) intentionally manipulated (optimization) the airborne angular momentum components. He manipulated only the minor components (a_y and a_z) (within ±55% of their respective SDs, with the increment being 1%) for two reasons: (1) since the minor components showed high SD-to-average ratios (Kwon, 1996), a more effective optimization was expected with the minor components; and (2) there was a need to limit the extent of optimization to prevent the nature of the trial from being altered extremely. The Y and Z angular momentum pair that provided the smallest combined simulation error (inclination + twist) was identified as the optimal angular momentum. The simulation errors obtained from the optimal angular momentum were regarded as the optimized simulation errors (Figure 1a and b).

It was reported that the angular momentum optimization produced mean decreases in the simulation errors of 11.9% (somersault), 28.1% (inclination), and 76.0% (twist). The optimized errors of the BSP estimation methods ranged 2.2–2.7% (somersault), 28.9–32.4% (inclination), and 3.6–4.7% (twist) showing no significant inter-method difference. All methods except C3, G1 and G2 showed significant decrease in the inclination error while all methods exhibited significant decrease in the twist simulation error. It was clearly demonstrated that the angular momentum optimization substantially improved the simulation accuracy.

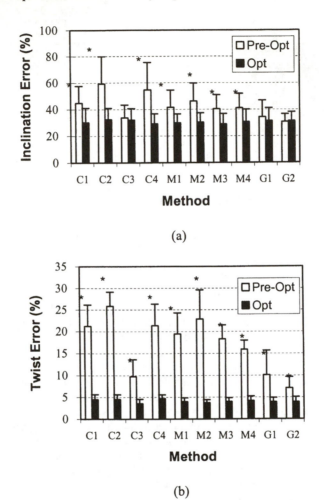

(a)

(b)

Figure 1 Comparison between the optimized and the pre-optimization simulation errors: (a) inclination, and (b) twist (Kwon, 2000). * Denotes a significant (p < .05) decrease in the simulation error due to the angular momentum optimization.

APPLICABILITY OF THE BSP ESTIMATION METHODS

Based on the results of a series of simulations with 10 BSP estimation methods, Kwon (2000) assessed the applicability of the BSP estimation methods. When the main focus of simulation is on the somersault, all methods are equally applicable.

The ratio methods (C1 and M1) and the simple regression methods (C2 and M2), however, are preferred since they require a considerably smaller number of anthropometric parameters (8–9), but still provide equally accurate simulation results. In simulating a complex motion with twist, the geometric models (G1 and G2) and the cadaver-based stepwise regression method (C3) are the only applicable methods. These methods require 67 (G2), 41 (G1) or 36 (C3) anthropometric parameters. The gamma mass scanning-based scaling method (M4) requires a smaller number of parameters (24) and may be used for the simulation of a complex movement of relatively short duration.

In methods C1 and C2, the anthropometric parameters were required to compute the BSPs of the subtrunk segments and to convert the BSP data compatible to the body model used by Kwon (1996, 2000). Similarly, 8–9 anthropometric parameters were required in methods M1 and M2 to secure the compatibility and to combine the BSPs of the thorax–abdomen. With additional modelling and/or assumptions, the number of required parameters can be reduced. Use of simple methods (C1, C2, M1 and M2) in conjunction with the angular momentum optimization strategy would substantially improve the flexibility of the experimental simulation approach.

SUMMARY

While most of the experimental simulation procedures can be incorporated into a well-structured user-friendly software package, one area that needs a special attention is the BSP estimation. The BSP estimation requires measurement of anthropometric parameters, and the complexity of the measurement and the method limits the flexibility of the experimental simulation approach. Among the 10 BSP estimation methods applicable in the experimental simulation of airborne movements, the geometric models and the cadaver-based stepwise regression method demonstrated superior applicability to others. All methods were equally applicable in simulating the somersault motion. The angular momentum optimization strategy developed by Kwon (2000), based on the minor angular momentum components, would substantially improve the applicability of the simpler methods such as the ratio and simple regression methods.

REFERENCES

Abdel-Aziz, Y.I. and Karara, H.M., 1971, Direct linear transformation from comparator coordinates into object space coordinates in close-range photogrammetry. In *Proceedings of the Symposium on Close-Range Photogrammetry* (Falls Church, VA: American Society of Photogrammetry), pp. 1-18.

Ackland, T.R., Henson, P.W. and Bailey, D.A., 1988, The uniform density assumption: its effect upon the estimation of body segment inertial parameters. *International Journal of Sport Biomechanics*, **4**, pp. 146-155.

Barter, J.T., 1957, *Estimation of the Mass of Body Segments* (WADC-TR-57-260) (Ohio: Aerospace Medical Research Laboratories, Wright-Patterson Air Force Base).

Chandler, R.F., Clauser, C.E., McConville, J.T., Reynolds, H.M. and Young, J.W., 1975, *Investigation of Inertial Properties of the Human Body* (AMRL-TR-74-137, AD-A016-485, DOT-HS-801-430) (Ohio: Aerospace Medical Research Laboratories, Wright-Patterson Air Force Base).

Clauser, C.E., McConville, J.T. and Young, J.W., 1969, *Weight, Volume and Centre of Mass of Segments of the Human Body* (AMRL-TR-69-70) (Ohio: Aerospace Medical Research Laboratory, Wright-Patterson Air Force Base).

Dapena, J., 1981, Simulation of modified human airborne movements. *Journal of Biomechanics*, **14**, pp. 81-89.

Dapena, J., 1978, A method to determine the angular momentum of a human body about three orthogonal axes passing through its centre of gravity. *Journal of Biomechanics*, **11**, pp. 251-256.

Dempster, W.T., 1955, *Space Requirements of the Seated Operator* (WADC-55-159, AD-087-892) (Ohio: Aerospace Medical Research Laboratories, Wright-Patterson Air Force Base).

Forwood, M.R., Neal, R.J. and Wilson, B.D., 1985, Scaling segmental moments of inertia for individual subjects. *Journal of Biomechanics*, **18**, pp. 755-761.

Hanavan, E.P., 1964, *A Mathematical Model of the Human Body* (AMRL-TR-64-102, AD-608-463) (Ohio: Aerospace Medical Research Laboratories, Wright-Patterson Air Force Base).

Hatze, H., 1975, A new method for the simultaneous measurement of the moment of inertia, the damping coefficient and the location of the centre of mass of a body segment in situ. *European Journal of Applied Physiology*, **34**, pp. 217-226.

Hinrichs, R.N., 1985, Regression equations to segmental moments of inertia from anthropometric measurements: an extension of the data from Chandler *et al.* 1975. *Journal of Biomechanics*, **18**, pp. 621-624.

Huston, R.L. and Passerello, C.E., 1971, On dynamics of a human body model. *Journal of Biomechanics*, **4**, pp. 369-378.

Jensen, R.K., 1978, Estimation of the biomechanical properties of three body types using a photogrammetric method. *Journal of Biomechanics*, **11**, pp. 349-358.

Kane, T.R. and Scher, M.P., 1970, Human self-rotation by means of limb movements. *Journal of Biomechanics*, **3**, pp. 39-49.

Kwon, Y.H., 1993, *The effects of body segment parameter estimation on the experimental simulation of a complex airborne movement*, Unpublished doctoral dissertation (Pennsylvania State University).

Kwon, Y.H., 1996, Effects of the method of body segment parameter estimation on airborne angular momentum. *Journal of Applied Biomechanics*, **12**, pp. 413-430.

Kwon, Y.H., 2000, Simulation of the airborne movement: applicability of the body segment parameter estimation methods. *Journal of Applied Biomechanics* (submitted for publication).

Kwon, Y.H. and Sung, R.J., 1994, Development of a software package for the experimental simulation of human airborne movement. *Korean Journal of Sport Science*, **6**, pp. 57-72.

McCrank, J.M. and Seger, D.R., 1964, *Torque Free Rotational Dynamics of a Variable-configuration Body (Application to Weightless Man)*, Unpublished

Master's thesis (GAW/Mech 64-19) (Ohio: Air Force Institute of Technology, Wright-Patterson Air Force Base).

Miller, D.I., 1970, *A Computer Simulation Model of the Airborne Phase of Diving*, Unpublished doctoral dissertation (Pennsylvania State University).

Mungiole, M. and Martin, P.E., 1990, Estimating segmental inertia properties: comparison of magnetic resonance imaging with existing methods. *Journal of Biomechanics*, **23**, pp. 1039-1046.

Passerello, C.E. and Huston, R.L., 1971, Human attitude control of a human body in free fall. *Journal of Biomechanics*, **4**, p. 95.

Pike, N.L., 1980, *Computer Simulation of a Forward, Full Twisting Dive in a Layout Position*, Unpublished doctoral dissertation (Pennsylvania State University).

Plagenhoef, S., Evans, F.G. and Abdelnour, T., 1983, Anatomical data for analyzing human motion. *Research Quarterly in Exercise and Sport*, **54**, pp. 169-178.

Ramey, M.R., 1973, A simulation of the running long jump. In *Mechanics and Sport*, edited by Bleustein, J.L. (New York, NY: American Society of Mechanical Engineers) pp. 101-113.

Ramey, M.R. and Yang, A.T., 1981, A simulation procedure for human motion studies. *Journal of Biomechanics*, **14**, pp. 203-213.

Rodrique, D. and Gagnon, M., 1983, The evaluation of forearm density with axial tomography. *Journal of Biomechanics*, **16**, pp. 907-913.

Yeadon, M.R., 1994, Twisting techniques used in dismounts from the rings. *Journal of Applied Biomechanics*, **10**, pp. 178-188.

Yeadon, M.R., 1993, Twisting techniques used by competitive divers. *Journal of Sports Sciences*, **11**, pp. 337-342.

Yeadon, M.R., 1990, The simulation of aerial movement – II. A mathematical inertia model of the human body. *Journal of Biomechanics*, **23**, pp. 67-74.

Yeadon, M.R., 1989, Twisting techniques used in freestyle aerial skiing. *International Journal of Sport Biomechanics*, **5**, pp. 275-281.

Yeadon, M.R., Atha, J. and Hales, F.D., 1990a, The simulation of aerial movement – IV. A computer simulation model. *Journal of Biomechanics*, **23**, pp. 85-89.

Yeadon, M.R., Lee, S.C. and Kerwin, D.G., 1990b, Twisting techniques used in high bar dismounts. *International Journal of Sport Biomechanics*, **6**, pp. 139-146.

Zatsiorsky, V.M. and Seluyanov, V.N., 1983, The mass and inertia characteristics of the main segments of the human body. In *Biomechanics VIII-B*, edited by Matsui, H. and Kobayashi, K. (Champaign, IL: Human Kinetics), pp. 1152-1159.

Zatsiorsky, V.M. and Seluyanov, V.N., 1985, Estimation of the mass and inertia characteristics of the human body by means of the best predictive regression equations. In *Biomechanics IX-B*, edited by Winter, D.A., Norman, R.W., Wells, R.P., Hayes, K.C. and Patla, A.E. (Champaign, IL: Human Kinetics), pp. 233-239.

Zatsiorsky, V.M., Seluyanov, V.N. and Chugunova, L., 1990, In vivo body segment inertial parameters determination using a gamma-scanner method. In *Biomechanics of human movement: Applications in rehabilitation, sports and ergonomics*, edited by Berme, N. and Cappozzo, A. (Worthington, OH: Bertec Corporation), pp. 187-202.

A Time-variant Forward Solution Model of the Bowling Arm in Cricket

Rene E. D. Ferdinands, Kevin A. Broughan[1] and Howell Round
Department of Physics and Electronic Engineering,
University of Waikato, Hamilton, New Zealand
[1]Department of Mathematics,
University of Waikato, Hamilton, New Zealand

INTRODUCTION

The function of bowling in cricket is to deliver the ball to the batter such that the ball first bounces once off the ground. The rules of cricket specify that the bowling arm must not be in the act of straightening after it has reached shoulder height. The basic bowling action is therefore characterized by the angular sweep of the bowling arm as it circumducts the glenohumeral joint (Figure 1).

Available work on bowling technique is based almost exclusively upon the observations of successful fast bowlers (Davis and Blanksby, 1976). There has been a need to analyse bowling from a scientific viewpoint. Most researchers, such as Elliott and Foster (1984) and Mason et al. (1989), have restricted their analyses to the kinematic and force plate data of bowlers. They identified potential causes of back injury, and found correlation between certain technical characteristics and ball release speed (Bartlett et al., 1996). However, from the available literature, there has been no attempt to produce a model of bowling based on dynamics.

In this paper, we model the bowling arm as a two-segment rigid body model. The system is considered an initial value problem with the initial conditions specifying the starting limb angles and velocities. These values and time-variant driving functions (torques and forces) are defined as the system inputs. Lagrangian mechanics, which provides a flexible technique for dealing with a wide range of physical situations (Marion and Thornton, 1988), is used to establish the system of ordinary differential equations. Then we used a forward solution to observe the system response.

Applications of Lagrangian mechanics to movement dynamics have been made previously. Onyshko and Winter (1980) developed a seven-link segment model to study human gait. This model successfully simulated the walking step, but did not completely satisfy the requirements of internal validity. Jorgensen (1970 and 1994) studied the dynamics of the swing of a golf club using a two-segment model. Many interesting findings resulted from this model, but only constant joint torques were used.

Figure 1 The basic bowling technique (right-hand bowler) has many characteristics: the run-up, leap, right foot contact, left arm motion, bowling arm rotation, left foot contact, ball release, and follow-through. A good technique allows the bowler to deliver a ball with speed at a chosen point on the pitch while maintaining a straight bowling arm. [Picture—Courtesy of The Crowood Press Ltd., Wiltshire.]

As the bowling arm makes a significant contribution (40–50%) to bowling speed (Elliot *et al.*, 1986), we are interested in the kinetics of the bowling arm. By specifying a range of input driving functions and initial arm positions, the forward solution model of the bowling arm developed here determines the combination of ball release speed and arm angle required to land a ball at a pre-determined position on the pitch. As fast bowlers are interested in delivering a ball at high speed, we investigate which trajectories of the bowling arm are more likely to result in an increased ball release speed.

MATERIALS AND METHODS

Link Segment Model

Using the approach of Winter (1990), a two segment link model of the bowling arm (upper arm and forearm) was constructed with respect to a global reference system and two local reference systems, along with three generalized coordinates: q_1 (linear shoulder displacement), q_2 (upper arm angular displacement), and q_3 (forearm angular displacement) (Figure 2b). Segment lengths are represented by l_j, distance to the centres of mass (from the proximal end) by r_j, segment masses by m_j, the horizontal force acting on the shoulder joint by F, and the shoulder and elbow torques by T_1 and T_2, respectively (Figure 2a and b). Flexion of the wrist is not considered, so m_2 includes the mass of the forearm, hand and ball. Also, the origins of the local reference systems are placed at the proximal ends of the segments.

The Lagrangian mechanics approach requires the formulation of the Lagrangian L, given by

$$L = T - V \tag{1}$$

where T and V are the kinetic and potential energies of the system, respectively, written in terms of the independent variables q_i.

The resulting system of differential equations of motion is generated using

$$\frac{d(\partial L / \partial \dot{q}_i)}{dt} - \frac{\partial L}{\partial q_i} = Q_i, \quad (i = 1, \ldots, 3) \tag{2}$$

where the Q_i are the virtual work expressions involving the joint torques and forces. The Lagrangian method does not require the specification of reaction forces at the joints. The bowling arm model is therefore completely specified by two local reference systems, two segments, three output displacement variables, two torques, and one force.

Projectile Study

Projectile equations that mimic the goal-oriented approach of the bowler—in this case, to hit a target on the pitch at a given distance from the bowler's end for a specified speed and trajectory—were linked to the Lagrangian solution.

Typical bowling actions comprise two phases of delivery: (1) the *pre-locked phase*, where the bowling arm begins its downward trajectory from an initial bent position around shoulder height to a position near the hips when the angle between the forearm and upper arm (elbow angle) becomes straight; and (2) the *locked phase*, when the elbow is locked and the straight arm is maintained throughout the remainder of its circular trajectory (Figure 2c). Ball release in cricket is performed during the locked phase, so the projectile equations are developed for the case of a straight segment, $l_1 + l_2$ in length, with the release height h_{ag} given by

$$h_{ag} = h_s + (l_1 + l_2) \sin(q_2) \tag{3}$$

where h_s is the height of the shoulder.

The standard projectile equation of motion for which the projection point is at a higher level than the impact point (de Mestre, 1990) is

$$R = \frac{u \cos \alpha \left(u \sin \alpha + \sqrt{u^2 \sin^2 \alpha - 2 g \, h_{ag}} \right)}{g} \tag{4}$$

where R is the range, g the gravitational acceleration, u the ball release speed, and α the *ball release angle*, which is related to q_2 by

$$\alpha = q_2 - \frac{\pi}{2} \tag{5}$$

If there are points on the bowling trajectory that satisfy a particular R, then equation (4) has solutions for

$$u = \dot{q}_2(l_1 + l_2) \tag{6}$$

There can be more than one solution pair (α, u) for a given range R (see Figure 2c).

use graph f3.

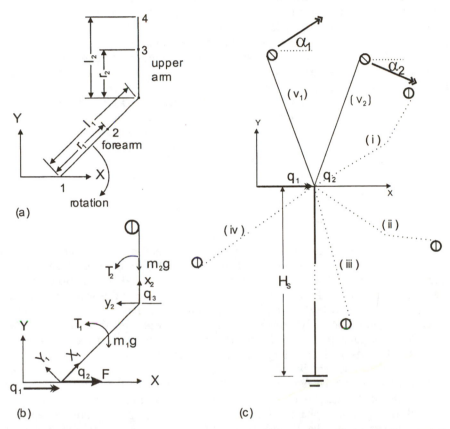

Figure 2 (a) Two segment link model of the upper arm and forearm representing the configuration of the bowling prior to locking (i.e. the point at which the arm is fully extended). The direction of rotation of the model is clockwise. (b) The link segment model of (a) showing the global reference system, two local reference systems, two joint torques (T_1, T_2), shoulder joint force F, and three output displacement variables (q_1, q_2, q_3). (c) The dotted stick figure sequence (i) to (v) shows how the rotation of the link segment model can represent the rotation of the bowling arm in cricket. Stage (i) and (ii) depict the bowling arm before locking, which occurs at (iii). (c) The projectile solution is sought after the arm is locked, so that the effective total segment length becomes $l_1 + l_2$. By simple geometry the relationship between α and q_2 can be established. There may be more than one combination of ball release angle and ball release speed for a specified range R. Release positions (v_1) and (v_2) represent two possible solutions at α_1 and α_2, respectively. However, the first release position generally does not yield practical solutions.

Data Collection

A Panasonic AG-188 NTSC video camera operating at 60Hz was used to film an elite fast bowler, bowling a series of balls on a synthetic cricket pitch in an indoor cricket net. The camera was placed perpendicular to the plane of motion in line with the bowling crease, and placed as far from the action as possible to reduce perspective error. The field of view was set to capture the performance area of the subject.

The subject performed two trial types. In the first trial type (Trial 1), the subject remained stationary in a side-on delivery position, and, using the bowling arm only, delivered twenty balls at maximum speed at a target 16 m in line with the wickets. Any run-up or motion of the non-bowling arm was disallowed. The intended objective of this exercise was to isolate the motion of the bowling arm for analysis. In Trial 2 the subject delivered the ball exactly as in Trial 1, but with the bowling arm locked 'as early as possible'.

Of the twenty balls bowled, we selected twelve based on their proximity to the target. The corresponding video footage was subsequently digitized and processed by an APAS motion analysis system (2-dimensional). To obtain a measure of digitizing accuracy, one recorded sequence was digitized three times, and the raw displacement data analysed. We found that the digitizing error was less than 5%. For data smoothing, we used cubic and quintic spline algorithms.

Inverse/Forward Solution

Data processing and numerical solving were performed by Mathematica Version 3.0, a symbolic manipulation software developed by Wolfram Research Ltd. As the link segment model is described by equations of motion that are functions of time, we used Mathematica's *Fit* function to yield simple fifth-order polynomial functions of time that best approximated the kinematic data. Then to calculate an inverse solution, the polynomial expressions for each of the kinematic data variables were substituted into the equations of motion (2), and the time-varying torques and forces on the bowling arm were calculated.

Once the initial conditions and driving functions $\{F, T_1, T_2\}$ were selected, Mathematica's *NDSolve* function could numerically solve the system of second-order differential equations (2). However, the solution process had to consider the pre-locked and locked phases of bowling. After *NDSolve* was run, the function *FindRoot* determined the "arm-locking" time (t_L) by searching the numerical solutions for the time when $q_2[t] = q_3[t]$. Then the *pre-locked* phase contains all the numerical solutions for $t \leq t_L$. Then, using the solutions $\{q_1[t_L], q_2[t_L], q_3[t_L], \dot{q}_1[t_L], \dot{q}_2[t_L], \dot{q}_3[t_L]\}$ as the initial conditions, and numerically solving (2) (by using *NDSolve* again) and imposing the constraint $q_2[t] = q_3[t]$ for $t \geq t_L$, we found solutions for the *post-locked* phase of bowling. Finally, to determine which points (if any) of the bowling trajectory satisfy a specified target range (R) on the pitch, *FindRoot* found solutions to (6) during the post-locked phase.

The advantage of a forward solution is that we can investigate the behaviour of the model resulting from any pattern of driving functions. To vary the pattern of joint torques, T_2 was multiplied by the factor γ. Any changes in γ would serve to predict how the model behaved in response to variation in the T_2 time-history. We were also interested in testing the model's response to changes in the time-history of F after the bowling arm had passed the horizontal. So F was split into two smaller functions, F_{BH} and F_{AH}, to describe the cases when the arm is below ($|q_2| < 180°$) and above (or equal to) the horizontal ($|q_2| \geq 180°$), respectively. The coefficient of the squared term in the polynomial expression, F_{AH}, was multiplied by the factor X_R, generating the new function F^ϕ_{AH}. Then, by varying X_R, and combining F_{BH} with F^ϕ_{AH} to create a new function F, we could test for changes in ball release speed.

RESULTS

The inverse solution for a typical ball (ball speed 65.1km/h, locking angle 120.4°) showed that the torques and forces on the bowling arm are time-varying and non-linear (Figure 3a and 3b). This was particularly apparent in the process of arm-locking (i.e. the period prior to $t_L = 0.28$s). After locking, all the driving functions, (T_1, T_2 and F), began to increase in magnitude with T_1 and T_2 accelerating the bowling arm in the clockwise direction, and F acting on the shoulder pulling it forwards. However, when the bowling arm had passed the horizontal (after 0.4s), the torques decreased in magnitude, and played a diminishing role in the angular acceleration of the bowling arm. This was compensated by a rapid change in the magnitude and direction of F, serving to decelerate the shoulder quickly prior to ball release (0.50s).

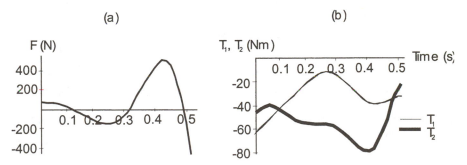

Figure 3 Inverse Solution for test bowl. (a) F represents the time-varying horizontal force on the shoulder joint. (b) Joint torques, T_1 and T_2, represent the time-varying torques on the upper arm and forearm, respectively. Arm-locking occurs at $t_L = 0.28$s.

An analysis of the trial-based kinematic data showed that there was correlation between decreased locking angle and increased ball speed. The mean locking angle for the subject in Trial 1 was ($-112\pm3.1°$), corresponding to an arm position behind the hips, with a mean ball speed of (23.1 ± 0.6 ms^{-1}). In Trial 2 the mean locking angle was ($-82.0\pm1.3°$), corresponding to an arm position in front of the hips, with a mean ball speed of (27.0 ± 0.2 ms^{-1}). This gives Trial 2 a 16.9% mean ball speed advantage over Trial 1.

The forward solution also showed that a decrease in locking angle caused an increase in ball speed. The initial conditions were: $q_1(0) = 0.000\,\mathrm{m}$, $q_2(0) = -0.247\,\mathrm{rad}$, $q_3(0) = 1.451\,\mathrm{rad}$, $\dot{q}_1(0) = 0.579\,\mathrm{ms}^{-1}$, $\dot{q}_2(0) = -2.115\,\mathrm{rad/s}$, $\dot{q}_3(0) = -5.043\,\mathrm{rad/s}$. Then using a range of locking angles from 120° to −80° approximating those recorded in the trials (i.e. −112° to 82.0°), we found that ball release speed increased almost linearly from 17.9 to 24.5 ms⁻¹, a 36.9% increase. This compares favourably with the trial-based percentage increase in speed (16.9%).

Also, selective decreases in the forearm torque in that period before arm locking could produce an increase in ball speed. By varying only γ from 0.95 to 1.01 in the forward solution, we calculated a 26.6% increase in ball release speed. This accompanied a decrease in locking angle from −179.4° to −140.0° (Figure 4d).

However, the forward solution calculated the most significant increases in ball release speed for selected changes in F. Using values of X_R, from 0.8 to 1.5 (Figure 4a), to increase the negative rate of change of F after the bowling arm passed the horizontal (i.e. after 0.4s), we produced a 41.0% increase in ball release speed (Figure 4b). Also, this corresponded with a 31.8° decrease in locking angle (Figure 4c).

DISCUSSION

In cricket matches, the quality and speed of the fast bowlers can often determine the outcome of a match. However, not all bowlers can bowl fast, and a large variety of techniques can be used to achieve high ball release speed. Therefore, in this study, we have developed a general approach which investigates how a range of joint torques and initial arm configurations can effect the ball release speed and arm angle required to land a ball on a predetermined position on the pitch.

We validated our model by comparing the results of the forward solution and the trials, both of which showed that ball speed increased with decreasing locking angle. This study indicates that a 'late' locking angle is a relatively inefficient method for the bowling arm alone to generate speed. But some of the world's fastest bowlers have successfully done the opposite, and locked the arm relatively late. Therefore, it is conceivable that bowlers locking the arm 'later' rely more heavily on the generation of speed from other parts of the body, such as the trunk or hips; whereas bowlers with 'early' locking arm angles generate much of their ball speed from the shoulder.

The model also predicted that decreasing the forearm torque in that period prior to locking could increase ball release speed. Normally, one would expect an increase in the forearm torque, or a decrease in upper arm torque to decrease the locking angle. But the bowling arm is actuated by non-linear torques, and the equations governing its trajectory are also non-linear, so it is sometimes impossible to predict what effect a change in inputs would have.

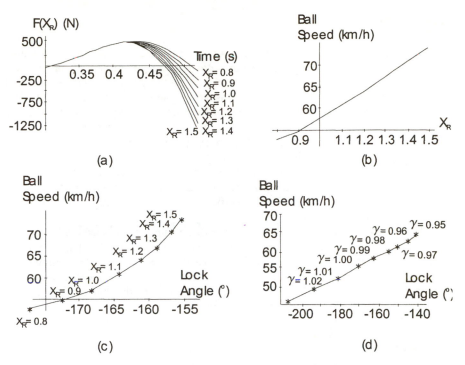

(a)

(b)

(c)

(d)

Figure 4 Forward Solution. (a) Time-varying force function F as a function of X_R. Increasing the coefficient X_R causes F to decrease more rapidly after the bowling arm has passed the horizontal i.e. after $q_2 = -180°$. (b) Velocity of ball release increases with X_R. (c) Shows relationship between ball release speed, X_R and locking angle. Locking angle decreases with ball release speed. (d) Shows relationship between ball release speed, and locking angle. Locking angle decreases with ball release speed.

— Bowling shoulder

We also found that when the bowling arm passes the horizontal, the force at the shoulder joint decreases sharply and then changes direction, effectively pulling the shoulder backwards, opposite to the intended direction of ball release. This is a direct result of Newton's third law. The force exerted backwards at the shoulder joint causes a clockwise reaction torque. In fact, this is the major process involved in accelerating the bowling arm above the horizontal, because at the corresponding time, the external joint torques (T_1 and T_2) are decreasing significantly. Also, a deceleration component in the motion of the trunk segment is primarily responsible for the process of shoulder deceleration. Many coaches encourage bowlers to 'bend the back' in order to generate more ball speed. This may be one of the factors that promote an increased risk of back injury. Instead, this study shows that the generation of ball speed is subtler: a faster delivery does not necessarily require more effort, but an increased sense of timing, particularly with an awareness of segmental deceleration.

Conclusion

CONCLUSION *use*

Bowling is technically a diverse art, and currently there is no consensus on which elements of bowling technique contribute most to the generation of ball release speed (Bartlett *et al.*, 1996). Even the simplified model presented here shows that the relatively simple motion of the bowling arm is subject to non-linear dynamic actuators. Coaches who attempt to improve bowling technique according to the standard textbook notions are not taking into account the underlying mechanics. This approach generally results in the prescription of unnaturally constrained techniques that are unlikely to improve performance, and may promote an increased susceptibility to injury. The development and validation of forward solution models of bowling will help prevent this situation by giving the coach a diagnostic tool to investigate how specific changes in technique will affect a particular bowler's performance.

Extension of our model to consider the three-dimensional case and include a larger number of segments would greatly increase its validity, and give a more accurate correlation between bowling performance and model simulation. However, the fact that good agreement was made between the locking angle and the trial data using reasonable assumptions, leads to considerable confidence that the results of this study are of interest to the bowler or coach.

REFERENCES

Bartlett, R.M., Stockhill, N.P., Elliott, B.C. and Burnett, A.F., 1996, The biomechanics of fast bowling in men's cricket: A review. *Journal of Sports Sciences*, **14**, pp. 403-424.

Davis, K. and Blanksby, B.A., 1976, Cinematographic analysis of fast bowling in cricket. *Australian Journal of Health Physical Education and Recreation*, **71** (March Supplement), pp. 9-15.

De Mestre, N., 1990, *The Mathematics of Projectiles in Sport* (Cambridge: University Press).

Elliott, B.C., Foster, D.H. and Gray, S., 1986, Biomechanical and physical factors influencing fast bowling. *The Australian Journal of Science and Medicine in Sport*, **18**(1), pp. 16-21.

Elliott, B.C. and Foster, D.H., 1984, A biomechanical analysis of the front-on and side-on fast bowling techniques. *Journal of Human Movement Studies*, **10**, pp. 83-94.

Jorgensen, T.P., 1970, On the dynamics of the swing of a golf club. *American Journal of Physics*, **38**, pp. 644-651.

Jorgensen, T.P., 1994, *The Physics of Golf* (New York: AIP Press).

Marion, J.B. and Thornton, S.T., 1988, *Classical Dynamics of Particles and Systems*, third ed. (Florida: Harcourt Brace Jovanovich).

Mason, B.R., Weissensteiner, J.R. and Spence, P.R., 1989, Development of a model for fast bowling in cricket. *Excel*, **6**(1), pp. 2-12.

Onyshko, S. and Winter, D.A., 1980, A mathematical model for the dynamics of human locomotion. *Journal of Biomechanics*, **13**, pp. 361-368.

Winter, D.A., 1990, *Biomechanics and Motor Control of Human Movement*, 2nd ed. (Toronto: John Wiley and Sons, Inc.).

Quantifying Judo Performance an Attempt to Judge the Effectiveness of Throwing Attacks

Manfred M. Vieten and Hartmut Riehle
Sports Department, University of Konstanz, Konstanz, Germany

INTRODUCTION

Jigoro Kano (1860–1938) is the founder of modern judo. He collected the knowledge of the old Japanese jujitsu schools and founded in 1882 the first school of judo. Judo was included in the Olympic Games for the first time at Tokyo in 1964 and held regularly since 1972. Women's Olympic competition began in 1992. Judo is a highly technical sport, which demands skill, strength, and fitness. Competitors (*judoka*) wear a judo suit (*judogi*), a loose-fitting garment of white or blue. The jacket is fastened by a belt, which goes twice round the body and is tied with a square knot. Fighters are judged on throwing technique (*nage-waza*), holding (*osae-komi-waza*), arm locking (*kansetsu-waza*), and choking (*shime-waza*).

In this paper we make an attempt to use momentum to judge the effectiveness of attacks for two different throws the *hane-goshi* (hip spring) and the *harai-goshi* (hip sweep). For details see Jigoro Kano's book "Kodokan Judo" published in 1994 (revised version).

METHODS

Four males and one female participated in this study. Their experience and main anthropometric data are shown in the following table (Table 1).

For each subject, 38 anthropometrical measurements were taken. Each participant performed 6 throws (3 *hane-goshis* and 3 *harai-goshis*) with each of the other participants. Altogether 120 throws were filmed. The throws were performed similar to an *uchi-komi* drill (pre-designed performance) at a given location on the judo mat (*tatami*). Movements were filmed using three 50Hz analogue cameras with a shutter speed of 1/1000 sec. A difficult step in the analysis was to select

those video sequences in which all the necessary landmarks on the bodies were visible
during the whole performance. For reasons of higher accuracy and better recognition of the lower extremities' joints participants wore tight fitting leggings instead of the traditional pants. The traditional jacket however was necessary to allow the judo throws to be performed. Fourteen throws (7 *hane-goshi* and 7 *harai-goshi*) were digitized manually using a Peak 5 system. For each person 16 coordinates (ears, shoulders, elbows, wrists, hips, knees, ankles, and toes) were selected. Therefore, 32 coordinates per frame and 38 anthropometric measurements per athlete were the input for the SDS simulation system. We used a digital filter that performed the smoothing by damping the FFT spectrum. SDS created the Hanavan model (Hanavan, 1964), see Figure 1 and calculated the inverse dynamics in accordance with the filmed movements. For technical details see Vieten (1999). No additional external forces was measured.

Table 1 Subjects information.

Participant	Age	Experience	Weight	Height
1	40	> 20 years (2. Dan)	75kg	1.75m
2	23	≈ 8 years (Kyu)	66kg	1.65m
3	25	≈ 1.5 years (Kyu)	75kg	1.79m
4	24	≈ 1.5 years (Kyu)	83kg	1.87m
5	30	≈ 1.5 years (Kyu)	54kg	1.60m

Figure 1 Hane-goshi (depicted using the Hanavan model).

RESULTS AND DISCUSSION

The horizontal momentum of the attacker (*tori*) as well as of the defender (*uke*) in x-direction (direction of movement) and the sum of these two momentums were calculated as functions of time (see Figure 2 *hane-goshi* and Figure 3 *harai-goshi*).

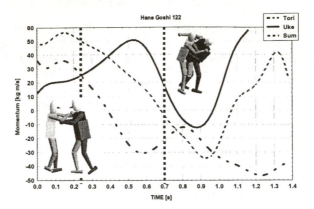

Figure 2 Momentum of a *hane-goshi throw*, *uke* pulling but moving forward.

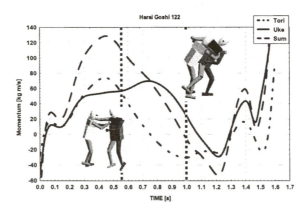

Figure 3 Momentum of a *harai-goshi throw*, *uke* pulling but moving forward.

The left vertical line marks the final sequence before throwing—denoted START. This sequence is either defined by the beginning of the last step or by *uke's* momentum increasing above *tori's* momentum (whatever comes last). The right vertical line marks the time when *uke's* feet are losing contact with the floor—denoted LIFT OFF. We calculated the following five parameters of which the results are shown in Figures 4 and 5:

The mean difference between *uke's* and *tori's* momentum

$$\left\langle p_{difference}\right\rangle = \left\langle p_{uke} - p_{tori}\right\rangle$$

for the time interval START to LIFT OFF. The maximum of the sum of *uke's* and *tori's* momentum between START and LIFT OFF. The sum of the two momentums at the START.

The mean value of the sum of the two momentums between START and LIFT OFF

$$P_{mean} = \langle p_{uke} + p_{tori} \rangle.$$

The momentum $p = p_{uke} + p_{tori}$ at LIFT OFF.

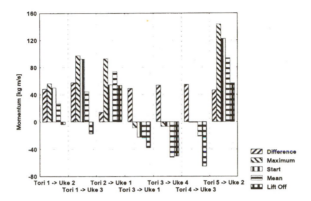

Figure 4 Momentums of the *hane-goshi throws*.

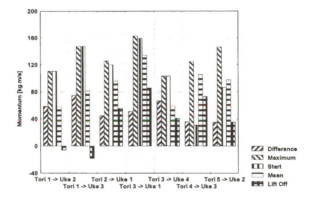

Figure 5 Momentums of the *harai-goshi throws*.

For all throws we found a momentum transfer from the attacker (*tori*) to the defender (*uke*) prior to the throw. This momentum is generated by *tori's* action. A *hane-goshi* is a throw where *tori* attacks the opponent's body from the shank up to the shoulder. A pulling action on arm and upper body is combined with a pushing/sweeping of one leg. At the same time *uke's* hip is being uplifted and as a result his or her standing stability is weakened. Therefore, this throw can be performed with a minimal initial momentum. This minimal momentum is necessary to get *uke* off-balance. In a *harai-goshi uke's* body is also attacked from leg up to the shoulder but the uplifting of *uke's* hip is not as prominent. Therefore, the *harai-goshi* needs more initial momentum to be successful. Our data shows the difference of initial momentum between *hane-goshi* and *harai-goshi* for all levels of experience. The initial momentum of the *hane-goshi* differs tremendously in-between the seven throws. In Figure 4 the first three throws and the seventh are performed with the *judokas* moving in the direction of the throw. The three other throws are performed from a static position. What is now the signature of a well-performed technique? In case of the *hane-goshi* the signature would be a high momentum transfer prior to the throw; in addition the next three parameters (see Figure 4) should contain positive values. The system's minimum momentum can approach small negative values. A *harai-goshi* should be performed with a high momentum transfer (parameter DIFFERENCE in Figure 5). MAXIMUM, START and MEAN should display significant higher values as in the case of the *hane-goshi*. The MINIMUM momentum can approach zero or small negative numbers but should not reach substantial negative values.

CONCLUSION

The above-described method allows discriminating diverse levels of performance quality. In addition, with this method we also established a monitoring tool, which quantifies the technical skill of a *judoka* during his or her training process. The method produces definite numbers, which need the interpretation of a coach with a scientific background. The interpretation depends on the situation the two competitors are in. If *uke* pushes *tori* an interpretation will look different compared to a situation in which *uke* pulls. The combination *tori 2* throws *uke 1* is an example for a pushing action for both *hane-goshi* and *harai-goshi*.

The decrease in the system's momentum during the period between START and LIFT OFF (Figures 6 and 7) is lower than in the above "pulling" example (Figures 2 and 4). Consequently the MEAN system momentum is higher and can elevate above the momentum at the START. The kind of motion, pulling, pushing or neutral is clearly identifiable in the momentum graphs (Figures 2, 3, 6, 7, 8 and 9).

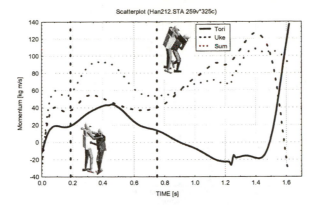

Figure 6 Momentum of a *hane-goshi throw*; *uke* pushing.

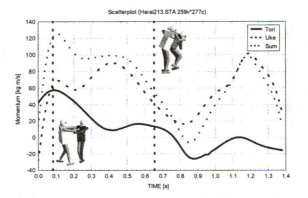

Figure 7 Momentum of a *harai-goshi throw*; *uke* pushing.

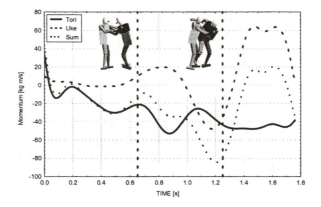

Figure 8 Momentum of a *hane-goshi throw*; *uke* standing.

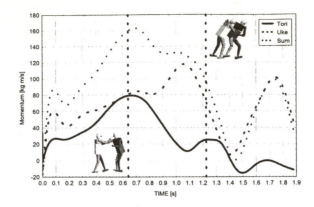

Figure 9 Momentum of a *harai-goshi throw*; *uke* pulling but moving forward.

The described method does not need external forces as input. Purely kinematical parameters are used. Therefore, a set of cameras and a digitizing system are sufficient to calculate the needed momentums. It is substantial for a tool monitoring the training process to deliver the data right away or at least at the end of a workout. The above-described instrumentation is not capable of delivering the data immediately. However, a modified equipment and a setting of markers (reflective elements on the *judogi* and on the lower extremities) would allow a real time capturing of the marker coordinates.

REFERENCES

Hanavan, E.P., 1964, *Mathematical Model of a Human Body* (AMRL-TR-64-102) (Ohio: Wright Patterson Air Force Base).

Kano, Jigoro, 1994, *Kodokan Judo* (Tokyo, New York, London: Kodansha International).

Vieten, Manfred, 1999, Inverse dynamics in sports biomechanics. In *Scientific Proceedings of the XVII International Symposium on Biomechanics in Sports*, edited by Sanders, R. and Gibson, B., pp. 219-230.

ACKNOWLEDGEMENTS

The raw data was taken from the "Zulassungsarbeit für das erste Staatsexamen" of Sabine Walter. The authors were supervising the project and one of them (MV) was actively involved in the whole process from data acquisition to preparation of the raw data.

Skill Evaluation of Rowers using Fuzzy Modelling

Kanta Tachibana, Takeshi Furuhashi[1], Manabu Shimoda[2],
Yasuo Kawakami[2] and Tetsuo Fukunaga[2]
Graduate School of Engineering, Nagoya University,
Japan and Bio-Mimetic Control Research Centre, Riken, Japan
[1]Graduate School of Engineering, Nagoya University, Japan
[2]Graduate School of Arts and Sciences, University of Tokyo, Japan

INTRODUCTION

It is the intention of rowers and their coaches to enhance the speed of their boat. Bio-mechanical efficiency should be increased in order to achieve an optimum performance. The boat speed is theoretically proportional to the cube root of the power supplied by rowers via oars. To enhance the production of power, the relationship between the rower's motion and his/her power must be explicitly clarified. Smith and Spinks (1995) used discriminate analysis to classify novice, good and elite rowers. This method distinguished each class with linear connection of the input of bio-mechanical factors. In this study, it was apparent that utilizing a nonlinear modelling method to describe the relationships was more accurate. Fuzzy modelling (Takagi and Sugeno, 1985) appears to be a promising technique with which to identify nonlinear system with multiple input variables. Furthermore, this method describes the input–output relationships with linguistic rules. Linguistic expressions are easy to understand for athletes and coaches.

The authors (Tachibana and Furuhashi, 1998) have proposed an automatic division method of input space for the fuzzy modelling. This paper presents a fuzzy modelling of relationships between bio-mechanical factors and power supplied to each oar. The authors (Shimoda et al., 1998) have developed a measuring device of forces and angles, which can be used while the rowers are actually on the water. The device measures the forces exerted on oars and the angles of oars. Effective advice according to the rower's output level is extracted from the obtained linguistic rules.

METHODS

The forces exerted on oars and the angles of oars were measured while women national team rowers were rowing in 100m runs. Using the measured data, the relationships were examined between the boat speed and the power. In addition, relationships were identified between the power and the skill parameters in a form of fuzzy model.

Subjects and Measurement

Six women rowers participated. Two of the subjects rowed a double scull as a crew. They rowed four runs of 100 metres. They were directed to row at 20, 24, 26 and 28 strokes per minute in the four runs, respectively. Other four crews carried out the same runs. During the runs, the forces exerted on oars were measured by strain gauges, and the angles by goniometers. The sampling frequency was 50Hz. The data were low-pass filtered with the cut-off frequency of 12.5Hz. An example of measured force and angle data is shown in Figure 1.

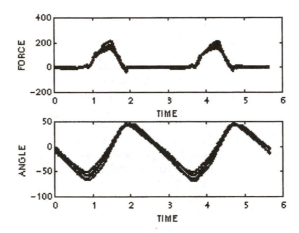

Figure 1 Example of data.

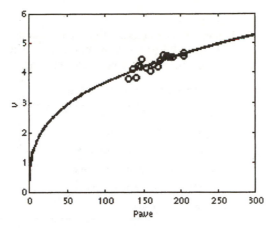

Figure 2 Boat speed dependence on power.

Boat Speed Dependence on Power

Power was calculated at each time step, by multiplying force $F_i(t)$, angular velocity $\omega_i(t)$ and outboard length of the oar. The angular velocity was the difference of the angle data $\omega_i(t)=(\theta_i(t)-\theta_i(t-1))/(\Delta t)$, where Δt is the sampling time).

$$P_i(t) = l_i F_i(t)\omega_i(t)$$

where the index i denotes each oar. A double scull has four oars, so ($i=1,...,4$).

The average power supplied by the four oars is:

$$Pave = \left(\sum_{t=1}^{T} \sum_{i=1}^{4} P_i(t)\right)\Big/T$$

where T is the final time step of the 100m run. The boat speed is: $v=100/T$.

It is a well-known theory that the resistance of a rigid bogy moving in a fluid is proportional to the square of the velocity. In this way, the power is proportional to the cube square of the velocity. Figure 2 shows the relationship between the boat speed and the average power. The curve in Figure 2 shows the cube root of the power. The coefficient was decided by the least square method. The main reason for the deviations was related to the disturbance of the wind.

Skill Parameters

Five parameters were calculated to characterize the force and angle data pattern for each stroke of each oar. Six specific times were defined as listed in Table 1 for each stroke of each oar to divide the driving phase into sections.

Table 1 Time steps to divide the driving phase.

t_1	The oar direction changes from negative to positive
t_2	The force becomes larger than 10% of the maximal force
t_3	The force becomes larger than 90% of the maximal force
t_4	The force becomes smaller than 90% of the maximal force
t_5	The force becomes smaller than 10% of the maximal force
t_6	The oar direction changes from positive to negative

The following are the parameters of rower's skill:

Maximal force:

$$F_M = \max_{t=t_1}^{t_6} F(t)$$

Wasted time:

$$t_w = (t_2 - t_1) + (t_6 - t_5)$$

Angular velocity in the beginning of effective driving:

$$\omega_B = (\theta(t_3) - \theta(t_2))/(t_3 - t_2)$$

Angular velocity in the middle of effective driving:

$$\omega_M = (\theta(t_4) - \theta(t_3))/(t_4 - t_3)$$

Angular velocity at the end of effective driving:

$$\omega_E = (\theta(t_5) - \theta(t_4))/(t_5 - t_4)$$

A rower can improve the performance more easily when she concentrates on one of these parameters rather than when she attempts to improve all of them. The relationships between these parameters and the output power are shown in Figure 3.

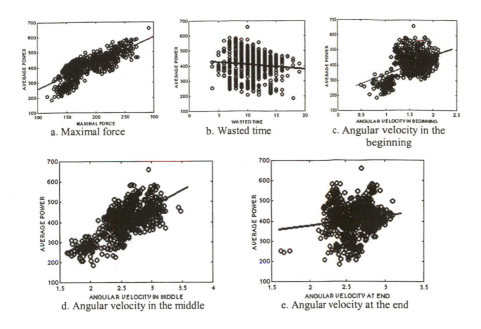

Figure 3 Relationships between skill parameters and average power.

USE OF FUZZY MODEL TO IDENTIFY THE DEPENDENCE OF POWER ON SKILL PARAMETERS

Distinct advantage of fuzzy modelling is the linguistic expression of nonlinear relationships with fuzzy rules. Suppose a system has M inputs $x=(x_1,x_2,...,x_M)$ and N outputs $y=(y_1,y_2,...,y_N)$, a fuzzy model describes the input–output relationships with linguistic rules such as: R^i: IF x is A^i, THEN y is B^i, where A^i and B^i are sets of membership functions for the i-th rule that have M and N elements, respectively. For details of fuzzy modelling, refer to Tachibana and Furuhashi (1998).

RESULTS AND DISCUSSION

The obtained fuzzy rules are shown in Table 2. They are listed and numbered in order of the output power. The relationships between the skill parameters and the power were described with 5-input plus 1-output rule. The rooted mean square error of the fuzzy model was 26W, which was 6.4% of the average output.

Table 2 Obtained Linguistic Rules with the Fuzzy Model.

Rule number	If part					Then part P
	F_M	t_w	ω_B	ω_M	ω_E	
1	Small	—	Small	—	—	253
2	Small	—	Large	—	Small	344
3	Very Small	—	Large	—	Large	362
4	Large	—	Large	Small	—	412
5	Medium Small	—	Large	—	Large	436
6	Large	Large	—	Large	—	469
7	Large	—	Small	Small	—	528
8	Medium Large	Small	—	Large	—	576
9	Very Large	Small	—	Large	—	617

Effective advice is extractable from this table. For example, Rule 8 has a difference in F_M from Rule 9. So "push strongly" is effective advice for a rower who can row about 570 watts in power. On examination of Rules 6 and 8, the difference is in t_w. "Reduce wasteful motion" is very good advice for a rower who outputs about 470 watts. There is also an apparent difference in ω_M between Rule 7 and Rule 8. For example, "speed up in the middle" is effective for a rower outputting about 530 watts.

CONCLUSION

Production of average power during the driving phase is important in order to enhance boat speed. Production of average power appears to depend on the rower's skill level nonlinearly. Fuzzy modelling revealed the nonlinear relationships, and effective advice for rowers in accordance with their skill level can be extracted from the obtained model.

REFERENCES

Shimoda, M., Kawakami, Y. and Fukunaga, T., 1998, *Japan Olympic Committee Report (in Japanese)*, **No. II**, pp. 341-349.
Smith, R.M. and Spinks, W.L., 1995, Discriminant analysis of biomechanical differences between novice, good and elite rowers. *Journal of Sports Sciences*, **13**(5), pp. 377-385.
Tachibana, K. and Furuhashi, T., 1998, A hierarchical fuzzy modelling using fuzzy neural networks which enable uneven division of input space. In *Proceedings of 14th Fuzzy System Symposium* (Japan Society for Fuzzy Theory and Systems), pp. 305-308.
Takagi, T. and Sugeno, M., 1985, Fuzzy identification of systems and its applications to modelling and control. *IEEE Transaction on System, Man and Cybernetics*, **15**(1), pp. 116-132.

Part Three

Biomechanics of the Neuro-Musculo-Skeletal System

Importance of Proprioceptive Activation on Functional Neuro-muscular Properties

Albert Gollhofer

Department of Sport Science, University of Stuttgart, Germany

INTRODUCTION

In strength training it has been shown that adaptation processes of the neuro-muscular system may be attributed to mechanisms based on either neuronal or muscular aspects (Sale, 1992). It is well agreed that the force capability of maximum voluntary contraction (MVC) is largely dependent on the cross sectional area of the muscle and that recruitment and firing rate of the active motoneurons determine the rate of force development (RFD) (Enoka and Fuglevand, 1993).

For strength adaptation most of the papers are related to the training induced changes in the basic strength of the maximum voluntary contraction (Garfinkel and Cafarelli, 1992; Jones and Rutherford, 1987; Häkkinen and Komi, 1986), only few approaches are investigating systematically the mechanisms underlying the alterations in the rate of force development.

Efferent and afferent contributions are determining the actual excitation of the motoneuron system. For strength training the efferent, voluntary controlled activation has been addressed to be responsible for neuronal adaptation in various training studies. The precise role of afferent contributions has been speculated primarily for a specific type of muscular action, the stretch-shortening cycle (Gollhofer, 1987; Komi, 1984).

In the present contribution the various possibilities of neuronal adaptation in strength training is addressed. Based on the potential possibilities of reflex induced activation in plyometric activities a training study is presented. Here, the combination of afferent and efferent activation processes is systematically trained on the basis of a proprioceptive training exercise. The final part concentrates on the problem to what extend the adaptations of afferent system may also influence voluntary muscular actions.

AFFERENT CONTRIBUTION IN STRETCH-SHORTENING CYCLE

Recent research work was concentrated on the activation characteristics in the natural combination of muscular action—in the stretch-shortening cycle (SSC). For those types the functional importance of stretch reflex activation has been controversially discussed (Van Ingen Schenau, 1997). Extensive literature provides evidence that stretch reflexes modulate the stiffness of the tendomuscular system in reactive and plyometric conditions. Both animal and human experiments were conducted to show whether afferent contribution in natural movement (i.e. locomotion) enhance the performance capability, especially when the system acts in the SSC (Gregor *et al.*, 1988; Komi and Gollhofer, 1997). Although it is not possible in natural human movement to separate methodologically afferent from efferent activation contributions, it has been argued that basically monosynaptic reflex activities contribute in SSC (Figure 1). Efficient stretch reflex contribution may be expected when the extensors are activated prior to the stretching phase after contact which is necessary to enlarge the range of short elastic stiffness, thus linearizing the stress-strain characteristics of the tendomuscular system (Nichols, 1987; Houk and Rhymer, 1981). Functionally these afferent contributions are necessary to compensate yield in the early impact phase and thus enhance the power output for the subsequent push-out phase. The reflex contribution, however, is highly sensitive to loading conditions (Gollhofer *et al.*, 1992) (Figure 1).

As the drop jump height is increased the amplitude of the reflex component is reduced suggesting a decreased reflex facilitation. This reduction has been interpreted to serve as a protection strategy to prevent excessive loading of the tendo-muscular complex. Thus, stretch reflexes may make a net contribution to muscle stiffness already during the eccentric part of the SSC. It is difficult to imagine that proprioceptive reflexes, the existence of which has been known for centuries, would not play any significant role in human locomotion including SSCs.

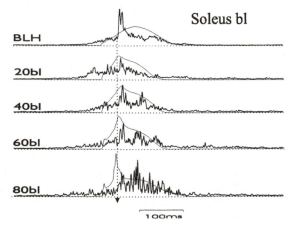

Figure 1 EMG-pattern of M. Soleus and vertical ground reaction force indrop jumps with increased stretch load (from top: BLH–both leg hopping, 20–80bl: Drop jumps from 20–80cm height. The vertical line indicates the instant 40ms after touching the force plates; 40ms after touch down, basically monosynaptic reflex contribution may be expected).

PROPRIOCEPTIVE TRAINING AS A MODEL OF EXERCISE AFFERENT ACTIVATION CONTRIBUTIONS

Theoretically promoted as proprioceptive facilitation of the neuronal contribution of the various receptor types in the joint complexes, in the tendon and in the muscular structures, proprioceptive training is frequently applied in rehabilitation. Similar to the argumentation in SSC, this type of training aims to improve the efficacy of the afferent contribution in the neuromuscular control, in order to attain better limb control and to achieve an early access to the muscles encompassing joint complexes. However, no controlled studies are available that demonstrate whether proprioceptive training improves the afferent contribution in general.

Thus, in a series of experiments we have investigated the effects of proprioceptive training interventions on the neuromuscular properties. Specific emphasis was given to the evaluation of afferent and efferent alterations. Additionally, it may be expected that augmentation of afferent input to the muscle should have also positive effects in the activation process under MVC conditions.

METHODS AND MATERIAL

Three experimental groups performed for four weeks (four times weekly) a specifically designed proprioceptive training programme. The training regimen consisted in postural exercises on tilt platforms or ankle pad (AIREX). The subjects (n=65) were instructed to perform all exercises as one-leg stance stabilization tasks. In order to differentiate the effects Group 1 (barefoot) exercised barefoot, Group 2 (AIRCAST®) with a semirigid ankle fixation and Group 3 (skiboot) trained with fixed ankle joint. The rationale for this selection was to separate the training effects according to the number of allowed degrees of freedom: the barefoot group was allowed to perform freely both the ankle and knee joint systems, whereas the skiboot group had to perform with mechanically blocked ankle systems.

Pre and post measurements comprised force examinations of the leg extension, postural stabilization carried out on a two-dimensional platform (POSTUROMED(®)), functional knee joint stiffness as well as inversion movements on a platform system. Tilt movements were designed to produce an unexpected valgus stress at the knee joint. The functional knee joint stiffness was assessed by a specifically designed apparatus that allowed to induce a mechanical displacement at the tibia relative to the thigh. Subjects were in the upright stance and loaded their legs equally. This mechanical stress produced an anterior drawer at the knee joint under functional, i.e. axial loaded conditions. Quantification of the mechanical parameters of the anterior drawer and determination of the neuronal response allows a comprehensive examination of the functional status of the knee joint complex (Bruhn, 1999).

Electromyographic activation was recorded from ankle and knee joint muscles: M. Gastrocnemius m.; M. Tibialis a.; M. Peronaeus; M. Vastus m.; M. Semitendinosus m. By means of twin-axis goniometers (PENNY and GILES(®)) the angular excursion in the ankle and knee joints was registered together with the relative torque between shank and thigh movement. All signals were A/D converted (1000Hz) and stored on a PC for off-line analysis.

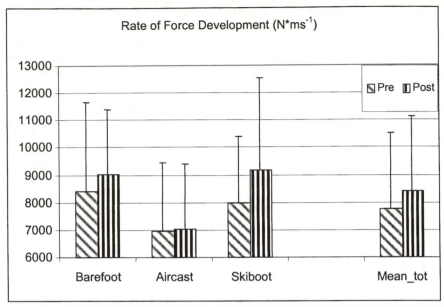

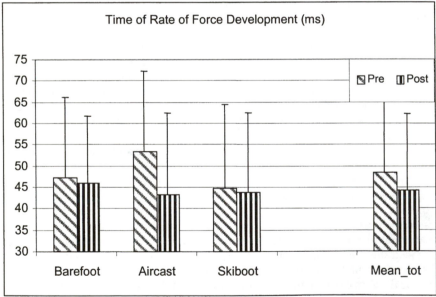

Figure 2 Mean values of the time to reach maximum rate of force development (RFD) in the isometric leg extension (upper part); mean values of the maximum RFD (lower part).

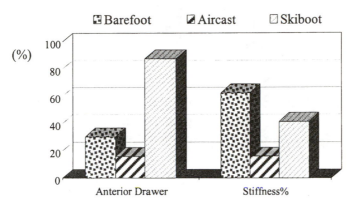

Figure 3 Training induced reductions of the anterior drawer and improvements od stiffness in the knee joint following mechanical displacement. The bars denote the mean values of the three experimental groups.

RESULTS

The EMG of the ankle joint muscles did not reveal statistical significance in the evaluation of the training effects. However, there was a significantly higher EMG activation for the skiboot group for the knee joint muscles. In all three training groups only small improvements in the leg extension force could be observed. However, the time to reach RFD was reduced while the mean rate of force development (RFD) was enhanced (Figure 2).

   In functional knee examination the anterior–posterior drawer was diminished (Figure 3) most pronounced in the skiboot group. The stiffness of the knee joint complex, determined as the ratio of induced drawer force and the resultant anterior drawer, was enhanced in all three groups by approximately 20 to 60% in the before/after comparison.

   In the stance stabilizing test the subjects were asked to maintain equilibrium while standing on one leg for 40sec on the two-dimensional unstable platform. Post training, the physical ability to stabilize in the upright stance was increased in all subgroups: Both medio-lateral component as well as anterio-posterior displacement of the integrated platform movement was drastically decreased. In line with these reductions the IEMG values of the ankle and knee joint muscles were diminished, respectively. However, the ratio "displacement necessary for stabilization divided by IEMG" was enhanced, both for the quadriceps muscle as well as for the hamstring muscles. Thus, the proprioceptive function expressed as the IEMG per sway was increased significantly in all three training groups.

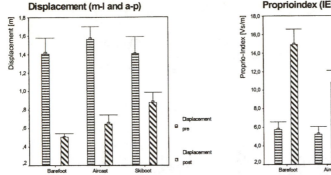

Figure 4 Pre/Post-Differences of the displacement in medio-lateral-direction and in anterior–posterior direction while the subjects performed free stance stabilization on a 2-dimersional unstable platform for 40secs (left part). Pre/post-Differences of the proprioceptive index, calculated as the ratio of displacement and integrated EMG (IEMG) of the quadriceps muscles (right part).

DISCUSSION

Despite the fact that proprioceptive training has loaded the knee joint muscles during training differentially, the functional adaptations were quite similar in all training groups. The mechanical stiffness of the joint complexes was increased, concomitant with a significantly enhanced proprioceptive control during dynamic stabilization. In-line with these findings the capability to produce the maximum rate of force development in shorter time was improved.

In previous studies on proprioceptive adaptation it has been observed that training induced proprioceptive gains in monosynaptic reflex behaviour are correlated with the improvements in explosive strength: subjects who performed in a four week training programme designed for proprioceptive joint stabilization enhanced their capability for explosive strength significantly compared to subjects who exercised pure isometric and concentric muscular performances. The group with the largest improvement in explosive strength showed the greatest gain in reflex contributions.

High Frequency Intermuscular Coordination, a Reflex Controlled Mechanism in Dynamic Stabilization

The mechanical importance of improvements in the proprioceptive gain reflects the changed ability of the neuromuscular system to activate the muscles more efficiently at the onset of force development (Dietz *et al.*, 1987). From a functional point of view quicker access to the muscle may be important in order to stiffen joint complexes in disturbance conditions. In rehabilitation, proprioceptive training programmes are employed to "teach" the agonist/antagonist muscles to stabilize a joint complex actively.

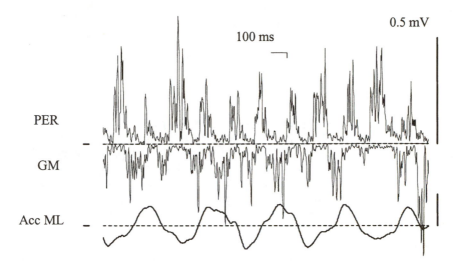

Figure 5 EMG Profile of Peroneus (PER) and Gastrocnemius (GM) muscle together with the medio-lateral component of the accelerometer signal (ACC ML) in a posture task on an unstable platform. The distinct bursts in the EMG patterns occur with a frequency of about 8Hz.

In order to verify this hypothesis a detailed electrophysiological analysis of the EMG profiles in dynamic stabilization control was performed. As an example the EMG patterns of one subject are depicted in Figure 5. Obviously, the dynamic stabilization task requires quick regulations in the muscular activation. This control is achieved by fast neuronal interactions of agonist and antagonist activation with high intermuscular frequency. The pattern of this neuronal communication consists of phasic bursts interacting with a frequency up to 8Hz.

Role of Ia-afferents in the Isometric Force Development

Macefield *et al.* (1991) demonstrated that the discharge rate is drastically reduced in isometric conditions when the afferent contributions are withdrawn. On the basis of frequency analysis on single motoneuron discharge rates they concluded that intact afferentation provides for adequate fusimotor drive. Higher discharge frequencies, however, are responsible for faster rates of force development of the motoneuron. Based on H-reflex data obtained in ramp contraction, several observations favour the hypothesis that afferent reflex contribution has also a gating effect on isometric strength development (Meunier/Pierrot-Designy, 1989). Comparing different ramp velocities and various levels of voluntary contraction (MVC) evidence exists that the sensitivity of the motoneuron pool is highest in the early phase of typically fast ramp velocities performed with high MVC percentages.

The results from proprioceptive adaptations emphasize the idea that based on these high frequencies and on the highly specific intermuscular coordination seen in postural performances (Figure 5) it is most likely that the neuromuscular activation observed in joint stabilization task is generated by reflex activation (Dietz and Noth, 1978). As the frequency of the observed intermuscular pattern is too high to assume regulation via central pathways, their control mechanisms must be assumed to be on the spinal level.

CONCLUSION

The mechanical importance of enhanced afferent gains in the neuromuscular control seems to reflect the changed ability of the neuromuscular system to activate the muscles more efficiently at the onset of force development. Especially in disturbance conditions quicker access to the muscles may be important to stiffen joint complexes. Not only in rehabilitation, even more pronounced in athletic training, i.e. in alpine skiing, proprioceptive training programmes may be an efficient tool to improve the agonist/antagonist intermuscular communication. This may have functional importance in all sport disciplines with explosive power demands.

From a physiological point of view, muscle spindle afferents are not simply stereotype responses to unexpected stretches. Embedded in the neuromuscular pattern they provide high stiffness in the tendomuscular system, not only in the SSC. Moreover, they are highly efficient in the isometric force development.

REFERENCES

Bruhn, S., 1999, *Funktionelle Stabilität am Kniegelenk* (Unpublished dissertation, University of Stuttgart).

Garfinkel, S. and Cafarelli, E., 1992, Relative changes in maximum force, EMG, and muscle cross-sectional area after isometric training. *Medicine and Science in Sports and Exercise,* **24**, pp. 1220-1227.

Enoka, R.M. and Fuglevand, A.J., 1993, Neuromuscular basis of maximum voluntary force capacity of muscle. In *Current Issues in Biomechanics*, edited by Grabiner, M. (Champaign IL, Human Kinetics), pp. 215-235.

Dietz, V., Quintern, J. and Sillem, M., 1987, Stumbling reactions in man. Significance of proprioceptive and pre-programmed mechanisms. *Journal of Physiology,* **386**, pp. 149-163.

Dietz, V. and Noth, J., 1978, Spinal stretch reflexes of triceps surae in active and passive movements. *Journal of Physiology,* **284**, pp. 180-181.

Gollhofer, A., 1987, Innervation characteristics of m. gastrocnemius during landing on different surfaces. In *Biomechanics X-B, International Series of Biomechanics*, (Champaign IL, Human Kinetics), pp. 701-706.

Gollhofer, A., Strojnik, V., Rapp, W. and Schweizer, L., 1992, Behavior of triceps surae muscle–tendon complex in different jump conditions. *European Journal of Applied Physiology and Occupational Physiology,* **64**(4), pp. 283–291.

Gregor, R.J., Roy, R.R., Whiting, W.C., Lovely, R.G., Hodgson, J.A. and Edgerton, V.R., 1988, Mechanical output of the cat soleus during treadmill locomotion. *Journal of Biomechanics*, **21**, pp. 721-732.

Häkkinen, K. and Komi, P.V., 1986, Training-induced changes in neuromuscular performance under voluntary and reflex conditions. *European Journal of Applied Physiology*, **55**, pp. 147-155.

Jones, D.A and Rutherford, O.M., 1987, Human muscle strength training. The effects of three different regimens and the nature of the resultant changes. *Journal of Physiology*, **391**, pp. 1–11.

Komi, P.V., 1984, Physiological and biomechanical correlates of muscle function. Effects of muscle structure and stretch-shortening cycle on force and speed. *Exercise and Sport Science Reviews*, **12**, pp. 81–121.

Komi, P.V. and Gollhofer, A., 1997, Stretch reflexes can have an important role in force enhancement during SSC exercise. *Journal of Applied Biomechanics*, pp. 451-460.

Houk, J.C. and Rhymer, W.Z., 1981, Neural control of muscle length and tension. Handbook of Physiology. *The Nervous System II* (Baltimore: Waverly Press), pp. 257-323.

Macefield, G., Hagbarth, K.E., Gorman, R., Gandevia, S.C. and Burke, D., 1991, Decline in spindle support to α-Motoneurons during sustained voluntary contractions. *Journal of Physiology,* **440**, pp. 497-512.

Meunier, S. and Pierrot-Deseilligny, E., 1989, Gating of the afferent volley of the monosynaptic stretch reflex during movement in man. *Journal of Physiology*, **419**, pp. 753-763.

Nichols, T.R., 1987, The regulation of muscle stiffness. *Medicine and Science in Sports and Exercise*, **26**, pp. 36-47.

Sale, D.G., 1992, *Strength and Power in Sport*, edited by Komi, P.V. (Oxford: Blackwell), pp. 249-265.

Van Ingen Schenau, G., 1997, Does elastic energy enhance work and efficiency in the stretch-shortening cycle? *Journal of Applied Biomechanics*, **13**(4), pp. 389-415.

The Significance of Titin Filaments to Resting Tension and Posture

Andreas Klee, Thomas Jöllenbeck and Klaus Wiemann
Bergische Universität–Gesamthochschule Wuppertal, Germany

INTRODUCTION

The theory of muscular balance is one of the most widely discussed topics in sport science over the past years. It is believed that a shortening of muscles which tilt the pelvis lead to a weak posture and backache (see Figures 1 and 2). There is a significant discrepancy between the accuracy of many statements on the theory of muscular balance that have been published and the small number of empirical studies in this field.

Furthermore it can be stated that in most of the empirical studies posture was examined by means of visual assessment or via the muscular function test according to JANDA. Neither of these methods comes up to the high standard demanded by empirical methods concerning validity, reliability and objectivity. Only two studies, up to the present time, have examined the correlation between muscular function (the maximal isometric force (MVC) of the back extensors and the abdominal muscles) and posture (the pelvic inclination and the shape of the spine) based on empirical methods (Asmussen and Heeboll-Nielson, 1959; Klausen et al., 1978). Neither study elucidated indisputable results in a way that could have been predicted by the publications on muscular balance.

In the field of "muscular balance, posture and exercise" only a small number of empirical studies have been presented so far. Consequently there is a high demand for empirically reliable data on this topic.

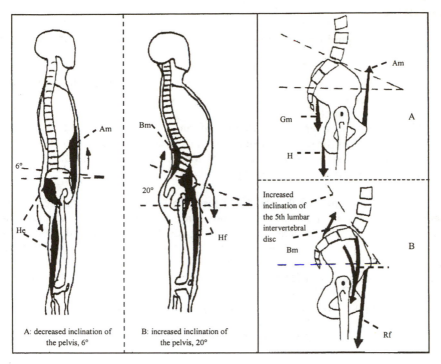

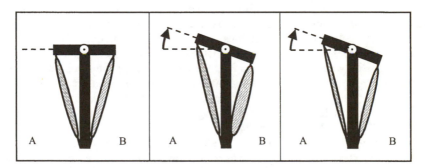

Figure 1 Muscle balance as a result of an equal pull of the antagonistic muscles A and B (muscle imbalance as a result of a short muscle B, muscle imbalance as a result of a weak muscle A).

Figure 2 Muscles which influence the pelvic inclination. On the right below: Increased inclination of the 5th lumbar intervertebral disc as a result of an increased inclination of the pelvis. Am: Abdominal muscles, Bm: Low back muscles, Hf: Hip flexors, He: Hip extensors, Gm: Gluteus maximus, H: Hamstrings, Im: Iliopsoas muscle, Rf: Rectus femoris.

METHODS

In this study, 53 pupils volunteered as subjects. The following parameters were determined:

1. The posture and the "Armvorhaltetest" according to Matthiaß by taking and evaluating photos (see Figures 3 and 5);
2. The muscular function;
3. The maximal isometric force (MVC) of the back extensors, the abdominal muscles, the hip flexors and the hip extensors (see Figure 4, above) and
4. The range of motion (ROM), end ROM torque and resting tension of the hip flexors and the hamstrings (see Figure 4, below).

Out of a total of 53 subjects, 40 of these volunteered to participate in a 10 week training experiment. They were divided into two groups of 20, according to their pelvic inclination whereas the remaining 13 pupils constituted the control group. Subjects with an above-average pelvic inclination took part in a training programme designed to straighten the pelvis. The programme included exercise to strengthen abdominal muscles and hip extensors. Stretching exercises for the back extensors and the hip flexors were also included. Pupils with an above-average pelvic inclination took part in a training programme designed to achieve the opposite effect (anterior tilt of the pelvis) by means of strengthening of the hip flexors and the back extensors and stretching of the hamstrings.

RESULTS

While examination of plausibility and stringency showed that the theory of muscular balance lacks an empirical basis, the present study disclosed a number of correlations between the variables of muscular function, between pelvic inclination, lordosis and kyphosis, and between muscular function and posture. The correlations between pelvic inclination, the inclination of the lumbo-sacral section of the spine and between pelvic inclination and the lordosis are in line with the current theory of the muscular balance: as the pelvis becomes more straight, the lordosis becomes less marked. On average subjects with a more inclined pelvis show more distinct lordosis and kyphosis.

Subjects with strongly developed abdominal muscles (in comparison with the hip flexors) show a smaller inclination of the sacrum, i.e. a more straightened lumbo-sacral section of the spine. If subjects have strongly developed hip flexors in relation to their weight, they show a more inclined pelvis if they stand in a form of resting posture. The results of the present study showed an increase of ROM and end ROM torque of the hip flexors and the hamstrings within the respective groups. The resting tension in an angle below ROM was not effected. There was no decline of resting tension by the long-term stretching exercises.

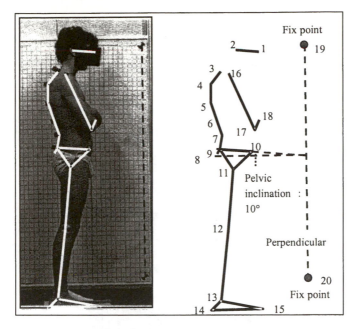

Figure 3 The photogrammetric measurement of the posture. Measuring points (Mp) 1–18: 1. Nose, 2. Ear, 3. Vertebrae prominens, 4-6. Spine between Mp 3 and Mp 7, 7. Max. lordosis, 8. Sacrum, 9. Spina iliaca post. sup., 10. Spina iliaca ant. sup., 11. Troch. major, 12. Epicondylus lat., 13. Malleolus lat., 14. Heel, 15. Fifth toe, 16. Acromion, 17. Elbow, 18. Wrist.

The study demonstrated that at the beginning of the "Armvorhaltetest", according to Matthiaß, tall, light people move their hip forward in a manner typical of persons with weak posture (Figure 5). Apart from the previously mentioned results only a weak correlation exists between the "Armvorhaltetest" and the MVC of the abdominal muscles. Furthermore, the expected correlation between the "Armvorhaltetest" and the force of the back extensors could not be established. These findings suggest that the applicability of the "Armvorhaltetest" as a method for diagnosis of posture faults in general, or to test the force of the back extensors in particular, has to be called into question.

The central aim of the training programme was to influence the degree of pelvic inclination. The results elucidated that the pelvic inclination was lowered significantly (2.16°, $p<0.01$) in the group participated in a training programme to straighten the pelvis. This is in line with the hypothesis.

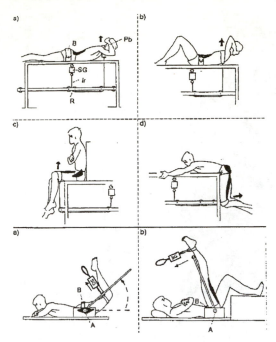

Figure 4 Above: Measurement of the maximal isometric force (MVC) of the (a) back extensors, (b) the abdominal muscles, (c) the hip flexors, (d) the hip extensors. B: Fastening belt, SG: Strain gauge, Ir: iron rope, R: roll, Pb: pulling belt. Below: Measurement of the flexibility (ROM, end ROM torque and resting tension) of the hip flexors (a) and the hamstrings (b). A: Axis of rotation with goniometer.

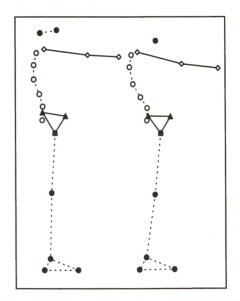

Figure 5 The "Armvorhaltetest" according to Matthiaß.

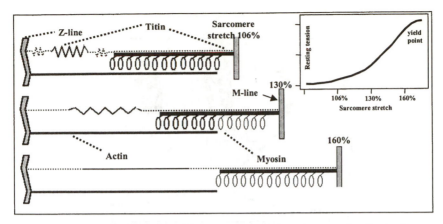

Figure 6 Model of titin extension with sarcomere stretch, inset: increase of resting tension.

DISCUSSION

Many questions for further investigation remain open. Before considering possibilities to influence posture by means of training, for example, it had to clarified which kind of posture can be defined as being healthy. The accepted methods to legitimate a norm or standard posture, i.e. calculating a mean value or evaluating according to theoretical–technical aspects can only be seen as a kind of guideline. The only way to legitimate standard values for factors which constitute posture is to prove a direct connection between the deviation of a defined standard value and backache. Until these questions have not been answered satisfactorily, it can only be stated that an extremely inclined pelvis bears potential risk for health. The results of this study suggest that a muscular training brings about a straightening of the pelvic inclination. We believe that the following factors are responsible for constancy of resting tension. Formerly, resting tension was attributed to elastic forces in the connective tissue and in the sarcolemma. Later on, it was demonstrated, that in intact muscles up to a stretching rate of 160%, resting tension arises from the elastic resistance of the myofibrils. Recently, the titin filaments have been identified as elastic molecular springs within the sarcomeres. They are responsible for the resting tension (Figure 6). Restoring sarcomere length after stretching appears to be the most important function of titin. This physiological function may be the reason for the finding that resting tension of human hamstrings could not be lowered by stretching exercises (Wiemann and Hahn, 1997). Since every single thick filament is associated with six titin filaments it can be suggested that hypertrophy leads to an increase of resting tension which brings about a change of posture (Figure 7). Therefore, muscular balance should not be treated with stretching but with resistance exercises (Wiemann *et al.*, 1998).

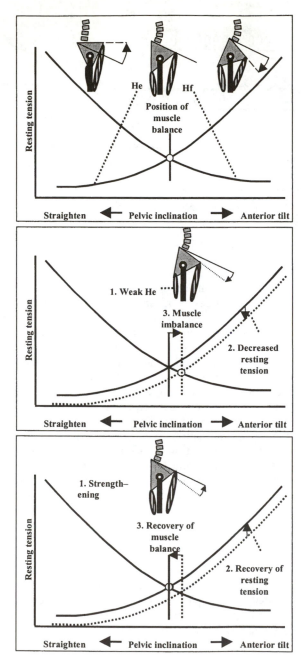

Figure 7 Correlation between resting tension of hip extensors (He) and hip flexors (Hf) and the degree of pelvic inclination.

REFERENCES

Asmussen, E. and Heeboll-Nielson, K., 1959, Posture, mobility and strength of the back in boys, 7 to 16 years old. *Acta Orthopaedica Scandinavica*, **28**, pp. 174-189.

Klausen, K., Jeppesen, K. and Mogenson, A., 1978, Form and function of the erect spine in young girls. *Biomechanics VI-B, International Series on Sport Science*, Volume 2B, edited by Asmussen, E. and Jorgenson, K. (USA, Baltimore), pp. 171-179.

Klee, A., 1995, *Haltung, Muskuläre Balance und Training. 2. unver.* (Auflage, Frankfurt a.M.: Verlag Harri Deutsch).

Klee, A., 1995, Muskuläre balance. *Sportunterricht*, **44**(1), pp. 12-23.

Klee, A., 1995, Zur Aussagefähigkeit des Armvorhaltetests nach Matthiaß. *Z Orthop*, **133**, 3, pp. 207-213.

Wiemann, K. and Hahn, K., 1997, Influences of strength, stretching and circulatory exercises on flexibility parameters of the human hamstrings. *International Journal of Sports Medicine*, **19**, pp. 340-346.

Wiemann, K., Klee, A. and Stratmann, M., 1998, Filamentäre quellen der muskelruhespannung und die behandlung muskulärer dysbalancen. *Dtsch Z Sportmed*, **44**(4), pp. 111-118.

The Coordination between Locomotion and Breathing during Treadmill Walking with Load Carriage in Children

Youlian Hong and Jing Xian Li
Department of Sports Science and Physical Education,
The Chinese University of Hong Kong, Hong Kong, China

INTRODUCTION

School children carrying heavy bags are a common phenomenon. The overloading of school bags has aroused the concern of communities in many countries. Reports from Europe and Asia have found that many students carry weights that are more than 10%, and in some cases even up to 20%, of their body weight (Sander, 1979; HKSCHD, 1988). However, compared with extensive studies on physiological and biomechanical responses to load carriage in adults, investigations on the influence of load carriage on growth and development in children are limited. Malhotra and Sen Gupta (1965) examined the metabolic cost to children associated with different ways of carrying schoolbags while walking. Pascoe *et al.* (1995) studied the kinematic impact on children's static postures and gait of walking under four different conditions: without a load; carrying a book bag weighing 17% of mean body weight in the form of a one-strap backpack; carrying the same load in a two-strap backpack; and carrying the load in a one-strap athletic bag. The one-strap backpack induced significant elevation of the strap-supporting shoulder and concomitant lateral bending of the spine. Hong *et al.* (1998) investigated the energy expenditure of children walking under four different load conditions—at 0%, 10%, 15%, and 20% of their body weight. The results showed that walking for 20 minutes under 15% and 20% load conditions produced significantly higher physiological strain than those measured under 0% and 10% load conditions. Recently, Hong and Brueggemann (2000) reported changes of gait patterns in ten-year-old boys carrying school bags of 0%, 10%, 15%, and 20% of their body weight while walking on a treadmill for 20 minutes. They found that the 20% load condition induced a significant increase in trunk forward lean, double support, and stance duration, as well as decreased trunk angular motion and swing duration; and the 15% load condition induced a significant increase in trunk forward lean.

As reported above, carrying loads that are equal to 15% or more of body weight will induce significantly increased physiological stain and abnormal gait and posture in children. The increased physiological strain is likely to demand more oxygen uptake for producing energy. Therefore respiratory system to load carriage during walking has to increase minute ventilation, which is achieved both by augmenting tidal volume (air volume breathed in or out during normal respiration) and raising breathing rate (breathing times per minute). Breathing rate and tidal volume, which are the two components of ventilation, as well as the ratio of breathing rate to tidal volume reflect the characteristics of respiratory activity and are often used to describe breathing pattern. Breathing pattern is affected by a lot of factors, such as exercise intensity, duration, and age. Additionally, it is known that respiratory activity is related to the movement of the thorax and the abdomen. Therefore, one question arises: what impact is placed on breathing activity as the load increases and the trunk position subsequently changes? No study has reported how breathing patterns—in terms of tidal volume respiratory frequency, ventilation, and the ratio of respiratory frequency to Tidal volume— alter in children under conditions of increased load carriage during walking. It is unknown whether trunk position, carried weight, and breathing patterns are associated. The purpose of the current project was to determine the impact of carrying differently weighted schoolbags on children's trunk position and breathing patterns while walking, and to examine possible associations between school bag weight, trunk position, and breathing patterns through an analysis of kinematics and pulmonary function.

METHODS

Twenty-five boys aged 10.31±0.26 years were selected from a primary school. The criterion of selection was that they best represented this age group in terms of mean Body Mass Index. The body mass and stature of the subjects were 33.60±3.62kg and 141.80±4.77cm respectively. Through medical examination and questionnaires, all subjects were determined to be free from cardiorespiratory and skeletal muscle diseases. Each subject participated in four walking trials on a treadmill: without a bag (0% of body weight), and with a school bag of 10%, 15%, and 20% of the child's body weight. Subjects walked at 1.1 m s^{-1} for 20 minutes on the treadmill. Their movement was recorded by one 3-CCD video camera (50Hz) positioned laterally to the subject with the lens axis perpendicular to the movement plane. The distance of the camera from the movement plane was 7.5m, and the shutter speed was set at 1/250s. The recorded videotapes were then digitized on a motion analysis system using a human body model consisting of 21 points, including the toes, heels, ankles, hips, shoulders, elbows, wrists, fingers, ears, and neck. In each trial, three complete gait cycles were taken for two time points: at the beginning of the test when the child's walking gait was observed to become consistent, and 20 minutes after the commencement of walking. For each complete gait cycle, the mean trunk inclination angle and the trunk motion range were calculated. "Trunk inclination angle" refers to the angle of the line connecting the shoulders and hips in relation to a horizontal line through the hips for each frame.

Values of less than 90° represent a forward lean of the trunk, while values greater than 90° represent a backward-leaning trunk position. "Trunk motion range" refers to the range of angular motion that was observed during the stride. Tidal volume and respiratory frequency were measured with a cardiopulmonary function system (Oxycon Champion, Yeager, Germany) before, during, and up to three minutes after the walk. All parameters measured were calculated automatically and continuously, and were averaged every 30 seconds by the cardiopulmonary function system. The data for Tidal volume and respiratory frequency that were recorded at the beginning of the test and 20 minutes after the commencement of walking were used for analysis. Vetilation values were calculated based on the obtained data of Tidal volume and respiratory frequency.

The values of Tidal volume and respiratory frequency measured at the commencement of walking under a 0% load condition served as baselines. Changes of Tidal volume in response to load carriage were then calculated as percentage increases compared to the baseline. A two-factor repeated measures analysis of variances was carried out on the Tidal volume, respiratory frequency, trunk inclination angle, and trunk motion range. A Pearson correlation was performed between the load condition, trunk inclination angle, Tidal volume, and respiratory frequency. A value of $\propto = 0.05$ was used for all tests as the criterion value in determining the presence or absence of significance.

RESULTS

Trunk Positions

Figures 1 and 2 illustrate the response of trunk position to different loads at the beginning of the test, and after 20 minutes of walking. No significant differences were found in trunk inclination angle and motion range between the different time for each load condition. Trunk inclination angle significantly increased under loads of 20% and 15% body weight, as compared to the 0% and 10% load conditions. Trunk motion range decreased significantly under a load of 20% body weight when compared to a 0% load condition.

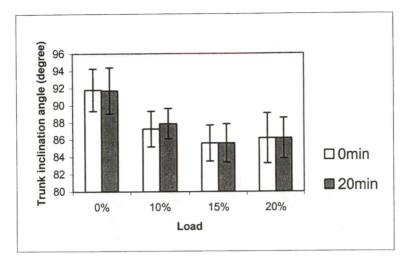

Figure 1 Mean trunk inclination angles under four load conditions, measured at the beginning of the test and after 20 minutes of walking.

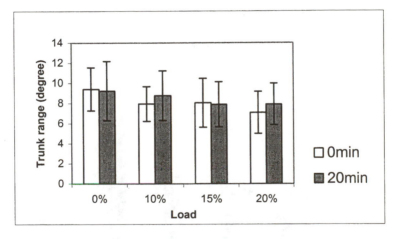

Figure 2 Mean trunk motion ranges under four load conditions, measured at the beginning of the test and after 20 minutes of walking.

Breathing Patterns

Analysis on the alteration of breathing patterns shows that ventilation increased with the load ($p < 0.05$). No significant difference was found in tidal volume among the four load conditions. The only significant difference in respiratory frequency ($p < 0.05$) was found between the 0% and 20% load conditions as shown in Figure 3. Figure 4 illustrates the changes in the ratio of respiratory frequency to tidal volume under each load condition at the beginning of the test and after 20 minutes of walking, and shows the highest increase in the ratio of respiratory frequency to tidal volume under the 20% load condition after 20 minutes. Comparing the percentage increase of tidal volume under each load condition after 20 minutes of walking shows that the lowest increase in tidal volume was associated with the 20% load condition.

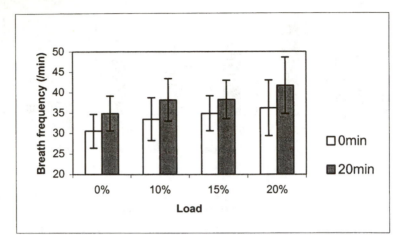

Figure 3 Mean breath frequency under four load conditions, measured at the beginning of the test and after 20 minutes of walking.

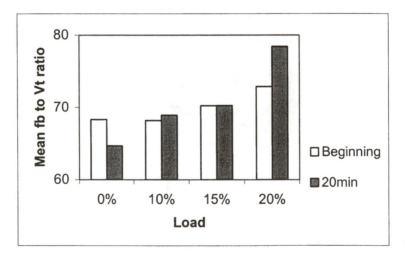

Figure 4 Ratio of respiratory frequency to tidal volume, measured at the beginning of the test and after 20 minutes of walking.

Association of Trunk Position, Load, and Breathing Patterns

An analysis of the data reveals that the Pearson correlation coefficients between load and trunk inclination angle, and between load and trunk motion range, were 0.674 and −0.282 respectively, with a significant difference at the 0.01 level. The trunk inclination angle increased linearly with the load weight, while the trunk motion range reduced linearly with the load weight. Weight carried was positively correlated with respiratory frequency, yielding a Pearson's correlation coefficient (0.360) which is significant at the 0.01 level.

DISCUSSION AND CONCLUSION

Changes of trunk position in children carrying loads have already been reported by several studies. Malhotra and Sen Gupta found that a load of 10% to 12% of the subjects' body weight did not produce appreciable trunk forward bend. Pascoe *et al.* (1995) found that carrying a two-strap backpack laden with 17% of body weight significantly promoted forward lean of the head and trunk in young subjects when compared to walking without a bag. The present study examined four different loads and found a positive linear relationship between trunk position and weight carried; a load equal to or greater than 15% of the subject's body weight resulted in significant trunk forward lean and reduced trunk motion range.

In this study, ventilation showed a trend increasing with load weight, which indicated an increased metabolic cost as the weight of a load grows. However, when we analysed Tidal volume and respiratory frequency, the two determinant factors of ventilation, considerable change was only found in respiratory frequency, which showed a positive linear relationship with load. The percentage increase of Tidal volume under the 20% load condition was even lower than that of other load conditions. These findings demonstrate that increased ventilation in children who walk under conditions of load carriage is mainly caused by the increase in respiratory frequency.

In the typical adult, increases in both Tidal volume and respiratory frequency contribute to the rise of ventilation that accompanies the onset of physical activity. However, as exercise intensity increases, the relative contribution of these two factors change (Pardy *et al.*, 1984). Above moderate intensity, Tidal volume tends to plateau, and subsequent improvement in ventilation is due solely to the influence of rising respiratory frequency. Some information suggests that this breathing pattern may be different in children. The experimental evidence provided by Boule *et al.* (1989) supports this hypothesis: the breathing rate was found to reach a plateau at 67% of maximum work in 6–15 year-old children, while Tidal volume rose linearly to exhaustion. Armstrong *et al.* (1997) demonstrated a steady increase of both Tidal volume and respiratory frequency in 11-year-old boys and girls throughout a maximal treadmill test. During this progressive test, the respiratory frequency to Tidal volume ratio rose, which is similar to the adult breathing pattern of the increasing importance of respiratory frequency at high exercise intensities. The results from Boule *et al.* (1989) and Armstrong *et al.* (1997) indicated that both Tidal volume and respiratory frequency increased as exercise intensity increased, while an increased respiratory frequency to Tidal volume ratio was only observed at high exercise intensity. Hong *et al.* (1998) demonstrated that working intensity linearly increases with the weight of load carried. The working intensity was at around 44.11% of VO_{2max} of the children when carrying a load of 20% of body weight, which indicates a moderate exercise intensity. According to the results obtained by Boule *et al.* (1989) and Armstrong *et al.* (1989), the rise of Ve in ten-year-old boys under load carriage while walking is attributable to increases of both Tidal volume and respiratory frequency. However, the present study not only showed a significant elevation of Tidal volume as the working intensity increased, but also the lowest rise in Tidal volume and highest rise in respiratory frequency under a 20% load condition when compared with other load conditions. This result indicates that there might be some factors that limited the increase of Tidal volume in the 20% load condition.

The present study reveals that there is a significantly positive correlation between load and trunk inclination angle, and between load and trunk motion range. Furthermore, weight carried is positively correlated with respiratory frequency. Thus, the changes of trunk position and motion range due to the load being carried might influence the response of Tidal volume to the increased working intensity. It is well known that the movement of respiratory muscles located in the thorax and the abdomen might contribute to the changing of Tidal volume. Increased trunk forward lean and limited trunk motion range can reduce the movement of respiratory muscles. Children carrying heavy loads have to bend their trunks forward to maintain body posture and balance while walking. Significantly increased forward lean might affect the movement of the chest and abdominal respiratory muscles. Thus, the only way that the subjects could increase oxygen uptake to support the increased metabolic cost was to breathe faster. According to Hong *et al.* (1998), the work intensity of ten-year-old children who walked for 20 minutes with a load equal to 20% of their body weight was low to medium (less than 50% VO_{2max}) and, to our knowledge, would not cause harmful strain on children. However, the present study showed that there is a positive linear relationship between load weight, trunk position, and breath frequency. Children who walked for 20 minutes while carrying a load approximate to 20% of their body weight were forced to lean their trunk forward and to breathe more rapidly with a stiffer upper body position, which results in physical strain. The ventilatory response in load carriage under the 20% load condition presented as the breathing pattern observed at high exercise intensity in children (Armstrong *et al.* 1997). Children at this age are experiencing significant growth and motor development. Carrying a bag of 20% of body weight for daily schooling will limit the movement of the thorax and abdominal muscles, and affect the response of Tidal volume to increased metabolic cost. Thus, load carriage of more than 20% of a child's body weight should be avoided.

REFERENCES

Armstrong, N., Kirby, B., McManus, A.M. and Welsman, J.R., 1997, Prepubescents' ventilatory responses to exercise with reference to sex and body size. *Chest*, **112**, pp. 1554-1560.

Boule, M., Gaultier, G. and Girard, F., 1989, Breathing pattern during exercise in untrained children. *Respiratory Physiology*, **75**, pp. 225-234.

Hong Kong Society for Child Health and Development, the Department of Orthopedic Surgery, University of Hong Kong, and the Duchess of Kent Children's Hospital (HKSCHD), 1988, *The Weight of School Bags and its Relation to Spinal Deformity.*

Hong, Y. and Brueggemann, G.P., 2000, Changes in gait pattern in 10-year-old boys with increased loads when walking on a treadmill. *Gait and Posture*, **11**, pp. 254-259.

Hong, Y., Li, J.X., Wong, A.S.K. and Robinson, P.D., 1998, Weight of schoolbags and the metabolic strain created in children. *Journal of Human Movement Studies*, **35**, pp. 187-200.

Malhotra, M.S. and Sen Gupta, J., 1965, Carrying of school bags by children. *Ergonomics*, **8**, pp. 55-60.

Pardy, R.L., Hussain, S.N.A and Macklem, P.T., 1984, The ventilatory pump in exercise. *Clinics in Chest Medicine*, **5**, pp. 35-49.

Pascoe, D.D., Pascoe, D.E., Wang, Y.T., Shin, D.M. and Kim, C.K., 1997, Kinematics analysis of book bag weight on gait cycle and posture of youth. *Ergonomics*, **40**(6), pp. 631-641.

Sander, M., 1979, Weight of schoolbags in a Freiburg elementary school: Recommendations to parents and teachers. *Offentliche Gesundheitswesen*, **41**, pp. 251-253.

ACKNOWLEDGEMENTS

The work described in this paper was fully supported by a grant from the Research Grants Council of Hong Kong Special Administrative Region (Project no. CUHK4122/99M).

Part Four

Biomechanics of Sports Injuries, Orthopaedics, and Rehabilitation

Biomechanics of Injury: Its Role in Prevention, Rehabilitation and Orthopaedic Outcomes

Bruce Elliott
Department of Human Movement and Exercise Science,
The University of Western Australia, Perth, Australia

INTRODUCTION

Seldom is a complex question dealing with injury answered by research based in a single science discipline. Previously, the sport biomechanist has been encouraged to combine with the exercise physiologist, the sport psychologist, the motor development specialist, and/or the physician or physiotherapist to structure appropriate research designs. Research into identifying key causal mechanisms associated with injury or rehabilitation processes inevitably requires the combined knowledge and skills of these professions.

Van Mechelen *et al.* (1992) reviewed risk factors involved in sport and suggested a four step prevention process. Researchers must:

1. Base research hypotheses on epidemiological data (nature, extent and severity of injury)
2. Identify the aetiology of the problem
3. Educate the relevant population as to the dangers inherent in that sport and the techniques needed to avoid these injuries
4. Evaluate the effectiveness of the preventative measures.

Winston *et al.* (1996) proposed that biomechanics should be an integral part of what they termed epidemiological research, if injury control mechanics were to be understood (Figure 1). This is essential as most injuries have a mechanically related aetiology (Whiting and Zernicke, 1998).

Therefore sport biomechanists must adopt a team approach for reducing sporting/physical activity based injuries. First, epidemiological data on the scope of the injury must clearly establish the "extent of the problem and the need for the research". Secondly, the aetiology of the injury must clearly be established. This could require collaboration with physicians, physiotherapists and/or radiologists. The choice of research design in studying the aetiology of sporting injuries will greatly influence the outcomes of such research. Only by relating injuries to corresponding populations can an estimate of injury ratio and risk factors be identified. Education and the assessment of the degree of success of the preventative strategies, might then require the assistance of professionals trained in health promotion.

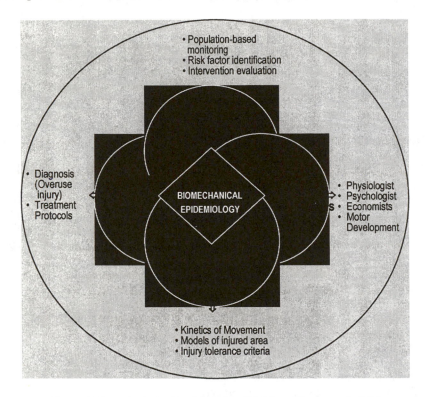

Figure 1 Biomechanical epidemiology (modified from Winston *et al.*, 1996).

Research projects discussed in this paper other than the golf case study, are from the biomechanics laboratory at the Department of Human Movement and Exercise Science at the University of Western Australia. These will be used to illustrate the model proposed by van Mechelen *et al.* (1992) and also to show where deficiencies in design might be improved.

THE REDUCTION OF BACK INJURIES DURING FAST BOWLING IN CRICKET: A GROUP APPROACH

1. Epidemiology: In the game of cricket, overuse back injuries to fast bowlers have been extremely common. Elliott *et al.* (1992) reported the incidence of bony abnormalities (spondylolysis and pedicle sclerosis) was 55%, while the prevalence of inter-vertebral disc abnormalities was 65% in a group of 18-year old high-performance fast bowlers. Furthermore, a group of young bowlers (mean age = 13.6 years) increased their incidence of disc degeneration from 21% to 58% over a 2.5 year period (Burnett *et al.*, 1996).

2. Aetiology: A prospective study of fast bowlers showed that counter-rotation of the shoulder alignment (line joining the two acromion processes) by greater than approximately 0.7 rad ($\approx 40°$) was related to an increase in spondylolysis and lumbar soft tissue injury over one year (Foster *et al.*, 1989). The incidence of bony abnormalities and disc degeneration in Elliott *et al.* (1992) and Burnett *et al.* (1996) were also found to be significantly related to counter-rotation of the shoulder alignment by greater than 0.35 rad ($\approx 20°$) in the bowling action. This movement is the key mechanical feature of the "mixed bowling action".

3. Education: This study examined whether supervised training (four group sessions per year) reduced the level of shoulder alignment counter-rotation during the bowling action as measured by an overhead camera operating at 50Hz. Levels of disc degeneration changes were measured from an MRI over a two year period. These sessions followed a seminar where all coaches, parents and fast bowlers were told of the dangers inherent in using a "mixed action" and provided with coaching literature to re-enforce "safe techniques".

4. Evaluation: After two years, the incidence of "mixed technique", defined as a shoulder counter-rotation of greater than 0.35rad decreased from 80% to 52% (n = 11 of 21 bowlers). The level of counter-rotation also reduced by 0.16 rad for the entire group. The level of lumbar disc degeneration increased from 17% (1997) to 33% (1999). This was a far better result than that reported by Burnett *et al.* (1996) over a similar period (21% to 58%) (Figure 2). The four bowlers, who showed a progression in degeneration from 1998 to 1999 all used the "mixed action". While these results are pleasing, the education procedures have been modified for the third year of the study to include more video sessions. Hence, each bowler will be treated more as an individual.

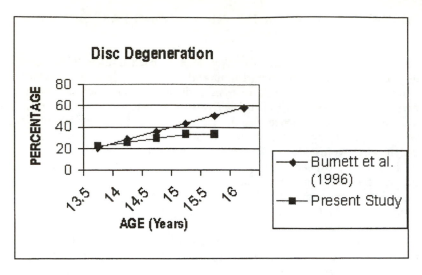

Figure 2 Disc degeneration of young fast bowlers over a 2-year period.

THE REDUCTION IN LOW BACK PAIN DURING GOLF: A CASE STUDY APPROACH

1. Epidemiology: The lower back is the site most commonly injured in both professional and amateur golf (Batt, 1992; McCarroll *et al.*, 1990).
2. Aetiology: Higher levels of torque, and shear and lateral bending forces in the lumbar spine have been identified as being related to these back injuries, particularly if these poor mechanics are linked to overuse (Hosea *et al.*, 1990). Grimshaw and Burden (2000) used 3-D videography of the trunk and para-spinal electromyography, in a case study design, to analyse potential causes of back pain. Their subject was a professional golfer suffering from low back pain. The low back pain was diagnosed by a general practitioner as deterioration of the ligaments and fibrous tissues around the lumbar spine (diagnoses supported by an MRI). The main aim of the education programme was to increase hip rotation whilst maintaining approximately the same rotation of the shoulder alignment during the swing (both measured from 3-D videography). This placed less torsional load on the lumbar spine. The level of para-spinal muscle activity was used as a measure of trunk torque.
3. Education: One coaching period per week was undertaken along with para-spinal muscle conditioning (3–4 times daily). This continued for a period of three months. The coaching intervention strategy consisted of exercises to reduce lateral hip slide by increasing the hip rotation during the backswing.
4. Evaluation: The re-test results showed that the golfer was standing in a similar position at the address and at impact. The golfer's lumbar movement was modified, particularly the hip to shoulder separation angle. This angle reached a maximum of 93.9° in test 1 (early in downswing) compared with

79.0° in the re-test. The activity level of the para-spinal muscles also was reduced during the swing and the low back pain ceased.

Therefore, technique modification and physical conditioning are potentially critical components in the control and reduction of low back pain in golf. While this case study design does not permit the results to be extended to the broader population it does provide a basic design upon which larger studies could be structured. These findings need to be presented to the broader golfing community and studies developed which evaluate the effectiveness of the programme in reducing back pain.

A REDUCTION OF KNEE INJURIES IN SPORTING MOVEMENTS

1. Epidemiology: The number of anterior cruciate ligament (ACL) injuries from sport cost Australia $100 million in 1990 (Egger, 1990). A high proportion of ACL injuries in sport are non-contact in nature and occur because of the increase in joint loading brought about by a combination of sudden changes in direction and acceleration of the body (Ryder *et al.*, 1997).
2. Aetiology: Reduced ligament loading is a critical factor in reducing the incidence of ACL injuries. Muscle activity has the potential to reduce ligament loading during extension at the knee (O'Connor, 1993), and during adduction or abduction at the knee (Lloyd and Buchanan, 1996). It also has been shown that muscle activation reduces ligament loading during static tasks (Lloyd and Buchanan, 1996) and preliminary work would indicate that this also is the case for selected dynamic tasks (Besier *et al.*, 1998).

Strength training has become an integral part of training throughout many levels of competition and in an effort to improve performance from enhanced size, strength and/or speed. Most strength training involves movement in one plane only, which is not relevant to the game situation. It is well known that strength training will affect the neural control needed to perform a movement or task. For example, leg flexion/extension strength training reduced the co-contraction of hamstrings and quadriceps, and optimizes co-ordination of synergist muscles (Carolan and Cafarelle, 1992). However, this reduced co-contraction also may diminish the activation patterns used to protect the ligaments of the ankle joint (Baratta *et al.*, 1988) and could be viewed as a possible negative outcome of strength training.

Re-training proprioception at the ankle and knee joint by using a wobble board has been an integral part of injury rehabilitation programmes for the past decade. However the use of the wobble board as a prophylactic modality is less common. The mechanisms underlying proprioceptive training are not well understood but recent evidence suggests wobble board training can alter the muscle activation patterns at the knee to counter external loads applied to the joint. Caraffa *et al.* (1996) showed that the incidence of ACL injuries at the knee in elite soccer players was dramatically reduced over two seasons following a wobble board training intervention.

Two questions arise regarding the incidence of knee ligament injuries. (1) Are there training methods that can reduce the incidence rates of knee and ankle joint injuries? (2) Do some of the current training methods increase the risk of knee and ankle injuries?

A randomized controlled field evaluation of three different conditioning programmes will be conducted over two seasons of play to determine the relative effectiveness of these types of programme for preventing injuries of the knee. Players will be randomized to one of four study arms: (1) proprioceptive training only; (2) strength training; (3) combined strength and proprioceptive training and (4) a control group. Ligament loading, pre- and post-training, will be assessed when running and side-stepping at 4 ms^{-1}. A model developed by Besier and Lloyd at the University of Western Australia will be used.

1. Education: A randomized control trial which has been structured by an exercise promotion specialist will be undertaken to investigate the effectiveness of the different training regimes following a season of injury surveillance. Teams of footballers from senior schools and district football teams will be invited to participate in the trial. Teams of players will be chosen as a sampling unit because they provide a natural grouping of players. Randomization of teams to the above groups will be made such that there is equal representation of each of the footballer codes (Australian rules, rugby) in each group.
2. Re-evaluation: The number of injuries to players for each training condition will be determined through injury surveillance and adjusted for exposure data.

CONCLUSION

Sport biomechanists interested in injury reduction must broaden their approach to research design. This will inevitably mean working with professionals not only from the medical and para-medical professions but also with health promotion professionals. Sport biomechanists must redefine the scope of their research. The ability to define techniques that allow the cricket fast bowler or golfer to remain injury free are clearly within the domain of the sport biomechanist. However, we must broaden the scope of our research to include the understanding of mechanisms involved in gait that will enable athletes of all ages to enjoy running again following knee surgery. We must also take more of an interest in veterans' activities so that the differentiation between sport and leisure becomes more closely aligned. Only then will sport biomechanics be able to maintain a valued position within universities and the community, thereby increasing the potential for growth in our profession.

REFERENCES

Batt, M.E., 1993, Golfing injuries: an overview. *British Journal of Sports Medicine*, **16**, pp. 64-71.
Baratta, R., Solomonow, M., Zhou, B., Letson, D. and Chuinard, R., 1988, Muscular coactivation. The role of the antagonist musculature in maintaining knee stability. *American Journal of Sports Medicine*, **16**(2), pp. 113-122.

Burnett, A., Khangure, M., Elliott, B., Foster, D., Marshall, R. and Hardcastle, R., 1996, Thoracolumbar disc degeneration in young fast bowlers in cricket: a follow-up study. *Clinical Biomechanics*, 11(6), pp. 305-310.

Besier, T., Lloyd, D., Cochrane, J. and Ackland, T., 1998, Muscle activation patterns at the knee during side-stepping and cross-over manoeuvres. In *Proceedings 12th Conference of the Australasian Society for Human Biology* (Perth, Australia).

Caraffa, A., Cerulli, G., Projetti, M., Asia, G. and Rizzo, A., 1996, Prevention of anterior cruciate ligament injuries in soccer. A perspective controlled study of proprioceptive training. *Knee Surgery in Sports Trauma and Arthroscopy*, 4(1), pp. 19-21.

Carolan, B. and Cafarelli, E., 1992, Adaptations in coactivation after isometric resistance training. *Journal of Applied Physiology*, 73(3), pp. 911-917.

Egger, G., 1990, Sports injuries in Australia: causes costs and prevention. *Commonwealth Report, Better Health Programme* (Sydney: Centre for Health Promotion and Research).

Elliott, B., Hardcastle, P., Burnett, A. and Foster, D., 1992, The influence of fast bowling and physical factors on radiologic features in high performance young fast bowlers. *Sport Medicine, Training and Rehabilitation*, 3, pp. 113-130.

Foster, D., John, D., Elliott, B., Ackland, T. and Fitch, K., 1989, Back injuries to fast bowlers in cricket: a prospective study. *British Journal of Sports Medicine*, 23(3), pp. 150-154.

Grimshaw, P. and Burden A., 2000, Case report: reduction of low back pain in a professional golfer. *Medicine and Science in Sport and Exercise*, 32(10), pp. 1667-1673.

Hosea, T., Gatt, C., Galli, K., Langrana, N. and Zawadsky, J., 1990, Biomechanical analysis of the golfer's back. In *Science and Golf: Proceedings of the First World Scientific Congress of Golf*, edited by A.J. Cochran (London: E. and F.N. Spon), pp. 43-48.

Lloyd, D.G. and Buchanan, T.S., 1996, A model of load sharing between muscles and soft tissues at the human knee during static tasks. *Journal of Biomechanical Engineering*, 118, pp. 367-376.

McCarrol, J.R., Rettig, A.C. and Shelbourne, K.D., 1990, Injuries in the amateur golfer. *The Physician and Sports Medicine*, 18, pp. 122-126.

O'Connor, J.J., 1993, Can muscle co-contraction protect knee ligaments' after injury or repair? *Journal of Bone and Joint Surgery*, 75(1), pp. 41-48.

Ryder, S., Johnson, R., Beynnon, B. and Ettlinger, C., 1997, Prevention of ACL injuries. *Journal of Sport Rehabilitation*, 6, pp. 80-96.

Van Mechelen, W., Hlobil, H. and Kemper, H., 1992, Incidence, severity, aetiology and prevention of sports injuries. *Sport Medicine*, 14(2), pp. 82-99.

Whiting, W. and Zernicke, R., 1998, *Biomechanics of Musculoskeletal Injury* (USA: Human Kinetics, Champaign).

Winston, F., Schwarz, D. and Baker, S., 1996, Biomechanical epidemiology: a new approach to injury control. *The Journal of Trauma, Injury, Infection and Critical Care*, 40, pp. 820-824.

Iliotibial Band Syndrome Injured Runners Increase Flexibility using Soft Tissue Mobilization and Increase Functional Strength using a Heat Pack-Implications for Faster Recovery

John M. MacMahon, Ajit M. Chaudhari, Mark A. Fadil[1]
and Thomas P. Andriacchi
Stanford Biomotion Laboratory, Stanford University,
Stanford, California
[1]Stanford Myofascial Institute, Palo Alto, California

INTRODUCTION

Iliotibial band syndrome (ITBS) injuries comprise as much as 22% of knee injuries (Ballas *et al.*, 1997). Rehabilitation may take as much as six weeks (Clancy, 1989). Termination of running, rest and ice are the more prevalent conservative treatments for this injury (Ballas *et al.*, 1997). With respect to recovery from ITB syndrome, there are two quantifiable measures that are hypothesized to correlate with ITBS recovery: Iliotibial band flexibility and increased hip abductor strength (Fredericson *et al.*, 1997).

Research has shown that an active programme of gluteus medius strength improvement correlates with ITBS recovery (Fredericson *et al.*, 2000). It is assumed that functional strength, and potential strength, a function of muscular cross section do not necessarily correlate in injured subjects. It is assumed that protective neuromuscular feedback guards injuries and thus reduces functional strength. An individual's functional strength can be quantified during an isometric contraction.

One local site of inflammation associated with ITBS is the lateral femoral epicondyle. The ITB traverses this region during 20–30° of knee flexion. Relaxation of the muscle–tendon complex may reduce the pressure between the ITB and the epicondyle by increasing flexibility. Since increased force development increases muscle–tendon relaxation, a stretch that increases the forces in the ITB will induce greater relaxation (Taylor *et al.*, 1997). In light of this, adduction moments at the hip and the knee are used to quantify the potential increased forces in the ITB.

Soft tissue mobilization treatments address tightness, trigger points and adhesions of muscle, tendons and fascia. Adhesions of the ITB layers can result in decreased flexibility and travel in the distal ITB. Given the multiple attachments of the distal ITB to the femur, there is ample fascia in the lateral distal femur to stimulate (Lobenhoffer, 1987).

Two hypotheses were investigated. Hypothesis I—Soft tissue mobilization significantly increases the flexibility of the ITB complex over a treatment of rest. Hypothesis II—A treatment of an ITB isolating heat pack increases functional abductor strength over a treatment of rest. These treatments may decrease recovery time for ITBS injured runners.

METHODS

The runners (N=5) had actively sought soft tissue mobilization treatment of ITBS. Inclusion in the study was based on the following criteria:

- Present Injury—ITBS presenting with pain at the lateral aspect of the knee
- Major Injuries—no lower limb surgeries or significant soft-tissue injuries
- Mileage before Injury— >20 mile/week.

Runners who matched the criteria were invited to the Biomotion Lab for three visits. The runners performed two independent measures before and after each treatment day.

Measure 1—Runners were asked to perform the standing ITB stretch four times (Figure 1). Each stretch was held for 30sec (data collected over last 5sec) followed by a rest period (<1min). Kinematics and kinetics of the stretch were analysed using seven retro-reflective markers, a four-camera system, and a force plate. Inverse dynamics were applied to determine abduction moments at the hip and knee during the stretch and then averaged over the 5sec trial.

Measure 2—Normalized isometric abductor strength measures were acquired using a test stand mounted dynamometer contacting the runner just proximal to the lateral malleolus. The test stand was adjusted to 20° of abduction (Figure 1). Runners performed the test four consecutive times: 3sec of isometric force development, followed by 20sec of rest. The runners were not coached during the tests. A moment arm length, the greater trochanter to lateral malleolus distance, was multiplied by the forces to get hip abduction moments and then normalized (%BW*HT) (Equation 1).

$$\text{Moment (\%BW}*\text{HT)} = \left(\frac{\text{Force (N)}*\text{Moment Arm(m)}}{\text{Body Weight(N)}*\text{Height(m)}} * 100\% \right) \tag{1}$$

It is assumed that increased adduction moments resulted in higher ITB forces.

Figure 1 Standing stretch of the right iliotibial band with the right foot upon the force plate.

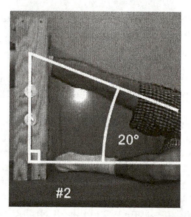

Figure 2 Isometric strength measure at 20° of abduction.

The three prescribed treatments were rest, a custom shaped heat pack, and soft-tissue mobilization. Both the STM treatment and the heat pack isolated the lateral femur distal to the greater trochanter and proximal to the lateral epicondyle. The heat treatment involved a microwaveable heat pack with a taper shape (~ 6in × 3in) to isolate the ITB. The treatment order was randomized.

ANALYSIS METHODS

The statistical analysis is based on before and after measures from each treatment. For each set of three trials, the trial with the peak hip adduction moment was chosen as representative. One-sided pair-wise t-tests were used to test for significance ($p<0.05$) between treatments and rest (Figure 3).

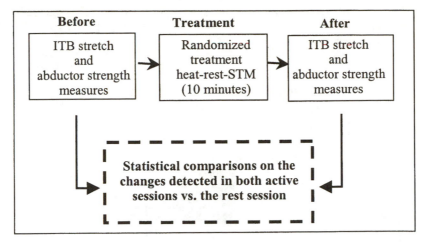

Figure 3 Experimental design to investigate statistical significance in changes from active treatments to changes resulting from rest.

RESULTS

When tested against a treatment of rest, soft tissue mobilization of the ITB increased flexibility significantly at both the hip and the knee (p<0.05) (Figure 4). When tested against a treatment of rest, a heat treatment of the ITB, increased peak abductor strength significantly (p<0.005) (Figure 5).

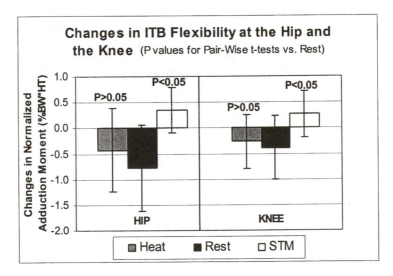

Figure 4 ITB flexibility changes—hip and knee ITB flexibility measured by the normalized adduction (N=5).

The protocol reduced runner strength, 0.62 (%BW*HT), and reduced flexibility, hip and knee moments were reduced by 0.98 (%BW*HT) and 0.53 (%BW*HT), respectively.

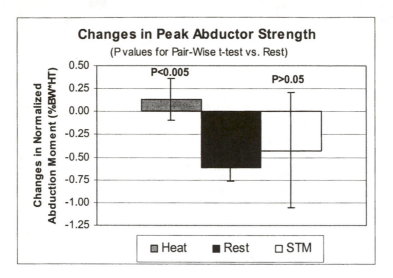

Figure 5 Strength changes—peak hip abductor strength measured by normalized abduction moment. (N=5).

DISCUSSION

The results support both hypotheses. The implications are that either of these two active treatments, a heat pack isolating the distal ITB and soft tissue mobilization, will aid in reducing recovery time for ITBS injured runners. The treatment of heat is envisioned to add functional strength that has been shown to correlate with ITB recovery. Soft tissue mobilization may reduce recovery time by increasing flexibility and muscle–tendon relaxation. The ability to generate greater moments allows greater potential force generation in the ITB complex. This will reduce lateral epicondyle pressure. This pressure is the presenting injury symptom.

Some physiologically limiting mechanism was overcome in response to these treatments. Either injury induced tightness, trigger points or soft tissue adhesions may be the cause. Taylor *et al.* (1997) hypothesized that viscous elements of the connective tissue will also be affected.

The major shortcoming of this effort is the influence of the protocol upon the runners. Also, normal soft tissue mobilization treatments are longer in duration (30–60min) than this 10min session, and they address the entire lower limb not just the distal ITB.

The resulting increased strength and flexibility are both beneficial to the ITBS injured runners.

REFERENCES

Ballas, M.T., Tytko, M.D. and Cookson, A.T.C., 1997, Common overuse running injuries: diagnosis and management. *American Family Physician*, **55**(5), pp. 2473-2480.

Clancy, W.G. Jr, 1989, Specific rehabilitation for the injured recreational runner. *Instructional Course Lectures*, **38**, pp. 483-486.

Fredericson, M., Guillet, M. and DeBenedictis, L., 2000, Innovative solutions for iliotibial band syndrome myofascial restrictions and hip abductor weakness can contribute to itbs but can be relieved by massage therapy, stretching, and strengthening. *The Physician and Sports Medicine*, **28**(2), pp. 53-68.

Fredericson, M., Dowdel, B., Oestreicher, N. *et al.*, 1997, Correlation between decreased strength in hip abductors and ITB syndrome in runners. *Archives of Physical Medicine and Rehabilitation*, **78**(9), pp. 1031.

Lobenhoffer, P., Posel, P., Witt, S., Piehler, J. and Wirth, C.J., 1987, Distal femoral fixation of the iliotibial tract. *Archives Orthopaedic and Trauma Surgery*, **106**(5), pp. 285-290.

Taylor, D.C., Brooks, D.E. and Ryan, J.B., 1997, Viscoelastic characteristics of muscle: passive stretching versus muscular contractions. *Medicine and Science in Sports and Exercise,* **29**(12), pp. 1619-1624.

ACKNOWLEDGEMENTS

Stanford Motion and Gait Analysis Lab, Kevin Rennert and Len DeBenedictus.

Skeletal Kinematics of the Anterior Cruciate Ligament Deficient Knee with and without Functional Braces

Dan K. Ramsey[1], Mario Lamontagne[2], Per F.Wretenberg[3] and Gunnar Németh[4]

[1]School of Human Kinetics, University of Ottawa, Ottawa, Canada
[2]School of Human Kinetics and Department of Mechanical Engineering, University of Ottawa, Ottawa, Canada
[1,3,4]Department of Orthopaedic Surgery, Karolinska Hospital, Stockholm, Sweden

INTRODUCTION

Functional knee braces are designed to stabilize anterior cruciate ligament (ACL) deficient knees by reducing pathological translations and rotations. Yet little research has examined the effects of these braces on three-dimensional osteokinematics and arthrokinetics during high dynamic activity. Braces are effective in reducing anterior translations when subjected to static or low anterior shear forces, but fail in situations where high loads are encountered or when the load is applied in an unpredictable manner (Cawley et al., 1991). Recent investigations have employed target markers affixed to intra-cortical pins implanted into the tibia and femur to describe skeletal tibiofemoral joint motion (Lafortune et al., 1992; McClay, 1990; Reinschmidt et al., 1997; Reinschmidt et al., 1997). However, activities were restricted to walking or light running. Since braces are designed for athletic activity, they should be evaluated under such conditions. The purpose of this investigation was to determine whether application of a functional brace reduced rotational and linear tibial displacements during the performance of a One Legged Jump (OLJ).

METHODS

Six young normal healthy males diagnosed with partial or complete ACL rupture and having no prior surgical treatment were selected for this investigation. The Ethics Committee of the Karolinska Hospital approved the surgery and experiment.

Steinmann traction pins were surgically implanted posterio-laterally into the femur and tibia with the knee flexed 45°. No flexion-extension impairments resulted from impingements between the iliotibial band and the femoral pin or the brace/pin interface. Stereophotogrammetric radiographs (RSA) were taken with the target markers affixed to the pins to identify the femoral and tibial anatomical reference points. The femoral anatomic reference point was defined as the deepest point of the intercondylar groove. The superior aspect of the medial intercondylar eminence was identified as the tibial anatomic reference point. Kinematics were recorded with the MacReflex motion analysis system sampling at 120Hz within a $0.25m^3$ measurement area (approximately 45cm off the floor). A Kistler force plate was synchronized to collect simultaneous ground reaction forces at 960Hz. Standard deviations less than 0.6° for rotations and translations less than 0.4mm have been reported when comparing RSA values and MacReflex data recorded in a volume of $0.25m^3$ (Lundberg *et al.*, 1992). To sufficiently stress the ACL, patients jumped for maximal horizontal distance. Subjects pushed off with their sound limb and landed onto the force platform with the contralateral deficient limb. The longest measurement was marked on the floor to determine the proper take off distance to the force platform. Subjects were then randomly assigned to start with either the braced or non-braced condition. Placement of the brace (DonJoy Legend) was applied by the researcher according to the specifications prescribed by the manufacturer. Target marker orientations were recorded during a neutral standing trial to define the tibial and femoral anatomical co-ordinate system. It was arbitrarily defined that the anatomical coordinate systems were aligned with the global co-ordinate system during neutral standing. Five measurement trials and two neutral standing trials were recorded for each brace condition. Skeletal tibiofemoral joint kinematics were computed employing coordinate transformation matrices (Lafortune *et al.*, 1992). Angular and linear motion was described as movement between the tibial anatomical reference frame relative to the femoral anatomical reference frame. Joint motion was referenced to Grood and Suntay's joint coordinate system (Grood and Suntay, 1983). Cardan angles were employed to describe sequence of rotations and were computed about y, x, z axes (Karlsson and Lundberg, 1994).

RESULTS AND DISCUSSION

No subjects experienced significant discomfort and all reported they could move their knees freely. Data is presented for only four subjects. One subject was excluded due to the femoral pin bent during flexion. The second subject was excluded due to significant marker dropout in the kinematic data. Each subject served as control with analysis focusing on differences in magnitudes and changes in the shape of the curves between bracing conditions. Averages were derived for each subject during non-braced and braced testing. All force data was associated with the coincident kinematic frame number.

KINETICS

Intra-subject peak vertical force and peak posterior shear force was generally consistent between unsupported and braced conditions. The result indicated that jumps onto the force platform were similar (Table 1). However, magnitudes varied across subjects. The differences between skeletal tibiofemoral kinematics across bracing conditions cannot be attributed to differences in jumping, but rather to the brace itself. Although the data recording system failed to store ground reaction force data for subject D, angular data was used to determine whether jumping styles were similar between conditions.

Table 1 Means of peak vertical and peak posterior ground reaction forces normalized to body mass and mass of the brace across subjects and conditions.

Subject	Trials	Peak vertical force (Fy)		Peak posterior shear force (Fx)	
		Unbraced	Braced	Unbraced	Braced
A	n = 5	2.947 (0.449)	2.612 (0.149)	-1.252 (0.174)	-1.109 (0.111)
B	n = 3	2.161 (0.266)	2.369 (0.079)	-0.637 (0.159)	-0.923 (0.090)
C	n = 5	3.409 (0.358)	2.638 (0.592)	-0.668 (0.067)	-0.603 (0.069)
D	n = 5	n/a	2.851 (0.301)	n/a	-1.102 (0.001)

KINEMATICS

As seen in Figure 1, an offset was evident between the unbraced and braced trials. This may be the result of the brace but is more likely the result of the different standing reference trials used for both test conditions. This created small deviations in alignment of the tibial and femoral anatomical co-ordinate systems. Therefore differences in movement patterns were reported rather than the absolute positions, i.e. the range from touchdown to maximum flexion instead of the (absolute) maximum flexion value. All subjects demonstrated fairly similar flexion patterns although flexion ranges of motion varied (Table 2). With respect to the origins of the anatomical co-ordinate systems, anteroposterior drawer curves were similar in shape between bracing conditions and fairly similar across subjects. The tibia exhibited a rapid anterior displacement with respect to the femur from footstrike to approximately peak Fz.

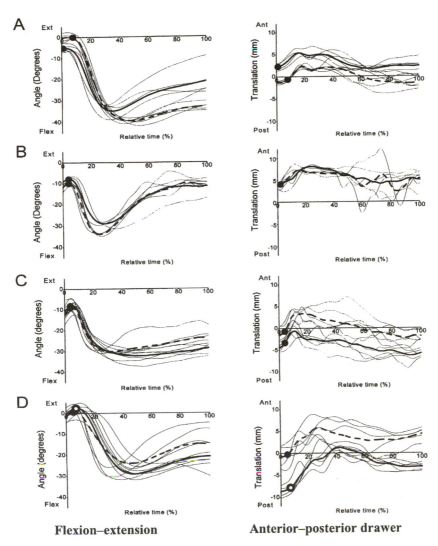

Flexion–extension   **Anterior–posterior drawer**

Figure 1 Each subject's flexion/extension and anterior drawer patterns derived from skeletal (femur, tibia) markers. Means are displayed in bold. The bold solid line represents the non-braced kinematics, the bold dashed line represents braced kinematics. Foot-strike is identified as an open circle derived from force platform. Closed circle derived from kinematics.

Table 2 Means of flexion and anterior translation ranges of motion.

Subject	Trials	Flexion		Anterior Drawer	
		Unbraced (degrees)	Braced (degrees)	Unbraced (mm)	Braced (mm)
A	n = 5	−29.9	−39.9	3.0	2.7
B	n = 3	−21.1	−23.7	3.5	2.4
C	n = 5	−24.2	−21.3	2.2	3.5
D	n = 5	−31.5	−24.6	8.8	5.7

(i)   A negative value indicates that flexion of the TFJ took place.
(ii)   A negative value indicates the tibia remained in a posterior position with respect to the femur even though it had moved in its most anteriorly located position.

Thereafter, the tibia was drawn posteriorly during flexion. However, differences in magnitudes between unbraced and braced patterns were small (Table 2). This may be due to the invasiveness of this protocol, landings are performed onto a deficient limb, or subjects jumped within their own comfort limits and did not maximally stress the ACL. Generally, intra-subject knee kinematics were very repeatable. Tibiofemoral rotations and translations show a general trend across conditions, i.e. the shape and amplitudes of the skeletal marker based curves were similar. As expected, inter-subject differences were typically much larger. Differences mainly concerned in amplitudes, orientation and position at footstrike. Additionally, patterns corresponded well with previous in-vivo tibiofemoral investigations although magnitudes differed. The discrepancies across investigations are likely the result of differences in locomotor activity and to differences in the placement of the segmental anatomical axes.

CONCLUSION

The negligible reductions in anterior tibial drawer indicate that the brace did not reduce translations during dynamic activity. From the lack of supportive evidence for bracing, a perceived improvement in performance may be the result of a proprioceptive feedback rather than the stabilizing effect of the brace. The patient's subjective approval for the brace may allow for the generation of larger forces during strenuous activity but not prevent abnormal tibial displacements. The increases in forces acting at the knee are thought to accelerate the degenerative joint disease as seen in ACL deficient knees. Therefore, athletes who wear the brace during strenuous physical activity are at greater risk of generating increased forces and theoretically increase the risk of joint damage.

REFERENCES

Cawley, P.W., France, E.P. and Paulos, L.E., 1991, The current state of functional knee bracing research. A review of the literature. *American Journal of Sports Medicine*, **19**, pp. 226-233.

Grood, E.W. and Suntay, W.J., 1983, A joint coordinate system for the clinical description of three dimensional motions: applications to the knee. *Journal of Biomedical Engineering*, **105**, pp. 97-106.

Karlsson D. and Lundberg A., 1994, In vivo measurement of the shoulder rhythm using external fixation markers. In *3rd International Symposium on 3-D Analysis of Human Movement* (Stockholm: Hasselbacken Conference Centre), pp. 69-72.

Lafortune, M.A., Cavanagh, P.R., Sommer, H.J. and Kalenak, A., 1992, Three-dimensional kinematics of the human knee during walking. *Journal of Biomechanics*, **25**, pp. 347-357.

Lundberg, A., Winson, I.G., Nemeth, G. and Josephson, A., 1992, In vitro assessment of the accuracy of opto-electric joint motion analysis. A technical report. *European Journal of Experiment Musculoskeletal Research*, **1**, pp. 217-219.

McClay, I.S., 1990, A Comparison of Tibiofemoral and Patellofemoral Joint Motion in Runners With and Without Patellofemoral Pain. Ph.D. Thesis (The Pennsylvania State University).

Reinschmidt, C., van den Bogert A.J., Nigg, B.M., Lundberg, A. and Murphy, N., 1997, Effect of skin movement on the analysis of skeletal knee joint motion during running. *Journal of Biomechanics*, **30**, pp. 729-732.

Reinschmidt, C., van den Bogert, A.J., Lundberg, A., Nigg, B.M., Murphy, N., Stacoff, A. and Stano, A., 1997, Tibiofemoral and tibiocalcaneal motion during walking: external vs. skeletal markers. *Gait and Posture*, **6**, pp. 98-109.

Quantification of the Dynamic Glenohumeral Stability Provided by the Rotator Cuff Muscles in the Late Cocking Phase of Throwing

Seok-Beom Lee, Shawn W. O'Driscoll[1], Bernard F. Morrey[1]
and Kai-Nan An[1]
Hallym University Sacred Heart Hospital, Pyungchon,
Kyunggi-do, Korea
[1]Department of Orthopedic Surgery,
Mayo Clinic and Mayo Foundation, Rochester, Minnesota, USA

INTRODUCTION

During the late cocking phase of throwing, the humerus maintains its level of abduction and moves into the scapular plane while externally rotating from 46° to 170°. In this position the head of the humerus is angled so that it can stretch the anterior structures. This creates the potential for anterior instability. Baseball pitchers with unstable shoulders demonstrated several significant differences from pitchers with normal shoulders during the late cocking phase. Jobe *et al.* (1983) reported that the player with unstable shoulder might begin with some compensatory mechanics, such as moving the humerus into the coronal plane. When the humerus moves into the coronal plane, the head of humerus angles even further anteriorly.

Both static (capsule and ligaments) and dynamic factors (muscle contraction) are responsible for glenohumeral joint stability. Many authors have noted that muscle activity across a joint leads to increased stability through concavity-compression mechanism (Matsen *et al.*, 1991; Lippitt *et al.*, 1993). The rotator cuff muscles are primarily dynamic stabilizer of the glenohumeral joint.

The purpose of this study was to twofold. First, we wanted to define a new biomechanical parameter which considered actual compressive and shear force vectors generated by each rotator cuff muscle and the concavity-compression mechanism, and thus could estimate quantitatively the dynamic glenohumeral stability provided by the rotator cuff muscles. Second, by calculating quantitatively the dynamic stability, we wanted to compare the dynamic stability provided by the rotator cuff muscles in the late cocking phase of throwing with the arm in the scapular plane with that in the coronal plane.

METHOD

Ten fresh-frozen shoulders (six right and four left) from human cadavers (age range 48 to 74 years) were prepared. The glenohumeral joint was disarticulated by resecting the gleno-humeral joint capsule after four rotator cuff muscles (subscapularis, supraspinatus, infraspinatus, and teres minor) were released from the scapula origin. The glenoid labrum was preserved. The glenoid neck was osteotomized 2.5cm medial to its articular surface. A specially designed Plexiglas frame was constructed to permit placement of the humerus in the desired glenohumeral position (Figure 1). The distal shaft of the humerus was fixed to the frame on which the load-cell (AMTI Model FS 160A-600; Barry Wright, Watertown, Massachusetts) was mounted. An anatomical neutral position was the position in which the humerus is unelevated (parallel to the medial border of the scapula) and in 0° of rotation (the elbow was flexed and the forearm was perpendicular to the coronal plane). The osteotomized glenoid was replaced back to the neck of the scapula and fixed temporarily for exact positioning of the humerus on the scapula. The scapula was rigidly fixed to the specially designed mounting device that permitted excursion of lines connected to each rotator cuff muscle around the scapula. The mounting device enabled the scapula and its glenoid to be anatomically aligned to the humeral head in any glenohumeral position. The glenoid piece was then taken out of the place before data collection to avoid bony contact between the humerus and scapula that could affect the measurement of force. Then, the position of the humeral head was maintained by secure fixation of the whole frame.

Muscle contraction was simulated by application of a constant force of 20N to each muscle individually by means of a hanging weight system. A six-degree-of-freedom electromagnetic tracking device (Fastrak, Polhemus Navigational Sciences Division, Colchester, VT) was used to measure position and orientation of the glenohumeral joint. The load-cell permitted accurate resolution of the forces that were applied to the humeral head by the rotator cuff muscle force across the joint. Anatomical axes for the measurement of force vectors were defined to be in line with the anterior/posterior and superior/inferior axes of the glenoid. The medial/lateral axis was defined as perpendicular to both axes.

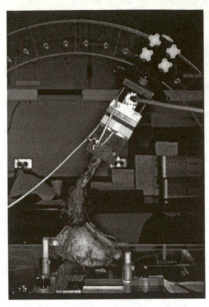

Figure 1 A specially designed Plexiglas frame.

DATA ACQUISITION AND ANALYSIS

To simulate the late cocking phase of throwing, testing was performed with the humerus (1) in the scapular plane and (2) in the 45° of extension (coronal plane), while glenohumeral joint was maintained in 60° of abduction, 90° of external rotation. The glenohumeral joint in 60° of abduction corresponded to the shoulder joint in 90° of abduction. The force components in the medial/lateral (compression), anterior/posterior (shear), and superior/inferior (shear) directions generated by each rotator cuff muscle/tendon unit were measured at both glenohumeral positions before and after application of the constant force of 20N to each muscle. Data measured before force application were used as the control. Raw load cell data were then transformed three dimensionally according to the defined anatomical axes. To verify the accuracy of measurement, vector summation of the three measured force components for each muscle was compared to the applied force in every glenohumeral position. The following calculations/derivations were made on the force vector data;

$$\text{Percent compressive force} = F_{comp} / \sqrt{(F_{comp}^2 + F_{A-P\,shear}^2 + F_{S-I\,shear}^2)} \times 100$$

$$\text{Percent anterior shear force} = F_{A-P\,shear} / \sqrt{(F_{comp}^2 + F_{A-P\,shear}^2 + F_{S-I\,shear}^2)} \times 100$$

$$\text{Percent superior shear force} = F_{S-I\,shear} / \sqrt{(F_{comp}^2 + F_{A-P\,shear}^2 + F_{S-I\,shear}^2)} \times 100$$

where F_{comp}, $F_{A-P\,shear}$, and $F_{S-I\,shear}$ denoted measured compressive, anterior shear, and superior shear forces, respectively. The denominator of the above equations represented a vector sum of the measured force vector.

A new biomechanical parameter, the dynamic stability index (DSI), was defined to represent the combined stabilizing effects of the rotator cuff muscle force vectors and the concavity-compression mechanism of the glenohumeral joint. The dynamic stability index in the anterior direction can be derived as;

Dynamic stability index (DSI) = (percent compressive force × stability ratio* in anterior direction) – percent anterior shear force

The stability ratio* is a concept describing the maximum dislocating force in a given direction that can be stabilized by the compressive muscle load on the glenoid fossa, assuming that frictional effect is minimal. From the published data regarding the concavity-compression mechanism, the stability ratio in the anterior direction was determined as 0.35 for glenohumeral joint with the labrum intact (Lippitt *et al.*, 1993). The unit of DSI is a percent magnitude of the minimal external anterior shear force that can dislocate the joint to the magnitude of contraction force of each cuff muscle. Thus the higher the DSI of a rotator cuff muscle, the greater the dynamic glenohumeral stability. All the percent force vectors and the dynamic stability index with the humerus in scapular and coronal plane were compared by analysis of variance (two-way layout with equal numbers of observations in the cells), for the force range that occurred in all specimens.

RESULTS

The rotator cuff muscles were primarily compressors as the compressive forces were far greater than the shear forces regardless of humeral position. The shear force vector generated by each rotator cuff muscle could either stabilize or destabilize the joint depending on its direction, directly affecting the dynamic stability.

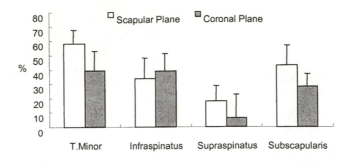

Figure 2 DSI with the arm in the coronal plane.

Dynamic Stability Index (DSI)

DSI of the teres minor, infraspinatus, supraspinatus, and subscapularis in the late cocking phase with the arm in the scapular plane was 58±9, 34±14, 18±10, and 43±14, respectively. DSI with the arm in the coronal plane was 40±13, 39±13, 6±16 and 28±9, respectively for each muscle (Figure 2). The supraspinatus was the least effective stabilizer in both positions (p<.05). Dynamic anterior stability provided by the teres minor and subscapularis decreased significantly when the arm moves from the scapular plane to the coronal plane in terms of DSI (p<.05)

DISCUSSION

All joint force vectors can be resolved into compressive and shear components. The compressive force component by the muscle stabilizes the glenohumeral joint by the mechanism referred to as concavity—compression, where the stability is related to the depth of concavity and the magnitude of the compressive force (Matsen *et al.*, 1991). We defined the dynamic stability index (DSI) to more realistically represent the biomechanical role of the force vectors providing dynamic glenohumeral stability. The DSI of a muscle comprised both the effects due to the concavity-compression mechanism and the shear force generated by a muscle itself. The subscapularis can stabilize the glenohumeral joint sufficiently to resist a dislocating anterior shear force of up to 43N, if DSI of the subscapularis in a specific humeral position were 43 per cent and the muscle force were 100N for example. The higher the DSI, the greater the dynamic glenohumeral stability.

Using the DSI as the most comprehensive way to analyse muscle effects on stability, the subscapularis (internal rotator) and infraspinatus and teres minor (external rotator) was found to provide greater dynamic stability in anterior direction than the supraspinatus in the late cocking phase. Gowan *et al.* (1987) analysed electromyographic signals during pitching and reported that, during late cocking, the subscapularis had the highest activity, followed by the infraspinatus and teres minor. The supraspinatus had the least activity in this position. The present study exactly shows the economy of the shoulder muscle activity in a physiological circumstance. Glousman *et al.* (1988) reported the patients who had chronic anterior instability of the shoulder had markedly lower electromyographic activities in the infraspinatus and subscapularis during late cocking. The levels of activity in the supraspinatus increased throughout the cocking phase. The authors, on the basis of our result, would be able to suggest that the patterns of altered electromyographic activity in anterior shoulder instability contributed to the instability.

Notably, in the present study, dynamic glenohumeral stability provided by the teres minor and subscapularis decreased significantly when the arm moves from the scapular plane to coronal plane (p<.05). The maximum muscle force may be estimated from the physiological cross-sectional area of each muscle (Ikai and Fukunaga, 1968). The subscapularis has the largest proportional physiological cross-sectional area among the cuff muscles and the decrease in the DSI of the subscapularis in the coronal plane would be able to have a more pronounced influence on the dynamic stability.

There are limitations in this study. First, simulation of muscle contraction by a single line of action might be different from that in vivo. However, we reproduced the line of action of a muscle that was determined previously by the anatomical and magnetic resonance imaging studies of shoulder (Blasier *et al.*, 1992). Second, the muscle length–tension relationships will differ according to shoulder position. To account for this, the force components and the DSI in this study were defined as percentage of the force applied to each muscle.

CONCLUSION

The rotator cuff muscle provided the glenohumeral joint with significant dynamic stability in the late cocking phase of throwing motion. But, force vectors generated by the cuff muscles with the arm in the coronal plane was less efficient to prevent anterior translation of the humeral head than those in the scapular plane.

Rehabilitation of the throwing athletes should emphasize strengthening of the external and internal rotators, which are efficient stabilizers in the late cocking phase, to enhance the dynamic stability. This study also shows that if a pitcher begins to move the arm into the coronal plane in the late cocking phase, then he can be pulled off the field and put on a specific strengthening programme of the scapular muscles to prevent further anatomic damage to the static stabilizers. Dynamic glenohumeral stability was successfully quantified by a new biomechanical parameter, dynamic stability index (DSI), defined in this study.

REFERENCES

Blasier, R.B., Guldberg, R.E. and Rothman, E.D., 1992, Anterior shoulder stability: contributions of rotator cuff forces and the capsular ligaments in a cadaver model. *Journal of Shoulder and Elbow Surgery*, **1**, pp. 140-150.

Glousman, R., Jobe, F., Tibone, J., Moynes, D., Antonelli, D. and Perry, J., 1988, Dynamic electromyographic analysis of the throwing shoulder with glenohumeral instability. *Journal of Bone and Joint Surgery*, **70**-A(2), pp. 220-224.

Gowan, I.D., Jobe, F.W., Tibone, J.E., Perry, J. and Moynes, D.R., 1987, A comparative electromyographic analysis of the shoulder during pitching. *American Journal of Sports Medicine*, **15**, pp. 586-590.

Ikai, M. and Fukunaga, T., 1968, Calculation of muscle strength per unit cross-sectional area of human muscle by means of ultrasonic measurement. *Internationale Zeitschrift fur Angewandte Physiologie Einschliesslich Arbeitsphysiologie*, **26**, pp. 26-32.

Jobe, F.W., Tibone, J.E., Perry, J. and Moynes, D., 1983, An EMG analysis of the shoulder in throwing and pitching. *American Journal of Sports Medicine*, **11**, pp. 3-5.

Lippitt, S.B., Vanderhooft, J.E., Harris, S.L., Sidles, J.A., Harryman, D.T., II and Matsen, F.A., III, 1993, Glenohumeral stability from concavity-compression: a quantitative analysis. *Journal of Shoulder and Elbow Surgery*, **2**(1), pp. 27-35.

Matsen, F.A., III, Harryman, D.T., II and Sidles, J.A., 1991, Mechanics of glenohumeral instability. *Clinics in Sports Medicine*, **10**, pp. 783-788.

ACKNOWLEDGEMENT

This study was supported by a grant from NIH, AR41171.

Part Five

The Application of Electromyography in Movement Studies

Application of Electromyography in Movement Studies

Mario Lamontagne
Department of Mechanical Engineering, School of Human Kinetics,
University of Ottawa, Ottawa, Canada

INTRODUCTION

The complexity of the biological system often introduces difficulties in the measurement and processing procedures. Unlike the physical systems, the biological system cannot be uncoupled like a subsystem that can be monitored and investigated individually. The signals produced by the system are influenced directly by the activity of the surrounding systems. The source of biological signals is the neural or muscular cell. These, however, do not function alone but in large groups. The accumulated effects of all active cells in the vicinity produce an electrical field which propagates in the volume conductor consisting of the various tissues of the body. The activity of a muscle can thus be indirectly measured by means of electrodes placed on the skin. The acquisition of this type of information is easy; electrodes can be conveniently placed on the skin. The information, however, is difficult to analyse. It is the result of all neural or muscular activity in unknown locations transmitted through an inhomogeneous medium. In spite of these difficulties, electrical signals monitored on the skin surface are of enormous clinical, physiological and kinesiological importance (Cohen, 1986). The electrical signal associated with the contraction of a muscle is called an electromyogram and the study of electromyograms is called electromyography (Winter, 1990). Electromyography (EMG) is a tool that can be very valuable in measuring skeletal muscle electrical output during physical activities. It is important that the EMG is detected correctly and interpreted in light of basic biomedical signal processing, and physiological and biomechanical principles (Soderberg, 1992). The usefulness of the EMG signal is greatly dependent on the ability to extract the information contained in it. EMG is an attractive tool because it gives easy access to physiological processes that cause the muscle to generate force and produce movement (De Luca, 1993a). Since the EMG tool is easy to use, it might be easily misused and the outcomes wrongly interpreted. Therefore, it is important to understand the principles of EMG signal detection and processing to optimize the quality of signal information.

The purpose of this paper is to provide sounded principles of EMG signal acquisition and processing in order to optimized the quality of signal and therefore leading to a better interpretation of mechanical muscle output during movement studies. In order to achieve this purpose, some background information will be provided on the origin of the EMG signal, factors affecting the quality of signal, recording techniques, signal processing, the fidelity and reproducibility of the signal, and a few applications in movement studies.

ORIGIN OF THE EMG SIGNAL

Muscle tissue conducts electrical potentials similarly to the way axons transmit action potentials. The muscle action potential (m.a.p.) can be detected by electrodes in the muscle tissue or on the surface of the skin. Several events must occur before a contraction of muscle fibres. Central nervous system (CNS) activity initiates a depolarization in the motoneuron. The depolarization is conducted along the motoneuron to the muscle fibre's motor end plate. At the endplate, a chemical substance is released that diffuses across the synaptic gap and causes a depolarization of the synaptic membrane. This phenomenon is called muscle action potential. The depolarization of the membrane spreads along the muscle fibres producing a depolarization wave that can be detected by recording electrodes (Figure 1). In a two electrode system placed over the muscle site, the m.a.p. waveform is represented by a triphasic potential which is the difference in potential between pole A and pole B. Once an action potential reaches a muscle fibre, it propagates proximally and distally. A motor unit action potential (MUAP) is a spatio-temporal summation of m.a.p.'s for an entire motor unit (MU). An EMG signal is the algebraic summation of many repetitive sequences of MUAP's for all active motor units in the vicinity of the recording electrodes. The order of MU recruitment is according to their sizes. The smaller ones are active first and the bigger ones are active last (Winter, 1990).

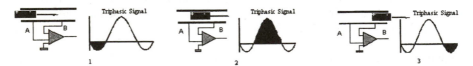

Figure 1 Propagation of a motor unit action potential waveform as it passes beneath the recording electrodes.

FACTORS AFFECTING THE QUALITY OF SIGNAL

Many factors may affect the quality of the EMG signal. They can be divided into physiological, physical, and electrical factors. Some factors are under the control of the investigator and some factors are not.

The physiological factors (such as the non-homogeneous medium between the muscle fibres—De la Barrera and Milner, 1994—and the electrodes, the non-parallel geometry and non-uniform conduction velocity of the fibres, and the physical and physiological conditions of the muscle) over which the investigator has no control, contribute to the random component (noise) of the signal. While it is not possible to remove this random component completely from the measurement, the user must be aware of its presence and how to reduce its effects (Harba and Teng, 1999). Other physiological factors (such as the number of active MU, the MU firing rate, the fibre type, and the fibre diameter) which are also not under the control of the investigator contribute to the signal.

The physical factors are those that are associated with the electrode structure and its location on the surface of the skin over the muscle. These factors include the area and shape of the electrodes, the distance between the electrodes, the location of the electrode in relation with the motor points in the muscle, the orientation of the electrodes with respect to the muscle fibres, and the types of electrodes (active, surface or indwelling). The investigator can manipulate these factors to improve the quality of the signal.

The electrical factors are those that are related to the recording system which is used to collect the signal. The fidelity and signal-to-noise ratio of the signal is based on the quality of the recording unit. The following factors are important for obtaining a reliable signal with the highest signal-to-noise ratio. The differential amplification with a common mode rejection ratio (CMMRR) greater than 80 (Winter, 1990) or 90 (De Luca, 1993a) is used to eliminate noise coming from the power line sources. The CMMRR represents the quality of the differential amplifier. The input impedance of the order of 10^9 ohms (Winter, 1990) or 10^{12} ohms (De Luca, 1993a) is recommended to prevent attenuation and distortion of the signal. According to Perreault *et al.* (1993), the skin preparation plays an important role to reduce the impedance input and therefore diminish the signal distortion.

Table 1 Minimum requirements for surface EMG amplifier.

Variables	Minimal Requirements
Input Impedance	$>10^{10}$ at DC[a,b] $>10^8$ at 100Hz $>10^{6}$ [c] $>10^{12}$ [d]
CMMRR	>80 dB[a,b] >90 dB[c]
Amplifier Gain	200–10,000[a,b,c]
Frequency Response	1–3000Hz[a] 1–1000Hz[b] 1–500Hz[d]
Input Bias Current	< 50 mA [a]
Noise	< 5 μV RMS with a 100KΩ resistance[a]

a: Recommended by ISEK
b: Recommended by Winter (1990)
c: Recommended by De Luca (1993a)
d: Recommended by Lamontagne (1992)

Finally, the frequency response of the differential amplifier is an important factor which insures that the signal is linearly amplified over its full frequency spectrum. The frequency response of the EMG signal is between 10 and 1000Hz as proposed by Winter (1990). Table 1 shows the recommended minimum specification for surface amplifier. The spectrum of the frequency can be narrower and this will be shown later in the paper.

RECORDING TECHNIQUES

A wide variety of electrodes are available to measure the electrical muscle output. Although microelectrodes and needle electrodes are available, they are not practical for movement studies (Soderberg, 1992). Surface electrodes (SE) (Németh *et al.*, 1990; Preece *et al.*, 1994; De Luca, 1993b; Ferdjallah and Wertsch, 1998; Kwatny *et al.*, 1970; McGill *et al.*, 1996; Merletti *et al.*, 1992) and Intramuscular wire electrodes (IWE) (Andersson *et al.*, 1997; Arokoski *et al.*, 1999; Davis *et al.*, 1998; Giroux and Lamontagne, 1990; Hagberg and Kvarnstrom, 1984; Kadaba *et al.*, 1985; Moritani *et al.*, 1985; Morris *et al.*, 1998; Park and Harris, 1996; Shiavi, 1974; Thorstensson *et al.*, 1982) are commonly used in movement studies. SEs are used mainly in a bipolar configuration along with a differential pre-amplifier to increase the signal. The differential preamplifier increases the amplitude of the difference signal between each of the detecting electrodes and the common ground. The advantage of the differential preamplifier is to improve the signal-to-noise ratio of the measurement. SE's are quick and relatively easy to use and have a fairly good reproducibility (Bilodeau *et al.*, 1994; Elert *et al.*, 1998; Elfving *et al.*, 1999; Giroux and Lamontagne, 1990; Mathieu and Aubin, 1999; Sinderby *et al.*, 1995). SE's detect the average activity of superficial muscles, however, they do not selectively record single MU's (Basmajian and De Luca, 1985). MU's that lie superficially in a muscle contribute more to the signal than the deeper MU's. In surface EMG, electrode size and the interelectrode distance should be proportional to the muscle size. IWE are known to be more selective in MU detection than SE. This type of electrode has a small leadoff area lying between 25µm and 100µm, therefore detecting fewer MU's. The advantages offered by intramuscular electrodes are the following: they are much less painful than needle electrodes, they rarely interfere with movement, they have a low sensitivity to movement artefacts (Notermans, 1984), and they can be easily implanted and withdrawn (Basmajian and De Luca, 1985). The active electrode consists of placing the differential amplifier as close as possible from the recording electrodes. This electrode reduces the noise from the cable motion (Hagemann *et al.*, 1985). Although, as reported by Nishimura *et al.* (1992), an active electrode was compared with a conventional one, and it was ascertained that the electrode could be replaced with the conventional one, and, moreover, it was preferable because it required less preparation time, and was less affected by environmental noise.

Of course an important question comes to mind: what should we use for kinesiological studies? This depends on the specific requirements for MU recording, reliability, reproducibility, and the interpretation of the muscle signal.

SIGNAL PROCESSING

As explained by Soderberg (1992), an analogy can be made between radio or television signals which are modulated, broadcast and demodulated at the destination and the EMG signal which undergoes the similar process. The detected EMG signal represents a modulation of the alphamotoneuron pool command. The rate of MU firings is frequency modulated by the neural command. The summation of the frequency modulated MU action potentials produces an amplitude modulated envelope representative of the recruitment and firing rates of the original neural command. Demodulation refers to processing techniques that extract the information related to the neural command.

The demodulation techniques commonly used in the time-domain are: full-wave rectification, linear envelope (Chen *et al.*, 1992; Kuster *et al.*, 1994; Shiavi *et al.*, 1992; Van Lent, 1994), integration of the full-wave rectification (Winter, 1990), and Root-Mean-Square Processing (Cook, 1992). The power spectral density (PSD) (Kwatny, 1970) is the function commonly used for frequency domain analysis of EMG signal. The parameters used from PSD are median (Sparto *et al.*, 1997) and mean frequency (Davis *et al.*, 1998; Elert *et al.*, 1998; Kwatny, 1970) of the EMG signal. EMG signal processing will provide information on the activation timing of the muscle, to estimate the force produced by the muscle, or to obtain an index of the rate at which a muscle fatigues obtained from the power spectral density.

FIDELITY AND REPRODUCIBILITY OF THE SIGNAL

The usefulness of the EMG signal is greatly dependent on the ability to extract the information contained in it. Moritani *et al.* (1985) studied different electromechanical changes in the gastrocnemius and soleus muscles with simultaneous recordings using SE and IWE. Bipolar IWE were inserted in each muscle and SEs were placed over the muscular group. The results demonstrated that when there was either a decrease or no EMG signal from the gastrocnemius or soleus there was still surface EMG activation. This result is acceptable since the surface EMG is representative of the whole EMG activity of the muscular group. Then, when the EMG signal is very low or when the EMG signal of one muscle is evident and the EMG on the other muscle of the group is not, intramuscular wire electrodes are preferable over surface electrodes. Kadefors and Herberts (1977) suggested that surface electrodes be avoided because of the movement between muscle tissue and the surface of the skin and the risk of crosstalk from muscles around or near the investigated area. Giroux *et al.* (1990) compared EMG surface electrodes (SE) and intramuscular wire electrodes (IWE) for isometric and dynamic contractions during a working task. Raw EMG signals from the middle deltoid, anterior deltoid and trapezius muscles were recorded by both IWE and SE for two conditions (isometric and dynamic contractions). Full-wave rectified and low-pass filtered EMG, and integrated EMG were processed from raw EMG signals. The statistical analysis performed on the integrated EMG was a factorial analysis model with repeated measures. Statistical results confirmed that EMG signals, from both SE and IWE, are reliable between trials on the same day. These statistical results also confirmed that SEs are more reliable than IWE on day-to-day investigations. Both electrodes recorded statistically similar signals, although the coefficient of variability between electrodes was very high (STDE%; 48% and 84%, for isometric and dynamic conditions respectively).

APPLICATIONS IN MOVEMENT STUDIES

Electromyography has been a subject of laboratory research for decades. Only with recent technological developments in electronics and computers has surface EMG emerged from the laboratory as a subject of intense research in particularly kinesiology, rehabilitation and occupational and sports medicine. Most of the applications of surface EMG (SEMG) are based on its use as a measure of activation timing of muscle, a measure of muscle contraction profile, a measure of muscle contraction strength (physical load or psychological stress), or as a measure of muscle fatigue.

Again the scope of this paper is not to present an exhaustive review of all various types of EMG applications but to expose a few sport and sport rehabilitation applications.

One of the important questions in SEMG consists of finding out the optimal sampling rate for dynamic contractions. If you must collect SEMG for long period of time or transmit the SEMG signal by telemetry, the sampling rate becomes an important issue, therefore the optimal sampling rate becomes an issue. Lamontagne *et al.* (1992) investigated the effects of different sampling rates on the power spectral density (PSD) and the integrated linear envelope (ILEEMG) of the raw surface EMG of the vastus lateralis during eccentric contractions at 60°/s. The results revealed that raw EMG can be sampled at less than 500Hz without significantly affecting the PSD and ILEEMG.

The following application illustrates the use of surface EMG as a measure of activation timing of muscle. Mâsse *et al.* (1992) investigated the pattern of propulsion for five male paraplegics in six seating positions. The positions consisted of a combination of three horizontal rear-wheel positions at two seating heights on a single-purpose-built racing wheelchair. At each trial, the propulsion technique of the subject was filmed at 50Hz with a high-speed camera for one cycle, and the raw electromyographic signal of the biceps brachii, triceps brachii, pectoralis major, deltoid anterior, and deltoid posterior muscles were simultaneously recorded for three consecutive cycles. The EMG signals were processed to yield the linear envelope (LE EMG) and the integrated EMG (IEMG) of each muscle. The kinematic analysis revealed that the joint motions of the upper limbs were smoother for the Low positions—since they reached extension in a sequence (wrist, shoulder, and elbow), when compared to the High positions. Also, the elbow angular velocity slopes were found to be less abrupt for the Backward–Low positions. It was observed that in lowering the seat position, less IEMG was recorded and the degrees of contact were lengthened. Among the seat positions evaluated, the Backward-Low position had the lowest overall IEMG and the Middle-Low position had the lowest pushing frequency. It was found that a change in seat position caused more variation in the IEMG for the triceps brachii, pectoralis major, and the deltoid posterior.

This next application is a good example of surface EMG as a measure of muscle contraction profile. Németh *et al.* (1997) studied six expert downhill skiers who had sustained anterior cruciate ligament injuries and had different degrees of knee instability. The electromyographic activity was recorded from lower extremity muscles during downhill skiing in a slalom course without and with a custom-made brace applied to the injured knee. Surface electrodes were used with an eight-channel telemetric electromyographic system to collect recordings from the vastus medialis, biceps femoris, semimembranosus, semitendanosus, and gastrocnemius medialis muscles from both legs. Without the brace, the electromyographic activity level of all muscles increased during knee flexion. The biceps femoris muscle was the most activated and reached 50% to 75% of the maximal peak amplitude. With the brace, the electromyographic activity increased in midphase during the upward push for the weight transfer and the peak activity occurred closer to knee flexion in midphase. Also, the uninjured knee was influenced by the brace on the injured leg, a decrease in electromyographic activity was seen during midphase. Spearman's rank correlation revealed a significant correlation between an increase in biceps femoris activity of the injured leg and increasing knee instability. We suggest that the brace caused an increased afferent input from the proprioceptors, resulting in an adaptation of motor control patterns secondarily modifying electromyographic activity and timing.

The surface EMG can also be used as a measure of muscle fatigue and recovery. Tho *et al.* (1997) investigated possible differences in muscle fatigue and recovery of knee flexor and extensor muscles in patients with a deficient anterior cruciate ligament compared with patients with a normal anterior cruciate ligament. Surface electromyography of 15 patients with anterior cruciate ligament deficiency was performed while the muscles were under 80% of maximum isometric contraction, and after 1, 2, 3, and 5 minutes of rest. During the first 60 seconds of contraction, all muscles recorded significantly decreased mean power frequency and increased amplitude. The rate of decrease of mean power frequency was significantly greater in the injured quadriceps and normal hamstrings. All muscles except two recovered to the initial mean power frequency level after 1 minute of rest. All but two muscles in the injured and normal limb recorded an overshoot of mean power frequency during the recovery phase. This overshoot phenomenon also was seen for some muscles in the amplitude analysis. The findings confirm the fatigue state in all the muscles, suggest recruitment of more Type II fibres as the muscles fatigues, and show the physiological adaptation of the quadriceps and hamstrings to anterior cruciate ligament insufficiency. The current study indirectly shows dissociation between low intramuscular pH and mean power frequency during the recovery phase. It also indirectly suggests that the atrophied thigh muscles have fibre type composition similar to that of the normal side.

The intramuscular and surface EMG can be used as a measure of activation timing, and muscle contraction profile. Lafrenière *et al.* (1997) studied the intramuscular EMG of the lateral pterygoid muscles (LPM), surface EMG of the temporalis and masseter muscles and force measurements of the temporomandibular joint (TMJ) for subjects with internal derangement (ID) of the TMJ. The analysis of variance results of the integrated linear envelope (LE) EMG showed no significant differences between the two groups for the masseter and temporalis muscles. Therefore, there is no apparent reason to believe that these muscles are hyperactive in TMJ ID. The integrated LE EMG of the SLP was significantly lower in the TMJ group during molar clenching. The superior head of the lateral pterygoid muscle (SLP) seemed to have lost its disc stabilizing function. The integrated LE EMG signals of the ILP were significantly higher in the TMJ ID group during rest, resisted protraction and incisor clenching. The ILP muscle has probably adapted to control the inner joint instability while continuing its own actions. The ILP muscle seemed to have lost its functional specificity. The results of the isometric forces showed that TMJ ID subjects exhibited significantly lower molar bite forces (297.1N over 419N, p=0.042) confirming that they have less muscle strength and tissue pain tolerance than subjects with healthy masticator muscle systems. A neuromuscular adaptation could be occurring in the TMJ ID masticator system affecting muscular actions and forces.

REFERENCES

Andersson, E.A., Nilsson, J. and Thorstensson, A., 1997, Intramuscular EMG from the hip flexor muscles during human locomotion. *Acta Physiologica Scandinavica*, **161**(3), pp. 361-370.

Arokoski, J.P., Kankaanpaa, M., Valta, T., Juvonen, I., Partanen, J., Taimela, S., Lindgren, K.A. and Airaksinen, O., 1999, Back and hip extensor muscle function during therapeutic exercises. *Archives of Physical Medicine and Rehabilitation*, **80**(7), pp. 842-850.

Basmajian, J. and De Luca, C., 1985, *Muscle Alive. Their Function revealed by Electromyography*, fifth ed. (Baltimore: Williams and Wilkins).

Bilodeau, M., Arsenault, A.B., Gravel, D. and Bourbonnais, D., 1994, EMG power spectrum of elbow extensors: a reliability study. *Electromyography and Clinical Neurophysiology*, **34**(3), pp. 149-158.

Chen, J.J., Shiavi, R.G. and Zhang, L.Q., 1992, A quantitative and qualitative description of electromyographic linear envelopes for synergy analysis. *IEEE Transactions on Biomedical Engineering*, **39**(1), pp. 9-18.

Cohen, A., 1986, *Biomedical Signal Processing, Vol. 1. Time and Frequency Domain Analysis* (Boca Raton: CRC Press).

Cook, T., 1992, EMG comparison of lateral step-up and stepping machine exercise. *JOSPT: Journal of Orthopaedic and Sports Physical Therapy*, **16**(3), pp. 108-113.

Davis, B.A., Krivickas, L.S., Maniar, R., Newandee, D.A. and Feinberg, J.H., 1998, The reliability of monopolar and bipolar fine-wire electromyographic measurement of muscle fatigue. *Medicine and Science in Sports and Exercise*, **30**(8), pp. 1328-1335.

De la Barrera, E.J. and Milner, T.E., 1994, The effects of skinfold thickness on the selectivity of surface EMG. *Electromyography and Clinical Neurophysiology*, **93**(2), pp. 91-99.

De Luca, C., 1993a, *The Use of Surface Electromyography in Biomechanics* (Paris: The XIVth ISB Congress).

De Luca, C.J., 1993b, Use of the surface EMG signal for performance evaluation of back muscles. *Muscle and Nerve*, **16**(2), pp. 210-216.

Elert, J., Karlsson, S. and Gerdle, B., 1998, One-year reproducibility and stability of the signal amplitude ratio and other variables of the electromyogram: test–retest of a shoulder forward flexion test in female workers with neck and shoulder problems. *Clinical Physiology*, **18**(6), pp. 529-538.

Elfving, B., Németh, G., Arvidsson, I. and Lamontagne, M., 1999, Reliability of EMG spectral parameters in repeated measurements of back muscle fatigue. *Journal of Electromyography and Kinesiology*, **9**(4), pp. 235-243.

Ferdjallah, M. and Wertsch, J.J., 1998, Anatomical and technical considerations in surface electromyography. *Physical Medicine and Rehabilitation Clinics of North America*, **9**(4), pp. 925-931.

Giroux, B. and Lamontagne, M., 1990, Comparisons between surface electrodes and intramuscular wire electrodes in isometric and dynamic conditions. *Electromyography and Clinical Neurophysiology*, **30**(7), pp. 397-405.

Hagberg, M. and Kvarnstrom, S., 1984, Muscular endurance and electromyographic fatigue in myofascial shoulder pain. *Archives of Physical Medicine and Rehabilitation*, **65**(9), pp. 522-525.

Hagemann, B., Luhede, G. and Luczak, H., 1985, Improved "active" electrodes for recording bioelectric signals in work physiology. *European Journal of Applied Physiology*, **54**(1), pp. 95-98.

Harba, M.I. and Teng, L.Y., 1999, Reliability of measurement of muscle fiber conduction velocity using surface EMG. *Frontiers of Medical and Biological Engineering*, **9**(1), pp. 31-47.

Kadaba, M.P., Wootten, M.E., Gainey, J. and Cochran, G.V., 1985, Repeatability of phasic muscle activity: performance of surface and intramuscular wire electrodes in gait analysis. *Journal of Orthopaedic Research*, **3**(3), pp. 350-359.

Kadefors, R. and Herberts, 1977, Single fine wire electrodes: properties in quantitative studies of muscle function. In *Biomechanics VI-A*, edited by E.A.J. Assmussen, K. (Baltimore: University Park Press).

Kuster, M., Wood, G.A., Sakurai, S. and Blatter, G., 1994, 1994 Nicola Cerulli Young Researchers Award. Downhill walking: a stressful task for the anterior cruciate ligament? A biomechanical study with clinical implications. *Knee Surgery, Sports Traumatology Arthroscopy*, **2**(1), pp. 2-7.

Kwatny, E., Thomas, D.H. and Kwatny, H.G., 1970, An application of signal processing techniques to the study of myoelectric signals. *IEEE Transactions on Biomedical Engineering*, **BME-17**(4), pp. 303-313.

Lafrenière, C.M., Lamontagne, M. and Elsawy, R., 1997, The role of the lateral pterygoid muscles in TMJ disorders during static conditions. *The Journal of Craniomandibular Practice*, **15**(1), pp. 38-52.

Lamontagne, M. and Coulombe, V.C., 1992, *The Effects of EMG Sampling Rate on the Power Spectral Density under Eccentric Contractions of the Vastus Lateralis* (Chicago: The Second North American Conference of Biomechanics).

Mâsse, L.C., Lamontagne, M. and O'Riain, M., 1992, Biomechanical analysis of wheelchair propulsion for various seating positions. *Journal of Rehabilitation Research and Development*, **29**(3), pp. 12-28.

Mathieu, P.A and Aubin, C.E., 1999, Back muscle activity during flexions/extensions in a second group of normal subjects. *Annales de Chirurgie*, **53**(8), pp. 761-772.

McGill, S., Juker, D. and Kropf, P., 1996, Appropriately placed surface EMG electrodes reflect deep muscle activity (psoas, quadratus lumborum, abdominal wall) in the lumbar spine. *Journal of Biomechanics*, **29**(11), pp. 1503-1507.

Merletti, R. Knaflitz, M. and De Luca, C.J., 1992, Electrically evoked myoelectric signals. *Critical Reviews in Biomedical Engineering*, **19**(4), pp. 293-340.

Moritani, T., Muro, M. and Kijima, A., 1985, Electromechanical changes during electrically induced and maximal voluntary contractions: electrophysiologic responses of different muscle fiber types during stimulated contractions. *Experimental Neurology*, **88**(3), pp. 471-483.

Morris, A.D., Kemp, G.J., Lees, A. and Frostick, S.P., 1998, A study of the reproducibility of three different normalisation methods in intramuscular dual fine wire electromyography of the shoulder. *Journal of Electromyography and Kinesiology*, **8**(5), pp. 317-322.

Németh, G., Kronberg, M. and Brostrom, L.A., 1990, Electromyogram (EMG) recordings from the subscapularis muscle: description of a technique. *Journal of Orthopaedic Research*, **8**(1), pp. 151-153.

Németh, G., Lamontagne, M., Tho, K.S. and Eriksson, E., 1997, Electromyographic activity in expert downhill skiers using functional knee braces after anterior cruciate ligament injuries. *American Journal of Sports Medicine*, **25**(5), pp. 635-641.

Nishimura, S., Tomita, Y. and Horiuchi, T., 1992, Clinical application of an active electrode using an operational amplifier. *IEEE Transactions on Biomedical Engineering*, **39**(10), pp. 1096-1099.

Notermans, S., 1984, *Current Practice of Clinical Electromyography* (New York: Elsevier).

Park, T.A. and Harris, G.F., 1996, "Guided" intramuscular fine wire electrode placement. A new technique. *American Journal of Physical Medicine and Rehabilitation*, **75**(3), pp. 232-234.

Perreault, E.J., Hunter, I.W. and Kearney, R.E., 1993, Quantitative analysis of four EMG amplifiers. *The Journal of Biomedical Engineering*, **15**(5), pp. 413-419.

Preece, A.W., Wimalaratna, H.S., Green, J.L., Churchill, E. and Morgan, H.M., 1994, Non-invasive quantitative EMG. *Electromyography and Clinical Neurophysiology*, **34**(2), pp. 81-86.

Shiavi, R., 1974, A wire multielectrode for intramuscular recording. *Journal of the International Federation for Medical and Biological Engineering*, **12**(5), pp. 721-723.

Shiavi, R., Zhang, L.Q., Limbird, T. and Edmondstone, M.A., 1992, Pattern analysis of electromyographic linear envelopes exhibited by subjects with uninjured and injured knees during free and fast speed walking. *Journal of Orthopaedic Research*, **10**(2), pp. 226-236.

Sinderby, C., Lindstrom, L. and Grassino, A.E., 1995, Automatic assessment of electromyogram quality. *Journal of Applied Physiology*, **79**(5), pp. 1803-1815.

Soderberg, G., 1992, *Selected Topics in Surface Electromyography for Use in the Occupational Setting: Expert Perspectives* (DHHS (NIOSH) 91-100), (National Institute for Occupational Safety and Health).

Sparto, P.J., Parnianpour, M., Reinsel, T.E. and Simon, S., 1997, Spectral and temporal responses of trunk extensor electromyography to an isometric endurance test. *Spine*, **22**(4), pp. 418-425.

Tho, K.S., Németh, G., Lamontagne, M. and Eriksson, E., 1997, Electromyographic analysis of muscle fatigue in ACL deficient knees. *Clinical Orthopedics and Related Research*, **340**, pp. 142-151.

Thorstensson, A., Carlson, H., Zomlefer, M.R. and Nilsson, J., 1982, Lumbar back muscle activity in relation to trunk movements during locomotion in man. *Acta Physiologica Scandinavica*, **116**(1), pp. 13-20.

Van Lent, M.E.T., Drost, M.R. and Wildenberg, F.A.J.M., 1994, EMG profiles of ACL-deficient patients during walking: the influence of mild fatigue. *International Journal of Sports Medicine*, **15**(8), pp. 508-514.

Winter, D., 1990, *Biomechanics and Motor Control of Human Motion*, second ed. (Toronto: John Wiley and Sons Inc.).

ACKNOWLEDGEMENTS

The travel expense has been funded by The Natural Sciences and Engineering Research Council of Canada (NSERC). The author would like to thank Dr Peter Stothart for his judicious comments on this paper.

Determination of the Onset of EMG and Force in EMG-based Motion Analysis: Methodological Problems and Limitations

Thomas Jöllenbeck
Bergische Universität–Gesamthochschule Wuppertal, Germany

INTRODUCTION

Electromyography and dynamography are the only basic methods in biomechanical motion analysis that provide information about non-visible activities and forces. For example, lifting a leg from a horizontal position requires the generation of a force greater than opposing force of gravity before motion becomes visible. While dynamography is usually limited to the description of a resultant force, electromyography is useful because it can show the time, duration and with some restrictions the degree of activity of a particular muscle participating in motion. Electromyography acquires special significance when dynamography is not applicable, e.g. during flight phase in sprint running. Thus exact knowledge of the electromechanical delay (EMD) as the distinct time shift between the onset of electrical activity (EMG) and the onset of the mechanical response (force) can provide important conclusions for the motion analysis of the mechanical effectiveness of a particular muscle whose activity is made evident via the corresponding EMG.

However, the exact value of EMD remains a matter of uncertainty because the reported values, e.g. for the KE, range between 18ms (Jöllenbeck and Wank, 1999) and 118ms (Horita and Ishiko, 1987). One possible explanation may be that different methods within different threshold values were used to identify the onset times of EMG and force and that so called methodological differences are responsible for the uncertainties in EMD (Corcos et al., 1992; Jöllenbeck, 1999).

Therefore it was the aim of the present study to investigate the influence of different methods on the identification of the onset times of EMG and force for determination of EMD and finally to show the method promising optimum results.

METHODS

For purposes of this study, data of about 800 explosive maximal isometric voluntary contractions of different investigations of elbow extensor muscles (EE), knee extensor muscles (KE) and knee flexor muscles (KF)—KE and KF in part additionally in up to eight different initial muscle length positions—of 140 male subjects were used (Figure 1).

The EMG-time-curves of EE (m. triceps brachii, TR), KE (m. vastus medialis, VM; m. vastus lateralis, VL; m. rectus femoris, RF) and KF (m. biceps femoris, BF; m. semitendinosus, ST) as well as the relevant force-time-curves were digitally recorded with a sampling rate of at least 1kHz.

Onset times of EMG and force were identified by means of the following methods found in literature: visual (VIS), fixed threshold values (FIX), percentage threshold values (PER), standard deviation above mean value as threshold value (STD), and an extreme low-pass filtering (ELF). Each method was applied with at least three different threshold levels. Additionally the advantages of previously filtered rectified EMG-data on FIX, PER and STD by a short-time weighted moving average (MA) and a moderate digital low-pass filtering (LF) procedure were tested (Table 1), each with two threshold levels. This analysis was carried out with the help of a specially designed computer programme.

It should be pointed out that the computer-aided visual method used here performs a zooming in a plane of about 300×150mm monitoring a data window of 300ms width and an extraction of 25% of the maximum values of both EMG and force to show the onsets as precisely as possible.

RESULTS

Despite identical input data, the results (Table 1, Figure 2) show muscle–independent wide–ranging EMD values that depend on the applied method ($12.3ms$, FLF_1–$128.3ms$, ELF_6). Overall, the shortest values of about 20ms and smallest standard deviations are to be found in VIS, longest values of about 130ms in ELF_5. But ELF clearly exceeds the levels of all other methods. Within a particular method, the shortest values are mostly to be found at lowest threshold values.

Comparing onset times of EMG and force, earliest times were found almost exclusive in VIS, indicating the comparatively lowest threshold values. Only a few pretreated methods show slightly earlier EMG-onsets (Figure 4).

Related to different initial muscle length positions (KE, KF), VIS is the only method showing the same constant course for all investigated muscles, with shortest EMD in optimal muscle length and an increment in direction of both stretched and destretched muscle (Figure 3).

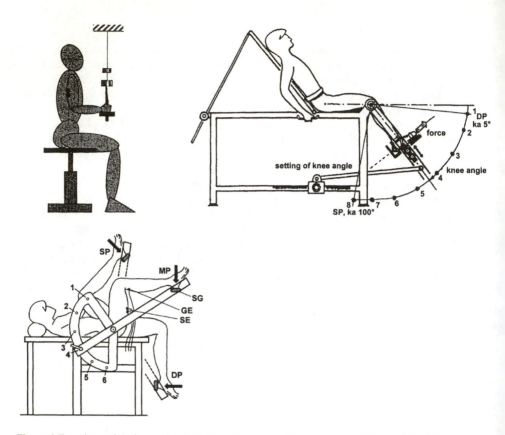

Figure 1 Experimental station to pick up the EMG- and force-time-curves of EE (left), KE (middle, modified by Tidow and Wiemann, 1993) and KF (right, modified by Wank *et al.*, 1998); SG–strain gauge; SE–surface electrode; GE–ground electrode; 1-8–position of muscle length; DP–destretched position; MP–median position; SP–stretched position.

Correlating EMD-values between and within methods, only in 6.4% of all cases an at least acceptable reliability of $r = 0.8$ (Willimczik, 1997) is reached, most within a method at different threshold values. An at least poor level of reliability ($r = 0.7$, Willimczik, 1997) is reached only in 12.3% of all cases. Related to the r^2-value, these results are to be interpreted as showing that in only 12.3% of all cases one method corresponds at least 50% with the results of another method. This value is absolutely unacceptable, given the identical input data. Further, no relation was found between similar EMD-values on the one side and correlation coefficient on the other side.

Table 1 Methods, pretreatments, threshold values and EMD, index *i* in ascending order related to threshold values.

Method / muscles	Pretreatment of EMG and force	EMG threshold	Force threshold	EMD [ms] (*stdev*) from / to
VIS		Zoomed Window of 300 ms width and 25% height (related to the maximum value of EMG and force), 'threshold' is determined by the first continuous onset		18.6 (*6.6*) / 22.0 (*8.5*)
FIX$_i$ KE, KF / EE		40 µV, 60 µV, 80 µV / 10 µV, 25µV, 50 µV	2 N, 5 N, 10 N / 1 N, 5 N, 10 N	14.5 (*9.1*) / 40.4 (*12.5*)
PER$_i$		3%, 5%, 5%, 10%, 10%, 20%	1%, 2%, 5%, 5%, 10%, 20%	24.4 (*8.4*) /43.9 (*12.7*)
STD$_i$		SD 3x, 4x, 5x above mean value		17.9 (*9.7*) / 29.8 (*14.9*)
ELF$_i$	3Hz low-pass	3%, 5%, 10%, 25%, 50%, 75%		70.9 (*11.4*) / 128.3 (*44.6*)
FMA$_i$ KE, KF / EE	EMG: MA 16ms, cos^2 weighted; force: LF 30Hz, hamming weighted	40 µV, 60 µV / 10 µV, 25µV	2 N, 5 N / 1 N, 5 N	12.5 (*5.8*) / 30.9 (*12.4*)
PMA$_i$		3%, 5%	1%, 2%	22.6 (*7.0*) /37.4 (*11.1*)
SMA$_i$		SD 3x, 4x above mean value		26.6 (*11.2*) / 45.3 (*16.1*)
FLF$_i$ KE, KF / EE	EMG and force: LF 30Hz, hamming weighted	40 µV, 60 µV / 10 µV, 25µV	2 N, 5 N / 1 N, 5 N	12.3 (*6.6*) / 32.4 (*12.1*)
PLF$_i$		3%, 5%	1%, 2%	24.6 (*6.6*) /42.4 (*12.0*)
SLF$_i$		SD 3x, 4x above mean value		27.3 (*12.7*) / 44.3 (*16.2*)

Related to VIS as the method with earliest onset-times, respectively lowest threshold values, the over-all standard-deviation at the 95% level (p = 0.05) as one indicator for the accuracy of the best fitting methods is at least about ±20ms (FIX1, FLF1, PLF1) for the EMG-onset (Figure 6) and about ±13ms (FMA1, FLF1, PLF1) for the force-onset (Figure 5). Correlating EMD by varying EMG-onsets and using constant force-onset of VIS, only doubtful reliabilities ($r \leq 0.7$) were reached (Figure 6). Conversely with varying force-onsets, only a few methods (FIX1, FMA1, FLF1, PLF1) show acceptable reliabilities ($r \geq 0.8$, Figure 5).

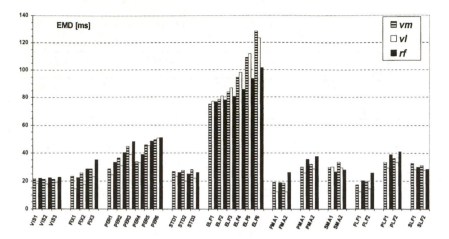

Figure 2 EMD of knee extensors identified by means of different methods and threshold values.

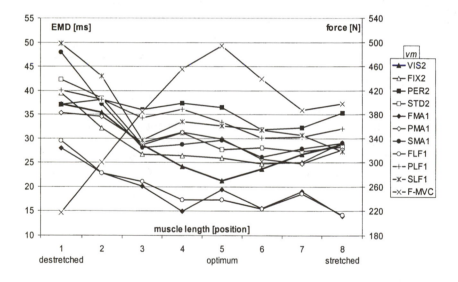

Figure 3 EMD of m. vastus medialis identified by means of selected methods in relation to different initial muscle length positions.

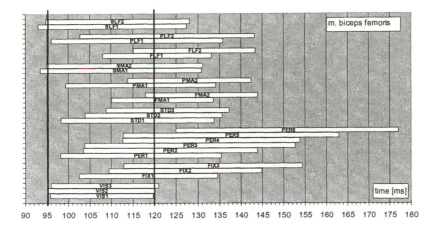

Figure 4 Time shift of EMD caused by different methods and threshold values exemplary using m. biceps femoris; left end of the beams represents the EMG onset the right end the force onset.

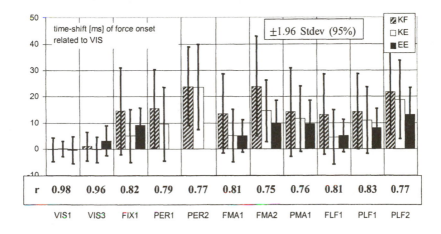

Figure 5 Time shift and correlation coefficient of force onset caused by different methods and threshold values related to VIS₂ additionally indicating standard deviation on 0.95 level (p=.05).

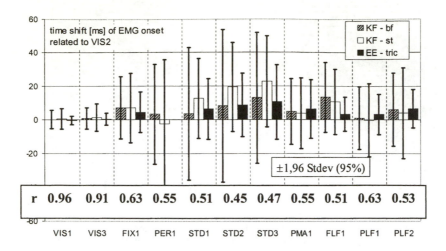

Figure 6 Time shift and correlation coefficient of EMG onset caused by different methods and threshold values related to VIS₂ additionally indicating standard deviation on 0.95 level (p=.05).

CONCLUSIONS

Using methods VIS, FIX, PER and STD, data are not treated or falsified apart from rectifying. The advantage of VIS is the PC-based free resolution of the displayed data. A zoomed data window of 300ms width and 25% height related to the maximum value of EMG and force represents the (subjective) optimum solution. The disadvantage is the great deal with time this method takes. A problem not only of this method is the uncertain identification of the beginning of a continuous activity when there is signal noise or disturbance. Therefore it is recommended that such cases be exluded from further analysis if possible.

The methods FIX, PER and STD are capable of running automatically, at least at higher threshold values. A disadvantage of Fix is that it lacks consideration of individual parameters. Therefore given two individuals with the same normalized force time characteristic, the one with the higher maximum force will cross a given threshold level earlier. This time shift problem is neutralized by PER. Using STD determination of mean value and standard deviation is to be done at a sufficient distance from the continuous onset of EMG and force. The advantage of STD is the independence from signal noise. The disadvantage is the dependence of the threshold value on signal noise and not on signal content. Therefore a higher noise level leads to a higher threshold and results in a time shift of the identified onset.

Because of the low pass filtering with 3Hz, ELF shows an extreme smoothing and with it falsification of input data. Especially in the case of EMG, there is a loss of input information. Subsequently the derived information is very doubtful. On the other hand this method is easy to use and runs automatically almost without any problem. But on whole this is not sufficient to compensate for the loss of input information.

By comparison, a moderate filtering or smoothing of data before using methods such as FIX, PER or STD may contribute to an improvement is ability to run automatically with a reduced threshold level at the same time. This is useful for the analysis of EMG because it removes short peaks from the signal without disturbing its real properties and content. Therefore automatic determination of onset becomes less trouble-prone.

Existing results confirm the assumption that the methods used and the different threshold values strongly affect the onset-times of EMG and force and therefore also the EMD. In most cases, the higher the threshold level the wider the time-shift and the later the identified onset-times.

However, what is surprising is the nonuniformity of the results, which was not expected to be so clear. It is true that results obtained by one method may be confirmed quantitatively by the results of another method, but there are no acceptable reliabilities. When comparing the results with absolutely the same input data but effected by different methods, it is to be pointed out that not any existing significance rather the amount of accordance, the acceptable level of reliability between two methods is of special interest. Exactly this level is missed in most cases. It seems that obviously different preconditions of analysis—the given method and within the selected value or level of threshold—lead to different results, independent whether the determined values are equal or not. So it is to be concluded that different methods for analysing the onset of EMG and force are not comparable, at least if time-sensitive data as the EMD are to be investigated. It may be speculated that this is a possible reason and explanation for some contradictory results or wrong conclusions in the past.

However, analysis of methods shows another surprising result. Only the non-automatic method in this comparison seems to be able to determine a natural and time-sensitive quantity as the EMD with sufficient accuracy and reliability. In the absence of an existing method of reference, some reasons are needed for this conclusion.

First, the visual method used here shows comparatively the earliest times of onset of both EMG and force. This should be equivalent to the lowest threshold values.

Second, this method is the only one showing the same muscle independent course of EMD related to the initial muscle length. This constancy is found with no other method. Since there is no reason to suppose that different muscles show different dependencies varying their initial muscle length, this result has to be considered as an important indicator for the accuracy of the visual method.

Third, unlike automatic methods, the visual method is not dependent on the contradictory preconditions of low threshold levels or values and the ability to run automatically with all data. This requires a compromise between both elements and leads to higher threshold levels, especially for signals as EMG, and therefore a distinct shift on the time scale. Furthermore the visual examination provides the basic information and preconditions for all automatic procedures and computer-aided analysis.

Ultimately the visual method seems able to decide accurately between individual conditions and signal characteristics caused by the individual orientated analysis in every single case. Especially given the stochastic character of EMG, this seem to be a performance that is unlikely to be matched by automatic methods.

Even if there seems to be no other possibility at applying an extensive time-consuming computer-aided visual method to get reliable and accurate results for the EMD, there may be other cases in biomechanical motion analysis or motor research which are not as time-sensitive as EMD. If a loss in accuracy of an order of about ±20–30ms is acceptable, automatic methods such as those presented here are applicable. Results show that force-onset, in spite of greater time-shifts, needs to be identified in a more accurate and reliable way as EMG-onset. For determination of force-onset methods with fixed and percentage values combined with lowest threshold levels of moderately pre–filtered data (lowpass 30Hz) show the optimum solution under the given restrictions. Showing the most constant results over all investigated muscles, FMA1 offers some advantages. For determination of EMG-onset, methods with lowest fixed values and lowest percentage values of moderately pre–filtered data are the solutions with the comparatively lowest scattering. But given there is no method with better than poor reliability related to the visual method in case of EMG-onset, it is not possible announce an "optimum" solution. On the method of lowest percentage values with moderate pre–filtered data is to be preferred with respect to ability to run automatically.

As a final conclusion in future work in the area of EMG-based motion analysis It is imprtant not to subordinate the EMG- and force-time-curves to the requirements of the preferential automatic method. Rather the methods to the real requirements and content of the EMG and force signal.

REFERENCES

Corcos, D.M., Gottlieb, G.L., Latash, M.L., Almeida, G.L. and Gyan, C.A., 1992, Electromechanical delay: An experimental artifact. *Journal of Electromyography and Kinesiology*, **2**, pp. 59-68.

Horita, T. and Ishiko, T., 1987, Relationships between muscle lactate accumulation and surface EMG activities during isokinetic contractions in man. *European Journal of Applied Physiology*, **56**, pp. 18-23.

Jöllenbeck, T., 1999, Unsicherheitsfaktor EMD–die auswirkungen unterschiedlicher analyseverfahren und möglichkeiten der verbesserung. In *Forschungsmethodologische Aspekte von Bewegung, Motorik und Training im Sport*, edited by Wiemeyer, J. (Hamburg: [in print]).

Jöllenbeck, T. and Wank, V., 1999, Electromechanical delay of the knee extensor muscles and relation to the initial muscle length. In *ISBS'99–XVI International Symposium of Biomechanics in Sports*, edited by Sanders, R.H. and Gibson, B.J. (Perth: Scientific Proceedings), pp. 125-128.

Tidow, G. and Wiemann, K., 1993, Zur Interpretation und Veränderbarkeit von Kraft-Zeit-Kurven bei explosiv-ballistischen Krafteinsätzen. *Deutsche Zeitschrift für Sportmedizin*, **44**, 3, pp. 92-103 und **44**, 4, pp. 136-150.

Wank, V., Wagner, H. and Blickhan, R., 1998, Muskelkraft und gelenkmoment– ein vergleich ausgewählter modelle zur berechnung der muskelmomenthebel für kniestrecker. *Sportwissenschaft*, **28**, 4, pp. 1-15.

Willimczik, K., 1997, Forschungsmethoden in der Sportwissenschaft. Band 1, *Statistik im Sport* (Hamburg: 3. Auflage, Czwalina).

Prediction of Net Ankle, Knee and Hip Joint Moments using an EMG-to-Force Model

Rod Barrett and Rob Neal[1]
School of Physiotherapy and Exercise Science,
Griffith University, Queensland, Australia
[1]Department of Human Movement Studies,
University of Queensland, Australia

INTRODUCTION

An emerging approach for determining subject specific tissue loads based on principles of inverse and forward dynamics is the EMG-to-force model (Hof and van den Berg, 1981). In this approach experimental measurements of normalized EMG for each muscle in the model are required together with kinematic data describing the relative joint angle of each joint under investigation. Normalized EMG data is assumed to be a measure of muscle stimulation from which the active state of the muscle (defined as the relative number of formed cross-bridges in the muscle) can be determined using a model of activation dynamics. Regression equations are used to estimate individual muscle-tendon lengths as a function of the relative joint angles for input into the model of contraction dynamics. This approach possesses features of the forward dynamics approach since the instantaneous length of the muscle fibres is determined from integration of the muscle fibre velocity which is itself predicted using the Hill based model of contraction dynamics. The EMG based modelling approach also possesses features of the inverse dynamics approach since estimates of muscle-tendon length based on experimental measurement of relative joint angles are required in order to estimate muscle-tendon forces in the model of contraction dynamics.

While EMG based muscle models have the advantage of being deterministic and able to account for antagonistic coactivity and individual muscle recruitment strategies, they can also been criticized for their inability to predict muscle forces that closely match joint torques measured using a dynamometer or estimated via inverse dynamics. One of the main reasons put forward to explain this discrepancy is that subject specific parameter values such as optimum muscle fibre lengths, tendon slack lengths and the maximum isometric force values for each muscle are difficult to determine. Other reasons include difficulties associated with normalizing EMG activity to a maximal contraction and questions concerning the validity of using EMG as a global measure of muscle stimulation. Depending on the application of the muscle model it may also be necessary to incorporate the effects of contraction history into simple Hill-based muscle models of contraction dynamics (Herzog and Leonard, 2000). To address problems associated with the poor predictive capacity of EMG-driven models, mathematical optimization schemes are commonly used to help select model parameter values that minimise error in model predictions. In this paper an EMG-to-force model with parameter values identified through mathematical optimization is used to predict net ankle, knee and hip joint torques for a range of common movement patterns. More specifically, the model was used to examine the mechanics of the semi-squat at two different loading conditions, and the countermovement and squat jump.

METHODS

Subjects and Experimental Procedures

Twelve physically active male subjects volunteered to participate in each experiment. In the semi-squat the knee joint was flexed to 90° at two different loading conditions, 25% and 75% of body weight (BW). The duration of each lift was set to 4 seconds (2 seconds each for the down and up phases) which was controlled using a metronome. For the vertical jumping experiment subjects were instructed to keep their hands on opposite shoulders, and to jump as high as possible while remaining side–on to the camera. During the SJ subjects were instructed not to make a countermovement. No constraints were placed on the extent to which the MCB was lowered in either jump.

Kinematics and Kinetics

Marker trajectories were recorded at 50Hz and marker coordinates were obtained using the Peak Motus Motion Measurement System. Simultaneous measurements of the vertical and fore–aft components of the ground reaction force and the centre of pressure were sampled at 200Hz using a Kistler (Type 9287A) force platform. Following synchronization of video and force plate data, a link segment model was used in an inverse dynamics approach to determine the net moments about the hip, knee and ankle joints. Position data were filtered using a Butterworth fourth order zero lag filter with a cutoff frequency of 16Hz prior to the calculation of linear and angular accelerations.

EMG

Pairs of silver–silver chloride surface electrodes were placed over the muscle belly of gastrocnemius (GAS), soleus (SOL), rectus femoris (RF), vastus medialis (VAS), biceps femoris (HAM) and gluteus maximus (GM). EMG signals were sampled at 1000Hz, amplified and transmitted telemetrically (Noraxon, Telemyo) to a PC for storage and subsequent analysis. All EMG signals were band pass filtered (20-500Hz) to reduce noise and were then rectified, low pass filtered (5Hz) and normalized relative to the activity associated with previously recorded maximum voluntary contractions. This normalized smoothed rectified EMG signal (NSREMG) was assumed to be a measure of muscle stimulation.

Model Description

The EMG-to-force model used in the present study was based on the model described by van Soest and Bobbert (1993) which can be conceptualized as a coupling between activation dynamics and contraction dynamics. Activation dynamics represents the process by which muscle stimulation is transformed to muscle activation. Activation can be considered to represent the proportion of formed cross-bridges in a muscle, with zero representing no attachments, and one representing full engagement of all cross-bridges. If it can be assumed that Normalized Smoothed Rectified EMG (NSREMG) can be used as a measure of muscle stimulation, then it is possible to estimate activation using relevant equations (e.g. Hatze, 1981). Hill-based models of muscle contraction dynamics attempt to represent the process by which muscle activation is transformed to muscle force and typically consist of a contractile component (CC), a series elastic component (SEC) and a parallel elastic component (PEC). The CC represents the effect of myofilament overlap and the velocity related effect of viscosity on the force generating capacity of muscle. The PEC is used to represent the passive force when inactive muscle is stretched in parallel with the CC and the SEC represents the elasticity of the myofilaments, aponeurosis and tendons in series with the CC. CC behaviour is characterized by the well-known force-length (FL) and force-velocity (FV) relations and the elastic components are typically represented by non-linear FL curves.

Overall, the model allowed the length, velocity and force in the contractile element (CC), series elastic element (SEC) and parallel elastic element (PEC) of six lower extremity muscles (GAS, SOL, VAS, RF, HAM and GM) to be calculated from input describing relative muscle stimulation levels and muscle–tendon complex lengths (LMTC). NSREMG was used as measure of muscle stimulation and LMTC for each muscle was determined from the regression equations of Jacobs and van Ingen Schenau (1992). Computationally, the model consisted of a set of uncoupled first order differential equations that were solved using a variable order Adams-Bashford-Moulton PECE ODE solver (Shampine and Reichelt, 1997). The solver implements numeric integration to compute the state variables as part of an initial value problem. Muscle specific parameter values for the optimum length of the CC (L_{CCOPT}), tendon slack length (L_{SLACK}) and percentage of slow twitch fibred (ST) were taken directly from Jacobs *et al.* (1996).

Optimization

Muscle specific values for maximum isometric force (FMAX) were assumed to correspond to the following ratios: SOL:GAS = 2:1, VAS:REC = 3:1, GM:HAM = 5:4, (Bobbert *et al.*, 1996) and were determined using multi-objective optimization

(Matlab Optimization Toolbox, Version 2.0, 1999). The optimization was formulated as a goal attainment problem in which the RMS difference between the peak torques determined using the muscle model and via inverse dynamics at each joint for the right side of the body were minimized.

RESULTS AND DISCUSSION

Output from the EMG-to-force model for the vastus femoris muscle from a representative subject is displayed in Figure 1. Variables plotted against time include NSREMG and active state (Q), normalized LMTC (L_{MTC}/L_{MTCOPT}), normalized velocity of the CC (L_{CCOPT}/s), force in the SEC (F_{SEC}/F_{MAX}), normalized length of the SEC (L_{SEC}/L_{SLACK}), and power in the CC, SEC and MTC (Watts). In addition, certain model variables are superimposed over plots of their known relationships with other variables. Calcium ion concentration ($[Ca^{2+}]$) is plotted over the length dependent sigmoidal relationship between $[Ca^{2+}]$ and Q, normalized CC length is superimposed over the isometric FL relation, normalized velocity of the CC is plotted over the FV relation, and normalized SEC and PEC length is plotted over the FL curves for the SEC and PEC. Instantaneous values of key variables are also presented (bottom right).

The model shows that the CC undergoes a period of active stretch prior to the shortening phase and that the CC operates primarily over the ascending limb of the FL relation. The decreased capacity of the muscle to produce force towards the end of the push-off phase is related to the decreased length of the CC (in accordance with the FL relation) and increased concentric contraction velocity of the CC (in accordance with the FV relation). The PEC was not recruited.

Despite the limited number of model parameters optimized, a close match was obtained between the net ankle, knee and hip joint torques predicted using the muscle model and measured using inverse dynamics for the semi-squat (Figure 2) and vertical jumping (Figure 3). As a check of the validity of the model prediction, the values for FMAX predicted by the optimization were compared with values for FMAX presented in the literature. FMAX values used in the present study were found to be in good general agreement with those reported by Bobbert *et al.* (1996), Jacobs *et al.* (1996), and van Soest and Bobbert (1993) (Table 1).

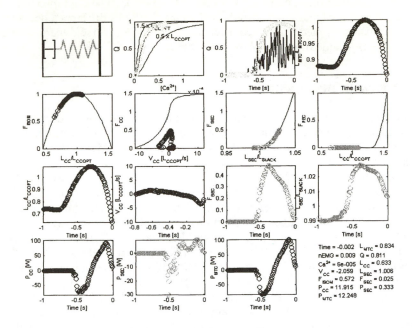

Figure 1 Activation and contraction dynamics for *m. vastus femoris* in a CMJ.

The slightly lower values used in the present study probably reflect that fact that the subjects used in the current study were not highly trained athletes. An alternative explanation is that NSREMG was overestimated causing the optimization procedure to yield lower values in order to ensure a good match between net joint torques predicted using the muscle model and estimated via inverse dynamics.

Table 1 Comparison of FMAX values used in the present study and those presented in the literature.

Muscle	Semi-squat	Jumping	Bobbert *et al.* (1996)	Jacobs *et al.* (1996)	Soest and Bobbert (1993)
SOL	2125	2667	2996	4235	4000
GAS	1062	1333	1496	2370	2000
VAS	4114	4500	5245	5400	4500
RF	1371	1500	1735	930	1500
HAM	1873	2178	2213	6000	2000
GM	2341	2722	2766	2650	2500

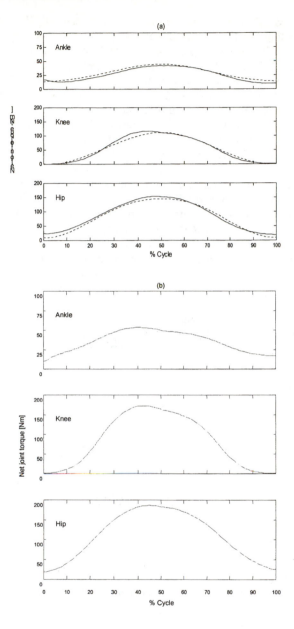

Figure 2 Mean net joint torque curves determined for the right side of the body from inverse dynamics (solid lines) and the muscle model (dashed lines) in (a) 25% BW condition; and (b) 75% BW condition.

In order to test the sensitivity of the muscle model to changes in NSREMG a simulation was performed whereby the NSREMG for the 25% loading condition for the semi-squat was increased by 20% and then the values for FMAX were re-optimized. FMAX values for each muscle were found to decrease by 12–18%

relative to the FMAX values from the original optimization. When the NSREMG for the 75% loading condition were increased by 20% the corresponding decrease in FMAX for each muscle was 5–14%. These results indicate that errors in estimating NRSEMG are at least partially compensated for by corresponding changes in FMAX. The smaller changes in FMAX when NSREMG was increased by 20% at the 75% compared to the 25% loading condition are explained by the sigmoidal relationship between calcium ion concentration and active state. Active state increases with calcium ion concentration at low levels of calcium ion concentration and saturates at higher levels of calcium ion concentration. Therefore a 20% increase in NSREMG at high levels of calcium ion concentration has only a small effect on active state, hence the amplitude of the muscle force is only marginally affected (although deactivation time is prolonged). Hence the amplitude of the net joint torques predicted via the muscle model are still in close agreement with the net joint torque estimated via inverse dynamics. At low levels of activation a 20% increase in NSREMG manifests in increased active state resulting in greater estimates of muscle force. Net joint torques predicted by the muscle model are overestimated resulting in lower estimates of FMAX from the optimization. It is concluded from this analysis that special attention must be paid to obtaining valid measures of maximal EMG activity with which to normalize the EMG data recorded during the task under investigation, especially when EMG activity in the task is high. This was not considered to be a problem in the vertical jumping experiment since differences in NSREMG were in timing rather than amplitude, and because only relative comparisons between jumps were made.

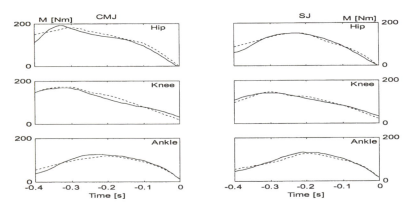

Figure 3 Mean values for moment of force curves determined from inverse dynamics (solid lines) and the muscle model (dashed lines) in (a) CMJ and (b) SJ.

REFERENCES

Bobbert, M.F., Gerritsen, K.G.M., Litgens, M.C.A. and van Soest, A.J., 1996, Why is countermovement jump height greater than squat jump height? *Medicine and Science in Sports and Exercise*, **28**(11), pp. 1402-1412.

Hatze, H., 1981, *Myocybernetic Control Models of Skeletal Muscle* (Pretoria: University of South Africa, Muckleneuk).

Herzog, W. and Leonard, T.R., 2000, The history dependence of force production in mammalian skeletal muscle following stretch-shortening and shortening stretch cycles. *Journal of Biomechanics*, **33**, pp. 531-542.

Hof, A.L. and van den Berg, J.W., 1981, EMG to force processing I: An electrical analogue of the Hill muscle model. *Journal of Biomechanics*, **14**(11), pp. 747-758.

Jacobs, R., Bobbert, M.F. and van Ingen Schenau, G.J., 1996, Mechanical output from individual muscles during explosive leg extensions: the role of biarticular muscles. *Journal of Biomechanics*, **29**(4), pp. 513-523.

Jacobs, R. and van Ingen Schenau, G.J., 1992, Intermuscular coordination in a sprint pushoff. *Journal of Biomechanics*, **25**, pp. 953-965.

Shampine, L.F. and Reichelt, M.W., 1997, The MATLAB ODE Suite. SIAM *Journal on Scientific Computing*, **18**(1), pp. 1-22.

van Soest, A.J. and Bobbert, M.F., 1993, The contribution of muscle properties in the control of explosive movements. *Biological Cybernetics*, **69**, pp. 195-204.

Part Six

Biomechanical Analysis of the Internal Load

20

Subject Specific Computer Simulations to Examine In-vivo Knee Joint Tissue Loading

David Lloyd
Department of Human Movement and Exercise Science,
University of Western Australia, Perth, WA, Australia

INTRODUCTION

"Only when the causal relations between applied forces and resultant injury are established and understood can appropriate programmes of intervention and prevention be designed and implemented" (Whiting and Zernicke, 1998). Moreover, if we are to prevent injury to ligaments, cartilage or bone then the forces experienced by these structures during tasks that cause the insult(s) must be determined. However, determining the actual loads sustained by tissues *in-vivo* is still a problem that is only starting to be resolved.

The methods that we have available to measure *in-vivo* tissue loads are direct measurement or indirect estimation using some form of modelling. Direct measurement is difficult, has obvious serious ethical considerations, and may modify the actual performance of the task. So modelling appears a logical choice, but there are many problems with this pathway.

First we must consider the factors that have to be accounted for in such models. Let's use the anterior cruciate ligament and the knee joint as an example. The important factors are: the anatomy of the knee, muscle, menisci, and ligaments; the strength of these tissues; the external loading; the static and dynamic joint posture; and the interactions between muscles, ligaments and articular surfaces in the joint. For example, even for the same joint position and load, muscles can be activated quite differently depending on the control task (Buchanan and Lloyd, 1995). Loading of the internal structures relies heavily on how muscles are activated, which is person and task specific. Last, but not least, the model must account for the indeterminate nature of the joint system.

Electromyograph (EMG) driven joint modelling can take into account all the above factors. EMG-driven models have been developed for the lower back (McGill, 1992; Thelen *et al.*, 1994; Nussbaum and Chaffin, 1998), elbow

(Buchanan *et al.*, 2000; Soechting and Flanders, 1997), shoulder (Laursen *et al.*, 1998) and knee (White and Winter, 1993; Lloyd and Buchanan, 1996). My colleagues and I have developed EMG-driven models of the knee to examine subject specific tissue loading in the joint. Two models have been developed, the first a static isometric model, and the second a dynamic model. The models have been developed for a continuing series of studies to determine the loading of the knee ligaments when the knee is loaded in varus and valgus. This loading direction was chosen as these loads, when coupled with anterior draw of the tibia, have the potential to subject the ligaments, particularly the anterior cruciate ligament, to high degrees of stress (Markolf *et al.*, 1995). In addition, muscular support of external varus-valgus (VV) moments controls the articular loading of the knee (Schipplein and Andriacchi, 1991).

This paper first briefly describes the models that we have developed. It then presents how these models have been used to evaluate the contribution of muscle to stabilize the knee during VV loading in static and dynamic conditions, briefly summarizing some of more important results. Finally, further refinements of the modelling methods and possible further uses are outlined.

THE MODELS

The EMG-driven joint model is a computer simulation in that it predicts the moments produced by the muscles that cross a joint (Lloyd and Besier, 2001; Besier and Lloyd, 1999; Lloyd *et al.*, 1996; Lloyd and Buchanan, 1996). The EMG-driven joint model can also be implemented to predict joint motion (see Buchanan *et al.*, 2000).

The model uses "real" data that is typically recorded in a motion analysis laboratory; electromyographs (EMG), 3-dimensional motion, and ground reaction force data. These data are recorded from subjects who perform different tasks that challenge knee stability. These tasks include static varus–valgus loads, dynamic tasks such as running and cutting, or isometric and isokinetic tasks on a dynamometer.

Both the static and dynamic model consists of four parts (1) an anatomical model, (2) an EMG-to-activation model, (3) a muscle model, and (4) calibration (see Figure 1). The EMG and motion data recorded during the various tasks serve as model inputs to enable prediction of the joint moments. Joint moments estimated using inverse dynamics are used to calibrate the model, and then to verify the model's performance following calibration. These various sub-components of the models are now discussed.

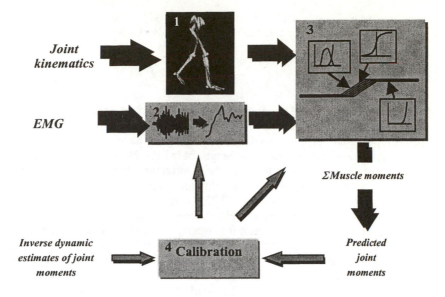

Figure 1 Propagation of a motor unit action potential waveform as it passes beneath the recording electrodes.

Anatomical Model

Software for Interactive Musculoskeletal Modelling (SIMM—Musculographics) is used to model the anatomy of the lower limbs and knee joint (Delp *et al.*, 1990). Using the motion or posture data collected during the trials as input, SIMM estimates the lengths, velocities, and moment arms of the musculotendon units that cross the knee. In the static model, only musculotendon lengths and moment arms are required.

EMG-to-Activation Model

The output of this model is muscle activation based on the recorded EMG of each muscle. EMG is first high pass filtered with a 30Hz zero lag Butterworth filter, full wave rectified and then low pass filtered with a 6Hz zero lag Butterworth filter.

In the *static model* the activation is just the average rectified and filtered EMG over the period of the isometric contraction, with a linear 1-to-1 relationship between processed EMG and activation. In the *dynamic model*, the rectified and filtered EMG is further processed using a similar scheme to the second-order discrete linear model proposed by Thelen *et al.* (1994) in which four coefficients shaped the response of this function. This model is also modified to account for the non-linear EMG to force relationship that has been reported by a number of researchers (e.g. Woods and Bigland-Ritchie, 1983). The reader is referred to Lloyd and Besier (2001) for full mathematical details of EMG-to-activation model.

Muscle Model

Muscle activation, musculotendon lengths and velocities, are used as inputs to determine muscle force employing a Hill-type muscle model similar to that proposed by Zajac (1989). Modifications to this model include (a) coupling between activation and optimal fibre length based on the work of Huijing (1996), (b) a passive elastic muscle force in the contractile element obtained from an exponential relationship, which allowed for passive forces to be obtained regardless of fibre length (Schutte, 1992), and (c) a passive parallel damping element added to the force–velocity relationship as suggested by Schutte (1992) to prevent any singularities of the mass-less model when activation or isometric force are zero. The full muscle model details are provided in Lloyd and Besier (2001).

The individual muscle FE moments generated by the muscles are estimated by multiplying the individual muscle forces with their FE moment arms. The predicted net flexion–extension (FE) joint moments are then calculated by summing the individual muscle FE moments.

Calibration

Calibration is performed for each subject using data from a number of different trials. Non-linear optimization is used to adjust the coefficients in the EMG-to-activation model and muscle model parameters. The optimization reduces the least-square error between the FE joint moments computed by the model and those estimated by inverse dynamics. Once the model is calibrated and the optimal parameters are obtained, the model is ready to predict individual muscle forces and joint torques.

APPLICATION OF THE STATIC MODEL

Muscular Support of Varus and Valgus Isometric Loads at the Human Knee

In this study, eight subjects were required to voluntarily generate various forces in a transverse plane just above their ankles, whilst sitting on their ischial tuberosities (Figure 2A). The forces were the same magnitude, but in different radial directions, which produced combinations of varus or valgus and flexion or extension moments at the knee (Figure 2B). The contributions of the subjects' muscles and non-muscular soft tissues (ligaments and joint capsule) to the support of the total external knee joint moment were determined by analysing the experimental data using the EMG-driven model of the knee.

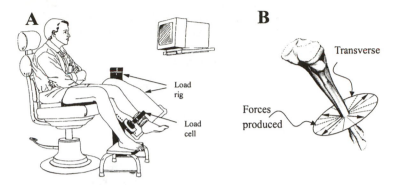

Figure 2 A) The seated subject generated forces in transverse plane at the shin. Subject was given visual display of the target forces and visual feedback of force they were producing. **B)** Schematic of the forces produced in the transverse load plane. These forces create combinations of VV and FE moments at the knee. For example, a force with a direction between pure extension and pure varus (from 90° to 180°) will produce a knee moment that has extension and varus components.

Specific Model Details and Performance

The model used in this study was a static version of the model (see Lloyd and Buchanan, 1996 for full details). The muscle parameters adjusted in the calibration were the global maximum flexor and extensor muscle specific stresses, and each muscle's optimal fibre length and tendon slack length. The model was calibrated to all trials recorded.

Following calibration, the static knee model was capable of predicting FE moments across all tasks. The model was able to predict FE knee moments with a mean (S.D.) coefficient of determination (R^2) of 0.99±0.01 across trials and mean residual error for these predictions was about 2Nm.

Muscular Contribution to the External Knee Moments

The calibrated model provides estimates of the muscular forces. The fundamental premise in the model is that the muscles contribute to 100% of the FE knee load; however, the muscular contribution to the external varus–valgus (VV) knee load has to be calculated. The total VV moment generated by muscles is determined by multiplying the individual muscle forces with their VV moment arms and summing the subsequent individual muscle VV moments.

The *residual load* constitutes the potential for non-muscular soft tissue loading. The residual load is difference between the internally generated muscle moments (determined from the model) and the external applied moments (determined using inverse dynamics). The *residual FE load* is, by assumption, equal to zero. However, the *residual VV load* is the difference between the externally applied VV moment from the internal VV moment generated by the muscles. If the VV moment generated by muscles is *greater than* that applied externally, then there is *no* residual load and *no* potential for soft tissue loading. If, however, the VV moment generated by muscles is *less than* that applied externally, then there is a residual VV load and potential for soft tissue loading. The *residual load ratio* is defined as the residual VV load expressed as a percentage of the magnitude of the combined FE and VV external moment.

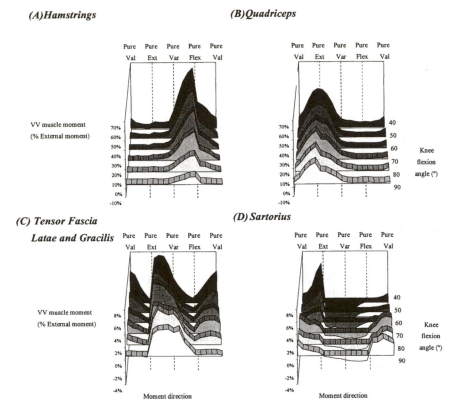

Figure 3 The subject average total muscle contribution to the external varus and valgus moment. These are plotted verses knee joint angle and moment direction. The varus and valgus muscle moment contribution shown is relative to the external varus–valgus moment. Value above 100% means that muscles support more than the external VV moment.

Static Muscular Support of Varus–valgus Knee Moments

The results showed that muscles were primarily used to support flexion and extension loads at the knee, but in so doing, were able to support some part of the varus or valgus loads (Figure 3). However, non-muscular soft tissue loading was still required. Soft tissues supported up to an average maximum of 83% of the pure varus and pure valgus external moments applied to the knee. Soft tissue loading in pure varus and valgus was less than 100% of the external load as the muscles, on average, were able to support 17% of the external load (Lloyd and Buchanan, 1996).

The hamstrings and quadriceps were specifically activated to support the flexion or extension moments respectively. However, it was found that the (1) co-contraction of the hamstrings and quadriceps, and (2) activation of the tensor fascia latae and gracilis were more tuned to the magnitude of the varus and valgus moments (Lloyd and Buchanan, 2001; Buchanan and Lloyd, 1997).

Compared to the tensor fascia latae and gracilis, the hamstrings and quadriceps supported most of the varus and valgus moments (Figure 3). In pure varus and pure valgus external loading hamstrings and quadriceps co-contraction (HAMs+QUADs) supported 8% to 12% of the external moment (Figure 4), significantly greater than that provided by the tensor fascia latae and gracilis (TFL+GR), and the gastrocnemi (GAS) (Lloyd and Buchanan, 2001).

Summarizing, in these static tasks the non-muscular soft tissues were required to support a large proportion of the VV load. Increasing muscular support of VV loads will increase the loading of the articular surfaces, so the activation patterns observed would definitely favour low articular loading. However, there were definite activation strategies to support VV moments, which suggest the muscles were activated to reduce the ligament loading to some degree. Therefore, the results support the premise that there are at least dual goals of the neuromotor system during the support of varus and valgus moments. How then does this pattern of support change in dynamic loading conditions? This will be addressed next.

APPLICATION OF THE DYNAMIC MODEL

Muscular Support of Varus and Valgus Loads at the Knee during Running and Cutting

The purpose of this study was twofold: (1) to determine if the dynamic version of the EMG-driven model of the human knee (as presented above) could be used to accurately and reliably estimate knee moments across a varied range of dynamic contractile conditions, and (2) to determine muscle contributions to dynamic varus and valgus loading.

Six subjects were tested (mean age: 20.5±2.9 years; mean mass: 74.6±8.6kg) and four of these six subjects were tested two weeks later to examine the test-retest reliability of the model across weeks. Subjects performed a series of tasks on a Biodex isokinetic dynamometer (Shirley, NY) and series of running and sidestepping manoeuvres in the three–dimensional gait analysis laboratory.

The Biodex tasks included: maximum isometric contractions for all muscles; passive FE at 60°/sec; eccentric hamstring and quadriceps contraction at 120°/sec; low effort FE at 120°/sec; combined FE with varus/valgus movements at 120°/sec; and maximal effort FE at 60 and 120°/sec. During these trials, knee FE torque, knee flexion angle, and EMG data from 10 knee muscles were collected at 2000Hz.

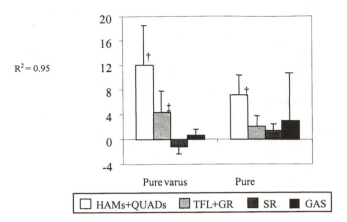

Figure 4 The VV muscle group moments (as a percent of the external moment) during pure varus and pure valgus loads. The values are the subject averages and standard deviations averaged across knee joint angle. †HAMs+QUADs VV moments significantly larger (p<0.001) than each of the SR, TFL+GR, and GAS. ‡TFL+GR VV moments significantly larger (p<0.001) than each of the SR and GAS.

The subjects performed a series of running and cutting manoeuvres at approximately 3 m/sec. The cutting tasks provided a dynamic challenge to knee joint stability in the VV, FE and internal–external rotation directions (Besier *et al.*, 2001). The cutting tasks were sidesteps to 60° (S60) and 30° (S30) from the direction of travel, and a crossover cut to 30° (XOV) from the direction of travel. Lower limb joint kinematic data were collected with a 6-camera 50Hz VICON Motion Analysis system (Oxford Metrics Inc.) using a VICON Clinical Manager (VCM) marker set (Kadaba *et al.*, 1990). Force data were collected simultaneously at 2000Hz using an AMTI force plate, and input into an inverse dynamic model to calculate knee FE moments across stance phase for each manoeuvre (Kadaba *et al.*, 1990). EMG data from the same ten knee muscles in the static experiments were also collected at 2000Hz. See Besier *et al.* (2001) for a full description of the experimental procedures.

The model was calibrated for each subject using five trials that were (1) a straight run, (2) a sidestep to 30°, (3) a crossover cut, (4) a passive (at rest) isokinetic on the Biodex dynamometer, and (5) an active concentric isokinetic task. The 18 model parameters were adjusted in the calibration. In the EMG-to-activation model the non-linear EMG-force relationship parameter and three coefficients in the second-order discrete linear model were adjusted, with the same parameters used for all muscles. In the muscle model each muscle's tendon slack length, and global flexor and extensor maximum muscle stresses were adjusted (Lloyd and Besier, 2001).

Once calibrated, the model was indirectly validated using the remaining ~30 tasks per person that were not used in the calibration. In this the predicted net FE muscle moments across were compared to the inverse dynamics estimates of the FE joint moments for these trials. We call this "an indirect validation" since we are not comparing the predicted muscle forces with actual measures of the muscle forces. Since this is really not possible this indirect validation is the best alternative at present.

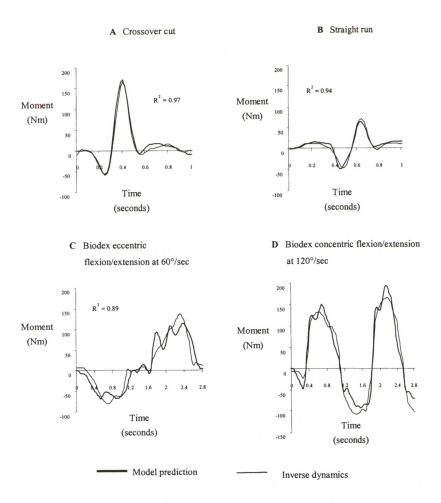

Figure 5 Typical results for one subject that compares the model predictions of knee flexion–extension muscle moments with FE knee joint moments determined using inverse dynamics. Extension moments are positive.

Dynamic Model Performance

Following calibration, the dynamic knee model was capable of predicting FE moments across a wide range of tasks from running, to crossover cutting and eccentric dynamometer tasks (Figure 5). The model was able to predict FE knee moments with a mean (S.D.) R^2 of 0.91±0.04 across 204 running, sidestepping and dynamometer trials not used to calibrate the model. Mean residual error for these predictions was about 12Nm, and when normalized to body weight was less than 0.03Nm/kg (Lloyd and Besier, 2001).

The model was retested on four subjects who returned for a repeat testing session two weeks later. It was assumed that the muscle model parameters should not change across this short period of time and thus the muscle model parameters from the first week's calibration were retained for the second week's model. However, it was considered that the new placement of the EMG electrodes would mean that the EMG-to-activation coefficients would be different, thus EMG-to-activation coefficients were recalibrated. The results revealed there was no decline in the accuracy of the model prediction of the FE joint moments across weeks (First week: R^2=0.91±0.018; Second Week: R^2= 0.91±0.031). This result provides further confidence in the model and parameters.

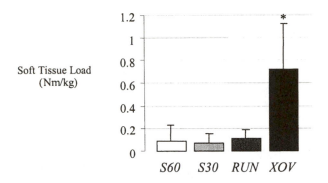

Figure 6 Peak residual load during running and sidestepping tasks. The crossover cut (XOV) task potentially placed significantly more load on soft tissues than the other tasks (*p < 0.01).

Dynamic Muscular Support of Varus and Valgus Knee Moments

In this study the residual loads were calculated the same as for the static case. However, this type of analysis does not consider the residual loads in the internal-external rotation and anterior–posterior draw, thus underestimate the possibility of soft tissue loading. This analysis is currently under way.

The residual VV loads measured across stance phase during the running and cutting tasks demonstrate that muscles were capable of resisting large VV external loads applied to the knee joint during the dynamic functional tasks (see Figure 6). Compared to the straight run (RUN) and side stepping tasks, the residual VV loading was greatest in the crossover cut, suggesting that people may be more at risk of ligament injury when performing these manoeuvres.

Comparing Static and Dynamic Muscular Stabilization of the Knee Joint

During the sidestepping tasks the residual load ratios were approximately 1%, the muscles being capable of resisting 99% of the combined FE and VV external load applied to the joint. During the run and crossover cutting tasks the residual load ratio was also only 1% and 5% respectively. In comparison, in the static joint stabilization tasks, when the external load had relative combinations of FE and VV moments and knee flexion angle that were similar to that seen in the running and cutting tasks, the residual load ratio was 50%. These results suggest that muscles relative contribution to the dynamic VV knee stabilization is far greater than that observed during static joint stabilization.

CONCLUSIONS

The static and dynamic EMG-driven models that were developed can estimate muscle forces at the knee validated against the model's ability to predict the knee flexion–extension moments during a range of static and dynamic tasks. This form of indirect validation provides confidence in the model and the muscle forces being estimated and that these are representative of the actual *in-vivo* forces.

The model has been useful in identifying the biomechanical results of the muscle activation patterns employed during these tasks that challenge knee stability in static and dynamic loading conditions. The technique has proven to be a very useful tool for investigating the potential for soft tissue loading during these tasks. When coupled with appropriate experiments the model can also be used in identifying relative risk of ligament injury when performing common sporting manoeuvres. Since the model implicitly incorporates the muscle activation patterns, it can be used to examine the way different groups of people stabilize the knee, and to assess changes in the muscle activation patterns that occur from different training studies.

Model Improvements

We are currently incorporating internal–external rotation and anterior–posterior draw as additional degrees of freedom in the anatomical knee model so the muscular contribution to these loading directions can be predicted. We are also developing more detailed anatomical models of the knee in which the muscles will be modelled as multiple line segments, especially for the vastus lateralis and vastus medialis, which originate over large areas on the femur. Ligaments, cartilage, and menisci are also being incorporated, and when these tissues have been included, it will be possible to estimate the loading of the articular surfaces.

Currently being tested are different forms of the EMG to activation model and the Hill-type muscle model. Specifically, we have been testing different ways to model the EMG to activation non-linearities, the time delay between activation and force, velocity history, and cross talk. We have also been examining the use of first order differential equations versus second–order discrete differential equations to characterize the muscle activation dynamics. Discrete versions of the muscle activation dynamics mean that these can be implemented in digital signal processing hardware for more rapid calculation of activation. Modifications to the Hill-type muscle model are being evaluated such as making the maximum contraction velocity dependent on activation and muscle fibre length (Hatze, 1977), and linking muscle fibre force output to work history (Herzog, 1998).

If this type of modelling is to be more routinely and widely adopted in biomechanical and epidemiological studies, then it must be simple and rapid to use. At the moment the calibration is time consuming, ranging from 2hr to 72hr (on a Silicon Graphics R10000 O2) depending on the number of calibration parameters included in the model. However once calibrated, the model could be implemented to work in real time.

The Future

EMG-driven models have been used sparingly but very effectively to date. With further refinement of such models and their widespread adoption, examination of issues that require *in-vivo* muscle–tendon forces will be possible. For example, the study of the energy flows across adjacent joints during different movements, or the in-depth study of the stretch-shorten cycle, will be possible. Greater use of these models will also mean that the investigation of *in-vivo* ligament and joint articular surface loads will be common place. It is then that we can start answering the questions of why and how tissue loading leads to injury or disease during physical activity.

REFERENCES

Ackland, T.R., Lloyd, D.G., Besier, T.F. and Cochrane, J.L., 2000, Soft tissue loads at the human knee during running and cutting manoeuvres. In *Proceedings of the XVIII International Symposium on Biomechanics in Sports*, edited by Hong, Y. and Johns, D. (Hong Kong: CUHK Press), pp. 853-856.

Besier, T.F. and Lloyd, D.G., 1999, A biomechanical knee model for the clinical prediction of *in vivo* tissue loads. In *Proceedings of Fifth International Olympic Commission World Congress on Sport Sciences* (Sydney, Australia).

Besier, T.F., Lloyd, D.G., Cochrane, J.L. and Ackland, T.R., 2001, External loading of the knee joint during running and cutting manoeuvres. *Medicine and Science in Sport and Exercise* (In Press).

Buchanan, T.S. and Lloyd, D.G., 1997, Muscle activation at the human knee during isometric flexion-extension and varus-valgus loads. *The Journal of Orthopaedic Research*, **15**, pp. 11-17.

Buchanan T.S., Manal K., Shen X., Lloyd D.G. and Gonzalez R.V., 2000, The virtual arm: estimating joint moments using an EMG-driven model. In *Proceedings of Congress of European Society of Biomechanics* (Dublin, Ireland).

Delp, S.L., Loan, J.P., Hoy, M.G., Zajac, F.E., Topp, E.L. and Rosen, J.M., 1990, An interactive graphics-based model of the lower extremity to study orthopaedic surgical procedures. *IEEE Transactions on Biomedical Engineering*, **37**, pp. 757-767.

Hatze, H., 1977, A myocybernetic control model of skeletal muscle. *Biological Cybernetics*, **25**, pp. 103-119.

Herzog, W., 1998, History dependence of force production in skeletal muscle: a proposal for mechanisms. *Journal of Electromyography and Kinesiology*, **8**, pp. 111-117.

Huijing, P.A., 1996, Important experimental factors for skeletal muscle modelling: non-linear changes of muscle length force characteristics as a function of degree of activity. *European Journal of Morphology*, **34**, pp. 47-54.

Kadaba, M.P., Ramakrishnan, H.K. and Wootten, M.E., 1990, Measurement of lower extremity kinematics during level walking. *Journal of Orthopaedic Research*, **8**, pp. 383-392.

Laursen, B., Jenson, B., Németh, G. and Sjogaard, G., 1998, A model predicting individual shoulder muscle forces based on relationship between electromyographic and 3D external forces in static position. *Journal of Biomechanics*, **31**, pp. 731-739.

Lloyd, D.G. and Buchanan, T.S., 1996, A model of load sharing between muscles and soft tissues at the human knee during static tasks. *Journal of Biomechanical Engineering*, **118**, pp. 367-376.

Lloyd, D.G. and Buchanan, T.S., 2001, Strategies of the muscular support of static varus and valgus loads at the human knee. *Journal of Biomechanics* (In press).

Lloyd, D.G. and Besier, T.F., 2001, An EMG-driven musculoskeletal model for estimation of the human knee joint moments across varied tasks. *Journal of Biomechanics* (Accepted).

Lloyd, D.G., Gonzalez, R.V. and Buchanan, T.S., 1996, A general EMG-driven musculoskeletal model for prediction of human joint moments. In *Proceedings of the Australian Conference of Science and Medicine in Sport* (Australia).

Markolf, K.L., Burchfield, D.M., Shapiro, M.M., Shepard, M.F., Finerman, G.A. and Slauterbeck, J.L., 1995, Combined knee loading states that generate high anterior cruciate ligament forces. *Journal of Orthopaedic Research*, **13**(6), pp. 930-935.

McGill, S.M., 1992, A myoelectrically based dynamic three-dimensional model to predict loads on lumbar spine tissues during lateral bending. *Journal of Biomechanics*, **25**, pp. 395-414.

Nussbaum, M. and Chaffin, D., 1998, Lumbar muscle force estimation using a subject-invariant 5-parameter EMG-based model. *Journal of Biomechanics*, **31**, pp. 667-672.

Schutte, L.M., 1992, *Using Musculoskeletal Models to Explore Strategies for Improving Performance in Electrical Stimulation-induced Leg Cycle Ergometry*, (PhD Thesis, Stanford University).

Schipplein, O.D. and Andriacchi, T.P., 1991, Interaction between active and passive knee stabilizers during level walking. *Journal of Orthopaedic Research*, **9**, pp. 113-119.

Soechting, J.F. and Flanders, M., 1997, Evaluating an integrated musculoskeletal model of the human arm. *Journal of Biomechanical Engineering*, **119**, pp. 93-102.

Thelen, D.G. Schultz, A.B., Fassois, S.D. and Ashton-Miller, J.A., 1994, Identification of dynamic myoelectric signal-to-force models during isometric lumbar muscle contractions. *Journal of Biomechanics*, **27**, pp. 907-919.

White, S.C., and Winter, D.A., 1993, Predicting muscle forces in gait from EMG signals and musculotendon kinematics. *Journal of Electromyography and Kinesiology*, **2**, pp. 217-231.

Whiting, W.C. and Zernicke, R.F., 1998, Biomechanics of musculoskeletal injury (Champaign, IL: Human Kinetic).

Woods, J.J. and Bigland-Ritchie, B., 1983, Linear and non-linear surface EMG/force relationships in human muscles. An anatomical/functional argument for the existence of both. *American Journal of Physical Medicine*, **62**, pp. 287-299.

Zajac, F.E., 1989, Muscle and tendon: properties, models, scaling, and application to biomechanics and motor control. *Critical Reviews in Biomedical Engineering*, **17**, pp. 359-411.

ACKNOWLEDGEMENTS

This work is the combined effort of a number of people. I would like to acknowledge the large contributions of Assoc. Prof. Tom Buchanan, Dr Roger Gonzalez, Dr Thor Besier, Assoc. Prof. Tim Ackland and Ms Jodie Cochrane. This work could not have been performed without the financial support of the NIH (USA), Arthritis Foundation (USA), NHMRC (Australia), AFL Research and Development Board (Australia) and the ARC (Australia). The kind support of Musculographics is also greatly appreciated.

21

Soft Tissue Loading of the Knee in Running and Side-stepping

Tim Ackland, David Lloyd, Thor Besier and Jodie Cochrane
Department of Human Movement and Exercise Science,
The University of Western Australia, Perth, Australia

INTRODUCTION

More than 5000 football-related anterior cruciate ligament (ACL) injuries occur annually in Australia. Around 60% of these injuries are non-contact and result from a landing, or when stopping, running, cutting and side–stepping. The tensile forces on the ACL can dramatically increase when the knee is more extended ($<30°$ flexion) and accommodating applied moments in flexion, combined with varus, valgus and/or internal rotation (Markolf et al., 1995). However, loading of the knee during the aforementioned sporting manoeuvres is largely unknown.

Many of these manoeuvres have to be performed "at the spur of the moment", leaving the player little time to prepare for the performance of the task. These unanticipated manoeuvres could place the knee at greater risk of injury than if they are pre-planned.

To better understand the mechanisms for non-contact knee ligament injury, the load sharing properties of muscle and other soft tissues during dynamic tasks that challenge the stability of the joint need to be determined. Forces produced by muscles during these tasks have the potential to counter the external loads applied to the joint, thereby reducing the potential loading of other knee joint soft tissues. The final part of this paper describes the estimation of varus/valgus (VV) moments supported by muscle in vivo, and the subsequent potential loading of other knee joint soft tissue structures during running and cutting tasks.

Therefore, the purposes of this paper are three-fold:

- to examine the external knee loading during side-stepping and cross-over cutting;
- to examine the external knee loads when side-stepping and cross-over cutting during unanticipated (UN) and pre-planned (PP) conditions; and
- to estimate the proportion of these loads accommodated by muscle activity during these tasks that challenge the stability of the knee joint.

METHODS

Loading of the knee during normal running (RUN), 30° sidestep (S30), 60° sidestep (S60) and 30° cross-over (XOV) was studied in ten subjects, running at a speed of 2.7±0.04m/s, and stepping off their preferred foot. Subjects knew which task was to be performed before they started the approach run under the PP condition. A set of LEDs, positioned within the subjects' fields of view, controlled the activity. In the PP condition the appropriate LEDs were illuminated early to inform the subject of the required manoeuvre before they started the approach run. However, in the UN condition, the LEDs were illuminated at the latest possible moment, so that the subject was just able to perform the manoeuvre. All cases were presented in random order.

Three dimensional (3D) motions were recorded using a 6-camera Vicon system employing a lower limb marker set (VCM), whilst ground reaction force (GRF) histories were collected synchronously using an AMTI force-platform. EMG recordings using surface electrodes for ten lower limb muscles were also made. Inter-segmental 3D knee joint moments were estimated using an inverse dynamic model of the lower limbs. The magnitude of resultant GRF was used to determine three phases during stance:

- weight acceptance (WA) (from heel strike to the first trough in the GRF history);
- peak push off (PPO) (time of peak push off force ±10% of stance time); and
- final push off (FPO) (last 15% of stance).

The externally applied flexion–extension (FE), VV, and internal-external rotation (IE) joint moments and the knee flexion angle were analysed during these phases. Running speed and cutting angle attained (direction following the manoeuvre with respect to the initial line of travel) were also determined from the trajectory of the pelvic centre. A repeated measures ANOVA was used to determine significant differences with a $p < 0.05$.

An electromyography (EMG)-driven Hill-type muscle model that can accurately predict joint moments during running and side–stepping ($r^2 = 0.91$) was developed (Lloyd and Besier, *in press*). This model takes muscle tendon length and EMG as input to determine *in vivo* forces for 13 muscles crossing the knee. Muscle tendon lengths and moment arms were determined using a 3D anatomical model, developed using Software for Interactive Musculoskeletal Modelling (SIMM©). To measure soft tissue loads, predicted muscle moments in varus/valgus were compared with those measured by inverse dynamics. If the external load applied to the knee was greater than the predicted muscle moments, then this residual had the potential to load the remaining soft tissue structures of the knee.

RESULTS AND DISCUSSION

During the performance of PP trials, knee moments during the PPO phase were generally larger than those recorded in the other phases ($p < 0.05$) (Figure 1). There were only very small or no differences between FE moments from the various manoeuvrers. Moving from S60 to XOV, externally applied moments changed from valgus to varus (p<0.05) (Figure 1A) and from internal to external rotation (Figure 1B).

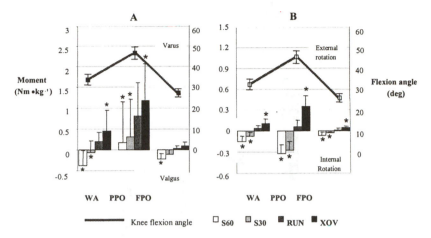

Figure 1 Varus–valgus and internal–external rotation moments at the knee (from Besier *et al.*, *in press*) (*Significantly different to RUN (p<0.05)).

During side-stepping there were substantial valgus moments in the WA and FPO phases (p<0.05), as well as notable internal rotation moments during WA and PPO (p<0.05). The varus moment of the knee during the XOV task was over 2 times larger than that recorded for running (p<0.05) during the WA and PPO phases.

The more extended knee angles during WA place the ACL at higher risk of injury, especially during side–stepping (S30 and S60) with increased valgus and internal rotation moments. A large varus moment at WA, combined with the applied flexion moment, could increase the risk of ACL injury in the XOV, however, the effect may be moderated due to a concurrent external rotation moment. Even though there is a very large varus moment during PPO the concurrently large applied flexion moment may, in part, reduce the risk of injury to the lateral collateral ligaments. There was no increase in the applied knee flexion moment during side-stepping and cross-over manoeuvres, but increases in the concurrent VV and internal rotation moments may place the ligaments, especially the ACL, at greater risk of injury.

Unanticipated Manoeuvres

In the UN tasks the subject ran marginally slower than for the PP tasks (2.62m/s vs 2.84m/s; p<0.05). The cutting angles attained during PP tasks were the same as for the UN tasks, with the exception of the S60 manoeuvre, where UN was smaller than PP (47.9° vs. 51.4°; p<0.05). There was a general increase in the magnitude of all moments, for each of the manoeuvres (all phases) in the UN compared to PP condition, with the most substantial differences being observed during XOV and S30 tasks. For example, when the knee was in an extended posture (31.26±6.9° of flexion) during the WA phase, there was at least a two-fold increase in the VV moments in the UN condition during the XOV and S30 manoeuvres (Figure 2).

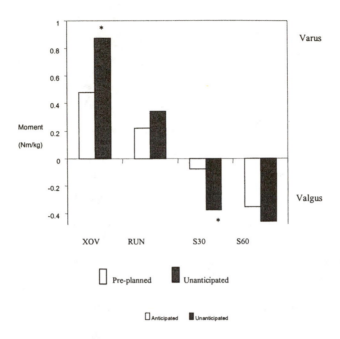

Figure 2 Varus–valgus moments in the weight acceptance phase.
(* UN different to PP; p<0.05).

   In the UN tasks the subjects experienced greater applied moments on the knee. Notable increases were observed in applied varus or valgus moments (during XOV and S30 respectively), and internal rotation (during S30). These applied moments have the potential to place large loads on the knee support structures, especially the ACL during side-stepping actions. Such differences were not generally observed in the S60 manoeuvres, because the subjects could not make the required cutting angle and so they performed the manoeuvre at a slower velocity during the UN condition. Since the magnitude of the cutting angle increased the load on the knee, were subjects able to perform this task under the same conditions as in the PP trials, then the applied knee moments would have been expected to rise accordingly. Therefore, in a game situation during "spur of the moment" changes in direction, athletes would appear to be at greater risk of knee ligament injury when attempting to perform dodging or evading moves compared to those that are pre-planned.

Soft Tissue Loads

Any externally applied VV load that is not countered by muscle has the potential to load the soft tissue structures of the knee, however it is important to note that the effects of joint reaction force have not been included in these calculations. The current model did not account for individual ligament, meniscus, or joint capsular forces, so the term "soft tissue" encompassed all non-muscular components that may contribute to the net VV moment about the knee. The potential VV load placed on soft tissues *in vivo* was therefore determined from the frontal plane joint kinetics.

Potential VV soft tissue load was calculated by subtracting the externally applied VV moment (from inverse dynamics) from the internal VV moment generated by muscle (from the model). If the moment generated by muscle matched that which was applied externally, then no contribution from other soft tissue structures was assumed. However, if the externally applied VV moment was greater than the VV moment generated by muscle, then soft tissue loading may be required to close the joint and a "residual load" was calculated.

For the run and side-step tasks, the VV moments generated by muscles were greater than the external load applied to the knee, thus no soft tissue loading was required. However, the large varus loads measured during the XOV exceeded the contribution from muscles by up to 1Nm/kg, thereby potentially loading the soft tissues (Figure 3). A lack of muscular stability when performing the XOV indicated that the ligamentous and meniscal tissues were at greater risk of injury when performing this task.

Furthermore, during a game situation where evading manoeuvres are performed at greater speeds and are often unanticipated, one might expect the applied loads to be greater than those reported in this study. Results from this investigation give us a better understanding of the aetiology of non-contact soft tissue knee injuries, and how muscle activation can assist in the protection of ligaments. Appropriate training methods might be used to alter muscle activation or movement strategies to reduce the load placed on soft tissues and prepare the athlete for these loads during game situations.

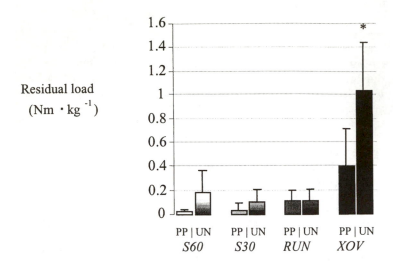

Residual load
$(\text{Nm} \cdot \text{kg}^{-1})$

Figure 3 Peak residual varus/valgus load for PP and UN tasks.

REFERENCES

Besier, T., Lloyd, D., Cochrane, J. and Ackland, T., External loading of the knee joint during running and cutting manoeuvres. *Medicine and Science in Sports and Exercise* (In press).

Lloyd, D. and Besier, T., Estimating in vivo muscle forces and knee joint moments using an EMG-driven musculoskeletal model. *Journal of Biomechanics (In press)*.

Markolf, K.L., Burchfield, D.M., Shapiro, M.M., Shepard, M.F., Finerman, G.A. and Slauterbeck, J.L., 1995, Combined knee loading states that generate high anterior cruciate ligament forces. *Journal of Orthopaedic Research*, **13**(6), pp. 930-935.

ACKNOWLEDGEMENT

We would like to acknowledge Musculographics Inc. for the use of SIMM©.

22

Estimating Lumbar Spinal Loads During a Golf Swing using an EMG-assisted Optimization Model Approach

Young-Tae Lim and John W. Chow[1]
Department of Physical Education, Yeungnam University,
Kyungsan, Korea
[1]Department of Kinesiology, University of Illinois,
Urbana, Illinois, USA

INTRODUCTION

A number of surveys have shown that the golf swing is increasingly being recognized as a potential cause of lower back injuries. Although many researchers have been interested in seeking a "perfect" golf swing to improve performance, surprisingly, few studies have investigated the potential causes of injury such as back pain. The forces generated by the musculature surrounding the lumbar spine often contribute a large part of spinal stresses. Tissue damage occurs when the force to which it is exposed to at a particular instant exceeds the tissue's tolerance. Therefore, large mechanical stresses on the lumbar spine are widely believed to be related to the development of low-back pain. During a golf swing, the L4-L5 disc as well as the lumbosacral (L5-S1) disc are subjected to large magnitudes of compressive loads in addition to the continuous static load due to the weight of the trunk. In order to explore the relationship between lumbar spinal loads and lower back injury, it is important to have knowledge of the lumbar spinal loads during a golf swing.

The purpose of this study was to estimate the loads acting on the spinal motion segment at the L4-L5 level (lower back) during a golf swing using an electromyography (EMG)-assisted optimization model (Cholewicki and McGill, 1994). It was expected that a golf swing would introduce large compressive, antero-posterior (A/P) shear, and medio-lateral (M/L) shear loads acting on the L4-L5 disc.

METHODS

Five male college golfers (age = 19.4±0.9 yrs, handicap = 0.8±1.1) served as the subjects. Each subject used his own driver (1-wood) and wore his own golf shoes during the tests.

Data Collection

Each subject performed ten trials (swings) in a laboratory setting and rated his own performance using a 5-point scale at the end of each trial. Four S-VHS camcorders (Panasonic AG455, 60Hz) were used to record the movement of trunk and lower extremities. Eight reflective markers were placed on the back of the subject in order to estimate the orientations of the middle and lower trunks and musculoskeletal parameters of the trunk musculature during a golf swing. Two AMTI force plates were used to record the ground reaction forces and moments acting on both feet. Ten pairs of surface EMG electrodes with on-site pre-amplification circuitry (Liberty Technology MYO115 and Therapeutic Unlimited D100) were placed on skin surfaces to record the activity of the left and right rectus abdominus, external oblique, internal oblique, erector spinae, and latissimus dorsi muscles.

The upper and lower four markers were used to define the middle and lower trunk reference frames, respectively. A calibration frame (PEAK Performance Technologies, USA, 25 control points, $2.2 \times 1.9 \times 1.6 \text{m}^3$) was videotaped prior to the trials for 3-D space reconstruction purposes. An event synchronization unit (PEAK Performance Technologies) and a microphone were used to synchronize the video, EMG, and force plate recordings. At the instant of impact during a golf swing, the sound captured by the microphone activated the event synchronization unit. As a result, two light emitting diodes (LEDs), which were visible to all camcorders, were turned on and a 3V signal was forwarded to the A/D converters of both EMG and force plates data collection systems simultaneously.

Data Reduction

The trial with the highest rating for each subject was selected for analysis. For each trial being analysed, six critical instants were identified from the video recordings: (1) ball address (BA)—initiation of backswing, (2) end of backswing (EB)—beginning of the downswing, (3) middle of downswing (MD)—the club at the horizontal position during the downswing, (4) ball impact (BI)—the instant of ball/driver impact, (5) middle of follow-through (MF)—the club at the horizontal position after impact, and (6) end of follow-through (EF)—the instant the club stopped its motion momentarily. For the purpose of this study, a golf swing was divided into five phases: (1) take away—from BA to EB, (2) forward swing—from EB to MD, (3) acceleration—from MD to BI, (4) early follow-through—from BI to MF, and (5) late follow-through—from MF to EF.

Two-dimensional coordinates of ten body landmarks and eight reference markers were extracted from video images using a Peak Motion Measurement System for each selected trial. The ten digitized body landmarks were the right and left hips, knees, ankles, heels, and toes. Using the KWON3D motion analysis software (V-tech, Korea), the Direct Linear Transformation (DLT) technique (Abdel-Aziz and Karara, 1971) was used to obtain 3-D coordinates of landmarks and markers relative to the reference frame defined by the calibration frame. The 3-D coordinates were smoothed and transformed to a global reference frame with principle axes parallel to the A/P, M/L, and vertical directions. Considering a free body diagram of the human body below the L5 level, the resultant force (F_r) acting on the L5 level was computed using the known segmental kinematic and inertial characteristics, and the ground reaction forces and moments.

The musculoskeletal parameters used in this study were based on the models of McGill (1992) and Cholewicki (1993). The musculoskeletal parameters included physiological cross-sectional area (PCSA) values of 22 muscles, 3-D coordinates of the origins and insertions of 22 muscles, and the proximal ends of individual lumbar vertebral bodies. The 22 muscles were the right rectus abdominus, external obliques (two parts), internal obliques (two parts), transverse abdominus, pars lumborum (five parts), quadratus lumborum, mulifidus (two parts), illiocostalis lumborum, longissimus thorasis, latissimus dorsi, and psoas (five parts). The musculoskeletal parameters of the corresponding muscles on the left side were obtained as the mirror image of the right side.

The muscle force at a given instant (F_m) was determined using a modification of a model from McGill and Norman (1986):

$$\mathbf{F}_m = g_m[(\sigma_m \mathbf{NEMG}_m A_m \Omega \delta + F_{pec})]\mathbf{e}_m$$

where g_m is a gain term, σ_m is the muscle stress which was set at 35N·cm^{-2}, NEMG$_m$ is the normalized EMG data, A_m is the PCSA of the muscle (cm^2), Ω is the coefficient of velocity modulation, δ is the coefficient of active length modulation, F_{pec} is the force due to passive elasticity, and $\mathbf{e}_m$ is a unit vector representing the line of action of the muscle. The gain term was obtained using an EMG-assisted optimization approach (Cholewicki and McGill, 1994). The contact force ($\mathbf{F}_c$) acting on the L4-L5 motion segment was estimated using the known $\mathbf{F}_m$ and $\mathbf{F}_r$ values:

$$\mathbf{F}_r = \mathbf{F}_c + \sum_{m=1}^{44} \mathbf{F}_m$$

Knowing the orientation of the L5 vertebra, $\mathbf{F}_r$ was resolved into compressive, A/P shear, and M/L shear forces.

DATA ANALYSIS

The lumbar spinal loads were normalized to the duration of a golf swing and mean and standard deviation values for all subjects were computed. In addition to absolute force values, loads were also normalized to the body weight (BW) of the subject.

RESULTS AND DISCUSSION

The lumbar spinal loads at the L4-L5 level during a golf swing are shown in Figure 1. The duration of a golf swing (from BA to EF) was normalized to 100% time. The dashed vertical lines represent the average times for different critical instants and the standard deviations are indicated as horizontal bars at the top of these lines.

Compressive Load

The mean average axial compression during the take away phase was about 370% BW. The compressive load increased steadily after EB and reached its maximum of 605% BW (or an average of approximately 4,300N) near IM. The mean average compressive loads were 531% BW and 298% BW for the early and late follow-through phases, respectively. The minimum mean compression of 202% BW (about 1,440N) was recorded at EF. The peak compressive load estimated in the present study was about 700% BW. However, Hosea *et al.* (1990) reported that both professional and amateur golfers generated peak compressive loads greater than 800% BW. They also found two major peaks and one minor peak in the compressive loading pattern during a golf swing. This three-peak pattern was not observed in the present study.

A/P Shear Load

The A/P shear loads were relatively small ($\cong$64 N) during the backswing but the mean A/P shear load increased gradually after EB and reached its peak of 124% BW (882N) at around 75% swing time (duration). The present study showed relatively large anterior shear loads throughout a golf swing except the small posterior shear loads ($\cong$ −21N) between 30 to 50% duration. An anterior shear load tends to displace the L4-L5 motion segment forward relative to the middle trunk. On the contrary, Hosea *et al.* (1990) reported large posterior shear loads during the forward swing and acceleration phases and the peak posterior shear load ($\cong$-596N) was recorded near IM. The differences could be due to the difference in modelling techniques. However, the hyperextension of the trunk, which was clearly observed during the follow-through phases, could produce large anterior shear loads. Thus, the results from the present study are more reasonable and accurate than those reported by Hosea *et al.*

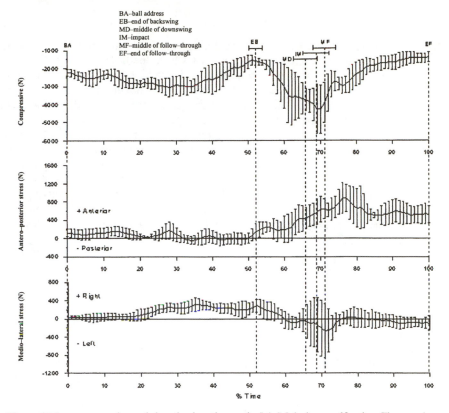

Figure 1 Mean compressive and shear loads acting on the L4–L5 during a golf swing. The error bars represent standard deviations.

M/L Shear Load

The mean M/L shear load was mostly acting toward the right during the take away phase. The direction was reversed during the early downswing and reached its peak (−252N) around MF. Relatively small M/L shear loads were observed during the late follow-through phase. Hosea *et al.* (1990) reported that professional golfers generated a mean peak M/L shear load (shear load to the right) of 530N while amateur golfers produced a mean peak of 960N. In their study, the amateurs exhibited a peak right M/L shear load during the forward swing phase and a peak left shear load in the acceleration phase. The two-peak loading pattern was also found in the professionals—a peak right M/L shear load near IM and a peak left shear load during the early follow-through phase. The present study predicted a mean peak right M/L shear load of 404N during the take away phase and a mean peak left M/L shear load of 463N during the early follow-through phase. However, the times of occurrence for the peak M/L shear loads were not comparable to those values reported by Hosea *et al.*

CONCLUSION

The present study demonstrated that the L4–L5 motion segment is subjected to considerable compressive, A/P shear, and M/L shear loads during a golf swing. However, the loads from a single swing seldom fall within the range of damaging loads. Thus, it seems that the magnitude of the load is not the primary factor for causing lower back injury. The repetitive changing direction of the shear load during a golf swing may increase the chance of fatigue fracture of pars interarticularis. In addition, the lumbar vertebra and disc are made of biological materials and the disc is viscoelastic in nature and consequently time rate dependent. Therefore, accumulated stress due to repeated golf swings may lead to disc degeneration, and even submaximal exertions may lead to structural deformation of the lumbar spine. A golf swing with shortened backswing and follow-through may reduce the risk of back injury because the smaller range of motion of the trunk reduces passive tensions of the lower trunk muscles and lumbar spinal loads.

REFERENCES

Abdel-Aziz, Y.I. and Karara, H.M., 1971, Direct linear transformation from comparator coordinates in object-space coordinates in close range photogrammetry. In *Proceedings of the ASP Symposium of Close-Range Photogrammetry* (Urbana: University of Illinois).

Cholewicki, J., 1993, *Mechanical stability of the in vivo lumbar spine.* Unpublished doctoral dissertation (University of Waterloo).

Cholewicki, J. and McGill, S.M., 1994, EMG assisted optimization: a hybrid approach for estimating muscle forces in an indeterminate biomechanical model. *Journal of Biomechanics*, **27**, pp. 1287-1289.

Hosea, T.M., Gatt, C.J., Galli, K.M., Langrana, N.A. and Zawadsky, J.P., 1990, Biomechanical analysis of the golfer's back. In *Science and Golf: Proceedings of the First World Scientific Congress of Golf*, edited by Cochran (London: E. and F.N. Spon), pp. 43-48.

McGill, S.M., 1992, A myoelectrically based dynamic 3-D model to predict loads on lumbar spine tissues during lateral bending. *Journal of Biomechanics*, **25**, pp. 395-414.

McGill, S.M. and Norman, R.W., 1986, Partitioning of the L4/L5 dynamic moment into disc, ligamentous, and muscular component during lifting. *Spine*, **11**, pp. 666-678.

ACKNOWLEDGEMENT

Supported in part by the UIUC Graduate College Research Grant.

23

Forces on the Lower Back during Rowing Performance in a Single Scull

Christie Munro and Toshimasa Yanai
School of Physical Education, University of Otago,
Dunedin, New Zealand

INTRODUCTION

The rowing technique used for a single scull requires repetitive flexion and extension of the trunk, upper and lower limbs. This technique predisposes the rower to injury to the structures of the lower back. In fact, the lower back has been the most common site of injury and pain for rowers (Motto, 1994; Reid, 1997; Soghikian, 1995). A number of factors have been proposed to explain why back pain has been a common complaint: (1) evolution of the modern style of rowing, which puts more strain on the back (Stallard, 1980), (2) introduction of continuous, high intensity training techniques (Stallard, 1980), (3) increased volume of training, (4) lack of proper supervision during weight training sessions, and (5) the introduction of bigger blades (Hatchet blades) for the oars. It has been speculated that the Hatchet blades increase the load on the lower back, particularly during the beginning of the stroke (Nolte, 1993), which has implications for injury. The purpose of this study was to determine the compressive force developed in the lower back during the rowing performance and compare the magnitudes between the trials with Macon sculling blades and with Hatchet sculling blades.

METHODS

Ten competitive single scull rowers at New Zealand national level participated in this study (mean age 18.8±2.20 years, mean height 1.71±.038m, and mean mass 66±5.97kg). Each rower was asked to perform ten 200m sprint trials at the maximum effort. Hatchet blades were used for five trials and Macon blades were used for the other five trials. A strain gauge was mounted on the shaft of the left oar to measure the magnitude of bending of the shaft, which was used to determine the normal component of the force exerted by the hand. The strain gauge was connected to a portable amplifier and a radio transmitter (Noraxon Telemyo

System, AZ, USA), both of which were carried by the rower. With this arrangement, the amplified data from the strain gauge were transmitted to the receiver device on shore as radio-waves and recorded digitally into the Peak Motus system (Peak Performance Technologies, Denver, CO, USA).

A two-dimensional videography technique was used to determine the position of each body segment of the left-hand side of each rower for one complete cycle of each trial. The video camera was fixed on a tripod on shore and was perpendicular to the movement of the boat. The videotapes of the performance were manually digitized using the Peak Motus System. In each digitized field, body landmarks were digitized. Assuming that the body was laterally symmetrical a 12-segment model of the human body was defined. Two fixed points on the boat were digitized to determine the scaling factor and the proximal and distal ends of the oar handle were digitized to determine the position and the orientation of the oar handle in three-dimensional space. The hand force was determined such that it could generate the magnitude of the normal component for every given instant. It was assumed that the hand force was directed posteriorly along the length of the forearm. The resulting sets of two-dimensional coordinate data were used as input to custom software that generated kinematic data (linear velocity, linear acceleration, angular velocity, angular acceleration), joint resultant forces, and joint resultant torques. Normalized and scaled anthropometric parameters (Clauser *et al.*, 1969; Hinrichs, 1990) were used to define the segmental parameters for each subject. The hip joint resultant torque and hip joint angle were used to determine the compressive force at the L5-S1 level in accordance with the low back model described by Chaffin and Andersson (1991).

In the present study, a "stroke" was defined as the period from the instant at which the blade made the first contact with the water to the instant at which the blade was completely extracted from the water. The stroke was subdivided into three phases (Redgrave, 1990) as shown in Figure 1: (a) the catch began when the tip of the blade made a contact with water at the beginning of the stroke and ended when the blade was completely immersed in the water; (b) the drive phase began when the catch finished and ended when the velocity of the trunk was zero, relative to the boat; and (c) the finish phase began when the drive phase finished and ended when the blade was completely extracted from the water.

For statistical analysis, the following variables were determined: (a) the maximum compressive force recorded in each phase; (b) the average compressive force over each phase. These variables were determined for each trial for each subject. A two-factor analysis of variance was used to test for the effects and the interaction of the blade type and the phase on the magnitude of compressive force. Post-hoc tests were then conducted to identify specific effect of blade type and the phase. The level of significance was set at 0.05.

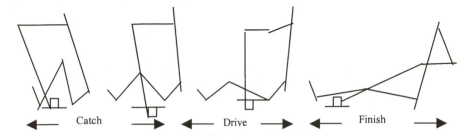

Figure 1 Catch phase, drive phase, and finish phase of the stroke cycle.

RESULTS

The time course of change in the compressive force for the two blades are presented in Figure 2, and the numerical results presented in Table 1. On average, the peak compressive force was developed 50±5.2% and 56±3.7% of the way through the stroke cycle for Hatchet blades and Macon blades.

Table 1 Mean value across the subjects for the peak compressive force [N] and the average compressive force [N].

	Catch	Drive	Finish	Overall
Peak–Macon	2490	5272	3371	5344
Peak–Hatchet	4099	4505	2789	4876
Average–Macon	1998	4039	1177	2396
Average–Hatchet	3142	3771	1267	2763

On average, the peak compressive force was developed, for Hatchet and Macon blades respectively at 96.8±7.6% and 100±0% of the way through the catch phase, at 63.2±22.3% and 69±20.5% of the way through the drive phase, and at 13±6.3% and 10±3% of the way through the finish phase. There was no difference in the peak and average compressive force between the trials with the Hatchet blade and the Macon blade, throughout the duration of the stroke (p>0.847). There was a difference in the peak and average compressive force between the trials with Hatchet blades and Macon blades, between the three phases (p<0.000). There is also a significant interaction effect of blade type and phase (p<0.000). The average compressive force over the catch phase was significantly greater (p<0.000) when the Hatchet blades were used than when Macon blades were used, whereas that over the drive phase was significantly greater (p<0.005) when the Macon blades were used than when the Hatchet blades were used. There was no difference (p>0.415) in the mean value for the average compressive force over the stroke (Macon: 2351N and Hatchet: 2463N).

There was no significant difference in the velocity of the boat (4.72s or 42s for 200m) for trials with Macon blades and Hatchet blades. There were no significant individual differences in boat velocity (Mean = 0.87±0.093).

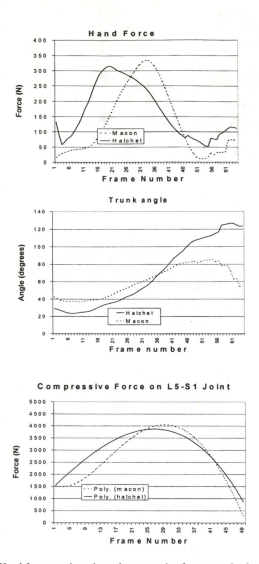

Figure 2 Hand force, trunk angle, and compressive force over the duration of the stroke.

DISCUSSION

There has been a postulation within the rowing community that the use of Hatchet blades may increase the risk of developing low back pain. An attempt was made in this study to determine the effect of blade types (Macon and Hatchet blades) on the compressive force developed in lower back during rowing performance.

The safe level for loads on the lower back, recommended by the National Institute of Safety and Health (NIOSH) is 3700N, which was exceeded in this study (Hatchet blades: 4876N and Macon blades: 5344N). The excessive amount of compressive force developed in rowing may lead to an injury to the structures of the lower back and cause low back pain. The values of the mean peak compressive force and the average value of the mean compressive force obtained in this study were comparable, but higher than the values obtained by Morris *et al.* (1996). The greater force values measured in this study may be due to the differences in the characteristics of the rowers used in each study. In the present study the rowers were of national level and were of a greater stature than those rowers who participated in the study by Morris *et al.* (1996). Morris *et al.* (1996) found the mean value for peak compressive force on the lower back was 4-5 times the bodyweight of the rowers, compared to six times the bodyweight of the rowers as was found in this study.

The results showed that blade type did not cause significant difference in the peak compressive force developed during the stroke cycle. However, the compressive force was increased immediately after the entry of the blade in the trials with Hatchet blades, whereas the increase in compressive force was delayed. This might explain the perception of rowers that there is a greater force on the lower back at the beginning of the stroke when the Hatchet blades are used. However, overall there is no significant difference in the peak and average compressive force throughout the duration of the stroke. This result does not support the guideline given by the Marlowe Rowing Club in England that the use of Hatchet blades may be linked to disc-related lower back problems, and thus there should be restrictions on their use by young rowers.

CONCLUSION

(1) The peak compressive force on the lower back was 4876N and 5344N for trials with Hatchet blades and Macon blades respectively. This degree of force is considered hazardous and may cause injury (NIOSH). (2) There is no difference in peak compressive force between Hatchet and Macon blades ($p > 0.847$). (3) With the Hatchet blades the compressive force increased immediately after the entry of the blade into the water.

REFERENCES

Boland, A.L. and Hosea, T.M., 1994, Injuries in rowing. *Clinical Practice of Sports Injury Prevention and Care*, **5**, pp. 624-632.

Chaffin, D.B. and Andersson, G.B.J., 1984, *Occupational Biomechanics* (New York: Wiley-Interscience Publication).

Clauser, Morris, P.L., Payne, W.R., Smith, R.M., Galloway, M.A. and Wark, J.D., 1996, Mechanical loading and bone mineral density in schoolgirl and lightweight rowers. *Unpublished transcript.*

Motto, S.G., 1994, Mechanical back pain in rowers. *Physiotherapy in Sport*, **19**, pp. 16-17.

Nolte, V., 1993, Do you need hatchets to chop your water? An analysis of big blades and how they work. *American Rowing*, **July/August**, pp. 23-26.

Pelham, T.W., Holt, L.E., Burke, D.G., Carter, A.G.W. and Peach, J.P., 1993, The effect of oar design of scull boat dynamics. In *Proceedings of the XIth Symposium of the International Society of Biomechanics in Sports* (Amherst, MA, USA).

Reid, D., 1997, *Injuries to New Zealand Rowers.*

Soghikian, G.W., 1995, Common injuries and how to treat them. *American Rowing*, **March/April**, pp. 24-43.

Stallard, M.C., 1980, Backache in oarsmen. *British Journal of Sports Medicine*, **14**, pp. 105-108.

ACKNOWLEDGEMENT

The present study was partially funded by Sports Science New Zealand.

Part Seven

Methods and Instrumentation in Sports Biomechanics

24

Instrumentation and Measurement Methods Applied to Biomechanical Analysis and Evaluation of Postural Stability in Shooting Sports

Kostas Gianikellis
Faculty of Sport Sciences, University of Extremadura, Spain

INTRODUCTION

Sport Biomechanics is one of the main fields of Biomechanics of Human Movement in continuous expansion and consolidation in the wide field of Sport Sciences. Nowadays, many applied research projects are orientated to the evaluation of the athletes' technique in the totality of sports and sport modalities. Also, scientific research has contributed to design sport equipment with the highest quality standards. Furthermore the evolution of measurement systems and/or instrumentation chains enables researchers to quantify with much more precision the biomechanical efficiency in sport activities, identifying the main characteristics of the most productive individual technique, the trainable factors that influence on the performance, and, the mechanical loads on the muscle–skeletal system. Finally, the conception and design of technical solutions and aids for the disabled help them to compete improving their quality of life. Methodological advances in Sport Biomechanics (photo-instrumentation techniques, force plates, EMG, modelling and simulation techniques, etc.) allow for reaching a considerable level of scientific knowledge respect to the motor patterns displayed in most sport activities. However, not so much research applied to the analysis and evaluation of sport technique in shooting sports, namely, shooting and archery. Even if more than a hundred medals are shared in the Olympics and Paralympics.

POSTURAL STABILITY

Shooting is a fine, steady and co-ordinated action of many physiological organs, like the visual organs, the proprioceptors, the motor effectors, and systems like the neurogenic, respiratory, cardiovascular, and locomotor system. Unlike most sport activities, target sports like shooting and archery require the elimination of any movement that could perturb the stability of the system shooter–gun/bow (S–G/B), to achieve the best performance on the target. Many trainers, athletes and training books consider postural stability as one of the most important factors that have influence on the performance. In its turn postural stability is the consequence of the interaction of the gravity with the mechanical properties of the locomotor system and the control process during aiming (Figure 1). Elite shooters and archers display high levels of precision. Experimental data proved that motor patterns in shooting sports are characterized by very slow movements with small amplitude where the range of movement is of the order of some mm. Also the posture adopted by athletes is mechanically unstable as consequence of interactions among the body segments (Gianikellis *et al.*, 1999). Therefore some kind of *"fine tuning"* of the movements at different joints is required in order to balance their posture with simultaneous reduction of the degrees of freedom at the joints. As far as it is known the most original scientific endeavour to contribute in improving postural stability in shooting is described in the book *On the centre of gravity of human body as related to the equipment of the German infantry soldier* (Braune and Fischer, 1895). However, up to now, there is no answer to the question *how the vertical posture is maintained and how it is related to voluntary limb movements.* In the research studies on the control of the vertical posture the human body is sometimes modelled as an inverted pendulum (Gurfinkel and Osovets, 1972; Hayes, 1982) that is not easy to equilibrate, especially in the presence of external perturbations (Figure 1). However the problem is much more complex due to the presence of a great number of joints and the direction of body segments oscillations. The *fine tuning* making sure that the projection of the centre of gravity is in the area of support is very close to the concept of *synergy,* defined as a fixed and reproducible interaction of the joints or groups of joints, developed as result of training or innate and organized and controlled by the CNS for effective solution of a specific motor problem. Also, Bernstein established some theoretical bases defining synergy as built-in co-ordinated sequences of motor commands to a number of joints leading to a desired common goal. The presence of synergies could be considered that simplify the control of the vertical posture and of the aiming process, solving (at least partially) the problem of mechanical redundancy. Postural synergies are frequently described as combinations of muscle activation patterns for a given perturbation and modulated by local sensory information.

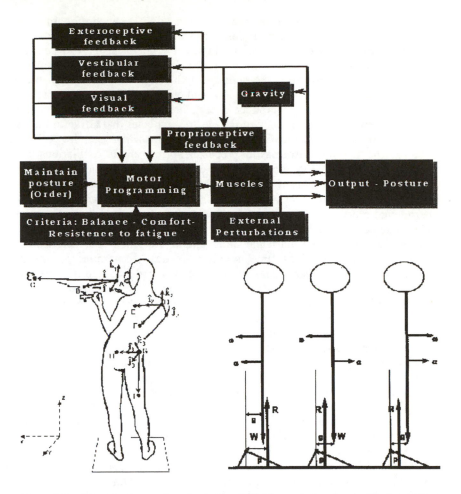

Figure 1 Control mechanisms and mechanical models of the vertical posture in rifle shooting.

Given that the number of degrees of freedom in a motor system is always excessive, control process can be regarded as overcoming the indetermination caused by redundant degrees of freedom (*Bernstein's problem*). For instance, the equilibrium–point hypothesis is an essentially single-joint model and cannot be directly generalized to multi-joint movements like postural synergies. In fact, as has been shown, seemingly different landmark trajectories do not necessarily imply an unsuccessful solution of the aiming problem. The main problem of sport technique in precision sports consists in maintaining the relative orientation of the body segments as stable as possible. On the other hand, shooters and archers try to make their posture more consistent and reproducible reducing the variability in the aiming. They align their eye with the rifle or bow and the target adopting a characteristic posture depending on the modality. In order to avoid or to limit the intervention of muscles that control the involved joints, shooters try to pass all mechanical loads across the passive structures and elements of the locomotor system. In air-rifle shooting, for instance, shooters adopt an uncomfortable posture characterized by a pronounced extension with simultaneous lateral bend and slight twist of the trunk respect to the pelvis (Figure 1). Their capacity to control the quasi-static motor patterns during the aiming has been proved to be fundamental to obtain good results. However, the activity of the involved muscles in order to maintain a desired posture is not continuous and only short duration contractions of the motor units contribute to produce a certain level of muscular tension. It is known that temporal inconsistency of the electric impulses that arrive to the motor units cause considerable fluctuations in the resultant muscular force level. This fact joined to the muscles viscoelastic properties bring about oscillations in the extremities of the S–G/B system and deviations of the aiming line from the target. After all these considerations it is clear that biomechanical analysis of technique, in shooting sports, requires: (1) *valid theoretical model* that is compatible with the experimental process and the system under study, (2) *very precise measurement chain* to obtain feasible information with respect to postural consistency and stability and to evaluate muscular intervention (technical characteristics and performance of electronic instruments will dramatically determine investigations results), (3) *adequate signal treatment techniques* in order to improve the signal–noise relationship and to calculate the time derivatives of the position–time data, (4) *correct parameterization of motor patterns* by means of "instability variables" to detect their influence on the performance, and, (5) *error analysis* that allows for knowing the errors magnitude. Many researchers have set up a variety of instrumentation chains and instruments in order to study shooting technique. Optoelectronic systems based on TV cameras, position-sensitive devices or mechano-optical scanners, photogrammetric techniques, sonic digitizing, accelerometry, ELG, laser beams, LVDT, force plates, EMG, etc., have been used to obtain biomechanical parameters related to performance (Zipp *et al.*, 1978; Nickel, 1981; Niinimaa, 1983; Dal Monte, 1983; Myllyla and Ky, 1986; Gajewski *et al.*, 1986; Gallozi *et al.*, 1986; Leroyer *et al.*, 1988; Iskra *et al.*, 1988; Larue *et al.*, 1989; Mason *et al.*, 1990; Stuart and Atha, 1990; Pekalski, 1990; Zatsiorsky and Aktov, 1990; Squadrone and Rodano, 1994; Gianikellis *et al.*, 1994). However, and in spite of the importance of the postural consistency most biomechanical studies have contributed in obtaining information merely with respect to the kinematics of the rifle or the bow neglecting the importance of postural consistency of the S-G/B system. Also it is worthwhile to mention that there is no relevant information about both the technical characteristics of the measurement systems and the quality of the obtained signals and signals processing. Thus, before making a decision with respect to the acquisition or use of a concrete measurement system for kinematic analysis of technique in precision sports a comparative evaluation of its performance must be done. The evaluation of a system with active or passive markers must be based on a standard test protocol and objective criteria (sampling rate, the resolution, precision, accuracy, linearity, spatio–temporal resolution, maximum amplitude error caused by the time skew in time-multiplexed sampling systems, maximum marker shift for a given aperture time, range of measurement, and calibration procedures).

A METHODOLOGY APPLIED TO THE BIOMECHANICAL ANALYSIS OF POSTURAL STABILITY

Elite shooters and archers display high levels of precision. In air-rifle shooting, for instance, the angular error to obtain a hit of "ten" must be no worse than 0.016° (Zatsiorsky and Aktov, 1990). The same respect to the torsion angle of the bow, from the distance of 30m in archery, should not exceed the value of 0.2° (Pekalski, 1990). These values give an idea of the order of magnitude of movements in shooting sports. As already has been mentioned shooters adopt a posture, characterized by an extension with simultaneous lateral bend and twist of the trunk (coupled joint motion) respect to the pelvic girdle. This mechanically unstable posture is a consequence of the shooters' adjustments to align their eye with the rifle or the bow and the target. These dynamic actions introduce oscillatory rotations of very small amplitude of the S-G/B system's parts. Therefore it is very important, for the analysis of motor patterns in shooting to describe in three dimensions the position and orientation of the body segments from an anatomical point of view, by means of three angles denoting flexion–extension, lateral bending and internal–external rotation.

The Theoretical Model

As far as it is known, several methods have been used to represent 3-D angular joint motion of a segment with respect to a global or local system of reference. This is directly possible, using triaxial ELGoniometry (Chao, 1980), or, indirectly, by means of the helical axis method (Spoor and Veldpaus, 1980), Cardan-Euler angles (Panjabi *et al.*, 1981), Joint Co-ordinate System (Grood and Suntay, 1983), and the attitude vector method (Woltring, 1991, 1992). For the particular case of coupled motions that take place in shooting sports both the attitude vector and the system of Cardan-Euler angles could be useful (Figure 2). However in this study the system of Cardan angles has been selected because rotations with respect to the global system of reference can be anatomically defined. Also, mathematical singularities (gimbal lock) are avoided, and, finally, because rotations are small ($< 10°$) and the established sequence of rotations do not affect the obtained results. In any case, it is possible to standardize this sequence.

It is known that three-dimensional rotations of the S-G/B system's parts with respect to the anatomical reference position are derived from the measured 3-D co-ordinates of three non-collinear markers fixed on every segment between their position registered at two consecutive instants (t_i) and (t_{i+1}). Also, local orthogonal frames are assigned to the segments and then the orientation of each segment with respect to the global system of reference is expressed by means of Cardan angles (Figure 1). The rotation matrix is parameterized in terms of three independent angles resulting from an ordered sequence of rotations with respect to the three axes of the global systems of reference. Thus, if the elements of the constructed orthogonal matrices $[T_{sti}]_{3\times3}$ and $[T_{sti+1}]_{3\times3}$ express the orientation of the local system of reference with respect to the global system of reference, at two consecutive instants, then the rotation matrix $[R_s]_{3\times3} = [T_{sti+1}]_{3\times3} \times [T^T_{sti}]_{3\times3}$ is calculated expressing the rotation of the segment(s) in the time interval $\Delta t = (t_{i+1}-t_i)$ with respect to the axes of the global systems of reference. Finally the Cardan angles are calculated according a standard sequence of rotations following the next steps:

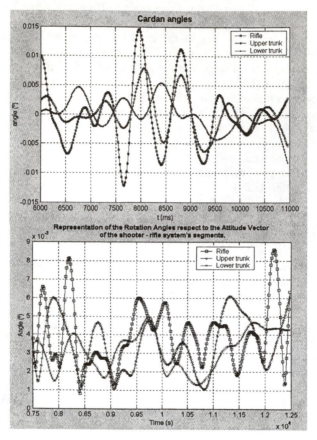

Figure 2 Representation of the Cardan angles and attitude vector of the shooter–rifle system segments.

$$\text{Given that } \left[\mathbf{T}_{st_i}\right]_{3x3} = \begin{vmatrix} \mathbf{i}_{st_ix} & \mathbf{j}_{st_ix} & \mathbf{k}_{st_ix} \\ \mathbf{i}_{st_iy} & \mathbf{j}_{st_iy} & \mathbf{k}_{st_iy} \\ \mathbf{i}_{st_iz} & \mathbf{j}_{st_iz} & \mathbf{k}_{st_iz} \end{vmatrix} \text{ and}$$

$$\left[\mathbf{T}_{st_{+1i}}\right]_{3x3} = \begin{vmatrix} \mathbf{i}_{st_{i+1}x} & \mathbf{j}_{st_{i+1}x} & \mathbf{k}_{st_{i+1}x} \\ \mathbf{i}_{st_{i+1}y} & \mathbf{j}_{st_{i+1}y} & \mathbf{k}_{st_{i+1}y} \\ \mathbf{i}_{st_{i+1}z} & \mathbf{j}_{st_{i+1}z} & \mathbf{k}_{st_{i+1}z} \end{vmatrix}$$

$$\left[\mathbf{R}_s\right]_{3x3} = \left[\mathbf{T}_{st_{i+1}}\right]_{3x3}\left[\mathbf{T}_{st_i}^{\mathbf{T}}\right]_{3x3} =$$

$$\begin{bmatrix} (c\varphi_{sz}c\varphi_{sy}) & (c\varphi_{sz}s\varphi_{sy}s\varphi_{sx}-s\varphi_{sz}c\varphi_{sx}) & (c\varphi_{sz}s\varphi_{sy}c\varphi_{sx}+s\varphi_{sz}s\varphi_{sx}) \\ (s\varphi_{sz}c\varphi_{sy}) & (s\varphi_{sz}s\varphi_{sy}s\varphi_{sx}+c\varphi_{sz}c\varphi_{sx}) & (s\varphi_{sz}s\varphi_{sy}c\varphi_{sx}-c\varphi_{sz}s\varphi_{sx}) \\ (-s\varphi_{sy}) & (c\varphi_{sy}s\varphi_{sx}) & (c\varphi_{sy}c\varphi_{sx}) \end{bmatrix}$$

where

$$\text{sen}\,\varphi_{sy} = -\mathbf{R}_{31}, \quad \text{sen}\,\varphi_{sx} = \frac{\mathbf{R}_{32}}{c\varphi_{sy}}, \quad \text{sen}\,\varphi_{sz} = \frac{\mathbf{R}_{21}}{c\varphi_{sy}}$$

$$\cos\varphi_{sy} = \sqrt{1-\text{sen}^2\varphi_{sy}}, \quad \cos\varphi_{sx} = \frac{\mathbf{R}_{33}}{\cos\varphi_{sy}}, \quad \cos\varphi_{sz} = \frac{\mathbf{R}_{11}}{\cos\varphi_{sy}}$$

In the case that this procedure is taking place to describe coupled motions in shooting sports it is very important to establish conveniently the global system of reference during the calibration procedure. In this way, rotational movements are clinically described. Also the model must be validated because rotational movements are very small and the propagated errors could be harmful for the obtained results. In rifle-shooting, an analysis of errors of the computed values of the Cardan angles, based on simulation procedures, yielded random relative errors ($p < 0.01$) that not exceed 5% of the mean values of the range of the real rotations (Gianikellis *et al.*, 1998).

The Measurement Chain

Even if measurement of the 3-D co-ordinates of a sufficient number of superficial landmarks, defining segments on the S-G/B, is necessary for analysis of postural consistency, shooter's postural stability can be evaluated on the basis of stabilometric measurements, using force plates to record the displacements of the Centre of Pressure on the horizontal plane as an integrator of the postural sway. Centre of Pressure (CoP) is defined as the point of application of the resultant of the external forces applied to the support area and its movements express the neuromuscular answer to the instantaneous position of the Body's Centre of Gravity in order to maintain the equilibrium (Figure3). Even if analysis of stabilometric data assumed random CoP migration recent research findings of prolonged unconstrained standing (PUS) (Duarte and Zatsiorsky, 1999) could justify the opposite idea. These authors considered that when the CoP migration is mapped in the anterior–posterior versus medial–lateral plane, two typical patterns are observed: the *multi-region pattern,* where subjects tend to change the average location of CoP several times during the trial and the *single-region standing.* Also, they maintain that specific and consistent patterns of the CoP migration can be recognized. In this way it is possible to detect fast step-like displacement of the average position of CoP from one region to another (*shifting*), fast large displacement and returning of CoP to approximately the same position (*fidgeting*), and, slow, continuous displacement of the average position of CoP (*drifting*).

Finally, the use of EMG for analysis of the muscular activity in shooting sports poses a very interesting question not only because in all modalities postural stability is the main objective of sport technique, but because in archery an intensive neuromuscular activity is necessary to draw the string and to withstand temporally the "*bow weight*" during the aiming. In that phase known as "*push–pull*" the bow's tension is balanced with the muscular force of the archer (Figure 4). Electromyography also enables the detection of the local muscular fatigue.

Therefore the measurement chain consists of a Sonic Digitizer, a strain-gauge force plate, a microphone sensor to detect the instant of triggering and an EMG system with surface electrodes (Figure 5).

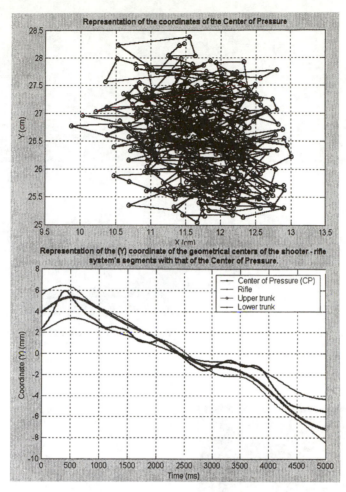

Figure 3 Representation of the CoP trajectory and of its (Y) co-ordinate.

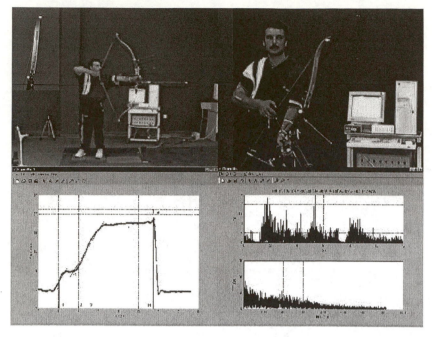

Figure 4 Representation of the bow's tension in the *"push–pul"* and rectified EMG signal with its spectrum.

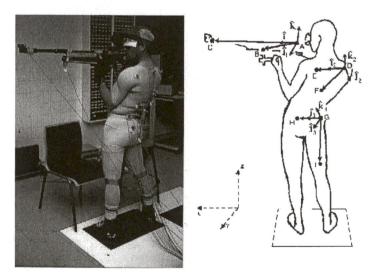

Figure 5 Measurement chain and mechanical model.

Sonic Digitizing consists of converting information with respect to the body landmark co-ordinates to digital values, using the properties of the sound propagation (Engin and Peindl, 1984; Hsiao and Keyserling, 1990; Worringham, 1991; Steffny and Schumpe, 1991; Charteris *et al.*, 1994; Herriots and Barret, 1994; Gianikellis *et al.*, 1994). It is a very efficient solution not only to quantify kinematics of the S-G/B but also to establish an on-line feedback loop providing to shooter information respect to his aiming quality. The sonic digitizer system (SAC, GP8-3D) includes sixteen sequentially activated ultrasound emitters (60kHz) connected to a multiplexer unit that are automatically identified. Four microphones fixed on a rigid frame receive the sonic waves of the sequentially fired emitters. The control unit connected to a PC by means of Parallel Interface Card (PIO12) for high data rate throughput in ASCII packed binary format. The system works counting the time that require the emitted sound waves to reach the microphones. Knowing the speed of the sound in still air, the time is converted in distances of the emitter to the four microphones and later in the 3-D co-ordinates of the emitters. All technical and performance characteristics of the Sonic Digitizer have been exhaustively evaluated according to a standard protocol (Stüssi and Müller, 1990) and the following have been obtained: *sampling rate* of the whole system 66.6Hz for an *active volume* of 1800mm × 1300mm × 1400mm. We have calculated that in rifle–shooting more than a 95% of the periodogram is contained up to 2.5Hz of the spectrum frequency. *Range of measurement* 2625 mm; *accuracy* 0.054 (A_x = .22, A_y = .038 y A_z = .032); *precision of the reconstructed 3-D co-ordinates* of the emitters .115mm (p_x=1:28125, p_y=1:26000, p_z=1:17073); *spatio-temporal resolution* of the system $(70.7Hz)^{1/2}$ mm^{-1}. The calibration is carried out knowing the position of at least three points (emitters) into the working volume to calculate the position of the four microphones by means of an iterative process of optimization (Newton-Raphson) (Gianikellis *et al.*, 1994, 1996). Given that the Sonic Digitizer is a multiplexing system there is a need of a data interpolation algorithm to obtain the co-ordinates at the same instant, and, a "smoothing" process to eliminate part of the contaminating high frequency "noise" before differentiation. Position-time data "smoothing" is carried out by quintic splines using the package "Generalized Cross-Validatory Spline" (Woltring, 1986), according to the "True Predicted Mean-squared Error" criterion (Craven and Wahnba, 1979), given the automatic identification of the markers (w_i = 1) and the known precision of the spatial co-ordinates (σ^2). This subroutine for smoothing and differentiation is based on the natural B-Spline functions. The strain-gauged Force Plate (DINASCAN-Ibv) is synchronized with the Sonic Digitizer. In this way stabilometric analysis, of the system's sway can be carried out. Strain gauges are highly linear sensors and their application to shooting sports measurements is particularly appropriate due to their good behaviour at low frequencies. The sampling rate is up to 1kHz for single force-plate. The precision respect to the position of the (CoP) is 2mm. The EMG system uses surface electrodes (Ag/AgCl) to transmit myoelectrical signals to a differential amplifier (input impedance 100Mohm) of variable gain (10–10000). CMRR is 90dB, and the frequency response 10 to 2000Hz. Data "filtering" is accomplished by "high pass filters" (10 or 100Hz), "low pass filter" (300, 1000 and 2000Hz) and "notch filter" to filter out the 50Hz power line noise. The resulting EMG signal is recorded and stored for further digital processing in a PC using a 12-bit acquisition card (DI-200/PGH).

The sampling rate of the system is 50kHz allowing the use of 16 channels. The processing of EMG signals and the calculation and graphical representation of all parameters take place in the MATLAB environment where data are exported in ASCII files. The measurement chain that is completed with a detector of the triggering instant makes it to carry out biomechanical analysis of technique in shooting sports. Finally, the methodological approach presented here to analyse sport technique in shooting sports, made possible the development of a system that generates on-line acoustical signals informing performers about the quality of their aiming. In this way, blind people could take up shooting sports once they made up for the lack of visual information by augmented concurrent acoustical feedback guiding them to move the aiming line close to the calibrated centre of the target. Sonic digitizer as measurement system provides information with respect to 3-D position and orientation of the rifle and the distance of the aiming–point to the centre of the calibrated target. The acoustical signal of variable intensity and frequency that is fed back by means of earphones allows the subject to adjust the rifle's position and orientation. The algorithm for calculation of the distance of the aiming line to the centre of the target is based on the definition of a local system of reference fixed on the rifle and the determination of the aiming line as invariant in the local system of reference which is continuously monitoring. This application is very useful for shooting simulation and dry training.

CONCLUSION

The methodology presented here can provide relevant and objective information on the motor patterns in the precision sports by identifying the nature of postural instability and its influence on the performance. Given that scoring is a consequence of the dynamic interactions of the system's parts, the shooter and his trainer have to look for aiming techniques that reduce all undesired oscillations and make possible the stabilization of the body segments.

REFERENCES

Clarys, J.P., Cabri, J., Bollens, E., Sleeckx, R., Taeymans, J., Vermeiren, M., Van Reeth, G. and Voss, G., 1990, Muscular activity of different shooting distances, different release techniques and different performance levels with and without stabilizers in target archery. *Journal of Sports Sciences*, **8**, pp. 235-257.

De Luca, C.J. and Knaflitz, M., 1990, *Surface Electromyography: What's New?* (Boston: Neuromuscular Research Centre).

Duarte, M. and Zatsiorsky, V.M., 1999, Patterns of centre of pressure migration during prolonged unconstrained standing. *Motor Control*, **3**, pp. 12–27.

Era, P., Konttinen, N., Mehto, P., Saarela, P. and Lyytinen, H., 1995, Postural stability in good and poor trials in rifle-shooting. A study on top level and naive shooters. In *Proceedings of XVth Congress of the International Society of Biomechanics*, edited by Häkkinen, K., Keskinen, K.L., Komi, P.V. and Mero, A. (Jyväskylä Finland), pp. 252-253.

Gallozi, C. *et al.*, 1986, A new method to measure lateral bow accelerations during shooting in archery. In *Biomechanics: Basic and Applied Research.* In *Proceedings of the 5th meeting of the European Society of Biomechanics*, edited by Bergmann, G., Kölbel, R. and Rohlmann, A. (Free University of Berlin), pp. 627-632.

Gianikellis, K., Dura, J.V. and Hoyos, J.V., 1994, A measurement chain applicable in the Biomechanics of shooting sports. In *Proceedings of the XIIth International Symposium on Biomechanics in Sports*, edited by Barabás, A. and Fabián, Gy. (Budapest, Hungary), pp. 266-269.

Gianikellis, K., Dura, J.V. and Hoyos, J.V., 1996, 3-D biomechanical analysis of the motor patterns observed during the 10 m rifle–shooting modality. In *Proceedings of the XIVth International Symposium on Biomechanics in Sports*, edited by Abrantes, J. (Madeira, Portugal), pp. 217-219.

Gianikellis, K., Maynar, M. and Dura, J.V., 1998, A mechanical model for measuring in three dimensions the small amplitude coupled motion that characterizes motor patterns in shooting activities. In *Proceedings of the XVIth International Symposium on Biomechanics in Sports*, edited by Riehle H.J. and Vieten, M.M. (Konstanz, Germany), pp. 330-333.

Iskra, L., Gajewski, J. and Wit, A., 1988, Spectral analysis of shooter-gun system. In *Biomechanics XI-B*, edited by de Groot, G., Holander, A.P., Huijing, P.A. and Ingen Schenau, G.J. (The Netherlands: Amsterdam Free University Press), pp. 913-919.

Larue, J., Bard, C., Otis, L. and Fleury, M., 1989, Stabilité en tir: influence de l'expertise en biathlon et en tir à la carabine. *Canadian Journal of Sport Sciences*, **14**, 1, pp. 38-45.

Leroyer, P., Van Hoecke, J. and Helal, J.N., 1993, Biomechanical study of the final push–pull in archery. *Journal of Sports Sciences*, **11**, pp. 63-69.

Mason, B.R., Cowan, L.F. and Gonczol, T., 1990, Factors affecting accuracy in pistol shooting. *Excel*, **6**(4), pp. 2-6.

Mason, B.R. and Pelgrim, P.P., 1990, Body stability and performance in archery. *Excel*, **3**(2), pp. 17-20.

Nishizono, H. *et al.*, 1987, Analysis of archery shooting techniques by means of electromyography. In *Proceedings of 5th Symposium of the International Society of Biomechanics in Sports*, edited by Tsarouchas, L., Terauds, J., Gowitzke, B.A. and Holt, L.E. (Athens), pp. 364-372.

Squadrone, R. and Rodano, R., 1994, Multifactorial analysis of shooting archery. In *Proceedings of the XIIth International Symposium on Biomechanics in Sports*, edited by Barabás, A. and Fabián, Gy. (Budapest, Hungary), pp. 270-273.

Squadrone, R., Rodano, R. and Gallozi, C., 1994, Fatigue effects on shooting archery performance. In *Proceedings of the XIIth International Symposium on Biomechanics in Sports*, edited by Barabás, A. and Fabián, Gy. (Budapest, Hungary), pp. 274–277.

Stuart, J. and Atha, J., 1990, Postural consistency in skilled archers. *Journal of Sports Sciences*, **8**, pp. 223-234.

Zatsiorsky, V.M. and Aktov, A.V., 1990, Biomechanics of highly precise movements: the aiming process in Air Rifle shooting. *Journal of Biomechanics*, **23**, supplementary I, pp. 35-41.

25

A Numerical Study of Magnus Force on a Spinning Soccer Ball

Takeshi Asai, Masahiro Masubuchi[1], Hiroyuki Nunome[2],
Takao Akatsuka[3] and Yoshiharu Ohshima[4]
Faculty of Education, Yamagata University, Japan
[1]Fluent Asia Pacific Co., Ltd, Shinjyuku, Tokyo, Japan
[2]Research Centre of Health, Physical Fitness and Sports,
Nagoya University, Nagoya, Japan
[3]Faculty of Engineering, Yamagata University,
Yonezawa, Japan
[4]Faculty of Education, Hirosaki University,
Hirosaki, Japan

INTRODUCTION

Today, many researchers are studying the aerodynamic force on balls used in sports (Briggs, 1959; Mehta *et al.*, 1983; Mehta, 1985; Watts and Bahill, 1990). We focused on determining the aerodynamic characteristics of a ball in a ball game. Lateral deflection in flight (otherwise known as curve, swing, or swerve) is well recognized in many sports. The curve is obtained by spinning the ball about an axis perpendicular to the line of flight, which gives rise to what is commonly known as the Magnus effect. However, there are few studies on the curve ball in soccer (Asai *et al.*, 1998a). Curve ball kicking is one of the most common techniques used today. The purpose of this study is to clarify the Magnus force on a curve ball in soccer using computational fluid dynamic analysis.

Figure 1 The 3–D soccer ball model with seams.

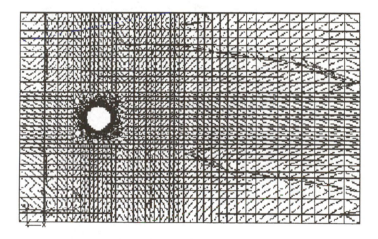

Figure 2 The Cartesian outer boundary of the analysis model.

METHODS

CFD analysis has the potential to clarify the flow characteristics around a soccer ball with seams (grooves). Complex shapes and physics like a soccer ball with seams require sophisticated geometry, meshing tools and physical models.

A 3–D soccer ball model with seams has been defined by a CAD system (MSC/PATRAN, MSC Inc.). The incompressible steady-state analysis was performed using finite volume method based on fully unstructured meshes with features such as hybrid mesh and non-conformal mesh interfaces for "parts-based" meshing using a commercial CFD code (FLUENT5, Fluent Inc.).

The diameter of the ball model was 0.23m. The depth of the seams on the soccer ball model was about 3mm. The cartesian outer boundary is defined as 2m height, 2m width and 3.25m length (Figure 2). The wedge mesh was described near the surface of the ball model, and approximately 200,000 tetrahedral cells were used to describe the solution volume that consisted of the ball model and the cartesian outer boundary (Figure 3). The spin wall (surface of the ball) was defined by the moving wall technique. Error minimization is the key to high-quality results, and this meshing technique is one of the most effective ways to minimize errors.

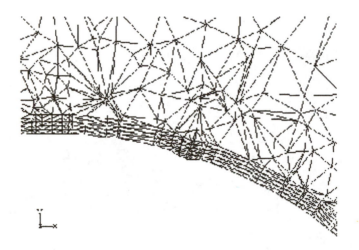

Figure 3 The wedge mesh near the surface of the ball model.

The calculations used the Renormalization Group (RNG) based on the k–εturbulent flow model. The RNG k–εturbulent flow model used in this study is based on the work of Yakhot and Orszag (1986). The RNG model equations look similar to the Standard k–εturbulent flow model equations. However, the constants in the RNG model equations assume slightly different values. Most importantly, the εequation in the RNG model has a source term, which is not in the standard k–εturbulent model. The initial velocity of the inlet boundary was 25 m/s and the exit boundary was defined by static pressure. In the early experimental study (Asai *et al.*, 1998b), the revolution ratio (spin ratio) of the curve ball in soccer was approximately from 6r/s to 10r/s. The spin ratio in this simulation was then defined for 5 cases from 30rad/s to 70 rad/s at intervals of 10rad/s.

RESULTS AND DISCUSSION

The static pressure contour on the lower surface of a soccer ball with seams (grooves) is shown in Figure 4. The air flow was defined from left to right at 25m/s. The spin of the ball was defined as 50rad/s, counter clockwise, about a horizontal axis at a right angle to the flow. The pressure near the seam was slightly higher than that of the other surfaces. It seems that this dip affects the boundary layer on the surface of the ball. In general, the addition of surface roughness reduces the aerodynamic drag coefficient and the critical Reynolds number. It is suspected that the seams on the surface of the soccer ball work similar to the dimples on a golf ball.

The contours of the velocity magnitude around the ball for the same case are shown in Figure 5. The separation points of the boundary layer were asymmetric. The effect of spin is to delay separation on the retreating side and to enhance it on the advancing side. So it produces the Magnus effect.

The aerodynamic lift coefficient increased as the spin ratio (revolution ratio) was increased at 25m/s in this simulation (Figure 6). In an experiment using a baseball, the lateral deflection is directly proportional to the spin rate (Briggs, 1959). In this study, it appears that the lateral force due to the Magnus effect is directly dependent on the spin ratio.

The aerodynamic lift coefficient decreased as the Reynolds number increased at 50rad/s in this simulation (Figure 7). Bearman and Harvey (1976) indicated that the aerodynamic lift coefficient of a golf ball increased as the spin parameter (v/U) increased (Equation 1).

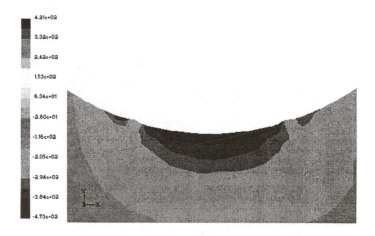

Figure 4 The contour of static pressure on the lower surface of a soccer ball with seams (grooves).

$$v \, / \, U = (r \times \omega) \, / \, U \tag{1}$$

where, v is the peripheral velocity (spin), U is the flow velocity, r is the radius of the ball, ω is the angular velocity of the ball.

In this study, the horizontal axis in Figure 7 indicated the Reynolds number (not the spin parameter), it is considered that these data have the same tendency as the data generated by Bearman and Harvey.

In the case of the spin ratio defined as 50rad/s and the ball velocity defined as 25m/s, the Magnus force on the ball was estimated to be 3.05N (Table 1). Therefore, the deflection of the ball trajectory in this case is about 3.4m sideways within 1 second.

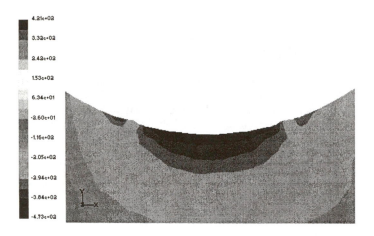

Figure 5 The contours of the velocity magnitude around the ball.

Table 1 Ball velocity, Magnus force and lift coefficient.

Ball velocity (m/s)	10	15	20	25	30	35
Magnus force (N)	0.64	1.38	2.26	3.05	4.08	5.20
Lift coefficient	0.26	0.24	0.22	0.19	0.18	0.17

(Spin ratio : 50 rad/s)

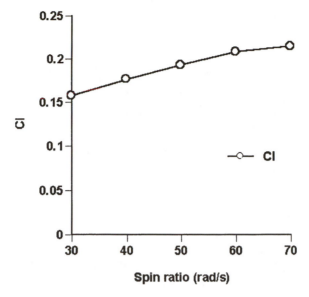

Figure 6 The relationship of the aerodynamic lift coefficient to the spin ratio.

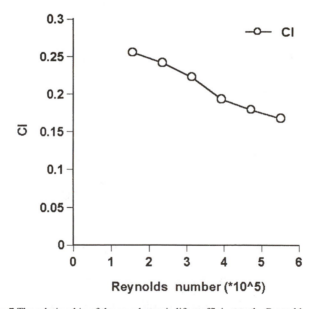

Figure 7 The relationship of the aerodynamic lift coefficient to the Reynolds number.

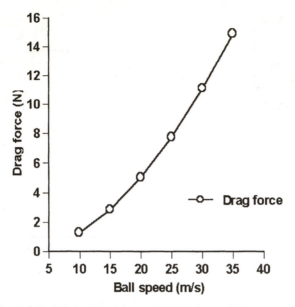

Figure 8 The relationship of the aerodynamic drag coefficient to the ball speed.

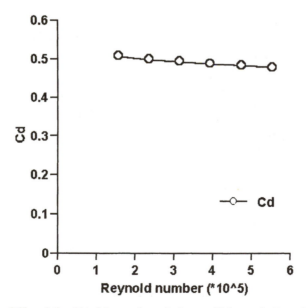

Figure 9 The relationship of the aerodynamic drag coefficient to the Reynolds number.

The aerodynamic drag force increased as the ball speed was increased at 50rad/s in this simulation (Figure 8). Moreover, the aerodynamic drag coefficient slightly decreased as the Reynolds number was increased at 50rad/s in this simulation (Figure 9).

Bearman and Harvey (1976) reported on the aerodynamic drag coefficient and the critical Reynolds number on a golf ball. As the computer simulation in this study used only the RNG k–εturbulent flow model, this simulation could not calculate the laminar flow and transition from the laminar flow to turbulent flow in boundary layers. Then, it is important to verify the critical Reynolds number on a soccer ball for further work.

CONCLUSION

The aerodynamic lift coefficient increased as the spin ratio (revolution ratio) was increased at 25m/s in this simulation. The aerodynamic lift coefficient decreased as the Reynolds number was increased at 50rad/s in this simulation. In the case of the spin ratio defined as 50rad/s and the ball velocity defined as 25m/s, the Magnus force on the ball was estimated to be 3.05N.

This study used the steady-state analysis on CFD. This technique is only useful when the side force is constant during flight. The real curve ball is more dynamic and complex. Hence, a more sophisticated computer model and transient analysis method are necessary for the accurate analysis of the curve ball trajectory in soccer.

REFERENCES

Asai, T., Akatsuka, T. and Haake, S.J., 1998a, Physics of football, *Physics World*, **Vol. 11-16**, pp. 25-27.

Asai, T., Akatsuka, T., Nasako, M. and Murakami, O., 1998b, Computer simulation of curve-ball kicking in soccer, *The Engineering of Sport*, edited by Haake, S.J. (Blackwell Science), pp. 433-440.

Bearman, P.W. and Harvey J.K., 1976, Golf ball aerodynamics. *Aeronaut. Q.* **27**, pp. 112-122.

Briggs, L.J., 1959, Effect of spin and speed on the lateral deflection (curve) of a baseball; and the Magnus effect for smooth spheres. *American Journal of Physics*, **27**, pp. 589-596.

Mehta, R.D., 1985, Aerodynamics of sports balls, *Annual Review of Fluid Mechanics*, **17**, pp. 89-151.

Mehta, R.D., Bentley, K., Proudlove, M. and Varty, P., 1983, Factors affecting cricket ball swing. *Nature*, Vol. 303-330, pp. 787-788.

Watts, R.G. and Bahill, T.A., 1990, *Keep your Eye on the Ball: the Science and Folklore of Baseball* (New York: W.H. Freeman and Company).

Yakhot, V. and Orszag, S.A., 1986, Renormalization group analysis of turbulence I basic theory. *Journal on Scientific Computing*, **1**, pp. 1-51.

26

Power in Rowing

Valery Kleshnev
Australian Institute of Sport, Canberra, Australia

INTRODUCTION

Measurements of an athlete's power in rowing are commonly used as the main tool for identification of the athlete's energy production and technique efficiency. The traditional method of rower's power (P) calculation consists of multiplying the momentum applied to the oar handle M by angular velocity of the oar rotation ω or handle force F by linear velocity v of the point of force application (e.g. Fukunaga *et al.*, 1986; Dal-Monte and Komor, 1989; Zatsiorsky and Yakunin, 1991):

$$P(t) = M(t) * \omega(t) = F(t) * R * \alpha(t) / dt = F(t) * v(t) \tag{1}$$

where R is the length of inboard oar radius between the gate pin and the point of force application. There are other modifications of this method when force was measured at the gate and handle moment was derived using inboard/outboard ratio (e.g. Staniak *et al.*, 1994).

Although this method is applicable to the stationary devices (rowing tanks, pools, stationary ergometers), it cannot be used in real on-water rowing because the reference point of the system (gate pin) moves with acceleration together with the boat shell and Newton laws are not applicable in this system.

Another method of rower's power calculation was introduced using power output at the oar blade (Kleshnev, 1997). It gave 11.2% higher power values in comparison with traditional methods, but it was developed on the special rowing simulator.

An interesting point is the power production of the body segments that can be used for identification of rowing styles and connected with strength and conditioning of the rowers. A number of studies consider transfer of internal energy between segments (e.g. Sanderson and Martindale, 1986), but only a few of them derived mechanical power of body segments (Kleshnev, 1995).

The purpose of this study is to introduce valid methods of the rowing power calculation and to give some example values of the total and body segments power in rowers' groups.

METHODS

The measurements were undertaken during on-water rowing in competitive singles, pairs and doubles using a radio telemetry system. Boat shell acceleration along horizontal axis was measured using a piezoresistive accelerometer. An electromagnetic sensor (Nielsen-Kellerman Co.) measured boat velocity.

The angle between oar and boat in a horizontal plane (α on Figure 1a) was measured using a servo potentiometer. Two forces applied to the oarlock were measured using instrumented gate: a perpendicular (*Fgp*) and an axial one (*Fga*) to the oar shaft. The perpendicular handle force (*Fhp*) was derived using *Fgp*, inboard and outboard length of the oar. The force applied to the footstretcher along the boat axis (*Ff*) was measured using special construction with strain gauges. Linear velocities of the seat (*Vseat*) and top of the trunk (*Vtrunk*) were measured using low stretchable fishing line and potentiometer devices (Figure 1b). The joint of *Sternum* and *Clavicle* was used as the point of top of the trunk. Linear velocity of the handle was calculated using angular velocity and the inboard radius of the oar.

The total number of 88 elite athletes took part in the measurements (Table 1). Every crew performed a set of the four–six test trials per one minute each with unlimited recovery time. The stroke rate increased in each trial on 4min^{-1} and was in a range of 16–40min^{-1} for the whole sample.

Table 1 Parameters of the rower's groups (mean± STD).

	Men sweep	Men scull	Women sweep	Women scull
N	28	20	24	16
Height (m)	1.91±0.06	1.88±0.05	1.80±0.03	1.76±0.07
Body mass (kg)	85.6±9.0	83.7±8.9	73.9±3.4	67.3±8.7

The data was collected and stored in a PC and then processed using special software. Typical patterns of biomechanical parameters of athlete's cyclic movements were produced. Then the patterns of derived parameters and the average patterns of the crew were calculated and used for analysis.

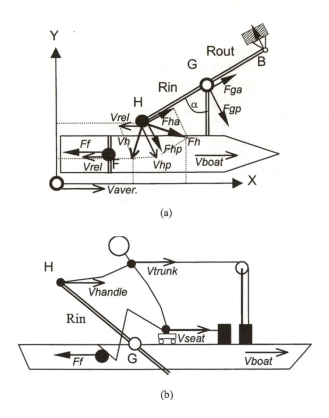

Figure 1 The simplified 2–D models of the oar–boat system in horizontal (a) and vertical (b) plane.

RESULTS AND DISCUSSION

Method of the Power Calculation

The rower's body was assumed as a rigid one. A 2–D coordinate system was chosen in the horizontal plane with the reference point that moves in parallel to the boat course at constant velocity equal to the average boat speed. The x-axis was directed parallel to the boat axis.

The rower applies power at two points only: at the oar handle (H) and at the footstretcher (F). The resulting handle force (Fh) was calculated as a vector product of the perpendicular (Fhp) and axial (Fha) forces. The resulting handle velocity was calculated as a vector product of the handle velocity perpendicular to the oar shaft (Vhp) and relative boat velocity ($Vrel$). The instantaneous handle power (Ph) was derived as a scalar product of Fh and Vh.

$$Ph = Fh * Vh * \cos(\varphi) \tag{2}$$

where φ is the angle between *Fh* and *Vh* vectors. Another method of *Ph* calculation could be used which is simpler in practice and gives the same results. It consists of deriving projections of forces and velocities vectors on axis x and y and of calculation of products of sums

$$Ph = Ph_x + Ph_y = (Php_x + Pha_x) * (Vh_x + Vrel) + (Php_y + Pha_y) * Vh_y \tag{3}$$

The footstretcher power (Pf) was calculated as a scalar product of the footstretcher force (*Ff*) and *Vrel*.

$$Pf = Ff * Vrel \tag{4}$$

The total power exerted by a rower into an external environment was derived as a sum of *Ph* and *Pf*:

$$P = Ph + Pf \tag{5}$$

The segments powers were derived as scalar products of corresponding force and velocity:

$$Plegs = Ff * Vseat \tag{6}$$

$$Ptrunk = Fhp * (Vtrunk - Vseat) \tag{7}$$

$$Parms = Fhp * (Vhp - Vtrunk) \tag{8}$$

Work done (*W*) and average power (*Pav.*) were derived using standard equations:

$$W = \int P(t)\, dt \tag{9}$$

$$Pav. = W / t \tag{10}$$

Power Patterns and Values

The difference between rowing power calculated using old and new methods could be explained by footstretcher power applied at the beginning of the drive phase (Figure 2a and 2c). On average the new method gave 16.8±7.0% higher power values and the difference did not depend on the boat type, rower's gender or stroke rate.

The patterns of the instantaneous powers of the body segments (Figure 2b and 2d) show examples of the rowing styles with sequential (upper row) and simultaneous segments work. The first one could be related to Rosenberg style (Klavora, 1976) and the second one to DDR style.

In the whole sample 47.2±4.1% of the total power applied to the footstretcher and 52.8±4.1% applied to the oar handle (Table 2). Sweep rowers applied more power at the footstretcher (48.5±3.8%) than scullers (45.2±3.8%, p < 0.01) and correspondingly less power at the handle. There was no difference in these parameters between male and female rowers.

Table 2 Footstretcher and handle shares in rowing power (mean± STD).

	Men sweep	Men scull	Women sweep	Women scull	All rowers
Footstretcher power (%)	48.9±3.5%	45.9±3.9%	48.2±4.1%	44.3±3.5%	47.2±4.1%
Handle power (%)	51.1±3.5%	54.1±3.9%	51.8±4.1%	55.7±3.5%	52.8±4.1%

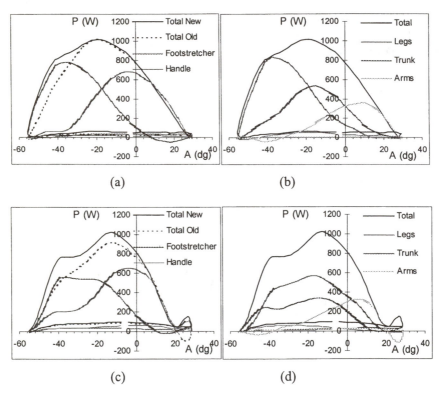

(a)   (b)

(c)   (d)

Figure 2 The typical patterns of the instantaneous powers applied by the rower at the handle and footstretcher (left column) and the segments powers (right). The *x*–axis is the oar angle relative to the boat perpendicular.

No significant differences were found in the segments shares between rowers' groups (Table 3) except male scullers that had lower trunk power share and higher arms power.

Table 3 Shares of body segments in rowing power (mean± STD).

	Men sweep	Men scull	Women sweep	Women scull	All rowers
Legs share (W)	45.4±4.5%	44.8±4.0%	45.7±6.4%	44.9±3.5%	45.2±4.9%
Trunk share (W)	32.5±5.9%	29.3±3.8%	33.5±6.8%	33.4±4.3%	32.2±5.8%
Arms share (W)	22.1±6.4%	25.9±3.8%	20.8±6.1%	21.7±4.6%	22.6±5.8%

In contradiction with previous studies (Dal-Monte and Komor, 1989) it was found that linear trend was the best approximation of power–rate dependence (Figure 3). Determination coefficient between predicted and actual data (R^2) was in the range 0.71–0.82.

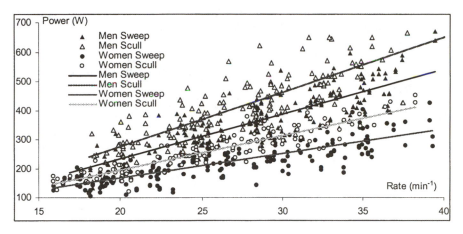

Figure 3 Dependence of rowing power on stroke rate in the rowers groups.

The equations of linear regression of rowing power (y) on stroke rate (x) had the following values in the different rowers' groups:

Men Sweep: $\qquad y = 15.3633\,x - 73.5170$ $\qquad\qquad$ (11)

Men Scull $\qquad y = 18.6887\,x - 98.6895$ $\qquad\qquad$ (12)

Women Sweep $\qquad y = 8.4722\,x - 2.6322$ $\qquad\qquad$ (13)

Women Scull: $\qquad y = 11.9570\,x - 45.1272$ $\qquad\qquad$ (14)

CONCLUSIONS

Calculation of the power during on-water rowing using handle force and oar angle cannot be valid due to non-stationary boat movement. It is necessary to take into account footstretcher force and boat velocity. The new method gives on average 16.8% higher rowing power.

Only around 53% of total rowing power was applied at the oar handle and the other 47% was applied at the footstretcher.

The main power in rowing executes by legs (around 45%); smaller power executes by trunk (~32%); the lowest power produces by arms (~23%).

REFERENCES

Dal-Monte, A. and Komor, A., 1989, Rowing and sculling mechanics. In *Biomechanics of Sport*, edited by Vaughan, C.L. (Boca Raton, Fla.: CRC Press), pp. 53-119.

Fukunaga, T., Matsuo, A., Yamamoto, K. and Asami, T., 1986, Mechanical efficiency in rowing. *European Journal of Applied Physiology and Occupational Physiology*, **55**, pp. 471-475.

Klavora, P., 1976, *Three Predominant Styles: the Adam style; the DDR style; the Rosenberg style* (Ottawa: Catch), **9**, p. 13

Kleshnev, V., 1995, *Relationship of total work performance with part performance of main body segments during rowing ergometry* (Annual Meeting of American College of Sport Medicine).

Kleshnev, V., 1997, The determination of total power during on-water rowing. In *XVI Congress of ISB* (Tokyo).

Sanderson, B. and Martindale, W., 1986, Towards optimizing rowing technique. *Medicine and Science in Sports and Exercise*, **18**, pp. 454-468.

Staniak, Z., Nosarzewski, Z. and Karpilowski, B., 1994, Computerized measuring set for rowing ergometry. *Warsaw: Biology of Sport*, **11**, pp. 271-282

Zatsiorsky, V.M. and Yakunin, N., 1991, Mechanics and biomechanics of rowing: a review. *International Journal of Sport Biomechanics*, **7**, pp. 229-281.

27

Symmetry of In-shoe Plantar Pressure during Running

Moshe Ayalon and David Ben-Sira
The Zinman College of Physical Education and Sport Sciences,
Wingate, Israel

INTRODUCTION

Running is an integral part of the physical activity habits of many people. Various studies suggest that injuries of the lower extremities may be a consequence of high ground reaction force and pressure overload at different locations on the underside of the foot (Winter *et al.*, 1992; Hennig and Milani, 1995; Beck, 1998). Despite an increased focus on the prevention of running injuries, injuries resulting from overuse are still rather frequent. It is important therefore, to identify the cause of the injury and treat the cause, not merely the symptoms. When injuries caused by overuse of the lower limbs are diagnosed in athletes, the structure and function of the foot should be examined. Many running injuries are manifestations of dysfunction of the kinetic chain especially among those patients with recurrent injuries. One of the suggested causes of such injuries is an asymmetric distribution of the external loads between the right and left lower extremities (Herzog *et al.*, 1989). Therefore, it is important to identify asymmetry during the stance phase, and to locate extreme forces or pressure imbalances.

A number of studies investigated the degree of symmetry during walking and running. Hamill *et al.* (1984), concluded that a high degree of symmetry in ground reaction forces exists between the preferred and non-preferred limb in running and walking. Herzog *et al.* (1989) found a deviation of less than 4% from zero in the mean symmetry index (SI) for the vertical ground reaction force (GRF). Bennell *et al.* (1999) reported a deviation of less than 6% from zero in the mean SI for all GRF parameters.

In-shoe plantar measurements have been used in numerous studies (Cavanagh *et al.*, 1992). No reference was found in the literature relating to the bilateral symmetry of plantar pressure in different areas of the foot across running velocities. The purpose of this study was two-fold: (1) to assess the influence of running velocity on the SI of plantar pressure at different areas of the foot and on the maximal vertical force, (2) to assess whether or not the SI of the maximal force can represent overall symmetry during contact in running.

METHODS

Eleven females (mean age = 24.8±1.3yrs, mean height = 167.5±4.7cm, mean weight = 60.2±6.7kg) and nine males (mean age = 25.3±1.5yrs, mean height = 176.4±8.2cm, mean weight = 71.1±4.6kg) volunteered to participate in this study. All subjects were physical education students. Only individuals with no history of lower extremity injuries were admitted into this study. PEDAR insoles (99 sensors each) were inserted into the left and right shoes. The insole size was individually adjusted to the participants' personal running footwear. The system was calibrated in accordance with the manufacturer's instructions. The sampling rate was 50Hz. The subjects ran on a treadmill at 8 and 14km/hr. The order of running velocities was randomized. After a warm up each subject ran at least 30 seconds before data were collected. This procedure enabled familiarization with the treadmill's velocity. Four right and left foot contacts were sampled at each running velocity. Three sets of sensors were defined to represent three area of the foot: six sensors under the centre of the heel, nine sensors under the centre of the forefoot and three sensors under the hallux. For each area the mean pressure was calculated and the peak value during the foot contact was selected for further analysis. In addition, maximal force (MF) was defined as the greatest force exerted on the insole at one instant during the step based on all 99 sensors.

Symmetry of all dependent variables was quantified using the symmetry index (SI) proposed by Robinson *et al.* (1987):

$$SI = (XR-XL) / [0.5(XR+XL)] * 100$$

where XR and XL are the dependent variable of the right and left foot, respectively. Four SI indices were calculated at each of the two velocities: heel, forefoot, hallux and MF Mean SI values were tested in relation to the null hypothesis of perfect symmetry (SI=0) by means of a t-test ($\alpha \leq 0.05$). Each area was tested for gender and velocity effects using a two way ANOVA with repeated measures ($\alpha \leq 0.05$). Bi-variate correlation coefficients were computed between all pairs of SI indices with α set as ≤ 0.01. The higher level for rejection of the null hypothesis for the correlation coefficients was adopted because of the large number (28) of hypotheses.

RESULTS

All mean plantar pressure values were higher while running at 14km/hr than at 8km/hr (39% at the heel, 24% at the forefoot, 23% at the hallux and 18% for MF) with marginal bilateral or gender differences. Descriptive statistics of the SI are presented in Table 1. The only mean that was significantly different from zero was that of the forefoot at 14 km/h (t_{19}=-2.76, p<0.05). A similar trend was also observed with regard to the SI of the forefoot at 8 km/h (t_{19}=-1.86, 0.05<p<0.10).

There were no significant gender or velocity effects with regard to the SI at any of the areas. Out of the 60 foot-pressure SIs (20 for each area), less than 10% difference between velocities was observed in 70% of the cases. In only 13% of cases the difference exceeded 15%. Frequency distributions of the magnitudes of the SIs are presented in Table 2.

Table 1 Descriptive statistics of symmetry indices.

Area	Velocity (km/hr)	Mean (%)	S.D (%)
Heel	8	2.2	16.9
	14	7.2	18.6
Forefoot	8	-5.0	12.0
	14	-6.9	11.2
Hallux	8	4.8	27.0
	14	8.9	25.1
Max. force	8	2.0	7.1
	14	1.5	8.2

Table 2 Frequency distribution of the symmetry index (n=20).

		Heel		Forefoot		Hallux		Max. force	
Velocity (km/hr)		8	14	8	14	8	14	8	14
	< 10 %	8	10	9	9	6	8	15	17
SI	10 % –15 %	6	1	4	5	4	2	5	2
	15 % –20 %	1	4	5	5	0	1		
	20% <	5	5	2	1	10	9		1

Bi-variate correlation coefficients between the all SIs of foot pressure reveal significant relationships between the two velocities at each of the areas (heel: r = 0.82, forefoot: r = 0.84, hallux: r = 0.86). There was a significant correlation (r = 0.71) between the SIs of the hallux and the forefoot at 8km/hr but not at 14km/hr. All other coefficients were in the low to moderate range and statistically insignificant. The correlation between MF and the three plantar pressure areas ranged between 0.12 and 0.39 except for a single higher correlation of 0.55 between the maximal force and forefoot at 8km/hr.

DISCUSSION

The SI that represents jogging and running paces is quite stable across the two velocities, as reflected by the high inter-velocity correlation for each area. The difference between velocities in mean SI did not exceed 5% (heel) and was as small as 0.5% for the MF. Moreover, most subjects did not exceed a difference in

SI of 10% between the two velocities. Only a small number of cases showed a substantial change in personal SIs as a result of increased velocity. The relative stability in symmetry is maintained in spite of a substantial increase in mean foot pressure and MF at the higher velocity. This characteristic of the SI suggests that it is not a velocity specific index and that increased velocity does not increase the risks attributed to the magnitude of asymmetry.

The lack of significant relationships between the SIs of the different areas of the foot (except for the hallux and forefoot at the slower velocity) supports the idea of area specificity of the SIs. The implication is that relative symmetry cannot be generalized for the whole foot. Subjects with low levels of SI in one area can exhibit different levels of symmetry in other areas of the foot and vice versa. This phenomenon may be explained by the different functions of each area during the stance phase (Hennig and Milani, 1995). Differences in the profiles of plantar pressure symmetry may be a consequence of between or within subject variability in parameters such as foot structure (Cavanagh *et al.*, 1997), shoe type (Hennig and Milani, 1995) and other anthropometric and neuromuscular factors (Vagenas and Hoshizaki, 1988). The low correlation between SI values of each of the plantar pressure areas and MF indicate that the latter is not a valid representative index of symmetry in local plantar pressure. No structural or functional explanation could be found for the exception of significant relationship between SIs of the forefoot and the hallux at the lower velocity. Because this relationship did not appear at the higher velocity it is assumed that this observation is an artifact. The results of area specificity in conjunction with the low relationships between the SI of the MF and those of the three areas suggest that using the SI based on MF may misrepresent specific foot pressure symmetry. This is a sound conclusion from a biomechanical point of view as well because the peak foot-pressure at the three sections of the foot takes place at different phases of the stance. None of these phases correspond to the temporal occurrence of the MF.

Most of the means of SI were not statistically different from zero. This trend is consistent with observations made by Herzog *et al.* (1989) and Bennel *et al.* (1999) for parameters of ground reaction forces namely that there is no lateral preference in the sampled subjects. The exception in the current study with regard to mean forefoot SI may well be a sample specific observation. The magnitude of this SI (−6.9%) only marginally deviates from the upper value for mean SI of 6.1% observed by Bennel *et al.* (1999).

There is a substantial difference between areas in SI variability. Herzog *et al.* (1989) documented different magnitudes of variability to different indices of ground reaction parameters during walking. The MF has the lowest variability with 80% of the subjects below a SI of 10%. The highest variability in SI was observed in the hallux with almost 50% of the subjects having SI greater than 20%. Blanc *et al.* (1999) reported similar observations with regard to temporal parameters of the foot roll-over during gait. The underlying mechanism of this result is not clear. It can be hypothesized that the hallux will be influenced by bilateral differences in foot orientation more than the forefoot and the heel. Full explanation of the differences in SI variability will require an integration of foot pressure data with kinematic and kinetic analysis.

CONCLUSION

SI indices are area specific but are not velocity specific. The implication is that symmetry should be evaluated separately for each area and that MF cannot reflect specific area symmetry. A general standard of symmetry cannot be assumed because of inter-area differences in variability. Therefore, individual SIs should be evaluated in relation to their specific measure of variability (sd).

REFERENCES

Bennell, K., Crossley, K., Wrigley, T. and Nitschke, J., 1999, Test–retest reliability of selected ground reaction force parameters and their symmetry during running. *Journal of Applied Biomechanics*, **15**, pp. 330-336.

Blanc, Y., Balmer, C., Landis, T. and Vingerhoets, F., 1999, Temporal parameters and patterns of the foot roll over during walking: normative data for healthy adults. *Gait and Posture*, **10**, pp. 97-108.

Cavanagh, P.R., Hewitt, F.G. and Perry, J.E., 1992, In-shoe plantar pressure measurement: a review. *The Foot*, **2**, pp. 185-193.

Cavanagh, P.R., Morag, E., Boulton, A.J.M., Young, M.J., Deffner, K.T. and Pammer, S.E., 1997, The relationship of static foot structure to dynamic foot function. *Journal of Biomechanics*, **30**(3), pp. 243-250.

Hamill, J., Bates, B.T. and Knutzen, K.M., 1984, Ground reaction force symmetry during walking and running. *Research Quarterly for Exercise and Sport*, **55**(3), pp. 289-293.

Hennig, E.M. and Milani, T.L., 1995, In-shoe pressure distribution for running in various types of footwear. *Journal of Applied Biomechanics*, **11**, pp. 299-310.

Herzog, W., Nigg, B.M., Read, L.J. and Olsson, E., 1989, Asymmetries in ground reaction force patterns in normal human gait. *Medicine and Science in Sports and Exercise*, **21**(1), pp. 110-114.

Robinson, R.O., Herzog, W. and Nigg, B.M., 1987, Use of force platform variables to quantify the effects of chiropractic manipulation on gait symmetry. *Journal of Manipulative Physiological Therapeutics*, **10**, pp. 172-176.

Vagenas, G. and Hoshizaki, B., 1988, Evaluation of rearfoot asymmetries in running with worn and new running shoes. *International Journal of Sport Biomechanics*, **4**, pp. 220-230.

Winter, D.A. and Bishop, P.J., 1992, Lower extremity injury: Biomechanical factors associated with chronic injury to the lower extremity. *Sports Medicine*, **14**(3), pp. 149-156.

28

Effect of Force Platform Surface on Ground Reaction Peak Force

Rosemary Dyson and Lee Janaway[1]
Faculty of Sciences, University College Chichester,
Chichester, West Sussex, UK
[1]Brunel Institute for Bioengineering, Brunel University,
Uxbridge, UK

INTRODUCTION

Force platforms are often used to assess the ground reaction forces occurring in sports performance. The top plate struck by the foot is usually constructed of metal. Although training shoes are often worn, there are many athletic and field sports which require the use of spiked shoes. To measure ground reaction force in athletic and field situations it is necessary to have a surface covering which allows the subject to use normal sports footwear. Knowledge of the effect of using an ecological surface cover upon primary ground reaction force measures is necessary to aid scientific experimental analysis. Although static electromechanical tests are used to assess force platform measurement performance, there is a role for dynamic ecological measurement studies (Nigg, 1990). The concept of population preferred cadence and associated speed (Murray *et al.*, 1966) was an underlying concept of the proposed study and was adopted in an effort to improve the reproducibility of ecological testing. However, in the experimental design it was also recognized that adoption of preferred cadence may result in individual preferred speeds which arise because of anthropometry and environmental factors. This study aimed to investigate the effect on peak ground reaction force measures of covering a force platform, mounted within a polyflex track, with a polyflex sports surface (International Amateur Athletic Federation standard) using an aluminium base plate interface. It was hypothesized that there would be no difference in the peak ground reaction force measures when the specially constructed polyflex cover was used in comparison to a metal top plate.

METHODS

Testing took place outdoors in fine weather on a 25m long polyflex track surface. Two 0.6m by 0.4m Kistler type 9851B piezoelectric force platforms (Kistler, Alton, UK) were located within a section of the track. A specially designed force platform mounting rig allowed the position of the force platforms to be moved relative to each other to account for the different stride lengths associated with individual gait characteristics and sports activities. The ability to adjust the platforms' positions to meet the needs of the individual subjects in this study allowed the ground reaction forces occurring during left and right foot strike to be measured within the same stride. During data acquisition the two force platforms were covered by either a polyflex surface cover, which consisted of a 0.017m polyflex layer upon a 0.004m aluminium sheet, or a 0.020m aluminium plate. The polyflex cover was exactly level with the track surface and was constructed at the time of the track. The aluminium plate was also machined to fit level within the track. The covers were fixed to the top of the Kistler force platforms with four M10 screws. Both types of platform cover were physically isolated from the surrounding track by a gap of approximately 0.003m.

The experimental design required the subjects to run and walk along the track at their own preferred running and walking speeds, within their natural stride pattern. During running and walking, ground reaction force measures were compared within each subject when the force platforms were covered with either the polyflex cover or aluminium plate cover. The ability to allow both the right and left foot strike, during the same stride, to be measured provided a check of the integrity of the data. In total, each subject was required to perform until five natural strides were recorded for both types of platform cover. For both running and walking this allowed five left and right foot strikes recorded with the polyflex cover to be compared to five strides recorded with the aluminium plate cover. Five male college students of mass 71.4±40.6kg (mean±S.D.) wearing their own training shoes gave informed consent to participate in the study. During a warm up and practice period each subject's stride length at preferred running and walking speed was visually assessed. Whether a subject performed the running or walking testing first was randomized. The approach speed to and through the measurement area was recorded by an infrared light multiple gate timing system (University College Chichester, Chichester, UK), which utilized 3m gate separations and detectors located at hip level. As a check for data integrity of platform strike a video camcorder was focused on each force platform mounting area 1m from the side of the track.

Ground reaction forces were sampled at 500Hz for each platform and stored using a 12 bit Amplicon analogue to digital converter (Amplicon, Brighton, UK) and Orthodata Provec software (MIE Medical Research Ltd., Leeds, UK) running on a Viglen 486 IBM compatible computer (Viglen, Alperton, UK). The acquired 3sec data sample was then printed and recorded from the computer screen trace data using cursor measurement to locate peak forces. For running the vertical peak impact, propulsive forces and peak braking force were compared. For walking the vertical landing and propulsion peak forces and peak braking force were compared for the two types of force platform cover. All peak forces were then expressed relative to each subject's body weight (BW), and standard errors calculated from

the standard deviation divided by the square root of the number of samples. Data was analysed using an analysis of variance model with two fixed factors (polyflex/ metal cover and first/second platform) and two random factors (variation between subjects and variation between five repeat trials by a subject). Significant differences were identified when $p<0.05$.

RESULTS AND DISCUSSION

As shown in Table 1, the approach speeds were very similar when both the polyflex and aluminium surfaces were under test. Table 2 indicated that when all subjects were considered there was no significant difference between the running speeds during the polyflex cover and aluminium plate cover tests.

Table 1 Preferred mean running and walking speeds (mean±s.e.) of the five subjects.

Subject	Running speed (ms^{-1})		Walking speed (ms^{-1})	
	Polyflex	Aluminium	Polyflex	Aluminium
1	3.669±0.013	3.693±0.02	1.450±0.009	1.443±0.003
2	3.717±0.22	3.724±0.021	1.734±0.007	1.742±0.012
3	3.772±0.040	3.809±0.078	1.371±0.017	1.333±0.017
4	4.749±0.035	4.703±0.014	1.967±0.018	1.945±0.013
5	3.499±0.035	3.568±0.365	1.518±0.015	1.539±0.003

Table 2 indicated that for all subjects during running, the mean peak vertical forces were almost the same when the two different surfaces were used; this was supported by comparison of the individual subject data shown in Table 3. However, for all the heel strike runners, greater mean peak braking force was achieved on the polyflex surface, though this was not statistically significant. The mean peak vertical propulsion achieved from the first and second platform in the same stride were similar and not significantly different ($p=0.984$) for polyflex (2.623BW and 2.619BW, respectively) and for aluminium (2.604BW and 2.610BW). There was also no significant difference in peak measures between the polyflex and aluminium covers ($p=0.826$). Overall the data suggests that for running activity the use of the polyflex surface cover with a 0.004m aluminium base plate did not appear to influence the measurement of peak vertical ground reaction force.

Table 2 Mean peak preferred running forces (±s.e.) for the left and right foot strike in the same stride expressed relative to body weight for all subjects.

	Vertical impact BW	Vertical propulsion BW	Braking BW	Speed (ms^{-1})
Polyflex	2.021±0.068	2.620±0.033	0.531±0.025	3.887±0.091
Aluminium	1.987±0.066	2.607±0.031	0.506±0.017	3.900±0.085
P value	0.354	0.388	0.072	0.598
Degrees of freedom	49	49	49	24

Table 3 Mean peak preferred vertical running forces (±s.e.) for the left and right foot strikes in the same stride for the five subjects.

Subject	Polyflex		Aluminium	
	Vertical impact BW	Vertical propulsion BW	Vertical impact BW	Vertical propulsion BW
1	2.380±0.046	2.903±0.028	2.253±0.030	2.832±0.016
2	1.621±0.036	2.508±0.029	1.653±0.019	2.525±0.037
3	1.617±0.069	2.290±0.017	1.515±0.044	2.264±0.024
4	2.652±0.105	2.759±0.046	2.673±0.053	2.736±0.032
5	1.851±0.090	2.642±0.018	1.842±0.117	2.678±0.026

For all subjects at the beginning of the foot contact in walking (Table 4) the mean peak vertical landing force and braking force were similar, and not significantly different, when the two different surfaces were used. This was supported by the individual subject data (Tables 5 and 6). Table 4 indicated that during walking greater mean peak propulsion was achieved from the polyflex surface than from the aluminium surface. This might have arisen because of reduced subject motivation during attention to the walking task, or it may have been associated with differences in the shoe sole and surface interface between the subjects as it was most notable in subjects 4 and 5. This effect was not observed in running which suggests that a motivational influence may have been involved. There was not a significant difference between the first and second platform measures ($p=0.356$).

Table 4 Mean preferred walking peak forces (±s.e.) for the left and right foot strike in the same stride for all subjects.

	Vertical landing BW	Vertical propulsion BW	Braking BW	Speed (ms^{-1})
Polyflex	1.255±0.024	1.187±0.012	0.265±0.009	1.619±0.046
Aluminium	1.255±0.024	1.166±0.012	0.271±0.010	1.611±0.045
P value	0.980	<0.001	0.409	0.871
Degrees of freedom	48	48	48	23

Table 5 Mean preferred walking peak forces (±s.e.) for the left and right foot strike in the same stride for five subjects.

Subject	Polyflex		Aluminium	
	Vertical landing BW	Vertical propulsion BW	Landing BW	Propulsion BW
1	1.183±0.009	1.218±0.012	1.166±0.007	1.218±0.008
2	1.156±0.007	1.308±0.012	1.180±0.008	1.282±0.015
3	1.150±0.013	1.093±0.009	1.153±0.028	1.087±0.006
4	1.564±0.025	1.148±0.017	1.564±0.023	1.107±0.012
5	1.212±0.009	1.159±0.006	1.201±0.009	1.129±0.007

Table 6 Mean peak braking forces (±s.e.) in a stride for each subject.

Subject	Running		Walking	
	Polyflex BW	Aluminium BW	Polyflex BW	Aluminium BW
1	0.452±0.010	0.434±0.015	0.220±0.006	0.205±0.006
2	0.397±0.006	0.407±0.003	0.223±0.003	0.260±0.003
3	0.459±0.019	0.451±0.013	0.236±0.010	0.230±0.014
4	0.820±0.064	0.705±0.024	0.372±0.017	0.380±0.015
5	0.527±0.019	0.534±0.020	0.270±0.005	0.273±0.006

CONCLUSION

In running the 0.017m of polyflex on the 0.004m aluminium base plate did not significantly attenuate peak vertical forces or braking force. Further testing of this type should involve a greater number of subjects wearing the same shoe type, and give consideration to using only running speed.

REFERENCES

Murray, M.P., Kory, R.C., Clarkson, B.H. and Sepic, J.B., 1966, Comparison of free and fast walking patterns in normal men. *American Journal of Physical Medicine*, **45**, p. 8.

Nigg, B.M., 1990, The validity and relevance of tests used for the assessment of sports surfaces. *Medicine and Science in Sports and Exercise,* **22**, pp. 131-139.

Part Eight

Biomechanics of Training

29

Task Specific Coordination of Leg Muscles during Cycling

Li Li and Graham Caldwell[1]
Department of Kinesiology, Louisiana State University, USA
[1]Department of Exercise Science, University of Massachusetts, USA

INTRODUCTION

The biomechanics of the cycling motion has been studied for decades by numerous researchers (see Gregor *et al.*, 1991, for review). Most of these studies have assumed that lower extremity motion is restricted to the sagittal plane with a fixed hip joint position for seated cycling (Hull and Jorge, 1985; Neptune and Hull, 1995). Both strain gauge and piezoelectric load washers have been used in instrumented pedals to measure pedal forces and moments (Hull and Davis, 1981; Broker and Gregor, 1990). The progress in force pedal design has greatly enhanced the mechanical analysis of cycling, permitting the estimation of joint forces, joint moments and joint powers (Redfield and Hull, 1986; Broker and Gregor, 1994). Electromyography (EMG) studies of cycling have demonstrated the degree of co-contraction of the muscles controlling the knee joint, and have shown the importance of two-joint muscles (Gregor *et al.*, 1985; Jorge and Hull, 1986; Ryan and Gregor, 1992; van Ingen Schenau, 1989). In order to study the contribution of specific muscle groups and their coordination, musculo-skeletal models have been used. For example, Hull and Hawkins (1990) studied muscle stretch/shorten cycles, while Yoshihuku and Herzog (1990) studied the relation between pedalling frequencies and maximum power output. The ongoing development of research methodologies and understanding of basic cycling motion provides us a good base to study cycling under different task constraints.

The most common changing task constraints in cycling competition are alterations in posture (seated, standing), grade (level, uphill, downhill), and pedalling frequency. Several studies have explored the biomechanics of uphill cycling in which standing posture is used often. Stone and Hull (1993) examined both pedal and handlebar forces in uphill standing cycling on an inclined treadmill for three subjects, and Alvarez and Vinyolas (1996) reported exemplar pedal force profiles from an instrumented bicycle in an actual hill climbing trial. The adaptation to different cycling cadences has generated more interest among researchers. Bolourchi and Hull (1985) reported that pedalling cadence had a significant effect on the measured pedal reaction forces. As cadence increased, the normal load decreased during the power phase (down-stroke) and increased during the recovery phase (up-stroke). However, cadence had no effect on temporal aspects of the load profiles, as peak pedal load was found between 90° and 110° of crank angle at all pedalling frequencies. Redfield and Hull (1984) reported that the peak hip extensor moment decreased from approximately 60Nm to 10Nm as the cadence increased from 63 to 100rpm. In contrast to the pedal force profiles, the peak knee flexor moments increased as cadence decreased, causing a shift in the transition from extensor to flexor knee moment to earlier in the down-stroke. Further, the relationship between cadence and lower extremity neuromuscular activity in cyclists has been investigated using surface EMG (Marsh and Martin, 1995; Neptune *et al.*, 1997). With increasing cadence, changes were observed in both magnitude and pattern of lower extremity EMG activity.

RESEARCH METHODS

In addition to the aforementioned studies, our research group has also investigated these task constraints during cycling. In general, we used sagittal plane kinematics, an instrumented force pedal, inverse dynamics modelling and electromyography to study cycling on the level versus uphill, seated versus standing, and at different cadences. Detailed descriptions of our methods can be found in Caldwell *et al.* (1998, 1999), Li and Caldwell (1998, 1999), and Li (1999).

In all studies, subjects rode on bikes mounted to a computerized Velodyne ergometer that provided controlled internal resistance to simulate cycling at different intensities and grades. To simulate uphill cycling, the Velodyne platform was tilted at 8% to provide the grade change. For the posture/grade study, data were collected in three different conditions: level seated (LS), uphill seated (US) and uphill standing (ST). For the cadence study, data were collected at high (HC, 95rpm) and low (LC, 65rpm) cadences.

Surface EMG data were collected at 1000Hz from selected lower extremity muscles, including gluteus maximus (GM), rectus femoris (RF), biceps femoris (BF), vastus lateralis (VL), gastrocnemius (GC) and tibialis anterior (TA). Raw EMG data were converted to linear envelopes by rectification and smoothing (zero-lag, low-pass digital filter). EMG activity differences were quantified by peak magnitude, integration, burst identification (onset and offset) and cross-correlation. Lower extremity kinematics and pedal force data were collected simultaneously. Sagittal plane inverse dynamics analysis was performed with a rigid link model of the thigh, leg and foot. Ankle, knee and hip joint moments and powers were calculated and compared across conditions.

RESULTS

Uphill Cycling with Different Posture—Kinetics

In this study, crank and lower extremity kinetics were investigated in three cycling conditions: level seated (LS), uphill seated (US) and uphill standing (ST). Eight national calibre cyclists were studied while riding their own bicycles mounted to the Velodyne at a power output of approximately 295W. The crank torque profiles were similar between level and uphill seated conditions. However, crank torque in the uphill standing condition was significantly altered from the seated trials (Figure 1). The higher and later occurrence of the peak crank torque was linked to changes in pedal orientation and pedal force vector direction throughout the crank cycle, and was associated with upward and forward movement of the rider's

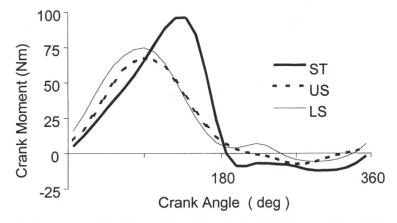

Figure 1 Crank moment profiles during cycling with level and uphill (8%) seated (LS and US) and uphill standing (ST) trials (Caldwell *et al.*, 1998).

centre of mass as the pelvis came off the saddle. Consequently, it was hypothesized that joint moments in the uphill standing condition would be altered in both magnitude and pattern. Overall, the joint moments were similar in the two seated conditions, with a modest increase in magnitude for US (Figure 2). The patterns for the hip displayed the most similarity across conditions. The hip moment profiles were predominately extensor, with a brief, low magnitude flexor burst at the end of recovery from 270° to top-dead-centre (TDC). The knee moment patterns were similar for the two seated conditions, with an extensor period that began near 270° before TDC, continued through the initial portion of the down-stroke until roughly 90°, followed by a flexor period from 90° to 270°. The uphill standing condition demonstrated   an   extended   bimodal   knee   extensor   phase,   with

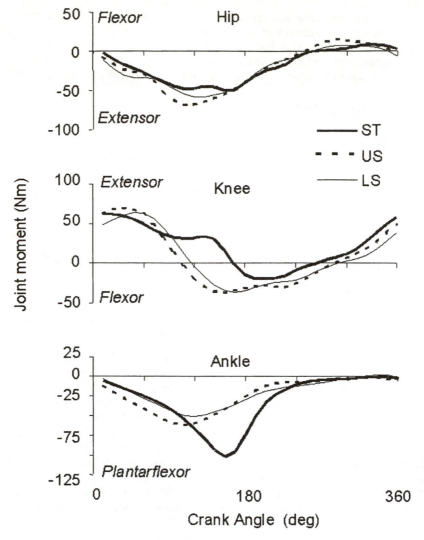

Figure 2 Joint moment profiles during cycling at level and uphill seated, and also uphill standing conditions (Caldwell *et al.*, 1999).

the extensor activity prolonged until near bottom-dead-centre (BDC). Because of this extended extensor period, the flexor period was more restricted, from 180° to 270° in ST. The ankle moment profiles for all conditions illustrated exclusively plantarflexor torque throughout the crank cycle, with the highest values after 90° in the latter part of the down-stroke. For the two seated conditions, the profiles had similar shapes but the peak moment was significantly higher in US. For the uphill standing condition (ST) the peak moment was much higher in magnitude and occurred much later in the down-stroke portion of the crank cycle. These moment changes in the standing condition can be explained by a combination of more forward hip and knee positions, increased magnitude of pedal force, and an altered pedal force vector direction. The data support the notion of an altered contribution of both muscular and non-muscular sources to the applied pedal force. In the next section we describe muscular coordination associated with postural and grade modifications.

Uphill Cycling with Different Posture—Muscular Activities

Recreational and club-level cyclists were tested under similar conditions as in the previous study: pedalling on a level surface (seated, LS), 8% up-hill (seated, US) and 8% up-hill (standing, ST), with a workrate of 250W (Li and Caldwell, 1998). High-speed video was taken in conjunction with surface EMG of six lower extremity muscles (GM, BF, RF, VL, GC and TA). Of these muscles, only GM and TA displayed significant differences in peak EMG between conditions (Figure 3). The peak EMG of GM in ST was nearly 50% higher than in LS and US conditions. To examine coordination among these muscles, important variables of interest are the starting (SMA) and ending (EMA) angles of the muscle activity bursts (Figure 4). Overall, Figure 3 and 4 illustrate that the two seated conditions (LS, US) had similar muscle activity patterns that differed from the standing uphill condition (ST). The muscle activity of GM started just before TDC for all conditions. However, the EMG of GM in ST displayed a longer duration, with activity well into late down-stroke (to approximately 160°). RF, which is both a hip flexor and knee extensor, also was active for a longer duration in ST. This increased duration had two components, as the muscle activity started earlier before TDC and continued later into the power stroke. The single joint knee extensor VL also displayed a greater duration of muscle activity in ST, even though the differences in SMA and EMA were not significant between conditions. The remaining three muscles, BF, GC and TA, had similar onset times and burst duration in the three conditions. The fact that three muscles had consistent patterns across conditions while three others showed altered ST profiles is indicative of a change in muscular coordination during the standing condition. The change of cycling grade from 0 to 8% did not induce a significant change in neuromuscular coordination. However, a postural change from seated to standing pedalling at 8% up-hill grade was accompanied by altered muscular activity of hip and knee extensors. The mono-articular extensor muscles (GM, VL) demonstrated the greatest change in activity patterns related to posture.

Mechanical Model of Pedalling at Different Cadences

In order to study the effect of inertial properties as influenced by altered pedalling cadence, a simple planar model of thigh motion during cycling (Figure 5) was proposed (Li and Caldwell, 1993). The hip joint torque was divided into three separate components associated with the inertial load (T_I), the gravitational load (T_{mg}) and the 'external' load on the distal end of the thigh (T_E) respectively. The equations governing each of these components are:

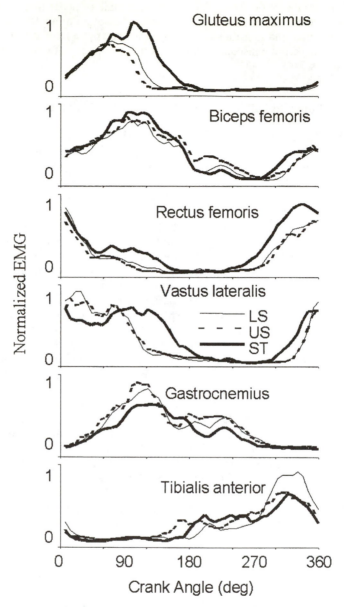

Figure 3 Normalized surface EMG profiles during cycling at three different conditions: level and uphill (8% grade) seated, and uphill standing postures (Li and Caldwell, 1998).

$$T_I = \theta_o I\left(\frac{2\pi}{P_t}\right)^2 \cos\left(\frac{2\Box t}{P_t}\right) \tag{1}$$

$$T_E = T_o \sin\left(\frac{2\pi t}{P_t}\right) \tag{2}$$

$$T_{mg} = -\frac{D}{2} mg\cos(\theta_o \cos\left(\frac{2\pi t}{P_t}\right)) \tag{3}$$

where P_t represents the period of the cycle, T_o represents the maximal external torque, which is assumed constant within a given pedalling revolution, $2*\theta_o$ represents the hip joint range of motion (θ_o is the maximum range in either direction), t is the time during the cycle, with the time at TDC represented by t = nP_t, (n = 0, 1, 2,...), I is the estimated moment of inertia, and D is the length of the segment. The total joint torque is the sum of these components, and is produced by the muscles crossing the hip. The model indicates (Figure 6) that T_{mg} puts additional load on the hip flexors, or reduces the load of hip extensors, throughout the crank cycle. T_I and T_E change in a sinusoidal pattern with 90° phase difference between them. The magnitude of T_I is very sensitive to changes of pedalling frequency (with the coefficient $4\pi^2/P_t^2$). With higher pedalling frequency, the cycle time P_t will be shortened, and the magnitude of T_I will increase dramatically. Since the magnitudes of the other torque components are not directly related to the pedalling cadence, increased pedalling frequency will lead to a larger T_I which, in turn, will lead to a greater hip extension torque, with an earlier occurrence in the crank cycle (toward the peak of T_I). Figure 6b shows the pattern of hip joint moment without the influence of the external component (Moment_No_E), which simulates a greater relative influence of the inertial component. This model predicts that the hip joint extensor moment would be changed by an increase in pedalling frequency. Therefore, the EMG pattern of a single joint hip extensor such as gluteus maximus is predicted to have an earlier appearance with high pedalling cadence, including advanced onset and offset times and an earlier occurrence of the peak EMG value.

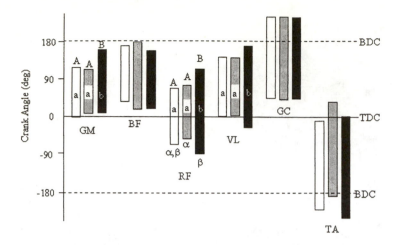

Figure 4 Higher levels of muscular activation displayed as a function of crank position. White, grey and dark bars indicate level seated (LS), uphill seated (US), and uphill standing (ST) conditions, respectively. Symbols α, β, A, B and a, b were employed to indicate homogeneous groups (LSD method with α=0.05) for start, end and duration of activation respectively (Li and Caldwell, 1998).

Different Pedalling Cadences—Muscular Coordination

Li (1999) examined the activity patterns of lower extremity muscles at different pedalling cadences and studied the predictions of the model presented above. The different functional roles of mono- and bi-articular muscles and the influence of the lower extremity inertial properties were investigated during cycling at 65 and 95 rpm. EMG activity of GM, RF, BF, VL, GC and TA was collected to examine neuromuscular coordination. Among the three one-joint muscles examined, GM demonstrated the greatest differences between conditions (Figure 7). The coordination of the mono- and bi-articular antagonist pair at the hip joint, GM and RF, displayed significantly greater change with cadence than the pair at the knee joint, VL and GC (Figure 8). One- and two-joint lower extremity muscles responded to the alteration in cadence differently, which provides insight to understanding their different functional roles. The results supported the hypothesis that the muscular coordination of the hip joint muscles would be affected by pedalling frequency more than knee joint muscles due to the greater inertial influence. This observation was further investigated using inverse dynamics to calculate joint kinetics.

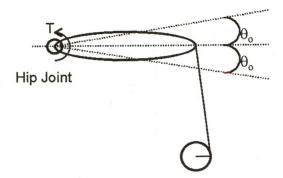

Figure 5 Mechanical model used to study the effect of inertial properties of lower extremity on hip joint moment. T: hip joint moment; θ_0 determine the range of motion at the hip joint (Li and Caldwell, 1993).

$m = 11.29\,kg;\ g = 9.81\,m/s/s;\ P_t = 0.8\,s;\ T_0 = 70\,Nm;\ \theta_0 = 0.3\,rad;\ I = 6.3\,Kgmm$

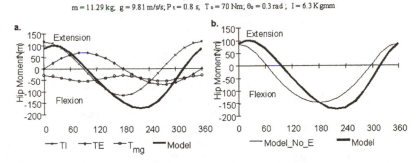

Figure 6 Predicted hip joint moment and its components. a. moment from the model and its three components. b. Moment from the model and Model_No_E is the moment without the contribution of its T_E component (Li and Caldwell, 1993).

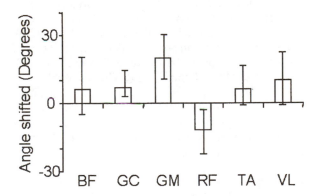

Figure 7 EMG pattern differences identified by cross correlation. GM and GC showed significant forward shifting while RF showed significant backwards shifting with increased pedalling frequency (Li, 1999).

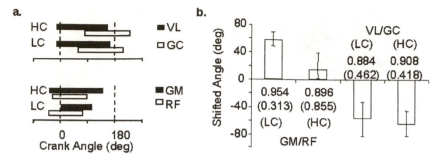

Figure 8 Differential adaptations of muscles adjacent to hip (GM-RF) and to knee (VL-GC) joint with different pedalling cadences. a. analysed by using burst duration; b. analysed by using cross correlation (Li, 1999).

Different Pedalling Cadences—Kinetics

Based on the mechanical model, it was hypothesized that joint moments and powers and their inertial, gravitational, and external components would change with pedalling cadence. Results showed that both the magnitude and patterns of joint moments and powers and their components changed as the pedalling cadence increased from 65 to 95rpm (Figure 9, hip joint moment patterns). As predicted, the relative inertial component contribution increased with pedalling cadence. The proportion of the inertial peak moments relative to the peak total joint moment increased from ≈ 12, 6 and 1% to ≈ 21, 17 and 2% for the hip, knee and ankle joint, respectively. The proportion of peak inertial joint power to peak total joint power increased from 8% to 27% for the hip and from 41% to 82% at the knee joint. The influence of the inertial properties on lower extremity joint kinetics can be seen from the hip joint time histories, where the greatest influence was observed. Figure 10 illustrates the relative proportion of the inertial contribution to the hip joint moment and power for the first half of the crank cycle (TDC to BDC) in both cadence conditions. The inertial component was less than 100% of total in LC for both hip joint moment and power, but increased to more than 300% in the HC condition between 45° and 90° of crank angle. The remarkable contribution of the inertial factor during the first quarter of HC pedalling coincided with decreased pedal force and greater downward acceleration of the lower extremity (Li, 1999). This indicates that during the first portion of the crank cycle in the HC condition, the effort of the hip joint neuromuscular mechanism was concentrated on moving the limb rather than pushing the pedal.

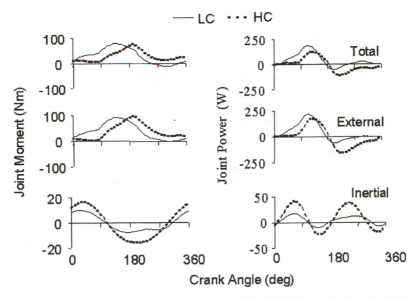

Figure 9 Hip joint moment and its components (external, inertial) during pedalling at low (LC) and high (HC) cadences (Li, 1999).

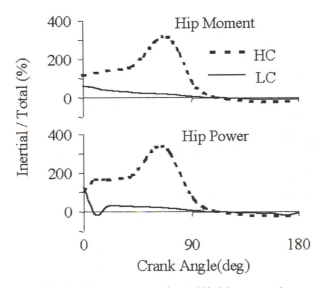

Figure 10 Percentage of the inertial components to the total hip joint moment (upper panel) and power (lower panel), respectively, within the first half of the crank cycle (Li, 1999).

DISCUSSION AND SUMMARY

Our cycling studies on grade, posture and cadence indicate that criterion measures change in a task-specific manner. With postural changes, muscular activities and kinetics display different trends. EMG was modified most at the hip and least at the ankle, whereas the ankle kinetics displayed the greatest changes. In contrast, alterations with cadence for both kinetics and EMG patterns were largest at the hip and least at the ankle. Those differences may be associated with different geometric configurations, which afforded more changes between different postures than different grades or cadences (van Ingen Schenau, 1989). The qualitative and quantitative differences that were observed in these studies could be applied to task specific cycling training.

REFERENCES

Alvarez, G. and Vinyolas, J., 1996, A new bicycle pedal design for on-road measurements of cycling force. *Journal of Applied Biomechanics*, **12**, pp. 130-142.

Bolourchi, F. and Hull, M.L., 1985, Measurement of rider induced loads during simulated bicycling. *International Journal of Sports Biomechanics*, **1**, pp. 308-329.

Broker, J.P. and Gregor, R.J., 1990, A dual piezoelectric force pedal for kinetic analysis of cycling. *International Journal of Sports Biomechanics*, **6**, pp. 394-403.

Broker, J.P. and Gregor, R.J., 1994, Mechanical energy management in cycling: source relations and energy expenditure. *Medicine and Science in Sports and Exercise*, **26**, pp. 64-74.

Caldwell, G.E., Li, L., McCole, S.D. and Hagberg, J.M., 1998, Pedal and crank kinetics in uphill cycling. *Journal of Applied Biomechanics*, **14**, pp. 245-259.

Caldwell, G.E., Hagberg, J.M., McCole, S.D. and Li, L., 1999, Lower extremity joint moments during uphill cycling. *Journal of Applied Biomechanics*, **15**, pp. 166-181.

Gregor, R.J., Broker, J.P. and Ryan, M.M., 1991, The biomechanics of cycling, *Exercise and Sports Sciences Reviews*, **19**, pp. 127-169.

Gregor, R.J., Cavanagh, P.R. and LaFortune, M., 1985, Knee flexor moments during propulsion in cycling: A creative solution to Lombard's paradox. *Journal of Biomechanics*, **18**, pp. 307-316.

Hull, M.L. and Davis, R.R., 1981, Measurement of pedal loading in bicycle: I. Instrumentation. *Journal of Biomechanics*, **14**, pp. 843-855.

Hull, M.L. and Hawkins, D.A., 1990, Analysis of muscular work in multisegment movements: application to cycling. In *Multiple Muscle Systems: Biomechanics and Movement Organization, Spinger-Verlag*, edited by Winters, J.M. and Woo, S.LY.

Hull, M.L. and Jorge, M., 1985, A method for biomechanical analysis of bicycle pedalling. *Journal of Biomechanics*, **18**, pp. 631-644.

Jorge, M. and Hull, M.L., 1986, Analysis of EMG measurements during bicycling pedalling. *Journal of Biomechanics*, **19**, pp. 683-694.

Li, L., 1999, The influence of the inertial properties of the human body: cycling at different pedalling speed (Doctoral dissertation, University of Massachusetts).

Li, L. and Caldwell, G.E., 1993, Effect of inertial loading on muscle activity in cycling, In *Biomechanics in Sports XI*, edited by Hamill, J., Derrick, T.R. and Elliott E.H. (Amherst, University of Massachusetts), pp. 120-125.

Li, L. and Caldwell, G.E., 1998, Muscular coordination in cycling: effect of surface incline and posture. *Journal of Applied Physiology*, **85**, pp. 927-934.

Li, L. and Caldwell, G.E., 1999, Coefficient of cross correlation and the time domain correspondence. *Journal of Electromyography and Kinesiology*, **9**, pp. 385-389.

Marsh, A.P. and Martin, P.E., 1995, The relationship between cadence and lower extremity EMG in cyclists and noncyclists. *Medicine and Science in Sports and Exercise*, **27**, pp. 217-225.

Neptune, R.R. and Hull, M.L., 1995, Accuracy assessment of methods for determining hip movement in seated cycling. *Journal of Biomechanics*, **28**, pp. 423-437.

Neptune, R.R., Kautz, S.A. and Hull, M.L., 1997, The effect of pedalling rate on coordination in cycling. *Journal of Biomechanics*, **30**, pp. 1051-1058.

Redfield, R. and Hull, M.L., 1984, Joint moments and pedalling rates in bicycling. *Biomechanics*, edited by Terauds, J., Barthtels, K., Kreghbaun, E., Mann, R. and Crakes, J. *Sports Mechanics* (New York: Academic Publishers), pp. 247-258.

Redfield, R. and Hull, M.L., 1986, On the relation between joint moments and pedalling rates at constant power in bicycling. *Journal of Biomechanics*, **19**, pp. 317-329.

Ryan, M.M. and Gregor, R.J., 1992, EMG profiles of lower extremity muscles during cycling at constant workload and cadence. *Journal of Electromyography and Kinesiology*, **2**, pp. 69-80.

Stone, C. and Hull, M.L. 1993, Rider/bicycle interaction loads during standing treadmill cycling. *Journal of Applied Biomechanics*, **9**, pp. 527-541.

Van Ingen Schenau, G.J., 1989, From rotation to translation: constraints on multi-joint movements and the unique action of biarticular muscles. *Human Movement Science*, **8**, pp. 301-337.

Yoshihuku, Y. and Herzog, W., 1990, Optimal design parameters of the bicycle-rider system for maximal muscle power output. *Journal of Biomechanics*, **23**, pp. 1069-1079.

30

Rapid Rotations in a "Somersault Simulator"

Juergen Krug, Falk Naundorf, Stefan Reiss and Klaus Knoll[1]
University of Leipzig, Faculty for Sport Science, Germany
[1]Institute for Applied Training Science, Leipzig, Germany

INTRODUCTION

The angular velocity of somersault rotations especially in diving, artistic gymnastics, and trampoline has increased in the last few years. Using own state-of-the-art analyses of the increase in the angular velocity in rapid somersault rotations in gymnastics and diving the highest level of this parameter was found with the 4½ somersaults forwards tucked in diving (approximately 1300 deg/s) and the handspring and double somersaults forwards tucked in gymnastics (approximately 1200 deg/s). This rapid somersault rotation is a high request on the visual control and motor coordination as well as induce load on the vestibular apparatus.

In diving competitions the 4½ somersaults forwards tucked (Figure 1) was seldom performed. Evidently, this dive with high speed rotation is an immense difficulty. In gymnastics many athletes demonstrated the handspring and double somersault forwards tucked on the vaulting horse at the World Championships and Olympic Games in the last few years (Figure 2). Not only the rapid somersault rotation is a high difficulty, but also the visual orientation and the motor control is very complicated in the rapid backward somersault rotation in diving. Additionally, to do an excellent entry into the water or an exact landing in gymnastics, athletes have to adapt to high speed rotations (Gundlach, 1985). Training, we assume, has positive effects on the adaptation of the vestibular apparatus during fast rotations

In the state-of-the-art analyses there are some dives and gymnastic elements with angular velocity higher than 1000 deg/s (Table 1). We identify these movements as a target to test new training methods.

Figure 1 4½ somersaults forwards tucked.

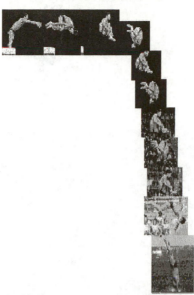

In the scientific literature air-borne human rotational movements represent a complicated problem of theoretical mechanics. Many studies have been presented during in recent years by Yeadon (1990) and Hildebrand (1997) and other authors to gain new knowledge on mechanical principles. In these studies the athlete was considered to be a multi-link system of rigid bodies.

The increase in the angular velocity at somersault rotations in gymnastics and diving in the last years was mainly connected with the question of finding out the increase in angular momentum. Therefore, the biomechanical analyses were directed towards the production of a higher level of angular momentum at the preparatory elements and the takeoff (Miller *et al.*, 1989, 1990; Brüggemann, 1994; Knoll, 1996; Murtaugh and Miller, 1998).

The scientific problem of coordination, especially of the motor control at rapid somersault rotations, was often neglected (Krug and Witt, 1996).

Figure 2 Handspring and double somersaults forwards tucked on the vaulting horse.

Table 1 Diving and gymnastic somersaults tucked with angular velocity higher than 1000 deg/s.

Diving	Gymnastics
Forward 4½ somersaults	Vaulting horse
Back 3½ somersaults	Handspring and double somersaults
	forwards
Reverse 3½ somersaults	Tsukahara with somersault backwards
Inward 3½ somersaults	Floor exercise
Armstand forward triple somersaults	Triple somersaults backwards
Armstand backward triple somersaults	

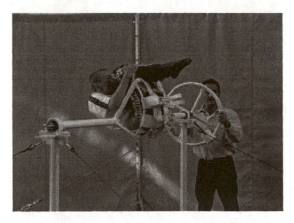

Figure 3 Athlete in the "somersault simulator".

Only in diving coaches discussed the teaching of spotting in back and reverse somersaults (De Mers, 1983a, 1983b). In the laboratory Stangl and Gollhofer (1998) investigated athletes in several kinds of sports concerning the spatial-dynamic precision of the vestibulo-ocular reflex. The athletes were trained to suppress this reflex in all of the three rotational directions. However, the angular velocity in this experiment was relatively slow (100 deg/s). The level of angular velocity at somersault rotations is tenfold higher than in this laboratory study. In order to reach more real conditions of the somersault rotations in the Institute for Applied Training Science a training device ("somersault simulator") was developed. In this study the training effects of rapid air-borne rotations in the "somersault simulator" were investigated. Young divers especially use this training apparatus to get experience of high quantity rotations.

METHODS

The athletes were fastened with the seatbelt of the training device "somersault simulator". With the help of the wheel the coach set in motion the athlete in the "somersault simulator".

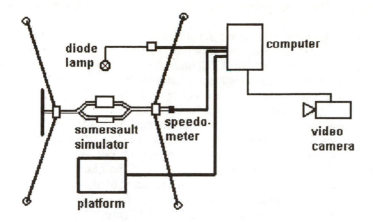

Figure 4 Schematic of the "somersault simulator".

In the training device the athletes were able during the rotation to perform tucked, piked, or stretched positions. On the axle of the training device a speedometer was set up to measure the angular velocity. The number of rotations and the angular acceleration were calculated with the computer. The diode lamp was used to test the visual orientation and perception. The video camera (synchronized with the speedometer) was placed rectangular to the movement plane. The force plate was integrated in this computer-aided measurement system for posturographic tests. This test was used before and after the rotational load. The athletes had to go as quickly as possible to the platform for the post-test. In this paper we focus on following investigations:

- Comparison between the somersault in the simulator and in the competition:

We used the videometric data recording and calculated the angular velocity concerning trunk and head. Additionally, we estimated the load on the vestibular apparatus with the following parameters:

Centrifugal force $\quad\quad\quad F_Z = m * \omega^2 * r \quad\quad\quad$ [N] $\quad\quad\quad$ (1)

Centrifugal acceleration $\quad a_Z = \omega^2 * r \quad\quad\quad\quad$ [deg/s^2] $\quad\quad\quad$ (2)

Coriolis force $\quad\quad\quad\quad F_C = 2 * m * v_r * \omega \quad\quad$ [N] $\quad\quad\quad$ (3)

- Analyses of the visual perception and motor control as well as vestibular load:

(1) In a quasi-experiment six female and male divers (13–15 years old) trained over six weeks in 12 sessions different rotational movements (2×1½; 2×2½; 2×3½ somersaults backwards) with orientation tasks. After the orientation tasks subjects had to perform 15 somersaults backwards. The training effects were analysed with a "One-Group Pretest–Posttest Design" (Campell and Stanley, 1963). For statistical analyses we applied the software package SPSS 8.0 for Windows (Friedman's Test–Non parametric repeated measures comparisons).

(2) We used the force plate (Kistler) for posturographic tests (Figure 4). The operationalization of the balance control was carried out as a function of force measurement. The force components F_x, F_y, F_z and the moment components M_x, M_y were recorded in this investigation. On the basis of these data the centre of pressure (CP) was calculated to operationalise the vestibular load with the parameters a_x and a_y. The equations (Rohrbach, 1967) are:

$$a_x = \frac{-M_y + F_x * a_z}{F_z} \tag{4}$$

$$a_y = \frac{M_x + F_y * a_z}{F_z} \tag{5}$$

where a_z is the space between the measure plane and the platform plane.

These analyses based on a pretest versus posttest design, the vestibular adaptation to angular velocity of 400–700deg/s was studied by means of posturographic methods. All experiments began with a pretest on the platform without any load. After a high quantity (10 or 15 rotations) of tucked passive somersaults in the "somersault simulator" the athlete had to go as quickly as possible to the platform for the post-test.

Subjects of different ages and different performance levels took part in a series of experiments (first experiment with youths: 13–15 years old female and male divers; second experiment with adults: female and male sport students; third experiment with children: 10–11 years old divers).

Different rotational movements (2×1½; 2×2½; 2×3½ somersaults backwards) with an orientation task (to test visual perception) around the transverse axle should be performed. After the orientation task, subjects (Ss) had to perform 15 somersaults backwards. Then the athletes had to go to the platform and remain standing for ten seconds.

In the second experiment 33 sport students had to perform only the second part of the experiment in the somersault simulator (no competition exercise and orientation tasks). They did only the rotational load of ten backward or forward somersaults. The main interest of the experiment was to show the influence of visual control in balance. To test the influence of visual control on balance, Ss were instructed to remain standing for 60 seconds on the platform with open eyes.

After a time interval the students had to do the same rotational load and remain standing on the platform without visual control (closed eyes).

The third experiment was developed to test the adaptation to the rotation load. Over a period about three months Ss had to come twice weekly for training in the somersault simulator. The aim was to examine the adaptation of visual orientation and control of balance over a longer time period. The time of remaining in the standing position was 30 seconds in this experiment.

To analyse the data a special software had to be developed on the basis of object oriented programming using the software HP VEE 5.0. Based on the developed programme the data listing was divided into three periods. A period of landing (only to get the time which athletes need from the somersault simulator to the platform), a period of regulation and the period of stability (Figure 5). To diagnose the period of landing, we use the force-curve of the component F_z. To divide the period of regulation and the period of stability we use the alteration of the component F_z. If the alteration of the component F_z located on the same level as in the pretest the athlete was in the period of stability.

For statistical analysis we used software package SPSS 8.0 for Windows. t–test, the analysis of variance, and correlation analysis have been carried out.

RESULTS AND DISCUSSION

We analysed the rotational load in competitions with two dives. The characteristic parameters are shown in Table 2.

Table 2 Parameters for rotational load in diving.

Dive	Max. angular velocity [deg/s]	Centrifugal force (on the head) [N]	Centrifugal acceleration (on the head) [m/s²]	Coriolis force [N]	Max. acceleration (on the head) [g]
Armstand triple somersaults bw tucked	900	360	90	101	9.2
Back 3½ somersaults tucked	1080	437	109	103	11.1

In the "somersault simulator" the angular velocity was approximately 700 deg/s. This corresponds to dives with 2½ somersaults and double somersaults in gymnastics. The training device is particularly well suited for age-group training. Additionally, the investigation showed the high load on the vestibular apparatus during rapid somersault rotations.

The advantage of the "somersault simulator" is that the athletes train a significantly higher number of rotations in relationship to real training situations. For that reason, the adaptation of the vestibular apparatus can be trained.

The analyses of the visual perception and motor control pointed out interesting facts. Divers use a spotting-technique for visual perception in rapid somersault rotations. This was identified with rhythmical head movements during the somersault. The characteristics are:

First, the head is moved before spotting in direction of rotation.

After that, the head is counter-rotated to the trunk for spotting.

In the experiment with the young divers we reached the following results:

The training with visual perception of the diode lamp produced significant improvements within the six weeks (p = 0.05). In the training sessions we used a randomized flash (but each time in the same angle) of the diode lamp. At the end of the experiment the recognition rate of the flash was very high. Obviously, in a relatively short interval the visual perception is well trainable in the "somersault simulator". Though, there are differences of the head movement in real somersaults and in the training device. In the "somersault simulator" the head movement was performed with a wider amplitude. It can be assumed that in the training device the athletes performed the somersaults without anxiety. Simultaneous psychological analyses demonstrated the advantage of the "somersault simulator".

In the first experiment there was no significant difference between the components of force (F_x, F_y) in the pre-test (youth divers). The expectation that the oscillation increases significantly from pre-test to post-test was confirmed. The increase of the oscillation was in forward and backward (F_x, a_x) direction higher than in left and right direction (F_y, a_y). The average force data were 6.1N in sagittal plane (F_x) and 4.8N in frontal plane (F_y).

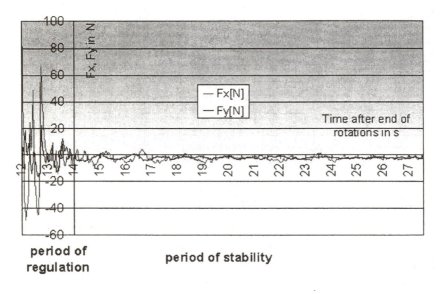

Figure 5 Example of a force-time curve (F_x, F_y) after ten rotations in the simulator.

In the second experiment, we used our own software to analyse the data. We compared the components in the period of regulation and the period of stability (Table 1 and Figure 5). The results were:

- There are significant differences between the data a_x and a_y for the CP in both periods.
- For the force data we had found only differences in the regulation period. These results were equal to the first experiment.

Table 3 Average data for experiment with sport students, N=57, sampling rate 0.02s.

Period	F_x [N]	F_y [N]	a_x [cm]	a_y [cm]
Regulation	15.60	12.10	0.820	0.410
Stability	2.35	2.49	0.064	0.023

To prove the validity of the software the period of stability in pre- and post-test had to be compared. There was no statistical difference between the two data.

For sport students the average time to reach the period of stability was 13, 7 seconds after the end of the rotation load.

If we compare the results of the experiments on the platform with and without visual control (open and closed eyes) we found interesting results (see Table 4):

1. In the period of regulation there was only a significant difference in the duration of this period.
2. The data for the components a_x, a_y, F_x and F_y in the period of regulation showed that there was no difference between the postural sway with and without visual control.
3. Like other authors (Hufschmidt *et al.*, 1980; Straube, 1996), we measured significant differences in the components a_x, a_y and F_x in the period of stability. Visual control had an important function for remaining in the standing position.

We assume that the balance control is strongly disturbed by the rotational load. The influence of visual control is less than the influence of the rotations in the period of regulation.

Table 4 t-test for depended measures (Student experiment with/without visual control).

Period	Component	Eyes open	Eyes closed	t	Sig. (2-tail)	
Regulation	Time interval [s]	2.655	4.386	−2.213	0.036	*
	a_x [cm]	0.862	0.754	1.108	0.278	
	a_y [cm]	0.417	0.397	0.322	0.750	
	F_x [N]	15.436	15.242	0.135	0.893	
	F_y [N]	12.391	11.323	0.567	0.576	
Stability	a_x [cm]	0.047	0.083	−4.906	0.000	*
	a_y [cm]	0.018	0.027	−4.223	0.000	*
	F_x [N]	2.151	2.455	−2.362	0.026	*
	F_y [N]	2.539	2.368	1.168	0.254	

Note: Degrees of freedom = 25
* significant difference ($p < 0.05$)

CONCLUSION

The "somersault simulator" is very helpful for special training sessions to extend the training duration for somersault rotations. The training device is particularly well suited for age-group athletes. The training load of rotational movements can be better organized and evaluated. The computer-aided simulator makes new training methods possible. The improvement of performance in the simulator was transferred into the competition.

Altogether we can report the rotational load had a significant effect on the control of balance. This can be explained by the perceived effort of the vestibular apparatus. A period of regulation of the balance was significantly to differ from a period of stability. But these effects were not measurable over a long period. The higher oscillation in sagittal plane is comparable to the rotation around transversal axis.

There was a first practical test for our system in a competition for the best age-group divers all over Germany. The test of visual orientation and the test of balance control after fast rotational movements were carried out. The results will help the national age-group coaches in their work with the young divers.

REFERENCES

Brüggemann, G.P., 1994, Biomechanics of gymnastic techniques. In *Sport Science Review*, **3**(2), pp. 79-120.

Campell, D.T. and Stanley, J.C., 1963, Experimental and quasi-experimental designs for research on teaching. In *Handbook of research on teaching*, edited by Gage, N.L. (Chicago), pp. 171-246.

De Mers, G.E., 1983, Utilizing visual reference points in springboard diving–1. article. *Swimming World.–Los Angeles*, **24**, pp. 38-41.

De Mers, G.E., 1983, Teaching spotting in back and reverse somersaulting dives– 2. article. Swimming World.–Los Angeles, **24**, pp. 46-48.

Gundlach, H.J., 1985, Posturographische untersuchungen zur differenzierung des quasi-statischen gleichgewichtverhaltens von sportlern verschiedener disziplinen. *Medizin und Sport*, **3**, pp. 69-72.

Hildebrand, F., 1997, *Eine biomechanische Analyse der Drehbewegungen des menschlichen Körpers* (Aachen: Meyer and Meyer).

Hufschmidt, A., Dichgans, J., Mauritz, K.H. and Hufschmidt, M., 1980, Some methods and parameters of body sway quantification and their neurological application. *Archiv für Psychiatrie und Nervenkrankheiten*, **228**, pp. 135-150.

Knoll, K., 1996, Analyses of acrobatic tumbling exercises on floor and balance beam. In *Proceedings XIV International Symposium on Biomechanics in Sports*, edited by Abrantes, J.M.C.S. (Madeira).

Krug, J. and Witt, M., 1996, Motor learning and muscular requests for rapid air-borne rotations of athletes. In *Proceedings XIV International Symposium on Bio-mechanics in Sports*, edited by Abrantes, J.M.C.S. (Madeira).

Miller, D.I., Hennig, E. and Pizzimenti, M.A., 1989, Kinetic and kinematic characteristics of 10m platform performances of elite divers: I. Back takeoffs. *International Journal of Sport Biomechanics,* **5**, 1, pp. 60-88

Murtaugh, K. and Miller, D.I., 1998, The Golden Armstand. North American Congress on Biomechanics 1998.
http://www.asb-biomech.org/NACOB98/122/index.html.

Riccio, G.E., 1993, Information in movement variability about the qualitative dynamics of posture and orientation. In *Variability and motor control*, edited by Newell, K.M. and Corcos, D.M. (IL, Champaign), pp. 317-358.

Rohrbach, C., 1967, Handbuch für elektronisches Messen mechanischer Größen (Düsseldorf).

Stangl, W. and Gollhofer, A., 1998, Räumlich-dynamische Präzision des vestibulo-okulären Reflexes im Sport. In *Bundesinstitut für Sportwissenschaft* (Hrsg.). BISp Jahrbuch 1997. S. (Köln), pp. 119-127,

Straube, A., 1996, Visuelle, vestibuläre und somatosensorische Interaktion in der Gleichgewichtsregulation und Raumperception. In *Aspekte der Sinnes- und Neurophysiologie im Sport,* edited by Bartmus, U., Heck, H., Mester, J., Schumann, H. and Tidow, G. (Hrsg.) (Köln), pp. 343-361.

Witte, K and Blaser, P., 1998, Die Dynamik des statischen Gleichgewichts aus nichtlinearer Sicht. *Psychologie und Sport*, **5**, 4, pp. 130-139.

Yeadon, M.R., 1990, The simulation of aerial movement. I. The determination of orientation angles from film data. *Journal of Biomechanics*, **23**, pp. 59-66.

Yeadon, M.R., 1990, The simulation of aerial movement. II. A mathematical inertia model of the human body. *Journal of Biomechanics*, **23**, pp. 67-74.

Yeadon, M.R., 1990, The simulation of aerial movement. III. The determination of the angular momentum of the human body. *Journal of Biomechanics*, **23**, pp. 75-83.

Zatsiorsky, V.M., 1998, *Kinematics of Human Motion* (Champaign).

ACKNOWLEDGEMENT

The investigation was supported by the Federal Institute of Sport Science (BISp), Cologne, Germany.

31

Forward Skating Mechanics of Ice Hockey Players Under Fatigued Conditions

G. Wayne Marino and Daniel Drouin
Department of Kinesiology,
University of Windsor,
Windsor, Canada

INTRODUCTION

It has been suggested (Green, 1987) that fatigue results in an inability to maintain a desired physical capability and that it is a persistent threat in ice hockey. As such, it has the potential to disrupt all aspects of performance and impact on both the players' effectiveness and risk of injury. In addition, since hockey involves alternating periods of high energy expenditure and rest, brief periods of fatigue can exist throughout the duration of a game and become even more prevalent during the later stages of the game when extraordinary efforts are often required to change the potential outcome of the game. Previous research has attempted to outline the basic mechanical aspects of maximum speed forward skating (Marino, 1977; Marino and Weese, 1978; Marino, 1984; McCaw and Hoshizaki, 1987; and Kirchner and Hoshizaki, 1989). In addition, Marino and Potvin (1989) and Marino and Goegan (1990) reported on several changes that take place in segmental kinetics of skating under fatigued conditions. These studies, however, did not deal extensively with kinematic descriptors of the movement pattern. To date, there is no evidence of research dealing with the effects of fatigue on skaters of different ability levels or on kinematic and postural aspects of the skating motion. In light of gaps in the literature, the purpose of the present study was twofold: first, to examine the differences in skating kinematics between skilled and less skilled performers; and, second to identify changes that occur in skating kinematics when an individual becomes fatigued during a maximum effort, anaerobic work bout.

METHODS

Fourteen subjects volunteered for participation in the study. Eight were considered highly skilled and had experienced ice hockey play at either university or major junior levels. Six were regarded as less skilled and, although all were proficient skaters, none of these had experiences similar to the skilled group. Each subject wore his own skates and was allowed sufficient time on the ice to warm up prior to the task performance. Subjects skated a predetermined route, including stops and starts, in a continuous task that was designed to last for approximately one minute. As such, the temporal aspect of the fatiguing task was designed to emulate the time of a "normal" shift experienced in ice hockey. The total distance covered during the task was 380m. Although a direct measure of fatigue was not recorded, based on previous research (Marino and Potvin, 1989) this time was believed to be sufficient to promote anaerobic fatigue. Subjective assessment through questioning of each subject after completion of the task confirmed this belief. Each subject was videotaped three times during the skating task. The first taping occurred early in the task in a non-fatigued condition and the second and third taping occurred late in the task when the subjects were fatigued. All video taped trials were recorded at the same location on the ice to eliminate the effects of prior stops, starts and turns. Also, an adequate distance to reach maximum speed was ensured. The subjects were fitted with reflective markers at appropriate joint centres and each trial was taped from two views using standard video cameras set at 45° angles from the path of motion. The video was subsequently subjected to three dimensional analysis using the Ariel Performance Analysis System (APAS). Direct Linear Transformation (DLT) processing was used for data transformation and the cubic spline curve fitting technique for data smoothing. Calibration was performed using a 12 control point cube which was video taped on the ice then removed prior to testing.

There were two independent variables in the study: subject performance level and state of fatigue. Skilled and less skilled subjects were subjected to repeated measures under a non-fatigued condition and two fatigued conditions. Both fatigued conditions were measured late in the skating task on consecutive passes through the video taping area. Thus, the two fatigued trials were meant to reflect two different levels of fatigue. Twenty-three postural and kinematic variables were chosen as dependent variables in an attempt to differentiate between skilled and less skilled skaters and between the fatigue conditions. Two way Analysis of Variance with repeated measures on fatigue was used to identify statistically significant differences at less than the .05 level of significance. Orthogonal means comparisons were used as a post-hoc multiple comparisons technique where warranted. Test, re-test confirmation and comparison with previous research was used to ensure the reliability and validity of the data.

RESULTS AND DISCUSSION

When test, re-test data were compared for several dependent variables, the results showed that errors were consistently less than 4 per cent. This was considered to be within the normal range of measurement error and the data were assumed to be reliable. The values recorded for the dependent variables, horizontal velocity, stride rate, and stride length were compared to the values reported in previous research on subjects of similar skill levels. Each of the variable means was found to be within the range reported by other researchers (Marino, 1977; McCaw and Hoshizaki, 1987) and the data, therefore, were considered to be valid representations of forward ice skating performance.

The total skating task times, recorded in seconds, were 57.1 (SD = 1.59) and 63.1 (SD = 2.34) for the skilled and less skilled groups respectively. The difference is statistically significant at p< .05. This confirms the validity of the assignment of subjects to the two groups. Although the non-fatigued skating velocities of the skilled group were somewhat higher than the less skilled group the differences were not statistically significant. This probably reflects the fact that the forward skating section of the course was the easiest section. The significant differences in total time to complete the course probably indicates the skilled subjects' higher ability to handle stops and starts and cornering. Like velocity, stride lengths and rates were somewhat different between skilled and less skilled groups but the differences were not statistically significant. Other postural variables did reveal statistically significant differences between skilled and less skilled groups. The skilled group was able to achieve better touchdown position of the foot relative to the centre of mass at the end of the recovery phase. In addition, the skilled group exhibited significantly more knee flexion at touchdown. This variable has been hypothesized by several researchers including Page (1979), Holt (1978) and McCaw and Hoshizaki (1987) to be important in preparing the skater for a forceful thrust during the subsequent propulsive phase of the stride. Overall, it appears that with only a couple of significant exceptions, skilled and less skilled maximum speed mechanics are approximately the same. For the most part, the skating techniques of the two groups did not vary significantly. In only a very few instances were significant differences found. This would corroborate the findings of McCaw and Hoshizaki (1989) who reported few differences in technique between intermediate and elite skaters. They did report several differences between novice skaters and these two groups but the current study did not employ novice subjects so that comparison was not possible.

The effects of fatigue were also monitored. The results of comparison of non-fatigued trials with the two fatigued trials are shown in Table 1. Since only minor between group differences were found, the data for the two groups were pooled in order to consider the effects of fatigue. Several important differences were found to occur for the whole group as a result of fatigue. The pooled velocity values reflected the effect of fatigue. In the non-fatigued condition, the mean velocity value was 9.2m/s. Velocity decreased to 7.71m/s and 6.97m/s respectively for the two subsequent fatigue trials (p< .01). It is interesting to note that the decreases in velocity were accompanied by decreases in the rate of striding. Stride rate declined from 2.57st/s in the non-fatigue trial to 2.03st/s and 1.92st/s in the fatigued trials (p < .05). Under conditions of fatigue, the muscular effort required to produce a high rate of striding is apparently difficult to achieve. These results tend to confirm the findings of Marino and Goegan (1990) that the primary changes in segment kinetics resulting from fatigue were in the work rates and energy transfer rates. Like stride rate, these variables are also time dependent. It is interesting to note that while the overall time of stride increased with fatigue, the two components of the stride time showed different trends. The single support time comprised 83.5% of the stride time in non-fatigued skating and this decreased to 78% in the fatigued trials. In contrast, double support increased from 16.5% of stride time to 21.0% as the skater became fatigued. In both instances, the differences in % times between non-fatigued and fatigued conditions were statistically significant. It is apparent, therefore, that when a skater becomes fatigued the ability to recover the leg quickly is diminished and the skater spends relatively more time with both skates on the ice. The second main component of velocity, stride length, showed no significant effects of fatigue. The values for this variable were 3.61m, 3.79m, and 3.63m respectively for the three fatigue conditions. As suggested in previous studies (Marino, 1977; McCaw and Hoshizaki, 1987; Marino and Potvin, 1989) the glide component of the stride ensures a fairly consistent stride length across a wide range of skating velocities. The longer stride times associated with fatigue would allow a longer period of time for the skater to glide. In conjunction with the minimal resistive forces from friction and air resistance, this would allow for a normal stride length.

Table 1 Mean values for selected kinematic and postural variables.
Pooled for skilled and less skilled skaters under Non-fatigued and Fatigued Conditions.

Variable	Non fatigued	Fatigued 1	Fatigued 2
Horizontal velocity (m/s)*	9.27	7.71	6.97
Stride length (m)	3.61	3.79	3.63
Stride rate (st/s)*	2.57	2.03	1.92
Single support time (%)*	83.5	78.5	78.6
Double support time (%)*	16.5	21.5	21.4
T. D. position (cm)*	11.3	7.1	4.5
T. D. knee angle (deg)*	102.3	110.9	16.4
Total knee ang. disp. (deg)*	60.6	51.0	45.1
Thigh ang. vel. (deg/s)*	169.0	112.5	101.3
Shank ang. vel. (deg/s)*	51.5	34.3	32.9

* Statistically significant differences at $p < .05$

In addition to the basic stride characteristic changes discussed above, several postural changes also accompanied the onset of fatigue. The touchdown position of the recovery skate, the knee angle at touchdown, the total range of motion of the knee, and the angular velocities of both the thigh and shank all changed significantly between the non-fatigued and fatigued conditions. Taken as a whole, these changes reflect the fact that when fatigued, the skater is not able to put the support leg in a favourable position to begin the subsequent support and thrust phase. Also, it appears that the skater is unable to generate the levels of angular velocity, in the leg segments, during a fatigued state that would produce velocities and stride rates similar to the non-fatigued state.

PRACTICAL APPLICATIONS

The results of this study indicate the importance of the time components in the ice skating stride. Players should be encouraged to emphasize a high stride rate without compromising the other thrust and glide aspects of the skating pattern. Sufficient knee bend at contact should be taught to ensure a full range of motion of the knee during the thrust phase of the support period. Conditioning exercises, both on and off ice, should emphasize increases in strength and power of the musculature responsible for both knee and hip extension. Such exercises should be performed at high velocity to mimic the action of the leg in skating. Finally, the observation of the onset of fatigue and its effects on basic skating mechanics in a relatively short period of time has several implications for the sport of hockey. Not only does the maximum velocity of skating decrease with fatigue, but other skills such as starting, stopping, accelerating and turning would also be expected to deteriorate under conditions of fatigue. The first fatigue trial in this study was recorded no longer than 42 seconds after the start of the task for any subject. This further supports the notion proposed by other researchers and by coaching practitioners that shift (on-ice) time should be kept below 45 seconds, especially if play is continuous and at high intensity.

REFERENCES

Green, H.J., 1987, Bioenergetics of ice hockey: consideration for fatigue. *Journal of Sports Sciences*, **5**, pp. 305-317.

Holt, L., 1978, Cinematographic analysis of skating. In *Proceedings: 1977 National Coaches Certification Programme. Level 5 Seminar*, edited by Almstedt, J. (Ottawa, Canada: Canadian Amateur Hockey Association).

Kirchner, G. and Hoshizaki, T.B., 1989, Kinematics of the ankle during the acceleration phase of skating. In *Biomechanics in Skiing, Skating, and Hockey*, edited by J. Terauds *et al.* (Del Mar, CA., USA: Academic Publishers).

Marino, G.W., 1977, Kinematics of ice skating at different velocities. *Research Quarterly*, **48**(1), pp. 93-97.

Marino, G.W. and Goegan, J., 1990, Work-energy analysis of ice skaters under progressive conditions of fatigue. In *Biomechanics in Sports VIII*, edited by Nosek, M. *et al.* (Prague, Cz: Charles University Press).

Marino, G.W. and Potvin, J., 1989, Effects of anaerobic fatigue on the biomechanics features of the ice skating stride. In *Biomechanics in Sports VII*, edited by Morrison, Wm. (Footscray, Victoria, Au.: Footscray Institute of Technology Press).

Marino, G.W. and Weese, R., 1978, A kinematic analysis of the ice skating stride. In *Science in Skiing, Skating and Hockey*, edited by Terauds, J. *et al.* (Del Mar CA Academic Publishers).

McCaw, S. and Hoshizaki, T.B., 1987, A biomechanical comparison of novice, intermediate, and elite ice skaters. In *Biomechanics X-B*, edited by Jonsson, B. (Champaign, IL, USA: Human Kinetics Press).

32

Improving the Swimming Start Technique using Biomechanics Feedback System

Raul Arellano, Susana Pardillo, Blança De La Fuente
and Francisco García[1]
Universidad de Granada, [1]CAR Sierra Nevada, Granada, Spain

INTRODUCTION

The starting time is one of the race components in swimming competition. Its importance is relatively greater during the shorter race distances (50 and 100m). The time that a swimmer spends starting is equal to the time from the starting signal being given until the feet leave the starting block (the block time), until first contact is made with the water (the flight time), plus the time from first contact with the water until the swimmer begins kicking and/or stroking (the glide time) (Hay, 1986). Starting times were recorded during international swimming competitions using fixed distances. The results showed the time spent from the starting signal until the head crossed the 10 or 15m line as was reported by Arellano *et al.* (1994) or more recently by Mason *et al.* (1998). The new F.I.N.A. rules put limits to the underwater starting distance (15m) and this length is now universally used to measure the total starting time. Some papers were published reporting data of the duration of the phases, centre of gravity trajectory, horizontal and vertical velocity of the body segments, force applied on the starting block and underwater propulsive actions (Zatsiorsky *et al.*, 1979; Lewis, 1980; Guimaraes and Hay, 1985; Pearson *et al.*, 1998). Our study aim was to develop a system to improve the swimmer's starting technique integrating force and video data from all the starting phases.

METHODS

Subjects

A group of swimmers (n=17) with different elite swimming skill levels (international and national) took part in an altitude training camp and in one technical evaluation session organized by the Technical Evaluation Staff of the Royal Spanish Swimming Federation in the Altitude Training Centre of Sierra Nevada. Each swimmer performed the 50m plus turn test (57.5m) with one all-out effort to record the split time for the 100m event. Each subject's trial was video-recorded with the Temporal Swimming Analysis System (TSAS) described by Arellano *et al.* (1999).

Table 1 Means for subject age, mass and height, correlation for subject mass and height with starting times.

	Mean	r with 5 m time	r with 10 m time
Age (years)	21		
Weight (kg)	72.3	−0.718***	−0.636**
Height (cm)	179	−0.580*	−0.501*

*** $p < 0.0011$, ** $p < 0.01$, * $p < 0.05$.

Instrumental

The TSAS was composed of five video cameras connected to a S-VHS video recorder (50Hz) through a video-timer and a video selector (see Figure 1). The image from the first two video cameras was mixed to see the over- and underwater phases of the start in the same frame (until 10m, see Figure 2). A third camera was used to measure the 15m time. A fourth camera was put in the middle of the swimming pool (25m) to record at least two complete underwater stroke cycles and the 25m time (with the head). The fifth camera was placed at the end of the swimming pool for video recording the turning phase. All the images from the cameras were recorded at a distance of 15m from the perpendicular plane of the swimmer displacement. The first camera was placed over the water. The rest of the cameras were placed 1m below the water-surface filming throught three different underwater windows. One reference system was put in the vertical plane of the swimmer's displacement and video-recorded before the swimmer's performance. Thanks to this reference, it was possible to draw vertical lines on the computer to measure the time where the swimmer's head crossed these reference lines. The assessment was carried out after a swimming start following the FINA rules. The starting signal was synchronized with the video-timer (time code) and the swimming pool electronic timing system. The 50m time was measured with this latter device when the swimmer touched the timing wall. After video recording, the timing data was collected directly from the tape, reading the time code recorded with a PC connected to the video player. A specific database was developed for collecting the data and to produce the printout with the analysis for information for coaches and swimmers. As our study aim was to analyse a set of variables related only to the start the data obtained from the first and second cameras were analysed (to the 10m line).

A force plate (Kistler model 9253) was adapted to the swimming starting block keeping the same height from the water (0.7m) and inclination (6°) as a standard starting block. The force plate was added to the TSAS system and was used to measure the forces applied by the swimmer during the block time. Both systems were synchronized thanks to a voltage change introduced by the starting switch to one of the recording channels of the A/D converter connected to the force plate and to the video timing system.

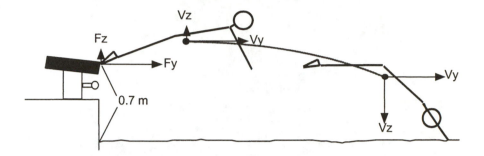

Figure 1 Graphical representation of the variables studied related with the force applied in the starting block and the parabolic trajectory during the flight.

Variables Measured

The start time was measured for 5m (T5) and 10m (T10) when the head of the swimmer crossed these reference lines (see Figure 2b). The duration of the block time (BT), flight time (FT) and entry time (ET) were measured as parts of the start time. Mean speed was measured between 0 and 5m, in order to compare the starting technique without the influence of the stroke selected for testing. Complementary data from 5 to 10m were analysed as well.

A bi-dimensional trajectory of the centre of mass (CM) was calculated during the block and flight time using the anthropometric data published by Donskoi and Zatsiorski (1988). Thanks to this trajectory it was possible to obtain the CM horizontal (Vy) and vertical (Vz) velocities during the take-off and during the first contact with the water surface (see Figure 2a). The parabolic equation was calculated using an algorithm developed by Dapena (1996). The resultant velocities during the take-off ($V0$) and during the first water contact (Ve), and the take-off angle (φ) were calculated as well. Horizontal (Fy) and vertical (Fz) peak forces during the block time were obtained from the force plate records. The resulting force data consider the weight of the swimmer as zero value.

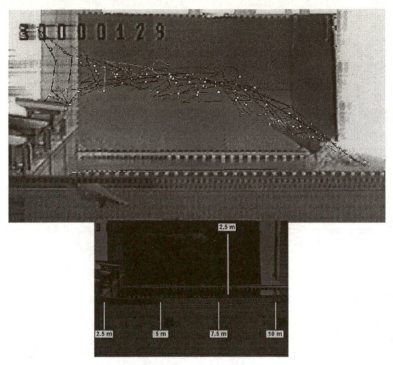

Figure 2 Digitized figures and centre of gravity trajectory during the flight phase. The video system let us see the entry phase over and underwater. Vertical line references are overlaid on the video image to measure the starting times.

The system developed let us integrate in real time the recorded force data with the video record of swimming start block phases. The recorded image can be visualized and it allows the observer to relate the impulse forces (Fy and Fz) with the body block actions just a few seconds after finishing the start (see Figure 3).

Statistical Analyses

The data from each performance were filed in a specifically designed database. Selected variables were exported to a statistical computer software (STATISTICA/Mac 4.1, Statsoft™) performing the calculations in a Macintosh computer. Averages were determined for all variables as presented in Tables 1 and 2. Partial correlation coefficients with subject mass partialled out was calculated between selected variables and shown in Table 2.

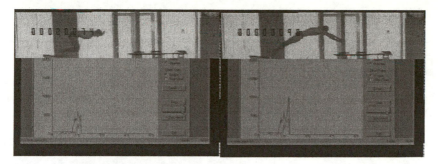

Figure 3 A sample of integration of video images with the video data.

RESULTS AND DISCUSSION

The mean data obtained in the timing analysis (see Table 2) are similar to those obtained in our previous studies. When the timing data phases are related to the force records, we found: (a) a negative value of Fz before the hands leave the block; (b) a progressive increase of Fy before the hands leave the block; (c) peak values of Fz just after the hands leave the block; (d) a rapid increase of Fy between the time the knees make an angle of almost 90° and the feet leave the block and; (e) Fy peak value is almost twice the Fz peak value and it is produced just before to leave the block (see Figure 4).

The Vy and Fy variables correlated between them ($r=0.863$, $p<0.01$) but each of them separately did not correlate with T5. Only Fy correlated significantly with T10 ($r=-0.522$, $p<0.05$). Our results were similar to those reported by Guimaraes and Hay (1985) that found very low correlation values between Vy and horizontal impulse with the starting time.

Only Ve showed a significant correlation with T5 ($r=-0.56$, $p<0.05$). The value of Vz is increased during the flight due to the external force gravity and when it is added to Vy (kept constant because it was assumed that air resistance was negligible) the result is a Ve higher than V_0 (nearly 25% more). Bowers and Cavanagh (1975) reported similar differences between V_0 and Ve.

The absolute values obtained for Fz are smaller than Fy as was shown in the recorded graph samples in Zatsiorsky *et al.* (1979). Different results were obtained by Pearson *et al.* (1998). Their results showed that Fz was surprisingly higher than Fy. This occurred because of the use of a special starting block with handles attached to the side of the block modifying the initial position of the body on the starting block and the forces applied on it. The values obtained in the take-off angle showed a high variability. The negative mean value produces a parabolic motion of the centre of mass forward and downward. A negative (φ) was also obtained by Bowers and Cavanagh (1975) in the two swimming starts compared in their study.

Table 2 Means, standard deviations and partial correlation coefficients with T5 for the variables analysed.

	Mean	SD	Partial *r*			Mean	SD	Partial *r*
BT (s)	0.850	0.112	ns		*V*y (m/s)	3.961	0.438	ns
FT (s)	0.387	0.146	ns		*V*z (m/s)	−0.225	0.568	ns
ET (s)	0.192	0.111	ns		*V*0 (m/s)	3.898	0.484	ns
T5 (s)	1.788	0.150	1		*V*e (m/s)	4.627	0.389	−0.56*
T10 (s)	4.506	0.546	0.85***		*F*y (N)	917.2	161.4	ns
V0_5 (m/s)	2.814	0.236	−0.99***		*F*z (N)	515.4	213.1	ns
V5_10 (m/s)	1.881	0.295	−0.78**		φ (deg.)	−3.26	8.55	ns

*** p<0.0011; ** p<0.01; * p<0.05.

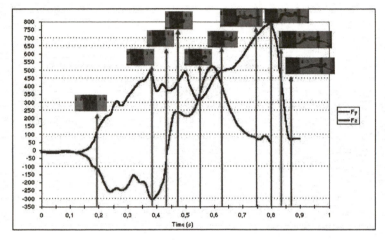

Figure 4 Sample of the records obtained from the force plate and pictures of the related movement phases.

The subjects (breast-strokers) of Table 3 obtained similar times in the block, flight and entry phases. S2 and S3 are swimmers of similar medium level. S1 is a Spanish elite swimmer. The differences in T5 and T7, 5 between S1 and S2–S3 are produced by higher value of Vz and Fz (more than 20% of related body weight force) and a better horizontal body position. The increase of the time difference at T10 is produced by a better propulsion obtained during the first underwater arm pull. The 15m time difference includes the first two or three strokes.

A new analysis of an experimental situation was carried out, comparing the recorded forces during (1) the vertical squat jump and the vertical counter-movement jump on land with (2) the horizontal and vertical starting block forces. When the absolute force values for the land jumps are compared, we found nearly double the peak forces were found for the land jumps. The effect of the body weight is greater during the vertical jump compared with the forces recorded during the dive action (see Figure 5). The pathways shown on the graph (see Figure 5) reveal different behaviour of the force application between horizontal block force and the vertical land forces, but the vertical forces look similar, especially during the impulsive phase (see parallel pathways on the graph).

Table 3 Shows the differences between three swimmers in their starting times, cinematic and kinetic data. You can see where a swimmer is gaining on the others.

	THLB	TFLB	T2.5m	THE	TFE	T5m	T7.5m	T10m	T15m
S1	0.48	0.86	1.02	1.22	1.54	1.60	2.62	4.04	7.82
S2	0.69	0.91	1.13	1.37	1.67	1.83	3.07	4.91	8.88
S3	0.57	0.85	1.06	1.27	1.67	1.81	3.01	4.80	8.66

THLB: Time hands leave the block. TFLB: Time feet leave the block. THE: Time hand entry. TFE: Time feet entry.

	Vz (m/s)	Vy (m/s)	Fz (N)	Fy (N)	φ (degrees)	$\%Fz/W$
S1	4.36	-0.20	1017	431	-2.67°	30%
S2	3.62	0.53	728	700	8.30°	6%
S3	3.60	0.01	647	647	0°	9%

V: velocity, z: horizontal, y: vertical, F: force, W: body weight. φ: take-off angle.

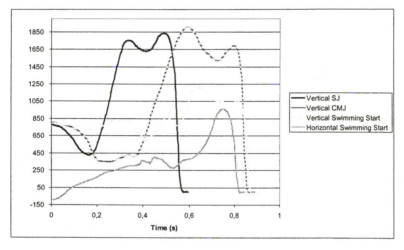

Figure 5 Comparison of forces recorded during vertical squat jump, vertical counter-movement jump and swimming start.

CONCLUSIONS

Combining the cinematic and kinetic information of the swimming start seems the only way to help the swimmer to improve the swimming start. The low correlation values obtained in this and previous studies between the kinetic, parabolic variables and the different starting times suggest the need to use a very individual analysis to provide appropriate start feedback. Analysing the vertical land forces, we can measure the improvement of the muscular power of the legs, so obtaining information about the effect of specific physical training. However, the extent to which this training is translated into making the start more efficacious you need to monitor the starting block forces. The transformation of the velocity components of the swimmer's centre of mass in the flight phase to the higher horizontal gliding speed seems the more complex problem to be resolved by the swimmer and where our research will be directed in the future.

REFERENCES

Arellano, R., Brown, P., Cappaert, J. and Nelson, R.C., 1994, Analysis of 50–, 100–, and 200–m freestyle swimmers at the 1992 Olympic Games. *Journal of Applied Biomechanics*, **10**, pp. 189-199.

Arellano, R., Pardillo, S. and García, F., 1999, A system for quantitative measurement of swimming technique. In *Biomechanics and Medicine in Swimming VIII*, 1st ed., edited by Keskinen, K.L., Komi, P.V. and Hollander, A.P. (Jyvaskyla [Finland]: Department of Biology of Physical Activity of the University of Jyvaskyla), pp. 269-275.

Bowers, J.E. and Cavanagh, P.R., 1975, *A biomechanical comparison of the grab and conventional sprint starts in competitive swimming* (Bruselas, Belgium: The Second International Symposium on Biomechanics in Swimming).

Dapena, J., 1996, Fortran algorithm to fit a parabola of second derivative ($=-9.81\text{m/s}^2$) to a series of n fit pairs of values of time (t) calculating the horizontal and vertical displacement and horizontal and vertical velocity at time zero.

Donskoi, D. and Zatsiorski, V., 1988, *Biomecánica de los Ejercicios Físicos* (Efremov, V. trans.) (Vol. 1). Moscú: Ed. Raduga.

Guimaraes, A. and Hay, J., 1985, A mechanical analysis of the grab starting technique in swimming, *International Journal of Sport Biomechanics*, **1**, pp. 25-35.

Hay, J.G., 1986, Swimming. In *Starting, Stroking and Turning (A Compilation of Research on the Biomechanics of Swimming, The University of Iowa, 1983-86)*, 1st edition, edited by Hay, J.G. (Iowa: Biomechanics Laboratory, Department of Exercise Science), pp. 1-51.

Lewis, S., 1980, Comparison of five swimming starting techniques. *Swimming Technique*, **16**(4), pp. 124-128.

Mason, B., Cossor, J., Daley, M., Page, K.A., Steinebronn, M., Cornelius, M., Lyttle, A. and Sanders, R., 1998, *1998 World Swimming Championships–Biomechanics Analysis* (Perth, Australia: Australian Institute of Sport).

Pearson, C.T., McElroy, G.K., Blitvich, J.D., Subic, A. and Blanksby, B.A., 1998, A comparison of the swimming start using traditional and modified starting blocks. *Journal of Human Movement Studies*, **34**, pp. 49-66.

Zatsiorsky, V.M., Bulgakova, N.Z. and Chaplinsky, N.M., 1979, *Biomechanical Analysis of Starting Techniques in Swimming* (Edmonton, Canada: the Third International Symposium of Biomechanics in Swimming).

ACKNOWLEDGEMENT

The development of the system and the research was developed thanks to a grant paid by "Convenio de Colaboración Científico-Educativa entre la Universidad de Granada y el Consejo Superior de Deportes en el CAR de Sierra Nevada".

33

Net Power Production and Performance at Different Stroke Rates and Abilities during Pair-oar Rowing

Richard Smith and Constanze Loschner[1]
University of Sydney, Faculty of Health Sciences, Australia
[1]New South Wales Institute of Sport, Sydney, Australia

INTRODUCTION

During on-water rowing, power developed by the rower may be delivered to the oars through the hands and to the foot stretcher through the feet. The proficiency of the rower will be partly determined by the effectiveness with which this power is coupled to boat propulsion. Sanderson and Martindale (1986) proposed that there were three components important to maximizing boat velocity: extraction the maximum amount of power from the rower's body; use of as much of this power to propel the boat; and use of this propulsive power in an efficient manner to move the boat at the greatest possible mean speed. Velocity cost, the ratio between the external power developed by the rower and the average velocity of the boat (the number of watts required to propel the boat for each ms^{-1}) is one effectiveness measure. Propulsion is defined as any action that directly affects the forward progression of the boat. For example, the transverse component of the handle force is a necessary accompaniment to the longitudinal component of the total handle force but has no effect on propulsion. The purpose of this paper was to develop the concept of velocity cost, measure it on-water with pair-oared boats and search for cause and effect links which explain the variability expected among rowers. Once these connections are found, they will comprise a useful tool for rowers and coaches in the improvement of rowing performance.

METHODS

Four male state level pairs rowed an instrumented pair boat at steady state cadences of 20, 24, 28, and 30 strokes per minute. Boat velocity was measured with a magnetic turbine and pickup coil, pin force with multi-component force transducers, stretcher forces with strain gauge transducers, and oar angles with servo potentiometers. The three-dimensional orientation of the boat was measured with gyroscopes. This information was sampled at 100Hz and telemetered to a laptop computer on the shore. Approximately twenty strokes were time normalized and averaged at each stroke rate. Power delivered to the boat by the rowers was calculated as the product of boat velocity and pin or stretcher force. Power delivered to the oar handle was calculated as the product of the handle force and handle velocity. Handle velocity was the result of the angular velocity of the oar and linear velocity of the boat. To calculate the handle forces from the pin forces, the oar was modelled as a simple lever with the water acting as a fulcrum. Motion in the horizontal plane only was considered.

The powers associated with each rower were summed. Total power was then integrated over the stroke to obtain the total external energy generated by the rowers at the oar handles and stretchers. This energy was then divided by the time per stroke to provide the average power for that stroke rate. The work effectiveness for each pair of rowers was calculated by dividing the pair's energy output in a propulsive direction by the total energy spent.

RESULTS AND DISCUSSION

The mean height and weight of the rowers was 186.5±0.8cm and 89.6±1.4kg respectively.

The patterns of power production involved both absorption and generation (Figure 1). During the drive phase the net propulsive power delivered by the pair was the balance between large amounts of power absorbed by the rower from the stretcher and high magnitudes developed at the stroke and bow oar handles. This balance is negative during the first 10% of the stroke then remains positive for the remainder of the drive phase. Towards the finish the propulsive power produced by the pair almost reaches zero but then climbs to a low positive level for the recovery phase up to 90% of the stroke. A small absorbing phase brings the net power up to the next catch. Although the rower experiences the greatest physiological stress during the drive phase, examination of the area under the net propulsive power curve (the energy) reveals that the net energy provided to the boat by the rower during the recovery phase is comparable to that of the drive phase.

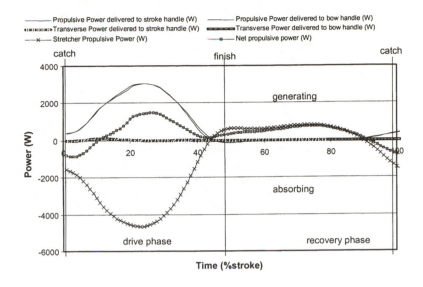

Figure 1 Ensemble average pair power output time series at 30 strokes per minute.

The mechanical effectiveness of the rowers was described by the velocity cost: the power expended by the rowers in producing each metre per second of velocity. It is also equivalent to the energy expended in moving the boat each metre. All rowers were of similar mass and rowed the same pair boat. Thus, potentially, each pair would encounter the same drag at the same velocity. Differences in the drag could be caused by unbalanced application of force causing the boat to yaw, pitch or roll and present changing cross-sections to the water and creating different amounts of wave drag.

Since drag is proportional to velocity squared it could be expected that the velocity cost would increase with boat speed. This is evident in the results (Table 1). Among the pairs, however, there was considerable variability in this relationship. Although the general trend was for increasing average powers being required for higher boat velocities ($r = 0.80$, $p < 0.001$) for each pair there were considerable differences in the amount of rower average power output expended in producing boat velocity (Figure 2). This afforded an opportunity to examine the reasons why pair A was able to attain different boat speeds for the same average power output (at 24 and 28 str min^{-1}). A further point of interest was why pair C used more average power to achieve the same boat velocity as pair A while both were rowing at the nominal 28 str min^{-1} level.

Table 1 Mean ±SD for the actual stroke rate and velocity cost at the four nominal stroke rates.

Stroke rate (min^{-1})	Actual stroke rate (min^{-1})	Boat velocity (ms^{-1})	Velocity cost W/ms^{-1}
20	20.3 ±1.3	2.8 ±0.2	152 ±23
24	25.3 ±1.9	3.1 ±0.1	198 ±23
28	27.5 ±1.3	3.1 ±0.1	214 ±31
30	30 ±1.2	3.3 ±0.3	241 ±21

In the first case pair A exhibited differences in the phasing and magnitude of the stroke- and bow-side pin forces. This in turn led to a larger yaw magnitude at 28 str min^{-1} than at 24 str min^{-1}. This would lead to a larger drag and thus higher velocity cost for the rowers performance at 28 str min^{-1}.

In the second case both stroke- and bow-side seat velocity ranges were higher for pair C than pair A. If the rower centre of mass position could be modelled as the seat position, a higher seat velocity would imply a higher centre of mass velocity and thus more kinetic energy stored. The boat velocity also had a larger range for pair C than for pair A, and the power expended moving the handle transversely was larger making propulsion less efficient for pair C. Finally, there was an underlying imbalance in the power developed by pair C. The ratio of stroke rower to bow rower power is usually within a few per cent of one but the value for pair C was 0.86. To keep the boat moving in the correct direction, the rudder would have to be offset from the centre line thus increasing the drag. A steady offset such as this would not be detected by the yaw sensor whose frequency response is 0.2–20Hz.

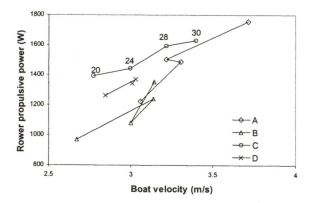

Figure 2 The average propulsive power output required of each pair to produce the resulting velocities. Each curve begins at the left with the data point for 20 str min^{-1} following the line for 24, 28 and 30 str min^{-1}.

This anecdotal evidence seems to suggest that the cause of ineffective rowing may be found in a number of variables: range of velocity for the seats and the boat, average power used to move the oar handle transversely, the range of boat yaw, pitch and roll, and the balance between the stroke and bow pin forces. A linear regression analysis (forward stepping) was carried out with velocity cost as the dependent variable. The first variable to be entered was boat velocity range ($p = 0.065$) then roll range ($p = 0.001$), average power to move the oar handle transversely ($p < 0.0001$), bow seat velocity range ($p = 0.006$), pitch range ($p = 0.0092$), stroke to bow propulsive pin force ratio ($p = 0.066$). The correlation coefficient was high at 0.99 ($p < 0.0001$).

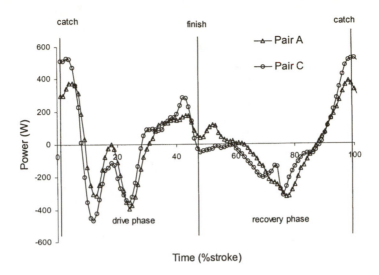

Figure 3 The power associated with changing the trunk and thigh kinetic energy. The centre of mass of these segments is modelled by seat position.

CONCLUSION

The variable velocity cost gave a numerical value to the effectiveness of the pair rowers performance. Clear differences were shown among the rowers using this variable. The differences were associated with a number of technique variables. Linear regression analysis used most of these in producing an equation which was able to explain 97% of the variance in velocity cost.

The data collection and analysis was carried out with just four pairs of rowers at four different stroke rates. Much larger numbers must be found and measured at predetermined boat velocities before the researchers can make valid extrapolations to the wider rowing community.

The velocity cost (for a given boat and boat velocity) is a single number which can alert the rower or coach to the effectiveness of the performance. Once a problem has been identified, the cause(s) can be sought out in a number of technique-related parameters.

REFERENCES

Dal Monte, A. and Komor, A., 1989, Rowing and Sculling Mechanics. In *Biomechanics of Sport*, edited by Vaughan, C. (Florida: CRC Press), pp. 54-117.
Sanderson, B. and Martindale, W., 1986, Towards optimizing rowing technique. *Medicine and Science in Sports and Exercise*, **18**, pp. 454-468.

Part Nine

Biomechanics of Paediatric and Geriatric Exercise

34

Biomechanics in Youth Sports

Eugene W. Brown
Department of Kinesiology, Michigan State University,
East Lansing, Michigan, USA

INTRODUCTION

Youth sports may be defined by the age of the athletes that participate in sport. Based on this approach, youth sports has been considered as the participation in sports by individuals approximately 18 years of age or younger. In the United States, the age generally corresponds with the age of students when they graduate from high school. To some, youth sports has a connotation that is associated with more of a recreational approach to athletic participation. However, the level of participation of youth in sport ranges from those who become occasionally involved in recreational activities to those who engage in heavy, year round training regimens.

How many youths participate in sports by age and level of competition? This is a difficult question to answer because it varies by country and by the structural organization of youth sports within various countries, and because there is a paucity of good data to answer this question. It has been estimated that 20 million children in the United States between the ages of 6 and 16 years are involved in sports that are organized and supervised by adults (Seefeldt, 1987). This implies that the participant count is even larger if non-organized youth sports participants were added to the total. A recent paper (Ewing *et al.*, 1999), commissioned by the Carnegie Corporation, documented the participation for specific categories of youth sports in the United States (Table 1).

The number of participants in sport, from youth to adulthood, can be represented by a pyramidal model (Figure 1). The greatest number of participants is evident at the youngest ages. The size of the population, for each age group, is represented by the area of the respective region of the pyramid. The slopes of the sides of the pyramid represent the drop out rate. It is likely that, in many countries, there is a rapid decline in sport participation from seven to 18 years of age and that this decline continues throughout adulthood.

Table 1 Estimated per cent of youth enrolled in specific categories of youth sports[a].

Category of activity	Estimated age range (yrs)	Per cent of eligible enrollees[b]	Approximate number of participants
Agency sponsored sports (i.e. Little League Baseball, Pop Warner Football)	5-17	45	22,000,000
Club sports (i.e. Pay for Services: Gymnastics, Ice Skating, Swimming)	5-17	5	2,368,700
Recreational sports programmes (everyone plays–sponsored by Recreational departments)	5-17	30	14,512,200
Intramural sports (Middle, Junior, Senior High Schools)	13-18	10	451,000
Interscholastic sports (Middle, Junior, Senior High Schools)	13-18	12[c] 40[d]	5,776,820 5,776,820

[a]Total population of eligible participants in the 5–17 year age category (1995) was estimated to be 48,374,000 by the National Centre for Educational Statistics, US Department of Education, 1989.
[b]Totals do not equal 100 per cent because of multiple-category participation by some athletes.
[c]Per cent of total population aged 5–17 years.
[d]Per cent of high school-aged population (N = 14,510,000).

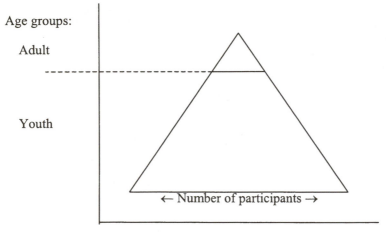

Figure 1 Schematic representation of the age and number of participants in sport.

What role does biomechanics have to play in youth sports? The answer to this question is "The same as it has in adult sports." Generally, biomechanics can contribute to sport in several ways: injury prevention, performance enhancement, equipment design, rule modifications, and instructional/coaching practices. Since the role of biomechanics is the same, irrespective of the age of the sport participant, one might be led to conclude that there would be more biomechanics activity associated with youth sports because of the disproportionate number of participants involved in this age group in comparison to adult athletes. This is not the case. In fact, a review of the published reports from three years (1995–97) of the *Journal of Applied Biomechanics* and the *1999 Proceedings of the International Society of Biomechanics in Sports* (Table 2) reveals proportionally few biomechanics studies of youth sports. The total number of studies and subjects (identified as under 18 years of age) reported were six and 70, respectively;

whereas, 388 subjects 18 years and older were reported to have participated in 33 studies.

What is behind this system of focusing the greatest effort in research and application on the smallest population of sports participants? The answer is organization, prestige, and money. Even though there are highly organized groups within various sports, much of youth sports tends to be recreational. Often, it is not until highly skilled youth athletes begin to emerge that coaches, the news media, and researchers begin to focus attention on them. With the exception of a few sports (e.g. women's gymnastics, figure skating, and swimming), where youth participants are also the top level competitors, proportionally little attention is given to research and application of biomechanics to youth sports. The professional sport model is driven by money. This money is often raised at the bottom of the pyramid of participants, through registration fees and the purchase of tickets for sporting events and sport paraphernalia, and is spent on the top levels of performers (e.g. prospective participants and participants of Olympic and professional sports). In general there is a void in the study of youth sport participants. Therefore, an opportunity exists for biomechanists to make widespread contributions at this level, especially when taking into consideration the greater number of youth sport participants and the relative longevity of sport participation of young athletes in comparison to adult athletes. The remainder of this paper will focus on two of the roles of biomechanics in youth sports—injury prevention and instructional/coaching practices.

INJURY PREVENTION

The epidemiology of sports injuries involves the study of the distribution and etiology (causes) of injuries for the purposes of reducing the severity and incidence of sports injuries in the future (Caine *et al.*, 1996). In general, there is a direct relationship between the age of athletes and level of their sport competition, and the incidence and severity of injury. Thus, on a per person basis, youth sports participants tend to have fewer and less severe injuries than their highly competitive and older counterparts. This may be a partial explanation for the tendency of youth sports to have fewer, if any, and less skilled medical personnel available at their practices and competitions to address their immediate injury needs.

Table 2 Number of biomechanics studies and subjects by sport and age group.

Sport	Age Group[a]				Age Group[b]			
	Youth (<18 yrs.)	Adult (≥18 yrs.)	Youth and Adult	No specific age information	Youth (<18 yrs)	Adult (≥18 yrs)	Youth and Adult	No specific age information
Alpine skiing		2:8						
Baseball					1:20	1:4		
Basketball								2:14
Crew								2:88
Cross country skiing		1:20						
Cycling		3:52		1:34				
Dance	1:2	2:14						
Diving			1:20					
Fencing							1:12	1:4
Figure skating			1:16					1:24
Football		1:12						
Football and baseball			1:52					
Golf		1:4						
Gymnastics	1:15	1:3		2:93				
Gymnastics and diving		1:6						
Karate								1:12
Kayak						1:10		
Martial arts								1:66
Rifle shooting								1:1
Rock climbing				1:6				
Roller skating					1:6			
Roller skiing			1:8					
Sailing								1:2
Ski jumping				1:20				
Softball						1:8	1:10	
Swimming			1:797	2:813		2:36		3:17
Tennis				2:23			1:8	5:85
Track and field	1:19	6:112	2:45	5:65		3:46		2:13
Trampolining	1:8	1:3				1:1		
Triathlon		1:11						
Volleyball						1:8		1:1
Water polo		2:26						
Weightlifting		1:4		2:32				
Sum	4:44	23:275	7:938	15:1086	2:26	10:113	3:30	21:327

[a]Data from the *Journal of Applied Biomechanics* (1995–97).
[b]Data from the *1999 Proceedings of the ISBS*.
[c]Data in table is reported as number of studies:total number of subjects.

Study of the etiology of sports injuries in youth is more difficult than in adult and highly skilled competitors because young athletes tend to be supervised less and the availability of trained medical personnel and other researchers to record the exact nature and mechanism of injury is often not available. There is a tendency for the study of injuries in young athletes to be retrospective, relying on the recall of children and their parents to elucidate the cause, type, and severity of injury. Under this approach, data that is collected is general (e.g. knee injury). On the other hand, more prospective studies take place in adult sports, providing better understanding of specific injuries (e.g. anterior cruciate injury of the knee) and their injury mechanisms.

By studying the mechanisms of injury in youth sports, the incidence and severity of injuries may be able to be reduced through rational decisions and recommendations regarding the (a) modification of sports rules; (b) design and use of sports equipment and personal protective supplies, devices, and clothing; (c) equation of competition; and (d) establishment of age requirements. The mechanisms of injury are the processes by which injuries occur in sport. These processes involve complex interactions among many factors associated with the performer (internal factors) and sport environment (external factors). Each athlete comes to the sport setting with his/her own set of physical, psychological, and cognitive characteristics. These characteristics are internal to the performer and are the result of past experiences and development. Therefore, they change over time. Examples of these characteristics are as follows: (a) physical characteristics— strength, somatotype, weight, gender, skeletal maturation; (b) psychological characteristics—trait anxiety, self-confidence, risk taking, state anxiety; and (c) cognitive characteristics—knowledge of rules, knowledge of safe performance, knowledge about the opponent, knowledge about how to use training equipment, strategy. Each specific characteristic may have an influence on an athlete's potential for injury. In studying injuries associated with youth involvement in sport, it is important to consider specific personal characteristics. Even though there are many specific characteristics associated with each athlete, coaches and biomechanists may have insight into the physical, psychological, and cognitive characteristics of athletes and thus be able to identify a few key characteristics to study as logically important contributors to injury.

Each sport setting, whether for training or actual sport competition, contains many environmental factors that can be contributors to injury. However, they can also change with time. These environmental factors are external to the athlete. They include items such as condition of the field, characteristics of implements used in sport, properties of protective equipment, and forces and torques' applied to the athlete. Similar to the specific characteristics of the performer, there are many specific characteristics associated with each sport environment. Insight into determining which of these are important factors in contributing to injury in sport requires the insight of coaches and biomechanists to selectively identify specific environmental factors to study.

An injury mechanism model (Brown, 1987) has been previously developed and modified (Brown and Learman, 1998) to include concepts related to the study of the biomechanics of injury in youth sports (Figure 2). Elements in this model include (a) a questionnaire to collect data on the athlete (performer) and the sport environment; (b) prospective research on injury mechanisms and the mechanics of performance to help understand the injury process; and (c) recommendations to prevent injuries and reduce their severity. The schematic model presented in Figure 2 suggests that injuries in sport result from interactions, on an individual level, between the athlete and the sport environment. The suggested relationship between performer and environment is in accord with Lysens *et al.* (1984) who stated that "sports injuries result from a complex interaction of identifiable risk factors at a given point in time".

A two stage process was developed to study the biomechanics of injury in youth sport athletes. The first stage involved the development of a questionnaire to collect retrospective information about the performer, sport environment, and interaction between the performer and sport environment. In general questionnaire items address the physical characteristics of young athletes, history of their sport participation, level and incidence of pain associated with their training and participation in sport, conditions under which their sport was conducted, and sites and types of injuries sustained. Questionnaire items must be specifically developed for each sport and rely upon the insight of knowledgeable coaches and sport biomechanists. A questionnaire was initially developed to specifically address injury mechanisms in teenage powerlifting (Brown and Kimball, 1983; Brown and Abani, 1985). This questionnaire has been modified to make it compatible with the specific terminology and sport involvement characteristics of other youth sport groups and its utility has been tested on these groups (Brown and McKeag, 1987; Brown *et al.*, 1996).

The second stage of this process involved drawing relationships between regions of the body with relatively high levels and incidences of pain (areas susceptible to overuse and acute injury), injury sites and types, and the kinetics of selected sport skills that were suspected of precipitating these problems. In powerlifting, for example, from the questionnaire administered to teenage subjects, it was learned that they experienced a relatively high level and incidence of pain in the low back region and that 50 % of their reported injuries occurred in this region (Brown and Kimball, 1983). Based on the questionnaire results, a kinetic model was developed to subsequently study the movement patterns in powerlifting (Brown and Abani, 1985) in order to more fully understand the injury mechanisms.

This process was successfully employed in collecting data on youth participants in powerlifting, pairs skating, gymnastics, and rowing. It has resulted in a strategy that can be used to collect similar information on other youth sport groups. It should be noted that this process is not as definitive in sports classified as "open" (sports in which the physical activities are somewhat unpredictable—e.g. soccer, American football, and basketball) in comparison to those that are classified as "closed" (e.g. shot put, weightlifting, and crew).

INSTRUCTIONAL/COACHING PRACTICES

In addition to injury prevention, another role of biomechanics in youth sports is relates to instructional and coaching practices.

Translating Principles of Biomechanics into Coaching Language

Many youth sport coaches are volunteers who become involved because of their enjoyment of and/or past participation in a particular sport. Others become involved as coaches because they want to share in the sport experience with their child who has signed up to play. Irrespective of the reasons why adults become involved, many lack formal coaching education, and they cannot be expected to contribute many hours beyond the time they train their team and guide their athletes in competition.

How can biomechanics be helpful to youth sports coaches when most coaches are not readily receptive to instruction on the centre of gravity of the human body, moments of inertia of body segments, conservation of linear and angular momentum, and the like? To reach them with these and other concepts, that may assist them to develop a better understanding of the performance of sport skills, there must be a translation of these principles of biomechanics into more practical concepts (bridging the gap between the science and practice of biomechanics). This type of translation should (a) use words that are more common to coaches, even if they may lack a precise physics definition, and (b) include visual support for understanding movement patterns (sequential drawings, video, CD, etc.). An example of this translation is drawn from an instructional manual in the sport of soccer (Brown and Williamson, 1992), specifically the skill of kicking. The approach, pre-impact, impact, and follow-through are four elements of the kick that are described. Focusing on the pre-impact phase, there are many translated statements and visual associations made (Table 3).

Teaching Youth Sports Coaches to Visually Evaluate Performance

Coaches of young athletes may know the skills they want to teach their athletes, but are often limited in their ability to observe their athletes' performances of skills and to subsequently provide suggestions as to how to correct performance errors and/or enhance performance. In addition, they may dedicate much of their time and effort in their coaching to organizational and administrative responsibilities. There are two general approaches that coaches employ to evaluate sport skills. The first, and least productive, is a product evaluation. It focuses on the results of performance. Telling an athlete, who finishes last in a 50 metre sprint to swim faster is stating the obvious. The important question involves the process of how to swim faster. Coaches need to learn ways to observe the performances of skills by their athletes in order to provide feedback on the form or process of performance. Therefore, an important ability that should be taught to coaches is visual evaluation techniques (Brown, 1982). These techniques involve the establishment of an observation strategy and use of simplified principles of biomechanics. Table 4 provides a listing of visual evaluation techniques and a brief explanation of each.

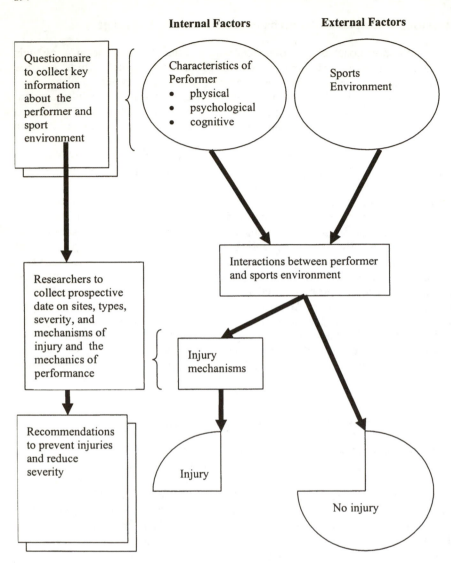

Figure 2 Schematic model for the study of injury mechanisms in youth sports.

Table 3 Soccer example of the translation of biomechanics into coaching language.

Components of kicking	Excerpted verbal description for coaches	Principles of Biomechanics
Approach	"A full-speed run to the ball is not usually desirable because a player will not likely be able to control the kick that follows."	• Speed versus accuracy
	"For maximum ball velocity, the hip of the kicking leg should be fully extended before swinging the leg forward."	• Stretch reflex • Elastic property of muscle • Application of force over a longer period of time

Pre-impact	"As the player contacts the ground, the support leg acts like a strut: to block the forward movement of its hip, to start the forward rotation of the other hip, and to initiate forward swing of the thigh of the kicking leg."	• Eccentric force causes rotation
	"Just before impact, the speed of the thigh's forward rotation should rapidly decrease. This is associated with a rapid extension of the knee of the kicking leg."	• Kinetic link principle • Conservation of angular momentum

Angled versus straight approach–hip rotation	"In the angled approach to the ball (B), because of the increased range to swing the hip of the kicking leg forward from the opened position, greater forward velocity can be achieved in the kicking leg."	• Application of force (torque) over a longer period of time

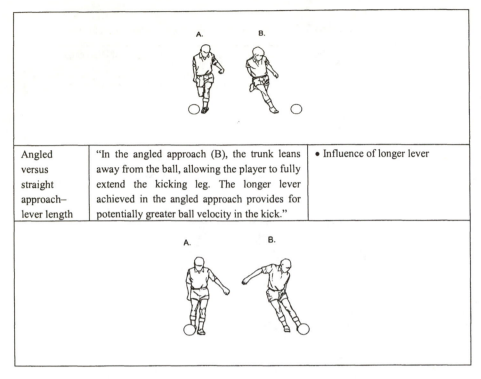

Angled versus straight approach– lever length	"In the angled approach (B), the trunk leans away from the ball, allowing the player to fully extend the kicking leg. The longer lever achieved in the angled approach provides for potentially greater ball velocity in the kick."	• Influence of longer lever

Schematically, Figure 3 highlights the observational strategy that accompanies these visual evaluation techniques. The coach is encouraged to use vantage point techniques whenever analysing sport techniques. During the initial observations, the movement simplification techniques should be employed to develop a general understanding of how the athlete performs the skill. Based on what is learned from the movement simplification techniques, the coach can concentrate on the specific observable problems and the nature of the skill (e.g. balance, projectile, maximum force and/or velocity, accuracy) to focus subsequent observation. These visual evaluation techniques have been taught to beginning and advanced coaches. At minimum, they provide an understanding that coaching should not be limited to organization and administration of their athletes.

Table 4 Visual evaluation techniques for coaches.

Visual evaluation categories and techniques	Explanations/comments
Vantage point techniques	The relative position of the coach and athlete determine what will be seen.
1. Select the proper observational distance.	Observe from afar to get an overall understanding and then move in closer to look at the specifics.
2. Observe the performance from different angles.	Each angle may provide additional information about performance.
3. Observe the performance from a carefully selected angle.	This is especially important when the coach may get only a few chances to observe.
4. Observe activities in a setting that is not distracting.	Observing an athlete in isolation may assist the coach in focusing on an individual performer.
5. Observe the performance in a setting with a vertical and/or horizontal reference line.	When the orientation of body parts are important, these references may be helpful.
6. Observe a skilled reference model.	This technique may provide insight, but should be used cautiously when athletes differ in size, strength, and maturation.
Movement simplification	Initial observations should attempt to simplify the movement. An understanding of performance in a simplified form will be helpful in subsequent observations.
7. Observe slower moving body parts.	The extremities and striking implements often move very fast. To gain initial understanding of the sport skill, coaches should focus on the slower moving body parts (usually the hip area).
8. Observe separate components of a complicated skill.	This involves breaking down a complex skill into component parts (e.g. preparatory phase, movement phase, and follow-through).
9. Observe the timing of performance components.	In order for a sport skill to be performed correctly, there is an appropriate sequencing that should be followed.
Balance and stability	Simplified concepts of balance, stability, centre of gravity, and base of support are introduced to assist the coach in understanding their relationships to stability and mobility.
10. Look at the supporting parts of the body.	This technique helps the coach focus on the base of support.
11. Look at the height of the body and body parts.	The concept of the centre of gravity in balance and stability is introduced indirectly.
Movement relationships	The motion of one or more body parts may influence the motion of other parts. These relationships may cause either desired or undesired performance of skills.
12. Look for unnecessary movement.	A waste of physical effort will be very costly in repetitive movements (e.g. running, swimming, or cycling) over the course of prolonged activity.
13. Look for movement opposition.	Structurally, the movements of the legs and arms are often used to counterbalance one another.
14. Observe the motion and direction of swinging body parts.	Sports skills (e.g. jumping activities) involve the transfer of momentum of the parts to the momentum of the whole.
15. Look at the motion of the head.	Anatomically, the motion of the head and neck through their connection with the spine provide insight into movement of the entire body.
16. Observe the location and direction of applied forces.	This observation technique is a simplification of the concepts of the effects of eccentric forces, forces through the centre of mass, and force couples.

Range of movement	Range of movement can be used to influence control and/or force and velocity.
17. Observe the range of movement of body parts.	The range of movement may influence the force and/or speed that the athlete attains in the sport skill.
18. Look for the stretching of muscles.	The concepts of stretch reflex and storage of elastic energy are important when attempting to achieve maximum force and/or velocity.
19. Look for a continuous flow of motion.	In most skills, smooth transition from one phase of movement to the next is essential.

Visual evaluation techniques   **Application**

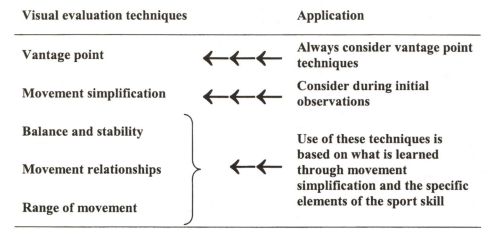

Figure 3 Schematic approach to the use of the visual evaluation techniques.

CONCLUSION

Even though youth sport participants far outnumber adult participants in sport, there is a paucity of biomechanics studies and application at the youth sport level. By bridging the gap between the science and practice of biomechanics, opportunities exist for biomechanists to make widespread contributions to youth sports in many ways: injury prevention, performance enhancement, equipment design, rule modifications, and instructional/coaching practices.

REFERENCES

Brown, E.W., 1982, Visual evaluation techniques for skill analysis. *Journal of Physical Education, Recreation and Dance*, **53**(1), pp. 21-26, 29.

Brown, E.W., 1987, Mechanisms of injury in young athletes. In *Competitive sports for children and youth–An overview of research and issues*, edited by Brown, E.W. and Branta, C. (Champaign, IL: Human Kinetics Publishers), pp. 107-113.

Brown, E.W. and Abani, K., 1985, Kinematics and kinetics of the dead lift in adolescent power lifters. *Medicine and Science in Sports and Exercise*, **17**(5), pp. 554-563.

Brown, E.W. and Kimball, R.G., 1983, Medical history associated with adolescent powerlifting. *Pediatrics*, **72**(5), pp. 636-644.

Brown, E.W. and Learman, J., 1998, Process for effectively studying the biomechanics of injury in youth sports. In *Proceedings II of the XVI International Symposium on Biomechanics in Sports*, edited by Riehle, H.J. and Vieten, M.M. (Konstanz, Germany: UVK- Universitatsverlag Konstanz), pp. 304-307.

Brown, E.W. and McKeag, D.B., 1987, Training, experience, and medical history of pairs skaters. *The Physician and Sports Medicine*, **15**(4), pp. 100-114.

Brown, E.W. and Williamson, G., 1992, Kicking. In *Youth soccer–A complete handbook*, edited by Brown, E.W. (Carmel, IN: Cooper Publishing Group), pp. 209-242.

Brown, E.W., Witten, W.A., Espinoza, D.M., Witten, C.X., Wilson, D.J., Wisner, D.M., Weise, M. and Learman, J., 1996, Attenuation of ground reaction forces in dismounts from the balance beam. In *Proceedings of the XIII International Symposium of the International Society of Biomechanics in Sports*, edited by T. Bauer, (Thunder Bay, Ontario, Canada: Lakehead University Press), pp. 114-117.

Caine, C., Caine, D. and Lindner, K., 1996, The epidemiologic approach to sports injuries. In *Epidemiology of sports injuries*, edited by Caine, D., Caine, C. and Lindner, K. (Champaign, IL: Human Kinetics), pp. 1-13.

Ewing, M., Seefeldt, V. and Brown, T., 1999, *Role of Organized Sports in the Education and Health of American Children and Youth* (New York, NY: Carnegie Corporation).

Lysens, R., Steverlynck, A., Auweele, Y., Lefevre, J., Renson, L., Claessens, A. and Ostyn, M., 1984, The predictability of sports injuries. *Sports Medicine*, **1**(1), pp. 6-10.

Seefeldt, V., 1987, Benefits of competitive sports for children and youth. In *Handbook for youth sports coaches*, edited by Seefeldt, V. (Reston, VA: American Alliance for Health, Physical Education, Recreation, and Dance), pp. 3-15.

35

Changes of Posture with Backpack Weight and Floor Walking in Children

Chi-kin Cheung and Youlian Hong
Department of Sports Science and Physical Education,
The Chinese University of Hong Kong, Hong Kong, China

INTRODUCTION

Concern has often been raised over the heavy school bags carried by children and the association between the loads carried and reports of spinal symptoms (Sander, 1979; The Hong Kong Society for Child Health and Development, 1988; Troussier *et al.*, 1994; Johnson and Knapik, 1995; Pascoe *et al.*, 1997; Grimmer *et al.*, 1999).

In recent years, a number of studies have investigated physiological responses to load carriage such as oxygen uptake and energy expenditure and heart rate (Hong *et al.*, 1999), or movement kinematic responses such as gait pattern and trunk posture (Pascoe *et al.*, 1997; Hong and Brueggemann, 2000). Heavy loads were found to induce physiological strain and the alteration of movement kinematics. However, most of the studies that focused on children carrying loads were conducted using treadmills. Little work has been devoted to the prolonged carriage of backpacks in a field setting, which is a more realistic method of simulating load carriage during a normal school day. Therefore, the present study examined the possible biomechanical and physiological stresses of prolonged load carriage upon children by quantifying the adaptations of stride and temporal parameters, trunk posture, and heart rate in an appropriate field setting.

METHODS

Twenty-three primary school boys aged between 9 and 10 years old were recruited as subjects. They were free from neuromuscular disorder. The mean age, body weight, and body height of the subjects were 9.43(0.51) years, 31.20(5.41)kg, and 134.52(6.00)cm respectively. The mean body weight and height of the subjects represented the 50th percentile of height and weight for 9 and 10 year old children in Hong Kong (Leung, 1994). The subjects and their parents were provided with all the information necessary to allow participation with informed consent. The experimental procedures were approved by the local Medical Ethics Committee.

The study took place in a university gymnasium. The subjects came to the gymnasium for four different days to complete the required four sessions. In each session, the subjects were assigned to carry backpack load that was equivalent to one of the following weight: 0%, 10%, 15%, or 20% of their body weight. The order of sessions was randomized using a Latin square design. In each session, the subject was walking around the perimeter of a basketball court (28m long and 15m wide) for 23 laps: i.e. a total of 1978m which was approximately the average distance of backpack carrying of Hong Kong children walking from home to school. Only 11 subjects completed the required four sessions and the data collected from these subjects were used for analysis.

At the beginning of each session, each subject was required to sit on the chair at the starting point of the walkways for 3 minutes, then stand with the backpack for 1 minute. Afterward, the subjects were required to walk at their natural cadence around the perimeter of the basketball court. The most popular school bag—a two straps backpack—was employed in this study.

A total of three gait cycles were filmed in two dimension for four different distances of total walking, with the first distance being one lap from the starting point of walking and the other distances having seven laps increment, i.e. 86 meter (Phase I), 688 metre (Phase II), 1290 metre (Phase III) and 1892 metre (Phase IV) from the starting point. A video camera (GY-X2BE, JVC, Japan) with a 50Hz filming rate and a 1/250 seconds shuttle speed was placed 12 metres to the sagittal plane of the subjects to record the locomotion. The filming field of 4 m provided at least one gait cycle for analysis. A 2–meter reference bar was placed on the subject movement position before and after the experiment for calibration purposes. The recorded video was digitized and analysed by a motion analysis system (Bewegungs Analyse System, Germany) to provide movement kinematics. A biomechanical model with 21 points and 15 segments was used in the digitization process. The mean of the kinematics parameters of the three cycles was then calculated and used to represent the gait cycle at this distance.

One gait cycle was deemed to contain the foot strike, opposite toe-off, opposite foot strike, toe-off, foot clearance, and the second strike. The stride length was measured as the distance between two consecutive heel strikes by the same foot, while the step length was the distance between two consecutive heel strikes (Wall *et al.*, 1987). Cadence was the number of steps per unit of time. Foot movement was divided into a stance phase and swing phase. The stance phase was measured as the period of time when the foot was in contact with the ground, while the swing phase was the period of time when the foot was not in contact with the ground. Double leg support duration was measured as the period of time when both feet were in contact with the ground, while single leg support duration was the period of time when only one foot was in contact with the ground (Sutherland *et al.*, 1994). Walking velocity was the average horizontal speed of the subject's centre of gravity along the plane of progression.

The mean and standard deviation of the stride parameters, including stride length, cadence, velocity, the normalized single leg support duration (% cycle time), double leg support duration (% cycle time), stance phase (% cycle time) and swing phase (% cycle time) were calculated by the motion analysis system. Furthermore, to compare gait characteristics across subjects, stride length and walking velocity were normalized according to body dimensions (Zatsiorsky *et al.*, 1994). A correction for differences in body height was made before the comparison of mean values of stride length and walking velocity (Hills and Parker, 1991).

The trunk inclination angle referred to the angle of the line connecting the shoulders and hips with the horizontal through the hips during all frames of one complete stride. Values greater than 0° represented a forward lean of the trunk, while values less than 0° represented a backward leaning trunk position. The trunk range of motion referred to the range of angular motion that was observed in one complete stride.

A heart rate monitor (Polar Electo, OY, USA) was used to monitor the heart rate of the subject in each session. Throughout the sessions, the subject's heart rate was recorded every 5 seconds. Polar heart rate software was employed to collect and analyse the data received. The mean values of initial heart rate and the heart rate at each phase were used to indicate the cardiovascular response of the subject during the test.

Two-way MANOVA (weight by phase) with repeated measures on the second independent variables were performed on the parameters of trunk posture and gait pattern. Gait pattern comprised walking velocity, stride length, cadence, stance phase, swing phase, single leg support duration and double leg support duration. Trunk posture consisted of the trunk inclination angle and range of motion. In addition, two-way ANOVA (weight by phase) with repeated measure on heart rate were performed. Provided the MANOVA was significant, a univariate two-way ANOVA was performed on each dependent variable to determine those which possessed significant variance. If a univariate two-way ANOVA showed significance for the main effect for phase and weight-by-phase interaction, then trend analysis was performed as a multiple comparison (Bock, 1985; Glass and Hopkins, 1996). For the significant main effect of weight, a Tukey post hoc test was used to identify the specific mean differences between weights. Statistical significance was accepted at the 0.05 level of confidence.

RESULTS

Gait Pattern

The means of the normal gait parameters obtained in this study are very close to those values reported by Waters *et al.* (1988), who derived data from the overground walking of 6–12 year old children.

The two-way MANOVA analysis revealed a significant overall Phase effect (Wilks' Lambda = 0.308, $p < 0.05$). This significant result allowed for further univariate analysis to determine which dependent variables were significant. The subsequent univariate ANOVA demonstrated a significant phase effect in walking velocity (F = 3.148, $p < 0.05$) and stride length (F = 3.693, $p < 0.05$). Trend analysis showed linear trends of walking velocity across the phases (F = 5.929, $p < 0.05$). Among all loads conditions, walking velocity increased from 1.40 m/s at Phase I to 1.47 m/s at Phase IV. A trend analysis for stride length showed that a quadratic trend was significant (F = 0.9864, $p < 0.005$). Table 1 demonstrates walking velocity as a function of phase.

Table 1 Mean and standard deviation of walking velocity (unit/s) under different load carrying conditions.

Weight	Phase				Mean
	I	II	III	IV	
0%	1.37	1.43	1.51	1.51	1.45
(N = 11)	(0.09)	(0.18)	(0.17)	(0.23)	(.14)
10%	1.40	1.43	1.48	1.52	1.46
(N = 11)	(0.13)	(0.12)	(0.16)	(0.14)	(.11)
15%	1.39	1.48	1.45	1.41	1.43
(N = 9)	(0.14)	(0.19)	(0.18)	(0.16)	(.14)
20%	1.45	1.45	1.44	1.42	1.44
(N = 10)	(0.19)	(0.16)	(0.20)	(0.18)	(.14)
Mean	1.40	1.45	1.47	1.47	
	(.14)	(.16)	(.17)	(.18)	

Note. Values enclosed in parentheses represent standard deviations. N stands for the number of subjects.

The main effects of weight on gait pattern and weight-by-phase interaction and their univariate ANOVA were not statistically significant. The gait pattern displayed during load carriage was similar to that of unloaded walking, and each weight displayed the same pattern of reactions to the phase. However, consistent but minor changes could be found in the gait parameters. The mean values of the cadence were similar at 0%, 10%, and 15% of body weight. Then there was a sudden reduction in cadence from 136.56 step/min at 15% body weight to 131 step/min at 20% of body weight. Likewise, stride length showed a similar trend across weight. Stride length decreased from 94.82 at 15% of body weight to 92.95 at 20%.

In terms of the temporal parameters, there were sudden changes during load carriage as compared to normal walking. The stance phase in normal walking was 61.98%. During load carriage with 10%, 15%, and 20% of body weight, the stance phase increased to 63.05%, 62.69%, and 63.40% respectively. Similar trends were found for double leg support duration, which increased from 24.14% in the unloaded condition to approximately 26% when a load was carried.

Trunk Posture

The two-way MANOVA with repeated measure performed on the trunk inclination angle resulted in significant main effects for weight and phase (Wilks' Lambda = 0.611, p < 0.005; Wilks' Lambda = 0.676, p < 0.05, respectively). Significant main effects and interaction were not found in trunk range of motion.

Table 2 shows the trunk inclination angle across phase and weight respectively. The mean trunk inclination angle increased with the weight carried. The Tukey post-hoc assessment indicated that there was a significant increase in trunk inclination angle for the 20% load as compared to those of 0%, 10%, and 15% of body weight. Moreover, there was also a significant main effect for phase in the trunk inclination angle (p < 0.05). A significant linear trend analysis (p < 0.005) indicated that the trunk inclination angle increased as the walking distance increased.

Table 2 Means and standard deviations of trunk inclination angle (degree) under different load carrying conditions.

Weight	Phase I	II	III	IV	Mean
0%	3.41	4.38	6.28	5.44	4.88
(N = 11)	(4.24)	(5.02)	(5.27)	(4.85)	(4.13)
10%	4.84	5.98	7.90	7.87	6.65
(N = 10)	(3.74)	(2.63)	(3.90)	(3.34)	(2.30)
15%	5.98	9.02	7.55	7.52	7.52
(N = 10)	(2.98)	(5.76)	(6.74)	(5.14)	(4.81)
20%	10.64	12.17	12.89	11.95	11.91
(N = 11)	(4.47)	(7.91)	(5.14)	(3.60)	(3.65)
Mean	6.25	7.91	8.70	8.22	
	(4.70)	(5.45)	(5.77)	(4.80)	

Note. Values enclosed in parentheses represent standard deviations. N stands for the number of subjects.

Heart Rate

Heart rate as a function of phase at the different weights is demonstrated in Table 3. Two-way ANOVA with repeated measures for heart rate showed that the main effect for phase was significant ($p < 0.05$); meanwhile the main effect for weight and weight-by-phase interaction were not significant. Moreover, trend analysis showed that the heart rate increased linearly with the phases ($p < 0.05$). As presented in Table 3, among all load conditions, the heart rate increased significantly in the first two laps ($p < 0.05$), and then gradually increased over time.

DISCUSSION

Gait Pattern

In this study, the effects of prolonged load carriage on stride and temporal parameters were investigated in a field situation. The study found that the walking pattern, including stride and temporal parameters, was not affected by the carriage of loads up to 20% of body weight.

Table 3 Means and standard deviations of heart rate (beats/minute) under different load carrying conditions.

Weight	Initial	Phase I	II	III	IV	Mean
0%	101.27	125.84	135.64	139.84	139.85	128.49
(N = 13)	(9.76)	(13.30)	(12.19)	(13.58)	(12.30)	(11.09)
10%	99.78	124.84	134.42	137.10	139.03	126.88
(N = 10)	(7.31)	(9.93)	(10.02)	(7.24)	(9.65)	(7.82)
15%	108.20	130.81	142.61	146.44	147.28	135.07
(N = 11)	(9.98)	(11.85)	(12.18)	(14.22)	(13.91)	(11.47)
20%	104.33	123.77	134.67	137.84	141.70	128.29
(N = 12)	(10.20)	(8.38)	(12.28)	(14.31)	(13.37)	(10.00)
Mean	103.40	126.10	136.79	140.30	141.70	
	(9.68)	(11.09)	(11.86)	(12.95)	(12.49)	

Note. Values enclosed in parentheses represent standard deviations. N stands for the number of subjects.

While walking velocity is an influential parameter in gait pattern, there has been little investigation regarding its adaptation when a backpack is carried. In the present study, the walking velocity did not change substantially even when subjects were carrying a load of up to 20% of their body weight. Most of the load carriage studies using backpacks have not yielded significant changes in stride length and cadence (Ghori and Luckwill, 1985; Charteris, 1998; Goh *et al.*, 1998; Hong and Brueggemann, 2000). Only Pascoe *et al.* (1997) found that there were significant decreases in stride length and increases in cadence with respect to normal walking when children walked overground with a backpack. However, it is difficult to compare this result with that of the present study because the walking distance and velocity were not reported by Pascoe *et al.* (1997).

The finding of the present study was in contrast to the speculation of Kinoshtia (1985), who proposed that if walking speed was self-determined by the subjects with heavy loads, then they would prefer to walk at a slower speed using a shorter stride length. Nottrodt and Manley (1989) provided evidence for Kinoshtia's speculation. Nottrodt and Manley found that when subjects carried loads of up to a self-determined maximum limit, the preferred walking speed relative to unloaded walking decreased, stride length decreased, and cadence increased. Since the heaviest backpack used in this study was 20% of body weight, the results of present study can be explained by assuming that the backpacks were not heavy enough to induce changes in walking velocity, stride length, or cadence.

It has been suggested that the aim of adjusting walking velocity under conditions of load carriage is to minimize energy expenditure. Minetti *et al.* (1995) pointed out that many biological systems associated with muscle activity are controlled under the criterion of minimum effort. The energy cost of walking with a load depends on the walking velocity and weight of the load (Datta *et al.*, 1973). It has been shown that the preferred walking speed is close to the most economical speed (Martin and Morgan, 1992). Thus, as the weight of load increases, the preferred velocity is expected to decrease to compensate for the additional energy expenditure required for load carrying. However, Hong *et al.* (2000) found that carrying a load of up to 20% of body weight did not induce a much higher workload in children than unloaded walking. Therefore, it was not surprising to find that walking velocity did not decrease substantially in this study. Not surprising was also the findings that walking velocity increased when distance increased.

Significant changes in the temporal parameters were not found in this study. The results of the present study were consistent with those of Charteris (1998), who determined the temporal parameters of gait pattern under incremental loads from 0% to 60% of body weight with self-determined constant walking velocity on a walkway. He found that the temporal parameters were not sensitive to the changes in the loads carried.

Although significant changes could not be observed in the present study, the temporal parameters seemed to change slightly according to the load carried. However, there was no further change when the weight of the load was increased. This result is similar to that of Pierrynowski *et al.* (1981), who described gait patterns in terms of mechanical energy.

However, the results of present study were inconsistent with most load carriage studies which used backpacks. Hong and Brueggemann (2000) found that walking on a treadmill with a load of 20% of body weight induced a significant increase in double leg support duration with a decrease in swing duration. Likewise *et al.* (1985) found that there was a significant decrease in swing duration when walking on a treadmill at a constant velocity with a load of 20, 30, 40 and 50% of body weight. Changes in the temporal parameters can be attributed to the employment of constant walking velocity in these studies. According to Winter (1991), the temporal parameters actually depend on walking velocity.

To conclude, gait pattern was not altered by load conditions of this study. It is possible that significant changes in gait pattern during load carriage are confined to situations where the weight is heavy enough or the walking velocity is constant.

Trunk Posture

The findings indicate that the children counterbalanced the load on their back by shifting their trunk forward, and this is in agreement with the findings from studies on adults (Kinoshita, 1985; Martin and Nelson, 1986) and children (Pascoe *et al.*, 1997; Hong and Brueggemann, 2000).

This trunk inclination can be explained by the motor control theory. One of the main functions of motor control is to orient the body with respect to the external world, which involves maintaining posture to minimize the disturbance of balance, thus stabilizing the whole-body centre of gravity.

When someone is loaded with a backpack, he/she will try to shift the centre of gravity of the body-backpack system back to that of an unloaded condition. This can be achieved by forward inclination (Bloom and Woodhull-McNeal, 1987), and such adjustment helps the body to minimize the energy expenditure and increase the efficiency of walking with weight.

Carrying a backpack induces deviations from natural postures, and increased the stress at the low back (Chaffin and Andersson, 1991). The prolonged postural strain caused by the trunk, which is greatly displaced from its normal position, may lead to postural discomfort and muscular pain in the shoulders, or lower back injury (Chaffin and Andersson, 1991). Goh *et al.* (1997) found that the maintenance of stability and effective forward progression resulted in increased peak lumbosacral forces when subjects carried a load in a backpack.

In a survey of 1,178 students conducted by Troussier *et al.* (1994), the risk factors of back pain in school children were investigated. The habitual or prolonged carriage of excessive loads was found to result in lower back pain, muscular-skeletal disorders, and related compensation costs.

Therefore, based on the results of the present study, load carriage of up to 15% of body weight would be acceptable because it does not exert significant forward inclination.

Heart Rate

Heart rate is a measure of the total work rate of the body (Bobet and Norman, 1984). As expected, the heart rate rose sharply in the first two laps (Phase I), and then increased gradually. These results indicate that external loads increase the energy costs of walking (Epstein *et al.*, 1988). However, there was no significant difference between the mean heart rates of the four loads from Phase I to Phase IV, which indicates that the work rate between loads was similar. This finding is consistent with those reported in the literature concerning load carriage by children (Hong *et al.*, 2000).

Borghols *et al.* (1978) suggested that a positive linear relationship between weight carriage and heart rate could only be found when subjects carried loads of up to approximately 40% of their body weight or above. The heart rate increase was a result of the greater demands of energy expenditure needed to sustain the load carried. In the present study, the heart rates that were recorded indicate that the cardiovascular response to load carriage was in a steady state. Astrand and Rodahl (1977) found that when an individual is exercising at less than 65% of Vo_{2max} cardiovascular response, their heart rate response is in a steady state. Moreover, the individuals can sustain activity for a prolonged duration without exhaustion (Waters *et al.*, 1988).

Andersson (1985) suggested that to achieve safe levels for materials handling, the load imposed on an individual should not damage their physical capabilities or the structural elements of their spine. Therefore, walking safely with a load should neither be too mechanically stressful on the back, nor should it create high physiological demands. Therefore, biomechanical and physiological strain should be considered together when determining a suitable backpack load for children.

According to physiological studies concerning load carriage, 10% of body weight is the recommended load for school children (Hong *et al.*, 1999). In this study, no significant effect of weight on gait pattern and heart rate was found, and significant changes in trunk posture were observed only when the loads were increased from 15% to 20% of body weight. The adaptation of trunk posture under the experiment condition showed that load carriage might induce musculoskeletal problems and low back pain. It has been suggested that discomfort, pain, and musculoskeletal disorders can be reduced through the prevention of postural deviations. Therefore, it can be concluded that 15% of body weight would be an acceptable load for children to carry in their school bags; and the permissible load should be between 15% and 20% of their body weight.

REFERENCES

Andersson, G.B., 1985, Permissible loads: biomechanical considerations. *Ergonomics*, **28**(1), pp. 323-326.

Astrand, P.O. and Rodahl, K., 1977, *Textbook of Work Physiology* (New York: McGraw-Hill).

Bloom, D. and Woodhull-McNeal, A.P., 1987, Postural adjustments while standing with two types of loaded backpack. *Ergonomics*, **30**(10), pp. 1425-1430.

Bobet, J. and Norman, R.W., 1984, Effects of load placement on back muscle activity in load carriage. *European Journal of Applied Physiology and Occupational Physiology*, **53**, pp. 71-75.

Bock, R.D., 1985, *Multivariate Statistical Methods in Behavioral Research* (USA: Scientific Software, Inc.).

Borghols, E.A.M., Dresen, M.H.W. and Hollander, A.P., 1978, Influence of heavy weight carrying on the cardiorespiratory system during exercise. *European Journal of Applied Physiology and Occupational Physiology*, **38**, pp. 161-169.

Chaffin, D.B. and Andersson, G.B.J., 1991, *Occupational Biomechanics*, second ed. (USA: John Wiley and Sons, Inc.).

Charteris, J., 1998, Comparison of the effects of backpack and of walking speed on foot-floor contact patterns. *Ergonomics*, **41**(12), pp. 1792-1809.

Datta, S.R., Chatterjee, B.B. and Roy, B.N., 1973, The relationship between energy expenditure and pulse rates with body weight and the load carried during load carrying on the level. *Ergonomics*, **16**(4), pp. 507-513.

Epstein, Y., Rosenblum, J., Burstein, R. and Sawka, M.N., 1988, External load can alter the energy cost of prolonged exercise. *European Journal of Applied Physiology and Occupational Physiology*, **57**, pp. 243-247.

Ghori, G.M.U. and Luckwill, R.G., 1985, Responses of the lower limb to load carrying in walking man. *European Journal of Applied Physiology and Occupational Physiology*, **54**, pp. 145-150.

Glass, G.V. and Hopkins, K.D., 1996, *Statistical Methods in Education and Psychology*, third ed. (MA: Allyn and Bacon).

Goh, J.H., Thambyah, A. and Bose, K., 1998, Effects of varying backpack loads on peak forces in the lumbosacral spine during walking. *Clinical Biomechanics*, 13(S1), S26-S31.

Grimmer, K.A., Williams, M.T. and Gill, T., 1999, The associations between adolescent head-on-neck posture, backpack weight, and anthropometric features. *Spine*, **24**(21), pp. 2262-2267.

Hills, A.P. and Parker, A.W., 1992, Locomotor characteristics of obese children. *Child Care, Health and Development*, **18**, pp. 29-34.

Hong, Y. and Brueggemann, G., 2000, Changes of gait pattern in 10 years old children during treadmill walking with increasing loads. *Gait and Posture*, **11**, pp. 254-259.

Hong, Y., Li, J.X., Wong, A.S.H. and Robinson, P.D., 2000, Effects of load carriage on heart rate, blood pressure and energy expenditure in children. *Ergonomics*, **43**(6), pp. 717-727.

Hong, Y., Li, J.X., Wong, A.S.H. and Robinson, P.D., 1999, Weight of schoolbags and the metabolic strain created in children. *Journal of Human Movement Studies*, **35**, pp. 187-200.

Hong Kong Society for Child Health and Development, 1988, *The weight of school bags and its relation to spinal deformity* (Hong Kong: The Department of Orthopaedic Surgery, University of Hong Kong, The Duchess of Kent Children's Hospital).

Johnson, R.F. and Knapik, J.J., 1995, Symptoms during load carrying: effects of mass and load distribution during a 20-km road march. *Perceptual and Motor Skills*, **81**, pp. 331-338.

Kinoshita, H., 1985, Effects of different loads and carrying systems on selected biomechanical parameters describing walking gait. *Ergonomics*, **28**(9), pp. 1347-1362.

Leung, S.S.F., 1994, *Growth Standards for Hong Kong: a territory wide survey in 1993* (Hong Kong: Department of Paediatrics, The Chinese University of Hong Kong).

Malhotra, M.S. and Sen Gupta, J., 1965, Carrying of school bags by children. *Ergonomics*, **8**, pp. 55-60.

Martin, P.E. and Morgan, D.W., 1992, Biomechanical considerations of economical walking and running. *Medicine and Science in Sports and Exercise*, **24**(4), pp. 467-474.

Martin, P.E. and Nelson, R.C., 1986, The effect of carried loads on the walking patterns of men and women. *Ergonomics*, **29**(10), pp. 1191-1202.

Minetti, A.E., Capelli, C., Zamparo, P., di Prampero, P.E. and Saibene, F., 1995, Effects of stride frequency on mechanical power and energy expenditure of walking. *Medicine and Science in Sports Exercise*, **27**(8), pp. 1194-1202.

Nottrodt, J.W. and Manley, P., 1989, Acceptable loads and locomotor patterns selected in different carriage methods. *Ergonomics*, **32**(8), pp. 945-957.

Pascoe, D.D., Pascoe, D.E., Wang, Y.T., Shim, D.M. and Kim, C.K., 1997, Influence of carrying book bags on gait cycle and posture of youths. *Ergonomics*, **40**(6), pp. 631-641.

Pierrynowsi, M.R., Norman, R.W. and Winter, D.A., 1981, Mechanical energy analyses of the human during load carriage on a treadmill. *Ergonomics*, **24**(1), pp. 1-14.

Sander, M., 1979, Weight of school bags in a Freibury elementary school: recommendations to parents and teachers. *Offentliche Gesundheitswesen*, **41**, pp. 251-253.

Sutherland, D.H., Kaufman, K.R. and Moitoza, J.R., 1994, Kinematics of normal human walking. In *Human Walking*, edited by Rose, J. and Gamble, J.G. second ed. (Baltimore: Williams and Wilkins).

Troussier, B., Davoine, P., De Gaudemaris, R., Fauconnier, J. and. Phelip, X., 1994, Back pain in school children: a study among 1178 pupils. *Scandinavian Journal of Rehabilitation Medicine*, **26**, pp. 143-146.

Wall, J.C., Charteris, J.C. and Turnbull, I.T.G., 1987, Two steps equals one stride equals what?: the applicability or normal gait nomenclature to abnormal walking patterns. *Clinical Biomechanics*, **2**, pp. 119-125.

Waters, R.L., Lunsford, B.R., Perry, J. and Byrd, R., 1988, Energy-speed relationship of walking: standard tables. *Journal of Orthopaedic Research*, **6**, pp. 215-222.

Winter, D.A., 1991, The Biomechanics and Motor Control of Human Gait: Normal, Elderly And Pathological, second ed. (Waterloo: University of Waterloo).

Zatsiorky, V.M., Werner, S.L. and Kaimin, M.A., 1994, Basic kinematics of walking: step length and step frequency. A review. *The Journal of Sports Medicine and Physical Fitness*, **34**(2), pp. 109-134.

ACKNOWLEDGEMENT

The work described in this paper was fully supported by a grant from the Research Grants Council of the Hong Kong Special Administrative Region (Project no. CUHK4122/99M).

36

Body Form Influences on the Drag Experienced by Junior Swimmers

Andrew Lyttle, Nat Benjanuvatra[1], Brian A. Blanksby[1]
and Bruce Elliott[1]
Western Australian Institute of Sport, Perth, Australia
[1]Department of Human Movement and Exercise Science,
The University of Western Australia, Perth, Australia

INTRODUCTION

Swimming is the interaction of propulsive and resistive forces. Understanding the relationship between human morphology and hydrodynamic resistance enables coaches to modify swimming strokes to improve performance. Total drag can be quantified with the body in a fixed position (passive drag), or while in motion (active drag).

Studies of hydrodynamic resistance (both passive and active drag) and body anthropometry have produced varying results (Clarys, 1978; Huijing et al., 1988). Generally, research has found that anthropometry influences passive drag, except for body surface area (Chatard et al., 1990; Lyttle et al., 1998). However, the link between morphology and active drag also has yielded contrasting results (Huijing et al., 1988; Kolmogorov et al., 1997). Huijing et al. (1988) found significant correlations between anthropometry and active drag, particularly maximal body cross-sectional area, but others have indicated that swimming mechanics, rather than body dimensions, have a greater influence on active drag.

Toussaint et al. (1990) examined the effects of growth on active drag in swimmers. They used the MAD system to longitudinally measure the change in active drag of children during front crawl swimming at 1.25ms[-1] over a 2.5 year period. Despite an 11% increase in height, 37% increase in mass and 16% increase in the body cross-sectional area, no differences were found in active drag at the above velocity. They suggested that the lack of change in active drag was due to a height increase. Theoretically, this reduced the wave drag component of the total drag in accordance with the Froude theory (Toussaint et al., 1990). That is, reduced wave-making resistance appeared to offset any increases in form and frictional drag. However, research has also shown that active drag is affected by swimming technique (Kolmogorov et al., 1997). Thus, changes in the stroke mechanics, skill and streamlining ability could have contributed to the lack of change in total drag found in the swimmers after 2.5 years of training and growth (Touissant *et al.*, 1990). This cross sectional study examined whether drag force was influenced by anthropometry, age, gender and kicking performance.

METHODS

Six males and six females aged 9, 11 and 13 years, participated in the study. Their height and mass measures were within ±1 standard deviation (SD) from the anthropometric means of Western Australian school children. Selected anthropometric variables were recorded and a maximal 25m freestyle flutter kick time was recorded as a performance measure. Subjects were towed along the surface of a 25m pool at 1.3, 1.6, 1.9, 2.2 and 2.5ms^{-1} while performing a prone streamlined glide and freestyle flutter kick at each velocity. Net force in the streamlined glide condition represented the resistance to towing the swimmer along the pool (passive drag) while the net force in the kicking trials was the interaction of the total resistance of the swimmer and the propulsive force created by the kick (total resistance minus propulsive force). Figure 1 outlines the experimental set-up and further details can be found in Lyttle *et al.* (1999). An underwater video camera, perpendicular to the swimmer's motion, ensured that the desired body position was maintained throughout the trial.

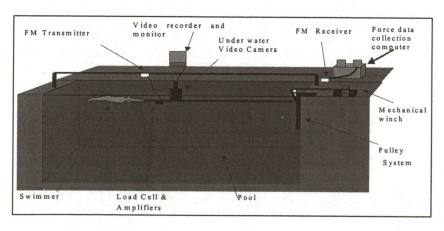

Figure 1 Schema of the experimental set-up for quantifying net forces.

RESULTS

A MANOVA revealed differences in the selected anthropometric variables between the three age groups (F = 11.877, p < 0.01). Males and females were also different across ages (F = 2.516, p < 0.05), but the age/gender interaction was not significant (F = 0.886, p = 0.58). A follow-up ANOVA examined each variable for each age group to ascertain the differences between males and females. The only significant gender difference was height for the 11 year olds (girls: mean = 151.48±3.04cm; boys: 147.37±1.49cm; F = 8.876, p < 0.05).

Force Analysis

The net force results are illustrated in Figure 2 for passive condition and in Figure 3 for active condition. A four way repeated measures MANOVA examined the differences in the net forces between the towing conditions, age groups and gender. Significant interactions were recorded between age groups and velocity ($F = 9.353$, $p < 0.01$), and between age groups and towing condition ($F = 17.199$, $p < 0.01$). However, the three way interaction between velocity, towing condition and age group was not significant ($F = 0.929$, $p = 0.45$).

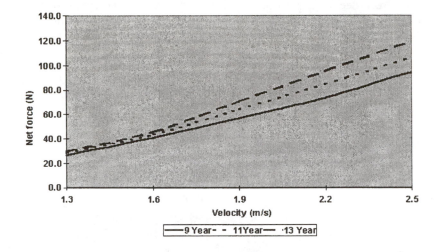

Figure 2 Mean net force during streamlined glide condition for the 9, 11 and 13 year age groups (n=12 per group).

The repeated measures MANOVA revealed no significant interaction effect for gender and any of the independent variables. However, tests of between-subjects effects revealed gender differences in the net force recorded ($F = 7.436$, $p < 0.05$). The repeated measure ANOVAs were conducted individually for each of the age groups and towing conditions to identify the age groups with a significant gender difference. Significant differences between gender occurred only in the 11 year age group where the girls created lower net drag forces than the boys in the streamlined glide condition ($F = 10.193$, $p < 0.05$) (Figure 4). Also, repeated measure ANOVAs found no significant interaction between gender and velocity, in the net force of both active and passive towing conditions in all age groups. The net forces from the passive and active conditions were compared via a four way repeated measures MANOVA. This revealed significant differences between the two conditions ($F = 7.033$, $p < 0.05$), as well as a significant velocity and towing condition interaction ($F = 58.614$, $p < 0.01$).

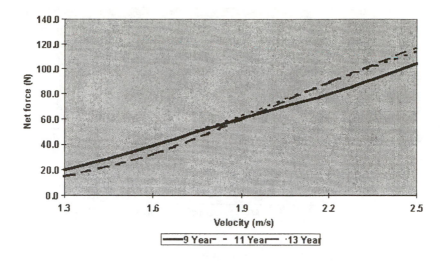

Figure 3 Mean net force during flutter kick condition for the 9, 11 and 13 year age groups (n=12 per group).

Relationships between the Net Forces and the Anthropometric Variables

Both height and 25m flutter kick time correlated significantly with most anthropometric variables and net forces. Partial correlations were constructed with the effects of height and 25m kick time held constant. Generally, the partial correlations revealed that no common variance was shared at 1.3 and 1.6ms^{-1}. However, at higher velocities, body indices and anthropometry correlated significantly with the flutter kick and streamlined glide.

Stepwise Multiple Regression

Stepwise multiple regression equations were developed to determine the best predictors of the net forces at each of the velocities in both the gliding and kicking conditions of the whole group (N = 36). At 1.3 and 1.6ms^{-1}, no regression equations could be computed for passive condition. Body mass was the best single predictor of the net force at 1.9, 2.2 and 2.5ms^{-1}. Passive drag at the faster velocities best predicted the net forces during the flutter kick.

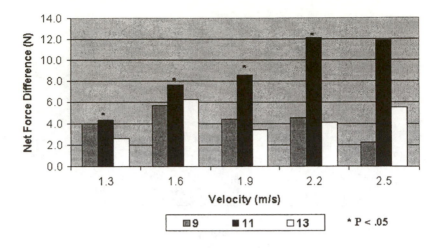

Figure 4 Gender comparison of the net force during the streamlined glide of each age group (Net force for boys minus net force for the girls).

DISCUSSION

Age Differences in Net Forces for the Streamlined Glide Condition

Lower velocities of 1.3 and 1.6ms^{-1} revealed similar drag values across the age groups. However, as the velocity increased, the 9 year old group recorded significantly lower drag forces than the 11 and the 13 year olds. At 2.2ms^{-1}, the three age groups differed significantly from one another with the 13 year age group recording the greatest amount of passive drag.

Toussaint *et al.* (1990) reported no change in active drag of young swimmers when swimming front crawl at 1.25ms^{-1} after a 2.5 year period, despite significant height (17cm) and mass (14.7kg) increases. They considered that increased height decreased the Froude number and reduced the wave-making drag component. This compensated for any increased frictional and form drag created by a larger body surface and cross sectional areas. No net changes in the drag force implied that the three age groups in the current study should record similar levels of passive drag. This was the case at the lower velocities of 1.3 and 1.6ms^{-1}, but not at the higher velocities.

Passive drag force at 1.9, 2.2 and 2.5ms^{-1} was significantly and positively correlated with the anthropometric variables except for sum of skinfolds. This agreed with other hydrodynamic studies that showed passive drag was highly influenced by body morphology (Clarys, 1978). Thus, at the higher velocities, differences in passive drag between the three age groups were due to increased body dimensions. However, it remains unclear as to why there was no significant difference at 1.3 and 1.6ms^{-1}. Frictional drag increases linearly with velocity, form drag increases with the square of the velocity and wave drag varies with the cube of velocity (Rushall *et al.*, 1994). Therefore, 1.3 and 1.6ms^{-1} might be too slow for body morphology to substantially influence passive drag.

Gender Differences in the Net Force during a Streamline Glide

There was no gender difference between the passive drag of 9 and 13 year olds, but the mean passive drag of the 11 year old girls was significantly less than that of the 11 year old boys. While the 9 and 13 year old boys and girls were similar in all of the selected anthropometric variables, the 11 year old girls were significantly taller than the 11 year old boys (151.5 and 147.4cm for girls and boys, respectively). As the other anthropometric variables for 11 year olds were similar across gender, the greater height of the girls was likely to be associated with reduced wave-making resistance. Similarity in all other anthropometric variables could lead one to assume that the frictional and form drag components also were similar.

Relationship between Anthropometry and Passive Drag

At 1.3 and 1.6ms^{-1}, this study agreed with Toussaint *et al.* (1990) that increased growth did not significantly influence drag. However, at the higher velocities, the increased body size with age also increased drag. Measures of slenderness, such as the Ponderal Index, H^2/BSA and H^2/X indices correlated significantly (p < 0.05), but negatively, with passive drag at 1.9, 2.2 and 2.5ms^{-1}, when height and kick time were held constant. Greater height per unit mass, greater height per unit surface area and greater height per unit body cross-sectional area all corresponded with lower passive drag, and supported the Froude number theory.

Therefore, anthropometric indices could explain how body morphology interacts with passive drag. Furthermore, the Ponderal Index is associated with the wave making component of drag (Lyttle *et al.*, 1998), while the H^2/BSA and the H^2/X are related to frictional and form drag, respectively (Clarys, 1978). In contrast to these authors, the significant correlations between passive drag and all of the three indices at the three highest velocities suggested similar contributions from wave making, friction and form components of drag.

The Influence of the Flutter Kick on Net Force

The mean kick time for 25m was significantly and negatively correlated with age and many anthropometric variables. Muscular strength and power of children increases with physical development and enables them to generate greater power. In combination with a better kicking technique, this could enhance kicking performance (Touissant *et al.*, 1990). The kick time of the 9 year olds did not differ significantly from the 11 year olds, but the 13 year olds were significantly faster.

Kicking performance did not correlated significantly with passive drag at any velocities. Clarys (1978) claimed that passive drag is not related to swimming performance, as swimmers do not stay in a rigid position. However, Chatard *et al.* (1990) found passive drag to be an important variable in the regression equations for predicting maximal swimming velocity for both males and females. Passive drag has also been shown to have a significant role in the starts and turns. Minimizing passive drag during the push-off phase after the turn has been shown to be a critical part of overall turning performance (Lyttle *et al.*, 1999).

Net force measured during active towing is the sum of active drag force and the propulsive force generated by the kick. If the active drag of the three age groups were similar (Toussaint *et al.*, 1990) and the propulsive kicking force for the 13 year olds was greater than the younger age groups, then the net force (in the kicking condition) for the 13 year olds would be less than the other two age groups. However, this was not the case which indicated that the mean net force produced by the three age groups during kicking were similar (Figure 3).

CONCLUSION

As the swimmers' ages increased, so too did the anthropometric variables and passive drag at velocities exceeding $1.9ms^{-1}$. Body mass was found to be the only predictor of passive drag at these velocities. Increased height was only associated with lower passive drag when all other anthropometric variables were similar. This study indicated that active drag during prone flutter kicking is related to passive drag and a number of anthropometric variables. This reinforces the importance of the streamline position adopted during the gliding and kicking phase after the turn to maximize velocity and distance.

REFERENCES

Chatard, J.C., Lavoie, J.M., Bourgoin, B. and Lacour, J.R., 1990, The contribution of passive as a determinant of swimming performance. *International Journal of Sports Medicine*, **11**, pp. 367-372.

Clarys, J.P., 1978, Relationship of human body form to passive and active hydrodynamic drag. In *Biomechanics VI-B*, edited by Asmussen, E. and Jørgensen, K. (Baltimore: University Park Press), pp. 120-125.

Huijing, P., Toussaint, H., Mackay, R., Vervoorn, K., Clarys, J., de Groot, G. and Hollander, A., 1988, Active drag related to the body dimensions. In *Swimming Science V B*, edited by Ungerechts, Wilke, K. and Reischle, K. (Champaign, IL: Human Kinetics), pp. 31-37.

Kolmogorov, S.V., Rumyantseva, O.A., Gordon, B.J. and Cappaert, J.M., 1997, Hydrodynamic characteristics of competitive swimmers of different genders and performance levels. *Journal of Applied Biomechanics*, **13**, pp. 88-97.

Lyttle, A.D., Blanksby, B.A., Elliott, B.C. and Lloyd, D.G., 1998, The effect of depth and velocity on drag during the streamlined glide. *The Journal of Swimming Research*, **13**, pp. 15-22.

Lyttle, A., Elliott, B., Blanksby, B. and Lloyd, D., 1999, An instrument for quantifying the hydrodynamic drag of swimmers: a technical note. *Journal of Human Movement Studies*, **37**, pp. 261-270.

Rushall, B.S., Sprigings, E.J., Holt, L.E. and Cappaert, J.M., 1994, A re-evaluation of forces in swimming. *The Journal of Swimming Research*, **10**, pp. 6-30.

Toussaint, H.M., de Looze, M., van Rossem, B., Leijdekkers, M. and Dignum, H., 1990, The effects of growth on drag in young swimmers. *International Journal of Sport Biomechanics*, **6**, pp. 18-28.

37

Why Tai Chi can Enhance Posture Control: Challenge to Biomechanics

Jing Xian Li, Youlian Hong and Paul D. Robinson[1]
The Chinese University of Hong Kong, Hong Kong, China
[1]University College Worcester, Worcester, UK

INTRODUCTION

In most English literature Tai Chi Chuan, abbreviated as TCC, is a traditional Chinese exercise form derived from martial arts folk traditions, handed down from generation to generation for more than 1,200 years. In the Chinese Phonetic Alphabet, this exercise form is expressed as Tai Ji Quan, or, by putting them together, Taijiquan. Here the word "Chuan" means boxing and in some literature this word has been omitted.

TCC was gradually and systematically developed to the point of formalization more than 300 years ago in the late Ming (1368–1644) and early Qing dynasties (1644–1911) of China. To understand TCC, which is a set of systematic calisthenic exercises, one must first understand the origin and meaning of the words Tai Chi. The words Tai Chi first appeared in the book "I Ching", where they refer to the creation of heaven and earth (the sky and the world). The state of the universe before the creation of heaven and earth is called Tai Chi. In simple terms, TCC firstly means, each movement is circular, as represented by the circle in the Tai Chi diagram. Within the circular movement are concealed many variations and changes; there is emptiness and fullness; there is movement and stillness; there is expressed strength and softness; there is forward and backward. All these are the meaning contained in the words Tai Chi. Secondly, TCC is the interplay of Yin and Yang. The theory of Yin and Yang is the theoretical basis of traditional Chinese Medicine. According to the principles of the Yin and Yang theory, in any thing or material are contained two aspects, Yin and Yang. Human beings can be expressed as Yin and Yang, the female as Yin, the male as Yang. Human physiological activity can be described as Yin and Yang, for example with digestion, the intake of nutrients as Yang and the excretion of metabolites as Yin. In traditional Chinese medicine, health is contingent upon the balance between Yin and Yang. Imbalances in these energy forces are thought to produce physical dysfunction that may lead to sickness. TCC is used to seek serenity in action and also to seek action in serenity. The emphasis is in the exercise of mind and consciousness. Lastly, movements of TCC are continuous, from beginning to end, from one posture to the next, the movement is never broken, it is a complete integrated circle.

A lot of TCC schools were devised and developed over the centuries, such as Chen, Yang, Sun and Wu. Among these schools, Chen's TCC is thought to be the earliest devised and has spread most widely. When performing TCC, each movement can be divided into two techniques depending on the height of the centre of gravity of the body. They can be performed with a high or a low centre of gravity. By 1956, a meeting of TCC masters, convened by the Chinese National Council of Sports and Physical Education, had produced a "combined style of TCC", namely the Simplified 24-forms TCC. This style of TCC was designed to convey the most representative components of various traditional TCC schools that had evolved over the previous centuries so as to maintain the main characteristics of TCC but make it easier to learn and to practice. The time required to practice a complete set of exercises has therefore been reduced (Mark, 1979). Today millions of people in China practice TCC, an activity that has become one of the most popular and favoured sports and exercise forms in China, especially among the older people.

During the past twenty years, TCC has spread widely in western countries. The observed beneficial effects of TCC on health, especially for older adults, evoked research interest from western scientists. To our knowledge, the first paper in English that presented an experimental study about TCC was published in China (Gong *et al.*, 1981). The same year, a paper about TCC was published in an international journal (Koh, 1981). With increasing numbers of older people and increasing expenditure for chronic disease and disability among this older population, TCC has drawn more and more attention from health related government organizations and research interests from scientists. Published results from well-controlled studies about the effects of TCC on health, particularly those focusing on the older population, have enriched the knowledge of TCC and added to the understanding of the characteristics of TCC movement and its impact on health.

Exercise has definite effects on the health of older people. However, the exercise forms that are suitable are relatively few because ageing is usually accompanied by a significant decline in organ function. It is well known that joint degeneration, poor eyesight, poor balance and loss of stamina are universal in the older population. Therefore, exercises with low velocity, low impact and high interest level, which also provide a good training effect, are preferred for older persons. Based on the published literature, TCC seemingly has provided all the demands that elderly people require from exercise. Additionally, TCC has the potential to offer more than a form of group exercise to obviate the expenditures associated with poor health since it facilitates a lifestyle that promotes wellness among people of all ages. Before endorsing these views, two relevant questions must be answered. What evidence exists that TCC affords any benefits? What are the underlying mechanisms of the benefits of TCC? The purpose of this article is firstly, to review the scientific studies, both Chinese and English, on the impact of this intriguing form of exercise on balance capacity, and secondly, to provide views on what should be done for the biomechanists in future TCC studies. This review is designed to provide a basis of reference for future biomechanical studies.

BIOMECHANICS STUDY IN TAI CHI CHUAN

There are a limited number of studies of the characteristics of muscular activity, movement kinematics and kinetics of TCC exercise. Zhang *et al.* (1989) reported an electromyography (EMG) study on Chen TCC. One of the later generations of the creator of Chen TCC and another eight Chen TCC masters participated in the study. Using surface electrodes, EMG activities of deltoideus, sacrospinalis (erector spinae), rectus femoris, and gastrocnemius on both sides of the body were recorded while performing the whole set of Chen TCC. The integrative EMG (iEMG) and power frequency EMG were employed for analysis. It was found that the iEMG pattern of the analysed movements showed alternation of higher amplitude and lower amplitude, and the high amplitude was accompanied by higher frequency while the lower amplitude was accompanied by lower frequency. Analysis of the movement "Ya shou hong chui" (one form in Chen TCC) showed that there was a time difference of 0.014sec in the muscle activity between the upper and lower body extremities. Also, the muscles of the upper extremity on the left side were activated first, then the lower extremity on this side, subsequently the muscles on the right side contracted with the sequence from upper to lower extremities. The EMG activity patters during TCC practice provided preliminary experimental evidence that TCC exercise demands the involvement and coordination of upper and lower extremities and unilateral and bilateral support. The power frequency EMG, however, did not show any evidence of muscle fatigue during TCC practice, indicating the mild exercise intensity of TCC practice.

Lu *et al.* (1991) published a biomechanical study on the kicking movement of Chen TCC which was thought to be more powerful than other TCC schools. The kicking movement of Chen TCC differs from the kicking movements of other TCC schools for it is characterized by a jump with high velocity and high power, and is considered as a representative movement of this school of TCC. One TCC master with twenty-four years of Chen TCC experience served as the subject. He was asked to perform twelve kicking movements on a force platform. EMG signals were collected for a total of nine pairs of muscles (deltoideus, biceps brachii, triceps, rectus femoris, biceps femoris, gastrocnemius, rectus abdominis, external oblique abdominis, and sacrospinals at L5). Ground reaction force and 3-D video filming were recorded synchronously with EMG throughout the performance of the kicking. The results showed that there was an appreciable change in both the centre of gravity of the body and the momentum of each body segment. The highest amplitude of the iEMG was found in the right rectus femoris, whereas the lowest amplitude of iEMG was recorded in the right biceps femoris among all EMG measurements during kicking. A recent biomechanical study (Lin *et al.*, 1999) examined the pressure distribution pattern and balance control during the kicking movement of TCC. The authors compared the pressure distribution patterns of the stable kick and unstable kick performed by a TCC athlete at national level. The mat pressure measurement system was used to collect the vertical reaction force and the pressure profile of the standing foot during a right kicking movement and a left kicking movement. The partial force and partial pressure were calculated. The pressure-time diagram of the phalanges, metatarsals and tarsals indicated that the pressure profiles or sequences tended to be stable each time the left kick was completed, and the phalanges produced "fragmented" and large pressure points acting on the ground. The evidence supported a key point of practicing TCC that "five toes grasping the ground to make us stable as a mountain".

These biomechanical studies mentioned above emphasized the profiling of some specific TCC movements. Only a few biomechanical studies have concentrated on explaining the mechanism of TCC exercise for improving functional capacity, particularly in posture control and balance. Forrest (1997) tried to explain the mechanism behind the positive effect of TCC exercise on balance control after examining the effects of a sixteen weeks TCC training programme on anticipatory postural adjustments. Eight subjects (average age 36.5 years) in good health, with no prior training in TCC were tested. The battery of tests included the dropping of a 2.2kg load onto an unstable board, on which the subject stood, which was also on a force platform. The level and direction of instability were varied. The results found counter intuitive reductions in the anticipatory postural adjustments of several muscle groups while the standing stability improved. The author stated that the findings from his study could be used as an indication that practising TCC leads to a greater use of the elasticity of the peripheral structures involving muscles, ligaments, and tendons while the participation of the central neural structures of postural equilibrium is decreased. In order to explore the mechanism of TCC exercise to improving posture control, more experimental evidence is needed.

BENEFICIAL EFFECTS OF TAI CHI CHUAN ON BALANCE CONTROL

TCC exercise demands precise joint movements, stability and balance. Performing TCC depends on either double-stance weight-bearing or single-stance weight-bearing manoeuvres, which further requires pivoting the whole body or twisting the trunk. In performing TCC, the roles of the muscles continually change between stabilizers and movers, between weight-bearing and non-weight-bearing and between contraction and relaxation. It has been suggested that the practice of TCC may enhance the repertoire of motor programmes stored in the brain (Tse and Bailey, 1992) and therefore may serve to train the various balance systems to promote greater steadiness. Numerous studies about the impact of TCC exercise on balance, muscle strength and flexibility have been reported and have demonstrated the beneficial effects of TCC exercise.

Cross-sectional Comparison

Cross-sectional studies provided positive evidence that TCC has beneficial effects on balance and flexibility. Tse and Bailey (1992) reported that TCC practitioners performed significantly better on right and left single leg stance with eyes open, and heel-to-toe walking than the non-practitioners. But this was not the case with single leg stance with eyes closed. Lan *et al.* (1996) found that long-term TCC practitioners showed better scores in the stand-and-reach test. Hong *et al.* (2000) supported the findings by Lan *et al.* by reporting that long-term (13.2 years) elderly TCC practitioners performed better in the tests of single leg stance with eyes closed (right and left), total body rotation (right and left), knee extension and ankle plantar flexion than the control group. These findings suggested that elderly people who exercise using TCC regularly and long-term, would improve their balance capacity with and without the help of vision.

TCC Intervention

Besides the cross-sectional studies, a number of TCC intervention studies on balance capacity and muscle strength in elderly people have been conducted. Schaller (1996) found that a 10-week exercise of an easy-to-learn westernized form of TCC resulted in a significant improvement in the scores of single leg stance with eyes open, but not in the single leg stance with eyes closed. Moreover, the scores of the sit-and-reach test for TCC practitioners were not improved. Wolf *et al.* (1996) demonstrated with a large sample size, that a moderate TCC intervention could impact favourably on some biomedical and psychosocial indices of frailty. The results indicated that TCC participants had a substantial reduction in risk of multiple falls by as much as 47.5%, in addition to other positive influences such as an increase in hand grip strength, and increased ambulating speed. Fear of falling was also reduced in the TCC group when compared with the non-exercise group. Jacobson *et al.* (1997) reported significantly better balance control (tilting board test), strength of knee extension (maximal voluntary extension test) and kinesthetic sense (gleno-humeral media rotation at 90°) in adult TCC participants than the sedentary control group after 12-week TCC intervention. Shih (1997) reported on the average velocity of sway in his study of a 16-week TCC intervention and stated that TCC exercise was associated with substantial reductions in anterio-posterior sway velocities between pre– and post–tests.

The beneficial effects of low intensity TCC exercise on the maintenance of gains in balance and strength in the health of older adults has also been demonstrated by Wolfson *et al.* (1996). TCC intervention has helped alleviate joint pain and has increased strength, flexibility, and balance in older patients with osteoarthritis (Lumsden *et al.*, 1998) and rheumatoid arthritis (Van Deusen and Harlowe, 1987; Kirsteins *et al.*, 1991). TCC exercise has had therapeutic effects on improving the range of motion of the upper extremities and in preventing further deterioration. Table 1 summarizes the experimental evidence of TCC studies on balance, muscle strength and flexibility.

PREVENTION OF FALLS

Falls, a real problem in public health, are the main cause of accidental death in the elderly according to data from the American National Safety Council (1988). Falls and subsequent fractures which occur in the elderly are a big medical and social problem throughout the world, increasing expenditure for chronic disease and disability. A poor balance capacity, decreased muscle strength and flexibility, and the changes of gait with aging are some of the risk factors related to falls in the elderly (Nickens, 1985; Perry, 1982). TCC exercise emphasizes continuous, slow movement with small to large expressions of motion, the shift of body weight from unilateral to bilateral, the progressive flexion of the knees, and rotation of the trunk, head and extremities. These movement components seemingly offer potential benefits in reducing the risk factors of falls. A study conducted by

Wolfson *et al.* (1996), with a relatively large sample size, provided important scientific evidence that TCC exercise could impact favourably on reducing falls in elderly individuals. Wolf *et al.* (1996) examined the effects of intervention with TCC exercise or computerized balance training on improving frailty or reducing falls in older people through physical, functional, behavioural, and environmental measures with an education group serving as the control for the study. They compared the specific biomedical changes among the three groups. Yang's 108-form TCC was simplified to ten forms for the TCC training. Each intervention lasted 15 weeks with hourly sessions for the education and balance training groups while the TCC group met for two hourly sessions but with a total instructional time equivalent to the other groups. All subjects were followed for four months after the 15 weeks of intervention. The results showed that TCC training reduced the number of falls by 47.5%, significantly attenuated the fear of falling, and improved physiological and psychosocial measures. These findings demonstrated the beneficial effects of TCC exercise on prevention of falling in elderly individuals. The changes of gait with aging are thought to be a factor related to falling in older persons. A preliminary study about the impacts of TCC exercise on gait in the elderly has been reported by Wolf and Gregor (1999). They examined the gait of 15 individuals from each of 20 independent living facilities. Each group experienced either 60–90 minutes of Tai Chi exercise classes twice a week for 48 weeks or received information on wellness behaviours for one hour per week over the same period. Three of the 15 volunteers from each facility were evaluated for strength and their gait analysed every four months for a period of two years. All subjects were tested for baseline measures at the start of the project and then three times during the first year (during the TCC or wellness classes) and three times during the second or follow-up year for a total of seven sessions. They calculated total body kinematics, lower extremity kinetics and centre of pressure during gait initiation. They studied normal walking at a preferred speed and situations during normal walking where the individual had to move unexpectedly to the right in the step cycle and had to make unexpected turns beginning with either the right or left foot. The exemplar data indicated that individual strategies were apparent during each of these movements and that each subject displayed a unique movement signature during both walking and turning. This study provided an indication that examined the changes in kinematics and kinetics in TCC practitioners and made a comparison with those sedentary older persons which might be helpful in exploring the scientific bases of the beneficial effects of TCC exercise in the prevention of falls in the elderly.

Exercise is a significant intervention for preventing falls and fall-related injuries. If falls occur at least in part because of physical deficits in balance, strength, reaction time, and flexibility, then it is plausible to believe that exercise targeted to improve these deficits might result in fewer falls or other injury events. In fact, many observational studies have demonstrated an association between low levels of some types of physical function or activity and increased risk of falls and some types of injuries (Blake *et al.*, 1988; Robbins *et al.*, 1989; Lord *et al.*, 1991). Some authors have suggested that among the physical deficits that appear with ageing in such areas as balance, strength, flexibility, and reaction time, balance deficits could have a more direct causal pathway to the generation of falls than deficits in other areas (Province *et al.*, 1995). It could also be that elderly people are more aware of their strength, flexibility, and endurance limitations than they are of balance problems. There are many signs that can warn an elderly person of any decline in strength, flexibility, and endurance (e.g. the inability to lift or reach while sitting or lying down and the like). Both the cross-sectional and longitudinal studies of TCC have demonstrated the effect of such exercise on improving physical deficits, particularly in balance capacity (Hong *et al.*, 2000; Tse and Bailey, 1992; Wolf *et al.*, 1996). TCC exercise should be replete with dynamic balance training components. TCC practitioners have to exercise control, adjust their posture, and maintain their balance during shifts in the body's centre of gravity from unilateral and bilateral at a smooth and slow movement speed. Movement during the performance of TCC is characterized as the transformation of open- and closed-kinetic-chain movements. The semi-squatting posture used in the performance of TCC allows practitioners to control their body's centre of gravity and remain very stable. Thus, the characteristics of TCC exercise might train the proprioception of the practitioners. Posture control during the practice of TCC forces the muscles involved in movement to work hard, which might lead to increased muscle strength. Moreover, it has been suggested that the practice of TCC may enhance the repertoire of motor programmes stored in the brain and therefore serve to train the various balance systems to promote greater steadiness (Tse and Bailey, 1992). However, the mechanism for improving balance capacity, and subsequently preventing falls, is still unclear. Experimental evidence about the characteristics of movement kinematics and kinetics and neuromuscular activity in TCC exercise has yet to be revealed. There should definitely be further investigation into the scientific basis of the way in which TCC exercise improves the physical deficits that are experienced due to aging.

CONCLUSION

Tai Chi Chuan is a time-honoured and life-time exercise that has gained recognition as an exercise form for people of a wide age range, for the younger and the older, for male and for female individuals. Studies have demonstrated that TCC may be classified as a moderate exercise, and its intensity does not exceed 55% of an individual's maximal oxygen intake (Zhuo *et al.*, 1984). The experimental evidence obtained from both cross-sectional and longitudinal studies suggested that TCC exercise has beneficial effects on musculoskeletal function, posture control capacity and reduction in falling in the elderly. This applied to either healthy people or patients with rheumatoid arthritis, or osteoarthritis. In consideration of the characteristics of TCC exercise and its valuable effect on improving the physical condition of human beings, at least in older people, TCC exercise has great potential value to health promotion and rehabilitation, particularly for the maintenance of balance control in the elderly.

Among the published literature biomechanical studies on TCC are limited. A few of the characteristics of muscular activity, movement kinematics and kinetics during the performance of TCC are understood but how TCC exercise helps to improve the human balance control has not yet been explained. This question provides a big challenge to the scientists of medicine and biomechanics.

Table 1 Summary of the studies of the effect of TCC exercise on balance control.

Reference	Subject	Test item	Measuring methods	Results
Tse and Bailey (1992) (CS)	N = 9 (TCC) N = 9 (Con) Age = 65 to 86 yrs	Questionnaire and balance	- Single leg stance with eyes open and closed - Heel-to-toe walking with eyes open	TCC group had significantly better posture control capacity with vision.
Schaller (1996) (10-wk IN)	N = 24 (TCC) N = 22 (Con) Age = 70 ± 5.9 yrs	Balance and flexibility	- Single limb stance with eyes open and eyes closed forms - Sit and reach test	Significantly improved the balance capacity with vision, did not change the flexibility.
Wolf *et al.* (1996) (15-wk IN and 4-m follow up)	N = 72 (TCC) N = 64 (BT) N = 64 (Education) Age = 76.2 yrs	Muscle strength and flexibility	- Isometric contractions about the hip, knee, or ankle - Grip strength - Fear of falling questionnaire	Fear of falling was reduced after the TCC intervention compared with Education group.
Wolfson *et al.* (1996) (6-m TCC IN after 3-m BT and strength training	N = 110 Age = 80 yrs (mean)	Balance and muscle strength	Loss of balance during sensory organization testing, single stance time, voluntary limits of stability, isokinetic torque of eight lower extremity movements, gait velocity	TCC training has the effects of maintenance for the significant gains of balance and strength.
Shih (1997) (16-wk TCC IN)	N = 110 Age = 30.8 ± 7.8 yrs	Balance	Velocity of sway in anterior and posterior at static and dynamic conditions	Significantly decreased the average velocity of sway on dynamic conditions, but not on static condition.
Jacobson *et al.* (1997) (12-wk TCC IN)	N = 12 (TCC) N = 12 (Con) Age = 30.4 ± 4.3 yrs	Stability, muscle strength and kinesthetic sense	Isometric muscle strength at 90°, Lateral body stability, kinesthetic sense in the glenohumeral joint at 30°, 45° and 60°	Lateral stability, kinesthetic sense at 60°, and strength of the knee extensor were significantly improved
Forrest (1997) (12-wk TCC IN)	N = 8 Age = 36.5 yrs	Anticipatory postural adjustments	Level and direction of instability on unstable board	Improved standing stability
Hong *et al.* (2000) (Case controlled study)		Balance capacity, trunk rotation, and flexibility	- Single limb stance with eyes open and eyes closed forms - Sit and reach test	

Note: CS: cross sectional study. IN: intervention. m: month. wk: week. Con: control. BT: balance training

REFERENCE

Blake, A.J, Morgan, J., Bendall, M.J., Dallosso, H., Ebrahim, S.B., Arie, T.H., Fentem, P.H. and Bassey, E.J., 1988, Falls by elderly persons at home: prevalence and associated factors. *Age and Aging*, **17**, pp. 365-372.

Forrest, W.R., 1997, Anticipatory postural adjustment and T'ai Chi Ch'uan. *Biomedical Sciences Instrumentation*, **33**, pp. 65-70.

Gong, L., Qian, J., Zhang, J., Yang, Q., Jiang, J. and Tao, Q., 1981, Changes in heart rate and electrocardiogram during Taijiquan exercise. *Chinese Medical Journal*, **94**(9), pp. 589-592.

Hong, Y., Li, J.X. and Robinson, P.D., 2000, Balance control, flexibility, and cardiorespiratory fitness among older Tai Chi practitioners. *British Journal of Sports Medicine*, **34**, pp. 29-34.

Jacobson, B.H., Chen, H.C., Cashel, C. and Guerrero, L., 1997, The effect of T'ai Chi Chuan training on balance, kinesthetic sense, and strength. *Perceptual and Motor Skills*, **84**(10), pp. 27-33.

Kirsteins, A.E., Dietz, F. and Hwang, S.M., 1991, Evaluating the safety and potential use of a weight-bearing exercise, Tai-Chi Chuan, for rheumatoid arthritis patients. *American Journal of Physical Medicine and Rehabilitation*, **70**(3), pp. 136-141.

Koh, T.C., 1981, Tai Chi Chuan. *American Journal of Chinese Medicine*, **9** (1), pp. 15-22.

Lan, C., Lai, J.S., Wong, M.K. and Yu, M.L., 1996, Cardiorespiratory function, flexibility, and body composition among geriatric Tai Chi Chuan practitioners. *Archive of Physical Medicine and Rehabilitation*, **77**(6), pp. 612-616.

Lin, Y., Lee, C., Tang, R., Huang, C. and Chen, C., 1999, Analysis of the pressure distribution pattern and the controlling balance during kick movement of Tai-Chi Chuan. In *International Symposium on Biomechanics in Sports '99 – Scientific Proceedings*, pp. 385-387.

Lord, S.R., Clark, R.D. and Webster, I.W., 1991, Postural stability and associated factors in a population of aged persons. *Journal of Gerontology*, **46**, M69-M76.

Lumsden, D.B., Baccala, A. and Martire, J., 1998, T'ai Chi for osteoarthritis: an introduction for primary care physicians. *Geriatrics*, **53**(2):84, pp. 87-88.

Lu, A.Y., Gang, T., A.J. and S, C., 1991, Biomechanical analysis of kicking movement in Chen Taijiquan, *Sports Science* (China), **5**, pp. 71-76.

Mark, B.S., 1979, *Combined Tai Chi Chuan*, (Chinese Wushu Research Institute).

National Safety Council, 1988, *National Safety Council Accidental Facts* (Chicago).

Nickens, H., 1985, Intrinsic factors in falling among the elderly. *Archives of Internal Medicine,* **145**, pp. 1089-1093.

Perry, B., 1982, Falls among the elderly: A review of the methods and conclusions of epidemiologic studies. *Journal of American Geriatrics Society*, **30**, pp. 367-371.

Province, M.A., Hadley, E.C., Hornbrook, M.C., Lipsitz, L.A., Miller, J.P., Mulrow, C.D., Ory, M.G., Sattin, R.W., Tinetti, M.E. and Wolf, S.L. 1995, The effects of exercise on falls in elderly patients. A preplanned meta-analysis of the FICSIT Trials. Frailty and Injuries: Cooperative Studies of Intervention

Techniques. *The Journal of the American Medical Association*, **273**, pp. 1341-1347.

Schaller, K.J., 1996, Tai Chi Chih: an exercise option for older adults. *Journal of Gerontology Nursing*, **22**(10), pp. 12-17.

Robbins, A.S., Rubenstein L.Z. and Josephson K.R., Schulman, B.L., Osterweil, D. and Fine, G., 1989, Predictors of falls among elderly people: Results of two population-based studies. *Archives of Internal Medicine*, **149**, pp. 1628-1633.

Shih, J., 1997, Basic Beijing twenty-four forms of T'ai Chi exercise and average velocity of sway. *Perceptual and Motor Skills*, **84**, pp. 287-290.

Tse, S.K. and Bailey D.M., 1992, Tai Chi and postural control in well elderly. *American Journal of Occupational Therapy*, **46**, pp. 295-300.

Van Deusen, J. and Harlowe, D., 1987, The efficacy of the ROM Dance Programme for adults with rheumatoid arthritis. *American Journal of Occupational Therapy*, **41**(2), pp. 90-95.

Wolfson, L., Whipple, R., Derby, C., Judge, J., King, M., Amerman, P., Schmidt, J. and Smyers D., 1996, Balance and strength training in older adults: intervention gains and Tai Chi maintenance. *Journal of American Geriatric Society*, **44**(5), pp. 498-506.

Wolf, S.L., Barnhart, H.X., Kutner, N.G., McNeely, E., Coogler, C. and Xu T.T, 1996, Reducing frailty and falls in older persons: an investigation of Tai Chi and computerized balance training. Atlanta FICSIT Group. Frailty and Injuries: Cooperative Studies of Intervention Techniques. *Journal of American Geriatric Society*, **44**(5), pp. 489-497.

Wolf, S.L. and Gregor, R.J., 1999, Exploring unique applications of kinetic analysis to movement in older adults. *Journal of Applied Biomechanics,* **15**, pp. 75-83.

Zhang, X.H., Huang, Z.Q., Hu, H.Z. and Gao, X., 1989, *Sports Science (Chinese)*, **1**, p. 64.

Zhuo, D., Shephard, R.J., Plyley, M.J. and Davis, G.M., 1984, Cardiorespiratory and metabolic responses during Tai Chi Chuan exercise. *Canadian Journal of Applied Sport Science*, **9**(1), pp. 7-10.

Author Index

Subject Index

KINANTHROPOMETRY AND EXERCISE PHYSIOLOGY LABORATORY MANUAL

SECOND EDITION

VOLUME 2: EXERCISE PHYSIOLOGY

This is the second edition of the highly successful *Kinanthropometry and Exercise Physiology Laboratory Manual*. Developed as a key resource for lecturers and students of kinanthropometry, sports science, human movement and exercise physiology, this edition is thoroughly revised and completely up-to-date. Now divided into two volumes – *Anthropometry and Exercise Physiology* – this manual provides:

- help in the planning and conduct of practical sessions
- comprehensive theoretical background on each topic, and up-to-date information so that there is no need for additional reading
- seven entirely new chapters providing a balance between kinanthropometry and physiology
- eleven self-standing chapters in each volume which are independent of each other, enabling the reader to pick out topics of interest in any order
- a wide range of supporting diagrams, photographs and tables

Volume 1: Anthropometry covers body composition, proportion, size, growth and somatotype and their relationship with health and performance; methods for evaluating posture and range of motion; assessment of physical activity and energy balance with particular reference to the assessment of performance in children; the relationship between anthropometry and body image; statistics and scaling methods in kinanthropometry and exercise physiology.

Volume 2: Exercise Physiology covers the assessment of muscle function including aspects of neuromuscular control and electromyography, the oxygen transport system and exercise including haematology, lung and cardiovascular function; assessment of metabolic rate, energy and efficiency including thermoregulation; and assessment of maximal and submaximal energy expenditure and control, including the use of heart rate, blood lactate and perceived exertion.

An entire one-stop resource, these volumes present laboratory procedures next to real-life practical examples with appropriate data. In addition, each chapter is conveniently supplemented by a complete review of contemporary literature, as well as theoretical overviews, offering an excellent basic introduction to each topic.

Dr Roger Eston is Reader and Head of the School of Sport, Health and Exercise Sciences, University of Wales, Bangor, and **Professor Thomas Reilly** is Director of the Research Institute for Sport and Exercise Sciences, Liverpool John Moores University. Both editors are practising kinanthropometrists and collaborate in conducting workshops for the British Association for Sport and Exercise Sciences.

KINANTHROPOMETRY AND EXERCISE PHYSIOLOGY LABORATORY MANUAL

SECOND EDITION

Volume 2: Exercise Physiology
Tests, procedures and data

Edited by Roger Eston and Thomas Reilly

London and New York

First edition published 1996 by E & FN Spon,
an imprint of the Taylor & Francis Group

Second edition published 2001 by Routledge
11 New Fetter Lane, London EC4P 4EE

Simultaneously published in the USA and Canada by Routledge
29 West 35th Street, New York, NY 10001

Routledge is an imprint of the Taylor & Francis Group

© 1996 E & F N Spon; 2001 Roger Eston and Thomas Reilly for selection and
editorial matter; individual contributors their contribution

Typeset in Palatino by Bookcraft Ltd, Stroud, Gloucestershire

Printed and bound in Great Britain by Bell and Bain, Glasgow

British Library Cataloguing in Publication Data
A catalogue record for this book is available from the British Library

Library of Congress Cataloging in Publication Data
A catalog record for this book has been requested

ISBN 0–415–251877 (hbk)
ISBN 0–415–251885 (pbk)

CONTENTS

CONTRIBUTORS

V. BALTZOPOULOS
Department of Exercise and Sport Science
Manchester Metropolitan University, UK

N.T. CABLE
Research Institute for Sport and Exercise
    Sciences
Liverpool John Moores University
Liverpool, UK

C.B. COOKE
School of Leisure and Sports Studies
Leeds Metropolitan University
Leeds, UK

J.H. DOUST
Department of Sports Science
University of Wales
Aberystwyth, UK

R.G. ESTON
School of Sport, Health and Exercise Sciences
University of Wales
Bangor, UK

N.P. GLEESON
School of Sport, Health and Exercise Sciences
University of Wales
Bangor, UK

M. GREAVES
Department of Medicine & Therapeutics
University of Aberdeen, UK

A.M. JONES
Department of Exercise and Sport Science
Manchester Metropolitan University, UK

J. LEIPER
Department of Biomedical Sciences
University of Aberdeen
Aberdeen, UK

D.P. MACLAREN
Research Institute for Sport and Exercise
    Sciences
Liverpool John Moores University
Liverpool, UK

R. MAUGHAN
Department of Biomedical Sciences
University of Aberdeen
Aberdeen, UK

T.P. REILLY
Research Institute for Sport and Exercise
    Sciences
Liverpool John Moores University
Liverpool, UK

J.G. WILLIAMS
Department of Kinesiology
West Chester University
West Chester, PA, USA

E.M. WINTER
Sport Science Research Institute
Sheffield Hallam University
Sheffield, UK

PREFACE

The subject area referred to as kinanthropometry has a rich history although the subject area itself was not formalized until the International Society for Advancement of Kinanthropometry was established in Glasgow in 1986. The Society supports its own international conferences and publication of Proceedings linked with these events. It also facilitates the conduct of collaborative research projects on an international basis. Until the publication of the first edition of *Kinanthropometry and Exercise Physiology Laboratory Manual; Tests, Procedures and Data* by the present editors in 1996, there was no laboratory manual which would serve as a compendium of practical activities for students in this field. The text was published under the aegis of the International Society for Advancement of Kinanthropometry in an attempt to make good the deficit.

Kinanthropometrists are concerned about the relation between structure and function of the human body, particularly within the context of movement. Kinanthropometry has applications in a wide range of areas including, for example, biomechanics, ergonomics, growth and development, human sciences, medicine, nutrition, physical education and sports science. Initially, the book was motivated by the need for a suitable laboratory resource which academic staff could use in the planning and conduct of class practicals in these areas. The content of the first edition was designed to cover specific teaching modules in kinanthropometry and other academic programmes, mainly physiology, within which kinanthropometry is sometimes subsumed. It was intended also to include practical activities of relevance to clinicians, for example in measuring metabolic functions, muscle performance,

physiological responses to exercise, posture and so on. In all cases the emphasis is placed on the anthropometric aspects of the topic. In the second edition all the original chapters have been updated and an additional seven chapters have been added, mainly concerned with physiological topics. Consequently, it was decided to separate the overall contents of the second edition into two volumes, one focusing on anthropometry practicals whilst the other contained physiological topics.

The content of both volumes is oriented towards laboratory practicals but offers much more than a series of laboratory exercises. A comprehensive theoretical background is provided for each topic so that users of the text are not obliged to conduct extensive literature searches in order to place the subject in context. Each chapter contains an explanation of the appropriate methodology and, where possible, an outline of specific laboratory based practicals. This is not always feasible, for example in studying growth processes in child athletes. Virtually all aspects of performance testing in children are reviewed and special considerations with regard to data acquisition on children are outlined in Volume 1. Methodologies for researchers in growth and development are also described in this volume and there are new chapters devoted to performance assessment for field games, assessment of physical activity and energy balance, and anthropometry and body image.

The last two chapters in Volume 1 are concerned with basic statistical analyses and scaling procedures which are designed to inform researchers and students about data handling. The information should promote proper use of common statistical techniques for analysing data obtained on human subjects as well as help to avoid common abuses of basic statistical tools.

The content of Volume 2 emphasizes physiology but includes considerations of kinanthropometric aspects of the topics where appropriate. Practical activities of relevance to clinicians are covered, for example in measuring metabolic and cardiovascular functions, assessing muscle performance, physiological and haematological responses to exercise, and so on. The chapters concerned with electromyography, haematology, cardiovascular function, limitations to submaximal exercise performance are new whilst material in the other chapters in this volume has been brought up to date in this second edition.

Many of the topics included within the two volumes called for unique individual approaches and so a rigid structure was not imposed on contributors. Nevertheless, in each chapter there is a clear set of aims for the practicals outlined and a comprehensive coverage of the theoretical framework. As each chapter is independent of the others, there is an inevitable re-appearance of concepts across chapters, including those of efficiency, metabolism, maximal performance and issues of scaling. Nevertheless, the two volumes represent a collective set of experimental exercises for academic programmes in kinanthropometry and exercise physiology.

It is hoped that the revised edition in two volumes will stimulate improvements in teaching and instruction strategies in kinanthropometry and physiology. In this way we will have made a contribution towards furthering the education of the next generation of specialists concerned with the relationship between human structure and function.

Roger Eston
Thomas Reilly

INTRODUCTION

The first edition of this text was published in 1996. Until its appearance, there was no laboratory manual serving as a compendium of practical activities for students in the field of kinanthropometry. The text was published under the aegis of the International Society for Advancement of Kinanthropometry, in particular its working group on 'Publications and Information Exchange' in an attempt to make good the deficit. The book has been used widely as the subject area became firmly established on undergraduate and postgraduate programmes. The necessity to update the content after a four-year period is a reflection of the field's expansion.

Kinanthropometry is a relatively new term although the subject area to which it refers has a rich history. It describes the relationship between structure and function of the human body, particularly within the context of movement. The subject area itself was formalized with the establishment of the International Society for Advancement of Kinanthropometry at Glasgow in 1986. The Society supports its own international conferences and publication of Proceedings linked with these events.

Kinanthropometry has applications in a wide range of areas including, for example, biomechanics, ergonomics, growth and development, human sciences, medicine, nutrition, physical education and sports science. The book was motivated by the need for a suitable laboratory resource which academic staff could use in the planning and conduct of class practicals in these areas. The content was designed to cover specific teaching modules in kinanthropometry and other academic programmes, such as physiology, within which

kinanthropometry is sometimes incorporated. It was intended also to include practical activities of relevance to clinicians, for example in measuring metabolic functions, muscle performance, physiological responses to exercise, posture and so on. In all cases the emphasis is placed on the anthropometric aspects of the topic.

In the current revised edition the proportion of physiology practicals has been increased, largely reflecting the ways in which physiology and anthropometry complement each other on academic programmes in the sport and exercise sciences.

The six new chapters have a physiological emphasis (focusing on electromyography, haematology, cardiovascular function, submaximal limitations to exercise, assessment of physical activity and energy balance), except for the final chapter on the links between anthropometry and body image. Of the fifteen chapters retained from the first edition, four have incorporated new co-authors with a view to providing the most authoritative contributions available.

As with the first edition, the content is oriented towards laboratory practicals but offers much more than prescription of a series of laboratory exercises. A comprehensive theoretical background is provided for each topic so that users of the text are not obliged to conduct extensive literature reviews in order to place the subject in context. Each chapter contains an explanation of the appropriate methodology and where possible an outline of specific laboratory-based practicals. This is not always feasible, for example in studying growth processes in child athletes. In such cases, virtually all aspects of performance testing in children are covered and special considerations with regard to data acquisition on children are outlined. Methodologies for researchers in growth and development are also described.

Many of the topics included in this text called for unique individual approaches and so it was not always possible to have a common structure for each chapter. In the majority of cases the laboratory practicals are retained until the end of that chapter as the earlier text provides the theoretical framework for their conduct. Despite any individual variation from the standard structure, together the contributions represent a collective set of exercises for an academic programme in kinanthropometry. The relative self-sufficiency of each contribution also explains why relevant concepts crop up in more than one chapter, for example, concepts of efficiency, metabolism, maximal oxygen uptake, scaling and so on. The last section contains two chapters which are concerned with basic statistical analysis and are designed to inform researchers and students about data handling. This advice should help promote proper use of common statistical techniques for analysing data obtained on human subjects as well as help to avoid common abuses of basic statistical tools.

It is hoped that this text will stimulate improvement in teaching and instruction strategies in the application of laboratory techniques in kinanthropometry and physiology. In this way we will have continued to make our contribution towards the education of the next generation of specialists concerned with relating human structure to its function.

Roger Eston
Thomas Reilly

PART ONE
NEUROMUSCULAR ASPECTS OF MOVEMENT

SKELETAL MUSCLE FUNCTION

Vasilios Baltzopoulos and Nigel P. Gleeson

1.1 AIMS

The aims in this chapter are to:
- describe specific aspects of the structure and function of the muscular system and the role of muscles in human movement,
- provide an understanding of how neuro-muscular performance is influenced by training, ageing and sex-related processes,
- provide an understanding of how neuro-muscular performance is influenced by joint angle and angular velocity,
- describe the assessment of muscle performance and function by means of isokinetic dynamometry,
- provide an understanding of the value and limitations of isokinetic dynamometry in the assessment of asymptomatic and symptomatic populations.

1.2 INTRODUCTION

Human movement is the result of complex interactions between environmental factors and the nervous, muscular and skeletal systems. Brain cell activities within the cerebral cortex are converted by supraspinal centre programming into neural outputs (central commands) that stimulate the muscular system to produce the required movement (Cheney, 1985; Brooks, 1986). In this chapter, specific aspects of the structure and function of the muscular system are considered as part of the process for producing movement. Knowledge of basic physiological and anatomical principles is assumed.

1.3 PHYSIOLOGICAL ASPECTS OF MUSCLE AND JOINT FUNCTION

1.3.1 BASIC STRUCTURE AND FUNCTION OF SKELETAL MUSCLE

Each skeletal muscle contains a large number of muscle fibres assembled together by collagenous connective tissue. A motoneuron and the muscle fibres it innervates represent a motor unit. The number of muscle fibres in a motor unit (innervation ratio) depends on the function of the muscle. Small muscles that are responsible for fine movements, such as the extraocular muscles, have approximately 5–15 muscle fibres per motor unit. Large muscles, such as the gastrocnemius, required for strength and power events, have innervation ratios of approximately 1:1800. A muscle fibre comprises a number of myofibrils surrounded by an excitable membrane, the sarcolemma. The basic structural unit of a myofibril is the sarcomere, which is composed of thick and thin filaments of contractile proteins. The thick filaments are mainly composed of myosin. The thin filaments are composed of actin and the regulatory proteins tropomyosin and troponin that prevent interaction of actin and myosin.

Nerve action potentials propagated along the axons of motoneurons are transmitted to the postsynaptic membrane (sarcolemma) by an electrochemical process. A muscle action potential is propagated along the sarcolemma at velocities ranging from 1 to 3 m s^{-1}. It has

Kinanthropometry and Exercise Physiology Laboratory Manual: Tests, Procedures and Data. 2nd Edition, Volume 2: Exercise Physiology Edited by RG Eston and T Reilly. Published by Routledge, London, June 2001

been reported, however, that the conduction velocity can be increased to approximately 6 m s^{-1} with resistance training (Kereshi *et al.*, 1983). The muscle action potential causes Ca^{2+} release that disinhibits the regulatory proteins of the thin filaments. This freedom from inhibition allows the myosin globular heads to attach to binding sites on the actin filaments and form cross-bridges. The interaction of the actin and myosin filaments causes them to slide past one another and generate force which is transmitted to the Z discs of the sarcomere. This is known as the sliding filament theory. The details of the exact mechanism responsible for the transformation of adenosine triphosphate energy from a chemical to a mechanical form in the cross-bridge cycle is not completely known (Pollack, 1983). For a detailed discussion of the electrochemical events associated with muscular contraction the reader is referred to the text by Gowitzke and Milner (1988).

1.3.2 MOTOR UNIT TYPES AND FUNCTION

Motor units are usually classified according to contractile and mechanical characteristics into three types (Burke, 1981).

- Type S: Slow contraction time, low force level, resistant to fatigue
- Type FR: Fast contraction time, medium force level, resistant to fatigue
- Type FF: Fast contraction time, high force level, fatiguable

Morphological differences are also evident between the different motor unit types. For example, motoneuron size, muscle fibre cross-sectional area and innervation ratio are increased in fast – compared to slow – type motor units.

Another scheme classifies motor units as Type I, IIa or IIb, based on myosin ATPase. An alternative subdivision is slow-twitch oxidative (SO), fast-twitch oxidative glycolytic (FOG) and fast-twitch glycolytic (FG), based on myosin ATPase and anaerobic/aerobic capacity (Brooke and Kaiser, 1974). The relative distribution of different motor unit types is determined by genetic factors. Elite endurance athletes demonstrate a predominance of slow or Type I fibres. Fast-twitch fibres predominate in sprint or power event athletes.

The muscle fibres in a motor unit are all of the same type, but each muscle contains a proportion of the three motor unit types (Nemeth *et al.*, 1986). Motor units are activated in a preset sequence (S–FR–FF) (orderly recruitment) that is determined mainly by the motoneuron size of the motor unit (size principle) (Henneman, 1957; Enoka and Stuart, 1984; Gustafsson and Pinter, 1985). The force exerted by a muscle depends on the number of motor units activated and the frequency of the action potentials (Harrison, 1983). The orderly recruitment theory, based on the size principle, indicates that recruitment is based on the force required, not the velocity of movement. Thus slow motor units are always activated irrespective of velocity. Most human movement is performed within the velocity range of the slow fibres (Green, 1986), although there is evidence of selective activation of muscles with a predominance of fast-twitch motor units during rapid movements (Behm and Sale, 1993).

1.3.3 TRAINING ADAPTATIONS

Resistance training results in neural and structural adaptations which improve muscle function. Neural adaptations include improved central command that generates a greater action potential (Komi *et al.*, 1978; Sale *et al.*, 1983) and a better synchronization of action potential discharge in different motor units (Milner-Brown *et al.*, 1975). Structural adaptations include increases in the cross-sectional area of muscle fibres (hypertrophy) and possibly an increase in the number of muscle fibres through longitudinal fibre splitting. There is no conclusive evidence for development of new fibres (hyperplasia) in humans. The structural changes that are induced by resistance training result in an overall increase in contractile proteins and therefore muscle force capacity (MacDougall *et al.*, 1982). Adaptation of specific motor unit types depends on resistance training that stresses their specific characteristics: this is known as the principle of specificity. For example, during fast high-resistance training movements, slow motor units are activated, but they do not adapt because their specific characteristics are not stressed. Recent evidence suggests that limited transformation between slow- and fast-twitch muscle fibres is possible with long-term specific training (Simoneau *et al.*, 1985; Tesch and Karlsson, 1985).

1.3.4 EFFECTS OF AGE AND SEX ON MUSCLE PERFORMANCE

Sex differences in muscle function parameters have been examined extensively. The absolute muscular force of the upper extremity in males is approximately 50% higher than in females (Hoffman *et al.*, 1979; Morrow and Hosler, 1981; Heyward *et al.*, 1986). The absolute muscular force of the lower extremities is approximately 30% higher in males (Laubach, 1976; Morrow and Hosler, 1981). Because of sex differences in anthropometric parameters such as body mass, lean body mass, muscle mass and muscle cross-sectional area that affect strength, muscular performance should be relative to these parameters. Research on the relationship between body mass and maximum muscular force or moment is inconclusive, with some studies indicating high significant correlations (Beam *et al.*, 1982; Clarkson *et al.*, 1982) and others no significant relationship (Hoffman *et al.*, 1979; Morrow and Hosler, 1981; Kroll *et al.*, 1990). Maximum muscular force expressed relative to body mass, lean body mass or muscle mass is similar in males and females, but some studies indicate that differences are not completely eliminated in upper extremity muscles (Hoffman *et al.*, 1979; Frontera *et al.*, 1991).

Maximum force is closely related to muscle cross-sectional area in both static (Maughan *et al.*, 1983) and dynamic conditions (Schantz *et al.*, 1983). Research on maximum force relative to muscle cross-sectional area in static or dynamic conditions indicates that there is no significant difference between sexes (Schantz *et al.*, 1983; Bishop *et al.*, 1987) although higher force:cross-sectional area ratios for males have also been reported (Maughan *et al.*, 1983; Ryushi *et al.*, 1988). However, instrumentation and procedures for measurement of different anthropometric parameters *in vivo* (for example, cross-sectional area, moment arms, lean body mass, muscle mass) are often inaccurate. Measurement of cross-sectional area in pennate muscles or in the elderly is inappropriate for the normalization of muscular force or moment. Muscle mass, determined from urinary creatinine excretion, is a better indicator of force-generating capacity and is the main determinant of age- and gender-related differences in muscle function (Frontera *et al.*, 1991). The findings of muscle function studies, therefore, must always be considered relative to the inherent problems of procedures, instrumentation and *in vivo* assessment of muscle performance and anthropometric parameters.

Muscular force decreases with advancing age (Dummer *et al.*, 1985; Bemben, 1991; Frontera *et al.*, 1991). This decline has been attributed mainly to changes in muscle composition and physical activity (Bemben, 1991; Frontera *et al.*, 1991). Furthermore, the onset and rate of force decline are different in males and females and in upper–lower extremity muscles (Dummer *et al.*, 1985; Aoyagi and Shephard, 1992). These differences are mainly due to a reduction in steroid hormones in females after menopause and involvement in different habitual-recreational activities. Generally there is a decrease of approximately 5–8% per decade after the age of 20–30 (Shephard, 1991; Aoyagi and Shephard, 1992).

1.4 MECHANICAL ASPECTS OF MUSCLE AND JOINT FUNCTION

1.4.1 MUSCULAR ACTIONS

Muscular activation involves the electrochemical processes that cause sliding of myofilaments, shortening of the sarcomere and exertion of force. The overall muscle length during activation is determined not only by the muscular force but also by the external load or resistance applied to the muscle. The ratio muscular force:external load determines three distinct conditions of muscle action:

1. *Concentric action*: muscular force is greater than external force and consequently overall muscle length decreases (i.e. muscle shortens) during activation.
2. *Isometric action*: muscular force is equal to external force, and muscle length remains constant.
3. *Eccentric action*: external force is greater than muscular force and consequently muscle length is increased (muscle lengthening) during activation.

During all three conditions, sarcomeres are stimulated and attempt to shorten by means of actin–myosin interaction (sarcomere contraction). The use of the term 'contraction' to mean shortening should be used only to describe the shortening of sarcomeres, not changes in length of the whole muscle. During eccentric activation, for example, the muscle is lengthened and therefore terms such as 'eccentric contraction' or 'isometric contraction' may be misleading (Cavanagh, 1988).

In attempting to examine whole muscle function it is important to consider the different component parts of the muscle, i.e. both the functional contractile (active) and the elastic (passive) components. A simplified mechanical model of muscle includes three components that simulate the mechanical properties of the different structures. The contractile component (CC) simulates the active, force-generating units (i.e. sarcomeres), the series elastic component (SEC) simulates the elastic properties of the sarcolemma, and the parallel elastic component (PEC) simulates the elastic properties of the collagenous connective tissue in parallel with the contractile component (Komi, 1984, 1986; Chapman, 1985).

Muscle architecture describes the organization of muscle fibres within the muscle and affects muscle function. The angle between the muscle fibres and the line of action from origin to insertion is defined as the pennation angle. The pennation angle and the number of sarcomeres that are arranged in series or in parallel with the line of action of the muscle are important factors affecting muscular force.

1.4.2 FORCE–LENGTH AND FORCE–VELOCITY RELATIONSHIPS IN ISOLATED MUSCLE

In muscles isolated from the skeletal system in a laboratory preparation, the force exerted at different muscle lengths depends on the properties of the active (CC) and passive components (SEC and PEC) at different muscle lengths. Force exerted by the interaction of actin and myosin depends on the number of the available cross-bridges, which is maximum near the resting length of the muscle. The force exerted by the passive elastic elements (SEC and PEC) is increased exponentially as muscle length increases beyond resting length (Figure 1.1). The total force exerted, therefore, is the sum of the active and passive forces. At maximum length, there is little force associated with active components because of minimum cross-bridge availability. However, force contributed by the elastic components alone may be even greater than the maximum CC force at resting length (Baratta and Solomonow, 1991).

The effect of the linear velocity during muscle shortening or lengthening on the force output has been examined extensively since the pioneering work of Hill (1938). With an increase in linear concentric velocity of muscle shortening, the force exerted is decreased non-linearly because the number of cross-bridges formed, and the force they exert, are reduced (Figure 1.2). Furthermore, the distribution of different motor unit types affects the force–velocity relationship. A higher output at faster angular velocities indicates a higher percentage of FF–FR motor units (Gregor *et al.*, 1979;

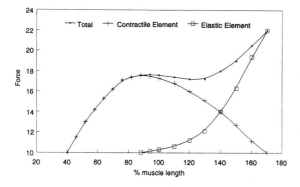

Figure 1.1 Force–length relationship in isolated muscle showing the contribution of the contractile and the elastic elements on total muscular force. Force units are arbitrary.

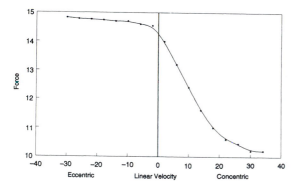

Figure 1.2 Force–velocity relationship of isolated muscle during concentric, isometric and eccentric muscle action. Force and velocity units are arbitrary and do not refer to specific muscles.

Froese and Houston, 1985). However, with an increase in linear eccentric velocity of muscle lengthening, the force exerted is increased (Wilkie, 1950; Chapman, 1976; Thorstensson *et al.*, 1976; Tihanyi *et al.*, 1987).

1.4.3 MUSCLE FUNCTION DURING JOINT MOVEMENT

Examination of the mechanical properties of isolated muscle is of limited use when considering how muscles function during movements in sports or other activities. Movement of body segments results from the application of muscular force around the joint axis of rotation. It is therefore important to consider the relationship between muscle function and joint position and motion (Bouisset, 1984; Kulig *et al.*, 1984). The movement of the joint segments around the axis of rotation is proportional to the rotational effect of the muscular force or moment. This is measured in newton metres (Nm) and is defined as the product of muscular force (in newtons) and moment arm, i.e. the perpendicular distance (in metres) between force line and the axis of rotation of the joint (Figure 1.3). Other physiological, mechanical and structural factors that were described earlier also affect muscle function in a joint system (Figure 1.4).

Joint motion results from the action of muscle groups. Individual muscles in the group may have different origin or insertion points, they may operate over one or two joints and have a different architecture. The moment arm of the muscle group is also variable over the range of motion of the joint. Assessment of dynamic muscle function, therefore, must consider these factors. It must be emphasized that relationships such as force–length or force–velocity refer to individual muscles, whereas moment–joint position and moment–angular joint velocity relationships refer to the function of a muscle group around a joint. For example, the moment of the knee extensor group (rectus femoris, vastus lateralis, vastus medialis, vastus intermedius) at different knee joint angular velocities and positions can be examined during voluntary knee extension using appropriate instrumentation. These terms must not be confused with the force–velocity and force–length relationships of the four individual muscles. These can be examined only if the muscles were separated from a cadaveric joint in the laboratory.

1.4.4 MEASUREMENT OF DYNAMIC MUSCLE FUNCTION – ISOKINETIC DYNAMOMETRY

The most significant development for the study of dynamic muscle and joint function was the introduction of isokinetic dynamometry in the 1960s (Hislop and Perrine, 1967; Thistle *et al.*, 1967). Isokinetic dynamometers have hydraulic or electromechanical mechanisms that maintain the angular velocity of a joint constant, by providing a resistive moment that is equal to the muscular moment throughout the range of movement. This is referred to as optimal loading. Passive systems (Cybex II, Akron, Merac) permit isokinetic concentric movements only, but more recently active systems (Biodex, Cybex 6000, KinCom, Lido) provide both concentric and eccentric isokinetic conditions, with maximum joint angular velocities up to 8.72 rad s^{-1} (500 deg s^{-1}) for concentric actions and 4.36 rad s^{-1} (250 deg s^{-1}) for eccentric actions (see Figure 1.5). It is important to note that it is the joint angular velocity that is controlled and kept constant,

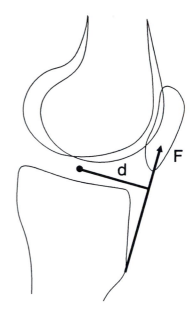

Figure 1.3 The moment arm (*d*) of the knee extensor group is the shortest or perpendicular distance between the patellar tendon and the joint centre. The muscular moment is the product of the force (*F*) along the patellar tendon and the moment arm (*d*).

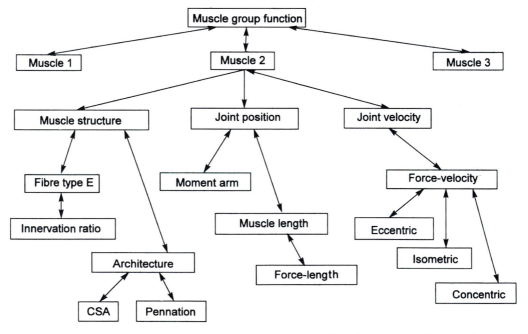

Figure 1.4 The main physiological and mechanical factors that affect the function of a muscle group. This simple model is not exhaustive and any interactions between the different factors are not indicated for simplicity.

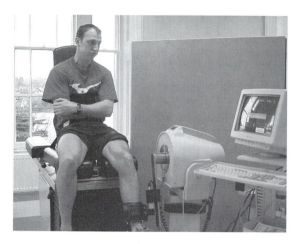

Figure 1.5 Measurement of knee extensor strength on an isokinetic dynamometer (KinCom 500H, Chattex, Chattanooga, TN, USA).

not the linear velocity of the active muscle group (Hinson *et al.*, 1979). Dynamometers that control the rate of change of joint angular velocity have also been developed (Westing *et al.*, 1991). Most commercial isokinetic systems have accessories that allow testing of all the major joints of the upper and lower limbs and the back. Apart from isolated joint tests, workplace manual activities, such as lifting and handling materials and equipment, can be simulated on adapted dynamometers using dedicated attachments. Methodological problems such as subject positioning and motivation during the test require standardized protocols. Mechanical factors such as the effect of gravitational moment or the control of the acceleration of the segment affect measurement of muscular moment but appropriate correction methods have been developed and used routinely (Baltzopoulos and Brodie, 1989). Excellent test reliability and computerized assessment of muscle function permit widespread application of isokinetics for testing, training and rehabilitation.

1.4.5 MOMENT–ANGULAR VELOCITY RELATIONSHIP

The moment exerted during concentric actions is maximum at slow angular velocities and decreases with increasing angular velocity. Some authors have reported a constant moment output (plateau) for a range of slow angular velocities (Lesmes *et al.*, 1978; Perrine and Edgerton, 1978; Wickiewicz *et al.*, 1984; Thomas *et al.*, 1987), whereas others have found a continuous decrease from slow to fast concentric angular velocities (Thorstensson *et al.*, 1976; Coyle *et al.*, 1981; Westing *et al.*, 1988). Although the plateau has been attributed to neural inhibition during slow dynamic muscular activation, it is also affected by training level and testing protocol (Hortobagyi and Katch, 1990). The rate of decrease at higher angular velocities is affected by activity, sex and the physiological/mechanical factors discussed above. The maximum concentric moment of the knee extensors decreases by approximately 40% from 1.05 to 4.19 rad s^{-1} (60 to 240 deg s^{-1}), whereas the knee flexor moment decrease varies between 25 and 50% (Prietto and Caiozzo, 1989; Westing and Seger, 1989). The eccentric moment remains relatively constant with increasing angular velocity and approximately 20% higher than the isometric moment. There are considerable differences in muscular moment measurements at different concentric–eccentric angular velocities between the large number of studies on dynamic muscle function. These result mainly from differences in methodology, anthropometric, physiological and mechanical parameters (Cabri, 1991; Perrin, 1993).

The moment–velocity relationship is influenced by the physiological principles of isolated muscular action and the mechanical factors affecting muscle function in a joint system. Figure 1.4 is a simple representation of the different mechanical and physiological factors that affect the function of a muscle group during joint movement. Direct comparisons of the moment–angular velocity relationship during isokinetic eccentric or concentric joint motion, with the force–linear velocity relationship of isolated muscle, is of limited use, given the number of variables affecting muscle and joint function (Bouisset, 1984; Bobbert and Harlaar, 1992).

1.5 ISOKINETIC DYNAMOMETRY APPLICATIONS

1.5.1 MEASUREMENT ISSUES: INDICES OF NEUROMUSCULAR PERFORMANCE AND RELATIONSHIPS TO FUNCTIONAL CAPABILITY

Applications of isokinetic dynamometry are manifold. Its deployment as a 'safe' tool for conditioning to enhance neuromuscular performance has been established in the literature. The most significant aspects of isokinetic training are velocity-specific adaptations and the transfer of improvements to angular velocities, other than the training velocity. Training at intermediate velocities 2.09–3.14 rad s^{-1} (120–180 deg s^{-1}) produces the most significant transfer to both slower and faster angular velocities (Bell and Wenger, 1992; Behm and Sale, 1993). Eccentric training at 2.09 rad s^{-1} improves muscle function in both slower (1.05 rad s^{-1}) and faster (3.14 rad s^{-1}) angular velocities (Duncan *et al.*, 1989). There is no conclusive evidence of improvements in eccentric muscle function after concentric training and vice versa.

Earlier studies reported no hypertrophy following isokinetic training (Lesmes *et al.*, 1978; Cote *et al.*, 1988) although more recent findings suggest isokinetic training can induce increases in muscle size (Alway *et al.*, 1990). Further research is required to examine the effects of both concentric and eccentric isokinetic training programmes on muscular hypertrophy.

Isokinetic dynamometry has also become a favoured method for the assessment of dynamic muscle function in both clinical, research and sports environments. Several indices, such as peak torque, are used in the

literature to characterize individual, group or larger population performance.

The relevance of isokinetic dynamometry may be better understood by consideration of the specificity of this mode of testing in relation to the criterial physical activity. This comparability may be achieved at different levels which include identification and assessment of the involved muscle group; simulation of the activity's movement pattern and muscle action type during testing; and simulation of the movement velocity during testing (Sale, 1991). The muscle group of interest may be tested using anatomical movements that employ this muscle group as an agonist. Further test specificity in terms of simulation of the movement pattern may be limited because, while commercially available isokinetic dynamometers are capable of testing unilateral single-joint movements, most are not suitable for testing the multi-joint movements common to many sports. Similarly, replication of the stretch–shortening cycle (eccentric–concentric) pattern of muscular action, which occurs in some sports and physical activities, is limited to those commercially available isokinetic dynamometers which offer assessment of both concentric and eccentric types of muscular action. This limitation may further extend to compromised replication of the temporal sequencing of these types of muscular action during testing.

Attempted replication of the eccentric component of sport-specific movements may offer increased potential for injury during the testing of symptomatic and asymptomatic individuals completing rehabilitation or conditioning programmes. Attempts to mimic aspects of sport-specific movement also demand greater attention be given by the test administrator to accommodation and habituation responses of the participant to the testing protocols. Isokinetic dynamometers are often compromised in their ability to replicate sport-specific movement velocities, for example, offering concentric muscle action test velocities up to only 58% (~7 rad s^{-1}) of the maximum unresisted knee extension velocity (~12 rad s^{-1})

(Thorstensson *et al.*, 1976) and up to 20% (~3.4 rad s^{-1}) of the maximal eccentric action velocity of the knee flexors during sprint running (~17 rad s^{-1}) (Sale, 1991).

The validity of isokinetic dynamometry is complicated by a myriad of factors that interact to influence the externally registered estimate of the net torque or work associated with a joint system. Strength performance constitutes only one aspect of the cascade of the neuromuscular and musculoskeletal machinery necessary to achieve temporal neuromuscular control and coordinated rapid force production. The relative importance of absolute strength to the sports-performance of interest will be influenced by torque–velocity and power–velocity relationships (Fenn and Marsh, 1935; Hill, 1938) interacting with sport-specific neuromuscular recruitment and activation patterns (Edman, 1992). The magnitude of the correlation between indices of isokinetic neuromuscular performance and functional performance has been shown to be variable and accounts for only low to moderate portions of the shared variance. During the rehabilitation of high-performance soccer players from musculoskeletal injury and dysfunction through to full functionality and return to match-play condition, absolute strength performance of the involved musculature varied relatively little across the period of rehabilitation (15–20% change relative to post-injury asymptomatic functional performance and time of return to match-play condition) (Rees and Gleeson, 1999). In contrast, indices of temporal neuromuscular control (electromechanical delay (see Chapter 2 by Gleeson), rate of force development, and static and dynamic proprioception (discussed later), demonstrated relatively dramatic performance changes over the same period (70–85%), suggesting a more potent role for the latter factors in functional performance. Assessment of strength using isokinetic dynamometry constitutes one component of a wider multivariate model of neuromuscular performance (Cabri, 1991; Perrin, 1993). In this respect, it may contribute partially to an

informed decision about the timing of a 'safe' return to play for the athlete rehabilitating from injury (Rees and Gleeson, 1999). However, the preceding discussion suggests that there are limitations associated with this mode of assessment and that it cannot be used unreservedly.

Sensitivity of a criterion test protocol may be defined as the ability to detect small changes in an individual's performance, or relative positional changes of an individual's performance within a sub-sample (Gleeson and Mercer, 1996). This ability to discriminate relates directly to the reliability and reproducibility characteristics of the isokinetic test protocol. Within the context of a given application, the selection of minimum or threshold reliability and reproducibility criteria to meet the demand for appropriate measurement rigour will in turn regulate the selection of suitable protocol characteristics (for example, required number of replicates, inter-replicate time duration and mode of action). In a 'case-study', less stringent sensitivity criteria may be appropriate for the discrimination of gross muscle dysfunction in the clinical setting, whereas relatively greater sensitivity may be needed to interpret correctly the effects of intervention conditioning in an elite strength-trained athlete, whose performance levels may vary by only ±5% over the competitive season (Gleeson and Mercer, 1992).

Once a mandate for the valid use of isokinetic dynamometry has been established within an intended measurement application, there are several competing demands within measurement protocol design which may affect the measurement of isokinetic strength and its subsequent suitability for meaningful evaluation and interpretation. The desire to increase measurement rigour, reliability and sensitivity to suit the intended application by using more elaborate multiple trials may be hampered by logistical and financial constraints or reduced subject compliance. The net effect of the interaction of such demands may be considered to be the utility of the isokinetic dynamometry protocol. Of the factors that impinge on utility, those relating to reliability afford the most control of measurement quality by the test administrator.

Research data suggest that, in many measurement applications, the reliability and sensitivity associated with many frequently-used indices of isokinetic leg strength which are estimated by means of single-trial protocols are not sufficient to differentiate either performance change within the same individual or between individuals within a homogeneous group. While such limitations may be addressed by the use of protocols based on 3–4 inter-day trials for the index of peak torque, other indices which demonstrate reduced reliability, for example, the ratio of knee flexion to extension peak torque, may require many more replicates to achieve the same level of sensitivity. Here, the measurement utility of the index may not be sufficient to justify its proper deployment. Such issues are important for the utility of all aspects of dynamometry, and the reader is directed to more complete reviews (for example, Gleeson and Mercer, 1996).

1.5.2 DATA COLLECTION AND ANALYSIS CONSIDERATIONS

One of the most important considerations in testing muscle function is the positioning of the subject. The length of the muscle group, contribution of the elastic components, effective moment arm, development of angular velocity and inhibitory effects by the antagonistic muscle groups are all influenced by positioning and segment–joint stabilization during the test. For these reasons, the above factors must be standardized between tests, to allow valid comparisons.

Isokinetic testing of an isolated joint does not employ a natural movement. Accurate instructions are required concerning the operation of the isokinetic dynamometers and the testing requirements, together with adequate familiarization. Eccentric conditions, particularly fast angular velocities, require special attention in order to avoid injury in novices or subjects with musculoskeletal weaknesses.

Simple isometric measurements can be performed using force transducers or cable tensiometers, hand dynamometers and simple free weights or resistive exercise equipment (Watkins, 1993). The force output using these devices depends on the point of attachment on the limb, moment arm of muscle group and the joint position. It is therefore essential to express joint function in terms of moment (N m), i.e. as the product of the force output of the measuring device (N) and the perpendicular distance (m) between the force line and the joint axis of rotation. Accurate determination of the joint centre is not possible without complicated radiographic measurements and therefore an approximation is necessary. An example is the use of the femoral epicondyle in the knee as a landmark.

Computerized, isokinetic dynamometers allow more accurate positioning of the subject and of the joint tested, and a more precise assessment of muscle function. However, the cost of these devices may prohibit their use as tools in teaching. The moment recorded by isokinetic dynamometers is the total (or resultant) moment exerted around the joint axis of rotation. The main component of this total joint moment is the moment exerted by the active muscle group. The contribution of other structures such as the joint capsule and ligaments to the total joint moment is minimal and therefore the moment recorded by isokinetic dynamometers is considered equal to the muscular moment. During testing of a knee extension, the moment exerted by the quadriceps is the product of the force exerted by the patellar tendon on the tibia and the moment arm, i.e. the perpendicular or shortest distance between the patellar tendon and the centre of the knee joint (Figure 1.3). The moment arm is variable over the range of movement (Figure 1.6), being least at full knee extension and flexion and greatest at approximately 0.78 rad of knee flexion (Baltzopoulos, 1995a). Moment arms at different joint positions are usually measured

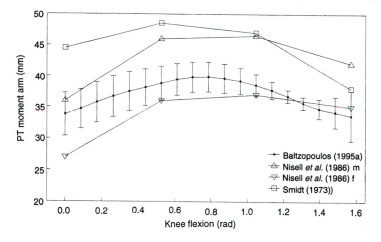

Figure 1.6 The patellar tendon moment arm during knee extension from different studies.

directly on the subject using radiography or derived indirectly from cadaveric studies. If the knee extensor isometric moment of a subject with body weight of 800 N (body mass 81.5 kg) is 280 N m at 0.87 rad (50 deg) of knee flexion, and assuming that the moment arm at this joint position is 0.035 m, then the muscular force exerted by the patellar tendon is 8000 N or 10 times the body weight (BW) of that subject. This method can be applied to the moment measurements from isokinetic or isometric tests in order to obtain the actual muscular force exerted. This is usually expressed relative to body weight to allow comparisons. Using a similar method, it was estimated that the maximum muscular force exerted during isokinetic knee extension ranged from 9 BW at 0.52 rad s^{-1} (30 deg s^{-1}) to 6 BW at 3.66 rad s^{-1} (210 deg s^{-1}) (Baltzopoulos, 1995b).

Another important aspect of muscle function assessment is the expression of maximum performance parameters, such as moment, force and power, as a ratio relative to different anthropometric parameters (e.g. body mass, lean body mass, cross-sectional area) without considering the underlying relationship between the two parameters. This ratio is usually obtained by dividing the mean force, for example, by the mean body mass, without considering the regression line between force and

body mass. A ratio relationship assumes that the regression line crosses the origin of the axes (or that the intercept is approximately zero). If, despite a high correlation, a ratio relationship does not exist between moment and body mass, then expressing the moment relative to body mass (N m kg^{-1}) is representative of subjects with body mass close to the mean body mass. This, however, will overestimate or underestimate the moment for subjects with body mass further away from the mean body mass. Indeed the magnitude of the error in estimating the maximum moment from the ratio, instead of the regression line, depends on the intercept (i.e. difference between regression and ratio lines) and the deviation of the subject's body mass from the mean body mass (see Volume 1, Chapter 11 by Winter and Nevill).

Another consideration when comparing muscle function between different groups over time is the use of an appropriate statistical technique. Analysis of covariance (ANCOVA) is necessary if the initial level of the dependent (measured) variable (e.g. maximum isokinetic moment) is different between the groups and the effects of training programmes over time are assessed. Multivariate ANOVA (MANOVA) or multivariate ANCOVA (MANCOVA) is necessary if a number of different muscle function parameters that are likely to affect each other are measured and compared simultaneously.

1.5.3 ASSESSMENT OF SHORT-TERM MUSCLE POWER AND FATIGUE USING ISOKINETIC DYNAMOMETRY

The work capacity of a muscle or muscle group may be determined by calculating the total area under one or a series of torque–angular position curves. Power is determined by assessing the time required to complete the relevant period of work. Many isokinetic dynamometry systems have software that is capable of determining these indices of performance. Protocols have been used to assess the capability of the neuromuscular system to produce all-out short-term work by means of varying simultaneous contributions from the ATP-PC and glycolytic energy pathways (Abernethy *et al.*, 1995; Kannus *et al.*, 1991). Depending on the methodology used for the assessment of power during single or repeated muscle actions, isokinetic indices of peak or mean power may be compromised by the intrusion of the effects of acceleration and deceleration periods associated with limitations of the angular velocity control mechanisms. Furthermore, limitations in the maximum sampling rates for data acquisition offered by commercially available dynamometers would tend to limit the accuracy of analogue-to-digital conversions and attenuate the highest frequencies of work patterns and associated power outputs.

Various isokinetic dynamometry protocols involving serial muscle actions have been used to assess the effects of fatigue on neuromuscular performance. Protocols have ranged from 50 unidirectional maximal voluntary actions of the knee extensor muscle group (Thorstensson *et al.*, 1976) to bidirectional (reciprocal) all-out exercise tasks consisting of 25–30 reciprocal maximal voluntary actions of the knee extensors and flexors of the leg at moderate movement velocities (3.14 rad s^{-1}) with no rest between movements (Burdett and van Swearingen, 1987; Baltzopoulos *et al.*, 1988; Montgomery *et al.*, 1989; Mathiassen, 1989; Gleeson and Mercer, 1992). In the case of bidirectional protocols, total work and indices of fatigue may be determined during both extension and flexion movements. The latter indices may be calculated automatically using the dynamometer's control software. A least-squares regression may be applied to the actual work done in all repetitions, and the index of fatigue can be determined as the ratio of the predicted work done in the last repetition compared to the first repetition and expressed as a percentage. Alternatively, Thorstensson *et al.* (1976) defined endurance as the torque from the last three contractions as a percentage of the initial three contractions of 50 contractions, and Kannus *et al.* (1992) reported that the work performed during the last 5 of 25 repetitions and the total work performed were valuable markers in the documentation of progress during endurance training. The isokinetic protocols may be designed to reflect the 'worst-case' scenario for fatiguing exercise within the context of the sport of interest (Gleeson *et al.*, 1997) or be associated with a particular duration in which a bioenergetic pathway is considered to have prominence (Sale, 1991).

Indices of leg muscular fatigue demonstrate significantly greater variability in inter-day assessments of reproducibility compared with indices of strength (9.1% vs. 4.3%, respectively) (Burdett and van Swearingen, 1987; Gleeson and Mercer, 1992). The ability to reproduce exactly the pattern of work output and fatigue responses over repeated day-to-day trials appears to be compromised. The latter trend may be due in part to an intrusion of conscious or unconscious work output pacing strategies as suspected for this and other exercise modalities during tests of similar duration (Perrin, 1986; Burke *et al.*, 1985). The inflated variability associated with the assessment of isokinetic endurance parameters may be explained by the problems of subjects having to sustain a higher degree of self-motivation to maximum effort throughout 30 repetitions lasting approximately 40 seconds, compared to the relatively short duration of 3 maximal voluntary muscle actions associated with strength assessment protocols. As the series of bidirectional agonist–antagonist muscle group actions associated with the fatigue test protocols progresses, it may be that inherently higher variability of the interaction of motoneuron recruitment, rate coding, temporal patterning and co-activation phenomena, and ultimately changes to the recorded net torque about the joint of interest (Enoka, 1994; Milner-Brown *et al.*, 1975) may underscore these findings. While the dynamometer provides a 'safe' environment in which to stress the musculoskeletal system with high-intensity fatiguing exercise tasks, the 'work–rest' duty cycles and motor unit recruitment patterns associated with the isokinetic testing cannot mimic faithfully the loading during the sports activity. The results from such isokinetic tests of muscle endurance must be interpreted cautiously.

1.5.4 CLINICAL APPLICATIONS OF ISOKINETIC DYNAMOMETRY

Isokinetic dynamometry provides a relatively 'safe' and controlled environment in which to stress the neuromuscular performance of a joint system. Clinical applications of isokinetic dynamometry include assessment of bilateral and agonist–antagonist muscle group performance ratios in symptomatic populations and prophylactic assessments of asymptomatic populations.

It is often assumed that net torque performance scores for the uninjured extremity can be used as the standard for return of the injured extremity to a normal state. This marker for a safe return to play may be compromised by the influence of limb dominance or the effect of neuromuscular specificity of various sport activities on bilateral strength relationships. Bilateral differences are minimal in healthy non-athletes or in participants in sports that involve symmetrical action. However, differences of up to 15% have been reported in asymmetrical sport activities (Perrin *et al.*, 1987). Importantly, in most circumstances involving

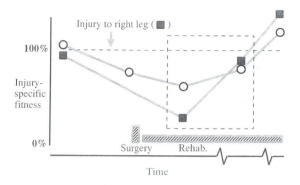

Figure 1.7 A schematic diagram illustrating the dilemma faced by the clinician in assessing safe return-to-play for the injured athlete. The figure shows the progression of performance associated with both the involved right leg (square markers) and contralateral (circular markers) leg prior to and following injury to the right leg. Pre-injury levels of performance are associated with injury. Post-injury conditioning should exceed pre-injury levels of performance for protection from the threat of injury. The clinician has data and contralateral leg comparisons within the dashed box available to help in the decision of when it is safe to return to play (see text).

sports injury, prospective pre-injury performance scores for both involved and contralateral limbs are unavailable to the clinician. Furthermore, the condition of the contralateral 'control' limb is often compromised substantively by deconditioning associated with changed motor unit recruitment patterns during reduced volume and intensity of habitual exercise and injury-related bilateral inhibitory effects. This often serves to lessen the utility of concurrent contralateral limb comparisons and effectively masks the pre-injury baseline performance of the contralateral limb. The latter may be compromised as an optimal marker for a safe 'return to play' because it was associated with the occurrence of the injury. Figure 1.7 illustrates the dilemma faced by the clinician in assessing a safe 'return to play' for the injured athlete.

The bilateral assessment of the injured athlete presents further issues that may hinder the

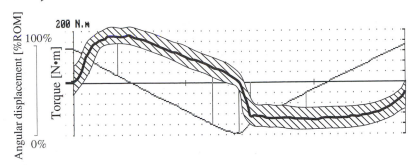

Figure 1.8 95% confidence limits constructed around a single torque–angular position curve derived from maximal voluntary muscle actions of the knee extensors and flexors at 1.05 rad s^{-1}. The *x* axis denotes the time over which the muscle actions take place (approximately 3 seconds).

proper interpretation of performance scores. The injury may cause unilateral restriction to the range of motion available for isokinetic assessment. While this may be an interesting clinical finding in itself, contralateral comparisons through unequal ranges of motion could be compromised by greater pre-stretch and metabolic potentiation to a muscle, enabling that muscle to produce a higher level of peak torque within the subsequent range of motion tested. Similarly, the differential movement patterns would confound contralateral comparisons of average torque and work values. Variations or modifications in placement of the fixation point between the dynamometer and the patient may affect the recorded peak or average torque. It is essential that appropriate anatomical measurements or mapping techniques be used in these circumstances to minimize the intrusion of these aspects of technical error (Gleeson and Mercer, 1996).

Reciprocal muscle group ratios (e.g. knee flexor/extensor) may indicate aspects of joint balance and possible predisposition to joint or muscle injury. Concentric knee flexion/extension moment ratios range from 0.4 to 0.6 and are mainly affected by activity, methodological measurement problems and gravitational forces (Appen and Duncan, 1986; Fillyaw *et al.*, 1986; Figoni *et al.*, 1988). Studies that use moment data uncorrected for the effect of gravitational forces demonstrate higher ratios and a significant increase in the ratio with increasing angular velocity. This increase is a

result of gravity. Gravity-corrected ratios are approximately constant at different angular velocities (Appen and Duncan, 1986; Fillyaw *et al.*, 1986; Baltzopoulos *et al.*, 1991). During joint motion in sport or other activities, concentric action of agonist muscles requires eccentric action of the antagonist muscles to control the movement and ensure joint stability. For this reason, ratios of agonist concentric to antagonist eccentric action (e.g. eccentric knee flexion moment/concentric knee extension moment) are more representative of joint function during sport activities.

It is intuitively appealing for isokinetic dynamometry to offer the capability to discriminate, and potentially diagnose, pathologies in muscle–tendon units and bony articulations of a joint system. Various artefacts in the torque–angular position curves have been attributed to conditions such as anterior cruciate ligament deficiency, and chondromalacia patella (Perrin, 1993). There are many factors, including subject–dynamometer positioning, limb fixation characteristics, the compliance of soft tissue, the compliance of padding and structures of the dynamometer, injury-related neuromuscular inhibitory and pain responses, differential accommodation, habituation and warm-up effects, that influence neuromuscular performance (Gleeson and Mercer, 1996). These factors contribute to the technical and biological variability in the recorded net torque associated with the interaction between a given

Side	Action	Parameter	Joint Angular Velocity (rad s^{-1})								
			Eccentric					Concentric			
			4.19	3.14	2.09	1.05	0	1.05	2.09	3.14	4.19
R	EXT	Maximum Moment (Nm)									
		Angular Position (rad))									
	FLX	Maximum Moment (Nm)									
		Angular Position (rad)									
		FLX/EXT Moment Ratio									
L	EXT	Maximum Moment (Nm)									
		Angular Position (rad)									
	FLX	Maximum Moment (Nm)									
		Angular Position (rad)									
		FLX/EXT Moment Ratio									
	L/R EXT Moment Ratio										
	L/R FLX Moment Ratio										

Figure 1.10 Data collection sheet (R = right, L = left, EXT = extension, FLX = flexion).

5. Position the subject on the dynamometer without attaching the input arm. A sitting position with the hips flexed at approximately 1.74 rad (100 deg) is recommended. A supine position may be preferable in order to increase muscular output and simulate movements where the hip angle is approximately neutral.
6. Carefully align the approximate joint axis of rotation with the axis of the dynamometer by modifying the subject's position and/or the dynamometer seat adjustments. For the knee test, align the lateral femoral epicondyle with the dynamometer axis and ensure that it remains in alignment throughout the test range of movement.
7. Attach the input arm of the dynamometer on the tibia above the malleoli and ensure that there is no movement of the leg relative to the input arm. Generally a rigid connection is required between the segment and the various parts of the input arm.
8. Secure all the other body parts not involved in the test with the appropriate straps. Ensure that the thigh, opposite leg, hips, chest and arms are appropriately stabilized. Make a note of the seat configuration and the joint positions in case you need to replicate the test on another occasion.
9. Provide written, clear instructions to the subject concerning the purpose of the test and the experimental procedure. Explain in detail the requirement for maximum voluntary effort throughout the test and the use of visual feedback to enhance muscular output. Allow the subject to ask any questions and be prepared to explain in detail the test requirements.
10. Familiarize the subject with the movement. Allow at least five submaximal repetitions (extension–flexion throughout the range of movement) at all the test angular velocities.

11. Allow the subject to rest. During this period, enter the appropriate data on the computer system, set the range of movement and perform the gravity correction procedure according to the instructions provided by the manufacturer of the dynamometer.
12. Start the test and allow 5–6 reciprocal repetitions (extension followed by flexion). The order of the test angular velocity should be randomized. Visual feedback and appropriate test instructions are adequate for maximum effort. If other forms of motivation are required (e.g. verbal encouragement) then make sure they are standardized and consistent between subjects.
13. After the test is completed, record on the data sheet the maximum moment for knee extension and flexion and the angular position where the maximum was measured. Allow the subject to rest for 1–2 minutes and perform the test at the other angular velocities. Repeat the procedure for the other side.

1.6.3 DATA ANALYSIS

1. Plot the maximum moment of the knee extensors and flexors against the angular velocity of movement (moment–angular velocity relationship).
2. Compare the increase/decrease of the moment during the eccentric and concentric movements with previously published studies examining this relationship.
3. Discuss the physiological/mechanical explanation for these findings.
4. Calculate the flexion/extension ratio by dividing the corresponding maximum moment recorded at each speed and plot this ratio against angular velocity. What do you observe? Explain any increase or decrease at the different eccentric and concentric velocities.
5. Plot the angular position (knee flexion angle) of the maximum moment at different angular velocities. Is the maximum moment recorded at the same angular position at different angular velocities? What is the physiological/mechanical explanation for your findings?
6. If data for both sides have been collected, then calculate the bilateral moment ratio (left joint moment/right joint moment) at the different angular velocities. See if you can explain any bilateral differences.
7. Establish the relationship between maximum moment, body mass and lean body mass. Can you express the maximum moment relative to body mass or lean body mass as a ratio? Explain the rationale for your answer.

1.7 PRACTICAL 2: ASSESSMENT OF ISOMETRIC FORCE–JOINT POSITION RELATIONSHIP

1.7.1 PURPOSE

The purpose of this practical is to assess the maximum isometric moment (static strength) of the knee extensor muscles at different knee joint positions. Isometric force can be measured using relatively inexpensive instruments that are commercially available.

1.7.2 PROCEDURE

Record all data on the data sheet for this practical (Figure 1.10).

1. Calibrate equipment according to the manufacturer's instructions. Record the date, the subject's name, gender, age, body mass, height and training status.
2. Measure or estimate other anthropometric parameters if required (for example lean body mass, cross-sectional area of muscle groups, segment circumference and volume, muscle mass etc.).
3. After some general warm-up/stretching exercises, position the subject on a bench lying on his/her side. A position with the hips flexed at approximately 1.74 rad (100 deg) is recommended. An extended position may be preferable to increase muscular output and simulate movements where the hip angle is approximately neutral.
4. Secure all the other body parts not involved in the test with appropriate straps. Ensure that the thigh, opposite leg, hips, chest and arms are appropriately stabilized. Make a note of the joint positions in case you need to replicate the test on another occasion. Attach the tensiometer or portable dynamometer to the limb near the malleoli. Ensure that the instrument is perpendicular to the tibia and on the sagittal plane (i.e. the plane formed by the tibia and femur). The movement must be performed on a plane parallel to the ground in order to avoid the effect of the gravitational force on the measurements. If the test is performed with the subject seated in a chair then the measurements of muscular moment are affected and must be corrected for the effect of the gravitational moment. For details of this procedure see Baltzopoulos and Brodie (1989).
5. Provide written, clear instructions to the subject concerning the purpose of the test and the experimental procedure. Explain in detail the requirement for maximum voluntary effort throughout the test and the use of feedback to enhance muscular output.
6. Familiarize the subject with the movement and allow at least two submaximal repetitions. An important aspect of isometric testing is the gradual increase of muscular force, avoiding sudden, ballistic movements. Allow the subject to ask any questions and be prepared to explain and demonstrate the test requirements.
7. Position the knee at approximately 90 degrees of knee flexion, start the test and maintain maximum effort for 5–7 seconds. Ensure that the presentation of test instructions and the use of verbal and visual feedback is standardized and consistent between subjects.
8. After the test is completed, record the maximum force measured. Measure the distance between the point of application and the joint centre of rotation and calculate the moment for knee extension as the product of force and moment arm. Record the isometric moment and the angular position where the maximum was measured, on the data sheet for this practical (Figure 1.10). Allow the subject to rest for 1–2 minutes and perform the test at angular position intervals of 10 degrees until full extension.

1.7.3 DATA ANALYSIS

1. Plot the maximum moment of the knee extensors against the angular joint position (moment–joint position relationship).

2. Explain the increase/decrease of the moment during the range of movement and compare these findings with previously published studies examining this relationship in other muscle groups.
3. Establish the physiological/mechanical explanation for these findings.
4. Calculate the muscular force from the equation: Force = Moment / Moment Arm. The moment arm of the knee extensors at different joint positions is presented in Figure 1.6. Is the force-position similar to the moment position relationship? What are the main determinants of these relationships during knee extension and other joint movements such as knee and elbow flexion?

1.8 PRACTICAL 3: ASSESSMENT OF KNEE JOINT PROPRIOCEPTION PERFORMANCE: REPRODUCTION OF PASSIVE JOINT POSITIONING

1.8.1 PURPOSE

The purpose of this practical is to assess the error associated with the passive reproduction of a series of blinded target knee flexion angles in a sagittal plane. Knee flexion angles can be measured using a isokinetic dynamometer goniometer system and movement of the lever input arm can be achieved manually or in an automated fashion under software control as appropriate.

1.8.2 PROCEDURE

1. Calibrate the equipment according to the manufacturer's instructions. Record the date, the subject's name, gender, age, body mass, height and training status.
2. Allow the subject to perform general warm-up/stretching exercises. Position the subject on the dynamometer without attaching the input arm. A sitting position with the hips flexed at approximately 1.74 rad (100 deg) is recommended. A supine position may be preferable in order to increase muscular output and simulate movements where the hip angle is approximately neutral.
3. Select a random assessment order for involved and contralateral limbs. Carefully align the approximate joint axis of rotation with the axis of the dynamometer by modifying the subject's position and/or the dynamometer seat adjustments. For the knee test, align the lateral femoral epicondyle with the dynamometer axis and ensure that it remains in alignment throughout the test range of movement.
4. Attach the input arm of the dynamometer on the tibia above the malleoli and ensure that there is no movement of the leg relative to the input arm. Generally a rigid connection is required between the segment and the various parts of the input arm.
5. Secure all the other body parts not involved in the test with the appropriate straps. Ensure that the thigh, opposite leg, hips, chest and arms are appropriately stabilized. Make a note of the seat configuration and the joint positions in case you need to replicate the test on another occasion.
6. Provide written, clear instructions to the subject concerning the purpose of the test and the experimental procedure. Explain in detail the requirement for a blinded

presentation of the target knee flexion angle (the participant should be blindfold or a screen should be placed so as to visually obscure the knee position). In the case of automated control of the input arm movement and associated knee flexion, the participant may need to wear ear-plugs in order to minimize the intrusion of the dynamometer's motor noise and potential cueing of knee position. Allow the subject to ask any questions and be prepared to explain in detail the test requirements.

7. Familiarize the subject with the procedures and allow at least three practice repetitions. Potential distractions to the participant should be minimized and a minimal number of investigators should be present in the laboratory during data capture.

8. The participant's musculature should remain passive throughout the test procedures.

9. Enter any preliminary information required by the data acquisition software and set the blinded target knee flexion angle. This can be achieved by using the on-screen visual display of knee flexion angle (which should be kept hidden from the participant) and either moving the input arm manually or using the control software to 'drive' the input arm into position. The specific target knee flexion angle may be selected from several angles spanning the knee range of motion, e.g. 15, 30, 45, 60, 75 and 90 degrees. Ensure that each movement is initiated from a different knee flexion angle which is selected at random to minimize potential cueing effects. Attempt to standardize the movement velocity of the input arm to 5 deg s^{-1} or to a value which is permitted by the dynamometer's control software. Once the blinded target knee flexion angle is achieved, maintain this target position for 5 seconds. Move the input arm to another position selected at random. After a 15 second period, initiate movement of the input arm at the standardized velocity throughout the knee joint range of movement. The initial direction of movement (either towards or further away from the target angle before returning from the extreme of the range of motion) should be selected at random. During this movement, the participant should indicate the position at which equivalence of knee joint angle with the blinded target angle is achieved.

10. Repeat the ipsilateral assessment process at the other knee flexion angles of interest in random order. Repeat the whole series of assessments.

11. Repeat the whole assessment protocol on the contralateral limb.

1.8.3 DATA ANALYSIS

1. Calculate the average error for joint position estimation across selected target knee flexion angles and duplicate trials.

2. Determine performance differences associated with contralateral limb comparisons.

3. Are there systematic differences in performance at the extremes and mid-range of the knee joint range of motion?

4. What improvements to the test procedures could be made to further limit the intrusion of potential cueing effects?

5. Discuss the physiological/mechanical basis for the findings.

6. On dynamometer systems which permit 'closed-chain' joint loading, repeat the above procedures. Discuss potential differences in responses between knee joint proprioception performance under 'closed-chain' (weight-bearing) and 'open-chain' (non-weight-bearing) joint loading conditions.

1.9 PRACTICAL 4: ASSESSMENT OF KNEE JOINT PROPRIOCEPTION PERFORMANCE: REPRODUCTION OF NET JOINT TORQUE

1.9.1 PURPOSE

The purpose of this practical is to assess the error associated with reproduction of a series of blinded target net torques in the knee flexors in a sagittal plane. This protocol was designed to assess the ability of the subject to actively regulate or control the force production in the knee flexors. Knee flexion torques can be measured using the isokinetic dynamometry system at 0 deg s^{-1} (static).

1.9.2 PROCEDURE

1. Calibrate equipment according to the manufacturer's instructions and record the date, the subject's name, gender, age, body mass, height and training status.
2. Allow the subject to perform general warm-up/stretching exercises.
3. Position the subject on the dynamometer without attaching the input arm. A sitting position with the hips flexed at approximately 1.74 rad (100 deg) may be used. A supine position may be preferable in order to increase muscular output and simulate movements where the hip angle is approximately neutral.
4. Select a random assessment order for involved and contralateral limbs. Carefully align the approximate joint axis of rotation with the axis of the dynamometer by modifying the subject's position and/or the dynamometer seat adjustments. For the knee test, align the lateral femoral epicondyle with the dynamometer axis and ensure that it remains in alignment throughout the test range of movement.
5. Attach the input arm of the dynamometer on the tibia above the malleoli and ensure that there is no movement of the leg relative to the input arm. Generally a rigid connection is required between the segment and the various parts of the input arm.
6. Secure all the other body parts not involved in the test with the appropriate straps. Ensure that the thigh, opposite leg, hips, chest and arms are appropriately stabilized. Make a note of the seat configuration and the joint positions in case you need to replicate the test on another occasion.
7. Assessments may be undertaken in random order at several knee flexion angles of interest (for example, 0.44 rad (25 deg), 0.87 rad (50 deg) and 1.31 rad (75 deg)).
8. Assess peak torque (PT) associated with maximal voluntary muscle actions of the knee flexors at each of the above knee flexion angles.
9. Provide written, clear instructions to the subject concerning the purpose of the test and the experimental procedure. Explain in detail the requirement for a blinded presentation of the target knee flexion torque. The participant should be blindfolded or a screen should be placed so as to visually obscure the knee musculature and any feedback from the computer control software. This minimizes the intrusion of the potential cueing of effort. Allow the subject to ask any questions and be prepared to explain in detail the test requirements.
10. Familiarize the participant with the procedures and allow at least three practice repetitions. Enter the appropriate data on the computer system.
11. Using the previously measured PT, ask the participant to produce muscle actions eliciting a blinded target knee flexion torque of 50% PT under verbal direction from the test

administrator. On attainment of the prescribed force level, ask the participant to maintain this prescribed torque for 3 seconds. The subject should then be requested to relax the involved musculature for a period of 15 seconds before reproducing the prescribed force within a period of 5 seconds. The participant should be requested to indicate perceived equivalence between the prescribed target torque and reproduced torque by relaxing the involved musculature immediately. The initiation of a rapid and sustained reduction in torque associated with muscle relaxation will effectively place a marker on the torque–time record. After allowing a 120-second recovery period, repeat this procedure.

12. Repeat the whole assessment protocol on the contralateral limb.

1.9.3 DATA ANALYSIS

1. The observed discrepancy between the prescribed and reproduced force levels may be expressed as a percentage of PT (torque error (TE%)). The TE% may be defined as the mean of the two intra-session replicates and calculated as the quotient of the difference between prescribed and perceived torque divided by the maximal voluntary knee flexion torque multiplied by 100.
2. Calculate the average torque error across selected knee flexion positions and duplicate trials.
3. Determine performance differences associated with contralateral limb comparisons.
4. Are there systematic differences in performance at the extremes and mid-range of the knee joint range of motion?
5. What improvements to the test procedures could be made to further limit the intrusion of potential cueing effects?
6. Discuss the physiological/mechanical basis for the findings.
7. Repeat the assessments at blinded target knee flexion torques of 75% peak torque and 25% peak torque in random order and suggest what effect this would have on torque error.

REFERENCES

Abernethy, P., Wilson, G. and Logan, P. (1995). Strength and power assessment. *Sports Medicine*, **19**, 401–17.

Alway, S., Stray-Gundersen, J., Grumbt, W. and Gonyea, W. (1990). Muscle cross-sectional area and torque in resistance trained subjects. *Journal of Applied Physiology*, **60**, 86–90.

Aoyagi, Y. and Shephard, R. (1992). Ageing and muscle function. *Sports Medicine*, **14**, 376–96.

Appen, L. and Duncan, P. (1986). Strength relationship of knee musculature: effects of gravity and sport. *Journal of Orthopaedic and Sports Physical Therapy*, **7**, 232–5.

Baltzopoulos, V. (1995a). A videofluoroscopy method for optical distortion correction and measurement of knee joint kinematics. *Clinical Biomechanics*, **10**, 85–92.

Baltzopoulos, V. (1995b). Muscular and tibio-femoral joint forces during isokinetic knee extension. *Clinical Biomechanics*, **10**, 208–14.

Baltzopoulos, V. and Brodie, D. (1989). Isokinetic dynamometry: applications and limitations. *Sports Medicine*, **8**, 101–16.

Baltzopoulos, V., Eston, R.G. and Maclaren, D. (1988). A comparison of power outputs on the Wingate test and on a test using an isokinetic device. *Ergonomics*, **31**, 1693–9.

Baltzopoulos, V., Williams, J. and Brodie, D. (1991). Sources of error in isokinetic dynamometry: effects of visual feedback on maximum torque output. *Journal of Orthopaedic and Sports Physical Therapy*, **13**, 138–42.

Baratta, R. and Solomonow, M. (1991). The effects of tendon viscoelastic stiffness on the dynamic performance of isometric muscle. *Journal of Biomechanics*, **24**, 109–16.

Beam, W., Bartels, R. and Ward, R. (1982). The relationship of isokinetic torque to body weight in athletes. *Medicine and Science in Sports and Exercise*, **14**, 178.

Behm, D. and Sale, D. (1993). Velocity specificity of resistance training. *Sports Medicine*, **15**, 374–88.

Bell, G. and Wenger, H. (1992). Physiological adaptations to velocity-controlled resistance training. *Sports Medicine*, **13**, 234–44.

Bemben, M. (1991). Isometric muscle force production as a function of age in healthy 20 to 74 yr old men. *Medicine and Science in Sports and Exercise*, **23**, 1302–9.

Bishop, P., Cureton, K. and Collins, M. (1987). Sex differences in muscular strength in equally trained men and women. *Ergonomics*, **30**, 675–87.

Bobbert, M. and Harlaar, J. (1992). Evaluation of moment angle curves in isokinetic knee extension. *Medicine and Science in Sports and Exercise*, **25**, 251–9.

Bouisset, S. (1984). Are the classical tension-length and force-velocity relationships always valid in natural motor activities? In *Neural and Mechanical Control of Movement*. ed. M. Kumamoto (Yamaguchi Shoten, Kyoto, Japan), pp. 4–11.

Brooke, M. and Kaiser, K. (1974). The use and abuse of muscle histochemistry. *Annals of the New York Academy of Sciences*, **228**, 121–44.

Brooks, V. (1986). *The Neural Basis of Motor Control*. (Oxford University Press, New York).

Burdett, R.G. and Van Swearingen J. (1987). Reliability of isokinetic muscle endurance tests. *Journal of Orthopaedic and Sports Physical Therapy*, **8**, 485–9.

Burke, E.J., Wojcieszak, I., Puchow, M. and Michael, E.D. (1985). Analysis of high intensity bicycle tests of varying duration. *Exercise Physiology: Current Selected Research*, **1**, 159–70.

Burke, R. (1981). Motor units: anatomy, physiology, and functional organization. In *Handbook of Physiology*. ed. V. Brooks (American Physiological Society, Bethesola, MD), pp. 345–422.

Cabri, J. (1991). Isokinetic strength aspects of human joints and muscles. *Critical Reviews in Biomedical Engineering*, **19**, 231–59.

Cavanagh, P. (1988). On muscle action versus muscle contraction. *Journal of Biomechanics*, **21**, 69.

Chapman, A. (1976). The relationship between length and the force-velocity curve of a single equivalent linear muscle during flexion of the elbow. In *Biomechanics IV*. ed. P. Komi (University Park Press, Baltimore, MD), pp. 434–8.

Chapman, A. (1985). The mechanical properties of human muscle. In *Exercise and Sport Sciences Reviews*. ed. L. Terjung (Macmillan, New York), pp. 443–501.

Cheney, P. (1985). Role of cerebral cortex in voluntary movements. A review. *Physical Therapy*, **65**, 624–35.

Clarkson, P., Johnson, J., Dexradeur, D., *et al.* (1982). The relationship among isokinetic endurance, initial strength level and fibre type. *Research Quarterly for Exercise and Sport*, **53**, 15–19.

Cote, C., Simoneau, J., Lagasse, P., *et al.* (1988). Isokinetic strength training protocols: do they include skeletal muscle fibre hypertrophy? *Archives of Physical Medicine and Rehabilitation*, **69**, 281–5.

Coyle, E., Feiring, D., Rotkis, T., *et al.* (1981). Specificity of power improvements through slow and fast isokinetic training. *Journal of Applied Physiology*, **51**, 1437–42.

Dummer, G., Clark, D., Vaccano, P., *et al.* (1985). Age related differences in muscular strength and muscular endurance among female master´s swimmers. *Research Quarterly for Exercise and Sport*, **56**, 97–102.

Duncan, P., Chandler, J., Cavanaugh, D., *et al.* (1989). Mode and speed specificity of eccentric and concentric exercise. *Journal of Orthopaedic and Sports Physical Therapy*, **11**, 70–5.

Edman, P.K.A. (1992). Contractile performance of skeletal muscle fibres. In *Strength and Power in Sport*. ed. P.V. Komi (Blackwell Scientific Publications, Oxford), pp. 96–114.

Enoka, R. and Stuart, D. (1984). Henneman's 'size principle': current issues. *Trends in Neurosciences*, **7**, 226–8.

Enoka, R.M. (1994). *Neuromechanical Basis of Kinesiology*. (Human Kinetics, Champaign, IL).

Fenn, W.O. and Marsh, B.S. (1935). Muscular force at different speeds of shortening. *Journal of Physiology*, **85**, 277–97.

Figoni, S., Christ, C. and Massey, B. (1988). Effects of speed, hip and knee angle, and gravity on hamstring to quadriceps torque ratios. *Journal of Orthopaedic and Sports Physical Therapy*, **9**, 287–91.

Fillyaw, M., Bevins, T. and Fernandez, L. (1986). Importance of correcting isokinetic peak torque for the effect of gravity when calculating knee flexor to extensor muscle ratios. *Physical Therapy*, **66**, 23–9.

Froese, E. and Houston, M. (1985). Torque-velocity characteristics and muscle fibre type in human vastus lateralis. *Journal of Applied Physiology*, **59**, 309–14.

Frontera, W., Hughes, V., Lutz, K. and Evans, W. (1991). A cross-sectional study of muscle strength and mass in 45- to 78-yr-old men and women. *Journal of Applied Physiology*, **71**, 644–50.

Fu, F.H. (1993). Biomechanics of knee ligaments. *Journal of Bone and Joint Surgery*, **75A**, 1716–27.

Gleeson, N.P. and Mercer, T.H. (1992). Reproducibility of isokinetic leg strength and endurance characteristics of adult men and women. *European Journal of Applied Physiology and Occupational Physiology*, **65**, 221–8.

Gleeson, N.P. and Mercer, T.H. (1994). An examination of the reproducibility and utility of isokinetic leg strength assessment in women. In *Access to Active Living: 10th Commonwealth and International Scientific Congress*. eds. F.I. Bell and G.H. Van Gyn (University of Victoria, Victoria, BC), pp. 323–7.

Gleeson, N.P. and Mercer, T.H. (1996). Influence of prolonged intermittent high intensity running on leg neuromuscular and musculoskeletal performance. *The Physiologist*, **39**, A–62.

Gleeson, N.P., Mercer, T.H., Morris, K. and Rees, D. (1997). Influence of a fatigue task on electromechanical delay in the knee flexors of soccer players. *Medicine and Science in Sports and Exercise*, **29**, S281.

Gleeson, N.P., Rees, D., Doyle, J., *et al*. The effects of anterior cruciate ligament-reconstructive surgery and acute physical rehabilitation on neuromuscular modelling associated with the knee joint. *Journal of Sports Sciences*. (In press).

Gowitzke, B. and Milner, M. (1988). *Scientific Basis of Human Movement*. (Williams and Wilkins, Baltimore, MD).

Green, H. (1986). Muscle power: fibre type recruitment metabolism and fatigue. In *Human Muscle Power*. eds. N. Jones, N. McCartney, and A. McComas (Human Kinetics, Champaign, IL), pp. 65–79.

Gregor, R., Edgerton, V., Perrine, J., *et al*. (1979). Torque velocity relationships and muscle fibre composition in elite female athletes. *Journal of Applied Physiology*, **47**, 388–92.

Gustafsson, B. and Pinter, M. (1985). On factors determining orderly recruitment of motor units: a role for intrinsic membrane properties. *Trends in Neurosciences*, **8**, 431–3.

Harrison, P. (1983). The relationship between the distribution of motor unit mechanical properties and the forces due to recruitment and to rate coding for the generation of muscle force. *Brain Research*, **264**, 311–15.

Hasan, Z. and Stuart, D.G. (1988). Animal solutions to problems of movement control: the role of proprioceptors. *Annual Reviews in Neuroscience*, **11**, 199–223.

Henneman, E. (1957). Relation between size of neurons and their susceptibility to discharge. *Science*, **126**, 1345–7.

Heyward, V., Johannes-Ellis, S. and Romer, J. (1986). Gender differences in strength. *Research Quarterly for Exercise and Sport*, **57**, 154–9.

Hill, A. (1938). The heat of shortening and the dynamic constants of muscle. *Proceedings of the Royal Society of London*, **126B**, 136–95.

Hinson, M., Smith, W. and Funk, S. (1979). Isokinetics: a clarification. *Research Quarterly*, **50**, 30–5.

Hislop, H. and Perrine, J. (1967). The isokinetic concept of exercise. *Physical Therapy*, **47**, 114–17.

Hoffman, T., Stauffer, R. and Jackson, A. (1979). Sex difference in strength. *American Journal of Sports Medicine*, **74**, 264–7.

Hortobagyi, T. and Katch, F. (1990). Eccentric and concentric torque-velocity relationships during arm flexion and extension. *European Journal of Applied Physiology*, **60**, 395–401.

Johannsen, H. (1991). Role of knee ligaments in proprioception and regulation of muscle stiffness. *Journal of Electromyography and Kinesiology*, **1**, 158–79.

Johannsen, H., Sjolander, P. and Sojka, P. (1986). Actions of γ-motoneurons elicited by electrical stimulation of joint afferent fibers in the hind limb of the cat. *Journal of Physiology (London)*, **375**, 137–52.

Kannus, P., Jarvinen, M. and Lehto, M. (1991). Maximal peak torque as a predictor of angle-specific torques of hamstring and quadriceps muscles in man. *European Journal of Applied Physiology and Occupational Physiology*, **63**, 112–8.

Kannus, P., Cook, L. and Alosa, D. (1992). Absolute and relative endurance parameters in isokinetic tests of muscular performance. *Journal of Sport Rehabilitation*, **1**, 2–12.

Kereshi, S., Manzano, G. and McComas, A. (1983). Impulse conduction velocities in human biceps brachii muscles. *Experimental Neurology*, **80**, 652–62.

Komi, P. (1984). Biomechanics and neuromuscular performance. *Medicine and Science in Sports and Exercise*, **16**, 26–8.

Komi, P. (1986). The stretch-shortening cycle and human power out-put. In *Human Muscle Power*. eds. N. Jones, N. McCartney, and A. McComas (Human Kinetics, Champaign, IL), pp. 27–39.

Komi, P., Viitasalo, J., Rauramaa, R. and Vihko, V. (1978). Effects of isometric strength training on mechanical, electrical and metabolic aspects of muscle function. *European Journal of Applied Physiology*, **40**, 45–55.

Krauspe, R., Schmidt, M. and Schaible, H.G. (1992). Sensory innervation of the anterior cruciate ligament. *Journal of Bone Joint Surgery (Am)*, **74**, 390 –7.

Kroll, W., Bultman, L., Kilmer, W. and Boucher, J. (1990). Anthropometric predictors of isometric arm strength in males and females. *Clinical Kinesiology*, **44**, 5–11.

Kulig, K., Andrews, J. and Hay, J. (1984). Human strength curves. In *Exercise and Sport Sciences Reviews*. ed. R. Terjung (Macmillan, New York), pp. 417–66.

Lattanzio, P.J. and Petrella, R.J. (1998). Knee proprioception: A review of mechanisms, measurements, and implications of muscular fatigue. *Othopaedics*, **21**, 463–70.

Laubach, L. (1976). Comparative muscular strength of men and women: a review of the literature. *Aviation, Space and Environmental Medicine*, **47**, 534–42.

Lephart, S.M., Kocher, M.S., Fu, F.H., *et al.* (1992). Proprioception following anterior cruciate ligament reconstruction. *Journal of Sports Rehabilitation*, **1**, 188–96.

Lesmes, G., Costill, D., Coyle, E. and Fink, W. (1978). Muscle strength and power changes during maximum isokinetic training. *Medicine and Science in Sports and Exercise*, **10**, 266–9.

MacDougall, J., Sale, D., Elder, G. and Sutton, J. (1982). Muscle ultrastructural characteristics of elite powerlifters and bodybuilders. *European Journal of Applied Physiology*, **48**, 117–26.

Mathiassen, S.E. (1989). Influence of angular velocity and movement frequency on development of fatigue in repeated isokinetic knee extensions. *European Journal of Applied Physiology and Occupational Physiology*, **59**, **1/2**, 80–8.

Maughan, R., Watson, J. and Weir, J. (1983).

Strength and cross-sectional area of human skeletal muscle. *Journal of Physiology*, **388**, 37–49.

Milner-Brown, H., Stein, R. and Lee, R. (1975). Synchronization of human motor units: possible roles of exercise and supraspinal reflexes. *Electroencephalography and Clinical Neurophysiology*, **38**, 245–54.

Montgomery, L.C., Douglass, L.W. and Deuster, P.A. (1989). Reliability of an isokinetic test of muscle strength and endurance. *Journal of Orthopaedic and Sports Physical Therapy*, **8**, 315–22.

Morrow, J. and Hosler, W. (1981). Strength comparisons in untrained men and trained women athletes. *Medicine and Science in Sports and Exercise*, **13**, 194–7.

Nemeth, P., Solanki, L., Gordon, D., *et al.* (1986). Uniformity of metabolic enzymes within individual motor units. *Journal of Neuroscience*, **6**, 892–8.

Perrin, D.H. (1986). Reliability of isokinetic measures. *Athletic Training*, **10**, 319–21.

Perrin, D. (1993). *Isokinetic Exercise and Assessment*. (Human Kinetics, Champaign, IL).

Perrin, D., Robertson, R. and Ray, R. (1987). Bilateral isokinetic peak torque, torque acceleration energy, power, and work relationships in athletes and nonathletes. *Journal of Orthopaedic and Sports Physical Therapy*, **9**, 184–9.

Perrine, J. and Edgerton, V. (1978). Muscle force-velocity and power-velocity relationships under isokinetic loading. *Medicine and Science in Sports and Exercise*, **10**, 159–66.

Pollack, G. (1983). The cross-bridge theory. *Physiological Reviews*, **63**, 1049–113.

Pope, M.H., Johnson, R.J., Brown, D.W. and Tighe, C. (1979). The role of the musculature in injuries to medial collateral ligament. *Journal of Bone and Joint Surgery (Am)*, **61**, 398–402.

Prietto, C. and Caiozzo, V. (1989). The in vivo force-velocity relationship of the knee flexors and extensors. *American Journal of Sports Medicine*, **17**, 607–11.

Rees, D. and Gleeson, N.P. (1999). The scientific assessment of the injured athlete. *Proceedings of the Football Association – Royal College of Surgeons Medical Conference*, Lilleshall Hall National Sports Centre, October.

Ryushi, T., Hakkinen, K., Kauhanen, H. and Komi, P. (1988). Muscle fibre characteristics, muscle cross-sectional area and force production in strength athletes, physically active males and females. *Scandinavian Journal of Sports Sciences*, **10**, 7–15.

Sale, D., McDougall, D., Upton, A. and McComas, A. (1983). Effect of strength training upon motoneuron excitability in man. *Medicine and Science in Sports and Exercise*, **15**, 57–62.

Sale, D.G. (1991). Testing strength and power. In *Physiological Testing of the High Performance Athlete*, 2nd edn. eds. J.D. MacDougall, H.A. Wenger and H.J. Green (Human Kinetics, Champaign, IL), pp. 21–106.

Schantz, P., Randal-Fox, A., Hutchison, W., *et al.* (1983). Muscle fibre type distribution of muscle cross-sectional area and maximum voluntary strength in humans. *Acta Physiologica Scandinavica*, **117**, 219–26.

Shephard, R. (1991). Handgrip dynamometry, Cybex measurements and lean mass as markers of the aging of muscle function. *British Journal of Sports Medicine*, **25**, 204–8.

Simoneau, J., Lortie, G., Boulay, M., *et al.* (1985). Human skeletal muscle fibre type alteration with high-intensity intermittent training. *European Journal of Applied Physiology*, **54**, 250–3.

Swanik, C. B., Lephart, S.M., Giannantonio, F.P. and Fu, F.H. (1997). Re-establishing proprioception and neuromuscular control in the ACL-injured athlete. *Journal of Sport Rehabilitation*, **6**, 182–206.

Tesch, P. and Karlsson, P. (1985). Muscle fibre type and size in trained and untrained muscles of elite athletes. *Journal of Applied Physiology*, **59**, 1716–20.

Thistle, H., Hislop, H., Moffroid, M. and Lohman, E. (1967). Isokinetic contraction: a new concept of resistive exercise. *Archives of Physical Medicine and Rehabilitation*, **48**, 279–82.

Thomas, D., White, M., Sagar, G. and Davies, C. (1987). Electrically evoked isokinetic plantar flexor torque in males. *Journal of Applied Physiology*, **63**, 1499–502.

Thorstensson, A., Grimby, G. and Karlsson, J. (1976). Force-velocity relations and fibre composition in human knee extensor muscle. *Journal of Applied Physiology*, **40**, 12–16.

Tihanyi, J., Apor, P. and Petrekanits, M. (1987). Force-velocity-power characteristics for extensors of lower extremities. In *Biomechanics X-B*. ed. B. Johnson (Human Kinetics, Champaign, IL), pp. 707–12.

Watkins, M. (1993). Evaluation of skeletal muscle performance. In *Muscle Strength*. ed. K. Harms-Ringdahl (Churchill Livingstone, London), pp. 19–36.

Westing, S. and Seger, J. (1989). Eccentric and concentric torque-velocity characteristics, torque output comparisons, and gravity effect torque corrections for the quadriceps and hamstring muscles in females. *International Journal of Sports Medicine*, **10**, 175–80.

Westing, S., Seger, J., Karlson, E. and Ekblom, B. (1988). Eccentric and concentric torque-velocity characteristics of the quadriceps femoris in man. *European Journal of Applied Physiology*, **58**, 100–4.

Westing, S., Seger, J. and Thorstensson, A. (1991). Isoacceleration: a new concept of resistive exercise. *Medicine and Science in Sports and Exercise*, **23**, 631–5.

Wickiewicz, T., Roy, R., Powell, P., *et al.* (1984). Muscle architecture and force velocity in humans. *Journal of Applied Physiology*, **57**, 435–43.

Wilkie, D. (1950). The relation between force and velocity in human muscle. *Journal of Physiology (London)*, **110**, 249–54.

ASSESSMENT OF NEUROMUSCULAR PERFORMANCE USING ELECTROMYOGRAPHY

2

Nigel P. Gleeson

2.1 AIMS

The aims of this chapter are to:
- describe the application of electromyography to the study of neuromuscular performance,
- describe the relationship between physiological and recorded electromyographic signals,
- provide an understanding of how the fidelity of the recorded electromyographic signal may be influenced by factors intrinsic to the muscle and by factors which may be controlled by the test administrator,
- describe some of the characteristics of the recording instrumentation associated with electromyography,
- evaluate the value and limitations of using electromyography in the assessment of temporal neuromuscular control,
- describe factors which affect the validity and reliability of measurements that are derived from electromyographic techniques.

2.2 INTRODUCTION

Muscle is an excitable tissue that responds to neural stimulation by contracting and attempting to shorten within its articular system. The many functions that are served by associated changes to the stiffness or movement of a joint system permit effective and safe interaction with our environment. Any mechanical response is preceded by an asynchronous pattern of neural activation and an electrical response from the muscle fibres. Electromyography (EMG) is a technique for recording the changes in the electrical potential of a muscle when it is caused to contract by a motor nerve impulse.

The fundamental structural and functional unit of neuromuscular control (Enoka, 1994; Aidley, 1998) is the motor unit which consists of a single motor nerve fibre (efferent α-motoneuron) and all the muscle fibres it innervates. Such fibres can be spread over a wide area of the muscle (Nigg and Herzog, 1994). Each muscle is composed of multiple motor units. The contractile force produced by the whole muscle is partly determined by the number of motor units that are activated by neural stimulation and by the rate at which stimulation occurs.

Stimulation of the muscle fibre at the neuro-muscular junction (motor end-plate) elicits a reduction of the electrical potential of the cell and propagation of the action potential throughout the muscle fibre. The waveform resulting from this depolarization is known as the motor (fibre) action potential (MAP). Each nerve impulse produces an almost simultaneous contraction in all the muscle fibres of the motor unit before being followed by a repolarization wave. The spatial and temporal summation of MAPs from the fibres associated with a given motor unit is termed a motor unit action potential (MUAP). Repeated neural stimulation elicits a train of MUAPs (MUAPT)

Kinanthropometry and Exercise Physiology Laboratory Manual: Tests, Procedures and Data. 2nd Edition, Volume 2: Exercise Physiology
Edited by RG Eston and T Reilly. Published by Routledge, London, June 2001

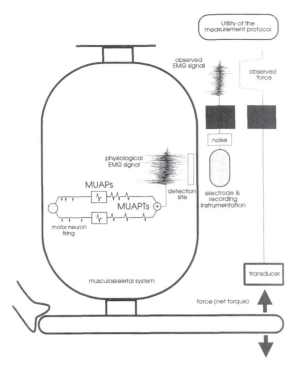

Figure 2.1 A schematic representation of the electromechanical sequelae of neural activation of the muscle.

(Basmajian and De Luca, 1985) and the summation over time of these trains from the various motor units is referred to as the physiological electromyographic signal (Figure 2.1). Of the electrical and mechanical events that follow neural activation, it may be somewhat easier to detect the electrical events. Electromyography is a fundamental tool in functional anatomy and clinical kinesiology. It offers the only method of objectively assessing when a muscle is active (Grieve, 1975) and is commonly used to evaluate the roles of specific muscles in movement situations (Basmajian and De Luca, 1985) and to present biological feedback for the improvement of motor performance. It has also been used to investigate the effects of neuromuscular conditioning.

While electromyography offers important and useful applications of kinanthropometric interest, it is also fraught with potential limitations which threaten to detract from its utility.

The recorded signal is an intrinsically complex history of the muscular electrical activity that can be influenced at any given time by many variables. It is thus a proxy of the physiological electromyographic signal. Its interpretation is considered to be even more complex.

2.3 FACTORS INFLUENCING THE ELECTROMYOGRAPHIC SIGNAL

The primary factors which have an influence on the recorded signal and ultimately its interpretation can be segregated into intrinsic and extrinsic factors. 'Intrinsic' factors reflect physiological, anatomical and biochemical characteristics within the muscle. 'Extrinsic' factors include the external system for detecting the electromyographic signals. In this respect, the quality of the recorded signal and its proper interpretation are very much dependent on the electrode structure and placement. However, depending on the application, the recorded electromyographic signal and its interpretation can also be influenced by other components of this system during modification of the signal (amplifier) and the storage of the resulting waveform (digital recording system).

2.3.1 THE MUSCULATURE AND INTRINSIC FACTORS INFLUENCING THE RECORDED ELECTROMYOGRAPHIC SIGNAL

This intrinsic group includes the number of active motor units at any specified time of the muscle action; fibre-type composition of the muscle; blood flow in the muscle; fibre diameter; depth and location of the active fibres within the muscle relative to the electrode detection surfaces; amount of tissue between the surface of the muscle and the electrode; firing characteristics of the motor units (firing rates of the motor units and potential for synchronization); and the motor unit twitch.

These factors contribute in various ways to changes in the amplitude and frequency content (spectrum) of the electromyographic signal by means of spatial filtering and changes to the conduction velocity. For example, the fibre diameter may influence the amplitude, shape and conduction velocity of the action potentials that constitute the signal; increased distance of the fibres of active motor units from the detection electrode hinders the detection of separate MUAPs. Also, the type and amount of subcutaneous tissue modifies the characteristics of the signal by rejecting some of the high-frequency components of the signal.

Limitations in current technology and knowledge mean that for the most part such intrinsic factors cannot be controlled. The contributions of some of the factors (for example, the depth and location of the active fibres within the muscle relative to the electrode detection surfaces) would be expected to add to the background experimental error (noise) associated with the measurement of the recorded signal. Others, for example, fibre diameter and firing characteristics of the motor units, may be influenced systematically by changes to the neuromuscular system associated with specific conditioning interventions. The relative importance of these factors to the utility of the electromyographic signal remains elusive.

2.3.2 THE SYSTEM FOR DETECTING THE ELECTROMYOGRAPHIC SIGNALS: EXTRINSIC FACTORS

Electrode configuration describes the shape and area of the electrode detection surfaces and determines the number of active motor units that are registered by the detecting electrodes. The distance between the electrode detection surfaces determines the bandwidth (the range of frequencies) that the differential electrode configuration will be capable of detecting. The location of the electrode with respect to the musculotendinous junction and the motor end-plates in the muscle moderates the amplitude and frequency characteristics of the detected signal. The location of the electrode on the surface of the muscle, with respect to the anatomical border of the muscle, regulates the potential for crosstalk (the term

crosstalk is used to describe the interference of electromyographic signals from muscles other than the ones under the electrode (Basmajian and De Luca, 1985). The orientation of the detection surfaces relative to the pennation characteristics of the muscle fibres influences the value of the measured conduction velocity of the action potentials and ultimately the frequency content and amplitude of the signal. Extrinsic factors such as those listed above can be controlled by the test administrator. Optimized practice should increase the utility, validity and reliability (reproducibility) of measurements involving electromyography.

Other aspects of the instrumentation associated with electromyography can contribute to the utility of the measurement. The following sections provide an overview of the key aspects of instrumentation used to optimize detection and recording of the signal.

2.4 ELECTRODES

The electromyographic signal can be recorded by means of invasive and surface electrodes. Invasive electromyography is necessary for recording activity in deep muscles but involves the use of indwelling (fine wire) electrodes which are inserted with a hypodermic needle. While the fine wire electrodes have a very small diameter (approximately 0.025 mm) which means that they are relatively painless in use, several problems limit the potential utility of such invasive procedures in sports medicine and science. These include ethical issues relating to possible breakage during dynamic manoeuvres and associated risks of infection. The method also requires clinical imaging techniques such as ultrasound to overcome the difficulties of locating deep muscles precisely. High electrode impedance, potential distortion of the recorded signal due to deformation and changes in the effective length of the electrode, and damage to adjacent muscle fibres during insertion are technical issues which have also contributed to the fact that these procedures are rarely deployed outside specialist research applications or where indicated clinically. Fine wire electrodes have been advocated clinically when the patient is obese, oedematous or in cold conditions but are rarely used even under such circumstances (Engbaek and Mortensen, 1994).

Surface electromyographic techniques generally permit access to electrical signals from superficial muscles only. Both active and passive surface electrodes require placement on the surface of the skin above the musculature of interest. Active surface electrodes require a power supply to operate and thus demand electrical isolation. This type of surface electrode has the advantage of not requiring any skin preparation or electrode gels but they are likely to increase the overall noise level during the amplification of the signal (De Luca and Knaflitz, 1990).

Passive surface electrodes are routinely used for monitoring neuromuscular transmission in a bipolar configuration in which the difference in potential between two adjacent electrodes is utilized to reduce mains-related interference during subsequent amplification (see later section). Paediatric electrodes are often recommended due to their increased current density. These are generally up to 10 mm in diameter although 10 mm × 1 mm rectangular-shaped electrodes are likely to interact with greater numbers of muscle fibres. Disposable, self-adhesive, surface electrodes are of the Ag/AgCl type consisting of a silver metal base coated electrolytically with a layer of ionic compound, silver chloride and pre-gelled with electrolyte gel. This type of electrode is electrochemically stable and reduces polarization potentials which cause signal distortion. A full discussion of electrode characteristics can be found in Geddes and Baker (1989).

Surface electrodes are subject to movement artefacts which in turn disturb the electrochemical equilibrium between the electrode and skin and so cause a change in the recorded electrode potential. Electrode gel minimizes this change by moving the metal and electrolyte away from the skin so that movement of the electrode does not disturb the metal–electrolyte junction and the potential is unaltered. Electrode gel contains Cl^- as the principal anion in order to maintain good contact. Lewes (1965) showed that electrolyte gel with high chloride and abrasive content is unnecessary with an amplifier input impedance in excess of 2 $M\Omega$. Reduction of impedance at the electrode–skin barrier is important to minimize induced currents from external electrical and electromagnetic sources. Without skin preparation, skin impedance can be in of the order of 100 $k\Omega$ depending on the measuring technique. Impedance has components of resistance, capacitance and inductance, making it frequency-dependent. In tissue such as muscle, fat and skin the capacitance and resistance are significant components (Basmajian and De Luca, 1985).

In most circumstances it is desirable to reduce skin impedance and contact resistance by means of appropriate skin preparation. Many techniques have been used to reduce electrode–skin impedance and motion artefacts. Medina *et al.* (1989) and Tam and Webster (1977) measured offset potential and showed a decrease with 'light' abrasive skin preparation. More invasive methods include a skin-puncture technique with a micro-lancet (Burbank and Webster, 1978) and scratching with a needle and the reverse side of a sterile lancet to break the superficial layer of dead skin (Okamoto *et al.*, 1987). De Talhouet and Webster (1996) suggested that motion artefact incurred by stretching of the skin could be reduced by stripping skin layers with adhesive tape. Degreasing the skin with acetone or alcohol is the least skin preparation technique employed prior to application of electrodes. Patterson (1978) found no significant difference between either solvent when considering impedance measurements. However, Almasi and Schmitt (1974) suggested differences between genders and, in addition, wide and systematic variation depending on where the electrodes were placed on the body. All strategies should aim to minimize (less than 10 kΩ and preferably less than 5 kΩ), standardize and maintain the measured impedance (measured across the expected signal frequency range) between sets of recording electrodes after the electrode sticker and sterilized electrode have been attached. These precautions will maximize the detected electromyographic signal compared to the noise inherent in the remainder of the recording instrumentation. The latter is particularly important where high performance (high-input impedance) amplifiers are not available.

2.4.1 POSITIONING OF THE ELECTRODES

Whatever the type of surface electromyographic electrode, the location of the electrodes is of fundamental importance. This should be away from the location of the motor end-plate (De Luca and Knaflitz, 1990). The amplitude and frequency spectrum of the signal are affected by the location of the electrode with respect to the innervation zone, the musculotendinous junction and the lateral edge of the muscle. The preferred location is in the mid-line of the belly of the muscle between the nearest innervation zone and the musculotendinous junction. In this location the electromyographic signal with the greatest amplitude is detected. The latter process requires the use of an external device to elicit activation of the muscle. Where a stimulator is not available, electrodes may be placed over the mid-point of the muscle belly (Clarys and Cabri, 1993), which may offer a reasonable approach to the standardization of the recorded signal. Further consistency is afforded to the recorded electromyographic signal by siting the two detector electrodes with the line between them parallel to the direction of the muscle fibres or pointing to the origin and insertion of the muscle where the muscle fibres are not linear or without a parallel arrangement (Clarys and Cabri, 1993).

Since surface electromyographic electrodes are susceptible to crosstalk, the separation of the electrodes determines the degree of localization of the detected signal. A standard electrode separation distance of 10 mm has been recommended (Basmajian and De Luca, 1985). Furthermore, as discussed previously, several factors have the potential to influence the spatial filtering, amplitude and frequency characteristics of the detected signal. These include the depth and location of the active fibres within the muscle with respect to the electrode detection surfaces, the amount of tissue between the surface of the muscle and the electrode, and the fibre diameter. Thus, even subtle deviations in the positioning of the detecting electrodes relative to the motor units and muscle fibres originally contributing to the physiological signal may alter the spatial filtering characteristics of the detection volume and may be sufficient to place a new set of active motor units within the detection volume of the electrode and to remove some of the motor units from the detection volume. Incorrect positioning would be expected to produce additional error or noise in the recorded electromyographic signal as well as in associated indices of neuromuscular performance. Under the most unfavourable circumstances of relative migration of the electrode and active fibres, this could actually invalidate the recorded electromyographic signal. This potential for error raises concern for inter-trial assessments of the same muscle where electrodes are re-affixed on each test occasion or during dynamic muscle actions. There is an inevitability about relative movement between detecting electrode and active muscle fibre population. Tattooing of the skin at the site of the electrode position or preserving the geography of the site by mapping on an acetate sheet the electrode position relative to moles, small angiomas and permanent skin blemishes would be expected to facilitate signal stability and comparability across inter-trial assessments of the neuromuscular performance of the same musculoskeletal system.

2.5 OVERVIEW OF HARDWARE

A typical physiological recording system will consist of an isolated connection to the participant, signal conditioning in terms of amplifiers and filters and an analogue-to-digital converter, before collection and storage on a PC.

As outlined earlier, where the electrode assembly connects directly to the participant circuit an isolation barrier is necessary for participant's electrical connection safety. These terms are defined under the relevant safety requirements for medical electrical equipment (see British Standards Institute documentation, BS/EN 60601–1: 1993, and international equivalents, International Electrotechnical Commission 60601–1). The safety implication for the amplifier circuitry is that the participant circuit is electrically isolated from the amplifying equipment and the connection provides no path to ground. This isolation barrier is often provided by an isolation transformer and a frequency modulator. After passing through a transformer with a low primary-to-secondary ratio, the modulated carrier is demodulated and the original signal is recovered. This isolated input demands that the electrical potential of the participant is floating, the participant is isolated from earth and the mains equipment is under a single fault condition and protected by an allowable participant leakage current.

2.5.1 SIGNAL AMPLIFICATION

The detected electromyographic signal will have an amplitude in the order of 5–9 mV with surface electrodes. This relatively low level signal typically requires amplification to match the electrical characteristics of a variety of suitable signal recording instrumentation systems. The gain describes this process and is calculated as the ratio of output to input voltages. The gains used in electromyography are typically high and vary in the range 10^2 to 10^4 depending on the instrumentation system and application.

There are several important aspects concerning design of amplifiers which are critical to the meaningful collection of the surface electromyographic signal and related physiological data (Basmajian and De Luca, 1985). The amplifier should be situated close to the participant during the recordings in order to minimize the potential intrusion of noise from many sources. This interference can be from the participant, from the environment, or from the instrumentation being used close to the participant. In particular, these sources can be due principally to electrostatic or electromagnetic induction from mains or radio-frequency sources.

In conjunction with other close equipment, the participant may contribute to the electrical capacitance associated with the assessment system. Capacitatively linked electrostatic potentials will vary as the potential path to ground varies with the object and they may appear at the input of the amplifier at the frequency associated with the alternating current of the mains. In addition, interference occurs close to cables carrying alternating current due to the constantly changing flux linkage across a conductor within its field. An electromagnetically induced current flowing at the same frequency as the source would be produced. Furthermore, mains-related interference can be introduced due to earth-loop interference where two earth points have slightly different potentials and a leakage current can flow due to the potential difference between the two. Finally, radio frequency, i.e. greater than 100 kHz, can enter the recording system by a number of routes. This may be through the mains mixed with the frequency of the alternating current, or directly propagated through the air. These interference effects can all be accentuated by high electrode impedance. If the electrode impedance is low then the induced current due to the interference will not cause a significant potential drop at the amplifier input. This will be exhibited as interference at the frequency of the alternating mains current on the input signal.

Good amplifier design aims to reduce interference; all amplifiers used in biological applications are of a differential type with a good Common Mode Rejection Ratio (CMRR). The CMRR is a measure of how well the amplifier rejects any interference or common-mode signal that will appear at both input terminals of a differential amplifier. The amplifier magnifies the difference between the voltages appearing at the two input terminals (a tri-phasic wave derived from the bi-phasic wave associated with each electrode from the bipolar electrode configuration) so that the common-mode signal is rejected (Basmajian and De Luca, 1985). The CMRR is defined as:

$$CMRR = \frac{differential\ voltage\ gain}{common\ mode\ voltage\ gain}$$

When expressed in decibels then:

$$CMRR\ (dB) = 20\log_{10}(CMRR)$$

Another feature of a biological amplifier that ensures faithful reproduction of the signal of interest is the high input impedance of the amplifier. The high input impedance ensures that most of the signal voltage is presented at the input of the amplifier. If the input impedance was similar to that of the skin and tissue impedance then a high proportion of the signal voltage would be lost due to the potential drop across the electrodes. The signal voltage at the input to the amplifier would be much less.

2.6 RECORDING OF DATA

Many systems have been used to record the amplified electromyographic signal. In contemporary practice, analogue-to-digital conversion and computer processing are the most commonly used recording methods. Where excessive connection cabling threatens to intrude on the ecological validity of the recording of electromyographic data during sports manoeuvres, radio telemetry and portable digital data loggers have also been used to transmit and provide intermediate storage for signals, respectively.

The highest frequency expected in the spectrum of the evoked muscle compound action potential is of the order of 500 Hz – 1 kHz when using surface electrodes. This will be higher when using wire electrodes (~1 kHz) and much higher with needle electrodes (10 kHz). In order to prevent erroneous measurement of the sampled signal (aliasing), the rate of digitization must be at least twice that of the highest frequency expected in the sample. This is termed the *Nyquist* frequency. Any frequency above the Nyquist frequency will be recorded as an artefact. This would suggest that an analogue-to-digital sampling rate of at least 2 kHz should be employed so as not to introduce additional error into the recorded signal during surface electromyography, for example. Ideally, the sampling rate should be several times higher than the Nyquist frequency (Basmajian and De Luca, 1985). However, depending on the application and the number of recording channels, the need to use such high sampling rates may exceed the capacity of some systems. An alternative strategy would be to digitally filter the signal with an anti-aliasing hardware filter in order to make sure only frequencies below this optimum frequency pass into the recording system. Wherever possible from a technical and logistical perspective, it may be prudent to attempt to record the electromyographic signal in an unadulterated fashion in the first instance. Recording in this way would involve maintaining the analogue-to-digital sampling rates at a level that ensures a significant margin of 'safety' between the highest frequency expected in the detected signal and the Nyquist frequency, and no additional filtering except for that intrinsically linked with the detection site. This procedure would preserve the integrity of the original recorded signal and make it available for a variety of appropriate subsequent manipulations involving software-derived digital filtering and data smoothing procedures.

The recorded electromyographic data offer potential utility when used in conjunction with other markers of neuromuscular and musculoskeletal performance to investigate the temporal and sequential activation of the musculature associated with exercise. A critical evaluation and comparison of all applications which have used electromyography in this way would be an impracticable task. In the next section selected applications will be described and potential limitations to their successful deployment highlighted.

2.7 SELECTED APPLICATIONS UTILIZING ELECTROMYOGRAPHIC TECHNIQUES

2.7.1 ASSESSMENT OF TEMPORAL MUSCULOSKELETAL AND NEUROMUSCULAR CONTROL

In many sports and daily activities, precise motor acquisition and rapid reaction time are as important as the capacity to produce force. This is perhaps best illustrated when considering the protection from injury offered to a joint system by the musculature associated with its movement. A conceptual model which defines the limits of normal joint movement comprises primary ligamentous restraints interacting with the other static stabilizers (osseous geometry, capsular structures, and menisci) and with the dynamic muscle stabilizers (Fu, 1993). An unfavourable interaction of the dynamic and static stabilizing factors may predispose sports participants to an increased threat of ligamentous disruption (Gleeson *et al.*, 1997a). The time-course of ligamentous rupture can be very rapid (300 ms; Rees, 1994). Optimal functioning of the dynamic muscle stabilizers of the joint system may be fundamental to the prevention or limiting of the severity of ligamentous injury. The neuromuscular system has a limited reaction time response to dynamic forces applied to the joint. Electromechanical delay (EMD) is defined as the time delay between the onset of muscle activity and the onset of force generation (Norman and Komi, 1979). The EMD may be associated with the unrestrained development of forces of sufficient magnitude to damage ligamentous tissue during exercise

(Mercer and Gleeson, 1996). The EMD is determined by the time taken for the contractile component to stretch the series elastic component of the muscle (Winter and Brookes, 1991). Exercise-related increases in connective tissue compliance have been observed and attributed to the visco-elastic behaviour of collagen under repetitive stress loading (Weisman *et al.*, 1980). The visco-elastic behaviour may be indicative of transient impairment to joint musculoskeletal robustness. According to this model, it is possible that fatigue-related slowing of excitation–contraction coupling or altered visco-elastic behaviour of collagen within the series elastic component of muscle and ligamentous structures of the knee may be reflected in an increased EMD. This alteration to temporal neuromuscular control has been observed in maximal voluntary actions of the musculature associated with the knee joint using EMG and static force assessment techniques. Studies involving acute bilateral cycling fatigue tasks (Zhou *et al.*, 1996), single-leg control trials involving prolonged cycling fatigue tasks (Mercer *et al.*, 1998), isokinetic fatigue trials (Gleeson *et al.*, 1997b) and under more ecologically-valid fatigue trials involving the simulation of metabolic and mechanical stresses of team games and high-intensity running (Gleeson *et al.*, 1998), have shown EMD latencies to have been increased by up to 60%. Alternative techniques for the assessment of voluntary EMD under dynamic muscle actions have been suggested (Vos *et al.*, 1991).

2.7.2 ASSESSMENT OF EMD INVOLVING STATIC AND DYNAMIC MUSCLE ACTIVATIONS

While EMD may offer potentially important insights into the neuromuscular and musculoskeletal performance of a joint system, attempts to estimate the precise time at which a muscle begins and ends being activated and at which net torque is provided by the joint system to do useful work are fraught with difficulties. The latter have not yet been completely resolved in the literature and offer a threat to the validity of the measurement. In addition, the protocols deployed to assess EMD are associated with technical and biological variability (noise) which may decrease measurement reproducibility and reliability and compromise ultimately the specificity, sensitivity and utility of the measurement. Nevertheless, the measurement of EMD serves as a useful model from which to appreciate some of the limitations associated with the assessment of neuromuscular performance by way of EMG.

2.7.3 MEASUREMENT TECHNIQUES

The validity of the measurement protocol used to assess EMD and other neuromuscular indices of performance may be inexorably linked to how well it mimics the stresses imposed on the neuromuscular system by the 'real-world' activity. In the case of ligamentous injury to the joint system, this has been observed in a spectrum involving high- and low-velocity episodes of joint movement (Rees, 1994). It may be appropriate therefore to attempt to assess EMD across this joint movement velocity-spectrum of joint movements. Of fundamental importance to the assessment of EMD involving both static and dynamic muscle actions is the determination of whether any segment of

the muscle in the vicinity of the electrode becomes active. This requires that the recorded surface EMG signal should not be substantively contaminated by crosstalk from adjacent muscles and that the amplitude of the EMG signal exceeds the amplitude of the noise in the detection and recording equipment. The issue of crosstalk is particularly important because the amplitude of the signal being analysed is relatively low at the initiation of muscular activity (Figures 2.2 and 2.3) and progressively emerges from the background noise level. Similar problems afflict the detection of significant force (net torque) generation relative to the electrical noise inherent in the transducer. While the placement of the electrode in the mid-line of the belly of the muscle may offer considerable protection against the intrusion of crosstalk in the detection of minimal signal, it may not always be a sufficient precaution (De Luca and Knaflitz, 1990). The assessment of EMD associated with dynamic muscle actions (for example, assessments involving isokinetic dynamometry; Vos *et al.*, 1991) may be more susceptible to issues such as crosstalk since there is a greater potential for repetitive deviations in the positioning of the detecting electrodes relative to the motor units and

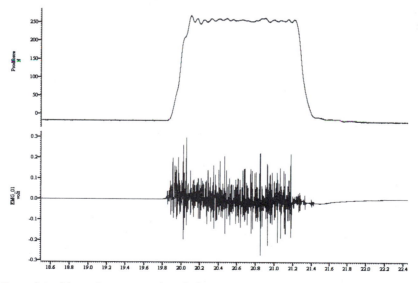

Figure 2.2 A time plot of force (upper trace) and electromyographic signal (lower trace) associated with a single static maximal voluntary muscle action of the m. biceps femoris at 0.44 rad of knee flexion.

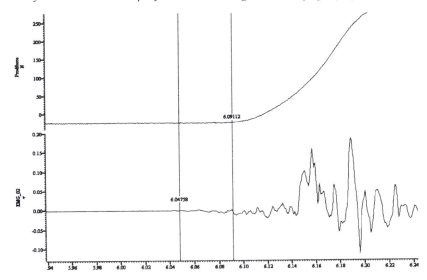

Figure 2.3 A time plot of force (upper trace) and electromyographic signal (lower trace) associated with the initial phase of a single static maximal voluntary muscle action of the m. biceps femoris at 0.44 rad of knee flexion. The time difference between left vertical line (muscle activation) and right vertical line (initiation of force response) may be defined as the electromechanical delay (EMD) (see text).

muscle fibres contributing to the physiological signal at any moment in time.

2.7.4 FACTORS INFLUENCING THE MEASUREMENT OF EMD

The delay between the detected EMG signal and the force would be expected to depend on several physiological and mechanical factors, including the fibre type composition and firing rate dynamics of the muscle and the visco-elastic properties of the muscle and tendon tissues. It may also be influenced by protective neuro-muscular inhibitory mechanisms associated with joint injury, deconditioning and limited motor unit recruitment patterns (Doyle *et al.*, 1999; Rees and Gleeson, 1999). In general, a muscle consisting of a greater percentage of fast-twitch muscle fibres may be expected to have a shorter time delay between the EMG signal and the registration of force. The estimate of EMD may be influenced also by the signal propagation velocity and its effect on differential positioning of the detection surfaces of the electrodes relative to the sites of innervation of the muscle. This may influence

inter-individual comparisons in particular. It may also contribute a limitation to the precision with which estimates of EMD can be made in intra-individual comparisons where the detection surfaces have been relocated and reference cannot be made to anatomical mapping of electrode positioning. A simple approach to the discrimination of the recorded EMG signal and joint net torque from background noise that has been adopted in the author's laboratory is to consider each recorded signal as a stochastic variable in which 95% confidence limits can be constructed around the mean noise amplitude. The time at which the EMG signal exceeds the 95% confidence limits associated with the background noise for a minimal period defined beforehand can be considered to indicate the initiation of activation of the muscle. The minimal amount of time can be based on the likely limits to the precision of EMD measurements considered earlier. In the absence of laboratory instrumentation to identify innervation points within the muscle of interest and thus physiological limits to the precision of the estimate of EMD, this period may need to be set to exceed 7 ms, given likely mean velocities of propagation through the muscle tissue (up to 6 m s^{-1}: Enoka, 1994) and possible distances between electrode positions (40 mm) and innervation points in large lower limb muscles. A similar approach can be deployed to detect significant force generation relative to the background noise of the transducer and associated instrumentation. The point of force generation may be defined as a sustained separation of confidence limits associated with the mean of the recorded force signal over and above those for the background noise. Alternatively, a criterion threshold for force generation may be set relatively to the peak force signal and which exceeds the likely confidence limits for the noise of the transducer system, for example, 1.0% of peak force.

2.7.5 ELECTROMECHANICAL DELAY AND FATIGUING EXERCISE

There are conflicting reports in the literature about the influence of fatiguing exercise on EMD. There is accumulating evidence from the recent literature (Horita and Ishiko, 1987; Mercer and Gleeson, 1996; Zhou *et al.*, 1996; Mercer *et al.*, 1998; Gleeson *et al.*, 1997b; Gleeson *et al.*, 1998) that EMD during maximal voluntary muscle actions in the knee extensors and flexors is influenced by fatiguing exercise. Other reports involving submaximal muscle actions suggest the opposite (Vos *et al.*, 1991).

The potential fatigue-related impairment of EMD may be attributed to a complex interaction of neuromuscular and biomechanical factors. The rate of shortening of the series elastic component of muscle may be the primary cause of EMD in a given muscle (Norman and Komi, 1979) and this compliance predominates over tendon compliance during movement requiring submaximal tension development (Alexander and Bennet-Clark, 1977). However, the limb segment orientation and moment of inertia and unfavourable joint position for net muscle torque development near to full knee extension may present substantive challenges to the whole musculotendinous unit. Thus,

any increases in compliance of the musculotendinous unit associated with the exercise would tend to increase the EMD. Increased muscle temperature may be an important moderator in the latter process. Such changes are associated with an increase in neural propagation velocity and an increase in compliance in the connective tissue (Shellock and Prentice, 1985). Since the time to shorten the series elastic component of muscle exceeds substantially the time leading to the activation of cross-bridges during concentric muscle actions (Norman and Komi, 1979), the influence of increased compliance may prevail and contribute to increase in EMD.

It is assumed that the asymptomatic, well-conditioned and motivated individual undertaking exercise involving maximal voluntary muscle actions is able to recruit heavily from populations of larger high-threshold fast-acting motor units to contribute to the measured neuromuscular performance. Larger high-threshold fast-contracting motor units have been observed to be recruited preferentially over slow-contracting in tasks demanding rapid ballistic muscle actions (Grimby and Hannerz, 1977; Sale, 1992) and it is known that normal recruitment order according to the 'size-principle' may be violated under some conditions (Enoka, 1994). This premise cannot be assured under all circumstances involving volitional efforts. For example, it is unclear how well orderly recruitment is preserved under conditions of fatigue (Enoka, 1994). It is possible that under conditions of fatigue or involving sub-maximal muscle actions, the determination of 'voluntary' EMD reflects variable contributions from slow-acting, fatigue-resistant motor units since these motor units are recruited first according to the 'size-principle' under most circumstances.

Although not yet widely used in contemporary clinical practice, evoked M-wave and fused tetanic responses from the knee extensor and flexor muscle groups by means of magnetic stimulation of the femoral nerve and anterior horn cells associated with the sciatic nerve (L4–L5), respectively, offer interesting insights into the ultimate physiological performance capability of these muscle groups (Figure 2.4). It is interesting to note that under conditions of muscle activation in which the musculature is not protected by central and peripheral nervous system inhibitory responses, EMD latency responses are significantly reduced compared to their volitional counterparts in all asymptomatic and symptomatic populations with musculoskeletal injury. The latter population has shown some of the greatest reductions in latency between volitional and evoked EMD performance (up to 70% relative to volitional performance) (Rees and Gleeson, 1999).

Other techniques for the estimation of temporal neuromuscular control have been proposed which offer utility under both static and dynamic assessment conditions. The estimation of EMD by means of cross-correlation techniques entails constructing a linear envelope without phase shift with respect to the raw, rectified EMG signal data. Subsequently the phase difference between the linear envelope and the force recorded during static or dynamic muscle actions is established by cross-correlation procedures (Vos *et al.*, 1990, 1991). The technique offers an estimate of EMD performance based on a large proportion of the rising phase of the force production and EMG response (for example, between 0% and 75% of peak force, Figure 2.5) and therefore provides a 'holistic' view of the muscle activation characteristics which may be averaged over several cycles of muscle activation and relaxation. The EMD may be defined

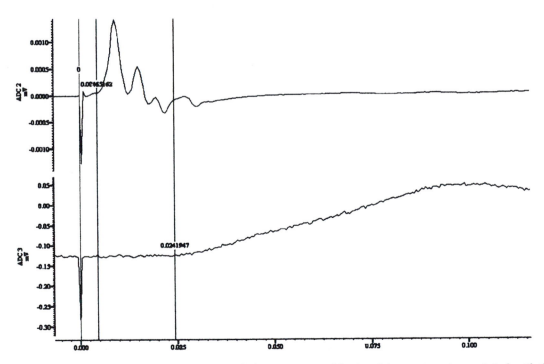

Figure 2.4 A time plot of force (lower trace) and electromyographic signal (upper trace) associated with the initial phase of a single evoked M-wave response from the knee flexor muscle group (m. biceps femoris) at 0.44 rad of knee flexion by means of magnetic stimulation of anterior horn cells associated with the sciatic nerve (L4–L5). The time difference between stimulation (0.0 ms) and middle vertical line (muscle activation) represents latency of neural propagation (4.6 ms). The time difference between muscle activation and the right vertical line (initiation of force response) may be defined as the electromechanical delay (EMD; 19.5 ms) (see text).

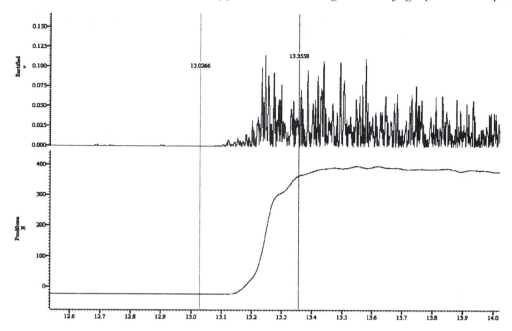

Figure 2.5 A time plot of force (lower trace) and electromyographic signal (rectified, raw, upper trace) associated with the initial phase (0% to 75% of peak force) of a single static maximal voluntary muscle action of the m. biceps femoris at 0.44 rad of knee flexion. The phase difference between muscle activation initiation of force response may be measured using cross-correlation techniques (see text).

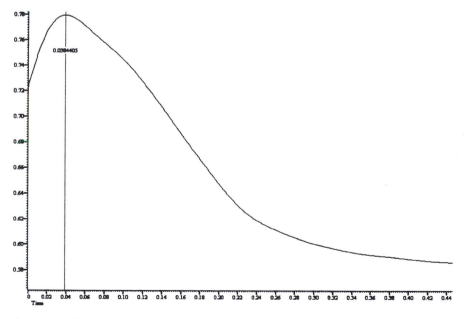

Figure 2.6 Cross-correlation (r, vertical axis) between force and electromyographic signal associated with the initial phase (0% to 75% of peak force) of a single static maximal voluntary muscle action of the m. biceps femoris at 0.44 rad of knee flexion. An index of EMD may be defined as the time (phase difference) at which the highest correlation is observed (vertical line, 38 ms).

as the delay at which the highest correlation is observed (Figure 2.6). It may be considered particularly effective in assessment conditions involving voluntary muscle activations and in which there are difficulties associated with precisely controlling the dynamic movements, for example in assessments involving bidirectional isokinetic dynamometry (Gleeson *et al.*, 1997b).

2.8 MEASUREMENT UTILITY: PRINCIPLES OF MEASUREMENT AND EVALUATION IN INDICES OF NEUROMUSCULAR PERFORMANCE INVOLVING EMG

While the appreciation of the factors which threaten to compromise the fidelity of the recorded EMG signal is fundamental to the integrity of the index of neuromuscular performance, other measurement issues contribute equally to the utility of the index within a specific measurement context. The assessment of indices of neuromuscular performance such as EMD has been deployed in a variety of measurement environments. The application continuum spans single-subject investigations in which the focus may be the rehabilitation or the monitoring of individual athletes, through use within relatively small-sample descriptive and intervention studies, and finally to a potential relevance within epidemiological studies involving relatively large sample populations. Each type of application presents unique demands in respect of an appropriate test protocol to achieve both acceptable utility and rigour during the data acquisition process.

(a) Reproducibility and reliability

Once repeated exposures to the criterion test elicit negligible increases in performance, subjects may be considered to have become habituated to the criterion test and its associated environment. This process may be verified using repeated-measures analysis of variance (ANOVA) techniques for sub-samples of appropriate size (Verducci, 1980; Kirkendall *et al.*, 1987; Thomas and Nelson,

1996). The process of learning will include an accommodation phase in which the specific movements, neuromuscular patterns and demands of the test will become familiar to the subject. Subsequent multiple measurements on the criterion test will be prone to random measurement variability or error, with smaller variations being indicative of greater reliability, consistency or reproducibility of the criterion test (Verducci, 1980; Sale, 1991; Thomas and Nelson, 1996).

(b) Variability in performance

The two principal sources of variability in the index of neuromuscular performance are biological variation, which is the relative consistency with which a subject can perform, and experimental error, which describes variations in the way the test is conducted (Sale, 1991). Examples of these categories of variation include time-of-day effects on indices of neuromuscular performance (Reilly *et al.*, 1993) and technological / instrumentation variation, respectively. Selected contributions to the latter sources of variation have been considered in the previous sections. The goal of the test administrator may be considered to be to dilute the error variance to best reveal the true performance score, consequently permitting the proper interpretation of the effects of physiological intervention or adaptation.

In situations where the assessment of reliability of the criterion test is intended to be reflected mainly in terms of the consistency or reproducibility of observed scores, reliability may be estimated effectively using the coefficient of variation ($V\%$), corrected for small-sample bias (Sokal and Rohlf, 1981). Such a process would allow the quantification of a test-response 'window of stability' for an individual and subsequently the minimum number of intra-subject replicates which are required to attain a criterial measurement error. Group mean estimates of the reproducibility of the index of EMD and related latencies of muscle activation have ranged between 3.2% and 6.9%

for repeated inter-day assessments (Viitasalo *et al.*, 1980; Gleeson *et al.*, 1998).

Reliability models relating to the fluctuations of a participant's repeated test scores within the context of sub-sample performance variability may be estimated using the intra-class correlation coefficient (r_i). This estimate of reliability is based on partitioning models in ANOVA but is susceptible to misinterpretation where significant inter-subject heterogeneity exists. For example, scores of greater than 0.80 have been considered acceptable in clinical contexts (Currier, 1984), whereas this criterion may be entirely inappropriate when attempting to discriminate amongst a group of high-performance athletes demonstrating homogeneous performance characteristics. Bland–Altman plots and the construction of 95% confidence limits associated with repeated measurements of EMD may also be useful in estimating the reproducibility responses in this context (Bland and Altman, 1986; Nevill and Atkinson, Volume 1, Chapter 10).

Sensitivity of a criterion test may be defined as the ability to detect small changes in an individual's performance, or relative positional changes of an individual's performance within a sub-sample. This discrimination ability relates directly to the reliability of the test and may be estimated and further quantified using standard error of measurement (SEM) in conjunction with r_i and the sub-population standard deviation (a measure of homogeneity/heterogeneity) (Gleeson and Mercer, 1992). For given levels of measurement reproducibility, greater heterogeneity amongst measurements would be expected to enhance measurement sensitivity. For example in 'case-study' interventions, assuming an appropriate current trainability phenotype, sensitivity should be enhanced in situations where there is greatest potential for improvement in performance. This would include situations in which the individual has undertaken limited prior strength conditioning or is rehabilitating following injury. The reader is directed to more complete reviews of measurement issues relating to the assessment of neuromuscular performance (Gleeson and Mercer, 1996).

(c) Measurement objectivity and standardization

Objectivity is the degree to which a test measurement is free from the subjective influences and concomitant additional variability due to the differential styles of test administrators (Thomas and Nelson, 1996). Standardization of all aspects of the test administration, including, for example, the test administrator, test instrumentation, calibration of the instrumentation, subject positioning and restraint, lever-arm length, delivery and content of test instructions, will minimize the intrusion of measurement error from extraneous variables and so enhance reliability (Sale, 1991).

(d) Measurement validity

A criterion test which does not yield consistent results is compromised in its validity because the results cannot be depended upon (Thomas and Nelson, 1996). As such, the identification of protocols that will confer appropriate test reproducibility and reliability is a prerequisite for establishing test validity. Validity of a test or measurement instrument refers to the degree of soundness or appropriateness of the test in measuring what it is designed to measure (Vincent, 1995). The validity of the index of EMD may be ascertained by a logical analysis of the measurement procedures, or an estimate of its concurrent validity may be obtained by correlating measurements with those from other established factors contributing to muscle contractile performance, such as predominance of a particular type of myofibrillar protein (Thomas and Nelson, 1996). The relevance and relative importance of the use of EMD within sports medical applications may be estimated by considering its likely predictive validity (Thomas and Nelson, 1996). The predictive validity of EMD as a discriminator of predisposition to musculoskeletal injury may be supported if individuals

who reported knee injury had demonstrated prior insufficiency in EMD capability compared to uninjured counterparts, or compared to their own uninjured limb.

(e) Utility of the protocol

A fundamental attribute of any assessment of EMD must be that it offers at least a minimal level of measurement rigour and integrity commensurate with its intended use, i.e. the utility of the test protocol may be considered to be the net outcome from several competing demands (Gleeson and Mercer, 1996).

Within the context of a given application, the selection of threshold reproducibility and reliability criteria to meet the demand for appropriate measurement rigour will in turn regulate the selection of suitable protocol characteristics (for example, required number of replicates, inter-replicate time duration and mode of action). The logistical constraints, time-related pressures and costs associated with replicate testing of the same individual may be considerable in the context of 'case-study' investigations. Furthermore, the concerns regarding the subject waning in motivation as a result of multiple replicate testing over protracted periods may compromise the validity of a test involving maximal voluntary muscle actions. The proper manipulation of the inter-replicate periods to minimize confounding physiological adaptation effects would tend to lengthen further the test period and exacerbate the problem.

Those factors which contribute to the measurement utility of EMD, and which may be directly manipulated by the test administrator, need to be fully appraised and optimized. This category includes factors such as electrode positioning, number of replicates, inter-replicate interval, presentation of test instructions, and isolation of the involved muscle groups. Other factors, such as the available EMG instrumentation, associated technological error, and biological variation in performance, are relatively immutable. The net overall effect of factors that tend to enhance measurement rigour but detract from ease of administration of testing and participant compliance may be to override any practical utility for the measurement in relation to its intended purpose. These issues remain a substantive challenge for the administrator of the test.

2.9 PRACTICAL 1: ASSESSMENT OF ELECTROMECHANICAL DELAY OF THE KNEE FLEXORS ASSOCIATED WITH STATIC MAXIMAL VOLUNTARY MUSCLE ACTIONS

Prior to conducting this practical, ensure that any conditions imposed by the local ethics committee for experimentation on humans have been met and that any participants are asymptomatic.

2.9.1 PURPOSE

The purpose of this practical is to assess the electromechanical delay (EMD) of the knee flexors associated with static maximal voluntary muscle actions and knee flexion angles at which key ligamentous structures are placed under mechanical strain and non-contact knee joint injuries have occurred (Rees, 1994). This practical requires appropriate surface electrodes, an electromyographic recording system as described previously and a dynamometry system permitting prone gravity-loaded knee flexion movements in the sagittal plane.

2.9.2 PROCEDURES

1. Test apparatus calibration. Prior to and repeatedly during testing, the technical error performance of the measurement instrument should be subject to validity assessments using inert gravitational loading. Experimentally recorded force transducer responses should be compared to those expected during the application of standard known masses through a biologically valid range (e.g. 0–600 N). Recorded forces should demonstrate an overall mean technical error (± standard error of the estimate) which is acceptable in the context of the assessment to be undertaken. For example, low technical error associated with the force transducer (0.2 ± 0.03 N across a total of more than 10 calibrations) facilitates the test administrator's ability to identify the point at which force generation is initiated. Similarly, where the appropriate instrumentation is available to generate known patterns of voltage potential, the calibration of the electromyographic signal voltage recording system can be verified.

2. Record the date, the participant's name, sex, age, relevant anthropometric details and training status.

3. The detected electromyographic signals may be recorded with bipolar surface electrodes (self-adhesive, silver–silver chloride, 10 mm diameter, inter-electrode distance 20 mm centre to centre) applied to the preferred leg following standard skin preparation (inter-electrode impedance < 5 kΩ). In the absence of muscle stimulation apparatus to identify sites of muscle innervation, electrodes should be placed longitudinally distal to the belly of the m. biceps femoris on the line between the ischial tuberosity and the lateral epicondyle of the femur. It may also be helpful if the participant were to perform a submaximal voluntary muscle action in the musculature of interest. This would facilitate the identification of the palpable part of the musculature and, by means of the appropriate surface anatomical landmarks, help to identify the longitudinal axis of the muscle. The reference electrode may be placed over the lateral femoral epicondyle, which is one of several possible anatomical sites that may be used for this purpose. The m. biceps femoris is of interest in this investigation as a contributor to the restraint of anterior tibio–femoral displacement in the knee joint and the restraint of the lateral rotation of the femur relative to the tibia, both of which are implicated in the disruption of the anterior cruciate ligament (Rees, 1994). As was discussed earlier, if further assessment trials are to be conducted on the same participant, it would be prudent to make a map of the thigh of each subject to ensure the same electrode placement in subsequent trials. This could achieved by marking on acetate paper the position of the electrodes, moles and small angiomas.

4. Following habituation to procedures, allow each participant to perform a standardized warm-up (5 minutes cycling at an exercise intensity of 120 W for males and 90 W for females, followed by 5 minutes of stretching of the involved muscles).

5. Position the participant in a prone position on the dynamometer with the knee flexed passively to 0.44 rad (25 deg) (0 deg = full knee extension). While seated positions can be used, a prone position may be preferable since it allows simulation of movements where the hip angle is approximately neutral. The lower leg should be supported at a position 0.1 m proximal to the lateral malleolus by a rigid adjustable system. The latter system should incorporate a load cell (range 2000 N) interfaced to a voltage signal recording system which provides appropriate signal amplification and analogue-to-

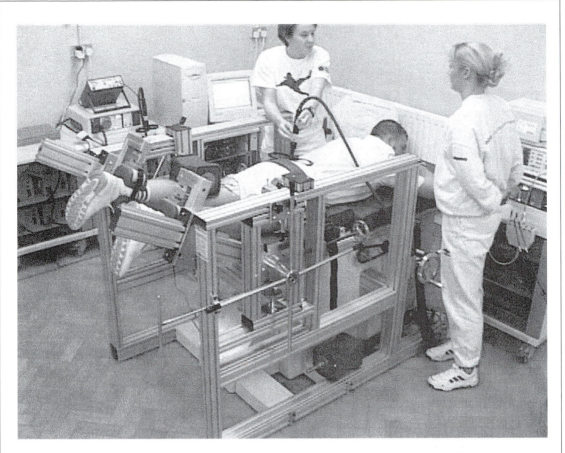

Figure 2.7 An example experimental set-up for the assessment of neuromuscular performance (EMD). The participant may be positioned prone on the dynamometer with the knee flexed passively to 0.44 rad (25°) (0° = full knee extension). The system incorporates a load cell (range 2000 N) interfaced to a voltage signal recording system which provides appropriate signal amplification and analogue-to-digital conversion of muscle force at more than 2 kHz and provides temporal synchronization of the load cell and EMG signal data.

digital conversion of muscle force at 2 kHz (see Figure 2.7). The signal recording system should provide temporal synchronization of the load cell and EMG signal data.

6. Carefully align the approximate joint axis of rotation with the axis of the dynamometer by modifying the participant's position and/or by adjusting the relative position of the dynamometer's seat and plinth. For this assessment involving the knee, align the lateral femoral epicondyle with the dynamometer's axis and ensure that it remains aligned throughout the participant's maximal intensity efforts.

7. Secure all the other body parts not involved in the test with the appropriate straps. Ensure that the thigh, contralateral leg, hips, chest and arms are appropriately stabilized. Record the seat configuration and the joint positions in case subsequent intra-participant comparisons are to be made.

8. Provide written, clear instructions to the participant concerning the purpose of the test and the experimental procedure. Explain in detail the requirement for muscular relaxation prior to the test and for maximum voluntary effort throughout the test, including the need to initiate the maximal force effort absolutely as rapidly as possible after receipt of the stimulus to start the muscle activation. Visual feedback may also be used to enhance muscular output. Allow the subject to ask any questions and be prepared to explain in detail the test requirements. Potential distractions to the participant should be minimized during data capture including the number of investigators present in the laboratory in addition to the participant.

9. Allow the participant to undertake a specific muscle warm-up against the resistance offered by the static immovable structure incorporating the load cell and allow at least five intermittent submaximal repetitions (nominally $3 \times 50\%$, $2 \times 75\%$ and $1 \times 95\%$ of maximal effort). It is worthwhile recording the latter trial as an estimate of the likely signal-to-noise ratios to be expected during the subsequent maximal voluntary assessments. Modifications to skin preparation, electrode to data acquisition system connections and potential intrusions from electromagnetic interference can be made at this juncture as appropriate.

10. Gravity moment correction. Compensation procedures for gravitational errors in recorded forces during maximal voluntary muscle actions in the vertical plane should be undertaken either immediately before or just after testing. Angle-specific torque data generated by the effect of gravity acting on the mass of the involved lower extremity of each participant and the weight of the relevant input accessories at the prescribed knee flexion angles of 0.44 rad (25 deg) should be recorded with the participant resting passively. These scores should then be used to correct all subsequent force measurements as appropriate.

11. Allow the participant to rest (more than 60 s).

12. After a verbal indication, an auditory signal should be given to the participant randomly within a 1–4 s period. On hearing the signal the participant should attempt to flex the knee joint as forcefully and rapidly as possible against the immovable restraint offered by the apparatus. After a suitable period of maximal voluntary muscle activation (~3 s) to elicit peak force (PF), another auditory signal should be given to cue the conscious withdrawal of muscle activation and associated neuromuscular relaxation by the participant as rapidly as possible. This procedure can be completed twice more with an appropriate inter-trial rest period (approximately 60 s or more). The electromyographic and force transducer signals should be saved to hard disk for subsequent software processing.

2.9.3 DATA ANALYSIS AND ADDITIONAL PRACTICAL ACTIVITIES

1. The EMD, in this practical, may be defined as the time interval from the onset of electrical activity of the biceps femoris muscle to the observed development of muscle force (Winter and Brookes, 1991). An example of the assessment output is displayed in Figure 2.2 (a time plot of a single maximal voluntary muscle action of the m. biceps femoris associated with the assessment protocol). Figure 2.3 shows a time plot of a single maximal voluntary muscle action from the onset of the electromyographic signal to the force generation (electromechanical delay, EMD).

2. Record the time at which the onset of electrical activity occurs in the m. biceps femoris and the development of force by means of visual inspection.

3. Using the relevant data capture and analysis software, identify and record the peak force from the data record as the highest force observed during the three muscle activations.

4. Compare the observed EMD for the m. biceps femoris with values from previously published studies examining this index of neuromuscular performance.

5. In order to assess the inter-tester reliability of the visual inspection method for the determination of EMD, perform 'blinded' assessments of a random sample of force–EMG records associated with single maximal voluntary muscle actions on three other test individuals. Undertake appropriate statistical analyses of the data (for example, intra-class correlation). Discuss factors that may contribute to measurement variability and error in the visual inspection method. For example, while the data presented in Figure 2.2 show relatively good signal-to-noise characteristics, how might responses in which greater noise levels have intruded be accurately assessed for the onset of the response of interest?

6. How might an objective determination of the onset of muscle electrical activity and force generation be achieved? Discuss the factors which may contribute to measurement error in the visual inspection method.

7. Repeat the experimental protocols with exercise intensities of nominally 50% and 75% of peak force. What differences, if any, would you expect to observe in EMD derived from maximal and submaximal voluntary muscle actions? Discuss the physiological basis for the recruitment of motor units during the onset of voluntary muscle activations.

8. Repeat the experimental protocols to assess EMD in the knee extensor muscle group (m. vastus lateralis or m. rectus femoris) associated with maximal voluntary muscle actions. Compare the observed EMD scores for the agonist–antagonist muscle groups. Discuss the physiological and mechanical basis on which EMD might contribute to joint stability and protection from injury. Similarly, assess this index of neuromuscular performance in the non-preferred leg and comment on ipsi- and contralateral performance differences. Sample data for contralateral leg comparisons are presented in Table 2.1.

9. Using the acetate sheet anatomical mapping of the electrode positions which was prepared earlier, select alternative electrode positions which should be 20 mm lateral and medial, and 40 mm proximal and distal, to the original detection site, respectively. Repeat the assessment of EMD derived from maximal and submaximal voluntary

muscle and discuss the physiological basis for any systematic changes that might be observed in EMD performance.

10. Repeat all or selected aspects of the above protocols at different times of the day matching those used in contemporary practice (e.g. 07 00 – 09 00 hr, 12 00 – 14 00 hr and 17 00 – 19 00 hr) to assess for variations in performance. Similarly, these protocols may be repeated on different days to assess the contributions of inter-day technical and biological variation to measurement error.

11. Repeat the experimental protocols to assess EMD in the knee flexor muscle group associated with maximal voluntary muscle actions before and after an acute fatiguing task. An example of a fatigue task may involve a 'work–recovery' cycle of 5 s static maximal voluntary exercise at the knee flexion angle used for the assessment followed by 5 s recovery which is repeated throughout a 60 s period. Investigate the effects of the acute fatigue task on the observed EMD scores for the muscle group of interest and the recovery. Data illustrating the effects of an acute fatigue task on the EMD values for the m. biceps femoris at 0.44 rad knee flexion are presented in Table 2.1.

Table 2.1 Example EMD data associated with static maximal voluntary muscle actions of the m. biceps femoris at 0.44 rad knee flexion in male high-performance soccer players ($n = 12$) presenting with unilateral recurrent m. biceps femoris injury (caput longus, greater than three episodes of serious injury (4 weeks absence from training or match-play))

Contralateral leg; pre-fatigue (ms)	Involved leg; post-fatigue (ms)	Contralateral leg; pre-fatigue (ms)	Involved leg; post-fatigue (ms)
45.4	56.1	78.5	88.2
39.2	49.8	67.8	73.2
30.5	37.5	56.8	64.2
37.6	45.2	89.7	102.3
52.5	60.4	63.2	73.3
47.5	52.1	58.2	64.8
34.7	39.9	41.7	48.8
36.7	47.8	51.3	60.0
47.8	55.0	64.5	69.8
45.7	48.9	72.1	73.7
37.9	54.2	56.2	59.3
40.9	46.1	49.6	55.5

Data were collected according to the procedures described in 'Practical activities' for the contralateral and involved legs, prior to and after an acute fatigue task (60 s duration, 5 s static maximal voluntary muscle action, 5 s passive recovery) (Gleeson and Rees, unpublished data).

2.10 PRACTICAL 2: ASSESSMENT OF ELECTROMYOGRAPHIC SIGNAL AMPLITUDE AND FORCE OF THE KNEE FLEXORS ASSOCIATED WITH STATIC VOLUNTARY MUSCLE ACTIONS

2.10.1 PURPOSE

The purpose of this practical is to assess the relationship between electromyographic signal amplitude and force of the knee flexors associated with static voluntary muscle. This practical requires appropriate surface electrodes, an electromyographic recording system as described previously and a dynamometry system permitting prone gravity-loaded knee flexion movements in the sagittal plane.

The previous practical activities show that the electromyographic signal can be detected with mimimal insult to the participant. Electromyography is therefore a favourable alternative for more direct methods of assessing muscular effort in many applications. However, considerable controversy exists in the contemporary literature regarding the description of the electromyographic signal–force relationship. This practical introduces the reader to the description of the electromyographic signal–force relationship in a relatively large muscle group (m. biceps femoris) associated with static muscle actions.

2.10.2 PROCEDURES

1. Test apparatus calibration should be undertaken in accordance with schedules described in the previous experimental procedures.
2. Record the date, the participant's name, sex, age, relevant anthropometric details and training status.
3. The detected electromyographic signals may be recorded with bipolar surface electrodes (self-adhesive, silver–silver chloride, 10 mm diameter, inter-electrode distance 20 mm centre to centre) applied to the preferred leg following standard skin preparation (inter-electrode impedance < 5 kΩ). Electrodes should be placed longitudinally distal to the belly of the m. biceps femoris on the line between the ischial tuberosity and the lateral epicondyle of the femur. The reference electrode may be fixed on the preamplifier and placed over the lateral femoral epicondyle. The m. biceps femoris is of interest in this investigation as a contributor to knee flexion performance.
4. Following habituation to procedures, allow each participant to perform a standardized warm-up (5 minutes cycling at an exercise intensity of 120 W for males and 90 W for females, followed by 5 minutes of stretching of the involved musculature).
5. Position the participant in a prone position on the dynamometer with the knee flexed passively to 0.44 rad (25 deg) (0 deg = full knee extension). While seated positions can be used, a prone position may be preferable since it allows simulation of movements where the hip angle is approximately neutral. The lower leg should be supported at a position 0.1 m proximal to the lateral malleolus by a rigid adjustable system. The latter system should incorporate a load cell (range 2000 N) interfaced to a voltage signal recording system which provides appropriate signal amplification and analogue-to-digital conversion of muscle force at 2 kHz (see Figure 2.7). The signal recording system should provide temporal synchronization of the load cell and electromyographic signal data.

6. Align carefully the approximate joint axis of rotation with the axis of the dynamometer by modifying the participant's position and/or the adjustments of the dynamometer's seat. For this assessment involving the knee, align the lateral femoral epicondyle with the dynamometer's axis and ensure that it remains aligned throughout the participant's efforts.

7. Secure all the other body parts not involved in the test with the appropriate straps. Ensure that the thigh, contralateral leg, hips, chest and arms are appropriately stabilized. Record the seat configuration and the joint positions in case subsequent intra-participant comparisons are to be made.

8. Provide written, clear instructions to the participant concerning the purpose of the test and the experimental procedure. Allow the subject to ask any questions and be prepared to explain in detail the test requirements. Potential distractions to the participant should be minimized during data capture including the number of investigators present in the laboratory in addition to the participant.

9. Allow the participant to undertake a specific muscle warm-up against the resistance offered by the static immovable structure incorporating the load cell and allow at least five intermittent submaximal repetitions (nominally $3 \times 50\%$, $2 \times 75\%$ and $1 \times 95\%$ of maximal effort). It is worthwhile recording the latter trial as an estimate of the likely signal-to-noise ratio to be expected during the subsequent maximal voluntary assessments. Modifications to skin preparation, electrode to data acquisition system connections and potential intrusions from electromagnetic interference can be made at this juncture as appropriate.

10. Gravity moment correction. Compensation procedures for gravitational errors in recorded forces during maximal voluntary muscle actions in the vertical plane should be undertaken just prior to testing. Angle-specific torque data generated by the effect of gravity acting on the mass of the involved lower extremity of each participant and the weight of the relevant input accessories at the prescribed knee flexion angles of 0.44 rad (25 deg) should be recorded with the participant resting passively. These scores should then be used to correct all subsequent force measurements as appropriate.

11. Allow the participant to rest (more than 60 s).

12. After a verbal warning, an auditory signal should be given to the participant. On hearing the signal the participant should attempt to flex the knee joint as forcefully as possible against the immovable restraint offered by the apparatus. After a suitable period of maximal voluntary muscle activation (~3 s) to elicit peak force, another auditory signal should be given to cue the conscious withdrawal of muscle activation and associated neuromuscular relaxation by the participant as rapidly as possible. This procedure can be repeated once more with an appropriate inter-trial rest period (approximately 60 s or more). The electromyographic and force transducer signals should be stored to hard disk for subsequent software processing. The recording of peak force as the average for the two trials serves as a reference from which various submaximal forces for each participant may be calculated (for example 10%, 20%, 30% of peak force).

13. Participants should be requested to produce in random order, muscle actions eliciting 'blinded' target knee flexion forces of 10%, 20%, 30%, 40%, 50%, 60%, 70%, 80% and 90% of peak force under verbal direction from the test administrator. The random ordering of the prescribed forces minimizes the potential for intrusion of fatigue and

other carry-over effects on the recorded scores. On attainment of the prescribed force level, the participant should be asked to maintain this prescribed net force for 3 seconds, before being requested to relax the involved musculature. Following a 120 s recovery period, this procedure should be repeated for the next target force prescribed at random. These procedures may be extended to include several efforts for each of the prescribed forces and several participants. The recorded force and corresponding electromyographic signal may be averaged over the number of repeated samples.

2.10.3 DATA ANALYSIS AND ADDITIONAL PRACTICAL ACTIVITIES

1. For each participant, plot the recorded force (as a percentage of peak force) against the normalized amplitude of the electromyographic signal in the m. biceps femoris (amplitude associated with peak force is recorded as 100%) for all of the prescribed force levels. Parameters that may be used to describe the amplitude of the electromyographic signal include mean rectified amplitude, mean-squared amplitude and versions of integrated amplitude (Basmajian and De Luca, 1985).

2. Describe the relationship between normalized force and electromyographic signal amplitude for these experimental conditions. Where appropriate, use statistical techniques to assist in the quantification of the relationship as linear or non-linear. An example relationship between signal amplitude and force normalized for their respective peak values is shown in Figure 2.8 for the m. biceps femoris.

3. Compare the observed relationship for the m. biceps femoris with those from previously published studies examining this aspect of neuromuscular performance. Further, examine interparticipant variability in the relationship between amplitude of the signal and force associated with static voluntary muscle actions. Example data illustrating the relationship between amplitude of the electromyographic signal and force associated with static voluntary muscle actions of the m. biceps femoris at 0.44 rad knee flexion in three male soccer players is presented in Table 2.2.

4. Where the appropriate experimental apparatus is available, repeat the whole assessment protocol on different muscle groups including, for example, smaller muscle

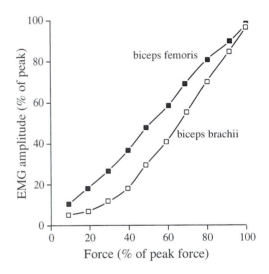

Figure 2.8 Amplitude of electromyographic signal–force relationship for m. biceps femoris and m. biceps brachii associated with static muscle actions. The electromyographic and force responses have been normalized to their respective peak values. Data points represent the mean response of six trials at each prescribed force (various percentages of peak force; see text) for a single participant. Standard error bars associated with electromyographic amplitude are omitted for visual clarity.

groups of the arm or hand. An example relationship between signal amplitude and force normalized for their respective peak values is shown in Figure 2.8 for the m. biceps brachii.

5. Discuss the factors which may moderate the relationship between the amplitude of the electromyographic signal and the force output associated with static muscle actions.

Table 2.2   Example data illustrating the relationship between amplitude of the EMG signal and force associated with static voluntary muscle actions of the m. biceps femoris at 0.44 rad knee flexion in three male soccer players

	Normalized EMG amplitude (%)		
Normalized force (%)	Participant 1	Participant 2	Participant 3
10	10.7 ± 2.2	9.2 ± 2.4	12.1 ± 3.8
20	17.9 ± 3.6	14.3 ± 3.7	16.1 ± 4.1
30	27.4 ± 5.1	24.4 ± 6.1	28.8 ± 5.5
40	38.1 ± 7.2	34.3 ± 8.6	40.1 ± 9.2
50	48.2 ± 7.3	44.2 ± 9.4	49.2 ± 7.9
60	57.9 ± 11.2	55.9 ± 12.7	58.9 ± 15.1
70	69.6 ± 12.8	66.1 ± 14.2	70.1 ± 12.3
80	81.7 ± 17.4	78.7 ± 18.3	82.4 ± 13.7
90	90.4 ± 19.1	91.3 ± 23.2	91.6 ± 19.3
100	98.9 ± 18.3	100.7 ± 24.1	99.4 ± 17.6

Data collected are from the preferred leg according to the procedures described in 'Practical activities'. The EMG and force scores have been normalised to their respective peak values.

REFERENCES

Aidley, D.J. (1998). *The Physiology of Excitable Cells*, 4th edn. (Cambridge University Press, Cambridge).

Alexander, R. McN. and Bennet-Clark, H.C. (1977). Storage of elastic strain energy in muscle and other tissues. *Nature*, **265**, 114–7.

Almasi, J.J. and Schmitt, C.H. (1974). Automated measurement of bioelectric impedance at very low frequencies. *Computing in Biomedical Research*, **7**, 449–56.

Basmajian, J.V. and De Luca, C.J. (1985). *Muscles Alive: Their Functions Revealed by Electromyography*, (Williams & Wilkins, Baltimore, MD).

Bland, J.M. and Altman, D.G. (1986). Statistical methods for assessing agreement between two methods of clinical measurement. *The Lancet*, **i**, 307–10.

Burbank, D.P. and Webster, J.G. (1978). Reducing skin potential motion artefact by skin abrasion. *Medical and Biological Engineering and Computing*, **16**, 31–8.

Clarys, J.P. and Cabri, J. (1993). Electromyography and the study of sports movements: a review. *Journal of Sports Sciences*, **11**, 379–448.

Currier, D.P. (1984). *Elements of Research in Physical Therapy*, 2nd edn. (Williams and Wilkins, Baltimore, MD).

De Luca, C.J. and Knaflitz, M. (1990). *Surface Electromyography: What's New?* Neuromuscular Research Centre, Boston, MA.

De Talhouet, H. and Webster, J.G. (1996). The origin of skin-stretch caused motion artefacts under electrodes. *Physiological Measurement*, **17**, 81–93.

Doyle, J., Gleeson, N.P. and Rees, D. (1999). Psychobiology and the anterior cruciate ligament (ACL) injured athlete. *Sports Medicine*, **26**, 379–93.

Engbaek, J. and Mortensen, C.R. (1994). Monitoring of Neuromuscular Transmission. *Annals Academy of Medicine*, **23**, 558–65.

Enoka, R.M. (1994). *Neuromechanical Basis of Kinesiology*. (Human Kinetics, Champaign, IL).

Fu, F.H. (1993). Biomechanics of knee ligaments. *Journal of Bone and Joint Surgery*, **75A**, 1716–27.

Geddes, L.A. and Baker, L.E. (1989). *Principles of Applied Biomedical Instrumentation*. (John Wiley & Sons, New York).

Gleeson, N.P. and Mercer, T.H. (1992). Reproducibility of isokinetic leg strength and endurance characteristics of adult men and women. *European Journal of Applied Physiology and Occupational Physiology*, **65**, 221–8.

Gleeson, N.P. and Mercer, T.H. (1996). The utility of isokinetic dynamometry in the assessment of human muscle function. *Sports Medicine*, **21**, 18–34.

Gleeson, N.P., Mercer, T. and Campbell, I. (1997a). Effect of a fatigue task on absolute and relativised indices of isokinetic leg strength in female collegiate soccer players. In *Science and Football III*. eds. T. Reilly, *et al.* (E & F.N. Spon, London), pp. 162–7.

Gleeson, N.P., Mercer, T.H., Morris, K. and Rees, D. (1997b). Influence of a fatigue task on electromechanical delay in the knee flexors of soccer players. *Medicine and Science in Sports Exercise*, **29(5)**, S281.

Gleeson, N.P., Mercer, T.H., Reilly, T., *et al.* (1998). The influence of acute endurance activity on leg neuromuscular and musculoskeletal performance. *Medicine and Science in Sports and Exercise*, **30**, 596–608.

Grieve, D.W. (1975). Electromyography. In *Techniques for the Analysis of Human Movement*. eds. D.W. Grieve, D.L Miller, D. Mitchelson, *et al.* (Lepus Books, London).

Grimby, L. and Hannerz, J. (1977). Firing rate and recruitment order of toe extensor motor units in different modes of voluntary contraction. *Journal of Physiology*, **264**, 865–79.

Horita, T. and Ishiko, T. (1987). Relationships between muscle lactate accumulation and surface EMG activities during isokinetic contractions in man. *European Journal of Applied Physiology*, **56**, 18–23.

Kirkendall, D.R., Gruber, J.J., and Johnson, R.E. (1987*). Measurement and evaluation for physical educators*, 2nd edn. (Human Kinetics, Champaign, IL).

Lewes, D. (1965). Electrode jelly in electrocardiography. *British Heart Journal*, **27**, 105–15.

Medina, V., Clochesy, J. M. and Omery, A. (1989). Comparison of electrode site preparation techniques. *Electromyography and Clinical Neurophysiology*, **18**, 456–60.

Mercer, T.H. and Gleeson, N.P. (1996). Prolonged intermittent high intensity exercise impairs neuromuscular performance of the knee flexors. *Physiologist*, **39**, A–62.

Mercer, T.H., Gleeson, N.P., Claridge, S. and Clement, S. (1998). Prolonged intermittent high intensity exercise impairs neuromuscular performance of the knee flexors. *European Journal of Applied Physiology and Occupational Physiology*, **77**, 560–2.

Nigg, B.M. and Herzog, W. (1994). *Biomechanics of the Musculoskeletal System*. (John Wiley, Chichester).

Norman, R.W. and Komi, P.V. (1979). Electromechanical delay in skeletal muscle under normal movement conditions. *Acta Physiologica Scandinavica*, **106**, 241–8.

Okamoto, T., Tsutsumi, H., Goto, Y. and Andrew, P. (1987). A simple procedure to attenuate artifacts in surface electrode recordings by painlessly lowering skin impedance. *Electromyography and Clinical Neurophysiology*, **27**, 173–6.

Patterson, R.P. (1978). The electrical characteristics of some commercial electrodes. *Journal Cardiology*, **11**, 23–6.

Rees, D. (1994). Failed ACL reconstructions. *Proceedings of the Football Association – Royal College of Surgeons, Edinburgh 6th Joint Conference on Sport Injury*, Lilleshall Hall National Sports Centre, 2nd–3rd July.

Rees, D. and Gleeson, N.P. (1999). The scientific assessment of the injured athlete. *Proceedings of the Football Association – Royal College of Surgeons Medical Conference*, Lilleshall Hall National Sports Centre, October.

Reilly, T., Atkinson, G. and Collwells, A. (1993). The relevance to exercise performance of the circadian rhythms in body temperature and arousal. *Biology of Sport*, **10**, 203–16.

Sale, D.G. (1991). Testing strength and power. In *Physiological Testing of the High Performance Athlete*, 2nd edn. eds. J.D. MacDougall, H.A. Wenger and H.J. Green (Human Kinetics, Champaign, IL), pp. 21–106.

Sale, D.G. (1992). Neural adaptations to strength training. In *Strength and power in sport*. eds. P.V. Komi (Blackwell Scientific Publications, Oxford), pp. 249–65.

Shellock, F.G. and Prentice, W.E. (1985). Warming-up and stretching for improved physical performance and prevention of sports-related injuries. *Sports Medicine*, **2**, 267–78.

Sokal, R.and Rohlf, F. (1981). *Biometry*, 2nd edn. (W.H. Freeman, Oxford).

Tam, H.W. and Webster, J.G. (1977). Minimising electrode motion artifact by skin abrasion. *IEEE Transactions of Biomedical Engineering*, **BME–24**, 134–9.

Thomas, J.R. and Nelson, J.K. (1996). *Research Methods in Physical Activity*, 3rd edn. (Human Kinetics, Champaign, IL).

Verducci, F.M. (1980). *Measurement Concepts in Physical Education*. (C.V. Mosby, St. Louis, MO).

Viitasalo, J.T., Saukkonen, S. and Komi, P. (1980). Reproducibility of selected neuromuscular performance variables in man. *Electromyography and Clinical Neurophysiology*, **20**, 487–501.

Vincent, W.J. (1995). *Statistics in Kinesiology*. (Human Kinetics, Champaign, IL).

Vos, E.J., Mullender, M.G. and Van Ingen Schenau, G.J. (1990). Electromechanical delay in vastus lateralis muscle during dynamic isometric contractions. *European Journal of Applied Physiology*, **60**, 467–71.

Vos, E.J., Harlaar, J. and Van Ingen Schenau, G.J. (1991). Electromechanical delay during knee extensor contractions. *Medicine and Science in Sports and Exercise*, **23**, 1187–93.

Weisman, G., Pope, M.H. and R.J. Johnson. (1980). Cyclic loading in knee ligament injuries. *American Journal of Sports Medicine*, **8**, 24–30.

Winter, E.M. and Brookes, F.B.C. (1991). Electromechanical response times and muscle elasticity in men and women. *European Journal of Applied Physiology*, **63**, 124–8.

Zhou, S., McKenna, M.J., Lawson, D.L., *et al.* (1996). Effects of fatigue and sprint training on electromechanical delay of knee extensor muscles. *European Journal of Applied Physiology*, **72**, 410–6.

OXYGEN TRANSPORT SYSTEM AND EXERCISE

LUNG FUNCTION

Roger G. Eston

3.1 AIMS

The aims of this chapter are to:
- provide students with an understanding of the assessment of lung function at rest and during different modes of exercise,
- describe the relevance of anthropometric, postural and environmental factors on lung function,
- outline practical exercises and data to exemplify techniques of assessing lung function using open and closed circuit spirometry procedures.

3.2 INTRODUCTION

3.2.1 PULMONARY VENTILATION AT REST AND DURING EXERCISE

Pulmonary ventilation refers to the mass movement of gas in and out of the lungs. It is regulated to provide the gaseous exchange necessary for aerobic energy metabolism. Inhaled volumes and exhaled volumes are usually not equal, since the volume of inspired oxygen is usually greater than the volume of expired carbon dioxide. Inspiratory volumes are therefore usually larger than expiratory volumes. **Pulmonary ventilation** is commonly assessed by measuring the volume of air that is exhaled per minute and is abbreviated $\dot{V}E$. It is dependent on the rate (frequency) and depth (tidal volume) of ventilation per breath. Under normal resting conditions, pulmonary ventilation varies between 4 and 12 litres per minute.

Naturally, this figure varies with body size and is smaller in women than in men. At rest, typical values for tidal volume and frequency are 400–600 ml and 10–20 breaths per minute, respectively.

3.2.2 FACTORS AFFECTING PULMONARY VENTILATION

Pulmonary ventilation varies with exercise intensity not only within the same individual, but also between individuals. Factors causing this variation mainly relate to body size, age and sex. Peak values for pulmonary ventilation are reached at about 15 years of age for females and 25 years of age for males. It then decreases with age when it declines to less than half the peak value (Figure 3.1). Increases in ventilation from young age to adulthood are caused primarily by physical maturation. As children grow in weight and particularly in stature, total lung capacity and pulmonary ventilation increase accordingly. However, adults over 25 years of age who have reached full physical growth experience reduced ventilation, even though body size remains the same or increases. The decline after young adulthood is due to a decrease in the inspiratory volumes and expiratory volumes as a consequence of physical inactivity and to a reduction of the elastic components in the wall of the thoracic cage. The greater pulmonary ventilation in males compared to females after the age of about 14 years is primarily the result

Kinanthropometry and Exercise Physiology Laboratory Manual: Tests, Procedures and Data. 2nd Edition, Volume 2: Exercise Physiology Edited by RG Eston and T Reilly. Published by Routledge, London, June 2001

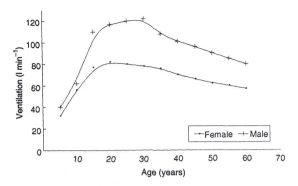

Figure 3.1 Relationship between pulmonary ventilation and age among males and females. (Data from Åstrand, 1952.)

of body size. When the male hormone testosterone is secreted in larger quantities, the skeletal and muscle mass of males increase rapidly. As the rib cage enlarges, the thoracic cavity can accommodate larger quantities of air, which increases pulmonary ventilation.

3.2.3 ALVEOLAR VENTILATION AND DEAD SPACE

Only part of the inspired tidal volume (V_T) of air reaches the alveoli where gaseous exchange takes place. This process is known as **alveolar ventilation** (V_A). The air that remains in the respiratory passages that do not participate in gaseous exchange is referred to as the **dead space volume** (V_D). The average resting value of the dead space volume is about 150 and 100 ml in men and women, respectively, although this depends on body size. The total expired gas is therefore a mixture of dead space and alveolar gas, or

$$V_T = V_A + V_D$$

If, at a ventilation of 6.0 l min^{-1}, the respiratory frequency is 10, and the dead space is 0.15 l, the alveolar ventilation is

$$60 - (10 \times 0.15) = 4.5 \; l \; min^{-1}$$

If the respiratory rate is 20, and the gross ventilation dead space is unchanged, the alveolar ventilation becomes

$$6.0 - (20 \times 0.15) = 3.0 \; l \; min^{-1}$$

During exercise, dilation of the respiratory passages may cause anatomical dead space to double, but since the tidal volume also increases, an adequate alveolar ventilation, and therefore gas exchange, is maintained. When submerged in water, breathing through a snorkel presents a considerable challenge to gaseous exchange. The snorkel represents an extension of the respiratory dead space, and the tidal volume has to be increased by an amount equal to the volume of the tube if alveolar ventilation is to be maintained unchanged. Although it is not possible to measure the dead space exactly, it is possible to estimate the dead space volume with the aid of Bohr's formula, which is explained in Practical 1 of this chapter.

3.3 EVALUATION OF PULMONARY VENTILATION DURING EXERCISE

In light to moderate exercise, ventilation increases linearly with oxygen consumption $\dot{V}O_2$, with a relatively greater increase at the heavier exercise intensities (Figure 3.2). It is notable from this relationship that pulmonary ventilation does not limit the maximal oxygen uptake. Maximal ventilation can reach values as high as 180 l min^{-1} and 130 l min^{-1} for male and female athletes, respectively. When pulmonary ventilation is expressed in relation to the magnitude of oxygen uptake, it is termed the **ventilatory equivalent** ($\frac{\dot{V}E}{\dot{V}O_2}$). It is maintained at about 20–25 litres of air breathed per litre of oxygen consumed. In non-steady-rate exercise, ventilation increases disproportionately with increases in oxygen consumption, and $\frac{\dot{V}E}{\dot{V}O_2}$ may reach 35–40. In children under 10 years of age, the values are about 30 during light exercise and up to 40 during maximal exercise (Åstrand and Rodahl, 1986). When the partial pressure of ambient oxygen is reduced,

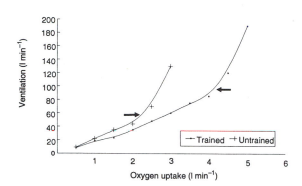
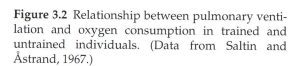
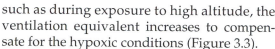

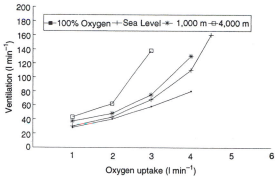

Figure 3.2 Relationship between pulmonary ventilation and oxygen consumption in trained and untrained individuals. (Data from Saltin and Åstrand, 1967.)

Figure 3.3 Pulmonary ventilation (BTPS) in relation to oxygen uptake at different altitudes. (Modified from Åstrand, 1954.)

such as during exposure to high altitude, the ventilation equivalent increases to compensate for the hypoxic conditions (Figure 3.3).

During exercise of low intensity, it is primarily the tidal volume rather than the breathing frequency that is increased. In many types of exercise, tidal volume may amount to approximately 50% of the vital capacity when the rate of exercise is moderately heavy or heavy. Children about 5 years of age may have a respiratory frequency of about 70 breaths min⁻¹ at maximal exercise, 12-year-old children about 55 breaths min⁻¹, and 25-year-old individuals 40–45 breaths min⁻¹. In well-trained athletes with high aerobic power, respiratory frequencies of about 60 breaths min⁻¹ are usual (Åstrand and Rodahl, 1986).

3.3.1 THE VENTILATORY THRESHOLD

As exercise intensity increases, the $\dot{V}O_2$ increases linearly, but the blood lactate level changes only slightly until about 60–80% of $\dot{V}O_2$ max is reached, depending on training status. After this, the blood lactate increases more rapidly (see Figure 10.2 in Chapter 10 by Jones and Doust). Because blood acidity is one of the factors that increases $\dot{V}E$, the abrupt increase in $\dot{V}E$ during exercise is often used to indicate the inflection point in the blood lactate

curve. This has been termed the **anaerobic threshold** and procedures for its derivation are explained in detail by Wasserman *et al.* (1987) and Jones and Doust (see Chapter 10). The concept is considered to be a misnomer by some experts as the physiological reasons for the rapid increase in $\dot{V}E$ beyond the inflection point are not necessarily due to metabolic acidosis. Consequently, the disproportionate rise in $\dot{V}O_2$ is preferably referred to as the **ventilatory threshold** (T_{vent}). The T_{vent} for the trained and untrained person is indicated in Figure 3.2 by the solid arrows.

One of the most pertinent refutations of the **anaerobic threshold** was the study by Hagberg *et al.* (1982) on patients with McArdle's syndrome. Victims of this disease lack the enzyme phosphorylase, which renders them incapable of catabolizing glycogen and forming lactate. Hagberg *et al.* (1982) showed that these patients possess ventilatory thresholds despite the fact that there is no change in blood lactate concentrations (Figures 3.4 and 3.5).

3.3.2 PULMONARY VENTILATION AND TRAINING

Endurance training reduces total ventilation volumes at given exercise intensities in

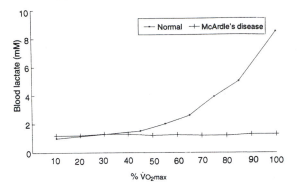

Figure 3.4 Blood lactate response in normal controls and in victims of McArdle's disease during continuous, progressive exercise on a cycle ergometer.

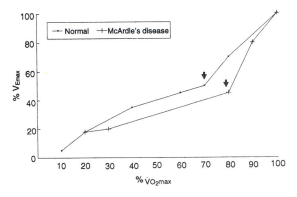

Figure 3.5 Both groups display a ventilatory threshold (arrow), despite the fact that there is no corresponding lactate threshold in the McArdle's patients. (Modified from Hagberg *et al.*, 1982.)

adolescents and adults (Jirka and Adamus, 1965; Tzankoff *et al.*, 1972; Fringer and Stull, 1974; Rasmussen *et al.*, 1975). In general, the tidal volume becomes larger and the breathing frequency is reduced with endurance training. Consequently, air remains in the lungs for a longer period of time between breaths. This results in an increase in the amount of oxygen extracted from the inspired air. The exhaled air of trained individuals often contains only 14–15% oxygen during submaximal exercise, whereas the expired air of untrained persons may contain 18% oxygen at the same workload

(McArdle *et al.*, 1996). The untrained person must therefore ventilate proportionately more air to achieve the same oxygen uptake (Figure 3.2). This is important for performing prolonged vigorous exercise because the lower breathing rate reduces the fatiguing effects of exercise on the ventilatory musculature and allows the extra oxygen available to be used by the exercising muscles.

Aerobic training also brings about changes in pulmonary ventilation during maximal exercise. Maximal ventilatory capacity increases with improvements in maximal oxygen uptake. This is an expected response, since an increase in maximal oxygen uptake results in a larger oxygen requirement and a correspondingly larger production of carbon dioxide that must be eliminated through increased alveolar ventilation (McArdle *et al.*, 1996).

3.3.3 ACUTE AND CHRONIC VENTILATORY ADAPTATIONS TO ARM AND LEG EXERCISE

Ventilatory adaptations appear to be specific to the type of exercise performed. The ventilatory equivalent is greater during arm exercise than during leg work (Rasmussen *et al.*, 1975; Eston and Brodie, 1986). As arm exercise elicits higher lactate levels for any given work-rate (Stenberg *et al.*, 1967), it is likely that this factor, in conjunction with the higher sympathetic outflow for arm work (Davies *et al.*, 1974) is the most likely reason for the higher ventilation during arm exercise. Bevegard *et al.* (1966) have suggested that the higher ventilation rate during arm exercise could be an important factor in maintaining ventricular filling pressures and stroke volume in the absence of the mechanical effect of the leg muscle pump. Additional factors which influence pulmonary ventilation during arm exercise may include (a) a mechanical limitation of tidal volume by static contractions of the pectoralis and abdominal musculature and (b) a metering or synchronization of respiratory rate caused by the rhythmic movement of the arms (Mangum, 1984).

The reduction in ventilatory equivalent that occurs through training is also dependent on the specificity of training. Rasmussen *et al.* (1975) observed that reductions in ventilatory equivalent occurred only when the mode of exercise training matched the activity. In a comparison of groups trained either by arm ergometry or leg ergometry, the ventilatory equivalent was reduced only in arm exercise for the arm-trained group (from 30 to 25) and only in leg exercise for the leg-trained group (from 26 to 23). Arm training did not reduce the ventilatory equivalent during leg exercise and vice versa.

3.4 POST-EXERCISE CHANGES IN LUNG FUNCTION

Changes in lung volumes and function occur *after* acute exercise. After all-out exercise, some people, particularly rowers (Rasmussen *et al.*, 1988) experience coughing with expectoration and dyspnoea. The cough may persist for several days. A decrease in the forced vital capacity (FVC) immediately following exercise (Miles *et al.*, 1991), reductions in peak expiratory flow rate (Rasmussen *et al.*, 1988) and increases in residual volume have been reported (Buono *et al.*, 1981). Shifts in central blood volume, changes in lung mechanics, respiratory muscle fatigue and the development of subclinical extravascular pulmonary fluid retention have all been suggested as contributing factors for the observed transitory changes in lung volume following exercise.

3.5 ASSESSMENT OF RESTING LUNG FUNCTION

Lung function tests are widely employed to assess respiratory status. In addition to their use in clinical case management, they are routinely used in health examinations in respiratory, occupational and sports medicine, and for public health screening. Assessment of lung function, particularly in the clinical and occupational health settings, is mostly concerned with the testing of lung volumes and capacities observed in the resting state. It is

common practice for the results of lung function tests to be interpreted in relation to reference values, and in terms of whether or not they are considered to be within the 'normal' range of values. Many published reference values and prediction equations are available for this purpose. The American Thoracic Society (1991) has summarized the most common equations for use with black and white adults. Some of these equations are shown in Tables 3.1–3.3. Equations for children and adolescents have also been provided by Cotes (1979) and Polgar and Promadhat (1971) (Table 3.4).

It is appropriate here to describe and distinguish the various volumes, capacities and peak flow rate classifications which are frequently measured. The lung volumes can be classified as either *static* – referring to the quantity of air with no relation to time – or *dynamic*, which are measured in relation to time.

3.5.1 STATIC LUNG VOLUMES

Lung volumes are measured by a spirometer (Figure 3.6). The bell of the spirometer falls and rises as air is inhaled and exhaled from it. As the bell moves up and down the movement is recorded on a rotating drum (kymograph) by a stylus or pen. This provides a record of the ventilatory volume and breathing frequency (spirogram), as depicted in Figure 3.7. The capacity of the spirometer is usually 9 litres or 13 litres. If it is to form part of a closed-circuit system to measure oxygen uptake, as in Practical 4, it should include a soda-lime canister on the inlet to absorb carbon dioxide.

The volume of air moved during a normal breath is the **tidal volume** (V_T). At rest V_T usually ranges between 0.4 and 0.6 litre per breath. During exercise it increases linearly with the ventilatory requirement of the subject up to a limiting value, which is about 50% of the vital capacity (Cotes, 1979). The reserve ability for inhalation beyond the tidal volume is termed the **inspiratory reserve volume** (IRV). This is the amount of air that can be inspired

Table 3.1 Predicted values for FEV_1 and FVC from selected regression equations for non-smoking Caucasian men and women (modified from American Thoracic Society (1991))

Source	Age	Number studied	FEV$_{1.0}$ for ht and age[a]	Regression coefficient Ht	Regression coefficient Age	SEE	FVC for ht and age[a]	Regression coefficient Ht	Regression coefficient Age	SEE
Men										
Morris et al. (1971)	20–84	517	3.63	3.62	−0.032	0.55	4.84	5.83	−0.025	0.74
Knudson et al. (1983)	25–84	86	3.81	6.65	−0.029	0.52	4.64	8.44	−0.030	0.64
Crapo et al. (1981)	15–91	125	3.96	4.14	−0.024	0.49	4.89	6.00	−0.021	0.64
Women										
Morris et al. (1971)	20–84	471	2.72	3.50	−0.025	0.47	3.54	4.53	−0.024	0.52
Knudson et al. (1983)	20–87	204	2.79	3.09	−0.020	0.39	3.36	4.27	−0.017	0.49
Crapo et al. (1981)	15–84	126	2.92	3.42	−0.026	0.33	3.54	4.91	−0.022	0.39

Format of equation

Men

Predicted $FEV_{1.0}$ or FVC = Predicted value[a] for: ht 1.75 m, Age 45 + {ht Coefficient × (ht − 1.75)} + {Age Coefficient × (Age − 45)}

Women

Predicted $FEV_{1.0}$ or FVC = Predicted value[a] for: ht 1.65 m, Age 45 + {ht Coefficient × (ht − 1.65)} + {Age Coefficient × (Age − 45)}

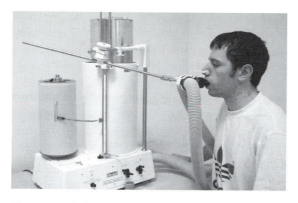

Figure 3.6 Subject breathing from a *Harvard* 9 Litre Spirometer (Harvard Apparatus Ltd, Kent, UK).

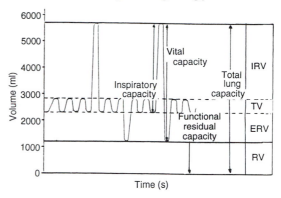

Figure 3.7 Spirogram showing the various lung volumes and capacities. IRV, inspiratory reserve volume; ERV, expiratory reserve volume; RV, residual volume; TV, tidal volume.

maximally at the end of a normal inspiration. At rest it is normally about 2.5–3.5 litres. The volume of air that can be expired maximally after normal expiration is the **expiratory reserve volume** (ERV), which ranges from 1.0 to 1.5 litres for the average-sized man. The IRV and ERV show large variations with posture on account of changes in the **functional residual capacity** (FRC). This function is defined as the volume of air in the chest at the end of a normal expiration when the elastic recoil of the lung and the thoracic cage are equal and opposite. In normal subjects the FRC is affected by posture, which affects the position of the chest wall and reduces FRC by about 25% in the supine position compared to the upright position. In the upright position, in healthy adults, FRC is in the range 0.8–5.5 and 0.7–4.9 litres for men and women, respectively. The FRC is increased in the presence of emphysema (a condition which causes an increase in the size of air spaces distal to the terminal bronchioles) when this is accompanied by a reduction in the elastic recoil of the chest wall. It is reduced when V_T is increased, such as during exercise, or by breathing a gas mixture of carbon dioxide in air. The **total lung capacity** (TLC) is defined as the volume of gas in the thorax at the end of a full inspiration. In healthy adults, depending on size, the TLC is in the range 3.6–9.4 and 3.0–7.3 litres for males and females, respectively. The TLC is reduced if there is a

decrease in the strength of the respiratory muscles, as in diseases such as interstitial fibrosis or muscular dystrophy. It is enlarged when the compliance of the lung is increased by emphysema or as a result of physical training. Hanson (1973) observed TLC values ranging from 7.0 to 9.8 litres in seven international cross-country skiers. During exercise, the IRV, particularly, and the ERV are reduced, which is a natural consequence of an increase in V_T.

The total volume of air that can be moved voluntarily from the lung from full inspiration to full expiration is the **vital capacity** (VC). It is the sum of V_T, IRV and ERV. In healthy adults, depending on age and size, VC is in the range 2.0–6.6 litres and 1.4–5.6 litres for males and females, respectively. It is reduced in emphysema and in other conditions which cause an increase in residual volume. Vital capacities of 6–7 litres are not uncommon for tall individuals and athletes. Ekblom and Hermansen (1968) observed a value of 7.7 litres in a champion male athlete. Although the size of the lung is influenced by the same anthropometric factors that may also predispose an individual to athletic success, VC can be increased by training, but this is only in certain circumstances and with special types of training. Cotes (1979) reported that training of the muscles of the shoulder girdle probably leads to an

Table 3.2 Predicted values for FEV$_{1.0}$ and FVC from selected regression equations for black men and women (modified from American Thoracic Society, 1991)

Source	Age	Number studied	FEV$_{1.0}$ FEV$_{1.0}$ for ht and age[a]	Regression coefficient Ht	Age	SEE	FVC FVC for ht and age[a]	Regression coefficient Ht	Age	SEE
Men										
Lapp et al. (1974)	34.9 ± 11.9	79	3.53	3.54	−0.025	0.23	4.11	3.94	0.021	0.32
Cookson et al. (1976)	43.6 ± 15.1	141	3.12	2.20	−0.024	0.50	3.74	3.90	0.017	0.65
Women										
Johannsen and Erasmus (1968)	20–50	100	2.25	2.18	−0.013	0.34	2.74	2.51	0.015	0.35
Cookson et al. (1976)	36.7 ± 11.6	102	2.35	2.35	−0.028	0.41	2.86	3.00	0.019	0.42

Format of equation
Men
Predicted FEV$_{1.0}$ or FVC = Predicted value[a] for: ht 1.75 m, Age 45 + {ht Coefficient × (ht − 1.75)} + {Age Coefficient × (Age − 45)}
Women
Predicted FEV$_{1.0}$ or FVC = Predicted value[a] for: ht 1.65 m, Age 45 + {ht Coefficient × (ht − 1.65)} + {Age Coefficient × (Age − 45)}

Table 3.3 Predicted values for total lung capacity (TLC) and residual volume (RV) from selected regression equations for men and women (modified from American Thoracic Society, 1991)

Source	Age	Number studied	TLC for ht and age[a]	Regression coefficient Ht	Regression coefficient Age	SEE	RV for ht and age[a]	Regression coefficient Ht	Regression coefficient Age	SEE
Men										
Boren et al. (1966)	20–62	422	6.35	7.80	—	0.87	1.62	1.90	0.012	0.53
Crapo et al. (1982)	15–91	123	6.72	7.95	0.003	0.79	1.87	2.16	0.021	0.37
Women										
Hall et al. (1979)	27–74	113	5.30	7.46	0.013	0.51	1.80	2.80	0.016	0.31
Crapo et al. (1981)	17–84	122	5.20	5.90	—	0.54	1.73	1.97	0.020	0.38

Format of equation
Men
Predicted TLC or RV = Predicted value[a] for: ht 1.75m, Age 45 + {ht Coefficient × (ht − 1.75)} + {Age Coefficient × (Age − 45)}
Women
Predicted TLC or RV = Predicted value[a] for: ht 1.65m, Age 45 + {ht Coefficient × (ht − 1.65)} + {Age Coefficient × (Age − 45)}

Table 3.4 Regression relationships for the prediction of indices of lung function from height and sitting height in healthy boys and girls of European descent (modified from Cotes, 1979)

Index	Sex	Height (H) Relationship	SD%	Sitting height (SH) Relationship	SD%
Cotes (1979)					
TLC (l)	M	$1.227\,H^{2.80}$	9	$7.242\,SH^{2.90}$	11
	F	$1.189\,H^{2.64}$	10	$6.554\,SH^{2.90}$	
VC (l)	M	$1.004\,H^{2.72}$	11	$5.641\,SH^{2.80}$	11
	F	$0.946\,H^{2.61}$	10	$5.053\,SH^{2.80}$	
FEV_1 (l)	M	$0.812\,H^{2.67}$	11	$4.807\,SH^{2.93}$	12
	F	$0.788\,H^{2.73}$	10	$4.527\,SH^{2.93}$	
RV (l)	M + F	$0.237\,H^{2.77}$	27	$1.448\,SH^{3.12}$	31
PEFR (l s^{-1})	M + F	$7.59\ H^{-5.53}$	13	$15.94\ SH^{-6.87}$	13
Polgar and Promadhat (1971)					
TLC (l)	M	$1.226\,H^{2.67}$	11.6		
	F	$1.153\,H^{2.73}$			
VC (l)	M	$0.963\,H^{2.67}$	13.0		
	F	$0.909\,H^{2.72}$			
FEV_1 (l)	M + F	$0.796\,H^{2.80}$	9.0		
RV (l)	M + F	$0.291\,H^{2.41}$	22.8		

increase in VC by virtue of the increased strength of the accessory muscles of inspiration. This is a feature of rowers, weightlifters and participants in archery and other sports in which these muscles are employed. When differences for body size and age are taken into account, middle-distance runners, cyclists and swimmers tend to have a higher than normal vital capacity. A larger lung leads to the V_T contributing more to the ventilation minute volume than in subjects with smaller lungs. The increased VC is not usually accompanied by a corresponding increase in the forced expiratory volume and thus the proportion of the VC which these subjects can expire in 1 s tends to be relatively low. In this respect, Hanson (1973) observed $FEV_{1.0\%}$ values ranging from 61 to 85% in male cross-country skiers whose VCs ranged from 4.8 to 7.3 litres. In swimmers, the increase in VC due to muscle training is superimposed on that associated with a long trunk length which probably also confers a competitive advantage (Cotes, 1979). Vital capacity is reduced by about 7% when the subject lies down. This change is due to the displacement of gas by blood which enters the thorax from the lower parts of the body.

The volume of air that cannot be exhaled after a maximal expiration is the **residual volume** (RV). Functionally, this makes sound physiological sense or there would be complete collapse (closure) of all airways as well as cessation of all gaseous exchange at the lung. In healthy adults, depending on size and age, the RV is in the range of 0.5–3.5 and 0.4–3.0 for males and females, respectively. The RV tends to increase with age, whereas the IRV and ERV become proportionately smaller. The loss in breathing reserve and the concomitant increase in RV with age are generally attributed to the loss of elasticity in the lung tissue (Turner *et al.*, 1968), although there is evidence to suggest that the effects of ageing on lung function can be altered with training (Hagberg *et al.*, 1988). As indicated previously, various studies have shown that RV is temporarily increased during and after recovery from acute bouts of exercise of both short- and long-term duration. The precise reason for an increase in RV with exercise is unknown, although it has been postulated that it is partially attributed to closure of the small peripheral airways and an accumulation of pulmonary extravascular fluid with exercise, which prevents a person from achieving a maximal exhalation (McArdle *et al.*, 1996).

3.5.2 DYNAMIC LUNG VOLUMES (INDICES OF MAXIMAL FLOW)

An important consideration is the individual's ability to *sustain* high levels of flow. This capability depends on the speed at which the volumes can be moved and the amount that can be moved in one breathing cycle. Dynamic function can be considered in terms of either a short period of hyperventilation or a single maximal respiratory effort. The term usually given to the former is maximal voluntary ventilation (MVV), which involves rapid and deep breathing for 15 s. The exact procedure for this measurement is explained in Practical 1. The MVV in adults, depending on age and size, is in the range of 47–253 and 55–139 l min^{-1} in males and females, respectively. The MVV is usually about 25% higher than the ventilation volume observed during maximal exercise $\dot{V}E$ max This is because the ventilatory system is **not** stressed maximally in exercise. Figure 3.2 clearly shows that the rate of ventilation ($\dot{V}E$) is not the limiting factor for maximal oxygen uptake, as $\dot{V}E$ continues to increase

Figure 3.8 Procedure for measuring maximal voluntary ventilation (MVV). The student photographed here (ht 1.97 m, mass 97 kg, age 24) had an abnormally high MVV of 294 l min^{-1} (BTPS).

when maximal oxygen uptake is reached. McArdle *et al.* (1996) have reported values of 140–180 and 80–120 l min^{-1} in college-aged males and females, respectively. Hanson (1973) reported average values of 192 l min^{-1} for the men's US Ski Team, with the highest value being 239 l min^{-1}. Figure 3.8 shows a young athletic male performing the MVV test. This subject, a former amateur boxer, had an abnormally high MVV, which was measured at 294 l min^{-1} (BTPS). Patients with obstructive lung disease can achieve only about 40% of the MVV predicted for their age and size (Levison and Cherniack, 1968).

The MVV can be increased by exercises that increase the strength of the respiratory muscles. This applies both to normal subjects and to pulmonary patients (Sonne and Davis, 1982; Akabas *et al.*, 1989).

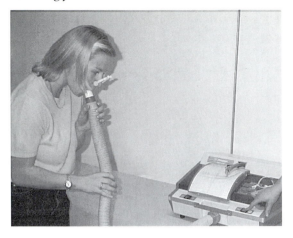

Figure 3.9 Subject performing a forced expiratory volume test on a Vitalograph spirometer.

When the ventilatory capacity is considered in terms of a single forced expiration or inspiration, it is expressed as either the maximal flow rate at a defined point in the respiratory cycle (e.g. the forced expiratory volume after the first or third second, $FEV_{1.0}$ and $FEV_{3.0}$ respectively, see below), the average over part of the breath, or portion of the vital capacity. This portion is usually the middle half (for example, $FEF_{25-75\%}$, see below).

The peak expiratory flow rate (PEFR) is the maximum flow rate that can be sustained for a period of 10 ms. The PEFR in healthy adults, depending on age and size, is in the range of 6–15 l s^{-1} and 2.8–10.1 l s^{-1} in males and females, respectively.

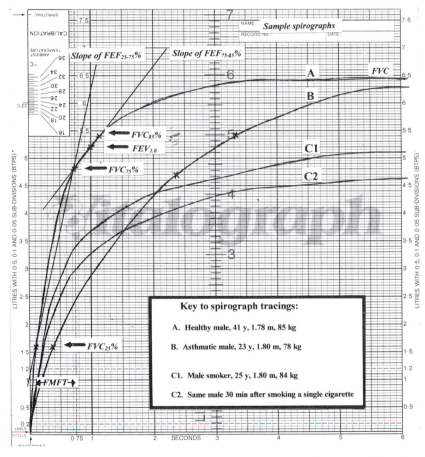

Figure 3.10 *Vitalograph* spirogram on a normal healthy male, an asthmatic male and a male smoker, which illustrates how the various static and dynamic lung function parameters can be calculated. (Vitalograph chart reproduced with permission of Vitalograph Ltd, Buckingham, UK.)

Table 3.5   Comparison of lung function values for the three spirograph tracings illustrated in Figure 3.10

Value		Subject A (Normal)	Subject B (Asthmatic)	Subject C Pre smoking	30 min after smoking
FVC	(l)	6.4	6.3	5.1	4.6
$FEV_{1.0}$	(l)	5.2	2.9	3.7	3.3
$FEV_{1.0\%}$	(l)	81	46	73	72
$FVC_{25\%}$	(l)	1.6	1.6	1.3	1.2
$FVC_{75\%}$	(l)	4.8	4.7	3.8	3.5
$FVC_{85\%}$	(l)	5.4	5.4	4.3	3.9
$FEF_{25-75\%}$	$(l\,s^{-1})$	5.1	1.6	2.5	2.0
$FEF_{75-85\%}$	$(l\,s^{-1})$	1.5	0.8	0.7	0.5
FMFT	(s)	0.65	2.0	0.95	1.05

Figure 3.9 shows a subject performing a forced expiratory volume test on a Vitalograph spirometer (Vitalograph Ltd., Buckingham, UK).

Figure 3.10 shows four spirometer tracings taken from a Vitalograph™ spirometer, to illustrate some of the static and dynamic characteristics of a single 6 s forced expiratory effort in a fit, healthy male, an asthmatic male and a regular smoker. The various lung function values are shown in Table 3.5.

The amount of air expired over a specific time period of a forced expiration is termed the forced expiratory volume qualified by the time over which the measurement is made, for example, $FEV_{1.0}$, $FEV_{3.0}$. In healthy adults, depending on age and size, the $FEV_{1.0}$ is in the range of 1.2–5.7 l and 0.8–4.2 l in males and females, respectively. In Figure 3.10, the $FEV_{1.0}$ for the healthy, non-smoking subject (A) and the asthmatic subject (B) is 5.2 and 2.9 l, respectively.

The forced mid-expiratory flow (FMF) is the average flow rate over the middle half of the FVC. It is also called the Forced Expiratory Flow (FEF) for the appropriate segment of the FVC, for example, $FEF_{25-75\%}$. Graphic analysis involves location of 25% and 75% volume points on the spirogram. The two points are then connected by a straight line and protracted to intersect the two time lines that are one second apart. The number of litres per second is then measured between the points of the intersection. This method is demonstrated for subject A in Figure 3.10. The 25%, 75% and 85% FVC values are shown on the time–volume curve. In this case, the $FEF_{25-75\%}$ was calculated by taking the difference between two intersection points at time lines 0 and 1 s, i.e. 1.1 and 6.2 l. The average flow rate between these two points is therefore 5.1 l s^{-1}. Alternatively, but less accurately, the FMF can be calculated by dividing the change in volume by the time period between FEV at 25% FVC ($FVC_{25\%}$) and at 75% FVC ($FVC_{75\%}$) on the Vitalograph. Another conventional flow rate is $FEF_{75-85\%}$, which is calculated in a similar manner. For subject A, it was calculated as the difference between 6.7 l (at 2 s) and 5.2 l (at 1 s). The 25%, 75% and 85% FVC values are also indicated for the asthmatic subject (B), as a further example of this procedure. The average flow for one litre of gas starting at 200 ml after the beginning of a forced expiration is also used as an index ($FEF_{200-1200}$).

A frequently used ratio is the forced expiratory volume in a second ($FEV_{1.0}$) expressed as a proportion of the vital capacity ($FEV_{1.0\%}$ = ($FEV_{1.0}$ / FVC) × 100). This value provides an indication of the respiratory power and the resistance to air flow. The ratio in healthy adults, depending on age and size, is 51–97% and 59–93% in males and females, respectively. Normally, the demarcation point for airway obstruction is the point at which less than 70% of the FVC can be expired in 1 s. It can be seen from Figure 3.10 and Table 3.5 that, although there is no difference between the FVC values for the healthy lung (A) and the asthmatic lung (B), the dynamic values for the latter are much lower. It is also interesting to note the acute increase in airway resistance after smoking a cigarette. In this example, the student, who was a regular smoker, was tested before (C1) and 30 minutes after smoking a cigarette (C2). Smoking resulted in a 10% reduction in FVC and a 20% reduction in the mid-expiratory flow rate.

3.6 PULMONARY DIFFUSING CAPACITY

The pulmonary diffusing capacity (D_L) is an indication of the rate of diffusion from the alveoli membrane to the pulmonary vascular bed. As greater volumes of air are brought into the alveoli during exercise, the increased volume is matched by a greater volume of pulmonary blood flow (ventilation:perfusion ratio). The rate of gaseous exchange is therefore increased considerably. The D_L therefore provides an indication of the available surface area interface of the alveolar and capillary membrane at any given point in time. It is theoretically dependent upon (a) the surface area of the pulmonary capillaries in contact with alveolar gas, (b) the thickness of the pulmonary membrane and (c) the specific resistance to gas diffusion of the tissue making up the membrane (Ogilvie *et al.*, 1957). It is commonly measured by a single breath-hold of a gaseous mixture of 0.03% CO, 10.0% He, 21% O_2 balanced with N_2. The technique is abbreviated as DL_{COsb}. A practical example of the method is described in Practical 3.

The measurement of D_L at rest provides an additional clinical measure which may be used in the diagnosis of disease, and which may not

be apparent from the normal FVC, $FEV_{1.0}$ and $FEV_{1.0\%}$ measurements. In normal subjects, values at rest range from about 20 to 30 ml CO min^{-1} $mmHg^{-1}$ but this is dependent on body size and sex, since oxygen consumption increases with body size. Ogilvie *et al.* (1957) observed that D_L was directly related to surface area and could be calculated by the equation:

$$D_L = \text{surface area (m}^2\text{)} \times 18.55 - 6.8 \ (r = 0.81),$$
$$SEE = 3.92 \text{ ml min}^{-1} \text{ mmHg}^{-1}$$

This equation was derived on subjects in the sitting position, since D_L, like residual volume, increases progressively as the person assumes a change in position from standing erect to supine. The increase in D_L is ascribed to a large pulmonary capillary blood volume and a more uniform balance between ventilation and perfusion in the supine position (Turino *et al.*, 1963).

Below-normal values are observed in patients who have suffered from such ailments as chronic obstructive emphysema, asthma, pulmonary arterial disease, pulmonary carcinoma and kyphoscoliosis, and in patients who have suffered chemical burns or who have been exposed to asbestos dust (refer to Ogilvie *et al.*, 1957, for specific examples).

3.6.1 EFFECTS OF EXERCISE ON PULMONARY DIFFUSING CAPACITY

An increase in D_L with exercise was first reported by Krogh (1915). Using the DL_{COsb} technique, the pulmonary diffusing capacity increases to about 55–70 ml min^{-1} $mmHg^{-1}$ (Turino *et al.*, 1963; Turcotte *et al.*, 1992), depending on the intensity of the exercise. Turino *et al.* compared the diffusing capacity of the lung during exercise in the upright and supine positions. Although they observed differences at rest, they showed that during exercise the body position has less of an effect on the determinants of D_L. They observed that D_L continued to increase as the intensity of the exercise increased and concluded that it was unlikely that D_L limited maximum oxygen uptake. This conclusion is consistent with the proposition that circulatory performance, rather than pulmonary diffusing capacity, sets the ceiling for physical exertion. There is also evidence to suggest that pulmonary diffusing capacity increases with training (Newman *et al.*, 1962).

3.7 SOURCES OF VARIATION IN LUNG FUNCTION TESTING

Measurements of pulmonary function are subject to a number of sources of variation. Variation can be attributed to technical factors, such as instrumentation, procedure, observer error, and so on. The variation could also be due to dysfunction, or disease, or a result of biological variation. The major focus here is on biological sources of variation within individuals and between individuals. For a more detailed discussion of all sources of variation in lung function testing, the reader is guided to the position statement of the American Thoracic Society (1991).

3.7.1 WITHIN-SUBJECT VARIATION

The main sources of within-subject variation in ventilatory parameters both at rest and during exercise that are not related to disease, environment, drugs or subject compliance are body position, head position and the degree of effort exerted during the test. There is also a circadian rhythm.

The FVC is 7–8% lower in the supine compared to the standing position and 1–2% lower in the sitting compared to the standing position (Townsend, 1984; Allen *et al.*, 1985). The standing position is also preferable for obese subjects. Systematic increases in maximal expiratory flows have been documented during neck hyperextension. This change may be due to elongation and stiffening of the trachea. Conversely, neck flexion may decrease peak expiratory flow rate and increase airway resistance (Melissinos and Mead, 1977). The $FEV_{1.0}$ may be 100–200 ml lower when the effort is maximal compared to submaximal, because the airway is narrower in relation to the exhaled volume (Krowka *et al.*, 1987). In some subjects,

repeated maximal efforts may trigger bronchospasm, resulting in a progressive decrease in FVC and $FEV_{1.0}$ (Gimeno *et al.*, 1972). Residual volume also increases by about 20% on changing from a standing to a sitting position and by about 30% on changing from a sitting to a supine position (Blair and Hickam, 1955).

Another source of intra-subject variation is the time of day due to circadian rhythms. For maximal expiratory flows, the lowest values are usually found in the morning (04:00 to 06:00 hours) and the largest values usually occur around midday (Hetzel, 1981). Guberan *et al.* (1969) observed significant increases in $FEV_{1.0}$ of 150 ml in the morning which decreased by 50 ml in the afternoon in nocturnal workers, demonstrating a disturbance of the normal circadian rhythm. Data on FVC from my laboratory on asthmatic and normal subjects were 7% higher at 16.00 hours compared to 08.00 hours ($p < 0.01$). The $FEV_{1.0}$ was also increased by about 200 ml ($p < 0.01$). In both studies the changes were more marked in the asthmatic subjects. Hetzel and Clark (1980) have reported that PEFR peak-to-trough amplitude of the circadian rhythm is about 8%. A rhythm in $\dot{V}E$ is also evident during submaximal exercise, and is closely related to the circadian curve in body temperature (Reilly, 1990).

3.7.2 BETWEEN-SUBJECT VARIATION

The main anthropometric factors responsible for inter-subject variation in lung function are sex, body size and ageing. These alone account for 30%, 22% and 8%, respectively, of the variation in adults (Becklake, 1986). Other factors are race and past and present health.

Although sitting height explains less of the variability in lung function than standing height (Ferris and Stoudt, 1971; Cotes, 1979), it may be a useful predictor when dealing with mixed ethnic origins due to the fact that blacks have a lower trunk-to-leg ratio than whites (Van de Wal *et al.*, 1971). It is also used to predict lung function in children, particularly during periods of rapid growth. Arm span measurements provide a practical substitute for stature in subjects unable to stand or those with a skeletal deformity such as kypho-scoliosis (Hibbert *et al.*, 1988). Measurements of chest circumference may also slightly improve the prediction of lung function (Damon, 1966). After correcting for body size, girls appear to have higher expiratory flows than boys, but men have larger volumes and flows than women (Schwartz *et al.*, 1988). With regard to *age*, after adult height is attained, there is either an increase (usually in young men) or little or no decrease in function (usu-ally in young women) after which lung func-tion decreases at an accelerating rate with increasing age (American Thoracic Society, 1991). *Race* is an important determinant of lung function (American Thoracic Society, 1991). Caucasians of European descent have greater static and dynamic lung volumes and greater forced expiratory flow rates than black people, but they have similar or lower $FEV_{1.0}$ / FVC ratios. In this respect, regression equations derived from white populations using stand-ing height as the measure of size usually over-predict values measured in blacks by about 12% for TLC, $FEV_{1.0}$ and FVC and by about 7% for FRC and RV (Cotes, 1979). Differences have been attributed to body build differences and frame size (Jacobs *et al.*, 1992). It has already been noted that blacks have a lower trunk:leg ratio than whites.

A factor related to the size of the lung is *growth in standing height*, as this affects lung function measurements in childhood and ado-lescence. Growth in stature is not in phase with lung growth during the adolescent growth spurt (DeGroodt *et al.*, 1986) and growth in chest dimensions lags behind that of the legs (DeGroodt *et al.*, 1988). In males, standing height and VC are often not maximal by the age of 17 years. The VC continues to increase after increases in height cease and may not be maximal until about 25 years of age. Girls, however, attain their maximal values around the age of 16 years (DeGroodt *et al.*, 1986).

The ratio $FEV_{1.0}$ / FVC and the ratio of maxi-mal expiratory flow (derived from flow–volume curves) to the FVC are almost constant from childhood to adulthood. Girls have larger expiratory flows than boys of the same age and stature (DeGroodt *et al.*, 1986). This is partly due to the fact that girls have a smaller VC for the same TLC than boys. It may also reflect the smaller muscle mass and the smaller number of alveoli found in girls (Thurlbeck, 1982). The American Thoracic Society (1991) recom-mended that such sex differences warrant the use of different prediction equations for boys and girls at all ages. Ideally, developmental rather than chronological age should be included in prediction equations for children and adolescents, although such equations are neither available nor practical.

The size of the lung determines the total lung capacity, its subdivisions and the indices that are dependent on lung size, for example, forced expiratory flow rates. In children up to the age of puberty, these indices are related to stature, usually in a curvilinear manner; the relationship is linear when height is raised to the power of about 2.6 (Cotes, 1979; Table 3.4).

After stature has been taken into account, the indices are independent of age and usually independent of body weight and sitting height. During the adolescent growth spurt, the rate of growth of the trunk and its contents, including the lungs, is relatively greater than that of the legs. It is therefore useful to use sit-ting height as an alternative reference variable during this stage of growth (Cotes, 1979; Cotes *et al.*, 1979). Equations which use stature and sitting height to predict lung function in child-ren are shown in Table 3.4. Relative to stature, boys and girls have similar values for residual volume, peak expiratory flow rate and flow rate at 50% of vital capacity. The ERV is slightly larger and the inspiratory capacity is about 12% larger for boys than for girls. Thus, boys have larger values for the functional residual capacity, the vital capacity and the total lung capacity. As a consequence of these differences in lung size, boys also have larger values for $FEV_{1.0}$.

3.8 LUNG FUNCTION IN SPECIAL POPULATIONS

3.8.1 HIGH-ALTITUDE NATIVES

Like the acclimatized visitor, the high-altitude native hyperventilates relative to a normal sea-level person. This increases alveolar ventilation and limits the fall in the partial pressure of oxygen in the alveoli which lessens the reduction in the oxygen pressure gradient across the alveolar membrane. At any given altitude, the ventilation of the acclimatized visitor is greater by about 20% than that of the native highlander (Minors, 1985). Thus, the high-altitude native seems to have lost some respiratory sensitivity to hypoxia.

Native highlanders developed certain anthropometric differences enabling them to tolerate the hypobaric conditions experienced at high altitude. They have a smaller stature than lowlanders of the same age. Although the difference in height varies by about 10%, the chest circumference of native highlanders is about 5% greater (Frisancho, 1975). This is accompanied by a larger vital capacity, larger lung volume and residual lung volume than sea-level subjects. In addition, morphometric measurements of the lungs of high-altitude natives resident at 4000 m have shown alveoli that are larger and greater in number than those in lowland natives of the same body size. The increased alveolar surface area in contact with functioning pulmonary capillaries, in combination with an increased pulmonary capillary blood volume, leads to an increased pulmonary diffusing capacity in the high-altitude native's lung. The combination of increased alveolar ventilation and pulmonary diffusing capacity increases the total alveolar gas exchange in the highlander.

3.8.2 LUNG FUNCTION IN DIVERS

Certain physical adaptations to long-term diving have been noted in US Navy Escape Training Tank Instructors (Carey *et al.*, 1956) and to a lesser extent in male recreational divers (Hong *et al.*, 1970). These changes include an increase in VC, a decrease in RV and a lowered RV / TLC ratio.

Differences have also been observed in the Korean diving women known as the *ama*. Before each dive an *ama* hyperventilates then dives between 5–18 metres for 20–40 s in repeated dives for approximately 3 h per day. Song *et al.* (1963) observed VC and MVV maximal volumes to be 125% and 128%, respectively, of predicted values. They also observed a higher inspiratory capacity, but no difference in ERV between the *ama* and a group of controls. The RV, expressed as a proportion of total lung capacity, was also lower in the *ama*.

The reason for the increased VC was attributed to the increased inspiratory capacity of the *ama*. This difference was attributed to better developed inspiratory muscles thought to be an adaptation to the constant hydrostatic pressure which the *ama* must overcome on inspiration before a dive. The lower RV / TLC ratio was considered to be important since it determines the maximal depth of diving.

3.9 PREDICTION OF LUNG FUNCTION

Reference equations provide a context for evaluating pulmonary function in comparison to the distribution of measurements in a reference population. Linear regression is the most common, but not the only model used to describe pulmonary function data in adults. These types of equations perform less well at the edges of the data distribution. Further, estimates are likely to be misleading if they go beyond the range of the independent variables used to create the equation. The most commonly reported measures of how well regression equations fit the data they describe are the square of the correlation coefficient (r^2) and the standard error of the estimate (SEE). The proportion of variation in the observed data explained by the independent variables is measured by r^2. The SEE is the average standard deviation of the data around the regression line. This will decrease and r^2 will increase as regression methods reduce the differences between predicted and observed values in the reference population. When the same equations are used to describe a different population, SEE will invariably be larger, and r^2 will be smaller.

Tables 3.1–3.4 contain a listing of various regression equations that predict the various lung function indices in black and white adults and children. The American Thoracic Society (1991) has recommended that, ideally, publications describing reference populations should also include a means of defining the lower limits of the regression equations. Nevertheless, it is possible to estimate lower limits of normal from a regression model.

3.9.1 ESTIMATION OF *LOWER* LIMITS OF NORMAL

Values below the 5th percentile are conventionally taken as below the expected range and those above the 5th percentile are taken as within the expected range (American Thoracic Society, 1991). It is possible to calculate percentiles if there are sufficient measurements within each category. The value of the 5th percentile can be roughly estimated as:

$$\text{Lower limit of normal} = \text{predicted value} - 1.645 \times \text{SEE}$$

For example, the predicted value of FVC for a 45-year-old male, stature 1.75 m (Table 3.1) is 5.83 l according to the prediction equation of Morris *et al.* (1971). The standard error of estimate is 0.74 l for this equation. Thus, the lower limit of normal (i.e. the lower 5% of the population) for a man of this age and stature would be 4.61 litres (5.83 l – (1.645 × 0.74)).

Defining a fixed $FEV_{1.0}$ / FVC ratio as a lower limit of normal (e.g. 80%) is not recommended in adults because $FEV_{1.0}$ / FVC is inversely related to age and stature (American Thoracic Society, 1991). The use of a fixed ratio will therefore result in an apparent increase in dysfunction associated with ageing. In addition, some athletes have values of FVC that are relatively larger than those for $FEV_{1.0}$, which

results in a lower $FEV_{1.0}$ / FVC ratio. Thus, the definition of the lowest 5% of the reference population is also the preferred method to predict abnormality in this parameter.

3.10 DEFINITION OF OBSTRUCTIVE AND RESTRICTIVE VENTILATORY DEFECTS

3.10.1 OBSTRUCTIVE DEFECT

An obstructive ventilatory defect is defined as a disproportionate reduction in maximal airflow from the lung with respect to the maximal volume (vital capacity) that can be displaced from the lung (American Thoracic Society, 1991). It implies narrowing of the airway during expiration.

Indications of an obstructive defect can be seen in the latter stages of a flow–volume curve. The slowing is reflected in a reduction in the instantaneous flow after 75% of the FVC has been exhaled ($FEF_{75-85\%}$) or in the $FEF_{25-75\%}$. In the event of airway disease becoming more advanced, the $FEV_{1.0}$ becomes reduced out of proportion to the reduction in VC.

3.10.2 RESTRICTIVE DEFECT

One may infer the presence of a restrictive ventilatory defect when VC is reduced and $FEV_{1.0}$ / FVC is normal or increased. A reduction in VC may occur because airflow is so slow that the subject cannot continue to exhale long enough to complete emptying or because airways collapse.

3.10.3 INTERPRETATION OF LUNG FUNCTION TESTS

The basic parameters used to interpret spirometry are the VC, $FEV_{1.0}$ and $FEV_{1.0}$ / FVC ratio (American Thoracic Society, 1991). Although FVC is often used instead of VC, it is preferable to use the largest VC, whether obtained on inspiration (IVC), slow expiration (EVC) or forced expiration (FVC) for clinical testing. The FVC is usually reduced more than IVC or EVC in airflow obstruction.

The $FEV_{1.0}$ / FVC ratio is the most important measurement for distinguishing an obstructive impairment. According to the American Thoracic Society (1991), expiratory flow measurements other than the $FEV_{1.0}$ and $FEV_{1.0}$ / FVC should be considered only after determining the presence and clinical severity of obstructive impairment using the basic parameters measured above. When $FEV_{1.0}$ and the $FEV_{1.0}$ / VC ratio are within the normal range, abnormalities in flow occurring late in the maximal expiratory flow–volume curve should not be graded as to severity and, if mentioned, should be interpreted cautiously. When there is a borderline value of $FEV_{1.0}$ / FVC, these values may help to confirm the presence of airway obstruction. The same is true for average flows such as $FEF_{25-75\%}$. It is important to note that there is wide variability of these measurements in healthy subjects and this variation must therefore be taken into account in the final interpretation.

3.11 PRACTICAL EXERCISES

In the following section four laboratory practicals are suggested. Lung function in the resting state is determined in Practical 1 and lung function during exercise is determined in Practical 2. Practical 3 describes a procedure for measuring D_L with examples of values and calculations. Practical 4 also describes how oxygen uptake may be demonstrated by the closed circuit system, during which lung function measures may also be demonstrated. Each practical contains actual data to exemplify the relationships between variables and provides examples and applications of the various formulae for assessing lung function.

3.12 PRACTICAL 1: ASSESSMENT OF RESTING LUNG VOLUMES

3.12.1 PURPOSE

* To measure static and dynamic lung volumes in the resting state
* To determine relationships between lung function and anthropometric variables
* To assess the effects of changes in posture on lung function.

Some data are presented in Table 3.6 to exemplify some of these measurements.

3.12.2 PROCEDURES

(a) Closed circuit spirometry

1. Record the subject's age, stature, mass, physical activity/training status.
2. Record ambient conditions (temperature, barometric pressure).
3. Record sitting height, arm span and chest circumference.
4. Measurement of inspired and expired volumes using a wet spirometer with kymograph.
   (a) Sanitize all equipment and mouthpiece.
   (b) The subject puts on a nose clip.
   (c) Procedure:
   (i) The recording pen is best placed just below half-way on the kymograph.
   (ii) Set the drum rotation speed to 10 mm s^{-1}.

Table 3.6 Assessment of resting lung volumes: example of lung volumes at rest in a 38-year-old active male

Descriptive data

Name	RGE	Age	38
Stature (m)	1.78	Mass (kg)	86.0
Sitting height (m)	0.91	Arm span (m)	1.84

Ambient conditions

Laboratory temperature (°C)	20	P_{Bar} (mmHg) 760

(a) Resting measurements (dry spirometer)[a]

	$FEV_{1.0}$ (l)	$FEV_{1.0}$%	$FEF_{25-75\%}$ ($l\,s^{-1}$)	$FEF_{75-85\%}$ ($l\,s^{-1}$)	$FEF_{0.2-1.2}$ ($l\,s^{-1}$)	FMFT (s)	MVV ($l\,min^{-1}$)
FVC (l)							
Standing							
6.65	5.41	81.2	5.37	1.2	13.0	0.62	230
Supine							
6.32	5.1	80.6	5.21	1.1	11.0	0.81	190
Predicted values							
5.02	4.04	80.0	4.60	1.27	9.00	0.73	200

(b) Resting measurements (wet spirometer)[a]

V_T (l)	IRV (l)	ERV (l)	FVC (l)	RV (l)	FRC (l)	TLC (l)
Measured						
0.60	3.20	1.65	6.65	1.80	3.45	8.45
Predicted values						
0.60	2.91	1.39	5.02	1.90	2.70	6.8

(c) Resting measurements (Douglas bag)[a]

$\dot{V}E$ ($l\,s^{-1}$)	f (breaths min^{-1})	V_T (l)	V_T as %FVC	MVV ($l\,min^{-1}$)
7.0	10.0	0.70	10.0	210.0

a All values should be recorded at BTPS.

3.14 PRACTICAL 3: MEASUREMENT OF PULMONARY DIFFUSING CAPACITY

3.14.1 PURPOSE

Pulmonary diffusing capacity (D_L) is commonly measured by the single-breath method. This technique requires the subject to inspire a mixture of 0.3% carbon monoxide (CO), 10% helium (He), 21% oxygen (O_2) and a balance of nitrogen (N_2). Specifically, the technique measures the rate of diffusion of CO from the alveoli to the pulmonary vascular bed in a single full 10 s breath-hold of the gas mixture and is hence abbreviated DL_{SOsb}. The rationale for its measurement was described in Section 3.6.

3.14.2 PROCEDURES

The method is described in detail by Ferris (1978) and is summarized here for ease of reference.

3.14.3 APPARATUS (FIGURE 3.11)

1. A 30 litre Douglas bag is flushed several times with the He–CO mixture.
2. Just before the test, the inspiratory tubing and valve section is also flushed with the He–CO mixture.
3. The subject is seated, fitted with a nose clip, and breathes ambient air (valve directed to A).
4. With the valve directed to A (ambient air), the subject is instructed to (1) exhale maximally to residual volume, signal by hand, and on instruction (2) inhale rapidly and maximally from the Douglas bag and hold the breath for 10 s. On a signal, the subject then exhales rapidly. The four-way valve is adjusted by the investigator to enable the subject to breathe normal air and exhale maximally to normal air (A), inspire from the bag (B), expire to space surrounding the bag (C, 1 litre wash-out) and to ensure 1 litre collection of alveolar air in the sampling bag (D).

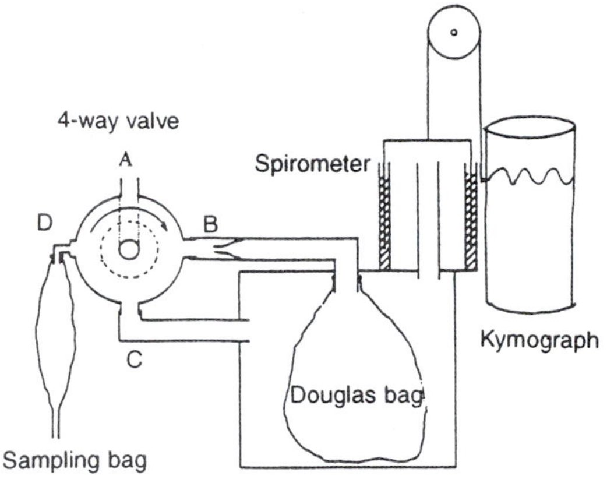

Figure 3.11 Conventional manual system for DL_{COsb}. (Modified from Ferris, 1978.)

5. The following values are recorded: (1) breath-hold time from mid-inspiration to beginning of the alveolar sampling (Figure 3.12), (2) the inspired volume (ATPS), (3) the final He concentration in the sampling bag and (4) the final CO concentration in the sampling bag.

It is important to note that a number of factors affect the calculation of DL_{COsb} such as the Valsalva manoeuvre, the method of measuring the breath-hold time, the actual breath-hold time and other factors. For more detail of these factors refer to the American Thoracic

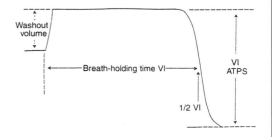

Society Epidemiology Standardization Project compiled by Ferris (1978). It is possible to reduce the breath-hold time to as low as 3 s with a minimum loss of accuracy during strenuous exercise (Turcotte *et al.*, 1992).

3.14.4 GAS ANALYSIS

The analysers for CO and He are connected in series, preceded by an H_2O absorber, CO_2 absorber, dust filter and a flow meter. A small pump should draw air through at a rate of 400 ml min^{-1} and a stable reading for CO and He is obtained in 30–40 s.

Figure 3.12 Standardized measurements from the spirographic tracing obtained during the single breath diffusing capacity maneouvre. The inspired volume is measured from the maximal expiration to the fullest inspiration. The breath-holding time is measured from the time when one-half of the inspiration is made to the time when washout has been completed and collection of alveolar gas has begun.

Example calculation of DL_{COsb}
  Equation:

$$DL_{COsb} = V_{A(STPD)} \times \frac{60}{\text{breath holding time}} \times \frac{1}{P_B - 47} \times \frac{CO_A}{CO_E}$$

where:
  DL_{COsb} = single breath diffusing capacity for CO
  P_B = barometric pressure
  CO_A = initial concentration of CO
  CO_E = expired concentration of CO
  V_A = alveolar volume (STPD) at which the breath was held

$$V_A = V_I (ATPS) \times (He_I / He_E) \times 1.05 \times STPD \text{ correction factor}$$

where:
  V_I = inspired volume (ATPS)
  He_I = inspired He
  He_E = expired He

$$CO_A = CO_I \times \frac{He_E}{He_I}$$

Sample data
  P_B = 754 mmHg He_E = 12.0%
  CO_I = 0.3%   T = 21°
  He_I = 10.0 %   STPD cf = 0.895
  V_I (ATPS) = 5000ml CO_E = 0.2%
  Breath-hold time = 10 s

Stage 1 (Solve for V$_{A(STPD)}$)

$$V_{A(STPD)} = 5000 \text{ ml} \times \frac{0.10}{0.12} \times 1.05 \times 0.895$$

$$V_{A(STPD)} = 3915 \text{ ml}$$

Stage 2 (Solve for CO$_A$)

$$CO_A = 0.003 \times \frac{0.12}{0.10} = 0.0036$$

Stage 3 (Solve for DL_{COsb})

$$DL_{COsb} = 3915 \text{ ml} \times \frac{60 \text{ s}}{10 \text{ s}} \times \frac{1}{754 - 47} \times \frac{0.0036}{0.0020}$$

$$DL_{COsb} = 33.8 \text{ ml CO min}^{-1} \text{ mm Hg}^{-1}$$

3.15 PRACTICAL 4: MEASUREMENT OF OXYGEN UPTAKE BY CLOSED-CIRCUIT SPIROMETRY

3.15.1 PURPOSE

Although the closed-circuit, indirect spirometry system is rarely used today, it can be used to exemplify some of the basic principles of measurement of oxygen consumption at rest and during exercise. Estimations of energy expenditure may be calculated using caloric equivalents for oxygen uptake for an RER of 0.83, i.e. 20.2 kJ l^{-1} (4.8 kcal l^{-1}). The following procedure should be used to produce the spirometry tracings as exemplified in Figure 3.13.

3.15.2 PROCEDURE FOR CLOSED-CIRCUIT OXYGEN UPTAKE

1. The spirometer is rinsed with 100% oxygen and then filled with 100% oxygen.
2. The subject is seated on the arm ergometer and connected to the spirometer and breathes atmospheric air for a few minutes to acclimatize to the mouthpiece and the resistance of the spirometer.
3. Expired air is directed through soda lime to remove CO_2.
4. The kymograph speed is set at 25 mm min^{-1}.
5. The subject then inspires oxygen from the spirometer. Initially, the expired air should be directed to the atmosphere. The spirometer should then be then closed so that oxygen is breathed from and back into the spirometer. Recordings can be made for several minutes, after which time the subject should breathe normal air.
6. After a warm-up the subject should then commence arm ergometry at 50 W for 3 minutes. Oxygen is inspired from the spirometer for the last minute. The spirometer is then refilled with oxygen.
7. After a 20 minute rest period the mode of ergometry is switched to cycling at 50 W and the above procedure is repeated.

8. Oxygen uptake at STPD may be calculated using the following formulae. The correction factor for converting ATPS to STPD volumes can be calculated from the formulae in Practical 2 or from Chapter 6, Table 6.2.

Calculation of $\dot{V}O_2$ at STPD (ml min^{-1})

$$\frac{y\,(\text{mm})\times 30\,(\text{ml mm}^{-1})\times \text{correction factor (CF)} \times 60\,(\text{s})}{x\,(\text{mm})\times 2.4\,(\text{s mm}^{-1})}$$

Sitting at rest $(20 \times 30 \times 0.919 \times 60) / (45 \times 2.4) = 306$ ml min^{-1}
Arm ergometry (50 W) $(50 \times 30 \times 0.919 \times 60) / (30 \times 2.4) = 1149$ ml min^{-1}
Cycling (50 W) $(48 \times 30 \times 0.919 \times 60) / (45 \times 2.4) = 735$ ml min^{-1}
NB: Paper speed = 25 mm min^{-1} or 1 mm = 2.4 s

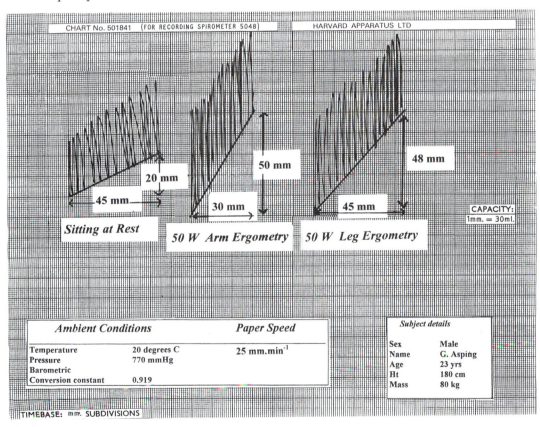

Figure 3.13 Closed circuit spirograph showing oxygen uptake at rest and during arm and leg exercise for a healthy, fit male student.

REFERENCES

Akabas, S.R., Bazzyar, A., Dimauro, S. and Haddad, G.G. (1989). Metabolic and functional adaptation of the diaphragm to training with resistive loads. *Journal of Applied Physiology*, **66**, 529–35.

Allen, S.M., Hunt, B. and Green, M. (1985). Fall in vital capacity with posture. *British Journal of Diseases of the Chest*, **79**, 267–71.

American Thoracic Society (1991). Lung function testing: selection of reference values and interpretation strategies. *American Review of Respiratory Disease*, **144**, 1202–18.

Åstrand, P.O. (1952). *Experimental Studies of Physical Work Capacity in Relation to Sex and Age*. (E. Munksgaard, Copenhagen).

Åstrand, P.O. (1954). The respiratory activity in man exposed to prolonged hypoxia. *Acta Physiologica Scandinavica*, **30**, 343–68.

Åstrand, P.O. and Rodahl, K. (1986). *Textbook of Work Physiology*. (McGraw-Hill, New York).

Becklake, M.R. (1986). Concepts of normality applied to the measurement of lung function. *American Journal of Medicine*, **80**, 1158–64.

Bevegard, S., Freyschuss, U. and Strandell, T. (1966). Circulatory adaptation to arm and leg exercise in supine and sitting position. *Journal of Applied Physiology*, **21**, 37–46.

Blair, E. and Hickam, J.B. (1955). The effect of change in body position on lung volume and intrapulmonary gas mixing in normal subjects. *Journal of Clinical Investigations*, **34**, 383–9.

Boren, H.G., Kory, R.C. and Syner, J.C. (1966). The Veterans Administration Army cooperative study of pulmonary function. *American Journal of Medicine*, **41**, 96–114.

Buono, M.J., Constable, S.A., Morton, A.R., *et al.* (1981). The effect of an acute bout of exercise on selected pulmonary function measurements. *Medicine and Science in Sports and Exercise*, **13**, 290–3.

Carey, C.R., Schaefer, K.E. and Alvis, H.J. (1956). Effect of skin diving on lung volume. *Journal of Applied Physiology*, **8**, 519–23.

Cookson, J.B., Blake, G.T.W. and Faranisi, C. (1976). Normal values for ventilatory function in Rhodesian Africans. *British Journal of Diseases of the Chest*, **70**, 107–11.

Cotes, J.E. (1979). *Lung Function: Assessment and Application in Medicine*. (Blackwell Scientific, Oxford).

Cotes, J.E., Dabbs, J.M., Hall, A.M., *et al.* (1979). Sitting height, fat-free mass and body fat as reference variables for lung function in healthy British children: comparison with stature. *Annals of Human Biology*, **6**, 307–14.

Crapo, R.O., Morris, A.H. and Gardner, R.M. (1981). Reference spirometric values using techniques and equipment that meet ATS recommendations. *American Review of Respiratory Disease*, **123**, 659–64.

Crapo, R.O., Morris, A.H., Clayton, P.D. and Nixon, C.R. (1982). Lung volumes in healthy non-smoking adults. *Bulletin European de Physiopathologie Respiratoire*, **18**, 419–25.

Damon, A. (1966). Negro–white differences in pulmonary function (vital capacity, timed vital capacity and expiratory flow rate). *Human Biology*, **38**, 381–93.

Datta, S.R. and Ramanathan, N.L. (1969). Energy expenditure in work predicted from heart rate and pulmonary ventilation. *Journal of Applied Physiology*, **26**, 297–302.

Davies, C.T., Few, J., Foster, K.G. and Sargeant, T. (1974). Plasma catecholamine concentration during dynamic exercise involving different muscle groups. *European Journal of Applied Physiology*, **32**, 195–206.

DeGroodt, E.G., Quanjer, P.H., Wise, J.E. and Van Zomeren, B.C. (1986). Changing relationships between stature and lung volumes during puberty. *Respiration Physiology*, **65**, 139–53.

DeGroodt, E.G., van Pelt, W., Quanjer, P.H., *et al.* (1988). Growth of lung and thorax dimensions during the pubertal growth spurt. *European Respiratory Journal*, **1**, 102–8.

Ekblom, B. and Hermansen, L. (1968). Cardiac output in athletes. *Journal of Applied Physiology*, **25**, 619–25.

Eston, R.G. and Brodie, D.A. (1986). Responses to arm and leg ergometry. *British Journal of Sports Medicine*, **20**, 4–7.

Ferris, A. (1978). Epidemiology standardization project (Part III), *American Review of Respiratory Disease*, **118**, 55–89.

Ferris, B.G. and Stoudt, H.E. (1971). Correlation of anthropometry and simple tests of pulmonary function. *Archives of Environmental Health*, **22**, 672–6.

Fringer, M.N. and Stull, G.A. (1974). Changes in cardiorespiratory parameters during periods of training and detraining in young adult females. *Medicine and Science in Sports*, **6**, 20–5.

Frisancho, A.R. (1975). Functional adaptation to high-altitude hypoxia. *Science*, **187**, 313–19.

Gimeno, F., Berg, W.C., Sluiter, H.J. and Tammeling, G.J. (1972). Spirometry-induced bronchial obstruction. *American Review of Respiratory Disease*, **105**, 68–74.

Guberan, E., Williams, M.K., Walford, J. and Smith, M.M. (1969). Circadian variation of FEV in shift workers. *British Journal of Industrial Medicine*, **26**, 121–5.

Hagberg, J.M., Yerg, J.E. and Seals, D.R. (1988). Pulmonary function in young and older athletes and untrained men. *Journal of Applied Physiology*, **65**, 101–5.

Hagberg, J.M., Coyle, E.F., Carroll, J.E., *et al.* (1982). Exercise hyperventilation in patients with McArdle's disease. *Journal of Applied Physiology*, **52**, 991–4.

Hall, A.M., Heywood, C., and Cotes, J.E. (1979). Lung function in healthy British women. *Thorax*, **34**, 359–65.

Hanson, J.S. (1973). Maximal exercise performance in members of the US Nordic Ski Team. *Journal of Applied Physiology*, **35**, 592–5.

Hetzel, M.R. (1981). The pulmonary clock. *Thorax*, **36**, 481–6.

Hetzel, M.R. and Clark, T.J.H. (1980). Comparison of normal and asthmatic circadian rhythms in peak expiratory flow rate. *Thorax*, **35**, 732–8.

Hibbert, M.E., Lanigan, A., Raven, J. and Phelan, P.D. (1988). Relation of armspan to height and the prediction of lung function. *Thorax*, **43**, 657–9.

Hong, S.K., Moore, T.O., Seto, G., *et al.* (1970). Lung volumes and apneic bradycardia in divers. *Journal of Applied Physiology*, **29**, 172–6.

Jacobs, D.R., Nelson, E.T., Dontas, A.S., *et al.* (1992). Are race and sex differences in lung function explained by frame size? *American Review of Respiratory Disease*, **146**, 644–9.

Jirka, Z. and Adamus, M. (1965). Changes of ventilation equivalents in young people in the course of three years of training. *Journal of Sports Medicine and Physical Fitness*, **5**, 1–6.

Johannsen, Z.M. and Erasmus, L.D. (1968). Clinical spirometry in normal Bantu. *American Review of Respiratory Disease*, **97**, 585–97.

Jones, N.L. (1984). Dyspnea in exercise. *Medicine and Science in Sports and Exercise*, **16**, 14–9.

Knudson, R.J., Lebowitz, M.D., Holberg, C.J. and Burrows, B. (1983). Changes in normal maximal expiratory flow–volume curve with growth and aging. *American Review of Respiratory Disease*, **127**, 725–34.

Krogh, M. (1915). Diffusion of gases through the lungs of man. *Journal of Physiology*, **49**, 271–300.

Krowka, M.J., Enright, P.L., Rodarte, J.R. and Hyatt, R.E. (1987). Effect of effort on forced expiratory effort in one second. *American Review of Respiratory Disease*, **136**, 829–33.

Lapp, N.L., Amandus, H.E., Hall, R. and Morgan, W.K.C. (1974). Lung volumes and flow rates in black and white subjects. *Thorax*, **29**, 185–8.

Levison, H. and Cherniack, R.M. (1968). Ventilatory cost of exercise in chronic obstructive pulmonary disease. *Journal of Applied Physiology*, **25**, 21–7.

McArdle, W., Katch, F.I. and Katch, V.L. (1991). *Exercise Physiology: Energy, Nutrition and Human Performance*. (Williams and Wilkins, Baltimore, MD).

Mangum, M. (1984). Research methods: application to arm crank ergometry. *Journal of Sports Sciences*, **2**, 257–63.

Melissinos, C.G. and Mead, J. (1977). Maximum expiratory flow changes induced by longitudinal tension on trachea in normal subjects. *Journal of Applied Physiology*, **43**, 537–44.

Miles, D.S., Cox, M.H., Bomze, J.P. and Gotshall, R.W. (1991). Acute recovery profile of lung volumes and function after running 5 miles. *Journal of Sports Medicine and Physical Fitness*, **31**, 243–8.

Minors, D.S. (1985). Abnormal pressure. In *Variations in Human Physiology*. ed. R.M. Case (Manchester University Press, Manchester, UK), pp. 78–110.

Morris, J.F., Koski, A. and Johnson, L.C. (1971). Spirometric standards for healthy non-smoking adults. *American Review of Respiratory Disease*, **103**, 57–67.

Newman, F., Smalley, B.F. and Thomson, M.L. (1962). Effect of exercise, body and lung size on CO diffusing capacity in athletes and non-athletes. *Journal of Applied Physiology*, **17**, 649–55.

Ogilvie, C.M., Forster, R.E., Blakemore, W.S. and Morton, J.W. (1957). A standardized breath holding technique for the clinical measurement of the diffusing capacity of the lung for carbon monoxide. *Journal of Clinical Investigations*, **36**, 1–17.

Polgar, G. and Promadhat, V. (1971). *Pulmonary Function Testing in Children: Techniques and Standards*. (W.B. Saunders, Philadelphia, PA), p. 272.

Rasmussen, B., Klausen, K., Clausen, J.P. and Trap-Jensen, J. (1975). Pulmonary ventilation, blood gases and pH after training of the arms and legs. *Journal of Applied Physiology*, **38**, 250–6.

Rasmussen, R.S., Elkjaer, P. and Juhl, B. (1988). Impaired pulmonary and cardiac function after maximal exercise. *Journal of Sports Sciences*, **6**, 219–28.

Reilly, T. (1990). Human circadian rhythms and

exercise. *Critical Reviews in Biomedical Engineering*, **18**, 165–80.

Saltin, B. and Åstrand P.O. (1967). Maximal oxygen uptake in athletes. *Journal of Applied Physiology*, **23**, 353–8.

Schwartz, J.D., Katz, S.A., Fegley, R.W. and Tockman, M.S. (1988). Analysis of spirometric data from a national sample of healthy 6–24-year-olds (NHANES II). *American Review of Respiratory Disease*, **138**, 1405–14.

Song, S.H., Kang, D.H., Kang, B.S. and Hong, S.K. (1963). Lung volumes and ventilatory responses to high CO_2 and low O_2 in the ama. *Journal of Applied Physiology*, **18**, 466–70.

Sonne, L.J. and Davis, J.A. (1982). Increased exercise performance in patients with severe COPD following inspiratory resistive training. *Chest*, **81**, 436–9.

Stenberg, J., Åstrand, P.O., Ekblom, B. *et al.* (1967). Hemodynamic response to work with different muscle groups, sitting and supine. *Journal of Applied Physiology*, **22**, 61–70.

Thurlbeck, W.M. (1982). Postnatal human lung growth. *Thorax*, **37**, 564–71.

Townsend, M.C. (1984). Spirometric forced expiratory volumes measured in the standing versus the sitting posture. *American Review of Respiratory Disease*, **130**, 123–4.

Turcotte, R.A., Perrault, H., Marcotte, J.E. and Beland, M. (1992). A test for the measurement of pulmonary diffusing capacity during high intensity exercise. *Journal of Sports Sciences*, **10**, 229–35.

Turino, G.M., Bergofsky, E.H., Goldring, R.M. and Fishman A.P. (1963). Effect of exercise on pulmonary diffusing capacity. *Journal of Applied Physiology*, **18**, 447–56.

Turner, J.M., Mead, J. and Wohl, M.E. (1968). Elasticity of human lungs in relation to age. *Journal of Applied Physiology*, **25**, 664–71.

Tzankoff, S.P., Robinson, S., Pyke, F.S. and Brown, C.A. (1972). Physiological adjustments to work in older men as affected by physical training. *Journal of Applied Physiology*, **33**, 346–50.

Van de Wal, B.W., Erasmus, L.D. and Hechter, R. (1971). Sitting and standing heights in Bantu and white South Africans – The significance in relation to pulmonary function values. *South African Medical Journal*, **45 (Suppl)**, 568–70.

Wasserman, K., Hansen, J.E., Sue, D.Y. and Whipp, B.J. (1987). *Principles of Exercise Testing and Interpretation*, (Lea and Febiger, Philadelphia, PA), pp. 33–6.

HAEMATOLOGY

Ron Maughan, John Leiper and Mike Greaves

4.1 AIMS

The aims of this chapter are to:
- describe practical issues and procedures relevant to blood sampling and handling,
- explain the rationale for haematology measurement procedures most widely used in the exercise science laboratory,
- describe some of the factors that influence haematological variables and their physiological significance.

4.2 INTRODUCTION

A high aerobic capacity is a prerequisite for success in all endurance-based sports, and many different factors contribute to the body's ability to derive energy from oxidative metabolism. Although maximum cardiac output is often considered to be the limiting factor to oxygen transport, this is true only in the absence of another limitation. For different individuals and in different situations, any of the steps in the chain of oxygen transport and use, from pulmonary function to mitochondrial enzyme activity, may determine this limit. This includes the transport of oxygen in the circulation, which in turn depends on the blood haemoglobin concentration and the total red blood cell mass. For this reason, athletes are often concerned to know their circulating haemoglobin concentration, as this is the most widely understood measure of adequacy or otherwise of an individual's iron status and is also the marker that is most closely related to exercise performance. Although it can be argued that other markers may be of more diagnostic use, it is generally accepted that some form of haematological assessment is an important part of any routine screening of athletes being carried out as part of a sports science or sports medicine athlete support programme.

A high circulating haemoglobin concentration can confer performance advantages, and abuse of erythropoietin, the hormone that stimulates red blood cell formation, is thought to be common in some groups of sportsmen and women. For this reason, the Governing Bodies of some sports have established an upper limit to the acceptable level of circulating red cells. In cycling, a rider with a haematocrit level of 52% or more is deemed to have committed a doping offence, and is liable to disqualification and suspension, even though this value is within the normal range for men (Table 4.1). Haematological assessment is thus also an essential part of doping control in many sports.

In the exercise laboratory, an individual's haematological profile can be seen as an important descriptor alongside other variables such as age, height, weight or body fat content. Measurement of changes in blood volume or plasma volume can also be important in assessing the significance of changes in the circulating concentration of a variety of hormones, substrates, metabolites and other organic and inorganic components. Haemoconcentration or haemodilution may cause or obscure changes in the

Kinanthropometry and Exercise Physiology Laboratory Manual: Tests, Procedures and Data. 2nd Edition, Volume 2: Exercise Physiology Edited by RG Eston and T Reilly. Published by Routledge, London, June 2001

Table 4.1 Normal values

	Units	Men	Women
Haemoglobin	g l^{-1}	13.5–17.5	11.5–15.5
Red cell count	$\times 10^{12}$ l^{-1}	4.5–6.5	3.9–5.6
Haematocrit (Hct, PCV)	l^{-1}, %	40–52	36–48
Mean cell volume	fl	80–95	80–95
Plasma volume	ml kg^{-1} body mass	45±5	45±5
Serum iron	µmol l^{-1}	10–30	10–30
Serum transferrin	g^{-1}	2.0–4.0	2.0–4.0
Total iron binding capacity	µmol l^{-1}	40–75	40–75
Serum ferritin	µg^{-1}	40–340	14–150

circulating concentration of the entity of interest (Kargotich *et al.*, 1998). Whether or not one should correct measured concentrations for changes in the volume of distribution depends on the question that is being asked.

This chapter will focus on a detailed description of the practical issues relevant to blood sampling and handling, and on those haematology measurement procedures most widely used in the exercise science laboratory. More sophisticated measures used in the clinical assessment of iron status and in the physiology research laboratory will be described more briefly as a full description of the methodology is outwith the scope of a single chapter.

4.3 BLOOD SAMPLING AND HANDLING

There are several different methods and sites of blood sampling that can be used in the collection of samples for analysis, and the results obtained will be affected by both sampling site and the procedures used in sample collection. The chosen procedures will be determined by the needs of the investigator and the facilities available. Whatever the method used, the safety of the subject and the investigator is paramount, and appropriate sterile or antiseptic precautions must be observed. Strict safety

precautions must be followed at all times in the sampling and handling of blood. It is wise to assume that all samples are infected and to treat them accordingly. This means wearing gloves and appropriate protective clothing and following guidelines for handling of samples and disposal of waste material. Used needles, cannulae and lancets must be disposed of immediately in a suitable sharps bin: re-sheathing of used needles must never be attempted. Sharps – whether contaminated or not – must always be disposed of in an approved container and must never be mixed with other waste. All other contaminated materials must be disposed of using appropriate and clearly identified waste containers. Any spillage of blood must be treated immediately.

The main sampling procedures involve collection of arterial, venous, arterialized venous or capillary blood. In most routine laboratory investigations of interest to the sports scientist, arterial blood sampling is impractical and unnecessarily invasive, and will not be considered in detail here. Where arterial blood is required, arterial puncture may be used, but in most situations, collection of arterialized venous blood as described below gives an adequate representation of arterial blood.

4.3.1 VENOUS BLOOD

Venous blood sampling is probably the method of choice for most routine purposes: sampling from a superficial forearm or ante-cubital vein is simple, painless and relatively free from risk of complications. Sampling may be by venous puncture or by an indwelling cannula. Where repeated sampling is necessary at short time intervals, introduction of a cannula is obviously preferred to avoid repeated venous punctures. Either a plastic cannula or a butterfly-type cannula can be used. The latter has obvious limitations if introduced into an ante-cubital vein, as movement of the elbow is severely restricted. However, because it is smaller and therefore less painful for the subject, as well as being very much less expensive, the butterfly cannula is often preferable if used in a forearm vein, provided that long-term access is not required. A 21 G cannula is adequate for most purposes, and only where large volumes of blood are required will a larger size be necessary. In most situations where vigorous movements are likely, the forearm site is preferred to the elbow (Figure 4.1). A disadvantage of

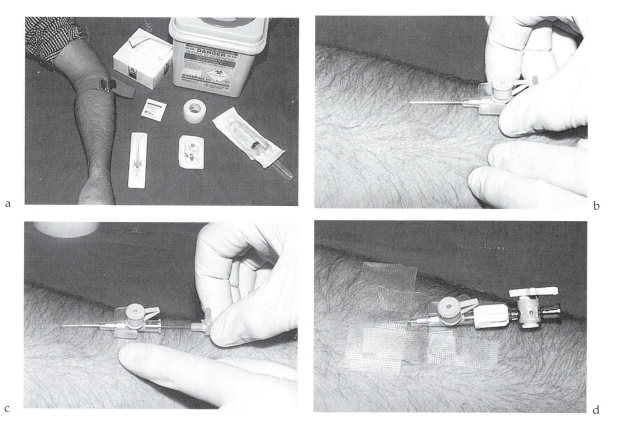

a   b   c   d

Figure 4.1 (a) Venous sampling from a superficial forearm vein is conveniently accomplished using an indwelling plastic cannula. (b) The cannula is inserted into the vein. If slight tension is applied to the skin, this should be completely painless. (c) The needle is withdrawn, leaving the plastic sheath in place. This is then advanced into the vein. (d) A three-way tap is attached to the end of the cannula, allowing samples to be withdrawn and the cannula to be flushed with saline as necessary.

venous cannulation is the need to ensure that clotting of blood in the cannula does not occur. This is easily avoided by flushing with sterile isotonic saline, but this in turn requires stringent hygiene procedures. Where intermittent sampling is performed, the cannula may be flushed with a bolus of saline to which heparin (10–50 IU ml^{-1} of saline) is added, allowing the subject freedom to move around between samples. Alternatively where the subject is to remain static, as in a cycle or treadmill exercise test, a continuous slow infusion (about 0.3 ml min^{-1}) of isotonic saline may be used, avoiding the need to add heparin. Collection of samples by venous puncture is not practical in most exercise situations, and increases the risk that samples will be affected by venous occlusion applied during puncture. If repeated venous puncture is used, care must be taken to minimize the duration of any occlusion of blood flow and to ensure that sufficient time is allowed for recovery from interruption of blood flow before samples are collected. The use of a butterfly cannula rather than a needle facilitates the collection of samples without the problems that arise from occlusion of the circulation, even when repeated sampling is not required.

The dead space of a 21 G butterfly cannula is small (about 0.4 ml), and even with the addition of a three-way tap does not exceed about 0.5 ml. It is, however, essential to ensure that the deadspace is completely cleared when taking samples. It is recommended that about 1–1.5 ml be withdrawn through the cannula before each sample is collected.

A disadvantage of the use of a superficial forearm vein is that flow through these veins is very much influenced by skin blood flow, which in turn depends on ambient temperature and the thermoregulatory strain imposed on the individual. In cold conditions, flow to the limbs and to the skin will be low, and venous blood will be highly desaturated. It is easy to observe that, where samples are taken progressively throughout an exercise task, the oxygen content of the venous blood increases progressively, reflecting the increased peripheral blood flow, especially the skin blood flow. Where sampling occurs over time, therefore, and where the degree of arterialization of the venous blood will influence the measures to be made, this may cause major problems. A good example of such a situation is where a tracer – deuterium oxide – is added to an ingested beverage, and the rate of rise of the blood deuterium concentration is used as an index of the combined rates of gastric emptying and intestinal absorption. Deuterium enters the vascular compartment as the blood passes through the gut, and leaves as it equilibrates with body water. The rate of equilibration with body water will depend on a number of factors, but it is clear that the arterial deuterium concentration will always be higher than the venous concentration, at least until all the ingested beverage has been absorbed and complete equilibration among all body water compartments has occurred. If peripheral venous blood sampling is used, and if these measurements are made during exercise or in a situation where ambient temperature changes, the degree of arterialization of the venous blood will change, and the values for deuterium accumulation will be meaningless. For some metabolites which are routinely measured, the difference between arterial and venous concentrations is relatively small and in many cases it may be ignored. Where a difference does occur and is of importance, the effect of a change in arterialization of the blood at the sampling site may be critical.

4.3.2 ARTERIALIZED VENOUS BLOOD

Where arterial blood is required, there is no alternative to arterial puncture, but for most practical purposes, blood collected from a superficial vein on the dorsal surface of a heated hand is indistinguishable from arterial blood. This reflects both the very high flow rate and the opening of arterio-venous shunts in the hand. Sampling can conveniently be achieved by introduction of a butterfly cannula into a suitable vein (Figure 4.2). The hand is

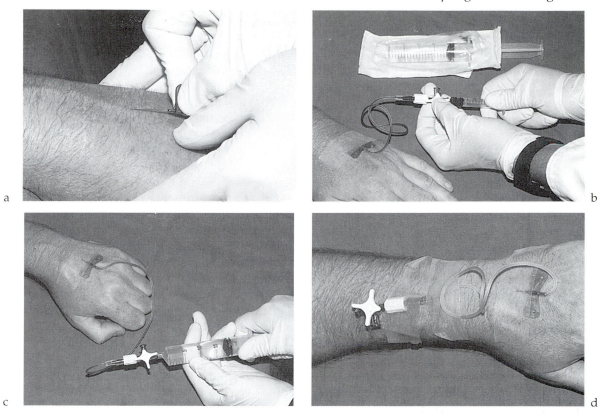

a   b   c   d

Figure 4.2 (a) A butterfly style cannula is convenient for sampling of arterialised venous blood from a dorsal vein in a hand that has been warmed by immersion for 10 minutes in warm (42°C) water. (b) Blood samples are withdrawn from the cannula as necessary via a syringe connected to the cannula by way of a three-way tap. (c) After sampling, the cannula is flushed with saline, which should be heparinized if there is more than a short time (1–2 minutes) between samples. (d) The cannula is taped in place, allowing the subject free use of the hand between sample collections.

first heated, either by immersion up to the forearm for at least 10 minutes in hot (about 42°C) water (Forster *et al.*, 1972) or by insertion into a hot air box (McGuire *et al.*, 1976). If hot water immersion is used prior to exercise, arterialization – as indicated by oxygen saturation – can be maintained for some considerable time by wearing a glove, allowing this technique to be used during exercise studies. This procedure allows large volumes of blood to be collected without problems. Capillary sampling by the 'finger prick' method cannot guarantee adequate volumes for many procedures.

4.3.3 CAPILLARY BLOOD

Where only small samples of blood are required, capillary blood samples can readily be obtained from a fingertip or ear lobe. The use of micromethods for analysis means that the limited sample volume that can be obtained should not necessarily be a problem in metabolic studies. It is possible to make duplicate measurements of the concentrations of glucose, lactate, pyruvate, alanine, free fatty acids, glycerol, acetoacetate and 3-hydroxybutyrate, as well as a number of other metabolites on a single 20 µl blood sample using routine laboratory methods (Maughan, 1982).

The sampling site should be arterialized, by immersion of the whole hand in hot (42°C) water in the case of the fingertip, and by the use of a rubefacient in the case of the ear lobe. Samples can be obtained without stimulating vasodilatation, but bleeding is slower, the volumes that can be reliably collected are smaller, and the composition of the sample is more variable. It is essential that a free-flowing sample is obtained. If pressure is applied, an excess of plasma over red cells will be obtained. Samples are most conveniently collected into calibrated glass capillaries where only small volumes are required (typically 10–100 µl). The blood must never be expelled from these tubes by mouth, because of the obvious risks involved.

Where larger volumes are required, a clean plastic or glass vessel may be used for collection and the blood then pipetted in the normal way using an automatic pipette. Use of suitable analytical methods allows most of the metabolites of interest to be measured on samples collected in this way. More difficulty arises when larger volumes are required. Nonetheless, a volume sufficient for the measurement of haematocrit, which is normally measured in triplicate and requires a blood volume of about 150 µl, and haemoglobin (2 × 20 µl) in addition to the metabolites referred to above is usually possible. Volumes greater than about 0.5 ml present real difficulties.

4.3.4 PROCEDURES FOR CAPILLARY BLOOD SAMPLING

As indicated above, capillary samples are commonly obtained from the ear lobe or from a digit. In most situations, the fingertip site is to be preferred. In order to ensure that a free-flowing sample can be obtained, it is helpful to immerse the hand to the wrist in hot (42°C) water or in a heated box for 10–15 minutes before the sample is collected. If necessary, the hand can be kept warm by continued immersion between samples where this is

practicable. Where this is not possible, some degree of arterialization can be maintained by wearing a glove. The degree of arterialization can be verified by measurement of blood gases.

A clean laboratory coat and disposable gloves must be worn during collection and handling of samples. The sampling kit – prepared in advance – will consist of:

- Lancets (a Lancer (B.D. Ltd., Dublin, Ireland) may be preferred)
- Sterile alcohol swabs
- Tissues
- Rubber gloves
- Disposal facility: sharps bin for used lancets and clear autoclavable bags for contaminated waste

For handling blood, collection into graduated glass capillaries is preferred. Larger volumes may be collected directly into disposable plastic beakers, but such volumes are difficult to collect reliably using the 'finger prick' technique, and there is a real danger that clotting will occur before sufficient volume is obtained. Suitably prepared and labelled tubes for sample reception should be prepared in advance if required. For most metabolite analysis where spectrophotometric or fluorimetric analysis is used, collection of 20 µl of blood into 200 µl of deproteinizing agent is appropriate. This may be facilitated by the use of heparinized capillary tubes, which will hold about 50 µl of blood. The blood can be ejected from the capillary and 20 µl aliquots transferred using a pipette.

Subjects should be instructed to wash their hands before the procedure begins. The sampling site should be swabbed with alcohol and wiped dry with a tissue, and the cleaned area stabbed with a single prick. It is essential to ensure a free-flowing sample: the puncture wound should not be squeezed. If pressure is applied, extracellular fluid will contaminate the sample collected, and some haemolysis is also inevitable. The results will therefore be invalid. The extent to which contamination with extracellular fluid will invalidate the results depends on the measurements to be made. The first drop of blood to appear should be wiped away with a clean tissue. The capillary should be filled to about 1 cm beyond the graduation mark: the outside of the capillary should then be wiped clean, and the end touched against a tissue until the bottom of the blood meniscus is aligned with the graduation mark. Transfer into the deproteinization agent is achieved by use of a rubber blow-bulb, with repeated aspiration and dispensing until all the residual blood is washed out of the capillary. Samples should always be collected in duplicate.

The site of the puncture wound should be wiped clean. If bleeding continues, a waterproof dressing should be applied. A new puncture must be made when repeated sampling is required, unless the time interval between samples is short. It is unwise to rely on continued bleeding from the same site.

4.4 BLOOD TREATMENT AFTER COLLECTION

Analysis of most metabolites can be carried out using either whole blood, plasma or serum. This requires a recognition of the differential distribution of most metabolites and substrates between the plasma and the intracellular space. It is important to recognize also that changes in the plasma volume during exercise or other situations may be quite different from the changes in the whole blood volume, and the effects of changes in the distribution space may require consideration. For most practical purposes, it is convenient to use whole blood for the measurement of most metabolites. The obvious exception is the free fatty acid concentration, which should be measured using plasma or serum. Glucose, glycerol and lactate are commonly measured on either plasma or whole blood. Most of the other metabolites of interest to the exercise physiologist are normally measured on whole blood. The differences become significant where there is a concentration difference between the intracellular and extracellular compartments, or where there is a change in

this distribution over the time course of an experiment.

If plasma is to be obtained by centrifugation of the sample, a suitable anticoagulant must be added. A variety of agents can be used, depending on the measurements to be made. The potassium salt of EDTA is a convenient anticoagulant, but is clearly inappropriate when plasma potassium is to be measured. Heparin is a suitable alternative in this situation. For serum collection, blood should be added to a plain tube and left for at least one hour before centrifugation: clotting will take place more rapidly if the sample is left in a warm place. If there is a need to stop glycolysis in serum or plasma samples (for example, where the concentration of glucose, lactate or other glycolytic intermediates is to be measured), fluoride should be added.

Where metabolites are to be measured on whole blood, the most convenient method is immediate deproteinization of the sample. The primary reason for deproteinization of whole blood is to inactivate the enzymes that would otherwise alter the concentrations of substances of interest after the sample has been withdrawn. A variety of agents can be used to achieve this: perchloric acid or trichloroacetic acid are equally effective. A 2.5% (0.3 N) solution of perchloric acid is recommended for general use. This can be prepared by adding 36 ml of the 70% acid to 964 ml of water.

Where blood samples are to be collected for analysis of glucose and lactate, it is convenient to add 100 µl of whole blood to 1 ml of 2.5% perchloric acid. Smaller volumes can be used, but pipetting and other measurement errors are reduced if the larger volume is used. The use of a 10:1 dilution reduces volumetric errors due to the presence of a substantial volume of precipitate. The tubes containing the acid should be prepared in advance and kept in iced water. Deproteinization should take place immediately upon collection of the sample. It is, however, recommended that an anticoagulant should be used. Blood should be transferred using an automatic pipette as described

106 *Haematology*

below. The deproteinized sample should be kept on ice until it can be centrifuged. A note of caution: glucose is not stable in this acid medium, even when frozen at −20°C. Lactate, pyruvate and other metabolites can be stored frozen, but glucose and ammonia should be analysed within a few hours of collection. If frozen samples are to be analysed, they must be centrifuged again after thawing.

4.5 MEASUREMENT OF CIRCULATING HAEMOGLOBIN CONCENTRATION

Haemoglobin is the porphyrin-iron-protein compound that binds with oxygen and gives blood its characteristic red colour. Many different methods have been developed to determine the concentration of haemoglobin and its derivatives in circulating and occult blood. The techniques usually depend on reactions involving the iron component of haemoglobin or the pseudoperoxidase activity of the haem. The two most common methods currently used are the oxyhaemoglobin and the cyanmethaemoglobin techniques. The oxyhaemoglobin method is currently mainly used in conjunction with automated or semi-automated haemoglobinometers, while the cyanmethaemoglobin method is the technique of choice for manual procedures.

4.5.1 THE CYANMETHAEMOGLOBIN METHOD

In 1966 the International Congress of Haematology recommended this method be the accepted routine manual procedure for measurement of haemoglobin in blood. The main reasons for adopting this as the standard technique were:

1. The method requires dilution of blood with a single reagent.
2. All forms of haemoglobin likely to occur in the circulation are determined.
3. The colour produced is suitable for measurement in filter photometers and narrow-band spectrophotometers because its absorption band at 540 nm is broad and relatively flat.

4. Standards prepared from either crystalline haemoglobin or washed erythrocytes when stored in brown glass containers and in sterile conditions are stable for at least 9 months (<2% change in absorbance).

(a) Principle

The iron of haem in haemoglobin, oxyhaemoglobin and carboxyhaemoglobin is oxidized to the ferric state by ferricyanide to form methaemoglobin. Methaemoglobin then combines with ionized cyanide to produce the stable, red cyanmethaemoglobin which is measured photometrically at 540 nm.

Cyanmethaemoglobin solutions generally obey Beer's Law within the concentration range of interest at a wavelength of 540 nm, and a calibration curve can therefore be constructed using a reagent blank as a zero standard and a single additional standard of known concentration. Secondary standards, prepared from blood and Drabkin's reagent, can be calibrated against the commercial standard and then used for construction of the calibration curve.

The method outlined below uses a sample volume of 10 μl and a reagent volume of 2.5 ml, and the reaction is always carried out in duplicate. Smaller sample volumes can be used, but the precision of the assay, which has a coefficient of variation of about 1–2% in the hands of an experienced operator, declines with very small volumes of blood. Larger volumes are wasteful of reagent.

(b) Procedure

Drabkin's Reagent: This reagent is stable for several months when stored in a brown bottle. As cyanide is a constituent of Drabkin's solution care must be taken in preparing and storing this reagent.
  1.0 g $NaHCO_3$
  0.2 g $K_3Fe(CN)_6$
  0.05 g KCN
Make up to 1 litre of solution.

Standard: 180 g l^{-1} human methaemoglobin

(available from Sigma Ltd (Poole, UK) or BDH (Poole, UK))

Calibrate: The calibration curve is prepared by measuring the optical density of the Drabkin's reagent (zero standard) and of the 180 g l^{-1} Sigma standard at 540 nm without dilution. Addition of other standards will only confirm the linearity of the calibration curve.

Sample assay: In duplicate, add 10 μl sample to 2.5 ml of Drabkin's reagent and mix thoroughly; incubate at room temperature for at least 10 minutes. Read samples at 540 nm. The colour is stable for several hours if kept in the dark. Standards should be exposed to the same conditions as the samples.

4.5.2 FACTORS AFFECTING MEASURED HAEMOGLOBIN CONCENTRATION

Many different factors – independent of the analytical method used – will affect the measured haemoglobin concentration. The sampling site and method can affect the haemoglobin concentration, as arterial, capillary and venous samples differ in a number of respects due to fluid exchange between the vascular and extravascular spaces and to differences in the distribution of red blood cells (Harrison, 1985). The venous plasma to red cell ratio is higher than that of arterial blood.

The measured haemoglobin concentration is also markedly influenced by the physical activity, hydration status and posture of the subject prior to sample collection, although the total body haemoglobin content is clearly not acutely affected by these factors. Posture is particularly important and should be standardized for a period of at least 15 minutes prior to sampling as plasma volumes will change significantly over this time (Figure 4.3a) (Harrison, 1985). This effect can be demonstrated reproducibly as a simple student laboratory class. Haemoglobin concentration is rather stable while a subject remains standing at rest, but increases promptly on assuming a seated or supine position. The time course of change is exponential and is largely complete within 15–20 minutes: it is then reversed with a similar time course on returning to the original posture.

Haemodynamic changes caused by postural shifts will alter the fluid exchange across the capillary bed, leading to plasma volume changes that will cause changes in the circulating haemoglobin concentration. On going from a supine position to standing, plasma volume falls by about 10% and whole blood volume by about 5% (Harrison, 1985). This corresponds to a change in the measured haemoglobin concentration of about 7 g l^{-1}. These

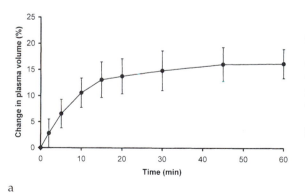
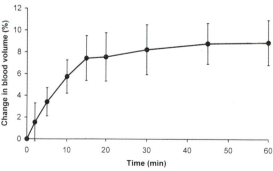

a

b

Figure 4.3 Calculated plasma volume (a) and blood volume (b) change on going from an upright to a supine position. The plasma volume change is relatively much greater than the change in blood volume: the entire blood volume change is accounted for by the changing plasma volume.

changes are reversed on going from an upright to a seated or supine position. These changes make it imperative that posture is controlled in studies where haemoglobin changes are to be used as an index of changes in blood and plasma volume over the time course of an experiment. It is, however, common to see studies reported in the literature where samples were collected from subjects resting in a supine position prior to exercise in a seated (cycling or rowing) or upright (treadmill walking or running) position. The changing blood volume not only invalidates any haematological measures made in the early stages of exercise; it also confounds cardiovascular measures, as the stroke volume and heart rate will also be affected by the blood volume.

Normal haemoglobin values for men are higher by about 20–40 g l^{-1} than those typically found in women, although it should be recognized that there is some overlap in the normal ranges for men and women. Many factors will affect the measured haemoglobin concentration. Many published reports, and most textbooks, describe a haemodilution as one of the characteristics of endurance-trained athletes. This is ascribed to a disproportionate expansion of the plasma volume relative to the red cell mass. In a comprehensive review of the published data, and of the methodology used in these studies, however, Sawka and Coyle (1999) concluded that the evidence is not as convincing as might be thought. There are also problems with sample collection from athletes in daily training because of the short-term changes that occur during and after a single exercise bout.

The circulating haemoglobin concentration generally increases during exercise, but the magnitude of the increase depends very much on the exercise intensity (Figure 4.4). At high exercise intensities, there is a marked fall in plasma volume due to the movement of water into the active muscle. Intracellular osmolality rises sharply due to the increased concentration of glycolytic intermediates. In prolonged exercise, at intensities of about 60–75% of maximum

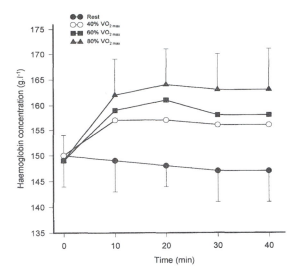

Figure 4.4 Effect of exercise intensity on measured haemoglobin (Hb) concentration. The circulating Hb concentration increases as a consequence of the plasma volume decrease: the rapid decrease in plasma volume at the onset of high-intensity exercise results from a redistribution of body water rather than a loss of water from the body.

oxygen uptake ($\dot{V}O_2$max) the initial fall in plasma volume that occurs within the first few minutes of exercise is smaller in magnitude and is often reversed with time as exercise progresses (Figures 4.5a and 4.5b; Maughan, Bethell and Leiper, 1996). After prolonged hard exercise, the haemoglobin concentration is likely to be elevated, and this will return to the pre-exercise level over the few hours following exercise, with the rate and magnitude of this change being influenced primarily by the volume and composition of fluids ingested, but also by activity, posture and other factors. If sampling continues beyond this time, however, a haemodilution will be observed, and this may persist for 2–3 days (Robertson *et al.*, 1988).

Hydration status clearly affects blood volume and therefore the concentration of all circulating variables, including haemoglobin concentration. The significance of this effect is clearly seen when comparing responses to exercise with and without fluid ingestion (Figure 4.5). The rise in haemoglobin concentration is smaller

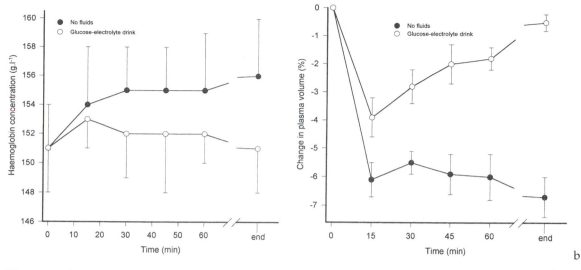

Figure 4.5 (a) Haemoconcentration in the later stages of exercise results from an interaction of two effects: a loss of body water due to sweat loss and a redistribution of fluid between the vascular and extravascular spaces. (b) Ingestion of fluids attenuates the change in plasma volume that occurs. These results are from a trial where fluid was ingested immediately before exercise and at intervals throughout the exercise period.

when fluid is ingested because of the better maintenance of blood volume. The dehydrated individual will have an elevated haemoglobin concentration, and care must therefore be taken to ensure euhydration if 'normal' values are to be obtained. These issues have been extensively debated in relation to the possibility that cyclists who have a high haematocrit level may find that this is further increased if they allow themselves to become dehydrated, leading to ejection from competition if the value exceeds 52%.

Other factors affecting the normal values include cigarette smoking, which causes a chronic elevation of the circulating haemoglobin concentration in part due to tissue hypoxia secondary to increased carbon monoxide levels and carboxyhaemoglobin formation. Ascent to high altitude also results in an increase in haemoglobin concentration. There is an initial fluid retention followed by diuresis. The latter may be sufficient to cause a reduction in plasma volume and a consequent increase in haemoglobin concentration and haematocrit through haemoconcentration. This is followed after a period of days to weeks by an erythropoietin-driven increase in the rate of erythropoiesis in response to hypoxia, and a true erythrocytosis with a raised haemoglobin concentration (polycythaemia). This adaptation confers a potentially increased oxygen-carrying capacity on return to sea level, but the evidence that it is this which translates to an improved exercise performance is not strong. Indigenous populations resident at an altitude of more than 1500 m have a chronic true polycythaemia.

Polycythaemia is occasionally constitutional, as a familial condition. This can arise through synthesis of a haemoglobin variant with increased oxygen affinity, through increased sensitivity to erythropoietin or through a genetically determined abnormality of the erythropoietin receptor which results in a loss of the 'off switch' for erythropoiesis. These erythropoietin-related familial polycythaemic conditions might be expected to confer increased oxygen-carrying capacity and a relative increase in endurance capacity in affected individuals. More commonly, in clinical practice, polycythaemia results from cardiac, respiratory or bone marrow disorders.

4.6 MEASUREMENT OF RED CELL PARAMETERS

4.6.1 PACKED CELL VOLUME (PCV) OR SPUN HAEMATOCRIT (HCT)

Packed cell volume is the measurement of the volume occupied by the erythrocytes compared with the overall volume of a column of the whole blood. Anticoagulated blood is spun at about 12000 g for 3–5 minutes in a glass capillary tube. The measured length of the column of packed erythrocytes is compared with that of the total length of the column of blood in the tube. Plain or heparinized micro-haematocrit capillary tubes can be used, but they must conform to the British Standard 4316 (1968) that stipulates that the capillary bore must be less than ±2% of the mean throughout the tube. Heparinized or EDTA-treated blood should be spun in plain capillary tubes, and heparinized tubes are used to collect capillary blood directly. Plain tubes may be used provided the sample is to be processed immediately, but the use of an anticoagulant is recommended in most situations to ensure that no clotting occurs. If there is any clotting of the sample, it must be discarded.

Method: Well-mixed blood is drawn into the tube by capillary attraction without the introduction of any air bubbles. The tube should be filled to approximately $2/3$ to $3/4$ of its length. Each blood sample should be measured in triplicate. The capillary end not dipped in blood is sealed by inserting that end into a block of 'Cristaseal' (clay-type sealant) (BDH Laboratories, Poole, UK) and twisting the tube into the clay. These tubes are fragile, so care must be taken to avoid breakages with the associated loss of sample and risk of injury. Haematocrit is normally measured in triplicate. After wiping the outside of the tube, place the capillary in the rotor of the micro-haematocrit centrifuge. The tube must lie in one of the channels in the rotor with the sealed end of the tube resting against the rubber rim. The safety cover is gently screwed down. The centrifuge lid is closed and the tubes spun for 5 minutes.

The spun tube is placed into the channel of the reader. The upper edge of the sealant plug is aligned with the black base line, and the meniscus of the column of blood plasma is aligned with the angled black upper line. The silver line of the movable slide on the reader is set at the level of the top of the packed erythrocyte column and the PCV reading is taken where the silver line cuts the scale on the right hand side of the instrument. It is not easy to measure more precisely than to the nearest 0.5%, and the three measurements should normally agree to within 1%. The mean of the three values should be used.

The PCV was traditionally expressed as a percentage of the whole blood volume (e.g. 45.3%), but it is now recommended that this value be expressed as litres of red cells per litre of whole blood (e.g. $0.453 \, 1 \, l^{-1}$).

Determination of the true proportions of red cells and plasma in the blood requires suitable correction for plasma trapped between the red cells. Corrections of 2–4% are widely used, but Dacie and Lewis (1968) suggested that 1–1.5% is a more realistic figure when the standard microhaematocrit method is used. There are also differences between the central and peripheral haematocrit due to differential distribution of the red blood cells in the circulation. This can cause practical difficulties if, for example, peripheral venous blood is sampled and the degree of arterialization changes due to changes in the distribution of cardiac output (see Harrison (1985) for a discussion of this).

4.6.2 ERYTHROCYTE (RED CELL) COUNT

The red cell count is seldom measured outwith a clinical setting, where it has diagnostic significance. Counting of red and white blood cells was, until recently, a standard laboratory practical class in most undergraduate physiology courses, but this seems now to be rare. Manual methods for cell counting involve counting individual cells in a known volume of diluted blood on a graduated microscope slide, and are tedious and time-consuming. These methods have also all but disappeared from the clinical laboratory, where they have been replaced by automatic cell counters.

The Coulter counter is the most widely known of the automated systems, and operates by passing diluted blood through a small aperture where electrical conductivity is measured. The cell membrane is an effective electrical insulator while the diluent is an electrolyte solution. Each particle displaces electrolyte, giving an electrical pulse proportional in amplitude to the cell volume: counting these signals gives a measure of cell number in the measured volume of sample and of the volume of each of the cells counted. These automated procedures are more reliable than the manual methods. A measure of total red cell volume is obtained from the mean cell volume and the total red cell count.

The modern Coulter counter incorporates an autosampler and spectrophotometer which permits automated measurement of haemoglobin concentration. While this automation has considerable attractions, including a high level of accuracy in the measures of red cell count and haemoglobin concentration, care must be taken in the interpretation of the measures of cell volume. The diluent commonly used in the preparation of samples for analysis is not isotonic with normal human blood plasma: Isoton II (Beckman Coulter Co., High Wycombe, UK) has an osmolality of about 340 mosmol kg^{-1}, compared with an osmolality of human plasma of about 285–290 mosmol kg^{-1}. Because the red cell membrane is freely permeable to water, a rapid equilibration will take place on mixing of blood with the diluent, leading to a change (in the case of Isoton II there will be a decrease) in the red cell volume. The measured volume is therefore different, by an amount proportional to the difference in osmolality between the plasma and the diluent, from the volume of the cells while in the circulation. In situations where the plasma

osmolality changes substantially, as during intense or prolonged exercise, this will invalidate measures made using automated cell-counting procedures.

4.7 ANAEMIA AND THE MEASUREMENT OF IRON STATUS

Athletes are often concerned about the possibility of anaemia, which will adversely affect exercise performance, and the usual measure used to assess this is the circulating haemoglobin concentration. This has some value, as iron deficiency does not adversely affect performance until it is sufficiently severe to cause a fall in the circulating haemoglobin level (Weight *et al.*, 1988). Haemoglobin concentration, however, is a poor index of an individual's iron status and more reliable measures should be used in any screening where there is reason to suspect that iron status might be suboptimal. The prevalence of iron deficiency anaemia is not different between the athletic population and the general population, but whereas mild anaemia may be of little consequence to the sedentary individual, it will have a negative effect on all exercise situations where oxygen transport is a factor.

4.7.1 ASSESSMENT OF IRON STATUS

When anaemia is due to iron deficiency, erythropoiesis is microcytic, and the mean cell volume (MCV) is therefore low. The adequacy or otherwise of the body's iron stores is most commonly assessed clinically by measurement of the serum concentration of ferritin. Ferritin is tissue storage iron and the small proportion present in blood generally reflects total body iron stores. A low serum ferritin concentration is therefore diagnostic of tissue iron deficiency and this reduction precedes any fall in MCV and haemoglobin concentration. This early warning of impending anaemia is clearly advantageous in any routine monitoring of athletes. However the serum ferritin concentration rises as a response to inflammatory and malignant conditions, and in such circumstances the serum concentration of ferritin may be misleadingly normal, or even raised, in the face of iron deficiency. This is not a significant problem in otherwise healthy subjects.

The serum iron concentration is also reduced in iron deficiency and this is accompanied by a rise in the total iron binding capacity, which represents transferrin, the principal iron transport protein in blood. Transferrin is normally around one-third saturated with iron, and a saturation of <15% is insufficient to support normal erythropoiesis, which becomes iron-deficient. Although low serum iron, low transferrin saturation and increased iron-binding capacity are typical of iron deficiency, the serum iron is also reduced in systemic disease even in the face of normal iron stores. This fall is usually accompanied by a reduced iron-binding capacity, in contrast to the typical increase in iron deficiency.

4.7.2 RED CELL TURNOVER AND CELL AGE

Erythropoiesis takes place in the red bone marrow in post-natal life. In adults, red marrow is restricted to the cavities of the flat and proximal long bones, especially the skull, sternum, ribs, vertebrae, pelvis and proximal ends of the femora. The released red cells circulate for 120 days and senescent cells are removed by macrophages of the reticuloendothelial system in liver, spleen and bone marrow. For the first 48 hours after this release, red cells contain residual ribonucleic acid (RNA) which gives these immature red cells a purple tinge on a stained blood film. These reticulocytes can be more readily identified and counted by staining of a spread blood film using a supravital stain. An absolute increase in reticulocytes, which normally represent less than 1% of red cells, is indicative of increased erythropoietic activity, typically in response to acute blood loss or shortened red cell life span due to haemolysis. A more accurate assessment of total erythropoiesis is best achieved through measurement of iron turnover. This can be measured using an isotope of iron, ^{52}Fe or ^{59}Fe, which binds to transferrin *in vivo*

and is cleared from plasma with a half-time of 60 to 120 minutes when erythropoiesis is in steady state and normal.

4.8 ALTITUDE TRAINING, BLOOD DOPING AND ERYTHROPOIETIN

Most endurance athletes are aware of the benefits of an elevated haemoglobin concentration, and can set about trying to achieve this in a number of ways. As indicated earlier, residence at high altitude results in a measurable increase in haemoglobin concentration due to an increase in body red cell mass in response to increased secretion of erythropoietin. This may be one mechanism for the perceived benefit of training at altitude. Historically, transfusion of red cells has been used to achieve an increase in body red cell mass, improved oxygen carriage and endurance performance. Transfusion of homologous blood (from a donor) carries many risks, including transfusion reactions and transmission of infections such as hepatitis. The same ends have been achieved more safely by transfusion of pre-donated autologous red cells. Because a donor who is iron-replete can replenish the red cells in a donated unit (around 400 ml of blood) in one week, and because the shelf life of blood or separated red cells under appropriate conditions is up to 5 weeks, it is possible to increase the haemoglobin concentration by up to 50 g l^{-1} from normal by transfusion of pre-donated autologous cells. Transfusion of as little as the equivalent of two units has been shown to improve aerobic work capacity and endurance performance under laboratory conditions. More recently erythropoietin has been employed to achieve the same ends as blood doping by transfusion. Erythropoietin manufactured by recombinant techniques has been and is readily available for clinical use, principally to treat the anaemia of chronic renal failure. When administered parenterally, along with intensive iron supplementation, to healthy individuals, it causes a predictable increase in body red cell mass, haemoglobin concentration and haematocrit which is likely to be performance-enhancing in endurance events. Should the haemoglobin be allowed to rise excessively, blood hyperviscosity results with reduced capillary perfusion. This situation, compounded by a further rise in haematocrit due to dehydration during competition, probably accounts for some cases of sudden death amongst competitive sportsmen using erythropoietin. Blood doping, by transfusion or pharmacological means, is banned under the International Olympic Committee (IOC) regulations. However, neither method can be detected by urine-testing and increased haematocrit can occur in other situations, as described earlier. This represents a difficult challenge for governing bodies in a range of sports.

4.9 BLOOD AND PLASMA VOLUME CHANGES

4.9.1 MEASUREMENT OF BLOOD AND PLASMA VOLUME

Many studies require the measurement of the blood and/or plasma volume. Blood and plasma volumes can be determined using a number of different dilution methods, but all of these are relatively invasive. They also require sophisticated labelling facilities and suffer from the problem of not being amenable to repeated measurements at short time intervals.

In many investigations, it is more important to know how these measurements change over the time course of a study than to know their absolute magnitude. Because of the practical difficulties, the indirect estimation of plasma or blood volume changes is more widely used in exercise physiology laboratories and will be discussed in greater detail here. First, however, a brief description of the methods for determination of blood and plasma volumes will be given.

Detailed descriptions of methods for measurement of red cell volume and plasma volume can be found in Dacie and Lewis (1984). In principle, a small volume of tracer material is injected intravenously and its dilution measured after allowing time for mixing in the circulation. The plasma volume can thus be measured using human albumin labelled with radioactive iodine (^{131}I or ^{125}I), although it should be noted that this has limitations as there is some interchange between albumin in plasma and that in extravascular extracellular fluids. There is also some concern regarding the small risk of contamination with infective agents, especially prions, of any product prepared from donor blood. Red cells can be easily labelled with radioactive chromium, technetium or indium (^{51}Cr, ^{99m}Tc, ^{111}In) and from the dilution of labelled injected autologous red cells and the haematocrit the total blood volume and red cell volume can be calculated.

4.9.2 ESTIMATION OF BLOOD AND PLASMA VOLUME CHANGES

Because of the difficulties outlined in the previous section, changes in blood volume are usually estimated without direct measurement of the absolute volume. Changes in the concentration of an endogenous marker can be used as an index of blood volume changes. Total plasma protein and plasma albumin have been used for this purpose, but some exchange of protein across the vascular endothelium does occur in exercise, making these markers unsuitable (Dill and Costill, 1974). Haemoglobin (Hb) is generally accepted as the most appropriate marker: Hb is contained within the red blood cell, and neither enters nor leaves the circulation in significant amounts over the timescale on which most exercise studies are conducted. Haemoglobin also has the added advantage of being easy and inexpensive to measure. It should be noted that the method is not suitable for use over long timescales where significant changes in the circulating Hb mass may occur or in experimental situations where there is a significant blood loss.

A change in haemoglobin concentration reflects, and can be used to calculate, a change in blood volume. Although the absolute plasma volume cannot be determined other than by dilution methods, changes in plasma volume can be calculated if both the Hb concentration and the haematocrit are known: various descriptions of the method have been published, but the most appropriate is that of Dill and Costill (1974). Use of changes in other circulating variables, such as total plasma protein, have been shown to be unreliable: proteins can enter and leave the vascular compartment during exercise (Harrison, 1985). Haemoglobin, which is trapped within the red cells, does not leave the circulation.

As mentioned above, it is not appropriate to use haematocrit (Hct) values derived from automated analysers (such as the widely used Coulter counter) to calculate changes in blood or plasma volume: these analysers rely on dilution of the blood in a medium with a constant osmolality prior to analysis. The osmolality of these solutions is often very different from plasma osmolality: Isoton II has an osmolality of about 340 mosmol kg^{-1}. Because plasma and intracellular osmolality are not the same as that of the diluent, the measured Hct will not reflect the true *in vivo* Hct due to changes in cell volume on being mixed with the diluent after collection. A more serious error arises if the osmolality of the plasma changes, as it almost invariably does when the plasma volume changes. In this situation, calculation of changes in plasma volume based on repeat measures of haematocrit have no validity, although there are many publications in the literature in which Coulter-derived values have been used inappropriately in this way.

4.9.3 CALCULATION OF VOLUME CHANGES

Changes in blood volume (BV), plasma volume (PV) and red cell volume (RCV) can be calculated from the changes in Hb and Hct. The subscripts B and A are used to denote the first (before) and second (after) samples in the following calculations.

$$BV_A = BV_B \times (Hb_B / Hb_A)$$

$$RCV_A = BV_A \times Hct_A$$

$$PV_A = BV_A - RCV_A$$

Percentage changes in BV, PV and RCV can be calculated even though the absolute values in the above equations remain unknown.

$$\Delta BV = 100 \, (BV_A - BV_B) / BV_B$$

$$\Delta RCV = 100 \, (RCV_A - RCV_B) / RCV_B$$

$$\Delta PV = 100 \, (PV_A - PV_B) / PV_B$$

Sample calculation: The calculations described above are demonstrated by a worked example based on the following data obtained before and after exercise:

Before: Hb = 151, Hct = 0.437

After: Hb = 167, Hct = 0.453

If the initial blood volume is assumed to be 100 ml, the blood volume after exercise is given by:

$$BV_A = 100 \, (151 / 167) \text{ ml} = 90.4 \text{ ml}$$

The decrease in blood volume (ΔBV) is therefore:

$$\Delta BV = ((90.4 - 100) / 100) \times 100 = -9.6\%$$

The red cell volume before exercise is 43.7 ml (Hct = 0.437): after exercise the red cell volume is given by:

$$RCV_A = 0.453 \times 90.4 \text{ ml} = 41.0 \text{ ml}$$

The decrease in red cell volume is therefore:

$$((41.0 - 43.7) / 43.7) \times 100 = -6.2\%$$

The plasma volume before exercise was (1 − Hct) × 100 ml, or 56.3 ml. After exercise, the plasma volume was (90.4 − 41.0) ml, or 49.4 ml. The decrease in plasma volume was therefore 6.9 ml, or:

$$((49.4 - 56.3) / 56.3) \times 100 = -12.3\%$$

Where some indication of the absolute magnitude of the volume shifts is required, an estimate of blood volume based on anthropometric data may be made. Several data sets are available, and a reasonable estimate may be that blood volume equals 75 ml kg^{-1} body mass in men and 65 ml kg^{-1} body mass in women (Åstrand and Rodahl, 1986).

REFERENCES

Åstrand, P.O. and Rodahl, K. (1986). *Textbook of Work Physiology*, 3rd edn. (McGraw Hill, New York).

Dacie, J.V. and Lewis, S.M. (1968). *Practical Haematology*. 4th edn. (Churchill, London). pp. 45–9.

Dacie, J.V. and Lewis, S.M. (1984). Blood volume, Chapter 9. In *Practical Haematology*, 6th edn. (Churchill Livingstone, London).

Dill, B.D. and Costill, D.L. (1974). Calculation of percentage changes in volumes of blood, plasma, and red cells in dehydration. *Journal of Applied Physiology*, **37**, 247–8.

Forster, H.V. and Dempsey, J.A., Thomson J., *et al.* (1972). Estimation of arterial PO_2, PCO_2, pH and lactate from arterialized venous blood. *Journal of Applied Physiology* **32**, 134–7.

Harrison, M. (1985). Effects of thermal stress and exercise on blood volume in humans. *Physiological Reviews*, **65**, 149–209.

Kargotich, S., Goodman. C., Keast, D. and Morton, A.R. (1998). The influence of exercise-induced plasma volume changes on the interpretation of biochemical parameters used for monitoring exercise, training and sport. *Sports Medicine*, **26**, 101–17.

McGuire, E.A.H., Helderman, J.H., Tobin, J.D., *et al.* (1976). Effects of arterial versus venous sampling on analysis of glucose kinetics in man. *Journal of Applied Physiology*, **41**, 565–73.

Maughan, R.J. (1982). A simple rapid method for the determination of glucose, lactate, pyruvate, alanine, 3-hydroxybutyrate and acetoacetate on a single 20μl blood sample. *Clinica Chimica Acta*, **122**, 232–40.

Maughan, R.J., Bethell, L.R. and Leiper, J.B. (1996). Effects of ingested fluids on exercise capacity and on cardiovascular and metabolic responses to prolonged exercise in man. *Experimental Physiology*, **81**, 847–59.

Robertson, J.D., Maughan, R.J. and Davidson, R.J.L. (1988). Changes in red cell density and related parameters in response to long distance running. *European Journal of Applied Physiology*, **57**, 264–9.

Sawka, M.N. and Coyle, E.F. (1999). Influence of body water and blood volume on thermoregulation and exercise performance in the heat. *Exercise and Sports Sciences Reviews*, **27**, 167–218.

Weight, L.M., Myburgh, K.H. and Noakes, T.D. (1988). Vitamin and mineral supplementation: effect on running performance of trained athletes. *American Journal of Clinical Nutrition*, **47**, 192–5.

CARDIOVASCULAR FUNCTION

Nigel T. Cable

5.1 AIMS

The aims of this chapter are to:
- provide students with an understanding of human cardiovascular control mechanisms during exercise,
- discuss techniques that are used for the measurement of blood pressure and peripheral blood flow,
- outline practical exercises that demonstrate the cardiovascular response to exercise, the reflexes involved in the cardiovascular response and the measurement of skin blood flow.

5.2 INTRODUCTION

During physical activity, several organs share the demand for increased perfusion. The heart must supply adequate blood to its own contracting muscle as well as to the contractile apparatus of skeletal muscle. Blood flow to the central nervous system must be maintained and skin perfusion augmented to allow for the dissipation of metabolic heat. During exercise, cardiac output, heart rate, oxygen consumption and systolic blood pressure are linearly related to the intensity of the activity performed. Indeed, during isotonic exercise in a thermally controlled environment, blood flow to skeletal muscle may be increased twenty-five-fold. Such an increase is mediated by means of an increase in cardiac output, a redistribution of the cardiac output and a reduction in muscle vascular resistance. According to the

Fick principle ($\dot{V}O_2$ = cardiac output (Q) × arteriovenous difference for oxygen (a–vO$_2$ diff)), oxygen consumption is also elevated by increasing oxygen extraction in the muscle (during exercise).

5.3 CARDIOVASCULAR ADJUSTMENTS DURING EXERCISE

5.3.1 HEART RATE

Cardiac output is a function of heart rate and stroke volume. During exercise, heart rate may increase 300% above that at rest; the actual increase being dependent upon the exercise intensity. At low workloads, this increase in heart rate is mediated through a withdrawal of vagal tone (Ekblom *et al.*, 1972). As exercise intensity is increased above a workload of 50% $\dot{V}O_2$max, the gradual rise in heart rate is mediated by both neural and humoral adrenergic activity, stimulating β_1 adrenoceptors. Evidence for such reciprocal control comes from studies in which atropine and propranolol have been infused (Ekblom *et al.*, 1972). Atropine is a competitive antagonist of acetylcholine and can therefore be used to block the action of the parasympathetic system. On the other hand, propranolol, which is a β_1 and β_2 receptor blocker, can be used to block sympathetic nervous activity to the heart. These drugs can therefore be used to examine the relative importance of parasympathetic and

Kinanthropometry and Exercise Physiology Laboratory Manual: Tests, Procedures and Data. 2nd Edition, Volume 2: Exercise Physiology
Edited by RG Eston and T Reilly. Published by Routledge, London, June 2001

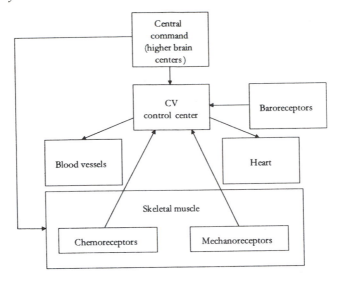

Figure 5.1 Reflexes responsible for cardiovascular control mechanisms.

sympathetic control of heart rate. Only at higher heart rates is the influence of vagal tone totally diminished. However, with β adrenergic blockade during exercise, the maximal heart rate achieved is some 40 beats min^{-1} below that normally attained. Adrenergic activity is therefore a prerequisite for the increase in heart rate during heavy exercise. The withdrawal of vagal tone and the initiation of sympathetic noradrenergic activity seen rapidly after the onset of exercise are probably mediated by central command, a resetting of the operating point of arterial blood pressure and a neural reflex mechanism originating in muscle and joint receptors (Group III fibre receptors). During longer-term exercise, heart rate responses are probably adjusted by means of a pressure 'error' signal and the stimulation of peripheral chemoreceptors (Group IV fibre receptors) following chemical changes in the extracellular fluid of active muscles (see Figure 5.1).

5.3.2 STROKE VOLUME

Stroke volume increases two-fold during dynamic exercise, with maximum stroke volume reached at an intensity of 50% $\dot{V}O_2$max

(Higginbotham *et al.*, 1986). The mechanisms that contribute to the increase in stroke volume include the Frank–Starling law of the heart and sympathetic neuronal activity. The Frank–Starling law of the heart states that the force of contraction is proportional to the initial length of the cardiac muscle fibres. Thus, the more blood that enters the ventricle during diastole, the greater the degree of stretch on the cardiac fibre and the greater the strength of contraction. The relationship only holds for work-rates up to 50% $\dot{V}O_2$max. Above this threshold, end diastolic volume (EDV) is reduced due to the increase in heart rate, which reduces cardiac filling time. Nevertheless, stroke volume is maintained in spite of the decreased EDV by a greater force of contraction of cardiac fibres mediated by stimulation of β_1 adrenoceptors arising from sympathetic noradrenergic activity. Such stimulation increases the contractility of the cardiac muscle as evidenced by a reduction in end systolic volume (ESV).

During exercise the stimulus that mediates the increased sympathoadrenal activity remains equivocal. There have been two major hypotheses (central command vs. peripheral command) generated to explain the control of the sympathoadrenal response to exercise. These hypotheses are not mutually exclusive and must be considered to be integrated in some manner. At the onset of exercise, it is thought that impulses from motor centres in the brain, as well as afferent impulses from inside the working skeletal muscle, are integrated to produce an increase in both noradrenergic and sympathoadrenal activity, which is dependent on work-rate. Throughout exercise the degree of this autonomic activity is continually adjusted by metabolic signals, and also by non-metabolic signals arising from the stimulation of pressure, volume, osmolality and temperature receptors (Galbo *et al.*, 1987).

During static isometric exercise there is a rapid pressor effect, an increase in mean arterial pressure (MAP) and an associated increase in heart rate. During dynamic exercise, there is a more gradual (depending upon intensity) increase in mean arterial pressure and heart rate, although the change in pressure is far less than that observed during static exercise. It has long been thought that these responses occur to maintain the close match necessary between blood flow and tissue metabolism.

5.3.3 CENTRAL COMMAND

Evidence that these haemodynamic responses are initiated by centrally generated motor command signals arises from studies in humans and animals that have used motor paralysis and partial neuromuscular blockade. In humans with the muscles of the forearm fully blocked by succinylcholine, an attempt to contract the paralysed muscle group was accompanied by approximately 50% of the increase in arterial pressure and heart rate reported under normal unblocked conditions (Frey-schuss, 1970). Therefore in the absence of peripheral feedback (i.e. from immobile muscle) the cardiovascular responses must have been mediated by central command. This suggestion is complemented by studies employing partial neuromuscular blockade using tubocurarine. This drug causes muscle weakness, and therefore in order to produce

the same absolute force of muscle contraction after blockade as that of before, a greater motor command signal is required. In studies in which maximum voluntary contraction (MVC) has been reduced by 50% with tubocurarine, arterial pressure rose more markedly at the same absolute force (Leonard *et al.*, 1985). However, at the same relative force before and after blockade (i.e. the same percent of pre-MVC and post-MVC, and presumably therefore the same degree of motor command) pressure changes were of a similar degree (Leonard *et al.*, 1985).

Mitchell (1990) suggested that the peripheral chemoreflex is also an important mediator of the exercise pressor reflex. This suggestion arose from studies using epidural anaesthesia, which not only reduces muscle strength by partial motoneuron blockade but also inhibits afferent feedback from the contracting muscle. When repeating the same experimental model described above, it was observed that at the same absolute force the pressor effect was similar. However, at the same relative force cardiovascular responses were less. In attempting to exert the same absolute force, which requires a greater central command signal, the expected elevation of cardiovascular response was not observed. Similarly at the same relative intensity, when central command and therefore the pressor response should have been similar, a reduced cardiovascular response was observed. Given that sensory afferents were inhibited, these studies indicate that the peripheral chemoreflex as well as central command have a role to play in generating the cardiovascular response to exercise.

In response to a powerful isometric contraction there is an immediate increase in arterial pressure and heart rate. The increase in arterial pressure is attributable to an immediate increase in cardiac output resulting from a rapid elevation of heart rate (Martin *et al.*, 1974). This tachycardia is governed by the removal of vagal tone rather than an increase in sympathetic activity, as the response is blocked by atropine and not propranolol

(Maciel *et al.*, 1987). In addition Maciel *et al.* (1987) found that the blockade of parasympathetic activity only influenced the first 10 s of very forceful isometric contractions at 50–70% MVC, whereas sympathetic blockade modified the heart rate response after 10 s.

It is clear, therefore, that central command governs the immediate cardiovascular response to exercise by the removal of vagal inhibition of heart rate. Following the initial 10 s of moderate to intense exercise, this response is increasingly controlled by augmented sympathetic nervous activity. Thus, it appears that central command plays a role in the removal of parasympathetic activity but not in the activation of the sympathetic nervous system (SNS).

5.3.4 PERIPHERAL COMMAND

The chemoreceptors located in muscle have been proposed as possible mediators of the increased activity of the sympathetic nervous system. These receptors are thought to be stimulated by the release of metabolites from exercising muscle in response to a mismatch between blood flow and metabolism. This response can be demonstrated during isometric muscle contraction by occluding the circulation to the muscle during and after exercise. The resultant post-exercise ischaemia maintains both the level of MAP (Alam and Smirk, 1937) and muscle sympathetic nerve activity (MSNA) (Seals *et al.*, 1988) that is observed during exercise. As this response persists, even during passive recovery (and therefore in the absence of any central command), it must be mediated by metabolite activation of muscle chemoreceptors, the leading candidates of which are lactate and changes in pH. The increase in MSNA observed during exercise is delayed for 0.5 to 2 minutes after the initiation of contraction, a time period required for the accumulation of metabolites needed to activate the chemoreflex. Thus, the current thinking is that cardiovascular responses to isometric exercise are governed by a central command-mediated withdrawal of vagal tone and a peripheral chemoreflex initiation of sympathetic activity.

It was indicated earlier that sympathetic nervous activity (as measured by MSNA and increased concentrations of circulating noradrenaline) begins to increase at a heart rate of approximately 100 beats min^{-1}. In sedentary populations, lactate accumulation is not evident until work-rates of about 50% $\dot{V}O_2$max are reached. In endurance-trained athletes this threshold may be 80% $\dot{V}O_2$max. These thresholds correspond to heart rates of approximately 140 and 170 beats min^{-1} respectively. Clearly at heart rates of 100 beats min^{-1} when SNS becomes active, sufficient lactate to stimulate the muscle chemoreceptors will not be present. It is therefore unlikely that the increase in sympathetic nervous activity observed during exercise of a moderate intensity is controlled by such chemoreceptor stimulation.

In summary, central command appears to govern the cardiovascular response to dynamic exercise at heart rates below 100 beats min^{-1} by the withdrawal of vagal tone. At higher work-rates, the haemodynamic response is mediated by the stimulation of peripheral chemoreceptors. The signal that initiates the increase in MSNA at moderate work-rates remains to be established.

5.3.5 RESETTING OF THE CAROTID SINUS BAROREFLEX

The rapid rise in arterial blood pressure and heart rate at the onset of exercise, has led to the conclusion that the arterial baroreflex is inactivated during exercise. This would therefore allow blood pressure to increase, without the baroreflex attempting to return it to a regulated value. Papelier *et al.* (1994) reported that the sensitivity of the baroreflex was unaltered during dynamic exercise in humans, but that the operating point (the value around which pressure is regulated) was shifted upwards in an intensity-dependent manner. That blood pressure may be regulated at a higher level immediately at the onset of exercise is supported by indirect evidence, showing that when the arterial baroreflex is denervated in exercising dogs, blood pressure falls (Melcher and Donald, 1981).

Rowell (1993) suggested that the resetting of the arterial baroreflex to a higher operating point during exercise is responsible for the increased activity seen in the sympathetic nervous system. Immediately at the onset of exercise, central command shifts the operating point of blood pressure to a higher level and withdraws vagal inhibition of heart rate. During mild exercise, the removal of vagal tone is sufficient to allow cardiac output to increase to a level that raises arterial pressure to the new regulated value, and there is therefore no perceived pressure 'error'. During more intense exercise, the vagally-induced increase in cardiac output is not sufficient to counteract the sudden vasodilation occurring in active muscle (i.e. a sudden fall in total peripheral resistance) and therefore according to the equation, MAP = Q × TPR (where MAP = mean arterial pressure (mmHg), Q = cardiac output ($l\,min^{-1}$) and TPR = total peripheral resistance ($mmHg\,l^{-1}$)), there is a mismatch between the new operating point of arterial pressure and the pressure detected. This pressure 'error' must be corrected by increased sympathetic nervous activity to the heart and vasculature, resulting in increased cardiac output and increased vasoconstrictor tone. Thus above a heart rate of 100 beats min^{-1} (when most vagal activity has been withdrawn), increased sympathetic activity is promoted in response to an arterial pressure error, rather than in response to metabolic changes occurring in the active muscle. At higher work-rates as lactate begins to accumulate, the muscle chemoreflex may become tonically active and increase sympathetic activity further (there is a close correlation between muscle sympathetic nerve activity and lactate accumulation). Rowell (1993) therefore proposed that cardiovascular adjustments observed during dynamic exercise resulted from pressure-raising reflexes secondary to the detection of arterial pressure errors, rather than a mismatch between blood flow and metabolism.

5.4 CONTROL OF BLOOD FLOW AT REST AND DURING EXERCISE

Regional blood flow is adjusted according to functional requirements of the tissue by changes in the resistance to flow through blood vessels. The resistance to flow through a given blood vessel varies inversely with the fourth power of the radius of the vessel, and therefore a relatively small change in the diameter of a resistance vessel initiates a dramatic fluctuation in blood flow through that tissue.

Depending on their functional requirements, tissues have varying ranges of blood flow. The rate of flow through organs such as the brain and liver remains relatively constant even when there are pronounced changes in both arterial blood pressure and cardiac output. In more compliant vascular beds such as skeletal muscle, skin and splanchnic regions, perfusion rates can vary markedly depending on the physiological conditions experienced.

5.4.1 LOCAL REGULATING MECHANISMS

There are various substances that are either required for cellular metabolism or are produced as a consequence of it, and that have a direct effect on the vasculature of muscle and therefore constitute the metabolic autoregulation of peripheral blood flow. This autoregulatory control is of great significance as it allows the matching of local blood flow to momentary nutritional requirements of the tissue. These local responses can completely override neurogenic constrictor effects which are mediated centrally.

Vasodilatation is evoked by a fall in partial pressure of oxygen in the local vascular bed. Thus, when arterial partial pressure of oxygen decreases as metabolic activity in the region is accelerated, vasodilatation occurs. Various mechanisms have been proposed to explain this process, including a direct effect of oxygen on vascular smooth muscle (Detar, 1980). In addition, as regional metabolism increases, there are local increases in the partial pressure of CO_2 and the concentration of H^+ which are also thought to cause vasodilatation. The accumulation of lactate in a vascular bed is associated with vasodilatation, but this effect is thought to be mediated indirectly by changes in plasma pH. It is unclear how these metabolites promote vasodilatation, but their release during contraction of muscle has a similar time course to the release of adenosine and its nucleotides, which are known to be potent vasodilator substances (Ballard *et al.*, 1985). Potassium is also a potent vasodilatory substance. Wilson *et al.* (1994) have reported a strong correlation between forearm vascular resistance and venous potassium concentration during potassium infusion into the brachial artery. The same authors reported relatively small changes in venous potassium during forearm exercise despite large decreases in forearm vascular resistance. During maximal whole-body exercise there were large changes in systemic potassium which might be expected to increase exercise hyperaemia (Wilson *et al.*, 1994).

It is now recognized that a substance released from the endothelium acts upon smooth muscle cells to produce relaxation. This substance was originally termed endothelium derived relaxing factor, but has since been identified as nitric oxide (Palmer *et al.*, 1987). It is produced from arginine in endothelial cells and stimulates cGMP (an intracellular second messenger signal) in smooth muscle cells to bring about relaxation (Collier and Vallance, 1989). Nitric oxide is now thought to be released continually from the vascular endothelium to exert a profound hypotensive effect.

In addition to a tonic release of nitric oxide from the endothelial cells at rest, blood flow through the lumen of blood vessels has been shown to stimulate the release of nitric oxide (Green *et al.*, 1996). This phenomenon is thought to be caused by shear stress on the endothelial cells, the stimulus for release being proportional to the magnitude of blood flow. With microvascular perfusion coupled to muscle fibre activity, muscle blood flow can be matched to metabolic demands. It has recently been observed, in an isolated electrically stimulated *in vitro* muscle preparation, that nitric oxide is released from muscle tissue itself. Thus, the possibility exists that, in response to exercise, the muscle cell produces endogenous nitric oxide which diffuses into the smooth muscle of the vasculature and decreases resistance. The resultant hyperaemia would presumably stimulate greater nitric oxide release via shear stress, thereby increasing blood flow further.

5.4.2 NEURAL REGULATION

The sympathetic nervous system influences vasomotor tone in a number of vascular beds. All blood vessels except capillaries are innervated, the result of stimulation dependent upon the distribution and density of the subclasses of adrenoceptors. The small arteries and arterioles of the skin, kidney and splanchnic regions receive a dense supply of sympathetic noradrenergic vasoconstrictor fibres, whereas those of skeletal muscle and the brain have a relatively sparse supply of these fibres. When stimulated, noradrenaline is released from postganglionic fibres which combines with α adrenoceptors to initiate constriction of the smooth muscle surrounding the lumen of the vessel, leading to increased resistance to blood flow and thereby reduced tissue perfusion.

As previously stated, the skeletal muscular, splanchnic, renal and cutaneous vascular beds are the major determinants of changes in systemic vascular resistance, which is under sympathetic noradrenergic control. If sympathetic activity to resting limb muscles is completely abolished there is a two- to three-fold increase in blood flow, and conversely when noradrenergic activity is maximal, resting blood flow is reduced by 75%. Although these changes only account for a small proportion of those observed during exercise, they nevertheless function to mediate important changes in total systemic vascular resistance due to the large proportion of muscle as a percentage of total body mass. The action of noradrenaline on α adrenoceptors may actually be modulated by the release of local factors from active skeletal muscle. Adenosine, adenine nucleotides, potassium, hydrogen ions and extracellular osmolarity may directly inhibit smooth muscle cell contraction by interrupting vasoconstrictor impulses of sympathetic nerves. Thus, during exercise muscle blood flow may be partially increased by the withdrawal of noradrenergic tone.

The resistance vessels in the arterial circulation of skeletal muscle possess β_2 adrenoceptors which have a high affinity for circulating adrenaline. As the exercise effort increases in duration and intensity, adrenaline concentration increases. This increase leads to stimulation of β_2 receptors, causing relaxation of the smooth muscle and a reduction of vascular resistance in skeletal muscle and therefore an increase in flow.

Controversy still exists as to the contribution of the cholinergic vasodilator pathway in exercise hyperaemia. Although reflex cholinergic vasodilator responses have been observed in humans during severe mental stress, it remains unclear whether such a mechanism exerts any influence on muscle blood flow during exercise. Cholinergic activity is thought to increase muscle blood flow during the initial 10 s of exercise, existing primarily as an anticipatory response to exercise initiated by the cholinergic vasodilatory pathway in the motor cortex.

5.5 CONTROL OF SKIN BLOOD FLOW DURING EXERCISE

Direct heating of the body or exercising, particularly in a warm environment, raises core temperature and results in a rapid increase in skin blood flow (SkBf) in an attempt to transfer this internal heat convectively away from the body. Such changes in SkBf are thought to be mediated by competition between vasoconstrictor and vasodilatory systems (Johnson, 1992). These systems are in turn regulated by a number of thermoregulatory and non-thermoregulatory reflexes.

All cutaneous resistance vessels receive a rich supply of sympathetic fibres, and therefore usually display tonic vasoconstriction. Additionally skin of the limbs and body trunk possesses an active vasodilator system. Therefore any increases in SkBf can be mediated by the removal of vasoconstrictor tone, an increase in active vasodilator activity, or both. Indeed, humans are the only species known to be dependent upon active vasodilation and sweating for their heat loss mechanisms. It is still not known whether vasodilation is mediated by specific vasodilator nerve fibres or is secondary to the effects of a neurohumoral compound co-released from sympathetic cholinergic nerve terminals which innervates sweat glands. The close association between active vasodilation and sweating is evident from studies indicating an inability to vasodilate in subjects that have a congenital absence of sweat glands (Brengelmann *et al.*, 1981). It has been proposed that sympathetic cholinergic nerves supplying the sweat gland co-release a potent vasodilator, along with acetylcholine. The identity and precise mode of action of this vasodilatory substance remain unknown, but possible candidates include vasoactive intestinal polypeptide and nitric oxide. Although the increases in sweating and SkBf are generally considered to be coincident, the temperature threshold at which both occur has been uncoupled (Kenney and Johnson, 1992), indicating that the control of sudomotor and vasodilator activity are independent of each other.

There are many complex interactions between thermoregulatory and non-thermoregulatory reflexes in the control of SkBf. The thermoregulatory reflexes are activated by an increase in both core and skin temperature, leading to the inhibition of vasoconstrictor tone and possibly the initiation of the active vasodilator system. Non-thermoregulatory reflexes include baroreceptor control of blood pressure and exercise reflexes associated with exercise itself (Rowell, 1993).

The cutaneous vascular response to exercise is as follows. Immediately at the onset of exercise there is a vasoconstrictor activity that causes SkBf to decrease below resting baseline values. Having reached its lowest value SkBf returns to pre-exercise values and increases markedly until a core temperature of 38°C is reached. Beyond this temperature SkBf attains a plateau or increases only by a small amount during prolonged endurance exercise (Kenney and Johnson, 1992). In addition, during exercise the threshold core temperature at which SkBf begins to increase is much greater than that observed in a warm environment at rest. Therefore, during exercise, SkBf at any given core temperature is much lower than at rest. The rate of increase in core temperature, once the threshold for vasodilation has been reached, is unaffected by exercise (see Figure 5.2).

Rowell (1983) hypothesized that the rightward shift of the SkBf–body temperature relationship is caused by a increased sympathetic vasoconstrictor activity during exercise, in response to a fall in resistance to blood flow in skeletal muscle (and therefore in order to maintain MAP, resistance in non-active circulation must be increased). Thus, SkBf was presumed to be limited by increased vasoconstrictor activity rather than a reduction in vasodilator activity, due to the fact that the vasodilator system was thought to be independent of non-thermal control systems (i.e. the baroreflex).

Kellogg *et al.* (1990) have shown that the baroreflex can decrease SkBf by the withdrawal of vasodilator activity. This phenomenon was demonstrated by blocking the release of noradrenaline and therefore vasoconstriction, whilst leaving the active vasodilator mechanism intact. Using this model, Kellogg *et al.* (1991) observed that the usual decrease in SkBf associated with the onset of exercise was mediated by sympathetic noradrenergic activity and not by the withdrawal of active

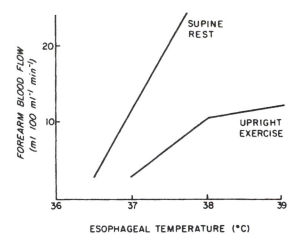

Figure 5.2 Skin blood flow (expressed as forearm blood flow) during passive whole-body heating and during upright exercise (adapted from Rowell, 1993).

vasodilation. In addition, it was observed that the delayed increase in SkBf during exercise, compared with heating at rest, was unaffected by adrenergic inhibition, and was therefore caused by a delayed onset in vasodilation outflow to the skin. Furthermore, Kenney and Johnson (1992) reported that the plateau in SkBf observed during prolonged exercise is not mediated by augmented vasoconstriction, but rather by a withdrawal of vasodilator activity. Kenney and Johnson (1992) therefore concluded that the control of SkBf is dominated by active vasodilation and that this system may be under non-thermal baroreflex control in an attempt to preserve arterial blood pressure.

5.6 MEASUREMENT OF BLOOD PRESSURE

Arterial blood pressures are most accurately measured through the use of rapidly responding pressure transducers located in the arterial circulation. Due to the invasive nature of this technique, its use is limited to a clinical environment. For this reason, blood pressure is not usually measured directly, but estimated using the auscultatory technique. This technique requires the use of a sphygmomanometer and stethoscope, and is dependent upon the observer detecting the characteristic 'Korotkoff sounds' that are produced following occlusion of the circulation to the forearm.

A cuff is inflated to supra-systolic pressure around the upper arm and then slowly deflated whilst simultaneously listening for the 'Korotkoff sounds' through a stethoscope which is placed over the brachial artery in the region of the antecubital fossa. At supra-systolic pressures, blood flow to the forearm is completely occluded. When the pressure in the occluding cuff is equal to systolic pressure in the cardiovascular system, blood forces its way back into the artery, creating turbulent flow and producing the so-called 'First Korotkoff sound'. The pressure cuff is connected to a mercury or aneroid manometer, allowing for the estimation of systolic blood pressure at this point. As pressure in the cuff is reduced further, blood flow entering the artery remains turbulent, until the diameter of the artery reaches its normal patency. This point reflects diastolic pressure and is indicated by the disappearance of the 'Korotkoff sounds' as the blood flow in the artery is now non-turbulent. When resting environmental conditions and measurement protocol are standardized, this indirect method gives reliable estimations of blood pressures, particularly when used by experienced personnel. In addition, this technique can be used during static and dynamic exercise in steady-state conditions. Indeed, when used to predict mean arterial pressure (diastolic pressure + $1/3$ (systolic – diastolic pressure)), this technique has been shown to provide a good estimation of blood pressure measured directly in the brachial artery during exercise (MacDougall *et al.*, 1999).

Until recently, beat-to-beat monitoring of blood pressure was only possible using the invasive technique of an intra-arterial catheter. Since the development of the photoelectric principle, it is now possible to demonstrate the full blood pressure waveform non-invasively from the finger during each cardiac cycle.

This measurement can be performed using the photoplethysmographic technique for measurement of the finger arterial pressure. The instrument (Ohmeda Finapres 2300, Englewood, Colorado, USA) comprises an electropneumatic transducer and an infrared plethysmograph within a small finger cuff. The transducer measures the absorption of light and links the plethysmograph to an air pressure source through a fast-reacting servo-mechanism. Air pressure in the finger cuff is then rapidly regulated to maintain the finger blood volume and plethysmographic light level equivalent to that detected at zero transmural pressure of the digital artery (unloaded arterial wall), thus reflecting the finger arterial pressure waveform. Measurement of blood pressure is fully automated using the Finapres device and the equipment is self-calibrating. A volume clamp level is established within 10 heart beats. Thereafter, blood pressure is continuously monitored except for a small interruption every 10 beats initially followed by 70-beat intervals. Such a device allows the immediate assessment of changes in blood pressure in response to various interventions (for example, upright posture, recovery from exercise), and provides an indication of the real-time change in pressure.

5.7 MEASUREMENT OF PERIPHERAL BLOOD FLOW

5.7.1 STRAIN GAUGE PLETHYSMOGRAPHY

Limb blood flow may be determined non-invasively by measurement of the volume change in a limb segment. Occlusion of the veins draining a limb to a pressure between venous and diastolic blood pressure allows continued arterial flow into the limb segment resulting in increased venous volume and limb volume. Changes in limb volume during venous occlusion may be determined by the displacement of water or air from a jacket secured around the limb or by the measurement of limb circumference changes using a mercury strain gauge. Whitney (1953) pioneered the mercury strain gauge technique

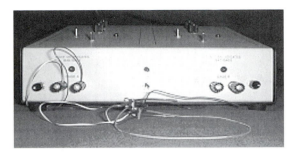

Figure 5.3 Mercury in silastic strain gauge connected to plethysmograph.

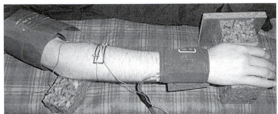

Figure 5.4 Measurement of forearm blood flow using strain gauge plethysmograph.

which is based on Ohm's law of electrical conductance (voltage = current × resistance). The principle of operation is related to the effect of changes in gauge length and diameter on the electrical resistance offered by the mercury thread within a silastic rubber tube (Whitney, 1953). This mercury thread forms one arm of a balanced Wheatstone bridge circuit which is housed within a plethysmograph device (Parks Medical Electronics Inc., OR, USA). Owing to the good linear correlation between voltage output from the bridge circuit and a change in strain gauge length (Whitney, 1953), the change in voltage may be used to reflect the change in limb circumference during venous occlusion (see Figure 5.3).

(a) Limb blood flow measurement protocol

The strain gauge is secured around the greatest circumference of the limb. In order to encourage rapid venous drainage during cuff deflation, the elbow and wrist or knee and ankle are comfortably elevated on foam supports to heights of 10 cm and 15 cm respectively. Circulation to the hand or foot is then occluded at a pressure of 200 mmHg for 1 minute before each venous occlusion cycle commences. Venous occlusion is achieved by inflating a collecting cuff, placed around the upper limb (e.g. immediately above the elbow or knee) to a pressure of 50 mmHg in a cycle of 10 s inflation – 5 s deflation for a total of 3 minutes using a rapid cuff inflator (see Figure 5.4).

(b) Calculation of limb blood flow

From the geometry of the circle and cylinder ($2\pi r$, πr^2, $\pi r^2 h$, where h = cylinder length), a percentage change in the volume of a cylinder is twice the percentage change in its circumference. Although limbs are not cylindrical, their length does not increase upon expansion with blood. The mathematical relationship between percentage changes in circumference and volume therefore holds (Whitney, 1953). Following calculation of the slope relating the changes between voltage and time during venous occlusion, the increase in gauge length is determined using the linear regression equation for each individually calibrated strain gauge. The change in gauge length is then expressed as a percentage of limb circumference according to the equation:

$$\text{Bloodflow} = \frac{\Delta\,\text{gauge length (mm)} \times 60\,(s) \times 100 \times 2}{\text{girth (mm)} \times 10\,(s)}$$

For example, for a change in gauge length of 1 mm in a forearm of girth 20 cm,

$$\text{Bloodflow} = \frac{1 \times 60 \times 100 \times 2}{200 \times 10}$$

$$= 6\ \text{ml 100 ml tissue}^{-1}\ \text{min}^{-1}$$

The percentage change in limb volume over time is then a direct indication of the rate of blood flow, expressed as ml 100 ml tissue^{-1} min^{-1}.

PART THREE

ASSESSMENT OF ENERGY AND EFFICIENCY

METABOLIC RATE AND ENERGY BALANCE

6

Carlton B. Cooke

6.1 AIMS

The aims in this chapter are to:
- describe methods of measuring metabolic rate and energy balance,
- describe methods of predicting resting metabolic rate,
- describe methods of measuring energy expenditure using expired air analysis,
- provide examples of the measurement of metabolic rate and energy balance.

6.2 BASAL METABOLIC RATE (BMR)

The main component of daily energy expenditure in the average person is the energy expenditure for maintenance processes, usually called basal metabolic rate (BMR). The BMR is the energy expended for the ongoing processes in the body in the resting state, when no food is digested and no energy is needed for temperature regulation. The BMR reflects the body's heat production and can be determined indirectly by measuring oxygen uptake under strict laboratory conditions. No food is eaten for at least 12 hours prior to the measurement so there will be no increase in the energy required for the digestion and absorption of foods in the digestive system. This fast ensures that measurement of BMR occurs with the subject in the postabsorptive state. In addition, no undue muscular exertion should have occurred for at least 12 hours prior to the measurement of BMR.

Normally, a good time to make a measurement of BMR is after waking from a night's sleep, and in a hospital situation BMR is typically measured at this time. In laboratory practicals and exercise physiology experiments involving volunteer subjects, it is often impossible to obtain the correct conditions for a true measure of BMR. It is likely that in a laboratory practical the subject will have eaten a meal in the preceding 12 hours, which will increase metabolism in certain tissues and organs such as the liver. This is known as the specific dynamic effect. Any measurement not made under the strict laboratory conditions already described is referred to as resting metabolic rate (RMR).

However, if the subject has only eaten a light meal some 3–4 hours prior to the experiment, and is allowed to rest in a supine position for at least 30 minutes, then the measurement of RMR will be elevated only slightly above the true BMR value. A description of the procedures for the measurement of RMR using the Douglas bag technique is given in Section 6.8. Although the Système International (SI) unit for rate of energy expenditure is the watt (W), RMR and BMR values are typically quoted in kcal min^{-1}. A calorie is defined as the amount of heat necessary to raise the temperature of 1 kg of water 1°C, from 14.5 to 15.5°C. The calorie is therefore typically referred to as the kilocalorie (kcal). To convert kcal into kilojoules (kJ) (the joule (J) is the SI unit of energy), multiply the kcal value by 4.2. To convert kcal min^{-1} into kilowatts (kW) multiply the kcal min^{-1} by 0.07.

Kinanthropometry and Exercise Physiology Laboratory Manual: Tests, Procedures and Data. 2nd Edition, Volume 2: Exercise Physiology
Edited by RG Eston and T Reilly. Published by Routledge, London, June 2001

(See the Appendix for a full list of conversion factors between different units of measurement.)

Estimates of BMR values can be used to establish an energy baseline for constructing programmes for weight control by means of diet, exercise, or the more effective and healthier option of combining both diet and exercise prescriptions. The measurement of BMR on subjects drawn from a variety of populations provides a basis for studying the relationships between metabolic rate and body size, sex and age.

6.2.1 BODY SIZE, SEX AND AGE EFFECTS ON BMR AND RMR

Since the time of Galileo, scientists have believed that BMR and RMR are related to body surface area. Rubner (1883) showed that the rate of heat production divided by body surface area was more or less constant in dogs that varied in size. He offered the explanation that metabolically produced heat was limited by ability to lose heat, and was therefore related to body surface area. This relationship between body surface area and basal and resting metabolic rate has since been verified for animals ranging in size from the mouse up to the elephant (Kleiber, 1975; McMahon, 1984; Schmidt-Nielsen, 1984) and is an important consideration when comparing children and adults. The 'surface area law' therefore states that metabolic rates of animals of different size can be made similar when BMR or RMR is expressed per unit of body surface area.

Table 6.1 shows that, related to body surface area, BMR is at its greatest in early childhood and declines thereafter (Altman and Dittmer, 1968; Knoebel, 1963). When RMR is based on oxygen uptake values the differences between a 10-year-old boy and a middle-aged man are of the order of 1–2 ml kg^{-1} min^{-1}, which amounts to a 25–35% greater metabolic rate in the child (MacDougall *et al.*, 1979). As can be seen from Table 6.1, BMR values are about 5% lower in women than in men. This does not reflect a true sex difference in the metabolic rate of specific tissues, but is largely due to the

differences in body composition (McArdle *et al.*, 1996). Women generally have a higher percentage of body fat than men of a similar size, and stored fat is essentially metabolically inert.

If the BMR values are expressed per unit of lean body mass (or fat-free mass) then the sex differences are essentially eliminated. Differences in body composition also largely explain the 2% decrease in BMR per decade observed through adulthood.

6.2.2 ESTIMATION OF BODY SURFACE AREA AND RESTING METABOLIC RATE

Using the mean BMR values (kJ m^{-2} h^{-1}) for age and sex from Altman and Dittmer (1968) shown in Table 6.1 it is possible to predict an individual's BMR value using an estimate of body surface area. The procedure is outlined in Section 6.4.

Table 6.1 Basal metabolic rate (kJ m^{-2} h^{-1}) as a function of age and sex (data from Altman and Dittmer, 1968)

Age (years)	Females	Males
5	196.7	205.1
10	178.0	183.3
15	163.2	177.9
20	152.4	165.8
25	151.5	162.0
30	151.1	157.4
35	151.1	155.7
40	151.1	156.1
45	150.3	155.3
50	146.5	154.5
55	142.7	152.4
60	139.4	149.4
65	136.9	146.5
70	135.6	144.0
75	134.8	141.5
80	133.5	139.0

6.3 MEASUREMENT OF ENERGY EXPENDITURE

Energy expenditure can be measured using either direct or indirect calorimetry. Both methods depend on the principle that all the energy used by the body is ultimately degraded into heat. Therefore the measurement of heat produced by the body is also a measure of energy expenditure (direct calorimetry). Direct measures of energy expenditure are made when a subject remains inside a chamber with walls specifically designed to absorb and measure the heat produced. This method is both technically difficult and costly. Since the energy provided from food can only be used as a result of oxidations utilizing oxygen obtained from air, measurement of steady-state oxygen uptake by the body is also used as a measurement of energy expenditure (indirect calorimetry). Detailed procedures for the measurement of oxygen uptake by means of the Douglas bag technique are given in Section 6.6.

6.4 PRACTICAL 1: ESTIMATION OF BODY SURFACE AREA AND RESTING METABOLIC RATE

With the mean BMR values (kJ m^{-2} h^{-1}) for age and sex from Altman and Dittmer (1968) shown in Table 6.1, it is possible to predict an individual's BMR value using an estimate of body surface area. The most commonly used formula is that of DuBois and DuBois (1916) which requires measures of stature and body mass only.

Subjects should remove their shoes for both the stature and body mass measures. Stature is measured to the nearest millimetre using a stadiometer. The subject should stand up as tall as he or she can, keeping the heels on the floor and maintaining the head position in the Frankfurt plane (i.e. the straight line through the lower bony orbital margin and the external auditory meatus should be horizontal). Mass should be measured on calibrated weighing scales to the nearest 0.1 kg. The subject should be wearing minimal clothing.

The formula for estimation of body surface area according to DuBois and DuBois (1916) is:

$$BSA = M^{0.425} \times H^{0.725} \times 71.84 \times 10^{-4}$$

where: BSA is body surface area in m^2, M is body mass in kg and H is stature in cm.

For example, a subject with a mass of 70 kg and stature of 177 cm will have a body surface area of

$$BSA = 70^{0.425} \times 177^{0.725} \times 71.84 \times 10^{-4}$$

$$= 6.0837 \times 42.6364 \times 71.84 \times 10^{-4}$$

$$= 1.86 \ m^2$$

If the subject is male aged 20 then according to the average values of BMR (kJ m^{-2} h^{-1}) of Altman and Dittmer (1968) (Table 6.1) he would have an approximate BMR value of 165.8 kJ m^{-2} h^{-1} (±10%). This would compute to a resting energy expenditure of 165.8 kJ m^{-2} h^{-1} × 1.86 m^2 = 308.4 kJ h^{-1}. Over a 24-hour period this would result in an estimated resting energy expenditure of 308.4 kJ h^{-1} × 24 h = 7401 kJ (1762 kcal).

Other sex-specific formulae based on body mass, stature and age have also been widely used for the estimation of BMR:

Harris and Benedict (1919)

$$103 \text{ lean females BMR} = 655 + 9.6(M) + 1.85(ht) - 4.68(age)$$

$$136 \text{ lean males BMR} = 66 + 13.8(M) + 5.0(ht) - 6.8(age)$$

Owen *et al.* (1986)

$$32 \text{ non-athletic females RMR} = 795 + 7.2(M)$$

Owen *et al.* (1987)

$$60 \text{ lean to obese males RMR} = 879 + 10.2(M)$$

Mifflin *et al.* (1990)

$$247 \text{ lean to obese females RMR} = -161 + 10(M) + 6.25(ht) - 5(age)$$

$$247 \text{ lean to obese males RMR} = 5 + 10(M) + 6.25(ht) - 5(age)$$

where: M = body mass (kg), ht = stature (cm), age = age (years), RMR and BMR are expressed in kcal day^{-1}.

Mifflin *et al.* (1990) provided the most general equations for age and weight. The equations of Harris and Benedict (1919) are shown to predict within 5% of RMR values, with the equations of Owen *et al.* (1986, 1987) performing even better (Cunningham, 1991).

6.5 PRACTICAL 2: ESTIMATION OF RESTING METABOLIC RATE FROM FAT-FREE MASS

The resting metabolic rate (RMR) can be estimated from fat-free mass (FFM) according to the following regression equation from Cunningham (1991):

$$\text{RMR (kcal day}^{-1}) = 370 + 21.6 \times \text{FFM}$$

This equation was derived from a review by Cunningham (1991) where all studies measured FFM according to the whole-body potassium K^{40} method and RMR, BMR and resting energy expenditure (REE) were considered to be physiologically equivalent. An equation was also presented for FFM estimated from triceps skinfold thickness:

$$\text{RMR (kcal day}^{-1}) = 261 + 22.6 \times \text{FFM}$$

Number of subjects = 77 and variance accounted for E (r^2) = 0.65.

Unfortunately, no reference to the specific source of the estimation of FFM from triceps skinfold thickness was given. However, values of fat-free mass from a variety of methods can be used in the estimation of RMR.

6.6 PRACTICAL 3: MEASUREMENT OF OXYGEN UPTAKE USING THE DOUGLAS BAG TECHNIQUE

Oxygen uptake can be measured using the open circuit Douglas bag technique. With this method the subject breathes from normal air into a Douglas bag, while wearing a nose clip. (All valve boxes, valves, tubing and Douglas bags should be routinely checked for wear and tear and leaks.) If subjects are exercising it is preferable to use a lightweight, low-resistance, low dead space valve box such as that described by Jakeman and Davies (1979). This is attached to lightweight tubing which is at least 30 mm internal diameter (e.g. Falconia tubing; Baxter, Woodhouse and Taylor Ltd., Macclesfield, UK), as these provide for some movement of the head and do not require fixed support, or the wearing of a headset. During gas collection the subject must also wear a nose clip (Figure 6.1).

Mouth pieces, valve boxes and tubing should be sterilized and dried prior to use by the next subject. Douglas bags must be completely empty before a collection of expired air is made. Ideally, they should be flushed out with a sample of the subject's expired air prior to data collection. For ease of data collection and long life, the Douglas bags should be hung on suitable racks and evacuated by means of vacuum cleaners, rather than rolling them out.

Naive subjects need habituating to breathing through a mouthpiece prior to data collection. At first, this should be done at rest, and then included in the habituation to ergometry prior to any exercise testing. For steady-state protocols, with 3-minute or 4-minute stages,

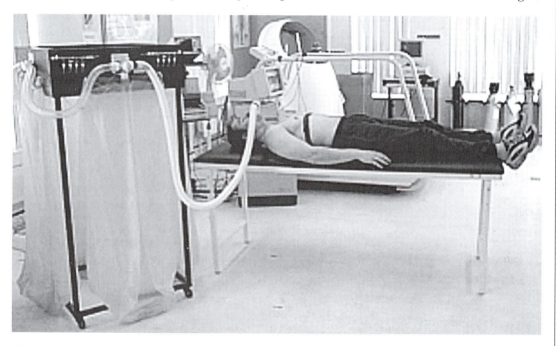

Figure 6.1 A subject lying in a supine position in a laboratory practical for the estimation of resting metabolic rate (RMR). Expired air collection is through a mouthpiece attached to a Salford valve (Cranlea and Company, Birmingham, UK) and lightweight tubing, which is connected to a Douglas bag. The subject is wearing a nose clip, and heart rate data are being recorded by a short-range radio telemeter (Polar, Finland).

the subject need only exercise with the mouthpiece in for 15–20 s before gas collection, as this gives ample time to clear any dead space in the tubing. In ramp protocols and in maximal testing during the latter stages it is necessary to keep the mouthpiece in all the time (Figure 6.2).

Prior to any measurements of gas concentration or volume of expired air, the O_2 and CO_2 analysers should be calibrated and the dry gas meters checked. Gas meters should be calibrated with a minimum of a three-point calibration. This is most conveniently achieved by using 100% nitrogen to set the zero for both analysers, and two known concentrations of O_2 and CO_2 which span the working range. If Haldane or Micro-Scholander apparatus (Rudolf Holker, Swathmore, PA, USA) is available then this can be used to check new standard gases before they are used for routine calibration

Figure 6.2 A subject on a standard Monark cycle ergometer (Monark Crescent AB, Varberg, Sweden), with expired air collection to a Douglas bag, and heart rate monitored by a short-range radio telemeter (Polar, Finland).

purposes. Room air can be used as a span gas for setting oxygen to 20.93%, but caution should be used in the site of collection of room air to ensure it will be valid as 20.93% (i.e. avoid any area where room air could be contaminated). Gas volume meters can be checked with a suitable calibration syringe or with a Tissot Spirometer (Collins Med Inc., Braintree, MA, USA).

6.6.1 SIMPLIFIED ESTIMATION OF OXYGEN UPTAKE

The most straightforward estimation of oxygen uptake ($\dot{V}O_2$) only requires the following measures to be made:

- Volume of expired air collected in the Douglas bag VE (litres)
- Temperature of air as volume is measured (°C)
- Barometric pressure (mmHg)
- Fraction of oxygen in expired air (F_EO_2 or $\%O_{2E}$)
- Time taken for collection of expired air in Douglas bag (s)

Oxygen uptake ($\dot{V}O_2$) is the volume of oxygen inspired minus the volume of oxygen expired, i.e.: $\dot{V}O_2 = (\dot{V}I \times F_IO_2) - (\dot{V}E \times F_EO_2)$
where:
  $\dot{V}O_2$ = oxygen uptake (l min^{-1})
  $\dot{V}I$ = volume of air inspired (l min^{-1})
  F_IO_2 = fraction of oxygen in inspired air = constant value of 0.2093 (i.e. 20.93%)
  $\dot{V}E$ = volume of air expired (l min^{-1})
  F_EO_2 = fraction of oxygen in expired air

6.6.2 TIMING GAS COLLECTIONS AND CORRECTION OF GAS VOLUMES

It should be noted that V stands for volume, whereas $\dot{V}$ stands for volume per unit of time, usually per minute.

$$VE = \text{volume of air expired in the Douglas bag}$$

$$\dot{V}E = \text{volume of expired air per minute (l min}^{-1})$$

$$\dot{V}O_2 = \text{volume of oxygen consumed per minute (l min}^{-1})$$

Expired air collections should always be timed accurately over a complete number of respiratory cycles, from end expiration to end expiration. Collection times are therefore rarely equal to 30 s or 1 minutes, but can be easily converted into minute ventilation values by the following general calculation:

$$\dot{V}E \text{ (l min}^{-1}) = (\text{volume of expired air collection} / 60 \text{ s})$$

End expiration can be judged by the following:
1. Watching for the closure of the expiratory valve in the valve box.
2. Feeling the air flow stop at the tap before turning it to fill the Douglas bag.
3. In strenuous exercise, listening for each breath of expired air rushing down the tubing into the Douglas bag.

A stop-watch should be used to time collections.

Gas volumes obtained in laboratory experiments are typically expressed in one of three ways.

$$ATPS = \text{ambient temperature, pressure and saturated}$$

$$STPD = \text{standard temperature, pressure and dry}$$

$$BTPS = \text{body temperature, ambient pressure and saturated}$$

The conditions at the time of the measurement of the volume of expired air in the Douglas bag are reflected in ATPS. It should be noted that the volume of gas varies with temperature and pressure, and its water content, even though the number of molecules in the gas does not change. More specifically, as the temperature of gas increases the volume increases proportionately and vice versa (i.e. if the pressure is constant then a doubling of the temperature will result in a doubling of the volume). This is known as Charles' Law. However, gas volumes vary inversely with pressure. Thus, an increase in pressure causes a proportionate decrease in volume, and vice versa (i.e. if temperature is constant then a doubling of pressure will cause a halving of volume). This is known as Boyle's Law. Finally, the volume of a gas increases with the amount of water content.

To compare measures of volume taken under different environmental conditions, there is a need for a standard set of conditions which are defined by STPD and BTPS. Standard temperature and pressure dry (STPD) refers to a gas volume expressed under *Standard Temperature* (273K or 0°C), *Pressure* (760 mmHg) and *Dry* (no water vapour). Volumes corrected to STPD conditions therefore allow comparison between values collected at different temperatures, altitudes and degrees of saturation. Values of $\dot{V}E$, $\dot{V}O_2$, and $\dot{V}CO_2$ are always expressed at STPD.

The formula for conversion of a volume of moist gas to STPD such as $\dot{V}_E$ is:

$$\dot{V}E_{STPD} = \dot{V}E_{ATPS} \times \frac{273}{273 + T^\circ C} \times \frac{P_B - P_{H_2O}}{760}$$

where $T^\circ C$ is the temperature of the expired air; P_B is barometric pressure; and P_{H_2O} is the water vapour pressure of the sample at the time volume is measured. The P_{H_2O} is not measured directly because conversion factors are tabulated for the normal range of temperatures of moist gas samples. Furthermore, none of the correction factors for volumes need to be calculated since tables for converting moist gas volumes into STPD conditions are readily available for the range of values of temperature and pressure normally experienced in most laboratories (Carpenter, 1964; McArdle *et al.*, 1996).

Body temperature and pressure saturated (BTPS) refers to a gas volume expressed at *Body Temperature* (273K + 37K), *Ambient* pressure and *Saturated* with water vapour with a partial pressure of 47 mmHg at 37°C. This is the conventional standard used for assessing lung function volumes (see Chapter 3 by Eston).

As with correction from ATPS to STPD, corrections from BTPS to STPD can be achieved by use of tabulated values of correction factors for a broad range of temperatures, or by using the formula:

$$\dot{V}E_{STPD} = \dot{V}E_{BTPS} \times (1 \,/\, \text{factor to convert ATPS to BTPS}) \times (\text{factor to convert ATPS to STPD}).$$

When using the simplified estimation of $\dot{V}O_2$ the composition of expired air remains relatively constant ($F_IO_2 = 0.2093$, $\%O_2I = 20.93\%$; $F_ICO_2 = 0.0003$, $\%CO_2I = 0.03\%$ and $F_IN_2 = 0.7904$, $\%N_2I = 79.04\%$).

Substituting the value for the fraction of O_2 in inspired air of F_IO_2 the expression becomes:

$$\dot{V}O_{2\ STPD} (l\ min^{-1}) = \dot{V}E_{STPD} (0.2093 - F_EO_2)$$

For example, given $\dot{V}E_{ATPS} = 60\ l\ min^{-1}$ (volume measured in Douglas bag), barometric pressure = 754 mmHg (measured by barometer), temperature of gas = 22°C (measured by thermometer as volume is measured), $F_EO_2 = 0.1675$ (measured by oxygen analyser), then

$$\dot{V}E_{STPD} = \dot{V}E_{ATPS} \times 0.891\ (\text{correction factor taken from Table 6.2})$$

$$\dot{V}E_{STPD} = 60 \times 0.891 = 53.46\ l\ min^{-1}$$

$$\dot{V}O_{2\ STPD} (l\ min^{-1}) = 53.46\ (0.2093 - 0.1675) = 2.23\ l\ min^{-1}$$

In summary, there are two steps to the calculation.

1. Correct the $\dot{V}E$ value from ATPS to STPD by multiplying by a correction factor from the appropriate table of values (Table 6.2).
2. Calculate the difference between the concentration of O_2 in inspired and expired air. Then all variables on the right of the equation are known and $\dot{V}O_2$ can be calculated.

6.6.3 CALCULATION OF OXYGEN UPTAKE ($\dot{V}O_2$) USING THE HALDANE TRANSFORMATION

In addition to the measurements required for the simplified calculation of $\dot{V}O_2$ a value for the fraction of carbon dioxide in expired air is also required (F_ECO_2).

Table 6.2 Conversion of gas volumes from ATPS to STPD (data from Carpenter, 1964; McArdle et al., 1996)

Barometric reading	Temperature (°C)																	
	15	16	17	18	19	20	21	22	23	24	25	26	27	28	29	30	31	32
700	0.855	851	847	842	838	834	829	825	821	816	812	807	802	797	793	788	783	778
702	857	853	849	845	840	836	832	827	823	818	814	809	805	800	795	790	785	780
704	860	856	852	847	843	839	834	830	825	821	816	812	807	802	797	792	787	783
706	862	858	854	850	845	841	837	832	828	823	819	814	810	804	800	795	790	785
708	865	861	856	852	848	843	839	834	830	825	821	816	812	807	802	797	792	787
710	867	863	859	855	850	846	842	837	833	828	824	819	814	809	804	799	795	790
712	870	866	861	857	853	848	844	839	836	830	826	821	817	812	807	802	797	792
714	872	868	864	859	855	851	846	842	837	833	828	824	819	814	809	804	799	794
716	875	871	866	862	858	853	849	844	840	835	831	826	822	816	812	807	802	797
718	877	873	869	864	860	856	851	847	842	838	833	828	824	819	814	809	804	799
720	880	876	871	867	863	858	854	849	845	840	836	831	826	821	816	812	807	802
722	882	878	874	869	865	861	856	852	847	843	838	833	829	824	819	814	809	804
724	885	880	876	872	867	863	858	854	849	845	840	835	831	826	821	816	811	806
726	887	883	879	874	870	866	861	856	852	847	843	838	833	829	824	818	813	808
728	890	886	881	877	872	868	863	859	854	850	845	840	836	831	826	821	816	811
730	892	888	884	879	875	871	866	861	857	852	847	843	838	833	828	823	818	813
732	895	890	886	882	877	873	868	864	859	854	850	845	840	836	831	825	820	815
734	897	893	889	884	880	875	871	866	862	857	852	847	843	838	833	828	823	818
736	900	895	891	887	882	878	873	869	864	859	855	850	845	840	835	830	825	820
738	902	898	894	889	885	880	876	871	866	862	857	852	848	843	838	833	828	822
740	905	900	896	892	887	883	878	874	869	864	860	855	850	845	840	835	830	825
742	907	903	898	894	890	885	881	876	871	867	862	857	852	847	842	837	832	827
744	910	906	901	897	892	888	883	878	874	869	864	859	855	850	845	840	834	829
746	912	908	903	899	895	890	886	881	876	872	867	862	857	852	847	842	837	832
748	915	910	906	901	897	892	888	883	879	874	869	864	860	854	850	845	839	834

continued on next page

Table 6.2 Conversion of gas volumes from ATPS to STPD (data from Carpenter, 1964; McArdle *et al.*, 1996) (cont.)

Barometric reading	Temperature (°C)																	
	15	16	17	18	19	20	21	22	23	24	25	26	27	28	29	30	31	32
750	917	913	908	904	900	895	890	886	881	876	872	867	862	857	852	847	842	837
752	920	915	911	906	902	897	893	888	883	879	874	869	864	859	854	849	844	839
754	922	918	913	909	904	900	895	891	886	881	876	872	867	862	857	852	846	841
756	925	920	916	911	907	902	898	893	888	883	879	874	869	864	859	854	849	844
758	927	923	918	914	909	905	900	896	891	886	881	876	872	866	861	856	851	846
760	930	925	921	916	912	907	902	898	893	888	883	879	874	869	864	859	854	848
762	932	928	923	919	914	910	905	900	896	891	886	881	876	871	866	861	856	851
764	936	930	926	921	916	912	907	903	898	893	888	884	879	874	869	864	858	853
766	937	933	928	924	919	915	910	905	900	896	891	886	881	876	871	866	861	855
768	940	935	931	926	922	917	912	908	903	898	893	888	883	878	873	868	863	858
770	942	938	933	928	924	919	915	910	905	901	896	891	886	881	876	871	865	860

Although the concentrations of oxygen (O_2), carbon dioxide (CO_2) and nitrogen (N_2) are constant for inspired air, the values recorded for expired air fractions will vary. The value for F_EO_2 will be less than F_IO_2 as some of the O_2 is extracted from the lungs into the blood capillaries. The F_EO_2 will range between approximately 0.15 and 0.185. The F_ECO_2 will increase in expired air since the body excretes CO_2 with the lungs from the blood by gas exchange. The F_ECO_2 will range from approximately 0.025 to 0.05. Although nitrogen is inert, i.e. the same number of molecules of N_2 exist in both the inspired and expired air, its concentration will change if the number of O_2 molecules removed from inspired air is not equal to the number of CO_2 molecules excreted in expired air. In simple terms, when the molecules of O_2 removed do not equal the molecules of CO_2 added, then the volume of inspired air (VI) will not equal the volume of air expired (VE), and the constant number of N_2 molecules will represent a different fraction or percentage of the inspired and expired volumes.

For example: inspired air constant fractions:

$$F_IO_2 = 0.2093, \text{ or } \%O_{2I} = 20.93\%;$$
$$F_ICO_2 = 0.003, \text{ or } \% CO_{2I} = 0.03\%;$$
$$\text{and } F_IN_2 = 0.7904, \text{ or } \%N_{2I} = 79.04\%$$

$$\%O_{2I} + \%CO_{2I} + \%N_{2I} = 100\%; (20.93 + 0.03 + 79.04 = 100)$$

Given expired air measured values from experiment:

$$\%O_{2E} = 16.75\%; \%CO_{2E} = 3.55$$
$$\%O_{2E} + \%CO_{2E} + \%N_{2E} = 100$$
$$\%N_{2E} = 100 - (\%O_{2E} + \%CO_{2E})$$
$$\%N_{2E} = 100 - (16.75 + 3.55)$$
$$\%N_{2E} = 79.7\%$$

Here the fraction of oxygen in inspired air has decreased from a value of 0.2093 to 0.1675 in expired air, whereas the concentration of carbon dioxide in inspired air has increased from a value of 0.0003 to 0.0355 in expired air. The decrease in oxygen concentration is therefore greater than the increase in carbon dioxide concentration in expired air. Therefore the fraction of nitrogen in inspired air ($F_IN_2 = 0.7904$) rises to a value of 0.7970 in expired air (the same number of molecules but increased in concentration).

The constant number of N_2 molecules representing a different percentage or concentration of inspired and expired volumes can be used to calculate VI from VE or vice versa. This is possible because the change in volume from inspired to expired is directly proportional to the change in nitrogen concentration:

$$\text{Mass of } N_2 \text{ inspired} = \text{Mass of } N_2 \text{ expired}$$

$$\text{As concentration} = \frac{\text{Mass}}{\text{Volume}}$$

$$\%N_{2I} = \frac{\text{Mass of } N_2}{\dot{V}I} \text{ and } \%N_{2E} = \frac{\text{Mass of } N_2}{\dot{V}E}$$

$$\dot{V}I_{STPD} = \frac{\dot{V}E_{STPD} \times \%N_{2E}}{\%N_{2I}}$$

Given the same values as for the simplified calculation, i.e. $\dot{V}E_{ATPS} = 60\ l\ min^{-1}$, temperature = 22°C, barometric pressure = 754 mmHg, correction factor from ATPS to STPD = 0.891, then $\dot{V}E_{STPD}$ will also be the same: $\dot{V}E_{STPD} = 53.46\ l\ min^{-1}$

Given that $\%N_{2E}$ was calculated from expired $\%O_{2E}$ and $\%CO_{2E}$ as 79.7% and $\%N_{2I}$ is constant at 79.04%, all the values on the right of the equation are known and can be used to calculate $\dot{V}O_{2\ STPD}$.

Oxygen uptake ($\dot{V}O_2\ l\ min^{-1}$) can now be calculated as the volume of oxygen removed from expired air per minute:

$$\dot{V}O_2 = \frac{[(\dot{V}E \times \%N_{2E} \times \%O_{2I}) - (\dot{V}E \times \%O_{2E})]}{\%N_{2I}} \div 100\ O_2 = [(\dot{V}I \times \%O_{2I}) - (\dot{V}E \times \%O_{2E})] \div 100$$

Substituting using the Haldane transformation $\dot{V}I = \dot{V}E \times \dfrac{\%N_{2E}}{\%N_I}$ we can replace $\dot{V}I$ by

our known expression $\dot{V}E \times \dfrac{\%N_{2E}}{\%N_I}$

$$\dot{V}O_2 = \frac{[(\dot{V}E \times \%N_{2E} \times \%O_{2I}) - (\dot{V}E \times \%O_{2E})]}{\%N_{2I}} \div 100$$

Substituting in constants for inspired air and simplifying the expression:

$$\dot{V}O_2 = \frac{[(\dot{V}E \times \%N_{2E} \times 20.93\%) - \%O_{2E})]}{79.04\%} \div 100$$

With the most simple form of the equation for computation being:

$$\dot{V}O_2 = \dot{V}E \times [(\%N_{2E} \times 0.265) - \%O_{2E}] \div 100$$

where $\dot{V}E$ is measured under ATPS conditions and corrected to STPD conditions before substitution into this equation, $\%O_{2E}$ is measured from O_2 analyser and $\%N_{2E} = 100 - \%O_{2E} - \%CO_{2E}$ ($\%CO_{2E}$ is measured from CO_2 gas analyser).

Inserting the example values into the simplified equation gives:

$$\dot{V}O_2\ (l\ min^{-1}) = 53.46\ [(79.7 \times 0.265) - 16.75\%] \div 100 = 53.46\ (4.3705) \div 100 = 2.34\ l\ min^{-1}$$

6.6.4 CALCULATION OF CARBON DIOXIDE PRODUCTION ($\dot{V}CO_2$)

The volume of carbon dioxide produced is calculated according to the following equation:

$$\dot{V}CO_2 = [\dot{V}E\ (\%\ CO_{2E} - \%\ CO_{2I})] \times 100$$

Where $\dot{V}E$ is measured and corrected to STPD conditions, $\%CO_{2I} = 0.03\%$ (constant for inspired air) and $\%CO_{2E}$ is measured from CO_2 gas analyser.

Since the fraction of CO_2 in inspired air is negligible, the Haldane transformation is unimportant in the calculation of $\dot{V}CO_2$. In many cases the fraction of CO_2 in inspired air is ignored altogether.

6.7 PRACTICAL 4: THE RESPIRATORY QUOTIENT

The respiratory quotient (RQ) is calculated as the ratio of metabolic gas exchange:

$$RQ = \frac{\dot{V}CO_2 \text{ (volume of carbon dioxide produced)}}{\dot{V}O_2 \text{ (volume of oxygen consumed)}}$$

The RQ gives an indication of what combination of carbohydrates, fats and proteins are metabolized in steady-state submaximal exercise or at rest. The specific equation associated with the RQ for oxidation of pure carbohydrates, fats and proteins is as follows:

(a) RQ for carbohydrates (glucose)

$$C_6H_{12}O_6 + 6O_2 + 6CO_2 + 6H_2O$$

Consequently, during the oxidation of a glucose molecule, six molecules of oxygen are consumed and six molecules of carbon dioxide are produced, therefore:

$$RQ = \frac{6CO_2}{6O_2} = 1$$

The RQ value for carbohydrate is therefore 1.

(b) RQ for fat (palmitic acid)

$$C_{16}H_{32}O_2 = 16CO_2 + 16H_2O$$

$$RQ = \frac{16CO_2}{23O_2} = 0.696$$

Generally, the RQ value for fat is taken to be 0.7.

(c) RQ for protein

The process is more complex for protein to provide energy as proteins are not simply oxidized to carbon dioxide and water, during energy metabolism. Generally, the RQ value for protein is taken to be 0.82.

McLean and Tobin (1987) published equations for the calculation of calorific factors from elemental composition, which included the following equation for respiratory quotient (RQ):

$$RQ = 1 \ / \ (1 + 2.9789 \, f_H \ / \ f_C - 0.3754 \, f_O \ / \ f_C)$$

where 1 g of a substance contains f_C, f_H and f_O g of carbon, hydrogen and oxygen respectively.

Given the formula for the chemical composition of carbohydrate, fat or protein, together with the atomic weights for carbon, hydrogen and oxygen (a_C = 12.011, a_H = 1.008 and a_O = 15.999) it is then possible to calculate f_C, f_H and f_O and solve the equation for RQ.

If we use the example of glucose ($C_6H_{12}O_6$):

$$C_6 \text{ gives } a_C \times 6 = 72.1$$

$$H_{12} \text{ gives } a_H \times 12 = 12.1$$

$$O_6 \text{ gives } a_O \times 6 = 96.0$$

The total is therefore 180.2, which gives fractions for each of 0.4, 0.067 and 0.533 for carbon, hydrogen and oxygen respectively. Substitution of these values in the equation above gives an RQ of 1 as previously derived.

As previously stated, the RQ calculated as the ratio of $\dot{V}CO_2$ and $\dot{V}O_2$ will reflect a combination of carbohydrates, fats and proteins currently being metabolized to provide energy. However, the precise contribution of each of the nutrients can be obtained from the calculation of the non-protein RQ.

(d) Non-protein RQ

This calculation of the non-protein RQ is based upon McArdle *et al*. (1996), where the procedures are discussed in more detail. Although this calculation is typical of the approach in most text books, Durnin and Passmore (1967) described the non-protein RQ as 'an abstraction which has no physiological meaning, as protein metabolism is never zero'. Durnin and Passmore (1967) preferred the four equations set out by Consolazio *et al*. (1963) which are used to define the metabolic mixture and calculate energy expenditure. The four equations are also based on oxidation of carbohydrates, fats and proteins and require the measurement of $\dot{V}CO_2$, $\dot{V}O_2$ and urinary nitrogen. Furthermore, they give the same answer as the classical method using non-protein RQ.

Approximately 1 g of nitrogen is excreted in the urine for every 6.25 g of protein metabolized for energy. Each gram of excreted nitrogen represents a carbon dioxide production of approximately 4.8 litres and an oxygen consumption of about 6.8 litres.

Example calculation:
A subject consumes 3.8 litres of oxygen and produces 3.1 litres of carbon dioxide during 15 minutes of rest, during which 0.11 g of nitrogen are excreted into the urine.

1. CO_2 produced in the catabolism of protein is given by $4.8\,l\,CO_2\,g^{-1} \times 0.11\,g = 0.53\,l\,CO_2$.
2. O_2 consumed in the catabolism of protein is given by $6.0\,l\,O_2\,g^{-1}$ protein $\times 0.11\,g = 0.66\,l\,O_2$.
3. Non-protein CO_2 produced $= 3.1 - 0.53 = 2.57\,l\,CO_2$
4. Non-protein O_2 consumed $= 3.8 - 0.66 = 3.14\,l\,O_2$
5. Non-protein RQ $= 2.57 / 3.14 = 0.818$

Table 6.3 shows the energy equivalents per litre of oxygen consumed for the range of non-protein RQ values and the percentage of fat and carbohydrates utilized for energy. As Table 6.3 shows 20.20 kJ per litre of oxygen are liberated for a non-protein RQ of 0.82 as calculated above. Thus, 59.7% of the energy is derived from carbohydrate and 40.3% from fat. The non-protein energy production from carbohydrate and fat for the 15 minute period is 63.42 kJ ($20.20\,kJ\,l^{-1} \times 3.14\,l\,O_2$), whereas the energy derived from protein is 12.71 kJ ($19.26\,kJ\,l^{-1} \times 0.66\,l\,O_2$). Therefore, the total energy for the 15 minute period is 76.13 kJ (63.42 kJ non-protein + 12.71 kJ protein).

In terms of carbohydrate and fat metabolism, for the non-protein RQ of 0.818, 0.454 g of carbohydrate and 0.313 g of fat were metabolized per litre of O_2 respectively (Table 6.3). This amounts to 1.43 g of carbohydrate ($3.14\,l\,O_2 \times 0.455$) and 0.98 g of fat ($3.14\,l\,O_2 \times 0.313$) in the 15 minute rest period.

Table 6.3 Thermal equivalent of O_2 for non-protein respiratory quotient, including percentage energy and grams derived from carbohydrate and fat

Non-protein RQ	Energy (kJ) per litre oxygen used	Percentage energy derived from		Grams per litre O_2 consumed	
		Carbohydrate	Fat	Carbohydrate	Fat
0.707	19.62	0	100	0.000	0.496
0.71	19.63	1.1	98.9	0.012	0.491
0.72	19.68	4.8	95.2	0.051	0.476
0.73	19.73	8.4	91.6	0.090	0.460
0.74	19.79	12.0	88.0	0.130	0.444
0.75	19.84	15.6	84.4	0.170	0.428
0.76	19.89	19.2	80.8	0.211	0.412
0.77	19.94	22.8	77.2	0.250	0.396
0.78	19.99	26.3	73.7	0.290	0.380
0.79	20.04	29.9	70.1	0.330	0.363
0.80	20.10	33.4	66.6	0.371	0.347
0.81	20.15	36.9	63.1	0.413	0.330
0.82	20.20	40.3	59.7	0.454	0.313
0.83	20.25	43.8	56.2	0.496	0.297
0.84	20.30	47.2	52.8	0.537	0.280
0.85	20.35	50.7	49.3	0.579	0.263
0.86	20.41	54.1	45.9	0.621	0.247
0.87	20.46	57.5	42.5	0.663	0.230
0.88	20.51	60.8	39.2	0.705	0.213
0.89	20.57	64.2	35.8	0.749	0.195
0.90	20.61	67.5	32.5	0.791	0.178
0.91	20.66	70.8	29.2	0.834	0.160
0.92	20.71	74.1	25.9	0.875	0.143
0.93	20.77	77.4	22.6	0.921	0.125
0.94	20.82	80.7	19.3	0.981	0.108
0.95	20.87	84.0	16.0	1.008	0.080
0.96	20.92	87.2	12.8	1.052	0.072
0.97	20.97	90.4	9.58	1.097	0.054
0.98	21.02	93.6	6.37	1.142	0.036
0.99	21.08	96.8	3.18	1.186	0.018
1.00	21.13	100.0	0	1.231	0.000

During rest or steady-state exercise such as walking or running slowly, the RQ does not reflect the oxidation of pure carbohydrate or fat, but a mixture of the two, producing RQ values which range between 0.7 and 1.00. As shown by the sample calculation of non-protein RQ, protein contributes only a minor amount of the total energy expenditure. For this reason the specific contribution of protein is often ignored, avoiding the monitoring of N_2 excretion together with the more complex and lengthy calculations. In most instances an RQ of 0.82 can be assumed (40% carbohydrate and 60% fat) and the energy equivalent of 20.2 kJ (5.6 kcal) per litre of oxygen can be used in energy expenditure calculations. The maximum error associated with this simplification in estimating energy expenditure from $\dot{V}O_2$ is only of the order of 4% (McArdle *et al.*, 1996).

Durnin and Passmore (1967) stated that in most studies of energy expenditure there is no need to find out how much carbohydrate, fat or protein is used. Furthermore, they advocated the use of Weir's (1949) formula for estimation of energy expenditure which negates the need for CO_2 measurement.

$$\text{Energy (kcal min}^{-1}) = \frac{4.92}{100} \dot{V}E_{\text{STPD}} (20.93 - \%O_{2E})$$

The advice of Durnin and Passmore (1967) is worth serious consideration, given the possible sources of error associated with the Douglas bag technique, gas analysis and volume measurement in unskilled hands.

6.7.1 RESPIRATORY QUOTIENT (RQ) AND RESPIRATORY EXCHANGE RATIO (RER)

Under steady-state conditions of exercise, the assumption that gas exchange at the lungs reflects gas exchange from metabolism in the cells is reasonably valid. When conditions are other than steady state, such as in severe exercise, or with hyperventilation, the assumption is no longer valid. Under such conditions the ratio of carbon dioxide production to oxygen consumption is known as RER even though it is calculated in exactly the same way.

6.8 PRACTICAL 5: ESTIMATION OF RMR USING THE DOUGLAS BAG TECHNIQUE

Under ideal conditions RMR should be estimated as soon as the person wakes up from an overnight sleep. This is not possible in most practical situations, but provided that the subject can rest in a supine position for a reasonable period of time a good estimate of RMR can be obtained. During the test the subject lies quietly in a supine position (Figure 6.1), preferably in a temperature-controlled room, thus ensuring a thermoneutral environment. After 30–60 minutes, the subject's oxygen uptake is measured for a minimum of 6–10 minutes, preferably 15 minutes. If O_2 and CO_2 concentrations are measured in expired air then the RQ, energy expenditure, and substrate utilization can be estimated according to the procedures outlined above. Values for oxygen uptake used as an estimate of BMR range between 160 and 290 ml min^{-1} (3.85–6.89 kJ min^{-1}), depending upon a variety of factors, but particularly on body size (McArdle *et al.*, 1996).

6.9 PRACTICAL 6: ENERGY BALANCE

This practical introduces the procedures for the measurement of energy balance, incorporating a simplified assessment of energy expenditure and food intake. In simple terms, if the total energy intake is repeatedly greater than the daily energy expenditure, the excess energy is stored as fat. In contrast, if daily energy expenditure is greater than energy intake the subject will lose weight. The aim of the laboratory practical is to calculate the energy expenditure and energy intake for a typical day. An understanding of key concepts in energy expenditure and intake is important for several areas of exercise physiology, such as the use of diet and exercise to alter body composition, thermoregulation and mechanical efficiency. Energy expenditure is calculated by a combination of measurements, using the Douglas bag technique or an automated gas analysis system (Figure 6.3), and estimations using generalized predictive equations and tables for a range of activities. Alternatively, if available, energy expenditure can be recorded for a range of activities using a portable gas analysis system, an example of which is shown in Figure 6.4 (this is a MetaMax II, Cortex GmbH, Leipzig, Germany). The estimation of energy intake is based on the energy value of food using standard reference tables. The subject should keep a diary of activities (duration and intensity) and food consumed (quantity and preparation) for a 24-hour period. Energy intake and expenditure can then be calculated from standard tables and from direct measures of energy expenditure completed in the laboratory.

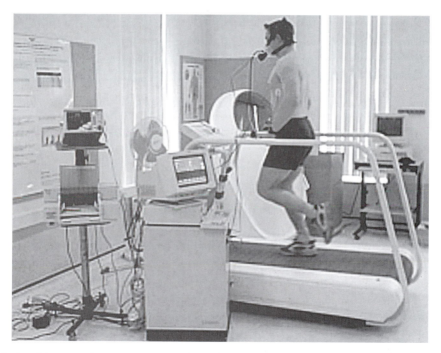

Figure 6.3 A subject running on a motorized treadmill, with expired air analysis through a face mask (Hans Rudolph Inc., KS, USA) connected to an on-line automated breath-by-breath gas analysis system (Oxycon Champion, Mijnhardt, Bunnik, Netherlands; Jaeger, Hoechberg, Germany) and a three-lead ECG through an ECG Oscillograph (CR7 Cardiorater, Cardiac Recorders, Enfield, UK).

Figure 6.4 A portable gas analysis system (MetaMax II, Cortex, Germany) to collect individual energy expenditure values for tennis. The left-hand photograph shows the system being initialised to work via telemetry, sending the signals from the device whilst the subject is playing tennis (right-hand photograph). Alternatively, the device can be used in data logging mode, with the data downloaded to the computer after the game has finished.

6.9.1 ENERGY EXPENDITURE

It is possible to measure oxygen uptake for a range of everyday activities, which should be ordered such that the least demanding are completed first. Oxygen uptake should be measured for RMR, and compared with RMR from the predictive formulae in Section 6.4. Oxygen uptake values can then be obtained for sitting, standing, self-paced walking, stair climbing and an appropriate form of exercise for the subject, such as running or cycling. If time permits, duplicate gas collections should be made. Most of the measurements can be made in the laboratory, but some may necessitate access to other buildings, such as stair climbing and descending, and self-paced walking. In such cases, the Douglas bag should be supported in some way. This is where purpose-designed portable gas analysis systems are most useful (Figure 6.4). All gas collections should be made under steady-state conditions for an appropriate length of time to analyse the expired air accurately (minimum of 10 minutes for RMR, dropping to 1 minute for the most strenuous exercise to ensure an accurately quantifiable volume).

Energy expenditure can then be calculated using the $\dot{V}O_2$, $\dot{V}CO_2$ and RQ values and their energy equivalents shown in Table 6.3 or Weir's formula presented in Section 6.7. A comparison of the two forms of calculation will indicate whether the extra precision associated with the measurement of carbon dioxide concentration and the calculation of RQ is warranted if the aim is to calculate energy expenditure.

The directly measured energy expenditure values can then be used in the calculation of the daily energy expenditure from the information recorded in the diary of activities. Where direct measurement was not possible, values for energy expenditure can be estimated from objective measures of physical activity such as heart rate. Heart rate telemetry systems, typically consisting of a chest strap, or electrodes, to detect heart rate and transmit the signal to a wrist-watch receiver with data storage (e.g. Polar, Finland), can be worn throughout the day, with data downloaded through an interface onto a computer for subsequent analysis. To use such heart rate data to estimate energy expenditure requires the relationship between heart rate and oxygen uptake to be established for the subject in the laboratory in a similar fashion to that described above for a range of everyday activities typical for the subject. Oxygen uptake and heart rate are related by a robust linear relationship which holds true throughout the submaximal range, especially when measured under controlled conditions. The heart rate values recorded throughout a typical day can be affected by a number of other factors, such as state of arousal, emotion, fatigue, stress, fever and other environmental factors such as temperature and humidity, which limits the validity of using heart rate for assessing energy expenditure and physical activity (Rowlands *et al.*, 1997). The nature of the linear relationship between heart rate and oxygen uptake will, however, be dependent upon the state of training of the subject. Remember that changes in heart rate response to a given workload or energy expenditure constitute a physiological response to endurance training. Heart rate recordings are therefore indicative of the individual, provided they are interpreted in terms of an equation relating heart rate and energy expenditure for that subject. Energy expenditure can then be estimated from the activity diary for the day using energy expenditure values estimated from the appropriate HR–VO$_2$ relationship and summed over the time period for which the particular activity was recorded.

Other objective measures of activity are also available, such as movement sensors based on mercury switches or accelerometers. These devices include a large range of relatively inexpensive pedometers to more sophisticated accelerometers that are capable of storing multi-dimensional data for subsequent computer analysis. Many devices will display a cumulative value for energy expenditure, most typically in kcal. However, it should not be assumed that such values are credible. These values are based on equations that link the direct measurement of steps, for example, to an estimate of energy expenditure based on an equation developed and validated on a particular population. It is not always possible to find out the equation used and therefore to understand the limitations of such values produced by the device. It is possible to use the raw data in the form of movement counts or steps, by calibration of the device with subjects prior to use, as exemplified in the study of habitual physical activity in children by Rowlands *et al.* (1999). These and other methods of estimating physical activity are described in more detail in Chapter 6 by Rowlands in Volume 1.

When either directly determined oxygen uptake or estimated oxygen uptake values are not available, estimates can be taken from mean values of energy expenditure published in the literature (e.g. Durnin and Passmore, 1967; Bannister and Brown, 1968; Ainsworth *et al.*, 1993; McArdle *et al.*, 1996). (Table 6.4 gives some examples of common activities.) The disadvantage of using mean values of energy expenditure taken from the literature is that they will not be specific to the individual, in terms of efficiency, and often are not very sensitive to the intensity of the activity.

156 Metabolic rate and energy balance

Table 6.4   Energy expenditure values for selected activities

Activity	kcal kg^{-1} min^{-1} [a]	METS [b]
Badminton	0.097	4.5 (general)
		7.0 (competitive)
Basketball	0.138	6.0 (general)
		8.0 (competitive)
Cycling	0.100 (15 km h^{-1})	6.0 (16–19 km h^{-1})
	0.169 (racing)	16.0 (racing >32 km h^{-1})
Dancing (aerobics)	0.135 (intense)	7.0 (high impact)
		5.0 (low impact)
		6.0 (general)
Home (cleaning general)	0.060	3.5 (general)
Home (play with child)		5.0 (run/walk – vigorous)
		2.5 (sitting)
Home (inactivity – quiet)	0.022 (lying)	1.0 (sitting)
Running	0.163 (cross-country)	9.0 (cross-country)
	0.193 (10.4 km h^{-1})	10.0 (9.6 km h^{-1})
	0.252 (16.0 km h^{-1})	16.0 (16 km h^{-1})
Squash	0.212	12.0
Swimming (crawl)	0.156 (fast)	11.0 (fast)
	0.128 (slow)	8.0 (slow)
Volleyball	0.050	4.0 (competitive)
	3.0 (non-competitive)	
Walking	0.080 (normal pace)	3.5 (4.8 km h^{-1})
		4.5 (6.4 km h^{-1})
		6.0 (backpacking)
		3.0 (downstairs)
		8.0 (upstairs)

a Values in kcal kg^{-1} min^{-1} are from McArdle *et al.* (1996).
b Values in METS are from Ainsworth *et al.* (1993).

Ainsworth *et al.* (1993) have presented a comprehensive compendium of physical activities classified in terms of intensity according to the number of METS of energy required. A MET is defined as the energy requirement for RMR. The most accurate way to compute the energy expenditure values for a given individual using their compendium is to measure the RMR and multiply it by the MET value associated with the physical activity of interest. For example, if the oxygen uptake measured as an estimate of RMR for a person of mass 70 kg was 270 ml min^{-1} with an RQ of 0.87 this would equate to an RMR value of 0.27 × 20.46 kJ l^{-1}, which equals 5.52 kJ min^{-1} (331 kJ h^{-1} or 7954 kJ day^{-1}) (1900 kcal day^{-1}). This value of RMR would represent one MET and could be multiplied by the appropriate MET value for a given physical activity. According to Ainsworth *et al.* (1993), fencing requires an energy expenditure equivalent to 6 METS. For the 70 kg individual this equates with an energy expenditure value of 6 × 5.52 kJ min^{-1}, which equals 33.1 kJ min^{-1} (7.91 kcal min^{-1}).

Table 6.5 Proforma for recording activity over a 24–hour period

	15–minute time periods			
Hour	1	2	3	4
1	Sleep	Sleep	Sleep	Sleep
2	Sleep	Sleep	Sleep	Sleep
3	Sleep	Sleep	Sleep	Sleep
4	Sleep	Sleep	Sleep	Sleep
5	Sleep	Sleep	Sleep	Sleep
6	Sleep	Sieep	Sleep	Sleep
7	Sleep	Sleep	Sitting	Eating
8	Walking	Walking	Walking	Typing
9	Typing	Typing	Typing	Typing
10	Sitting	Sitting	Sitting	Sitting
11	Typing	Typing	Typing	Typing
12	Typing	Typing	Typing	Typing
13	Walking	Eating	Eating	Typing
14	Typing	Typing	Typing	Typing
15	Typing	Typing	Walking	Walking
16	Walking	Sitting	Play child	Play child
17	Cooking	Cooking	Cleaning	Cleaning
18	Eating	Sitting	Walking	Sitting
19	Aerobics (general)	Aerobics	Aerobics	Aerobics
20	Walking	Sitting	Eating	Sitting
21	Sitting	Sitting	Sitting	Sitting
22	Sleep	Sleep	Sleep	Sleep
23	Sleep	Sleep	Sleep	Sleep
24	Sleep	Sleep	Sleep	Sleep

(Short intensive activity should be noted separately)

In the absence of a measure or prediction of RMR, diaries of self-reported physical activity can be conveniently assessed for energy expenditure based on a mean estimate of RMR of 1 kcal kg^{-1} h^{-1}. For a body mass of 70 kg this value would produce an energy expenditure value of (6 METS × 70 kg × 1 kcal kg^{-1} h^{-1} / 60 min = 7.00 kcal min^{-1} (29.3 kJ min^{-1})) for fencing. This value represents 88% of the value calculated from the measured RMR value.

The diary of physical activities for the day should be broken down into periods of the order of 10–15 minutes, with high intensity activities of a short duration, such as stair climbing, also recorded as these events can have a significant cumulative effect on the total energy expenditure for the day. Table 6.5 shows an example of such a diary which has been completed by a young female (age 24 years; mass 57 kg) who has a sedentary desk job. The data indicate that this person spends much of her time sitting, but walks to work, walks the children home from school, and attends an aerobics class in the evening. Using the appropriate MET values from Ainsworth *et al.* (1993), the daily energy expenditure can be estimated using a mean estimated RMR of 1 kcal kg^{-1} h^{-1}. For a body mass of 57 kg, this value would produce the following estimates of energy expenditure for Table 6.5:

Sleep = (57 kg × 0.9 MET × 1 kcal kg^{-1} h^{-1} × 38 (15 min periods))/4 = 487 kcal

Walking = (57 × 3.5 × 1 × 9)/4 = 449 kcal

Typing = (57 × 1.5 × 1 × 20)/4 = 428 kcal

Sitting = (57 × 1 × 1 × 14)/4 = 200 kcal

Play = (57 × 5 × 1 × 2)/4 = 143 kcal

Eating E = (57 × 1.5 × 1 × 5)/4 = 107 kcal

Cooking = (57 × 2.5 × 1 × 2)/4 = 71 kcal

Cleaning = (57 × 3.5 × 1 × 2)/4 = 100 kcal

Aerobics = (57 × 6 × 1 × 4)/4 = 342 kcal

Total = 2327 kcal (9773 kJ)

This fictitious young female subject therefore expended 2327 kcal of energy on this particular day. Table 6.6 shows an example of an alternative data collection form for recording physical activity (Ainsworth *et al.*, 1993) for a few activities for the same person (57 kg).

Table 6.6 Example of recording form for physical activities (Ainsworth *et al.*, 1993)

	Type of activity	METS	Duration (h:min)	Energy expended (kcal kg^{-1}h^{-1})
1	Sitting	1.0	8:0	456
2	Walking	3.5	2:0	399
3	Swimming fast	11.0	0:30	313
			Total	1 168 (in a 10.5 h period)

6.9.2 MEASURING ENERGY INTAKE

A set of calibrated kitchen weighing scales should be used to weigh all food that is consumed in the 24-hour period under examination. The weight of the food, its form of preparation (e.g. fried, boiled) and the amount and type of fluid drinks should be recorded in the 24-hour food diary. An example of a 24-hour diet for the young female subject for whom a 24-hour activity diary was analysed is shown in Table 6.7. The diet can then be analysed for energy intake using standard tables for common foods (e.g. McArdle *et al.*, 1996; Holland *et al.*, 1992). For the example shown in Table 6.7, using COMPEAT software (Nutrition Systems, Grantham, UK), the total energy intake is calculated to be 8346 kJ (1994 kcal).

This means that for this particular day the young female subject would be in negative energy balance, expending 1629 kJ (389 kcal) more energy than she consumes. The dietary analysis can easily be extended to a seven-day weighed food intake, with a more accurate dietary analysis of nutrients and percentages of recommended daily allowances of fat, carbohydrate and protein which can be performed using commercially available software (e.g. COMPEAT, based on Holland *et al.*, 1992).

Table 6.7 Example of a 24-hour diet record sheet

Food description	Mass (g)
Special K	50.0
Skimmed milk	150.0
Water	1 700.0
Indian tea	520.0
Meat paste	30.0
Wholemeal bread	76.0
Tomatoes (raw)	65.0
Eating apples (Cox's Pippin)	100.0
Crisps	25.0
Chocolate digestive biscuits	51.0
Cheese and tomato pizza	365.0
Hot cross bun	50.0
Ribena (undiluted)	30.0

6.10 SUMMARY

This chapter has set out a small selection of laboratory practicals which will give an introduction to the measurement of metabolic rate and energy balance. These procedures form the basis of many aspects of experimental work in a variety of areas of study, such as kinanthropometry, nutrition and exercise physiology, and can easily be adapted to the specific requirements of a large number of experiments using different items of equipment.

REFERENCES

Ainsworth, B.E., Haskell, W.L., Leon, A.S., *et al.* (1993). Compendium of physical activities: classification of energy costs of human physical activities. *Medicine and Science in Sports and Exercise*, **25**, 71–80.

Altman, P.L. and Dittmer, D.S. (1968). *Metabolism*. (FASBEB, Bethesda, MD).

Bannister, E.W. and Brown, S.R. (1968). The relative energy requirements of physical activity. In *Exercise Physiology*. ed. H.B. Falls (Academic Press, New York).

Carpenter, T.M. (1964). *Tables, Functions, and Formulas for Computing Respiratory Exchange and Biological Transformation of Energy*, 4th edn. (Carnegie Institution of Washington, Publication 303C, Washington, DC).

Consolazio, C.F., Johnson, R.E. and Pecora, L.J. (1963). *Physiological Measurements of Metabolic Functions in Man*. (McGraw-Hill, New York).

Cunningham, J.J. (1991). Body composition as a determinant of energy expenditure: a synthetic review and a proposed general prediction equation. *American Journal of Clinical Nutrition*, **54**, 963–9.

DuBois, D. and DuBois, E.F. (1916). Clinical calorimetry. A formula to estimate the approximate surface area if stature and weight are known. *Archives of Internal Medicine*, **17**, 863–71.

Durnin, J.V.G.A. and Passmore, R. (1967). *Energy, Work and Leisure*. (Heinemann, London.)

Harris, J. and Benedict, F. (1919). *A Biometric Study of Basal Metabolism in Man*. (Carnegie Institution, Publication 279, Washington, DC).

Holland, B., Welch, A.A., Unwin, I.D., *et al*. (1992). *McCance and Widdowson's The Composition of Foods*, 5th edn. (The Royal Society of Chemistry and Ministry of Agriculture, Fisheries and Food, Richard Clay Ltd, UK).

Jakeman, P. and Davies, B. (1979). The characteristics of a low resistance breathing valve designed for measurement of high aerobic capacity. *British Journal of Sports Medicine*, **13**, 81–3.

Kleiber, M. (1975). *The Fire of Life. An Introduction to Animal Energetics*. (Kreiger, New York).

Knoebel, L.K. (1963). *Energy metabolism, in Physiology*. ed. E.E. Selkurt. (Little, Brown, Boston, MA), pp. 564–79.

McArdle, W.D., Katch, F.I. and Katch, V.L. (1996). *Exercise Physiology, Energy Nutrition and Human Performance*, 4th edn. (Williams and Wilkins, Baltimore, MD).

MacDougall, J.D., Roche, P.D., Bar-Or, O. and Moroz, J.R. (1979). Oxygen cost of running in children of different ages; maximal aerobic power of Canadian school children. *Canadian Journal of Applied Sports Sciences*, **4**, 237–41.

McLean, J.A. and Tobin, G. (1987). *Animal and Human Calorimetry*. (Cambridge University Press, Cambridge).

McMahon, T.A. (1984). *Muscles, Reflexes and Locomotion*. (Princeton University Press, Princeton, NJ).

Mifflin, M.D., St Jeor, S.T., Hill, L.A., *et al*. (1990). A new predictive equation for resting energy expenditure in healthy individuals. *American Journal of Clinical Nutrition*, **51**, 241–7.

Owen, O.E., Kavle, E. and Owen, R.S. (1986). A reappraisal of the caloric requirements in healthy women. *American Journal of Clinical Nutrition*, **44**, 1–19.

Owen, O.E., Holup, J.L. and D'Allessio, D.A. (1987). A re-appraisal of the caloric requirements of healthy men. *American Journal of Clinical Nutrition*, **46**, 875–85.

Rowlands, A.V., Eston, R.G. and Ingledew, D.K. (1997). Measurement of physical activity in children with particular reference to the use of heart rate and pedometry. *Sports Medicine*, **24**, 258–72.

Rowlands, A.V., Eston, R.G. and Ingledew, D.K. (1999). The relationship between activity levels, aerobic fitness, and body fat in 8- to 10-yr-old children. *Journal of Applied Physiology*, **86**, 1428–35.

Rubner, M. (1883). Über den Einfluss der Körpergrösse auf Stoff- und Kraftwechsel. *Z. Biology. Munich*, **19**, 535–62.

Schmidt-Nielsen, K. (1984). *Scaling: Why is Animal Size so Important?* (Cambridge University Press, Cambridge).

Weir, J. B. De V. (1949). New methods for calculating metabolic rate with special reference to protein metabolism. *Journal of Physiology*, **109**, 1–9.

MAXIMAL OXYGEN UPTAKE, ECONOMY AND EFFICIENCY

7

Carlton B. Cooke

7.1 AIMS

The aims in this chapter are to:
- define the measurements of maximal oxygen uptake, economy and efficiency,
- describe procedures for the direct determination of maximal oxygen uptake,
- consider methods and limitations of predicting maximal oxygen uptake,
- describe procedures for assessing the economy of movement,
- discuss the concept of 'efficiency' and describe the limitations of various measurements for assessing the efficiency of human movement,
- describe the effects of load carriage on the economy, posture and kinematics of walking.

7.2 INTRODUCTION

Measurements of maximal oxygen uptake, economy and efficiency of different forms of exercise are important in gaining an understanding of the differences between groups of athletes, and the requirements of sporting, recreational and occupational activities. They also serve to help highlight effects of sex, age and size differences.

Maximal oxygen uptake and economy are commonly measured in studies in which the aerobic performances of different individuals or groups of athletes are compared. Defining the current training status of an elite runner, or comparing the physiological profiles of different standards of athlete are examples. Efficiency measures, other than average values for estimating oxygen uptake from external work done, are less often quoted in the literature due to problems of measurement which are often exacerbated by the use and abuse of different definitions (Cavanagh and Kram, 1985).

Load carriage is an activity that provides an appropriate focus for the study of economy, including the need to consider energy expenditure, posture and kinematics. Load carriage is of interest from both occupational and recreational perspectives. The efficacy of rucksacks as a means of load carriage is important for trekkers as well as soldiers, both of which may have to carry relatively heavy loads for prolonged periods of time.

7.3 DIRECT DETERMINATION OF MAXIMAL OXYGEN UPTAKE

7.3.1 RELEVANCE

There is an upper limit to the oxygen that is consumed during exercise requiring maximal effort. This upper limit is defined as maximal oxygen uptake ($\dot{V}O_2$max), which is the maximum rate at which an individual can take up and utilize oxygen while breathing air at sea level (Åstrand and Rodahl, 1986). It has traditionally been used as the criterial standard of cardiorespiratory fitness, as it is considered to be the single physiological variable that best

Kinanthropometry and Exercise Physiology Laboratory Manual: Tests, Procedures and Data. 2nd Edition, Volume 2: Exercise Physiology
Edited by RG Eston and T Reilly. Published by Routledge, London, June 2001

defines the functional capacity of the cardio-vascular and respiratory systems. However, it is more accurate to consider it as an indicator of both potential for endurance performance and, to a lesser extent, training status. Even though the physiological basis of $\dot{V}O_2$max has been established for a considerable time, there has recently been some robust debate based on a challenge of A.V. Hill's paradigm by Noakes (1997, 1998) which has been refuted by Bassett and Howley (1997) and others.

At any given time the $\dot{V}O_2$max of an individual is fixed and specific for a given task, e.g. running, cycling, rowing and so on. The $\dot{V}O_2$max can be increased with training or decreased with a period of enforced inactivity, such as bed rest. Changes of up to 100% in $\dot{V}O_2$max have been reported after a period of training following prolonged bed rest (Saltin *et al.*, 1968). Pollock (1973) published a review in which the effect of endurance training is reported to have produced changes in $\dot{V}O_2$max which ranged from 0 to 93%. The initial level of fitness (a reflection of an individual combination of endowment and habitual activity), intensity, frequency and duration of training are factors that will influence the effects of endurance training on $\dot{V}O_2$max. The age and sex of the individual are relevant considerations also. It is, therefore, not surprising that training studies carried out on habitually active endurance athletes have produced non-significant changes in $\dot{V}O_2$max, of the order of only 2–3%, whereas endurance performance has dramatically increased. Training programmes carried out on previously sedentary subjects can produce significant changes in $\dot{V}O_2$max values, usually of the order of 20–30%.

Measurements of $\dot{V}O_2$max indicate aerobic potential and to a lesser extent, training status. The sensitivity of $\dot{V}O_2$max to changes in training or the establishment of regular habitual physical activity is strongly related to the degree of development in $\dot{V}O_2$max that may be ultimately realized, which reflects a combination of endowment and habitual physical activity. Although it is generally agreed that

genetic factors play an important role in defining the potential for development of physiological variables such as $\dot{V}O_2$max, the extent to which $\dot{V}O_2$max is determined by endowment has been adjusted downwards in more recent studies from 90% to something of the order of 40–70% (Bouchard and Malina, 1983).

The maximal oxygen uptake ($\dot{V}O_2$max) is also important as a baseline measure to be used with other measures of endurance performance, such as fractional utilization (%$\dot{V}O_2$max that can be sustained for prolonged periods), onset of blood lactate accumulation (OBLA) and running economy (see Chapter 10 by Jones and Doust). A high $\dot{V}O_2$max may be considered to be a prerequisite for elite performance in endurance sport, but does not guarantee achievement at the highest level of sport. Technique, state of training and psychological factors also have positive and negative modifying effects on performance. It is for these reasons that measures of $\dot{V}O_2$max do not allow an accurate prediction of an individual's performance potential in aerobic power events. Shephard (1984) reviewed 37 studies reporting correlation coefficients between all-out running performance and measured $\dot{V}O_2$max, and found coefficients ranging from 0.04 to 0.90.

(a) Age, sex and $\dot{V}O_2$max

A combination of cross-sectional and longitudinal studies provides a reasonably clear picture of the development of $\dot{V}O_2$max during childhood and adolescence and its decline during adulthood (Bar-Or, 1983; Krahenbuhl *et al.*, 1985; Åstrand and Rodahl, 1986; Allied Dunbar National Fitness Survey, 1992). Absolute $\dot{V}O_2$max values increase steadily prior to puberty with the growth of the pulmonary, cardiovascular and musculoskeletal systems. At the onset of puberty the curves relating age and $\dot{V}O_2$max values for males and females begin to diverge and continue to do so during adolescence. After the acceleration of $\dot{V}O_2$max values in males at puberty which reflects the increased muscle mass, and given that $\dot{V}O_2$max in females remains virtually unchanged after early teens, females' $\dot{V}O_2$max values are on average 65–75% of those of males.

In both sexes there is a peak in $\dot{V}O_2$max values at 18–20 years of age followed by a gradual decline with increasing age. The results of the Allied Dunbar National Fitness Survey (1992), where $\dot{V}O_2$max was estimated for over 1700 men and women, produced average values of 55 and 40 ml kg^{-1} min^{-1} for men and women aged 16–24 years, respectively. After this time, $\dot{V}O_2$max declined steadily with increasing age, resulting in average values of about 30 and 25 ml kg^{-1} min^{-1} for men and women aged 65–74 years, respectively. In contrast, $\dot{V}O_2$max values for elite endurance athletes may exceed 80 ml kg^{-1} min^{-1}. Data from a variety of population studies indicate that at the age of 65 the average $\dot{V}O_2$max value is approximately 70% of that of a 25-year-old of the same sex.

(b) Body size and $\dot{V}O_2$max

Comparisons of physiological measurements between subjects of different size are common-place, especially in the case of children versus adults. These comparisons are made in both cross-sectional and longitudinal studies, which in the latter case include comparisons of the same subjects during the growing years.

In the case of $\dot{V}O_2$max there is a strong positive relationship between body size and absolute $\dot{V}O_2$max (l min^{-1}). Generally speaking, the larger the subject the larger the $\dot{V}O_2$max in absolute terms (l min^{-1}). In an attempt to overcome the effects of differences in body mass when comparing $\dot{V}O_2$max values, the latter are often divided by body mass prior to comparison. The $\dot{V}O_2$max (ml kg^{-1} min^{-1}) is therefore considered to be a weight-adjusted expression of $\dot{V}O_2$max where the effects of differences in body mass have been factored out.

However, $\dot{V}O_2$max expressed in ml kg^{-1} min^{-1} correlates negatively with body mass. Far from eliminating the effect of body mass, this form of expression converts a positive relationship between $\dot{V}O_2$max (l min^{-1}) and body mass into a negative one between $\dot{V}O_2$max (ml kg^{-1} min^{-1}) and body mass. Therefore, this common form of weight correction does not eliminate the effects of body mass or weight at all.

Nevertheless, $\dot{V}O_2$max has probably continued to be related to body mass in the form ml kg^{-1} min^{-1} because body mass is easily obtained. It also correlates well with most measures of cardiorespiratory function. There is also a strong positive relationship with performance in weight-bearing activities such as running, so expressing the power output per kilogram of body mass would seem appropriate where the body mass has to be carried in the activity.

If dividing $\dot{V}O_2$max by body mass does not factor out the effects of body mass on $\dot{V}O_2$max (l min^{-1}), then the question arises as to what form of expression of $\dot{V}O_2$max is independent of body mass and can therefore allow meaningful comparisons among individuals differing in body size?

Theoretically, since maximal force in muscle is dependent on cross-sectional area, muscle force will be proportional to length^2 (L^2), the squared function representing an area. Similarly, work or energy is based on force × distance, therefore work done or energy expended is proportional to $F \times L$ or L^3 (on a cubic function). As $\dot{V}O_2$max is an expression of energy expenditure per unit of time or power output, which is $(F \times L) / t$, and time is proportional to L then $\dot{V}O_2$max (l min^{-1}) is proportional to $L^3 L^{-1}$ or L^2.

Since mass (M) is proportional to volume which is proportional to L^3, then $\dot{V}O_2$max (l min^{-1}) should be proportional to $M^{2/3}$ (since M is proportional to L^3, $\dot{V}O_2$max is proportional to L^2 and $M^{2/3} = L^2$). A more detailed discussion of the scaling effects of body size and dimensional analysis can be found in Schmidt-Nielson (1984), McMahon (1984) and Åstrand and Rodahl (1986).

The theoretical expectation that $\dot{V}O_2$max (l min^{-1}) should be proportional to L^2 or $M^{2/3}$ is true for well-trained adult athletes (Åstrand and Rodahl, 1986) and recreationally active adult males and females (Nevill *et al.*, 1992). However, longitudinal studies of children's $\dot{V}O_2$max (l min^{-1}) have identified exponents of L which range from 1.51 to 3.21 (or M from 0.503 to 1.07) (Bar-Or, 1983).

In the case of active adults and athletes, expressing $\dot{V}O_2$max in ml kg$^{-2/3}$ min^{-1} would appear to eliminate the confounding effects of body mass on $\dot{V}O_2$max (l min^{-1}). It therefore provides a more meaningful index than the more conventional expression of $\dot{V}O_2$max in ml kg^{-1} min^{-1}, which disadvantages heavier individuals.

Besides demonstrating the superiority of the expression of $\dot{V}O_2$max in ml kg$^{-2/3}$ min^{-1}, in adjusting for differences in body mass, Nevill *et al.* (1992) also showed that the more conventional expression of $\dot{V}O_2$max in ml kg^{-1} min^{-1} held true in terms of predicting ability to run 5 km expressed as a function of average running speed. This supports the use of the conventional expression of $\dot{V}O_2$max in ml kg^{-1} min^{-1} for weight-bearing activities, which are highly dependent on body size. It is therefore important to be clear on the aim of comparing different forms of expression, since performance and physiological function do not always use the same criteria. Further discussion on the principles of scaling physiological and anthropometric data is presented in Volume 1, Chapter 11 by Winter and Nevill.

7.3.2 PROTOCOLS

There is a large number of protocols reported in the literature for the direct determination of $\dot{V}O_2$max. These range from short, single-load protocols performed at so-called 'supra-maximal' workloads, lasting no longer than 6 minutes, to relatively long discontinuous protocols where the subject exercises for anything from 3 to 6 minutes at each workload and then rests for about 3 minutes between increments (Åstrand and Rodahl, 1986).

One of the general recommendations for the assessment of $\dot{V}O_2$max is that subjects should perform rhythmic exercise which requires a large muscle mass. This ensures that the cardiorespiratory system is taxed and the test is not limited by local muscular endurance. The muscle mass engaged explains why simulated cross-country skiing produces the highest $\dot{V}O_2$max values, followed by graded treadmill running, flat treadmill running and cycle ergometry. The specificity of the activity of the subject undergoing assessment should take precedence if the aim is to produce meaningful values for interpretation of aerobic potential or current training status. For example, canoeists should be tested on a canoe ergometer, but will generally produce lower $\dot{V}O_2$max values than if they were running on a treadmill. It has been known, in exceptional cases, for a subject only used to strenuous exercise in canoeing to produce a higher $\dot{V}O_2$max value than when running on a treadmill.

Given the plethora of protocols for the direct determination of $\dot{V}O_2$max, it is worthwhile to consider attempts at standardization through guidelines such as those published by the British Association of Sports Sciences (1992) in its 'Position Statement on the Physiological Assessment of the Elite Competitor'. These guidelines contain tables for establishing the appropriate exercise intensities for the direct determination of $\dot{V}O_2$max using leg and arm cycling and graded treadmill running (Tables 7.1 and 7.2).

The British Association of Sports and Exercise Sciences (BASES) (1997) have recommended the following criteria for establishing maximal oxygen uptake in adult subjects:

1. A plateau in the oxygen uptake–exercise intensity relationship. This has been defined as an increase in oxygen uptake of less than 2 ml kg^{-1} min^{-1} or 3% with an increase in exercise intensity. If this plateau is not achieved, then the term $\dot{V}O_2$peak is preferred.
2. A final respiratory exchange ratio of 1.15 or above.
3. A final heart rate of within 10 beats min^{-1} of the predicted age-related maximum. (Maximum heart rate can be estimated from the

Table 7.1 Guidelines for establishing exercise intensity for the determination of maximal oxygen uptake during leg or arm cycling in adults

	Warm-up (W)	Initial work-rate (W)	Work-rate increment (W)
Leg cycling (pedal frequency 60 min^{-1})			
Male	120	180–240	30
Female	60	150–200	30
Arm cycling (pedal frequency 60 min^{-1})	60	90	30
Elite cyclists (pedal frequency 90 min^{-1})			
Male	150	200–250	35
Female	100	150	35

Table 7.2 Guidelines for establishing exercise intensity for the determination of maximal oxygen uptake during treadmill running in adults

	Warm-up speed (m s^{-1})	Test speed (m s^{-1})	Initial grade (%)	Grade increment
Endurance athletes				
Male	3.13	4.47	0	2.5
Female	2.68	4.02	0	2.5
Games players				
Male	3.13	3.58	0	2.5
Female	2.68	3.13	0	2.5

formula: Maximal heart rate = 220 – age (years) if the maximum value is unknown.)
4. A post-exercise (4–5 minutes) blood lactate concentration of 8 mmol l^{-1} or more.
5. Subjective fatigue and volitional exhaustion.
6. A rating of perceived exertion (RPE) of 19 or 20 on the Borg 6 to 20 rating of perceived exertion scale.

The third edition of the BASES guidelines has been considerably developed and includes much more useful information than the second edition, including sport-specific testing guidelines and considerations for testing children. Nevertheless, the tables presented above still provide useful guidance for testing maximal oxygen uptake in adult subjects. Considerations for testing children are presented in Volume 1, Chapter 8 by Boreham and Van Praagh.

(a) Example treadmill protocol (continuous protocol)

The protocol in Table 7.2 is based on that of Taylor *et al.* (1955) and is suitable for the habitually active and sports participants. The recommended exercise intensities should produce volitional exhaustion in 9–15 minutes of continuous exercise, following a 5 minute warm-up. Thus, unless steady-state values are required, 2-minute increments are recommended.

(b) Example cycle ergometer protocol (discontinuous protocol)

A detailed description of such a protocol and associated procedures is given in Section 7.8.

7.3.3 RESULTS

Table 7.3 shows a completed pro forma for the discontinuous cycle ergometer protocol. It can be used for most protocols involving expired air collection and analysis using the Douglas bag technique, but is easily adapted for variations in data collection or experimental protocols. Figure 7.1 shows the results from a $\dot{V}O_2$max test performed on the treadmill by a trained male runner aged 21. Data for the

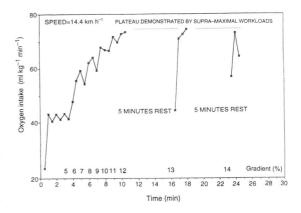

Figure 7.1 Results of a $\dot{V}O_2$max test performed by a 21-year-old male runner on a motorized treadmill.

Table 7.3 Douglas bag data collection during an intermittent cycle ergometer protocol

Subject: J. Bloggs	Date: 30–9–1993	Time: 2.00	Mass (kg): 81
Age: 21	DoB: 7.12.71	PB (mmHg): 753.5	Ht (cm): 180
Temp. (°C): 21	Humidity (%) 65	Protocol: Discontinuous	Ergometer: Cycle (3 min work, 3 min rest)

Bag no.	1	2	3	4	5
Work-rate (W)	200	250	300	350	400
Exercise time (min)	2–3	5–6	8–9	11–12	14–15
Collection time (s)	60	60	60	60	60
Temperature of expired air (°C)	24.0	24.0	23.8	24.0	24.0
Volume (l) (ATPS)	68.60	93.75	125.5	162.1	170.3
Volume of sample (l)	2.0	2.0	2.0	2.0	2.0
$\dot{V}E$ ATPS (l)	70.60	95.75	127.5	164.1	172.3
$\dot{V}E$ STPD (l min^{-1})	62.44	84.68	113.1	145.1	152.4
F_EO_2 (%)	16.13	17.03	17.37	17.71	17.82
F_ECO_2 (%)	4.30	3.46	3.34	3.25	3.22
$\dot{V}O_2$ (l min^{-1})	3.09	3.41	4.10	4.69	4.73
$\dot{V}CO_2$ (l min^{-1})	2.66	2.91	3.74	4.69	4.86
RER	0.863	0.852	0.913	1.00	1.03
Borg RPE	13	15	16	19	20
Heart rate (beats min^{-1})	154	168	183	197	198

treadmill test were collected using an Oxycon 5 automated gas analysis system (Mijnhardt Oxycon Champion, Bunnik, Netherlands). The test was continuous until volitional exhaustion, after which the subject attempted two further workloads to demonstrate a plateau in oxygen uptake.

7.4 PREDICTION OF MAXIMAL OXYGEN UPTAKE

Although a direct determination of maximal oxygen uptake is feasible with well-conditioned and highly motivated individuals, provided there is access to appropriate laboratory facilities, it is often only possible to conduct either a submaximal exercise test, or a maximum performance test in the field. The results from many such tests are then used to estimate maximal oxygen uptake (Åstrand and Ryhming, 1954; Siconolfi *et al.*, 1982; Åstrand and Rodahl, 1986).

Probably the most widely used procedure for predicting maximal oxygen uptake is the Åstrand–Ryhming (1954) nomogram. Use of the nomogram in submaximal field tests is based on measuring the heart rate response to a quantifiable form of external work for which the mechanical efficiency is known. Thus, the oxygen uptake elicited by the external work can be estimated (i.e. cycle ergometry, treadmill walking and running, stepping). The nomogram consists of scales for work-rate in cycle ergometry, and steps of 33 cm and 40 cm in height, which are located alongside a scale for oxygen uptake. Therefore, if the appropriate step height or cycle ergometry is used, then a prediction of maximal oxygen uptake can be obtained from the measured heart rate response. The value can then be age-adjusted based on empirically derived age-correction factors. Shephard (1970) produced an algorithm for a computer solution of the Åstrand–Ryhming nomogram which is easily programmed in most computer languages.

Åstrand and Rodahl (1986) described a simple submaximal cycle ergometer test which when used in conjunction with the nomogram will provide an estimate of maximal oxygen uptake. For women a work-rate of 75–100 W has been suggested, and for men 100–150 W. If the heart rate exceeds 130 beats min^{-1} the test is stopped after 6 minutes. If the heart rate is lower than 130 beats min^{-1} after a couple of minutes of exercise, the work-rate should be increased by 50 W. The steady-state heart rate response, taken as the mean of the value at 5 and 6 minutes, together with the work-rate, can then be used to predict the maximal oxygen uptake. There is error associated with the prediction of $\dot{V}O_2$max using the Åstrand–Ryhming nomogram and associated submaximal test procedures. Some of the reasons for this are: assumptions of linearity in the heart rate–oxygen uptake relationship for all subjects, decline and variation in maximum heart rate with increasing age and variations in mechanical efficiency. In addition, there are factors which affect the heart rate response to a given exercise intensity, but not maximal oxygen uptake, such as anxiety, dehydration, prolonged heavy exercise, exercise with a small muscle mass and exercise after consumption of alcohol.

The standard error for predicting maximal oxygen uptake from the studies used to validate the nomogram is 10% in relatively well-trained individuals of the same age as the original sample, but up to 15% in moderately trained individuals of different ages when the age correction factors are used. Values for untrained subjects are often underestimated, whereas elite athletes are often overestimated (Åstrand and Rodahl, 1986). This limitation in accuracy for estimation of maximal oxygen uptake is an important consideration, especially when dealing with repeated measures of subjects participating in a training study. The authors concluded that 'this drawback (in accuracy) holds true for any submaximal cardiopulmonary test'.

Another common form of submaximal test using a step or a cycle ergometer is to exercise the subject at four different exercise intensities and measure the heart rate (HR) and oxygen uptake at each work-rate (Wyndham *et al.*, 1966; Harrison *et al.*, 1980). Using linear regression, the HR–$\dot{V}O_2$ relationship is extrapolated to a predicted maximum heart rate value (e.g. maximum heart rate = 220 – age in years) to obtain an estimate of maximal oxygen uptake.

The Physical Work Capacity (PWC) test is also a popular form of submaximal exercise test, and was adopted as the cycle ergometer test for use with children in the Eurofit initiative (Council of Europe, 1988). The relationship between heart rate and work-rate is established using three or four submaximal work-rates and the PWC is calculated by extrapolation to a specific heart rate, which is most commonly 170 beats min^{-1}; hence the score is called a PWC$_{170}$. However, if the oxygen uptake can be measured directly, then it is preferable to do so, as the PWC procedure takes no account of individual variations in mechanical efficiency. This test has also been used with adults in an adjusted form where the target heart rate for the final workload was 85% of predicted maximum heart rate. Whether or not this heart rate value is achieved during the test, it is used as the criterion value for the extrapolation or interpolation of the PWC value.

There are also a large number of field tests which include an equation for the prediction of maximal oxygen uptake, such as a one-mile-walk test (Kline *et al.*, 1987), a 20 m multistage shuttle test (Léger and Lambert, 1982; Paliczka *et al.*, 1987; Boreham *et al.*, 1990), and Cooper's 12 minute walk–run test (Cooper, 1968). All these tests are maximal in that the subjects have to go as fast as possible in the walk and run tests, and for as long as possible in the multistage shuttle test. They are therefore dependent on subjects being well motivated and used to strenuous exercise. However, they are acceptable as indicators of current training status as they are all performance tests, irrespective of their accuracy in the prediction of maximal oxygen uptake. The reliability and validity of run–walk tests have been reviewed by Eston and Brodie (1985).

In conclusion, whatever form of submaximal test is adopted, whether it is based on either the work-rate–heart rate relationship or the oxygen uptake–heart rate relationship, extreme caution should be used in the interpretation of predicted maximal oxygen uptake values.

7.5 ECONOMY

7.5.1 INTRODUCTION

Economy of energy expenditure is important in any endurance event which makes demands on aerobic energy supply. If a lower oxygen uptake can be achieved through the optimization of skill and technique for a given exercise intensity, be it cross-country skiing, kayaking or running, then, all other things being equal, performance can be maintained for a longer period of time at a given exercise intensity, or at a slightly increased exercise intensity for the same period of time. Although the measurement of economy of energy expenditure described here is that of running economy, similar principles, procedures and protocols also apply to other activities. One such activity that is also considered is that of load carriage, which may have an effect on economy, kinematics and efficiency of movement.

Running economy can be defined as the metabolic cost, measured as oxygen uptake per kilogram per minute for a given treadmill speed and slope. A lower oxygen uptake for a given running speed is therefore interpreted as a better running economy.

There is a strong correlation between $\dot{V}O_2$max and distance running performance in studies based on a wide range of running capabilities (Cooper, 1968; Costill *et al.*, 1973). This relationship is not evident in a homogeneous sample of elite runners (Conley and Krahenbuhl, 1980). However, running economy is correlated significantly with distance running performance (Costill, 1972; Costill *et al.*, 1973; Conley and Krahenbuhl, 1980) and therefore may, in part, account for why $\dot{V}O_2$max is not a good predictor.

7.5.2 METHODOLOGY

Running economy is measured by means of establishing the oxygen cost to running speed (or speed and gradient) relationship. Many of the studies in the literature have entailed comparisons of measures of running economy for a single running speed (e.g. equivalent to race pace and/or training pace). Nevertheless, there is value in measuring oxygen uptake over a range of running speeds, especially if comparing the performance of children and adults.

In order to obtain a 'true' measure of running economy at a range of running speeds the oxygen uptake must be measured under steady-state conditions. The subject should be exercising in the aerobic range (i.e. no significant contribution to metabolic energy from anaerobic sources). Åstrand and Rodahl (1986) suggested that $\dot{V}O_2$max protocols based on work-rates where a steady state of oxygen uptake is achieved have the advantage of simultaneously establishing relationships between submaximal oxygen cost and speed of performance. Similarly, measures of running economy can be made at the same time as the establishment of blood lactate responses (see Chapter 10 by Jones and Doust). When the $\dot{V}O_2$max of the subject is known, it is common practice to select four running speeds which are predicted to elicit 60%, 70%, 80% and 90% of $\dot{V}O_2$max.

(a) Protocol

A protocol for measurement of running economy is described in section 7.9. This protocol and associated procedures can easily be adapted for other forms of ergometry.

7.5.3 RESULTS

Figure 7.2 shows the relationships between oxygen cost and running speed for three groups of adult male runners: 10 elite, 10 club and 10 recreational runners. There was a significant increase ($p < 0.001$) in the oxygen cost of running over the range of speeds analysed

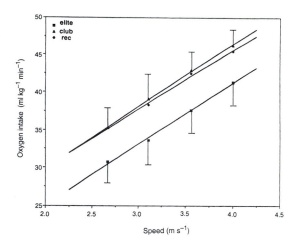

Figure 7.2 Oxygen cost to running speed relationship for three groups of ten adult male runners: elite, club and recreational.

($2.67–4.00$ m s^{-1}) in all three groups. Linear regression equations for the three groups are:

Elite $\dot{V}O_2$ (ml kg^{-1} min^{-1}) $= 8.07 \times$ SPEED (m s^{-1}) $+ 8.87$

$$(r = 0.99; r^2 = 0.98)$$

Club $\dot{V}O_2$ (ml kg^{-1} min^{-1}) $= 8.27 \times$ SPEED (m s^{-1}) $+ 13.27$

$$(r = 0.99; r^2 = 0.98)$$

Rec $\dot{V}O_2$ (ml kg^{-1} min^{-1}) $= 7.80 \times$ SPEED (m s^{-1}) $+ 14.35$

$$(r = 0.99; r^2 = 0.98)$$

There was a significant difference ($p < 0.001$) in the oxygen cost of running in the three groups. The elite group required significantly lower ($p < 0.001$) oxygen uptakes than either the club or recreational runners (mean difference of 4.7 ml kg^{-1} min^{-1}; 11.5%). The recreational runners appeared to have slightly better running economy at the higher running speeds than the club runners (Figure 7.2). Blood lactate values revealed that not all the recreational runners were meeting the energy requirements by aerobic sources alone, which would account for the less steep slope of their regression line. It is therefore important to ensure that comparisons of running economy are made on subjects who are exercising aerobically so that steady-state oxygen uptake values reflect the energy requirements of the exercise.

Figure 7.3 shows the relationships between oxygen cost and running speed for two groups of male runners: adults aged 21.3 ± 2.3 years and children aged 11.9 ± 1.0 years (Cooke *et al.*, 1991). There was a significant increase ($p < 0.001$) in the oxygen cost of running over the range of speeds studied (2.67, 3.11, 3.56 and 4.0 m s^{-1}) in both the children and adults. The children required a significantly greater ($p < 0.001$) $\dot{V}O_2$, on average 7 ml kg^{-1} min^{-1} (18.5%), for any given running speed. The divergence of the two regression lines shows the significant difference (ANCOVA; $p < 0.05$) in the $\dot{V}O_2$ response of the children and the adults over the range of speeds. Slopes of 10.87 for the children and 9.05 for the adults equate to a difference of 5.8 ml kg^{-1} min^{-1} at 2.67 m s^{-1} and 8.6 ml kg^{-1} min^{-1} at 4.0 m s^{-1}.

As the correlation between oxygen uptake and body mass is non-significant when oxygen uptake is expressed in ml kg$^{-0.75}$ min^{-1} (Kleiber, 1975), the ANCOVA was repeated with $\dot{V}O_2$ expressed in ml kg$^{-0.75}$ min^{-1} to establish whether the group differences in the oxygen cost of unloaded running could be accounted for by

differences in body mass. Figure 7.4 shows that there was no significant difference between the groups, as the regression lines became similar. For an explanation of the analysis of covariance procedure and its application, see Volume 1, Chapter 11 by Winter and Nevill).

7.5.4 DISCUSSION

(a) Adult running economy values

The running economy results for the three groups of adult male runners reflect that elite runners have trained themselves in the technique of running, optimizing their running style to produce significantly lower oxygen uptake values for any given running speed. This finding is in agreement with other cross-sectional studies which have generally reported that highly-trained distance runners have better running economy than runners of club and recreational standard, but there is variation in economy within each standard of running (Costill and Fox, 1969; Costill, 1972; Pollock, 1973; Bransford and Howley, 1977; Conley and Krahenbuhl, 1980; Morgan *et al.*, 1995). Longitudinal studies have also shown that running economy can

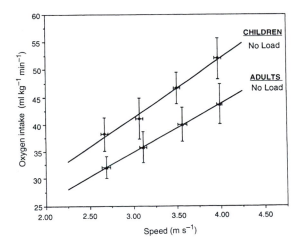

Figure 7.3 Oxygen cost (ml kg^{-1} min^{-1}) to running speed relationship for two groups of well-trained male runners: 8 boys and 8 men (Cooke *et al.*, 1991).

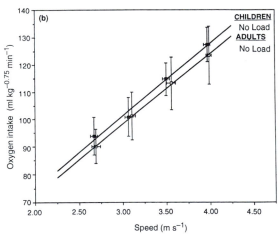

Figure 7.4 Oxygen cost (ml kg$^{-0.75}$ min^{-1}) to running speed relationships for two groups of well-trained male runners: 8 boys and 8 men (Cooke *et al.*, 1991).

be improved with training (Conley *et al.*, 1981).

It is fairly well established that there is a U-shaped relationship between stride length or stride frequency and energy cost at a given unloaded walking or running speed (Cavanagh and Williams, 1982). Moreover, it appears that the curve is relatively flat near to the optimum stride length / stride frequency combination (Cavanagh and Williams, 1982). As a result small deviations from the normal pattern have little or no effect on energy cost. Freely chosen stride length / stride frequency combinations are known to be close to optimum (Cavanagh and Williams, 1982). However, variations in stride length and stride frequency have been shown to increase the oxygen uptake for a given running speed, thereby making the movement less economical. This has been found in experiments where runners have made acute adjustments to their running technique by either deliberately overstriding or understriding. Both forms of adjustment therefore decrease economy, which led researchers to the conclusion that runners adopt a stride length / stride frequency combination that best suits them in terms of running economy. However, the research that has led to this viewpoint is based on experiments that incorporate acute rather than chronic changes to running kinematics. In the case of competitive athletes, the stride length / stride frequency combination has developed as a result of long-term training. The effect of stride manipulation on running economy can be demonstrated easily in the laboratory.

The effect of posture on running economy can be assessed by altering head position. In one study, runners were required to run with their eyes focussed on a target 2 m in front of them at eye level, to produce an upright posture, or 1 m in front of them at floor level to induce a bent-over posture. Running economy was lower in the bent-over position (Jordan and Cooke, 1998). The protocol outlined in Section 7.9 can be used to evaluate the effects of the adjustments of either head position or stride length. When altering stride length it is necessary to measure stride frequency using a stopwatch to time a set number of stride cycles. Changes in stride length (SL) can then be calculated from the stride frequency (SF) and speed of the treadmill, using the formula SL (m) = SPEED (m s^{-1}) / SF (str s^{-1}). If required, a video camera can be set up perpendicular to the line of running to record the runner. This allows the changes in posture to be checked by simple measurements taken from the video images.

One criticism of comparing weight-corrected oxygen uptake values between individuals or groups is that oxygen uptake per kilogram body mass is not itself independent of body mass. Since the elite subjects had a lower mean body mass, the differences between the elite, club and recreational runners would be increased only slightly if oxygen uptake was expressed in ml kg$^{-0.75}$ min^{-1}.

(b) Child and adult running economy values

The mass-specific equations relating oxygen uptake to running speed for both children and adults shown in Figure 7.3 are similar to others reported in the literature (Åstrand, 1952; Margaria *et al.*, 1963; Davies, 1980). Some variation in equations due to population bias, treadmill type, and measurement techniques is to be expected. However, the mean difference between children and adults of 8 ml kg^{-1} min^{-1} in oxygen uptake is similar to that of other studies.

Smaller animals are metabolically more active than larger ones. This difference is also apparent in a comparison of mass-specific resting metabolic rates of children and adults. If the estimated resting metabolic rate is subtracted from the gross oxygen cost of running shown in Figure 7.3 then the difference between the regression lines decreases by 1.8 ml kg^{-1} min^{-1} (25%). Resting metabolic rate was estimated from the data of Altman and Dittmer (1968) using the formula of DuBois and DuBois (1916) for estimating body surface area.

The correlation between metabolic rate per

unit of body size and body mass is non-significant when metabolic rate is divided by body mass to the power of 0.75 (Kleiber, 1975). The data for boys and men shown in Figure 7.4 are consistent with this established comparative measure of metabolic body size.

The data also agree closely with a power function developed to predict the mass-specific oxygen cost of running from body mass and running speed in over 50 animal species (Taylor *et al.*, 1982). The power function was indicated by:

$$\frac{\dot{V}O_2}{M} = 0.533 \times M^{-0.316} \times V + 0.300 \times M^{-0.303}$$

where $\dfrac{\dot{V}O_2}{M}$ = oxygen cost (ml kg^{-1} s^{-1})

V = velocity (m s^{-1})

M = body mass (kg)

The analogy between animals of different mass (from the flying squirrel with a mass of 0.063 kg to zebu cattle with a mass of 254 kg) would appear to suggest that differences in the relationship between oxygen cost and running speed in children and adults might be expected. However, Eston *et al.* (1993) showed that when body mass was used as a covariate (i.e. the dependent variable of oxygen uptake was linearly adjusted such that comparisons were made as if all subjects had the same body mass) differences between the oxygen uptake of boys and men running at the same speeds were non-significant. The use of scaling techniques to partition out the effects of size is currently an area of renewed interest and investigation, and is discussed in greater detail in Volume 1, Chapter 11 by Winter and Nevill.

Rowland (1990) has suggested a number of factors that might explain the differences in running economy between children and adults:

1. Ratio of surface area to mass: as discussed previously, differences in BMR may account for something of the order of 25% of the greater oxygen cost of running in children compared with adults. This difference in BMR is based on the surface area law as described in Chapter 6 of this text.

2. Stride frequency: the higher oxygen uptake for a given running speed in children may be partly explained by the necessarily higher stride frequency, resulting in the more frequent braking and acceleration of the centre of mass of the body, and the increased metabolic cost of producing more muscle contractions (Unnithan and Eston, 1990).

3. Immature running mechanics: the running styles of children are different from those of adults, with changes occurring through the growing years to adulthood (Wickstrom, 1983). However, the extent to which variations in running style with age might explain the differences between adults and children in the relationship between oxygen uptake and running speed is as yet unknown.

4. Speed–mass mismatch: the speed at which a muscle contracts is inversely related to the force generated. Thus, as muscles contract more quickly they produce less force (Hill, 1939). Davies (1980) suggested that an imbalance of these two factors might help to explain the differences between children and adults in running economy. This suggestion was based on observations that when children were loaded with a weight jacket their oxygen uptake per kilogram total mass decreased, and approached adult values. However, similar experiments have revealed different results, suggesting that children and adults may be equally efficient at running with different forms of loading (Thorstensson, 1986; Cooke *et al.*, 1991).

5. Differences in anaerobic energy: it is well established that children are unable to produce anaerobic energy as effectively as adults. It is therefore important that subjects are exercising aerobically to prevent any inflation of child–adult differences in running economy values due to anaerobic energy contributions in the adult subjects.

6. Less efficient ventilation: children need to ventilate more than adults for each litre of oxygen consumed (i.e. $\dot{V}E/\dot{V}O_2$, the ventilatory equivalent for oxygen is greater in children). These differences in ventilation patterns in children and adults may contribute to the differences in economy, since during maximal exercise the oxygen cost of ventilation may reach 14–19% of total oxygen uptake.

Sex differences in the running economy of six-year-old children have been reported in terms of absolute and mass-specific oxygen uptake values, but oxygen uptake values expressed relative to fat-free mass were not different. The conclusion was that the sex differences in running economy may reflect an increase in aerobic energy demands associated with the greater muscle mass of the boys (Morgan *et al.*, 1999). For anyone interested in running economy it is worthwhile to read the collection of papers from a symposium on this topic that are introduced by Morgan (1992).

7.6 EFFICIENCY

7.6.1 INTRODUCTION

Efficiency is defined as:

$$\%\text{Efficiency} = \frac{\text{output}}{\text{input}} \times 100$$

In order to produce an efficiency ratio, both the numerator and the denominator have to be measured. With regard to activities such as walking, running and load carriage, there are several definitions of efficiency which are based on different forms of numerator and denominator in the efficiency equation (Whipp and Wasserman, 1969; Gaesser and Brooks, 1975). However, the numerator is always based on some measure of work done (either internal, external or both) and the denominator is based on some measure of metabolic rate (oxygen uptake).

These efficiency ratios are defined as:

Gross efficiency

$$\%\text{Efficiency} = \frac{\text{Work accomplished} \times 100}{\text{Energy expended}}$$

$$= \frac{W \times 100}{E}$$

Net efficiency

$$\%\text{Efficiency} = \frac{\text{Work accomplished} \times 100}{\text{Energy expended above that at rest}}$$

$$= \frac{W \times 100}{E - e}$$

Apparent or work efficiency

$$\%\text{Efficiency} = \frac{\text{Work accomplished} \times 100}{\text{Energy expended above unloaded}}$$

$$= \frac{W \times 100}{EL - EU}$$

Delta efficiency

$$\%\text{Efficiency} = \frac{\text{Delta work accomplished}}{\text{Delta energy}}$$

$$= \frac{DW \times 100}{DE}$$

where:

W = caloric equivalent of mechanical work done

E = gross caloric output

e = resting caloric output

EL = caloric output loaded condition

EU = caloric output unloaded condition

DW = caloric equivalent of increment in work performed above previous work-rate

DE = increment in caloric output above that at previous work-rate.

These definitions of efficiency are not a complete set and have received criticism by several authors (e.g. Stainsby *et al.*, 1980; Cavanagh and Kram, 1985).

Muscle efficiency is the efficiency of the conversion of chemical energy into mechanical energy at the cross-bridges and is based on phosphorylative coupling and contraction coupling, which are essentially linked in series. Phosphorylative coupling efficiency, which is defined as:

$$\frac{\text{Free energy conserved as ATP}}{\text{Free energy of oxidized food}} \times 100$$

has been estimated to be between 40 and 60% (Krebs and Kornberg, 1957). Contraction coupling, the conversion of energy stored as phosphates into tension in the muscle, is of the order of 50% efficient, giving an overall theoretical maximum muscle efficiency of 30% (Whipp and Wasserman, 1969; Wilkie, 1974; Gaesser and Brooks, 1975). Given a maximum value of only 30% for muscle efficiency, it is of interest to examine why gross efficiency values quoted in the literature for activities such as running are often considerably higher, and can even exceed 100% using certain forms of calculation in the estimation of mechanical work done (Norman *et al.*, 1976).

Measures of whole-body efficiency or implied changes based on the different $\dot{V}O_2$ responses of children and adults to unloaded running (Davies, 1980) do not indicate the efficiency of muscle. The different definitions of efficiency quoted above are therefore important when trying to compare values from various sources.

The efficiency experiment which will be described in detail is that originally proposed by Lloyd and Zacks (1972). It was designed to measure the mechanical efficiency of running against a horizontal impeding force.

7.6.2 METHODOLOGY

The problem of accurately measuring external work in horizontal running was overcome, to a large extent, by Lloyd and Zacks (1972), who reported an experimental procedure in which they used a quantifiable external workload in the form of a horizontal impeding force, on adult subjects running on the treadmill. Loaded running efficiency (LRE) was then calculated for a given running speed from the linear relationship between metabolic rate (oxygen uptake) and external work-rate. The

value of LRE is therefore consistent with apparent or work efficiency as defined by Whipp and Wasserman (1969). This method was also used by Cooke *et al.* (1991) to test the hypothesis that there are differences in LRE between children and adults.

Protocol

The protocol and procedures for the LRE experiment are described in detail in Section 7.10.

7.6.3 RESULTS

The results presented here are from a comparison of LRE values between a group of well-trained boys and men (Cooke *et al.*, 1991). Figure 7.5 shows that no significant differences were found between the two groups in terms of LRE and the effects of speed. The mean LRE was 43.8% for the boys and 42.9% for the men.

7.6.4 DISCUSSION

The major finding from the horizontal impeding force experiment on boys and men is that there is no significant difference between the LRE values. The mean LRE values quoted in the results fall between the small number of values published in the literature (36%, Lloyd

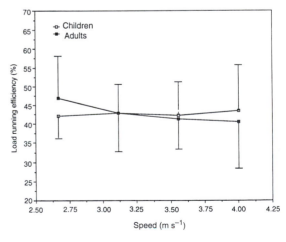

Figure 7.5 Loaded running efficiency values (means ±SD) for two groups of well-trained male runners: 8 boys and 8 men (Cooke *et al.*, 1991).

and Zacks, 1972; 39.1%, Zacks, 1973; 53.8%, Asmussen and Bonde-Peterson, 1974). These data support the hypothesis that there is no significant difference in efficiency between children and adults in the performance of external work.

Measures of mechanical efficiency for other forms of ergometry such as the cycle or the step are necessary for the estimation of energy expenditure from mechanical work done when $\dot{V}O_2$ is not measured. For example, such values form the basis of the Åstrand–Ryhming (1954) nomogram, when only the mechanical work done is known. Oxygen uptake is estimated from the work performed in stepping or cycling, which together with the heart rate response can be used to estimate $\dot{V}O_2$max. A description of how to measure mechanical efficiency in both stepping and cycle ergometry is given in Section 7.11.

7.7 LOAD CARRIAGE

7.7.1 EFFECTS ON ECONOMY

Load carriage is an activity that provides an appropriate focus for the study of economy, including the need to consider energy expenditure, posture and kinematics. Load carriage is of interest from both an occupational and recreational perspective, where relatively heavy loads are carried for prolonged periods of time. The physiology of load carriage has been extensively studied, with the effect of the position of the carried load on energy expenditure receiving particular attention. Carrying loads on the head is a common method of load carriage in both Africa and Asia (Datta and Ramanathan, 1970; Maloiy *et al.*, 1986). Maloiy *et al.* (1986) found that African women could carry loads of up to 20% body weight with no increase in energy cost and that thereafter oxygen uptake rose proportionately with added load, i.e. an added load of 30% body weight produced a 10% increase in oxygen uptake, an added load of 40% body weight produced an increase in oxygen uptake of 20%.

It would seem then that the energy cost of carrying loads is not fixed but can be affected by the position of the load. This fact may have implications for different load carriage systems. Again many comparative studies have been undertaken. Datta and Ramanathan (1971) compared seven modes of carrying loads. The results indicated the best economy for a double pack system, where the load was shared between the back and front of the trunk. The order in terms of energy cost from lowest to highest was: double pack, load carried on basket on head, rucksack, load supported by strap on forehead, rice bag, yoke and finally load in canvas bags carried by hands. The oxygen uptake associated with the double pack was significantly lower than that associated with all of the other methods except for the load carried in a basket on the head. Legg and Mahanty (1985) compared five modes of carrying loads close to the trunk. No significant differences were found between any of the load carriage systems but there was a consistent trend for the double pack to be associated with the lowest physiological cost. Lloyd and Cooke (2000) also observed that the economy of level and inclined walking was greater when wearing a rucksack which distributed the weight around the front and back of the trunk, compared to a traditional rucksack (Figure 7.6).

Kirk and Schneider (1992) compared the performance of internal and external frame packs. The results indicated no significant difference in economy between the two packs, although there was a consistent trend for the internal frame pack to elicit lower oxygen uptake values than the external frame pack. The postulated advantage for the internal frame pack is that the load can be carried closer to the body.

7.7.2 EFFECTS ON STRIDE PATTERN

The majority of previous studies relating to the kinematics of load carriage have been concerned with alterations to stride length and frequency. Theoretically, changes in stride length / stride frequency associated with acute responses to load carriage may lead to an increased energy cost, therefore changing both economy and efficiency. The studies reported, however, all deal with acute perturbations to the walking gait. The effect of chronic changes are less well known, but given the long term changes in stride length / stride frequency achieved by athletes it is possible that adaptation may take place.

There is no consensus concerning the effect of load carriage on stride length / stride frequency. Martin and Nelson (1986) observed an increase in stride frequency, 2% for men and a 5% for women, when carrying a load of 36 kg, made up of military clothing, waist belt and rucksack, at 6.34 km h^{-1}. Cooke *et al.* (1991) reported a significant difference in stride frequency when loads of 5 and 10% body weight were carried around the trunk. The magnitudes of the increases were 1.5 and 5% above the unloaded condition. Thorstensson (1986) found significant differences in stride frequency for both boys and men when carrying a load of 10% body weight around the trunk at 10 km h^{-1} for the boys and 11 km h^{-1} for the men. The percentage increases were 1.5% and 1.9% for the men and boys respectively. Kram *et al.* (1987) reported a significant increase in stride frequency when 60% body weight was carried at 10.8 km h^{-1} using a method in which the load is attached to either end of a bamboo pole which is carried across the shoulders. They found no significant difference in stride frequency when the same load was carried in a traditional rucksack. A number of other studies, covering a wide range of loading conditions and speeds, have reported no significant changes in stride frequency. These include Robertson *et al.* (1982) (loads of 0–15% body weight carried at speeds between 3.2 and 8.1 km h^{-1}), Maloiy *et al.* (1986) (34 kg carried on the head) and Kinoshita (1985) (loads of 20 and 40% body weight carried at 4.5 km h^{-1} in a traditional rucksack and a double pack system).

7.7.3 EFFECTS ON TRUNK ANGLE

It would seem that the alterations to stride length / stride frequency elicited by load carriage are relatively small and, on their own, unlikely to have a significant effect on energy cost. It is possible, however, that these small alterations may either contribute to, or combine with, changes in other variables and thus have a significant effect on the economy of load carriage. One of the most important changes in kinematics associated with load carriage is an alteration in trunk angle. This is an aspect of load carriage that has received scant attention.

Kinoshita (1985) found that both back and front/back load carriage systems were associated with increased forward lean but that the forward lean associated with the back system, (11°), was considerably greater than for the double pack system. Bloom and Woodhull-McNeal (1987) observed increased forward lean whilst standing for both an internal and an external frame pack loaded with 27% body weight, but did not quantify it. Martin and Nelson (1986) showed that forward lean increased when a load was carried on the back but not when distributed about the waist. When carrying a total of 36 kg (19 kg on the back) forward lean was increased by approximately 10°. Gordon *et al.* (1983) also noted that forward lean increased with the addition of load but did not quantify this.

Another form of measurement that has been used to make comparisons between different load carriage systems, loads, speeds and gradients is the extra load index (ELI) (Taylor *et al.*, 1980). This is a measure of relative economy, which is calculated by dividing the oxygen consumption when carrying a load (ml kg total mass^{-1} min^{-1}) by the oxygen consumption for no load (ml kg body mass^{-1} min^{-1}). An ELI of 1 indicates that the energy cost of carrying 1 kg of extra load is the same as that of 1 kg of live mass; a value >1 indicates a reduction in the economy of load carriage; a value <1 indicates an increased economy. Using this technique, the results of Lloyd and Cooke (2000) suggested that the energy cost of carrying a kilogram of extra load is greater than that of carrying a kilogram of live mass.

7.7.4 METHODOLOGY

Numerous protocols have been used to assess the effects of load carriage on economy and efficiency. Various treadmill walking and running speeds and both uphill and downhill gradients have been used to compare a variety of different forms of load carriage. The methodology for assessing the effects of load carriage on economy is very similar to that described for running economy in section 7.9. The protocols typically consist of steady state exercise, walking or running at each speed and gradient combination for a period of a minimum of three minutes.

Protocol

A protocol for investigating the effects of load carriage on economy is described in detail in Section 7.10.

The experimental protocol and results presented here are based on the work of Lloyd and Cooke (2000). The protocol involved walking downhill at a speed of 3 km h^{-1} for 3 minutes at gradients of 27%, 22%, 17%, 12% and 5%. Subjects were then given a rest of 20 minutes, after which they walked uphill at a speed of 3 km h^{-1} for 3 minutes at gradients of 0%, 5%, 10%, 15% and 20%. Expired air was collected throughout both the downhill and uphill sections. The protocol was completed three times. On each occasion the subjects completed one of three conditions in random order: unloaded, loaded with a traditional rucksack and loaded with a rucksack that incorporated front pockets. This distributed the load around the front and back of the trunk. The mass of both 65 litre packs and contents was 25.6 kg. All the treadmill tests were filmed with a video camera.

7.7.5 RESULTS

(a) Economy

Statistical analysis (3 × 10 repeated measures ANOVA) of the data indicated that unloaded walking requiring a significantly lower ($p < 0.05$)

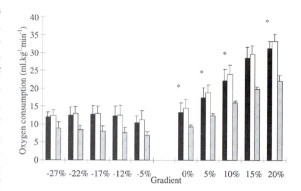

Figure 7.6 Oxygen uptake values (means ±SD) for walking with rucksack with front and back pockets (■), traditional rucksack (□) and unloaded conditions (▨)(* denotes $p < 0.05$ between the two rucksacks).

$\dot{V}O_2$ than either of the loaded conditions. On average the extra oxygen cost, above that for unloaded walking, associated with the front and back loading rucksack was 5.4 ml kg^{-1} min^{-1} (45.1%), whilst that associated with the traditional rucksack was 6.3 ml kg^{-1} min^{-1} (52.8%). The $\dot{V}O_2$ was also about 8% lower ($p < 0.05$) for the front and back loading rucksack on the uphill gradients (Figure 7.6).

(b) Stride length

Mean values of stride length (m) and percentage changes from the unloaded condition at each gradient are shown in Table 7.4. Changes in stride length were greater in the loaded condition ($p < 0.05$). Across the whole protocol, the traditional rucksack and the front and back loading rucksack were associated with, on average, 3.2 cm (3%) and 5.1 cm (5%) shorter stride lengths, respectively, although there was no significant difference ($p > 0.05$) in stride length for the two conditions. The reduction in stride length associated with both rucksacks was slightly more marked during the uphill section than the downhill section.

Table 7.4 Mean stride length (m) (±SD) and meanpercentage change (±SD) from the unloaded condition at each gradient

		Gradient									
		−27%	−22%	−17%	−12%	−5%	0%	5%	10%	15%	20%
Front and back	Mean stride length (±s)	0.86	0.88	0.89	0.95	1.04	1.12	1.13	1.14	1.11	1.08
		0.07	0.06	0.07	0.08	0.08	0.08	0.09	0.12	0.11	0.11
	Mean	−5.4	−5.4	−5.8	−4.0	0.1	0.5	−5.7	−5.0	−5.7	−7.8
	% change (±s)	5.8	5.4	5.9	5.8	4.6	4.2	5.5	4.1	5.7	5.6
Traditional	Mean stride length (±s)	0.86	0.89	0.91	0.99	1.06	1.14	1.17	1.15	1.12	1.08
		0.07	0.07	0.06	0.12	0.10	0.11	0.15	0.14	0.13	0.13
	Mean	−5.1	−4.3	−3.7	−0.4	1.9	1.6	−2.0	−3.6	−4.8	−7.6
	% change (±s)	6.5	4.5	4.4	4.8	7.1	7.2	6.0	8.3	8.0	5.9
Unloaded	Mean stride length (±s)	0.91	0.93	0.95	0.99	1.04	1.12	1.19	1.20	1.18	1.18
		0.07	0.08	0.08	0.11	0.11	0.09	0.13	0.13	0.13	0.13

(c) Trunk angle

The increase in forward lean was greater whilst wearing the traditional rucksack when standing still and walking ($p < 0.001$). The increases amounted to about 4° and 14° for the front and back loading and traditional rucksacks, respectively. The extra forward lean induced by the traditional rucksack also tended to increase as the slope increased, whereas it remained relatively constant in the front- and back-loaded condition.

7.8 PRACTICAL 1: DIRECT DETERMINATION OF $\dot{V}O_2$ USING A DISCONTINUOUS CYCLE ERGOMETER PROTOCOL

7.8.1 PROTOCOL

1. Warm-up: cycle for 3 minutes at 50 W for females or 100 W for males.
2. Rest: 2 minutes.
3. Initial work-rate: 50–150 W for females, 100–200 W for males, depending on type of subject, e.g. lighter less active subjects would be set lower work-rates (heart rate response during warm-up is a good guide to selection of appropriate work-rate). Record heart rate every 30 s. Collect expired air for last 30 s of work-rate.
4. Rest: 3 minutes (during which time team members can analyse expired air).
5. Increase work-rate by 50 W and repeat stages 3 and 4 of the protocol.
6. At higher workloads increments of 25 W may be used. If the subject cannot complete a 3- minute workload then a gas collection can be made on a signal from the subject (minimum 30 s, preferably 1 minute).
7. Recovery: at the end of the test the subject should continue to pedal gently at a low work-rate of the order of 25–50 W.

The subject should be closely monitored at all times, both during the test and recovery, since the probability of some sort of cardiac episode occurring is higher at exercise intensities above 80% of age-related maximum heart rate and during the 20 minutes or so following the cessation of the test. The subject may need verbal encouragement to complete the latter stages of the test in order to attain a maximal oxygen consumption.

Although heart rate can be monitored effectively by radio telemetry, it is preferable to use chest electrodes linked to an oscilloscope and/or chart recorder. This enables the shape of the electrocardiogram (ECG) to be observed. In the event of a gross abnormality or arrhythmia occurring, the test can be stopped and the hard copy of the ECG examined by a qualified person. Clearly the more sophisticated the ECG equipment used, the more objective will be the ECG analysis. It is possible to see arrhythmias such as ventricular ectopics with a simple three-lead system, which is available in most laboratories.

7.8.2 PROCEDURES

The procedures for the cycle ergometer protocol are as described, but they can be generalized in most cases to any direct determination of $\dot{V}O_2$max using the Douglas bag technique.

1. The procedures and protocol should be explained to the subject, and should include a statement that he or she can stop the test at any time.

2. The subject should sign an informed consent form.
3. The name, age and sex of the subject should be recorded.
4. The stature (m) and body mass (kg) of the subject should be measured.
5. The heart rate measuring device or ECG electrodes should be attached and a check made that a good signal is being recorded or displayed.
6. The handlebar and saddle positions should be adjusted to suit the size of the subject, especially as subjects can become uncomfortable during the latter stages of the test, resulting in the premature cessation of the test. If the saddle is too low, the subject may experience undue fatigue in the quadriceps muscles and possibly pain in the knee joint. If the saddle is too high, the subject will have to raise and lower his/her left and right hips repeatedly in order to maintain effective contact with the pedals. The recommended position is obtained by placing the middle of the foot on the pedal at the bottom of its travel. If the saddle height is correct the leg will be very slightly flexed. More sophisticated guidelines are available in the literature, but the simple procedure described here works well in most cases. Competitive cyclists will have their own measures for obtaining an optimal saddle height and handlebar position. They also prefer their own bicycles mounted on turbo-trainers. More sophisticated examples, such as the King Cycle (High Wycombe, UK) have gained wider acceptance in exercise physiology laboratories.
7. The respiratory value and mouthpiece should be connected to allow room air to be inspired and then expired into the Douglas bag.
8. The nose clip should be placed on the subject's nose so that all the expired air passes into the Douglas bag.
9. The warm-up and the test proper should be completed according to the protocol described above.

With respect to the control of cycle ergometers, the following points should be considered.

1. All cycle ergometers should be calibrated regularly according to the manufacturer's instructions.
2. Recommended pedalling frequencies for mechanically-braked cycle ergometers are traditionally of the order of 50–60 rev min^{-1}. Although a frequency of 60 rev min^{-1} is comfortable and efficient for low work-rates, it is recommended that the pedalling frequency be increased above work-rates of the order of 200 W to 70–80 rev min^{-1}. This will decrease the force required per pedal revolution, thus decreasing the strength component of the pedalling action and the probability of cessation of the test due to fatigue in the quadriceps.
3. It is always important to inform the subject in advance of alterations in work-rate in continuous protocols. This is especially important in the use of electronically-braked cycle ergometers, which automatically alter the resistance at the pedals to accommodate changes in pedalling frequency, thus keeping the power output constant. A tired subject pedalling at 200 W with an unexpected increase of 50 W, and who is already pedalling at the lower end of the pedalling frequency range (approximately 50 rev min^{-1}) may well let the cadence drop still further with the increase in load. This will result in a further increase in resistance offered at the pedals. The result could then be that the

subject terminates the test, so a warning of pending increases in workload should always be given, together with encouragement to pedal faster to accommodate the increase in work-rate on an electronically-braked cycle ergometer.

4. Mechanically-braked cycle ergometers of the type used in most laboratories require the subject to pedal at a constant frequency in order to maintain a constant power output. To help maintain a constant pedalling frequency the subject may pedal in time to a metronome and/or use the digital display of pedalling frequency which is now fitted to most new cycle ergometers. Another alternative is to mount small mechanical cams or optoelectric devices on the flywheel to count the number of revolutions during each workload. Use of these suggestions should help ensure that quantification of external power output is as objective as possible.

7.8.3 CALCULATIONS

Gas analysis, volume measurement, $\dot{V}O_2$, $\dot{V}CO_2$ and respiratory exchange ratio calculations should be performed in accordance with the procedures outlined in Chapter 6 of this text.

7.8.4 RESULTS

Table 7.3 shows a completed pro forma for the discontinuous cycle ergometer test described above.

Some questions to consider for the measurement of maximum oxygen uptake:

- What day-to-day variability might you expect in repeated measures of maximum oxygen uptake and what might be the factors that contribute to this variability?
- What are the ethical implications and methodological limitations of using direct measurements of maximal oxygen uptake on subjects who are not well accustomed to strenuous exertion?
- What are the apparent contradictions in considering the general principles of testing for maximal oxygen uptake, such as using a large muscle mass in a rhythmic movement pattern, and testing sports performers from a particular sport?
- Should maximal oxygen uptake be considered the criterion standard measure of aerobic or endurance fitness?
- What are the practical and theoretical factors that might effect whether a plateau in oxygen consumption is measurable or not?

7.9 PRACTICAL 2: MEASUREMENT OF RUNNING ECONOMY

7.9.1 PROTOCOL

The protocol outlined here is recommended by The British Association of Sport and Exercise Sciences. Where the $\dot{V}O_2$max of the subject is known, an appropriate generalized equation relating $\dot{V}O_2$ to running speed can be used to predict the running speeds that should elicit 50–90% of $\dot{V}O_2$. For example, PE Students (British Association of Sport Sciences, 1992):

| Males | $n = 58$ | $Y = 11.6\,X + 0.72$ |
| Females | $n = 44$ | $Y = 10.7\,X + 3.30$ |

where:

$Y = \dot{V}O_2$ (ml kg^{-1} min^{-1}) and X = running speed (m s^{-1})

or those cited in Section 7.5.3. However, the selection of the running speeds should take into account the state of training of the subjects, since only well-conditioned athletes can cope with running speeds that elicit 90% of $\dot{V}O_2$max

1. Warm-up: no warm-up other than gentle jogging and stretching is required, since the first workload represents a running speed approximately equivalent to 60% $\dot{V}O_2$max. Ideally, naive subjects should be habituated to treadmill running on a previous occasion so $\dot{V}O_2$ values will be a true reflection of running economy.
2. Test: the protocol consists of 16 minutes of running on a level treadmill during which running speed is increased every 4 minutes. For children aged less than 15 years, a 3-minute interval is recommended.
3. Expired air should be collected for the 4th, 8th, 12th and 16th minute for adults, and for the 3rd, 6th, 9th and 12th minute for children.

7.9.2 DATA COLLECTION, GAS ANALYSIS AND CALCULATIONS

Follow the procedures outlined in Chapter 6 for the collection and analysis of expired air using the Douglas bag technique, and the calculation of oxygen uptake. Alternatively an automated gas analysis system can be used to collect and analyse the expired air (as in Figure 6.3).

7.9.3 RESULTS

The results from the experiment should be plotted with oxygen uptake on the y axis and running speed on the x axis. The method of least squares can then be used to establish the extent to which the data conform to the expected linear relationship, with the production of a linear regression equation, correlation coefficient (r) and coefficient of determination (r^2 = variance accounted for) (see Volume 1, Chapter 10 by Nevill and Atkinson). Group data can then be compared using appropriate statistical techniques such as ANOVA or ANCOVA. Examples of group comparisons for both equations and graphs appear in Sections 7.5.3 and 7.5.4.

Some questions to consider on running economy and related areas of study include:

• Is it appropriate to be totally confident in extrapolating forwards or backwards using an individual subject's equation that allows you to predict oxygen uptake from running speed?
• What applications might make use of extrapolations from such equations?
• What happens to the oxygen uptake / speed relationship when the subject walks instead runs?

7.10 PRACTICAL 3: MEASUREMENT OF LOADED RUNNING EFFICIENCY (LRE)

7.10.1 PROTOCOL

For each running speed the subject should run unloaded for 3 minutes. A horizontal impeding force is then exerted via weights attached to the subject by a cord running over a pulley (Figure 7.7). A total of three increasing loads can then be added to the system, one every 3 minutes (a total of 12 minutes continuous running including the 3 minutes unloaded), followed by 5 minutes rest. Weights should be individually selected such that the maximum external load applied to the system does not elicit a $\dot{V}O_2$ greater than 85% of $\dot{V}O_2$max in well-trained subjects (this value would have to be adjusted down for less active individuals as it is important that the energy expenditure is derived from aerobic metabolism and therefore reflected in the measured $\dot{V}O_2$ values). Even increments in $\dot{V}O_2$ can be achieved by predicting the increase in $\dot{V}O_2$ per kilogram of mass added to the pulley, on the basis of a mean LRE value from the literature of approximately 40%. Running speeds and weight increments can then be individually tailored to the subject in terms of $\dot{V}O_2$max and running economy. Where subjects represent a homogeneous sample it is better in terms of experimental design to have all subjects run at the same speeds with the same increments. Typical values for weights to be added to the pulley would be 1, 2 and 3 kg for adults and 0.5, 1 and 1.5 kg for children.

7.10.2 PROCEDURES

Collection and analysis of expired air can be performed either according to the procedures outlined for the Douglas bag technique in Chapter 6, or using an automated gas analysis system. The data presented in Figure 7.5 and discussed in Section 7.6.4 were collected using an Oxycon 5 system). A full description of the experimental procedures can be found in Cooke *et al.* (1991).

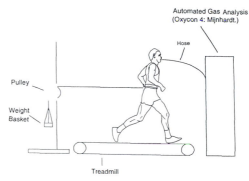

Figure 7.7 Diagram of the horizontal impeding force experiment used to calculate loaded running efficiency (Lloyd and Zacks, 1972).

7.10.3 CALCULATION OF LRE

Metabolic work-rate is calculated from steady-state $\dot{V}O_2$ for each load condition. A value of 20.9 kJ min^{-1} (5.0 kcal min^{-1}, 348.8 W) can be used as the energy equivalent for one litre of oxygen since this will cause no more than a 4% variation based on observed respiratory exchange ratios.

External work-rate is calculated as the product of the force exerted by the weight over the pulley and the distance moved per unit of time by the treadmill belt. A linear regression equation is then fitted to the data, with metabolic rate as the dependent variable and external work-rate as the independent variable. Apparent efficiency of running against a horizontal load, or LRE, is then calculated for each speed of running by taking the inverse of the slope of the regression equation, as shown in Figure 7.8. For example, given the raw data that form the basis for Figure 7.8, the calculations are as follows:

Running speed constant at 11.2 km h^{-1} = 3.11 m s^{-1}

The calculation of metabolic work-rate (MWR) in watts is given by:

$$\text{MWR (W)} = \dot{V}O_2 \, (\text{l min}^{-1}) \times 348.8$$

where: $\dot{V}O_2$ = measured oxygen uptake for each load condition = 20.9 kJ min^{-1} = 348.8 W = 5 kcal min^{-1} = 1 litre of oxygen

The calculation of external work-rate (EWR) in watts is given by:

$$\text{EWR (W)} = M \times g \times D$$

where: M is mass (kg) applied to runner acting over pulley, g is acceleration due to gravity (m s^{-2}), D is distance moved by treadmill belt in 1 s = velocity of treadmill (m s^{-1}).

Given the following oxygen uptake values for each of four external loads measured as mass applied to the pulley the metabolic work-rate and external work-rate can be calculated according to the formulae above. These are shown in Table 7.5.

The EWR and MWR values are plotted in Figure 7.8, which also shows the linear regression equation fitted by the method of least squares. Given that EWR is the independent variable it has to be plotted on the x axis, and the dependent variable, MWR, is plotted on

Table 7.5   Example of metabolic work-rate and external work-rate results

Mass on pulley (kg)	EWR (W)	$\dot{V}O_2$ (l min^{-1})	MWR (W)
0	0.00	2.01	701.1
1	30.51	2.22	774.3
2	61.02	2.43	847.6
3	91.53	2.63	917.3

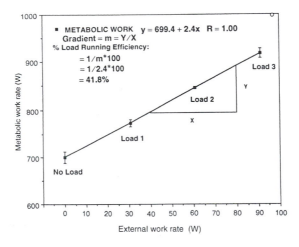

Figure 7.8 Calculation of loaded running efficiency (LRE) in the horizontal impeding force experiment for a subject running at 11.2 km h^{-1}. Values are means ± SD for data collected in two experiments completed by the same subject on different days (Cooke *et al.*, 1991).

the *y* axis. Loaded running efficiency expressed as a percentage is therefore given by the reciprocal of the gradient of the linear regression equation multiplied by 100:

$$\% \text{ Loaded running efficiency} = (1 / 2.4) \times 100 = 41.7\,\%$$

- What are the limitations involved in the measurement of loaded running efficiency?
- The example discussed in the text for this practical is concerned with a comparison of children and adults. What other applications and research questions can this procedure be used to investigate?

7.10.4 RESULTS

The results can be reported in terms of individual LRE values for each speed of running, and combined in a variety of ways depending on the aim of the experiment (e.g. either to investigate the effects of running speed on LRE or to compare the apparent efficiency of horizontal treadmill running against other forms of ergometry).

7.11 PRACTICAL 4: MEASUREMENT OF THE EFFICIENCY OF CYCLING AND STEPPING

7.11.1 CYCLE ERGOMETRY

In mechanical cycle ergometry the external power output (W) or mechanical work-rate is quantified as the product of the frictional force (N) or resistance applied to the flywheel and the distance travelled (m) by one point on the circumference of the flywheel, which gives the work done (J), divided by the time to do the work (s):

$$\text{External power output (W)} = \frac{\text{Force (N)} \times \text{Distance (m)}}{\text{Time (s)}}$$

Most cycle ergometers allow the work-rate to be set in watts, whether they are mechanically or electronically braked.

As with the LRE experiment, metabolic work-rate is calculated from steady-state $\dot{V}O_2$:

$$\text{Metabolic work-rate (W)} = (\dot{V}O_2\, \text{l min}^{-1}) \times 348.8$$

A gross measure of efficiency can then be calculated by dividing the external power output by the metabolic power output:

$$\%\text{Gross efficiency} = \frac{\left[(\text{Force} \times \text{Distance})\, \text{Time}\right]}{\dot{V}O_2\ (\text{l min}^{-1}) \times 348.8} \times 100$$

Net efficiency can be calculated by dividing the external power output by net metabolic power, the latter being obtained by subtracting an estimate of resting $\dot{V}O_2$ (see Chapter 6) from the gross measured value. Provided that both the numerator and denominator are in the same units (watts, kJ min^{-1} or kcal min^{-1}) the correct ratio will be calculated and when multiplied by 100 will give percentage net efficiency.

7.11.2 STEPPING

For stepping, the external work-rate (W) is calculated as a function of the vertical height that the centre of mass of the body is raised (m). This is estimated by multiplying the step height (m) by the number of complete step cycles performed. The total vertical height is then multiplied by the force (body weight (N)), and divided by the duration (s) of the stepping exercise:

$$\text{External power output } (W) = \frac{\text{Step height (m)} \times \text{No. steps} \times \text{Weight (N)}}{\text{Time (s)}}$$

The gross and net efficiency ratios can then be calculated using the external work-rate and metabolic work-rate as for cycle ergometry.

The net efficiency of stepping is of the order of 16% (Shephard *et al.*, 1968).

7.11.3 EXPERIMENTAL PROCEDURES AND PROTOCOLS

Gross and net efficiency ratios can be calculated over the submaximal range of exercise intensities, provided that the energy demands of the exercise are matched by a steady state of oxygen uptake. Efficiency values calculated for high-intensity exercise, where anaerobic sources make a significant contribution to the energy demands, will be higher than expected since under such conditions oxygen uptake will not reflect the energy demands of the exercise.

For stepping on a double 'nine-inch' step (total vertical height 45 cm) the oxygen uptake can be estimated to be:

$$\dot{V}O_2 \text{ (ml kg}^{-1} \text{ min}^{-1}) = 1.34 \times n$$

where n = number of step cycles per minute.

For example, stepping on a double step requires a six-beat cadence. Therefore stepping to a metronome set at 120 beats per minute would result in the completion of 20 step cycles per minute, giving an estimated oxygen uptake of 26.8 ml kg^{-1} min^{-1}.

A suitable submaximal range of work-rates for the above step would consist of four by three minute work-rates with metronome cadences set at 60, 90, 120 and 150 beats min^{-1}. Expired air can be collected during the third minute of each work-rate and analysed according to the methods described in Chapter 6.

Although stepping is considered to be a simple inexpensive form of ergometry, every effort must be made to ensure that the subject keeps in time with the metronome and that he/she stands up straight on a flat foot with full knee extension.

For cycle ergometry a suitable range of submaximal exercise intensities would consist of 50–150 W depending on the age, sex and condition of the subjects. As a guide, heart rate response should not exceed 85% of age-related maximum heart rate during a submaximal test. Traditionally a pedal frequency of 50 rev min^{-1} has been used in submaximal exercise tests using mechanically-braked cycle ergometers. However, 60 rev min^{-1} is often a more comfortable pedalling frequency.

Shephard *et al.* (1968) showed that over a range of submaximal loads the mean net mechanical efficiency for stepping and cycle ergometry was 16% and 23% respectively.

7.11.4 DISCUSSION

The values quoted from Shephard *et al.* (1968) represent group means for subjects performing repeated experiments in both stepping and cycling to a random design. There was more variability in stepping (coefficient of variation approximately 10%) than cycling (coefficient of variation approximately 7%). There was also some variation in mechanical efficiency values associated with loading.

Individual values for mechanical efficiency can be used as calibration factors for estimating oxygen uptake from work done, rather than having to use estimates from the literature. There are several experiments that can be conducted with either stepping or cycle ergometry to investigate variations in mechanical efficiency values. For example, the effects of pedalling frequency, stepping frequency, work-rate, saddle height, single or double step, step height and leg length in relation to step height can all be investigated.

Consider the effects that the variability in efficiency across subjects might have on estimating energy expenditure for a given task, predicting fitness (e.g. maximum oxygen uptake) and predicting performance without reference to measures of economy, based on assumptions of constant mechanical efficiency.

7.12 PRACTICAL 5: THE EFFECTS OF LOAD CARRIAGE ON THE ECONOMY OF WALKING

7.12.1 PROTOCOL

The experimental protocol involves walking at a speed of 3 km h^{-1} for 3 minutes at each selected gradient. The gradients used in the study discussed above were downhill at 27%, 22%, 17%, 12%, and 5%, which was completed first. Subjects were then given a rest of 20 minutes. After the rest subjects walked uphill at a speed of 3 km h^{-1} for 3 minutes at gradients of 0%, 5%, 10%, 15% and 20%. This gives a total test time of 50 minutes (30 minutes walking and 20 minutes resting) per subject per load condition, but allows the data to be compared directly to the results presented above. In terms of a single practical, reasonable results could be obtained for one subject using one downhill gradient of 20%, level walking and one uphill gradient of 20%. For the purpose of comparing unloaded and loaded walking it is only necessary to use two conditions, one without a rucksack and one carrying a loaded rucksack. Clearly, different rucksacks, load carriage systems or loads can be used, but this would only be practical for project work. The practical could also be adapted by looking at different walking speeds, or running with a daysack.

7.12.2 MEASUREMENTS

Follow the procedures outlined in Chapter 6 for the collection and analysis of expired air using the Douglas bag technique, and the calculation of oxygen uptake. Alternatively use an automated gas analysis system, making sure that you calibrate each system carefully before you start your testing. If you are using an automated gas analysis system it is worthwhile ensuring that you include minute ventilation, breathing frequency and tidal volume in your configuration of the system as well as oxygen consumption and carbon dioxide production.

Although not essential for the comparison of economy between unloaded and loaded walking, it is also worthwhile timing a set number of stride cycles at each workload using a stopwatch to assess whether there is any difference in stride length and frequency between the two conditions. If you have a video camera available, it is also worthwhile setting up one with the axis of the lens perpendicular to the plane of walking (about 5–6m away from the side of the treadmill should suffice). This will facilitate measurement of the forward lean of the trunk (touch-down, toe-off and mid-stance are good points for comparison) in both conditions, as well as allowing checks on the stride length and stride frequency calculations. Rating of perceived exertion and heart rate can also be recorded for each stage of the protocol.

7.12.3 RESULTS

1. Draw a graph of the results for the following variables for every stage of the protocol for each of the two (or more) loading conditions (use mean and standard deviations if you have more than one subject): oxygen consumption, minute ventilation, breathing frequency, tidal volume, heart rate, stride length, stride frequency, stride length and forward lean. Use values from the Douglas bag collected in the third minute, or the last two 30 s values from the automated gas analysis system for expired air variables.
2. Calculate ELI values for your data and compare them with the mean values presented above.
3. Compare all of your results with those presented above and, more importantly, evaluate the differences between the results for the two loading conditions. It may be worthwhile to consider whether there are any associations between changes in certain variables with loading, which might suggest some explanation of some of the physiological effects of load carriage.
4. Consider the implications, in terms of different types of validity and reliability, for designing an appropriate protocol to be used in comparing different load carriage systems. What would you need to add to the experiment in order to measure the efficiency of different load carriage systems? How might you go about doing this?

REFERENCES

Allied Dunbar National Fitness Survey (1992). *Main Findings*. Sports Council and Health Education Authority.

Altman, P.L. and Dittmer, D.S. (1968). *Metabolism* (FASBEB, Bethesda, MD).

Asmussen, E. and Bonde-Peterson, F. (1974). Apparent efficiency and storage of elastic energy in human muscles during exercise. *Acta Physiologica Scandanavica*, **92**, 537–45.

Åstrand, P.O. (1952). *Experimental Studies of Physical Working Capacity in Relation to Sex and Age*. (Munksgaard, Copenhagen).

Åstrand, P.O. and Ryhming, I. (1954). A nomogram for the calculation of aerobic capacity (physical fitness) from pulse rate during submaximal work. *Journal of Applied Physiology*, **7**, 218.

Åstrand, P.O. and Rodahl, K. (1986). *Textbook of Work Physiology, Physiological Bases of Exercise*, 3rd edn. (McGraw-Hill, New York).

Bar-Or, O. (1983). Pediatric sports medicine for the practitioner. In *Physiological Principles to Clinical Application*. (Springer, New York).

Bassett. D.R., and Howley, E.T. (1997). Maximal oxygen uptake: 'classical' versus 'contemporary' viewpoints. *Medicine and Science in Sport and Exercise*, **29**, 591–603.

Bloom, D. and Woodhull-McNeal, A.P. (1987). Postural adjustments while standing with two types of loaded backpack. *Ergonomics*, **30**, 1425–30.

Boreham, C.A.G., Paliczka, V.J. and Nichols, A.K. (1990). A comparison of PWC$_{170}$ and 20-MST tests of aerobic fitness in adolescent schoolchildren. *Journal of Sports Medicine and Physical Fitness*, **30**, 19–23.

Bouchard, C. and Malina, R.M. (1983). Genetics of physiological fitness and motor performance. *Exercise and Sport Sciences Reviews*, **11**, 306–39.

Bransford, D.R. and Howley, E.T. (1977). Oxygen cost of running in trained and untrained men and women. *Medicine and Science in Sports and Exercise*, **9**, 41–4.

British Association of Sport and Exercise Sciences (1997). *Guidelines for the Physiological Testing of Athletes*. eds. S. Bird and R. Davison (British Association of Sport and Exercise Sciences, Leeds, UK).

British Association of Sports Sciences (1992). *Position Statement on the Physiological Assessment of the Elite Athlete*. (British Association of Sports Sciences. Physiology Section).

Cavanagh, P.R. and Williams, K.R. (1982). The effect of stride length variation on oxygen uptake during distance running. *Medicine and Science in Sports and Exercise*, **14**, 30–5.

Cavanagh, P.R. and Kram, R. (1985). The efficiency of human movement – a statement of the problem. *Medicine and Science in Sports and Exercise*, **17**, 304–8.

Conley, D.L. and Krahenbuhl, G. (1980). Running economy and distance running performance of highly trained athlete. *Medicine and Science in Sports and Exercise*, **12**, 357–60.

Conley, D.L., Krahenbuhl, G. and Burkett, L. (1981). Training for aerobic capacity and running economy. *Physician and Sportsmedicine*, **9 (4)**, 107–15.

Cooke, C.B., McDonagh, M.J.N., Nevill, A.M. and Davies, C.T.M. (1991). Effects of load on oxygen intake in trained boys and men during treadmill running. *Journal of Applied Physiology*, **71**, 1237–44.

Cooper, K.H. (1968). A means of assessing maximal oxygen intake, correlation between field and treadmill testing. *Journal of American Medical Association*, **203**, 201–4.

Costill, D.L. (1972). Physiology of marathon running. *Journal of the American Medical Association*, **221**, 1024–9.

Costill, D.L. and Fox, E.L. (1969). Energetics of marathon running. *Medicine and Science in Sports*, **1**, 81–6.

Costill, D.L., Thomson, H. and Roberts, E. (1973). Fractional utilisation of the aerobic capacity during distance running. *Medicine and Science in Sports and Exercise*, **5**, 248–52.

Council of Europe (1988). *Testing Physical Fitness*. (Eurofit, Strasbourg).

Datta, S.R. and Ramanathan, N.L. (1970). Ergonomical studies on load carrying up staircases. Part 1 – effect of external load on energy cost and heart rate. *Indian Journal of Medical Research*, **58**, 1629–35.

Datta, S.R. and Ramanathan, N.L. (1971). Ergonomic comparison of seven modes of carrying loads on the horizontal plane. *Ergonomics*, **14**, 269–78.

Davies, C.T.M. (1980). Metabolic cost of exercise and physical performance in children with some observations on external loading. *European Journal of Applied Physiology*, **45**, 95–102.

DuBois, D. and DuBois, E.F. (1916). Clinical calorimetry. A formula to estimate the approximate surface area if height and weight are known. *Archives of Internal Medicine*, **17**, 863–71.

Eston, R.E. and Brodie, D.A. (1985). The assessment of maximal oxygen uptake from running tests. *Physical Education Review*, **8(1)**, 26–34.

Eston, R.G., Robson, S. and Winter, E. (1993). A comparison of oxygen uptake during running in children and adults, in *Kinanthropometry IV*. eds. W. Duquet and J.A.P. Day (E & FN Spon, London), pp. 236–41.

Gaesser, G.A. and Brooks, G.A. (1975). Muscular efficiency during steady-rate exercise: effects of speed and work rate. *Journal of Applied Physiology*, **38**, 1132–9.

Gordon, M.J., Goslin, B.R., Graham, T. and Hoare, J. (1983). Comparison between load carriage and grade walking on a treadmill. *Ergonomics*, **26**, 289–98.

Harrison, M.H., Bruce, D.L., Brown, G.A. and Cochrane, L.A. (1980). A comparison of some indirect methods of predicting maximal oxygen uptake. *Aviation Space and Environmental Medicine*, **51**, 1128.

Hill, A.V. (1939). The mechanical efficiency of frog's muscle. *Proceedings of the Royal Society of London*, **127**, 434–51.

Jordan, C.D. and Cooke, C.B. (1998). The effects of upper posture on horizontal running economy. *Journal of Sports Sciences*, **16**, 53–4P.

Kinoshita, H. (1985). Effects of different loads and carrying systems on selected biomechanical parameters describing walking gait. *Ergonomics*, **28**, 1347–62.

Kirk, J. and Schneider, D.A. (1992). Physiological and perceptual responses to load carrying in female subjects using internal and external frame backpacks. *Ergonomics*, **35**, 445–55.

Kleiber, M. (1975). *The Fire of Life. An Introduction to Animal Energetics.* (Kreiger, New York).

Kline, G.M., Porcari, J.P., Hintermeister, R., *et al.* (1987). Estimation of $\dot{V}O_2$ max from a one-mile track walk, gender, age, and body weight. *Medicine and Science in Sports and Exercise*, **19**, 253–9.

Krähenbuhl, G.S., Skinner, J.S. and Kohrt, W.M. (1985). Developmental aspects of maximal aerobic power in children. *Exercise and Sport Sciences Reviews*, **13**, 503–38.

Kram, R., McMahon, T.A. and Taylor, C.R. (1987). Load carriage with compliant poles – Physiological and/or biomechanical advantages. *Journal of Biomechanics*, **20**, 893.

Krebs, H.A. and Kornberg, H.L. (1957). *Energy Transformations in Living Matter.* (Springer, Berlin).

Léger, L. and Lambert, J. (1982). A maximal multi-stage 20 m shuttle run test to predict $\dot{V}O_2$ max. *European Journal of Applied Physiology*, **49**, 1–12.

Legg, S.J. and Mahanty, A. (1985). Comparison of five modes of carrying a load close to the trunk. *Ergonomics*, **28**, 1653–60.

Lloyd, B.B. and Zacks, R.M. (1972). The mechanical efficiency of treadmill running against a horizontal impeding force. *Journal of Physiology (London)*, **223**, 355–63.

Lloyd, R. and Cooke, C.B. (2000). The oxygen consumption associated with unloaded walking and load carriage using two different backpack designs. *European Journal of Applied Physiology*, **81**, 486–92.

McMahon, T.A. (1984). *Muscles, Reflexes and Locomotion.* (Princeton University Press, Princeton, NJ).

Maloiy, G.M.O., Heglund, N.C., Prager, L.M., *et al.* (1986). Energetic cost of carrying loads: have African women discovered an economic way? *Nature*, **319**, 668–9.

Margaria, R., Cerretelli, P., Aghemo, P. and Sassi, G. (1963). Energy cost of running. *Journal of Applied Physiology*, **18**, 367–70.

Martin, P.E. and Nelson, R.C. (1986). The effects of carried loads on the walking patterns of men and women. *Ergonomics*, **29**, 1191–202.

Morgan, D.W. (1992). Introduction: economy of running: a multidisciplinary perspective. *Medicine and Science in Sports and Exercise*, **24**, 454–5.

Morgan, D.W., Tseh, W., Caputo, J.L., *et al.* (1999). Sex differences in running economy of young children. *Pediatric Exercise Science*, **11**, 122–8.

Morgan, D.W., Bransford, D.R., Costill, D.L., *et al.* (1995). Variation in the aerobic demand of running among trained and untrained subjects. *Medicine and Science in Sports and Exercise*, **27**, 404–9.

Nevill, A.M., Ramsbottom, R. and Williams, C. (1992). Scaling physiological measurements for individuals of different body size. *European Journal of Applied Physiology*, **65**, 110–17.

Noakes, T.D. (1997). Challenging beliefs: ex Africa semper aliquid novi. *Medicine and Science in Sport and Exercise*, **29**, 571–90.

Noakes, T.D. (1998). Maximal oxygen uptake: 'classical' versus 'contemporary' viewpoints: a rebuttal. *Medicine and Science in Sport and Exercise*, **30**, 1381–98.

Norman, R., Sharrat, M., Pezzack, J. and Noble, E. (1976). Re-examination of the mechanical efficiency of horizontal treadmill running. *Biomechanics*, **7**, 87–98.

Paliczka, V.J., Nichols, A.K. and Boreham, C.A.G. (1987). A multi-stage shuttle run test as a predictor of running performance and maximal oxygen uptake in adults. *British Journal of Sports Medicine*, **21**, 163–5.

Pollock, M.L. (1973). The quantification of endurance training programmes. In *Exercise and Sport Sciences Reviews.* ed. J.H. Wilmore (Academic Press, New York), pp. 155–88.

Robertson, R.J., Caspersen, C.J., Allison, T.G., *et al.* (1982). Differentiated perceptions of exertion and energy cost of young women while carrying loads. *European Journal of Applied Physiology and Occupational Physiology*, **49**, 69–78.

Rowland, T.W. (1990). *Exercise and Childrens Health.* (Human Kinetics, Champaign, IL).

Saltin, B., Blomquist, G., Mitchell, J.H., *et al.* (1968). Response to exercise after bed rest and after training. *Circulation*, **38 (suppl. 7)**, 1–78.

Schmidt-Nielsen, K. (1984). *Scaling: Why is Animal Size so Important?* (Cambridge University Press, Cambridge).

Shephard, R.J. (1970). Computer programs for solution of the Åstrand nomogram and calculation of body surface area. *Journal of Sports Medicine and Physical Fitness*, **10**, 206–12.

Shephard, R.J. (1984). Tests of maximum oxygen intake: a critical review. *Sports Medicine*, **1**, 99–124.

Shephard, R.J., Allen, C., Benade, A.J.S., *et al.* (1968). Standardization of submaximal exercise tests. *Bulletin of the World Health Organization*, **38**, 765–75.

Siconolfi, J.F., Cullinane, E. M., Carleton, R.A. and Thompson, P.D. (1982). Assessing in epidemiologic studies: modifications of the Astrand–Ryhming test. *Medicine and Science in Sports and Exercise*, **14**, 335–8.

Stainsby, W.N., Gladden, L.B., Barclay, J.K. and Wilson, B.A. (1980). Exercise efficiency: validity of baseline subtractions. *Journal of Applied Physiology*, **48**, 518–22.

Taylor, C.R., Heglund, N.C. and Maloiy, G.M.O. (1982). Energetics and mechanics of terrestrial locomotion I. Metabolic energy consumption as a function of speed and body size in birds and mammals. *Journal of Experimental Biology*, **97**, 1–22.

Taylor, C.R., Heglund, N.C., McMahon, T.A. and Looney, T.R. (1980). Energetic cost of generating muscular force during running. *Journal of Experimental Biology*, **86**, 9–18.

Taylor, H.L., Buskirk, E. and Henschel, A. (1955). Maximal oxygen uptake as an objective measure of cardiorespiratory performance. *Journal of Applied Physiology*, **8**, 73–7.

Thorstensson, A. (1986). Effects of moderate external loading on the aerobic demand of submaximal running in men and 10-year-old boys. *European Journal of Applied Physiology and Occupational Physiology* , **55**, 569–74.

Unnithan, V.B. and Eston, R.G. (1990). Stride frequency and submaximal treadmill running economy in adults and children. *Pediatric Exercise Science*, **2**, 149–55.

Whipp, B.J. and Wasserman, K. (1969). Efficiency of muscular work. *Journal of Applied Physiology*, **26**, 644–8.

Wickstrom, R.L. (1983). *Fundamental Motor Patterns.* (Lea and Febiger, Philadelphia).

Wilkie, D.R. (1974). The efficiency of muscular contraction. *Journal of Mechanochemistry and Cell Motility*, **2**, 257–67.

Wyndham, C.H., Strydom, N.B., Leary, W.P. and Williams, C.G. (1966). Studies of the maximum capacity of men for physical effort. *Internationale Zeitschrift für Angewandte Physiologie*, **22**, 285–95.

Zacks, R.M. (1973). The mechanical efficiencies of running and bicycling against a horizontal impeding force. *Internationale Zeitschrift für Angewandte Physiologie*, **31**, 249–58.

THERMOREGULATION

8

Thomas Reilly and Nigel T. Cable

8.1 AIMS

The aims of this chapter are to:
- provide students with an understanding of human thermoregulation, at rest and during exercise,
- describe the relevance of anthropometric factors in maintaining heat balance,
- outline practical exercises for the acquisition of techniques to monitor physiological responses to heat loads.

8.2 INTRODUCTION

The human is homoeothermic, meaning that body temperature is maintained within narrow limits independently of fluctuations in environmental temperature. For thermoregulatory purposes the body can be regarded as consisting of a core within which the temperature is 37°C and an outer shell where the ideal average temperature is 33°C, although this value is largely dependent on environmental factors. The precise temperature gradient from core to skin depends on the body part, but generally speaking the size of the gradient that exists between the skin and the environment will determine the amount of heat that is lost or gained by the body.

8.3 PROCESSES OF HEAT LOSS / HEAT GAIN

Normally the body is maintained in thermoequilibrium or heat balance. Heat is produced by metabolism and the level of heat production can be increased dramatically by physical exercise. The processes of conduction, convection and radiation allow for either heat loss or heat gain (depending on environmental conditions) with evaporation being a major avenue of heat loss when body temperature is rising.

The heat of basal metabolism is about 1 kcal kg^{-1} h^{-1}. One kcal (4.186 kJ) is the energy required to raise 1 kg of water through 1°C. The specific heat of human tissue is less than this figure, 0.83 kcal of energy being needed to raise 1 kg of tissue through 1°C. Thus if there were no avenue of heat loss, the temperature of the body would rise by 1°C per hour in an individual with body mass of about 72 kg, and within 4–6 hours death from overheating would follow. The process would be accelerated during exercise, when energy expenditure might approach 25 kcal min^{-1} (105 kJ min^{-1}). This value might include 1 kcal min^{-1} for basal metabolism and 6 kcal min^{-1} for producing muscular work. The remaining 18 kcal is dissipated as heat which builds up within the body. In this instance the theoretical rise in body temperature would be 20°C in just over one hour. Obviously maintaining life depends on the ability to exchange heat with the environment.

A number of factors contribute to heat production and heat loss (Figure 8.1). The maintenance of a relatively constant core temperature is frequently expressed in the form of a heat balance equation:

Kinanthropometry and Exercise Physiology Laboratory Manual: Tests, Procedures and Data. 2nd Edition, Volume 2: Exercise Physiology
Edited by RG Eston and T Reilly. Published by Routledge, London, June 2001

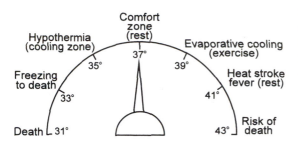

Figure 8.1 The body temperature range.

Heat stored = Metabolic rate – Evaporation
± Radiation ± Convection ± Conduction
– Work done

Heat may be gained from terrestrial sources of radiation or from solar radiation, while the body radiates heat to its immediate environment. In physical terms the human body can be regarded as a black box, the body surface being a good absorber of radiant heat and also a good radiator.

Convection refers to transfer of heat by movement of gas or fluid. The barriers to convective heat exchange include subcutaneous adipose tissue, clothing and films of stationary air or water in immediate contact with clothing.

Conduction describes heat transfer from core through body fluids to the surface of the body and exchange with the environment by direct contact of the skin with objects, materials or surfaces.

Evaporative heat loss includes vaporization of water from moist mucous membrane of the upper respiratory tract with breathing, insensible perspiration through the skin and evaporation of sweat from the surface of the body. When water evaporates from any surface, that surface is cooled. When sweat droplets fall from the skin, no heat is exchanged. At rest in a room temperature of 21°C the heat lost by a nude human would be about 60% from radiation, 25% evaporation from lungs and skin, 12% by means of convective air currents and 3% by means of conduction from the feet. During exercise the main mechanism for heat

loss is evaporation of sweat. This mechanism will be less effective when the air is highly humid, 100% relative humidity meaning that the air is already totally saturated with water vapour and can take up no more at the prevailing temperature.

The rate of evaporative heat loss is dependent on the vapour pressure gradient across the film of stationary air surrounding the skin and on the thickness of the stationary film. It is influenced also by air movement over the skin surface. Evaporative loss from the lungs depends on minute ventilation, dryness of the atmosphere and the barometric pressure. Consequently, dry nose and throat are experienced at altitude, where the atmospheric pressure is lower than at sea level.

8.4 CONTROL OF BODY TEMPERATURE

Body temperature is regulated by temperature-sensitive neurons located in the anterior and posterior hypothalamus. These cells detect the temperature of the circulating blood, with the cells in the anterior hypothalamus responding to an increase in body temperature and those in the posterior portion triggering the effector response to a decrease. These areas also receive afferent input from peripheral warm and cold receptors located in the skin and therefore receive information about changes in the body's immediate environment. Warm receptors in the skin are stimulated in the temperature range of 28–45°C. Paradoxically, above this level the cold receptors begin to fire, particularly if the skin is subjected to a rapid increase. This is called paradoxical inhibition and gives the sensation of cold in very hot surroundings (e.g. in a shower).

During exposure to cold, or when body temperature decreases, the posterior hypothalamus initiates a number of responses. This activity will be neurally mediated via the sympathetic nervous system, and will result in a generalized vasoconstriction of the cutaneous circulation. Blood will be displaced centrally away from the peripheral circulation, promoting a fall in skin temperature which will ultimately increase the temperature gradient between the core and the skin. Importantly, however, this reduction in skin temperature will decrease the gradient that exists between the skin and the environment, and therefore reduce the potential for heat loss from the body. Superficial veins are also affected such that blood returning from the limbs is diverted from them to the vena comitantes that overlie the main arteries. The result is that arterial blood is cooled by the venous return almost immediately it enters the limb by means of the countercurrent heat exchange mechanism.

The reduction in blood flow is not uniform throughout the body, its effects being most pronounced in the extremities. Severe cold may decrease blood flow to the fingers to 2.5% of its normal value whereas, in contrast, blood flow to the head remains unaltered. There are no vasoconstrictor fibres to the vessels of the scalp, which seem to be slow in responding to the direct effect of cooling (Webb, 1982). As heat loss from the head can account for up to 25% of the total heat production, the importance of covering the head to protect against the cold is clear. This would equally apply to the underwater swimmer and to the winter jogger or skier. Froese and Burton (1957) showed that there is a linear relationship between heat loss through the head and ambient temperature within the range −20°C to +32°C, emphasizing the need to insulate the top of the head in extreme cold.

Paradoxically, if the environment is extremely cold, there may be a delayed vasodilation of the blood vessels in the skin which alternates with intense vasoconstriction in cycles of 15–30 minutes and leads to excessive heat loss. This has been described as a hunting reaction in the quest for an appropriate skin temperature to achieve the best combination of gradients between core, shell and environment. The vasodilation may be the result of accumulated vasoactive metabolites arising from increased anaerobic metabolism in local tissues which is associated with the reduced blood flow. The explanation by Keatinge (1969) is that the smooth muscle in the walls of peripheral blood vessels is paralysed at temperatures of 10°C; as the muscles cannot then respond to noradrenaline released by vasoconstrictor nerves, the muscles relax to allow a return of blood flow through the vessels, thus completing the cycle. This alternation of high and low blood flow to local tissue produced by ice-pack application is exploited in the treatment of sports injuries by physiotherapists. The phenomenon is also well recognized by runners and cyclists if they train in cold conditions without wearing gloves; the fingers are initially white but become a ruddy colour as blood enters the digits in increased volumes. Blood flow to the skin may also be influenced by alcohol, which has a vasodilator effect. Though alcohol can make a person feel more comfortable when exposed to cold, it will increase heat loss and so may endanger the individual. Consequently, drinking alcohol is not recommended when staying outdoors overnight in inclement weather conditions and the customary hip-flask of whiskey serves no useful protective function for recreational skiers or mountaineers.

Shivering represents a response of the autonomic nervous system to cold. It constitutes involuntary activity of skeletal muscles and the resultant heat production may be as large as three times the basal metabolic rate. Indeed, metabolic rates five times that at rest have been reported (Horvath, 1981), though such values are rare. Shivering tends to be intermittent and persists during exercise until the exercise intensity is sufficient on its own to maintain core temperature. The piloerection response to cold that is found in animals is less useful to the human who lacks the furry overcoat to the skin that cold-dwelling animals possess. Contraction of the small muscles attached to hair roots causes air to be trapped in the fur and this impedes heat loss. The pilomotor reflex in humans has little thermal impact but is reflected in the appearance of goose pimples. Paradoxically, the 'gooseflesh syndrome' is sometimes found in marathon runners during heat stress when heat loss mechanisms begin to fail, the condition being accompanied by a sensation of coldness (Pugh, 1972).

Elevation of basal heat production may be brought about by the neuroendocrine system in conditions of long-term cold exposure. The hypothalamus stimulates the pituitary gland to release hormones that affect other target organs, notably the thyroid and adrenal glands. Thyroxine causes an increase in metabolic rate within 5–6 hours of cold exposure. This elevation will persist throughout a sojourn, the metabolic rate at rest being greater in cold than in temperate climates and elevated over that of tropical residents. Adrenaline and adrenocortical hormones may also cause a slight increase in metabolism, though the combined hormonal effects are still relatively modest. Brown fat, so-called because of its iron-containing cytochromes active in oxidative processes, is a potential source of thermogenesis. This form of fat is located primarily in and around the kidneys and adjacent to the great vessels, beneath the shoulder blades and along the spine. It is evident in abundance in infants but its stores decline during growth and development. Its high metabolic rate has been presented as an explanation of why some individuals fail to increase body weight despite appearing to overeat, though this point is highly contentious.

The anterior hypothalamus initiates vasodilation of the cutaneous circulation in response to an increase in body temperature. This results in an expansion of the core and ultimately increases the temperature gradient between the skin and the environment, allowing for greater heat exchange. Cutaneous vasodilation is initiated by a removal of vasoconstrictor tone in the skin, and enhanced by the release of vasodilator substances (bradykinin and vasoactive intestinal polypeptide) from the sweat glands following stimulation via sympathetic cholinergic fibres. These substances are thought to cause the smooth muscle of the cutaneous blood vessels to relax and allow total peripheral resistance to decrease, thereby increasing blood flow. Evidence for this response comes from individuals with a congenital lack of sweat glands, who are not able to increase skin blood flow when body temperature increases.

It is, therefore, evident that the process of thermoregulation is subserved by the cardiovascular system. That is to say, heat is gained or lost by changes in blood flow. Such changes in blood flow must obviously have ramifications for the control of blood pressure. If total peripheral resistance is increased (i.e. when body temperature falls and skin blood flow is restricted), blood pressure will increase. Conversely with peripheral vasodilation skin blood flow is enhanced and blood pressure may fall. Thus thermoregulatory responses can initiate changes in non-thermal control mechanisms. Examples of this include the increased diuresis seen in cold weather. As total peripheral resistance increases, antidiuretic hormone secretion is reduced and therefore less fluid is reabsorbed from the kidney; ultimately some blood volume is lost, which returns blood pressure to normal. Conversely, the soldier who stands on parade for a number of hours in the heat will, following increases in skin blood flow, no longer be able to maintain blood pressure sufficiently to perfuse the cerebral circulation, and therefore may faint to allow blood flow to return to normal.

8.5 THERMOREGULATION AND OTHER CONTROL SYSTEMS

During exercise, particularly in the heat, sweating becomes the main mechanism for losing heat. Sweat is secreted by corkscrew-shaped glands within the skin and it contains a range of electrolytes as well as substances such as urea and lactic acid. Its concentration is less than in plasma and so sweat is described as hypotonic. Altogether there are about 2 million eccrine sweat glands in the human body, though the number varies between individuals; the other type, apocrine sweat glands, are found mainly in the axilla and groin and are not important in thermoregulation in the human.

Table 8.1 The 24-hour water balance in a sedentary individual

Intake (ml)		Output (ml)	
Solid and semi-solid food	1 200	Skin	350
Water released in metabolism	300	Expired air	500
Drinks (water, tea, fruit juice, coffee, milk and so on)	1 000	Urine	1 500
		Faeces	150
Total	2 500		2 500

While exercising hard in hot conditions, the amount of fluid lost in sweat may exceed $2 \, l \, h^{-1}$ so athletes may lose 5–6% of body weight as water within 2 hours of heavy exercise. This loss would amount to over 8% of body water stores and represent a serious level of dehydration. The normal body water balance is illustrated in Table 8.1.

As thermoregulatory needs tend to override the physiological controls over body water, sweat secretion will continue and exacerbate the effects of dehydration until heat injury is manifest. Costill (1981) demonstrated how losses are distributed among body water pools during prolonged exercise. Muscle biopsies were taken before, during and after exercise in active and non-active muscles, and blood samples were also obtained. It was calculated that extracellular and intracellular and total body water values decreased by 9, 3 and 7.5%, respectively. The conclusion was that electrolyte losses in sweat did not alter the calculated membrane potential of active and inactive muscles sufficiently to be the cause of cramp suffered in such conditions.

Effects of dehydration are manifest at a water deficit of 1% of body weight in a sensation of thirst. This is due to a change in cellular osmolarity and to dryness in the mucous membrane of the mouth and throat. The sensation can be satisfied long before the fluid is replaced so that thirst is an imperfect indication of the body's needs. As fluid may be lost at a greater rate than it can be absorbed, regular intakes of water, say 150 ml every 10–15 minutes, are recommended in events such as marathon running. This can halt the rise in heart rate and body temperature towards hyperthermic levels that might otherwise have resulted. Energy drinks have no added value for thermoregulatory purposes, though hypotonic solutions have marginal benefits in terms of the speed at which the ingested fluid is absorbed. Indeed, in hot conditions, it is sound practice to start contests well stocked up with body water and then take small amounts of fluid frequently en route. However, in prolonged endurance events care must be taken not to over-hydrate as this can lead to the development of hyponatraemia or water toxicity, which if severe may need hospitalization. This condition usually only presents itself in avid water drinkers, but is becoming more common during events such as 'ironman' triathlons and 'ultramarathons'.

Boxers and wrestlers are known to use dehydrating practices to lose weight before their events and stay within the limit of their particular weight categories. In many cases the use of diuretics for the purpose of body water loss has been suspected. The practice is dangerous, especially if the impending contest is to be held in hot conditions and severe levels of dehydration have been induced prior to weighing-in. It was soundly condemned in a position statement of the American College of Sports Medicine in 1976 which was updated in 1984.

Effects of dehydration on performance vary with the amount of fluid lost and the nature of the activity being performed. These are compounded when accompanied by imminent hyperthermia due to a combination of high humidity and high ambient temperature. Throughout the history of sport there are many dramatic examples of competitors suffering from heat stress. Television audiences witnessing transmission of the first Women's Olympic Marathon in 1984 empathized with the struggle of the Swiss competitor to complete the course. The Irish professional boxer, Barry McGuigan, lost his world title in the heat of Las Vegas, having had difficulty in making the scheduled weight limit before the fight. Examples of less fortunate victims of heat stress were the deaths of a Danish cyclist (Knud Jensen) at the Rome Olympics in 1960 and later that of the British professional cyclist, Tommy Simpson. In both cases the use of amphetamines was allegedly implicated, these having an enhanced effect on performance but a deleterious effect on thermoregulatory mechanisms.

The fact that body water content is variable should be taken into account when body composition is assessed from measurements of body water. This applies to chemical methods for measuring body water and predicting body fat values from the measurements. It applies also to the use of bioelectric impedance analysis (BIA) methods, which record conductance or resistance of the whole body in response to a low-voltage electrical signal administered to the subjects. The resistance is dependent on water content, and estimates of body fat will be affected by the state of the subject's hydration (Brodie *et al.*, 1991, Lemmey *et al.*, 2000).

Women are often reputed to have inferior thermoregulatory functions to men during exercise in the heat. It seems that the early studies reporting women to be less tolerant of exercise in the heat ignored the low fitness levels of the women who were studied. Though women tend to have more body fat than men and so greater insulation properties, their larger surface area relative to mass gives them an advantage in losing heat. There appears to be no sex difference in acclimatization to heat, and the frequency of heat illness in road races in the USA is approximately the same for each sex (Haymes, 1984).

There are, however, differences between the sexes that should be considered when body temperature is concerned. The greater subcutaneous tissue layers in females should provide them with better insulation against the cold. In females the set point is not fixed at 37°C but varies with the menstrual cycle. In mid-cycle there is a sharp rise of about 0.5°C which is due to the influence of progesterone and this elevation is indicative of ovulation.

There is also a circadian rhythm in body temperature that is independent of the environmental conditions (Reilly, 1990). Core temperature is at a low point during sleep and is at its peak at about 18:00 hours (Figure 8.2). The peak-to-trough variation is about 0.6°C and this applies to both males and females. The amplitude is less than this in aged individuals (Reilly *et al.*, 1997). There is a wealth of evidence intimating that many types of sports performance follow a curve during the day that is closely linked to the rhythm in body temperature (Reilly *et al.*, 2000).

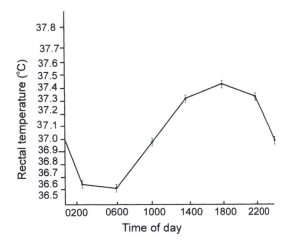

Figure 8.2 Circadian variation in core temperature.

8.6 MEASUREMENT OF BODY TEMPERATURE

Core temperature refers to the thermal state of essential internal organs such as heart, liver, viscera and brain. Although it is normally considered that core temperature is regulated about an internal temperature of 37°C, this value varies depending on the site of measurement. There are also rhythmic changes in the temperature set point, which varies during exercise and in fever.

Rectal temperature is the most commonly used site for indicating core temperature in athletes. The probe should be inserted to a depth of 10 cm beyond the external anal sphincter if reliable measures are to be obtained. Care is also necessary that probes are sterilized and treated with HIV risk in mind. Rectal temperature is not the best measure of core temperature in situations where temperature is changing rapidly. For this reason oesophageal temperature is preferred in some exercise experiments. This entails inserting a probe through the nose and threading it into the oesophagus.

An alternative is tympanic temperature where a sensor is placed adjacent to the tympanic membrane. Caution is necessary as it is easy to damage the membrane and also the ear must be completely insulated to avoid environmental influences. External auditory meatus temperatures can also be measured by inserting a probe 1 cm inside the ear canal and insulating the ear. However, with this measurement and those of rectal and oesophageal temperatures, it is best to represent data as a change from a baseline, since a temperature gradient exists down these tissues.

Oral or sublingual temperatures, typically measured with a mercury thermometer, are used in clinical rather than exercise contexts and give values about 0.4°C lower than rectal temperature. Oral temperature is of little use in swimmers, for example, whose mouths are affected by surrounding water and high ventilation rates. Similarly measurement of axilla or groin temperatures in athletic subjects gives a poor indication of their thermal status. A temperature-sensitive pill which can be swallowed and then monitored by radio-telemetry has been used in occupational contexts. Difficulties include the necessity for accurate calibration, differences in temperature between the internal organs adjacent to the passage of the pill, the influences of recently digested food on core temperature and the possible unsavoury task of its retrieval once the pill has traversed the full course of the digestive tract. A more acceptable alternative is to measure the temperature of mid-stream urine which gives a reasonable indication of internal body temperature.

Skin temperature has conventionally been measured by thermistors and thermocouples. Optoelectronic devices are now also available. The common method is to place thermistors over the surface of the skin and tape over them. From measurements of a number of designated skin sites, a mean skin temperature may be calculated. The formulae that require the least number of observations are;

$$MST = 0.5\, T_c + 0.36\, T_l + 0.14\, T_a$$
$$\text{(Burton, 1935)}$$

$$MST = 0.3\, T_c + 0.3\, T_a + 0.2\, T_t + 0.2\, T_l$$
$$\text{(Ramanathan, 1964)}$$

where: MST is mean skin temperature, T_c is temperature of the chest, juxta-nipple, T_l is leg temperature measured over the lateral side of the calf muscle, T_a is lower arm temperature and T_t is anterior thigh temperature. Mean body temperature (MBT) may then be calculated by weighting rectal temperature (T_r) and MST in the ratio 4:1. In other words: $MBT = 0.8\, T_r + 0.2\, MST$.

8.7 THERMOREGULATORY RESPONSES TO EXERCISE

Exercise implies activity of skeletal muscle and this demands energy. Most of the energy utilized is dissipated as heat, a small amount contributing towards mechanical work. The muscular efficiency represents the work performed as a percentage of the total energy expenditure. For cycle ergometry this value is about 22%, depending on whether or not the resting energy expenditure is taken into consideration. In swimming, this figure is much lower; in weight lifting, it has been calculated to be about 12% (Reilly, 1983). It is acknowledged that the mechanical efficiency is difficult to estimate in activities such as running.

During sustained exercise the cardiac output supplies oxygen to the active muscles but also distributes blood to the skin to cool the body. In cases where cardiac output is maximal, the exercise performance is impaired by thermoregulatory needs. Since the maximal cardiac output determines how well blood can be distributed for peripheral cooling, the heat load induced by exercise is a function of the percentage of maximal oxygen uptake rather than the absolute work rate engaged.

The body acts as a heat sink in the early minutes of exercise and blood is shunted from viscera and other organs to the exercising muscles. Blood flow to the brain remains intact although there seems to be differential distribution to areas within the brain. If exercise imparts a severe heat load, the sweat glands are activated and droplets appear on the skin surface after about 7 minutes. The extent to which body temperature rises then depends on the exercise intensity and the environmental conditions.

8.8 ENVIRONMENTAL FACTORS

Heat exchange with the environment is influenced by a number of environmental variables as well as individual characteristics. The clothing and equipment used also affect heat exchange. Thus some background is provided on relevant interactions with the environment in this section before progressing to anthropometric considerations in the next.

Athletic contests are sometimes held in conditions that challenge the body's thermoregulatory system. Cold is less of a problem than heat since athletes usually choose to avoid extremes of cold. Exceptions are winter sports such as mountaineering, where it is imperative to protect the individuals against the cold. Outdoor games, such as American football, are also sometimes played in freezing conditions.

Experiments in cold air close to freezing have not consistently shown a significant effect on the maximal oxygen uptake. The effects are more marked in the periphery of the body, where the drop in temperature of tissues is more pronounced. Normally the mean skin temperature is about 33°C and extreme discomfort is felt when this drops below 25°C. As skin temperature of the hand falls below 23°C, movements of the limb begin to get clumsy, and finger dexterity is severely affected at skin temperatures between 13°C and 16°C. This is especially critical in winter sport activities that require fine manipulative actions of the fingers, which are impaired because of numbness in those digits. Tactile sensitivity of the fingers is also affected for the worse to the extent that an impact on the skin at 20°C has to be about six times greater than normal for usual sensations to be felt. The skeletal muscles function at an optimal internal temperature and when this drops to about 27°C, the muscle's contractile force is much impaired. This can be demonstrated by the progressive decline in grip strength with increased cooling of the arm. In sports such as downhill skiing, the performer could be cooled during the chair lift to the top of the ski run and must therefore take steps to keep the limb muscles warm prior to skiing. Synovial fluid in the joints also becomes colder and more viscous, thus increasing the stiffness of the joints. The fatigue curve of muscle also deteriorates due to a combination of factors such as impaired strength, lower blood flow, increased resistance of connective tissue and increased discomfort.

One of the most important consequences of sports participation outdoors in the cold is the poorer neuromuscular co-ordination that may result. As temperature in nervous tissue falls, conduction velocity of nerve impulses is retarded and this slows reaction time. If the slide in temperature is not reversed, eventually complete neural block occurs. Co-ordination is also impaired by the effect of cold on the muscle spindles which, at 27°C, respond to only 50% of normal to a standardized stimulus. Consequently, the stumbling and poor locomotion of climbers in the cold may be due to impairments in peripheral nerves.

Such an effect is particularly evident during cold water immersion. When swimming in water temperatures below 10°C there is a progressive reduction in swimming efficiency that appears to be related to local cooling in the arm muscles, rather than whole-body hypothermia. Arm cooling tends to result in local muscle weakness and even paralysis, which results in increasing drag and risk of sinking. This coupled with the hyperventilation often seen during cold immersion makes a co-ordinated swimming stroke virtually impossible, and may be a reason why many drowning deaths occur in cold water, even in cases where the victim is very close to land and safety (Tipton *et al.*, 1999).

Some protection against this risk is offered by a greater subcutaneous fat layer around the arm muscles to restrict heat loss. In addition, lean individuals acutely exposed to cold water immersion should restrict body movement in order to prevent hypothermia. Whilst this manoeuvre may limit heat production, it will allow heat loss to be markedly restricted. This is because both fat and inactive muscle act as good insulators. However, when muscle becomes active, blood flow is dramatically increased, which ultimately changes a good insulator under resting conditions into a very effective heat conductor.

Frostbite is one of the risks of recreational activities in extreme cold. This can occur when the temperature in the fingers or toes falls below freezing and at −1°C ice crystals are formed in those tissues. The results can be a gangrenous extremity, often experienced by mountaineers in icy conditions when their gloves or boots fail to provide adequate thermal insulation. Recent clinical experience is

that amputation of damaged tissue is not a necessary consequence of frostbite and prognosis tends to be more optimistic than thought in previous decades. Of more serious consequence is a fall in the body's core temperature. The cold stress is progressively manifested by an enlargement of the area of the shell while the area of the core becomes smaller until its temperature ultimately begins to fall dangerously. A core temperature of 34.5°C is usually taken as indicative of grave hypothermic risk, though there is no absolute consensus of a critical end point. Some researchers assume that a rectal temperature of 32–33°C is a critical end point, though the exact value of hypothalamic temperature for fatality is subject to controversy.

Scientists have used metaphorical models to predict survival time by extrapolating from initial rates of decline in core temperature to an arbitrary value of 30°C (Ross *et al.*, 1980). This avoids the need to take subjects too close to a risk of hypothermia. Researchers in Nazi concentration camps were not so considerate to their prisoners, who were cooled to death at core temperatures of about 27°C. An example was given by Holdcroft (1980) of an alcoholic woman exposed overnight in Chicago to sub-freezing temperatures and whose rectal temperature was reported to be 18°C when she was found in a stupor. In hindsight it is doubtful if this was representative of core temperature in these conditions. Happily, she survived after being re-warmed in a hospital room temperature of 20°C. Death usually occurs at a much higher core temperature than that reported for the fortunate Chicago woman, shivering being usually replaced by permanent muscle rigidity, then loss of consciousness at core temperatures of 32°C and heart failure may follow. The range of clinical symptoms associated with hypothermia is presented in texts such as Holdcroft (1980).

Behavioural strategies and proper clothing can safeguard individuals in cold environments. Enormous strides have been made in the provision of protective equipment against the cold for sports participants. Major advances have been made in clothing design and in the reliability and durability of tents. A similar systematic improvement is noted in the provision of first-aid and rescue services for most outdoor pursuits. The specially treated sheets of foil paper readily availed of by recreational marathon runners to safeguard against rapid heat loss on cessation of activity are an example.

Existence of good rescue facilities is no excuse for climbing parties to take risks in inclement weather. Early warning systems used by rangers on mountainsides must be heeded if they are to be effective, and this inevitably means consumer education. Otherwise, the safety of the rescue team in addition to that of the climbing party may be jeopardized if weather conditions further deteriorate. Assessment of the risk involves some calculations of the magnitude of cold stress. On the mountainside the wind velocity may be the most influential factor in cooling the body, so that the ambient temperature alone would grossly underestimate the prevailing risk. The wind-chill index designed by Siple and Passel (1945), and widely used by mountaineers and skiers, provides a method of comparing different combinations of temperature and wind speed. The values calculated correspond to a caloric scale for rate of heat loss per unit body surface area; they are then converted in to a sensation scale ranging from hot (about 80) through cool (400) to bitterly cold (1200) and on to a value where exposed flesh freezes within 60 s. The cooling effects of combinations of certain temperatures and wind speeds are expressed as 'temperature equivalents' and are estimated with a nomogram. Use of the wind-chill index enables sojourners to evaluate the magnitude of cold stress and take appropriate precautions. Wet conditions can exacerbate cold stress, especially if the clothing worn begins to lose its insulation. Attention to safety may be even more important in water sports since, apart from the risk of drowning, body heat is lost much more rapidly in water than in air.

The formula of Siple and Passel (1945) for calculating heat loss is:

$$K_o = \left(\sqrt{100V} + 10.5 - V \right)\left(33 - T \right)$$

where: K_o = heat loss in kcal m^{-2} h^{-1}; V = wind velocity in m s^{-1}; T = environmental temperature in °C; 10.5 = a constant; 33 = assumed normal skin temperature in °C

For example, if wind velocity is 14 m s^{-1} and the ambient temperature is 2°C, the rate of heat loss is:

$$K_o = \left(\sqrt{100 \times 14} + 10.5 - 14 \right)\left(33 - 2 \right) = (33.9)(31)$$
$$= 1051 \, \text{kcal} \, \text{m}^{-2} \, \text{h}^{-1}$$

Water has a much greater heat conduction capacity than air, and so heat is readily exchanged with the environment when the human body is immersed. Though mean skin temperature is normally about 33°C, a bath at that temperature feels cold, yet if the water temperature is elevated by 2°C, the temperature of the body will begin to rise. This suggests that the human is poorly equipped for spending long spells in the water. Finding the appropriate water temperature is important for swimming pool managers who have to cater for different levels of ability. The preferred water temperature for inactive individuals is 33°C, for learners it is about 30°C, for active swimmers it is in the range of 27–29°C, whereas competitive swimmers are more content with temperatures around 25°C. Generally the water is regulated to suit the active users. Indeed, the whole environment of the swimming pool must be engineered for the comfort of users. Condensation in the arena may not be welcomed by spectators, but the high humidity in the swimming pool militates against heat loss when the swimmer is out of the water. Engineering may involve double glazing of the surround to avoid losing radiant heat outwards from the building as well as provision of supplementary radiant heating. Permissible indoor dew points can be calculated from temperature differences between outdoors and inside the pool to avoid high condensation risks, these being the points where moisture is deposited. Air ventilation rates inside the building may reduce the moisture content of indoor areas to decrease the discomfort of spectators, but this will cool the bather and call for increased heating costs. A practical compromise is to have air temperatures in the region of 28–30°C, which are much warmer than normal office room temperatures.

In hot conditions, heat stroke is a major risk and should be classed as an emergency. It reflects failure of normal thermoregulatory mechanisms. It is characterized by a body temperature of 41°C or higher, cessation of sweating and total confusion. Once sweating stops, the body temperature will rise quickly and soon cause irreversible damage to liver, kidney and brain cells. In such an emergency immediate treatment is essential.

Calculating the risk of heat injury requires accurate assessment of environmental conditions. The main factors to consider are dry bulb temperature, air velocity and cloud cover. Dry bulb temperature can be measured with a mercury glass thermometer, whereas relative humidity can be calculated from data obtained from a wet bulb thermometer used in either a sling psychrometer or a Stevenson screen. The dew point temperature, the point at which the air becomes saturated, is a measure of absolute humidity and it can be measured with a whirling hygrometer. Radiant temperature is measured by a globe thermometer inserted into a hollow metal sphere coated with black matt paint. Air velocity can be measured by means of a vane anemometer or an alcohol thermometer coated with polished silver. Cloud cover will protect against solar radiation and may provide some intermittent relief to the athlete. More details of the measuring devices and their operations are contained in the classic publication by Bedford (1946).

A problem for the sports scientist is to find the proper combination of factors to reach an integrated assessment of the environmental heat load. Many equations have been derived

for this purpose and three-quarters of a century of research to this end were reviewed by Lee (1980). Most of the formulae incorporate composites of the environmental measures, whereas some, such as the predicted 4-hour sweat rate (P4SR), predict physiological responses from such measures. Probably the most widely used equation in industrial and military establishments has been the WBGT Index, WBGT standing for wet bulb and globe temperature. The US National Institute of Occupational Safety and Health recommended it as the standard heat stress index in 1972. The weightings (beta weights) underline the importance of considering relative humidity:

$$WBGT = 0.7 \, WBT + 0.2 \, GT + 0.1 \, DBT$$

where: WB represents wet bulb; G indicates globe; DB represents dry bulb; T indicates temperature.

A comprehensive selection of indices derived in the United Kingdom and the USA was given by Lee (1980). A later development is the Botsball which was validated by Beshir *et al.* (1982). It combines the effects of air temperature, humidity, wind speed and radiation into a single reading. It got its name from its designer, Botsford, and the WBGT can be reliably predicted from it if necessary.

Heat stress indices provide a framework for evaluating the risk of competing in hot conditions and for predicting the casualties. The American College of Sports Medicine (1984) set down guidelines for distance races, recommending that events longer than 16 km should not be conducted when the WBGT Index exceeds 28°C. This value is often exceeded in distance races in Europe and in the USA during the summer months, and in many marathon races in Asia and Africa. It is, however, imperative in all cases that the risks are understood and that symptoms of distress are recognized and promptly attended to. The plentiful provision of fluids en route and facilities for cooling participants are important precautionary steps.

8.9 ANTHROPOMETRY AND HEAT EXCHANGE

The exchange of heat between the human and the environment is affected by both body size and weight composition. Age, sex and physique of the individual are relevant considerations also.

The exchange of heat is a function of the body surface area relative to body mass. The dimensional exponent for this relation is 0.67. The smaller the individual, the easier it is to exchange heat with the environment. Consequently children gain and lose heat more quickly than do adults, and marathon runners on average tend to be smaller than those specialising in shorter running events. It is important to recognize that children are more vulnerable than adults in extremes of environmental conditions.

It is thought that elderly people living alone prefer warmer environments than younger individuals due to their lower metabolic rate. This is countered by a decrease in insensible perspiration due to a change in the vapour diffusion resistance of the skin with age. There is a higher incidence of death from hypothermia in old people living alone in the European winter than in the general population. These deaths are more likely to be due to socio-economic conditions and physical immobility than to thermoregulatory changes with age.

Physiological thermoregulatory responses, notably skin blood flow and sweat rates, to heat stress tend to diminish with increasing age. This is probably due to age-related changes in the skin. Nevertheless, changes in core temperature and heat storage often show only marginal age-related effects if healthy men and women preserve a high degree of aerobic fitness. The ability to exercise in hot conditions is more a function of the status of the oxygen transport system (especially maximal oxygen uptake and cardiac output) than of chronological age.

Differences between the sexes in heat exchange are largely explained by body composition, physique and surface-to-volume ratios. These predominate once differences in fitness levels are taken into account.

Adipose tissue layers beneath the skin act to insulate the body and are protective in cold conditions. The degree of muscularity or mesomorphy can add to this. Ross *et al.* (1980) demonstrated that prediction of survival time in accidental immersion in water should take both endomorphy and mesomorphy into consideration, and the best prediction was when the entire somatotype was taken into account. Pugh and Edholm (1955), in their classical studies of English Channel swimmers, showed that the leaner individuals suffered from the cold much earlier than did those with high proportions of body adiposity. They compared responses of two ultra-distance swimmers in water of 15°C. The larger and fatter individual showed no decrease in rectal temperature for 7 hours, after which his radial pulse was impalpable for 50 minutes. The lighter and leaner swimmer was taken from the water after half an hour when his rectal temperature had dropped from 37°C to 34.5°C. In their studies in a swimming flume, Holmer and Bergh (1974) found that oesophageal temperature was constant at a water temperature of 26°C in subjects operating at 50% $\dot{V}O_2$ max, except for a decrease in those with low body fat. They would be at an even greater disadvantage in colder water.

Racial differences in thermoregulatory response to heat seem to reflect physiological adjustments to environmental conditions more than genetic factors. Acclimatization to heat occurs relatively rapidly, a good degree of adaptation being achieved within two weeks. Sweating capacity is increased, concentrations of electrolytes in sweat are reduced due to an influence of aldosterone and there is an expansion of plasma volume. The sensitivity of the sweat glands is altered so that more sweat is produced for a given rise in core temperature. It is less clear how genetic and acclimatization factors are separated for cold exposure, since diet, activity, living conditions and so on are confounding factors. Studies of the ama, professional pearl divers of Korea and Japan, suggest a mild adjustment to chronic cold water exposure occurs (Rahn and Yokoyama, 1965). Thermal conductance in a given water temperature was found to be lower for diving than for non-diving women matched for skinfold thickness. These divers were also reported to have higher resting metabolic rates, which would help them to preserve heat. A similar vasoconstriction to reduce thermal conductance of tissues was reported by Skreslet and Aarefjord (1968) in subjects diving with self-contained underwater breathing apparatus (SCUBA) in the Arctic for 45 days.

The elevation of metabolic rate is also found in Eskimos when their thermal values are compared to Europeans. To what extent this can be attributed to diet and the specific dynamic activity of food is not clear. Adaptive vasoconstriction is most pronounced in Aborigines sleeping semi-naked in near-freezing temperatures in the Australian outback. By restricting peripheral circulation, they can tolerate cold conditions that would cause grave danger to sojourners similarly exposed. This circulatory adjustment occurs without an increase in metabolic rate.

8.10 PRACTICAL EXERCISES

It is easier to demonstrate thermoregulatory factors using single-case studies as examples. Experiments require controlled laboratory conditions and usually prolonged exercise is involved. In the absence of an environmental chamber, three different laboratory demonstrations are suggested.

8.11 PRACTICAL 1: MUSCULAR EFFICIENCY

This practical entails exercise under steady-rate conditions on a cycle ergometer with work-rate being controlled and metabolic responses measured. From these measurements the muscular efficiency of exercise can be calculated.

8.11.1 AIM

To examine the efficiency of various cycling cadences

8.11.2 EQUIPMENT

- Electronically-braked cycle ergometer
- Oxygen consumption measuring device (e.g. on-line system or Douglas bags and oxygen and carbon dioxide analysers)

8.11.3 PROTOCOL

An electronically-braked ergometer maintains work-rate (power output) independent of changes in pedal cadence. In this instance the work-rate chosen was 120 W. The subject has $\dot{V}O_2$ measured whilst sitting still, then commences exercise pedalling at a frequency of 50 rev min^{-1} for 20 minutes with $\dot{V}O_2$ measured during the last 2 minutes. This is followed by a 10 minute rest period and then this regimen is performed twice more using exactly the same work-rate but with new pedalling frequencies of 70 and 100 rev min^{-1}.

8.11.4 CALCULATIONS

$$\text{Work efficiency} = \frac{\text{work done (kJ min}^{-1})}{\text{energy expended (kJ min}^{-1})}$$

where: 1 watt = 0.06 kJ min^{-1}

Energy expended = $\dot{V}O_2$ (l min^{-1}) × caloric equivalent (see Table 6.3)

Net efficiency; as above, except that resting $\dot{V}O_2$ must be subtracted from the exercise value. (Note: If an electronically-braked cycle ergometer is not available, use a mechanically-braked ergometer and exercise entailing a steady-state protocol.)

8.11.5 EXAMPLES OF CALCULATIONS

Efficiency
e.g. Work-rate = 120 W = 7.2 kJ min^{-1}
      Resting $\dot{V}O_2$ = 0.25 l min^{-1}
      Exercise $\dot{V}O_2$ = 2.0 l min^{-1}
      RER = 0.85
      Energy equivalent for 2.0 l min^{-1} at RER = 0.85 = 20.3 kJ min^{-1}

$$\text{Therefore: Gross efficiency} = \frac{7.2}{2.0 \times 20.3} \times 100 = 17.74\%$$

$$\text{Net efficiency} = \frac{7.2}{(2.0 - 0.25) \times 20.3} \times 100 = 20.3\%$$

8.12 PRACTICAL 2: THERMOREGULATORY RESPONSES TO EXERCISE

The laboratory exercise involves recordings of rectal and skin temperatures at regular intervals during sustained performance. Exercise may be undertaken on either a motor-driven treadmill or a cycle ergometer. The purpose is to demonstrate physiological responses to exercise using thermoregulatory variables.

An example is shown in Figure 8.3. The exercise intensity was 210 W sustained for 60 minutes. Rectal temperature and skin temperatures were measured. The rectal temperature rose by 2°C during the experiment.

8.12.1 AIM

To investigate the thermoregulatory response to steady state and incremental exercise

8.12.2 EQUIPMENT

- Cycle ergometer
- Weighing scales
- Rectal thermistor (e.g. Grant Instruments, Royston, UK)
- Analogue or digital temperature monitor
- Electrocardiogram or short-range radio telemetry (e.g. Sport Tester, Polar Electro, Kempele, Finland)

8.12.3 PROTOCOL

Two subjects are required for this test. The subjects should place the rectal thermistor 10 cm beyond the external anal sphincter and attach skin thermistors on the sternum, on the medial forearm midway between elbow and wrist, on the anterior surface of the thigh midway between hip and knee and on the lateral surface of the lower leg between knee and ankle. Measure the subject's body mass immediately prior to exercise. One subject exercises at 70% maximum heart rate for 60 minutes with measurements of all variables taken at 3 minute intervals. The other subject exercises at 60 W for 5 minutes with the work-rate increased by 30 W each subsequent 5 minutes until exhaustion. Variables should be measured every minute. At the completion of exercise subjects should be weighed immediately (without drying the skin) to obtain an index of sweat evaporation rate.

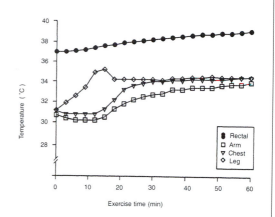

Figure 8.3 Temperature changes during exercise at 70% maximal heart rate.

8.12.4 CLEANING OF PROBES

Rectal probes should be washed in warm soapy water and then immersed in a 1:20 concentration of sterilization fluid for at least 30 minutes. On removal from the solution, the probes should be left to dry completely in room air before further use. Skin probes can be washed and immersed in a 1:40 solution of sterilization fluid for 10 minutes and left to dry.

8.13 PRACTICAL 3: ESTIMATION OF PARTITIONAL HEAT EXCHANGE

8.13.1 AIM

To examine the effect of different environmental conditions on evaporative and partitional heat exchange during exercise

8.13.2 EQUIPMENT

- Cycle ergometer
- Weighing scales
- Oxygen consumption measuring device (e.g. on-line system or Douglas bag method)
- Rectal thermistor
- Four skin thermistors
- Analogue or digital temperature monitor

8.13.3 PROTOCOL

One of the subjects exercises on two separate occasions, once in normal ambient conditions (21°C) and again in a hotter environment at the same work-rate. Immediately prior to exercise the individual is weighed (with all probes and clothes) and then completes 30–60 minutes of exercise followed by rapid re-weighing. All temperatures are measured every 5 minutes and $\dot{V}O_2$ is measured at 20-minute intervals.

8.13.4 CALCULATIONS

Heat balance equation

$$HS = M \pm (R \pm C \pm K) - E - W$$

Where:

$$\text{Metabolic Rate (M)} = \frac{\dot{V}O_2(1\,\text{min}^{-1}) \times \text{caloric equivalent} \times 60}{\text{Body Surface Area } (BSA)}$$

$$\text{Metabolic Rate (M)} = \frac{(\text{pre}-\text{exercise mass} - \text{post}-\text{exercise mass})(\text{kg}) \times 2430\,(\text{kJ}\,1^{-1}\,\text{sweat loss})}{\text{Time of exercise (h)} \times BSA}$$

$$Work\,(W) = \frac{\text{Work - rate (kJ min}^{-1} \times 60)}{BSA}$$

$$\text{Stored heat} = \frac{(\text{post}-\text{exercise } T_B - \text{pre}-\text{exercise } T_B) \times 3.47\,(\text{kJ kg}^{-1}\,\text{h}^{-1} \times \text{mass})}{\text{Time (h)} \times BSA}$$

All units are kJ m^{-2} h^{-1}

Examples of calculations using the following data:

  $\dot{V}O_2 = 2.0\,1\,\text{min}^{-1}$
  RER = 0.85
  Pre-exercise rectal temperature = 36.5°C
  Post-exercise rectal temperature = 38.0°C
  Pre-exercise skin temperature = 33.0°C
  Post-exercise skin temperature = 33.9°C
  Pre-exercise body mass = 72.0 kg
  Post-exercise body mass = 71.5 kg
  Body surface area = 1.8 m^2
  Work-rate = 120 W
  Duration of exercise = 60 minutes

$$\text{Metabolic rate (M)} = \frac{\dot{V}O_2 \times \text{caloric equivalent} \times 60}{\text{BSA}} = \frac{2 \times 20.3 \times 60}{1.8} = 1353.33 \text{ kJ m}^{-2} \text{ h}^{-1}$$

$$\text{Evaporation (E)} = \frac{\text{weight loss} \times 2430}{\text{time} \times \text{BSA}} = \frac{(72.0 - 71.5) \times 2430}{1 \times 1.8} = 675 \text{ kJ m}^{-2} \text{ h}^{-1}$$

$$\text{Work (W)} = \frac{72 \times 60}{1.8} = 240 \text{ kJ m}^{-2} \text{ h}^{-1}$$

$$\text{Stored heat} = \frac{(\text{post-exercise } T_B - \text{pre-exercise } T_B) \times 3.47 \times 72}{\text{Time (h)} \times \text{BSA}}$$

Where $T_B = (0.65 \text{ rectal}) + (0.35 \text{ skin})$

$$= \frac{(36.57 - 35.28) \times 3.47 \times 72}{1 \times 1.8} = 179.1 \text{ kJ m}^{-2} \text{h}^{-1}$$

Heat balance HS = M – E ± (R ± C ± K) – W
Therefore rearranging:
Partitional heat exchange = HS – M + E + W
$$= 179.1 - 1353.3 + 675 + 240$$
$$= -259.2 \text{ kJ m}^{-2} \text{ h}^{-1}$$

Therefore in the above example 259.2 kJ m^{-2} h^{-1} is lost from the body by the combined processes of radiation, conduction and convection.

REFERENCES

American College of Sports Medicine (1984). Position Statement. Prevention of thermal injuries during distance running. *Physician and Sportsmedicine*, **12** (7), 43–51.

Bedford, T. (1946). Environmental warmth and its measurement. *Medical Research Council War Memorandum no. 17.* (HMSO, London).

Beshir, M.Y., Ramsey, J.D. and Burford, C.L. (1982). Threshold values for the Botsball: a field study of occupational heat. *Ergonomics*, **25**, 247–54.

Brodie, D.A., Eston, R.G., Coxon, A., *et al.* (1991).The effect of changes of water and electrolytes on the validity of conventional methods of measuring fat-free mass. *Annals of Nutrition and Metabolism*, **35**, 89–97.

Burton, A.L. (1935). Human calorimetry. *Journal of Nutrition*, **9**, 261–79.

Costill, D.L. (1981). Muscle water and electrolyte distribution during prolonged exercise. *International Journal of Sports Medicine*, **2**, 130–4.

Froese, G. and Burton, A.C. (1957). Heat loss from the human head. *Journal of Applied Physiology*, **10**, 235–41.

Haymes, E.M. (1984). Physiological responses of female athletes to heat stress: a review. *Physician and Sportsmedicine*, **12**, no.3, March, 45–50.

Holdcroft, P. (1980). *Body Temperature Control.* (Baillière Tindall, London).

Holmer, I. and Bergh, U. (1974). Metabolic and thermal responses to swimming in water at varying temperatures. *Journal of Applied Physiology*, **37**, 702–5.

Horvath, S.M. (1981). Exercise in a cold environment. *Exercise and Sport Science Reviews*, **9**, 221–63.

Keatinge, W.R. (1969). *Survival in Cold Water.* (Blackwell, Oxford).

Lee, D.H.K. (1980). Seventy five years of searching for a heat index. *Environmental Research*, **22**, 331–56.

Lemmey, A., Eston, R.G., Moloney, S. and Yeomans, J. (2000). The effects of hydration state and rehydration method on bioelectrical impedance analysis. *South African Journal of Sports Medicine*, **7**, 8–12.

Pugh, G. (1972). The gooseflesh syndrome in long distance runners. *British Journal of Physical Education*, March, ix-xii.

Pugh, L.G.C. and Edholm, O.G. (1955). The physiology of channel swimmers. *Lancet*, **ii**, 761–8.

Rahn, H. and Yokoyama, T. eds. (1965). *Physiology of Breathold Diving and the Ama of Japan.* (National Academy of Sciences, Washington, DC).

Ramanathan, N.L. (1964). A new weighting system for mean temperature of the human body. *Journal of Applied Physiology*, **19**, 531–3.

Reilly, T. (1983). The energy cost and mechanical efficiency of circuit weight training. *Journal of Human Movement Studies*, **9**, 39–45.

Reilly, T. (1990). Human circadian rhythms and exercise. *Critical Reviews in Biomedical Engineering*, **18**, 165–80.

Reilly, T., Waterhouse, J. and Atkinson, G. (1997). Ageing, rhythms of physical performance, and adjustment to changes in the sleep-activity cycle. *Occupational and Environmental Studies*, **54**, 812–6.

Reilly, T., Atkinson, G. and Waterhouse, J. (2000). Chronobiology and physical performance, in *Exercise and Sport Science*. eds. W.E. Garrett Jr. and D.T. Kirkendall (Lippincott, Williams and Wilkins, Philadelphia, PA), pp. 351–72.

Ross, W.R., Drinkwater, D.T., Bailey, D.A. *et al.* (1980). Kinanthropometry; traditions and new perspectives. In *Kinanthropometry II.* eds. M. Ostyn, G. Beunen and J. Simons (University Park Press, Baltimore, MD), pp. 3–27.

Siple, P.A. and Passel, C.F. (1945). Measurement of dry atmospheric cooling in sub-freezing temperatures. *Proceedings of the American Philosophical Society*, **89**, 177–99.

Skreslet, S. and Aarefjord, F. (1968). Acclimatisation to cold in man induced by frequent scuba diving in cold water. *Journal of Applied Physiology*, **24**, 177–81.

Tipton, M., Eglin, C., Gennser, M. and Golden, F. (1999). Immersion deaths and deterioration in swimming performance in cold water. *Lancet*, **354**, 626–9.

Webb, P. (1982). Thermal problems. In *The Physiology and Medicine of Diving*. eds. O.G. Edholm and J.S. Weiner (Baillière Tindall, London), pp. 297–318.

PART FOUR

ASSESSMENT AND REGULATION OF ENERGY EXPENDITURE AND EXERCISE INTENSITY

CONTROL OF EXERCISE INTENSITY USING HEART RATE, PERCEIVED EXERTION AND OTHER NON-INVASIVE PROCEDURES

Roger G. Eston and John G. Williams

9.1 AIMS

The aims of this chapter are to:
- review and apply common non-invasive methods of determining exercise intensity,
- review relationships between heart rate, rating of perceived exertion, oxygen uptake and exercise intensity,
- assess the reliability of ratings of perceived exertion and evaluate the validity of such methods in controlling exercise intensity.

9.2 INTRODUCTION

People participate in physical exercise to improve general health, to improve performance-related fitness for a particular sport, and/or for recreation and relaxation. Improved fitness results from adaptation and improvement of cardiovascular, respiratory, and metabolic function as well as local responses in the muscle groups engaged. The nature and magnitude of any training effect are influenced by the frequency, duration, and intensity of exercise. The process of determining and controlling appropriate exercise intensity presents a challenge, which has implications related to both physiological changes and to individual compliance within an exercise programme.

9.3 NON-INVASIVE METHODS OF DETERMINING EXERCISE INTENSITY

An important principle to be assimilated at the outset is that intensity is interpreted by the person engaged in the exercise. No matter how sophisticated the physiological measurements, the psychological interpretation of cardio-respiratory, metabolic, and musculoskeletal functions will play a major role in this process. The psychological component of how 'hard' or 'easy' people perceive their physical efforts to be has been emphasized by Gunnar Borg for exercise testing and prescription since the 1960s (e.g. Borg, 1962). It is now included in mainstream guidelines for the conduct of exercise testing and prescription (American College of Sports Medicine, ACSM, 1995; British Association of Sport and Exercise Sciences, BASES, 1997).

However perceptive an individual's judgements of exercise intensity may be, accurate determination is enhanced by assessment of functional capacity and monitoring to ensure that optimal intensity is not exceeded. The acquisition of such data is only possible in a fully equipped exercise physiology laboratory using trained personnel. Plainly, this requirement invokes considerable practical limitations for many categories of participant. The

Kinanthropometry and Exercise Physiology Laboratory Manual: Tests, Procedures and Data. 2nd Edition, Volume 2: Exercise Physiology
Edited by RG Eston and T Reilly. Published by Routledge, London, June 2001

ACSM (1995) and BASES (1997) have provided concise guidelines for the conduct of such assessments.

9.4 PHYSIOLOGICAL INFORMATION

Several measurements for gauging exercise intensity for various exercise modalities have been devised and applied. These include proportion of maximal oxygen uptake (%$\dot{V}O_2$ max), proportion of maximal heart rate (%HR_{max}), proportion of maximal heart rate reserve (%HRR_{max}), and blood lactate indices. The following will cover the main principles of predicting and controlling exercise intensity by extrapolation from the relationships between oxygen uptake, heart rate, power output and running speed. For a detailed review of the application of metabolic and ventilatory measures for controlling exercise intensity, refer to Chapter 10 by Jones and Doust.

9.4.1 USING OXYGEN CONSUMPTION ($\dot{V}O_2$) TO PRESCRIBE EXERCISE INTENSITY

Exercising at a high (or moderate) intensity for a sustained period of time requires the ability to deliver oxygen to the active muscles. The most frequently cited criterion of maximal functional capacity for sustained exercise is the maximal oxygen uptake ($\dot{V}O_2$ max). Acquisition of this information requires appropriately equipped facilities and expert personnel as well as a high degree of compliance on the part of the participant. The method is explained in Chapter 7 by Cooke. Ideally, proportions of the $\dot{V}O_2$ max are used to specify exercise intensity levels. The recommended intensity range is normally between 40% and 85% depending on the health and training status of the individual (ACSM, 1995).

(a) Prediction of oxygen consumption levels using a multi-stage test

Although the measurement of $\dot{V}O_2$ is preferred, it is possible to predict $\dot{V}O_2$ max using the equations suggested by the ACSM (1995) for cycling, running, walking, stepping and rowing. Oxygen uptake can be predicted for any speed of walking and running on the level and uphill, as well as for cycling, stepping and rowing at specific work rates. In this way, the submaximal, predicted oxygen uptake values can be compared against the subject's heart rate and extrapolated to the maximal heart rate to predict $\dot{V}O_2$ max. With knowledge of the subject's $\dot{V}O_2$ max, it is then possible to prescribe speeds/work-rates that correspond to a given exercise intensity (%$\dot{V}O_2$ max values), using the ACSM formulae. The following examples are for running and cycling.

The formula used to predict $\dot{V}O_2$ at any given speed and gradient is:

$$\dot{V}O_2 \text{ (ml kg}^{-1} \text{ min}^{-1}\text{)} = \text{horizontal component} + \text{vertical component} + \text{resting component}$$

For running

$$\dot{V}O_2 \text{ (ml kg}^{-1} \text{ min}^{-1}\text{)} = (\text{speed (m min}^{-1}) \times 0.2 \text{ ml kg}^{-1} \text{ min}^{-1}) + (\text{gradient} \times \text{m min}^{-1} \times 0.9 \text{ ml kg}^{-1} \text{ min}^{-1}) + 3.5 \text{ ml kg}^{-1} \text{ min}^{-1}$$

For cycling

$$\dot{V}O_2 \text{ (ml min}^{-1}\text{)} = (\text{work rate (kg m min}^{-1}) \times 2 \text{ ml kg}^{-1} \text{ min}^{-1}) + (\text{mass} \times 3.5 \text{ ml kg}^{-1} \text{ min}^{-1})$$

(Note: 1 W = 6.12 kg m min^{-1}; an alternative and simpler formula is: $\dot{V}O_2$ (ml min^{-1}) = (12 × W) + 300)

In a multi-stage test the subject runs or cycles at two levels. When two submaximal $\dot{V}O_2$ values are calculated, the slope of the $\dot{V}O_2$ regression line is obtained and this is used to predict the $\dot{V}O_2$ max by extrapolation of one of the multi-stage $\dot{V}O_2$: HR values.

Calculation of the 'slope' of the $\dot{V}O_2$: HR relationship is determined by:

$$\text{Slope (b)} = \frac{(\dot{V}O_2 \text{ stage 2} - \dot{V}O_2 \text{ stage 1})}{(\text{HR stage 2} - \text{HR stage 1})}$$

$$\dot{V}O_2 \text{ max} = \dot{V}O_2 \text{ stage 2} + b\,[(220 - \text{age}) - \text{HR stage 2}]$$

It is important to note that HR values must be at steady state. Thus, the subject must exercise for at least 3 minutes. If the HR is not at steady state (i.e. it is still increasing) it will predict an unrealistic overestimation of the $\dot{V}O_2$ max and be inaccurate for prescription of subsequent exercise intensity. What follows is an example of the method used to predict $\dot{V}O_2$ max using actual data derived from an exercise test on one of the authors (RGE, age 38, mass 86 kg) a few years ago!

Prediction of $\dot{V}O_2$ max (treadmill protocol)

Treadmill data of the example are shown in Table 9.1.

Table 9.1   Treadmill data

	Stage 1	*Stage 2*
Speed (mph)	6	8
Gradient (%)	4	8
HR	134	172

Calculation of submaximal $\dot{V}O_2$
Stage 1:

$$\dot{V}O_2 \text{ (ml kg}^{-1}\text{ min}^{-1}) = (160.8 \text{ m min}^{-1}$$
$$\times\, 0.2 \text{ ml kg}^{-1}\text{ min}^{-1} + (0.04 \times 160.8 \text{ m min}^{-1}$$
$$\times\, 0.9 \text{ ml kg}^{-1}\text{ min}^{-1}) + 3.5 \text{ ml kg}^{-1}\text{ min}^{-1}$$
$$= 41.4 \text{ ml kg}^{-1}\text{ min}^{-1}$$

Stage 2:

$$\dot{V}O_2 \text{ (ml kg}^{-1}\text{ min}^{-1})$$
$$= (214.4 \text{ m min}^{-1} \times 0.2 \text{ ml kg}^{-1}\text{ min}^{-1})$$
$$+ (0.08 \times 214.4 \text{ m min}^{-1} \times 0.9 \text{ ml kg}^{-1}\text{ min}^{-1})$$

$$+ 3.5 \text{ ml kg}^{-1}\text{ min}^{-1}$$
$$= 61.8 \text{ ml kg}^{-1}\text{ min}^{-1}$$

(Note: 1 mph = 26.8 m min^{-1} = 0.45 m s^{-1})

Calculation of slope (b)

$$b = (61.8 - 41.4)\,/\,(172 - 134) = 0.54$$

Calculation of $\dot{V}O_2$ max

$$\dot{V}O_2 \text{ max (ml kg}^{-1}\text{ min}^{-1})$$
$$= 61.8 + 0.54\,((220 - 38) - 172) = 67$$

Prediction of $\dot{V}O_2$ max (cycle ergometry protocol)

Cycle ergometry data of the example are shown in Table 9.2.

Table 9.2   Cycle ergometry data

	Stage 1	*Stage 2*
Work rate (kg m min^{-1})	900 (147 W)	1200 (196 W)
Heart rate	124	138

Calculation of submaximal $\dot{V}O_2$
Stage 1:

$$\dot{V}O_2 \text{ (ml)} = (900 \text{ kg m min}^{-1} \times 2 \text{ ml kg min}^{-1}) +$$
$$(86 \text{ kg} \times 3.5 \text{ ml kg}^{-1}\text{ min}^{-1}) = 2101$$

$$\dot{V}O_2 \text{ (ml kg}^{-1}\text{ min}^{-1}) = 2101 \text{ ml}\,/\,86 \text{ kg} = 24.4$$

Stage 2:

$$\dot{V}O_2 \text{ (ml min}^{-1}) = (1200 \text{ kg m min}^{-1} \times 2 \text{ ml kg}^{-1}\text{ min}^{-1})$$
$$+ (86 \text{ kg} \times 3.5 \text{ ml kg}^{-1}\text{ min}^{-1}) = 2701$$

$$\dot{V}O_2 \text{ (ml kg}^{-1}\text{ min}^{-1}) = 2701 \text{ ml}\,/\,86 \text{ kg} = 31.4$$

Calculation of slope (b)

$$b = (31.4 - 24.4)\,/\,(138 - 124) = 0.50$$

Calculation of $\dot{V}O_2$ max for cycle ergometry

$$\dot{V}O_2 \text{ (ml kg}^{-1}\text{ min}^{-1})$$
$$= 31.4 + 0.50\,((220 - 38) - 138) = 53$$

(b) Determining the exercise prescription

Once a maximal aerobic capacity has been determined, it is possible to prescribe a running speed/work-rate that corresponds to a given exercise intensity. In the following example, the exercise intensity corresponding to 70% $\dot{V}O_2$ max is determined, for running and for cycling for RGE.

For running

In the above example the $\dot{V}O_2$ max was determined to be 67 ml kg^{-1} min^{-1}; 70% of this is 46.9 ml kg^{-1} min^{-1}.

By substitution into the formula:

$$\dot{V}O_2 = (\text{m min}^{-1} \times 0.2 \text{ ml m}^{-1} \text{ min}^{-1}) + 3.5$$

The running speed (m min^{-1})
$$= (\dot{V}O_2 - 3.5) / 0.2 = (46.9 - 3.5) / 0.2$$
$$= 217 \text{ m min}^{-1} (3.61 \text{ m s}^{-1})$$

This equates to a running speed of 13 km h^{-1} (8.1 mph) or a running pace of 4 min 36 s per km or 7 min 24 s per mile on a level gradient.

For cycling

In the above example the $\dot{V}O_2$ max was determined to be 53 ml kg^{-1} min^{-1}; 70% of this is 37.4 ml kg^{-1} min^{-1}. This value is multiplied by mass (86 kg) to give an absolute $\dot{V}O_2$ = 3216 ml.

By substitution into the formula

$$\dot{V}O_2 \text{ (ml min}^{-1}) = (\text{kg m min}^{-1} \times 2 \text{ ml kg}^{-1}) + (3.5 \text{ ml kg}^{-1} \text{ min}^{-1} \times \text{mass})$$

The work rate (kg m min^{-1})

$$= (\dot{V}O_2 - (3.5 \times \text{mass})) / 2$$
$$= (3216.4 - (3.5 \times 86)) / 2$$
$$= 1457.7 \text{ kg m min}^{-1} (238 \text{ W})$$

The next thing to decide is the preferred cycling frequency. Clearly, the higher the pedal frequency, the lower the load. If we assume that one pedal revolution is equal to a forward motion of 6 m (as per a Monark cycle ergometer; Monark Exercise AB, Varberg, Sweden), the loading can be calculated by the formula:

$$\text{Load (kg)} = (\text{kg m min}^{-1}) / (6 \text{ m} \times \text{rev min}^{-1})$$

Thus, for a pedal frequency of 50 rev min^{-1} the loading will be 4.86 kg, and for a pedal frequency of 70 rev min^{-1} it would be 3.47 kg. At both pedalling speeds, the power output = 1457 kg m min^{-1} or 238 W.

(c) Estimation of energy expenditure

The concept of energy expenditure and metabolic rate is reviewed by Cooke in Chapter 6. The total energy expenditure can be calculated on the basis that 1 MET (3.5 ml kg^{-1} min^{-1}) is equivalent to an energy expenditure of approximately 4.2 kJ kg h^{-1} (1 kcal kg^{-1} h^{-1}). Thus, an 86 kg person would expend approximately 361 kJ min^{-1} (86 kcal min^{-1}) at rest. In the above example, to run at a pace equal to 70% $\dot{V}O_2$ max, the metabolic equivalent is about 13.4 METs. Thus, the energy expenditure per hour is 86 kg × 13.4 kcal kg^{-1} h^{-1} = 1152 kcal h^{-1} (4817 kJ h^{-1}). If the person runs for 30 minutes, the theoretical energy expenditure at this level can be calculated by the appropriate time proportion, i.e. 30 / 60 = 576 kcal (2409 kJ). This method is sometimes used to estimate a predicted weight loss. For example, on the basis that 1 g of substrate of mixed carbohydrate and fat (assuming an RER of 0.85) yields an energy content of 7.2 kcal (30 kJ), the weight loss in the above example would be about 2409 kJ / 30 kJ g^{-1} (576 kcal / 7.2 kcal g^{-1}) which equals 80 g. This may not seem much for all that effort, but an energy deficit of this magnitude for 7 days a week over one month would lead to a weight loss of (7 d × 80 g × 4.2 wk) about 2352 g (5.2 lb).

9.4.2 USING HEART RATE TO PRESCRIBE EXERCISE INTENSITY

The advent of non-encumbering telemetry methods has made the accurate measurement of heart rate a relatively straightforward process. Since heart rate and oxygen uptake share a positive, linear relationship regardless of age and sex, target heart rate ranges may be selected to correspond with $\dot{V}O_2$ max values (Karvonen and Vuorimaa, 1988). This method is used in a variety of field tests and exercise protocols to approximate and monitor exercise intensity.

As a general rule, maximal aerobic power improves if exercise is sufficiently intense to increase heart rate to about 70% of maximum; equivalent to about 50–55% of $\dot{V}O_2$ max. This is a level of intensity thought to be the minimal stimulus required to produce a training effect (Gaesser and Rich, 1984), which will vary according to initial fitness status. Estimation of $\dot{V}O_2$ max from percentage HR is subject to error in all populations because of the need for a true maximal heart rate value. This can be attained from 2–4 minutes of 'all-out' exercise in the activity of interest. Such a procedure demands sound health coupled with a high level of commitment from an individual and is only really appropriate for competitive athletes. For this reason, maximum heart rate is usually arrived at by subtracting an individual's age from a theoretical maximum of 220 beats min^{-1} regardless of gender and age.

Although all people of the same age (or gender) do not possess the same maximal heart rate, the loss in accuracy for individual variation of approximately ±10 beats min^{-1} as one standard deviation at any age-predicted heart rate is usually considered to be of small significance in establishing an effective exercise programme for healthy individuals. Nevertheless, caution is required with this predictive procedure because, within normal variation, only 68% of 20-year-olds will have a heart rate maximum between 190 and 210 beats min^{-1} (i.e. 220 – 20 ±10 beats min^{-1}). This formula is also inappropriate for certain types of activity such as swimming, because flotation in the supine position and the cooling effect of water reduce heart rate values to an average of about 10–13 beats min^{-1} lower than in running. The assessment of intensity for swimming should therefore be at least 10 beats min^{-1} lower than the age-predicted maximum heart rate (McArdle *et al.*, 1991).

A preferred method to prescribe exercise intensity is the percentage maximal heart rate reserve method (%HRR$_{max}$) as described by Karvonen and Vuorimaa (1988). This method uses the percentage difference between resting and maximal heart rate added to the resting heart rate. When compared to the %HR$_{max}$ method, %HRR$_{max}$ yields at least a 10 beat min^{-1} higher training heart rate when calculated for exercise intensities between 60% and 85% $\dot{V}O_2$ max. This method equates more closely with given submaximal $\dot{V}O_2$ max values in both healthy adults and cardiac patients (Pollock *et al.*, 1982).

The procedure for calculating %HRR$_{max}$ values to determine exercise heart rates and the method of calculating %HRR$_{max}$ from exercise heart rates is shown below.

To calculate %HRR$_{max}$ from an exercising heart rate the following formula is used:

$$\%HRR_{max} = \frac{\text{Exercise HR} - \text{RHR}}{HR_{max} - \text{RHR}}$$

$$e.g. \frac{154 - 60}{195 - 60} = 70\% HRR_{max}$$

where:
RHR = resting heart rate
HRR = heart rate reserve
%HRR$_{max}$ = percentage maximal heart rate reserve
HR$_{max}$ = 220 – age (e.g. at age 25 the predicted HR$_{max}$ = 195 beats min^{-1})
HRR = HR$_{max}$ – RHR (e.g. if RHR = 60 then HRR=195 – 60 = 135 beats min^{-1})
%HRR$_{max}$ = (training intensity (% of maximum) × HRR) + RHR

The training intensity at 70% of HRR$_{max}$ is therefore ((0.7 × 135) + 60) = 154 beats min^{-1}.

Table 9.3 provides data in support of the %HRR$_{max}$ method. Oxygen uptake and HR data were collected on RGE during a graded exercise test to maximum for treadmill running. The %HRR$_{max}$ values (column 1) correspond very closely to the %$\dot{V}O_2$ max values (column 7), and may be used to prescribe exercise intensity at a given %$\dot{V}O_2$ max. The %HRmax values tend to

Table 9.3 A comparison of %$\dot{V}O_2$ max at equivalent %HRRmax and %HRmax levels

%HR level	HR at %HRmax	$\dot{V}O_2$ (ml kg^{-1} min^{-1})	%$\dot{V}O_2$ max	HR at %HRRmax	$\dot{V}O_2$ (ml kg^{-1} min^{-1})	%$\dot{V}O_2$ max
40	73	8	13	105	26	41
50	91	21	33	118	33	52
60	109	28	44	131	38	60
70	127	37	59	144	46	73
80	140	43	68	157	52	82
90	164	56	89	169	58	92
100	182	63	100	182	63	100

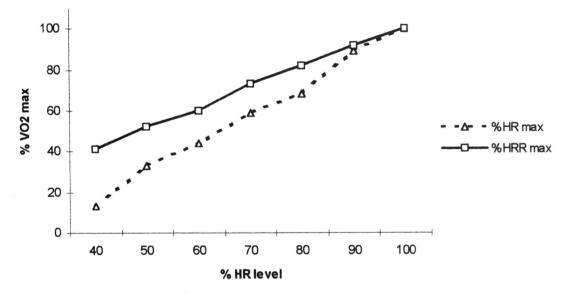

Figure 9.1 A comparison of %$\dot{V}O_2$ max values at equivalent %HRRmax and %HRmax levels for RGE.

underestimate the %$\dot{V}O_2$ max values (column 4), as exemplified in Figure 9.1.

9.4.3 RATING OF PERCEIVED EXERTION (RPE)

(a) The concept of effort perception

The realization that physical performance emanates from a complex interaction of both perceptual, cognitive, and metabolic processes occurred a long time ago (see discussion by Borg, 1998, pp. 2–6). Perceived exertion is known to play an important role in the

regulation of exercise intensity. Use of the Rating of Perceived Exertion Scale was first adopted as a principle in the exercise testing guidelines of the ACSM in 1986. Since then more detail has been added on the use of this important tool by both the ACSM (1995; 1998), BASES (1997) and of course by Borg (1998) himself.

The reasoning behind the use of what appears to be 'cardboard technology' is that humans possess a well-developed system for sensing the strain involved in physical effort.

This system is in constant use. A person can sense whether he/she is able to continue during vigorous exercise. Furthermore, during a bout of exercise, one is able to report both current, overall feelings of exertion and the locus of particular strain (say, in the chest or arms). With some experience of various levels of exercise, people have little difficulty in numerically scaling or at least ordering samples of exercise to which they have been subjected.

(b) Rating of perceived exertion scales

Attempts have been made to establish a basis for interpreting bodily sensations during exercise. By applying established principles of psychophysics (Stevens, 1957; Ekman, 1961) to gross motor action, Borg determined relative stimulus–response (S–R) functions and then developed two rating scales, the 6–20 Category Scale (RPE, Borg, 1970) and the Category-Ratio 10 Scale (CR10, Borg, 1982). Both scales have been revised since their inception. The latest revisions documented by Borg (1998) are used here. By far, the most commonly used device is the RPE Scale (RPE, Table 9.4). With this scale, the RPE increases linearly as exercise intensity increases. It is most closely correlated with the physiological responses that increase linearly, for example, heart rate and oxygen consumption. The CR10 Scale (Table 9.5) was constructed by Borg to take advantage of the properties of Stevens's ratio scaling (Stevens, 1957, 1971) and category scaling, so that verbal expressions and numbers could be used in a way that is congruent with the non-linear characteristics of sensory perception and physical stimulation. Basically, the psychophysical characteristics of the relationship between perceived exertion (Response, R) and exercise intensity (Stimulus, S) can be described as $R = c \times S^n$, where n is the exponent which reflects the growth function. The CR10 Scale may therefore be considered more appropriate to reflect the psychophysical characteristics of those variables which increase as a curvilinear

Table 9.4   The Borg 6 to 20 RPE Scale (Borg, 1998)

6	No exertion at all
7	
8	Extremely light
9	Very light
10	
11	Light
12	
13	Somewhat hard
14	
15	Hard (heavy)
16	
17	Very hard
18	
19	Extremely hard
20	Maximal exertion

function of power output, such as blood lactate and ventilation.

In both scales, numbers are anchored to verbal expressions. However, in the Category-Ratio Scale, unlike the 6–20 Category Scale, the numbers are not fixed. Half numbers or decimals can be used, e.g. 0.7 or 2.3. The numerical values also have a fixed relation to one another. For example, an intensity (I) judgement of 5 would be gauged to be half that of 10. It is important to note that in the CR10 Scale, a rating of 10 is not truly maximal. Borg (1998) indicated that this level is 'as hard as most people have ever experienced before in their lives'. If during the exercise test the subjective intensity exceeds this level, the person is free to choose any number in proportion to 10 that describes the proportionate growth in the sensation of effort. For example if the exercise intensity feels 20% harder than 10, the RPE would be 12. Instructions and rationale for using the two RPE Scales are provided in more detail by Borg (1998).

Table 9.5 The Borg CR10 Scale (Borg, 1998)

0	Nothing at all	'No I'
0.3		
0.5	Extremely weak	Just noticeable
0.7		
1	Very weak	
1.5		
2	Weak	Light
2.5		
3	Moderate	
4		
5	Strong	Heavy
6		
7	Very strong	
8		
9		
10	Extremely strong	'Max I'
11		
⤢		
●	Absolute maximum	Highest possible

(c) Exercise intensity and effort perception

Investigators who have examined the relationship between perceived exertion ratings and the indices of relative intensity discussed above (%$\dot{V}O_2$ max, %HR_{max} and so on) for graded exercise testing have generally reported high and positive correlation values ($r = 0.85$ and above). Also, perceived exertion, HR, and blood lactate La, for cycling, running, walking and arm ergometry are related in a consistent manner in that the incremental curve for perceived exertion can be predicted from a simple combination of HR and La (Borg *et al.*, 1987). Furthermore, criterion group differences (such as trained versus untrained, lean versus obese) observed at equivalent absolute work-rates diminish at the same %$\dot{V}O_2$ max. These results apply to both intermittent and continuous protocols.

Pollock *et al.* (1982) compared the validity of the RPE scale for prescribing exercise intensity with the two HR methods in young adult, old adult and cardiac patients. They observed that the %HRR_{max} method coupled with RPE was a much better indicator of exercise intensity and that the differences in RPE were greatly diminished at equivalent %HRR_{max} levels.

The empirical evidence supporting the notion that the regulation of exercise intensity is a psychophysiological process has led to the assertion that perceived exertion alone may be a sufficient basis for gauging exercise intensity (Borg, 1971). Ratings of 12 to 13 on the Borg 6 to 20 scale correspond to about 60–80% of $\dot{V}O_2$ max during treadmill running in most individuals (Eston *et al.*, 1987; Lamb *et al.*, 1999) and ratings of 16 to 17 are approximately 90% $\dot{V}O_2$ max (Eston *et al.*, 1987). For cycle ergometry the exercise intensities elicited at RPEs 13 and 17 tend to be somewhat lower, ranging from about 45% to 80% $\dot{V}O_2$ max, respectively (Eston and Williams, 1988; Parfitt *et al.*, 1996; Eston and Thompson, 1997).

(d) Applications for preferred exercise intensity

Although the association between RPE and preferred exercise intensity was included in Borg's published PhD thesis (Borg, 1962, pp. 31–32), it is only fairly recently that the use of RPE in this way has been applied in studies on preferred exercise intensity (Dishman *et al.*, 1994; Eston *et al.*, 1998; Parfitt *et al.*, 2000). Parfitt *et al.* (1996) investigated the differences in psychological affect and interest–enjoyment between prescribed treadmill intensity (based on 65% $\dot{V}O_2$ max) and preferred intensity exercise sessions, each of 20 minutes. Participants exercised at a higher intensity in the preferred versus a prescribed exercise condition, although there were no differences in RPE. It seems that the participants perceived that they were exercising at the same level in both conditions. This may indicate a positive perception for the preferred exercise intensity session as the participants worked harder but reported similar RPEs. In addition, work-rate and RPE increased over the duration of the exercise session. The apparent warm-up strategy during the preferred exercise intensity session confirmed findings from a previous study by Eston *et al.* (1998). In the latter study, preferred exercise intensity during a 30 minute cycle ride with both active and inactive healthy men, equated with a mean RPE of 13.

(e) Prediction of maximal heart rate

Often, it is not possible to measure maximal heart rate (HR_{max}) for practical or medical reasons. In such circumstances, prediction from the formula 220 beats min^{-1} minus age is used, although it has been indicated that this is only a rough estimate. As the relationship between RPE, VO_2 and HR is linear over most of its range, it is theoretically possible to estimate maximal heart rate on the basis of submaximal RPE:HR responses, because RPE has a maximal value of 20. In fact, in our experience, a rating of 20 is rarely given by the subject. It is more common to record RPEs of 18 or 19, 'which for most people is the most strenuous exercise they have ever experienced' (Borg, 1998). The prescription of appropriate exercise intensities on the basis of this relationship, i.e. prediction of maximal heart rate from the linear extrapolation of submaximal RPEs, taken from a graded exercise test, has been applied in a number of studies (e.g. Wilmore *et al.*, 1986; Eston and Williams, 1986). Although less frequently used, perhaps indicating a short-sighted approach by researchers in the field, the prediction of HR_{max} can be derived from an effort-production rather an effort-estimation procedure. With this method an effort level of perceived magnitude to points on the RPE scale is produced. Eston and Thompson (1997) used this method to predict maximal heart rate in patients receiving beta blockade treatment to help quantify appropriate exercise intensity levels. Prediction of HR_{max} from RPE estimation and production protocols is demonstrated using data from RGE in the laboratory practical later in this chapter.

(f) Reliability of RPE production and estimation procedures

A worthwhile practical application is to use the rating scale as a frame of reference for regulating various intensities of exercise. Such an approach is clearly applicable to endurance training in various sports, but also applies to the attainment of general fitness and rehabilitation. As a rule it seems sensible to encourage people to 'tune' to their effort sense and develop sufficient awareness for determining an appropriate exercise intensity without recourse to external devices.

Several studies have confirmed the validity of self-regulation guided by effort rating procedures. In other words, the rating of perceived exertion can be used to regulate exercise intensities by enabling a subject to repeat a given physiological measure or exercise level from trial to trial. This has been demonstrated for treadmill running in adults (Smutok *et al.*, 1980; Eston *et al.*, 1987; Dunbar *et al.*, 1992; Glass *et al.*, 1992), cycling (Eston and Williams, 1988; Dunbar *et al.*, 1992; Buckley *et al.*, 2000), wheelchair exercise in children (Ward *et al.*, 1995) and cycling in children (Eston and Williams, 1986; Williams *et al.*, 1991; Eston *et al.*, 2000). This approach has also been used to predict VO_2 max or maximal work-rate (e.g. Eston and Thompson, 1997).

An important consideration of the plausibility of determining exercise intensity through perceived exertion is that much of the research in this area has been undertaken in controlled laboratory conditions. As indicated above, a number of studies employing the RPE production mode have evaluated the reliability of RPE during treadmill exercise, track walking and running and/or cycle ergometry. With the exception of the study by Eston and Williams (1988), the target production mode RPE levels were determined from a passive estimation protocol measured during an initial graded exercise test (GXT). Byrne and Eston (1997) recommended caution when inferring a target production RPE from GXT estimation mode responses. They reported a mismatch of exercise intensities at a given RPE between estimation and production modes. Eston and Williams (1988) evaluated multiple-trial production mode reliability using pre-selected, randomly assigned RPEs of 9, 13 and 17 during cycle ergometry, and concluded that reliability improves after a period of initial practice. Such an application would seem relevant for field-work, where the practical problems and safety issues of administering an initial GXT are alleviated. Although this study has been widely cited when RPE reliability is discussed, it has only recently been replicated (Buckley *et al.*, 2000). The study by Eston and Williams (1988) and more recent studies by Lamb *et al.* (1999), Buckley *et al.* (2000) and Eston *et al.* (2000), which have used more rigorous measures for assessing reliability, provide evidence that the accuracy of effort perception is dependent on familiarization and practice for both production and estimation procedures.

If exercise prescription is to be based on RPE, then the exercise mode must be specified because the source of the effort percept varies and influences the magnitude of the rating (Pandolf, 1983). When different modes of exercise are performed, the RPE is greater for work involving small muscle groups (Berry *et al.*, 1989). The classic study by Ekblom and Goldbarg (1971) which differentiated between local and central effort percepts showed that the RPE for a given submaximal oxygen uptake or heart rate was higher for cycling compared to running. Also, Eston and Williams (1988) showed that RPE was higher for a given %$\dot{V}O_2$ max value for cycling compared to running, when RPE was used to self-regulate exercise intensity. In addition, local and central factors are influenced by pedalling rate on a cycle ergometer (Robertson *et al.*, 1979). Higher RPE values were reported for pedalling rates of 40 rev min^{-1} compared to 80 rev min^{-1}. Furthermore, the timing of the measurement of RPE has been found to be an important consideration. For example, Parfitt and Eston (1995) observed that RPEs measured during cycle ergometry were significantly higher in

the final 20 s of a 4-minute exercise bout, compared to the same point 2 minutes into the exercise bout for both men and women.

Dunbar *et al.* (1992) observed that there was greater test–retest reliability when RPE was estimated during cycle ergometry compared to treadmill running. This was attributed to the greater localization of muscle fatigue during cycle ergometry, allowing for a more accurate assessment of the intensity of the peripheral signal. They reported that a comparatively greater attentional focus on these intense regionalized perceptual signals might sharpen input to the perceptual cognitive framework. It follows from this finding that the production of a target RPE on the cycle should be facilitated. Another possible explanation advanced by Dunbar *et al.* (1992) was that the more stable position of the subject during cycle ergometry results in greater consistency in the RPE estimation. They postulated that the task of maintaining balance on a moving belt, as on a treadmill while running, may distract the individual from the quantity and intensity of the perceptual signals.

Although the process is not the same, the role of dissociation, as a method of alleviating the discomfort associated with exercise-induced fatigue, has been the subject of interest for some time (Benson *et al.*, 1978). It has been claimed to be a useful coping mechanism (Morgan *et al.*, 1983), although Rejeski (1985) has reported that theoretical explanations of why and how it works are lacking. He suggested that dissociative strategies provide a relief from fatigue by occupying limited channel capacity critical to bringing a percept into focal awareness. In addition, the subject is faced with the task of regulating speed and gradient of the treadmill and it is likely that the perception of speed is fundamentally different from the perception of exertion for whole-body exercise.

Those involved in assessing and giving advice on exercise prescription should be aware of the numerous factors that might influence this process. Apart from gender and age, contrasting styles of sensory processing may predispose individuals to modulate intensity (Robertson *et al.*, 1977). Furthermore, perceptual reactance mediated by sensory processing probably interacts with personality traits (characteristic ways of behaving). Whereas such variables may well be randomized out in general in research on perceived exertion, these are important considerations for individual exercise prescription. Reference should be made to Morgan (1981), Williams and Eston (1985, 1986, 1989), Cioffi (1991) and Watt and Grove (1993) for discussions of these variables.

9.5 EFFORT PERCEPTION IN CHILDREN

Consideration of the validity and reliability of an RPE scale for children should not ignore age, reading ability, experience, and conceptual understanding. The latter is a developmental issue, influenced by the extent of children's experiences of exercise, which was recognized some time ago by two of the leading proponents of RPE (Bar-Or, 1977; Borg, 1977). In recognition of the difficulties associated with the application of Borg's 6 to 20 Rating of Perceived Exertion (RPE) scale with children (Williams *et al.*, 1991), Williams *et al.* (1993, 1994) proposed and validated a 1–10 scale (Children's Effort Rating Table, CERT, Table 9.6) which contained fewer possible responses, a range of numbers more familiar to children, and more simple verbal expressions identified by children through a series of exercise sessions. Although CERT appears to have acceptable validity (Eston *et al.*, 1994; Lamb, 1995, 1996), it nevertheless requires the child to interpret words and numbers alone.

For a child to perceive effort accurately, and subsequently to produce exercise intensity level from a predetermined RPE, it is logical to assume that learning must occur. A production protocol was incorporated into the early research procedures during the development of CERT (Williams *et al.*, 1993) and it was found that children in the 6- to 8-year age range were

Table 9.6 Children's Effort Rating Table (CERT) (Williams *et al.*, 1994)

1	Very, very easy
2	Very easy
3	Easy
4	Just feeling a strain
5	Starting to get hard
6	Getting quite hard
7	Hard
8	Very hard
9	Very, very hard
10	So hard I am going to stop

unable to gauge even roughly intermediate levels of exercise intensity. Learning is a more or less permanent change in behaviour which is reflected by a change in performance brought about by practice as well as maturation (Buskist and Gerbing, 1990). Thus, the child must have developed the relevant cognitive capacity to comprehend the task as well as the direct experience and practice of the activity. According to Piaget's (1972) stage model of development, children around the age of 7–10 years can understand categorization, but find it easier to understand and interpret pictures and symbols rather than words and numbers. Contemporary paediatric exercise research has addressed this problem.

Recently, investigators have incorporated a variety of symbols and pictures to represent categories of effort in paediatric versions of effort perception scales. These developments recognize the need for verbal descriptors and terminology that are more pertinent to a child's cognitive development, age, and reading ability. The first published attempt was by Nystad *et al.* (1989) who depicted various stages of fatigue with stick figures to improve understanding of the Borg 6 to 20 scale in a group of 10–12-year-old asthmatic children. However, they still observed that children had difficulty interpreting the scale. Robertson *et al.* (2000) have produced the 0–10 Omni Scale, which depicts a child on a bicycle, at various stages of physical exertion, on a uniform gradient set at about 45°. This study validated the scale on separate ethnic groups of children.

As a consequence of reviewing the existing scales and concern with their limitations, Eston *et al.* (2000) proposed a symbolic Cart and Load Effort Rating scale (CALER, Figure 9.2). The CALER scale presents a child on a bicycle, at various stages of exertion, pulling a cart that is loaded progressively with bricks along a non-incremental path. The number of bricks in the cart corresponds with the numbers on the scale. The wording on the scale has been selected from the CERT. Other variants, including a four effort level scale anchored with versions of the well-known 'smiley' face and scaled directly from CERT and RPE, have been developed. Early research with 7-year-olds in the USA indicates that children readily identify and discriminate effort level with the various facial expressions (Williams and O'Brien, 2000).

As previously indicated, data on adults suggest that the accuracy of repeated effort production procedures is improved with practice. Eston *et al.* (2000) assessed the reliability of effort production at CALER 2, 5 and 8 across four occasions separated by one to two weeks in 20 boys and girls aged 7–10 years. A 'levels of agreement' and correlation analysis (for a discussion of these procedures, refer to Volume 1, Chapter 10 by Nevill and Atkinson) provided strong evidence that practice improves the reliability of effort perception and preliminary evidence for the validity of the CALER Scale. A more detailed discussion of effort perception in children, with examples of symbolic scales, is provided by Eston and Lamb (2000).

The next stage for the reader is to gain practical experience of determining exercise intensity which involves the measurement of perceived exertion and heart rate. Three practical exercises, an effort estimation, a heart rate production, and effort production protocol, are described. The data shown in Tables 9.7, 9.8 and 9.9 were taken on RGE over three consecutive days in 1994.

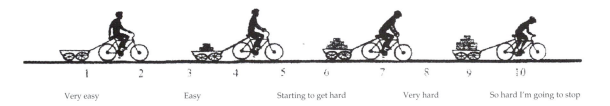

Figure 9.2 The Cart and Load Effort Rating Scale (Eston *et al.*, 2000).

9.6 PRACTICAL 1: USE OF RATINGS OF PERCEIVED EXERTION TO DETERMINE AND CONTROL THE INTENSITY OF CYCLING EXERCISE

9.6.1 ESTIMATION PROTOCOL

(a) Purpose

To determine the relationships between heart rate (HR), rating of perceived exertion (RPE), and power output for cycle ergometry

(b) Procedure

The subject is prepared for exercise with a heart rate monitoring device and informed that consecutive bouts of exercise will be performed on a cycle ergometer for 4 minutes. In the last 15 s of each 2-minute period the HR is recorded and the subject is requested to provide a rating of how hard the exercise feels. After the 4-minute period the resistance is increased by 25 W and the procedure repeated. The subject continues exercising in this way until 85% of the predicted maximal heart rate (220 minus age) is reached. At this point the resistance is removed and the subject is allowed a 5-minute warm-down period. All data are recorded as in Table 9.7.

Table 9.7   RPE estimation protocol

| Name | Roger Eston | Age | 38 | HT 1.78 m |
| Body mass | 83 kg | Date | 21st Sept '94 | Rest HR 45 beats min^{-1} |

Power (W)	Time (min)	HR	RPE	$\%HR_{max}$	$\%HRR_{max}$
50	2	67	6	37	16
	4	73	7	40	20
75	2	81	7	44	26
	4	82	7	45	27
100	2	86	9	47	30
	4	92	10	50	34
125	2	96	10	53	37
	4	97	10	53	38
150	2	117	11	64	53
	4	122	12	67	56
175	2	135	12	74	66
	4	140	13	77	69
200	2	148	14	81	75
	4	153	15	84	79
225	2	157	15	86	82
	4	160	16	88	84
250	2	163	16	90	86
	4	165	17	91	88

Immediately prior to exercising, each subject is introduced to Borg's 6 to 20 Rating of Perceived Exertion Scale. It is essential that the subjects clearly understand that an accurate interpretation of the overall feeling of exertion brought about by the exercise is required when requested by the investigator. To do this, the participant uses the verbal expressions on the scale to provide a numerical rating of effort during exercise. It is recommended that standardized instructions are used to introduce the scale, as described in Borg (1998) and that complete comprehension of the process is checked during a brief warm-up period. Customized instructions may be needed for special applications of RPE. We have found that the perceptual 'anchoring' of the scale can be facilitated by manipulating the work-rates so that the participant experiences how hard the exercise feels at RPEs of 8–9 and RPEs of 16–17.

9.6.2 PRODUCTION PROTOCOL

(a) Purpose

To use heart rate and a given perceived exertion rating to produce exercise intensity levels on a cycle ergometer

(b) Procedure

The subjects, apparatus, exercise mode and general organization remain the same as in the Estimation Protocol (Section 9.6.1). However, in this task the approach is quite different. Two protocols are followed. Both are representative of procedures used in the determination of exercise intensity. The investigator should register the results into a record as shown in Tables 9.8 and 9.9, which also serves as a guide to each step in the process.

(c) HR Production Test: use of heart rate to produce selected levels of exercise intensity (Table 9.8)

The subject is allowed a brief period to habituate and warm-up for exercise. Following this the investigator increases power output randomly to elicit steady-state heart rate levels of 110, 130, 150 and 170 beats min^{-1} for between 3 and 4 minutes. The RPE (Category Scale) is applied in the final 15 s of the exercise period.

Table 9.8   Using heart rate to control exercise intensity

HR	Power output (W)	RPE	%HRR$_{max}$
110	159	11	47
130	188	12	62
150	223	14	77
170	260	18	91

Table 9.9   Using RPE to control exercise intensity

RPE	Power output (W)	HR	%HRR$_{max}$
11	105	107	45
13	182	135	66
15	217	150	77
17	253	165	88

(d) RPE Production Test: use of RPE to produce selected levels of exercise intensity (Table 9.9)

The subject uses Borg's 6 to 20 category scale as a frame of reference to determine selected levels of exercise intensity using only his or her bodily sensations arising from the exercise. All visual (except pedalling frequency, which is constant) and auditory information feedback is removed. The subject exercises and self-adjusts power output until steady-state levels of RPE 11, 13, 15 and 17 are established and maintained for between 3 and 4 minutes. The investigator records power output at steady state and heart rate in the final 15 s of exercise, when the subject is confident that he or she is exercising at a constant RPE.

(e) Tasks/questions

1. Using linear regression analysis on data from the estimation protocol at minute 4, comment on the relationship between power output, heart rate and the rating of perceived exertion.
2. Using related *t* tests, compare the HR and RPE data from minute 2 and 4. How could this difference affect the prediction of maximal values for power output and HR?
3. Draw a simple graph to compare the relationship between HR and RPE for each of the three protocols. Put HR on the *x* axis so that the relationships can be directly compared.
4. Compare / correlate the power output and RPE values predicted from the estimation test at HR 110, 130, 150, 170 to the actual RPE and power output values produced in the HR production test.
5. Using RPEs of 19 and 20, predict the HRmax from both the estimation and production protocol. How does this compare to 220 – age?

9.7 BRIEF ANALYSIS OF THE EFFORT ESTIMATION AND PRODUCTION TEST DATA SHOWN IN TABLES 9.7, 9.8 AND 9.9

9.7.1 RPE ESTIMATION TEST

Table 9.7 contains an example of data collected during an 'estimation test' on one of the authors (RGE). It is possible to determine relationships between power output, heart rate and the rating of perceived exertion. It is evident from these data that there is a strong correlation between HR, RPE and power output, with correlations around 0.98. The importance of allowing sufficient time to adapt to the work-rate is also evident. A related *t* test indicates a significantly lower HR and RPE at minute 2 compared to minute 4 ($p < 0.01$).

The data from the estimation test can be compared with data derived from the production test. As already indicated above, the high correlations between HR, power output and RPE allow predictions of HR and power output to be made from RPE in both the estimation protocol (Table 9.8) and the effort production test (Table 9.9). The following section provides an example of such calculations. Note that only steady-state values have been used. The RPE data for each protocol could also be plotted against HR to compare the relationship.

In the estimation test, the regression equation for HR and power output is: power output = 1.9 (HR) – 79 ($r = 0.99$, SEE = 12 W). Thus, with prescribed heart rates of 110, 130, 150 and 170 beat min^{-1} the predicted power output values are 130, 168, 206 and 244 W respectively. A similar analysis on HR:RPE reveals that the predicted RPEs at these heart rates are 10.8, 12.9, 14.9 and 17 (RPE = 0.102 (HR) – 0.4; $r = 0.98$, SEE = 0.7). These values compare fairly well to the obtained values in the production test.

9.7.2 RPE PRODUCTION TEST

To compare how well the manipulation of RPE in the effort production protocol was at producing target heart rates, it is necessary to re-compute the linear regression equation for RPE:HR, with RPE as the predictor variable. The regression equation for RPE and HR is: $HR = 9.47 (RPE) + 7.8$ ($r = 0.98$, SEE = 11 beats min^{-1}). Thus, for an RPE of 11, 13, 15 and 17, the predicted HR values are 112, 131, 150 and 169, which compare extremely well with the target heart rates used to prescribe exercise intensity in Table 9.8. A similar analysis reveals that the predicted power output values at these RPEs are 134 W, 171 W, 208 W and 244 W, respectively. The regression equation for this prediction is: power output = 18.4 (RPE) − 68.4 ($r = 0.99$, SEE = 22 W). The reliability of the predicted versus actual HR and power output values at the prescribed RPEs is 0.99 and 0.98, respectively. Related t tests revealed no significant difference between the means.

As subjects rarely report a maximal RPE of 20, it is recommended that an RPE of 19 and 20 is inserted into the regression equation to predict a HR$_{max}$ range. The predicted HRmax is 188 to 197 for RPE 19 and 20, respectively. A HR$_{max}$ of 192 (RPE 19) was recorded on RGE one year later during a graded exercise test on the treadmill. This value compares to an age-predicted HR$_{max}$ of $(220 − 39) = 181$. For this individual therefore, the RPE estimation of maximal heart rate is closer.

For RGE the exercise test provided useful data which enabled him to regulate subsequent exercise intensities using both RPE and HR information obtained in the estimation test. One should remember, however, that the subject was an experienced user of the RPE scale and that practice improves the reliability of RPE for prescribing exercise intensities (Eston and Williams, 1988; Buckley *et al.*, 2000; Eston *et al.*, 2000).

9.8 PRACTICAL 2: RELATIONSHIP BETWEEN POWER OUTPUT, PERCEIVED EXERTION (CR10), HEART RATE AND BLOOD LACTATE

9.8.1 PURPOSE

To determine the relationship between perceived exertion (R), using Borg's CR10 Scale, with equal and gradual increments in exercise intensity (Stimulus, S) of 30–40 W. The psychophysical characteristics of the relationship can primarily be described as $R = c \times S^n$, where n is the exponent which reflects the growth function.

9.8.2 PROTOCOL

After explanation of the procedures, exercise intensity commences at 30–40 W and increases by similar increments until the participant responds at about 8 on the CR10 Scale. The participant should be reminded that he/she does not have to stick to the numbers on the scale. The scale is continuous and decimals (e.g. 0.8 or 2.3) can be used. If the participant is able, he/she should continue to maximal volitional exhaustion. The predicted maximal work-rate from extrapolation of the 'curve of best fit' can then be compared to the actual maximal work-rate.

9.8.3 TO DO

1. Plot the raw values of power output against the CR10 Scale on the vertical axis. You should observe that the relationship is curvilinear in nature.

2. *Calculation of the exponent by log-log regression analysis.* The curve of best fit can be calculated by performing a simple linear regression analysis on the natural log values (ln) from the CR10 Scale and the power output (PO) values. Table 9.10 gives an example using the sample class data: The ln:ln regression equation for the above data is R = −5.496 + S (1.42). In this case, the exponent is 1.42.

3. *Prediction of maximal work rate using CR10 as the independent variable.* Using a similar procedure, in Table 9.10 it should be possible to predict the maximal work rate from the above submaximal data by entering a CR10 value of 10. The ln:ln regression equation for the above, using R as the x value is:
   S = 3.872 + 0.703(R). The antilog of 3.872 is 48.04. The exponent is 0.703.
   Then from the equation $y = bx^a$:
   Maximal power output at CR10 = b
   $CR10^{0.703} = 48.04 \times (CR10)^{0.703} = 242$ W

Table 9.10 Example data for Practical 2

Stimulus (S in watts)	Response (R, CR10)
40	0.8
80	2.0
120	3.5
160	5.5
200	8.0

Table 9.11 Relationship between power output, perceived exertion (CR10), heart rate and blood lactate (female aged 24, 182 cm, 78 kg)

Power output (W)	CR10 value	HR	La
40	0.5	94	2.5
80	1.0	102	2.4
120	2.5	135	1.9
160	3.5	154	3.9
200	4.5	166	4.1
240	7.5	184	6.1
280	9.5	191	10.1
320	11.0	193	12.9
3 min post			12.1

As a check, enter ln 250 into the equation in paragraph 2, which uses PO as the independent factor, i.e., R = −5.496 + 1.42 (5.52) = ln 2.344. Antilog of 2.344 = 10!

4. It would be interesting to compare the predicted maximal power output to the actual maximum obtained. The data in Table 9.11 were derived from a female participant (Elaine) during a workshop with Gunnar Borg at the University of Wales, Bangor in April 2000. You could compare the power output versus lactate relationship using similar procedures.

The ln : ln regression equation (of values up to CR 7.5) to calculate exponent:
$$R = −4.871 + S (1.18) \qquad \text{Exponent} = 1.18$$

The ln: ln regression equation using CR10 as the independent variable:
$$\text{Max S at CR10} = 4.271 + R (0.64) \quad \text{Exponent} = 0.64 \quad \text{Antilog of intercept} = 71.6$$

The equation of the curve to predict maximal power output (POmax) at CR10 ($y = bx^a$):
$$71.6 \times CR10^{0.64}$$

Predicted POmax at CR10 = 313 W   Actual POmax at CR11 = 320 W

What does this indicate about the efficacy of the CR10 Scale to predict maximal functional capacity?

9.9 PRACTICAL 3: THE BORG CYCLING STRENGTH TEST WITH CONSTANT LOAD

9.9.1 PURPOSE

To determine the maximal power output that can be sustained for a period of 30 s, using the Borg RPE Scale. The rationale and development of this test, which could be considered as the forerunner to the well-established Wingate Test (described in Chapter 11 by Winter and Maclaren) is presented in greater detail by Borg (1998, pp. 57–58).

9.9.2 PROTOCOL

In this laboratory experiment, the participant cycles for a series of 30 s bouts at constant work rates of 50, 100, 150, 200, 250, 300 … W, to an RPE of about 16–17. Pedalling speed should be kept constant at 60 or 70 rpm. The work intervals are separated by 2 minutes rest/active recovery. RPE and HR are recorded in the final 5 s. The predicted maximal work-rate range is calculated by extrapolating to RPE 19–20. This can be done by linear regression or pen and paper. After five minutes the subject cycles at the predicted work rate (W1) that he/she can sustain for 30s. The time is recorded. This is T1. The load is then adjusted using time to exhaustion (T1) at W1 using the formula in the next section. See data in Table 9.12.

9.9.3 TO DO

1. Plot the raw values of PO versus RPE and HR for each increment.
2. Extrapolate the PO:RPE and the PO:HR relationships to RPE = 20 and HR = maximal heart rate, respectively.
3. Compare the predicted work rates from the perpendicular at RPE (20) and the predicted HR_{max}.
4. The equation describing the curvilinear relationship for this kind of exercise is:
   Time on task = $c \times W^{-4}$
   (see Borg, 1998, pp. 57–58)
5. In Borg's example (1998, p. 58), the predicted maximal work rate that can be sustained for 30 s is 275 W. This is W1. The subject now pedals at this level for as long as possible, which in Borg's example is 44 s (T1). The power output is then corrected according to the formula:

$$W2 = W1 \times (T1/30s)^{0.25}$$

i.e. $W2 = 275 \times (44/30)^{0.25} = 302$ W.

Table 9.12 Data example from the Borg Cycling Strength Test with constant load

Power output (W)	RPE value	HR
50	7	94
100	7	109
150	11	131
200	11	134
250	13	146
300	14	151
350	14	152
400	15	170
450	16	178

After a rest of 5 minutes the subject pedals as close to the desired 30 s PO (W2) and the time is recorded. Table 9.12 contains data from a female participant (Elaine, age 24, ht 182 cm, 78 kg) collected during the RPE Symposium at Bangor in April 2000 to exemplify the procedure.

Regression analysis for RPE (x) and W (y) produced the following equation:

$$W = -231 + 40 \text{ (RPE)} \quad (r = 0.96) \quad \text{Predicted} \quad PO_{max} \text{ at RPE } 19 - 20 = 529 - 569W$$

Regression analysis for HR (x) and W (y) produced the following equation:

$$W = -446 + 4.95 \text{ (HR)} \quad (r = 0.98) \quad \text{Predicted} \quad PO_{max} \text{ at } HR_{max} (196) = 524 \text{ W}$$

Trial 1. Time (s) at predicted PO_{max} using RPE = 46 s
Trial 2. Time (s) at 'corrected PO_{max}' based on formula: $W2 = W1 \times (T1/T2)^{0.25}$

$$W2 = 569 \times (46/30)^{0.25} = 633 \text{ W}$$

After a 5-minute recovery Elaine managed to sustain the above power output for 29 s. For Elaine, therefore, the procedure seems to have worked well.

9.10 SUMMARY

1. Beneficial effects of exercise accrue when individuals engage in activity with appropriate frequency, duration, and intensity. The interplay of all three dimensions is important, but the determination of appropriate intensity requires careful consideration because of the impact of numerous variables.

2. One approach to determining intensity is to base judgements on physiological information. The usual method is to recommend intensity levels relative to actual or predicted maximal capacity based on measures of heart rate response, oxygen utilization, ventilation and blood lactate.

3. A comprehensive approach to setting exercise intensity is desirable. This requires the coupling of indices of bodily response during exercise with information on how hard the individual perceives the exercise to be. The most commonly used perceived exertion device used in this process has been the Borg 6 to 20 Category Scale. The Category Ratio 10 Scale deserves greater attention than it has previously received, particularly as it tends to reflect a classical stimulus–response pattern for perceived exertion and exercise intensity. For young children, the Children's Effort Rating Table (CERT) has been recommended. More recently, pictorial scales such as the CALER and OMNI Scales have been suggested.

4. Perceived exertion ratings have been mainly used in two ways, namely the response or estimation method and the production method. In the former, the subject provides a rating for a power output selected by the investigator. In the latter, the subject is requested to produce a power output which is judged to correspond with a given RPE.

5. The predictions of exercise intensity and maximal functional capacity using the RPE must consider the process by which it is used, owing to the essential differences in the process of estimation and production.

6. Whilst the correlation between physiological information and perceived exertion ratings measured in an exercise physiology laboratory for both response and production methods is usually high, 25% of the variance in the relationship between the two methods remains unaccounted for. The remnant is probably due to individual differences which predispose people to modulate their interpretation of intensity. Thus, the fine-tuning of exercise intensity within an exercise programme comes down to

individual decision-making emanating from effort sense. The exercise scientist's role is to arrive at balanced judgements from a psychophysiological perspective by taking into account the variables discussed.

The purpose of this chapter has been to introduce the reader to the concept of exercise intensity determination as a multifaceted process which requires consideration of both physiological and psychological information about the individual relative to specific activities. Through reading the introductory material, following up some of the primary reference material and undertaking the practical tasks which were suggested, a sound knowledge base for decision-making in this area should have been acquired.

REFERENCES

American College of Sports Medicine (1995). *Guidelines for Exercise Testing and Prescription*, 5th edn. (Williams and Wilkins, Baltimore, MD).

American College of Sports Medicine Position Stand (1998). The recommended quantity and quality of exercise for developing and maintaining cardiorespiratory and muscular strength and flexibility in healthy adults. *Medicine and Science in Sports and Exercise, 30*, 975–91.

Bar-Or, O. (1977). Age-related changes in exercise perception. In *Physical Work and Effort*. ed. G. Borg (Pergamon Press, Oxford), pp. 255–66.

Benson, H., Dryer, T. and Hartley, H. (1978). Decreased consumption during exercise with elicitation of the relaxation response. *Journal of Human Stress, 4*, 38–42.

Berry, M.J., Weyrich, A.S., Roberts, R.A., *et al.* (1989). Ratings of perceived exertion in individuals with varying fitness levels during walking and running. *European Journal of Applied Physiology, 58*, 494–9.

Borg, G.A.V. (1962). *Physical performance and perceived exertion.* Studia Psychologica et Paedagogica. Series altera, Investigationes XI. (Gleerup, Lund, Sweden).

Borg, G.A.V. (1970). Perceived exertion as an indicator of somatic stress. *Scandinavian Journal of Rehabilitation Medicine, 2*, 92–8.

Borg, G.A.V. (1971). La sensation de fatigue consécutive au travail physique. *Psychologie Médicale, 3*, 761–73.

Borg, G.A.V. (1977). *Physical Work and Effort.* (Pergamon Press, Oxford), pp. 289–93.

Borg, G.A.V. (1982). Psychophysical basis of perceived exertion. *Medicine and Science in Sports and Exercise, 14*, 377–81.

Borg, G.A.V. (1998). *Borg's Perceived Exertion and Pain Scales.* (Human Kinetics, Champaign, IL).

Borg, G.A.V., Van de Burg, M., Hassmen, P., *et al.* (1987). Relationships between perceived exertion, HR, and La in cycling, running, and walking. *Scandinavian Journal of Sports Science, 9*, 69–77.

British Association of Sports & Exercise Sciences. (1997). *Physiological Testing Guidelines.* 3rd edn. eds. S. Bird and R. Davison (BASES, Leeds, UK).

Buckley, J.P., Eston, R.G. and Sim, J. (2000). Ratings of perceived exertion in Braille: validity and reliability in 'production' mode. *British Journal of Sports Medicine, 34*, 297–302.

Buskist, W. and Gerbing, D.W. (1990). *Psychology: Boundaries and Frontiers.* (Harper Collins, New York), pp. 376–414.

Byrne, C. and Eston, R.G. (1997). Use of ratings of perceived exertion to regulate exercise intensity: a study using effort estimation and effort production (abstract). *Journal of Sports Sciences, 16*, 15P.

Cioffi, D. (1991). Beyond attentional strategies: a cognitive-perceptual model of somatic interpretation. *Psychological Bulletin, 109*, 25–41.

Dishman, R.D., Farquhar, K.P. and Cureton, K.J. (1994). Responses to preferred intensities of exercise in men differing in activity levels. *Medicine and Science in Sports and Exercise, 26*, 780–3.

Dunbar, C., Robertson, R., Baun, R., *et al.* (1992). The validity of regulating exercise intensity by ratings of perceived exertion. *Medicine and Science in Sports and Exercise, 24*, 94–9.

Ekblom, B. and Goldbarg, A.N. (1971). The influence of physical training and other factors in the subjective rating of perceived exertion. *Acta Physiologica Scandinavica, 83*, 399–406.

Ekman, G. (1961). A simple method for fitting psychophysical power functions. *Journal of Psychology, 51*, 343–50.

Eston, R. and Williams, J.G. (1988). Reliability of ratings of perceived effort for the regulation of exercise intensity. *British Journal of Sports Medicine, 22*, 153–4.

Eston, R., Davies, B. and Williams, J.G. (1987). Use of perceived effort ratings to control exercise intensity in young, healthy adults. *European Journal of Applied Physiology*, **56**, 222–4.

Eston, R., Lamb, K.L., Bain, A., *et al.* (1994). Validity of CERT: a perceived exertion scale for children: a pilot study. *Perceptual and Motor Skills*, **78**, 691–7.

Eston, R.G. and Williams, J.G. (1986). Exercise intensity and perceived exertion in adolescent boys. *British Journal of Sports Medicine*, **20**, 27–30.

Eston, R.G. and Thompson, M. (1997). Use of ratings of perceived exertion for prediction of maximal exercise levels and exercise prescription in patients receiving atenolol. *British Journal of Sports Medicine*, **31**, 114–9.

Eston, R.G. and Lamb, K.L. (2000). Effort Perception. In *Paediatric Exercise Science and Medicine*. eds. N. Armstrong and W. Van Mechelen (Oxford University Press, Oxford), pp. 85–91.

Eston, R.G., Parfitt, G. and Tucker, R. (1998). Ratings of perceived exertion and psychological affect during preferred exercise intensity in high- and low-active men. *Journal of Sports Sciences*, **16**, 82–3.

Eston, R.G., Parfitt, C.G., Campbell, L. and Lamb, K.L. (2000). Reliability of effort perception for regulating exercise intensity in children using the Cart and Load Effort Rating (CALER) Scale. *Pediatric Exercise Science*, **12**, 388–97.

Gaesser, G.A. and Rich, E.G. (1984). Effects of high performance and low intensity training on aerobic capacity and blood lipids. *Medicine and Science in Sports and Exercise*, **16**, 269–74.

Glass, S., Knowlton, R. and Becque, M.D. (1992). Accuracy of RPE from graded exercise to establish exercise training intensity. *Medicine and Science in Sports and Exercise*, **24**, 1303–7.

Karvonen, J. and Vuorimaa, T. (1988). Heart rate and exercise intensity during sports activities. *Sports Medicine* **5**, 303–12.

Lamb, K.L. (1995). Children's ratings of effort during cycle ergometry: an examination of the validity of two effort rating scales. *Pediatric Exercise Science*, **7**, 407–21.

Lamb, K.L. (1996). Exercise regulation during cycle ergometry using the CERT and RPE scales. *Pediatric Exercise Science*, **8**, 337–50.

Lamb, K.L., Eston, R.G. and Corns, D. (1999). The reliability of ratings of perceived exertion during progressive treadmill exercise. *British Journal of Sports Medicine*, **33**, 336–9.

McArdle, W.D., Katch, F. and Katch, V.L. (1991).

Exercise Physiology: Energy, Nutrition and Human Performance. (Lea & Febiger, Philadelphia, PA).

Morgan, W. (1981). Psychophysiology of self-awareness during vigorous physical activity. *Research Quarterly for Exercise and Sport*, **52**, 385–427.

Morgan, W.P., Horstman, D.J., Cymerman, A. and Stokes, J. (1983). Facilitation of physical performance by means of a cognitive strategy. *Cognitive Therapy and Research*, **7**, 251–64.

Nystad, W., Oseid, S. and Mellbye, E.B. (1989). Physical education for asthmatic children: the relationship between changes in heart rate, perceived exertion, and motivation for participation. In *Children and Exercise XIII*. eds. S. Oseid and K. Carlsen (Human Kinetics, Champaign, IL), pp. 369–77.

Pandolf, K.D. (1983). Advances in the study and application of perceived exertion. In *Exercise and Sport Sciences Reviews*. ed. R. L. Terjung (Franklin Institute Press, Philadelphia, PA), pp. 118–58.

Parfitt, G. and Eston, R.G. (1995). Changes in ratings of perceived exertion and psychological affect in the early stages of exercise. *Perceptual and Motor Skills*, **80**, 259–66.

Parfitt, G., Eston, R.G. and Connolly, D.A. (1996). Psychological affect at different ratings of perceived exertion in high- and low-active women: a study using a production protocol. *Perceptual and Motor Skills*, **82**, 1035–42.

Parfitt, G., Rose, E. and Markland, D. (2000). The effect of prescribed and preferred intensity exercise on psychological affect and the influence of baseline measures of affect. *Journal of Health Psychology*, **5**, 231–40.

Piaget, J. (1972). Intellectual evolution from adolescence to adulthood. *Human Development*, **15**, 1–12.

Pollock, M.L., Foster, C., Rod, J.L. and Wible, G. (1982). Comparison of methods of determining exercise training intensity for cardiac patients and healthy adults. In *Comprehensive Cardiac Rehabilitation*. ed. J. J. Kellermann (S Karger, Basel, Switzerland), pp. 129–33.

Rejeski, W.J. (1985). Perceived exertion: an active or a passive process. *Journal of Sport Psychology*, **7**, 371–8.

Robertson, R.J., Gillespie, R.L., Hiatt, E. and Rose, K.D. (1977). Perceived exertion and stimulus intensity modulation. *Perceptual and Motor Skills*, **45**, 211–18.

Robertson, R.J., Gillespie, R.L., McArthy, J. and Rose, K.D. (1979). Differentiated perceptions of exertion: Part 1: mode of integration and regional signals. *Perceptual and Motor Skills*, **49**, 683–9.

Robertson, R.J., Goss, F.L., Boer, N.F., *et al.* (2000). Children's OMNI Scale of perceived exertion: mixed gender and race validation. *Medicine and Science in Sports and Exercise*, **32**, 452–8.

Smutok, M.A., Skrinar, G.S. and Pandolf, K.B. (1980). Exercise intensity: subjective regulation by perceived exertion. *Archives of Physical Medicine and Rehabilitation*, **61**, 569–74.

Stevens, S.S. (1957). On the psychophysical law. *The Psychological Review*, **64**, 153–81.

Stevens, S.S. (1971). Issues in psychophysiological measurement. *The Psychological Review*, **78**, 426–50.

Ward, D. S., Bar-Or, O., Longmuir, P. and Smith, K. (1995). Use of RPE to control exercise intensity in wheelchair-bound children and adults. *Pediatric Exercise Science*, **7**, 94–102.

Watt, B. and Grove, R. (1993). Perceived exertion: antecedents and applications. *Sports Medicine*, **15**, 225–42.

Williams, J.G. and Eston, R.G. (1985). Personality and effort perception in adolescent males. *Journal of Sports Sciences*, **3**, 228–9.

Williams, J.G. and Eston, R.G. (1986). Does personality influence the perception of effort? *Physical Education Review,* **9, 2**, 94–9.

Williams, J.G. and Eston, R.G. (1989). Determination of the intensity dimension in vigorous exercise programmes with particular reference to the use of the Rating of Perceived Exertion. *Sports Medicine*, **8**, 177–89.

Williams, J.G. and O'Brien, M. (2000). A Children's Perceived Exertion Picture Scale. Unpublished data. University of West Chester, PA, USA.

Williams, J.G., Eston, R. and Stretch, C. (1991). Use of the Rating of Perceived Exertion to control exercise intensity in children. *Pediatric Exercise Science*, **3**, 21–7.

Williams, J.G., Eston, R. and Furlong, B.A.F. (1994). CERT: a perceived exertion scale for young children. *Perceptual and Motor Skills*, **79**, 1451–8.

Williams, J.G., Furlong, B., Mackintosh, C. and Hockley, T.J. (1993). Rating and regulation of exercise intensity in young children. *Medicine and Science in Sports and Exercise*, **5 (Suppl. 25)**, S8.

Wilmore, J.H., Roby, F.B., Stanforth, M.J., *et al.* (1986). Ratings of perceived exertion, heart rate and power output in predicting maximal oxygen uptake during submaximal bicycle riding. *The Physician and Sports Medicine*, **14**, 133–43.

LIMITATIONS TO SUBMAXIMAL EXERCISE PERFORMANCE

Andrew M. Jones and Jonathan H. Doust

10.1 AIMS

The aims of this chapter are to:
- describe the three domains of submaximal exercise in terms of changes in acid-base status and respiratory gas exchange,
- review the methods that have been used to delineate the transition from moderate to heavy submaximal exercise, in particular the lactate and ventilatory thresholds,
- review the methods that have been used to delineate the transition from heavy to severe submaximal exercise, in particular the direct measurement or estimation of the maximal lactate steady-state,
- highlight the importance of a knowledge of the exercise domains in predicting the physiological response to exercise, and in prescribing and regulating exercise intensity within endurance training programmes,
- provide a series of practical exercises which explore the methods that have been used to identify the boundaries between the various domains of submaximal exercise.

10.2 INTRODUCTION

Maximal exercise is defined here as exercise of an intensity that requires 100% of the maximal oxygen uptake ($\dot{V}O_2$ max). Exercise that has an oxygen requirement above an individual's $\dot{V}O_2$ max (and that therefore is associated with an obligatory anaerobiosis to meet the energy demand) can thus be described as supramaximal, while exercise that requires an oxygen uptake below $\dot{V}O_2$ max can be termed submaximal. Maximal exercise can be sustained for only about 4–8 minutes before exhaustion occurs (Billat *et al.*, 1994b). Therefore, most forms of recreational exercise, and indeed many sports, can be considered to be submaximal. Continuous submaximal exercise can also be termed endurance exercise. The causes of fatigue during submaximal exercise are manifold and complex but may depend upon whether the exercise is of a sufficiently low intensity that adenosine triphosphate (ATP) resynthesis is almost completely aerobic or whether supplementary anaerobiosis is required, resulting in a progressive accumulation of blood lactate. For low-intensity submaximal exercise, fatigue may result from substrate depletion, dehydration, hyperthermia, or loss of motivation associated with central fatigue (Newsholme *et al.*, 1992). For high-intensity submaximal exercise, fatigue may result from the effects of acidosis on muscle contractile function or on inhibition of key glycolytic enzymes (Edwards, 1981). Understanding the physiological limitations to submaximal exercise is important in developing training programmes to enhance endurance performance.

10.3 EXERCISE DOMAINS

Three domains of intensity have been identified during submaximal exercise based on the characteristic responses of blood acid-base status and pulmonary gas exchange (Whipp

Kinanthropometry and Exercise Physiology Laboratory Manual: Tests, Procedures and Data. 2nd Edition, Volume 2: Exercise Physiology
Edited by RG Eston and T Reilly. Published by Routledge, London, June 2001

and Mahler, 1980; Whipp and Ward, 1990). These are moderate exercise, heavy exercise, and severe exercise (Figure 10.1). The metabolic, physiological and perceptual responses to exercise differ considerably according to the exercise domain that is studied. The boundaries between these different domains can be demarcated by the physiological 'landmarks' of the 'lactate threshold', and the maximal lactate steady state or critical power, while the $\dot{V}O_2$ max marks the boundary between severe submaximal exercise and supramaximal exercise. The lactate threshold (T_{lac}), which marks the transition between moderate and heavy intensity exercise, can be defined as the $\dot{V}O_2$ above which blood [lactate] exceeds the resting concentration during incremental exercise (Wasserman *et al.*, 1973). The maximal lactate steady state (MLSS) or critical power (P_{crit}), which mark the transition between heavy and severe intensity exercise, can be defined as the highest exercise intensity that allows blood [lactate] to be stabilized during long-term exercise (Poole *et al.*, 1988; Beneke and Von Duvillard, 1996).

If constant-load *moderate* exercise (below the T_{lac}) is commenced from a resting baseline, pulmonary $\dot{V}O_2$ rises in a mono-exponential fashion to attain a steady-state value within 2–3 minutes. The deficit between the energy demand and the oxygen uptake during this initial period of exercise is covered by intramuscular oxygen stores, depletion of phosphocreatine, and a small and transient increase in the rate of anaerobic glycolysis resulting in 'early lactate'. This lactate is rapidly cleared as exercise proceeds so that blood [lactate] will remain at or close to resting values during continuous moderate-intensity exercise.

If constant-load *heavy* exercise (i.e. above the T_{lac} but below the MLSS) is commenced from a resting baseline, $\dot{V}O_2$ rises to attain its predicted steady-state value within 2–3 minutes. As exercise is sustained, $\dot{V}O_2$ continues to rise until it reaches a steady-state value that is higher than the expected value. This continued increase in $\dot{V}O_2$, until a delayed and elevated steady state is attained, is due to the emergence of the $\dot{V}O_2$ 'slow component' (Whipp and Ward, 1990). If serial blood samples are taken and analysed for lactate concentration during continuous heavy exercise, it is seen that, following a transient overshoot in the first 5 minutes, blood [lactate] will eventually stabilize at an elevated level of around 2–5 mM.

In the transition from rest to severe exercise (i.e. above the MLSS but below $\dot{V}O_2$ max), the development of the $\dot{V}O_2$ slow component after 2–3 minutes also causes $\dot{V}O_2$ to rise above the expected steady-state value. In contrast to

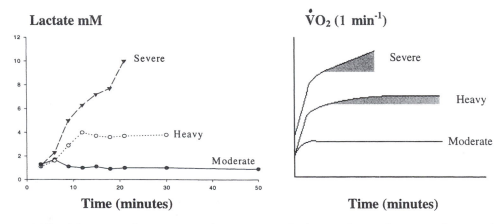

Figure 10.1 Blood lactate and oxygen uptake responses during moderate, heavy, and severe intensity submaximal exercise. The shaded areas in the oxygen uptake panel represent the increase in $\dot{V}O_2$ above the expected steady-state level.

heavy exercise, however, during *severe* exercise, $\dot{V}O_2$ will not attain a steady state but will continue to rise until the exercise is terminated and/or $\dot{V}O_2$ max is attained (Poole *et al.*, 1988). The $\dot{V}O_2$ slow component can account for as much as $0.5–1.0\,l\,min^{-1}$ of $\dot{V}O_2$ and result in the attainment of $\dot{V}O_2$ max during high-intensity *submaximal* exercise. The physiological mechanisms responsible for this reduction in efficiency (i.e. an increased oxygen cost for the same external power output) during sustained exercise above T_{lac} are not known with certainty. However, it has been demonstrated that ~86% of the $\dot{V}O_2$ slow component can be attributed to increased oxygen utilization in the exercising limbs (Poole *et al.*, 1991). This suggests that motor unit recruitment patterns and the increased energetic cost of contraction of type II muscle fibres might be important in the mediation of the $\dot{V}O_2$ slow component (Whipp, 1994; Barstow *et al.*, 1996). If severe exercise is continued and blood [lactate] is determined at regular intervals, it can be observed that blood [lactate] never attains a steady state but continues to increase with time. Typically, the exercise is terminated by the subject when the blood [lactate] reaches 8–12 mM.

During *supramaximal* exercise (exercise that requires a $\dot{V}O_2$ above the $\dot{V}O_2$ max), the exercise duration (1–5 minutes) is often too short to discern a $\dot{V}O_2$ slow component, and $\dot{V}O_2$ appears to project mono-exponentially to $\dot{V}O_2$ max. Likewise, the increased contribution of anaerobic glycolysis to ATP resynthesis in this domain causes lactate to accumulate very rapidly in the blood as lactate production outstrips its removal.

The profound differences in the physiological responses to moderate, heavy, and severe exercise make it essential that the boundaries that demarcate these intensities can be accurately measured. This is important not only in terms of exercise and training prescription but also for the prediction of functional or performance capability. It should be recognized that setting exercise intensity in relation to $\dot{V}O_2$ max

alone may result in vastly different responses to exercise even in individuals with identical $\dot{V}O_2$ max values (Katch *et al.*, 1978). This is because exercise at, for example, 65% $\dot{V}O_2$ max may be above the T_{lac} in some subjects but below this threshold in others. Likewise, exercise at 85% $\dot{V}O_2$ max will be above T_{lac} in most subjects but it could be above the MLSS in some subjects and below MLSS in others. Therefore, setting exercise intensity relative to $\dot{V}O_2$ max alone is unlikely to 'normalize' exercise stress across a group of subjects. If an equivalent exercise intensity is required in a group of subjects, then this should, ideally, be calculated using measurements of T_{lac}, MLSS and $\dot{V}O_2$ max. Exercise physiologists have acknowledged this and their attempts to gain greater precision in the prescription and control of exercise intensity have led to the evolution of numerous methods to determine the boundaries between moderate, heavy and severe exercise in different population groups and in different settings (for example, field vs. laboratory).

10.4 FROM MODERATE TO HEAVY EXERCISE: THE LACTATE / VENTILATORY THRESHOLD

10.4.1 THE LACTATE THRESHOLD

The lactate threshold (T_{lac}) was originally defined as the first increase in blood [lactate] above resting values during incremental exercise (Figure 10.2; Wasserman *et al.*, 1973). The exercise intensity at the T_{lac} is associated with a non-linear increase in $\dot{V}_E$ (the ventilatory threshold, T_{vent}) due to bicarbonate buffering of the lactic acidosis (see below). As outlined previously, constant-intensity exercise below T_{lac} can be sustained without an appreciable increase in blood [lactate]. Heart rate and ventilation reach an early steady state and subjects perceive the exercise to be relatively easy. Exercise below T_{lac} can be sustained for several hours but will eventually be terminated by substrate depletion, dehydration, musculoskeletal injury or by psychological factors. If exercise at a constant intensity just above the T_{lac} is performed, blood [lactate] increases above resting levels, eventually stabilizing at 2–5 mM. Exercise above T_{lac} is associated with a non-linear increase in metabolic, respiratory and perceptual stress (Katch *et al.*, 1978; Whipp and Ward, 1990). Furthermore, exercise above T_{lac} is associated with more rapid fatigue, either through the effects of metabolic acidosis on contractile function or through an accelerated depletion of muscle glycogen (Jones *et al.*, 1977; Roberts and Smith, 1989).

The exercise intensity at the T_{lac} / T_{vent} is a powerful predictor of endurance exercise performance (Farrell *et al.*, 1979; Fay *et al.*, 1989). Numerous studies also testify to the sensitivity of the T_{lac} and T_{vent} to endurance training. A rightward shift of the T_{lac} / T_{vent} to a higher power output or running speed is characteristic of successful endurance training programmes (Henritze *et al.*, 1985; Weltman *et al.*, 1992; Carter *et al.*, 1999b). This adaptation allows a higher absolute (running speed or power output) and relative (%$\dot{V}O_2$ max) exercise intensity to be sustained without the accumulation of blood lactate as a result of training. In athletes who have trained for competition for several years, the T_{lac} (and performance) may continue to improve despite a relatively stable $\dot{V}O_2$ max (Pierce *et al.*, 1990). Furthermore, endurance training is associated with a reduction in the degree of lactacidaemia for any given absolute or relative exercise intensity. This means the power output or running speed corresponding to arbitrary 'blood lactate reference values' such as 2 mM or 4 mM blood lactate is increased following a period of endurance training (Farrell *et al.*, 1979; Hurley *et al.*, 1984). An improvement in the T_{lac} / T_{vent} with training is therefore a clear marker of an enhanced endurance capacity. The T_{lac} / T_{vent} is typically found at 60–80% $\dot{V}O_2$ max even in highly trained subjects, and it therefore occurs at a lower exercise intensity than is maintained by endurance athletes during most forms of endurance competition. The maximal lactate steady state (MLSS), which is the highest exercise intensity at which blood lactate does not

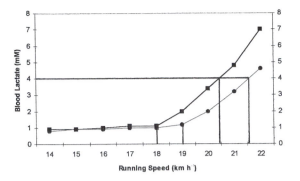

Figure 10.2 Determination of exercise intensity at lactate threshold (T_{lac}, first increase in blood lactate above resting values) and at 4 mM blood lactate ('OBLA') from an incremental treadmill test before (squares) and after (circles) a period of endurance training.

accumulate over time, may be of more importance to success in these events.

Several authors have hypothesized that T_{lac} represents the optimal intensity for improvement of endurance fitness (Weltman *et al.*, 1990; Mader, 1991). Training at T_{lac} should provide a high-quality aerobic training stimulus without the accumulation of lactate that would compromise training duration (Weltman, 1989). The effect of training intensity on improvements in the T_{lac} / T_{vent} has recently been reviewed (Londeree, 1997). In general, it appears that training at intensities close to or slightly above the existing T_{lac} / T_{vent} is important in eliciting significant improvements in this parameter (Henritze *et al.*, 1985; Acavedo and Goldfarb, 1989; Weltman *et al.*, 1992). For example, increasing training intensity through the use of fartlek training on three days per week (Acavedo and Goldfarb, 1989) or adding a 20-minute run at speed corresponding to T_{lac} to the weekly training programme (Sjodin *et al.*, 1982) caused an improvement in T_{lac} with no change in $\dot{V}O_2$ max in runners. Athletes with access to heart rate telemetry can regulate their training intensity in relation to their T_{lac} by recording the heart rate at T_{lac} measured during an incremental exercise test in a physiology laboratory (Jones, 1996).

The physiological mechanisms responsible for the increase in blood [lactate] at the T_{lac} have been much debated (Walsh and Banister, 1988). It was originally considered that muscle hypoxia was the main cause of this increase (Wasserman *et al.*, 1973). Despite the possibility that there may be regional inequalities in muscle perfusion, it is hard to accept that O_2 availability may be limited at the submaximal exercise intensities associated with the T_{lac}. Indeed, some studies have demonstrated an increase in lactate production without any evidence for the existence of hypoxic loci in the contracting muscle tissue (Jobsis and Stainsby, 1968; Connett *et al.*, 1984). It has been proposed that lactate produced in muscle during submaximal exercise may be important as a cytosolic reserve for carbohydrate and reducing equivalents, thereby maintaining optimal coupling of cytosolic supply to mitochondrial utilization (Connett *et al.*, 1985; Honig *et al.*, 1992). The effect of catecholaminergic stimulation of glycolysis should also be considered. Some studies have shown similar patterns of increase and simultaneous 'thresholds' in plasma lactate and plasma catecholamines (Mazzeo and Marshall, 1989). Greater oxidative enzyme activity following training may reduce lactate production by limiting the ability of the enzyme lactate dehydrogenase (LDH) to compete with the mitochondria for pyruvate and reducing equivalents. An augmented rate of entry of pyruvate into the mitochondria would diminish the possibility of a mass action effect, although study of the lactate / pyruvate ratio has indicated no role for mass action in lactate production at T_{lac} (Wasserman *et al.*, 1985). It is possible that T_{lac} represents a transient imbalance between mechanisms of lactate production and lactate removal from the blood (Brooks, 1991). Certainly, the rate of blood lactate accumulation should be considered to be the difference between the rate of lactate production and the rate of lactate clearance in tissues such as red skeletal muscle fibres, and the heart, liver and kidneys (Donovan and Pagliassotti, 1990; MacRae *et al.*, 1992). It has been suggested that lactate produced in type II muscle fibres might be used as a fuel by adjacent type I muscle fibres before lactate ever reaches the bloodstream, and that net lactate release by less active muscle during exercise may provide a convenient method to distribute carbohydrate stores from glycogen-replete to glycogen-depleted areas (Talmadge *et al.*, 1989; Brooks, 1991). Finally, the close correlation between the percentage of type I fibres in the active muscles and the T_{lac} (Ivy *et al.*, 1980) suggests that T_{lac} may coincide with a greater recruitment of type II fibres as exercise intensity increases (Nagata *et al.*, 1981).

The notion of a 'threshold' in lactate accumulation is not universally accepted. Some groups believe that blood [lactate] increases as a continuous function of exercise intensity (Hughson *et al.*, 1987). Although lactate may increase exponentially above T_{lac}, an exponential curve does not provide a good fit to exercise data in the region of interest (1–4 mM) (Wasserman *et al.*, 1990). The exercise protocol is also of importance if a clear identification of T_{lac} is required. Firstly, it is critical that the exercise test is started at a sufficiently low exercise intensity so that the baseline blood [lactate] can be established. If precision is required in the identification of T_{lac} then numerous stages (7–9) with small increments between incremental stages are recommended (Jones and Doust, 1997a). The $\dot{V}O_2$ at T_{lac} is independent of the rate at which the exercise intensity is increased during incremental or ramp exercise tests. Yoshida (1984) demonstrated that the $\dot{V}O_2$ at T_{lac} was the same when exercise was increased by 25 W every 1 minute or by 25 W every 4 minutes. However, the exercise intensity (power output or running speed) at the T_{lac} depends upon the incremental rate used (Ferry *et al.*, 1988), so if the identification of power output or running speed at T_{lac} is required for training prescription, then a protocol using 'steady state' stages of at least 3–4 minutes duration is recommended. The 'real' exercise intensity at T_{lac} can be estimated from ramp or incremental tests if the data are corrected for the lag time in $\dot{V}O_2$ at the onset of exercise. This is generally equivalent to subtracting 75% of the ramp rate from the measured value. For example, if the power output at T_{lac} is 200 W when using a ramp exercise test with a ramp rate of 20 W min^{-1}, then the 'corrected' power output at T_{lac} = 200 − (0.75 × 20) = 185 W.

The T_{lac} is routinely used in laboratory-based physiological assessments of endurance capacity. Subjects commonly perform a single incremental protocol involving a number of short (3–5 minute) stages of increasing intensity. Blood samples for the determination of blood [lactate] are obtained at the end of each stage before the exercise intensity is increased. Assessment of T_{lac} is usually by scrutiny of data plots by one or more reviewers. While this practice has been shown to be highly reliable both within and between reviewers (Davis, 1985), some authors have criticized this approach for its subjectivity (Yeh *et al.*, 1983). Until relatively recently, the measurement of blood lactate was confined to the exercise laboratory. However, the advent of portable and robust blood lactate analysers has enabled blood [lactate] and the T_{lac} to be assessed in field conditions (Figures 10.3a and 10.3b).

10.4.2 REFERENCE BLOOD LACTATE CONCENTRATIONS

To circumvent problems associated with the subjective assessment of T_{lac}, some authors have chosen to define T_{lac} as the $\dot{V}O_2$, power output or running speed at which an absolute blood lactate concentration is reached. Examples of this are interpolation to blood [lactate] of 2 mM (Lafontaine *et al.*, 1981), 2.5 mM (Hurley *et al.*, 1984) and 1 mM above resting lactate levels (Coyle *et al.*, 1983). It should be borne in mind that absolute blood lactate concentrations are affected by factors such as the incremental rate used in the exercise protocol (Foxdal *et al.*, 1994), muscle glycogen levels (Hughes *et al.*, 1982), the blood sampling site (artery, vein, or fingertip) and the choice of assay (whole blood, lysed blood, or plasma) (Robergs *et al.*, 1990; Williams *et al.*, 1992). Despite these limitations, the reduction in blood [lactate] for a given absolute exercise intensity following endurance training means that this method can be useful in demonstrating

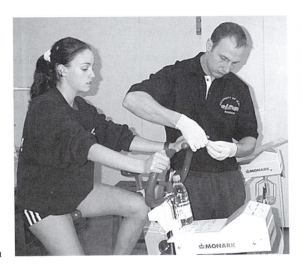

a   b

Figure 10.3a and b Lactate measurement in the laboratory and in the field on two members of the British Figure Skating team.

an improved endurance capacity provided that the same methods are used longitudinally. Another method that has been used to increase objectivity of T_{lac} assessment is the D_{max} method (Cheng *et al.*, 1992). This procedure involves fitting a curve to the blood lactate response to exercise and then drawing a line between the first and the last data points. The 'T_{lac}' is defined as the running speed that is furthest away from this line. A problem with the D_{max} method is that determination of the 'T_{lac}' may be skewed by error in either the first or last blood [lactate] measurement.

10.4.3 THE VENTILATORY THRESHOLD

The T_{lac} can be assessed non-invasively by consideration of the gas exchange responses to exercise. Due to its low pK, lactic acid will be almost completely dissociated on formation. The liberated protons will be buffered predominantly by intracellular and plasma bicarbonates, resulting in the liberation of large amounts of 'non-metabolic' CO_2. This is detected by the peripheral chemoreceptors and causes a disproportionate increase in $\dot{V}_E$ and $\dot{V}CO_2$ at what is known as the ventilatory threshold (T_{vent}) (Figure 10.4). The most sensitive approaches to the measurement of the T_{vent} is the disproportionate increase in $\dot{V}CO_2$ known as the V-slope method (Beaver *et al.*, 1986), and the increase in the ventilatory equivalent for O_2 ($\dot{V}_E / \dot{V}O_2$) without a concomitant increase in the ventilatory equivalent for CO_2 ($\dot{V}_E / \dot{V}CO_2$) (Caiozzo *et al.*, 1982). While it is possible to dissociate the T_{lac} from the T_{vent} by using a variety of manipulations of protocol and dietary status owing to the complexity of both lactate accumulation and ventilatory control, in most situations the T_{lac} and T_{vent} are coincident.

The T_{vent} can be measured during multistage exercise protocols with stage durations of 3–4 minutes, but ventilatory breakpoints are sharper when fast incremental or ramp protocols are used to bring subjects to exhaustion in

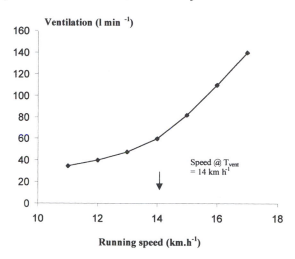

Figure 10.4 Determination of exercise intensity at ventilatory threshold (T_{vent}) from an incremental treadmill test.

around 10 minutes. It is possible to measure T_{vent} by collecting expired air into Douglas bags during each stage of an incremental test but breath-by-breath gas analysis allows a greater density of respiratory gas exchange measures and a more reliable assessment of the T_{vent}. During fast incremental or ramp exercise tests, a second ventilatory breakpoint known as the respiratory compensation threshold can be identified. For a short period of time during incremental exercise above the T_{vent}, there is an 'isocapnic buffering' region in which $\dot{V}_E$ increases in direct proportion to $\dot{V}CO_2$. Above this point, $\dot{V}_E$ increases at a faster rate than $\dot{V}CO_2$ to achieve respiratory compensation for the metabolic acidosis. The respiratory compensation threshold can be observed as a second breakpoint in $\dot{V}_E$ when plotted against $\dot{V}O_2$, or, more easily, as a single breakpoint when $\dot{V}_E$ is plotted against $\dot{V}CO_2$. While measurement of the T_{vent} can be convenient, the requirement for sensitive and sophisticated gas analysis equipment means that it is limited to laboratory use.

10.4.4 BREATHING FREQUENCY THRESHOLD

The increase in $\dot{V}_E$ during incremental exercise is caused by changes in tidal volume (breathing depth) and ventilatory frequency (breathing rate). Tidal volume typically attains a plateau at ~50% $\dot{V}O_2$ max, so that further increases in $\dot{V}_E$ are mediated mainly by changes in ventilatory frequency. It has been suggested that a non-linear increase in ventilatory frequency might be used to determine T_{vent} without the requirement for the analysis of expired air (James *et al.*, 1989). This would allow for the T_{lac} / T_{vent} to be determined non-invasively outside the laboratory and for exercise intensity to be prescribed and/or monitored using ventilatory frequency. However, factors such as the entrainment of ventilatory frequency to exercise rhythm (cadence) and disruption of the ventilatory pattern by coughing, swallowing, and speech limit the utility of monitoring breathing frequency to give information on the proximity to T_{vent} in the field situation (Jones and Doust, 1998a).

10.5 FROM HEAVY TO SEVERE EXERCISE: THE MAXIMAL LACTATE STEADY STATE

10.5.1 THE MAXIMAL LACTATE STEADY STATE

The maximal lactate steady state (MLSS), the exercise intensity above which blood [lactate] (and $\dot{V}O_2$) will rise continuously during continuous exercise, demarcates the boundary between heavy and severe exercise and it is considered by some to be the criterion measure of endurance fitness. Measurement of the MLSS requires that subjects perform a series of prolonged constant-intensity exercise bouts with blood [lactate] determined serially over a range of exercise intensities. As an example, a subject may be required to complete five treadmill runs each of 30 minutes duration at different running speeds on separate days (see Figure 10.5). The MLSS is defined as the highest running speed or power output at which blood [lactate] will stabilize during prolonged exercise (Beneke and von Duvillard, 1996;

Jones and Doust, 1998b). Measurement of MLSS, however, is not suitable for routine diagnostic use. Measurement of MLSS is time-consuming, requiring several days to complete the series of exercise bouts. Additionally, a large number of blood samples must be taken in order to define MLSS accurately (e.g. 30 samples for 5 × 30 minute exercise bouts with blood samples taken at rest and then every 5 minutes during exercise). This is unpleasant for the subject and is expensive in costs of consumables. Another problem is the precise definition of MLSS. While several methods have been used to define MLSS, Londeree (1986) recommended an increase of no more than 1 mM in blood [lactate] measured between 10 and 30 minutes of a sustained exercise bout and this criterion has been applied by other authors (Snyder *et al.*, 1994; Beneke and Von Duvillard, 1996; Jones and Doust, 1998b). This criterion would appear to be reasonable given the small error inherent in capillary blood sampling and assay and the changes in muscle substrate and plasma volume that might be expected with exercise of this duration and intensity.

For exercise above the MLSS, the time to exhaustion will be a function of the rate at which $\dot{V}O_2$ increases towards $\dot{V}O_2$ max and the rate at which muscle and blood [lactate] rises to fatiguing levels. Therefore, it is not surprising that the MLSS has been shown to be an important predictor of endurance exercise performance. Jones and Doust (1998b) demonstrated that the MLSS was better correlated with 8 km running performance ($r = 0.92$) than a number of other physiological measures including T_{lac}, T_{vent}, blood [lactate] reference values, and $\dot{V}O_2$ max. Theoretically, the exercise intensity at the MLSS can be sustained for one hour during competition, but under laboratory conditions an exercise duration of 40–50 minutes is more common. Therefore, it appears that the MLSS dictates the running speed that can be sustained during competition in running races at distances of 10 km to 10 miles.

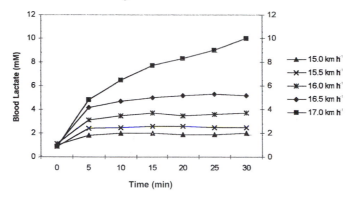

Figure 10.5 Determination of the running speed at the maximal lactate steady state (MLSS) from 5 treadmill runs of 30 minutes duration at different speeds. In this example, the MLSS occurs at 16.5 km h^{-1}.

Despite the great theoretical and practical interest in the direct determination of the MLSS, the requirement for several laboratory sessions and numerous blood samples has led exercise physiologists to devise simpler tests for the estimation of the MLSS.

10.5.2 CRITICAL POWER

Monod and Scherrer (1965) noted a hyperbolic relationship between power output and time to exhaustion in isolated muscle groups and transformed this into a linear relationship between total work done and time to exhaustion. The critical power (P_{crit}) was later defined as the slope of the regression of work done on time to exhaustion, and was considered to represent the highest exercise intensity that could be sustained for long periods without fatigue (Moritani *et al.*, 1981). The critical power can also be defined as the intercept of the regression equation describing the relationship between power output and the inverse of time to exhaustion (1 / *t*), (Figure 10.6). The P_{crit} concept has also been applied to other sports including running (Hughson *et al.*, 1984; Pepper *et al.*, 1992) and swimming (Wakayoshi *et al.*, 1992), but in these sports the term critical velocity is used. The measurement of P_{crit} requires that subjects exercise to exhaustion at several (ideally 4–6) constant power outputs on separate days. In theory, the P_{crit} should represent the same

exercise intensity as the MLSS and provide a direct measure of the boundary between heavy and severe exercise. Poole *et al.* (1988) demonstrated that blood lactate and $\dot{V}O_2$ attained steady-state values below the P_{crit} but rose over time during exercise above the P_{crit}. It has also been demonstrated that P_{crit} is sensitive to endurance training (Poole *et al.*, 1990; Jenkins and Quigley, 1992) and that the $\dot{V}O_2$ slow component which is most evident for exercise

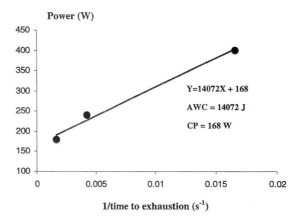

Figure 10.6 Determination of the critical power (P_{crit}). In this example, the subject performed three exercise bouts to exhaustion at three power outputs on a cycle ergometer. The intercept of the regression equation relating power output to the inverse of time to exhaustion is the P_{crit}, while the anaerobic work capacity (AWC) is given by the gradient of the regression line.

above the P_{crit} is attenuated with endurance training (Casaburi *et al.*, 1987; Womack *et al.*, 1995). However, time to exhaustion at the P_{crit} has varied considerably between studies and it has been reported that exercise at P_{crit} cannot be sustained beyond about 45 minutes (Poole *et al.*, 1988; Housh *et al.*, 1989; Jenkins and Quigley, 1990; Overend *et al.*, 1992). The differences in time to exhaustion at the P_{crit} noted in different studies may relate to the range of exercise intensities that are used to calculate the P_{crit}. Exhaustive trials of less than 3 minutes duration may not sufficiently tax the aerobic system, while trials requiring greater than 15 minutes may be prematurely curtailed as subjects lose motivation (Hill, 1993).

The critical power has obvious relevance as a theoretical construct. However, the necessity for subjects to perform a number (3–6) of exhaustive efforts on separate days precludes its routine use as means of identifying the boundary between heavy and severe exercise.

10.5.3 NEUROMUSCULAR FATIGUE THRESHOLD

The neuromuscular fatigue threshold (NFT) was first described by De Vries *et al.* (1982). Determination of the NFT requires subjects to exercise at a number of severe and supra-maximal power outputs while electromyographic activity (EMG) in the working muscles is measured continuously. The slope of the increase in the integrated EMG (iEMG) over time in each of these exercise bouts is recorded. Subsequently, the slope of the iEMG is plotted against the respective power output and the intercept of this relationship is defined as the NFT (i.e. the NFT therefore represents the highest power output at which iEMG will remain stable over time). The NFT has been shown to occur at a similar power output to the P_{crit} (Housh *et al.*, 1991a; Housh *et al.*, 1991b). This coincidence may indicate that the transition from heavy to severe exercise is associated with an increased firing frequency of already recruited muscle fibres or with a progressive recruitment of low-efficiency type II muscle fibres as fatigue ensues. The latter scenario

may also explain the increase in blood [lactate] over time and the emergence of the $\dot{V}O_2$ slow component for exercise above the P_{crit} / MLSS (Poole *et al.*, 1988; Barstow *et al.*, 1996).

Measurement of the NFT has not proved popular as a method for defining the boundary between the heavy and severe exercise intensity domains due to the requirement for subjects to complete several exercise bouts and for equipment to measure and analyse electromyographic activity.

10.5.4 LACTATE TURNPOINT

During multistage and incremental exercise tests, some authors have identified two lactate thresholds from plots of blood [lactate] against $\dot{V}O_2$ or exercise intensity (Ribeiro *et al.*, 1986; Aunola and Rusko, 1992; Hofmann *et al.*, 1994). These correspond to the traditional *first* lactate threshold where blood [lactate] first increases above baseline, and a *second* 'sudden and sustained' lactate threshold or lactate turnpoint at around 2.5–4.0 mM. Skinner and McLellan (1980) first argued for the existence of two transition points in both the blood lactate and ventilatory responses to incremental exercise, and these authors also speculated on the possible physiological mechanisms that may underpin these phenomena. It has been noted that the lactate turnpoint may be more meaningful in terms of the endurance race performance characteristics of highly trained subjects than is the T_{lac} (Ribeiro *et al.*, 1986; Aunola and Rusko, 1992; Hoffman *et al.*, 1994). It is not known whether any similarity between the exercise intensity at the lactate turnpoint and the P_{crit} / MLSS is coincidental or whether both are related to the same underlying mechanism. If incremental exercise tests utilize stage durations that are sufficiently long and intensity increments that are sufficiently small to allow the measured blood [lactate] to reflect entry of lactate and its removal from the blood, it is possible that the lactate turnpoint can provide a reasonable estimate of the MLSS. Identification of the lactate turnpoint is subjective and it is often impossible to identify a *second* lactate threshold.

10.5.5 FIXED BLOOD LACTATE CONCENTRATIONS (OBLA)

Mader *et al.* (1976) defined the 'aerobic–anaerobic transition' as the point at which blood [lactate] reached 4 mM in an incremental exercise test (Figure 10.2). This rationale may have been based on the suggestion that muscle lactate transporters become saturated at approximately 4 mM muscle [lactate] (Jorfeldt *et al.*, 1978). Support for the 4 mM concept was provided by Kindermann *et al.* (1979) and Heck *et al.* (1985) who demonstrated that the *mean* blood [lactate] at MLSS was approximately 4.0 ± 0.7 mM (range: 3.1–5.5 mM). Jones and Doust (1998b) also recently reported that the mean blood [lactate] at MLSS in a group of runners was close to 4 mM, but noted that individual values could be as low as 2.5 mM or as high as 6.0 mM. The 4 mM blood [lactate] reference value evaluated during incremental exercise was termed the 'onset of blood lactate accumulation' (OBLA) by Sjodin and Jacobs (1981). This is something of a misnomer given that 4 mM blood [lactate] is reached at a significantly higher exercise intensity than the T_{lac} (Jones and Doust, 1994).

The use of OBLA, and other fixed values such as 3 mM (Borch *et al.*, 1993), certainly improves the objectivity with which exercise lactate data can be evaluated and may be useful in demonstrating a reduced reliance on anaerobic metabolism during submaximal exercise following training. This procedure takes no account of inter-individual differences in the rate of blood lactate accumulation, and the dependency of blood [lactate] on substrate availability (Ivy *et al.*, 1981), exercise protocol (Ferry *et al.*, 1988), and on the site of blood sampling and the assay medium (Williams *et al.*, 1992) brings the validity of this practice into question. Coincidentally, the exercise intensity at 4mM blood [lactate] may be similar in some subjects to the exercise intensity at the lactate turnpoint, which, in turn, may provide a good estimate of the MLSS. It should be remembered, however, that blood lactate responses during incremental exercise tests rarely allow the blood lactate response during prolonged exercise at a constant intensity to be predicted (Orok *et al.*, 1989; Aunola and Rusko, 1992). If subjects are asked to exercise continuously at the exercise intensity corresponding to 4 mM blood [lactate] derived from an incremental test, blood [lactate] rises throughout the exercise bout and exhaustion occurs relatively quickly (Mognoni *et al.*, 1990; Oyono-Enguille *et al.*, 1990). This suggests that, in most subjects, the exercise intensity at which 4 mM blood [lactate] is reached in an incremental test overestimates the exercise intensity at the MLSS. This may be especially true in elite subjects who may not increase their blood [lactate] to greater than 4 mM until they reach $\geq 95\%$ $\dot{V}O_2$ max (Jones and Doust, 1994).

10.5.6 INDIVIDUAL ANAEROBIC THRESHOLD

Investigations by Stegmann *et al.* (1981) and Stegmann and Kindermann (1982) into individual blood lactate kinetics during exercise and recovery led to the concept of the individual anaerobic threshold (IAT). The calculation of IAT involves the measurement of blood [lactate] during a standard incremental exercise test and during the subsequent recovery period. The IAT concept makes several important assumptions including that the lactate clearance kinetics during recovery reflect those that are operating during exercise. An exponential curve is fitted to the blood [lactate] response to exercise and a third-order polynomial is fitted to the data for blood [lactate] during the recovery period. Then, a horizontal line is drawn to connect the peak exercise blood [lactate] to the equivalent blood [lactate] in recovery. A second line is then drawn from this point on the 'recovery blood [lactate] curve' tangential to the 'exercise blood [lactate] curve'. The point at which this line cuts the 'exercise blood [lactate] curve' is defined as the IAT and is assumed to represent the exercise intensity at which the elimination of blood lactate is both maximal and equal to the rate of diffusion of lactate from working muscle to blood (Stegmann *et al.*, 1981). The physiological rationale for this approach has never been transparent, and misgivings exist as to the validity of a number of the assumptions made in the IAT concept, including that the rate of blood lactate clearance reaches a plateau during submaximal exercise. Although the IAT is sensitive to endurance training (Keith *et al.*, 1992), the time to exhaustion at IAT varied considerably in different studies. Stegmann *et al.* (1981) reported that exercise at IAT could be sustained for 50 minutes in all subjects tested , whereas Orok *et al.* (1989) found that exercise at IAT could only be sustained for 3–36 minutes. Jones and Doust (1998c) reported that in well-trained runners, the IAT overestimated the running speed at both T_{lac} and at 4 mM blood [lactate]. The differences between studies may be related to variations in the protocols used to derive IAT including the incremental rate and stage duration employed in the incremental test, whether the exercise test is continued to exhaustion, and the use of a passive or active recovery period (McLellan and Jacobs, 1993). The requirement for complex data analysis in the determination of IAT precludes routine use of IAT by athlete and coach, and the method has not proved popular.

10.5.7 LACTATE MINIMUM SPEED

Tegtbur *et al.* (1993) suggested that the point at which blood [lactate] reaches a minimum before beginning to rise during an incremental exercise test initiated during lactacidosis provides a valid estimate of MLSS. The lactate minimum speed test requires subjects to perform: (1) two supramaximal exercise bouts for 60 s and 45 s (separated by a 60 s recovery period) at an intensity of ~120% $\dot{V}O_2$ max; (2) an 8 minute walk to allow blood [lactate] to reach a peak in the blood; and (3) an incremental exercise test using ~3-minute stages with blood [lactate] measured at the end of each stage. The blood [lactate] response during the incremental portion of the test, which should be described using a cubic spline function, is characteristically U-shaped and the nadir on this curve can be termed the lactate minimum speed (LMS),

(Figure 10.7). Tegtbur *et al.* (1993) suggested that the decreasing blood [lactate] during the early stages of the incremental test indicated that the rate of blood lactate clearance was greater than the rate of lactate production, while the increasing blood [lactate] during the latter part of the test indicated that lactate production outstripped its removal. On this basis, the point at which blood [lactate] reaches a minimum should reflect the point at which lactate production and lactate clearance rates are equal, i.e. the MLSS. Tegtbur *et al.* (1993) showed that when 25 endurance runners ran for 8 km at the LMS they exhibited elevated but stable blood [lactate] values. When the subjects ran at a speed only 0.68 km h^{-1} above the LMS, there was a significant accumulation of blood lactate which caused 11 subjects to terminate the exercise bout before 8 km had been completed. The LMS test is attractive in that the LMS may be determined objectively, is robust to variations in stage duration during the incremental test provided that stages are of at least 800 m in length (or 2.5–3 minutes in duration), and is claimed not to be affected by glycogen depletion (Tegtbur *et al.*, 1993).

Several recent studies indicate that the LMS may not be valid for the estimation of MLSS. Jones and Doust (1998b) reported that the LMS was not significantly different from the running speed at T_{lac} but that it was significantly lower than the running speed at the MLSS in 10 trained runners. The LMS had poor discriminatory power between subjects, was poorly correlated with MLSS, and provided the worst estimate of the MLSS out of a range of other physiological measures including T_{lac}, T_{vent}, and OBLA. Carter *et al.* (1999a) have shown that the LMS is profoundly influenced by the exercise intensity at which the incremental portion of the lactate minimum test is started. These authors reported a positive linear relationship between the starting speed used in the incremental test and the speed at which the lactate minimum was found. Although it would be possible to choose a starting speed that would provide a reasonable value for LMS, this requirement for manipulating the test protocol does not inspire confidence in the validity of the LMS concept. In another study, Carter *et al.* (1999b) measured T_{lac} and the blood lactate response to a standard incremental treadmill test, the LMS, and $\dot{V}O_2$ max in 16 subjects before and after they completed a 6-week endurance training programme and in a further 8 subjects who acted as controls. In the control group, there were no changes in the running speeds at T_{lac} or 3 mM blood [lactate], LMS or $\dot{V}O_2$ max. In the experimental groups, there were significant improvements in the running speeds at T_{lac} and 3 mM blood [lactate], and a significant increase in $\dot{V}O_2$ max. However, despite this clear evidence of improvement in endurance fitness in the training group, the LMS was not significantly different before or after training. Although further work is needed, this lack of sensitivity to training, along with the protocol-dependency of the lactate minimum test, suggests that the LMS does not provide a valid estimate of MLSS.

10.5.8 HEART RATE DEFLECTION POINT

Conconi *et al.* (1982) reported that the speed at which the linearity in the heart rate (HR)–running speed relationship was lost in an incremental field test in runners, i.e. the heart rate deflection point, was highly correlated with ($r = 0.99$) and not significantly different from the running speed at T_{lac}. Droghetti *et al.* (1985) confirmed this relationship in a number of other sports and activities. Conconi *et al.* (1982) hypothesized that the $\dot{V}O_2$ spared by the increased anaerobic contribution to the total energy cost of exercise beyond T_{lac} would be reflected by a reduced rate of increase in HR above T_{lac}. Conconi's original method required subjects to run around an athletic track initially at a slow speed. Thereafter, there was a progressive increase in running speed every 200 m with HR recorded using an HR monitor at the end of each stage until athletes reached exhaustion. When HR is plotted against running speed, a deviation of heart rate at high speeds can sometimes be seen (Figure 10.8). Conconi *et al.*

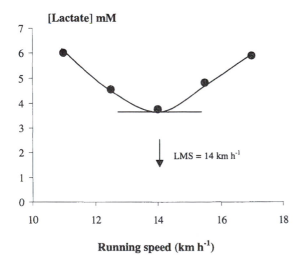

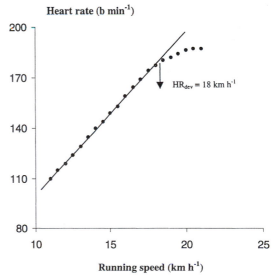

Figure 10.7 Determination of the lactate minimum speed (LMS). In this example, an incremental treadmill test involving five exercise stages has been completed following prior sprint exercise. The blood lactate data are fitted with a cubic spline and the minimum point on the curve is termed the LMS.

Figure 10.8 Determination of the heart rate deflection point. The heart rate deflection point is the running speed at which heart rate begins to deviate from linearity.

(1982) claimed that the deflection point in HR could be observed in all subjects and that it occurred at the same running speed as the T_{lac}. However, the protocol used to assess T_{lac} was unusual and it was later suggested that the deflection in HR corresponded to the lactate turnpoint (Ribeiro *et al.*, 1985) or the MLSS (Hofmann *et al.*, 1994). Recently, Conconi's research group has modified the original Conconi test protocol (Grazzi *et al.*, 1999) in the face of criticism from the scientific community.

The interest in the possibility of a non-invasive field test for MLSS led to a large number of investigations into the validity of Conconi's method. Most of these studies have cast great doubt upon the validity, reliability, and underpinning theory of the Conconi test (Kuipers *et al.*, 1988; Tokmakidis and Leger, 1992; Jones and Doust, 1995; Jones and Doust, 1997b), although other groups have maintained that the test is valid and useful (Hofmann *et al.*, 1994; Bunc *et al.*, 1995). The physiological rationale for the existence of a deflection in heart rate and for its mechanistic link to increased blood lactate accumulation has never been clear. Conconi's original hypothesis that increased anaerobic metabolism spares $\dot{V}O_2$ is, however, untenable. The increased rate of ATP resynthesis through anaerobic glycolysis above the T_{lac} appears to supplement rather than spare the rate of ATP production through oxidative metabolism. During incremental tests which bring subjects to exhaustion in 8–12 minutes, a reduced rate of increase in $\dot{V}O_2$ during submaximal exercise has never been demonstrated, although there is generally a plateau in $\dot{V}O_2$ at maximal exercise ($\dot{V}O_2$ max). Rather, with longer stage durations, $\dot{V}O_2$ may demonstrate an upward curvilinearity as the $\dot{V}O_2$ slow component develops (Jones *et al.*, 1999). It has been suggested that the deflection in heart rate is an artefact of the specifics of the Conconi test protocol (Jones and Doust, 1997b). The increase in running speed every 200 m means that the time between increases in exercise intensity becomes progressively shorter as the test proceeds. This may have two important effects. Firstly, measurements of HR become more frequent as HR approaches its maximum. When plotted against running speed, this will elongate the region at HR max and lead to the artificial appearance of a deflection point. Secondly, the decreasing exercise stage durations in the face of similar or slowed HR response kinetics may not allow sufficient time for HR to rise to its 'steady state' level.

Pokan *et al.* (1993) demonstrated that the existence of a deflection in HR depends on increases in the left ventricular ejection fraction. The same group have acknowledged that a deflection in HR is not always found because the HR response to incremental exercise may be perfectly linear up to HR_{max} or may even exhibit an upward deflection point (Pokan *et al.*, 1995). Difficulty in observing a deflection in HR in all subjects has been recognized as a limitation to the Conconi test (Kuipers *et al.*, 1988; Jones and Doust, 1995; Jones and Doust, 1997b) and these difficulties persist even when mathematical approaches to the identification of a deflection in HR are utilized (Tokmakidis and Leger, 1992). Jones and Doust (1995) assessed the test–retest reliability of the Conconi test in 15 subjects and reported that a deflection in HR was found in both tests in only 6 individuals. The deflection in HR has also been shown to occur at rather high submaximal exercise intensities, i.e. 90–95% HR_{max}, that are above both the T_{lac} and OBLA (Tokmakidis and Leger, 1992; Jones and Doust, 1997b). Two studies of running (Jones and Doust, 1997b) and cycling (Heck and Hollmann, 1992) have shown that the exercise intensity at the deflection in HR cannot be sustained without appreciable accumulation of blood lactate and premature fatigue. These studies suggest that a deflection in HR, when it can be determined, overestimates the exercise intensity at MLSS in most subjects.

10.5.9 OTHER ESTIMATES

Recently, other approaches have been used to estimate the boundary between heavy and severe exercise. Snyder *et al.* (1994) proposed that the exercise intensity at 85% HR_{max} provides a close estimate of the exercise intensity at MLSS. While this may be generally true, dangers in non-individual evaluation of the physiological response to exercise have been highlighted previously (Katch *et al.*, 1978). For example, in elite distance runners, exercise at the MLSS requires approximately 90% HR_{max} (Jones, 1998). Billat *et al.* (1994a) estimated the power output at MLSS during cycling by analysing the change in blood [lactate] between 20 and 30 minutes at two levels corresponding to ~65% and ~80% $\dot{V}O_2$ max. Effectively, these authors interpolated between a power output which incurred a decreased or constant blood [lactate] with time, and a power output which incurred an increased blood [lactate] with time, to predict a power output at which blood [lactate] would be maximal but stable. Clearly, there will be inherent error in using interpolation as opposed to direct measurement of MLSS and some precision will be lost. Nevertheless, this type of approach would seem to have some potential, since it might permit a working estimate of MLSS from two short exercise bouts performed on the same day. Further research is required to determine a simple and practical procedure for determination of MLSS or critical power that does not unduly sacrifice accuracy.

10.6 FROM SEVERE TO SUPRAMAXIMAL EXERCISE: THE $V - \dot{V}O_2$ max

The boundary between severe submaximal exercise and supramaximal exercise (exercise having an energy cost greater than the $\dot{V}O_2$ max) is, by definition, the $\dot{V}O_2$ max. The $\dot{V}O_2$ max represents the maximal rate at which ATP can be generated aerobically. Numerous studies have shown that $\dot{V}O_2$ max is an excellent predictor of endurance performance in heterogeneous groups (e.g. Costill *et al.*, 1973).

Although a high $\dot{V}O_2$ max (>70 ml kg^{-1}min^{-1} for males, >60 ml kg^{-1} min^{-1} for females) is necessary for elite-level performance, other factors such as T_{lac}, MLSS, and exercise economy can discriminate performance differences in athletes with similar $\dot{V}O_2$ max values. In terms of the control of physical training, and the definition of exercise intensity domains, however, it is not the absolute or relative value of $\dot{V}O_2$ max (in units of l min^{-1} or ml kg^{-1} min^{-1}) that is important but rather the 'functional expression' of $\dot{V}O_2$ max in units of velocity or power output. In order to estimate the running velocity at $\dot{V}O_2$ max ($V - \dot{V}O_2$ max) it is necessary to make measurements of both $\dot{V}O_2$ max and the running economy characteristics of the subject. The latter is best done by measuring the steady-state $\dot{V}O_2$ at several sub-T_{lac} running speeds. A regression equation describing the relationship between $\dot{V}O_2$ and submaximal running speed can then be solved for $\dot{V}O_2$ max to give the estimated $V - \dot{V}O_2$ max (Morgan *et al.*, 1989). Two individuals with the same $\dot{V}O_2$ max values may have different $V - \dot{V}O_2$ max values if one subject is more economical than the other (Figure 10.9). In this example, the subject with the better economy

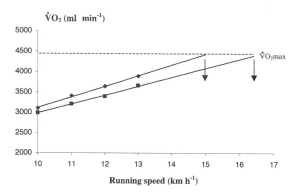

Figure 10.9 Determination of the running velocity at maximal oxygen uptake ($V - \dot{V}O_2$ max). This involves regressing $\dot{V}O_2$ on exercise intensity for submaximal exercise and extrapolating this relationship to $\dot{V}O_2$ max. The $V - \dot{V}O_2$ max can differ in two individuals with the same $\dot{V}O_2$ max (in ml kg^{-1}min^{-1}) if exercise economy differs in the two individuals.

would be able to run at a higher speed for the same exercise intensity such as 100% $\dot{V}O_2$ max. The $V-\dot{V}O_2$ max is highly correlated with endurance performance (Jones, 1998; Jones and Doust, 1998b). This is due, in part, to the fact that athletes sustain similar percentages of their $\dot{V}O_2$ max for given durations of exercise (Londeree, 1986). The $V-\dot{V}O_2$ max has also been shown to be sensitive to endurance training (Jones, 1998; Billat *et al.*, 1999). It has been suggested that the $V-\dot{V}O_2$ max represents an important exercise intensity if the goal is to improve $\dot{V}O_2$ max and endurance fitness (Billat and Koralsztein, 1996; Hill and Rowell, 1997).

10.7 CONCLUSION

This chapter has demonstrated the existence of several 'domains' of submaximal exercise (Figure 10.1). These are referred to as moderate exercise, heavy exercise and severe exercise. Moderate exercise is that performed below the lactate threshold. During moderate exercise, $\dot{V}O_2$ attains an early steady state and blood [lactate] remains close to resting levels. Heavy exercise is that performed above the lactate threshold but below the maximal lactate steady state or critical power. In this domain, both $\dot{V}O_2$ and blood lactate will attain a delayed but elevated steady state. Severe exercise is that performed above the maximal lactate steady state but below the exercise intensity corresponding to $\dot{V}O_2$ max. In the severe domain, both $\dot{V}O_2$ and blood [lactate] will rise continuously over time until $\dot{V}O_2$ max is reached and/or fatigue resulting from the metabolic acidosis terminates exercise. In the severe submaximal exercise domain, the time to exhaustion is predictable based upon the critical power and the anaerobic work capacity.

In order to define exercise intensity accurately, it is important to delineate the boundaries between the various exercise domains. In this chapter, the variety of methods that have been employed to measure or estimate the physiological parameters that define the

transition from one domain to another have been reviewed. These methods differ in the degree to which the scientific literature supports their validity, reliability, and sensitivity to change following physical training. The possible advantages of practicality and simplicity of a method must be secondary to the principles of good scientific measurement. None of the measures reviewed above has received universal acceptance, but the weight of evidence suggests that the lactate threshold and MLSS are the criterial standards in terms of defining the boundaries between the submaximal exercise intensity domains. The $V-\dot{V}O_2$ max is widely accepted as a useful parameter that separates submaximal from maximal / supramaximal exercise. Table 10.1 summarizes the validity, reliability, sensitivity, objectivity, practicality, and acceptability of the methods that are most commonly used for evaluating endurance fitness.

Direct measurements (or estimates) of T_{lac}, MLSS, and $V-\dot{V}O_2$ max in an individual athlete allow for endurance performance capability and/or times to exhaustion at particular running speeds or power outputs to be estimated. This information can also be used to help in the prescription of a structured, balanced and appropriate training programme. For example, an individual who is new to regular exercise may initially be prescribed only moderate-intensity exercise because higher intensities ($>T_{lac}$) may be perceived to be unpleasant and stressful and this experience may adversely affect adherence to the exercise programme. In contrast, elite endurance athletes will generally perform exercise sessions at moderate, heavy, severe, and supramaximal intensities during a normal training week. The relative proportions of these sessions will depend on current fitness status, age, aspirations, training preferences, the time in the training macrocycle, and the specialist event. Excessive severe intensity exercise may impair recovery and eventually contribute to overtraining, while if moderate-intensity exercise is performed almost exclusively in a training

Table 10.1 The validity, reliability, sensitivity, objectivity, practicality and acceptability of the methods that are most commonly used for evaluating endurance fitness

Test	Strong evidence for validity?	Strong evidence for reliability?	Strong evidence for sensitivity?	Objective?	OK for field testing?	Athlete friendly?
Tlac	√	√	√	x	√	√
Tvent	√	√	√	x	x	√
MLSS	√	√	√	√	x	x
Pcrit	?	√	√	√	x	x
TlacP	?	?	?	x	x	√
OBLA	x	x	√	√	√	√
IAT	x	?	√	√	x	√
LMS	x	√	x	√	√	√
HRD	x	x	x	x	√	√
$\dot{V}-\dot{V}O_2$ max	√	√	√	√	x	√

programme then 'underperformance' may result. The training intensity can be regulated if an athlete has a portable heart rate monitor and knows his or her heart rate at the lactate threshold and at maximal lactate steady state as well as the maximal heart rate (Figure 10.10). The balance of training intensities (and hence durations) in a training programme can be specified and controlled with this systematic approach. Over time, this should maximize the effectiveness of training and result in improved performance.

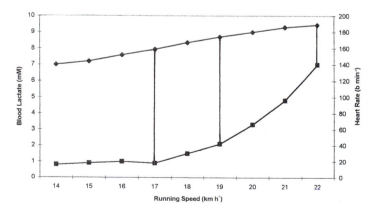

Figure 10.10 Use of heart rate to regulate training intensity. The vertical lines represent the heart rate at lactate threshold, the heart rate at the lactate turnpoint (which may provide a reasonable estimate of the maximal lactate steady state) and the maximal heart rate. These heart rates and the corresponding running speeds can be used to prescribe and regulate training intensity within the moderate, heavy, severe, and supramaximal domains.

10.8 PRACTICAL EXERCISES

10.8.1 GENERAL GUIDELINES

Subject preparation: Subjects should be well rested, hydrated, and with full glycogen stores to ensure that the responses to exercise are not influenced by acute changes in physiological status. The following procedure is recommended.

- 48 hours before testing: Refrain from heavy exercise. Light exercise can be undertaken. A high-carbohydrate diet should be consumed.
- 24 hours before testing: No exercise should be undertaken. A high-carbohydrate diet should be consumed.
- The day of testing: No exercise should be undertaken. A light-carbohydrate meal 2 to 4 hours before testing should be consumed but nothing thereafter. Adequate fluids should be taken but no caffeine or high (>12%) carbohydrate drinks should be consumed in the four hours prior to testing.

Subjects should wear appropriate athletic clothing and training shoes. The laboratory should be well ventilated and at a comfortable temperature for exercise (17–20°C). Appropriate informed consent and pre-exercise health questionnaires should be completed (see Jones and Doust, 1997a).

10.8.2 ESTIMATING CAPABILITY

In a number of the experiments, an estimate of the subject's likely performance is required to guide the intensity of exercise in an incremental test. Prior testing for maximal oxygen uptake provides the best guidance, although estimations can be made based on knowledge of the subject's sporting performance. Table 10.2 offers guidance.

10.8.3 GENERAL METHODS

Heart rate is best obtained from a portable heart rate telemeter (Polar Sport Tester, Polar Electro Oy, Finland) or similar device set to 5 s recording intervals for immediate playback after exercise. Interpretation of data can be enhanced if the subject is instructed to press the electronic marker button at the commencement of each level of a staged protocol.

Oxygen uptake can be obtained from an on-line system or from Douglas bags. The former allows observation in real-time. If using Douglas bags, expired air should be collected for a whole number of breaths over a timed period of about 45 s during the final minute of each level of a staged protocol. Rating of perceived exertion can be obtained during the period of expired air collection.

Blood sampling can take place immediately after collection of air is completed. During

Table 10.2 Estimation of speed and work rate increments for graded exercise testing according to fitness status.

Standard	Running (male) (km h⁻¹)	Running (female) (km h⁻¹)	Cycling (male) (W)	Cycling (female) (W)
Fair	9, 10.5, 12, 13.5, 15	7, 8.5, 10, 11.5, 13	50, 80, 110, 140, 170	50, 75, 100, 125, 150
Average	11, 12.5, 14, 15.5, 17	9, 10.5, 12, 13.5, 15	110, 140, 170, 200, 230	80, 110, 140, 170, 200
Good	13, 14.5, 16, 17.5, 19	11, 12.5, 14, 15.5, 17	180, 210, 240, 270, 300	110, 140, 170, 200, 230
Excellent	15, 16.5, 18, 19.5, 21	13, 14.5, 16, 17.5, 19	250, 280, 310, 340, 370	140, 170, 200, 230, 260

Fair would be a typical student who keeps fit but does not take part in competitive sport
Average would be a typical student who plays team sports
Good would be a typical student endurance athlete
Excellent would be a competitive endurance athlete

treadmill running, blood sampling is most easily achieved by the subject jumping astride the moving belt at the end of each stage. This allows a finger to be held stable for sampling. During the sampling period the treadmill speed can be increased to the next level and once sampling is complete the subject can recommence running. The advantages of achieving a quick and neat sample from a stationary hand outweigh the disadvantages of the short (~30 s) interruption to exercise which, given the slow kinetics of lactate change, is unlikely to significantly influence the data (Gullstrand *et al.*, 1994). In cycling exercise, a finger can easily be stabilized and no interruption to exercise is required. Laboratory health and safety guidelines must be adhered to when handling blood (see Chapter 4 by Maughan *et al.*).

Fingertip capillary sampling is the most convenient method for blood collection although the ear lobe is preferred by some. Lactate concentration is affected by the site of sampling and the post-sampling treatment (see Williams *et al.*, 1992). The general pattern of change will be similar whatever the method used but absolute values will differ.

Treadmill grade should be set to 1% to reflect the energetic cost of outdoor running (Jones and Doust, 1996). An electronically braked cycle ergometer, where power is kept constant even if pedalling rate changes, will allow superior results to those obtained with a friction-braked cycle ergometer.

Where a laboratory practical is being undertaken with inexperienced students to show the basic phenomena, the use of larger increments (1.5 km h^{-1} or 30 W) will provide clear data and allow easy understanding but poor precision. More precise identification of the T_{lac} requires smaller step changes and the guidance given in the Guidelines of the British Association of Sport and Exercise Sciences (Jones and Doust, 1997a) should be followed.

10.8.4 GENERAL FURTHER ANALYSIS OPPORTUNITIES

If more than one of the following practicals can be completed over the course of a teaching unit, the running speed or power output obtained by the different methods can be ranked and cross-correlated. This would allow discussion of how the data fit into the theoretical framework (see main text) and the extent of similarity between the parameters.

Confirmation (or otherwise) of the validity of any of the parameters can be shown by a 'verification' test. Following identification of the running speed or power output at T_{lac}, subjects may undertake constant load exercise at this intensity on a separate day. Heart rate, oxygen uptake and blood [lactate] can be determined at 5-minute intervals. This test can be undertaken on a running track with heart rate monitored continuously and a blood sample taken every 800 m (running) or 2400 m (cycling) for analysis of blood [lactate].

10.9 PRACTICAL 1: T_{LAC} (LACTATE THRESHOLD) AND OBLA (ONSET OF BLOOD LACTATE ACCUMULATION)

10.9.1 GENERAL PROTOCOL (CYCLING OR RUNNING)

Following a 5-minute jogging or cycling warm-up, the subject completes an incremental test of five 4-minute stages. Oxygen uptake is measured over the final minute of each stage. A blood sample is taken at the end of each stage for the determination of lactate concentration. The intensities can be estimated from Table 10.2.

10.9.2 ADDITIONAL HINTS

- This practical can be performed equally well on a treadmill or a cycle ergometer.
- Only a short warm-up is required due to the early, sub-threshold stages of the protocol.
- A resting blood [lactate] value may give some insight into carbohydrate status.

10.9.3 DATA ANALYSIS

Blood lactate concentration should be plotted against exercise intensity (speed or power output). The data points may be joined by straight lines. If available, a cubic spline program provides the best form of curve fitting. It is not recommended that any form of best-fit polynomial curve is used since there is no physiological justification for such an approach.

The OBLA is determined as the exercise intensity at a blood lactate concentration of 4 mM. The lactate threshold is judged by visual inspection as the exercise intensity at which the blood [lactate] data show a sudden and sustained increase above baseline levels.

10.9.4 FURTHER ANALYSIS OPPORTUNITIES

- Determine inter-reviewer reliability by coding plots. Each person in a class can then be asked to identify T_{lac}.
- Does [lactate] at T_{lac} equal [lactate] at OBLA?

10.10 PRACTICAL 2: VENTILATORY THRESHOLD

10.10.1 GENERAL PROTOCOL (CYCLING OR RUNNING)

Following a 5-minute jogging or cycling warm-up, the subject completes an incremental test of seven 2-minute stages. Oxygen uptake is measured over the final minute of each stage. The exercise intensities can be estimated from Table 10.2.

10.10.2 ADDITIONAL HINTS

- This practical can be performed equally well on a treadmill or a cycle ergometer.
- Only a short warm-up is required due to the early, sub-threshold stages of the protocol.
- A ramp protocol can be used (20 W min^{-1} or 1 km h^{-1} min^{-1}) with oxygen uptake being measured continuously with an on-line system or with 45 s sequential Douglas bag collections.

10.10.3 DATA ANALYSIS

Ventilation (l min^{-1} STPD) should be plotted against exercise intensity (running speed or cycling power output). The data points may be joined by straight lines. If available, a cubic spline program provides the best form of curve fitting. It is not recommended that any form of best-fit polynomial curve is used since there is no physiological justification for such an approach.

Ventilatory threshold is judged as the intensity at which the linear relationship between $\dot{V}_E$ and exercise intensity is lost.

10.10.4 FURTHER ANALYSIS OPPORTUNITIES

- Plotting the ventilatory equivalent for oxygen (that is, $\dot{V}_E / \dot{V}O_2$) against exercise intensity may make the threshold clearer.
- Ventilatory parameters may be plotted against $\dot{V}O_2$ rather than speed or power output.
- Plotting three lines ($\dot{V}_E$, RER and $\dot{V}CO_2$) against exercise intensity offers the opportunity to discuss potential underlying physiological mechanisms associated with the respiratory compensation for metabolic acidosis.
- Determine inter-reviewer reliability by coding plots. Each person in a class can then be asked to identify T_{vent}.

10.11 PRACTICAL 3: CRITICAL POWER

10.11.1 GENERAL PROTOCOL (CYCLE)

Three tests to exhaustion are completed on three separate days. Each test is undertaken at a constant intensity and cadence. The intensity is set so that time to exhaustion is between 1 and 10 minutes. After a 5-minute submaximal warm-up, the intensity is increased to the desired value and the subject continues until unable to maintain the required cadence (>5 rev min^{-1} decrease for >5 s). Since the tests are maximal, strong verbal encouragement is appropriate.

The intensities can be judged from Table 10.2 by taking the fifth-stage intensity and cycling at this intensity (likely duration about 10 minutes), + 15% (likely duration about 6 minutes), and + 30% (likely duration about 1 minute).

10.11.2 ADDITIONAL HINTS

- Attempting to complete three tests on one day will not yield reliable results. Tests can be completed on consecutive days but should be given in a random order.
- Note the saddle height so this may be kept constant between tests.
- The exact intensities chosen for the three bouts are not critical since, in principle, exhaustion times anywhere between 1 and 30 minutes will be linearly related. However, the variability in time to exhaustion is greater with durations above 10 minutes.
- Ideally the intensities should be given in random order. If little is known about the subject, give the middle intensity first and the intensities for the subsequent two bouts can be adjusted to ensure the data span an adequate range of exercise intensity.
- The equivalent to critical power, the critical velocity, can be determined on the treadmill using three bouts of exhaustive running at different speeds. However, running to exhaustion on a fast-moving treadmill is a potentially dangerous procedure and not advisable as a student practical.

10.11.3 DATA ANALYSIS

The inverse of time to exhaustion (i.e. $1/t$) is plotted against power output and a linear regression line is fitted. The intercept of the line gives critical power (P_{crit}) and the slope of the line gives anaerobic work capacity.

10.11.4 FURTHER ANALYSIS OPPORTUNITIES

Adjusting one of the times to exhaustion by ~10% and recalculating P_{crit} and anaerobic work capacity will allow discussion of the sensitivity of these parameters to methodological variation due to subject's motivation to exercise to exhaustion.

10.12 PRACTICAL 4: LACTATE MINIMUM SPEED

10.12.1 GENERAL PROTOCOL (RUNNING)

The subject should warm up with 5 minutes of jogging, some stretching and three acceleration sprints where the treadmill speed is raised over 30 s from slow jogging to sprinting speed and back down again.

The test begins with two pre-test sprints at a speed that is 120% of the running speed at $\dot{V}O_2$ max. The subject should stand with legs astride the treadmill belt. The treadmill speed is increased to the required level and the subject lets go carefully and begins running. The first sprint is for 60 s and the second is for 45 s with a 60 s rest given between sprints. The treadmill speed is lowered to 4 km h^{-1} and the subject walks for 8 minutes, with a capillary blood sample taken after 7 minutes for the determination of lactate concentration. Five 3-minute incremental stages are then completed. The intensities can be judged from Table 10.2.

A capillary sample is obtained at the end of each stage for the determination of lactate concentration.

10.12.2 DATA ANALYSIS

Capillary lactate concentration is plotted against running speed for the five incremental stages. A cubic spline is fitted and the lactate minimum speed determined as the speed at which the lowest point occurs (i.e. a zero-gradient tangent) by visual inspection or mathematically. If a spline-fitting algorithm is not available the data may be connected by straight lines.

10.12.3 ADDITIONAL HINTS

- The lactate concentration after walking for 7 minutes allows confirmation that the pre-test sprints have induced a significant lactacidosis. If the value is < 5 mM the sprints were insufficiently intense and the test should be stopped and repeated on another day.
- The exact sprinting speed and the exact lactate concentration after the sprints is not important in illustrating the principle of the lactate minimum speed test.
- If running speed at $\dot{V}O_2$ max is not known, the speeds for the initial sprints can be estimated by adding 4 km h^{-1} to the fifth-stage speed shown in Table 10.2.

- It is not recommended that any form of best-fit polynomial curve is used since there is no physiological justification for such an approach.
- The test can be undertaken on a cycle ergometer. The sprint power can be estimated as 125% of the fifth-stage power output in Table 10.2. The same table gives estimates for the power output during the subsequent five stages.
- The test can be undertaken in the field using a running track. A pre-recorded tape and loudspeaker system is needed to control the running pace (see Tetgbur *et al.*, 1993).

10.13 PRACTICAL 5: HEART RATE DEFLECTION POINT (CONCONI TEST)

10.13.1 GENERAL PROTOCOL (RUNNING)

Following a 3-minute warm-up jog and some stretching, the subject completes an incremental protocol to maximal effort. The starting intensity is the lowest intensity shown in Table 10.2. Treadmill velocity is increased by 0.5 km h^{-1} every 200 m. Heart rate is recorded throughout using a short-range radio telemeter (Polar Sport Tester, Polar Electro Oy, Finland) or similar device set to 5 s recording intervals for immediate playback after exercise. The subject should press the electronic marker button on the telemeter at the end of each stage.

10.13.2 DATA ANALYSIS

Heart rate at the end of each 200 m stage is plotted against running speed. Heart rate deflection point is identified as the running speed at which linearity is lost in the HR–speed relationship.

10.13.3 ADDITIONAL HINTS

The test can be undertaken in the field using a running track. A pre-recorded tape and loudspeaker system are needed to control the running pace. The intensity should be increased according to distance covered (i.e. every 200 m) not according to time to remain true to Conconi's original work.

10.13.4 FURTHER ANALYSIS OPPORTUNITIES

- Determine inter-reviewer reliability by coding plots. Each person in a class can then be asked to identify the heart rate deflection point.
- Compare the heart rate deflection point determined by visual inspection with the same point determined using the software provided with the Polar Sport Tester radio telemetry unit.

ACKNOWLEDGEMENT

The authors would like to record their thanks to Dr Helen Carter for her help in the preparation of this chapter.

REFERENCES

Acavedo, E.O. and Goldfarb, A.H. (1989). Increased training intensity effects on plasma lactate, ventilatory threshold, and endurance. *Medicine and Science in Sports and Exercise,* **21**, 563–8.

Aunola, S. and Rusko, H. (1992). Does anaerobic threshold correlate with maximal lactate steady state? *Journal of Sports Sciences,* **10**, 309–23.

Barstow, T.J., Jones, A.M., Nguyen, P. and Casaburi, R. (1996). Influence of muscle fiber type and pedal frequency on oxygen uptake kinetics of heavy exercise. *Journal of Applied Physiology,* **81**, 1642–50.

Beaver, W.L., Wasserman, K. and Whipp, B.J. (1986). A new method for detecting anaerobic threshold by gas exchange. *Journal of Applied Physiology,* **60**, 2020–7.

Beneke, R. and Von Duvillard, S.P. (1996). Determination of maximal lactate steady state response in selected sports events. *Medicine and Science in Sports and Exercise,* **28**, 241–6.

Billat, V., Blondel, N. and Berthoin, S. (1999). Determination of the longest time to exhaustion at maximal oxygen uptake. *European Journal of Applied Physiology,* **80**, 159–61.

Billat, V.L. and Koralsztein, J.P. (1996). Significance of the velocity at $\dot{V}O_2$ max and time to exhaustion at this velocity. *Sports Medicine,* **22**, 90–108.

Billat, V.L., Dalmay, F., Antonini, M.T. and Chassain, A.P. (1994a). A method for determining the maximal steady state of blood lactate concentration from two levels of submaximal exercise. *European Journal of Applied Physiology,* **69**, 196–202.

Billat, V.L., Renoux, J.C., Pinoteau, J., *et al.* (1994b). Times to exhaustion at 100% of velocity at $\dot{V}O_2$max and modelling of the time-limit / velocity relationship in elite long-distance runners. *European Journal of Applied Physiology,* **69**, 271–3.

Borch, K.W., Ingjer, F., Larsen, S. and Tomten, S.E. (1993). Rate of accumulation of blood lactate during graded exercise as a predictor of "anaerobic threshold". *Journal of Sports Sciences,* **11**, 49–55.

Brooks, G.A. (1991). Current concepts in lactate exchange. *Medicine and Science in Sports and Exercise,* **23**, 895–906.

Bunc, V., Hofmann, P., Leitner, H. and Gaisl, G. (1995). Verification of the heart rate threshold. *European Journal of Applied Physiology,* **70**, 263–9.

Caiozzo, V.L., Davis, J.A., Ellis, J.F., *et al.* (1982). A comparison of gas exchange indices used to detect the anaerobic threshold. *Journal of Applied Physiology,* **53**, 1184–9.

Carter, H., Jones, A.M. and Doust, J.H. (1999a). Effect of incremental test protocol on the lactate minimum speed. *Medicine and Science in Sports and Exercise,* **31**, 837–45.

Carter, H., Jones, A.M. and Doust, J.H. (1999b). Effect of six weeks of endurance training on the lactate minimum speed. *Journal of Sports Sciences,* **17**, 957–67.

Casaburi, R., Storer, T.W., Ben-Dov, I. and Wasserman, K. (1987). Effect of endurance training on possible determinants of $\dot{V}O_2$ during heavy exercise. *Journal of Applied Physiology,* **62**, 199–207.

Cheng, B., Kuipers, H., Snyder, A.C., *et al.* (1992). A new approach for the determination of ventilatory and lactate thresholds. *International Journal of Sports Medicine,* **13**, 518–22.

Conconi, F., Ferrari, M., Ziglio, P.G., *et al.* (1982). Determination of the anaerobic threshold by a non-invasive field test in runners. *Journal of Applied Physiology,* **52**, 869–73.

Connett, R.J., Gayeski, T.E.J. and Honig, C.R. (1984). Lactate accumulation in fully aerobic, working, dog gracilis muscle. *American Journal of Physiology,* **246**, 120–8.

Connett, R.J., Gayeski, T.E.J. and Honig, C.R. (1985). Energy sources in fully aerobic work-rest transitions: a new role for glycolysis. *American Journal of Physiology,* **248**, 922–9.

Costill, D.L., Thomason, H. and Roberts, E. (1973). Fractional utilisation of the aerobic capacity during distance running. *Medicine and Science in Sports.* **5**, 248–52.

Coyle, E.F., Martin, W.H., Ehsani, A.A., *et al.* (1983). Blood lactate threshold in some well-trained ischemic heart disease patients. *Journal of Applied Physiology,* **54**, 18–23.

Davis, J.A. (1985). Anaerobic threshold: review of the concept and direction for future research. *Medicine and Science in Sports and Exercise,* **17**, 6–18.

De Vries, H.A., Moritani, T., Nagata, A. and Magnussen, K. (1982). The relation between critical power and neuromuscular fatigue as estimated from electromyographic data. *Ergonomics,* **25**, 783–91.

Donovan, C.M. and Pagliassotti, M.J. (1990). Enhanced efficiency of lactate removal after endurance training. *Journal of Applied Physiology*, **68**, 1053–8.

Droghetti, P., Borsetto, C., Casoni, I., *et al.* (1985). Non-invasive determination of the anaerobic threshold in canoeing, cross-country skiing, cycling, roller and ice-skating, rowing and walking. *European Journal of Applied Physiology*, **53**, 299–303.

Edwards, R.H.T. (1981). Human muscle function and fatigue. In *Human Muscle Fatigue: Physiological Mechanisms*. eds. R. Porter and J. Whelan (CIBA Foundations Symposium No. 82, Pitman Medical, London), pp. 1–18.

Farrell, P.A., Wilmore, J.H., Coyle, E.F., *et al.* (1979). Plasma lactate accumulation and distance running performance. *Medicine and Science in Sports*, **11**, 338–44.

Fay, L., Londeree, B.R., Lafontaine, T.P. and Volek, M.R. (1989). Physiological parameters related to distance running performance in female athletes. *Medicine and Science in Sports and Exercise*, **21**, 319–24.

Ferry, A., Duvallet, A. and Rieu, M. (1988). The effect of experimental protocol on the relationship between blood lactate and workload. *Journal of Sports Medicine and Physical Fitness*, **28**, 341–7.

Foxdal, P., Sjodin, B., Sjodin, A. and Ostman, B. (1994). The validity and accuracy of blood lactate measurements for prediction of maximal endurance running capacity: dependency of analysed blood media in combination with different designs of the exercise test. *International Journal of Sports Medicine*, **15**, 89–95.

Grazzi, G., Alfieri, N., Borsetto, C., *et al.* (1999). The power output / heart rate relationship in cycling: test standardization and repeatability. *Medicine and Science in Sports and Exercise*, **31**, 1478–83.

Gullstrand, L., Sjodin, B. and Svedenhag, J. (1994). Blood sampling during continuous running and 30-second intervals on a treadmill: effects on the lactate threshold results? *Scandinavian Journal of Science and Medicine in Sports*, **4**, 239–42.

Heck, H. and Hollmann, W. (1992). Identification, objectivity, and validity of Conconi threshold by cycle stress tests. *Osler Journal Sportsmedizin*, **22**, 35–53.

Heck, H., Mader, A., Hess, G., *et al.* (1985). Justification of the 4 mmol/l lactate threshold. *International Journal of Sports Medicine*, **6**, 117–30.

Henritze, J., Weltman, A., Schurrer, R.L. and Barlow, K. (1985). Effects of training at and above the lactate threshold on the lactate threshold and maximal oxygen uptake. *European Journal of Applied Physiology*, **54**, 84–8.

Hill, D.W. (1993). The critical power concept: a review. *Sports Medicine*, **16**, 237–54.

Hill, D.W. and Rowell, A. L. (1997). Response to exercise at the velocity associated with VO_2 max. *Medicine and Science in Sports and Exercise*, **29**, 113–6.

Hofmann, P., Bunc, V., Leinter, H., *et al.* (1994). Heart rate threshold related to lactate turnpoint and steady-state exercise on a cycle ergometer. *European Journal of Applied Physiology*, **69**, 132–9.

Honig, C.R., Connett, R.J. and Gayeski, T.E.J. (1992). O_2 transport and its interaction with metabolism: a systems view of aerobic capacity. *Medicine and Science in Sports and Exercise*, **24**, 47–53.

Housh, D.J., Housh, T.J. and Bauge, S.M. (1989). The accuracy of the critical power test for predicting time to exhaustion during cycle ergometry. *Ergonomics*, **32**, 997–1004.

Housh, T.J., De Vries, H.A., Housh, D.J., *et al.* (1991a). The relationship between critical power and the onset of blood lactate accumulation. *Journal of Sports Medicine and Physical Fitness*, **31**, 31–6.

Housh, T.J., Johnson, G.O., McDowell, S.L., *et al.* (1991b). Physiological responses at the fatigue threshold. *International Journal of Sports Medicine*, **12**, 305–8.

Hughes, E.F., Turner, S.C. and Brooks, G.A. (1982). Effects of glycogen depletion and pedalling speed on "anaerobic threshold". *Journal of Applied Physiology*, **52**, 1598–607.

Hughson, R.L., Cook, C.J. and Staudt, L.E. (1984). A high velocity treadmill running test to assess endurance running potential. *International Journal of Sports Medicine*, **5**, 23–5.

Hughson, R.L., Weisiger, K.H. and Swanson, G.D. (1987). Blood lactate concentration increases as a continuous function in progressive exercise. *Journal of Applied Physiology*, **62**, 1975–81.

Hurley, B.F., Hagberg, J.M., Allen, W.K., *et al.* (1984). Effect of training on blood lactate levels during submaximal exercise. *Journal of Applied Physiology*, **56**, 1260–4.

Ivy, J.L., Withers, R.T., Van Handel, P.J., *et al.* (1980). Muscle respiratory capacity and fiber type as determinants of the lactate threshold. *Journal of Applied Physiology*, **48**, 523–7.

Ivy, J.L., Costill, D.L., Van Handel, P.J., *et al.* (1981). Alteration in the lactate threshold with changes in substrate availability. *International Journal of Sports Medicine*, **48**, 523–7.

James, N.W., Adams, G.M. and Wilson, A.F. (1989). Determination of the anaerobic threshold by breathing frequency. *International Journal of Sports Medicine*, **10**, 192–6.

Jenkins, D.G. and Quigley, B.M. (1990). Blood lactate in trained cyclists during cycle ergometry at critical power. *European Journal of Applied Physiology*, **61**, 278–83.

Jenkins, D.G. and Quigley, B.M. (1992). Endurance training enhances critical power. *Medicine and Science in Sports and Exercise*, **24**, 1283–9.

Jobsis, F.F. and Stainsby, W.N. (1968). Oxidation of NADH during contractions of circulated mammalian skeletal muscle. *Respiration Physiology*, **4**, 292–300.

Jones, A.M. (1996). Heart rate, lactate threshold and endurance training. *Coaching Focus*, 12–13.

Jones, A.M. (1998). A five year physiological case study of an Olympic athlete. *British Journal of Sports Medicine*, **32**, 39–43.

Jones, A.M. and Doust, J.H. (1994). Disparity between exercise intensity at lactate threshold and at the 4 mM blood lactate reference value increases with maximal aerobic power in runners (abstract). *Journal of Sports Sciences*, **12**, 141.

Jones, A.M. and Doust, J.H. (1995). Lack of reliability in Conconi's heart rate deflection point. *International Journal of Sports Medicine*, **16**, 541–4.

Jones, A.M. and Doust, J.H. (1996). A 1% treadmill grade most accurately reflects the energetic cost of outdoor running. *Journal of Sports Sciences*, **14**, 321–7.

Jones, A.M. and Doust, J.H. (1997a). Specific considerations for the assessment of middle distance and long distance runners. In *British Association of Sport and Exercise Sciences Physiological Testing Guidelines*, 3rd edn. eds. S. Bird and R. Davison (BASES, Leeds, UK), pp. 108–11.

Jones, A.M. and Doust, J.H. (1997b). The Conconi test is not valid for estimation of the lactate turnpoint in runners. *Journal of Sports Sciences*, **15**, 385–94.

Jones, A.M. and Doust, J.H. (1998a). Assessment of the lactate and ventilatory thresholds by breathing frequency in runners. *Journal of Sports Sciences*, **16**, 667–75.

Jones, A.M. and Doust, J.H. (1998b). The validity of the lactate minimum test for determination of the maximal lactate steady state. *Medicine and Science in Sports and Exercise*, **30**, 1304–13.

Jones, A.M. and Doust, J.H. (1998c). The relationship between the individual anaerobic threshold, the lactate threshold, and the 4 mM blood lactate reference value during incremental treadmill exercise (abstract). *Journal of Sports Sciences*, **16**, 53.

Jones, A.M., Carter, H. and Doust, J.H. (1999). A disproportionate increase in VO_2 coincident with lactate threshold during treadmill exercise. *Medicine and Science in Sports and Exercise*, **31**, 1299–306.

Jones, N.L., Sutton, J.R., Taylor, R. and Toews, C.J. (1977). Effect of pH on cardiorespiratory and metabolic responses to exercise. *Journal of Applied Physiology*, **43**, 959–64.

Jorfeldt, L., Juhlin-Dabbfelt, A. and Karlsson, J. (1978). Lactate release in relation to tissue lactate in human skeletal muscle during exercise. *Journal of Applied Physiology*, **44**, 350–2.

Katch, V., Weltman, A., Sady, S. and Freedson, P. (1978). Validity of the relative percent concept for equating training intensity. *European Journal of Applied Physiology*, **39**, 219–27.

Keith, S.P., Jacobs, I. and McLellan, T.M. (1992). Adaptations to training at the individual anaerobic threshold. *European Journal of Applied Physiology*, **65**, 316–23.

Kindermann, W., Simon, G. and Keul, J. (1979). The significance of the aerobic-anaerobic transition for the determination of work load intensities during endurance training. *European Journal of Applied Physiology*, **42**, 25–34.

Kuipers, H., Keizer, H.A., De Vries, T., *et al.* (1988). Comparison of heart rate as a non-invasive determinant of anaerobic threshold with the lactate threshold when cycling. *European Journal of Applied Physiology*, **58**, 303–6.

Lafontaine, T.P., Londeree, B.R. and Spath, W.K. (1981). The maximal steady state versus selected running events. *Medicine and Science in Sports and Exercise*, **13**, 190–3.

Londeree, B.R. (1986). The use of laboratory test results with long distance runners. *Sports Medicine*, **3**, 201–13.

Londeree, B.R. (1997). Effect of training on lactate / ventilatory thresholds: a meta-analysis. *Medicine and Science in Sports and Exercise*, **29**, 837–43.

McLellan, T.M. and Jacobs, I. (1993). Reliability, reproducibility and validity of the individual anaerobic threshold. *European Journal of Applied Physiology*, **67**, 125–31.

MacRae, H., Dennis, S.C., Bosch, A.N. and Noakes, T.D. (1992). Endurance training vs. lactate production and removal. *Journal of Applied Physiology*, **73**, 2206–7.

Mader, A. (1991). Evaluation of the endurance performance of marathon runners and theoretical analysis of test results. *Journal of Sports Medicine and Physical Fitness*, **31**, 1–19.

Mader, A., Liesen, H., Heck, H., *et al.* (1976). Zur Beurteilung der sportartspezifischen Ausdauerleistungsfähigkeit im Labor. *Sport und Medizin*, **27**, 80–112.

Mazzeo, R.S. and Marshall, P. (1989). Influence of plasma catecholamines on the lactate threshold during graded cycling. *Journal of Applied Physiology*, **67**, 1319–22.

Mognoni, P., Sirtori, M.D., Lorenzelli, F. and Cerretelli, P. (1990). Physiological responses during prolonged exercise at the power output corresponding to the blood lactate threshold. *European Journal of Applied Physiology*, **60**, 239–43.

Monod, H. and Scherrer, J. (1965). The work capacity of a synergic muscle group. *Ergonomics*, **8**, 329–38.

Morgan, D.W., Baldini, F.D., Martin, P.E. and Kohrt, W.M. (1989). Ten kilometer performance and predicted velocity at $\dot{V}O_2$ max among well-trained male runners. *Medicine and Science in Sports and Exercise*, **21**, 78–83.

Moritani, T.A., Nagata, A., De Vries, H.A. and Muro, M. (1981). Critical power as a measure of physical work capacity and anaerobic threshold. *Ergonomics*, **24**, 339–50.

Nagata, A., Muro, M., Moritani, T. and Yoshida, T. (1981). Anaerobic threshold determination by blood lactate and myoelectric signals. *Japanese Journal of Physiology*, **31**, 85–97.

Newsholme, E.A., Blomstrand, E. and Ekblom, B. (1992). Physical and mental fatigue: metabolic mechanisms and importance of plasma amino acids. *British Medical Bulletin*, **48**, 477–95.

Orok, C.J., Hughson, R.L., Green, H.J. and Thomson, J.A. (1989). Blood lactate responses in incremental exercise as predictors of constant load performance. *European Journal of Applied Physiology*, **59**, 262–7.

Overend, T.J., Cunningham, D.A., Paterson, D.H. and Smith, W.D.F. (1992). Physiological responses of young and elderly men to prolonged exercise at critical power. *European Journal of Applied Physiology*, **64**, 187–93.

Oyono-Enguille, S., Heitz, A., Marbach, J., *et al.* (1990). Blood lactate during constant-load exercise at aerobic and anaerobic thresholds. *European Journal of Applied Physiology*, **60**, 321–30.

Pepper, M.L., Housh, T.J. and Johnson, G.O. (1992). The accuracy of the critical velocity test for predicting time to exhaustion during treadmill running. *International Journal of Sports Medicine*, **13**, 121–4.

Pierce, E.F., Weltman, A., Seip, R.L. and Snead, D. (1990). Effects of training specificity on the lactate threshold and $\dot{V}O_2$ peak. *International Journal of Sports Medicine*, **11**, 267–72.

Pokan, R., Hofmann, P., Preidler, K., *et al.* (1993). Correlation between inflection of heart rate / work performance curve and myocardial function in exhausting cycle ergometer exercise. *European Journal of Applied Physiology*, **67**, 385–8.

Pokan, R., Hofmann, P., Lehmann, M., *et al.* (1995). Heart rate deflection related to lactate performance curve and plasma catecholamine response during incremental cycle ergometer exercise. *European Journal of Applied Physiology*, **70**, 175–9.

Poole, D.C., Ward, S.A. and Whipp, B.J. (1988) The effects of training on the metabolic and respiratory profile of high-intensity cycle ergometer exercise. *European Journal of Applied Physiology*, **59**, 421–9.

Poole, D.C., Ward, S.A., Gardner, G.W. and Whipp, B.J. (1990). Metabolic and respiratory profile of the upper limit for prolonged exercise in man. *Ergonomics*, **3**, 1265–79.

Poole, D.C., Schaffartzik, W., Knight, D.R., *et al.* (1991). Contribution of exercising legs to the slow component of oxygen uptake kinetics in humans. *Journal of Applied Physiology*, **71**, 1245–53.

Ribeiro, J.P., Fielding, R.A., Hughes, V., *et al.* (1985). Heart rate breakpoint may coincide with the anaerobic and not the aerobic threshold. *International Journal of Sports Medicine*, **6**, 224–34.

Ribeiro, J.P., Hughes, V., Fielding, R.A., *et al.* (1986). Metabolic and ventilatory responses to steady state exercise relative to lactate thresholds. *International Journal of Sports Medicine*, **6**, 220–4.

Robergs, R.A., Chwalbinska-Moneta, J., Mitchell, J.B., *et al.* (1990). Blood lactate threshold differences between arterialised and venous blood. *International Journal of Sports Medicine*, **11**, 446–51.

Roberts, D. and Smith, D.J. (1989). Biochemical aspects of peripheral muscle fatigue: a review. *Sports Medicine*, **7**, 125–38.

Sjodin, B. and Jacobs, I. (1981). Onset of blood lactate accumulation and marathon running performance. *International Journal of Sports Medicine*, **2**, 23–6.

Sjodin, B., Jacobs, I. and Svedenhag, J. (1982). Changes in onset of blood lactate accumulation

(OBLA) and muscle enzymes after training at OBLA. *European Journal of Applied Physiology*, **49**, 45–57.

Skinner, J.S. and McLellan, T.H. (1980). The transition from aerobic to anaerobic metabolism. *Research Quarterly for Exercise and Sports*, **51**, 234–48.

Snyder, A.C., Woulfe, T., Welsh, R. and Foster, C. (1994). A simplified approach to estimating the maximal lactate steady state. *International Journal of Sports Medicine*, **15**, 27–31.

Stegmann, H., Kindermann, W. and Schnabel, A. (1981). Lactate kinetics and individual anaerobic threshold. *International Journal of Sports Medicine*, **2**, 160–5.

Stegmann, H. and Kindermann, W. (1982). Comparison of prolonged exercise tests at the individual anaerobic threshold and the fixed anaerobic threshold of 4 mmol/l lactate. *International Journal of Sports Medicine*, **3**, 105–10.

Talmadge, R.J., Scheide, J.I. and Silverman, H. (1989). Glycogen synthesis from lactate in a chronically active muscle. *Journal of Applied Physiology*, **66**, 2231–8.

Tegtbur, U., Busse, M.W. and Braumann, K.M. (1993). Estimation of an individual equilibrium between lactate production and catabolism during exercise. *Medicine and Science in Sports and Exercise*, **25**, 620–7.

Tokmakidis, S.P. and Leger, L. (1992). Comparison of mathematically determined blood lactate and heart rate 'threshold' points and relationship with performance. *European Journal of Applied Physiology*, **641**, 309–17.

Wakayoshi, K., Yoshida, T., Udo, M., *et al.* (1992). The determination and validity of critical speed as an index of swimming performance in the competitive swimmer. *European Journal of Applied Physiology*, **64**, 153–7.

Walsh, M.L. and Banister, E.W. (1988). Possible mechanisms of the anaerobic threshold – a review. *Sports Medicine*, **5**, 269–302.

Wasserman, K., Beaver, W.L. and Whipp, B.J. (1990). Gas exchange theory and the lactic acidosis (anaerobic) threshold. *Circulation*, **81 (Suppl II)**, 14–30.

Wasserman, K., Whipp, B.J., Koyal, S.N. and Beaver W.L. (1973). Anaerobic threshold and respiratory gas exchange during exercise. *Journal of Applied Physiology*, **35**, 236–43.

Wasserman, K., Beaver, W.L., Davis, J.A., *et al.* (1985). Lactate, pyruvate, and the lactate-to-pyruvate ratio during exercise and recovery. *Journal of Applied Physiology*, **59**, 935–40.

Weltman, A. (1989). The lactate threshold and endurance performance. *Advances in Sports Medicine and Fitness*, **2**, 91–116.

Weltman, A., Snead, D. and Seip, R. (1990). Percentages of maximal heart rate, heart rate reserve and $\dot{V}O_2$ max for determining endurance training intensity in male runners. *International Journal of Sports Medicine*, **11**, 218–22.

Weltman, A., Seip, R.L., Snead, D., *et al.* (1992). Exercise training at and above the lactate threshold in previously untrained women. *International Journal of Sports Medicine*, **13**, 257–63.

Whipp, B.J. (1994). The slow component of O_2 uptake kinetics during heavy exercise. *Medicine and Science in Sports and Exercise*, **26**, 1319–26.

Whipp, B.J. and Mahler, M. (1980). Dynamics of pulmonary gas exchange during exercise. In *Pulmonary Gas Exchange (Vol. II)*. ed. J.B. West (Academic Press, New York), pp. 33–96.

Whipp, B.J. and Ward, S.A. (1990). Physiological determinants of pulmonary gas exchange kinetics during exercise. *Medicine and Science in Sports and Exercise*, **22**, 62–71.

Williams, J.R., Armstrong, N. and Kirby, B.J. (1992). The influence of the site of sampling and assay medium upon the measurement and interpretation of blood lactate responses to exercise. *Journal of Sports Sciences*, **10**, 95–107.

Womack, C.J., Davis, S.E., Blumer, J.L., *et al.* (1995). Slow component of O_2 uptake during heavy exercise: adaptation to endurance training. *Journal of Applied Physiology*, **79**, 838–45.

Yeh, M.P., Gardner, R.M., Adams, T.W., *et al.* (1983). 'Anaerobic threshold': problems of determination and validation. *Journal of Applied Physiology*, **55**, 1178–86.

Yoshida, T. (1984). Effect of exercise duration during incremental exercise on the determination of anaerobic threshold and the onset of blood lactate accumulation. *European Journal of Applied Physiology*, **53**, 196–9.

ASSESSMENT OF MAXIMAL-INTENSITY EXERCISE

Edward M. Winter and Don P. MacLaren

11.1 AIMS

The aims in this chapter are to:
- provide students with an understanding of techniques for assessing maximal-intensity exercise,
- describe the development of cycle ergometer-based assessments of peak power output,
- describe the concept of anaerobic capacity,
- describe techniques for direct (invasive) and indirect (non-invasive) estimation of anaerobic metabolism.

11.2 INTRODUCTION

Maximal-intensity exercise refers to exercise that is performed 'all-out'. It should not be confused with intensities of exercise which elicit a maximal physiological response. For instance, maximal oxygen uptake (VO_2 max) can be elicited by intensities of exercise that are only a third or quarter of maximal-intensity exercise (Williams, 1987).

Movement does not always occur during maximal-intensity exercise. The scrum in rugby and maintenance of the crucifix and balance in gymnastics are examples where maximal force production occurs during isometric muscle activity. Durations of exercise are short and range from approximately 1 to 2 seconds in discrete activities like the shot-put and golf swing to 20 to 45 seconds of sprinting during running and cycling. Even in these latter activities, there is probably an element of pacing rather than genuinely all-out effort. Also,

associated mechanisms of energy release are predominantly anaerobic but they are not exclusively so. During 30 s of 'flat out' cycling, for example, 13–29% of energy provision could come from aerobic sources (Inbar *et al.*, 1976; Bar-Or, 1987).

The purpose of this section is to outline current developments in assessments of maximal-intensity exercise. Special attention is given to those that use cycle ergometry, and investigations into accompanying metabolism.

11.3 TERMINOLOGY

Maximal-intensity exercise can be assessed in different ways, and care should be taken to ensure that descriptions of performance adhere to principles of mechanics. These descriptions can be categorized into one of three broad groups. First, and the most basic, are scalar quantities such as time (s), distance (m) and speed (m s^{-1}). In the field, time is probably the most widely used measure and is employed to assess performance in activities such as running, swimming and cycling; distance is used to assess performance in activities which involve throwing and jumping, either for height or distance; and speed can be used to assess performance when both time taken and distance moved are known.

Next are vector quantities such as force (F), impulse (N s) and momentum (kg m s^{-1}), which are assessments that tend to be laboratory,

Kinanthropometry and Exercise Physiology Laboratory Manual: Tests, Procedures and Data. 2nd Edition, Volume 2: Exercise Physiology Edited by RG Eston and T Reilly. Published by Routledge, London, June 2001

rather than field, based. Thirdly, there are measures of energy which also tend to be laboratory-based and concern either energy expended (J) or mechanical power output (W). Clearly, power output is only one measure of maximal-intensity exercise, yet there is a tendency to assume it is the only measure of this type of performance. Indeed, Adamson and Whitney (1971) and Smith (1972) addressed this point in detail and suggested that, in explosive activities such as jumping, the use of power is meaningless and unjustified. Horizontal velocity in sprinting and vertical velocity in jumping are determined by impulse. Consequently, it is the impulse-generating capability of muscle, not its power-producing capability, that is the determinant of effective performance.

Unless the units of performance are watts, performance cannot be described as power. Even when these units are used and the description appears to be sound, underlying theoretical bases might not be sustainable.

These considerations are important because they influence the purpose of assessments. Performance per se could be the focus in studies that investigate the effects of training. An assessment could also be used to investigate changes in metabolism brought about by training or growth. The integrity of the procedure has to be sound, otherwise the insight into underlying mechanisms could be obscured. An understanding of principles of mechanics is a prerequisite of effective test selection and subsequent description of measures.

11.4 HISTORICAL BACKGROUND

Concerted interest in maximal-intensity exercise has a long history which can be traced back to 1885, when Marey and Demeney introduced a force platform to investigate mechanisms that underpinned jumping (Cavagna, 1975). Investigations into how muscle functions were based on studies of isolated mammalian and amphibian tissue (Hill, 1913). Attention turned to humans and investigations into $\dot{V}O_2$ at running speeds that were in excess

of those that could be maintained at steady state (Hill and Lupton, 1922; Sargent, 1926; Furusawa *et al.*, 1927) and attempts to determine mechanical efficiency and equations to describe motion during maximal-intensity exercise (Lupton, 1923; Best and Partridge, 1928, 1929).

In 1921 D.A. Sargent introduced a jump test which is still used today. Shortly afterwards, L.W. Sargent (1924) suggested that the test could be used as a measure of power, and the Lewis nomogram (Fox *et al.*, 1988) has been suggested as a means to estimate power output from vertical jump data in spite of the forcible objections stated earlier by Adamson and Whitney (1971) and Smith (1972).

Investigations into the mechanics of bicycle pedalling during high-intensity exercise also have a long history (Dickinson, 1928; Fenn, 1932; Hill, 1934). So too have attempts to increase the sensitivity of assessment in this type of exercise. Kelso and Hellebrandt (1932) introduced an ergometer that used a direct current generator to apply resistive force, and Tuttle and Wendler (1945) modified the design so that alternating current could be used. It was not until Fleisch (1950) and Von Döbeln (1954) introduced their forerunners that inexpensive friction-braked devices became available commercially. It was a further twenty or so years before these types of ergometer had a marked impact on studies into maximal intensity exercise (Cumming, 1974). Moreover, developments in microprocessor-based data logging systems (McClenaghan and Literowitch, 1987) improved the sensitivity and practicality of assessments.

In 1938 Hill published one of the most influential reports on muscle function ever written, in which he described the relationship between the force a muscle can exert and the accompanying speed with which it can shorten. This has become known as the muscle force–velocity relationship. Hill was remarkably modest about this work and claimed later that he 'stumbled upon it' (Hill, 1970, p. 3) and that Fenn and Marsh (1935) had actually outlined a similar relationship already. A major point to be emphasized here is that peak power output is produced by an optimum load; if the load is either too great or too low, a muscle or group of muscles will not exert peak power output. This presents major implications for meaningful assessments of peak power output during maximal-intensity exercise.

11.5 SCREENING

Tests of maximal-intensity exercise are strenuous and might produce feelings of nausea or giddiness. It is important that potential subjects are recruited by means of suitable pre-test medical questionnaires.

11.6 PROCEDURES FOR ASSESSING MAXIMAL-INTENSITY EXERCISE

There is a variety of procedures for assessing maximal-intensity exercise. Cycle ergometer tests are the most common and these can be categorized into one of four groups; (a) 'Wingate' type procedures, (b) optimization procedures, (c) correction procedures, (d) isokinetic procedures. The first three of these procedures use friction-braked devices, whereas the isokinetic group uses more elaborate control systems which restrain pedalling to constant velocity. Other procedures include other forms of isokinetic testing, treadmill and field assessments. Details of laboratory procedures for the above tests are outlined at the end of this chapter.

11.6.1 WINGATE-TYPE PROCEDURES

The Wingate Anaerobic Test, so named because it was developed at the Wingate Institute in Israel, was introduced as a prototype by Ayalon *et al.* (1974). Since then it has been refined and a comprehensive description was published later (Bar-Or, 1981) and subsequently reviewed (Bar-Or, 1987). Its use has become widespread. Subjects have to pedal flat out for 30 s on a cycle ergometer against an external resistive load which usually is equivalent to 7½% of body weight for Monark-type ergometers and 4% on Fleisch systems (see Practical 1).

In the original Wingate Anaerobic Test, three measures of performance were recorded: peak power output, mean power output and power decay. For the purposes of recording, the test was subdivided into six 5-s blocks and peak power output invariably occurred in the first 5 seconds. Although mean power output was demonstrated to be a robust measure and could withstand variations above and below the proposed optimum (Dotan and Bar-Or, 1983), reservations were expressed about the integrity of peak power output. Sargeant *et al.* (1981) suggested that the fixed load of 7½% of body weight was unlikely to satisfy Hill's force–velocity relationships, so casting doubt on this particular measure. Later, Bar-Or (1987) acknowledged that this might be the case, and confirmation was provided by Winter *et al.* (1987, 1989). Consequently, it is advisable to omit this measure from data summaries.

Time to peak power can be of interest, although the importance placed upon this particular measure depends to a large extent on the timing system that is used. With rolling starts, the precise beginning of the test is difficult to identify. While a stationary start would resolve this issue, it is difficult to set the system in motion from standstill.

After the highest value of power output is produced, and although maximal effort is continued, performance begins to deteriorate as fatigue sets in. At first sight it is tempting to suggest that mechanisms of adenosine triphosphate (ATP) synthesis are being demonstrated and that performance can be partitioned into alactic and lactacid phases. However, studies that have used muscle biopsy techniques have demonstrated clearly that lactic acid is produced from the moment all-out exercise begins, not when phosphocreatine stores are depleted (Boobis, 1987). Consequently, use of the terms alactacid and lactacid should be avoided.

Blood lactate provides some insights into underlying metabolism, although there are some points of caution that have to be considered. Peak blood lactate concentration [HLa] occurs some minutes after exercise has ended and, coincidentally, tends to correspond with feelings of nausea. Efflux of lactic acid from muscle cells into interstitial fluid and then into blood takes time, and not all of the lactic acid that is produced enters the circulation. Some of it is used by muscle cells as substrate (Brooks, 1986) and some is removed from the circulation before subsequent sampling occurs. This is a timely reminder that, although blood lactate can be a useful indicator of metabolism, when non-steady-state exercise is under examination, it might well provide a less than clear window through which mechanisms can be viewed.

Differences in performance are partly attributable to differences in body size between subjects, so ways to partition out size have to be introduced. This scaling, as it is called, is currently an area of renewed interest (Nevill *et al.*, 1992; Winter, 1992) although early considerations date back more than forty years ago (Tanner, 1949). It is now appreciated that the construction of straightforward ratio standards, in which a performance variable is simply divided by an anthropometric characteristic such as body mass, probably misleads by distorting the data under investigation. Comparisons between subjects, especially when there are marked differences in size – say, between men and women, or adults and children – should be based on *power function ratios* (Nevill *et al.*, 1992; Welsman *et al.*, 1993; Winter *et al.*, 1993; Eston *et al.*, 1997) that are obtained from the allometric relationship between performance and anthropometric variables (Schmidt-Nielsen, 1984). This issue is discussed in more detail in Volume 1, Chapter 11 by Winter and Nevill.

Another feature that appears to be clear, but upon further investigation is seen to be more complicated, is the expression of fatigue profiles. It would be tempting to suggest that after training, the difference between peak power output and the succeeding lowest value would

decrease, but this is not necessarily the case (Bird and Davison, 1997). Training can produce a higher peak so that fatigue appears actually to increase, and there is no clear explanation for this observation. Possibilities could be a change in force–velocity characteristics of muscle that are not accommodated by the fixed resistive load, technicalities over the way in which performance is expressed, or other as-yet-unidentified factors associated with the skill required to perform the test. This is a rich area for further research.

In summary, the Wingate Anaerobic Test is a useful laboratory procedure to demonstrate how fatigue occurs. The fixed external resistive force might not satisfy muscle force–velocity relationships, so values of peak power output are probably affected adversely. Blood lactate does not necessarily provide a full insight into the underlying metabolism. Fatigue profiles are ambiguous. Differences in the size of subjects should be scaled out using allometry (see Volume 1, Chapter 11 by Winter and Nevill).

11.6.2 OPTIMIZATION PROCEDURES

Anxieties about the potential inability of fixed external loads to satisfy muscle force–velocity relationships led to the development of alternative procedures which provide theoretically sound indications of peak power output. The concern is not simply with a single isolated muscle, but groups of muscles *in vivo* whose leverage characteristics undergo constant change throughout a complete mechanical cycle.

The availability of 'drop-loading' basket ergometers has played a key role in developments whose origins date back over seventy years to when Dickinson (1929) identified an inverse linear relationship between peak pedalling rate and applied load. Vandewalle *et al.* (1985) and Nakamura *et al.* (1985) used the principle to calculate optimized peak power output on the basis of flywheel-derived data. Acknowledging the reservations about the use of instantaneous values of power output expressed by Adamson and Whitney (1971) and Smith (1972), Winter *et al.* (1991) modified the protocol and recorded movements of the pedals.

The relationship between peak pedalling rate in rev min^{-1} (R) and applied load (L) is in the form:

$$R = a + bL$$

where:

a = intercept of the line of best fit
b = slope of the line of best fit.

On Monark ergometers, one revolution of the pedal crank moves a point on the flywheel a distance of 6 m. Consequently, an expression for power output (W) can be produced as:

$$1\,W = 1\,J\,s^{-1} = 1\,N\,m\,s^{-1}$$

$$\text{then Power} = \frac{R}{60} \times 6\,m \times L\,(\text{newtons})$$

$$\therefore \text{Power} = \frac{(a+bL)}{60} \times 6\,m \times L\,(\text{newtons})$$

$$\therefore \text{Power} = \frac{aL}{10} + \frac{bL^2}{10}$$

We can use differential calculus to help us interpret the relationship. By differentiating the power / load expression, which is a quadratic relationship, the gradient at any point on the curve can be identified:

$$\frac{dW}{dL} = a + 2bL$$

At the top of the curve, the gradient is zero:

$$\therefore 0 = a + 2bL$$

$$\therefore L = \frac{-a}{2b}$$

Substituting this value of L in the original equation yields the optimized peak power output:

$$\text{Optimized peak power} = \frac{a\left(\frac{-a}{2b}\right)}{10} + \frac{b\left(\frac{-a}{2b}\right)^2}{10}$$

$$= \frac{-0.025a^2}{b}$$

Thus, three key measures of performance can be identified: the optimized peak power output; the load corresponding to the optimized peak power output, and the pedalling rate corresponding to optimized peak power output. Assessment of these measures is exemplified in Practical 2.

Seemingly, optimization procedures are useful and they increase the sensitivity with which maximal intensity exercise can be assessed. However, the protocols are considerably longer than the Wingate Anaerobic Test, even if, as Nakamura *et al.* (1985) suggested, only three loads are used to establish the regression equation that provides the basis for calculating the optimized peak power output. Furthermore, while peak values are identified, the protocols do not assess fatigue profiles, and this is a distinct limitation. Nevertheless, the protocols have one distinct advantage; because body weight is supported, they isolate activity to the legs and remove potentially contaminating effects from the trunk, head and arms. Similarly, they could be applied to investigations of performance characteristics of the arms. Coupled with this is an especially useful anthropometric technique that can assess the total and lean volume of the leg (Jones and Pearson, 1969) and meaningful comparisons of performance capabilities between groups can be made.

Winter *et al.* (1991) and Eston *et al.* (1997) compared maximal-intensity exercise of men and women and found that there were distinct differences in performance that were independent of differences in the size of the leg. These studies also demonstrated the importance of applying correct scaling procedures. Similarly, the techniques have been used to compare children and adults (Winter *et al.*, 1993) where it is suggested that traditional ratio standard measures overestimate children's maximal intensity exercise.

In summary, optimization procedures appear to satisfy muscle force–velocity relationships and produce theoretically sound assessments of peak power output. Useful studies can be performed when optimization is coupled with anthropometric procedures that assess limb volumes. Optimization procedures do not produce valid fatigue profiles.

11.6.3 CORRECTION PROCEDURES

Optimization procedures are not the only tests that have been proposed for friction-braked cycle ergometers. The completeness of calculations that are used to determine the optimized peak power output have been questioned by Lakomy (1986) who pointed out that the external resistive load does not necessarily account for all the forces applied to the pedals and transmitted to an ergometer's flywheel. Clearly, as the flywheel is accelerated, a force greater than the resistive load is applied to the system and this extra force is ignored in traditional calculations of mechanical work done and hence power output.

Lakomy (1986) determined an 'acceleration balancing load' (*EL*) which was identified by plotting deceleration of the flywheel from 150 rev min^{-1} against the conventional resistive force. As a result, the effective load, i.e. the actual force applied could be calculated as:

Effective load (*F*) = resistive load (*RL*) + excess load (*EL*)

The value of *F* could then be multiplied by the velocity of the flywheel to provide an instantaneous value of power output. By introducing this correction, Lakomy (1985) demonstrated that the lightest loads produced peak power output. A commercially available kit (Concept II, Nottingham, UK) which contains a fly-wheel-mounted generator and related computer software can be used with Monark friction-braked ergometers. A similar system was developed by Bassett (1989). By using the kit, simultaneously data can be logged from the flywheel to calculate corrected peak power output, and from the pedals to calculate the optimized peak power output.

As can be seen from the data generated in Practical 3, although the relationship between data generated by optimization and correction procedures is high, the two methods can produce different results. The explanation for this could be technical in that it is associated with the precision of measurement, but the sensitivity of measurement procedures suggests that this is unlikely. The reason could still be technical because of the procedures for calculating power output which are, of course, distinctly different. The value for the optimized peak power output is calculated at peak velocity for a complete mechanical cycle of activity, whereas the corrected peak power output is based on products of force and instantaneous velocity. This latter procedure has been questioned by Adamson and Whitney (1971) and Smith (1972). While these products yield the units of power, the meaningfulness of using W is still not clear. Correction procedures are based on systems in which acceleration occurs, and in Section 11.3 it was pointed out that acceleration and hence change in momentum is attributable not to power but to preceding impulse. Hence, it is the impulse-generating capability of muscle that is manifest, but it is described in terms of power. Nevertheless, although there is a difference between the optimized peak power output and the corrected peak power output, the difference is systematic and the association between the variables is particularly strong.

Clearly, this unresolved debate impacts directly on our understanding of how muscle functions and, in particular, how it functions in concert with skeletal, neurophysiological and metabolic systems *in vivo*. Winter *et al.* (1996) have compared the optimized peak power output and the corrected peak power output, but no studies have been undertaken to compare the way in which these values reflect changes in performance brought about by training. From a practical point of view, correction procedures are easier to administer than optimization tests because only one bout of exercise has to be performed. On the other hand, optimization procedures satisfy muscle force–velocity relationships and appear to be sound theoretically. This area is still a rich field for further investigation.

11.6.4 ISOKINETIC SYSTEMS

Before the advent of optimization and correction procedures, isokinetic systems were introduced to assess peak power output in a way that satisfied muscle force–velocity relationships.

Sargeant *et al.* (1981) designed an ergometer in which the pedals were driven at constant angular velocity by an external electric motor and forces applied to the pedals were detected by strain gauges attached to the pedal cranks. By altering pedalling rate externally, force–velocity relationships were explored. McCartney *et al.* (1983) developed a similar system but, in this case, the pedals of the ergometer are driven by the subject until an electric motor restricts any further acceleration of the system.

The acquisition of data from these systems is demanding. Data have to be transmitted from a rotating device via a slip ring, and this can introduce noise into the signals which can be difficult to suppress. Also, previously questioned instantaneous values of power output are calculated from the products of force and velocity. Conversely, calibration is easier than in friction-braked systems. In the latter, frictional losses from the chain and bearing assemblies are not usually considered, whereas in the former, especially with the motor-driven version, these losses are irrelevant. The assessment of peak power output using a conventional isokinetic dynamometry system has also been compared to the traditional Wingate test (Baltzopoulos *et al.*, 1988).

11.6.5 NON-MOTORIZED TREADMILLS

While cycle ergometry has a number of key advantages, there is one major limitation: it is task-specific and does not necessarily reflect performance in running. Within the last decade attempts have been made to redress this problem by means of non-motorized treadmills in which the subject drives the belt of the treadmill. These systems can be used to assess power output whilst running horizontally (Lakomy, 1984). Subjects are tethered to the apparatus by a suitable harness that contains a force transducer that registers the horizontal forces exerted. These forces and the treadmill speed provide the basis for calculation.

It has been reported that substantial periods of habituation are required before valid data can be obtained (Gamble *et al.*, 1988). Nevertheless, this type of assessment has been used successfully to examine mechanical characteristics of running (Cheetham and Williams, 1985; Cheetham *et al.*, 1986).

Recent developments in the design of treadmills have renewed interest in the use of this form of ergometry to assess exercise capabilities of humans (Jaskólski *et al.*, 1996; Jaskólska *et al.*, 1999). Jaskólski *et al.* (1996) attempted to identify optimal resistances that maximized external peak power output, and Jaskólska *et al.* (1999) compared muscle force–velocity relationships during treadmill running and cycling. The improved sensitivity of these systems and their continued development suggest that they will be used in further studies of exercise performance and underlying metabolism.

11.6.6 MULTIPLE-SPRINT TYPE PROTOCOLS

Maximal-intensity exercise might have to be performed in repeated bouts interspersed with periods of rest. This intermittent form of exercise is typified in what have been termed multiple-sprint sports (Williams, 1987) such as soccer, hockey and racket games, and is probably the most common type of activity in sport. Common though it is, this type of activity is difficult to model, but the challenge has been met by proposals of field-based and laboratory-based procedures.

Léger and Lambert (1982) devised a shuttle running type protocol in which subjects ran 20 m lengths in time to a metronome. Running speed increased progressively until volitional exhaustion occurred. Since then this system has been commercialized (Brewer *et al.*, 1988).

Wootton and Williams (1983) used cycle ergometry, and subjects performed 5 bouts of exercise, each of which lasted 6 s with a 30 s rest between bouts. Bird and Davison (1997) suggested 10 × 6 s sprints and outlined other field- and laboratory-based procedures. Non-motorized treadmills have been used (Hamilton *et al.*, 1991; Nevill *et al.*, 1993) in which up to 30 repeated sprints are required. By various means, there have been concerted attempts to develop protocols that model multiple-sprint activities in controlled ways.

Studies have investigated the effects of: hot environments on shuttle running performance (Morris *et al.*, 1998); creatine supplementation in repeated sprint swimming (Peyrebrune *et al.*, 1998); and branched-chain amino acids and carbohydrate on fatigue during intermittent, high-intensity running (Davis *et al.*, 1999). Muscle soreness induced by shuttle running has also been examined (Thompson *et al.*, 1999), as has the effect of intermittent high-intensity exercise on neuromuscular performance (Mercer *et al.*, 1998). It is likely that these types of assessment will be used increasingly as investigations into metabolism and mechanisms of fatigue continue.

11.7 ASSESSMENT OF METABOLISM

There have been developments in procedures for assessing maximal-intensity exercise, and both the sensitivity and integrity of measures have been improved in recent years. While performance can be quantified and underlying metabolic processes demonstrated, quantification of this underlying metabolism is still a considerable challenge. By way of comparison, the criterial standard for aerobic exercise is maximum oxygen uptake ($\dot{V}O_2$ max), but as Williams (1990) queried: why should this be so? The problem is to measure the contribution from anaerobic energy releasing mechanisms up to and including the maximum contribution, i.e. a person's anaerobic capacity. Immediately a dilemma is presented: anaerobic capacity could be expressed as an amount, but the concern is more likely to be with the rate at which energy can be released and the length of time for which this release can be sustained. Furthermore, it was reported in Section 11.2 that, even in a short-duration test like the Wingate Anaerobic Test, aerobic mechanisms account for ~20% of total energy provision. We have also already seen that previous suggestions that maximal-intensity exercise could be

partitioned into alactacid and lactacid phases are now known to be simplifications; energy release from high-energy phosphagens and glycolysis occurs simultaneously, not sequentially.

In spite of these difficulties, techniques that attempt to assess anaerobic capacity have been devised and can be categorized into 'direct' and 'indirect' determinations (Bangsbo, 1997). The direct measures include the use of muscle biopsies before and immediately after any form of muscle contractions, or the use of ^{31}P magnetic resonance spectroscopy if the muscle is electrically stimulated or made to perform isometrically. Indirect measures, on the other hand, are based on the concept of the oxygen deficit.

11.7.1 DIRECT ESTIMATION OF ANAEROBIC METABOLISM

During maximal- and high-intensity exercise, decreases in muscle ATP and in phosphocreatine (PCr) are observed along with an increase in lactate. It is possible therefore to quantify the anaerobic energy production if determinations of the changes in these metabolites are made immediately following the exercise. This quantification has only been made possible after the introduction of the muscle biopsy technique (Bergström, 1962). In essence, the process requires the muscle under investigation to be identified before a small area on the surface is sterilized and then a local anaesthetic injected beneath the surface of the skin. A small incision of the skin and subcutaneous tissue is made initially before cutting through the muscle fascia. A hollow biopsy needle can then be inserted through the incision to the depth required before aspiration is applied. Aspiration causes a small portion of the muscle to 'bulge' into a small window at the side of the biopsy needle where it is cut by a sharp blade inside the hollow of the needle. The needle is then withdrawn and the sample is immediately frozen in liquid nitrogen. When this process is used for the determination of phosphagen stores (i.e. ATP + PCr) following high-intensity exercise, speed of sampling and freezing the muscle tissue is necessary since some resynthesis is possible.

Table 11.1 provides data from selected studies in which the muscle biopsy technique has been used for the estimation of anaerobic energy production from phosphagens and glycolysis before and immediately after maximal-intensity exercise of varying time periods. The findings are based on calculations of the decrease in muscle ATP and PCr, and the increase in muscle lactate from muscle samples taken both at rest and immediately after exercise. The highest rates of anaerobic energy production for PCr and for glycolysis during dynamic exercise lasting up to 10 s are 5·1 and 9·3 mmol kg^{-1} s^{-1} respectively. When the dynamic exercise is increased to 30 s, the highest rates of ATP produced anaerobically from PCr and glycolysis are 1.9 and 5·9 mmol kg^{-1} s^{-1} respectively. These values are mean rates over the 10 or 30 s exercise bouts, and the actual peak rates would be expected to occur within the first second or so. Indeed the change in power output during a 30 s Wingate test reflects the maximal rates of ATP being engendered within the muscle from these anaerobic sources as well as the aerobic contribution.

There are problems with the estimations calculated from the muscle biopsy data. First, there is the time delay in getting the muscle sample frozen following exercise. This procedure involves stopping the activity, immobilizing the leg, taking the biopsy, and then transferring the sample to the liquid nitrogen; a series of events that can take between 10 and 20 s. Nevertheless, Soderlund and Hultman (1986) have shown that ATP and PCr concentrations in muscle biopsy samples are not significantly affected by a delay in freezing. A second problem is the difficulty in determining the muscle mass involved in whole-body exercise, and therefore the metabolic response of the biopsied muscle may not be representative of all those muscles engaged in the exercise. Finally, the amount of energy related to the release of lactate into the blood from the

muscle is not taken into account in the calculations presented in Table 11.1, so the anaerobic energy production from glycolysis is underestimated. It is difficult to determine the volume in which lactate is diluted. Bangsbo (1997) suggested that the likely underestimation for a 75 kg individual is between 5.2% and 25.6% for maximal-intensity exercise of 30 s duration. The lower value is based on a dilution volume of 6 litres (i.e. blood volume), whereas the higher value is based on a dilution volume of 30 litres (i.e. total body fluids). Even these calculations do not take account of the lactate metabolized by inactive muscles and by the heart.

In spite of these limitations outlined above, there is a consistency in the data on rates of anaerobic ATP production during maximal-intensity exercise from the various studies. Indeed, the data from a recent study involving twenty electrically evoked maximal isometric actions of the anterior tibialis muscle using both magnetic resonance spectroscopy and muscle biopsy demonstrated that there was little difference in the muscle concentration of PCr, although differences were found in the estimates of ATP and changes in lactate (Constantin-Teodosiu *et al.*, 1997). The significantly higher muscle lactate concentrations estimated using magnetic resonance spectroscopy accounted for ~30% greater estimation of ATP turnover.

All the studies reported so far have documented the metabolic response of mixed muscle to maximal intensity exercise without recourse to possible variations in fibre type. Some recent investigations have separated single fibres and measured ATP, PCr, and glycogen of one fibre type at rest, during muscle action and in recovery (Soderlund *et al.*, 1992; Greenhaff *et al.*, 1994; Casey *et al.*, 1996). The conclusions from these studies are that during maximal-intensity exercise, type II fibres compared with type I fibres produce a greater rate of PCr degradation, a greater rate of glycolysis and a slower rate of resynthesis of PCr.

As many sports can be classified as multiple-sprint sports, there have been developments in

Table 11.1 Estimated total anaerobic ATP production, rate of anaerobic ATP production and % contribution from PCr and glycolysis during dynamic exercise

Reference	Type of exercise	Duration (s)	Total ATP produced ($mmol\,kg^{-1}$)	Rate of ATP produced ($mmol\,kg^{-1}\,s^{-1}$) PCr	Rate of ATP produced ($mmol\,kg^{-1}\,s^{-1}$) Glycolysis	% contribution PCr	% contribution Glycolysis
Boobis et al. (1982)	Cycle	0–6	63	4.9	4.8	47	53
		0–30	189	1.9	4.0	30	64
Jones et al. (1985)	Isokinetic cycle 60 rpm	0–10	166	5.1	8.0	42	58
		0–30	291	1.4	5.8	21	79
	140 rpm	0–10	173	4.4	9.3	35	65
		0–30	240	0.7	6.5	11	89
McCartney et al. (1986)	Isokinetic cycle 100 rpm	0–30	228	1.4	5.9	23	77
Cheetham et al. (1986)	Run	0–30	183	1.9	3.8	38	62
Nevill et al. (1989)	Run	0–30	186	1.9	4.1	33	67

assessing the metabolic requirements of repeated high-intensity exercise. Casey *et al.* (1996) reported metabolic responses of different fibre types during repeated bouts of maximal isokinetic cycling. Exercise consisted of two bouts of 30 s cycling with a 4-minute passive recovery between bouts. The authors reported that a 4-minute recovery period was insufficient to allow total resynthesis of ATP and PCr in type II muscle fibres although recovery was complete in type I fibres. Furthermore, utilization of ATP and PCr was less in type II fibres during the second bout of exercise without a corresponding change in type I fibres. Performance was also significantly reduced.

A major reason for performing tests of anaerobic capacity, speed, power output and the like is to examine the effect of training on these parameters. Sprint training normally results in an increase in the ability to perform maximal intensity exercise. Are these performance changes reflected in an enhanced capacity for generation of anaerobic ATP production? Boobis *et al.* (1983) trained subjects for 8 weeks by means of sprinting on a cycle ergometer and analysed muscle samples at rest and after 30 s of maximal cycling before and after the training programme. Training increased the mean power output by 8%, a change mirrored by an increase in anaerobic energy production from glycolysis. The energy produced anaerobically from PCr and ATP was not significantly affected. Similar results were obtained in a study in which recreational runners were sprint-trained for 8 weeks (Nevill *et al.*, 1989). A 6% increase in mean power output was matched by a 20% increase in anaerobic energy production from glycolysis but not from the phosphagen stores.

11.7.2 INDIRECT ESTIMATIONS OF ANAEROBIC METABOLISM

Direct measures of metabolites in muscle are needed to determine anaerobic capacity accurately, but owing to the invasive nature of this approach an alternative technique is often desirable. The most commonly used indirect estimation of anaerobic capacity is maximal accumulated oxygen deficit (MAOD) during short, intense exercise. This measure arose from the original idea of the oxygen deficit and was first proposed by Hermansen (1969). The method requires establishing a linear relationship between oxygen uptake and exercise intensity over a number of visits (since oxygen uptake is measured over a 4 to 10 minute period for each intensity), then extrapolating the line beyond maximal oxygen uptake to a value corresponding to 120% $\dot{V}O_2$ max. The subject then exercises at this intensity to exhaustion. The MAOD is calculated as the difference in oxygen estimated as needed to exercise at that intensity (from the extrapolated data) and the actual oxygen consumed during the exercise corresponding to 120% $\dot{V}O_2$ max (see Medbø *et al.*, 1988). Although there appears to be similarity in the estimation of anaerobic energy provision between the MAOD and data from muscle biopsies in isolated muscle groups (Bangsbo *et al.*, 1990), there are conflicting views about the implications for whole-body exercise. For details of the debate taking place in the literature readers are advised to consult Bangsbo (1996a, 1996b) and Medbø (1996a, 1996b). Practical 4 provides a modified version of the MAOD assessment procedure.

11.7.3 AEROBIC CONTRIBUTION

The data presented above are exclusively concerned with rates of anaerobic energy production, with no recourse to aerobic contribution. Indirect estimates of the anaerobic and aerobic contribution to intense isolated knee extension exercise of 30 s are 80% and 20% respectively (Bangsbo *et al.*, 1990). These values change to 45%:55% and 30%:70% anaerobic:aerobic as the exercise duration increases from 60 to 90 s and 120 to 192 s. During the first 10 s of a 30 s Wingate test, the estimated contribution from aerobic metabolism is 3% (Serresse *et al.*, 1988), whereas the mean values of the aerobic contribution for the 30 s Wingate test have been reported as being between 16% and 28% (Serresse *et al.*, 1988; Smith and Hill, 1991).

Even if a subject does not breathe, myoglobin and haemoglobin stores can provide oxygen for aerobic energy provision and assessment of anaerobic capacity needs to take account of the likely aerobic energy contribution.

11.7.4 POSSIBLE RELATIONSHIP BETWEEN METABOLISM AND FATIGUE

The power output profile of an individual undergoing a 30 s Wingate test shows a peak in the first few seconds followed by a decline. This profile has a parallel in the decrease in rate of ATP production from both PCr and glycolysis (Table 11.1). It should also be recognized that aerobic contribution increases with time. The greatest rate of decrease in energy production is attributable to the depletion of PCr stores. This is noticeable in the type II muscle fibres, where after 10 s of activity 70% of these stores are used and after 20 s they are nearly depleted. The maximal rate of ATP production from glycolysis probably occurs at around 20 s and is maintained thereafter until the build-up of lactate and inorganic phosphate inhibit glycolytic enzyme activity. The switch from generation of ATP from PCr predominantly to glycolysis and then to aerobic metabolism necessitates a decrease in the maximal rate of ATP production. If ATP can only be generated at given (reducing) rates, then power output must decrease in a like manner. So the power output profile over 30 s is a function of maximal rate of ATP production from a changing energy source and is unlikely to be due solely to increases in lactate production and concomitant increases in hydrogen ions.

11.8 SUMMARY AND CONCLUSION

There has been considerable progress in assessments of maximal intensity exercise that involve brief single and repeated bouts of exercise. Similarly, successful field- and laboratory-based attempts have been made to model multiple-sprint type sports. Unequivocal quantification of accompanying metabolism is a challenge that has yet to be met.

11.9 PRACTICAL 1: WINGATE TEST

11.9.1 AIM

The aim of this practical is twofold: first, to describe external power output characteristics during the Wingate anaerobic test and, second, to examine changes in blood lactate concentration.

11.9.2 EQUIPMENT

A Monark 824E (Monark Exercise AB, Varberg, Sweden) basket-loading cycle ergometer with microprocessor-linked data logging facilities is used to record movements of either the flywheel or pedals; a separate ergometer can be used during the warm-up. Figure 11.1 shows the general arrangement for the test, and Figures 11.2 and 11.3 illustrate detection systems for logging data from movements of the flywheel and pedals respectively.

11.9.3 METHODS

1. Subjects should wear shorts and a T-shirt.
2. Take a finger-prick blood sample at rest. Collect the blood in duplicate, i.e. in two microcapillary tubes. One tube is labelled *a*, the other *b*, (see Chapter 4 by Maughan *et al.* for details on blood sampling).

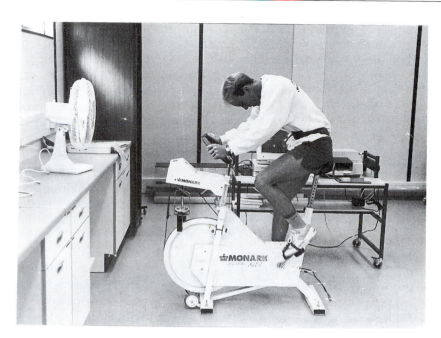

Figure 11.1 General layout of the equipment used in the Wingate Anaerobic Test. The cycle ergometer is bolted to the floor and has a modified load hanger. Note also the use of toe clips and a restraining belt.

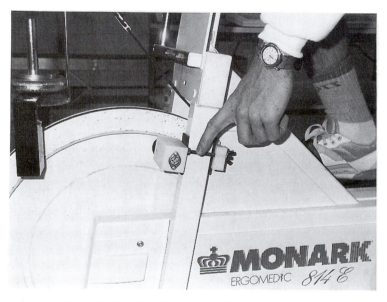

Figure 11.2 Data logging from the flywheel by means of a precision DC motor (Lakomy, 1986).

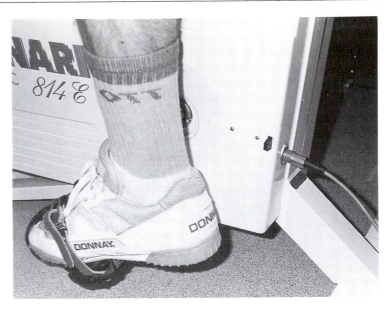

Figure 11.3 Data logging from the passage of the left pedal by means of a optoelectronic sensor housed in the chain guard (Winter *et al.*, 1991; Winter *et al.*, 1996).

3. Subjects have a 5-minute warm-up at 100 W with a flat-out sprint for 5 s at 3 minutes, followed by a 5-minute rest.
4. During this time subjects transfer to the test machine. Seat height is adjusted for comfort (Hamley and Thomas, 1967; Nordeen-Snyder, 1977), toe clips are secured (La Voie *et al.*, 1984), the resistive load (usually 7.5% ± 0.5 N of body weight) is positioned and a restraining harness should be fixed to ensure that the subject cannot rise from the saddle.
5. Subjects pedal at 50–60 rev min^{-1} with the external load supported. Upon the command, '3, 2, 1, go!' the load is applied abruptly, subjects begin to pedal flat out and data logging is started.
6. Subjects pedal for 30 s.
7. At the end of the test subjects undertake a suitable warm-down, e.g. two minutes of cycling at 100 W.
8. Take blood samples as in step 2 immediately at the end of exercise, and 7½ minutes and 12½ minutes later, and determine blood lactate concentration (HLa). This can be done by means of fast-response analysers but this practical uses Maughan's (1982) fluorimetric technique, which has greater control over the precision of measurement.
9. Complete the results sections (Tables 11.2–11.5).

11.9.4 SAMPLE RESULTS

Plot the calibration curve including the regression analysis.

The regression equation for the data in Table 11.3, which minimizes the sum of squares of residuals about the regression line in a *horizontal* direction, is equal to:

$$x = 0.015 + 0.139\, y$$

Table 11.2 Raw data for WAnT on a small sample of 20-year-old male college students

Subject	Time to peak power (s)	Mean power (W)	Decay (W)
1	4.50	635	456
2	2.87	806	538
3	3.45	745	426
4	5.34	813	562
5	3.83	830	446
Mean	4.00	766	486
SD	0.96	80	60

Mean power output ranges from 400 to 900 W, although differences in participant size account for some of the variation. Other factors such as muscle fibre type and training status are also influential. Time to peak power output ranges approximately from 2 to 6 s, very early in the test, and decay, the difference between the highest value of peak power output and the subsequent lowest value is approximately 40–60 % of the mean value. Blood lactate concentrations tend to peak some 7 to 8 minutes after exercise has ended.

Table 11.3 Calibration data for blood lactate (Hla). This is a six-point calibration, i.e. a blank and five standards are used. Each is analysed in duplicate.

Standards						
Tube	Blank	2.5	5.0	7.5	10.5	12.5
1	0	18	35	53	70	91
2	0	18	37	54	72	90
Mean	0	18.0	36.0	53.5	71.0	90.5

Standards $(mmol\, l^{-1})$

Table 11.4 Samples (fluorimeter reading). Note how each of the capillary tubes is analysed in duplicate.

Tube	Rest a	b	0 a	b	7.5 min PE a	b	12.5 min PE a	b
1	5	6	64	66	75	75	68	61
2	5	6	62	64	76	75	70	62

Table 11.5 Blood lactate values in mmol l^{-1}. Use the regression data from Table 11.3 to convert the instrument readings in Table 11.4. Note how each blood sample is analysed in quadruplicate.

Tube	Rest a	b	0 a	b	7.5 min a	b	12.5 min a	b
1	0.71	0.85	8.92	9.19	10.45	10.45	9.47	8.50
2	0.71	0.85	8.64	8.92	10.58	10.45	9.75	8.64
Mean	0.71	0.85	8.78	9.06	10.52	10.45	9.61	8.57
Mean	0.78		8.92		10.49		9.09	

Table 11.6 Sample results for WAnT

	Mean	SD	Range
Time to peak power (s)	3.6	1.2	2–6
Mean power (W)	650	80	400–900
Decay (W)	300	50	150–500

Table 11.7 Sample results for blood lactate following performance of the Wingate Anaerobic Test (values are mean, SD).

	Blood lactate (mmol l^{-1})
Rest	0.70, 0.15
Immediately post-exercise	9.6, 2.1
7.5 min post-exercise	12.5, 2.4
12.5 min post-exercise	11.0, 2.1

11.10 PRACTICAL 2: OPTIMIZATION PROCEDURES

11.10.1 AIMS

The purposes of this practical are
- to assess optimized peak power output, optimized load and the optimized pedalling rate
- to compare these measures with Wingate-derived data
- to establish the extent to which muscle force–velocity relationships are not satisfied by the Wingate Anaerobic Test.

11.10.2 EQUIPMENT

The same as for the Wingate Anaerobic Test.

11.10.3 METHODS

1. Dress, warm-up and screening procedures are the same as for the Wingate Anaerobic Test.
2. After a 5-minute warm-up, subjects perform four bouts of all-out exercise against randomly assigned loads. Each bout lasts 10 s and is followed by 1 minute of warm-down. A period of rest is allowed such that each exercise bout is separated in total by 5 minutes. Each bout is started in the same way as for the Wingate Anaerobic Test. Loads are assigned according to body mass, and guidelines are given in Table 11.8. These loads should produce peak pedalling rates within the range 100–200 rev min^{-1}.

Table 11.8 Suggested loads in newtons for the optimization procedure according to body mass (9.81 N = 1 kg force)

Load	Body mass (kg)					
	< 50	50–59.95	60–69.95	70–79.95	80–89.95	> 90
1	20.0	25.0	25.0	25.0	30.0	30.0
2	30.0	35.0	37.5	40.0	45.0	47.5
3	Wingate	Wingate	Wingate	Wingate	Wingate	Wingate
4	50.0	55.0	62.5	70.0	75.0	82.5

3. The order for applying the loads is: Wingate (i.e. 7½% of body weight), load 2, load 4 and finally load 1.
4. Record peak pedalling rate for each load and calculate the optimized peak power output, optimized load and optimized pedalling rate.
5. Compare the Wingate-derived values of peak power output and peak pedalling rate with the optimized values.

11.10.4 SAMPLE RESULTS

Table 11.9 gives peak pedalling rate and applied load data for a female sports studies student. Pearson's product-moment correlation coefficient and regression data are as follows:

$r = -0.998$

$R = 212.5 - 1.969\,L$

i.e. $a = 212.5$

$b = -1.97$

Substituting these values of a and b:

$$\text{Optimized peak power output} \; = \; \frac{-0.025a^2}{b} = 573\,\text{W}$$

$$\text{Optimised load} \; = \; \frac{-a}{2b} = 53.9\,\text{N}\,(5.49\,\text{kg force})$$

Optimized pedalling rate $= a + bL = 106.2$ rev min^{-1}

The relationship between peak pedalling rate, applied load and power output is illustrated in Figure 11.4. Tables 11.10 and 11.11 illustrate some typical results. The calculation of the optimized peak power output, optimized load and optimized pedalling rate depends on the linearity of the relationship between peak pedalling rate and applied load. In this example, r was -0.996 ± 0.005 for the men and -0.996 ± 0.006 for the women, so the required linearity is clearly illustrated. Values of peak power output derived from the Wingate Anaerobic Test were only ~88% of the optimized peak power output in men and ~90% in women. In addition, the reductions were not consistent. Although values of r were significant ($p < 0.001$), ~20% of the variance of the optimized peak power output in men and ~16% in women is not accounted for by the relationship with Wingate-derived peak power output values.

Table 11.9 Sample results for peak pedalling rate and applied load

Load (N)	Peak pedalling rate (rev min^{-1})	Peak power output (W)
44.1	128	564
34.3	144	493
53.9	105	566
24.5	164	402

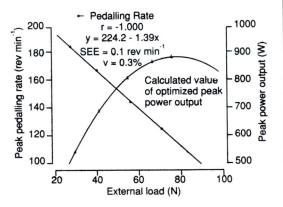

Figure 11.4 An example of the way in which peak pedalling rate and power output are related to the applied braking force.

The results demonstrate clearly that the optimized peak power output is greater than Wingate-derived peak power output (WPP) and that the pedalling rate that accompanied WPP is greater than the pedalling rate that accompanied the optimized peak power output. Consequently, these data confirm the suggestion (Sargeant *et al.*, 1981) that the Wingate load of 7½% of body weight does not necessarily satisfy muscle force–velocity relationships. Optimized pedalling rate is ~115 rev min^{-1} in men (Sargeant *et al.*, 1984; Nakamura *et al.*, 1985; Winter *et al.*, 1991) and ~105 rev min^{-1} in women (Sargeant *et al.*, 1984; Winter *et al.*, 1991). Pedalling rate at WPP is some 15–20 % higher in each case. The higher pedalling rate is at the expense of effective force production and hence power output. This reduction in effectiveness is also illustrated by OL (optimized load), which is ~11% of body weight in both men and women, and considerably higher than the Wingate value.

Table 11.10 Sample results for optimized and WAnT-derived data in men, $n = 19$. Values are mean, SEM (Winter *et al.*, 1987)

	Optimum	*Wingate*	*r*	*t*	*V%*
Peak power (W)	1 012, 30	883, 21	0.898[a]	−9.029[a]	5.8
Pedal rate	118.4, 1.8	155.9, 2.5	0.589[b]	−19.078[a]	5.4

[a] $p < 0.001$.
[b] $p < 0.01$.

Table 11.11 Sample results for optimized and WAnT-derived data in women, $n = 28$. Values are mean, SEM (Winter *et al.*, 1987)

	Optimum	*Wingate*	*r*	*t*	*V%*
Peak power (W)	640, 20	579, 17	0.918[a]	9.22[a]	6.8
Pedal rate	103.8, 1.6	134.5, 1.7	0.582[b]	−22.571[a]	6.7

[a] $p < 0.001$.
[b] $p < 0.01$.

11.11 PRACTICAL 3: CORRECTION PROCEDURES

11.11.1 AIMS

The purpose of this practical is to compare optimized peak power output values to corrected values for peak power output, as suggested by Lakomy (1985).

11.11.2 METHODS

1. Warm-up procedures as for Practical 1.
2. Subjects perform the optimization procedure outlined in Practical 2.

3. During the 'Wingate Load' bout, i.e. bout one, data are also recorded using the Concept II system and the corrected peak power output is calculated.
4. Record the corrected peak power output, the optimized peak power output and the pedalling rates for both.

11.11.3 SAMPLE RESULTS

Table 11.12 Sample data for optimized and corrected peak power output in men, $n = 19$, women $n = 18$. Values are mean, SEM (Winter *et al.*, 1996)

	Optimized	Corrected	r	t	V%
Men					
Peak power (W)	915, 35	1 005, 32	0.92[a]	−6.79[a]	5.6
Pedal rate (rev min^{-1})	111, 2	128, 2	0.64[b]	−11.77[a]	5.1
Women					
Peak Power (W)	673, 33	777, 39	0.96[a]	−9.38[a]	5.8
Pedal rate (rev min^{-1})	101, 1	111, 2	0.51[b]	−4.71[a]	7.9

[a] $p < 0.001$.
[b] $p < 0.01$.

The important points to note are that the corrected peak power output is greater than the optimized peak power output and similarly, pedalling rate is higher for the corrected peak power values.

The value for the corrected peak power output is ~10% greater than the optimized peak power output, although the relationship between the measures is strong, with 85% of the variance in the corrected peak power output accounted for by its relationship with the optimized peak power output. Similarly, the pedalling rate for the corrected peak power output is ~15% greater, but in this case only 41% of the variance in this value is accounted for by its relationship with the optimized equivalent. However, the coefficient of variation is smaller than for the optimized peak power output and this is a good example of the caution that has to be taken when r is interpreted. The magnitude of r is influenced by the range in the data and it does not necessarily give a clear indication of the relationship between variables. This is a reminder of the care that has to be taken when using r (Sale, 1991).

11.12 PRACTICAL 4: ASSESSMENT OF MAXIMAL ACCUMULATED OXYGEN DEFICIT (MAOD)

The original method for the determination of MAOD as described by Medbø *et al.* (1988) required subjects to perform ~20 runs on a treadmill at varying speeds up to a speed corresponding to maximal oxygen uptake. Each run lasted for 10 minutes, with the treadmill gradient set at 10.5%. Oxygen uptake was determined in the last two minutes of each run, and because only one run was performed on a particular day, the whole process took three weeks. Clearly this would be impractical for testing athletes or for student laboratory classes. However, to illustrate the principles a scaled-down version can be used over two testing sessions as follows:

11.12.1 METHODS

1. The subject runs at 4 submaximal speeds on a treadmill with a gradient set at 10.5% for 4 minutes each during which oxygen uptake is measured in the last two minutes. From these data, it is possible to establish a linear relationship between oxygen uptake and running speed.
2. After the final 4-minute run, the treadmill speed is progressively increased every minute until volitional exhaustion occurs, so that maximal oxygen uptake can be determined.
3. Produce graph of $\dot{V}O_2$ vs. running speed and determine the oxygen demand and running speed equivalent to 120% of $\dot{V}O_2$ max. This is achieved by extrapolating the straight line relationship beyond $\dot{V}O_2$ max. Alternatively, it may be predicted from the regression equation derived from the relationship between oxygen uptake (x) and running speed (y).
4. On a separate day, the subject runs to exhaustion on the treadmill (set at 10.5% gradient) at the speed corresponding to 120% $\dot{V}O_2$ max. Oxygen uptake is monitored throughout this test, which normally results in fatigue between 2 and 6 minutes.
5. The MAOD is calculated from the difference between the oxygen demand for that running speed (i.e. time to fatigue × $\dot{V}O_2$ extrapolated to 120% $\dot{V}O_2$ max) and the actual total oxygen consumption during the run.

Using this brief method, it is possible to distinguish between sprint-trained and endurance-trained populations, but it is probably not sensitive enough to distinguish subtle changes due to training. The use of four 4-minute bouts of running in one session as well as continuing to $\dot{V}O_2$ max might account for this lack of sensitivity.

11.12.2 SAMPLE RESULTS

The following data provide an example of oxygen uptake values collected on a male college sprinter using the above protocol.
(i) Day One (Table 11.13)
  120% of $\dot{V}O_2$ max (1.2 × 69) = 83 ml kg^{-1} min^{-1}
  Regression equation for $\dot{V}O_2$ (x) versus speed (y):
  Speed (m min^{-1}) = 23.2 + 2.758 ($\dot{V}O_2$) r = 0.99
  Therefore, the speed corresponding to 120% $\dot{V}O_2$ max = 251.5 m min^{-1}

Table 11.13 Running speeds and equivalent oxygen uptake values

Run	Speed $(m\ min^{-1})$	$\dot{V}O_2$ $(ml\ kg^{-1}min^{-1})$
1	161	49
2	174	56
3	188	60
4	201	64
5	214	69

Table 11.14 Oxygen uptake at specific times while running at 251.5 m min^{-1} at a gradient of 10.5%

Time (s)	$\dot{V}O_2$ $(ml\ kg^{-1}min^{-1})$
30	27
60	49
90	55
120	60
150	62

(ii) Day Two (Treadmill speed = 251.5 m min^{-1} at a gradient of 10.5%) (Table 11.14)

$$\text{Calculation of MAOD} = (2.5\ min \times 83\ ml\ kg^{-1}) - ((27 + 49 + 55 + 60 + 62)/2)$$
$$= 207.5 - 126.5 = 81\ ml\ kg^{-1}$$

$$\text{Aerobic contribution} = (126.5\ /\ 207.5) \times 100 = 61\%$$

The following are typical values for MAOD (ml kg^{-1}):

Before training (males)	66.4
After training (males)	79.8
Before training (females)	69.6
After training (females)	80.9

(Ramsbottom *et al.*, 1991)

Values of 55 ml kg^{-1} and 72 ml kg^{-1} have been observed for endurance-trained and sprint-trained men in the exercise physiology laboratory in Don MacLaren's laboratory.

REFERENCES

Adamson, G.T. and Whitney, R.J. (1971). Critical appraisal of jumping as a measure of human power. In *Medicine and Sport 6, Biomechanics II.* eds. J. Vredenbregt and J. Wartenweiler (S. Karger, Basel, Switzerland), pp. 208–11.

Ayalon, A., Inbar, O. and Bar-Or, O. (1974). Relationships among measurements of explosive strength and anaerobic power. In *International Series on Sport Sciences (Vol. I, Biomechanics IV).* eds. R.C. Nelson and C.A. Morehouse (University Press, Baltimore, MD), pp. 572–7.

Baltzopoulos, V., Eston, R.G. and Maclaren, D.A. (1988). A comparison of power measures between the Wingate test and tests of using an isokinetic device. *Ergonomics*, **3**, 1693–9.

Bangsbo, J. (1996a). Oxygen deficit: a measure of the anaerobic energy production during intense exercise? *Canadian Journal of Applied Physiology*, **21**, 350–63.

Bangsbo, J. (1996b). Bangsbo responds to Medbø's paper. *Canadian Journal of Applied Physiology*, **21**, 384–8.

Bangsbo, J. (1997). Quantification of anaerobic energy production during intense exercise. *Medicine and Science in Sports and Exercise*, **30**, 47–52.

Bangsbo, J., Gollnick, P.D., Graham, T.E., *et al.* (1990). Anaerobic energy production and the O deficit-debt relationship during exhaustive exercise in humans. *Journal of Physiology*, **422**, 539–59.

Bar-Or, O. (1981). Le test anaérobie de Wingate: caractéristiques et applications. *Symbioses*, **13**, 157–72.

Bar-Or, O. (1987). The Wingate Anaerobic Test: an update on methodology, reliability and validity. *Sports Medicine*, **4**, 381–94.

Bassett, D.R. (1989). Correcting the Wingate Test for changes in kinetic energy of the ergometer flywheel. *International Journal of Sports Medicine*, **10**, 446–9.

Bergström, J. (1962). Muscle electrolytes in man. *Scandinavian Journal of Clinical Laboratory Investigation*, **14**, (**Suppl 68**), p. 110.

Best, C.H. and Partridge, R.C. (1928). The equation of motion of a runner exerting maximal effort. *Proceedings of the Royal Society Series B*, **103**, 218–25.

Best, C.H. and Partridge, R.C. (1929). Observations on Olympic athletes. *Proceedings of the Royal Society Series B*, **105**, 323–32.

Bird, S. and Davison, R. (1997). *Physiological Testing Guidelines*, 3rd edn. (British Association of Sport and Exercise Sciences, Leeds).

Boobis, L.H. (1987). Metabolic aspects of fatigue during sprinting. In *Exercise: Benefits, Limitations and Adaptations.* eds. D. Macleod, R. Maughan, M. Nimmo, *et al.* (E. and F.N. Spon, London), pp. 116–43.

Boobis, L.H., Williams, C. and Wootton, S.A. (1982). Human muscle metabolism during brief maximal exercise. *Journal of Physiology*, **338**, 21P–22P.

Boobis, L.H., Williams, C. and Wootton, S.A. (1983). Influence of sprint training on muscle metabolism during brief maximal exercise in man. *Journal of Physiology*, **342**, 36P–37P.

Brewer, J., Ramsbottom, R. and Williams, C. (1988). *Multistage Fitness Test – a progressive shuttle-run test for the prediction of maximum oxygen uptake.* National Coaching Foundation, Leeds, UK.

Brooks, G.A. (1986). The lactate shuttle during exercise and recovery. *Medicine and Science in Sports and Exercise*, **18**, 355–64.

Casey, A., Constantin-Teodosiu, D., Howell, S., *et al.* (1996). Metabolic response of type I and II muscle fibres during repeated bouts of maximal exercise in humans. *American Journal of Physiology*, **271**, E38–E43.

Cavagna, G.A. (1975). Force platforms as ergometers. *Journal of Applied Physiology*, **39**, 174–9.

Cheetham, M.E. and Williams, C. (1985). Blood pH and blood lactate concentrations following maximal treadmill sprinting in man. *Journal of Physiology*, **361**, 79P.

Cheetham, M.E., Boobis, L.H., Brooks, S. and Williams, C. (1986). Human muscle metabolism during sprint running in man. *Journal of Applied Physiology*, **61**, 54–60.

Constantin-Teodosiu, D., Greenhaff, P.L., McIntyre, D.B., *et al.* (1997). Anaerobic energy production in human skeletal muscle in intense contraction: a comparison of ^{31}P magnetic resonance spectroscopy and biochemical techniques. *Experimental Physiology*, **82**, 593–601.

Cumming, G. (1974). Correlation of athletic performance and anaerobic power in 12–17-year-old children with bone age, calf muscle and total body potassium, heart volume and two indices of anaerobic power. In *Paediatric Work Physiology*. ed. O. Bar-Or (Wingate Institute, Isreal), pp. 109–34.

Davis, J.M., Welsh, R.S., DeVolve, K.L. and Alderson, N.A. (1999). Effects of branched-chain amino acids and carbohydrate on fatigue during intermittent, high-intensity running. *International Journal of Sports Medicine*, **20**, 309–14.

Dickinson, S. (1928). The dynamics of bicycle pedalling. *Proceedings of the Royal Society Series B*, **103**, 225–33.

Dickinson, S. (1929). The efficiency of bicycle pedalling as affected by speed and load. *Journal of Physiology*, **67**, 242–55.

Dotan, R. and Bar-Or, O. (1983). Load optimization for the Wingate Anaerobic Test. *European Journal of Applied Physiology*, **51**, 409–17.

Eston, R.G., Winter, E. and Baltzopoulos, V. (1997). Ratio standards and allometric modelling to scale peak power output for differences in lean upper leg volume in men and women. *Journal of Sports Sciences*, **15**, 29.

Fenn, W.O. (1932). Zur Mechanik des Radfahrens im Vergleich zu der des Laufens. *Pflügers Archiv für gesante Physiologie*, **229**, 354–66.

Fenn, W.O. and Marsh, B.S. (1935). Muscular force at different speeds of shortening. *Journal of Physiology*, **85**, 277–97.

Fleisch, A. (1950). Ergostat à puissances constantes et multiples. *Helvetica Medica Acta Series A*, **17**, 47–58.

Fox, M.L., Bowers, R.W. and Foss, M.L. (1988). *The Physiological Basis of Physical Education and Athletics*, 4th edn. (Saunders, Philadelphia, PA).

Furusawa, K., Hill, A.V. and Parkinson, J.L. (1927). The energy used in "sprint" running. *Proceedings of the Royal Society Series B*, **102**, 43–50.

Gamble, D.J., Jakeman, P.M. and Bartlett, R.M. (1988). Force velocity characteristics during non-motorised treadmill sprinting. *Journal of Sports Sciences*, **6**, 156.

Greenhaff, P.L., Nevill, M.E., Soderlund, K., *et al.* (1994). The metabolic responses of human type I and II muscle fibers during maximal treadmill sprinting. *Journal of Physiology*, **478**, 149–55.

Hamilton, A.L., Nevill, M.E., Brooks, S. and Williams, C. (1991). Physiological responses to maximal intermittent exercise: differences between endurance-trained runners and games players. *Journal of Sports Sciences*, **9**, 371–82.

Hamley, E.J. and Thomas, V. (1967). Physiological and postural factors in the calibration of the bicycle ergometer. *Journal of Physiology*, **193**, 55P–57P.

Hermansen, L. (1969). Anaerobic energy release. *Medicine and Science in Sports*, **1**, 32–8.

Hill, A.V. (1913). The absolute mechanical efficiency of the contraction of an isolated muscle. *Journal of Physiology*, **46**, 435–69.

Hill, A.V. (1934). The efficiency of bicycle pedalling. *Journal of Physiology*, **82**, 207–10.

Hill, A.V. (1938). The heat of shortening and the dynamic constants of muscle. *Proceedings of the Royal Society Series B*, **126**, 136–95.

Hill, A.V. (1970). *First and Last Experiments in Muscle Mechanics*. (Cambridge University Press, London).

Hill, A.V. and Lupton, H. (1922). The oxygen consumption during running. *Journal of Physiology*, **56**, xxxii–xxxiii.

Inbar, O., Dotan, R. and Bar-Or, O. (1976). Aerobic and anaerobic components of a thirty-second supramaximal cycling task. *Medicine and Science in Sports*, **8**, 51.

Jaskólska, A., Goossens, P., Veenstra, B., *et al.* (1999). Comparison of treadmill and cycle ergometer measurements of force-velocity relationships and power output. *International Journal of Sports Medicine*, **20**, 192–7.

Jaskólski, A., Veenstra, B., Goossens, P., *et al.* (1996). Optimised resistance for maximal power during treadmill running. *Sports Medicine and Training Rehabilitation*, **7**, 17–30.

Jones, N.L., McCartney, N., Graham, T., *et al.* (1985). Muscle performance and metabolism in maximal isokinetic cycling at slow and fast speeds. *Journal of Applied Physiology*, **59**, 132–6.

Jones, P.R.M. and Pearson, J. (1969). Anthropometric determination of leg fat and muscle plus bone volumes in young male and female adults. *Journal of Physiology*, **204**, 63P–66P.

Kelso, L.E.A. and Hellebrandt, F.A. (1932). The recording electrodynamic brake bicycle ergometer. *Journal of Clinical and Laboratory Medicine*, **19**, 1105–13.

Lakomy, H.K.A. (1984). An ergometer for measuring the power generated during sprinting. *Journal of Physiology*, **354**, 33P.

Lakomy, H.K.A. (1985). Effect of load on corrected peak power output generated on friction loaded cycle ergometers. *Journal of Sports Sciences*, **3**, 240.

Lakomy, H.K.A. (1986). Measurement of work and power output using friction loaded cycle ergometers. *Ergonomics*, **29**, 509–17.

La Voie, N., Dallaire, J., Brayne, S. and Barrett, D. (1984). Anaerobic testing using the Wingate and Evans-Quinney protocols with and without toe stirrups. *Canadian Journal of Applied Sport Sciences*, **9**, 1–5.

Léger, L.A. and Lambert, J. (1982). A maximal multistage 20m shuttle run test to predict O$_2$ max. *European Journal of Applied Physiology*, **49**, 1–5.

Lupton, H. (1923). An analysis of the effects of speed on the mechanical efficiency of human muscular movement. *Journal of Physiology*, **57**, 337–53.

McCartney, N., Heigenhauser, G.J.F. Sargeant, A.J. and Jones, N.L. (1983). A constant-velocity cycle ergometer for the study of dynamic muscle function. *Journal of Applied Physiology: Respiratory, Environmental and Exercise Physiology*, **55**, 212–17.

McCartney, N., Spriet, L.L., Heigenhauser, G.J.F., *et al.* (1986). Muscle power and metabolism in maximal intermittent exercise. *Journal of Applied Physiology*, **60**, 1164–9.

McClenaghan, B.A. and Literowitch, W. (1987). Fundamentals of computerised data acquisition in the human performance laboratory. *Sports Medicine*, **4**, 425–45.

Maughan, R.J. (1982). A simple rapid method for the determination of glucose, lactate, pyruvate, alanine, b hydroxybutyrate and acetoacetate on a single 20 ml blood sample. *Clinica Chimica Acta*, **122**, 231–40.

Medbø, J.I. (1996a). Medbø responds to Bangsbo's paper. *Canadian Journal of Applied Physiology*, **21**, 364–9.

Medbø, J.I. (1996b). Is the maximal accumulated oxygen deficit an adequate measure of the anaerobic capacity? *Canadian Journal of Applied Physiology*, **21**, 370–83.

Medbø, J.I., Mohn, A., Tabata, I., *et al.* (1988). Anaerobic capacity determined by the maximal accumulated oxygen deficit. *Journal of Applied Physiology*, **64**, 50–60.

Mercer, T.H., Gleeson, N.P., Claridge, S. and Clement, S. (1998). Prolonged intermittent high intensity exercise impairs neuromuscular performance of the knee flexors. *European Journal of Applied Physiology*, **77**, 560–2.

Morris, J.G., Nevill, M.E., Lakomy, H.K.A., *et al.* (1998). Effect of a hot environment on performance of prolonged, intermittent, high-intensity shuttle running. *Journal of Sports Sciences*, **16**, 677–86.

Nakamura, Y., Mutoh, Y. and Miyashita, M. (1985). Determination of the peak power output during maximal brief pedalling bouts. *Journal of Sports Sciences*, **3**, 181–7.

Nevill, A.M., Ramsbottom, R. and Williams, C. (1992). Scaling measurements in physiology and medicine for individuals of different size. *European Journal of Applied Physiology*, **65**, 110–7.

Nevill, M.E., Boobis, L.H., Brooks, S. and Williams, C. (1989). Effect of training on muscle metabolism during treadmill sprinting. *Journal of Applied Physiology*, **67**, 2376–82.

Nevill, M.E., Williams, C., Roper, D., *et al.* (1993). Effect of diet on performance during recovery from intermittent sprint exercise. *Journal of Sports Sciences*, **11**, 119–26.

Nordeen-Snyder, K. (1977). The effect of bicycle seat height variation upon oxygen consumption and lower limb kinematics. *Medicine and Science in Sports and Exercise*, **9**, 113–17.

Peyrebrune, M.C., Nevill, M.E., Donaldson, F.J. and Cosford, D.J. (1998). The effect of oral creatine supplementation on performance in single and repeated sprint swimming. *Journal of Sports Sciences*, **16**, 271–9.

Ramsbottom, R., Nevill, A.M., Nevill, M.E. and Williams, C. (1991). Effect of training on maximal accumulated oxygen deficit and shuttle run performance. *Journal of Sports Sciences*, **9**, 429–30.

Sale, D.G. (1991). Testing strength and power. In *Physiological Testing of the High-Performance Athlete*, 2nd edn. eds. J.D. MacDougall, H.A. Wenger and H.A. Green (Human Kinetics, Champaign, IL), pp. 21–106.

Sargeant, A.J., Hoinville, E. and Young, A. (1981). Maximum leg force and power output during short term dynamic exercise. *Journal of Applied Physiology: Respiratory, Environmental and Exercise Physiology*, **53**, 1175–82.

Sargeant, A.J., Dolan, P. and Young, A. (1984). Optimal velocity for maximal short-term (anaerobic) power output in cycling. *International Journal of Sports Medicine*, **5**, 124–5.

Sargent, D.A. (1921). The physical test of a man. *American Physical Education Review*, **26**, 188–94.

Sargent, L.W. (1924). Some observations on the Sargent Test of Neuromuscular Efficiency. *American Physical Education Review*, **29**, 47–56.

Sargent, R.M. (1926). The relation between oxygen requirement and speed in running. *Proceedings of the Royal Society Series B*, **100**, 10–22.

Schmidt-Nielsen, K. (1984). *Scaling: why is animal size so important?* (Cambridge University Press, Cambridge).

Serresse, O., Lortie, G., Bouchard, C. and Boulay, M.R. (1988). Estimation of the contribution of the various energy systems during maximal work of short duration. *International Journal of Sports Medicine*, **9**, 456–60.

Smith, A.J. (1972). *A study of the forces on the body in athletic activities, with particular reference to jumping*. Unpublished Doctoral Thesis, University of Leeds, UK.

Smith, J.C. and Hill, D.W. (1991). Contribution of energy systems during a Wingate power test. *British Journal of Sports Medicine*, **25**, 196–9.

Soderlund, K. and Hultman, E. (1986). Effects of delayed freezing on content of phosphagens in human skeletal muscle biopsy samples. *Journal of Applied Physiology*, **61**, 832–5.

Soderlund, K., Greenhaff, P.L. and Hultman, E. (1992). Energy metabolism in type I and II human muscle fibres during short term electrical stimulation at different frequencies. *Acta Physiologica Scandinavica*, **144**, 15–22.

Tanner, J.M. (1949). Fallacy of per-weight and per-surface area standards and their relation to spurious correlation. *Journal of Applied Physiology*, **2**, 1–15.

Thompson, D., Nicholas, C.W. and Williams, C. (1999). Muscular soreness following prolonged intermittent high-intensity shuttle running. *Journal of Sports Sciences*, **17**, 387–95.

Tuttle, W.W. and Wendler, A.J. (1945). The construction, calibration and use of an alternating current electrodynamic brake bicycle ergometer. *Journal of Laboratory and Clinical Medicine*, **30**, 173–183.

Vandewalle, H., Pérès, G., Heller, J. and Monod, H. (1985). All out anaerobic capacity tests on cycle ergometers: a comparative study on men and women. *European Journal of Applied Physiology*, **54**, 222–9.

Von Döbeln, W. (1954). A simple bicycle ergometer. *Journal of Applied Physiology*, **7**, 222–4.

Welsman, J., Armstrong, N., Winter, E. and Kirby, B.J. (1993). The influence of various scaling techniques on the interpretation of developmental changes in peak O_2. *Pediatric Exercise Science*, **5**, 485.

Williams, C. (1987). Short term activity. In *Exercise: Benefits, Limits and Adaptations*. eds. D. Macleod, R. Maughan, M. Nimmo, *et al*. (E and F.N. Spon, London), pp. 59–62.

Williams, C. (1990). Metabolic aspects of exercise. In *Physiology of Sports*, eds. T. Reilly, N. Secher, P. Snell and C. Williams (E. and F.N. Spon, London), pp. 3–40.

Winter, E.M. (1992). Scaling: partitioning out differences in body size. *Pediatric Exercise Science*, **4**, 296–301.

Winter, E.M., Brookes, F.B.C. and Hamley, E.J. (1987). A comparison of optimized and non-optimized peak power output in young, active men and women. *Journal of Sports Sciences*, **5**, 71.

Winter, E.M., Brookes, F.B.C. and Hamley, E.J. (1989). Optimized loads for external power output during brief, maximal cycling. *Journal of Sports Sciences*, **7**, 69–70.

Winter, E.M., Brookes, F.B.C. and Hamley, E.J. (1991). Maximal exercise performance and lean leg volume in men and women. *Journal of Sports Sciences*, **9**, 3–13.

Winter, E.M., Brookes, F.B.C. and Roberts, K.W. (1993). The effects of scaling on comparisons between maximal exercise performance in boys and men. *Pediatric Exercise Science*, **5**, 488.

Winter, E.M., Brown, D., Roberts, N.K.A., *et al*. (1996). Optimized and corrected peak power output during friction-braked cycle ergometry. *Journal of Sports Sciences*, **14**, 513–21.

Wootton, S. and Williams, C. (1983). The influence of recovery duration on repeated maximal sprints. In *Biochemistry of Exercise*. eds. H.G. Knuttgen, J.A. Vogel and J. Poortmans (Human Kinetics, Champaign, IL), pp. 269–73.

APPENDIX: RELATIONSHIPS BETWEEN UNITS OF ENERGY, WORK, POWER AND SPEED

Table A.1 Energy and work units (The joule is the SI unit for work and represents the application of a force of 1 newton (N) through a distance of 1 metre. A newton is the force producing an acceleration of 1 metre per second every second (1 m s^{-2}) when it acts on 1 kg.)

1 joule (J)	=	1 newton metre (N m)
1 kilojoule (kJ)	=	1000 J
	=	0.23892 kcal
1 megajoule (MJ)	=	1000 kJ
1 kilocalorie (kcal)	=	4.1855 kJ = 426.8 kg m

Table A.2 Relationships between various power units (The watt is the SI unit for power and is equivalent to 1 J s^{-1}.)

	W	$kcal\ min^{-1}$	$kJ\ min^{-1}$	$kg\ m\ min^{-1}$
1 watt (W)	1.0	0.014	0.060	6.118
1 kcal min^{-1}	69.77	1.0	4.186	426.78
1 kJ min^{-1}	16.667	0.2389	1.0	101.97
1 kg m min^{-1}	0.1634	0.00234	0.00981	1.0

Table A.3 Conversion table for units of speed (m s^{-1} is the SI unit for speed.)

$km\ h^{-1}$	$m\ s^{-1}$	mph
1	0.28	0.62
2	0.56	1.24
3	0.83	1.87
4	1.11	2.49
5	1.39	3.11
6	1.67	3.73
7	1.94	4.35
8	2.22	4.98
9	2.50	5.60
10	2.78	6.22

INDEX

£=18-70

8

Therapeutics
Through Exercise

The Fifty-first Hahnemann Symposium

Therapeutics Through Exercise

Edited by

DAVID T. LOWENTHAL, M.D.

Professor of Medicine and Pharmacology
Director, Division of Clinical Pharmacology
William Likoff Cardiovascular Institute
Hahnemann Medical College and Hospital
Philadelphia, Pennsylvania

KRISHAN BHARADWAJA, M.D.

Associate Professor of Medicine
Hahnemann Medical College and Hospital
Philadelphia, Pennsylvania

WILBUR W. OAKS, M.D.

Professor of Medicine
Chairman, Department of Medicine
Hahnemann Medical College and Hospital
Philadelphia, Pennsylvania

GRUNE & STRATTON
A Subsidiary of Harcourt Brace Jovanovich, Publishers
New York   London   Toronto   Sydney   San Francisco

Library of Congress Cataloging in Publication Data

Main entry under title:

Therapeutics through exercise.

(Hahnemann symposium)
Includes bibliographical reference and index.
1. Exercise therapy.   2. Exercise—
Physiological aspects.   I. Lowenthal, David T.
II. Bharadwaja, Krishan.   III. Oaks, Wilbur W.,
1928–   IV. Series. [DNLM: 2. Exertion—
Congresses.   2. Exercise Therapy—Congresses.
WB541 T3982 1977]
RM725.T48   615′.82   79-19682
ISBN 0-8089-1209-7

Grune & Stratton, Inc.
111 Fifth Avenue
New York, New York 10003

Distributed in the United Kingdom by
Academic Press, Inc. (London) Ltd.
24/28 Oval Road, London NW 1

Library of Congress Catalog Number 79-19682
International Standard Book Number 0-8089-1209-7

Printed in the United States of America

Contents

Preface

Traditionally, the Hahnemann Symposia have dealt with topical subjects of both clinical and research interest. In keeping with this custom, the 51st Hahnemann Medical College and Hospital Symposium on *Therapeutics Through Exercise* has attempted to combine both research and clinical information related to basic principles of exercise physiology, environmental adaptation, environmental stresses, and the application of these principles to patients with chronic illnesses. Since the "Marathon," published by the New York Academy of Science in 1977, there has not appeared a compendium of information dealing with exercise physiology and especially its application to patients with various chronic illnesses. The "Marathon" addressed the physiological changes associated with distance running. This compilation attempts to address exercise regardless of the type employed.

Americans are more conscious of exercise and all its phases than ever before. Doctors George Sheehan and Gabe Mirkin have labored arduously to make Americans aware of the benefits and pitfalls of exercise, primarily aerobic and especially running. These authors have dealt mostly with normal subjects. In an attempt not to duplicate their fine efforts, we have made the effort in this publication to deal not only with basic principles of exercise physiology but also to delineate such information as it applies to patients with chronic illness, information that in some areas is meager and in others vast. The implication is that even patients who have various diseases can also exercise. Much work needs to be done, i.e., clinical investigation in order to document the various changes that may accrue to patients with chronic musculoskeletal, neurological, chronic renal and chronic cardiopulmonary-renal diseases. Significant contributions have been made in the fields of endocrinology and metabolism as they apply to diabetes and obesity. Presently, a considerable number of clinical studies are being channeled into adolescent and adult hypertension as this disease relates to exercise. It is hoped that adequate clinical studies will dispel many of the myths and anecdotes that have been the subjects of dogma amongst the laity and of consternation amongst exercise physiologists.

The editors of this volume are indebted to Mr. Robert Schaefer, his capable staff in the Department of Continuing Medical Education at Hahnemann Medical College and Hospital, and to Mrs. Janice Chancey for her devoted secretarial assistance in the compilation of these manuscripts. Finally, those clinical studies which are referred to in this manuscript would not have been possible without the participation of those normal volunteers and patients who have provided us with substantive information. To these people we are also indebted.

David T. Lowenthal, M.D.
Krishan Bharadwaja, M.D.
Wilbur W. Oaks, M.D.

Contributors

Gideon B. Ariel, Ph.D.
Vice President and Director of Research
Computerized Biomechanical Analysis, Inc.
Amherst, Massachusetts

Toby B. Bedford, M.S.
Exercise Science Program
The University of Iowa
Iowa City, Iowa

Krishan Bharadwaja, M.D.
Associate Professor of Medicine
Hahnemann Medical College and Hospital
Philadelphia, Pennsylvania

Alfred A. Bove, M.D., Ph.D.
Associate Professor of Medicine and
   Physiology
Section of Cardiology
Philadelphia, Pennsylvania

Warren S. Chernick, D.Sc.
Professor and Chairman
Department of Pharmacology
Hahnemann Medical College and Hospital
Philadelphia, Pennsylvania

Joseph R. DiPalma, M.D.
Professor of Pharmacology
Vice President and Dean
Hahnemann Medical College and Hospital
Philadelphia, Pennsylvania

Arnold R. Eiser, M.D.
Fellow, Division of Nephrology
Hahnemann Medical College and Hospital
Philadelphia, Pennsylvania

Philip M. Felig, M.D.
C.N.H. Long Professor and Vice Chairman
Department of Medicine
Chief, Section of Endocrinology
Yale University School of Medicine
New Haven, Connecticut

Allan P. Freedman, M.D.
Assistant Professor of Medicine
Division of Pulmonary Diseases
Hahnemann Medical College and Hospital
Philadelphia, Pennsylvania

Dennis I. Goldberg, M.A.
Temple University
Biokinetics Research Laboratory
Philadelphia, Pennsylvania

Allan H. Goldfarb, M.Ed.
Temple University
Biokinetics Research Laboratory
Philadelphia, Pennsylvania

Martin Grabois, M.D.
Associate Professor and Chairman
Department of Physical Medicine
Baylor College of Medicine
Houston, Texas

Dorothy V. Harris, Ph.D.
Professor, Physical Education
Director, Research Center for Women and
   Sport
Pennsylvania State University
University Park, Pennsylvania

Veikko Koivisto, M.D.
Department of Internal Medicine
Yale University School of Medicine
New Haven, Connecticut

Robert L. Lavine, M.D.
Assistant Professor of Medicine
Divison of Endocrinology and Metabolism
Hahnemann Medical College and Hospital
Philadelphia, Pennsylvania

Ronald M. Lawrence, M.D., Ph.D.
Assistant Clinical Professor of Psychiatry
U.C.L.A. School of Medicine
Los Angeles, California

Joel R. Leininger, DVM, Ph.D.
Assistant Professor of Preventive Medicine
Comparative Medicine Section
The Institute for Agricultural Medicine
    and Environmental Health
The University of Iowa
Iowa City, Iowa

David T. Lowenthal, M.D.
Professor of Medicine and Pharmacology
Director, Division of Clinical Pharmacology
William Likoff Cardiovascular Institute
Hahnemann Medical College and Hospital
Philadelphia, Pennsylvania

Ronald D. Matthes
Supervisor
Exercise Physiology Laboratory
Exercise Science Program
The University of Iowa
Iowa City, Iowa

Loretta J. Miller, M.T.
Exercise Physiology Laboratory
Exercise Science Program
The University of Iowa
Iowa City, Iowa

Wilbur W. Oaks, M.D.
Professor of Medicine
Chairman, Department of Medicine
Hahnemann Medical College and Hospital
Philadelphia, Pennsylvania

Robert A. Oppliger, M.S.
Exercise Science Program
The University of Iowa
Iowa City, Iowa

Warren K. Palmer, Ph.D.
Assistant Professor
Exercise Physiologist, Department of
    Physical Education
University of Illinois at Chicago Circle
Chicago, Illinois

Leslie I. Rose, M.D.
Professor of Medicine
Director, Division of Endocrinology and
    Metabolism
Hahnemann Medical College and Hospital
Philadelphia, Pennsylvania

Stuart Snyder, M.D.
Assistant Professor of Medicine
Hahnemann Medical College and Hospital
Philadelphia, Pennsylvania

Charles Swartz, M.D.
Director, Divison of Nephrology and
    Hypertension
Professor and Vice Chairman, Department
    of Medicine
Hahnemann Medical College and Hospital
Philadelphia, Pennsylvania

Charles M. Tipton, Ph.D.
Professor, Department of Physical
    Education and Physiology and Biophysics
Director, Exercise Science Program
The University of Iowa
Iowa City, Iowa

Mitchell S. Whiteman
Thomas Jefferson University School of
    Medicine
Philadelphia, Pennsylvania

William W. Winder, Ph.D.
Assistant Professor of Preventive Medicine
Washington University School of Medicine
St. Louis, Missouri

Vincent J. Zarro, M.D., Ph.D.
Director, Division of Rheumatology
Associate Professor of Medicine
Hahnemann Medical College and Hospital
Philadelphia, Pennsylvania

Therapeutics Through Exercise

Part I

Applications of Exercise Physiology

The Metabolic Response to Exercise: Implications for Diabetes

PHILIP FELIG, M.D.,
VEIKKO KOIVISTO, M.D.

Augmented fuel utilization during acute exercise necessitates a variety of metabolic changes to secure adequate substrate availability. In addition, regular exercise or training can lead to long-term alterations in fuel homeostasis and hormonal regulation which are present in the resting state as well as during exercise. These exercise–induced changes in metabolism and its regulation may have therapeutic value in the management of metabolic disorders such as diabetes mellitus. This review will focus on the exercise–induced alterations in fuel metabolism in normal man and diabetes, and discuss some of the potential beneficial effects of exercise in the management of diabetes.

NORMAL SUBJECTS

Substrate Turnover during Exercise

Muscle glycogen, blood-borne glucose, and free fatty acids (FFA) are the main sources of energy during exercise, the relative contribution of each of these substrates depending on the intensity and duration of muscular work. Figure 1 demonstrates the relative contribution of these fuels to oxidative energy production at various stages of

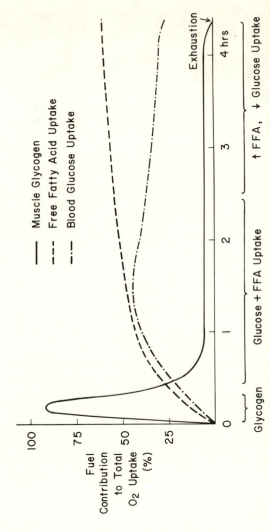

Fig. 1. The relative contribution of muscle glycogen and blood-borne glucose and free fatty acids on fuel utilization at various stages of prolonged exercise in normal man.

submaximal exercise. Muscle glycogen is the main source of energy during the first five to ten minutes of exercise, the rate of glycogen breakdown being particularly rapid during exercise of high intensity.[1] As exercise continues, muscle glycogen stores become depleted, and, although they still provide energy to a small extent, blood-borne substrates, glucose, and FFA become increasingly important fuels. During 60 to 90 minute exercise at a submaximal intensity corresponding to 30 percent of subject's maximal aerobic power ($\dot{V}O_2$ max), glucose uptake by the exercising muscle increases markedly above the resting level (Fig. 1).[2] As a consequence, glucose utilization corresponds to 40 percent of oxidative fuel after 90 minutes of exercise. When exercise is continued, the contribution of glucose to energy production begins to fall. Nevertheless, after four hours of exercise the rate of glucose oxidation is still markedly above resting level (Fig. 1).

Despite the marked stimulation of glucose utilization, blood glucose levels remain virtually unchanged during the first 40 minutes of exercise or may increase slightly.[3] The blood glucose pool is replenished continuously by a three- to five-fold increase in glucose release from the liver during exercise.[3,4,5] During the first 40 minutes of exercise, 75 percent of liver glucose production is derived from hepatic glycogenolysis and 25 percent from gluconeogenesis.[3] Since estimated liver glycogen stores in postabsorptive man are only 75–90 g,[6] prolonged exercise necessitates increased reliance on gluconeogenesis. Accordingly, by the end of four hours of exercise, 75 percent of glycogen stores are mobilized and gluconeogenesis from various precursors (lactate, pyruvate, glycerol, and aminoacids, mainly alanine) is increased to the extent that 45 percent of the splanchnic glucose production is derived from gluconeogenesis.

If exercise is continued beyond 40–60 minutes, blood glucose level begins to fall despite enhanced gluconeogenesis because augmented glucose utilization by exercising muscle exceeds the rate of splanchnic glucose production. To prevent an excessive fall in glycemia, a gradual shift in energy metabolism from carbohydrate to fat utilization occurs. While after 60 to 90 minute exercise glucose and FFA are employed to the same extent as an oxidative fuel, between 90 and 240 minutes of exercise the uptake of FFA by muscle rises by 70 percent while glucose uptake falls by 30 percent (Fig. 1). Thus, after 240 minutes of continuous muscular work, the contribution of FFA to total oxygen uptake is twice that of glucose.[2] With respect to the mechanism of enhanced FFA utilization during prolonged exercise, a direct relationship has been observed between the level of plasma FFA and its uptake by exercising muscle.[2,7] Thus, a high rate of FFA oxidation during prolonged exercise is, at least partly, a consequence of enhanced lipid mobilization resulting in increased FFA presentation to the exercising muscle. The possibility also exists that some of the utilized FFA are derived from intramuscular triglycerides.[8]

A variety of hormonal changes are involved in the regulation of fuel homeostasis during muscular work. Exercise causes a fall in plasma insulin[9,10] and a rise in the level of plasma glucagon,[10,11,12,13] catecholamines,[13] and cortisol.[14] These changes are dependent on both the duration and the intensity of exercise. A fall in plasma insulin and a rise in catecholamines stimulates lipid mobilization in adipose tissue, resulting in the enhanced availability of FFA. In addition, hypoinsulinemia in association with elevated levels of glucagon, catecholamines, and cortisol is a potent stimulus for hepatic glycogenolysis and gluconeogenesis during exercise.[15]

In well trained athletes, fuel metabolism during exercise differs from that in sedentary individuals. Athletes demonstrate a lower respiratory exchange ratio and a smaller rise in lactate in response to exercise than untrained subjects.[1] These observations indicate that athletes use more fat and less carbohydrate as a fuel than sedentary persons. As a consequence, during prolonged exercise athletes can better maintain euglycemia than untrained subjects,[16,17] which may contribute to their better performance. During exercise, however, lipid mobilizaation and plasma FFA levels tend to be lower in athletes than in untrained subjects,[17] suggesting that factors other than substrate presentation may regulate fat oxidation in athletes. As compared to the untrained state, muscular tissue in trained individuals has a greater capacity for fat oxidation.[18,18a] Thus, the higher rate of FFA uptake in athletes may be, at least partly, due to their increased oxidative capacity. An increase in fat oxidation may, in turn, decrease carbohydrate utilization in muscle by reducing glycolysis and pyruvate oxidation.[19,20]

In addition, during prolonged exercise athletes have demonstrated a fall in insulin binding to receptors in contrast to a rise in insulin binding observed in untrained subjects. Thus, athletes may have a decrease in insulin action, which may further diminish glucose uptake by exercising muscle.[16]

Effects of Glucose Ingestion prior to Exercise

Despite a progressive increase in FFA utilization as exercise is prolonged, glucose oxidation continues, and may finally result in the depletion of muscle glycogen stores and hence exhaustion. Glucose administration before exercise can markedly enhance body carbohydrate stores as well as alter fuel metabolism during exercise. Ingestion of 200 g glucose raises blood glucose level two-fold above baseline 50 minutes after administration.[21] If exercise is then initiated at an intensity corresponding to 30 percent of maximal oxygen uptake, the blood glucose level declines. At the end of the four hour exercise period, however, the blood glucose concentration is 30 to 40 percent higher than in fasted control subjects. Furthermore, after glucose administration, glucose uptake by the exercising leg is 40 to 100 percent greater than in controls. Blood-borne glucose can thus account for 48 to 58 percent of total oxidative fuel as compared to 27 to 41 percent in unfed subjects (Figure 2).[21] Reflecting this augmented glucose uptake, the respiratory exchange ratio is increased during exercise in glucose fed subjects, while plasma FFA levels are decreased.

With respect to the mechanism of enhanced glucose and decreased fat utilization after glucose feeding, plasma insulin may play the key regulatory role. After glucose ingestion, plasma insulin levels were two to three-fold higher than in control subjects throughout the four hour exercise period.[21] Thus, hyperinsulinemia during exercise may stimulate glucose uptake by the exercising leg. In addition, by decreasing lipid mobilization, hyperinsulinemia reduces plasma FFA levels, and this leads to a decline in fatty acid uptake by the exercising muscle.

In addition to enhanced muscle glucose utilization, splanchnic glucose output

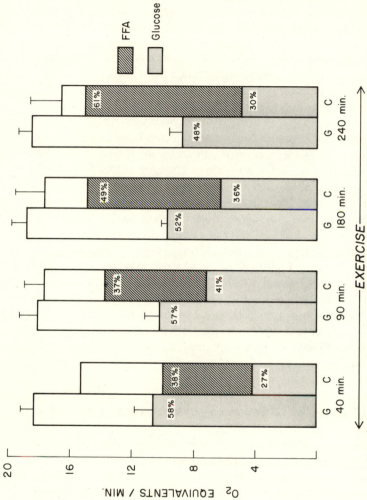

Fig. 2. Leg uptake of oxygen and substrates during exercise in glucose fed (G) and fasted control subjects. Height of bar represents man ± SE oxygen uptake. (From Ahlborg and Felig.)[21] Reprinted with permission from Am J Physiol 233: E188, 1977.

after glucose ingestion is 80 to 140 percent greater than in nonfed controls during exercise. This rise in hepatic glucose release is due to a diminished retention of ingested glucose in the liver rather than enhanced hepatic gluconeogenesis. During four hours of exercise, the uptake of gluconeogenic precursors (lactate, pyruvate, glycerol) is reduced by 65 to 100 percent after glucose feeding as compared to controls. This fall in splanchnic uptake of glucose precursors is comparable to that found in nonexercising subjects after oral[22] or intravenous[23] glucose administration. Thus, prolonged exercise at moderate intensity fails to overcome the inhibitory effect of glucose administration on hepatic gluconeogenesis.

Regarding the mechanism of decreased gluconeogenesis during exercise preceded by glucose ingestion, hyperinsulinemia, changes in plasma glucagon levels, and elevated plasma glucose may be of importance. After 200 g glucose ingestion, plasma glucagon levels were 60 to 75 percent lower than in control subjects throughout the four hours of exercise.[21] Thus, relative hypoglucagonemia, particularly in the presence of hyperinsulinemia, may contribute to the decline in splanchnic uptake of gluconeogenic precursors. In addition, recent studies have indicated that hyperglycemia per se, in the absence of changes in glucoregulatory hormones, can diminish hepatic glucose production.[24] Thus, elevated plasma glucose levels in glucose–fed subjects may have further inhibited gluconeogenesis during exercise.

Although glucose ingestion before moderate exercise (at 30 percent of $\dot{V}O_2$ max) helps to avoid exercise–induced hypoglycemia, the same may not be the case if exercise is performed at high intensities. During severe exercise (at 75 percent of $\dot{V}O_2$ max) preceded by glucose ingestion, blood glucose may fall within the first 10 to 20 minutes to or near hypoglycemic levels.[25,26] Concerning the mechanism of this acute fall in glycemia, both the high intensity of exercise and hyperinsulinemia may be of importance. Since glucose uptake by the exercising muscle is proportional to the intensity of work performed, strenuous exercise together with hyperinsulinemia accompanying glucose ingestion may stimulate glucose uptake to levels which exceed the rate of splanchnic glucose release. As a result, a rapid fall in plasma glucose level may ensue.[25,26]

Influence of Glucose Ingestion during Exercise

Whether glucose administration during exercise (rather than before exercise) can similarly alter fuel metabolism, has been studied by Ahlborg and Felig.[27] Glucose was given at a dose of 200 g after 90 minutes of exercise, which was then continued for two and half hours at 30 percent of $\dot{V}O_2$ max. Glucose administration reversed the decline in glycemia and increased arterial glucose levels by 35 percent. Simultaneously, glucose uptake by the exercising leg rose to levels twice those observed in unfed control subjects. Blood-borne glucose could thus account for over 60 percent of the oxygen consumption at the end of four hours of exercise in glucose–fed subjects as compared to only 30 percent in fasted controls. A greater dependence on carbohydrate as a fuel was also reflected by a higher respiratory exchange ratio in the glucose–fed as compared to the control group during exercise. In addition, glucose ingestion during exercise resulted in a marked inhibition of exercise–induced lipid mobilization, as indicated by a 60 to 70 percent decline in plasma FFA and glycerol.[27] Thus, a fall in FFA availability may have contributed to the decreased fat oxidation during exercise.

The rise in carbohydrate utilization after glucose ingestion could be attributed mainly to changes in plasma insulin concentrations. Following glucose feeding, plasma insulin rose two to three-fold above that in control subjects indicating that glucose administration can overcome the inhibitory effect of exercise on insulin secretion.[9,10]

Following glucose ingestion during exercise, net splanchnic glucose release was two-fold greater than that observed in fasted subjects.[27] This, again, was due to an escape of ingested glucose rather than enhanced glucose synthesis (gluconeogenesis) in the liver, since in the fed group the uptake of lactate, pyruvate, and glycerol at four hours of exercise was 70 to 100 percent below that in the fasted controls. The fall in gluconeogenesis in the glucose–fed subjects can be accounted for by the rise in plasma insulin and the failure to observe any increase in glucagon during exercise, as contrasted with the fall in insulin and the rise in glucagon observed in the control group.[27]

Taken together, the metabolic and hormonal response to exercise appears to be similarly altered when glucose is ingested prior to or during exercise. Following glucose administration, hyperglycemia, hyperinsulinemia, and hypoglucagonemia ensue; fuel utilization by muscle shifts from fat to carbohydrate, and splanchnic gluconeogenesis is decreased.

Glucose Disposal after Exercise

In the basal, postabsorptive state, a major proportion of ingested glucose is metabolized in the liver. During the first three hours after ingestion of a 100 g oral glucose load, 60 percent is utilized by the splanchnic bed, 25 percent is delivered to the brain, while only 15 percent is made available for insulin–dependent uptake by muscle and adipose tissue.[28] Prior exercise, which causes depletion of muscle as well as liver glycogen, has the effect of markedly altering the sites of disposal of oral glucose so as to favor repletion of muscle as compared to liver glycogen. When 100 g of glucose is ingested immediately or 14 to 15 hours after the termination of exhaustive exercise, splanchnic glucose release is 50 to 100 percent greater than in nonexercised subjects (Figure 3). Thus, total splanchnic glucose output (over a 135 minute period after glucose ingestion) accounts for 60 percent of the ingested glucose load in the exercised group as compared to less than 30 percent in resting controls.[29] Despite the doubling of splanchnic glucose escape in the exercised individuals, their blood glucose, insulin, and glucagon levels after glucose ingestion are comparable to those of control subjects.[29] This finding thus suggests that prior exercise decreases hepatic while enhancing peripheral glucose utilization.

With respect to the site of the enhanced extrahepatic uptake of glucose, it is noteworthy that during exhaustive exercise muscle glycogen stores are depleted by

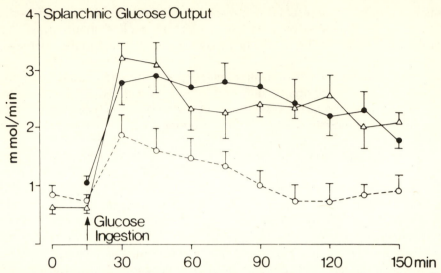

Fig. 3. Splanchnic glucose output following the ingestion of 100 g glucose immediately after exercise (•–•), 14–15 hours following exercise (Δ-Δ) and in nonexercised control subjects (O--O). (From Maehlum et al.)[29] Reprinted with permission from Am J Physiol 235: E255, 1978.

60 to 70 percent.[5] After glucose feeding, the repletion of muscle glycogen can account for 66 percent of the glucose which is ingested immediately prior to exercise. Similarly, when glucose is administered 14 to 15 hours after the completion of exercise, approximately 50 percent of the ingested glucose can be accounted for by repletion of muscle glycogen. Thus, regardless of whether the exercise is performed immediately prior to glucose feeding or 14 to 15 hours before the glucose ingestion, a major part of the administered glucose is released to the systemic circulation and is used for resynthesis of muscle glycogen.[29] Similar observations have been made in the rat, demonstrating accelerated muscle glycogen repletion in the postexercise recovery period.[30]

These findings thus indicate the primary importance of repletion of muscle rather than liver glycogen after glucose administration during the postexercise recovery period. Furthermore, even in the absence of glucose feeding, muscle glycogen stores are partially repleted (30–35 percent) during a 14 to 15 hour recovery, presumably at the expense of hepatic glycogenolysis and gluconeogenesis.[29] The regulatory mechanisms responsible for the enhanced splanchnic escape of glucose and for the primary resynthesis of muscle rather than liver glycogen during recovery remain to be established. As noted above, the changes in the major glucoregulatory hormones, insulin and glucagon, after glucose feeding were comparable in the exercised and control subjects after oral glucose.[29] It is possible, however, that exercise causes changes in the sensitivity of specific tissues to these hormones and thus affects their action at the cellular level.

DIABETIC SUBJECTS

Diabetic Control and the Metabolic Response to Exercise

A beneficial effect of exercise on diabetes has been long recognized, and exercise is generally recommended as an important component of the treatment in diabetes. Clinical evidence available even before the introduction of insulin therapy, however, suggested that strenuous exercise may be harmful in some patients, increasing hyperglycemia, glycosuria, and hyperketonemia.[31,32] It is only recently that the basis for this discrepancy has been examined in detail. It appears that the metabolic response to exercise in juvenile–onset diabetes depends not only on the intensity and duration of exercise, but primarily on the state of diabetic control. In moderately well controlled diabetic patients, blood glucose falls during exercise, the fall being generally greater and more rapid than in nondiabetic subjects (Figure 4). If the fasting blood glucose level is above 300 to 350 mg/dl 17–20 mmol/l, however, and the patients have hyperketonemia (2 mM or more) indicating the presence of severe insulin deficiency, a rise rather than fall in the blood glucose level is observed.[33,34,35,36] Since both hepatic glucose production and peripheral utilization are, at least partly, regulated by circulating insulin,[37,38] the rise in blood glucose in insulin–deficient patients could be a consequence of overproduction or underutilization of glucose, or both. The absolute uptake of glucose by muscle, as well as its relative contribution to total oxidative fuel metabolism during short-term exercise, is virtually identical in poorly and moderately well controlled diabetes and in healthy subjects (27 percent). These observations suggest that the rise in plasma glucose in poorly regulated diabetics is largely due to overproduction of glucose. Excessive glucose production in insulin deficiency may be further stimulated by the excessive rise in glucagon, growth hormone, and cortisol observed in ketotic subjects during exercise.[35]

With respect to lipid metabolism, exercise causes a greater rise in plasma FFA levels in ketotic patients than in nonketotic subjects or healthy individuals.[34,35] As a consequence of greater substrate availability, FFA uptake by the exercising muscle is two-fold higher in ketotic than nonketotic diabetics. Hyperketonemic subjects also demonstrate a substantial rate of muscle uptake of ketone acids. In mildly hyperketonemic patients, a seven-fold increase in ketone body utilization is observed during a 40 minute exercise period.[34]

With regard to overall muscle fuel metabolism during exercise, the relative contribution of blood-borne fuels is similar in nonketotic diabetics and normal man, but differs in ketotic diabetic patients. During 40 minute exercise, blood-borne glucose contributes 25 to 30 percent of oxidative fuel, and a similar proportion is provided by FFA in normal subjects and nonketotic diabetics. In contrast, in ketotic subjects 60 to 65 percent of oxidative fuel is derived from lipids, 56 percent being from FFA and 6 percent from ketone bodies.[34,36] Thus, while the contribution of blood glucose to oxidative energy does not decrease during exercise in ketotic diabetics, FFA utiliza-

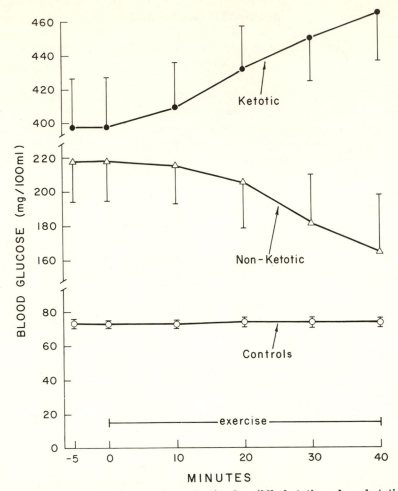

Fig. 4. Changes in arterial glucose concentration in mildly ketotic and nonketotic diabetic patients and healthy subjects during exercise. Insulin was withdrawn 24 hours prior to the exercise. The intensity of exercise corresponded to 60 percent of subjects' maximal aerobic power. (From Wahren et al.)[36] Reprinted with permission from Diabetologia 14:213, 1978.

tion is two-fold higher than in controls and 70 percent above FFA oxidation in nonketotic diabetics. The augmented rate of FFA utilization in ketotic subjects is presumably a consequence of augmented lipolysis, and possibly decreased availability of muscle glycogen observed in insulin deficiency.[39]

With respect to hepatic metabolism, the diabetic state increases the gluconeogenic response to exercise. Short-term exercise (40 minutes) in normal subjects fails to increase the rate of gluconeogenesis above resting levels. In contrast, in diabetics the absolute rate of gluconeogenesis is increased two-fold. This is due to increased hepatic uptake of virtually all gluconeogenic substrates (lactate, pyruvate, alanine, and glycerol). The overall effects of short-term (40 minutes) exercise in the diabetic patient are thus comparable to those of prolonged (four hours) exercise in normal subjects: augmented muscle utilization of FFA and increased hepatic consumption of gluconeogenic precursors. Furthermore, diabetic patients demonstrate a consistent uptake of branched chain amino acids (valine, leucine, and isoleucine) by the exercising leg after 40 minutes, whereas normal subjects demonstrate a similar uptake only after four hours. Thus, the effect of diabetes is to accelerate the metabolic adaptation to exercise.

The disparate responses of poorly controlled and well controlled diabetics to exercise are not only apparent with respect to changes in plasma glucose but also with regard to hepatic metabolism of FFA and ketones. In ketotic diabetics, short-term exercise results in a 50 percent increase in splanchnic uptake of FFA, which contrasts with a decline in FFA utilization in nonketotic diabetics.[34] Furthermore, in the poorly controlled diabetics, hepatic production of ketone acids (β–hydroxy-butyrate and acetoacetate) rises to values two to three-fold the basal rate. In contrast, exercise fails to stimulate hepatic ketogenesis in the nonketotic diabetics.[34] Nevertheless, circulating (arterial) ketone acids remain unchanged from resting levels in both groups because muscle utilization of ketone acids keeps pace with hepatic ketone production.

Concerning the overall clinical effects of exercise on diabetes, it is obvious that utilization of glucose, FFA, and ketone bodies during exercise is augmented in virtually all patients. In adequately treated patients, exercise results in a fall in blood glucose levels because the stimulatory effects on glucose utilization exceed the increase in glucose production. In addition to the acute effect, depletion of muscle and liver glycogen during exercise results in a prolonged enhancement of peripheral glucose utilization,[29] as described in the previous section. As a consequence, postexercise glucose tolerance improves,[40] and insulin requirements may decline in diabetics.[41] In circumstances of insulin deficiency and poor metabolic control, however, the production of glucose, FFA, and ketone bodies may exceed their peripheral utilization during exercise, thus further increasing hyperglycemia and ketogenesis. Acidosis due to ketone body accumulation may be further intensified by the rise in blood lactic acid concentrations during strenuous exercise.[42] These findings indicate that exercise in controlled diabetes has beneficial metabolic effects but may worsen the diabetic state in ketonemic diabetes and thus underscore the importance of adequate insulin treatment in diabetic patients involved in exercise.

The Route of Insulin Administration and
Exercise–induced Hypoglycemia

Hypoglycemia during or after vigorous muscular work has long been recognized as a possible adverse effect of exercise in insulin–treated diabetic subjects.[43] The mechanism of this excessive fall in blood glucose level has only recently been studied in detail, however. When insulin–dependent diabetic patients[44] or pancreatectomized dogs[45] were infused with insulin to maintain basal plasma insulin levels, blood glucose concentration remained unchanged during short-term (45–60 minutes) exercise. If insulin was injected subcutaneously before exercise, however, a

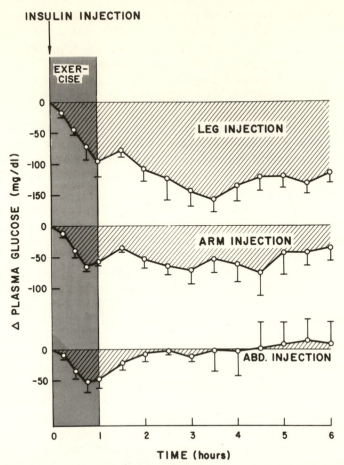

Fig. 5. Plasma glucose response to leg exercise after insulin injection into leg, arm, or abdomen. The shaded areas represent the changes in plasma glucose levels (mean ±SE) induced by leg exercise as compared to the nonexercise control day. The area above the curve for leg injection was 57 percent greater than that observed for arm injection (p<0.02) and 89 percent greater than after abdominal injection (p<0.005). (From Koivisto and Felig.)[50] Reprinted by permission from N Eng J Med 298:79, 1978.

marked fall in blood glucose occurred during exercise.[44,46] These findings suggested that exercise may stimulate the absorption of insulin from the subcutaneous injection site, thus raising plasma insulin levels. This hypothesis was supported by findings in three newly diagnosed diabetics who demonstrated an increase in plasma insulin during exercise preceded by subcutaneous injection of insulin.[46,47] In addition, in normal humans[48] and rats[49] injected with subcutaneous insulin, exercise has been shown to increase plasma insulin levels.

The effects of exercise on insulin absorption in the insulin dependent diabetic was further examined by injecting ^{125}I–labeled insulin subcutaneously and measuring the disappearance rate of labeled insulin during exercise.[50] As compared to a resting, control day, insulin disappearance from the leg increased by 135 percent during the first 10 minutes of leg exercise, and at 60 minutes of exercise was 50 percent above the resting level. In contrast, leg exercise had no effect on insulin disappearance from the arm, and actually reduced the rate of insulin absorption from the abdomen during the postexercise recovery period.[50] Changes in blood glucose caused by exercise were proportional to the alterations in insulin absorption rate. Thus, the exercise–induced fall in blood glucose was greatest when insulin was injected into the leg and least when injected into the abdomen. As compared to the leg injection, after arm or abdominal injection the hypoglycemic effect of leg exercise was reduced by 57 and 89 percent respectively, during a six hour follow-up period (Figure 5).[50] These findings thus indicate that exercise accelerates insulin absorption from the exercising limb, whereas injection into a nonexercising area does not result in enhanced insulin delivery during exercise. These observations have clinical implications in the management of insulin–dependent diabetic subjects; by the use of a nonexercised injection site (e.g., arm or abdomen with leg exercise), exercise–induced hypoglycemia can be reduced.

Exercise and Insulin Sensitivity

ACUTE EXERCISE

In obese, nondiabetic subjects, 60 minutes of submaximal exercise decreases the insulin response to an oral or intravenous glucose load without impairing glucose tolerance.[51] This effect may persist up to four to six days after exercise, suggesting that muscular work may increase body sensitivity to insulin. In insulin–treated diabetic subjects, acute exercise can increase the disposal of glucose which is administered intravenously immediately after the exercise.[40] The improvement in the glucose disappearance rate is proportional to the intensity of exercise, and it may rise from 0.4 mg/kg/min in the resting state to levels of 0.8–0.9 mg/kg/min (i.e., close to normal) after intensive exercise.[40] Consequently, the dose of exogenous insulin can be reduced in some diabetic patients involved in exercise.[41,43]

The mechanism of augmented glucose uptake and insulin sensitivity during and after exercise is not completely understood. Although an increase in insulin delivery to the muscle vascular bed,[37] as well as the depletion of glycogen stores,[29] may promote glucose uptake during and after muscular work, they may not fully explain the improved insulin sensitivity which follows exercise. Recent studies have indicated that alterations in insulin sensitivity correlate with changes in insulin binding to monocytes in a variety of conditions, such as obesity,[52,53] growth hormone deficiency,[54] and maturity onset diabetes.[55] Consequently, the effect of acute exercise on insulin binding to monocytes was examined. In a recent study, we observed a 36 percent rise in insulin binding to monocytes after a three hour period of exercise (Figure 6).[56] This rise was due to a rise in receptor affinity rather than an increase in the number of receptors. Furthermore, the augmentation in insulin binding was proportional to a fall in plasma glucose level during exercise. These findings thus suggest that enhanced insulin binding may contribute to augmented glucose uptake and insulin sensitivity caused by acute exercise.

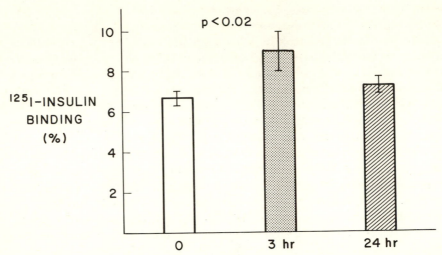

Fig. 6. Specific binding of ^{125}I–insulin to monocytes in normal man prior to, immediately after, and 24 hours after a three hour ergometric exercise. During exercise, insulin binding rose by 36 percent, but was returned to the baseline 24 hours later.

PHYSICAL TRAINING

Since acute exercise can improve insulin sensitivity, one might postulate that regularly repeated exercise or training can result in an even greater improvement of body sensitivity to insulin. In obese subjects, an eight week training program, involving exercise three to four hours per day three to five days a week, did not change the plasma glucose response to oral glucose load. The rise in plasma insulin after glucose ingestion was 40 to 50 percent less after the training program, however, suggesting enhanced insulin sensitivity.[57] More recently, the glucose and insulin response to an intravenous glucose load was studied in "world–class" long–distance runners.[58] After intravenous glucose, the plasma glucose response was comparable to that in sedentary controls. In the athletes, however, both the basal insulin concentration and the insulin response to glucose was 50 to 70 percent lower than in control subjects. Thus, physical training in obese subjects as well as athletes has a hypoinsulinemic effect yet causes no deterioration in glucose tolerance. On the other hand, physical inactivity, such as two weeks of bedrest, causes hyperinsulinemia in association with a deterioration of glucose tolerance, suggesting the development of insulin resistance.[59]

We have recently examined the mechanism of the augmented insulin sensitivity in athletes by determining the specific binding of insulin to monocytes.[16] In well trained long–distance runners ($\dot{V}O_2$max 66±1 ml/kg/min) insulin binding was 69 percent higher than in sedentary controls ($\dot{V}O_2$max 43± ml/kg/min). Furthermore, in athletes insulin binding was proportional to their maximal aerobic power. In other recent studies, we noted that when previously sedentary subjects were studied after a six week training program, insulin binding to monocytes, as well as insulin-stimulated glucose uptake (as determined by the euglycemic insulin clamp technic), rose by 35 to 40 percent.[59a] Thus augmented insulin binding to receptors may constitute the mechanism of enhanced insulin sensitivity induced by physical training. It is of interest that in well trained long-distance runners the activity of lipoprotein lipase both in muscle and adipose tissue is 1.5 to 2.3 fold higher than in sedentary subjects.[60] Similarly, in rats subjected to a 12 week training program, lipoprotein lipase activity is elevated two to three-fold.[61] Since functional lipoprotein lipase is highly sensitive to insulin, its enhanced activity in trained individuals could be explained, at least partly, by augmented insulin action in muscle tissue.

These findings, indicating that acute exercise and particularly physical training can improve insulin sensitivity in the resting state, may have implications in the management of diabetes mellitus. In maturity-onset diabetes, insulin resistance rather than insulin deficiency is often the major reason for hyperglycemia.[55,62] Furthermore, insulin resistance in these patients is closely proportional to a reduction in insulin binding to monocytes.[55] Since training can augment insulin binding and insulin sensitivity, regular exercise may provide a means to reverse or ameliorate abnormalities in insulin binding and sensitivity in patients with maturity-onset diabetes.

REFERENCES

1. Saltin B, Karlsson J: Muscle glycogen utilization during work of different intensities. in: *Muscle Metabolism during Exercise*, Pernow B, Saltin B (eds). New York, Plenum Press, 1971, p 289
2. Ahlborg G, Felig P, Hagenfeldt L, et al: Substrate turnover during prolonged exercise in man. *J Clin Invest* 53:1080, 1974
3. Wahren J, Felig P, Ahlborg G, et al: Glucose metabolism during leg exercise in man. *J Clin Invest* 50:2715, 1971
4. Rowell LB, Masoro EJ, Spencer MJ: Splanchnic metabolism in exercising man. *J Appl Physiol* 20:1032, 1965
5. Bergstrom J, Hultman E: A study of glyogen metabolism during exercise in man. *Scand J Clin Lab Invest* 19:218, 1967
6. Hultman E, Nilsson LH: Liver glycogen in man. Effect of different diets and muscular exercise. in: *Muscle Metabolism during Exercise*, Pernow B, Saltin B (eds). New York, Plenum Press, 1971, p 143
7. Hagenfeldt L, Wahren J: Metabolism of free fatty acids and ketone bodies in skeletal muscle. in: *Muscle Metabolism during Exercise*, Pernow B, Saltin B (eds). New York, Plenum Press, 1971, p 153
8. Fröberg SO, Carlsson LA, Ekeland LG: Local lipid stores and exercise. in: *Muscle Metabolism during Exercise*, Pernow B, Saltin B (eds). New York, Plenum Press, 1971, p 307
9. Pruett EDR: Plasma insulin concentrations during prolonged work at near maximal oxygen uptake. *J Appl Physiol* 29:155, 1970
10. Felig P, Wahren J: Fuel homeostasis in exercise. *N Engl J Med* 293:1078, 1975

11. Felig P, Wahren J, Hendler R, et al: Plasma glucagon levels in exercising man. *N Engl J Med* 287:184, 1972
12. Böttger I, Schlein EM, Faloona GR, et al: The effect of exercise on glucagon secretion. *J Clin Endocrinol Metab* 35:117, 1972
13. Galbo H, Holst J, Christensen NJ: Glucagon and plasma catecholamine responses to graded and prolonged exercise in man. *J Appl Physiol* 38:70, 1975
14. Few JD: Effect of exercise in the secretion and metabolism of cortisol in man. *J Endocrinol* 62:341, 1974
15. Galbo H, Richter EA, Hilsted J, et al: Hormonal regulation during prolonged exercise. *Ann NY Acad Sci* 301:72, 1977
16. Koivisto VA, Soman V, Conrad P, et al: Insulin binding to monocytes in trained athletes: Changes in the resting state and after exercise. *J Clin Invest* in press
17. Johnson RH, Walton JL, Krebs HA, et al: Metabolic fuels during and after severe exercise in athletes and nonathletes. *Lancet* 2:452, 1969
18. Fitts RH, Booth FW, Winder WW, et al: Skeletal muscle respiratory capacity, endurance and glycogen utilization. *Am J Physiol* 228:1029, 1975
18a. Holloszy JO, Booth FW: Biochemical adaptations to endurance exercise. *Ann Rev Physiol* 38:273, 1976
19. Neely JR, Morgan HE: Relationship between carbohydrate and lipid metabolism and the energy balance of heart muscle. *Ann Rev Physiol* 36:413, 1974
20. Paul P, Issekutz B, Miller HI: Interrelationship of free fatty acid and glucose metabolism in the dog. *Am J Physiol* 211: 1313, 1966
21. Ahlborg G, Felig P: Substrate utilization during prolonged exercise preceded by ingestion of glucose. *Am J Physiol* 233:E188, 1977
22. Felig P, Wahren J, Hendler R: Influence of oral glucose ingestion on splanchnic glucose and gluconeogenic substrate in man. *Diabetes* 24:468, 1975
23. Felig P, Wahren J: Influence of endogenous insulin secretion on splanchnic glucose and amino acid metabolism in man. *J Clin Invest* 50:1702, 1971
24. Sacca L, Hendler R, Sherwin RS: Hyperglycemia inhibits glucose production in man independent of changes in glucoregulatory hormones. *J Clin Endocrinol Metab* 47:1160, 1978
25. Böje O: Der Blutzucker während und nach körperlicher Arbeit. *Skand Arch Physiol* 74:1, 1936
26. Costill DL, Coyle E, Dalsky G, et al: Effects of elevated plasma FFA and insulin on muscle glycogen usage during exercise. *J Appl Physiol* 43:695, 1977
27. Ahlborg G, Felig P: Influence of glucose ingestion on fuel–hormone response during prolonged exercise. *J Appl Physiol* 41:683, 1976
28. Felig P, Wahren J, Hendler R: Influence of oral glucose ingestion on splanchnic glucose and gluconeogenic substrate metabolism in man. *Diabetes* 24:468, 1975
29. Maehlum S, Felig P, Wahren J: Splanchnic glucose and muscle glycogen metabolism after glucose feeding during postexercise recovery. *Am J Physiol* 235:E255, 1978
30. Terjung RL, Baldwin KM, Winder WW, et al: Glycogen repletion in different types of muscle and in liver after exhausting exercise. *Am J Physiol* 226:1387, 1974
31. Allen FM, Stillman E, Fitz R: Total dietary regulation in the treatment of diabetes. Monograph No. 11, the Rockefeller Institute of Medical Research, New York, 1919, p 468
32. Barringer TB: The effect of exercise upon carbohydrate tolerance in diabetes. *Am J Med Sci* 151:181, 1961
33. Sanders CA, Levinson GE, Abelman WH, et al: Effect of exercise on the peripheral utilization of glucose in man. *N Engl J Med* 271:220, 1964

34. Wahren J, Hagenfeldt L, Felig P: Splanchnic and leg exchange of glucose, amino acids, and free fatty acids during exercise in diabetes mellitus. *J Clin Invest* 55:1303, 1975
35. Berger M, Berchtold P, Cuppers HJ, et al: Metabolic and hormonal effects of muscular exercise in juvenile type diabetics. *Diabetologia* 13:355, 1977
36. Wahren J, Felig P, Hagenfeldt L: Physical exercise and fuel homeostasis in diabetes mellitus. *Diabetologia* 14:213, 1978
37. Vranic M, Kawamori R, Pek S, et al: The essentiality of insulin and the role of glucagon in regulating glucose utilization and production during strenuous exercise in dogs. *J Clin Invest* 57:245, 1976
38. Berger M, Hagg S, Ruderman NB: Glucose metabolism in perfused skeletal muscle. Interaction of insulin and exercise on glucose uptake. *Biochem J* 146:231, 1975
39. Roch-Norlund AE, Bergstrom J, Castenfors H, et al: Muscle glycogen in patients with diabetes mellitus. Glycogen content before treatment and the effect of insulin. *Acta Med Scand* 187:445, 1970
40. Maehlum S, Pruett EDR: Muscular exercise and metabolism in male juvenile diabetics. II. Glucose tolerance after exercise. *Scand J Clin Lab Invest* 32:149, 1973
41. Engerbretson DL: The effects of exercise upon diabetic control. *J Assoc Phys Ment Rehab* 19:74, 1965
42. Koivisto VA, Akerblom HK, Kiviluoto MK: Metabolic and hormonal effects of exercise in the severely streptozotocin–diabetic rat. *Diabetologia* 10:329, 1975
43. Lawrence RD: The effect of exercise on insulin action in diabetes. *Br Med J* 1:648, 1926
44. Murray FT, Zinman B, McClean PA, et al: The metabolic response to moderate exercise in diabetic man receiving intravenous and subcutaneous insulin. *J Clin Endocrinol Metab* 44:708, 1977
45. Kawamori R, Vranic M: Mechanism of exercise–induced hypoglycemia in depancreatized dogs maintained on long-acting insulin. *J Clin Invest* 59:331, 1977
46. Zinman B, Murray FT, Vranic M, et al: Glucoregulation during moderate exercise in insulin treated diabetics. *J Clin Endocrinol Metab* 45:641, 1977
47. Albisser AM, Leibel BS, Zinman B, et al: Studies with an artificial endocrine pancreas. *Arch Intern Med* 137:639, 1977
48. Dandona P, Hooke O, Bell J: Exercise and insulin absorption from subcutaneous tissue. *Br Med J* 1:479, 1978
49. Berger M, Halban BA, Muller WA, et al: Mobilization of subcutaneously injected tritiated insulin in rats: effects of muscular exercise. *Diabetologia* 15:133, 1978
50. Koivisto VA, Felig P: Effects of leg exercise on insulin absorption in diabetic patients. *N Engl J Med* 298:79, 1978
51. Fahlen M, Stenberg J, Björntorp P: Insulin secretion in obesity after exercise. *Diabetologia* 8:141, 1972
52. Olefsky JM: Decreased insulin binding to adipocytes and circulating monocytes from obese subjects. *J Clin Invest* 57:1165, 1976
53. DeFronzo R, Soman V, Sherwin RS, et al: Insulin binding to monocytes and insulin action in human obesity, starvation and refeeding. *J Clin Invest* 62:204, 1978
54. Soman V, Tamborlane W, DeFronzo R, et al: Insulin binding and insulin sensitivity in isolated growth hormone deficiency. *N Engl J Med* 299:1025, 1978
55. DeFronzo R, Deibert D, Hendler, et al: Insulin sensitivity and insulin binding to monocytes in maturity onset diabetes. *J Clin Invest,* in press
56. Soman VR, Koivisto VA, Grantham P, et al: Increased insulin binding to monocytes after acute exercise in normal man. *J Clin Endocrinol Metab* 47:216, 1978
57. Björntorp P, DeJounge K, Sjöstrom L, et al: The effect of physical training on insulin production in obesity. *Metabolism* 19:631, 1970

58. Lohman D, Liebold F, Heilman W, et al: Diminished insulin response in highly trained athletes. *Metabolism* 27:521, 1978

59. Lipman RL, Raskin P, Love T, et al: Glucose intolerance during decreased physical activity in man. *Diabetes* 21:101, 1972

59a. Felig P, Koivisto V, Soman V, et al: Increased sensitivity to insulin and increased insulin binding induced by physical training. *Diabetes* 28:suppl 2, 37

60. Nikkila EA, Taskinen M-R: Lipoprotein lipase activity in adipose tissue and skeletal muscle of runners: relation to serum lipoproteins. *Metabolism* 27:1661, 1978

61. Borensztajn J, Rone MS, Babirak SP, et al: Effect of exercise on lipoprotein lipase activity in rat heart and skeletal muscle. *Am J Physiol* 229:394, 1975

62. Reaven GM, Berstein R, Davis B, et al: Nonketotic diabetes mellitus: insulin deficiency or insulin resistance. *Am J Med* 60:80, 1976

Heart and Circulatory Function in Exercise

ALFRED A. BOVE, M.D., PH.D.

Although exercise is generally considered to be an undertaking reserved for the athlete who is usually young or for those few individuals who are willing to undertake exercise programs in later years, in essence it is part of the daily life of all individuals. The body's response to even minimal changes in physical activity such as walking, climbing stairs, lifting moderately heavy objects, avoiding injury or danger by rapid locomotion, and many other examples, are characteristic of the exercise response.

Not only man but most other animal species are adapted to perform exercise to preserve safety, provide for survival, and often to obtain food. In all cases, exercise is associated with increased metabolism and increased performance of skeletal muscle. This increased metabolic activity allows for rapid locomotion when it is needed for rapid mobility, as well as for increased physical strength and for the performance of structured athletic activities. In all cases, the increased activity in skeletal muscle ultimately results in an increase in skeletal muscle blood flow.[1,2] This increase in blood flow to the skeletal muscle causes a change in peripheral vascular resistance which is sensed and responded to by the circulation in such a way that the blood flow demands are met. This typical blood flow response is found in most mammalian species, including man. According to the specific need, exercise may require different muscle groups, but in all cases a common response is increased activity of the sympathetic nervous system.[2,3] The increased activity of the sympathetic nervous system occurs in response to central perception of the need for exercise, such as a dangerous situation which requires rapid physical motion or, in the animal world, the sensing of a natural enemy nearby. The response in all cases causes an increase in sympathetic outflow, a rise in blood pressure, an increase in heart rate, an increase in myocardial contractility, changes in the peripheral vascular system, and a number of other changes which will be outlined below. Thus, exercise represents one of the many stimuli for activity of the sympathetic system and, as such, the understanding of the hemodynamic changes which are induced by exercise are founded on a general understanding of the effect of the sympathetic nervous system on the heart and circulation.

Exercise can be divided into two types: aerobic (isotonic) and anaerobic (isometric). Many activities are a combination of the two types, but many activities are primarily one or the other.

AEROBIC EXERCISE

This type of exercise is represented by jogging, swimming, or bicycling, for example. It involves moving the extremities or working the muscles on a continuous basis in such a way that a steady state balance is achieved between oxygen utilization and oxygen supply to skeletal muscle. Thus, aerobic exercise induces an increase in the rate of respiration and in the flow of blood to working skeletal muscle to meet the needs for oxygen and metabolic fuels. When the workload in this steady state mode is increased, cardiac output and respiratory minute volume also increase, but in general a balance is maintained between oxygen utilization and oxygen uptake.[2,4,5] As the workload is increased to near maximal levels, however, a significant component of anaerobic metabolism occurs in skeletal muscle and the steady state balance may be upset. Indeed, at maximal workloads the activity no longer is aerobic but primarily anaerobic.[5] At this point the exercising subject develops rapid fatigue.

As discussed above, the sympathetic nervous system is activated by both the centrally mediated perception of the need for exercise and circulatory responses which most likely are subservient to the needs of skeletal muscles for blood flow. When the sympathetic system is activated, the state of activation of the brain itself is increased,[3] which in turn causes the individual to become more alert, to have quicker reflexes, and to be more responsive to external stimuli, Sympathetic outflow to the heart causes an increase in the heart rate, an increase in the force of contraction, and an increase in contractility.[6] Stroke volume and heart rate variation can alter cardiac output and since heart rate initially increases more rapidly than cardiac output with increasing workloads, the stroke volume tends to fall early in exercise. As the workload increases and heart rate reaches maximum, the stroke volume then contributes more to cardiac output reserve. In a study by Stone[7] using chronically implanted ultrasonic crystals, the cardiac dimensions were noted to fall slightly early in exercise; and as workload and heart rate increased, the cardiac dimensions which are indicators of left ventricular volume showed a slight increase as exercise progressed. Heart rate, on the other hand, is known to rise continuously with workload.[11,5] This linear relationship has been noted by several investigators when comparing heart rate with workload measured in some standard fashion.[5,7] Thus, for example, using an exercise treadmill and a standard stress test protocol such as that described by Bruce,[4] one notes a linear increase in heart rate as workload rises above resting levels (Figure 1). The same phenomenon can be found in experimental ani-

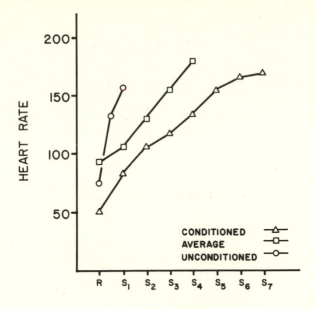

Fig. 1. Heart rate response to a graded treadmill workload in three healthy individuals with different levels of conditioning. The conditioned individual shows the lowest heart rates at each workload. R, rest; S1, S7, stages of a standard Bruce protocol.

mals and is a typical response to increasing loads.[7] A response of this type can be used to characterize the state of physical condition of an individual or an animal. Early in exercise, left ventricular end diastolic pressure usually falls and the ventricular function curve indicates that a decreased end diastolic volume results from the combination of increased contractility and increased heart rate induced by exercise (Figure 2). When this pattern of change is followed from the normal to the increased contractility curve, it is evident that left ventricular end diastolic volume and left ventricular end diastolic pressure should fall. Myocardial blood flow increases with exercise and may reach levels of three to five times resting values with exercise.[8,9] Myocardial blood flow and blood flow distribution have been studied in our laboratory, using the radioactive microsphere technique,[10] and we found an increase in myocardial blood flow with exercise. The distribution of flow as measured by endocardial to epicardial flow ratio has recently been of interest because of its relationship to ischemic heart disease. We found this ratio was unchanged in the normal heart during exercise in experimental animals (Table 1). Thus, endocardial blood flow is not compromised and does not fall during exercise in normal animals. Indeed, endocardial blood flow rises in a fashion similar to blood flow in other regions of the myocardium during aerobic exercise.

Generally, skeletal muscle is controlled by the sympathetic nervous system at rest.[1,2,11] Thus, when the sympathetic nervous system is activated in the absence of

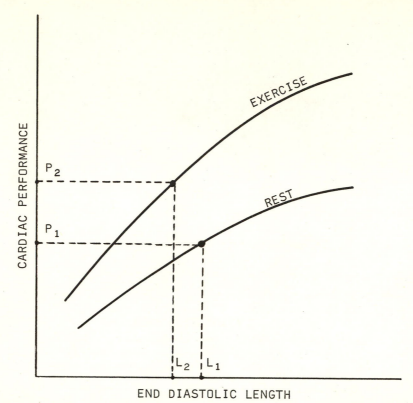

Fig. 2. Ventricular function (Starling) curves for rest and exercise. Due to increased contractility in the exercise curve, end diastolic length will fall even though performance is increased.

exercise or increased skeletal muscle metabolism, there is a reflex vasoconstriction in the skeletal muscle. On the other hand, during exercise skeletal muscle is primarily regulated by local metabolic control of blood vessels.[1,11] Thus, during exercise, changes in sympathetic activity will not affect skeletal muscle blood flow. Rather the workload which the muscle experiences in some way causes increased demands for blood. These demands are manifested by vasodilation and reduced vascular resistance in the specific muscle bed which is exercising. During exercise, cardiac output is responsive to the needs of skeletal muscle. In response to the reduced peripheral

TABLE 1 Endocardial/Epicardial Blood Flow Ratio in 6 Dogs at Rest and during Exercise

	Rest	Exercise
Heart Rate	98	175
	+6	+3
E/E Ratio	1.216	1.265
	+.07	+.07

resistance, the heart, circulation, and sympathetic system are activated to increase cardiac output and supply the skeletal muscle demands. It is reasonable to expect that cardiac output would rise linearly with workload. This is indeed the case. One can find a linear relationship between cardiac output and workload up to maximal workload levels.[5,12,13] This response is of interest in regard to the heart which is impaired by chronic disease, for example. In patients who have mild degrees of left ventricular failure from any cause, the skeletal muscle functions normally during exercise. When an individual with heart failure exercises, the skeletal muscle vascular beds dilate, the peripheral resistance falls, and the sympathetic system is stimulated to increase the cardiac output. However, if the heart is abnormal, this increased stimulus may not produce an appropriate cardiac output increase. If cardiac output does not rise appropriately, blood pressure will not be maintained in the presence of the dilated peripheral vascular beds and the individual will experience syncope.[14]

Alterations Induced by Training

Although exercise itself produces acute changes within the cardiovascular system in response to the increased demands of skeletal muscle, it is also evident that chronic endurance exercise produces changes in the heart and circulation which adapt the organism to the demands of the chronic exercise.[2,7,19,20,21,22,23,24,25,26] The adaptation of the circulation includes an increase in the circulating blood volume.[15,18,19,23,24] This increase is primarily an increase in blood plasma; however some investigators have suggested an increase in the red cell or hemoglobin content as well. The increase in blood volume would provide more blood flow to the peripheral circulation and, in addition, it appears to produce increased heart size. This response is thus equivalent to a volume overload. Heart rate in the endurance-trained person is usually slower at rest.[2,18,19,26,27] Studies by numerous authors indicate that this is a consistent finding among males and females and in a variety of age groups.[30,31] The cause for this reduced heart rate is not clear. Tipton et al[29] have found increases in acetylcholine in the atrial tissues of rats and dogs exercised to a level which improved their state of conditioning. The resting bradycardia may indeed be an effect of adaptive change within the nervous system. For example, it is possible that the increased circulating blood volume stimulates the baroreceptors and causes reflex bradycardia. None of these hypotheses, however, have been well substantiated, and at present the precise mechanism for the resting bradycardia of training remains unclear. Heart size in endurance-trained athletes is known to be increased.[30,32] This increase was first noticed on the standard chest x-ray and was initially considered to represent an abnormal condition.[33] Thus, the "athlete's heart," a heart which is larger than normal in size, was considered in the past to function abnormally. However, it is now evident that this concept of abnormal function is erroneous. The heart of the endurance-trained athlete functions normally and indeed may demonstrate above normal function. The change in heart size is mediated by an increase in end diastolic volume[20] with an associated increase in stroke volume. The increase in end diastolic volume is considered to be a result of the bradycardia which, in the face of maintaining a normal resting cardiac output, would induce a larger stroke volume and end diastolic volume. Studies in our laboratory on trained dogs,[20] as well as echocardiographic studies on humans, however,[32] have shown that when heart rate is held constant there is still an increase in end diastolic volume as a result of endurance training. The increase in heart size, therefore, is not entirely dependent on the reduced heart rate at rest but indeed may also be a function of other factors such as increased blood volume. A third possibility, which is as yet unexamined, is that an alteration in the compliance of the left ventricle has allowed the ventricle to attain a larger volume at the same diastolic filling pressures.

A variety of animal studies using different species has shown that exercise produces cardiac hypertrophy.[15,20,22,30,34] Hypertrophy in this case is defined as an increase in muscle mass of the heart (usually in relation to body weight). Studies in exercising rats have demonstrated cardiac hypertrophy of the left and right ventricles on the order of 40 to 50 percent.[19,28,35] In canine studies of chronic endurance exercise, cardiac hypertrophy has been found to vary between 8 and 30 percent. From these studies, it is clear that increase in mass or muscle weight of the heart relative to body size is known to occur in response to chronic endurance exercise. Several studies examining the performance of such mildly hypertrophied hearts indicate that they function in either a normal or above normal way. Studies by Scheuer and coworkers[17,22,35] have shown that the rat heart hypertrophied from exercise functions on a higher ventricular function curve when examined in the isolated perfused heart preparation. Studies from our laboratory on intact dogs indicate that the left ventricle functions along the same Starling Curve when stroke volume is compared to end diastolic volume before and after training. When pressure is considered in performance, however, the left ventricle demonstrates an increased performance compared to the heart of untrained control animals.[20] An interesting response of the myocardium to exercise concerns the distribution of blood capillaries in the myocardium in response to exercise. Several studies[9,36] have shown that total capillary blood volume is increased in the exercise-trained heart, while others[37,38] have demonstrated that the number of capillaries per unit of myocardium is increased. A study in our laboratory examining the distribution of myocardial blood flow in exercise-trained animals under several loads[10] indicates that blood flow distribution under acute loads may be somewhat more uniform in the exercise-trained heart.

An important adaptation of the heart and circulation to chronic-endurance exercise occurs in the factors making up cardiac output. Cardiac output is controlled primarily by the needs of tissues and organs for oxygen and metabolic fuels. The oxygen demands of tissue, however, can also be met by increasing oxygen extraction. Indeed, in trained subjects the arteriovenous O_2 difference during exercise is increased, as compared to sedentary controls.[2] This change comes about because of adaptation in the skeletal muscle which allows the muscle to utilize oxygen at a more rapid rate. The changes in skeletal muscle have been recently identified as an increase in cytochrome oxidase which is a respiratory enzyme residing within the mitochondria.[39] This enzyme activity increases because of both an increase in mitochondrial density in trained skeletal muscle and an increase in the specific enzyme activity per gram of mitochondria.[39] With an increased oxidative capacity in skeletal muscle, more oxygen can be extracted per unit of blood flowing through the muscle; thus the arteriovenous O_2 difference will be increased. Since the blood flow to skeletal muscle during exercise is regulated by oxygen demand, it is clear that an increased arterial venous oxygen difference results in a reduced cardiac output in a trained subject, as compared to an untrained subject under the same workload. In trained subjects or experimental animals, both heart rate and cardiac output are lower than non-trained controls subjected to the same workload. The net result is an equivalent delivery of oxygen to the working muscles which must produce the same amount of work whether the subject is trained or untrained.

Several studies have shown that resting blood pressure is lower in trained subjects. The cause for this change is unclear but may be related to an alteration in overall autonomic balance as a result of endurance training. In addition to the reduced resting blood pressure found in trained subjects at rest, blood pressure during exercise in trained subjects does not attain levels as high as sedentary controls.[2] Mild hypertension may be amenable to treatment with aerobic training as an adjunct to more standard forms of therapy.[40,41]

Finally, it is well accepted that physical performance is improved as a result of exercise training. Thus, the individual who trains vigorously with daily endurance exercise is noted to have the capability of maintaining high workloads over long periods of time. This adaptation comes about because of the combination of changes which occur in the circulation and skeletal muscle. These changes provide the trained individual with greater circulatory reserve which is not taxed as severely for a given workload as in the untrained individual. Thus, at a given workload lactic acid levels are lower, heart rate is lower, cardiac output is lower, and blood pressure is lower. Myocardial oxygen demands are reduced and myocardial blood flow is lower, thus providing a significant reserve. All of these factors in combination with adaptive changes in lung function tend to provide a greater overall performance reserve and allow the trained individual to tax less of this reserve at a given workload. Indeed, the converse of this statement is also true. A lack of adequate conditioning and a lack of adequate physical activity causes alterations in the heart and circulatory system, as well as the lungs, blood volume, and skeletal muscle, which are the opposite of those found in endurance training.[16,21,42] Thus, during prolonged bed rest, for example, blood volume is reduced, heart size is smaller, myocardial mass falls, blood pressure response to exercise is higher, and physical performance capability is markedly reduced; so that from the standpoint of physical performance, the detrained individual is physically inferior to the well-trained one. This reduced capacity is manifest both in the objective tests of physical capacity and the subjective sensations which the detrained subject experiences when physical activity is required.

Isometric Exercise

The second type of exercise to be considered is isometric or anaerobic exercise. Exercise of this type usually involves exertion which is of a brief duration but which is undertaken against a heavy load. In isometric exercise the individual usually is required to lift, push, or pull very heavy loads in a manner which requires no motion or very little motion of the exercising muscles. The skeletal muscle in this case is required to produce high force or tension but little or no external shortening.

Because of the large forces generated in the skeletal muscle, interstitial tissue pressures are high and often result in obstruction of blood flow to the muscle.[43] With absence or significant diminution of blood flow to the skeletal muscle during work, metabolism is primarily anaerobic and results in accumulation of lactic acid. This type of exercise and the response which it induces in the skeletal muscle results in a different adaptive change than that found with chronic endurance exercise. In addition to the skeletal muscle changes which occur during acute isometric exercise, most individuals who experience or undertake this exercise perform a valsalva maneuver during the straining or lifting phase. The combination of skeletal muscle blood flow restriction and the valsalva maneuver tend to raise arterial blood pressure to high levels during the performance of the isometric workload. Thus, with isometric work, both systolic and diastolic pressure rise because of the significant rise of vascular resistance.[43,44] Changes of this type within the circulation produce excessive demands on the myocardium because of the high cost of pressure work in terms of myocardial oxygen utilization.[43,44] Thus, isometric exercise produces significant hypertension during exercise. This response produces excessive elevation of myocardial oxygen demand and in the presence of coronary artery disease, for example, can produce symptoms during this type of exercise. The cardiac response to acute isometric exercise includes a rapid rise in heart rate during the acute exercise state.[43] This response is reflex in nature and appears to be independent of the intensity of the workload.[43] An increase in cardiac output is also found with isometric exercise. In the presence of reduced muscle flow, the distribution must include increased flow to other tissues. Cardiac output returns toward baseline once skeletal muscle metabolites generated by anaerobic metabolism regain a steady state balance. Even low intensity isometric exercise induces a sympathetic response. Indeed an isometric hand grip can be used to raise arterial blood pressure. When exercise is confined to forearm muscle activity, the hypertensive response cannot be explained purely on the basis of increased peripheral vascular resistance from increased interstitial muscle tissue pressure, but must in addition include a component of sympathetic vasoconstriction during the isometric activity. All of these responses cause significant rises in both systolic and diastolic blood pressure and may result in detrimental responses in the myocardium.

The chronic response to isometric exercise is also different from the chronic response to long term endurance exercise. Skeletal muscle hypertrophies to a greater degree in isometric exercise. Thus, the typical weight lifter has a markedly increased skeletal muscle mass which is produced in response to the chronic isometric loads. These skeletal muscles, however, are not adapted for increased oxygen utilization to the degree found with long term endurance training. Rather, the muscles are trained for large loads and short durations of activity.

As a result of chronic isometric exercise training, the heart is usually hypertrophied to some degree.[36] In a study of weight lifters in our laboratory,[45] we found a 30 percent increase in ventricular muscle mass in a group of competitive weight lifters compared to normals. The hypertrophy is not a concentric hypertrophy but appears to be an increase in myocardial mass with maintenance of essentially normal intracavitary volume. There have been few useful experimental studies on intrinsic cardiac performance after isometric conditioning. An echocardiographic study performed by Morganroth[32] has shown essentially unchanged performance characteristics in shot-putters who train primarily by weight lifting. The reason for the lack of performance information in this type of exercise is the difficulty in developing an adequate means of producing chronic isometric exercise loads in controlled experimental models. A recent study in cats by Muntz et al,[46] however, has to some degree overcome this deficit. They trained cats to perform isometric exercise to obtain food rewards. In their study, 40 percent left ventricular hypertrophy was found after two to nine months. Further experimental studies are needed to better understand acute and chronic isometric exercise effects on the heart and circulation.

CONCLUSIONS

It is evident from the data presented above that exercise is an important component of the normal activity of all persons. This concept is supported by the presence in man of an active autonomic system which provides protection against adversity by generating an adequate circulatory response for the supply of skeletal muscle with oxygen and metabolic substrates as the need arises. In modern society, man utilizes this response minimally unless he undertakes appropriate exercise. It is evident from studies on detraining effects that inadequate utilization of this response blunts the ability of the sympathetic system to respond properly to exercise demands, so that non-exercising man becomes unable to exercise even when required to do so. This inherited sympathetic system is the prime mediator of the responses to exercise and is activated both by central stimulation arising from the perception of the need for exercise and by local skeletal muscle blood flow demands which are generated by products of metabolism within the exercising skeletal muscle. As a result of a number of animal studies undertaken in the laboratory of this author as well as those of others, it appears from adaptations of blood volume, heart size, heart rate, blood pressure, tissue vascularity, skeletal muscle metabolic properties, and the overall hemodynamic responses to exercise that modern man exists in a chronically detrained state. Even a moderate degree of continuous and routine exercise will produce a significant change in the above mentioned aspects of the blood and circulation. Indeed, these changes may be useful in the rehabilitation of cardiac patients. Although one may argue that modern man does not need to be an athlete, it is important to point out that exercise does not necessarily mean competitive athletics or a routine program of daily jogging or other structured activity. The important concept to maintain is the fact that exercise is performed whenever an individual walks, climbs stairs, lifts or carries any object, or participates in any recreational activity. Although individuals with normal cardiovascular systems do not feel seriously stressed by average day-to-day activity, the same activity can stress the individual with serious heart or lung disease to levels near maximal capacity, producing an exercise response similar to that found in a normal person working at extremely high workloads. A better understanding of the adaptation which the blood, heart, and circulation undergo in response to exercise will provide a better understanding of the response to exercise of patients with chronic heart disease or other abnormalities of the circulation, and may provide insight into therapy for improvement of physical capacity.

REFERENCES

1. Bevegard S, Shepherd JT: Regulation of the circulation during exercise in man. *Physiol Rev* 47:178, 1967
2. Clausen JP: Effect of physical training on cardiovascular adjustments to exercise. *Physiol Rev* 37:779, 1977
3. Bove AA: The cardiovascular response to stress. *Psychosomatics* 18:13, 1977
4. Bruce RA, Kusumi F, Hosmer D: Maximal oxygen intake and monographic assessment of functional aerobic impairment in cardiovascular disease. *Am Heart J* 85:546, 1973
5. Astrand PO, Saltin B: Maximal oxygen uptake and heart rate in various types of muscular activity. *J Appl Physiol* 16:977, 1967
6. Vatner SF, Braunwald E: Cardiovascular control mechanisms in the conscious state. *New Engl J Med* 293:970, 1975
7. Stone L: Cardiac function and exercise training in conscious dogs. *J Appl Physiol* 42:824, 1977
8. Sonnenblick EH, Ross J, Braunwald E: Oxygen consumption of the heart: new concepts of its multifactorial determination. *Am J Cardiol* 22:328, 1968
9. Terjung RL, Spear KL: Effects of exercise training on coronary blood flow in rats. *Physiologist* 18:419, 1975
10. Bove, AA, Hultgren PB, Ritzer TF, Carey RA: Myocardial blood flow and hemodynamic responses to exercise training in dogs. *J Appl Physiol* 46:571, 1979
11. Brundin T, Cernigliaro C: The effect of physical training on the sympatho-adrenal response to exercise. *Scan J Clin Lab Inv* 35:525, 530, 1975
12. Ekblom B, Hermansen L: Cardiac outputs in athletes. *J Appl Physiol* 25:619, 1968
13. Saltin B, Astrand P: Maximal oxygen uptake in athletes. *J Appl Physiol* 23:353, 1967
14. Zelis R, Longhurst J, Capone RJ, et al: Peripheral circulatory control mechanisms in congestive heart failure. in: Mason DT (ed): *Congestive Heart Failure*. Dun. Donnelley, New York, 1976, p 129
15. Grande F, Taylor HL: Adaptive changes in the heart, vessels and patterns of control under chronically high loads. in: Hamilton WF, Dow P (eds): *Handbook of Physiology*. Circulation. Proc. Washington, D.C. Vol. 3, p 2615
16. Saltin B, Blomquist G, Mitchell JH, et al: Response to exercise after bed rest and after training. *Circulation* 38: suppl 7, 1
17. Scheuer J: Physical training and intrinsic cardiac adaptations. *Circulation* 47:677, 1973
18. Holmgren A, Mossfeldt F, Sjostrand T, et al: Effect of training on work capacity, total hemoglobin, blood volume, heart volume, and pulse rate in recumbent and upright positions. *Acta Physiol Scan* 50:72, 1960
19. Scheuer J, Tipton CM: Cardiovascular adaptations to physical training. *Ann Rev Physiol* 39:221, 1977
20. Ritzer TF, Bove AA, Lynch PR: Left ventricular size and performance following long term endurance exercise in dogs. *Fed Proc* 36:447, 1977
21. Erick H, Knottinggen A, Sarajas SH: Effects of physical training on circulation at rest and during exercise. *Am J Cardiol* 12:142, 1963
22. Wyatt HL, Mitchell JH: Influence of physical training in the heart of dogs. *Circ Res* 35:883, 1974
23. Brotherhood J, Brozovik B, Pugh LGC: Hematologic status of middle and long distance runners. *Clin Sci Mol Med* 48:139, 1975
24. Miller PB, Johnson RL, Lamb LE: Effects of moderate exercise during four weeks of bed rest on circulatory function in man. *Aerosp Med* 38:1077, 1965

25. Oscai LB, Williams BT, Hertig BA: Effect of exercise on blood volume. *J Appl Physiol* 24:622, 1968
26. Hanson JS, Tabakin BS, Levy AM, Nedde W: Long term physical training and cardiovascular dynamics in middle aged men. *Circulation* 38:783, 1968
27. Ehblom B, Kilbom A, Soltysiak J: Physical training, bradycardia and the automanic nervous system. *Scan T Clin Lab Inv* 32:251, 1973
28. Tipton CM: Training and bradycardia in rats. *Am J Physiol* 209:1089, 1965
29. Tipton CM, Bernard RJ, Tchang T: Resting heart rate investigations with trained and non-trained hypophysectomized rats. *J Appl Physiol* 26:585, 1969
30. Zelis SM, Morganroth J, Rubler S: Cardiac hypertrophy in response to dynamic conditioning in female athletes. *J Appl Physiol: Resp Environ Exercise Physiol:* 44:849, 1978
31. Bevegard S, Holmgren A, Johnson B: Circulatory studies in well trained athletes at rest and during heavy exercise, with special reference to stroke volume and influence of body position. *Acta Physiol Scan* 57:26, 1963
32. Morganroth J, Moran DJ, Henry WL, Epstein SE: Comparative left ventricular dimensions in trained athletes. *Ann Int Med* 85:521, 1975
33. Wenger NK, Gilbert CA: Athlete's Heart in: Logue RB, et al: *The Heart.* McGraw Hill Co., New York, 1978, p 1706
34. Riedhammer HH, Rafflenbeul W, Weihe WH, Krayenbuhl HP: Left ventricular contractile function in trained dogs with cardiac hypertrophy. *Basic Res Cardiol* 71:297, 1976
35. Penpargkul S, Scheuer J: The effect of physical training upon mechanical and metabolic performance of the Rat heart. *J Clin Inv* 49:1859, 1970
36. Nakkila J: Studies on the myocardial capillary concentration in cardiac hypertrophy due to training. *Ann Med Exp Biol Fin* 33:7, 1955
37. Tomanek RJ: Effects of age and exercise on the extent of the myocardial capillary bed. *Anat Rec* 167:55, 1969
38. Bloor CM, Leon AS: Interaction of age and exercise on the heart and its blood supply. *Lab Inv* 22:160, 1970
39. Holloszy JO, Booth FW: Biochemical adaptations to endurance exercise in muscle. *Ann Rev Physiol* 38:273, 1976
40. Boyer JL, Kasch FW: Exercise therapy in hypertensive men. *JAMA* 211:1668, 1970
41. Choquette G, Ferguson RJ: Blood pressure reduction in borderline hypertensives following physical training. *Can Med Assn J* 108:699, 1973
42. Saltin B, Blomquist G, Mitchell JH, et al: Responses to exercise after bed rest and after training. *Circulation* 38:Suppl 8:1, 1968
43. Nutter DO, Schlant RO, Hurst JW: Isometric exercise and the cardiovascular system. *Mod Concepts Cardiovasc Dis* 41:11, 1972
44. Petrofsky JS, Lind AR: Aging, isometric strength and endurance, and cardiovascular responses to static effort. *J Appl Physiol* 38:91, 1975
45. Menapace FJ, Hammer WJ, Kessler KK, et al: Echocardiographic measurements of left ventricular wall thickness in weight lifters. *Am J Cardiol* 39:276, 1977
46. Muntz KM, Gonyea WJ, Mitchell JH: The effect of chronic isometric exercise on heart mass. *Anat Rec* 190:488, 1978

Adaptation of Skeletal Muscle to Exercise

WILLIAM W. WINDER, PH.D.

Regular endurance exercise training as exemplified by long-distance running, long-distance swimming, or bicycling causes major physiological adaptations which result in an increase in the capacity to do prolonged strenuous work. We have been interested in studying the adaptations that occur in muscle in response to regular prolonged exercise training that are responsible for the increase in endurance and maximal exercise capacity. That is, what adaptations are responsible for the fact that marathoners can run 26 miles at a five minute mile pace when most people cannot run one five minute mile?

PHYSIOLOGICAL MANIFESTATIONS OF TRAINING

It has been known for many years that endurance exercise training causes an increase in an individual's maximum oxygen consumption and in his maximal work capacity. The rate of muscle lactate formation is lower after training when subjects are tested at the same submaximal workload.[1] There also appears to be a shift in the substrate oxidation mixture in muscle after training so that a greater proportion of the energy requirement is met by fat oxidation, thereby sparing muscle and liver glycogen stores during prolonged submaximal work.[1] This results in a lower respiratory quotient (R.Q.) during prolonged work after a period of training. The practical adaptation of interest to the athlete is that he becomes capable of working longer at higher workloads.

It was previously assumed that these physiological manifestations of endurance exercise training were due to improved delivery of substrates and oxygen to the working muscle, which in turn was a result of the improvement in cardiovascular performance induced by training. It was assumed that the rate of lactate production by the working muscle is a reflection of the degree of hypoxia at the muscle site. The available experimental evidence does not support this concept, however. It is well documented that trained muscles consume the same amount of oxygen as non-trained muscles at the same submaximal work load.[2] If the muscle were hypoxic during work, the oxygen consumption by that muscle should be higher after training if the oxygen supply were increased. In reality, blood flow to muscle working at the same submaximal intensity is decreased after training.[2] The arterio-venous O_2 difference increases to maintain the same O_2 consumption at the same submaximal work rate.[2]

Since oxygen utilization by skeletal muscle during submaximal exercise is not increased by training, it was reasoned that other adaptations, perhaps in the muscle itself, are responsible for the lower blood lactate levels, the slower rate of glycogen depletion, the lower R.Q., and the greater endurance seen after training.

Comparative studies indicate that a good correlation exists between the ability of muscle to perform prolonged exercise and its mitochondrial enzyme content. Breast muscle of the domestic chicken has a low capacity to oxidize α-ketoglutarate and succinate whereas breast muscle of mallard ducks and pigeons, which can fly long distances, are rich in mitochondria.[3] Similarly, cytochrome oxidase and succinate oxidase activities are one-third to one-half as high in muscles of sedentary laboratory rabbits as in wild rabbits.[3] It seemed possible, then, that an important component of the adaptation to endurance training might be an increase in the amount of mitochondrial enzymes in the muscle.

Intramuscular Adaptations

In a study designed to test this possibility, rats were taught to run on a motor-driven small-animal treadmill. The speed and duration of daily running bouts were gradually increased until at the end of three months rats were running 120 minutes a day at 31 meters a minute up an 8° incline, five days a week. This running program resulted in a dramatic increase in the endurance of these animals. It was shown that leg muscles do not hypertrophy with this type of training.

This training program causes a two-fold increase in oxygen uptake by muscle mitochondria in the presence of non-limiting amounts of ADP, pyruvate, and malate.[3] The respiratory control index and P:O ratio are not affected, which implies that the increase in respiratory capacity is accompanied by an increase in the capacity to form ATP. The total mitochondrial content is increased, as estimated by measurements of protein yield of isolated mitochondrial pellets.[3] Succinate oxidase and cytochrome oxidase are approximately twice as high in whole homogenates in the gastrocnemius muscles of trained rats as in those of non-trained rats, which provides evidence that differences seen in isolated mitochondria are not due to differences in the percentage yield of mitochondria. Cytochrome C and other components of the electron transport chain increase approximately two-fold in gastrocnemius muscle in response to this training program.[4] Citrate synthase, aconitase, NAD-specific isocitrate dehydrogenase, and succinate dehydrogenase, all components of the citric acid cycle, increase approximately two-fold in the gastrocnemius.[4] Malate dehydrogenase and α-ketoglutarate dehydrogenase increased only 50 to 60 percent.

This treadmill running program also results in an increase in the capacity of muscle mitochondria to oxidize fatty acids in the presence of non-limiting amounts of carnitine, coenzyme A, and ADP.[4] Production of $^{14}CO_2$ from ^{14}C-labeled fatty acids and from carnitine and CoA deriviitives of fatty acids is also twice as high in the whole muscle homogenates of trained animals as in those of non-trained animals.[4] Levels of the enzymes involved in activation, transport, and oxidation of long-chain fatty acids are increased approximately two-fold in the gastrocnemius muscle in response to training.[4]

The enzymes specifically involved in oxidation of 3-hydroxybutyrate and acetoacetate, the ketone bodies, are increased in the muscle of trained rats.[4]

With the exception of hexokinase, the muscle glycolytic enzymes and total phosphorylase are affected very little by endurance exercise training.[4] Hexokinase increases in parallel with the mitochondrial enzymes.[4] Total glycogen synthetase has been reported to be increased in trained skeletal muscle.[5]

Myoglobin, the oxygen carrying pigment of muscle fibers, is increased approximately 80 percent in response to the training program. This increase in myoglobin may facilitate the transport of O_2 through the cytoplasm to the mitochondria.[4]

In summary, endurance training results in an increase in the capacity of muscle to oxidize pyruvate, fatty acids, and ketones in the mitochondria. This adaptation has been shown to occur in humans as well as in experimental animals. One-leg training experiments in human subjects show that an increase in mitochondrial oxidative enzymes occurs in the trained muscle, but not in the untrained muscle of the same individual.[6] Electron microscopic studies have demonstrated that endurance training causes increases in both the size and number of muscle mitochondria.[6,7] Biochemical studies have also demonstrated a change in the composition of mitochondria in trained muscle.[4]

Skeletal Muscle Fiber Types

The rodent has three different types of muscle fibers. Fast-twitch white fibers have a low respiratory capacity, a high glycogenolytic capacity, a low myoglobin content, and a high myosin ATPase activity. Fast-twitch red fibers have a high respiratory capacity, a high glycogenolytic capacity, a high myoglobin content, and a high myosin ATPase activity. Slow-twitch red fibers have a moderately high respiratory capacity, a low glycogenolytic capacity, high myoglobin content and low myosin ATPase activity.[cf8] In rodents, distinct regions of the muscle consist of predominantly one type of fiber. For example, the superficial region of the quadriceps muscle of the rat consists almost entirely of white fibers, whereas the deep portion near the bone consists predominantly of fast-twitch red fibers. The soleus of the rat has primarily slow-twitch red fibers. These specific regions of muscle have been studied to determine the effects of training on the different types of muscle fibers.

All three fiber types show increases in mitochondrial oxidative enzymes in response to training.[8] The extent to which mitochondria increase in white muscle fibers, however, depends on the nature of the training. White fibers appear to be recruited only during very strenuous work or at the end of a prolonged exercise bout when red fibers fatigue.[8] If the mitochondrial content of white fibers is to be increased by training, the training program must be designed to cause the white fibers to be recruited during the training sessions. That is, interval running consisting of high-speed sprints, or hill running separated by jogging or rest periods would be more effective in training white muscle fibers than would prolonged running at low intensity. Baldwin et al were able to induce a two-fold increase in citrate synthase in white muscle of rats when they used a training program of interval running consisting of two to three minute high-speed sprints separated by periods of running at a lower intensity.[8] With a steady-state training program, wherein rats ran at a constant speed with no sprints, the mitochondrial enzyme citrate synthase increased 45 percent by the end of two weeks of training and then returned toward control levels as the training program continued.[8] This finding suggests that trained animals rely less on white fibers than do nontrained animals during submaximal exercise and that high workloads are required to cause white fibers to be trained.

PHYSIOLOGICAL IMPLICATIONS OF THE ADAPTIVE INCREASE IN MITOCHONDRIA

The increase in mitochondrial enzymes is proportional within limits to the duration of the daily exercise sessions.[9] The mitochondrial content of muscle may thus be varied over a wide range to enable correlation of mitochondrial content with physiological responses to exercise. Using this technique, Fitts et al found that the run time to exhaustion is directly proportional to muscle content of the mitochondrial oxidative enzymes.[9] He also found that the amount of muscle and liver glycogen utilized during an exercise bout of fixed time and duration is inversely proportional to muscle mitochondrial content.[9] In other words, the higher the content of mitochondria in working muscles, the lower the glycogen utilization rate during work. This implies that the animal is obtaining more of his energy from fat oxidation during work and less from carbohydrate oxidation, an observation that is consistent with measurements of R.Q. on human subjects.[1] In work that can be maintained for one to two hours, there is a correlation between the time of glycogen depletion in muscle and the time required to reach exhaustion.[1] Thus, it appears that any adaptation that results in glycogen sparing during exercise will increase endurance.

If increased fatty acid oxidation is responsible for increasing endurance, then if we could artificially enhance the rate of muscle fatty acid oxidation in a relatively untrained animal, his endurance should be increased. Two factors have been identified as being important in determining the rate of fatty acid oxidation in muscle. The first is the capacity of the muscle to oxidize fatty acids. The higher the content of mitochondria, the greater will be the rate of fat oxidation when respiration is turned on.[10,11] The second important factor is the fatty acid concentration. Within the limits of 0.1 and 0.75 mM, the higher the fatty acid concentration, the greater will be the rate of oxidation.[10] Hickson et al were able to increase fatty acid concentration artificially by feeding corn oil to rats by stomach tube and then giving heparin by injection to activate lipoprotein lipase. Rats treated in this manner show a spectacular increase in endurance. These corn oil-fed rats can run an hour longer (three hours vs two hours) than the controls.[12] They also show a reduction in the rate of glycogen utilization during prolonged bouts of exercise.[12,13]

Trained animals or trained human subjects do not have higher plasma fatty acids than corresponding untrained controls during prolonged bouts of submaximal exercise.[11] The increased rate of fat oxidation which occurs as a result of training is probably due to the increase in fatty acid oxidizing enzymes of the mitochondria.

Some work has been done on the question of how the increased rate of fat oxidation slows the utilization of glycogen. Rennie et al showed that muscle citrate and glucose–6–phosphate levels are higher in hindlimb muscles perfused with a medium containing 1.8 mM oleate compared to muscles perfused with a fatty acid free medium.[14] Citrate inhibits phosphofructokinase, the rate-limiting enzyme of the glycolytic pathway, and glucose–6–phosphate inhibits hexokinase.[cf11] The net result of inhibition of these two enzymes is reduction in glucose uptake from the blood and reduction in the rate of utilization of endogenous carbohydrate.[14]

As mentioned previously, trained individuals have lower blood and muscle lactate during submaximal exercise than do nontrained individuals. The increase in muscle mitochondrial oxidative enzymes is also probably responsible for this adaptation to training.[cf11] With twice as many mitochondria, at the same absolute work load, each mitochondrion has to produce only half as much ATP after training as before training. The total ATP production rate is determined by the ADP/ATP ratio in the mitochondria, which in turn is determined by the rate of ATP utilization for muscle contraction and other cellular processes. That is, the higher the ADP/ATP ratio in the mitochondria, the more respiration is turned on to meet the increased demands for ATP. Creatine phosphate (CP) is utilized in the creatine phosphokinase reaction to buffer the change in ATP concentration in muscle during work. The concentrations of ATP and CP drop and the concentrations of ADP and inorganic phosphate increase until the production of ATP balances the rate of ATP utilization. With twice as many mitochondria, however, the steady-state ATP and CP concentrations required to turn on respiration sufficiently to balance ATP production with utilization would be expected to be higher and the concentrations of ADP and Pi lower than before training when the muscle had fewer mitochondria. ATP and CP are inhibitors of phosphofructokinase and ADP, Pi, AMP, and ammonia counteract this inhibition. Thus, the concentrations of these compounds in the sarcoplasm determine the rate of glycolysis.[cf11] With a smaller drop in ATP and CP concentrations and a smaller rise in ADP and Pi concentrations, phosphofructokinase would be inhibited to a greater degree after training than before, thus resulting in a lower rate of lactate production at the same submaximal work load. In addition, the average diffusion distance of the high energy phosphates to and from the mitochondria would be less in trained muscle, thus resulting in a lowering of the requirement for high localized concentration gradients between sites of production and sites of utilization. This may contribute to the lower rate of lactate production as well.

Time Course of Intramuscular Adaptation to Training

The time course of the increase in muscle mitochondrial proteins has been studied for the purpose of determining whether the increase is due to an increased rate of protein synthesis or a reduced rate of enzyme degradation. One way to approach this question was outlined by Shimke.[15] An increase in enzyme concentration is induced by using a constant stimulus for induction. The time course to the new steady state is determined. Then the inducing stimulus is removed and the time course of the return of enzyme activity to baseline steady state levels is determined. The time course to the new steady state is a function only of the degradation rate constant during induction. The time course of the decline in enzyme levels after removal of the stimulus can be used to estimate the normal degradation rate constant. If the half-time ($t_{1/2}$) is the same for both processes, then the higher steady state enzyme levels are due primarily to increased synthesis of the enzyme. If the $t_{1/2}$ is longer for the upslope than for the downslope, the higher steady state enzyme levels are due at least in part to a reduced rate of degradation.

Booth and Holloszy used this model to study the adaptation to training.[16] A group of rats were taught to run on a treadmill for five to ten minutes a day until they were well accustomed to running. Then the running time was increased from 10 to 100 minutes per day and was maintained constant for the duration of the study. Rats were killed and muscle mitochondrial levels were determined at intervals to define the time course of the approach to the higher steady state. The half-time for this process was five to eight days for several mitochondrial proteins. Another group of rats was trained by the usual program. When they were fully trained, the daily training sessions were eliminated and muscle mitochondrial levels were determined at intervals after cessation of training to define the time course of the return to a lower steady state. The half-time for this process was also in the range of six to eight days. Since the degradation rate constant was found to be approximately the same during induction as following removal of the exercise stimulus, it was concluded that the increase in mitochondrial enzymes with training is due to an increase in the rate of mitochondrial enzyme synthesis.

As pointed out by Booth, knowledge of the half-times for the induction and decay processes for the muscle mitochondrial enzymes may be important for design of training programs.[17] For example, if an individual begins running three miles each day and maintains his training bouts constant from day to day, assuming a $t_{1/2}$ of 7 days for mitochondrial proteins in muscle, half the total increase in mitochondria will occur in the first week; three-fourths will occur in two weeks; seven-eighths will occur in three weeks; and fifteen-sixteenths in four weeks. Thus, as far as muscle mitochondria are concerned, essentially all the adaptation that is going to occur will have occurred within a month of the beginning of training. If a larger increase in mitochondria is to occur, the individual must increase the intensity and duration of his training sessions.

The experimental model described here, where the training stimulus is suddenly increased in a stepwise fashion, is not the usual way of training. The time course of the increase in muscle mitochondria is much different for a progressive program where the intensity and duration of daily work bouts are gradually increased.[17] In a progressive program, the theoretical steady state value for the higher levels of mitochondrial enzymes is continually being increased as the daily work bouts become more prolonged and more intense. The final theoretical steady state is not set until the duration and intensity of training sessions is constant from day to day. The one-step training program is much more efficient in terms of inducing rapid changes in mitochondrial enzyme content, particularly in the first two weeks of the program. The degree of discomfort and potential for injury, however, is much greater than with milder progressive programs.

Another practical advantage of the knowlege of the half-lives of mitochondrial proteins is that it enables us to predict the magnitude of effects of detraining, as for example during periods following injury or illness.[17] How fast does the training effect wear off and how long does it take to come back to peak endurance after a period of detraining? Suppose, for example, an athlete trained vigorously for two months and induced a two-fold increase in skeletal muscle mitochondria. Then the individual contracted an illness that prevented him from training for one week. With a half-life of seven days, muscle mitochondrial enzymes would decrease to a value half way between the training steady state and the sedentary level the first week. If detraining continued, three-fourths would be lost in two weeks, seven-eighths in three weeks, and fifteen-sixteenths in four weeks. Assuming the athlete is able to resume training at the end of one week of bed rest, how long is required to regain what he lost? If he can train at the same intensity and duration as he would prior to bedrest, he will regain half of what he lost in a week, three-fourths in two weeks, seven-eighths in three weeks, and so on.[17] If he is unable to train at the same intensity and duration, then longer periods will be required.

SUMMARY

Endurance exercise training induces increases in the capacity of skeletal muscle to oxidize pyruvate, fatty acids, and ketone bodies. These adaptations are probably responsible for the lower exercise muscle and blood lactates, the shift in substrate oxidation mix from carbohydrate to fat, and the increased endurance developed in response to training. These adaptations occur in all three types of skeletal muscle fibers if the intensity of the training bouts is high enough to recruit white fibers. If the intensity and duration of the daily training sessions are suddenly increased to a high level and held constant, mitochondrial respiratory enzymes increase with a half-time of five to eight days. When a sedentary life is resumed following a period of training, levels of the mitochondrial enzymes return to normal with a half-time of six to eight days.

REFERENCES

1. Saltin B, Karlsson J: Muscle glycogen utilization during work of different intensities. in: Pernow B, Saltin B (eds): *Muscle Metabolism during Exercise*. Plenum, New York, 1971, p 289

2. Scheuer J, Tipton CM: Cardiovascular adaptations to physical training. *Ann Rev Physiol* 39:221, 1977
3. Holloszy JO: Biochemical adaptations in muscle. *J Biol Chem* 242:2278, 1967
4. Holloszy JO, Booth FW: Biochemical adaptations to endurance exercise in muscle. *Ann Rev Physiol* 38:273, 1976
5. Jeffress RN, Peter JB, Lamb DR: Effects of exercise on glycogen synthetase in red and white skeletal muscle. *Life Sci* 7:957, 1968
6. Morgan TE, Cobb LA, Short FA, Ross R, Gunn DR: Effects of long-term exercise on human muscle mitochondria. in: Pernow, B, Saltin B (eds): *Muscle Metabolism during Exercise*. Plenum, New York, 1971, p 87
7. Gollnick PD, King DW: Effect of exercise and training on mitochondria of rat skeletal muscle. *Am J Physiol* 216:1502, 1969
8. Baldwin KM, Winder WW: Adaptive response in different types of muscle fibers to endurance exercise. *Ann NY Acad Sci* 301:411, 1977
9. Fitts RH, Booth FW, Winder WW, Holloszy JO: Skeletal muscle respiratory capacity, endurance and glycogen utilization. *Am J Physiol* 228:1029
10. Molé PA, Oscai LB, Holloszy JO: Adaptation of muscle to exercise. *J Clin Invest* 50:2323, 1971
11. Holloszy JO, Rennie MJ, Hickson RC, Conlee RK, Hagberg JM: Physiological consequences of the biochemical adaptations to endurance exercise. *Ann NY Acad Sci* 301:440, 1977
12. Hickson RC, Rennie MJ, Conlee RK, Winder WW, et al: Effects of increased plasma fatty acids on glycogen utilization and endurance. *J Appl Physiol* 43:829, 1977
13. Rennie MJ, Winder WW, Holloszy JO: A sparing effect of plasma fatty acids on muscle and liver glycogen content in the exercising rat. *Biochem J* 156:647, 1976
14. Rennie MJ, Holloszy JO: Inhibition of glucose uptake and glycogenolysis by availability of oleate in well-oxygenated perfused skeletal muscle. *Biochem J* 168:161, 1977
15. Schimke RT: Regulation of protein degradation in mammalian tissues. in: Munro HN (ed): *Mammalian Protein Metabolism*. Academic, New York, 1970, p 177
16. Booth FW, Holloszy JO: Cytochrome c turnover in rat skeletal muscles. *J Biol Chem* 252:416, 1977
17. Booth FW: Effects of endurance exercise on cytochrome c turnover in skeletal muscle. *Ann NY Acad Sci* 301:431, 1977

Endocrine Aspects of Strenuous Exercise

LESLIE I. ROSE, M.D., ROBERT L. LAVINE, M.D.

This chapter will concentrate on the response of the adrenal cortex to acute exercise. To review very briefly, there are three zones in the adrenal cortex—the outer, zona glomerulosa, producing the mineralocorticoid, aldosterone; the middle, zona fasiculata, producing glucocorticoids, predominately cortisol; and the inner, zona reticularis, predominately producing androgens.

GLUCOCORTICOID RESPONSE TO EXERCISE

Glucocorticoids are extremely important in almost every reaction in the body. They play a role in carbohydrate, fat, and protein metabolism and thus directly pertain to the athletic performance of the individual. Glucocortocoids are responsible for the release of amino acids from protein during exercise. They increase hepatic glycogenolysis and also increase gluconeogenesis, thereby elevating the blood sugar and maintaining it at a normal level. Glucocorticoids also play a role in other important functions, such as maintaining normal blood pressure (see chapters nine and ten in this symposium). Without glucocorticoids the blood pressure will fall, since glucocorticoids themselves play a role in salt and water metabolism; however, the predominent control of salt and water metabolism by the adrenal gland is via aldosterone, a mineralocorticoid. Thus, one can see that the glucocorticoids affect many body functions. Therefore, the question has arisen as to whether glucocorticoids increase in response to the stress of exercise.

Many animal studies have been done in an attempt to answer this question, but these studies must be carefully evaluated. For example, studies reporting changes in glucocorticoid levels in the exercising rat may not be completely valid. Rats are made to exercise by being thrown in water and made to swim. This produces a psychic stress phenomenon in the rat which in itself will stimulate the adrenal cortex. Thus, caution must be "exercised" in interpreting exercise studies in rats. If one examines these studies, however, it is apparent that the adrenal cortex is larger in exercising rats and that corticosterone, which is the glucocorticoid in the rat, rises. The data imply that with exercise glucocorticoids increase, at least in the rat. There are also scattered dog treadmill studies showing a rise in glucocorticoids. The following data will summarize our predominant interest in studying the human during exercise.

Throughout the literature, the cortisol response in exercising humans will be found to range from a decrease in plasma cortisol to a rise in plasma cortisol. It is very important when looking at these studies to consider the condition of the subjects. Were the subjects well conditioned or poorly conditioned? What was the duration of the exercise stress? Many studies fail to indicate exactly how long a person was exercised or what relationship this exercise had to his maximum O_2 consumption. One must carefully search for these details in evaluating a paper.

Nine normal volunteers of varying ages were studied before and after a mile run.[1] A sample of blood for plasma cortisol assay was obtained before the mile run and immediately upon completion of the run. The object was to find out what happened to plasma cortisol. The second thing we wanted to know was whether there would be any correlation between an individual's plasma cortisol response and his maximum O_2 consumption. There was no significant change in the plasma cortisol in response to a mile run in these individuals. Therefore, it is not surprising that there was no correlation between changes in plasma cortisol and the maximum O_2 consumption, nor any correlation between the absolute level of plasma cortisol and the maximum O_2 consumption. This demonstrates that in a mile run little if any change occurs in zona fasiculata activity.

Plasma cortisol concentration is dependent upon the rate at which the adrenal gland secretes cortisol into the blood and how rapidly it is catabolized. To further investigate cortisol metabolism in exercise, we elected to investigate a rather prolonged stress, such as the effects of a marathon run on highly conditioned men.[2] A sample for plasma cortisol was obtained before and immediately after the run as the subjects crossed the finish line, arms extended for immediate blood sampling. We discovered that in a marathon run the plasma cortisol does significantly rise. This tells us that the adrenal cortex does respond with an increased secretion of plasma cortisol in response to exercise. If one evaluates short exercising periods only, one might miss an increase but in a prolonged run cortisol clearly increases.

What is the clinical significance of knowing that plasma cortisol increases during exercise? If a patient who is engaged in athletics has adrenocorticoid insufficiency or hypopituitarism, he should be given supplemental glucocorticoids during his training and running periods. Remember, he is supposed to increase his output of cortisol, but he cannot due to disease. Therefore, the patient requires exogenous glucocorticoids. Should we consider giving glucocorticoids to the healthy athlete who is exercising? I would not. There is no evidence that by exogeneously giving glucocorticoids any benefit will result. As a matter of fact, chronic prolonged increase in glucocorticoid concentrations causes the breakdown of muscles, and thus results in a weaker individual. The adrenal exhaustion phenomenon occurs when the adrenal gland is supposedly working to extremes and then suddenly stops. This interesting phenomenon was studied during the Korean war. What was done was to fly a group of volunteers, in whom the pituitary–adrenal axis had been found to be normal, into the front lines to expose them to the stress of battle. The plan was to bring these volunteers out in a couple of weeks, and to then retest the adrenal gland to see if the axis was intact. The study was begun, but after a couple of days the Red Chinese crossed the Yalu River. The stress was great and 50 percent of the volunteers were killed. The survivors were stressed with ACTH stimulation and there was no glucocorticoid response. One would expect cortisol to rise but it remained at base level. This study has never been repeated; however, this does imply that individuals under prolonged stress may need glucocorticoid supplementation. By comparison, a marathon run is not an abnormally prolonged adrenocortical stress when related to people with adrenocortical insufficiency engaged in the same physical activity.

MINERALOCORTICOID RESPONSE TO EXERCISE

It was also noted that following a marathon run plasma aldosterone significantly rose.[3] What is this compound and what does it do? Aldosterone is the primary salt and water regulator in the body. It enables the body to retain sodium and water and to lose potassium and hydrogen. Why does it go up in exercise? To answer this question, one must consider the known causes of aldosterone stimulation. The predominant stimulus to aldosterone secretion is thought to be via the renin angiotensin system. This system operates via the juxtaglomerular apparatus in the kidney which releases renin under appropriate stimuli. The enzyme, renin, is released into the blood. It acts on a circulating alpha 2 globulin, a large protein made in the liver and sometimes referred to as angiotensinogen. Renin degrades this large protein into angiotensin I, a decapeptide. This then circulates through the lungs where two amino acids are removed, giving us angiotensin II, an octapeptide. Angiotensin II directly stimulates the adrenal gland to release aldosterone. Aldosterone circulates, acting on the kidney, where it promotes sodium and water retention with loss of potassium and/or hydrogen, and on the sweat glands. It is in the latter system that the importance of aldosterone in exercise lies. Aldosterone causes us to retain sweat sodium but to lose sweat postassium and magnesium. It also acts on salivary glands, but for our purposes this is of lesser importance.

Potassium is also a stimulus to aldosterone secretion. Large infusions of potassium do not result normally in hyperkalemia because the adosterone secretion stimulated by potassium results in potassium excretion by the kidney. ACTH also stimulates aldosterone secretion but to a lesser extent than its influence on cortisol secretion. It is known from the cortisol studies mentioned above that ACTH increases in exercise. Therefore, this certainly plays a role in the stimulation of aldosterone normally seen in exercise.

In exercise, even in marathon running, the loss of electrolytes through the kidney is minimal because blood is shunted away from the kidney and most people do not have to stop to urinate. In marathon races (42 km) the sweat glands become the major excretory organs. Prolonged and profuse sweating leads to sodium retention and, as a result, potassium and magnesium depletion.

To study electrolytes and aldosterone in exercise, eight normal, healthy male volunteers were studied at sea level, after acute exposure to high altitude, (Pike's Peak), and after living on Pike's Peak for 11 days.[3] The design of the study was as follows. A glucose infusion was started two hours before obtaining any samples (this manipulation will increase ACTH, stimulating both cortisol and aldosterone). The volunteers were then exercised on a treadmill for 20 minutes at 45 percent of their maximum O_2 consumption. This was followed by an hour of rest after which they were exercised for 20 minutes at 75 percent of their maximum O_2 consumption. This was followed by another hour of rest, and again they were exercised for 20 minutes at 75 percent of their maximum O_2 consumption. Blood samples were drawn before and immediately after each exercise period. This study was done on all subjects at sea level, at acute high altitude exposure, and at chronic high altitude exposure. The results were quite interesting. It had already been demonstrated in the marathon run that plasma aldosterone rises with exercise, and this study shows that it rises linearly with increasing exercise at sea level. At acute high altitude exposure, there was a significantly lower response of aldosterone to the same exercise stress in the same individual than at sea level. After the subjects had been in the hypoxic environment for 11 days, however, aldosterone returned to a level that really did not differ from its performance at sea level. This demonstrates that aldosterone rises in response to exercise, decreases with acute high altitude exposure, but then returns to its sea level values with chronic high altitude exposure. To determine the control of the plasma aldosterone changes, plasma renin levels were analyzed. At sea level, the response of plasma renin to increasing exercise showed a linear rise. Renin also showed a fall at acute high altitude exposure similar to that seen with plasma aldosterone. After 11 days of high altitude acclimatization, aldosterone virtually returned to higher sea level values. This implies that a decrease in renin due to hypoxia is one cause for the decrease in aldosterone seen at acute high altitude exposure. The renin pathway was further evaluated by measuring angiotensin II. This was necessary to demonstrate that there was not a problem in converting angiotensinogen to angiotensin I and then to angiotensin II. There was no significant difference in angiotensin II levels between rest and under acute high altitude exposure. Total plasma catecholamines were also measured in these subjects. With increasing exercise a rise in plasma catecholamines was found. In contrast to the plasma aldosterone effect which decreased upon acute hypoxia, the catecholamines increased and continued to rise even after ten days of chronic hypoxia. Thus, the catecholamine response rose with acute hypoxia and went even higher with chronic hypoxia.

From these studies, it is our opinion that the changes in renin are predominantly responsible for the decrease in plasma aldosterone seen in acute hypoxia, although there is also an effect of ACTH. In addition to changes in ACTH and renin, there are also serum potassium changes associated with exercise. Unfortunately, for experimentation purposes it has been found that changes in serum potassium below the sensitivity of the ability to measure may induce significant changes in aldosterone secretion. Thus, one must remember that in exercise of almost any kind there is a rise in serum potassium and that this also stimulates aldosterone. Skeletal muscle breakdown most likely contributes to these small increases in serum potassium.

To understand the clinical significance of the aldosterone changes in exercise, the electrolytes in eight individuals before and after a marathon run were measured.[4] There was a significant increase in serum sodium, which correlated with changes in serum proteins. In a marathon run, the subjects usually lose anywhere from one to five kilograms of weight. This loss, which is almost all via sweat, results in a contracted plasma volume. One way of quantifying the contraction of the plasma volume is to measure the protein changes or the osmolar changes. When one corrects the serum sodium for the total protein changes, there is no significant difference in serum sodium. Serum potassium significantly rose, even after correcting for the changes in total protein. It did not rise to toxic levels. Calcium decreased slightly but not significantly. Serum magnesium significantly fell. In every physiological state potassium and magnesium are lost from the cells together. Therefore, one might ask why serum potassium rose and magnesium fell as a result of exercise. The answer lies in the electrolyte composition of sweat. Sweat magnesium, in prolonged exercise, markedly increases. The potassium in sweat is also high but does not reach the levels of the magnesium. This has been confirmed by others who have shown that, as one keeps on exercising, sweat magnesium continues to increase. Sweat sodium actually decreases with continued sweating. Therefore, one is left with the interesting paradox that this is the only physiological state where there is a diversion of serum potassium and serum magnesium. Total body potassium (lost from cells through skeletal muscle breakdown) and magnesium (lost from sweat) fall. This is important to keep in mind when one thinks about the type of electrolytes to give athletes. Aldosterone will lead to retention of sodium, and in exchange for the sodium will excrete potassium and magnesium. Therefore, the worst type of electrolyte replacement to give an athlete would be salt tablets. With more sodium available, the body must excrete more potassium and magnesium. Therefore, I think if given the choice between nothing and salt tablets, I would choose nothing. For safe electrolyte replacement, it is impor-

TABLE 1   Plasma Hormonal and Electrolyte Changes from Baseline following a Marathon Run

Na - Cl[1]	increase
K[2]	increase
Total Protein[1]	increase
Magnesium[3]	decrease
Cortisol	increase
Aldosterone	increase
Norepinephrine	increase

[1]Related to extracellular fluid volume contraction.

[2]Related to skeletal muscle breakdown with release of intracellular potassium.

[3]The decrease in plasma Mg^{++} is due to greater quantity of Mg^{++} being lost in sweat.

tant to look at the commercial electrolyte solutions to see how much potassium and magnesium are contained. Magnesium must be taken by the exercising athlete along with potassium in a water or glucose vehicle.

This review stresses the importance and relevance of the adrenal cortex in relation to exercise. The changes described here are summarized in Table 1.

REFERENCES

1. Rose LI, Friedman HW, Beering SC, Cooper KH: Plasma cortisol changes following a mile run in conditioned subjects. *J Clin Endocrinol Metab* 31:339, 1970
2. Newmark SR, Himathongkam T, Martin RP, Cooper KH, Rose LI: Adrenocortical response to marathon running. *J Clin Endocrinol Metab* 42:393, 1976
3. Maher JT, Jones LG, Hartley LH, Williams GH, Rose LI: Aldosterone dynamics during graded exercise at sea level and high altitudes. *J Appl Physiol* 39:18, 1975
4. Rose LI, Carroll DR, Lowe SL, Peterson EW, Cooper KH: Serum electrolyte changes following marathon running. *J Appl Physiol* 29:449, 1970

Hematological Changes during Exercise

WARREN K. PALMER, PH.D., DENNIS I. GOLDBERG, M.A.

The blood is the medium in which many physiological compounds are transported throughout the mammalian body for the purpose of metabolic control, fuel supply, and cellular waste removal. The function of numerous physiological systems is mediated by alterations in blood components. Thermal regulation is, in part, mediated by the heat transfer of the blood. Osmotic balance of body fluids is reflected in changes in the blood components. Internal and external respiration, as well as the cardiovascular system, are influenced by alterations that occur in blood gases. The blood is all important in mediating the body's immune system through the action of specific plasma proteins and white blood cells. The blood itself controls blood volume loss during hemorrhage through the coagulation process.

During an acute bout of exercise the internal environment becomes disrupted. To meet the demand of the increased muscular work, the systems whose functions are mediated by the blood respond to the stress by altering the consistency of the blood dramatically. Changes in endocrine and neural functions are reflected by elevated circulating hormonal and neurotransmitter concentrations. Increases in substate concentrations occur as well as elevations in organic metabolites. A brief summary of alterations in concentrations occurring in plasma are briefly summarized in Table 1.

If an individual is exposed to chronic bouts of exercise (physical training), changes occurring in the blood as a result of the bout of physical stress will differ significantly from those seen when a non-trained individual is exercised. For example, blood hormone concentration changes are different in the trained and non-

TABLE 1   Effect of Exercise on Plasma Concentrations

Metabolites		Hormones		Other	
Glucose[3]	↓	Human growth hormone (HGH)[2]	↑	Pv O_2[1]	↓
Lactate[3]	↑	Immunoreactive insulin (IRI)[2]	↓		
Pyruvate[3]	↑	Glucagon[2]	↑	Pv CO_2[1]	↑
Glycerol[3]	↓				
FFA[3]	↑	Norepinephrine	↑	pH[1]	↓
Ketone bodies[3]	↑	Epinephrine	↑		
Alanine[4]	↑				

trained subject subjected to equivalent bouts of exercise.[1] Differences also occur in the levels of substrates[2] and metabolites[3] measured in the two groups during exposure to work.

While alterations in blood constituents specific to other systems occur in response to exercise and training, dramatic changes are seen in the blood components and their hematological functions as a result of exercise and training. This paper will specifically address the literature related to the alterations and mechanisms associated with changes in blood volumes, coagulation activity, and thrombocytotic activity.

EXERCISE AND BLOOD VOLUME

Numerous experimental studies exist in the literature attempting to answer questions relating the influence of exercise and physical training upon total blood, red cells, and/or plasma volume. Changes in hematocrit ratio have often been used as an index of hemodilution or hemoconcentration of the blood, while plasma protein concentrations have been used as an indirect index of altered plasma volume. Astrand and Saltin[4] studied the influence of prolonged work upon various vascular volumes. Following a cross-country ski race of long duration plasma volume was elevated 11.4 percent and red cell volume was decreased 3.2 percent. During submaximal work of 75 minutes duration, van Beaumont and co-workers[5] found that, in normally hydrated subjects, plasma volume was increased 5.4 percent, as was plasma protein concentrations, while the hematocrit ratio was unchanged.

With high intensity work of short duration, a different response occurs. Following 1.75 minutes of exhaustive arm exercise, Joye and Poortmans[6] have shown that hematocrit is increased by three percent above the control. Exhaustive bicycle ergomerty of trained men showed a 6 percent elevation in hematocrit.[7] These data were supported by other investigators using intense work in males,[5,8,9] and we have obtained a similar trend with exhaustive exercise in females (Figure 1). The summary of published results presented in Table 2 suggests that during submaximal work

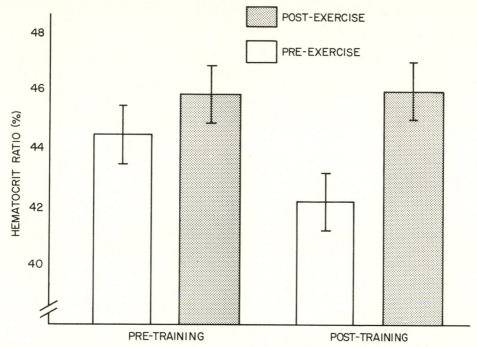

Fig. 1. Alterations in total blood volume as determined indirectly by the measurement of hematocrit. Hematocrit ratio was measured in mixed venous blood taken prior to (open bar) and following (stippled bar) a graded exercise bout to exhaustion before and after a training program. The exercise bout was a continuous treadmill test run at a speed of 6 mph at grade increases of 3 percent each 4 minutes. The test went until subject could not continue.

TABLE 2 Reported Effects of Exercise Upon Blood Volumes

Type of exercise	PV	HcT%	TBV	Ref.
8 min. Stair Climb	↓	↑	↓	Nylan[10]
Submax. (32–64% max.)	↑	↔	↑	Van Beaumont et al[5]
Max. Bicycle	↓	↑	↓	Van Beaumont et al[5]
85 Km cross-country Skiing	↑	↔	↑	Astrand and Saltin[4]
Progressive Bicycle Ergometry to Exhaustion	↓	↑	—	Poortmans[7]
Exhaustive Arm Work	↓	↑	↓	Joye and Poortmans[6]
4 hr Step Test	↓↑	↑↓	↓↑	Senay and Kok[11]

where there is adequate fluid replacement there is an actual increase in plasma volume or even a hemodilution of the blood. On the other hand, in maximal exercise there is a hemoconcentration of the blood.

During short term, high intensity work there seems to be no significant alteration in the red cell volume.[4,10] The hemoconcentration influence seems to be associated with a decrease in plasma volume due to the increase in capillary filtration which is in turn a result of the exercise-induced elevation in arterial pressure.[4,10] This hypothesis, however, does not seem to completely explain the hemoconcentration seen in the plasma proteins accompanying exercise. A number of studies report that during exercise the proportional changes seen in hematocrit are significantly less than the changes seen in plasma protein content. Joye et al[6] have reported a 3.3 percent increase in hematocrit accompanied by a 7.0 percent increase in plasma protein concentration. Saltin,[8] studying the combined effects of exercise and heat, has reported a 8.5 percent increase in hematocrit in conjunction with a 25.7 percent increase in plasma proteins. He found no significant correlation between hematocrit change and plasma protein change. Similar findings have been reported by Poortmans[7] using trained subjects. Senay and Kok[11] have investigated this phenomenon and have reported that there is actually a protein loss from the vascular bed in unfit working subjects, while there is an addition of protein to the vascular compartment when trained individuals exercise.

Studies have been undertaken to determine the plasma protein components contributing to the increase. Poortmans and Jeanloz[12] have found that the increase is due primarily to increased amounts of albumin, haptoglobin, α_2-macroglobin, transferrin, β_1A-globin, γ A-globin, and γ G-globin. Although it has been speculated that the plasma protein increase may be related to tissue damage,[7,13] it is also possible that rapidly exchangeable extravascular plasma protein pools are mobilized whenever large changes in total peripheral resistance occurs—such as during exercise or heat exposure.

The elevated plasma protein concentration may explain, in part, the elevated plasma volumes that have been reported[4,5] during submaximal exercise. A plasma protein shift to the intravascular space could elevate capillary osmotic pressure, thus offsetting any change in arterial blood pressure and possibly causing increased water movement into the capillary.

Reports comparing endurance athletes with sedentary individuals suggest that one of the results of a program of chronic exercise is an increase in TBV.[14,15,16] These types of experiments, however, stimulate the age-old question: Are these individuals athletes because they have a larger than normal blood volume, or is the enhanced blood volume a function of exercise training? Studies which have investigated blood volume prior to and following training have shown elevations in TBV. Oscai et al[17] found a 5.9 percent increase in blood volume resulting from 16 weeks of endurance training. When individuals who are already physically fit undergo training, however, there does not seem to be an enhancement of blood volume.[18] The actual component changes that occur in response to training have been investigated both by comparing athletes to non-athletes and by measuring various parameters before and after training. Kjeldberg et al[16] have reported that trained subjects have significantly more hemoglobin than nontrained individuals. Holmgren et al[19] have substantiated these findings by testing subjects before and after a chronic exercise training program. Other studies have shown that trained individuals have lower hematrocrit ratios[14,15] and protein concentrations[14] than the nontrained individual. This phenomenon is illustrated by the data in Figure 1. While relative protein and hemoglobin concentrations are lowered, total amounts of these constituents are increased.[14,18,19] It seems to be generally accepted that training is associated with a "thinning of the blood."

The elevation in TBV that has been seen to occur as a result of training can partly be explained by the acute increase in antidiuretic hormone[20] accompanying acute exercise. This hormone, released from the posterior pituitary during each work bout, stimulates water absorbtion by the collecting tubules of the kidneys. Rocker et al [21] have also shown that there is an increase in several specific liver-synthesized proteins in the plasma of trained individuals. These proteins contribute to the capillary osmotic pressure, thus effectively retaining intravascularly much of the water retained by the kidney. Although these proteins do not completely explain osmotic pressure differences seen in the plasma of trained and nontrained individuals, this diluted blood syndrome in trained athletes enables an athlete to lose approximately 200 ml of plasma water before his hemotocrit and protein concentrations are equal to those found in sedentary individuals.[15] This could be advantageous for thermoregulatory and cardiovascular purposes. There would be more water available for evaporative cooling. Decreased viscosity would be associated with a decreased resistance to flow. Possibly the redistribution of blood flow seen during exercise would not compromise tissue function with an enhanced blood volume.

The elevated hematocrit ratios seen following exercise have stimulated investigators to study erythropoiesis in exercise.[22,23] In rats performing long duration walking at a rate of two meters a minute at normal atmospheric pressure, no change in erythropoietin titers were measured. When rats were exposed to exercise at an atmospheric pressure equivalent to an elevation of 400 m or higher, however, the exercise did stimulate elevations in erythropoietin.[24] Unfortunately, it is hard to draw conclusions from studies utilizing such low work loads. These workloads would not be expected to alter blood gas concentrations significantly, and it seems that depressed arterial pO_2 is the primary stimulus for erythropoietin release from renal tissue.

While exercise may not influence erythropoiesis, it is postulated that long term-endurance exercise may, in fact, cause red cell destruction or hemolysis. In 1953, Gilligan et al [24] investigated the effect of runs of various distances on the red cell fraction of the blood and found that runs of long duration were accompanied by hemoglobinemia and hemoglobinuria. A study of RBC fragility, however, showed no effect of exercise. These researchers concluded that the hemolysis seen during work was physiological and not a pathological event. It is interesting to note that hemoglobinuria occurring as a result of exercise only occurs when work is performed in an erect position.[25] A number of theories have been put forward to explain hemolysis accompanying exercise. Hemolytic agents have been investigated during and following exercise but none have been found.[26,27] Artifical elevation of body temperature did not cause hemoglobinuria.[26] Venous stasis, the circulatory interference in the spleen, liver, or kidneys, has been considered a possible cause of hemolysis, but limb exercise during venous occlusion was not accompanied by cell destruction.[26] Reticuloendothelial blockade interferring with plasma clearance of hemoglobin derived from the breakdown of aging erythrocytes has been proposed,[26] but this hypothesis is not reasonable when the long life-span of the red cell is considered. Davidson[28] has found that hemoglobinuria occurs more frequently when runs are performed on hard surfaces. Running on roadways was associated with a decrease in plasma haptoglobin* concentration.[29] These results have led Davidson[25] to propose that mechanical trauma leads to erythrocyte destruction. The older red cells are destroyed owing to a positive relationship existing between cell fragility and age.[30] From this conclusion the excretion of hemoglobin can be considered a passive event secondary to intravascular hemolysis. In a recent presentation by Hansen and colleagues,[31] supportive data was given suggesting that in response to jogging, occult hemolysis and hypohaptoglobinemia result.

COAGULATING ACTIVITY

A blood clot forms in response to hemorrhage to stop bleeding and, in effect, acts as a homeostatic mechanism conserving blood volume. A simplified scheme of clot formation is presented in Figure 2. A well documented hematologic effect of exercise is the enhancement of coagulability. In 1927, Hartman[32] using cats, Miles and Necheles[33] using humans and dogs, and Schneider and Zangari[34] using humans, reported this decrease in clotting time following exercise. Rizza,[35] on the other hand, reported no change in clotting time as a result of 1.2 kilometer run. However, a specific protein termed the antihemophilic globulin (AHG) increased markedly in all subjects irregardless of sex or age in Rizza's study. A 4.8 kilometer walk did not affect AHG concentration. A number of studies[36,37,38] were subsequently undertaken to further investigate the relationship between exercise and coagulation. In general, the data support the concept that clotting is potentiated by exercise. Further experiments have been performed to ascertain the mechanism of this potentiation. There are a number of exercise-related factors that would accelerate the clotting sequence, including the following: (1) altered membrane permeability and tissue damage causing release of tissue of thromboplastin thus activating the extrinsic pathways;[39] (2) increased coagulation with lactate accumulation;[40] (3) increased concentration of plasma proteins owing to the previously mentioned hemoconcentration; (4) increased concentration of specific clotting factors (factor VIII[35,36,37,38], fibrinogen,[41] factor V,[40] and factor VII[37]); and (5) alterations in platelet function. Consistent increases are reported in clotting factor VIII as a result of exercise, while the other reports of alterations in clotting factors are equivocal.

The mechanism for this elevation in factor VIII is yet unknown. Rizza and Eipe,[43] using splenectomized subjects, have reported that the spleen does not play a role in the factor increase. The involvement of the neuroendocrine system is suggested as a

---

*A class of plasma proteins that specifically bind hemoglobin. The bound form of haptoglobin is not detected in the assay.

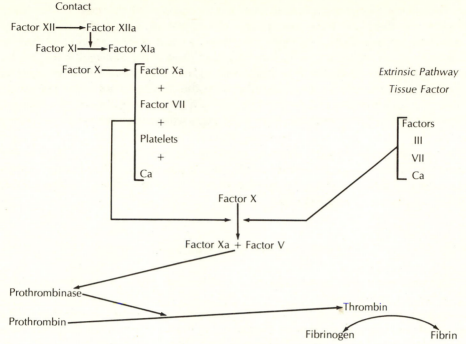

Fig. 2.   Pathways of blood coagulation.

mechanism through which factor VIII is increased because epinephrine infusion mimics the exercise-coagulation response.[41,44] Propranolol, the beta-receptor blocking agent, blocks the formation of factor VIII during both exercise and epinephrine infusion.[46] Platelets play a significant role in clot formation. Catacholamine effect upon platelet function has also been reported.[46,47,48] Platelets contribute to the function of the intrinsic clotting system by sticking to the edges of vessel walls and each other to form a hemostatic plug in the wound.[49] Exercise has been shown to increase platelet number.[47,48,49,50,51,52,53] The magnitude of the increase seems to vary in proportion to the intensity of the exercise. Following heavy exercise, not only are there more platelets but large "stress platelets" are present.[52] The source of the platelets that increase during exercise is not known, but Sarajas and coworkers[54] and Sarnoff[55] have suggested that platelets are washed from the pulmonary circulation (a platelet storage area).

Platelet function, which is determined by measurement of adhesiveness and aggregation, may be affected by exercise. An increase in platelet function as a result of intense work has been reported by some studies,[46,48,53] while others have reported no change or even decrease in platelet function with exercise.[41,51,56,57] It has been reported that catecholamines increase platelet plug formation;[46] however, the equivocal nature of platelet function in response to exercise negates the formulation of an elaborate hypothosis.

The coagulation response of the trained individual following an acute bout of exercise may differ from the response seen in the nontrained subject. While the clotting time is significantly reduced following a bout of exercise in both the trained and nontrained individual, the much quoted data of Ferguson and Guest[42] suggest that the acceleration in coagulation is less in the trained individual. Unfortunately, it is difficult to generalize from these data because the relative work loads before and following training have not been calculated as a proportion of maximal capacity. There is evidence available, however, that suggests that an epinephrine-mediated mechanism is responsible for the difference between trained and nontrained individuals. If the elevated concentration in clotting factor VIII as a result of exercise is adrenergically mediated, evidence exists[58] that catecholamine release is significantly depressed in trained subjects in comparison to nontrained subjects when both are working at comparable workloads.

FIBRINOLYSIS

There is significant clinical interest in processes associated with the degradation of thrombus as an aid to tissue repair. An attempt to accomplish increased thrombus degradation has been made through artificial stimulation of fibrinolysis. A system of proteolytic enzymes is involved in the degradation of the fibrin clot (Figure 3). Very simply, the proteolytic enzyme, plasmin, hydrolyzes specific peptide bonds of fibrin. Inactive plasminogen is found in the circulation and is converted to plasmin by chemical and physiological activators. Tissue activators have been extracted from various cell types while a humeral activator stimulated by plasma factor XII is present in the blood.[59]

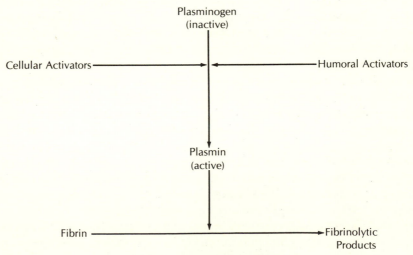

Fig. 3. Fibrinolytic pathway.

In 1947, Biggs et al[60] reported that human fibrinolytic activity increased with anxiety and exercise. These findings have since been substantiated in a number of laboratories.[61,62,63,64,65,66] The discrepancies in the relationship between the intensity of exercise and proteolytic activity that have been reported, however, are confusing. In a study[62] in which post-excercise fibrinolysis in response to an unspecified moderate workload was examined, there was no relationship between heart rate and lysis clot rate. Hawkey et al,[41] using bicycle ergometry, reported a positive linear relationship between heart rate and post-exercise fibrinolysis. Davis' group[64] found that an exponential relationship between heart rate elevated on a bicycle ergometer and clot lysis activity existed. Rapid rates of clot breakdown occurred only after 70 to 80 percent of maximal oxygen consumption was reached.

To ascertain the mechanisms involved in this enhanced proteolysis, Bennett and co-workers[67] investigated the blood levels of components of the fibrinolytic system following walking exercise. They found no alteration in plasma content of plasminogen, fibrinogen, or serum inhibitors that slow the degradation process. There was a time-related increase in plasminogen activator (PA) concentration through the first three hours of work. These findings are in agreement with those of other investigations of exercise induction of PA.[68,69]

To ascertain the influence of local metabolites upon the exercise-enhanced increase in PA, Rennie et al[70] studied the effect of local exercise and vessel occlusion on clot lysis. Exercise with venous occlusion was associated with increased PA levels. No change in PA concentration occurred with arterial occlusion. These results suggest that venous distension and not metabolite accumulation may stimulate activator release from vascular endothelium. In support, Holemans[71] has found that vasodilator drugs stimulate a ten-fold increase in PA titers.

Cash, Woodfield, and Allan[72] reported only a 30 percent inhibition of andrenalin-stimulated PA release by propranolol. They hypothesized that a portion of the activator release is dependent upon vasomotor activity while the remainder of the adrenergic effect acts through some other undefined mechanism. Cohen et al[45] found no propranolol effect on the exercise-stimulated PA release. In support, Hawkey and co-workers[41] found no correlation between work-induced epinephrine and PA concentrations. These studies suggest that PA release may not be mediated by the beta-adenergic system.

Although variables such as the intensity of exercise and the state of subject training leave many unanswered questions, data from two laboratories[42,63] suggest that exercise training has no significant influence upon the resting or post-work fibrinolytic response.

In summary, it can be concluded that reported data suggest some trends in hemotoglogical effects of exercise. Unfortunately the lack of quantitative control of exercise intensity and duration make interpretation difficult. The functional, physiological, and clinical significance of the exercise-induced alterations that have been reported are yet to be determined. For such determinations to be made, the mechanisms associated with these hemotological alterations must be investigated. The following is a list of generalizations related to the effect of exercise upon the blood that are supported by the literature:

1. Strenuous exercise will cause a decrease in blood volume that is due primarily to loss of plasma H_2O. This is associated with a hemoconcentration effect.
2. There is an alteration in the total amount of plasma protein following exercise. The direction and magnitude of change seems dependent upon the intensity of work and the physical condition of the subject.
3. Intravascular hemolysis results from physical trauma caused by long runs on hard surfaces.
4. Training causes an overall "thinning of the blood." There is increased total blood volume, increased plasma volume, and no appreciable change in red cell volume with training.
5. An acute bout of exercise increases both the clotting and fibrinolytic activity of the blood.
6. Exercise causes increased platelet number and may alter platelet function.

REFERENCES

1. Rennie MH, Johnson RH: Alteration of metabolic and hormonal responses to exercise by physical training. *Euro J Appl Physiol* 33:215, 1974
2. Galbo H, Host JJ, Christensen NJ: Glucagon and plasma catecholamine responses to graded and prolonged exercise in man. *J Appl Physiol* 38:70, 1975
3. Rennie MJ, Parks DM, Sulaiman WR: Uptake and release of hormones and metabolities by tissues of exercising leg in man. *Amer J Physiol* 231:967, 1976
4. Astrand PO, Saltin B: Plasma and red cell volume after prolonged severe exercise. *J Appl Physiol* 19:829, 1964
5. van Beaumont W, Greenleaf JE, Jubos L: Disproportional changes in hematocrit, plasma volume, and proteins during exercise and bed rest. *J Appl Physiol* 33:55, 1972
6. Joye H, Poortmans J: Hematocrit and serum proteins during arm exercise. *Med Sci Sports* 2:187, 1970
7. Poortmans JR: Serum protein determination during short exhaustive physical activity. *J Appl Physiol* 30:190, 1971
8. Saltin B: Circulatory response to submaximal and maximal exercise after thermal dehydration. *J Appl Physiol* 19:1125, 1964
9. Kaltreider NL, Meneely CR: The effect of exercise on the volume of blood. *J Clin Invest* 19:627, 1940
10. Nylan G: The effect of heavy muscular work on the volume of circulating red corpuscles in man. *Amer J Physiol* 149:180, 1947
11. Senay LC, Kok R: Effects of training and heat acclimatization on blood plasma contents of exercising men. *J Appl Physiol* 43:591, 1977
12. Poortmans J, Jeanloz RW: Quantitative immunological determination of 12 plasma proteins excreted in human urine collected before and after exercise. *J Clin Invest* 47:386, 1968
13. Haralambie G: Serum seromucoid and physical exercise. *J Appl Physiol* 27:669, 1969
14. Rocker L, Kirsch KA, Stoboy H: Plasma volume, albumin and globulin concentrations and their intravascular mass. *Euro J Appl Physiol* 36:57, 1976
15. Dill DB, Braithwaite K, Adams WC, Bernauer EM: Blood volume and middle-distance

runners: effect of 2,300-m altitude and comparison with non-athletes. *Med Sci Sports* 6:1, 1974

16. Kjellberg SR, Rudhe V, Sjostrand T: Increase in the amount of hemoglobin and blood volume in connection with physical training. *Acta Physiol Scand* 19:146, 1949

17. Oscai LB, Williams BT, Hertig BA: Effects of exercise on blood volume. *J Appl Physiol* 24:622, 1968

18. Glass HI, Edwards RHT, DeGarreta AC, Clark JC: [11]CO red cell labeling for blood volume and total hemoglobin in athletes: effect of training. *J Appl Physiol* 26:131, 1969

19. Holmgren A, Mossfeldt F, Sjostrand T, Strom G: Effect of training on work capacity, total hemoglobin, blood volume, heart volume and pulse rate in recumbent and upright positions. *Acta Physiol et Biochim* 12:840, 1976

20. Kozlowski S, Szczepansica E, Zielinski A: The hypothalamo-hypophyseal antidiuretic system in physical exercise. *Arch Inter de Physiol et Biochim* 75:218, 1967

21. Rocker L, Kirsch K, Wicke J, Stoboy H: Role of proteins in the regulation of plasma volume during heat stress and exercise. *Isr J Med Sci* 12:840, 1976

22. Zinvy J, Travnicek T, Neuwirt J: Effect of exercise on production of erythropoietin in normal and hypoxic rats. *Am J Physiol* 220:329, 1971

23. Zinvy J, Neuwirt J, Travnicek T: The effect of lactic acid on erythropoietin production and the rate of disappearance of erythropoietin from rat plasma during exercise. *Life Sci* 10:11, 1971

24. Gilligan DR, Altschule MD, Katersky EM: Hemoglobinemia and hemoglobinuria following cross-country runs. *J Clin Invest* 22:859, 1943

25. Davidson RJL: March on exertional haemoglobinuria. *Semin Hematol* 6:150, 1969

26. Palmer RA, Mitchell HS: March haemoglobinuria. *Can Med Assn J* 49:465, 1943

27. Lowbury EJL, Blakely APL: Exertion haemoglobinuria: report on a case. *Br Med J* 1:12, 1948

28. Davidson RJL: Exertion haemoglobinuria: report on three cases with studies on the hemolytic mechanism. *J Clin Path* 17:536, 1964

29. Allison AC, Rees W: The binding of haemoglobin by plasma proteins (Haptoglobins). *Br Med J* 2:1137, 1957

30. Stewart WB, Stewart JM, Izzo MJ, Young LE: Age as affecting the osmotic and mechanical fraility of dog erythrocytes tagged with radioactive iron. *J Exp Med* 91:147, 1950

31. Hanson PG, Buhr B, Sarnwick R, Shahidi NA: Exercise hemolysis in trained and untrained runners. *Med Sci Sports* 10:48, 1978 (abst)

32. Hartman F: Changes in the clotting time of the blood of cats as a result of exercise. *Am J Physiol* 80:716, 1927

33. Mills CA, Necheles H: Variations in the coagulability of the blood normally and after food ingestion. *Clin J Physiol* 2:19, 1928

34. Schneider RA, Zangari VM: Variations in clotting time, relative viscosity, and other physiochemical properties of the blood accompanying physical and emotional stress in the normotensive and hypertensive subject. *Psychosom Med* 13:289, 1951

35. Rizza CR: Effect of exercise on the level of antihaemophilic globulin in human blood. *J Physiol* 156:128, 1961

36. Egeberg O: Changes in the activity of antihemophilic A factor (F. VIII) and in bleeding time associated with muscular exercise and adrenalin function. *Scand J Lab Clin Invest* 15:539, 1963

37. Iatridas SG, Ferguson JH: Effect of physical exercise on blood clotting and fibrinolysis. *J Appl Physiol* 18:337, 1963

38. Ikkala E, Myllyla IG, Sarajas HSS: Haemostatic changes associated with exercise. *Nature* 199:459, 1963

39. Fowler WM, Showdbury SR, Pearson CH, Gardner G, et al: Changes in serum enzyme levels after exercise in trained and untrained subjects. *J Appl Physiol* 17:943, 1962

40. Crowell JW, Houston B: Effect of acidity on blood coagulation. *Am J Physiol* 201:379, 1961

41. Hawkey CM, Britton BJ, Wood WG, Peele IM, et al: Changes in blood catecholamine levels and blood coagulation and fibrinolytic activity in response to graded exercise in man. *Br J Haematol* 29:377, 1975

42. Ferguson EW, Guest MM: Exercise, physical conditioning, blood coagulation, and fibrinolysis. *Thromb Diath Haemorrh* 31:63, 1974

43. Rizza CR, Eipe J: Exercise factor VIII and the spleen. *Br J Haematol* 20:629, 1971

44. Cash JD, Allan AGE: The fibrinolytic response to moderate exercise and intravenous adrenaline in the same subjects. *Br J Haematol* 13:376, 1967

45. Cohen RJ, Epstein SE, Cohen LS, Dennis LH: Alterations of fibrinolysis and blood coagulation induced by exercise and the role of beta-adrenergic receptor stimulation. *Lancet* 2:1264, 1968

46. Simpson MT, Howes CG, Olewine DA, Ramsey FH, et al: Physical activity, catecholamines, and platelet stickiness. *Recent Advances in Studies on Cardiac Structure and Metab* 1:742, 1972

47. Dawson AA, Ogston D: Exercise-induced thrombocytosis. *Acta Haematol* 42:241, 1969

48. Warlow CP, Ogston D: Effect of exercise on platelet count, adhesion, and aggregation. *Acta Haematol* 52:47, 1974

49. Chandler AB: The platelet in thrombus formation. in: Brinkhous KM, et al (eds): *The Platelet*. Williams and Wilkins, Baltimore, 1971, p 183

50. Wachholder K, Parchwitz E, Egili H, Kessler K: Der einfluss körperlicher arbeit auf die zahl der thrombocyten und auf deren haftneigung. *Acta Haematol* 18:59, 1957

51. Lee G, Amsterdam EA, DeMaria AN, Davis G, et al: Effects of exercise on hemostatic mechanisms. in: Amsterdam EA, et al (eds): *Exercise in Cardiovascular Health and Disease*. York Medical Books, New York, 1977, p 122

52. Sarajas HSS: Reaction patterns of blood platelets to exercise. *Adv Cardiol* 18:176, 1976

53. Dimitriadov C, Dessypris A, Louizov C, Mandalaki T: Marathon run II: Effects on platelet aggregation. *Thrombos Haemostas* 37:451, 1977

54. Sarajas HSS, Konttinen A, Frick MH: Thrombocytosis evoked by exercise. *Nature* (London) 192:721, 1961

55. Sarnoff JG: Alterations in fibrinolysis and blood coagulation. *Lancet* 1:259, 1969

56. Bennett PN: Effect of physical exercise on platelet adhesiveness. *Scand J Haematol* 9:138, 1972

57. Pegrum GD, Harrison KM, Shaw S: Effect of prolonged exercise on platelet adhesiveness. *Nature* 213:301, 1967

58. Hartley I, Mason J, Hogan R, Jones L, et al: Multiple hormonal responses to graded exercise in relation to physical training. *J Appl Physiol* 33:602, 1972

59. Astrup T: An overview. in: Davidson JR, et al (eds): *Progress in Chemical Fibrinolysis and Thrombolysis*. Raven Press, New York, 1978, p 1

60. Biggs R, McFarlane RG, Pilling J: Observations on fibrinolysis. *Lancet* 1:402, 1947

61. Ogston D, Fullerton HW: Changes in the fibrinolytic activity produced by physical activity. *Lancet* 2:730, 1961

62. Cash JD: Effect of moderate exercise on the fibrinolytic system in normal young men and women. *Br Med J* 2:502, 1966

63. Moxley, RT, Brackman P, Astrup T: Resting levels of fibrinolysis in blood in inactive and exercising men. *J Appl Physiol* 28:549, 1970

64. Davis GL, Abildgaard CF, Bernauer EM, Britton M: Fibrinolytic and hemostatic changes during and after maximal exercise. *J Appl Physiol* 40:287, 1976

65. Mandalaki T, Dessypris A, Louizov K, Bossinakov I, et al: Marathon run I: effects on blood coagulation and fibrinolysis. *Thrombos Haemostas* 37:444, 1977

66. Rosing DR, Brakman P, Redwood DR, Goldstein RE, et al: Blood fibrinolytic activity in man. *Circ Res* 27:171, 1970

67. Bennett NB, Ogston CM, Ogston D: The effect of prolonged exercise on the components of the blood fibrinolytic enzyme system. *J Physiol* 198:479, 1968

68. Sherry S, Lindemeyer RI, Fletcher AP, Alkjaersig N: Studies on enhanced fibrinolytic activity in man. *J Clin Invest* 38:810, 1959

69. Sawyer WD, Flectcher AP, Alkjaersig N, Sherry S: Studies on the thrombolytic activity of human plasma. *J Clin Invest* 39:426, 1960

70. Rennie JAN, Bennett B, Ogston D: Effect of local exercise and vessel occlusion on fibrinolytic activity. *J Clin Path* 30:350, 1977

71. Holemans R: Enhancing the fibrinolytic activity of blood by vasoactive drugs. *Med Exper* 9:5, 1963

72. Cash JD, Woodfield DG, Allan AGE: Adrenergic mechanisms in the systemic plasminogen activator response to adrenaline in man. *Br J Haematol* 18:487, 1970

The Female in Exercise

DOROTHY V. HARRIS, PH.D.

While females generally are five inches shorter, 30 to 40 pounds lighter, and ten percent fatter on the average than males, they respond and adapt to chronic exercise and physical training in much the same manner. Efforts to determine quantitative and qualitative differences in response to physical training between males and females have generally demonstrated that observed differences are not mediated by sex but by the level of physical fitness. In short, the differences are influenced by factors other than one's biological sex. There are more differences within a sex than between the sexes when fitness levels are controlled.

In spite of the fact that the female does respond to exercise in much the same pattern as the male, she performs at a substantially lower level than he does in almost all athletic contests. In running events (based on 1977 records), the percentage of difference in performance is 9.62 percent in the 100 meters, 11.02 percent in the 400 meters, 13.0 percent in the 1,000 meters, 15.3 percent in the 2,000 meters, 18.15 percent in the 10,000 meters and 17.0 percent in the marathon. Are these differences truly biological ones, are they only the result of sex differences, or are they reflective of social and cultural restrictions and expectations placed on the female?

Smaller, slower, and weaker individuals are discriminated against when it comes to selection for sports. Only about 20 percent of the body types are represented in the Olympics. Generally, there is less difference in the body types of males and females who excel in the same athletic events than there is between males and females in general or perhaps between males who are selected and males who are not. In other words, the high jumper, male or female, who uses the Fosbury Flop will be quite similar in body type. Much the same can be said about the basketball player, the marathoner, and so on.

The female matures sooner than the male; twenty weeks after conception she is two to three weeks more mature and at birth her level of maturation may be as much as 20 weeks ahead of the male's. This is due to the fact that the male must wait for "something to be added"—the Y chromosome—to indicate that the gonads will be testicles. These cells must mature and multiply sufficiently to begin to produce androgen, the male hormone which will then begin to differentiate to male development. This lag behind the female in development is not closed until the male has reached approximately 20 years of age. There is great variation in the maturation rate, with this being more pronounced in the male. Seefeldt[1] reported that there was as much as 40 months difference in maturation among six year-old boys and 72 months difference in 13 year-old boys. Such a wide variation in maturation is not observed among females, most of whom have reached their mature height and growth soon after the onset of menarche. One cannot recruit a girl from high school for basketball and assume that she will grow several more inches while in college; however, most males will continue to grow during those years.

During late childhood the female may be bigger than her male counterpart as a result of reaching her growth spurt sooner. During this time she may be faster and stronger than boys and may outperform them in athletic feats, provided she has had the opportunity to learn skills and has been reinforced in a positive manner for her performance and involvement. Once physical maturity has been reached, there are average differences between males and females that have specific implications for athletic performance.

Males mature later, and therefore grow longer than females, and are thus generally bigger than females. The higher levels of androgens (male hormones) in the male also influence development. Males have longer extremities in relationship to their trunk length, broader shoulders, greater muscle development in the shoulder area, and less body fat. Higher estrogen levels (female hormones) in the female close off the epiphyses of the long bones sooner and this results in shorter height. Body fat is increased in the female who is 10 percent fatter than the male. Her hips are broader in relation to her shoulders, she has less muscle mass in the shoulder girdle, and her trunk tends to be longer in relation to her leg. Body type is also influenced by genetics, nutrition, exercise, and other factors beyond those of the endocrine system.

As indicated, there are average differences between males and females that have specific implications for performance in sports. Twelve of the 78 female distance runners studied by Wilmore and Brown[2] had 10 percent body fat, 32 of them had less than 15 percent body fat indicating that well over half of these female distance runners were less fat than the average college male who is 15 percent fat. These trained women were significantly less fat than their untrained female peers who have approximately 25 percent body fat. While low body fat may be a genetic endowment, high intensity endurance type exercise is also a significant factor. It appears that with strenuous training females can reduce the percentage of fat content in their bodies to levels that are comparable to that of male athletes. It also appears that the average percentage of fat in untrained females is higher than ideal; regular exercise could reduce those stores.

A greater percent of body fat in the female provides her with advantages for some activities. She is more buoyant in water and has better insulation in cold temperatures. This combined advantage has allowed females to better the world records in long distance open water swimming. A young Canadian woman swam the English Channel round trip in the fall of 1977 and knocked over ten hours off the previous record, which had been held by a male. Dr. Joan Ullyot[3] has reported that women "run off their fat"—that the additional fat that women have provides them with extra fuel for energy. Ullyot suggested that women may be able to use their fat stores more efficiently than men. It is possible that they burn a higher percentage of fat mixed with glycogen; if so, their glycogen would tend to last longer and make them feel better after running a marathon than do men. While the biochemical mechanisms have not been isolated, there appears to be a difference in the adaptation to strenuous endurance type exercise between males and females.

Strength differences between males and females have traditionally been acknowledged. However, Wilmore[4] has reported that leg strength is nearly identical in the two sexes and that when expressed relative to body size it is identical. In fact, when expressed relative to lean body mass, the females are slightly stronger! The difference between males and females in strength is greatest in the shoulders, less pronounced in the trunk, and apparently nonexistent as far as leg strength is concerned. The female responds to strength training in much the same manner as the male from a developmental point of view. While weight training produces large gains in strength in the female, concomitant gains in muscle bulk do not result. In the fall of 1977, a 114 pound female broke the men's lift record in that weight class by lifting 225 pounds. There is much to learn about factors relating to strength, strength development, and the maximizing of potential strength development.

Efforts to determine qualitative and quantitative differences in the aerobic capacity of males and females have demonstrated that the female has a maximal oxygen uptake that is less than that of the male. In general, however, the level of physical fitness overrides the effect of sex. Hermanson and Andersen[5] have reported that female cross country skiers had an average aerobic capacity of 55 ml/kg min while the average male had 44 ml/kg min. Female athletes have higher oxygen-carrying capacity than untrained male peers. While athletic males are noticeably superior, trained females are 25 percent more efficient than untrained males. Body composition and training level generally explain the observed differences between males and females. Whether the lean body mass of the female can approach that of the male with the same training as a moot point. The female must deliver oxygen to her fat tissue as well as her working muscle as part of her work load; she cannot leave her fat tissue in the locker room!

In addition to body composition and training level, other factors influence the capacity of oxygen uptake. The female generally has a smaller heart, smaller lungs, chest muscles, blood volume, and so forth. She compensates for these average differences with the ability to increase her heart rate to levels higher than those observed in most males. Another significant difference is observed in the percent of hemoglobin with the female having as much as ten percent less than the male.[6] No significant differences are observed until puberty between males and females. The assumpton has been that the female's hemoglobin is reduced through blood loss with menstruation. However, Lamb[7] reported a 20 percent increase in hemoglobin in castrated male animals when testosterone was injected, and concluded that testosterone promoted red blood cell production. It appears that males significantly increase their hemoglobin as testosterone increases and that females do not necessarily reduce theirs through normal menstruation. Males, however, have approximately 1,000,000 more red blood cells than females and can store 850 mg of iron as compared to the female's 250 mg. Compensatory factors do not appear to adjust for this difference in males and females; therefore, some type of iron supplement is frequently recommended for the female athlete.

Menstruation and factors relating to that process have probably produced more concern and misinformation than any other difference in males and females. Females have made and broken their own personal best performances at all phases of the menstrual cycle. It appears that menstruation produces no diminution in the performance of females who have made a serious commitment to athletic pursuits; however, it is possible that the female athletic population is biased toward those women who experienced no impairments. Those who had performance fluctuations coinciding with the menstrual cycle may have been systematically eliminated.

During the 1970s an awareness of another pattern of response in females who are training strenuously has developed.[8,9] It has been estimated that perhaps 15 to 20 percent experience secondary amenorrhea or cessation of menstruation. There are several theories that attempt to explain this response. Most hinge on the percent of body fat. Ullyot[3] suggests that the cessation of menstruation is Mother Nature's way of protecting the female. Because of reduced body fat, for whatever reasons (starvation, disease, exercise, etc.), the body does not have sufficient fat storage to support a pregnancy so the system "shuts down." Frisch[10] supports this theory to some extent. She has developed a method for predicting the age of onset of menarche by charting the height and weight of girls every year during their 9 to 13 age span, and has concluded that the ratio of lean body weight to fat is an important determinant of sexual maturation in the female. This is not a simple cause-effect relationship, however, since increasing levels of estrogen, as well as triggering the menstrual cycle, cause the female to begin to store body fat. In essence, body fat and menarche are both caused by elevating levels of estrogen; therefore, increased body fat is not the cause of the onset of menarche. They coincide!

There are several situations in which a significant decrease in body fat does appear to be related to secondary amenorrhea. Starvation, anorexia nervosa, and a drastic reduction in caloric intake, resulting in a significant weight loss in a short period of time, produce secondary amenorrhea. At the same time, obesity can also lead to the cessation of menstruation. Other stressful situations, such as being in a concentration camp, entering college, experiencing the loss of a loved one, divorce, fear of failure, and so forth can also alter the menstrual cycle.

Since reduced body fat is not a factor in all of the reported cases of secondary amenorrhea, other explanations have to be explored. Females on the same training program, who have no significant differences in percent body fat, and who have not lost a significant amount of body fat, can be on the same track team. Some of these women will experience secondary amenorrhea while others will not. The fact that different individuals respond differently to stress may be the explanation for this. Why some endure stress without any noticeable changes while others do not is currently a medical mystery, as far as I know. As Selye[11] suggests, "Stress is stress." This may be the case whether that stress is a result of exercise, reduction of body fat in a short period of time, emotional factors, competition, or whatever. It will be necessary to examine a whole array of responses to understand why secondary amenorrhea occurs in some women.

The magnitude of the problem has not actually been established. It appears that several different patterns occur. First, those who have had normal cycles and who have then experienced secondary amenorrhea with an increase in physical training and exercise, generally resume normal cycles with detraining. In many cases individuals did not menstruate for two or more years, stopped hard training, resumed their cycles, and had normal pregnancies and deliveries of healthy babies.

Secondly, some women who experienced the cessation of menstruation did not alter their training programs or replace the lost fat tissue, yet resumed their cycles after a period of time. This would suggest that the body adapted to the stresses placed upon it and accommodated them without long term endocrine alteration. A 1978 survey study completed by Feicht and Johnson[12] at Boulder, Colorado suggests that the percent of those experiencing secondary amenorrhea increases significantly as mileage increases. Running 60 or more miles a week may be the critical factor. At this point no one knows for sure whether exercise per se or low body fat causes the condition. As Dr. John Marshall, co-chairman of New York Medical Society's Committee on the Medical Aspects of Sports, has said, "The body-fat percentage is not the cause, all kinds of things we don't know about the delicate balance of hormones have an effect. It may have to do with the kind of training, it may be psychological."[9] Certainly, the medical profession does not know.

In response to an article I wrote on the topic for *WomenSports,*[8] nearly 200 letters relating case studies were received. I must say that I was appalled at the medical treatment and guesswork that some women were subjected to, not to mention the almost total lack of consideration of the fact that vigorous exercise might have something to do with their secondary amenorrhea. One woman spent six years with different physicians experimenting with various tests and theories—everything from brain scans, hormone injections, oral hormone medication, and exploratory surgery—finally came to the conclusion that she was "having identity problems and denying her femininity" since nothing showed up that was irregular or abnormal beyond the fact that she did not menstruate!

While alterations and changes in the female cycle are obvious, males may have similar alterations and not even know about them. Bloom[13] cited a little known Finnish study conducted in 1973 and reported in the 1976 British Journal of Steroid Biochemistry which involved hormonal assays in males before and after running a marathon. Statistically significant changes were observed in several hormones which have an impact on male sexuality. A rise or fall in their levels can adversely affect fertility, both in decreasing sex drives and lowering sperm count. Almost no one has examined this relationship. Dr. Mona Shangold,[13] physician-endocrinologist, has suggested, "There may be a relationship between reproductive problems and chronic exercise such as extensive training done by long distance runners." She has suggested further that if there is a correlation between very low body fat levels and fertility problems, this may mean that runners of both sexes will have to decrease their running if they wish to have children: in the case of women, until their cycles return; in the case of men, who knows? Shangold has suggested that a male with a low sperm count who wishes to restore it to normal may have to stop running for 74 days because it takes that long for sperm to mature.

To date there is nothing in the literature to support the belief that there is a high infertility rate among runners, male or female. The problem may be on a very small scale indeed because of great individual differences and responses to exercise and stress. The cardiovascular, psychological, and other benefits of running far outweigh potential adverse effects on reproduction. Furthermore, there is no evidence to suggest that reproductive problems that may develop during training are irreversible.

Another concern that even less is known about is the possibility of strenuous exercise delaying the onset of menarch. The *New York Times*[9] quoted Dr. Jack Wilmore as saying, ''We know there is a tendency for girls who participate in heavy competition before menarch to have onset delayed until they are 17 or 18 but we do not know whether that is good or bad.'' The average age of onset is between 12 and 13 years; however, beginning menstruation at age 15 or 16 is still considered normal. At a discussion of the issue at the American College of Sports Medicine meeting in Chicago in May 1977, physicians could not agree as to the age at which one should become concerned if the female has not begun to menstruate. At this point it is not known whether or not strenuous training prior to puberty can be detrimental to normal development of the endocrine or reproductive systems. No one knows whether it is possible to delay development and then make up for that delay with a decrease in training routine.

Apparently there is little reason to drastically alter one's exercise pattern with pregnancy if that pattern has been a part of one's lifestyle for some time. There are many case studies in which pregnant athletes have accomplished all sorts of athletic feats during the early stages of their pregnancies. Lynn Blackstone, during her ninth month, ran twice around Central Park's reservoir, which is approximately three miles, each evening. She finished 58th out of 102 women in the 1977 Boston marathon. Mary Jones ran a half marathon race at the Dallas White Rock Marathon in two hours and five minutes in December 1976, when she was nearly nine months pregnant. She returned to marathon running ten weeks after giving birth, saying, ''Pregnancy is not a disease. I listened to my body and let it dictate what I could do, and I'm healthier for it.'' Many others report the same experience. Trina Hosmer, U. S. Olympic cross-country skier, in 1972 ran four miles two hours before her first child was born. She barely had time to get changed and get to the hospital for delivery. While Trina may be exceptional, there is no evidence that regular exercise and running during pregnancy has to be discontinued if the woman is used to regular exercise.

Osteoporosis is far more prevalent among women than men; this may be the case for several reasons. In the first place, growing girls are not generally socialized to participate in vigorous exercise during those years when bones are developing and growing so that stresses placed on them during this time can result in stronger, more dense bones. Secondly, estrogen levels decrease with age and the onset of menopause, so the effect that estrogen has in stimulating bone maintenance is lost to some degree. Thirdly, females do not exercise enough throughout their lives to stimulate bone maintenance. Running, jogging, or other types of regular exercise are especially important for aging women, yet the emphasis has been on males getting exercise. The harmful effects of inactivity on bone tissue are well documented; long term bed rest can lead to early osteoporosis. Even bones that are in a plaster cast for a short duration tend to become lighter due to mineral loss. The astronauts experienced alteration in bone metabolism during periods of weightlessness and physical confinement.

On the other hand, exercise stimulates bone growth and maintenance; one has only to compare one's dominant arm with one's lesser used arm to see that this is so. The prevention of osteoporosis appears to be related to vigorous exercise during the growing years to maximize the skeletal development, then continued exercise throughout one's lifetime with some attention paid to the amount of calcium in the diet.

Females may be more or less efficient in heat dissipation than males, depending on how the research is interpreted. Studies show that males do sweat sooner and more profusely than females in response to increased body temperatures. On the other hand, males may sweat prolifically and wastefully. The female may adjust her sweat rate more efficiently; that is, she can compensate for the observed differences. On the average, females have more sweat glands than males. Generally, her body temperature gets two to three degrees warmer than that of the male's before she begins to sweat. Females sweat less than males and can accomplish the same work loads with less water loss. Both males and females acclimatize to work or exercise in heat, but females are able to do so without increasing their sweat rates. There may be some factors that have not been examined. For one thing, higher levels of estrogen in females tend to provide greater vascularization; therefore the female may be able to get more blood to the surface of her body for cooling and thus delay the sweating process. This may allow her to compensate for her additional fat insulation and smaller body surface. Moreover, since the female has more active sweat glands than the male, her sweat is distributed more evenly over her body, which allows for maximal cooling by evaporation and compensates for her smaller body surface.

While the male sweats sooner, the female may sweat better! Wells,[14] as a result of her research in heat environments, has suggested that women may regulate their body temperature more effectively than men. Perhaps it is time to examine this response more carefully and to stop perpetuating the notion that females may be less effective in heat dissipation. Once the next generation has been educated out of the notion that men sweat, gentlemen perspire, and ladies glow, we may observe a different response to heat stress!

In summary, it appears that while the male and female do differ in many respects in terms of their response to vigorous exercise, there are more differences within a sex than between the sexes. The level of physical fitness mediates the difference to a greater extent than sex. Further, when differences are observed in trained males and females, in most cases the response is one of adapting and conditioning to chronic exercise. In many situations the female adapts differently in that she compensates for these differences. Or, we could say that the male compensates, as in the case of his having to sweat sooner in order to cool his body.

When training and conditioning are equal, there appears to be no difference in the injury predisposition between males and females. Statistics suggest that females are more vulnerable to leg and knee injuries. Again, the level of physical conditioning and fitness is more important than one's sex with regard to injury predisposition. As increasing emphasis is placed on conditioning for female athletes, the injury statistics reflect the type of sport played rather than the sex of the player. In short, individuals who play basketball will experience similar types and rates of injuries that will not be linked to sex. A great deal of research is needed before there can be full understanding and insight into just what differences do exist between the response of males and females to long term strenuous exercise. At this point in time it appears that the sauce for the gander is sauce for the goose. The female gains all the benefits and pleasure of having a body as healthy and fit as the male, and certainly the joys and challenges of participation and competition in sports are not linked to sex. From everything available in the literature, the responses are all positive in physiological and psychological ways.

REFERENCES

1. Seefeldt D: Scope of youth sports programs in the state of Michigan. in: Smoll L, Smith E (eds): *Psychological Perspectives in Youth Sports*. New York, John Wiley & Sons, 1978
2. Wilmore H, Brown C: Physiological profiles of women distance runners. *Med Sci Sports* 6(3):178, 1974
3. Ullyot J: *Women's Running*. Mountain View, CA, World Publications, 1976
4. Wilmore H: The female athlete. *J Sch Health* 47(4):227, 1977
5. Hermanson L, Andersen KL: Aerobic work capacity in young Norwegian men and women. *J App Physiol* 20:425, 1965
6. Harris DV: The anemic athlete. *WomenSports* 4(12):52, 1977
7. Lamb DR: Androgens and exercise. *Med Sci Sports* 7(1):1, 1975
8. Harris V: The monthly mystery. *WomenSports* 4(9):49, 1977
9. Brozan N: Training linked to disruption of female reproductive cycle. *The New York Times,* April 17, 1978
10. Frisch RE: A method of prediction of age of menarche from height and weight at ages 9 through 13 years. *Pedatrics* 53(3):384, 1974
11. Selye H: *The Stress of Life*. New York: McGraw-Hill, 1976
12. Feicht C, Johnson TS: Secondary amenorrhea in athletes. *The Lancet,* Nov. 25, 1978
13. Bloom M: Running as birth control? *The Runner* 1(1):21, 1978
14. Wells CL: Sexual differences in heat stress response. The *Physician and Sportsmedicine* 5(9):79, 1977

Peripheral Vascular Changes during Exercise

JOSEPH R. DiPALMA, M.D.

It is generally agreed that certain changes associated with exercise occur in the peripheral circulation. There is an increase in pulse rate and an increase in both systolic and diastolic blood pressure. The systolic rise is greater than the diastolic and this causes an increase in pulse pressure[1] (Figure 1). Venous pressure also rises during exercise.[2] It is also generally agreed that while the total changes in peripheral resistance may not be dramatic, there are profound readjustments in the flow of various peripheral organs. Obviously the flow to skeletal muscles is markedly increased while the flow to abdominal organs is decreased.[3] The kidney for example suffers a decrease in flow of from 50 to 80 percent during exercise.[4]

In acute exercise there are marked shifts in fluid balance. The increased concentration of erythrocytes, hemoglobin, and plasma proteins indicates hemoconcentration with a loss of blood volume. This is partially the result of an increased venous pressure which causes an increased capillary filtration and loss of fluid from the blood into the interstitial tissues.[3] Sweating, of course, accounts for additional fluid loss. As moderate exercise is continued, eventually compensatory mechanisms limit the shift of fluids.[5]

It is thus obvious that complicated events contribute to the changes in blood flow in any organ during exercise. These changes are largely mechanical but also involve the control of vasculature by central reflexes mediated through the autonomic nervous system, as well as local control involving tissue substances such as potassium concentration, serotonin, bradykinin, and prostaglandins. Finally, circulating hormones such as norepinephrine and the renin-angiotension system undoubtedly also contribute to the local vascular responses.[6] As of yet, no group has succeeded in unraveling all these factors in any organ during rest, much less during

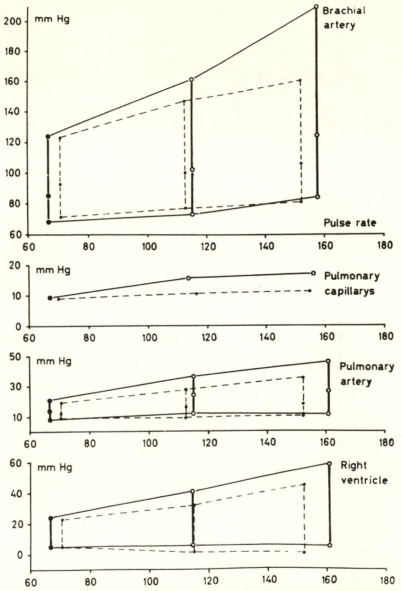

Fig. 1. Response of blood pressure in the brachial artery, pulmonary capillary (wedge pressure), pulmonary artery, and right ventricle to graded exercise (pedaling bicycle in supine position). Solid lines are trained athletes; broken lines, nonathletes. (From Bevegard S, Holmgren A, Jonsson B: Acta Physiol Scand 57:26, 1963. Used with permission.)

exercise. There is, however, an approach to this problem by the study of the response to local ischemia or reactive hyperemia. The skin is the most convenient organ to study these changes as it is easily accessible and visible. Moreover, during exercise the skin has the important function of temperature control and fluid balance.

The physiological changes observed in this study, as well as other changes in the peripheral circulation that have been documented, might serve as a basis for predicting the value or danger of exercise in various diseases. Most recent evaluations of the value of exercise in disease prevention have focused on cardiac function. It would appear desirable to study, as well, any exercise predictive features of peripheral vascular changes which might influence disease processes.

METHODS

The method of measuring cutaneous reactive hyperemia must be briefly described in order to interpret the results obtained in exercise. The volar surface of the forearm is used. Weights are applied whose application surface is a smooth rubber ring. Local ischemia is thus caused, which, on lifting the weight results in a ring of hyperemia. This ring can be read quite reliably by a trained observer to constitute an end point of hyperemia response (a complete ring without a flare response). This end point is called the "threshold" and is the least duration in seconds required to produce the standard response. "Clearing time" is the time in seconds for the complete disappearance of the reactive hyperemia produced by the occlusion of threshold duration. It has been shown that this method yields results which indicate that the threshold is related to the tone of the small blood vessels of the skin (subpapillary venous plexus). The clearing time, on the other hand, is related to the rate of blood flow in these vessels.[7] For the purpose of avoiding artifacts from changes in venous pressure, the method was modified to apply to the elevated forearm so that subjects could still conveniently run on the treadmill.[8,9]

The study was done on six male subjects in good physical condition ranging in ages from 20 to 45. Graded exercise was given on a motor driven treadmill in consecutive ten minute periods at speeds ranging from 1.5 to 3.0 miles per hour and at grades of from 0° to 10°. Venous pressure (mm saline) was measured in the forearm using a zero point corresponding to the level of the xiphoid process. Skin temperatures were recorded from the forearm, pulp of the forefinger, and the forehead. Rectal temperatures were also recorded in most experiments. In some experiments the respiratory rate and minute volume were recorded.[8]

OBSERVATIONS

A representative experiment is shown in Figure 2. Incremental increases in exercise over a 50 minute period caused marked changes in pulse rate as expected. The venous pressure did not change appreciably until work was intensified by increasing the grade. Cutaneous reactive hyperemia also did not change with mild exercise.

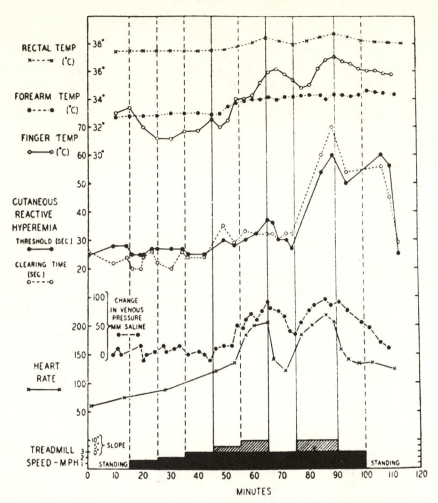

Fig. 2. Representative experiment showing relationships of graded exercise to exhaustion on venous pressure, cutaneous reactive hyperemia, heart rate, skin and rectal temperatures. (From Barger AC, Greenwood WF, DiPalma JR, et al: J Appl Physiol 2, 81, 1949. Reprinted with permission.)

When the grade was increased, however, an increase in threshold and clearing time occurred, indicating some vasoconstriction and some slowing of blood·flow in the forearm skin. Skin temperature in the finger, however, indicated at first a vasoconstriction, then a vasodilation as the rectal temperature rose.

The subject was then returned to a zero degree slope and, as seen in Figure 2, all modalities tended to return to normal except rectal and skin temperatures. This may indicate that it is not so much the duration of exercise but the intensity of work that brings about the changes in peripheral circulation. At 75 minutes after the start of the experiment the subject was again exercised at a high intensity. Now the pulse rate, venous pressure, and cutaneous reactive hyperemia showed marked increases. Exhausting exercise is thus shown to cause severe vasoconstriction in the skin and slowing of blood flow as studied in the smallest blood vessels. It is interesting that this occurs at a time when the forearm temperature is elevated. Skin temperature measurements thus do not always reliably indicate relative changes in blood flow. Recovery of all modalities occurred over a 10 to 15 minute period once exercise was terminated.

Naturally, different subjects showed some variations in response but all of these were in the same direction. Figure 3 shows comparative experiments on four dif-

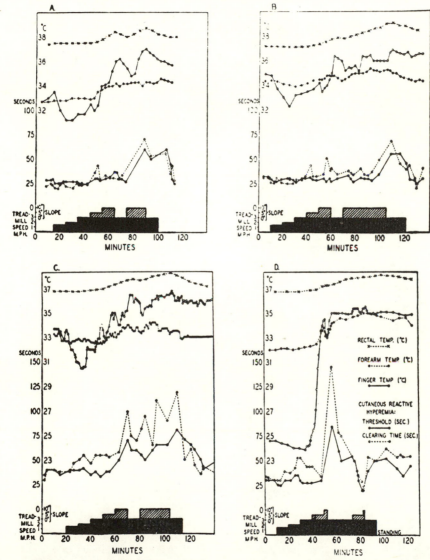

Fig. 3. Selected experiments to demonstrate variation in different subjects charting cutaneous reactive hyperemia, finger, forearm, and rectal temperatures in relationship to graded exercise. (From Barger AC, Greenwood WF, DiPalma JR, et al: J Appl Physiol 2, 81, 1949. Reprinted with permission.)

ferent subjects. A striking response was obtained in subject D who was older and in poorer physical condition. Only three minutes at 10° caused marked changes in cutaneous reactive hyperemia, indicating vasoconstriction and slowing of peripheral blood flow with only moderate degrees of exertion.

The other striking change is in venous pressure. Mild exercise shows no significant change, although the actual figures may show a decrease. Significant changes occur as soon as the grade is increased from the base level. Severe exercise (10° grade at 3 mph) for ten minutes raised venous pressure by 50 to 90 mm H_2O. This was accompanied by visible distension of the neck veins.

The tone of the vessels and rate of blood flow in the skin showed little direct correlation with the other modalities. As might be expected, however, there was excellent correlation between venous pressure, the heart rate, and the increase in respiratory minute volume (Figures 4 and 5). This confirms some older observations of Bainbridge and Bock and Dill.[10] Venous pressure is undoubtedly one of the strongest determinants of central reflexes which control heart rate, cardiac output and respiratory volume.

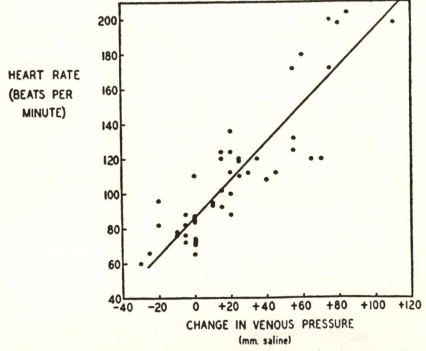

Fig. 4.   The relationship between peripheral venous pressure and heart rate. Venous pressure is charted as the difference between resting values and those at the end of each 10 minute period of graded exercise. (From Barger AC, Greenwood WF, DiPalma JR, et al: J Appl Physiol 2, 81, 1949. Reprinted with permission.)

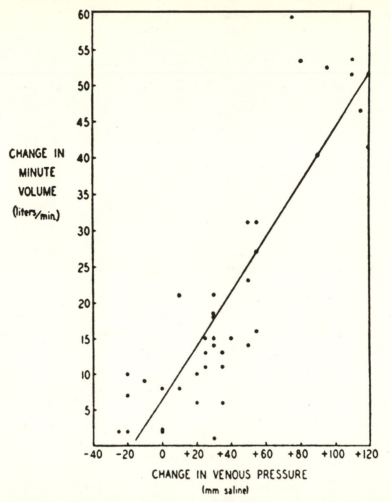

Fig. 5.   The relationship between peripheral venous pressure and respiratory minute volume during graded exercise. The differences are plotted as those existing between resting values and those at the end of each 10 minute period of exercise. (From Barger AC, Greenwood WF, DiPalma JR, et al: J Appl Physiol 2, 81, 1949. Reprinted with permission.)

DISCUSSION

The constriction and slowing of blood flow which occurs in the skin with exhausting exercise must be caused by a powerful stimulus because at this time the skin is warm and the thermoregulatory mechanism is usually dominant. The high venous pressure present at this time may contribute to the stimulus. This in turn causes hemoconcentration because elevation of venous pressure greatly increases fluid loss from the blood stream into the interstitial tissues.[3] With exhausting exercise a time eventually comes when venous return to the heart fails because of hemoconcentration, and this may be the signal by a central nervous reflex to cause intense vasoconstriction. Eventually this may involve the adrenal medulla with secretion of norepinephrine. Apparently other organs are more sensitive to this stimulus than the skin. Lesser grades of exercise definitely reduce renal plasma flow.[11]

Other obvious factors are the production of lactic acidosis and anoxemia in exhausting exercise.[3] Both of these factors affect cutaneous reactive hyperemia by raising threshold and clearing time.[12] Thus they would augment the changes seen in exhausting exercise.

The hyperemia seen in skeletal muscle has been extensively studied.[3] Here the peripheral resistance is reduced in proportion to the degree of exercise. This affects mainly the precapillary resistance vessels (sphincters). Actually this results in a rise in pressure in postcapillary vessels which in turn causes an outward filtration. Potassium ions released into the intercellular space reach a high concentration, and some attribute the vasodilation seen in muscle tissue to this factor.

CONCLUSIONS

These studies confirm the rise in venous pressure which occurs in exercise, particularly in higher degrees of work performance. As studied in the skin, mild exercise does not affect the small blood vessels, and this is shown by their ability to respond to local ischemia. Severe exercise causes vasoconstriction and slowing of blood flow. Thus this study finds no changes in the peripheral circulation which would preclude mild exercise in any individual. Exhausting exercise, however, places severe strains on the peripheral circulation and might well lead to peripheral circulatory failure.

REFERENCES

1. Bevegard S, Holmgren A, Jonsson B: Circulatory studies in well trained athletes at rest and during heavy exercise, with special reference to stroke volume and the influence of body position. *Acta Physiol Scand* 57:26, 1963
2. Schneider EC, Collins T: Venous pressure responses to exercise. *Am J Physiol* 121:574, 1938
3. Kjellmer I: Studies on exercise hyperemia. *Acta Physiol Scand* 64: Supplement 244, 1965
4. White HL, Rolf D: Effects of exercise and of some other influences on the renal circulation in Man. *Am J Physiol* 155:505, 1948
5. Karpovich PV, Sinning EW: *Physiology of Muscle Activity*. Philadelphia, W. B. Saunders Co., 1971
6. Kosunen KJ, Pakarinin AJ: Plasma renin, angiotension II and plasma and urinary aldosterone in running exercise. *J Appl Physiol* 41, 26, 1976
7. DiPalma JR, Reynolds SRM, Foster FI: Quantitative measurement of reactive hyperemia in human skin: individual and season variations. *Am Heart J* 23:377, 1942
8. Greenwood WF, Barger AC, DiPalma JR, et al: Factors affecting the appearance and persistence of visible cutaneous reactive hyperemia in Man. *J Clin Invest* 27:187, 1948

9. Barger AC, Greenwood WF, DiPalma JR, et al: Venous pressure and cutaneous reactive hyperemia in exhausting exercise and certain other circulatory stresses. *J Appl Physiol* 2:81, 1949

10. Bainbridge FA: *The Physiology of Muscular Exercise,* Rewritten by AV Bock and DB Dill, London, Longmans, Green and Co., 1931

11. Chapman CB, Henschel A. Minckler J, et al: The effect of exercise on renal plasma flow in normal male subjects. *J Clin Invest* 27:639, 1948

12. DiPalma JR: Quantitative alterations in the hyperemia responses to local ischemia of the smallest blood vessels of the human skin following systemic anoxemia, hypercapnia, acidosis and alkalosis. *J Exp Med* 76:401, 1942

Part II

The Individual in
His Environment

Climate and Exercise

ALLAN P. FREEDMAN, M.D.

EXTREMES OF TEMPERATURE

Internal Climate

Heat is produced by muscular effort. Muscular effort is less than 25 percent efficient, the other 75+ percent of energy expended being converted to heat. Every liter of oxygen consumed results in the production of 4.9 k cal of heat.[1,2] Heat production can range from 1.25 k cal per minute at rest to over 25 k cal per minute during exercise in a trained individual.[3] Despite this, the body's core temperature (measured by rectal, esophageal, or tympanic membrane probes) never rises more than several degrees even with vigorous exercise.[4]

At rest, evaporation of water from the skin and mucous membranes dissipates one-quarter of the heat produced.[3,5] The rest is lost via radiation and convection, provided that the environment is at a lower temperature. During exercise, the increased heat production is mainly dissipated by evaporation.[3] The evaporation of 1 liter of water cools the body by 580 k cal.[3] This can occur even where ambient temperature exceeds skin temperature, if relative humidity is less than 100 percent.

Warm up periods before maximal effort have been reported to increase work capacity by several percentage points.[3] This is due to increased muscular efficiency rather than an increase in maximal oxygen consumption ($\dot{V}_{O_2\,max}$). It is caused by the small rise that occurs in muscle temperature. Factors accounting for this include the temperature-related increase in cellular metabolism and nerve conduction.[3] Also the rightward shift of the oxyhemoglobin dissociation curve that occurs with elevated temperature can enhance oxygen release to the tissues.[6] Five to fifteen minutes of exercise at 60 percent $\dot{V}_{O_2\,max}$ will raise core temperature to approximately 38.5°C and muscle temperature to 39°C, but will not result in significant lactate build up.[7] Warm clothing will hasten the rise in core temperature during warm-up.

Exercise in Warm Environments

At rest, vasodilitation of skin vessels and increased sweating will occur.[8] Blood is an excellent heat carrier, having a specific heat greater than body tissue.[9] Radiation and convection become less effective as ambient temperature approaches body temperature and evaporation of sweat assumes greater importance at rest. Both redistribution of blood flow and an increase in cardiac output provide the necessary increase in skin blood flow.[8] The increase in cardiac output is mostly mediated by an increase in heart rate, and in fact stroke volume may decrease.[8,9,10]

During exercise, cardiac output to the skin may increase from 5 percent to over 20 percent of total output.[8] Total cardiac output at each work level increases to supply this added requirement during mild exercise.[8,9] At heavy exercise levels, however, cardiac output may fall significantly as a result of a marked fall in stroke volume. This is probably a result of further skin vasodilitation with consequent decline in venous return.[8,11]

Evaporative losses may exceed two liters an hour.[3] An increase in relative humidity impairs evaporation, thus decreasing the body's ability to lose heat. An increase in air flow, however, will increase evaporation by removing the thin layer of humidified air overlying the skin.[5,12]

The net effect of exercise in a warm environment is to reduce work capacity. Maximal cardiac output is reached at lower work levels because of redistribution of blood away from muscles to skin. Therefore, muscles must shift to anaerobic metabolism earlier. $\dot{V}_{O_2 \, max}$ may also be reduced for similar reasons, but it may be normal if the duration of work is brief and skin vasodilitation does not fully develop.[8]

After several days of exposure to a warm environment, adaptation or acclimatization begins. At rest, both heart rate and stroke volume return toward normal, and cardiac output is only mildly increased.[9] Blood volume may temporarily increase.[13]

TABLE 1   Physiologic Changes during Exercise in a Warm Environment

Acute:	↑↑ Vasodilitation
	↑↑ Sweating
	↑↑ Cardiac Output*
	↑ Rate
	↓→ Stroke volume
Chronic:	↑ Vasodilitation
	↑↑↑ Sweating
	↑→ Cardiac Output
	↑→ Rate
	↑→ Stroke volume

*Cardic output is reduced at heavy work levels

With exercise, sweating begins at a lesser elevation of core temperature.[14] Sweating is more copious and skin vasodilitation is less marked at any given exercise level.[14,15] Similar changes may occur with physical conditioning at more comfortable temperatures if work levels are adequate to raise core body temperature.[10,16] Ascorbic acid has been found to enhance heat tolerance, but experimental data is scanty.[17]

PATHOLOGIC STATES DUE TO HEAT STRESS

Heat stroke represents a failure in temperature regulation, with a cessation of sweating and a consequent marked rise in core temperature.[18] This may be an accentuation of the normal fatiguing of sweating in a hot environment.[19] Drugs with anticholingergic effects, old age, and alcohol may be predisposing factors.[20] With heat stroke, the skin is hot and dry. Rectal temperatures up to 43°C have been reported. Central nervous system changes range from mental confusion to seizuring. Shock may be present due to the marked vasodilitation and associated dehydration.[21] Rapid cooling with water immersion is therapeutic, though heat stroke can progress to metabolic acidosis, disseminated intravascular coagulation, neurologic damage, and death.[18,20]

Heat syncope or exhaustion refers to orthostatic hypotension from vasodilitation and either relative or absolute hypovolemia. Treatment is by fluid and salt repletion.

Exercise in Cold Environments

At rest, without protective clothing, the cold produces skin vasoconstriction.[5] Shivering (actually massive isometric contractions[5]) increases heat generation up to threefold.[5] Paradoxically, in cold water heat conduction is so high that shivering and even exercise may increase heat loss from the extremities.[22] Work capacity and exercise ability may be impaired from decreased nerve conduction and muscle coordination at lower temperature.[23] Additional clothing will prevent body cooling but increase the resistance to motion. However, $\dot{V}_{O_2 max}$ is preserved with adequate caloric intake.[24]

With repeated exposure and consequent acclimatization, shivering decreases.[25] This may be maladaptive, as there is no other source of heat production in man to offset this. It may merely represent suppression of an uncomfortable sensation. With repeated exposure, the skin vasoconstriction becomes more selective, sparing the hands and to some extent the face.[5,25]

TABLE 2   Physiologic Changes during Exercise in a Cold Environment

Acute:	Vasoconstriction
	Shivering
Chronic:	Selective Vasoconstriction
	Less Shivering

Exercise in High Altitudes

At altitudes above sea level, the barometric pressure (P_B) is reduced because the column of overlying atmosphere is shorter and gravitational pull is less. Though oxygen still comprises approximately 0.21 of the total gases ($F_{1O_2} = 0.21$), its partial pressure is proportionately reduced. Alveolar and arterial oxygen tension will fall. Though arterial P_{O_2} falls linearly with altitude, hemoglobin saturation and consequently blood oxygen content remain at safe levels until arterial P_{O_2} falls to quite low levels because of the sigmoid shape of the oxghemoglobin dissociation curve. This is shown in Table 3.

Heart rate and minute ventilation are both increased for any given level of work to maintain oxygen supply to tissues.[26] This hyperventilation reduces alveolar P_{CO_2}, thus increasing alveolar P_{O_2} and improving oxygenation. The increase in heart rate may have a variable effect on oxygen delivery, since stroke volume and cardiac output may decrease.[27,28] This reduction in cardiac output has not been clearly related to either myocardial hypoxia or the hypoxemic increase in pulmonary vascular resistance, and may be secondary to increased peripheral vascular resistance.[29,30]

The lowered tissue oxygen pressure enhances unloading of oxygen from hemoglobin.[31] During exercise, the rightward shift in the oxyhemoglobin saturation curve from the tissue acidosis of anaerobic metabolism may also enhance oxygen unloading.[31]

Additional stresses at high altitudes occur from reduced temperature and humidity. There is a 6.5° C fall in air temperature with each 1000 meter ascent, and the reduction in humidity with altitude enhances evaporative water loss.[3] During vigorous exercise, these changes in environment may enhance heat loss at moderate elevations in altitude. At more extreme elevations, however, the cold may reduce coordination and work capacity.

There are some interesting, though minor, beneficial effects from high altitude. The decreased gas density at high altitude decreases the work of breathing through lowered airway resistance.[32] Also, reduced air friction will enhance speed events such as sprinting, skiing and skating.[3] Finally, the slight decrease in gravitational pull

TABLE 3   Changes in Blood Oxygenation with Altitude*

Altitude	Barometric Pressure	Predicted** Arterial P_{O_2}	Hemoglobin Saturation
sea level	760 mmHg	94 mmHg	97%
1000 meters	674 mmHg	77 mmHg	95%
3000 meters	526 mmHg	50 mmHg	85%
5000 meters	405 mmHg	27 mmHg	50 %

*Based on data for P_{Bar} in: Altman PL, Dittmer DS: *Respiration and Circulation*. Bethesda, Federation of American Society for Experimental Biology, 1971; and data for alveolar P_{CO_2} in: Department of the Air Force: Flight Surgeon's Manual. Air Force Manual 160–5, 1954.

**Assuming a constant alveolar-arterial oxygen gradient of 15 mmHg and ignoring the Bohr effect of the lowered arterial P_{CO_2} from hyperventilation.

because of increased distance from the earth's center of mass can improve performance in jumping and throwing activities.[3]

The net effect of these changes will be a decreased performance in distance events, as aerobic capacity is impaired. The lowered arterial oxygen content also impairs $\dot{V}_{O_2 max}$ and endurance time at submaximal levels.[32-35] Lactate production and fatigue occur at a lower work rate, and recovery time is increased from the reduced oxygen delivery.[33] Performance in sprint-type events, jumping, and throwing, which rely on short-term anaerobic metabolism, may actually be improved from the reduction in air friction and gravitational pull at high altitude.

Acclimatization takes several weeks to significantly develop and will improve performance in distance events, though it will still be below sea level performance.[30,33] Hemoglobin concentration will increase causing a secondary polycythemia. Red cell 2,3 DPG increases, facilitating unloading of oxygen from hemoglobin at the tissue level (a rightward shift of the oxyhemoglobin saturation curve).[29,36] Muscle myoglobin and, probably, capillary density in muscle both increase, allowing better supply of arterial blood and improved muscle oxygen storage respectively.[37,38] Additionally, the pulmonary diffusing capacity may be increased, thus decreasing the difference between alveolar and arterial oxygen tensions.[39]

Environmental Pollutants

Carbon monoxide in cigarette smoke and car exhaust binds to hemoglobin and decreases the oxygen carrying capacity of blood.[40] This can lower $\dot{V}_{O_2 max}$ and cause an increase in cardiac output and minute ventilation for any given level of work.[41] The cumulative exposure of the airways and pulmonary parenchyma to atmospheric toxins such as ozone, sulfur dioxide, nitrous dioxide, and so forth increases with exercise due to the increased minute ventilation, but rarely assumes clinical importance.[42-44]

REFERENCES

1. Asmussen E: Muscular exercise. in: *Handbook of Physiology,* Vol 1, Section 3, Washington, American Physiologic Society, 1965, p 939
2. Weir JB de V: New methods for calculating metabolic rate with special reference to protein metabolism. *J Physiol* 109:1, 1949
3. Astrand P, Rodahl K: *Textbook of Work Physiology* ed 2. New York, McGraw-Hill, 1977, p 525
4. Saltin B, Hermansen L: Esophageal, rectal, and muscle temperature during exercise. *J Appl Physiol* 21:757, 1966
5. Burton AC, Edbolm OG: *Man in a Cold Environment.* London, Arnold, 1955, p 29
6. Asmussen E, Bøje O: Body temperature and capacity for work. *Acta Physiol Scand* 10:1, 1945
7. Davies CTM, Brotherhood JR, Zeidifard E: Temperature regulation during severe exercise with same observations on effects of skin wetting. *J Appl Physiol* 41:772, 1976

8. Rowell LB: Human cardiovascular adjustments to exercise and thermal stress. *Physiol Rev* 54:75, 1974
9. Wyndham CH, Rogers GG, Senay LC, Mitchell D: Acclimatization in a hot, humid environment: cardiovascular adjustments. *J Appl Physiol* 40:779, 1976
10. Wyndham CH: The physiology of exercise under heat stress. *Ann Rev Physiol* 35:193, 1973
11. Rowell LB, Marx HJ, Bruce RA, et al: Reductions in cardiac output, central blood volume, and stroke volume with thermal stress in normal men during exercise. *J Clin Invest* 45:1801, 1966
12. Nelson NA, Shelley WB, Horvath SM, et al: Thermal exchanges in man at various hot environments. *J Clin Invest* 27:209, 1948
13. Senay LC, Mitchell D, Wyndham CH: Acclimatization in a hot humid environment: body fluid adjustments. *J Appl Physiol* 40:786, 1976
14. Wyndham CH: Effect of acclimatization on the sweat rate/rectal temperature relationship. *J Appl Physiol* 22:27, 1967
15. Roberts MF, Wenger CB, Stolwijk JAJ, et al: Skin blood flow and sweating changes following exercise training and heat acclimation. *J Appl Physiol: Respirat Environ Exercise Physiol* 43:133, 1977
16. Henane R, Flandrois R, Charbonnier JP: Increase in sweating sensitivity by endurance conditioning in man. *J Appl Physiol: Respirat Environ Exercise Physiol* 43:822, 1977
17. Kotze MF, Van Der Walt WM, Rogers GG, et al: Effects of plasma ascorbic acid levels on heat acclimatization in man. *J Appl Physiol: Respirat Environ Exercise Physiol* 42:711, 1977
18. Clowes GHA, O'Donnell TF Jr: Heat stroke. *N Engl J Med* 291:564, 1974
19. Cabanac M: Temperature regulation. *Ann Rev Physiol* 37:415, 1975
20. Gottschald PG, Thomas JE: Heat stroke. *Mayo Clin Proc* 41:470, 1966
21. O'Donnell TF, Clowes GHA Jr: The circulatory abnormalities of heat stroke. *New Engl J Med* 287:734, 1972
22. Keatinge WR: *Survival in Cold Water*. Oxford, Blackwell, 1969, p 31
23. Vanggaard L: Physiological reactions to wet-cold. *Aviat Space Environ Med* 46:33, 1975
24. Rodahl K, Horvath SM, Birkhead NC, et al: Effects of dietary protein on physical work capacity during severe cold stress. *J Appl Physiol* 17:763, 1962
25. Keatinge WR: Acclimatization to cold. *J Physiol* 157:209, 1961
26. Stenberg J, Ekblåm B, Messin R: Hemodynamic response to work at simulated altitude, 4,000 m. *J Appl Physiol* 21:1589, 1966
27. Alexander JK, Hartley LH, Modelski M, et al: Reduction of stroke volume during exercise in man following ascent to 3100 m altitude. *J Appl Physiol* 23:849, 1967
28. Hoon RS, Balasubramanian V, Mathew OP, et al: Effect of high-altitude exposure for 10 days on stroke volume and cardiac output. *J Appl Physiol: Respirat Environ Exercise Physiol* 42:722, 1977
29. Grover RF, Lufschanowski R, Alexander JK: Alterations in the coronary circulation of man following ascent to 3,100 m altitude. *J Appl Physiol* 41:832, 1976
30. Vogel JA, Hartley LH, Cruz JC, et al: Cardiac output during exercise in sea level residents at sea level and high altitude. *J Appl Physiol* 36:169, 1974
31. Hartley LH, Vogel JA, Landowne M: Central, femoral, and brachial circulation during exercise in hypoxia. *J Appl Physiol* 34:87, 1973
32. Luft UC: Aviation physiology—the effects of altitude. in: Fenn WO, Rahn H (eds): *Handbook of Physiology*, Vol 1, Section 3, Washington, American Physiologic Society, 1964, p 1099

33. Raynaud JR, Martineaud JP, Bordachar, J, et al: Oxygen deficit and debt in submaximal exercise at sea level and high altitude. *J Appl Physiol* 37:43, 1974

34. Maher JT, Jones LG, Hartley LH: Effects of high-altitude on submaximal endurance capacity of men. *J Appl Physiol* 37:895, 1974

35. Jokl E, Jokl P: The effect of altitude on athletic performance. in: Jokl E, Jokl P (eds): *Exercise and Altitude,* Basel, Karger, 1968, p 28

36. Morpurgo G, Battaglia P, Carter ND, et al: The Bohr effect and the red cell 2-3 DPG and Hb content in Sherpas and Europeans at low and at high altitude. *Experientia* 28:1280, 1972

37. Reynafarje B: Myoglobin content and enzymatic activity of muscle and altitude adaptation. *J Appl Physiol* 17:301, 1962

38. Hurtado A: Animals in high altitudes: resident man. in: Dill DB, Adolph EF, Wilber CG (eds): *Handbook of Physiology,* Vol 1, Sec 4, Washington, American Physiologic Society, 1964, p 843

39. Tenney, SM: Physiological adaptations to life at high altitude. in: Jokl E, Jokl P (eds): *Exercise and Altitude,* Basel, Karger, 1968, p 60

40. Root WS: Carbon monoxide. in: *Handbook of Physiology,* Vol 1, Sec 3, Washington, American Physiologic Society, 1965, p 1087

41. Ekblåm B, Huot R: Response to submaximal and maximal exercise at different levels of carboxyhemoglobin. *Acta Physiol Scand* 86:474, 1972

42. DeLucia AJ, Adams WC: Effects of O_3 inhalation during exercise on pulmonary function and blood biochemistry. *J Appl Physiol:* Respirat Environ Exercise Physiol 43:75, 1977

43. Folinsbee LJ, Silverman F, Shephard RJ: Exercise responses following ozone exposure. *J Appl Physiol* 38:996, 1975

44. Holland GJ, Benson D, Bush A, et al: Air pollution simulation and human performance. *Am J Pub Health* 58:1684, 1968

Fatigue and Overtraining

WARREN K. PALMER, Ph.D.,
ALLAN H. GOLDFARB, M.Ed.

In 1971, Simonson[1] compiled a monograph on physiological fatigue which encompassed approximately 1400 references. He was clear to point out that the numerous semantic problems in the literature relating to fatigue created ambiguities. Therefore, prior to any discussion of the topics alluded to in the title of this presentation, a few ground rules must be set to define a framework within which to work. Because of the equivocal nature of the literature relating to fatigue, the following terms are operationally defined:

1. *Fatigue* – a transitory loss of work capacity owing to work already accomplished.
2. *Exhaustion* – synonymous with fatigue as a result of the lack of consistency found in the literature in establishing sound criteria.
3. *Overtraining* – a layman's term denoting an incomplete recovery from prior work bouts causing a decline in work capacity.

Because of the scope of the topic, no attempt will be made to cover all factors and possible mechanisms thought to contribute to fatigue. Evidence will be reported which implicates specific intracellular alterations that have been related to a deterioration in muscle cell function. Events occurring outside the cell as a result of increased muscle work which may result in decreased muscle function will only be discussed in relation to intracellular effects. The section on overtraining is concerned primarily with the return of work-limiting parameters to a pre-exercise "optimal" level following a bout of muscle activity.

When discussing skeletal muscle, its heterogeneity must be considered for a more complete understanding of its function. A qualitative difference in skeletal muscle is quite obvious upon visual inspection. The darker red portion of the muscle is high in myoglobin content while the pale white muscle has a low myoglobin concentration. Recently, investigators[2,3] have classified skeletal muscle fibers histochemically, biochemically, and physiologically into three categories. A summary of the fiber types and their characteristics are given in Table 1. We have taken the liberty to simplify the sometimes confusing disagreements found in the literature. The fast-twitch red fiber (FOG) has a rapid speed of contraction, high oxidative (mitochondrial) capacity, and relatively high glycolytic enzyme activity. The fast-twitch white fiber (FG) has high contractile velocity and high glycolytic activity, but a low oxidative capacity. The slow-twitch red fiber (SO) develops tension slowly as denoted by the relatively low myosin ATPase activity, and has a low glycolytic capacity. The oxidative capability of this fiber type is high. For the purpose of expedience and clarification, reference will be made to only two classifications of muscle fibers: slow-twitch (SO) and fast-twitch (FOG and FG). We feel justified in doing this because of reports of significant increases in oxidative capacity in the adaptation of fast-twitch white fibers to chronic exposure to endurance work.[4]

Human skeletal muscle seems to be a homogeneous mixture of fiber types, unlike patterns reported for lower mammals.[4] Each motor unit, however, is composed of only one type of fiber. (For further review of skeletal muscle function, refer to the study by Close.[5]) The varied physiological and biochemical capacities exhibited by the different fiber types suggest that when the energy requirement of muscle work exceeds the specific metabolic capacity of a particular fiber type fatigue will follow. This is, in part, counteracted by the ability of the nervous system to recruit specific fiber types, depending upon the intensity of work performed.[6]

It is intuitively evident, even to the layman, that there must be different types of fatigue. One can maintain supramaximal effort for only short periods of time. As the intensity of work is reduced, the time required for the individual to reach exhaustion is increased. Reported results show significant differences in the internal environment of the cell at exhaustion resulting from the different exercise modes. This suggests that there may be different mechanisms mediating fatigue, depending upon

TABLE 1   Biochemical and Physiological Characteristics of Muscle Fibers

Fiber Classification	Twitch Time	Mitochondrial Content	Glycolytic Capacity	Myosin ATPase
Red SO I A	Slow	High	Low	Low
Intermediate FOG IIa B	Fast	High	High	High
White FG IIb C	Fast	Low	High	High

the type of work performed. For this reason the duration and type of work performed must be characterized when discussing fatigue.

The muscle must have an immediate available supply of chemical energy to function properly. The compound synonymous with energy necessary for contraction is adenosine triphosphate (ATP). Davies et al[7] have shown that when ATP synthesis is blocked, only three maximal contractions can be elicited. All subsequent contractions exhibit reduced tension until the muscle ceases to function. At that point ATP concentration is reduced significantly. From these data it is reasonable to start the investigation as to the mechanism of fatigue by identifying malfunction of the synthesis of ATP. The chemical energy (ATP) necessary for muscle contraction comes primarily from three sources within the cells, as illustrated by Equations 1–3.

$$ADP^* + \text{Creatine Phosphate} \rightarrow ATP + \text{Creatine} \qquad \text{(equ.1)}$$

$$\text{Glycogen} + ADP \rightarrow ATP + \text{Lactate} \qquad \text{(equ. 2)}$$

$$C_6 H_{12} O_6 + O_2 \xrightarrow{\quad ADP \rightarrow ATP \quad} H_2O + CO_2 \qquad \text{(equ. 3)}$$

The reactions denoted in Equations 1 and 2 result in the production of ATP in the absence of O_2, while the reactions of Equation 3 require O_2 for the complete oxidation of substrate.

The first two (anaerobic) sources of energy supply a rapid but limited amount of ATP to the contractile elements, while the aerobic production of ATP occurring in the mitochondria is capable of supplying large quantities of energy. The demand upon specific biochemical pathways described is a function of the intensity of the work performed. As the intensity of work increases, the portion of energy derived from anaerobic sources is increased.[8]

During long-term endurance work, when subjects work at approximately 75% V_{O2max}, the time when work must cease is coincident with the depletion of glycogen in the muscle.[9] Bergstrom and associates[10] have reported a positive linear correlation between resting skeletal muscle glycogen content and endurance work time to exhaustion. Dietary manipulation of muscle glycogen concentrations affects work times. Elevations of muscle glycogen content enhance work times, while decreased glycogen decreases work capacity.[10] Evidence supporting this relationship between fatigue and glycogen depletion has been reported by groups using both experimental animals and humans.

The oxidation of glycogen by contracting skeletal muscle is the primary source of energy-yielding ATP in work bouts of high intensity where oxygen supply to the muscle is not sufficient to meet the tissue demand. As the intensity of the work is reduced, the proportion of fat oxidation to carbohydrate oxidation is increased with lipid supplying as much as 70 percent of the energy to skeletal muscle.[11] As the

---

*Adenosine diphosphate

availability of fatty acid to skeletal muscle through intracellular degradation of stored triglyceride–by lipolysis of adipocyte-stored triglyceride or by lipoprotein lipase hydrolysis of circulating lipid–increases during endurance exercise, the rate of glycogen catabolism is reduced. Glycogen sparing through the elevation of plasma lipids has been shown to increase endurance work-time significantly.[12] Rennie and co-workers[13] have obtained data suggesting that the slowing of glycogen degradation may be due to the acetate residues originating from lipid competing for entrance into oxidative pathways of the mitochondria, causing an elevation in the production of the metabolic intermediate, citrate, a potent inhibitor of the key glycolytic enzyme, phosphofructokinase. Costill and associates[14] have shown that the fatty acid sparing phenomenon exists in humans, with a decreased rate of glycogen degradation.

An additional piece of evidence supporting glycogen influence on endurance work was presented by Ivy et al.[15] Ingestion of caffeine, a phosphodiesterase inhibitor that promotes lipolysis, was associated with an increased work capacity and an inhibited glycogen catabolic rate. Because adipose tissue phosphodiesterase inhibition was not demonstrated, the mechanism for the caffeine effect can only be hypothesized.

The correlations existing between work-time, onset of fatigue, and muscle glycogen content permit us to speculate about the cause for fatigue at submaximal workloads. These findings have proposed one more link in the chain of events associated with fatigue. Unfortunately, however, we are still a long way from determining the specific biochemical site in skeletal muscle where glycogen (or ATP derived from glycogen) is an absolute requirement for continued function. An alternative to the breakdown of a single intracellular site is the possibility that glycogen depletion of a particular muscle fiber type necessitates shut down of glycolysis in that fiber. Although alternative oxidative pathways are still available for mitochondrial oxidation of lipid, the failure of glycolytic production of ATP may result in numerous alterations in cytoplasmic and/or plasma membrane function. This hypothesis is based upon the concept of intracellular compartmentalization.

Glycogen depletion in skeletal muscle is not the only cause of fatigue during exercise. Exhaustion resulting from short bouts of intense work at loads between 90 and 120 percent of maximal oxygen consumption reduces muscle glycogen by only about 25 percent.[16] Consequently there must be other factors to be considered in the determination of mediators of fatigue.

An immediate source of energy is depicted in Equation 1. With the hydrolysis of ATP forming ADP, there is a rapid resynthesis of ATP by the transfer of phosphate from creatine phosphate (CP). Danforth[17] has shown that under anaerobic conditions, frog sartorius muscle could perform work for only 20–30 seconds when solely dependent upon intracellular stores of ATP and CP. If resynthesis of these compounds is inhibited, the ability to contract is reduced. Tension development of muscle is dependent upon ATP content. Reductions in its content result in decreased tension development.[18]

The amount of muscle CP hydrolyzed during a bout of exercise is directly proportional to the intensity and duration of work performed.[19] The CP concentration can approach complete depletion with heavy work, at which time tension development becomes impaired. In fatigued isolated muscle preparations where ATP resynthesis is blocked, no further contraction can be elicited even when 1 mM ATP is still present. However, a ten minute rest will be accompanied with a contraction upon stimulation.[20] These results suggest intracellular compartmentalization, with an ATP lack at the site of action—at the contractile elements. Although analysis of intracellular localization of the specific biochemical events at precise points in time is necessary information for the explanation of physiological phenomena, technical capacity is only now becoming sophisticated enough to address this topic.

Fatigue during intense exercise has long been related to the production of anaerobic glycolysis, lactic acid (Equation 2). The transfer of electrons from NADH* to form lactic acid regenerates NAD^+, a necessary coenzyme in glycolysis. Lactic acid is readily diffusable from the cell into the circulation. At a work intensity of approximately 60 percent of maximal oxygen consumption, blood lactic acid concentration increases, with the increase proportional to exercise intensity.[21] As the concentration of lactic acid in the blood increases, the buffer systems present in the vascular compartment become progressively bound to H^+. Once saturated, excess free H^+ disrupts homeostasis and the pH of the plasma decreases. While the relationship between decreasing blood pH and increasing lactic acid concentration has been reported on numerous occasions,[22,23] it cannot be concluded that similar alterations are occurring within the cell. Buffering systems that may be present in the cell maintain an optimal intracellular pH. Excess hydrogen ions could be compartmentalized in one or more organelles capable of dealing with elevated levels of H^+ (lysozome). Recently, studies have been reported attempting to determine the influence of exercise upon the intracellular pH and the influence of altered pH on muscle function.

Fitts and Holloszy[24] have investigated the relationship between lactic acid concentration and twitch-tension development in frog sartorius muscle. In muscles stimulated under anaerobic conditions, a 15.4 mM increase in lactate corresponded with a 36 percent decrease in tension development. A systematic study of the relationship between lactate and tension yielded a significant negative correlation (r = −0.99), while a similar correlation (r = −0.92) existed during recovery.

Fretthold and Garg,[25] on the other hand, used an isolated hemidiaphragm preparation to investigate the effect of acid-base changes on muscle-twitch tension. They found that decreasing the pH of the bathing medium through the reduction of bicarbonate (or the elevation of CO_2) produced a decrease in intracellular pH, potassium, and muscle-twitch tension. At a constant extracellular pH, however, increased CO_2 (bicarbonate compensated) produced increased intracellular potassium and twitch tension with a decrease in intracellular pH. These authors concluded that there is no consistent relationship between intracellular pH and twitch tension in the diaphragm.

Recently, Steinhagen and co-workers[26] have used a glass mini-electrode to measure interstitial pH in working isolated dog gastronemius muscle. At rest, a pH gradient existed between the interstitial and venous fluid compartments. The gradient was evident at rest, work, and recovery. Lactate release corresponded with increased

---

*Nicotinamide adenine dinucleotide (reduced)

interstitial pH changes. Electrical stimulation of muscle was associated with a rapid increase in interstitial and venous (H^+). During induction of metabolic acidosis (arginine-hydrochloride infusion), pH and lactate changes were more pronounced during work, while metabolic alkalosis (bicarbonate infusion) caused smaller changes in pH during contraction. Lactate release was significantly higher during exercise in metabolic alkalosis than in metabolic acidosis. Muscle fatigue of the gastrocnemius occurred most rapidly during metabolic acidosis.

Utilizing the needle biopsy to obtain tissue from exercising humans, a study was performed[27] that measured the relationship of tissue homogenate pH and tissue lactate and pyruvate concentrations. The relationship between muscle pH and the content of lactate and pyruvate measured immediately after dynamic exercise was r = −0.92. Analagous measurements made during recovery exhibited a similar relationship (r = −0.93). Calculation of NADH/NAD at exhaustion showed the ratio to be increased significantly above resting values. While the above two studies have shown very nice relationships between lactic acid and pH, analysis of true pH during exercise in the area of the contractile apparatus is yet to be determined.

Although conclusive evidence has not been presented showing an altered intracellular pH in exercising muscle, the evidence that has been reported warrants speculation as to the events involved in the contractile process that would be affected by the altered environment. Hill[28] has shown that lactic acid formation ceases to respond to stimulus when pH drops to 6.3. In vitro analysis of numerous enzyme systems shows significant pH dependence. An excellent example of this phenomenon is phosphorylase *b* kinase, which is completely active at pH 8.2 while only minimally active at pH 6.8.[29] Phosphofructokinase, another important enzyme in the glycolytic pathway, is sensitive to pH.[30] Myocardial ($Na^+ + K^+$) −ATPase is more sensitive to calcium inhibition in acidic environments.[31] Muscle sarcoplasmic reticulum uptake of calcium is inhibited at a pH below 6.4 but is not significantly influenced by pH changes between 6.5 and 7.2.[32]

Reports on the H^+ ion effect upon the myosin ATPase have been presented independently by Kentish and Nayler[33] and Schadler.[34] Myofibrils isolated from heart and skeletal muscle are characterized by a progressive decrease in ATPase sensitivity to Ca^{++} and an increase in H^+ concentration. Coffelt et al[35] have shown a sharp pH optimum at 7.5 for the divalent cation activation of skeletal muscle myosin ATPase. Also, at pH levels below 7.5 the affinity of myosin for ATP in the presence of divalent cations was decreased. Troponin is a regulatory protein found that is associated with actin and that binds Ca^{++}. Decreases in pH decrease the affinity of Ca^{++} for purified troponin,[36] a consequence which could significantly affect actin-myosin interaction.

While speculation is intriguing, the relationship between pH and biochemical events occurring in vitro may be unrelated to those taking place in vivo.

The complete recovery from a bout of fatiguing exercise will depend upon such factors as recovery time, the type of activity causing fatigue, nutritional status during recovery period, and activity during recovery. When the effect on muscle glycogen of an endurance run of ten miles performed on three successive days was studied,[37] it was found that prior to the run on day 2, glycogen was only 75 percent of that measured before the run on day 1. Only about 50 percent of the original amount of glycogen measured before the start of the experiment was present prior to the run on the third day. Five days following the last exercise bout, muscle glycogen levels were not back to pre-experiment levels. From the previously mentioned discussion regarding the relationship between glycogen content and fatigue from endurance work, it can be seen that the above results hold significant implications for those who must exercise to exhaustion on successive days. Under such conditions, rest and dietary modification must be provided to facilitate total glycogen resynthesis.

The data indicate that recovery from high-intensity work is a more rapid process than recovery from work that depletes muscle glycogen. In frog sartarius muscle that had a 64 percent decrease in twitch-tension development and an 85 percent decrease in creative phosphate induced by exercise, Fitts and Holloszy[24] showed a return of CP levels to normal within the first ten minutes. The contractile integrity of the muscle, however, did not return to normal until 50 minutes of recovery. Harris et al[38] have measured CP resynthesis in exercised human quadriceps muscle. Following exhaustive dynamic exercise, CP levels were back to normal after eight minutes of recovery. Unfortunately, no report on the relationship between CP synthesis and muscle tension development was made.

While creatine phosphate resynthesis is rapid, return of intracellular pH to normal is not as rapid. The time course of attaining an optimal homeostatic environment may be a function of the amount of anaerobic work performed and the amount of lactic acid produced. In exhausted frog sartorius, 50 minutes were required for lactate and contractile capacity to return to prestimulation levels. In exercise bouts where exhaustion was reached in six minutes, correlating with a 0.6 unit decrease in pH and a greater than 100 mM increase in muscle lactate content, the half time of lactate decrease was approximately 9.5 minutes. While intracellular pH had returned to control levels 20 minutes following exercise, the NADH/NAD ratio was still elevated, a factor that might well influence performance in subsequent bouts of exercise.

Although the concept of fatigue seems clear, the mechanisms involved in mediating its effects are numerous and complex. With techniques available for the study of events occurring at the subcellular level, data will gradually appear delineating "fatigue" in greater detail.

REFERENCES

1. Simonsen E: *Physiology of Work Capacity and Fatigue.* Springfield, IL, Charles C. Thomas, 1971
2. Barnard RJ, Edgerton VR, Peter JB: Effects of exercise on skeletal muscle: I. Biochemical and histochemical properties. *J Appl Physiol* 28:762, 1970
3. Barnard RJ, Edgerton VR, Peter JB: Effects of exercise on skeletal muscle: II. Contractile properties. *J Appl Physiol* 28:767, 1970
4. Essen B, Jansson E, Hendriksson J, et al: Metabolic characteristics of fiber types in human skeletal muscle. *Acta Physiol Scand* 95:153, 1975
5. Close RI: Dynamic properties of mammalian skeletal muscles. *Physiol Rev* 52:129, 1972
6. Gollnick PD, Piehl K, Saltin B: Selective glycogen depletion pattern in human skeletal

muscle fibers after exercising of varying intensity and at varying pedal rates. *J Physiol* (London) 241:45, 1974

7. Cain DR, Davies RE: Breakdown of adenosine triphosphate during a single contraction of working muscle. *Biochem Biophys Res Commun* 8:361, 1962

8. Astrand PO: *Textbook of Work Physiology.* New York, McGraw-Hill Book Co., 1970

9. Hermansen L, Hultman E, Saltin B: Muscle glycogen during prolonged severe exercise. *Acta Physiol Scand* 71:129, 1967

10. Bergstrom J, Hermansen L, Hultman E, et al: Diet, muscle glycogen and physical performance. *Acta Physiol Scand* 71:140, 1967

11. Havel RJ, Naimark A, Borchgrevink CR: Turnover rate and oxidation of free fatty acids of blood plasma in man during exercise: Studied during continuous infusion of palmitate-1-C^4. *J Clin Invest* 42:1054, 1963

12. Hickson RC, Rennie MJ, Conlee RK, et al: Effect of increased plasma fatty acids on glycogen utilization and endurance. *J Appl Physiol* 43:829, 1977

13. Rennie MJ, Winder WW, Holloszy JO: A sparing effect of increased plasma fatty acids on muscle and liver glycogen content in the exercising rat. *Biochem J* 156:647, 1976

14. Costill DL, Coyle E, Dalsky G, et al: Effects of elevated plasma FFA and insulin on muscle glycogen usage during exercise. *J Appl Physiol* 43:695, 1977

15. Ivy JL, Costill DL, Fink WJ, et al: Influence of caffeine and carbohydrate feedings on endurance performance. *Med Sci Sports* 11:6, 1979

16. Saltin B, Karlsson J: Muscle glycogen utilization during work of different intensities. in: *Muscle Metabolism During Exercise.* Pernow B, et al (eds): New York, Plenum Press, 1971, p 289

17. Danforth WH: Control of energy metabolism activation of glycolytic pathway in muscle. in: *Control of Energy Metabolism.* Chance B, et al (eds): New York, Academic Press, 1965, p 287

18. Murphy RA: Correlations of ATP content with mechanical properties of metabolically inhibited muscle. *Am J Physiol* 211:1082, 1966

19. Hultman E, Bergstrom J, Anderson N: Breakdown and resynthesis of phosphorylcreatine and adenosine triphosphate in connection with muscular work in man. *Scand J Clin Lab Invest* 19:56, 1967

20. Hohorst HJ, Reims M, Bartels H: Studies on the creatinekinase equilibrium in muscle and the significance of ATP and ADP levels. *Biochem Biophys Res Commun* 7:142, 1962

21. Karlsson J, Diamant B, Saltin B: Muscle metabolites during submaximal and maximal exercise in man. *Scand J Clin Lab Invest* 26:385, 1970

22. Visser BF, Kreukniet J, Maas AHJ: Increase of whole blood lactic acid concentration during exercise as predicted from pH and CO_2 concentration *Pflugers Arch* 281:300, 1964

23. Hermansen L: Anaerobic energy release. *Med Sci Sports* 1:32, 1969

24. Fitts RH, Holloszy JO: Lactate and contractile force in Frog muscle during development of fatigue and recovery. *Am J Physiol* 231:430, 1976

25. Fretthold DW, Garg LC: The effect of acid-base changes on skeletal muscle twitch tension. *Can J Physiol Pharmacol* 56:543, 1978

26. Steinhagen C, Hirche HJ, Nestle HW, et al: The interstitial pH of the working gastrocnemius muscle of the Dog. *Pflugers Arch* 367:151, 1976

27. Sahlin K, Harris RC, Nylind B, et al: Lactate content and pH in muscle samples obtained after dynamic exercise. *Pflugers Arch* 367:143, 1976

28. Hill AV, Kupalov P: Anaerobic and aerobic activity in striated muscles. *Proc Soc Lond* (Ser B) 103:313, 1929

29. Krebs EG, Love DS, Bratvold GE, et al: Purification and properties of rabbit skeletal muscle phosphorylase *b* kinase. *Biochem* 3:1022, 1964

30. Trivedi B, Danforth WH: Effect of pH on kinetics of frog muscle phosphofructokinase. *J Biol Chem* 241:4110, 1966

31. Godfraind T, DePover A, Verbeke N: Influence of pH and sodium on the inhibition of Guinea-pig heart $(Na^+ + K^+)$ -ATPase by calcium. *Biochem Biophys Acta* 481:202, 1977

32. Berman MC, McIntosh DB, Kench JE: Proton inactivation of Ca^{2+} transport by sarcoplasmic reticulum. *J Biol Chem* 252:994, 1977

33. Kentish J, Nayler WG: Effect of pH on the Ca^{2+}- dependent ATPase of rabbit cardiac and white skeletal myofibrils. *J Physiol* (Lond) 265:18, 1977

34. Schadler M: Proportionale activierung von ATPase- activitat und kontvaktionsspannung durch calciumionen in isolierten contractilen strukturen verschiedener muskelarten. *Pflugers Arch* 296:70, 1967

35. Wikman-Coffelt J, Fenner C, Zelis R, et al: Effects of variations in pH on kinetics of myosin. in: *Recent Advances in Studies on Cardiac Structure and Metabolism* Vol. 8. Roy PE, et al (eds): Baltimore, University Park Press, 1975, p 47

36. Fuchs F, Reddy Y, Briggs FN: The interaction of cations with the calcium-binding site of troponin. *Biochem Biophys Acta* 221:407, 1970

37. Costill DL, Bowers R, Branam G, et al: Muscle glycogen utilization during prolonged exercise on successive days. *J Appl Physiol* 31:834, 1971

38. Harris C, Edwards RHT, Hultman E, et al: The time course of phosphorylcreatine resynthesis during recovery of the quadriceps muscle in Man. *Pflugers Arch* 367:137, 1976

Elementary Biomechanics

GIDEON B. ARIEL, PH.D.

How to explain movement and change is a problem that has attracted the attention of men since the time of the Anicent Greeks, and the ideas which the Greeks put forward dominated thinking for some 2000 years. The explanations adopted in the Middle Ages were largely based upon the writings of Aristotle, who lived from 384 to 322 B.C. Though some of Aristotle's views had been questioned earlier, it was not until the sixteenth and seventeenth centuries that the problems of movement came to be seen from the modern point of view. Many were involved in the preliminary discussions leading to this development, but the two most outstanding invididuals in what came to be a scientific revolution were Galileo and Sir Isaac Newton. It was the great change in the theory of movement, initiated by these men, which has since formed the basis for the modern scientific age. Alfonso Borelli, who studied under Galileo, theorized mathematically that bones serve as levers and that muscles function according to mathematical principles.

In perhaps the most powerful and original piece of scientific reasoning ever published, Sir Isaac Newton laid the foundation of modern dynamics.[1] Particularly important to the future of biomechanics was his formulation of the three laws of motion, which express the relationships between forces and their effects. These laws are as follows:

1. *Law of Inertia*—Every body continues in its state of rest, or in uniform motion in a straight line, unless it is changed by forces acting upon it.
2. *Law of Momentum*—A change in motion is proportional to the force causing the change, and the direction is in the same line as the impinging force.

3. *Law of Interaction*—For every action there is always an equal and opposite reaction.

Mechanics is that branch of the science of physics that encompasses the action of forces on material bodies. It deals with motion and includes the general principles and laws which make possible the applied science of biomechanics. Biomechanics is the study of the motion of living organisms including man. The field of mechanics may be divided into statics, which considers rigid bodies in a state of static equilibrium, and dynamics, which studies objects in motions. Dynamics may be further subdivided into kinematics, the geometry of motion, which includes displacement, velocity, and acceleration without regard for the forces acting on a body, and kinetics, which incorporates the concepts of mass, force, and energy as they affect motion.

For the coach, examination of a football place kicker presents a complex performance of interacting limbs and dynamic forces. While watching the kicker, the coach can ask a variety of questions:

1. What are the force-counterforce components between the upper and lower body segments of the kicker?
2. Was conservation of angular momentum utilized at the knee joint within the kicking limb?
3. Was an optimum position of the foot applied to the ball at the point of contact for force to be transferred from the kicking limb to the ball?
4. Was transformation of linear motion of the body and angular motion of the kicking limb adequate to effectively execute the skill?
5. What was the angle of projection and subsequent trajectory and flight pattern of the ball?

For the purpose of mechanical analysis, the individual performer—regardless of whether it is an athlete, a child at play, a doctor performing an operation, or a factory worker on the job—can be accurately represented mechanically as a series of interconnected rigid segments which comprise a complex link system. The primary complexity of such a link system is a function of the number of segments. Because any change in the state of rest or motion of a biomechanical system is governed by the action of external forces, it is important to identify these forces, their magnitudes, directions, and points of application. To facilitate this process, a free body diagram is constructed with all of the forces affecting the system. The system is thus analyzed taking into consideration the mass of each segment and its action, either acceleration or deceleration, through the sequence of the activity. Unfortunately, to process such a mathematical enormity by hand with paper and pencil would be prohibitively time-consuming. With the advent of computer technology and its accompanying peripherals, the millions of calculations could be more readily processed.

Kinematic and kinetic analysis of human motion has been expanded by the computer-digitizer complex so that analyses of total body motion can be accomplished through the use of slow motion cinematography, special tracing equipment for data acquisition, and the high-speed computer for computations.[2] Appropriate programming results in a segmental breakdown of information of the whole motion including the total body center of gravity, segment velocities and accelerations, horizontal, vertical, and resultant forces, moments of force, and the timing between the body segments. This analysis provides a quantitative measure of the motion and allows for perfection and optimization of human performance at a speed which can reasonably be incorporated into any athletic training program or rehabilitative regimen. An additional advantage is that reduction of the motion system to a mechanical problem permits an objective, quantitative assessment of performance, replacing the uncertainty of trial and error, eliminating doubt, and providing a realistic opportunity for improved performance.

The analysis involves the following steps:

1. Obtaining cinematographic data.
2. Digitizing the data.
3. Measuring and utilizing anatomical data.
4. Utilizing computer software for the manipulations of the equations of motions.
5. Interpreting the results.

Slow motion cinematography is used to record the desired motions. This technique permits an undetected recording of an individual's performance under actual conditions—an advantage over accelerometers or force transducers with their accompanying wires. Film speed must, of course, be fast enough so that actions are not blurred, and therefore most human activity is recorded at speeds of 64 to 200 frames per second.[3]

The second step in data processing involves a composite tracing of the joint centers of the body. This is accomplished by locating the joint centers with a sonic pen-microphone arrangement so that x and y coordinates are represented within the computer memory for each joint and each position for the entire movement sequence.

Calculation of forces and moments of force requires knowledge of the mass of each segment as well as its center of gravity. These parameters are available from NASA research, and tables of body segment percentages of total body weight, specific gravity, and segment lengths as percentages of total height may be used when data is not available on the specific performer.[4,5] There are, however, various methods for calculation of the weight, volume, and the center of mass of segments of the body when the subject is available. In order to calculate the forces, it is necessary to know the radii of gyration which may be calculated from Dempster's data on moments of inertia.[6]

After the joint centers are acquired and stored in the computer, the segment lengths and angles can be ascertained while calculations of the segment masses, centers of gravity, and radii of gyration are obtained from the anatomical data. Knowledge of the film speed and the displacement of the joint centers enables calculation of the velocities of the body segments, and from the velocities it is then possible to calculate segment accelerations. Segment masses are utilized in the calculation of forces and moments of force. Appropriate computer software yields a segmental breakdown of information of the whole motion, including; the total body center of gravity; segment velocities and accelerations; horizontal, vertical, and resultant forces; angle of the resultant force application; moments of force, which indicate the magnitude of the muscle action at each joint; the vertical and horizontal forces at the ground contact points; the timing or coordination of motion between the body segments; and the differences due to discrepancies in body builds.[2] A quantitative measure of the motion results from the combination of the moments of force, the interrelated patterns of the body segments, and the task performed. Following these calculations, it is possible to alter various positions of the body segments in order to determine the effects on the motion that such hypothetical changes would cause or for optimization of the activity.

An example of this optimization procedure can be illustrated using patterns of the velocity curves for each segment in a golf swing.[7] A typical professional golfer will produce a sequential arrangement of the timing of the peak velocity for each segment of the heavier segments, such as the thighs and trunk, slowing down so that they "stop" at a point immediately before impact occurs. The arms and club segments, on the other hand, reach peak velocity prior to impact with the club velocity being the greatest at or near impact. This type of coordination of velocities and their resultant accelerations is typical of most athletic events which are ballistic in nature. If a less skilled golfer is examined, his patterns may not conform to such a sequential arrangement, and with the computer software, the performance of this individual could be altered to determine the optimized results.

Research and opportunity continue to reveal new applications for biomechanical analysis of human performance. The application of the scientific tools of mechanics and the speed of computer technology offer refreshing opportunities for quantification of motion and the removal of trial and error.

REFERENCES

1. Sears F, Zemansky MW: *University Physics*, ed 4. Reading, Mass, Addison-Wesley, Inc, 1973
2. Ariel GB: Computerized Biomechanical Analysis of Human Performance. in: *Mechanics and Sport*. The American Society of Mechanical Engineers, 1973, Vol 4, p 301
3. Mascelli JV, Miller A: *American Cinematographer Manual*. Hollywood, American Society of Cinematographers Holding Corp, 1966
4. Clauser CE, McConville JT, Young, JW: *Weight, Volume, and Center of Mass of Segments of the Human Body*. Wright Air Development Center, AMRL-TR-69-70, Ohio, Wright-Patterson Air Force Base, 1969
5. Krogman WM, Johnston FE: *Human Mechanics: Four Monographs Abridge*, AMRL Technical Documentary Report No. AMRL-TDR-63-123, 1963
6. Dempster WT: *Space Requirements of the Seated Operator*. Wright Air Development Center TR-55-159, Ohio, Wright-Patterson Air Force Base, 1955
7. Ariel GB: Comparative Biomechanical Analyses of the Golf Swings of President Gerald R. Ford and Jack Nicklaus. Technical Report Conducted for *Golf Magazine* 20(10):56, 1978

The Psychology of Sports Competition

RONALD M. LAWRENCE, M.D., PH.D.

The title of this paper encompasses a broad topic which in no way can be covered in the amount of time and with the depth of introspection that the subject requires. Moreover, very little information in the literature deals with this most important topic. Our purpose will be to broadly define the psychological forces at work in all sports but particularly in the field of long distance running. By long distance running we mean distances over six miles. This is certainly an arbitrary definition since a short time ago top coaches considered distances between two and six miles to be long distance running.[1] Certainly since the evolution of the great interest in the marathon distance (26 miles, 385 yards), the concept of distance running has changed. It is entirely possible that within the remainder of the century distance running may imply covering the space between 50 and 100 miles, although this seems unlikely at present.

We shall also, by way of investigating this area, discuss some aspects of the psychology of winning as well as the effects of distance running on the psyche. There has been a great deal of interest during the last two years and particularly during the last year in the entire area of the use of endurance exercise (particularly long distance running) for the treatment of psychological and psychiatric disorders.[2,3,4] The psychological substrate in sports competition may appear to be markedly different in those sports that might be grouped as individual and those that might relate to a group endeavor. This might not necessarily be true, however, since the mere introduction of a competitive element into the sports activity tends to mobilize psychological mechanisms which are common to all competitive sports. Francis J. Ryan has analyzed this relationship in an excellent fashion.[5] He has stated that a good competitor casts his opponent in the role of a "temporary enemy." Poor competitors, however, rather than dealing with their opponent in a strenuous emotional manner which incites their anger, approach their opponents in an atmosphere of friendliness. They in fact downplay the competitive aspect of their encounter. Poor competitors, according to Ryan, are "peace makers." If the good competitor (as classed by Ryan) performs poorly, he becomes angry at himself, depressed, uses many verbal expletives, and generally becomes distasteful to those around him. The poor competitor approaches his loss or poor performance in the opposite manner; he accepts his defeat with a philosophical attitude. He acts rather cheerful and supportive of those around him. It is almost as if the poor competitor has a "compulsion to lose." Ryan therefore reaches the conclusion that competition in sports requires that aggression (both occult and overt) be directed toward the goal of victory at all costs. The poor competitor has learned, again either consciously or unconsciously, to suppress this aggression mostly for fear of it. He actually "defuses" this aggressive spirit and, in doing so, reduces his need to be victorious. Many consistent losers, who otherwise would appear to have the capabilities of being winners, undergo this process of suppression of the aggressive spirit.

We have had the opportunity to informally analyze the motivation to win in a group of physician runners (American Medical Joggers Association) who were known for their excellence in long distance running and their ability to win races or to place among the top runners. Often these competitors used language before their races that made it seem as if they wanted to inflict mayhem on their opponents. Some of these winning competitors would state that they would "run the so-and-so into the ground" or that they would "kill" their opponents. These are not uncommon statements made before athletic events; we have all heard them used, we accept them in the light of the situation in which they are being used. When one analyzes these statements, however, one can get some inkling of what is going on in the athlete's mind. Beisser labels this "the killer instinct."[6] Although this is usually taken to mean that an athlete is able, relentlessly and without inner prohibition or a sense of guilt, to keep the pressure on his opponent while achieving victory, the language chosen to describe it suggests a criminal act rather than a sportsmanlike activity. Kopelman and Pantaleno,[7] in a paper entitled "Rejection, Motivation and Athletic Performance: Is There A Traded Player Syndrome?" state that "it is widely held that the professional athlete who is traded tends to perform better against the trading team than against other teams." Two psychological explanations for this hypothesis were advanced (a separation-hostility mechanism and an esteem loss-counteraction mechanism). Data were analyzed for 47 professional baseball players over a two-year period. Support for the hypothesis was weak across the entire sample; however, some support appeared among players who: (a) were traded for the first time; (b) had a long tenure with the trading team; (c) were young; and (d) had outstanding ability. Somewhat stronger positive results were found for individuals who met two or more of the conditions favorable to this hypothesis. As predicted, results became attenuated over the course of time. So far, this general aspect of aggression associated with competitiveness does not seem to have penetrated into the ranks of women athletes to the same extent that it has with male athletes. Balazs and Nickerson,[8] in a study entitled

"A Personality Needs Profile of Some Outstanding Female Athletes," administered the Edwards Personal Preference Schedule (EPPS) to 24 outstanding U.S. female athletes who were competitors in the 1972 Olympic Games. The results of the EPPS Group Profile strongly points to the essential normality of these competitors. Within the framework of a well-balanced needs profile, the two highest group needs scores were in the realm of achievement and autonomy. Thus, these prominent athletes demonstrated the kind of seemingly high needs for achievement and self-accomplishment.

All of this information relating to aggressiveness is particularly interesting in view of the fact that Morgan and Pollock,[9] reporting on a group of world class athletes, have observed that they resemble the general population in most psychological traits. They have concluded further that the major distinguishing psychological dimension of the elite marathoners is in the "effort sense" that these runners employ as an associative cognitive strategy during competition. The obvious normality of these competitors at all times except when they are actually competing fits in well with other studies that report the positive mental health (from an affective standpoint) of such classes of athletes. The classification of cognitive strategy, as used by Morgan and Pollock, is based upon the two categories of dissociative and associative strategies. Dissociative strategy is related to reducing sensory input because of the discomfort it creates, while the associative aspect deals with "paying attention to bodily signals." We shall discuss the importance of pain in sports competition later on in this paper.

Fixx[10] states that "running changes our attitude concerning defeat. When we run, even in competition, we compete not so much against others as against ourselves." Most runners, however, do not accept their performances with such a philosophical attitude. It is not uncommon to hear many of these athletes (who are running against themselves) actually curse themselves or use language addressed to themselves in which it appears that they are addressing another individual. Perhaps this goes along with the depersonalization that accompanies many athletic events. I recently talked to one of the leading football linebackers in the country today. He told me that when he observes films of the football action on the day after it has occurred, he wonders how he can take the "beating" that he undergoes and yet survive. He stated that he does not feel the impact of the injuries sustained at the time that they are happening. In fact, he only feels, for the most part, a slight aching or pain on the day following a particularly difficult game. This ability to abstract oneself from the action perhaps explains why football players and other athletes who sustain rather severe impact injuries while competing seem to survive their daily routine and in fact return to the game so readily. This goes along with Morgan and Pollock's hypothesis of dissociative cognitive strategy. In their paper, however, Morgan and Pollock seem to feel that distance runners and particularly elite marathoners deal with their problems during competition by employing an associative cognitive strategy, by which they become more attuned to their internal body signals. This may explain, to a small degree, why some athletes choose one sport over another. The evolution of this type of thinking probably relates to a long-term process beginning in the early stages of life and perhaps even in the womb that develops as the individual matures. This deals not only with maturational factors but genetic factors as well.

The limitations of athletic ability are usually considered to be physical, but in actuality they may relate more to a psychological substrate than a physical one. Over and over in sports competition one hears athletes saying that they were feeling particularly good on a certain day or that their body was functioning in a fashion which would mean a chance to break a record or to definitely win an event. Most of these feelings are based on psychological rather than on physical factors. Athletic coaches who implant a sense of the winning spirit into their team or into their individual athletes usually are of the type that inspire psychological enforcement. To lose is unconscionable. Lazlo Tabori, who has been track coach to some of the leading women distance runners, as well as other track champions, is an example of such a "stern father" image. I have often watched him work, and have observed that he places great psychological and physiological demands on his trainees. Beneath the hard exterior which he exhibits, however, there is a reservoir of understanding, particularly for the athlete who tries to comply with his rigorous training schedules. When such athletes are exposed to competition, they think back to their training with Tabori, and they just "cannot lose" because it would be so disappointing to their "father." This, of course, brings up another aspect of the competitive sports scene: the role played by the Oedipal complex. Most male athletes are in strenuous unconscious or subconscious competition with their fathers. They want to exceed the prowess of their fathers and one of the best ways to do it is on the athletic fields. Of all the concepts that Sigmund Freud expounded, it is the Oedipal theory that has been most widely accepted, even by those who criticize Freudian theories. Frequently, the depression which follows winning an event, in a male athlete, can be traced to the sense of guilt in defeating the father or the "father image." Deep Oedipal conflict can be elicited during psychoanalytic questioning, as has been done by many investigators in the past. Beisser[6] states that "unconsciously the aggression is often tantamount to violent destruction of the opponent." So "the athlete, although he basks in the glory of victory, also unconsciously stands convicted of murder." I doubt whether things are as serious as this but there certainly are elements of these complexes to be considered.

Roger Bannister,[11] when discussing his conquest of the four minute mile with me and also when writing about it in his book, makes it very clear that he feels that his feat was more a psychological one than a physical one. It is not that he downplays the physical aspect of this great event but he states that his running faster than a four minute mile was because of the way he handled the problem psychologically. He actually divided the mile into four parts, each of which consisted of one quarter mile, and he viewed each quarter of a mile separately. In this manner he attempted to divorce from his mind the fact that he was running an entire mile. He instead set out to run each quarter at a time of one minute or less. He has aptly expressed the experience in his book, *The Four Minute Mile:* "I had a moment of mixed joy and anguish, when my mind took over. It raced well ahead of my body and drew my body compellingly forward. I felt that the moment of a lifetime had come. There was no pain, only a great unity of movement and aim. The world seemed to stand still, or did not exist." Bannister stated to me personally that he appreciated the fact that the four minute mile barrier had stood for so long because of psychological reasons. He felt that there were numerous runners who could have broken the barrier if they could only have believed that they could. Their mistake was to view the mile as one continuous event rather than break it down, as he had done, into four parts. The fact that this was true is evidenced by the number of runners who within one year also "broke the barrier" after Bannister had. Once he had proven to them that it could be done from the psychological point of view, the others were able to use this fact to perform their wonderful feats.

The situation has reached the point where world records have been studied in a mathematical fashion, and such formulas are fascinating.[12] Even these equations do not tell the whole story, however. Ernst Jokl[13] writes of the "once-in-a-lifetime" accomplishment of Bob Beamon's world record long jump at the Mexico City Olympics in 1968. Jokl also writes about Beamon's collapse immediately after the event. He describes it as a "cataplectic collapse." He defines it as an "atonic state of somatic muscles which developed suddenly on the heels of emotional excitement." Jokl also states that Beamon's jump has "revolutionized exercise physiology. It corroborates the view that laboratory studies are of little value for understanding of athletic performances. Even more important is the conclusion that the massive evidence derived from the analysis of the improvement of records can no longer be considered a reliable basis for the prediction of things to come. The Beamon jump has projected a new kind of bud into the future."

Jokl also states that "the same phenomenon played a part in Bob Seagren's victory in the pole vault competition in Mexico City." Seagren said, "If I had known the metric system better, I would not have passed that high. To me 5.35 meters did not sound as high as 17 feet, 6¾ inches." Jokl then further states: "Symbolic stimuli derive their force from the special significance they have to the individual, not from their intrinsic qualities. Their sequelae cannot be explained through the analyses of the physical factors involved in the performance."

George Sheehan[14] quotes William James as saying that "pain and wrong and death must be fairly met and overcome, or the sting remains unbroken." Sheehan also quotes psychiatrist Viktor Frankl as another who speaks of "the need to confront this tragic triad of human existance: guilt for our past, pain in the present and death in the future." These realities, they both warn us, must be neither ignored nor evaded but squarely faced and conquered. But where can this encounter be sought? Where can pain be found on demand? Where can we meet guilt head on and cleanse ourselves? Where can we experience death and then return? The best answer, according to Sheehan, is in sport. There can be no denying that pain is linked with death, and this brings us to the importance of pain in athletic events and particularly in the competitive area which we are dealing with. How can the competitive athlete deal with the rather severe pain he must be forced to live with so many times during the course of these events? D. M. Ewin[15] notes that "there is a special psychological meaning to the complaint of constant pain." I feel that his statement, although relating to chronic pain syndromes, can be applied to the athlete and particularly to the endurance athlete who must undergo great pain in order to compete successfully in his or her events. This applies particularly to long distance running. When the chronic pain patient states, upon being queried about his pain, "I live with it," he is often expressing the subconscious corollary, "If I don't have it I'm dead." Ewin further states: "Investigation of this complaint under hypnosis will frequently uncover an initial trauma associated with mental disorientation during which the experience of pain was reassuring to the subconscious that the organism was still alive. Obviously if the pain proves he's [the patient] alive it cannot be relinquished for even five minutes. Cure of this complaint is effected by uncovering its origin and pointing out to the patient that it may have been useful at the time, but is no longer necessary to prove he's still alive." We feel that the athlete, particularly after events that elicit great pain which lasts for more than a few moments, frequently makes statements which support the fact that pain "proves that he is alive." Perhaps this feeling is responsible for the great elation which endurance athletes experience after their events. Roger Bannister makes this statement about pain: "This psychological factor is beyond the ken of physiology which sets the razor's edge between victory and defeat and which determines how closely the athlete comes to the absolute limits of performance."[10] Pain therefore brings us to the brink of life and back again so that the appreciation of life is never greater than when it is realized in this manner. This may also be the psychological source behind the Indian fakir's using his "bed of nails" or walking over "hot coals." Certainly no one wants to live in a state of chronic pain, but the fact that pain exists proves again and again that one is indeed alive! This is especially true for the athlete. Sheehan remarks that "not to yield says it all. The enduring, the surviving, does not stop with age. We may even grow more skillful at it as the years pass. So we do not envy youth. We ask no quota of life. We accept no favors. We are men following virtue and knowledge." Bob Glover,[16] after experiencing his marathon pain, writes: "I ran across the finish line—and kept going until someone finally made me stop after an unforgetable journey of agony and ecstasy." Here again we have an explicit statement of the association between pain and pleasure. Thomas Szasz,[17] in his book *Pain and Pleasure,* states that pain and suffering may ennoble us, change "our notions of work and play, spur us on to constructive action," and "keep us 'usefully' alive." The absence of pain may mean inactivity and death. Szasz's statements reinforce the theory that pain is associated with "life," and "life" is enhanced by experiences gained in endurance sports.

From a psychological point of view, one must certainly consider the importance of obtaining immortality as part of the reward for the expenditure of effort in athletic competition. Otto Rank[18] writes: "Only through the will-to-self-immortalization, which arises from the fear of death, can we understand the interdependence of production and suffering and the definite influence of this on positive experience." Here, then, is a relationship between suffering (pain) and a "positive experience" (sports competition). Where can mere mortal man obtain a better crack at immortality than on the sporting field? Even the use of the word "longevity" implies a certain immortality. The recent popularity of Pritikin's Longevity Research Institute and the implication of the statement of his book *Live Longer Now* again implies a sense of gaining immortality. I am always amused, as many of you are, by the number of runners who quickly seek out books, magazines, and periodicals that mention their records and athletic accomplishments. In fact, several publications are designed to do just that, to take advantage of our desires to see our names in print, especially in regard to some particular sporting feat. These pastimes are certainly aimed at our subconscious or unconscious desires to attain immortality. Rank[18] tells us that there seems to be a "common impulse in all creative types to replace collective immortality" (sexual propagation) by "deliberate self-perpetuation"—individual immortality. This late development in the concept of immortality, Rank continues, follows efforts to form conceptions of collective immortality, most importantly through religion.

In this day and age when religion has lost many of its adherents,[19] participation by the masses in athletic events is gaining each day. New adherents are appearing faster than individuals are leaving the various churches and religions. As a substitute for the collective immortality that Rank writes about, we have moved into the age of individual immortality, as he conceptualizes it. The way many of the endurance athletes, particularly long distance runners, approach their sport does in fact put one in mind of a religious ritual.[20]

Lastly, we must consider the crowd. For it is the crowd, in the final analysis, that spurs many an athlete on to be a winning performer and frequently improves the performance of even a mediocre sports competitor. Beisser[6] states that "among the other forces that may play a decisive role in an athlete's ability to win is the crowd. It is well known that if the crowd is with a team or a player, there is an advantage for that team or player. So widely recognized is this fact that in making up the season's schedules in sports, careful attention is paid to giving the teams equal numbers of home games. Sports experts say that a football team playing at home has a seven point advantage and a basketball team playing at home has a five–to–ten point advantage." From personal experience, we have noticed that although the course of the Boston Marathon is more difficult than most marathon courses, and although the weather is frequently not as satisfactory as during many other marathons, many of the Boston Marathon competitors do their best at the time of this well known annual race. One of the major reasons, if not the major reason, for this is the crowds. The attendance has often ranged into the millions. *The New York Times* has estimated that between one and two million spectators have attended the Boston Marathon during the last few years. The crowds file along the entire race route and give encouragement to all of the runners—not only the leaders, but also the sluggards. Here we see a psychological principle clearly in action every year. Every runner that is interviewed at the end of the race states, without prompting, that it was the spectators that made the "whole thing worthwhile." Many a tired and almost beaten runner is stimulated to complete the 26 mile distance by the exhortations of the crowd.

We must also remember that the players' teammates also form part of this crowd. An athlete's teammates sometimes become more important to the performance that he or she delivers than the spectators in the stands or on the field. There is an allegiance that grows up between the individual athlete and his teammates. Having worked out together and having participated in many events together, a comradeship is born which has great psychological thrust. "The need to be loved" is strong in all of us[21] and it is particularly reinforced by such groups of spectators at sporting events and also by fellow teammates as well. This need is a basic biological one and is firmly rooted in the soul. There is a symbiotic relationship between the participant and the observer. Each obtains from the other the necessary psychic ingredient of being needed and loved. In imagination and fantasy, the observer or spectator takes an active role, identifying with the participant. In our study of the marathons throughout the country we have found that those who have better than average spectator qualities usually are productive of better than average sports performances.

Even if no spectators are actually present, many sports competitors fantasize their existence. Many athletes, when queried about their fantasies during sporting events, frequently state that they can "hear the sound of the cheering crowd" as they excel at their performance, even when there are few or no spectators. Certainly in the sport of mountain climbing, when the peak is reached one does not usually have a group of spectators present. The one Great Spectator, which many men feel is the Ultimate One, is frequently there, however. Tenzing Norgay (better known as Tenzing of Everest) has stated that

> . . . on the top of Everest I did not see anything supernatural or feel anything superhuman. What I felt was a great closeness to God, and that was enough for me. In my deepest heart I thanked God. And as we turned to leave the summit I prayed to Him for something very real and practical: that having given us victory, He would get us down off the mountain alive.[22]

In summary, I would like to talk about the three A's that I feel are concerned with the psychology of all sports competition. These are aggressiveness, the ability to handle pain, and the adulation of the crowd. Learning how to handle aggressiveness in a constructive fashion is one of the most difficult problems for all athletes. An athlete's ability to integrate or to manage painful stimuli and overcome a subconscious fear of pain and death is a key to his ultimate performance. The adulation of the crowd, which consists not only of the visible group of spectators but also of the player's or participant's teammates or fellows as well as the coach, who frequently has become part of the psyche of the participant, is also of great importance. Perhaps a greater understanding of how a coach, be he official or unofficial, incorporates himself into the psyche of the participant is needed to better understand the entire problem of sports competition. Proving to oneself that the adulation of the crowd is deserved and that it is given to reward the participant for his constructive aggressive actions forms the basis for the competitive spirit. These three A's represent the summarized ultimate of a complex interplay of forces and factors which influence the total outcome.

REFERENCES

1. Jordan P, Spencer B: *Champions in the Making*. Englewood Cliffs, N.J.: Prentice-Hall, 1968
2. Eischens R, Greist J, McInvaille T: *Run To Reality*. Madison Running Press, 1978
3. Kostrubala T: *The Joy of Running*. J. B. Lippincott, 1976
4. Sheehan G: *Dr. Sheehan on Running*. Mountain View, Calif., World Publications, 1975
5. Ryan F: An investigation of personality differences associated with competitive ability in psychosocial problems of college men. Bryant M (ed): New Haven, Wedge Yale University Press, 1958
6. Beisser A: *The Madness in Sports*. Baltimore, Md., Charles Press, 1977
7. Kopelman RE, Pantaleno JJ: Rejection, motivation and athletic performance: Is there a traded player syndrome? *Percept Mot Skills* 45(Pt3 1):827, 1977
8. Balazs E, Nickerson E: A personality needs profile of some outstanding athletes. *J Clin Psychol* 32(1):45, 1976

9. Morgan WP, Pollock ML: The psychological characterization of the elite distance runner. in: Milvey P (ed): *The Marathon: Physiological, Medical, Epidemiological, and Psychological Studies.* New York, Academy of Sciences, 1977, p 382
10. Fixx JF: *The Complete Book of Running.* New York, Random House, 1978
11. Bannister R: *The Four Minute Mile.* New York, Dodd-Mead, 1955
12. Ryder HW: Future performance in footracing. *Sc Am* 234:109, 1976
13. Jokl E: Athletic performance. *Olympic Review.* Nov–Dec 1973, p 189
14. Sheehan G: *Running and Being.* New York, Simon and Schuster, 1978
15. Ewin DM: Constant pain: its psychological meaning and cure using hypnosis. in: Liebeskind JC, et al (eds): *Pain Abstracts.* Second World Congress on Pain. Montreal, 1978
16. Glover B, Shepherd J: *The Runner's Handbook.* New York, Penguin Books, 1978
17. Szasz, TS: *Pain and Pleasure.* New York, Basic Books, 1957
18. Rank, O: *The Myth of the Birth of the Hero and Other Writings.* New York, Vintage Books, 1959
19. Kolb LC: *Modern Clinical Psychiatry.* Philadelphia, W. B. Saunders Co., 1977
20. Shainberg D: Long distance running as meditation. in: Milvey P (ed): *The Marathon: Physiological, Medical, Epidemiological, and Psychological Studies.* New York, New York Academy of Sciences, 1977, p 1002
21. Reik T: *The Need to be Loved.* New York, Bantam Books, 1964
22. Ullman JR: *Tenzing of Everest.* London, Oxford University Press, 1958

Part III

The Effects of Exercise on Disease

Exercise, Hypertension, and Animal Models

CHARLES M. TIPTON, PH.D.,
RONALD D. MATTHES,
TOBY B. BEDFORD, M.S.,
JOEL R. LEININGER, DVM, PH.D.,
ROBERT A. OPPLIGER, M.S.,
LORETTA J. MILLER, M.T.

Symptoms associated with changes in blood pressure have been described since 2600 B.C., strokes have been known since 5 A.D., and the disease of hypertension has been observed since 1655.[1] Even so, this disease remains a major medical problem because one in every five individuals over 17 years of age is considered to be hypertensive.[2] This means that more than 20 million Americans face the dangers and complications associated with cerebral lesions, myocardial lesions, nephrosclerosis and strokes.[3,4] Equally important is the finding that many Americans (50%) are unaware they are hypertensive.[3,5]

Supported in part by funds from HL #21245-01 and GM 07045-01.

The principal investigator is deeply indebted to Mr. Arthur Vailas for his fine and scholarly presentation of this manuscript at the Philadelphia conference.

Since the pathophysiologic mechanisms for 80 to 90 percent of the hypertensive population are unknown,[3,6] it is essential that resources of private and federal agencies be utilized to find solutions for the problems associated with this disease.

The emphasis of this symposium is "Therapeutics Through Exercise"; therefore, it is important to examine the overall aspects of the problem before attempting to define the specific roles of exercise. For purposes of discussion, we have arbitrarily delineated the problems of hypertension into the following five categories:

A.   Detection
B.   Treatment and Management
C.   Pathophysiologic Mechanisms
D.   Prevention
E.   Education

Each category is important in its own right, all are interrelated, and progress in one should facilitate advancement in the others.

One would have to concede at this time that there is very little "official or unofficial" support for exercise as being essential in any one of the five categories listed. The reasons can be best summarized by the recent statement from the Task Force on Blood Pressure Control in Children, concerning the advisability of physical exercise and sports by hypertensive children: "While much is known regarding the effects of exercise on the cardiovascular system, extrapolations to hypertension, although reasonable, are not yet fully documented."[7]

Those results or reviews from human and animal studies that are documented,[8-12] show contradictory findings. Some of the reasons for the controversy can be seen in Figure 1, which shows data obtained from the same general population but reduced in number for different experimental purposes. Frequently overlooked in a discussion of hypertension is the effect of exercise on the lowering of the fat content of humans and animals.[12-14] Recommendation Eight from the Task Force on Blood Pressure Control in Children states that hypertensive children should receive long-term follow-up programs which could include "counseling covering weight control, salt intake, exercise and smoking, and anti-hypertensive pharmacotherapy when indicated."[7]

It has been reported that hypertension develops more frequently in overweight adults and that there is a strong relationship between hypertension and body weight.[3,5,15] We feel that this aspect of the therapeutic use of exercise should receive more attention. It is unlikely, however, that this procedure alone will be adequate for normalization purposes of hypertensive individuals because studies of families with natural and adopted children living in the same household indicate that approximately 94 percent of the relationship between body weight and blood pressure is genetic in origin.[15]

From a small percentage of the voluminous literature on hypertension[3-7,16-18] we have selected the major factors associated with this disease:

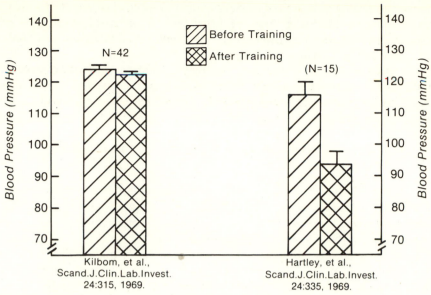

Fig. 1. The influence of training on the sitting blood pressure of humans. These results were calculated from published data in Scand J Clin Lab Invest 24:315 and 335, 1969 on the same patient populations used for different studies. Means and SE are listed.

A.   Structural changes
B.   Autonomic nervous system changes
C.   Alterations in baroreceptor sensitivity
D.   Changes in the renin-angiotensin system
E.   Hemodynamic changes
F.   Elevated blood volumes
G.   Corticosteroid changes

Investigators have utilized horses, sheep, pigs, dogs, cats, rabbits, rats, and other animals to study mechanisms which could increase our understanding of the rise in blood pressure of humans with age. Of these species, the rat has been the one that has received the most emphasis.[3,4]

Rapp[19] notes that four strains of rats have been selectively bred for studying hypertension because each strain exhibits elevated blood pressures before maturity. Two of the strains (Dahl's salt-sensitive and Branchi's Milan Hypertensive strain) are primarily used to study kidney, salt, and water balance mechanisms. The other two strains (Okamoto-Aoki's spontaneously hypertensive rats and Smirk's New Zealand Rats) are employed for their neurogenic contribution to the hypertensive state. However, more information is available on SHR groups than the others mentioned.[4] They are useful experimental models because:

A.   They exhibit familial traits in the progression of the disease.[4]
B.   They demonstrate a rise in pressure with age.[4]

C. They demonstrate the same cardiovascular complications (left ventricle enlargement and dilation, congestive heart failure, hemorrhagic strokes, nephrosclerosis, fibrinoid necrosis of arterioles and small arteries) as commonly found in human hypertensive populations.[4]
D. They show similar hemodynamic changes as humans in cardiac output and total peripheral resistance with the progression of the disease.[4]
E. They exhibit increases or decreases in blood pressure with elevations or reductions in salt intake.[4]
F. They respond to antihypertensive drug therapy and are protected from the complications of untreated hypertension in the same manner as humans.[20-22]

With a short lifespan (18 months) and increased availability to investigators, the SHR is a convenient and useful model to study the pathogenesis of hypertension. It is important to realize, however, that only the Wistar-Kyoto is an appropriate "normotensive" control for this strain of hypertensive rats.[4]

There is considerable confusion as to what systolic or diastolic blood pressure limits constitute normotensive, borderline, or hypertensive populations.[2,3,16] The problem becomes more confused when the terms "juvenile" or "labile" hypertension are included or used.[16] With rats, the problem becomes somewhat simplified because most of the unanesthetized readings are systolic blood pressures as recorded by the tail cuff method from the caudal artery.[4,9,10] For this presentation, normotensives are 140 mmHg or less and borderline hypertensives are between 140–170 mmHg, whereas hypertensive animals are those in excess of 170 mmHg.

METHODS AND RESULTS

To obtain experimental data on the role of exercise in hypertension, we initiated and are currently conducting a series of short-term (50–84 days)[9] or long-term (300–400 days) training studies. In each study a progressive training program is used that has been effective in significantly increasing muscle cytochrome oxidase activity, reducing adipocyte diameters and lowering submaximal exercise rats.[9,23,24] We have also demonstrated in Wistar-Kyoto and Sprague-Dawley male rats that training caused statistically significant differences in resting blood pressures[9] (Figures 2 and 3) of unanesthetized animals. Previously,[25] we reported that daily injections of deoxycorticosteroid acetate (DOCA) combined with a one percent saline drinking solution produced hypertensive animals within three weeks; therefore, we reduced the frequency of DOCA injections to three per week and eliminated the one percent saline drinking solution to produce a borderline hypertensive animal. The findings presented in Figure 4 showed that at 12 weeks the trained rats had means that were not significantly higher than the saline injected controls. This finding was similar, but not identical, to the one noted by Critz and associates.[26] Of interest were the findings that the DOCA injected animals consumed more water per day than the saline injected

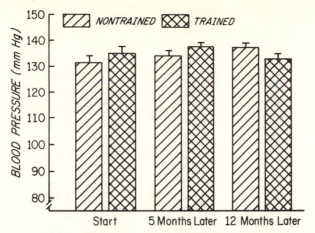

Fig. 2. Unpublished results showing the influences of nine months of moderate exercise on resting caudal artery blood pressure of unanesthetized Sprague-Dawley male rats. Means and SE are listed. There were 14 animals in each group. Covariance analysis indicated that the differences noted when the animals were one year old were statistically significant.

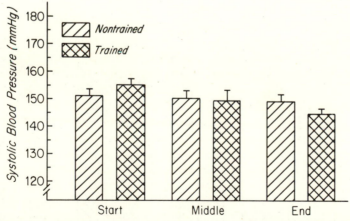

Fig. 3. The influence of short-term training on the resting caudal artery pressure of Wistar-Kyoto male rats. Means and SE are listed. The differences noted at the end of the experimental period were statistically significant at the .05 probability level. These data were summarized in Table 4 of reference 9.

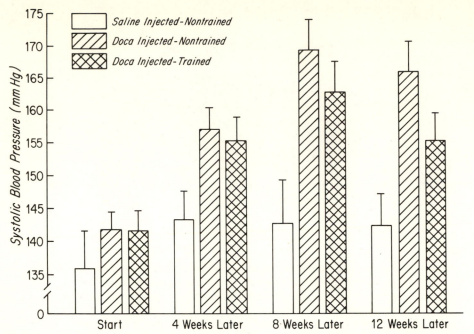

Fig. 4. The influence of saline and DOCA injections (5 mg/rat, 3 times weekly) on resting caudal artery systolic blood pressure of male Sprague-Dawley rats. Means and SE are listed. Co-variance of the differences noted after 12 weeks were not statistically significant between the saline injected and the DOCA injected trained group. There were 11, 15, and 15 male rats respectively in the saline injected, DOCA-injected nontrained, and DOCA-injected trained rats. Additional information can be obtained from Table 6 of reference 9. This figure is reprinted with permission from Tipton CM, et al: The role of chronic exercise on resting blood pressures of normotensive and hypertensive rats. Med Sci Sports 9:168, 1977.

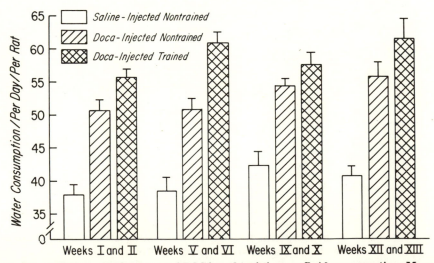

Fig. 5. The influence of injections of DOCA and training on fluid consumption. Means and SE are listed. The differences observed for the trained at weeks 5 and 6 were statistically significant at the .05 probability level.

controls and that the trained consumed more fluid than the nontrained group (Figure 5). This same trend was exhibited with the hypertensive runners (Figure 6) and indicated a source for a potential problem when pharmacological compounds were to be added to the drinking water for antihypertensive purposes.

To determine whether genetic hypertensives would respond to short and long-term training, we initiated a series of experiments with animals obtained from the colony maintained by Dr. M. J. Brody of the Department of Pharmacology. Results recorded before and prior to sacrifice[9] (Figures 7–10) showed that the animals had changed according to a variety of anatomical, biochemical, and physiological parameters. Resting blood pressure measurement obtained before and after the animals became hypertensive revealed that short-term training attenuated the rise in pressure that occurred with time (Figure 11). It must be emphasized, however, that the exercise program could not and did not normalize resting systolic blood pressures. The classic studies associated with Fries et al[20-22] demonstrated that a combination of chlorothiazide, resperine, and hydralazine would normalize hypertensive animals and human populations. When this approach was followed with trained and nontrained rats,[9] the findings confirmed the earlier ones by Fries[20] and others,[4] but did not exhibit any advantages for the trained group (Figure 12).

Because the previous findings evolved from essentially short-term experiments, we initiated a long-term study that currently has been underway for approximately one year. The animals are born, weaned, raised, and exercised in animal quarters located within the Exercise Physiology Laboratory, and litter mates are assigned by

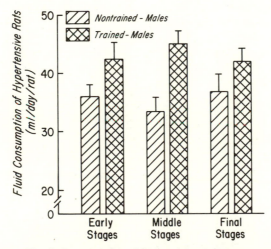

Fig. 6. The influence of training on the fluid consumption of male hypertensive rats. Means and SE are shown. The experimental period was 10–12 weeks long and there were 16 rats in each of the nontrained and trained categories. Early stages (week 3) and middle stages (week 6) revealed differences that were statistically significant at the .05 probability level.

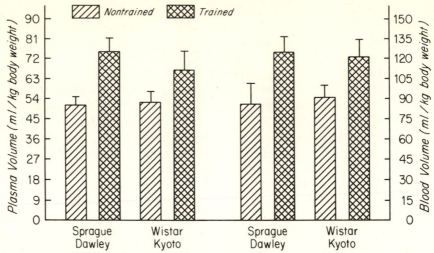

Fig. 7. The influence of training on plasma and blood volumes of male normotensive Sprague-Dawley and Wistar-Kyoto male rats. Means and SE are listed. There were 24 nontrained and 12 trained Wistar-Kyoto rats. Further details can be obtained from Table 9 of reference 9. This figure is reprinted with permission from Tipton CM, et al: The role of chronic exercise on resting blood pressures of normotensive and hypertensive rats. Med Sci Sports 9:168, 1977.

sex into trained and nontrained categories. Training is initiated when the animals are approximately 55 days old and will continue until they are more than one year of age. Once the study was underway, it was apparent that long-term exercise studies could not be conducted in the same manner as the ones of shorter intervals. Unlike Sprague-Dawley animals,[27] genetic hypertensive rats die sooner,[4] with some differences existing between trained and nontrained populations as well as between males

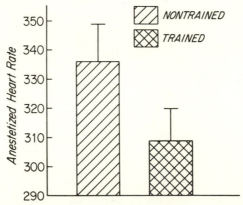

Fig. 8. The influence of training on the anesthetized heart rates of 16 nontrained and 16 trained spontaneously hypertensive male rats. Means and SE are listed. The differences noted were statistically significant at the .05 probability level.

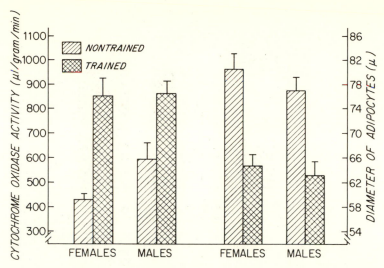

Fig. 9. The influence of training on gastrocnemius muscle cytochrome oxidase activity and adipocyte diameter of genetic hypertensive rats. Means and SE are listed. There were 16 males and 20 females in each of the nontrained and trained groups. Additional details can be obtained from Table 2 of reference 9.

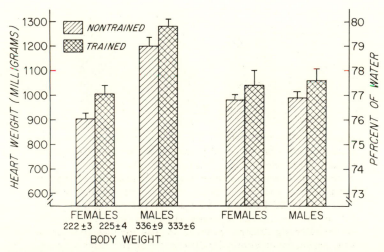

Fig. 10. The influence of training on wet heart weights of nontrained and trained genetic hypertensive rats. Means and SE are listed. Results were obtained from 16 males and 17 females in the nontrained and trained groups respectively. Additional details can be obtained from Table 8 of reference 9.

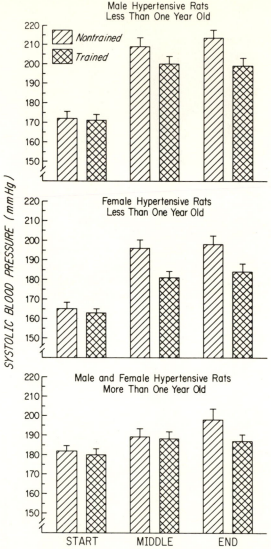

Fig. 11. The influence of short-term training on resting caudal artery systolic blood pressures from male and female genetic hypertensive rats. Means and SE are listed. There were 16 males and 20 females in each nontrained and trained group of the younger animals. There were 7 males and 10 females in each of the older groups. For the younger animals, the differences noted for males at the terminal stages were statistically significant, whereas for the females the middle time period was statistically different. For the older animals, the differences observed after 10-12 weeks of training were statistically significant at the .05 probability level. Information on the younger animals can be obtained from reference 9. Parts of this figure is reprinted with permission from Tipton CM, et al: The role of chronic exercise on resting blood pressures of normotensive and hypertensive rats. Med Sci Sports 9:168, 1977.

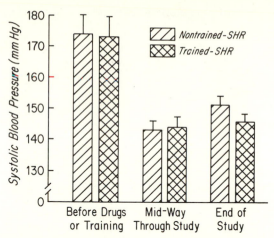

Fig. 12. The influence of short term-training combined with anti-hypertensive medication (added to the drinking water) on SHR groups. Means and SE are listed. There were no group differences that were statistically significant at the .05 probability level. Additional information can be obtained from Table 7 on reference 9.

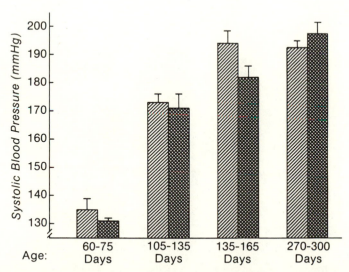

Fig. 13. The influence of long-term physical training on the resting caudal artery systolic blood pressures of unanesthetized female rats (N-31). Means and SE are listed. The differences noted after 135–165 days were statistically significant at the .05 probability level. This figure is reprinted with permission from Tipton CM, et al: The role of chronic exercise on resting blood pressures of normotensive and hypertensive rats. Med Sci Sports 9:168, 1977.

TABLE 1   Mortality Results on Nontrained and Trained SHR Groups

Group	Sex	Activity Status	Initial Number	Remaining Number	Percentage That Died
WKY	Males	Nontrained	13	11	13.4
SHR	Males	Nontrained	14	11	21.4
SHR	Males	Trained	17	15	11.8
WKY	Females	Nontrained	12	11	8.3
SHR	Females	Nontrained	15	12	20.0
SHR	Females	Trained	15	11	26.7

These data were tabulated on August 1, 1978 and represent a time interval of approximately 330 days. Tissues from 9 SHR and 3 WKY, collected at post mortem were examined. They revealed multi-organ congestion that was especially prominent in the lungs, livers and kidneys of SHR groups. Both SHR and WKY had inflammatory lung lesions that varied from mild interstitial pneumonia to severe bronchiectasis. Heart lesions in the SHR animals consisted of acute terminal hemorrhage, and in one rat, multiple foci of necrosis with histiocytic or fibrocytic replacement.

and females (Table 1). Resting blood pressures showed a trend to decrease in the females (Figure 3) but this reduction was not present in male runners. The reasons for these differences are not apparent. Some possibilities are that the rats became more "hyperresponsive" than normal groups[28] to the long-term stress of exercise or that we were exercising them too strenuously for their respective ages.[29,30] Our maximum oxygen consumption results[29,30] (Figures 14 and 15) indicated that they were exercis-

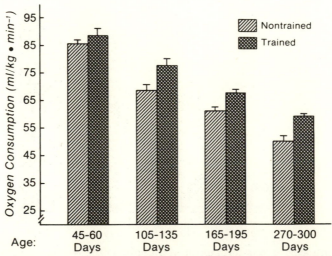

Fig. 14.   Maximum oxygen consumption results of 15 male nontrained and 17 trained hypertensive rats measured at different time periods. Means and SE are listed. The differences noted after the initial time periods were statistically significant at the .05 probability level.

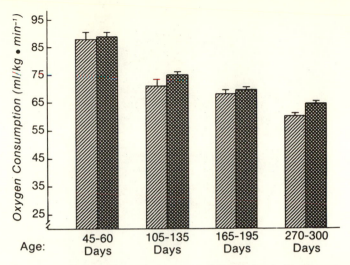

Fig. 15. Maximum oxygen consumption results of female hypertensive rats. Results were obtained from nontrained and trained female rats at various time periods. Means and SE are listed. The differences noted at the 270–300 day time period were statistically significant at the .05 probability level.

Fig. 16. Histological profile of a male Wistar-Kyoto middle caudal artery. The animal was six months old, and the perfusion pressure of the fixative was 120mm Hg. The section has been magnified approximately 126 times.

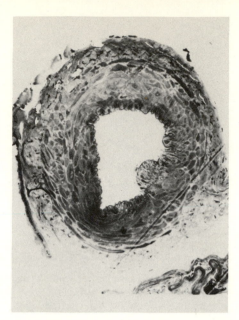

Fig. 17. Histological profile of a male spontaneously hypertensive middle caudal artery. The animal was six months old, and the perfusion pressure of the fixative was 180mm Hg. The section has been magnified approximately 126 times.

ing between 70 to 90 percent of their maximal work capacity. Recent studies conducted at Iowa[10] with isolated hind limb preparations suggest that training might alter the myogenic properties of vascular smooth muscle. Preliminary histological studies (Figures 16 and 17) show the marked differences that exist between caudal arteries obtained from SHR and WKY animals. It remains to be determined whether training will have any influence on wall–lumen ratios and related indices.

DISCUSSION AND CONCLUSIONS

The basic issue is the role of exercise in the various categories associated with the hypertension problem. Although few would dispute the advantages of regular exercise for weight control or improving one's psychological or physiological well-being, the controversy rages as to whether regular exercise will change the resting blood pressure of humans.[3,7-9,11] We feel that much of the controversy can be reduced if it is recognized that the documented benefits of exercise are more advantageous to populations that are overweight, past thirty years of age, and in the borderline hypertensive category.[9] Some current findings[8,9,31,32] suggest that exercise can have a normalizing effect on these populations. With essential hypertensive populations, young or old, there is little evidence available to support a definitive statement on the contribution(s) of exercise.[8,9,33-35] Animal results on this specific problem have not been exceedingly helpful, as contradictory[8,9,11,26] results from different animal models have been published. Extrapolations from short-term results (Figure 12 and 13) showed that chronic exercise could attenuate the rise in pressure, but not to the degree of normalization. The long-term findings from SHR groups complicate this interpretation because of their hyperresponsiveness,[28] their susceptibility to diseases,[4] their shorter lifespans,[4] the possibility that we overtrained them, and their deficiencies in temperature regulation[36] (Table 2).

During the course of our long-term experiments, it became obvious that the exercise capability or the exercise tolerance of older rats (> 5 months) was limited by their temperature regulation ability. Although trained rats were capable of achieving significantly higher core body temperatures (Table 2), the rats were exercising at the upper limits of their thermal tolerance. In fact, three deaths occurred during maximal exercise testing and the symptoms clearly suggested that this was due to heat stroke. Rectal temperatures in those situations were in excess of 41°C. The finding that SHR groups have an impaired temperature regulating system is not new.[36] From a practical point of view, it means that SHR animals should be exercised or stress-tested in cool ambient conditions, that females need to be watched more closely than males, and that constant monitoring of core body temperatures is necessary to avoid potential heat disorders. These findings also raise many questions concerning the responses of hypertensive populations to elevated ambient temperatures.

As noted earlier, hypertension is associated with a myriad of pathological changes which include cardiac enlargement, myocardial infarction, congestive heart failure, nephrosclerosis, fibrinoid necrosis of arterioles and small arteries, hemorrhages, cerebral micro-aneurysms, stroke, and so forth.[3,4,17,19] Some, but not all, of these conditions were observed in those animals (Table 1) that died during the long-term studies. The most prevalent condition was pulmonary inflammation which ranged from acute interstitial pneumonia to chronic bronchiectasis. This condition is probably not specific to the hypertensive state, but rather, a result of the domestication and selective breeding required to produce a hypertensive animal. Since our results are limited in number and scope, it is difficult to state whether training had any influence on the mortality rate. The one surprising trend was that female rats appeared to have higher rates than males.

Although extrapolation of training results from one species to another are sub-

TABLE 2 Rectal Temperature Measurements Obtained Before and After the Maximum Oxygen Consumption Tests

Group	Sex	N	Age in Days	T_r Before °C Exercise	T_r After °C Exercise	Change in T_r °C
Nontrained	Males	75	106 ± 7	37.72 ± .11	40.19 ± .12	2.44 ± .08
Trained	Males	71	138 ± 7*	37.90 ± .09	40.76 ± .12*	2.89 ± .11*
Nontrained	Females	47	97 ± 7	38.22 ± .13	40.37 ± .13	2.13 ± .11
Trained	Females	62	113 ± 7	38.04 ± .11	40.76 ± .12	2.62 ± .12*

Means and SE are listed. Asterisk denotes a group difference that was statistically significant at the .05 probability level.

ject to error,[37] we are currently advocating that exercise be combined with anti-hypertensive medication.[3,7,16,20-23] The hypothesis is that lower dosages would be associated with normalized resting blood pressures. A similar effect was noted with one group of asthmatics[38] but more research is required before credence can be given to this concept. Whether such an approach would be useful for juvenile or labile hypertensive populations[16] remains to be determined.

The mechanisms responsible for the pressure changes associated with training are obscure. Since training is generally associated with significantly higher resting blood volumes in both animals[9] (Figure 7) and humans,[8,9] it is unlikely that elevated blood volumes per se are directly responsible for the rise in resting pressures. It is possible, however, that an impairment of the fluid volume mechanisms is intimately involved with the disease process. Of the possibilities previously listed, we believe that reductions in resting sympathetic tone,[8,9,39] decreases in baroreceptor sensitivity,[8,40,41] changes in myogenic structures, tone, or relationships,[10] and/or decreases in resting cardiac output are the most important.[42-43] Figure 18 shows that training can have this latter effect; in the specific populations studied, however, there were no significant changes in resting blood pressures.[42-43]

To return to the purposes of this symposium and to the five categories concerned with the problem of hypertension, we believe that exercise can play an important role in many of those listed. Furthermore, animal models can be extremely helpful in defining that role. It is essential to realize, however, that the purposes of the study should dictate the animal model to be used. To employ a single animal model for every factor identified with the complex problem of hypertension will increase, rather than decrease, the confusion on the subject.

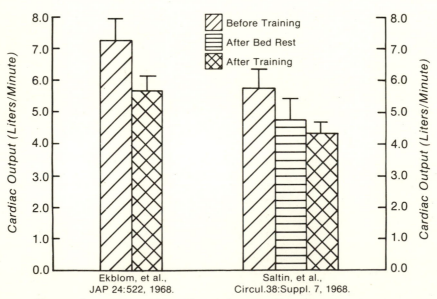

Fig. 18.   Changes in cardiac output with training. The figure has been drawn from calculations of the raw data published in references 42 and 43. Means and SE are listed.

REFERENCES

1. Ruskin A: *Classics in Arterial Hypertension*. Springfield, Charles C. Thomas, 1956, p 356
2. Advance Data, Hypertension: United States, 1974, HEW: 2:1, 1976
3. Arteriosclerosis, Report of National Heart and Lung Task Force on Arteriosclerosis. DHEW Publication (NIH) 72–219, 2871–79, 1971
4. Committee on Care and Use of Spontaneously Hypertensive (SHR) Rats. Spontaneously Hypertensive (SHR) Rats: Guidelines for Breeding, Care and Use. ILAR News 19: G3, 1976
5. Paul O: A survey of the epidemiology of hypertension. *Mod Concepts Cardiovasc Dis* 43:99, 1974
6. Neufeld, HN: Precursors of coronary arteriosclerosis in the pediatric and young adult age groups. *Mod Concepts Cardiovasc Dis* 43:93, 1974
7. Report of the task force on Blood Pressure Control in Children, *Pediatrics Suppl* 59:797, 1977
8. Scheuer J, Tipton CM: Cardiovascular adaptations to training. *Annu Rev Physiol* 39:221, 1977
9. Tipton CM, Matthes RD, Callahan A, et al: The role of chronic exercise on resting blood pressures of normotensive and hypertensive rats. *Med Sci Sports* 9:168, 1977
10. Edwards MT, Diana JN: Effect of exercise on pre- and postcapillary resistance in the spontaneously hypertensive rat. *Am J Physiol* 234:H439, 1978
11. Buucks RJ: Effect of exercise on hypertension. *Med Sci Sports* 10:37, 1978
12. Åstrand PO, Rodahl K: *Textbook of Work Physiology*, ed 2. New York, McGraw-Hill, 1977, p 391
13. Parizkova J: Body fat and physical fitness. The Hague, Martinus Nijhoff, 1977, p 279
14. Oscai LB, Babirak SP, McGarr, JA, et al: Effect of exercise on adipose tissue cellularity. *Fed Proc* 33:1956, 1974
15. Mongeau J-G, Biron P, Bertrand D: Familial aggregation of blood pressure and body weight. in: New MI, Levine LS (eds): *Juvenile Hypertension*, New York, Raven Press, 1977, p 39
16. New MI, Levine LS: *Juvenile Hypertension*, New York, Raven Press, 1977, p 230
17. Hollander W: Role of hypertension in arteriosclerosis and cardiovascular disease. *Am J Cardiol* 38:786, 1976
18. Spontaneous Hypertension: Its Pathogenesis and Complications. Proceedings of the Second Symposium on the Spontaneously Hypertensive Rat. DHEW Publication (NIH) 77–1179, 1976, p 500
19. Rapp JP: Hypertension in the young rat. in: New MI, Levine LS (eds): *Juvenile Hypertension*. New York, Raven Press, 1977, p 79
20. Freis ED, Ragan D, Pillsbury H, et al: Alteration of the course of hypertension in the spontaneously hypertensive Rat. *Circ Res* 31:1, 1972
21. Veterans Administration Cooperative Study Group on Antihypertensive Agents. Effects of treatment on morbidity in hypertension. Results in patients with diastolic blood pressures averaging 115 through 129 mmHg. *JAMA* 202:1028, 1967
22. Veterans Administration Cooperative Study Group on Antihypertensive Agents. Effect of treatment on morbidity in hypertension. II: Results in patients with diastolic blood pressure averaging 90 through 114 mmHg. *JAMA* 213:1143, 1970
23. Tipton CM, Struck PJ, Baldwin KM, et al: Response of adrenalectomized rats to chronic exercise. *Endocrinology* 91:573, 1972
24. Palmer WK, Tipton CM: Influence of hypophysectomy and training on size of isolated fat cells. *Am J Physiol* 224:1206, 1973

25. Dowell RT, Tipton CM, Tomanek RJ: Cardiac enlargement mechanisms with exercise training and pressure overload. *J Mol Cell Cardiol* 8:407, 1976
26. Critz JB, Lipsey P: Relationships between physical training and DOCA hypertension in rats. *Proc Soc Exp Biol Med* 151:552, 1976
27. Tipton CM, Matthes RD, Martin RK: Influence of age and sex on the strength of bone ligament junctions in knee joints of rats. *J Bone Joint Surg* 60–A; 230, 1978
28. Chiveh CC, Kopin IJ: Hyperresponsivity of spontaneously hypertensive rats to indirect measurement of blood pressure. *Am J Physiol* 234:H690, 1978
29. Wilson NC, Bedford TG, Tipton CM, et al: The maximum aerobic capacity of nontrained Rats. *Med Sci Sports* 10:58, 1978
30. Bedford TG, Wilson NC, Tipton CM, et al: Influence of age, sex, training and pregnancy on the oxygen consumption of rats. *Physiologist* 2187, 1978
31. Boyer JL, Kasch FW: Exercise therapy in hypertensive Men. JAMA 211:1668, 1970
32. Choquette G, Ferguson RJ: Blood pressure reduction in "borderline" hypertensives following physical training. *Can Med Assoc J* 108:699, 1973
33. Hanson JS, Nedde WH: Preliminary observations on physical training for hypertensive Males. *Circ Res* 26–27: (Suppl 1), 49, 1970
34. Pyorala K, Karava R, Punsar S, et al: A controlled study of the effects of 18 months' physical training in sedentary middle-aged Men with high indexes of risk relative to coronary heart disease. in: Larson OA, Malmborg RO (eds): *Coronary Heart Disease and Physical Fitness.* Baltimore, University Park, 1971, p 261
35. Johnson WP and Grover JA: Hemodynamic and metabolic effects of physical training in four patients with essential hypertension. *Can Med Assoc J* 96:842, 1967
36. Wilson JR, Wilson LM, DiCarra, LV: Evidence for an elevation in thermoregulatory setpoint in the SHR. Proceedings of the Second International Symposium on the Spontaneously Hypertensive Rat, Newport Beach, CA, 1976, p 477
37. Tipton CM, Matthes RD, Vailas AC, et al: The response of the Galago senegalensis to physical training *Comp Biochem Physiol* 63A:29, 1979
38. Fitch KD, Morton AR, Blanksby BA: Effects of swimming training on children with asthma. *Arch Dis Child* 51:190, 1976
39. Tipton CM, Matthes RD, Tcheng T-K, et al: The use of the Langendorff preparation to study the bradycardia of training. *Med Sci Sports* 9:220, 1977
40. Paynter DE, Tipton CM, Tcheng T-K: Response of immunosypathectomized Rats to training. *J Appl Physiol* 42:935, 1977
41. Tipton CM, Matthes RD, Gross PM, et al: The effect of lower body negative pressure on blood pressure changes in Rats. *Physiologist* 19:250, 1976
42. Ekblom B, Astrand PO, Saltin B: Effect of training on circulatory response to exercise. *J Appl Physiol* 24:518, 1968
43. Saltin B, Blomquist G, Mitchell JH, et al: Response to exercise after bed rest and after training. A longitudinal study of adaptive changes in oxygen transport and body composition. *Circulation* Suppl 7; 38:1, 1968

Hypertension and Exercise

DAVID T. LOWENTHAL, M.D., MITCHELL S. WHITEMAN

It is now well accepted that sustained elevation of blood pressure for a long enough period results in significant vascular damage throughout the body and early death from hypertensive cardiovascular disease.[1,2,3] Lowering the blood pressure with pharmacologic agents is effective in reducing morbidity and mortality not only in patients with malignant and severe hypertension but also in patients with moderately severe and mild blood pressure elevation.[4,5,6] Furthermore, in the absence of drug therapy, borderline hypertensives have experienced a fall in blood pressure following physical training with aerobic (isotonic) activities.[7]

Since precise knowledge of the mechanisms responsible for elevation of blood pressure is still lacking, the therapeutic and exercise approaches to essential hypertension must remain empirical. Our challenge is to reduce elevated blood pressure effectively without producing side effects that would make the therapy essentially counterproductive and to incorporate a program of physical activity which would synergistically act with drug therapy to reduce blood pressure.

HEMODYNAMICS OF HYPERTENSION

Although the etiology of essential hypertension remains undefined, extensive hemodynamic studies have elucidated the alterations of the circulation in these patients.[8] In hemodynamic terms, the blood pressure is related both to cardiac output (the flow of blood through the general circulation) and to the resistance offered to the

TABLE 1   Hemodynamic Changes with Age in Essential Hypertension

Ages 17–29		CO↑, HR↑, TPR-N, A-VO$_2$↑; systolic ↑; diastolic-N-SI↑
Ages > 30	< 50	CO-N, HR-N, TPR-↑; systolic and diastolic ↑.
Ages > 50		CO↓, TPR↑↑; systolic and diastolic ↑↑.

blood flow by the peripheral arterioles (total peripheral vascular resistance). This relationship is expressed by the formula BP=CO x TPR. The hemodynamics of hypertension change with age (Table 1). Thus, between the ages of 17 and 29, essential hypertension may be characterized by an elevation in heart rate and in cardiac output with a normal total peripheral resistance and an increase in the arterial-venous oxygen consumption by the body. It must be understood that along with this increase in cardiac output (which occurs early) there is a relative increase in total peripheral vascular resistance, but, clinically, diastolic pressure is normal. Since norepinephrine and renin may increase in borderline hypertension (genetic and labile) under conditions of exercise, low-salt diet, and mental stress, there may be some abnormal response within the autonomic nervous system (possibly an increase in sympathetic or a decrease in parasympathetic response).[8a] From age 30 to less than age 50, the cardiac output and heart rate revert to normal, but characteristic of fixed essential hypertension is an absolute increase in total peripheral vascular resistance and an increase in diastolic blood pressure. Beyond age 50, cardiac output may decrease with greater increases in total peripheral vascular resistance. When hypertension has become well established, the peripheral resistance is uniformly elevated in different areas of the circulation—except in the kidneys where it appears to be slightly higher. Therefore, the kidneys probably play a fundamental role in the long-term maintenance of the hypertensive state.

It is now well accepted that most patients with sustained hypertension have elevated blood pressure with normal cardiac output and an elevated total peripheral vascular resistance (the indicator of peripheral arterial vasoconstriction). It is desirable, from a therapeutic standpoint, to correct the hypertension by correcting the hemodynamic derangement of the disease—that is, to lower total peripheral vascular resistance and maintain cardiac output. In this way blood flow to the vital organs and systems can be maintained.

Hemodynamics of Hypertension During Exercise

The hemodynamic derangements of hypertension should be controlled 24 hours a day whether the patient is supine, sitting, or standing, whether resting or exercising. Lund-Johansen[8] has characterized the normotensive and hypertensive patient's response to exercise (Table 2). Hypertensive patients who have trained in aerobic exercise programs have had hemodynamic studies performed on a bicycle ergometer at 300, 600, and 900 kpm/minute.

TABLE 2   Hemodynamic Effects in Exercise (Trained Individuals)

	Normotensive	Hypertensive
HR	↑	↑↑ — (probably due to greater adrenergic response and higher A-VO$_2$ differences)
SV	↑↑	↑ — (progressively falls with age and leads to subnormal cardiac output)
CI	↑↑	↑ — (decreases significantly with age in the hypertensives)
TPR	± or *↓	↑↑ — (higher at all ages and at all levels of work)
BP	↑*	↑↑ — (res ipsa locquitor)
LVSW	↑	↑ — (higher with light and moderate work because of hr. no difference when severe work is done because of lower SV)
A-VO$_2$	↑	↑↑ — ("safety mechanism" for hypertensives to meet O$_2$ demands from tissue, A-VO$_2$ difference increases with age)

*During aerobic activity, systolic pressure rises; diastolic pressure is either unchanged from control or it decreases.
±No change

It should be noted that the heart rate response is greater in the hypertensive and is probably related to a greater underlying adrenergic sympathetic response and a higher arterio-venous oxygen difference. Simultaneously, however, there is less of an increase in stroke volume and in the cardiac index. The stroke volume tends to fall progressively with age and this is linked directly to a smaller rise in the cardiac index which likewise decreases significantly with age. Total peripheral resistance is higher at all ages and at all levels of work in the hypertensive trained individuals, thus leading to a greater blood pressure response both in the systolic and diastolic components. Left ventricular stroke work is increased in both normotensive and hypertensive groups, but in the hypertensive group it is higher with light and moderate work because of an increase in heart rate. There is no difference, however, when severe work is done, probably because of a lower stroke volume. Finally, the arterio-venous oxygen difference is significantly higher in hypertensives, as this is a safety mechanism for hypertensives to meet oxygen demands from the tissue. This arterio-venous oxygen difference increases with age. Exercise has been shown to normally increase muscle blood flow in both normotensive and hypertensive subjects.[9] At rest, both muscle blood flow and resistance are increased in hypertensives—as compared to normotensives—indicating that muscle blood vessels share the increase resistance, though probably to a lesser extent than the total circulation. In the upright position, muscle blood flow determined after ischemic exercise decreases in normal subjects; this change has been shown to be even more pronounced in hypertensive subjects. It may be concluded, however, that during periods of high flow after ischemic exercise hypertensive subjects are able to decrease their resistance in the muscles that are stressed during the exercise procedure, but it continues to remain higher than in normotensive controls. Thus, aerobic exercise may be used synergistically (i.e. in addition to a diuretic in mildly hypertensive patients, i.e., diastolic blood pressure less than 105 mmHg) or by itself in an attempt to reduce total peripheral vascular resistance.[7,10] On the contrary, anaerobic exercises, e.g., weight lifting, hand gripping, and wrestling, are associated with increases in diastolic blood pressure. Such activity should be minimized and discouraged in hypertensive patients.

This chapter presents a simple, satisfactory therapeutic regimen for the long-term management of the ambulatory patient with uncomplicated diastolic hypertension. In addition, this review will emphasize the alterations in hemodynamic responses to exercise in patients receiving antihypertensive drug therapy.

Hemodynamic Response To An Exercise-Diuretic Program

Drastic reduction of dietary sodium chloride is quite effective in reducing the blood pressure in patients with essential hypertension.[11] In order to be clinically effective, however, the restriction must be in the range of 25–35 mEq/24 hours. Implementation of this form of dietary restriction may be fraught with non-compliance especially if during exercise one experiences severe weakness as a consequence of inadequate caloric and sodium consumption.

In 1957, Novello and Sprague synthesized chlorothiazide,[12] a compound that marked the beginning of a new era in therapeutics. The availability of oral diuretics made the treatment of hypertension easier and did not impose an extreme restriction on dietary salt. From chlorothiazide, several members of the thiazide family were derived, including chlorthalidone (a phthalimidine derivative), a long-acting diuretic. Other types of diuretics were also developed—for example, metolazone (a quinazoline derivative), which also is long-acting (18–20 hours) and can be administered once a day. Furosemide and ethacrynic acid are potent diuretics that act on the ascending limb of the loop of Henle and are reserved for hypertension which is complicated by heart failure and/or renal insufficiency. Further discussion of these latter two drugs is beyond the scope of this review.

Twenty years of clinical experience have clearly demonstrated that the use of a diuretic is safe and effective in combating hypertension in both the supine and standing positions. The hemodynamic response to a diuretic when studied over the first four to six weeks of administration is characterized by a fall in blood pressure, which is due to acute volume contraction (decrease in plasma volume), and a resultant fall in cardiac output. Peripheral resistance rises. After six to eight weeks of diuretic therapy, the blood pressure remains decreased but cardiac output is restored to baseline; yet plasma volume never really returns to pretreatment control. Total peripheral vascular resistance, however, falls. Studies from the laboratory of Lund-Johansen[13] have shown that as a result of most diuretic therapy, normal cardiovascular responses occur in the hypertensive patient during exercise (Table 3). When hypertensive patients received chlorthalidone, polythiazide, or hydrochlorothiazide were studied at work loads of 300, 600, and 900 kpm/minute, the patients were able to maintain a reduced mean arterial pressure. Total peripheral resistance was re-

TABLE 3   Hemodynamic Changes during Exercise after One Year of Antihypertensive Therapy

	HR	SI	CI	TPR	BP
Hydrochlorothiazide	sl↑	↑	↑	↓	sl↑
α-Methyldopa	↑	±	↑	↓	↑
Clonidine	↑	↑	↑	↓	↑
β-blocker	±	sl₁↑	sl₁↑	↓**	sl↑
Prazosin	↑	↑	↑	↓	sl↑

ϑ increases; ς decreases; ±, no significant change; **, At rest, TPR is increased–TPR decreases with exercise but still remains above baseline; slϑ slight increase; slς slight decrease.

*The responses are related as increase, decrease or no change as compared with those responses to antihypertensive therapy at rest.

duced during exercise with hydrochlorothiazide and with polythiazide but not with chlorthalidone. There was a significant reduction in the cardiac index with chlorthalidone administration and it was this parameter that accounted for the reduction in mean arterial blood pressure. Arteriovenous oxygen difference was not increased with hydrochlorothiazide or polythiazide but was significantly greater in the hypertensive patients receiving chlorthalidone. Chlorthalidone produced the most pronounced antihypertensive effect, but the pressure reduction was due mainly to a decrease in cardiac output rather than in vascular resistance. From a practical as well as a theoretical point of view, the response to chlorthalidone is not the ideal way to reduce blood pressure and is reminiscent of the effect of beta blockade at rest and during exercise. In any event, the final hemodynamic effect from oral diuretics, especially hydrochlorothiazide and polythiazide, is a decrease in total peripheral vascular resistance.[14] Thus, long-term diuretic therapy results in peripheral arteriolar dilatation which can lead to the correction of the hemodynamic derangement of hypertensive disease regardless of whether the patient is studied at rest or during exercise. The side effects of diuretics include hyperuricemia, hypokalemia, and possible aggravation of diabetes mellitus. Recent, albeit controversial, evidence suggests that side effects may include the development of hypercholesterolemia and hypertriglyceridemia.[15] In light of these side effects with diuretics in the exercising hypertensive, various drug-exercise interactions must be considered.

Based on the elegant studies of Knochel et al,[16,17,18] it appears that muscle blood flow is increased when potassium is in adequate concentration in the blood which perfuses the muscle. In potassium-depleted animals, muscle blood flow is diminished, so that stressed muscles may become significantly ischemic and necrotic. Rhabdomyolysis may be brought on by intense exercise in the unconditioned subject, especially as a result of intense heat, alcohol, viral infection, trauma, and (in this context) possibly diuretic-induced hypokalemia. In addition, during extreme conditions of heat, volume contraction through sweating can induce secondary hyperaldosteronism and also hyperuricemia (contributed by muscle catabolism as well) which, if already increased with diuretic therapy, may lead to significant problems with regard to urate deposition. Therefore, potassium retaining diuretics, e.g., spironalactone and triamterene are useful when given in combination with the thiazide diuretic for the purpose of maintaining potassium balance. Ordinarily, potassium supplementation need not be administered unless the patient is on digitalis, is a diabetic with hypokalemia in whom glucose homeostasis may be upset, is a patient undergoing surgery in whom hypokalemia may unmask the arrhythmogenic effect of general anesthesia, and lastly is exercising vigorously. Diuretics may be used adjunctively to inhibit the sodium retention induced by sympathetic-inhibiting antihypertensives (vide infra).

Hemodynamics of Sympathetic-Inhibiting Drugs

When a blood pressure is not normalized by the oral diuretic alone, a second antihypertensive agent is added. Again, any second step drug requires the concomitant administration of a diuretic in order to produce a full therapeutic effect and avoid the phenomenon of pseudoresistance.

CLONIDINE

Clonidine lowers blood pressure effectively by decreasing sympathetic outflow from the vasomotor centers in the brain. The systemic hemodynamic effects include a decrease in both cardiac output and total peripheral vascular resistance.[19,20,21] With prolonged administration, the decrease in total peripheral vascular resistance becomes more pronounced, whereas cardiac output may return to pretreatment levels.[22] As a result of clonidine stimulating central adrenergic receptor sites within the vasomotor center, vagal outflow is enhanced and thus leads to a transient decrease in heart rate. Clonidine does not interfere with the physiologic increase in cardiac output, systolic blood pressure, and oxygen consumption induced by exercise.[23] But the *acute* oral administration of clonidine given to eight subjects with moderate to severe hypertension during exercise on the bicycle ergometer produced results compatible with a decrease in maximal oxygen consumption, cardiac output, heart rate, and blood pressure—after treatment, at rest, as well as during exercise.[23] Lund-Johansen has studied the *long-term* effect of clonidine given in dose ranges between 0.3 and 0.6 mgs a day to 13 subjects who were studied at rest and during steady-state muscular exercise sitting on a bicycle ergometer at work loads of 300, 600 and 900 kpm per minute (Table 3). The changes during muscular exercise are related to those alterations before and after one year of clonidine treatment. Thus, mean arterial blood pressure was reduced by approximately 9 percent at 300 and 600 kpm per minute, but at 900 kpm a minute the blood pressure response was unchanged when compared to pretreatment values. Similar results were observed with the heart rate. For reasons that were not apparent, the stroke volume during exercise tended to be higher after therapy than before but the changes were not statistically significant. Cardiac index increased during exercise but was unchanged when compared to pretreatment values. This is explainable by the fact that the fall in heart rate at the lower work levels and the increase in stroke volume during exercise together result in no change in cardiac output. Total peripheral vascular resistance tended to be decreased during exercise but the changes were not influenced by clonidine treatment. It is apparent that at submaximal levels of work, the central effects of clonidine are overridden by peripheral mechanisms (alpha vasoconstriction) that control blood flow and peripheral vascular resistance. This would lead to a decrease in both skin blood flow and muscle blood flow in hypertensive patients. The decrease in skin blood flow may be due to a predominant vasoconstricting effect of the drug in the cutaneously vascular bed, and the decrease in muscle blood flow may be related to the decrease in cardiac index which occurs both at rest and during exercise in patients receiving long-term clonidine therapy; yet these results in cardiac index are not statistically different from the resting state to the exercise state.[24] The most important feature to consider is that, in contrast to diuretics, beta-adrenergic blocking drugs, and prazosin, clonidine did not decrease blood pressure at *submaximal work levels*. This is probably related to the fact that clonidine exerts its main antihypertensive effect via the central (as opposed to the peripheral) nervous system.

The most important side effects of clonidine are drowsiness and dryness of the mouth which occur in approximately 25 to 35 percent of patients and are transient in duration. These effects have been shown to be related to peak plasma clonidine concentration.[25] In less than 1 percent of patients there is a symptomatic return to pretreatment control, especially in those patients who abruptly discontinue the medication. This is reversible with 0.1 mgs of clonidine. Predictably, patients in whom this symptomatic return to control may be found are those in whom the pretreatment diastolic pressure has been 120 mmHg or more or those requiring at least 1.2 mgs of clonidine per day. Whitsett et al have recently documented that although clonidine produces no rise in blood pressure beyond pretreatment levels, the withdrawal of the drug may result in an increase in plasma norepinephrine and urinary catecholamine excretion.[26]

The important therapeutic advantages of clonidine are its versatility, easy titration, and virtual freedom from orthostatic hypotension. It may therefore be used in mild, moderate, or severe hypertension and in the patient who is on an exercise program since the response to exercise is not significantly blunted.[27,28]

ALPHAMETHYLDOPA

Although the major site of action of alphamethyldopa is through the central nervous system, peripheral sympathetic inhibition also occurs and is probably responsible for the predominance of orthostatic hypotension. Methyldopa lowers blood pressure by decreasing peripheral vascular resistance in both the supine and standing positions.[29,30] Furthermore, although the hypotensive effect of alphamethyldopa is more pronounced in the upright position, the difference between supine and standing blood pressures is less with methyldopa than with other sympathetic inhibitors.[29,30,31] Methyldopa produces a consistent decrease in cerebral vascular resistance and a slight but significant increase in cerebral blood flow when blood pressure is reduced to normal levels.[32] On the basis of these hemodynamic considerations, prudent reduction of blood pressure with methyldopa is desirable in the hypertensive patient with cerebral vascular disease. Furthermore, methyldopa does not impair perfusion to the myocardium and the renal vascular bed.

With regard to exercise (Table 3), patients on methyldopa therapy show a normal rise in cardiac output with no tendency to post-exercise hypotension.[30] The rise in cardiac index has been demonstrated by Lund-Johansen to be significant with exercise during methyldopa therapy but *not* greater than the treated pre-exercise state. Similarly, although heart rate does increase with exercise involving graded increases in workload, it is less than the treated pre-exercise levels. Systolic and diastolic and mean arterial pressure remain reduced in the treated group during exercise at all work loads when compared with the group before treatment during exercise.There is a fall in total peripheral resistance during exercise before and after treatment. Overall, both at rest and during exercise, the drop in blood pressure with methyldopa is associated with a drop in cardiac output and practically no change in total peripheral resistance. The drop in cardiac output is mostly due to a reduction in heart rate. There is also a small drop in maximum oxygen consumption at rest with methyldopa, and this is most likely due to the sedating effect of the drug on the central nervous system. During muscular exercise, the maximum oxygen consumption after treatment is also lower than before, particularly at the 900 kpm per minute workload. It is difficult to explain why there was no decrease in total peripheral vascular resistance after treatment with methyldopa at rest—this is in contrast to previous studies[29,31]—but the study by Lund-Johansen did not include any observations on regional blood flow. To accomplish a reduction in peripheral resistance with a group of such patients, it would seem prudent to add hydrochlorothiazide to the regimen.[33] Side effects attributable to methyldopa therapy include drowsiness, dry mouth, positive Coomb's test, hemolytic anemia, hepatotoxicity, impotence, and methyldopa fever. Running can elevate SGOT and LDH enzymes. Patients receiving methyldopa may have increases in these enzymes. To avoid confusing the elevation of enzymes with hepatotoxicity, isoenzyme fractionation is critical.

BETA BLOCKADE

Lund-Johansen studied the hemodynamic response to alprenolol, a beta blocker similar to propranolol, and found that the *posttreatment resting* cardiac index, mean arterial pressure, and heart rate were significantly lower than pretreatment levels and that this was associated with a higher total peripheral resistance after treatment (Table 3). Increasing the workload during treatment with beta blockade caused a progressive fall in peripheral resistance, although it remained elevated when compared to pre-exercise treatment conditions. With increased workload during treatment, there was a slight progressive increase in cardiac index, mean arterial pressure, and heart rate, but at all levels of workload in the treated group these values were lower than before treatment. There was no significant difference in stroke index at the lower workload, but at the higher work levels there was a significant increase. Therefore, at all levels of work (300, 600, and 900 kpm per min) cardiac hemodynamics in general are suppressed with beta blockade. It is obvious, therefore, from these results that beta blockade blunts to a significant degree the normal exercise response.[34] The effects of propranolol during exercise in hypertensive and ischemic heart disease has been studied for the patients' response to exercise on a treadmill, and similar effects to those described with alprenolol were observed but were more striking in the hypertensive patients than in those with ischemic heart disease.[35] Contraindications to nonselective beta blockade have been amply described in the literature.[27] Finally, beta blockers may lead to hyperkalemia during exercise and can block free fatty acid utilization during stress.

PRAZOSIN

Prazosin is primarily an alpha-receptor blocking agent, but it differs from the classical alpha blockers, phenoxybenzamine and pentolamine, in a number of respects. The latter two not only cause an orthostatic fall in blood pressure, but due to the fact that norepinephrine can no longer inhibit its own release, the adrenergic stimulus to norepinephrine release remains in effect and tachycardia and renin release are prominent when these two drugs are given. When prazosin is administered, on the other hand, norepinephrine release permits itself to be inhibited due to excitation, and thus the adrenergic stimuli of tachycardia and renin release are not found. In patients studied at rest, prazosin produces a negligible increase in heart rate and in cardiac index; there is a fall in peripheral resistance and in mean arterial blood pressure. When compared to the response of pretreatment exercise group, the treated group demonstrates a greater increase in cardiac index, stroke volume, and heart rate, but in the latter category the changes were not significant. Mean arterial blood pressure and total peripheral resistance were significantly lower after treatment as compared with the same workloads before treatment. Thus, with prazosin therapy (1 mg, three times a day) the cardiac response remains intact, whereas blood pressure and peripheral resistance are decreased with exercise[36] (Table 3).

The overall therapeutic to toxicity ratio with prazosin is quite high and the highest precautions must be observed with the first dosage of prazosin—the first mg can produce significant orthostatic response and, in rare cases, syncope.

DISCUSSION

The hemodynamic response to exercise is dependent on the type of drug used. No generalities can be made which are applicable to all drugs. It is apparent, however, that all drugs reduce mean arterial blood pressure at rest and during exercise. The mechanisms differ, however. All drugs except prazosin reduce cardiac index at rest, in the sitting position. The reduction induced by hydrochlorothiazide is only about 5 percent, whereas that induced by beta blockade with alprenolol is approximately 23 percent. Where prazosin causes a significant decrease in peripheral resistance, beta blockade will increase peripheral vascular resistance at rest. Of further significance is the individualized response to the hemodynamic effects of these drugs with exercise. The hemodynamic response to exercise after long-term therapy with clonidine differs from treatment with other antihypertensive drugs, such as the diuretics, beta adrenergic blockade, and prazosin. With these latter three drugs the posttreatment blood pressure is significantly reduced at submaximal work levels, whereas the pressure response with clonidine following submaximal work—i.e., 900 kpm per minute—is no different than before treatment during exercise. When compared with the resting blood pressure after treatment, however, blood pressure increases slightly and variably as does cardiac output following exercise in the treated group.

In conclusion, those drugs with the best hemodynamic profile in relation to exercise are hydrochlorothiazide, clonidine, methyldopa, and prazosin.[36] Oxprenolol and pindolol are investigational beta-adrenergic blockers with intrinsic sympathomimetic activity, i.e., they induce an increase in cardiac output and heart rate.

Eventually, they may become useful in exercise states when beta blockers are indicated.

Whether exercise will be of benefit in the early, neurogenic form of hypertension as described by Esler[37] in protecting against the development of fixed hypertension remains to be determined. It is well appreciated that mental stress and isometric exercise (as opposed to isotonic exercise) will provoke an increase in blood pressure in those with neurogenic or labile hypertension.[37,38] Exercise of the dynamic or isotonic variety, such as distance running, may induce sufficient parasympathomimetic influence to decrease the neurogenic and/or adrenergic component of blood pressure control and thus alter the evolution of fixed diastolic hypertension.

REFERENCES

1. Dublin LJ, Lotka AJ, Spiegelman M: *Length of Life: A Study of The Life Table,* ed 2. New York, Ronald Press, 1949
2. Hamilton M, Thompson EN, Wisniewski TKM: The role of blood pressure control in preventing complications of hypertension. *Lancet* 1:235, 1964
3. Hodge JV, Smirk FH: The effect of drug treatment of hypertension on the distribution of deaths from various causes. A study of 173 deaths among hypertensive patients in the years 1959 to 1964 inclusive. *Am Heart J* 73:441, 1967
4. Moyer JH, Heider C, Pevey K, Ford RV: The effect of treatment on the vascular deterioration associated with hypertension, with particular emphasis on renal function. *Am J Med* 24:177, 1958
5. Veterans Administration Cooperative Study Group on Antihypertensive Agents: Effects of treatment on morbidity in hypertension. Results in patients with diastolic blood pressures averaging 115 through 129 mmHg. *JAMA* 202:1028, 1967
6. Veterans Administration Cooperative Study Group on Antihypertensive Agents: Effects of treatment on morbidity in hypertension. II. Results in patients with diastolic blood pressures averaging 90 through 114 mmHg. *JAMA* 213:1143, 1970
7. Choquette G, Ferguson RJ: Blood pressure reduction in "borderline" hypertensives following physical training. *Can Med Assoc J* 108:699, 1973
8. Lund-Johansen P: Hemodynamics in early hypertension. *Acta Med Scand* 181 (Suppl 482):1, 1967
8a. Robertson D, Shand DG, Mollifield JW, et al: Alterations in the responses of the sympathetic nervous system and renin in borderline hypertension. *Hypertension* 1:118, 1979
9. Amery A, Bossaert H, Verstraete M: Muscle blood flow in normal and hypertensive subjects. Influence of age, exercise and body position. *Am Heart J* 78:211, 1969
10. Amery A, Julius S, Whitlock LS, et al: Influence of hypertension on the hemodynamic response to exercise. *Circ.* XXXVI:231, 1967
11. Grollman A, Harrison TR, Mason MF, et al: Sodium restriction in the diet for hypertension. *JAMA* 129:533, 1945
12. Novello FC, Sprague JM: Benzothiadiazene and diazoxide as novel diuretics. *J Am Chem Soc* 79:20, 1957
13. Lund-Johansen P: Hemodynamic changes in long-term diuretic therapy of essential hypertension. *Acta Med Scand* 187:509, 1970
14. Villarreal H, Exaire JE, Revollo A, et al: Effects of chlorothiazide on systemic hemodynamics in essential hypertension. *Circulation* 26:405, 1962

15. Ames RP, Hill P: Elevation of serum lipid levels during diuretic therapy of hypertension. *Am J Med* 61:748, 1976

16. Knochel JP, Schlein EM: On the mechanism of rhabdomyolysis in potassium depletion. *J Clin Invest* 51:1750, 1972

17. Knochel JP, Vertel RM: Salt loading as a possible factor in the production of potassium depletion, rhabdomyolysis and heat injury. *Lancet* 1:659, 1967

18. Knochel JP, Dotin LN, Hamburger RJ: The pathophysiology of intense physical conditioning in a hot climate. I. The mechanisms of potassium depletion. *J Clin Invest* 51:242, 1972

19. Onesti G, Schwartz AR, Kim KE, et al: Antihypertensive effects of clonidine. *Circ Res* 23(Suppl II):53, 1971

20. Onesti G, Bock KD, Heimsoth V, et al: Clonidine: A new antihypertensive agent. *Am J Cardiol* 28:76, 1971

21. Lund-Johansen P: Hemodynamic changes in long-term therapy of essential hypertension. A comparative study of diuretics, alphamethyldopa and clonidine. *Clin Sci Mol Med* 45:199, 1973

22. Schneider KW, Gattenlohner W: Hamodynamische utersuchungen nach ST-155 2-(2,6-dichlorphenylamino)-2-imidazolin-hydrochlorid beim menschen. *Dtsch Med Wochenschr* 91:1533, 1966

23. Stenberg J, Holmberg S, Maets E, et al: The hemodynamic effects of catapresan. Central circulation at rest. Circulation at rest and during exercise. in: Heilmeyer L, Holtmeyer, HJ, Pfeiffer E (eds): *Hochdrucktherapie*. Stuttgart, Thieme, 1968, p 68

24. Lund-Johansen P: Hemodynamic changes at rest and during exercise in long-term clonidine therapy of essential hypertension. *Acta Med Scand* 195:111, 1974

25. Dollery CT, Davies DS, Draffan GH, et al: Clinical pharmacology and pharmacokinetics of clonidine. *Clin Pharmacol Ther* 19:11, 1976

26. Whitsett TL, Chrysant SG, Dillard BL, et al: Abrupt cessation of clonidine administration: a prospective study. *Am J Cardiol* 41:1285, 1978

27. Onesti G, Martinez EW, Fernandes M: Alphamethyldopa and clonidine: Antihypertensive agents with action on the central nervous system. in: Onesti G, Lowenthal DT (eds): *The Spectrum of Antihypertensive Drug Therapy*. New York, Biomedical Information Corp., 1976, p 47

28. Onesti G, Bock KD, Heimsoth V, et al: Clonidine, a new antihypertensive agent. *Am J Cardiol* 28:74, 1971

29. Onesti G, Brest AN, Novack P, et al: Pharmacodynamic effects of alphamethyldopa in hypertensive subjects. *Am Heart J* 67:32, 1964

30. Sannerstedt R, Bojs G, Varnauskas E, et al: Alphamethyldopa in arterial hypertension. *Acta Med Scand* 174:53, 1963

31. Cannon PJ, Whitlock RT, Morris RC, et al: Effect of alphamethyldopa in severe and malignant hypertension. *JAMA* 179:673, 1962

32. Meyer JS, Sawada T, Kitamura A, et al: Cerebral blood flow after control of hypertension in stroke. *Neurology* 18:772, 1968

33. Lund-Johansen P: Hemodynamic changes in long-term methyldopa therapy of essential hypertension. *Acta Med Scand* 192:221, 1972

34. Lund-Johansen P: Hemodynamic changes at rest and during exercise in long-term beta blocker therapy of essential hypertension. *Acta Med Scand* 195:117, 1974

35. Shinebourne E, Fleming J, Hamer J: Effects of beta-adrenergic blockade during exercise in hypertensive and ischemic heart disease. *Lancet* 2:1217, 1967

36. Lund-Johansen P: Hemodynamic changes at rest and during exercise in long-term prazo-

sin therapy for essential hypertension. *Postgraduate Medicine Symposium on Prazosin.* Nov. 1975, p 45

37. Esler M, Julius S, Zqeifler A, et al: Mild high-renin essential hypertension. A neurogenic human hypertension? *N Eng J Med* 296:405, 1977

38. Nyberg G: Blood pressure and heart rate response to isometric exercise and mental arithmetric in normotensive and hypertensive subjects. *Clin Sci Mol Med* 51:681, 1976

Renal and Electrolyte Alterations during Exercise

ARNOLD R. EISER, M.D.,
CHARLES SWARTZ, M.D.

Renal function and electrolyte balance during exercise may mimic pathologic states, represent supernormal function, or exemplify normal physiology. This chapter will examine the relationships between kidney function, electrolyte homeostasis, and exercise.

RENAL HEMODYNAMICS DURING EXERCISE

In the normal resting state, 20 percent of the total cardiac output perfuses the kidneys. With physical exertion, the renal perfusion is diminished as blood is shunted from the splanchnic circulation to the exercising muscles. Renal plasma flow as measured by clearance of paraaminohippurate (PAH) is decreased proportionately with increasing strenuousness of the exercise until the maximum pulse is obtained.[1] At this level of maximum exertion, renal plasma flow is decreased approximately 50 percent from the resting level. After heavy supine exercise, the renal plasma flow returns to normal within one hour.

Although renal plasma flow is decreased 50 percent during and immediately subsequent to heavy exercise, the reduction in the glomerular filtration rate is only on the order of 30 percent. As a consequence, filtration fraction is increased to approximately 25 percent. This relative preservation of glomerular filtration is apparently accomplished by efferent arteriolar vasoconstriction. This alteration in the renal microcirculation may have consequences on the kidney in exercise other than those on the glomerular filtration rate. It may be an important factor in the mechanism of exercise proteinuria, as will be detailed later.

The decrease in the glomerular filtration rate is maximal during exercise of moderate intensity and, unlike renal plasma flow, does not correlate with heart rate. The state of hydration of the exercising subject can modify the decrease in glomerular filtration rate during exercise, with dehydration further reducing glomerular filtration rate.

With sustained repetitive exercise, such as marathon training, a new phase of alteration of the glomerular filtration rate occurs after the initial decline. Beginning at the end of a week of heavy physical exertion, the glomerular filtration rate increases to levels 20 percent above resting normal.[2] This increase coincides with an increase in total body water and plasma volume. A causal relationship between increased plasma volume and the increase in the glomerular filtration rate probably exists, although other non-volume factors, such as a neurogenic mechanism, may also play a part in the increase of the glomerular filtration rate.

ANTIDIURESIS DURING EXERCISE

The urine flow rate decreases during strenuous exercise such as cross country skiing or marathon running, frequently falling below 0.5 ml a minute.[1,3] The magnitude of antidiuresis not only depends upon the degree of exertion but also on the state of hydration of the exercising subject. There is marked individual variation in the decrease in urine flow.

Four factors which apparently underlie the phenomenon of antidiuresis during exercise are decreased free water clearance, increased sodium reabsorption, decreased osmolar clearance, and decreased glomerular filtration rate. The factor which correlates best with diminished urine flow is the reduction in free water clearance.[4] It has been suggested that enhanced antidiuretic hormone (ADH) release and/or production underlies the decrease in free water clearance. Enhanced ADH may be elicited by neurogenic factors as well as the hyperosmolality and hypovolemia which develop during exercise.

Increased sodium reabsorption is a second factor in antidiuresis during exercise. Reduction in urine sodium excretion occurs briefly after the onset of heavy exercise. As will be discussed below, it appears to occur as a result of both renin–aldosterone activation as well as other mechanisms. The decrease in osmolar clearance which occurs during exercise is not only due to the decrease in urine sodium excretion but also to the decrease in the concentration of urea, phosphate, and chloride.[5] This impaired concentrating ability may be the result of impaired delivery of solute out of the proximal tubule as proximal reabsorption increases for several solutes. The fourth factor in the reduction in urine flow during prolonged heavy exercise is the reduction in the glomerular filtration rate. Although this is not always evident in the early stages of exercise, there is a significant correlation of GFR decrease in urine flow during prolonged exercise and associated dehydration.[1]

SODIUM BALANCE DURING EXERCISE

The net sodium balance during exercise is predominantly a function of sodium loss through sweat and urine since minimal intake generally occurs during exercise. As mentioned above, reduction in urine sodium excretion occurs briefly after the onset of heavy exercise. Although renin mediated aldosterone elevation has been documented in exercise[3,11,12] and most probably is a factor in enhanced sodium reabsorption, the rapidity of onset of antinatriuresis at a time before aldosterone elevation can be detected suggests an alternate mechanism is acting. Brod has suggested that a neural mechanism mediates this rapid increase in tubular sodium reabsorption.[6]

The sodium concentration of sweat varies with the rate of sweat production. Although levels of sweat sodium concentration approximate 20 mEq/L at basal condition, with maximal sweat flow rate sodium concentration reaches 50 mEq/L.[3] Hence the main route of sodium loss during heavy exercise is through enhanced sweating. However, even when dehydration during exercise is as much as six percent, the reduction in total interstitial sodium is substantially less then the reduction in interstitial water.[7] As a consequence, the serum sodium concentration rises on an average of 6 mEq/L.[9] Sodium concentration within exercising muscle cell water is unchanged.[7]

CHANGES IN TOTAL BODY WATER DURING EXERCISE

Acute Changes

The quantative changes in total body water during exercise are a complex combination of transmembrane movement as well as net water loss to the environment. With initiation of heavy exercise, water moves out of the vascular space into the active muscle cell, as demonstrated by muscle biopsy techniques.[9] Tissue hyperosmolality generated by active metabolism initiates this movement of water out of the interstitium and plasma.[7] The plasma volume is decreased and plasma osmolality is increased early in exercise. This decline plateaus within the first half hour of exercise, however, apparently as a result of the increased plasma osmolality. Further water losses are then derived from interstitial and/or intracellular spaces. At a level of approximately six percent dehydration as measured by weight loss, the plasma osmolality will rise an average of 20 mOsm/L.[7] At levels of dehydration of three percent, the bulk of the water loss comes from the interstitial space.[7] At greater levels of dehydration, the intracellular space becomes the major compartment for water loss. Some of this water is released during the process of glycolysis while some is produced from oxidative reactions.

Chronic Changes

In chronic, repetitive heavy exertion such as marathon training, alterations occur in plasma volume, total body water, and total body sodium that are the opposite of those which occur during the acute phase of exercise. After a week of heavy training, total body sodium, total body water, and plasma volume are increased above resting values.[3] This effect persists for several days after the cessation of exercise. This hypervolemia is the factor responsible for the so-called "athlete's anemia" since hemodilution of the red cell mass does occur.

POTASSIUM BALANCE IN EXERCISE

Potassium homeostasis during exercise involves several mechanisms involving the kidneys, sweat glands, and transcellular movement. In mild exercise, a slight increase in urine potassium excretion is observed, while during brief heavy exercise diminished potassium excretion occurs.[1] During prolonged athletic training, several environmental factors affect potassium balance. Reduction of potassium in the diet during training results in a decrease of urinary potassium excretion, although a moderate potassium body deficit may develop (approximately 70 mEq in four days).[3] In addition, potassium restriction per se will lead to a decrease in urine flow rate during exercise.[3] Reduction of urinary potassium excretion occurs despite the elevation of circulating aldosterone levels, which by itself would favor potassium excretion.

Knochel offers evidence that heavy physical training in a hot, humid climate leads to significant abnormality of potassium homeostasis. He demonstrated using a K^{42} method that subjects training under hot, humid conditions developed reduced total body potassium when compared with similar trainees in a cooler climate.[2] The trainees in the hot climate developed total body potassium deficits of approximately 500 mEq. Potassium efflux from active muscle cells has been demonstrated by muscle biopsy techniques to occur early in acute exercise. Much of the average 13 percent rise in serum potassium concentration, however,[8] can be accounted for by the contraction of the plasma volume as a result of the loss of plasma water. The rise in serum potassium after a marathon run is on the order of 0.5 mEq/L. The report of Makechnie, however, that serum potassium rose to 7.2 mEq/L after a 50 mile run[10] suggests that potentially fatal hyperkalemia may develop in the most severe forms of physical exertion.

ALTERATIONS IN OTHER SERUM CATIONS

In contrast to sodium and potassium, serum magnesium levels are decreased after prolonged heavy exercise by a mean of approximately 0.4 mEq/L.[8] Most of the loss of magnesium from the body during exercise is through increased quantities of sweat. Magnesium concentration in sweat approximates 4.5 mEq/L and does not vary with the rate of sweat production.[3] In addition, a 12 percent reduction in muscle magnesium concentration has been observed and denotes efflux of magnesium out of muscle cells.[3] Changes in serum magnesium during exercise do not appear to be of the magnitude that would have clinical importance.

Serum calcium concentration is unchanged after heavy exertion.[8] This lack of change in serum concentration probably reflects concomitant hemoconcentration and moderate calcium losses in urine and sweat. The concentration of calcium in sweat actually decreases as the quantity of sweat produced increases.[3]

THE RENIN ANGIOTENSIN SYSTEM IN EXERCISE

Several studies[3,11,12,13,14] have demonstrated that plasma renin activity is significantly elevated during exercise. This has been demonstrated not only during prolonged heavy exercise in the erect posture but also during brief exercise in the supine position.[14] Plasma renin and aldosterone levels rise after brief heavy exercise with both the rise in plasma aldosterone and plasma renin activity being approximately twice control values.[11] The elevation in plasma aldosterone may persist for several hours to several days depending on the duration of exercise. The maximum for the plasma renin activity is reached shortly after cessation of exercise.

The mechanism of renin activation during exertion has been the subject of some study. The administration of ethacrynic acid during supine exercise increased plasma renin activity over exercising controls.[12] This tends to contradict the thesis that renin released during exercise was a response to diminished sodium delivery to the distal tubule. Administration of dihydralazine which minimizes renal vasoconstriction did not diminish exercise-induced plasma renin activity enhancement.[1] Hence, renal vasoconstriction per se is not likely to be a factor initiating renin activity elevation. Some evidence does exist that renin elevation of exercise was mediated by autonomic nervous system mechanisms. The administration of ganglionic blockers prevent renin elevation from occurring in exercising rats.[15] Furthermore, it has been shown that exercising humans have prominent rises in plasma norepinephrine levels as well as plasma renin levels.[13] This data is by no means conclusive but suggests that autonomic nervous system may mediate exercise-induced renin release. The rapid time course of the elevation of renin is consistent with such a neural mechanism.

PROTEINURIA RELATED TO EXERCISE

The occurrence of increased urinary excretion of protein during exercise has been known for a century, yet the etiology of this phenomenon remains uncertain. Castenfors describes total protein excretion after prolonged heavy exercise rising threefold to 150 mg/gram of creatinine excreted.[16] The magnitude of proteinuria during exercise is small. Only about 20 percent of exercising subjects tested reach a level of proteinuria that can be detected by usual clinical tests. After short, heavy exertion, protein excretion returns to normal within an hour, while after prolonged exercise proteinuria persists as long as ten hours.[16]

The analysis of the composition of the protein excreted in the urine during exercise reveals that albumin accounts for approximately 45 percent while the remainder consist of alpha, beta, and gamma globulins. The average molecular weight of the protein excreted is on the order of 50 to 60,000 daltons. There is a great deal of individual variation in the protein excretion, and in a few cases the predominant protein excreted were globulins.

The occurrence of proteinuria during exercise could be the result of either (1) enhanced glomerular filtration of protein; (2) diminished reabsorption by the proximal tubule; or (3) enhanced secretion of protein distally. The composition of the constituents of urinary protein in exercise is consistent with an origin as filtered plasma protein. While Tamm-Horsfall protein has been observed to be increased,[17] this increase is too small to account for the proteinuria of exercise.

The integrity of proximal tubular reabsorptive function during strenuous exercise has been assessed by measurement of excretion of glucose, alpha amino acids, and the low molecular weight enzyme, ribonuclease. These substances are normally reabsorped in significant quantities in the proximal tubule, and their normal excretion rate during exercise support the notion that proximal tubular reabsorption is intact at this time.[16]

The observed increase in plasma renin activity during exercise raises the possibility that alterations in their renin angiotensin system may be a factor in exercise proteinuria. Castenfors was unable to demonstrate a correlation between urine protein excretion and plasma renin activity during exercise, however, although such a relation was present before exercise was begun.[16] This apparent inconsistency may be understood if renin angiotensin activation is but one of several factors that modify renal hemodynamic changes during exercise and indirectly alter protein excretion. Norepinephrine and other vasoconstrictive substances may contribute to hemodynamic changes and proteinuria in the exercising human.

Perhaps the mechanism of exercise proteinuria may best be understood in light of the recent knowledge of the hydrodynamic forces across the glomerular membrane. Studies by Brenner[18] and Bohrer[19] show that when there is an elevation of the filtration fraction, the glomerulary–capillary flow rate can be diminished while the single nephron glomerular filtration rate is unchanged, and that such changes can result in an increase in the concentration of plasma protein along the glomerular wall. Enhanced glomerular passage of plasma protein can subsequently occur without an alteration in membrane permeability characteristics or structure.

In fact, angiotensin II has been shown to produce proteinuria in an experimental model.[19] In addition, a number of other vasoactive substances which can elevate filtration fraction may also result in increased protein excretion.

Exercise proteinuria may be the result of increased production of vasoactive substances, including angiotensin, which alter glomerular microhemodynamics and raise filtration fraction. Proteinuria then ensues through alterations of convective forces rather than a change in the glomerular membrane.

RHABDOMYOLYSIS AND ACUTE NEPHROPATHY AS A CONSEQUENCE OF SEVERE EXERCISE

Knochel and associates[20] and other investigators[21] have offered evidence that exercise in a hot, humid environment is a significant cause of rhabdomyolysis and acute renal failure. This is an unusual occurrence in athletes and appears to be confined to poorly trained subjects suddenly undergoing heavy exertion particularly in hot, humid climates.

A fundamental concept in the pathogenesis of heat–exercise induced rhabdomyolysis is the occurrence of potassium deficiency. As noted above, potassium deficits may develop during heavy training in hot, humid climates. Knochel, in experiments with laboratory dogs, shows that the efflux of potassium out of contracting muscle cells appears to provide an important vasodilatory effect on those vessels supplying the active muscles.[22] Furthermore, the study showed that potassium deficiency diminished the potassium release and blunted the increase in blood flow and produced necrosis of muscle cells. If an analogous mechanism is functional in the human, hypokalemia and potassium depletion may render exercising subjects, particularly prone to muscle injury.

Potassium deficiency may mediate or predispose to muscle injury by an additional mechanism. The muscles of potassium-depleted laboratory animals show an abnormal glycogen content. Since glycogen is an important fuel source for the exerting muscle, a glycogen deficiency may predispose muscle cells to injury during exercise.[23]

When muscle cells lyse, myoglobin is liberated into the circulation and subsequently filtered at the glomerulus. While myoglobin per se is nontoxic to renal tubular cells, it is metabolized to hematin, a breakdown product toxic to tubular cells.[23] The conversion of myoglobin to the hematin byproduct is enhanced in an acidic environment. The urine of the exercising subject usually has a pH of less than 5.0 and hence will be predisposed to the conversion of hematin.

Rhabdomyolysis may result in the release of yet another nephrotoxic substance into the circulation. As has long been noted, serum uric acid levels can be markedly elevated after exercise.[24] Injured muscle cells release purines into the circulation and the uric acid is the metabolic end product. Since uric acid must compete with lactic acid for excretion and the lactate levels will be elevated during exercise, impaired excretion of uric acid combines with increased production of uric acid to lead to dangerously high levels of uric acid in the renal interstitial fluid. Furthermore, the acid pH of the urine would favor precipitation of uric acid in the tubule and interstitium. This can produce acute renal failure if the uric acid levels of the interstitium exceed critical levels.

The occurrence of acute rhabdomyolysis in acute renal failure is exceptionally uncommon in the well-trained athlete. It may be that the enhanced glomerular filtration previously described is a factor that provides a measure of protection from these potentially nephrotoxic substances released by muscle injury. In addition, the well trained athlete may sustain significantly less muscle injury during the same degree of exertion. The clinical syndrome of exercise-induced acute rhabdomyolysis and acute renal failure is predominantly limited to untrained subjects, such as military recruits, who suddenly undergo heavy exertion. A hot, humid climate is also an important predisposing factor for this clinical phenomenon.

EXERCISE HEMOGLOBINURIA

It is almost a century since Fleischer described hemoglobinuria occurring subsequent to a prolonged march.[25] Since then, several cases of hemoglobinuria occurring subsequent to running or marching for a prolonged distance on hard surfaces have been reported. Repetitive traumatic exercise of the upper extremities, such as karate or congo drumming, have also been reported to result in hemoglobinuria.[26] The syndrome of exercise hemoglobinuria is characterized by the voiding of urine darkened by its content of hemoglobin subsequent to the inciting exercise. In addition, evidence of intravascular hemolysis is present, namely elevated serum-free hemoglobin, methemalbuminemia, and decreased serum haptoglobin. In addition, the urinalysis frequently reveals granular casts suggesting that some tubular injury may be sustained. Cases of acute renal failure resulting from exercise hemoglobinuria are exceptional but have been reported.[27]

There have been some studies of exercise hemoglobinuria which support the thesis that hemolysis is the result of mechanical trauma to circulating erythrocytes while they circulate through the plantar vessels during hard impact on hard surfaces. Davidson compared the hemolysis of blood from both patients suffering from exercise hemoglobinuria and control subjects.[28] The blood from both the control and patient groups showed greater hemolysis when running was done on a hard surface, although blood from the patient suffering from exercise hemoglobinuria showed relatively greater hemolysis on both surfaces. Spicer[29] showed that cases suffering from march hemoglobinuria had a low grade hemolytic state with the minor trauma of normal activity. Routine laboratory tests of erythrocyte fragility in these patients are normal, however. A particular susceptibility of erythrocyte to hemolysis cannot be excluded. It should be noted that soft surfaces as well as the use of properly padded soles can substantially reduce the occurrence of exercise hemoglobinuria in susceptible individuals.

CONCLUSIONS

The changes that occur in renal function and fluid and electrolyte balance in acute exercise appear to be counterbalanced by changes that occur during the repetitive heavy exertion which occurs during physical training. The fall in glomerular filtration, total body water, and total body sodium appears to be counterbalanced by the rise of these factors during repetitive exercise. These adaptations appear to be a fundamental part of the "training" process.

Alterations in the renin aldosterone angiotensin system appear to be part of the physiological adaptation to exercise but may also account for some of the "abnormalities"—such as proteinuria—seen in subjects undergoing heavy exertion. Maintenance of relatively normal water and electrolyte balance appears to be important in prevention of untoward effects on the kidney of heavy exercise, namely rhabdomyolosis and subsequent acute renal failure.

Exercise hemoglobinuria appears to be related to traumatic sheering forces of hard surfaces, but may be confined to particularly susceptible individuals.

REFERENCES

1. Castenfors J: Renal function during exercise. *Acta Physiol Scand* 70:(Suppl 293)1, 1967
2. Knochel JP: Potassium deficiency during training in the heat. *Ann NY Acad Sci* 170:175, 1977
3. Costill DL: Sweating: its composition and effects on body fluids. *Ann NY Acad Sci* 170:160, 1977
4. Castenfors J: Renal clearance and urinary sodium and potassium excretion during supine exercise in normal subjects. *Acta Physiol Scand* 70:207, 1967
5. Refsan, NE, Stroinic SB: Relationship between urine flow, glomerular filtration and uri-

nary solute concentration during prolonged heavy exercise. *Scand J Clin Lab Invest* 35:775, 1975

6.   Brod J: *Die Nieren, Physiologie, Klinische Physiologie und Klinik.* Berlin, Veb. Verlag Volk und Gesundheit, 1964

7.   Costill DL, Cote R, Fink W: Muscle water electrolytes following varied levels of dehydration in man. *J Appl Physiol* 40(1):6, 1976

8.   Rose LI, Carroll DR, Lore SL, et al: Serum electrolyte changes after marathon running. *J Appl Physiol* 29(4):449, 1970

9.   Bergstan J: Muscle electrolyte in man. Determination by neurton activate analysis on needle biopsy specimen. *Scand J Clin Lab Invest* 18:16, 1962

10. McKechni JK, Leary WP, Jourbet SM: Some electrocardiographic and biochemical changes recorded in marathon runners. *S Afr Med J* 41:722, 1967

11. Bozovic L, Castenfors J, Piscator M: Effects of prolonged, heavy exercise on urinary protein excretion and plasma renin activity. *Acta Physiol Scand* 70:143, 1967

12. Castenfors J: Effect of ethacrynic acid on plasma renin activity during supine exercise in normal subjects. *Acta Physiol Scand* 70:215, 1967

13. Chodahons K, Nazas K, Mocial B, et al: Plasma catecholamines and renin activity in response to exercise in patients with essential hypertension. *Clin Sci Mol Med* 49:511, 1975

14. Collier JG, Keddie J, Robinson BT: Plasma renin activity during and after dynamic and status exercise. *Cardiovasc Res* 9:323, 1975

15. Bozovic L, Castenfors J: Effect of ganglionic blocking on plasma renin activity in exercising and pain-stressed rats. *Acta Physiol Scand* 71:253, 1967

16. Castenfors J, Mossfeld F, Piscator M: Effect of prolonged heavy exercise on renal function and urinary protein excretion. *Acta Physiol Scand* 70:194, 1967

17. Patel R: Urinary casts in exercise. *Aust Ann Med* 13:170, 1964

18. Brennan BM, Bohrer MP, Boylis C, et al: Determinants of glomerular permeability: insight derived from observation in vivo. *Kidney Int* 12:229, 1977

19. Bohrer MP, Dean WM, Robertson CR, et al: Mechanism of angiotensin II—induced protein in the rat. *Am J Physiol* 2:F13, 1977

20. Knochel JP, Dotin NH, Haburger RJ: Heart stress, exercise, and muscle effects on urate metabolism and renal function. *Ann Intern Med* 81:321, 1974

21. Schrier RW, Henderson HS, Tischer CC, et al: Nephropathy associated with heart stress and exercise. *Ann Int Med* 67:356, 1967

22. Knochel JP, Schlein EM: On the mechanism of rhabdomyolosis in potassium depletion. *J Clin Invest* 51:1750, 1972

23. Knochel JP, Carter, NW: The role of muscle cell injury in the pathogenesis of acute renal failure after exercise. *Kidney Intern* 10:558, 1976

24. Cathcart EP, Kernanny EL, Leather JB: On the origin of endogenous uric acid. *Q J Med* 1:416, 1908

25. Fleischer R: Ueber eine nene form von hemoglobinuria bein menshen. *Klin Wochenschr,* 47:691, 1881

26. Caro XJ, Sathetlard PW, Mitchel DB, et al: Traumatic hemoglobinuria associated with congo drums. *West J Med* 123:141, 1975

27. Pollard TD, Weiss IW: Acute tubular necrosis in a patient with march hemoglobinuria. *N Eng J Med* 283:803, 1970

28. Davidson RJ: Exertional hemoglobinuria: a report of three cases with studies on the hemolytic mechanism. *J Clin Path* 17:536, 1964

29. Spicer AJ: Studies on March hemoglobinuria. *B Med J* 1:115, 1970

Drugs and Exercise

DAVID T. LOWENTHAL, M.D., WARREN CHERNICK, D.Sc., MITCHELL S. WHITEMAN

It is a great misfortune that pharmacological agents, henceforth referred to as drugs, must permeate the environment of athletic competition. Because of this problem the International Olympic Committee has mandated the medical commission to test for psychomotor stimulants, sympathomimetic amines, narcotic analgesics, miscellaneous central nervous system stimulants, anabolic steroids, and alcohol (see Table 1). These drugs are consumed by presumably healthy competitors. They are taken with the presumption that they will enhance athletic performance. Much research has been performed in the areas of the psychomotor stimulants, anabolic steroids, and alcohol which refutes the contention that these drugs have a salutary effect on athletic performance. One does not have to be athletically inclined to appreciate the negative features of chronic narcotic addiction. This paper will address several of these categories and in addition briefly refer to an entity called "Drug Exercise In-

TABLE 1 Categories of Drugs Tested for by the Medical Commission of the International Olympic Committee

Psychomotor (CNS) Stimulants—amphetamines, cocaine
Sympathomimetic amines—ephedrine
Nacotic analgesics—heroin, morphine, methadon
Miscellaneous CNS stimulants—nikethamide, bemegride, pentylenetetrazol
Anabolic steroids
Alcohol

teractions" that may exist in patients who are exercising and consuming various categories of drugs which in this case would be referred to as medicines.

ANABOLIC STEROIDS

The Press sisters from the Soviet Union were the first athletes in Olympic competition (Melbourne, 1956) who were alleged to have been "primed" with androgenic agents. Twenty years later (Montreal, 1976) the International Olympic Committee (IOC) inaugurated tests for anabolic steroids when urine specimens were submitted for specific radioimmunoassay.[1,2] Prior to 1976 the IOC began testing for "doping" drugs at the winter and summer Olympic games of 1968.

Androgens have been given to victims of starvation and to debilitated patients with chronic disease to help induce a state of positive nitrogen balance. The anabolic steroids are less virilizing drugs and are used today by weight lifters, shot putters, discus throwers, wrestlers, and football players. The rationale for their use is that they enhance performance by increasing muscle mass, strength, and body weight, especially if consumed with a diet high in protein.[3-6] Since many of these studies were poorly controlled, there is ample evidence which negates these contentions.[7,8] Golding et al[9] have amply demonstrated no change in body weight or strength with dianabol, whether or not it is accompanied by high dietary protein. Casner[10] demonstrated that the increase in weight was due primarily to water retention.[4] Carefully controlled studies in male albino rats[11] found no change in body weight or performance, but did find an increase in SGOT with high doses of nandrolone deconate.

Several factors may account for the conflicting data. Testosterone is the only androgen capable of enhancing muscle mass, strength, and body weight. The type and degree of response to synthetic anabolic steroids depend largely on the age of the subject. Increased muscle strength occurs to a greater extent when the drugs are administered before puberty or after the age of 50, as a result of decreased testosterone production in both instances. The dosage of the drug and regularity with which it is administered also influence the results. The usual recommended dosage of methandrostenolone (Dianabol) is 10 mg per day for 6 to 12 weeks. This may be enormously exceeded (two to three times) by ill-advised athletes.[12,13] Is it any wonder that there is a conflict between subjective impressions of an increase in strength and the lack of confirmation by scientific evidence?

The adverse effects of anabolic steroids should suffice to warn athletes against their use. Most notable among these adverse effects are the following: hepatic dysfunction, including cirrhosis of the liver and hepato–cellular carcinoma (seen in aplastic anemia); decreased libido, testicular atrophy; gynecomastia; salt and water retention; and hypertension. Anabolic steroids may also cause premature closure of the epiphyses.[7,14]

In women, anabolic agents may produce such signs of virilization as beard, increased body hair, male escutcheon, increased musculature, and receding hair line. Amenorrhea and sterility are also noted. Therefore, anabolic steroids play no role in maintaining the health of the athlete and are of questionable benefit as aids to enhanced performance.[13]

ALCOHOL

Recently there has been a furor over the supposedly salutary effects of beer consumption during long-distance races, especially marathons (42 km). Felig et al[15] have demonstrated the dependence on free fatty acids for energy utilization during exercise in non-exercise inhibitors. Alcohol will raise the levels of circulating fatty acids but will also inhibit the oxidation for substrate utilization.[16,17] Indeed, since the metabolizing ethanol oxidizing system accounts for 20 to 30 percent of alcohol metabolism without generating any energy source, Lieber[16] has termed alcohol an "energy waster." From a caloric aspect, the alcohol plus an accumulation of reduced NADH (as a result of which hypoglycemia may occur) prevents gluconeogenesis.[16] The formation of lactate occurs under anaerobic conditions which exist initially during long-distance races and through the duration of a short sprint. As the runner proceeds, the lactate concentration decreases and aerobic metabolism supports the needs of the competitor.[15] Why, then, give beer or any alcoholic beverage under conditions of aerobic demand when glucose and fatty acids are what is needed and not lactate? Lactate accumulation secondary to alcohol will block uric acid secretion. In the state of volume contraction and renal hypoperfusion experienced by distance runners, uric acid retention with or without alcohol may be a consequence of muscle catabolism and may play a pathogenetic role in rhabdomyolysis.[18] (See Table 2.)

Assuming steady consumption of alcoholic beverage prior to and during a race, the metabolic consequences of alcohol ingestion are impaired gluconeogenesis and possibly hypoglycemia (especially, if glycogen depletion occurs during a marathon), hyperuricemia, an increase in free fatty acids, an increase in ketones, and lactate.[16]

TABLE 2   Metabolic Effects of Alcohol While at Rest

Increased blood lipids (due to depressed oxidation of FFA)
Increased serum lactate
Increased serum uric acid
Increased serum ketones
Decreased blood glucose (due to decreased gluconeogenesis)
Increased activity of smooth endoplasmic reticulum of liver resulting in:
    increased activity of drug metabolizing enzymes
    increased testosterone reductase, which causes an increase in testosterone catabolism
        resulting in decreased serum testosterone
Functional alterations in mitochondria result in an accumulation of acetaldehyde which can
    be toxic to brain, heart, and liver

Unfortunately, the hypermetabolic state of exercise will *not* accelerate the metabolism of alcohol,[19] and in fact the elimination of alcohol from the blood may be slow owing to lactate accumulation.[20]

Alcohol consumption will influence the metabolism of many drugs.[21] It can impair the breakdown or accelerate the elimination of various drugs by its influence on the microsomal oxidizing system. Alcohol can convert drugs to active or toxic metabolites (carbon tetrachloride).[16] Testosterone reductase activity is increased by alcohol, and this results in an increase in testosterone metabolism causing a decrease in plasma testosterone concentration (Table 3).[22]

During strenuous exercise, drugs which are depressant to any organ system must be avoided. Alcohol, in the form of beer, is now considered by some distance runners to be of help in enhancing performance. Thus, it is consumed with meals (during the carbohydrate loading period) and during the race.

The initial stimulation from alcohol may *not* be a result of catecholamine release but may be due to unrestrained activity of the lower centers of the brain which are released from the depression of the higher inhibitory control mechanisms.[23] Alcohol does nothing to increase mental or physical capabilities. The subjective sense of heightened performance, as determined by minor effects on respiration, circulation, and skeletal muscle activity, may be due to a lessened awareness of fatigue.

Mild stimulants, such as amphetamines, methylphenidate, caffeine, and nicotine not only have a limited degree of pharmacological antagonism to the depressing effects of alcohol, but also have a synergistic effect in increasing the deterioration of performance with smaller doses of alcohol.[21]

Trained runners utilize free fatty acids (FFA) for energy sources, a reflection of aerobic metabolism. Untrained runners depend on carbohydrate for substrate.[15,24] In so doing, the low FFA in the untrained individual is associated with high serum lactate concentrations, a manifestation of anaerobic metabolism.

The skeletal muscle of trained athletes responds to increased plasma concentrations of FFA by increasing the activity of the cytochrome c system and the rate of oxidation of FFA.[24] The consumption of alcohol is related to an increase in lactate, a depression of FFA oxidation, and, consequently, hypertriglyceridemia.[16] Coincidentally, carbohydrate loading stimulates insulin release. Insulin inhibits lipolysis.[15] Thus, the fashionable practice of carbohydrate loading and beer drinking can lead to poor FFA utilization even in the trained athlete. Whether the caffeine[25] component of various beverages may make them more sensible potions (if one in fact needs an oral boost to ensure better pedal performance) depends on one's cardiac sensitivity to the arrhythmogenic effects of caffeine.

TABLE 3   Effects of Alcohol on GI Tract While (at Rest)

Impairment to intestinal transport of vitamins, minerals
Decrease hepatocyte uptake and storage of absorbed nutrients
Impaired conversion of food stuffs into active metabolites, i.e. thiamine

Cardiovascular Effects of Alcohol

Alcohol is a myocardial depressant (Table 4). Regan[26,27] has demonstrated impaired myocardial performance when dogs are given alcohol acutely and when alcoholic man is given alcohol both *acutely* and *chronically*. When compared to glucose and saline controls, alcohol caused a progressive fall in stroke work as left ventricular end diastolic pressure increased. In chronic alcoholics, angiotension infusion impairs the anticipated rise in stroke work that is observed in nonalcoholic controls. This may reflect underlying alcoholic cardiomyopathy. Biochemical evidence of myocardial necrosis (reversible) has been observed in both dog and man by an increase in coronary sinus potassium, phosphate, and serum glutamic oxalacetic transaminase. In dogs, triglyceride accumulation in the myocardium indicating an alcohol–related depression of FFA oxidation has been observed.

Conway[28] confirmed the data of Regan et al in eight patients with coronary heart disease. Despite the administration of one-third to one-half less alcohol in these patients, Conway demonstrated a decrease in MAP at rest and at exercise (through 350 kpm/min), a fall in cardiac output (significant only at 150 kpm/min), and no change in peripheral resistance. Left ventricular work and time tension index fell. Electrocardiographic changes associated with ischemia and angina following alcohol during exercise was experienced in five of eight patients. The fact that peripheral resistance did not change confirms the studies of Gillespie[29] and Fewings et al,[30] who demonstrated an increase in only skin blood flow with either *no* increase or an actual decrease in muscle blood flow in nonischemic and ischemic upper and lower extremities.

TABLE 4   Effects of Alcohol on Cardiovascular System (Acute and Chronic Dosing)

Decrease in stroke work with concomitant increase in LVEDP, especially in subjects with hypertension, coronary artery disease, and chronic alcohol ingestion. Cardiac output and heart rate may rise in healthy, young subjects given alcohol and stressed.

Alcohol increases total peripheral vascular resistance.

No overall change in mean arterial blood pressure.

Alcohol increases blood flow to skin but decreases blood flow to skeletal muscle.

Increase in sweating during exercise following alcohol consumption.

Early, significant increase in heart rate with heavy work load following alcohol.

Increased total and myocardial oxygen uptake (at rest) after small doses of ethanol given by mouth or intravenously.

In subjects with grossly normal cardiac function, the acute effect of alcohol on coordination will be more evident than electrocardiographic changes associated with exercise. Conversely, underlying heart disease due to hypertension or coronary artery disease will manifest the alcohol effect by reducing cardiac output, and consequently the exercise response will be reduced.[28] If a patient or a normal subject consumes large amounts of alcohol, even if no underlying heart disease is recognized, abnormalities may be observed on the EKG. Healthy, young subjects given 81 grams of 90 percent proof bourbon (dosage was not on a weight basis) showed an increase in cardiac output and in heart rate within 30 minutes after the dose when exercised for *only* five minutes at 100 watts.[31]

Finally, the hemodynamic responses in healthy, young men differ according to whether the work load is submaximal or maximal. Heart rate and cardiac output at rest and during submaximal exercise was higher after ingestion of alcohol whereas the total arteriovenous oxygen difference and the total peripheral resistance decreased. During maximal work, pulmonary ventilation was reduced but the circulatory response was not affected by alcohol. The enigma is why healthy men exhibit hemodynamic changes with submaximal stress when with maximal workloads these cardiac parameters are unchanged from control. It is likely that motivational and other sympathetically derived compensatory factors override the effects of alcohol during maximal stress.[32,33]

Renal Effects of Alcohol

During exercise, glomerular filtration and renal blood flow decrease.[34] Alcohol may improve renal hemodynamics by inhibiting vasopressin (ADH), but the positive effect is transient and can be associated with an annoying diuresis which may occur at a crucial period during a distance race.

In addition, alcohol can decrease muscle blood flow by increasing peripheral resistance.[29,30,35] Just when the demand for FFA utilization for energy is maximal, alcohol consumption will prevent its oxidation, and theoretically the decrease in flow during demand can result in myoglobin release. Klatskin[36] has demonstrated that the direct toxic effect of alcohol on skeletal muscle results in muscle necrosis, which may ultimately lead to myoglobin nephrotoxicity, if exercise-induced renal hypoperfusion is present. Swartz and Eiser have reviewed the subject of rhabdomyolysis in this text (see pp. 150–151).

Musculo-Skeletal Effects of Alcohol

The effects of alcohol on the musculo-skeletal system are confined primarily to skeletal muscle. Rhabdomyolysis is a known occurrence which has been alluded to above under the renal effects of alcohol and has also been addressed in the section on diuretic usage in the hypertensive athlete with regard to hypokalemia.

AMPHETAMINES AND RELATED STIMULANTS

It is well known that amphetamines and related stimulants are consumed in large dosages by professional athletes, but their effects are controversial.[37,38] Their original medical indication was for weight control, but they are no longer recommended for this purpose. They have been found more useful, however, in the treatment of narcolepsy and hyperactivity in children. The customary dosage of benzadrine or dexadrine is 15 mg, but, according to a recent publication in *Sports Illustrated,* professional football players may consume 150 mgs of amphetamines per game.[39] The short-term effects of the average dose (15 mg) (Table 5) include a decrease in appetite, a dramatic increase in alertness and confidence, an elevation in mood, an improvement in physical performance and concentration, and a decrease in the sense of fatigue; yet associated with this is the feeling of anxiousness or of generally being on "a high."

TABLE 5   Amphetamines: Short-term Effects of Average Dose (15 mg)

Decrease in appetite
Increase in alertness and confidence
Improved physical performance and concentration
Lessened sense of fatigue
Feeling of anxiousness

On the other hand, the short-term effects of large amounts (150 mg) (Table 6) of amphetamines are profound overstimulation, acute paranoia, agitation, insomnia, fear, irritability, a sharp rise in blood pressure, fever, chest pain, headaches, chills, stomach distress, rhabdomyolysis due to a direct toxic effect of the amphetamine on the skeletal muscle, and, rarely, death. For those who depend on the long-term effects of chronic abuse, tolerance develops rapidly. Psychological dependence on and preoccupation with these drugs is customary. The user may suffer from paranoia, auditory and visual hallucinations, and formication. Withdrawal syndrome is very well appreciated. It would be senseless to belabor the issue that amphetamines are in fact deleterious to the athlete as well as to the nonathlete when improperly consumed.

Cocaine has an effect similar to the amphetamines, but the subjective symptoms of the drug are more intensely felt. This may be due to the fact that the way in which cocaine is taken results in a more rapid onset of action and a shorter duration of effect

TABLE 6   Amphetamines: Short-term Effects of Large Dose (150 mg)

Acute paranoia, agitation, fear
Irritability
Sharp rise in blood pressure
Fever, chills, Headache
Chest pain
Rarely, death

for the average dosage. Short-term effects of large amounts of cocaine are similar to amphetamines, however; an initial tachycardia may become slow and weak and the tachypnea may become shallow and slow.

DRUG–EXERCISE INTERACTIONS IN PATIENTS
(Table 7)

Diuretics

This subject has been addressed in the section on hypertension and exercise in this text (see pp. 136–137). Diuretic therapy forms the cornerstone of antihypertensive regimens. There is in general no need to give supplemental potassium when a diuretic is given alone. During the summer months, however, this may be necessary because, as Knochel[40] has described, aldosterone affects the sweating mechanism and results in a loss of potassium not only through the urine but through the sweat. Thus, potassium supplementation may be necessary. In addition, the extracellular fluid volume which is already contracted from chronic diuretic administration may need supplementation of salt, water, and potassium during periods of exercise during the hot summer months.

Digitalis

Patients taking only digitalis may not need potassium supplementation. During exercise, especially in the hot summer months when potassium loss through the skin may increase, there may be a requirement for supplemental potassium administration to prevent the arrhythmogenic effects of hypokalemia.

Antiarrhythmic Drugs

In general, patients with arrhythmias who are being treated with drugs such as procainamide, quinidine, phenytoin, and disopyramide (Norpace®) may not be able to perform strenuous forms of exercise owing to significant cardiovascular disease. In

TABLE 7   Drug–Exercise Interactions in Patients

Diuretics
Digitalis
Antiarrhythmics
β-blockers
Cortico-steroids
Insulin and oral hypoglycemics
Anticholinergics
Antiasthmatics
Oral contraceptives

addition, antiarrhythmics may speed conduction through the AV node, and exercise in association with the antiarrhythmics may set up the patient for significant tachyarrhythmias.

Beta-Blockers

This subject has been addressed in the hypertension section. Beta-adrenergic blockade curbs the subject's normal hemodynamic responses to exercise. The subject cannot develop an increase in heart rate or in cardiac output to supply the exercising muscle with the necessary increase in blood flow. In fact, these drugs increase peripheral vascular resistance and thus negate the normal findings of a decrease in resistance.

Corticosteroids

This class of drugs, when taken systemically, may have an effect that encompasses adverse responses to the cardiovascular system, metabolic–endocrine system, and renal function. A complete review of corticosteroid pharmacology is beyond the scope of this particular discussion, but suffice it to say that pharmacological doses of corticosteroids may be deleterious to the exercising individual, especially with regard to their effects on potassium, bone, and skeletal muscle.

Insulin and Oral Hypoglycemics

This subject has been addressed by Drs. Felig and Koivisto with regard to the effects of insulin on the exercising diabetic and nondiabetic. (See chapter by Drs. Felig and Koivisto, this text.)

Anticholinergics

These drugs tend to have a direct pharmacological effect on patients who are not exercising by causing dryness of the mouth as well as impaired sweating and urinary retention. Thus, fluid balance can certainly be altered in the person who is strenuously exercising, especially during the hot summer days. Therefore, caution must be taken to supply extra quantities of fluids for patients who require anticholinergic medication.

Antiasthmatics

The asthmatic patient has received particular attention with regard to exercise physiology. He has even been the subject of the withdrawal of an Olympic Gold Medal.[41] Asthmatic patients require bronchodilator therapy. Some bronchodilators, such as isoproteronol and ephedrine, have a profound effect on the cardiovascular system because they are nonspecific. Recent evidence shows that terbutaline and metoproterenol have a more specific effect on bronchial smooth muscle and a less specific effect on cardiovascular function.[42,43] Thus, these two drugs are acceptable in international competition and have been approved by the International Olympic Committee for being administered to asthmatic competitors. Exercise-induced asthma may be treated by these drugs as well as with cromolyn sodium. This subject has been reviewed in greater detail by Dr. Allan Freedman in this symposium (see pp. 176–177).

Oral Contraceptives

See chapter by Drs. Oaks and Lowenthal.

ASSAY METHODOLOGY

Samples of blood, urine, and parotid saliva (obtained by suction from Stenson's duct) may be obtained for detection and quantification of the drug categories shown in Table 1. Once collected the sample may be assayed by spectrophotometric, spectrophotofluorometric, chromatographic (thin layer, gas liquid, high pressure liquid) and more conventional radioimmunoassay techniques.

REFERENCES

1. Percy EC: Athletic aids: fact or fiction. *Can Med Assoc J* 117:601, 1977
2. Dugal R, Dupuis C, Bertrand MJ: Radioimmunoassay of anabolic steroids: an evaluation of three antisera for the detection of anabolic steroids in biological fluids. *Br J Sports Med* 11:162, 1977
3. Tahmindjis AJ: The use of anabolic steroids by athletes to increase body weight and strength. *Med J Aust* 1:991, 1976
4. Johnson LC, Fisher G, Sylvester LJ, et al: Anabolic steroids: effect on strength, body weight, oxygen uptake and spermatogenesis upon mature males. *Med Sci Sports* 4:43, 1972
5. Johnson LC, O'Shea JP: Anabolic steroids—effects on strength development. *Science* 164:957, 1969
6. O'Shea JP, Winkler W: Biochemical and physical effects of an anabolic steroid in competitive swimmers and weight lifters. *Nutr Report Int'l* 6:351, 1970
7. Shepard RJ, Killinger D, Fried T: Responses to sustained use of anabolic steroids. *Br J Sports Med* 11:170, 1977
8. Hervey GR, Hutchinson I, Knibbs AV, et al: "Anabolic" effects of methandienone in men undergoing athletic training. *Lancet* 2:699, 1976
9. Golding LA, Freydinger JE, Fishel SS: The effect of an androgenic anabolic steroid and a protein supplement on size, strength, weight and body composition in athletes. *Proceedings of the 15th National Conference on the Medical Aspects of Sports.* Craig TT (ed): 1974, p 25
10. Casner SW, Early RG, Carlson BR: Anabolic steroid effects on body composition in normal young men. *J Sports Med Phys Fitness* 11:98, 1971
11. Young M, Crookshant HR, Ponder L: Effects of an anabolic steroid on selected parameters in male albino rats. *Res Q Am Assoc Health Phys Educ* 48:653, 1977

12. News and Comment. Anabolic Steroids: Doctors denounce them but athletes aren't listening. *Science* 176:1399, 1972
13. Darden E: Drugs and athletic performance: facts and fallacies. *Clinical Medicine* 79:25, 1972
14. Johnson FL, Feagler JR, Lerner KG: Association of adrenergic anabolic steroid therapy with development of hepatocellular carcinoma. *Lancet* 2:1273, 1972
15. Felig P, Wahren J: Fuel homeostasis in exercise. *N Engl J Med* 293:1078, 1975
16. Lieber CS: Pathogenesis and early diagnosis of alcoholic liver injury. *N Engl J Med* 298:888, 1978
17. Fleming CR, Higgins JA: Alcohol: nutrient and poison. *Ann Intern Med* 87:492, 1977
18. Knochel JP: Renal injury in muscle disease. in: *The Kidney in Systemic Disease.* New York, Wiley, 1976, p 129
19. Pawan GLS: Physical exercise and alcohol metabolism in man. *Nature* 218:966, 1968
20. Krebs HA, Cunningham DJC, Stubbs M, et al: Effect of ethanol on post-exercise lactacidemia. *Isr J Med Sci* 5:959, 1969
21. Seixas, FA: Alcohol and its drug interactions. *Ann Intern Med* 83:86, 1975
22. Gordon GG, Altman K, Southren AL, et al: Effect of alcohol (ethanol) administration on sex-hormone metabolism in normal man. *N Engl J Med* 295:793, 1976
23. Garlind T, Goldberg L, Graf A, et al: Effect of ethanol on circulatory, metabolic and neurohormonal function during muscular work in men. *Acta Pharmacol Toxicol* 17:106, 1960
24. Van Handel PJ, Sandel WR, Mole PA: Effects of Exogenous cytochrome c on respiratory capacity of heart and skeletal muscle. *Biochem Biophys Res Commun* 74:1213, 1977
25. Asmussen E, Boje O: The effect of alcohol and some drugs on the capacity for work. *Acta Physiol Scand* 15:109, 1948
26. Regan TJ, Weisse AB, Moschos CB, et al: The myocardial effects of acute and chronic usage of ethanol in man. *Trans Assoc Am Phys* 78:282, 1965
27. Regan TJ, Koroxenidis G, Moschos CB, et al: The acute metabolic and hemodynamic responses of the left ventricle to ethanol. *J Clin Invest* 45:270, 1966
28. Conway N: Haemodynamic effects of ethyl alcohol in patients with coronary heart disease. *Br Heart J* 30:368, 1968
29. Gillespie JA: Vasodilator properties of alcohol. *Br Med J* 2:274, 1967
30. Fewings JD, Hanna MJD, Walsh JA, et al: The effects of ethyl alcohol on the blood vessels of the hand and forearm in man. *Br J Pharmacol* 27:93, 1966
31. Riff DP, Jain AC, Doyle JT: Acute hemodynamic effects of ethanol on normal human volunteers. *Am Heart J* 78:592, 1969
32. Blomqvist G, Saltin B, Mitchell JH: Acute effects of ethanol ingestion on the response to submaximal and maximal exercise in man. *Circulation* XLII:463, 1970
33. Ikai Michio, Steinhaus AH: Some factors modifying the expression of human strength. *J Appl Physiol* 16:157, 1961
34. Castenfors J: Renal function during exercise. *Acta Physiol Scand* Suppl 293, Vol. 70, 1967
35. Graf K, Strom G: Effect of ethanol ingestion on arm blood flow in healthy young men at rest and during leg work. *Acta Pharmacol Toxicol* 17:115, 1960
36. Perkoff GT, Dioso MM, Bleisch V, et al: A spectrum of myopathy associated with alcoholism. I. Clinical and laboratory features. *Ann Intern Med* 67:481, 1967
37. Smith GM, Beecher HK: Amphetamine sulfate and athletic performance. *JAMA* 170:542, 1959
38. Karpovich PV: Effect of amphetamine sulfate on athletic performance. *JAMA* 170:558, 1959

39. Underwood J: Brutality: Part 3. Speed is all the rage. *Sports Illustrated,* August 28, 1978, p 30
40. Knochel JP, Vertel RM: Salt loading as a possible factor in the production of potassium depletion, rhabdomyolysis and heart injury. *Lancet* 1:659, 1967
41. Frazier CA: Asthma, ephedrine and olympic eligibility. *JAMA* 236:2942, 1976
42. Morse JLC, Jones NL, Anderson GD: The effect of terbutaline in exercise-induced asthma. *Am Rev Respir Dis* 113:89, 1976
43. Allegra J, Field J, Trantlein J, et al: Oral terbutaline sulfateamelioration of exercise-induced bronchospasm. *J Clin Pharmacol* 16:367, 1976

Rehabilitation of Musculoskeletal and Neuromuscular Disorders by Exercise

MARTIN GRABOIS, M.D.

Therapeutic exercise is a prescription of bodily movement to correct an impairment, improve musculoskeletal function, or maintain a state of well being.[1] In neuromuscular and musculoskeletal disorders, all of these aspects of therapeutic exercise must be utilized in the rehabilitation of the patient. This paper will attempt to discuss these exercises and their use in clinical practice.[2]

TYPES OF MUSCLE FUNCTION

For clinical purposes, we may differentiate three basic qualities of muscle function:

1. *Strength*—the ability of the muscle to contract.
2. *Elasticity*—the ability of the muscle to give up contraction and to yield to passive stress.
3. *Coordination*—the ability of muscle to cooperate with other muscles in proper timing and with appropriate power and elasticity.

The physiological mechanism for increasing strength is to increase tension, whether by isometric or isotonic exercises. Increasing strength over a period of time will ultimately lead to increased endurance. On the other hand, strength may be lost by inactivity, overstretching, and lesions of nerve or muscle which can ultimately lead to atrophy. If decrease in strength is noted, exercises that overcome resistance are indicated. If the resistance is too little, however, no increase in strength will develop. If the resistance is excessive, fatigue will be seen which could lead to a decrease in strength also. Aggressive resistive exercises, as developed by DeLorme and modified by others and brief maximal isometric exercises are the two most common forms of exercise prescribed to increase strength.[3]

Physiological and mechanical elasticity are two forms of elasticity that will influence muscle function. Physiological elasticity is the ability of the muscle to surrender contraction, or relax, and mechanical elasticity is the ability of the muscle to yield to passive stretching.[2]

A decrease in elasticity may be caused by faulty management of muscle, such as fatigue, or impaired physiological function, such as muscle contracture. The method used to develop elasticity will depend on the type of loss and on the cause of this loss. Relaxation training and muscle stretching are the most common exercises prescribed to increase elasticity.

Coordination requires well-timed, well-balanced function of several muscles acting together, usually mediated through postural and conditioning reflexes. If one sees a decrease in strength or elasticity of a minor degree, coordination problems will often be hidden by the use of compensatory mechanisms. When seen, poor coordination is usually manifested because of incorrect timing of muscle contractions, incorrect quality of cooperation between muscles, and/or forgotten or nonestablished motor patterns. The use of simple patterns that are made more complicated in a step by step manner and the use of skills within the capacity of the muscle are recommended in treating patients with coordination problems. In addition, development of strength and/or elasticity, if either are impaired, may also be a necessary part of the program in improving the coordination process.

CLINICAL EVALUATION

In planning an exercise program, it is essential to keep certain basic considerations in mind. In patients with a disability, the clinical reason for ordering a therapeutic program is usually to correct an impairment or improve musculoskeletal function. In the normal patient population, it is to maintain or improve a state of well being.

With regard to the clinical evaluation of the patient, it is of the utmost importance that not only the patient's deficiencies but his remaining abilities be examined. Evaluation of the general physical and mental state, the available motor and sensory pathways, and the joint and skeletal alignment, is necessary before an exercise program can be established. Following the evaluation, goals are established and a planned, graduated exercise program is prescribed. Reevaluations are undertaken to see that goals established are being attained. A therapeutic exercise program for patients with neuromuscular and musculoskeletal disorders cannot be a cookbook approach but requires knowledge and understanding of the clinical conditions of individual patients as well as exercises available.

Goals and Sequence of Treatment Program

Goals in treating neuromuscular and musculoskeletal disorders involve developing motor awareness and voluntary response, strength and endurance in acceptable patterns, and motor patterns that minimize musculoskeletal deformity that may lead to abnormal stress and strain.[4] Prefunctional goals, such as increasing the range of motions, balance, coordination, and strength, are often necessary to establish before vital functional areas relating to acitivities of daily living, transfer, and ambulation can be accomplished. The program can often begin at the bedside, immediately after the disability is incurred, with a passive type of program which will often advance to an intermediate program in which exercises are performed with assistance. Finally, a long-term therapeutic program that involves active exercises can be established. Treatment should be terminated when no further improvement has been obtained for a period of time or when full function has been restored.

General Principles of Treatment

Rusk, in his study of physical therapy, describes general principles applicable to all forms of exercise.[5] The patient should be placed in a position of comfort with proximal joints stabilized to eliminate undesired motions. Short, frequent sessions of exercise are better than more intense, prolonged treatment sessions. An increase in pain lasting longer than three hours and/or a decrease in range of motion or strength may indicate overdosage. If this occurs, the patient should be put at rest for a short period of time and the exercise restarted at a lower intensity level. The intensity of exercise should be sufficient, however, to enable the patient to exceed his present capacities in order to obtain improvement. The patient must be made part of the treatment program, and accurate periodic measurements of improvements are necessary.

CASE REPORT

This is a case history that illustrates how a therapeutic program of exercise is undertaken for a person with a diagnosis of cerebral vascular accident.

HISTORY. Mrs. S. is a 55 year old female who suffered right sided weakness and slurred speech on October 1, 1973. She was admitted to The Methodist Hospital for evaluation and rehabilitation.

Past medical history revealed patient had mild hypertension controlled with a diuretic and mild diabetes mellitus controlled by diet.

Social history revealed patient lived with husband in a one-story house. She worked part-time as a cashier. She was independent in all activities prior to admission, but now is dependent in all activities except feeding herself.

Laboratory evaluation shows an EKG which has some S-T inversion, stroke workup compatible with CVA and a right shoulder subluxation.

The hospital course has been uneventful except that the patient required catheterization and is occasionally incontinent of bowel.

PHYSICAL EXAMINATION.   Positive physical findings show a mild receptive and expressive aphasia with a right homonymous hemianopsia and right 7th central palsy. Deep tendon reflexes were increased on the right compared to the left with a positive right babinski. Evaluation of the right upper extremity revealed a +1 shoulder subluxation, slight decrease range of motion (ROM) at the shoulder, mild spasticity, and a flexor synergy pattern. The right lower extremity showed slight spasticity with fair proximal muscle power and poor distal muscle power.

PLAN OF TREATMENT.   To therapy daily by wheelchair; *precautions:* Cardiac; *goal:* Independent ambulation, transfer and ADL activities

THERAPY

1. Evaluate ROM and strength, right side, and follow
2. Hot pack to right shoulder for 20 minutes
3. Active assisted ROM to RUE; active assisted ROM to right lower extremity
4. Progressive resistive exercises to left side
5. Neuromuscular facilitate/reeducate to right side
6. Transfer and balance activities
7. Stand and ambulate starting in parallel bars—use training short leg brace as necessary
8. Wheelchair instruction
9. ADL evaluation and training followed by housekeeping training
10. Sling for right upper extremity
11. Instruct to overcome visual field deficit, energy conservation technique

REFERENCES

1. Kraus H: Musculo-skeletal apparatus: Indications for therapeutic exercises. in: Kraus H (ed): *Therapeutic Exercise.* ed 2. Springfield IL, Thomas, 1963, p 91
2. Kraus H: Clinical patho-physiology of muscle exercises. in: Kraus H (ed): *Therapeutic Exercise.* ed 2. Springfield, IL, Thomas, 1963, p 5
3. Kottke F: Therapeutic exercise. in: Krusen F, Kottke F, Ellwood P (eds): *Handbook of Physical Medicine and Rehabilitation,* ed 2. Philadelphia, WB Saunders Co, 1971, p 385
4. Bennett R: Principles of therapeutic exercise. in: Licht S (ed): *Therapeutic Exercise.* ed 2. Revised, Baltimore, Waverly Press, Inc, p 472
5. Rusk H: Principles of physical therapy. in: Rusk H (ed): *Rehabilitation Medicine* ed, 3. St. Louis CV Mosby Co, 1971, p 77

Pulmonary Aspects of Exercise

ALLAN P. FREEDMAN, M.D.

NORMAL PULMONARY RESPONSE TO EXERCISE

During exercise, $\dot{V}_E$ (minute ventilation) increases to supply the extra oxygen required and remove the carbon dioxide generated. It can increase from a resting ventilation of about five liters per minute to well over 100 liters per minute. This provides the body's oxygen requirement which ranges from a $\dot{V}_{O_2}$ (minute oxygen consumption) of 250 cc per minute at rest to over 5000 cc per minute during exercise in a fit individual.[1]

With the initiation of exercise, there is an abrupt increase, perhaps reflex, of $\dot{V}_E$.[1,2] The increase in respiratory depth or tidal volume is much greater than the increase in respiratory rate at this stage. $\dot{V}_E$ increases linearly with the $\dot{V}_{O_2}$ as the work level increases, until about 60 percent of the maximal working capacity.[3,4] The $\dot{V}_E$ needed for a given $\dot{V}_{O_2}$ is the ventilatory equivalent, $\dot{V}_E/\dot{V}_{O_2}$. It is 20 to 30 liters/liter in the normal individual.[5]

During exercise, the amount of wasted ventilation decreases for two reasons. First, alveolar ventilation but not anatomic dead space increases with larger tidal volumes, resulting in a reduction of the fraction of dead space ventilation ($\dot{V}_D/\dot{V}_{Total}$).[6] Second, the relatively overventilated apical areas are better perfused when pulmonary artery pressure rises with exercise, resulting in a reduced physiologic dead space.[7] Similarly, the increased diffusing capacity from capillary bed expansion caused by raised pulmonary artery pressure and increased stroke volume also reduces physiologic dead space. These adaptations are summarized in Table 1.

The linear relationship of $\dot{V}_E$ to total body oxygen consumption holds only until approximately 60 percent of maximal oxygen consumption is reached. At this point,

Table 1 Reduction of Wasted Ventilation during Exercise

↓ Anatomic $\dot{V}_D/\dot{V}_{Total}$: → $\dot{V}_D$
  ↑ $\dot{V}_{Total}$ as tidal volume increases

↓ Physiologic $\dot{V}_D/\dot{V}_{Total}$: Better perfusion of apices
  ↑ Diffusing capacity

anaerobic metabolism in muscle starts to become significant.[1,3,4] The rising lactic acid level in blood produced by anaerobic metabolism is partially neutralized by serum bicarbonate, resulting in CO_2 production:

$$H^+ lactate^- + Na^+HCO_3^- = Na^+ lactate^- + H_2O + CO_2.$$

This CO_2 production is over and above the CO_2 produced from aerobic metabolism.[8] Therefore, $\dot{V}_E$ increases at a faster rate than $\dot{V}_{O_2}$ to blow off this extra CO_2, as shown in Figure 1, an increase in respiratory rate is the major mediator of the increased $\dot{V}_E$ at this stage of exercise. The point at which anaerobic metabolism becomes significant is termed the anaerobic threshold. It is quite useful, as it can be used to predict

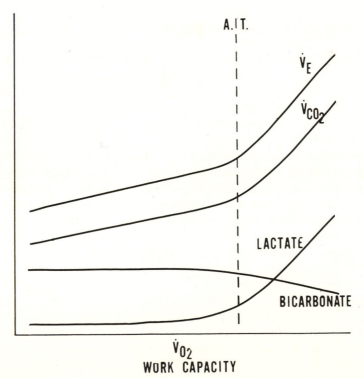

Fig. 1. The relationship of ventilation to oxygen consumption and work level during progressive exercise, and the concept of anaerobic threshold.

maximal oxygen consumption ($\dot{V}_{O_2\,max}$). Whether $\dot{V}_{O_2\,max}$ is reduced by disease or increased by training, the anaerobic threshold occurs at approximately 60 percent $\dot{V}_{O_2\,max}$.[3,4]

In contrast to the cardiovascular or musculo-skeletal systems, the lungs operate at near maximal efficiency in even the untrained, unfit individual. The work of breathing can be expressed as pressure $\times$ volume, since force/cm^2 $\times$ cm^3 equals force $\times$ distance, the units of work. This work normally requires only five percent or less of total $\dot{V}_{O_2}$, equivalent to 0.5–1.0 cc O_2/liter $\dot{V}_E$.[5]

EXERCISE LIMITATION IN PULMONARY DISEASE

Whether we are dealing with alveolar destruction and bronchiolar dysfunction from emphysema, lessened alveolar volume and airway closure from restrictive lung disease, or loss of perfusion in ventilated areas from vascular disease, dead space ventilation comprises a greater fraction of total ventilation. $\dot{V}_D/\dot{V}_{Total}$ is normally approximately 1:3 but may rise to greater than 1:2 of total ventilation with pulmonary disease.[1] The ventilatory equivalent, $\dot{V}_E/\dot{V}_{O_2}$, rises as a result of the wasted ventilation. Consequently a higher $\dot{V}_E$ is required to supply the necessary $\dot{V}_{O_2}$ for any level of work. With normal lungs, the maximal breathing capacity is not reached at $\dot{V}_{O_2\,max}$.[1,9,10] With pulmonary pathology, ventilation becomes a limiting factor. Exercise must stop at a lower work level. $\dot{V}_E$ is inappropriately high for this work level, yet heart rate is appropriately low.

Often, the anaerobic threshold is not evident due to early cessation of exercise from dyspnea. Since dyspnea limits exercise, the exercise level at which anaerobic threshold occurs may not be reached.[10-12] If this is the case, lactate concentration at the individual's maximal exercise level, oxygen debt, and recovery time will all be less.[1,13]

The work of breathing at rest may require over 10 cc O_2/liter $\dot{V}_E$, which represents more than 20 percent of total body $\dot{V}_{O_2}$.[14] During exercise, even a greater percentage of the $\dot{V}_{O_2}$ may be used by the respiratory muscles. It is interesting that work capacity is more limited in pure panlobular emphysema (type A, "pink puffer"), where the pathophysiology includes both reduced capillary bed and airway closure on expiration, than in pure centrilobular emphysema (type B, "blue bloater"), where perfusion of unventilated areas is the major problem. During exercise, the type A patient experiences a decline in PaO_2 while the type B patient often experiences an increase in PaO_2.[12,15] This difference is probably due to the limited pulmonary capillary bed in the type A patient.[16]

PULMONARY REHABILITATION

As Petty points out, pulmonary rehabilitation "attempts to return the patient to the highest possible functional capacity allowed by his pulmonary handicap and overall life situation."[17] In patients with pulmonary disease, exercise training only sometimes produces the up to 16 percent increase in $\dot{V}_{O_2\,max}$ that occurs in normal subjects.[18,19,20] This is because maximal breathing capacity is reached during exercise and limits it. Increased oxygen extraction by muscles, such as occurs in normal trained individuals, is only sometimes observed and has not been clearly related to exercise level achieved or degree of anaerobic metabolism reached.[21,22] Surprisingly, cardiac function has not been found to show a consistent training effect in emphysema even when heart rates reach 70 percent of the maximum level.[21,22] As expected, pulmonary function shows no improvement.[18,20,22,23] Ventilatory efficiency is related to the underlying pathology, and does not show a measurable training effect.

Musculo-skeletal efficiency does show a training effect, however, depending on what exercise levels can be reached. The body becomes more efficient, decreasing the $\dot{V}_{O_2}$ and $\dot{V}_E$ needed for any given level of exercise. This results in an increase in the maximal work level, as well as an increase in endurance and a decrease in dyspnea at submaximal levels.[1,18,20-22] Because of this decrease in the oxygen cost of work, patients can do more longer, with the pulmonary function they have, as shown in Table 2.

Steady state techniques are usually used for exercise training, though intermittent short periods of exercise separated by rest periods have been successfully employed.[9,18] Running, however, is often beyond the capability of patients with pulmonary disease. Walking protocols have resulted in training effects that markedly improve life style and psychological outlook.[24]

In patients whose arterial P_{O_2} is low enough to cause a significant reduction in oxygen saturation and content, the use of supplemental oxygen improves exercise tolerance.[25,27] The improvement may be much greater than the less than 10 percent increase in work capacity that supplemental oxygen causes in normal individuals, as little increase in oxygen content occurs if the hemoglobin is already saturated.[28] The increased $\dot{V}_{O_2}$ given to these patients with supplemental oxygen not only allows greater activity, but may enable exercise to proceed to a level where a musculo-skeletal training effect develops. This would in turn improve exercise ability without oxygen. The increase[9] in arterial P_{CO_2} that may occur is usually well tolerated.[25,26]

The use of low-flow nasal oxygen to bring arterial P_{O_2} at rest to over 50 mm Hg increases oxygen content enough to reduce hypoxemic pulmonary hypertension—because of the sigmoid nature of the oxyhemoglobin dissociation curve. When used for 15 hours daily, cor pulmonale and secondary polycythemia are markedly improved.[29,30] Additionally, hypoxemic left ventricular function is alleviated. Oxygen can be supplied from stationary pressurized tanks, dewars of liquid oxygen, or a

---

TABLE 2   Exercise Training in Pulmonary Disease

↑ Work/ $\dot{V}_{O_2}$ from enhanced musculoskeletal efficiency

↓ Dyspnea
↑ Endurance   at Submaximal $\dot{V}_{O_2}$

↑ Work at Maximal $\dot{V}_{O_2}$

TABLE 3   Home Oxygen

Benefits:
   ↓ Pulmonary vascular resistance
   ↓ Cor pulmonale
   ↓ Secondary polycythemia
   ↑ Left heart function
   ↑ Exercise tolerance

Modalities:
   Pressurized tanks, stationary and portable
   Liquid oxygen dewars, stationary and portable
   Molecular sieve concentrator

molecular sieve concentrator. Extention tubing facilitates household activity, but true mobility can be best achieved through use of small tanks or dewars with handles, carrying straps, or wheels. These aspects of oxygen use are summarized in Table 3.

Many methods have been used to try to lessen the work of breathing, improve ventilatory efficiency, and increase ventilatory capacity (Table 4). Breathing exercises stressing slow, deep inspiration and passive expiration through pursed lips reduce the airway closure that occurs with active expiration when bronchioles are poorly supported. This lessens the work of breathing.[27,31] Additionally, the larger tidal volumes may result in a reduction of the fraction of wasted ventilation ($\dot{V}_D/\dot{V}_{Total}$).[27] Tidal respiration at higher lung volumes also reduces airway closure, but may reduce inspiratory muscle efficiency as well.[32] Diaphragmatic strengthening exercises are not of proven value.[27] In normal individuals, it is possible to show a small training effect on respiratory force (pressure generated) and endurance (maximal voluntary ventilation), and a similar effect has been demonstrated in patients with cystic fibrosis.[33,34]

Avoiding panic and high expiratory pressures is critical, and patient education and confidence is extremely important. Bronchial irritants must be avoided. Standard modalities such as bronchodilators, chest physiotherapy and postural drainage, early treatment of chest colds with antibiotics, and influenzal prophylaxis all help maintain optimal pulmonary function.[35] The use of pneumococcal vaccine has recently been added to our prophylactic regimen.

Patients in programs using all of these methods have fewer symptoms, an increased sense of well being, increased exercise tolerance, and fewer hospitalized

TABLE 4   Breathing Training

Reduced work of breathing and airway closure
   slow, deep, diaphragmatic inspiration
   pursed lip, passive exhalation
Avoiding panic

± Diaphragmatic strengthening
± Increase in maximal breathing capacity

days.[29,36] Some patients may return to gainful employment. Mortality is significantly reduced only in cases where home oxygen reverses hypoxemic and pulmonary hypertensive cardiac dysfunction.[17,37]

EXERCISE-INDUCED ASTHMA

This phenomenon may be demonstrated in the majority of asthmatics if sensitive tests of airway function are performed.[38,39] Increases in residual volume from air trapping and specific conductance are the most sensitive indicators but are of little clinical significance in terms of exercise limitation.[39,40] Reduction in the one-second forced expiratory volume, peak expiratory flow rate, and mid expiratory flow rate are the parameters usually monitored, as they correlate with an increase in ventilatory equivalent ($\dot{V}_E/\dot{V}_{O_2}$) that can cause clinical symptoms.[39] It is important to note that mild exercise-induced bronchoconstriction occurs in normal individuals and may cause a 10 percent reduction in peak expiratory flow rate.[41,42]

There are many interesting observations regarding exercise-induced asthma. Running has the greatest propensity to elicit bronchospasm, while cycling is less likely and swimming least likely to provoke this response.[42,43] Exercise levels above the anaerobic threshold cause the most severe attacks, though unrelated to blood pH and lactate.[44,45] The onset of bronchospasm often occurs after the cessation of exercise, with maximal bronchoconstriction occurring three to five minutes after exercise.[42] Since exercise must be performed for a minimum of several minutes to induce an attack, however, intermittent work–rest protocols have been advocated as non-competitive training programs for asthmatics who desire to exercise by running.[46-50]

If steady state exercise is carried out longer than six to eight minutes, the optimal period for induction of asthma, the severity of the attack diminishes.[42] It has also been noted that a refractory or protective period of reduced susceptibility exists for a half hour or more after an attack.[44] Finally, though there is a correlation between baseline bronchial tone and the severity of the attack, this may merely be an artifact due to the greater fall possible if baseline function is near normal.[38,39,42]

The etiology of exercise-induced asthma is still uncertain. Its association with positive histamine challenge, the "running through" phenomenon with continued exercise, and the period of refractoriness after an attack all suggest a chemical mediator that can be depleted.[38,47-49] Though attacks are related to work level, they are not induced by the products of anaerobic metabolism.[42,45] The hypothesis that a given level of exercise is needed to maximize bronchoconstricting factors, while the loss of countering sympathetic discharge after cessation of exercise precipitates the attack, seems to best explain the observed phenomena.[42]

Post-exercise hyperventilation, with a low P_{CO_2} causing bronchoconstriction, has been demonstrated in a subset of the asthmatic population,[50] but does not seem to be a major factor.[51] Cold air that is unwarmed by the nasopharynx because of mouth breathing is the initiator or enhancer of some attacks.[52-54] Cold air appears to act via upper airway receptors, being abolished by lidocaine but not by atropine.[52-54]

β agonists such as isoproterenol, isoetharine, metaproterenol, and terbutaline are very effective in prophylaxis.[42,43,56] Inhalation seems preferable to oral medication, as the effect is more prdictable.[41] The more specific β_2 agents are preferable to isoproterenol, as excess cardiac stimulation is undesirable. Phosphodiesterase inhibitors such as theophylline are effective, but long-term administration or a loading dose is needed to achieve therapeutic levels.[43,56]

Disodium cromoglycate inhalation to block mediator release from mast cells is also effective prophylactically.[49,57] The variable effect of atropine inhalation may be due to exercise-induced asthma's having a variable effect on small and large airways, with atropine being most effective when small airway bronchoconstriction predominates.[49,52-57] Steroids used alone are not effective in prophylaxis.[41,58]

REFERENCES

1. Dempsey JA, Rankin J: Physiologic adaptations of gas transport systems to muscular work in health and disease. *Am J Phys Med* 46:582, 1967
2. Dejours P: Control of respiration in muscular exercise. in: *Handbook of Physiology,* vol 1, section 3. Washington, American Physiological Society, 1965, p 631
3. Wasserman K: Breathing during exercise. *N Engl J Med* 298:780, 1978
4. Wasserman K, Mc Ilroy MB: Detecting the threshold of anaerobic metabolism in cardiac patients during exercise. *Am J Cardiol* 14:844, 1964
5. Otis AB: The work of breathing. in: *Handbook of Physiology,* vol 1, section 3. Washington, American Physiological Society, 1965, p 463
6. Asmussen E: Muscular exercise. in: *Handbook of Physiology,* vol 2, section 3. Washington, American Physiological Society, 1965, p 939
7. West JB: Topographical distribution of blood flow in the lung. in: *Handbook of Physiology,* vol 2, section 3. Washington, American Physiological Society, 1965, p 1437
8. Naimark A, Wasserman K, Mc Ilroy MB: Continuous measurement of ventilatory exchange ratio during exercise. *J Appl Physiol* 19:644, 1964
9. Astrand P, Rodahl K: *Textbook of Work Physiology,* ed 2. New York, McGraw Hill, 1977, p 235
10. Jones NL, Jones G, Edwards RHT: Exercise tolerance in chronic airway obstruction. *Am Rev Respir Dis* 103:477, 1971
11. Cotes JE: Response to progressive exercise. A three-index test. *Br J Dis Chest* 66:169, 1972
12. Wasserman K, Whipp BJ: Exercise physiology in health and disease. *Am Rev Respir Dis* 112:219, 1975
13. Astrand, *op cit,* p 313
14. Cherniack RM: The oxygen consumption and efficiency of the respiratory muscles in health and emphysema. *J Clin Invest* 38:494, 1959
15. Jones NL: Pulmonary gas exchange during exercise in patients with chronic airway obstruction. *Clin Sci Mol Med* 31:39, 1966
16. Burrows B, Fletcher CM, Heard BE, et al: The emphysematous and bronchial types of chronic airways obstruction. A clinico–pathological study of patients in London and Chicago. *Lancet* 1:830, 1966
17. Petty TL: Pulmonary rehabilitation. *Basics of Resp Dis* 4:1, 1975
18. Pierce AK, Taylor HF, Archer RF, et al: Responses to exercise training in patients with emphysema. *Arch Intern Med* 113:28, 1964

19. Ekblom B, Astrand P, Sattin B, et al: Effect of training on circulatory response to exercise. *J Appl Physiol* 24:518, 1968
20. Vyas MN, Banister EW, Morton JW, et al: Response to exercise in patients with chronic airway obstruction. I Effects of exercise training. *Am Rev Respir Dis* 103:390, 1971
21. Degre S, Sergysels R, Messin R, et al: Hemodynamic responses to physical training in patients with chronic lung disease. *Am Rev Respir Dis* 110:395, 1974
22. Chester EH, Belman MJ, Bahler RC, et al: The effect of physical training on cardio-pulmonary performance in patients with chronic obstructive pulmonary disease. *Chest* 72:695, 1977
23. Paez PN, Phillipson EA, Masangkay M, et al: The physiologic basis of training patients with emphysema. *Am Rev Respir Dis* 95:944, 1967
24. McGavin CR, Gupta SP, Lloyd EL, et al: Physical rehabilitation for the chronic bronchi-tic. Results of a controlled trial of exercises in the home. *Thorax* 32:307, 1977
25. Vyas MN, Banister EW, Morton JW, et al: Response to exercise in patients with chronic airway obstruction. II Effects of breathing 40 percent oxygen. *Am Rev Respir Dis* 103:401, 1971
26. Block AJ: Low flow oxygen therapy. *Am Rev Respir Dis* 110 (Suppl):71, 1974
27. Lertzman MM, Cherniack RM: Rehabilitation of patients with chronic obstructive pul-monary disease. *Am Rev Respir Dis* 114:1145, 1976
28. Margaria R, Camporesi E, Aghemo, et al: The effect of O_2 breathing on maximal aerobic power. *Pflegers Arch* 336:225, 1972
29. Petty TL: *Intensive and Rehabilitative Respiratory Care,* ed 2. Philadelphia, Lea and Febiger, 1974, p 301
30. Stark RD, Finnegan P, Bishop JM: Daily requirement of oxygen to reverse pulmonary hypertension in patients with chronic bronchitis. *Br Med J* 3:724, 1972
31. Petty, op cit, p 110
32. Derenne JPH, Macklem PT, Roussos CH: The respiratory muscles: mechanics, control, and pathophysiology. *Am Rev Respir Dis* 118:119, 1978
33. Leith DE, Bradley M: Ventilatory muscle strength and endurance training. *J Appl Physiol* 41:508, 1976
34. Keens TG, Krostins IRB, Wannamaker EM, et al: Ventilatory muscle endurance training in normal subjects and patients with cystic fibrosis. *Am Rev Respir Dis* 116:853, 1977
35. Hodgkin JE, Balchum OJ, Kass I, et al: Chronic obstructive airway diseases. Current concepts in diagnosis and comprehensive care. *JAMA* 232:1243, 1975
36. Hudson LD, Tyler ML, Petty TL: Hospitalization needs during an outpatient rehabilitation program for severe chronic airway obstruction. *Chest* 70:606, 1976
37. Neff TA, Petty TL: Long-term continuous oxygen therapy in chronic airway obstruction. *Ann Int Med* 72:621, 1970
38. Mellis CM, Kattan M, Keens TG, et al: Comparative study of histamine and exercise challenges in asthmatic children. *Am Rev Respir Dis* 117:911, 1978
39. Haynes RL, Ingram RH Jr, McFadden ER Jr: An assessment of the pulmonary response to exercise in asthma and an analysis of the factors influencing it. *Am Rev Respir Dis* 114:739, 1976
40. Buckley JM, Souhrada JF, Kopetzky, MT: Detection of airway obstruction in exercise-induced asthma. *Chest* 66:244, 1974
41. Anderson SD, Seale JP, Rozea P, et al: Inhaled and oral salbutamol in exercise-induced asthma. *Am Rev Respir Dis* 114:493, 1976
42. Anderson SD, Silverman M, König P, et al: Exercise-induced asthma. *Br J Dis Chest* 69:1, 1975

43. Fitch KD, Godfrey S: Asthma and athletic performance. *JAMA* 236:152, 1976
44. Anderson SD: *Physiological Aspects of Exercise-Induced Bronchoconstriction,* doctoral thesis. University of London, 1972. Quoted in Fitch KD, Godfrey S: Asthma and athletic performance. *JAMA* 236:152, 1976
45. Strauss RH, Ingram RM jr, McFadden ER Jr: A critical assessment of the roles of circulating hydrogen ion and lactate in the production of exercise-induced asthma. *J Clin Invest* 60:658, 1977
46. Edmunds AT, Tooley M, Godfrey S: The refractory period after exercise-induced asthma. Its derivation and relation to the severity of exercise. *Am Rev Respir Dis* 117:247, 1978
47. Racaniello AF: Prevention of exercise-induced asthma. *N Engl J Med* 299:1193, 1978
48. Report of the Committee on Rehabilitation Therapy. Exercise and Asthma. *J Allergy Clin Immunol* 54:396, 1974
49. McFadden ER Jr, Ingram RH Jr, Haynes RL, et al: Predominant site of flow limitation and mechanisms of postexertional asthma. *J Appl Physiol:* Respirat Environ Exercise Physiol 42:746, 1977
50. Ferguson A, Addington WW, Gaensler EA: Dyspnea and bronchospasm from inappropriate postexercise hyperventilation. *Ann Int Med* 71:1063, 1969
51. McFadden ER Jr, Stearns DR, Ingram RH Jr, et al: Relative contributions of hypocarbia and hyperpnea as mechanisms in postexercise asthma. *J Appl Physiol:* Respirat Environ Exercise Physiol 42:22, 1977
52. Deal EC Jr, McFadden ER Jr, Ingram RH Jr, et al: Effects of atropine on potentiation of exercise-induced bronchospasm by cold air. *J Appl Physiol:* Respir Environ Exercise Physiol 45:238, 1978
53. Strauss RH, McFadden ER Jr, Ingram RH Jr, et al: Enhancement of exercise-induced asthma by cold air. *N Engl J Med* 297:743, 1977
54. Shturman-Ellstein R, Zeballos RJ, Buckley JM, et al: The beneficial effect of nasal breathing on exercise-induced bronchoconstriction. *Am Rev Respir Dis* 118:65, 1978
55. Rodriguez-Martinez F, Mascia AV, Mellins RB: The effect of environmental temperature on airway resistance in the asthmatic child. *Pediatr Res* 7:627, 1973
56. Bierman CW, Pierson WE, Shapiro GG: Exercise-induced asthma. Pharmacological assessment of single drugs and drug combinations. *JAMA* 234:295, 1975
57. Rachelefsky GS, Tashkin DP, Katz RM, et al: Comparison of aerosolized atropine, isoproterenol, atropine plus isoproterenol, disodium cromoglycate and placebo in the prevention of exercise-induced asthma. *Chest* 73(Suppl):1017, 1978
58. König P, Jaffe P, Godfrey S: Effect of corticosteroids on exercise-induced asthma. *J Allergy Clin Immunol* 54:14, 1974

Treatment of Pain Syndromes through Exercise

MARTIN GRABOIS, M.D.

Pain is an unpleasant sensation which is usually evoked by a noxious stimulus, generally accompanied by psychological reactions, and often followed by automatic responses.[1] Thus, it is apparent that when dealing with pain, we are dealing not only with physical but also with psychosocial factors.

Pain syndromes can be divided into three phases: acute, subacute, and chronic (Table 1). Acute pain lasts a few days and is often of great intensity associated with swelling and tenderness. During this phase, therapeutic exercises are usually contraindicated except, perhaps, for maintaining an active range of motion. Restoring the affected area to full and perfect function and eliminating the pain in a short period of time is a realistic goal for the physician.

Subacute pain lasts from a few days to six months. It is less intense than the acute

TABLE 1   Pain Syndromes

Pain Type	Time	Symptoms	Goal	Therapeutic Exercises
Acute	Few days	Intermittent pain	Full restoration	Rest; ROM
Subacute	Till 6 months	Intermittent pain	Full restoration between episodes	Conservative program
Chronic	>6 months	Chronic pain	Learn to tolerate	Behavior modification program

pain syndrome and is often intermittent in character. During this phase, a conservative program including therapeutic exercises is highly desirable. Restoring the affected area to almost full and perfect function and eliminating the pain for extended periods of time is a realistic goal. The treatment time usually requires a few weeks and can be accomplished with an outpatient treatment program in a physical medicine and rehabilitation department followed by a home program. Emphasis should be made on teaching the patient how to handle recurring pain problems.

Chronic pain is pain lasting greater than six months, and is often associated with a large psychosocial component. During this phase of pain, a conservative therapy program combined with new techniques in treating chronic pain such as biofeedback, transelectrical nerve stimulation (TENS), and vibration are indicated. In addition, a behavior modification program of treatment with a large psychosocial component will probably be necessary. Full or perfect function and elimination of pain may not be a realistic goal. One may expect only modest gains such as a slight reduction in pain intensity, an improvement in the quality of life, a reduction in the pain associated with medication, an increase in the exercise level, and an increased ability to live with pain. While acute and subacute pain syndromes require a short period of time for treatment, chronic pain programs require a relatively long period of treatment time in terms of weeks or months, and usually an in and outpatient therapeutic program. The program usually must be continued indefinitely.

It should be noted that in some cases acute and subacute pain problems become chronic pain syndromes because of either inadequate management leading to residual weakness, stiffness and trigger points or repeated, injury.

INDICATIONS AND CONTRAINDICATIONS

In prescribing therapeutic exercises for the patient with pain, one attempts to relieve pain by a combination of therapeutic exercises that increase muscle elasticity and strength. Increased elasticity is obtained by therapeutic exercises that decrease tension, spasm, and contracture, while increased strength and endurance are obtained as a result of an exercise program that emphasizes progressive resistive exercises.

Relative contraindications in prescribing a therapeutic exercise include acute or chronic inflammation, cardiovascular inability to tolerate a therapeutic program, infection of a joint, and bony or ligamentous or tendon instability.

Complications

Complications resulting from a therapeutic exercise program can either be due to trauma or overexertion.[2] It is estimated that 15 to 20 percent of patients engaged in a therapeutic program have to discontinue to decrease the exercise program because of injuries even when these therapeutic programs are under professional supervision. These injuries usually result from incorrect or too intensive a load on the musculoskeletal complex. One sees stiffness of muscle, muscle or tendon ligamentous inflammation, muscle rupture, and injured joints or fractures. If any of these complications arise, they must be treated. If they are minor in character, however, a period of rest followed by a resumption of the therapeutic program at a lower dose level is usually satisfactory.

Clinical Evaluation

A clinical and laboratory evaluation is not only necessary to obtain a diagnosis for pain states but also to investigate the ability of the patient to participate in an exercise program. Evaluation is also necessary to determine if the patient is motivated to participate in such a program. Specific evaluations of range of motion, strength, elasticity, and body mechanisms are necessary.

Pain syndromes usually result in loss of elasticity with muscle spasm. Muscle spasm is usually caused by increased contracture of muscle because of inability to give up this permanent state of contraction. This results eventually in an impaired physiological elasticity. Muscle tension can aggravate and potentiate muscle spasms. It is a result of an individual's inability to discharge energies accumulated in a preparation for the "flight or fight" situation. If muscle tension remains, it leads to physical discomfort and ultimately loss of muscle length and muscle spasms.

Modalities of Treatment

Physical modalities that decrease pain and muscle spasms are necessary so that an effective therapeutic exercise program can be accomplished to return muscles to normal length and relaxation. In the acute stages of pain, immobilization or rest of the painful region of the body will produce a reduction of afferent stimuli by diminishing activity. In addition, reducing the metabolic requirements of the painful portion of the body by immobilization may reduce the passive vascular engorgement which might also be responsible at least in part for the pain state.[3] Immobilization may be accomplished by elevation and non-movement of the area involved or by the use of devices such as corsets or braces. The rest period must be for a limited period of time because if it is prolonged, there will be a further decrease in strength and elasticity. Therapeutic exercises should not be performed during the acute phase of pain, except perhaps for those involving an active range of motion.

Treatments involving heat and cold are the most commonly used physical modalities prior to a therapeutic exercise program. Both heat and cold can cause analgesia as well as sedation or muscle relaxation. Using cold is indicated for acute pain syndromes while heat is used for subacute and chronic pain states. These modalities are primarily used to decrease pain and increase relaxation so a therapeutic exercise program can be carried out. Massage, whether manual or mechanical, will affect the elasticity of muscle by increasing relaxation so once again a therapeutic exercise can be performed. Massage is usually used in the subacute state and occasionally with chronic pain syndrome, but because it often leads to increased pain in acute pain states it is contraindicated at this stage.

Certain new techniques in treating pain such as TENS, biofeedback, and vibration have been indicated in treating subacute and chronic pain syndromes. Transelectrical nerve stimulation produces electrical stimulation that reduces pain based on the Gate Theory. Biofeedback is a technique that combines electric technology with meditation and psychology to allow the patient to get feedback on techniques that affect bodily function. Biofeedback, when used in pain states, can lead to relaxation of muscle and a decrease in pain from muscle spasm and tension. It is probably most useful in chronic pain states. Vibration, like transelectrical nerve stimulation, theoretically can decrease afferent inflow into the spinal cord, and thus decrease pain.

A therapeutic exercise program is the cornerstone treatment of subacute and chronic pain syndromes. Once the acute phase is passed and physical modalities have been given to decrease the pain syndrome, a therapeutic exercise program that emphasizes increase in elasticity by decreasing tension, spasm, and contracture followed by a program increasing strength and endurance by progressive resistive exercises or isometric exercises is indicated. Kraus and Krusen in separate publications describe specific exercise programs that can be of assistance in both of these two areas.[4,5]

Behavior Modification Programs

Historically, because of the large psychosocial component of chronic pain, conservative treatment programs have been totally successful in treating this syndrome. Fordyce describes a relatively new approach to treating chronic pain called behavior modification.[6] Behavior modification applies learning principles to modifying the pain state by a contingency management or operant conditioning program. This program is base on three strategies: pain behavior may be reduced by withdrawing positive reinforcers; activity may be increased by attaching positive reinforcers; and finally (if the treatment gains are to be maintained) the natural environment of the patient must be modified from a sick to a well contingency situation. The program combines medicine management, an increase in exercise level, and a psychosocial awareness of factors that influence pain behavior.

Pain medication is shifted from a pain contingency (PRN) to a time contingency basis. Thus, medication is given independently of how the patient feels and no longer serves as a contingent reinforcer for pain behavior. Gradually the pain medication is reduced to a low dose nonnarcotic analgesic agent. The patients and their families are taught to change or reprogram their behavior to a healthy behavior approach from a program that is usually potentially reinforcing for pain behavior. Patients are introduced to socializing and to vocational placement.

Most chronic pain patients move in guarded manners and restricted activity to avoid pain. The behavior modification program rearranges contingencies to deal with this restricted process. Patients are allowed to engage in activities that are relevant to a tolerance level. Once this is obtained a quota of exercises is then established and started at a lower level and gradually increased to pass the previous tolerance level. Rest and attention are made positive reinforcers contingent upon completing the exercise program and not on pain symptoms. Fordyce and others have shown that this type of program with proper patient selection is generally successful in reducing chronic pain but more important in changing patients' life style in response to their pain syndromes.[7]

CASE REPORT

The following case shows how a therapeutic exercise program can be utilized in a patient with acute or subacute pain syndrome:

HISTORY.   Mrs. S. is a 39 year old patient who injured her back in April 1978, when she slipped on the floor. She experienced similar episodes in January 1975 and February 1977.

PHYSICAL EXAMINATION.   Physical examination is within normal limits (WNL) for motor and sensory systems with deep tendon reflex WNL in the lower extremities. There was a negative straight leg raising sign. Tenderness in low back paraspinal muscles with moderate amount of muscle spasm was noted with poor abdominal muscles strength and tight hamstring muscles.

PLAN OF TREATMENT.   To therapy daily as outpatient; *precautions:* None; *Goal:* Relief of pain and improved body mechanics.

THERAPY

1. Hot pack 20 minutes lumbosacral (L/S) area
2. Ultrasound 1.5–2.5 watt cm² for 3–5 minutes to trigger area
3. Massage to L/S area
4. Instruction in posture techniques
5. Williams' Flexion Exercises

SUMMARY

This article has attempted to show that pain is both a physical and psychological phenomenon, and therefoe, if exercise is to be useful in treating pain, it must attack both problems.

REFERENCES

1. Corbin K: Symposium on management of pain problems. Proc of Mayo Clinic 31:205, 1956
2. Liljedahl S: Common injuries in connection with conditioning exercises. *Scand J Rehabil Med* 3:1, 1971
3. Krusen F: The role of the physiatrist in management of pain. Proc of Mayo Clinic 31:219, 1956
4. Kraus H: Clinical patho–physiology of muscle exercises. in: Kraus H (ed): *Therapeutic Exercise,* ed 2. Springfield, Thomas, 1963, p 5
5. Krusen F: Therapeutic exercise. in: Krusen F, Kottke F, Ellwood P (eds): *Handbook of Physical Medicine and Rehabilitation,* ed 2. Philadelphia, W. B. Saunders, Co, 1971, p 385
6. Fordyce WE: *Behavior Methods for Chronic Pain and Illness.* St. Louis, C. V. Mosby Co, 1976
7. Fordyce W: Treating chronic pain by contingency management. in: Bonica JJ (ed): *Advances in Neurology,* vol 4. New York, Raven Press, 1974, p 583

Part IV

Exercise and Environmental Stresses

Effect of Age on Exercise Performance

STUART SNYDER, M.D.

Cardiac performance is known to be markedly decreased in subjects as they age. In many cases, the cause of the decreased cardiac performance is rather obvious since many patients develop coronary artery disease or valvular disease such as calcific aortic stenosis or cardiomyopathy. In these cases, the pathophysiology behind their decreased ability to exercise is a result of their underlying heart disease. On the other hand, many subjects will age and not develop any apparent heart disease but still suffer impaired exercise tolerance. In various studies of myocardial function, it can be seen that cardiac function and cardiac reserve are markedly decreased with age.

ETIOLOGIES

There are many possible etiologies[1,2] for the cause of decreased cardiac function in the aged, in the absence of apparent cardiac disease. Many subjects develop amyloidosis. This appears to be present in approximately two percent of hearts between the ages of 70 and 80, but increases to approximately 50 percent of hearts between the ages of 90 and 100. Secondly, intracellular brown pigment, which is called lipofuscin, may accumulate in aged hearts. It is not certain whether this may interfere with myocardial function, but in any case it is a pathological finding. In certain hearts there is adipose infiltration. In contrast, in other hearts there is diffuse impairment of function without any anatomical cause seen at necropsy. This would be known as presbycardia, and this is a change in functional capacity without any change in anatomy.[1,2]

There may be certain other additional biochemical factors which might not necessarily be apparent on routine pathological examination, such as myocardial enzyme deficiency, altered mitochondrial ultrastructure, or perhaps neural atrophy that also might account for decreased cardiac function with aging. These have not been well demonstrated, however.

This change in cardiac function with aging may have several manifestations. First of all, it may affect the person's ability to exercise and, secondly, it may affect his ability to respond to certain illnesses such as pneumonia or acute myocardial infarction.

EFFECT OF AGE AT REST

Age has a number of effects upon an electrocardiogram and upon cardiac function that may be seen at rest and independent of exercise. The heart rate does not appear to be changed, but there appears to be a small increase in the P–R interval, the QRS duration, and the Q–T interval. In addition, the QRS amplitude appears to be decreased, and there is a shift of the axis to the left.[3] In addition, other reviews[4] on the effect of age changes at rest have shown that there appears to be a slight prolongation in left ventricular ejection time, a increase in pre-ejection period, and an increase in isovolumetric relaxation time. Moreover, there appears to be a decrease in resting cardiac output, which is approximately a one percent decline per year. The etiology of the change in resting cardiac output appears to be somewhat controversial, but it seems to be due to a decrease in preload rather than a decrease in actual contractility.

EFFECT OF AGE ON EXERCISE

When the effects of exercise are studied in patients with normal hearts,[5] it is observed that there is a marked increase in exercise cardiac output which is often four to five times the baseline. This increase in cardiac output seems to be mostly due to an increase in heart rate. There is often an increase in stroke volume due to an increase in contractility, but the effect of this in producing the change in cardiac output is much less than that for heart rate. Intracardiac pressures do not change very much in the normal subject, although a slight increase in left ventricular end diastolic pressure and left ventricular size may occasionally be noticed. There is an increase in systolic arterial pressure in the normal subject, however.

In order to best comprehend the effects of aging on exercise performance, the concept of maximum oxygen consumption needs to be invoked. This refers to the maximum amount of oxygen that can be utilized by the subject in any one time period. This is a function of three physiological parameters: the maximal heart rate that can be developed, the maximum stroke volume that can be developed, and the maximal oxygen extraction that may occur by the tissues, which would be equated with the maximal A–V, O_2 difference. This maximal oxygen consumption should directly correlate with the maximal exercise ability. In normal subjects, the most important determinant of the maximal exercise ability or maximal oxygen consumption is the maximal heart rate that can be developed by the subject.

Aging persons, it has been shown[4,5,6,7,8] experience a significant decrease in maximal oxygen consumption that corresponds to a decrease in the maximal exercise performance of approximately 20 to 50 percent. Whereas the main reason appears to be a decrease in maximal heart rate development, there also is a smaller increase in stroke volume due to a deterioration of the ability of aged persons to maximize contractility in comparison to younger subjects. In addition, there is also a decrease in the maximal oxygen extraction by peripheral tissues, compared to younger subjects. Therefore, it may be concluded that all three determinants of maximum oxygen consumption are decreased in the aged subject when compared to younger subjects, but the most important determinant that is affected is the maximal heart rate that the subject is capable of developing.

Not only is the exercise performance affected, but there seems to be a concomitant change in intracardiac pressures in aged subjects when compared to younger subjects during exercise. In younger individuals, the most apparent change is an increase in systolic pressure. In contrast, older subjects tend to develop an increase in pulmonary capillary wedge pressure, left ventricular end diastolic pressure, right ventricular end diastolic pressure, and systolic blood pressure. In addition, their peripheral resistance seems to be significantly increased when compared to exercising young subjects, and much the same is true for their pulmonary vascular resistance. Therefore, not only are they not able to perform as well as younger subjects, but there is a significant change in intracardiac pressure. While this change may be a compensatory effect—i.e. by increasing preload, cardiac function may increase—it may also produce a detrimental effect on lung function, since higher intracardiac pressure results in pulmonary congestion with more shortness of breath.

Whereas this change in maximal exercise performance occurs in nearly all individuals with aging, and does not seem to be reversible by itself, some of the other factors that may alter the maximal oxygen consumption can be manipulated. These are obesity, smoking, and training. The older subject can be advised to lose weight, to stop smoking, and to embark on a training program. By these means, he may be able to increase his exercise performance and more than compensate for the deterioration that occurs with aging.

TRAINING AND AGE

Training is a process by which the exercise ability is improved. In the course of the normal training program in healthy young subjects, it may be observed that not only is resting heart rate significantly decreased but also the change in heart rate during submaximal exercise is likewise significantly decreased.[9] In addition, the maximal oxygen consumption or maximal exercise performance may be increased in normal subjects by a training program. This increase in exercise performance is not due to any change in the maximal heart rate, but rather is due to an increase in the maximal stroke volume that the subject is generating as the result of greater increases in contractility. In addition, the subject may likewise increase his $AV-O_2$ difference with exercise even more than before the training program. Training, therefore, can increse exercise performance, but not by virtue of any change in the maximal heart rate development. Furthermore, the effects of training in any one individual appear to be limited.

Just as with younger subjects, training increases the maximal oxygen utilization and maximal exercise performance of other subjects. Likewise, there does not appear to be an effect on maximal heart rate development of older subjects. The maximal exercise performance of aged subjects after training appears to be less than that of younger subjects, however.

OTHER EFFECTS OF EXERCISE

The purpose of an exercise program for an older individual, therefore, would be to improve his exercise performance and his work capacity. In addition, numerous studies have shown that people undergoing exercise programs tend to feel better, tend to have a more positive outlook on life, and, even as they get older, tend to be more active. There may be certain beneficial health effects beyond that of just exercise performance, moreover. Exercise has been shown to decrease triglycerides, and this could be beneficial in reducing the incidence of vascular disease. In addition, exercise has also been shown to raise high–density lipoprotein levels,[10] and this could mitigate against the tendency towards atherosclerosis in older people.

To date, however, there has been no study that clearly demonstrates that exercise programs—whether they involve older or younger subjects, with or without coronary heart disease, have any beneficial effect on subsequent mortality or morbidity rates in terms of cardiovascular events. In fact, for patients who already had suffered an acute myocardial infarction, exercise was not shown to affect longevity or recurrence of infarction.[11] We, therefore, would encourage older subjects to participate in exercise programs, but there is no substantial evidence that life is prolonged or that the recurrence of heart attacks or strokes is mitigated by such programs.

REFERENCES

1. Dock W: Cardiomyopathies of the senescent and senile. *Cardiovas Clin* 4:362, 1972
2. Dock W: How some hearts age. *JAMA* 195:148, 1966
3. Simonson E: The effect of age on the electrocardiogram. *Am J Cardio* 29:64, 1972
4. Gerstenblith G, Lakatta EG, Weisfeldt ML: Age changes in myocardial function in exercise response. *Prog Cardiovasc Dis* 19:1 1976
5. Vatner SF, Pagani M: Cardiovascular adjustments to exercise: Hemodynamics and mechanisms. *Prog Cardiovasc Dis* 19:91, 1976
6. Julius S, Amery A, Whitlock LS, et al: Influence of age on the hemodynamic response to exercise. *Circulation* 36:222, 1967
7. Granath A, Jonsson B, Strandell T: Healthy old men studied by right heart catheterization

at rest and during exercise in supine and sitting position. *Acta Med Scand* 176: suppl 4, 425, 1964

8. Skinner JS: The cardiovascular system with aging and exercise. *Medicine in Sport,* Vol 4, Physical activity in aging. Karger, S Basel, 1970, p 100

9. Clausen JP: Circulatory adjustments to dynamic exercise and effect of physical training in normal subjects and in patients with coronary artery disease. *Prog Cardiovasc Dis* 18:459, 1976

10. Lopez SA, Vial R, Balart L, et al: Effect of exercise and physical fittness on serum lipids and lipoproteins. *Atherosclerosis* 20:1, 1974

11. Wilhelmsen L, Sanne L, Elmfeldt H, et al: A controlled trial of physical training after myocardial infarction: Effects on risk factors, non-fatal reinfarction and death. *Prev Med* 4:491, 1975

The Effect of Exercise on the Skeletal System

VINCENT J. ZARRO, M.D., PH.D.

While there is a wealth of information on the topic of acute and chronic cardiovascular, pulmonary, musculoskeletal injury, biochemical and other organ system changes induced by exercise, little is know of the actual bone and joint changes affecting physiology and biochemistry as altered by acute and long-term exercise. Studies during space flight, however, have added to the knowledge of the effect of weightlessness and lack of exercise on the bone.

In the natural state, bone is continually undergoing reabsorption by osteoclastic activity and deposition by osteoblastic activity. By this activity, bone may increase or decrease in size and continually change its shape. There is substantial evidence that stress or lack of stress (more or less exercise) markedly affects the shape and density of bone. The piezo—electric effect can explain this mechanism. At the point of increased stress, a negative action potential develops in relation to bone mass elsewhere. Flow of electric current stimulates osteoblastic activity at the negative pole.[1]

Lack of stress and exercise, such as occurs during space flight, has effects on the musculoskeletal system and in particular calcium metabolism.[2,3] Calcium balance studies as well as sophisticated techniques to measure bone density of subjects undergoing prolonged space flight were studied and compared to groups of people on prolonged bed rest. Both groups showed a negative calcium balance as well as loss of density of the os calcis.

As would be expected from results of studies of patients on bed rest, muscle deconditioning also occurs. Muscle atrophy is reversible to a large extent by proper exercising; however, the effect of exercise on reducing the negative calcium balance is not entirely established.[4] Continued conditioning exercise does increase bone mass, probably as a result of stress causing an increase in osteoblastic activity as

TABLE 1   Skeletal and Lean Body Mass in 18 Post Menopausal Women
Following 1 year of Sedentary and Exercise Periods (3 times per week for
1 hour)*

	Total Body Calcium	Total Body Potassium	Bone Mineral Content
Sedentary (9♀)	Decrease	Unchanged	Unchanged
Exercise (9♀)	Increase	Unchanged	Unchanged

*Adapted from reference 5

described above. Post menopausal women who exercise for one hour three times per week showed a significant increase in total body calcium after one year of aerobic activity[5] (see Table 1).

Aside from the obvious effect of injury to a joint and periarticular structures, exercise probably has little significant effect on articular physiology. The claim that there is an increase in the amount of synovial fluid is not well established. On the other hand, immobolization of rabbit joints does produce thinning of cartilage and narrowing of joint spaces. Further studies are required to evaluate changes in normal articular physiology caused by exercise.

REFERENCES

1. American Academy of Orthopedic Surgeons: *Symposium on Sports Medicine*. Saint Louis, C. V. Mosby, 1969
2. Johnston RS, Laurence FD (eds): *Biomedical Results From Skylab*. Washington, National Aeronautics and Space Administration, 1977
3. Mack PB, La Chance PA, Vose CP: Bone demineralization of foot and hand of Gemini–Titan IV, V, VII astronauts during orbital flights. *Am J Roentgenol* 100:3, 1967
4. Browse NL: *The Physiology and Pathology of Bed Rest*. Springfield, Charles C. Thomas, 1965
5. Aloia JF, Cohn SH, Ostuni JA: Prevention of involutional bone loss by exercise. *Ann Int Med* 89:356, 1978

Equipment Safety and Effectiveness

GIDEON B. ARIEL, PH.D.

Biomechanics is the study of the structure and function of biological systems by means of the methods of mechanics. Mechanics deals with the description of motion as well as the forces that act on objects to cause motion. Therefore, mechanics is divided into two sub disciplines: kinematics and kinetics. Kinematics deals with the description of motion and kinetics deals with forces.

The three factors underlying all human movement are displacement, duration of movement, and forces. All of these are equally important in human performance. In all motor skills, muscles provide the forces to move the body through the activity, while the displacement of the body parts and their speeds are important in the coordination of the activity. Direction and speed are directly related to the forces produced.

In order to measure human movement, there is a need for either a measuring device attached to the body or the utilization of cinematographical techniques. An unfortunate limitation to the attachment of transducers to the human body is the chance that the body movement may be impaired. In addition, a transducer necessitates wires or telemetry electronics which are usually cumbersome or lacking in accuracy. It is possible to record motion on film by means of film recording techniques, and then reduce the data into a coordinate system for further calculation of displacement, velocity, and acceleration of the body segments by means of digitizers. In the past, this procedure was very laborious and extensive. Recently, however, the biomechanics of human motion has been aided by computer technology, which has resulted in the feasibility of rapid calculations of large quantities of data. The computer–digitizer complex has reduced the long, tedious hours of tracing and hand calculations to a matter of minutes, and thus complex whole body motion analysis can be easily obtained.[1, 2]

The laws of physics apply to any system in motion regardless of whether the system is a living organism or a machine. The human body may be likened to a machine made up of mechanical members: the joints serve as fulcrums and the contracting skeletal muscles exert forces on the segments. The segments of the human body form a link system consisting of segments such as the foot, shank, thigh, trunk, shoulders, upper-arm, forearm, and hand. In order to perform a biomechanical analysis of the human body, the following steps are necessary: obtaining cinematographic data by utilizing high speed cameras; digitizing the data; measuring and utilizing anatomical data; utilizing the computer programs for kinematic and kinetic measurements; and interpretating the results.[3, 4]

The purpose of the present paper is not to derive the equations of motion since these equations can be found in any physics textbook, but to illustrate the significant contribution of biomechanics to optimizing human performance. In appreciation of the genius of humans, Ben Franklin wrote: "Man is a tool–making animal." Tools are implements that assist us in our life. A shovel facilitates snow removal. A shoe protects the foot. A golf club drives a ball towards the green. Stairs provide an economical way to overcome gravity. In a modern technological society, indeed in any but the most primitive societies, we are tied to an almost infinite variety of simple and complicated machines.

Human beings seem to have become so infatuated with their ability to invent things, however, that they have concentrated almost exclusively upon improving the efficiency and safety, adding to the durability, reducing the cost, or enhancing the aesthetic appeal of the device in question. Badly neglected has been the key tool, the most versatile instrument of all, the human body, with its own marvelously sophisticated capacity to grip, lift, push, carry, and manipulate. It can perform wonders by itself and is even more effective when connected with one of its own innovations, the tool.

Unfortunately, in spite of their inventiveness, human beings often studiously ignore their own reality as a set of arms and a torso at the end of the working shovel. The shovel alone moves no snow. Inside the shoe is a foot that is attached to the body. The shoe does not become a working tool until the foot employs it. The dynamic properties of the golf club undergo a radical change when it leaves the bag and becomes a tool swung by the arms of a particular individual.

But other forces have continued to compose the tunes played by designers and producers of tools. Vanity decrees that women wear high heels, a threat to both their immediate and long-term health.[5] Tradition dictates the dimensions of stairs, one of the greatest hazards in buildings. Ignorance guides the design of furniture so that even a Bauhaus giant such as Mies Van Der Rohe creates an aesthetically breathtaking chair that is a sure contributor to the potential for backache and varicosities. Common household books of matches become tiny incendiary bombs because of a failure to consider the dynamics of striking a match. Automobiles continue to be an uneasy marriage of economics and safety without any true appreciation for the human factor.

The drive to defeat physical decay and postpone death dances to the beat of hucksters pushing exercise programs and equipment that may not suit the individual. The current mania is jogging. Because too little attention is being paid to what is actually a foot in jogging, the activity may prove to be another DDT—the miracle pesticide—until 20 years later we discover that along with the bugs, it has been killing us. Immediate gains can have far off costs. Only in the most intricate technological systems, those that are enormously expensive and life threatening, such as space missions or highly sophisticated weapons systems, is there serious attention paid by the builders of tools and machinery to how the human body moves, applies force or pressure, reacts to resistance.

A full cure for the wasteful assault upon nature's most noble invention, the human body, is the application of the science of biomechanics. This is the discipline that concerns itself with environmental effects of forces, velocities, and accelerations upon living organisms and, most particularly, homo sapiens. Biomechanics covers the mechanical actions of humans, whether they are simply using their own bodies or whether they are relating to other objects, devices, or persons.

Biomechanics also includes biocybernetics—the systems of control and communication within a human.[6] Simple biomechanics deals only with the calculation of forces, masses, acceleration, velocity, and movement of segments of the body. But something must coordinate all of the body's forces if one is to achieve an optimum performance, the best that he or she can accomplish under the circumstances, whether it is in an Olympic event or in shoveling out a snow-filled driveway.

Biomechanics in its widest sense seeks to find the principles that organize the interaction of the nervous system with the musculature. Coaches, trainers, physicians, physiologists, biochemists who ignore the control and communication apparatus, indeed anyone who doesn't include biocybernetics in the explanation of human movement, limits the discussion to vague superficialities.

The spiritual father of biomechanics is Leonardo da Vinci, who wrote: "Mechanical science is the noblest and above all others the most useful, seeing that by means of it all animated bodies which have movement perform all their actions." Others in the century or so after Leonardo echoed his thinking. An early 18th Century Italian Professor of Anatomy, Giorgio Baglivi, described the entire human body as a mechanical system: ". . . a complex of chemico–mechanical motions, depending upon such principles as are purely mathematical. For whoever takes an attentive view of its fabric, he'll really meet with shears in the jaw–bones and teeth . . . hydraulic tubes in the veins, arteries and other vessels . . . a pair of bellows in the lungs, the power of a lever in the muscles, pulleys in the corners of the eyes. . . ."

Apart from space missions, however, biomechanics appears to have made inroads into the consciousness of only one modern form of human endeavor, sports. Unfortunately, even there the vision of biomechanics seems to be clouded, suggesting that the use of the science's language is less a concern for integrating the human more efficiently into the relationship with equipment than it is to use the imprimatur of biomechanics as one more hype for selling.

For example, ads for a brand of tennis shoes brag, "extra deep, extra soft padding and cushioning, over 200 individual pads to grip the playing surface like the claws of a cat for instant starts and stops and lightning moves." There is not a shred of scientific evidence to show that piles of padding in a shoe absorb the shock to the body when a human runs during a tennis game. Tests show that the "200 individual pads" do not provide any more traction than any other contours of a sole bottom. Furthermore, humans do not move the way cats do. The hyerboles of advertising have become so accepted that one is tempted to ignore the outrageous claims, but if biomechanics is going to have any effect it must begin to shout about the emperor's nudity.

"A larger sweet spot," claims another tennis ad, this one by the manufacturer of a racket with an oversized face. In scientific terms, the sweet spot is the center of percussion. That is the point where any effective application of force will be completely counteracted by the mass acting upon that point. That means that for a rigid rod, such as a tennis racket or a baseball bat, the impulse or force transmitted through the racket or bat at the point of contact would not be felt at the point of the rod's suspension, which in the case of a racket or bat would be the hand or hands. But the makers of the racket determined the sweet spot or center of percussion on the basis of the instrument alone. They omitted the key element—the player. Unfortunately, in spite of the brochures issued by manufacturers, tennis also follows the laws of physics. In a player's hand the racket is no longer an independent rod with is suspension point located at the end of the handle. It is instead a piece of a lever that stretches from the shoulder through the hand to the tip of the racket. The true point of suspension is the shoulder joint. When biomechanial analysis was conducted and the data analyzed utilizing computer technology, the racket as part of a lever that included the entire arm, the center of percussion, or sweet spot, in the buzz word of the industry, was in the player's wrist. It would indeed be a triumph if a racket could be designed so that the center of percusion lay in the racket strings because that would go a long way towards the elimination of tennis elbow. If one consistently struck the ball on a center of percussion within the racket strings, no forces would be transmitted up the shaft of the racket to injure tendons, ligaments, or muscles.

Currently, jogging is another sports growth industry in the United States. The number of runners is surpassed only by the vast quantities of products for joggers and the claims made for these items. In particular, manufacturers, eager to cash in on the popularity of jogging, have created zippy-looking shoes decorated with flashy colors and stripes. All are allegedly endowed with special constructions that make the jogging go better. There is little actual biomechanical science behind any of these shoes. Jogging merits much more attention from a biomechanical viewpoint than it currently receives. It apparently does benefit the cardiovascular system under some circumstances. But what profits a man or woman with a healthy heart if at age 40 or 50 they are crippled by ankle and knee pains, shin splints, degeneration of disks and cartilege, and chair bound by traumatic arthritis? They may indeed be the biomechanical price for jogging in the modern urban environment.

Walk into any quality sporting goods store and look at the golf clubs. For sale to all comers are sticks bearing the autographs of Jack Nicklaus, Johnny Miller, Jerry Pate, or whoever happens to have scored well on the pro golf tour during the year. Obviously, Jack Nicklaus's golf clubs serve his game well. He has had them built to fit his specifications, the dynamics of his swing, and his particular body interacting with these special clubs. The weekend hacker who lays out several hundred dollars for a set of clubs designed by and for Jack Nicklaus ignores a basic component in his golf game—himself and his own biomechanical functioning. He may well fall into the percentile of the population that does not match the Niclaus somatype.

To summarize, the age of biomechanics which is dawning now offers much larger and more positive opportunities than just a kind of consumer's guide to sports and recreation equipment and techniques. Biomechanics can literally improve life from cradle to grave. If properly applied, biomechanics can aid newborns to explore their environment and develop their muscles better. The young can be taught how to get off on the right foot when they begin to walk. Much of what surfaces as a health problem with middle age begins during the early years of life. At the other end of the spectrum, biomechanics possesses the means to supply programs that will preserve the strength and the flexibility of aging bodies ravaged by time or even illness. Years of life may be added or, at the very least, older people will be able to enjoy more active, more comfortable lives.

REFERENCES

1. Ariel GB: Computer Analysis of Track Biomechanics. *Track Technique* 50:1597, 1972
2. Ariel GB: Computerized Biomechanical Analysis of Track and Field Atheltics Utilized by the Olympic Training Camp for Throwing Events. *Track and Field Quarterly Review* 72:99, 1972
3. Ariel GB: Computerized Biomechanical Analysis of Human Performance. *Mechanics and Sport,* The American Society of Mechanical Engineers 4:301, 1973
4. Ariel GB: Method for Biomechanical Analysis of Human Performance. *Res Quart* 45:72, 1974
5. Ariel GB: Computerized Biomechanical Analysis of Athletic Shoe. *V. International Congress of Biomechanics Abstracts,* Jyvaskyla, Finland, 1975
6. Arbib, MA: *The Metaphorical Brain.* New York, Wiley-Interscience, 1972

The Relationship between Sexual Activity and Athletic Performance

WILBUR W. OAKS, M.D., DAVID T. LOWENTHAL, M.D.

The relationship between sex and athletic activity is of concern to many people, and yet there is very little objective data published on this subject. In fact, much of it turns out to be more myth than fact.

The mystique of sexual activity and athletic performance or exercise evokes memories of coaches telling players not to engage in sexual performances for a prescribed period of time before competition. This concept has survived, unfortunately, throughout modern day sports. Daily medical myths are exchanged for facts derived from clinical investigation in virtually all disciplines of medicine. This chapter about sexual activity and exercise is not as replete with hard data as the preceding chapters. There is a need for carefully gathered facts rather than anecdotal medicine.

CARDIOVASCULAR EFFECTS OF SEX AND EXERCISE

The role of exercise on blood pressure regulation has been covered in two previous chapters. Several points of emphasis need to be considered which are germane to sexual activity.

During isotonic or dynamic (aerobic) exercise—such as jogging, walking, swimming, cycling, crosscountry skiing—there is an increase in systolic but not diastolic pressure. In association with a rise in heart rate and in cardiac output (see pages 133–144 of this text), the hypertensive patient exhibits a greater increase in mean arterial blood pressure. Following a period of training, the rise in arterial pressure and in heart rate is less marked. Isotonic (or aerobic) activities induce far better cardiovascular–pulmonary fitness than isometric or static activities.

Isometric or static exercises—such as pushing, pulling, and lifting—induce increases in both systolic and diastolic pressure in addition to the rise in heart rate. As a result of these forms of exercise, vagal tone is reduced and peripheral resistance is increased. Poorly treated hypertensive patients may have significant increases in blood pressure. The sustained muscular contractions of isometrics produce very high pressures which may precipitate angina, congestive heart failure, and cerebral hemorrhage.

Sexual intercourse is a form of isometric activity (muscular contractions of voluntary and involuntary types and increased sympathetic nervous system activity), which can lead to marked rises in heart rate and blood pressure.

From a physiological standpoint, the sexual act itself is a form of exercise akin to walking two to three flights of stairs. In a controlled setting, the maximal heart rate usually attained during orgasm with the same partner is equivalent to Stage I of the Bruce Exercise Test; that is 115–120 beats per minute. The physiological events during sexual intercourse relate to changes in cardiopulmonary function. During intromission, the heart rate can rise to greater than 100 beats per minute, and during orgasm to above 120 beats per minute. Systolic and diastolic pressures can increase by 51 mm Hg and 15 mm Hg respectively, thereby increasing the myocardial oxygen requirements for a brief period of time (Table 1).[1] The increase in myocardial oxygen consumption may lead to symptoms in patients with coronary artery disease and poorly controlled hypertension. Changes in pulmonary function are due to hyperventilation, which leads to slight respiratory alkalosis. All of these alterations are transient and the recovery period is rapid. In general, however, from a purely physiological standpoint, it would seem that ordinary sexual activity of brief duration and with the same partner would not be deleterious to one's health or psyche.

TABLE 1   Changes in Blood Pressure and Pulse Rate during Stages of Intercourse

Change in Blood Pressure	Rest	Intromission	Orgasm	Rest—Two Min Later
Man on top*	———	+36/+13	+51/+15	+6/+3
Man on bottom*	———	+30/+4	+48/+7	+8/+1
% change in pulse rate from resting state		↑35%	↑48%	↑13%

*P, N.S.

TABLE 2   Changes in Hemodynamics with Exercise during Oral
Contraceptive Use

Blood volume	– Increased*
Cardiac output	– Increased*
Stroke volume	– Increased*
Heart rate	– Unchanged*
Systolic pressure	– Unchanged*
Diastolic pressure	– Unchanged*

*Increased or unchanged refer to change in status under conditions of exercise alone before oral contraceptive.

REPRODUCTIVE ENDOCRINE CHANGES WITH EXERCISE

The female athlete until recently has been neglected in terms of her physiological changes before and during exercise. Women runners do have subtle menstrual irregularities which simulate anovulatory cycles. This may be due to changes in luteinizing hormone (LH) and follicle stimulating hormone (FSH) as well as to changes in plasma estrodial and progesterone levels.[2]

The hemodynamic effects of oral contraceptives during exercise in trained women is known. The increase in blood volume, stroke volume, and cardiac output during acute exercise on an ergometer is greater during combined oral contraceptive therapy than when the patients were not taking the pill. In fact, the use of combined pill with exercise may be advantageous to the physical fitness of female athletes (Table 2).[3]

One step beyond the "pill," aerobic exercise has been shown to have salutary effect both during and after pregnancy. A more encompassing review of this subject has been offered by Dr. Dorothy Harris (see pages 61–68 of this text).

Whether myth or fact, the issues of self-image, fidelity, sobriety, tenderness and aggressiveness are realistic considerations and all play some role in the relationship between the psychology of sex and the psychology of athletic performance. The AMA Committee report on the medical aspect of sports states that if sexual activity is performed regularly with a regular partner, it does not detract from athletic performance and may actually be extremely helpful.

SUMMARY

In summary, scant data exist which directly or tangentially relate sexual activity to exercise. The brevity of this paper reflects the need for additional scientific data to dispel the mythical contentions that "sex weakens legs" as well as other bodily functions, and is a deterent in athletic performance.

REFERENCES

1. Nemec ED, Mansfield L, Kennedy JW: Heart rate and blood pressure responses during sexual activity in normal males. *Am Heart J* 92:274, 1976
2. Lehtovirta P, Kuikka J, Pyorala T: Hemodynamic effects of oral contraceptives during exercise. *Int J Gynecol Obstet* 15:35, 1977
3. Jurkowski JE, Jones NL, Walker WC, et al: Ovarian hormonal responses to exercise. *J Appl Phys* 44:109, 1978

Epiloque: The Role of the Physician in Exercise

RONALD M. LAWRENCE, M.D., PH.D.

HISTORICAL BACKGROUND OF AMERICAN MEDICAL JOGGERS ASSOCIATION

The history of the American Medical Joggers Association (AMJA) may offer more light and information relating to this topic than anything that I can think of in my limited experience. In 1968, when I conceptualized the development of such an organization as the American Medical Joggers Association, I felt that the main reason to bring it into existence would be to interest the physician in participating in sporting events. We were primarily interested in having the physician become interested in an endurance type of exercise. The presence of other paramedical organizations such as the American Medical Tennis Association was known to me at that time. There were very few of these organizations in existence in 1968, however. The American Medical Tennis Association was one of the few successful ones that dealt with sports in any manner. Most of the existing paramedical organizations dealt with non-strenuous leisure activities, such as in the arts. The concept of an organization which would engage the physician in a rather strenuous endurance type of exercise such as jogging or running had not been evolved at that time. It was felt, and I really believed it, that such an organization would not attract too many physicians. We actually began the organization in 1969 with five physicians. The year 1979 therefore marks the tenth anniversary of the AMJA, and today the membership is over 3800 and is rapidly approaching the 4000 mark. The majority of the members are physicians, although we do have paramedical personnel such as rehabilitation nurses, hospital administrators, and scientists who are Ph.Ds working in the field of medical research.

Recently we started a subdivision of the Association for lay people whom we call supporting members. These people, for the most part, have some connection with medicine, but they do not have any of the privileges in the organization which are accorded to the regular members who are physicians. Most of these physician members are MDs and DOs, but we also have almost 100 podiatrists in the organization (or "podiatric physicians" as they are now known the state of California and elsewhere). Although it was given very little chance for long life, the AMJA is now coming into its eleventh year, and it is clear that the organization should survive for a long time to come. The concept that the physician has an important role in exercise might have been new ten years ago but it certainly is not new today. One of the reasons for that is the American Medical Joggers Association, which we feel is perhaps behind the present trend toward jogging and running, involving millions of people in the United States and Canada. It is probable that in our own way we have helped to prolong the lives of many of our patients by interesting them in this type of activity. Even if this is not true, we know we have at least enhanced the quality of their lives.

THE PHYSICIAN IMAGE

It was one of our concepts in establishing this organization and engaging the interest of physicians to participate that we should overcome the old image of the obese, unhealthy physician who stated to his patients, "Do as I say and not as I do." I recall, with great love I might add, our family practitioner, an obese individual with scarlet-complexion who died at a young age and who looked like he was old before his time. He was a lovely man who served his community well and for very little economic recompense, but he fit the image of the practicing physician that prevailed for many years, if not through most of the early part of this century. That image was depicted by Norman Rockwell on the cover of the *Saturday Evening Post,* in which a doctor is examining the small doll of a beautiful little female patient. He sat in his chair with his large protruding abdomen, wearing a vest which was expanding to the point that you expected a button to pop off any minute. His eyeglasses were down on his nose, and he leaned forward from his desk to examine the girl's little dolly. This image was known to millions of Americans and, in fact, formed the idealized conception of the family physician and indeed of all physicians. This is not true today. It is not true because the image no longer fits the younger physicians who now occupy those same chairs in offices throughout the country. The image of the physician is now of an individual who, however hirsute he may be, is at least fifty to seventy five pounds lighter, whose complexion has a healthier glow, and whose buttons don't look as though they are going to pop off at any minute. This is the way it should be, for as much as we love the old man, we must love and cherish the new man more.

CHANGING LIFE STYLES

There has been a great disillusionment of the American public relating to medical care and delivery, particularly during the last decade. There has been a flow away from organized medicine and organized physicians towards care by individuals who are outside of the mainstream of medicine. This attitude, for the most part, is not due to those members of the American Medical Joggers Association or to those members of the medical profession who are active sports participants and transmit this on to their patients. Indeed, the new hope for medicine lies with those physicians who are showing the way to their patients, and we know that patients appreciate their example. Although the original concept of the AMJA was to preserve and to help improve the quality of life of our patients, the Association has found that the physician himself is perhaps the greatest beneficiary of these efforts. The average life span of physicians who have participated in the endurance sports has been increased. This statement is based upon personal observation, but I think it will be borne out by scientific study within the next few years. We do know that physicians who participate in endurance sports such as running and jogging will reduce the likelihood of their experiencing a myocardial infarction, which had been called the "physician's disease." Most of us recall the epidemic of myocardial infarction and coronary artery disease that struck the country and particularly the medical profession through the 1960s and into the 1970s. According to the statistics given, there has now been a decrease in the number of these cases and we feel that exercise has something very important to do with this, not only because of the exercise but because the physicians and patients who participate in such forms of exercise change their lifestyles as well. They turn to better nutrition, they lead a more healthful life.

From a study of the obituary columns of the medical journals, we see over and over again the great numbers of physicians who die in their forties, fifties, and early sixties from coronary artery disease and its concomitant myocardial infarction. We also see the great numbers who die from diabetes mellitus and the other degenerative diseases brought about by sedentary activities, by poor dietary habits, and by poor lifestyle. Therefore, the physician is one of the greatest beneficiaries of the improvement that goes along with exercise and particularly endurance exercise. The type of exercise that we recommend for the physician is one of continued endurance activity, such as running, jogging, bicycling, or swimming. We do not feel, from the evidence presented to this date, that such exercises as tennis, golf, or exercises that require spurt-like activity rather than sustained physical activity, do in the long run produce the benefits of which we speak. This might be open to dispute by many here since there is certainly a psychological advantage to getting out in the fresh air and doing any form of exercise and getting away from tensions. But is that advantage great enough to produce a long-lasting change in the quality of life and, more importantly, in the length of life? This remains as a question to be answered, we hope within this next decade.

WALKING IS AEROBIC, TOO

I do not want to forget the importance of walking and particularly sustained walking for long distances. We believe that there is a three to one relationship between running and walking. In other words you must walk approximately three times farther than you would run in order to obtain similar benefits. One thing that has always disturbed patients, as well as physicians, is the fact that in walking one mile exactly the same number of calories are expended as in running one mile. In other words, since running or jogging one mile takes less time, the advantage gained is in time—not in calories expended. The cardiovascular effects may be different, but the cardiovascular effect of long distance walking is excellent and certainly better than many of the spurt-like activities that are engaged in by individuals who feel that they cannot take the time to do long distance walking.

RUNNING MANIA

I want to take a few moments to talk about the physician and the current running and jogging craze, which some have estimated involves at least 20,000,000 Americans and perhaps more. The fact that books such as Jim Fixx's *Complete Book of Running* and George Sheehan's *Running and Being* are on the best seller lists for many months is evidence of the fact that there is an interested public out there. 1976 *Runner's World Magazine* estimated that there were approximately 1,000,000 to 1,500,000 Americans who would buy these books, and now it is found that this number has been exceeded, much to the delight of the authors as well as the publishing houses. New books are "popping out" every day. I receive at least four books per week to review for our publication, the Newsletter of the American Medical Joggers Association, and this represents only the tip of the iceberg in regard to publications dealing with running, jogging, and endurance exercise. In our opinion the physicians of the American Medical Joggers Association are among those who are most directly responsible for the present popularity of running and jogging. Each one of these individuals influences many hundreds of patients, so that together their influence runs into the millions. They are to be commended for what they have done for this country. Perhaps what they have done is as important a contribution to the health of this nation as has been made by many a drug or many a therapy that has evolved within the last 50 years. This may sound like a grandiose statement, but if you think about it, I think that you will see what I mean. I think that we are only at the beginning, however, of this entire movement and I think it will grow during the next several years to a point where it will involve even larger numbers of people in these healthful activities. Many think that this is a passing fad, but so far this does not appear to be so. A fad is something that springs up suddenly and then subsides just as suddenly. If one were to draw it on a graph, there would be many peaks and many valleys in the line that is used to depict the growth or the attrition of the activity. In the case of running and jogging, however, this has not been true. The graph shows that there is a steady crescendo line that has not peaked and that is representative of a continual positive growth curve. We look forward to the outcome of this situation.

OCCIDENTAL MEDITATION

I spent the month of April 1978 in the People's Republic of China. I can assure you that there is a great interest in physical activity as an important part of maintaining health in that country. The Chinese spend a portion of every day in organized sports or in organized healthful activity. In all of the large cities I found great numbers of people who participated in exercise programs such as jogging or running or in the very popular Chinese exercise of Tai Chi. Tai Chi is a strenuous form of endurance exercise. It does not look strenuous, but if you attempt it you will find that it requires movement of all the body muscles. It also requires increased respiratory activity and it satisfies the criteria for a beneficial endurance type of exercise when done properly. We must reach a health level in this country that the 900,000,000 people of China are reaching. It is rare that you see an obese person in China today. It is still rarer that you see an early demise or death of a patient in China from the degenerative diseases we see so much of in this country. The statistics that the Chinese offer—which appear to coincide with the evidence when one visits China—indicate that there has been a decrease in the degenerative diseases that were in existence before 1949. Since 1949, as a result of the health philosophies developed by the incoming powers at that time, there appears to have been a marked improvement in the general health of the population, particularly of the older portion of the population. Several physicians who were with our group and who had been in China in the 1930s have verified that statement. This is a result not only of the improvement in nutrition and the alleviation of many of the infectious and contagious diseases but also, no doubt, of the inculcation of exercise in daily life activities. Exercise is an important part of that whole program. Children are started on endurance type exercises, even consisting of strenuous dancing and acrobatics, at an early age. This concept is built into their lives and into their lifestyle; it is continued as they become older. I saw groups of soldiers and civilians running through the streets of various cities in an organized fashion every morning, and they were jogging for long distances. When I questioned them, I found out that they would spend at least one hour in jogging or running every day. I saw numerous high school children and public school children, as well as college students, running on tracks and performing road running exercise throughout the entire country, even in the smaller villages.

I am sure that this interest in running and jogging in the United States has spread to Europe also and to the other nations in the Western Hemisphere. Thoughout the world today, more and more people are jogging and running than ever before. In all of the major cities of the world, one sees people of different nationalities going out in their jogging suits and participating in endurance exercise. To give an example of what can happen with physician participation, at the first AMJA meeting at the time of the Boston Marathon in 1970 approximately 15 physicians ran the marathon. At the last meeting in 1978, approximately 750 physicians ran the race and completed it. Many of these physicians are in the over-50 age group.

WHAT IS SUFFICIENT EXERCISE?

Now let me say something about what has been considered as a base level for athletic programs that might ensure cardiovascular and cardiorespiratory benefit as well as improve the quality of life generally. This is something that has interested me very much since the founding of the American Medical Joggers Association in 1969. We have asked the authorities who are in the organization and many who are not in the AMJA to give us their opinion as to what they would consider the minimal amount of exercise that would at least ensure some form of cardiovascular and cardiorespiratory protection as well as reduce detrimental factors in the lifestyle of individuals, not only physicians but also patients. We have kept a record of these opinions for many years now and find that there is a general consensus that exercising in a sustained fashion for one hour every other day or running or jogging for 60 minutes every other day in a continual fashion with no breaks is considered by all of these experts as a way of obtaining these benefits. There seems to be a general agreement among 90 to 95 percent of these specialists that this appears to be the minimal level for obtaining these benefits. This means that for the jogger the suggested level is a ten minute-a-mile pace for six miles, which amounts to one hour, every other day at least. Now, anything that exceeds this contributes to more benefit then this base level. This, I think, is the kernel of something we can offer to our patients. It is the first actual agreement among those who are engaged in research in this area as to where exercise starts to produce its really beneficial effects.

PSYCHIATRY BENEFITS, TOO

It is about 100 years since Silas Weir Mitchell expounded his theory of rest therapy for mental disorders. It is most interesting that at this time we stand on the threshhold of an advance in the treatment of mental illness that might appear at first to offer a completely opposite therapy to what Mitchell originally suggested. Today the use of endurance exercise, particularly running and jogging, is being strenuously investigated by psychiatrists as a treatment not only for mental depression and psychoneuroses but also for the treatment of schizophrenia. This field of research is being explored vigorously, and indeed I would expect that within the next three to five years there is going to be a lot of activity in this area. There are very competent psychiatrists and psychologists engaged in this field of endeavor today. In my investigation of this area during the last five to six months, I have found, indeed, that there are larger number of investigators than I had originally thought. At first I believed that there were only two, or perhaps three at most, psychiatrists and psychologists investigating this relationship. I now find that there are several dozen investigators. I think that this is one of the most exciting new areas in the field of the beneficial effects of exercise. It is entirely possible that the results of the investigation may show that the beneficial effects of exercise on mental disease exceed those that have been found to be the case for cardiorespiratory disease. Many feel that this exploration into the effect of endurance exercise on mental disease is going to open a field that will exceed anything being done in cardiovascular and cardiorespiratory relationships to exercise today. This may be so, for the preliminary studies have shown that there is a definite measurable change that has been rendered in certain mental patients and groups of mental patients. Work done by Kavanagh and Sheppard at Toronto Rehabilitation Centre, in conjunction with their use of running as a therapy for the rehabilitation of patients who suffer from coronary artery disease and myocardial infarction, showed definite improvement in the depression indices of the Minnesota Multiphasic Inventory (MMPI) testing. Work done by Dr. John Griest and his associates at the University of Wisconsin has shown that running as a form of therapy has exceeded the classical psychotherapeutic measures in controlling and in improving patients who have certain types of mental disorders, particularly mild depression. Other investigators have produced a great deal of important data in these areas. Dr.

Robert Brown and his associates in Washington, D.C. have shown actual central nervous system chemical changes that occur in this form of therapy. Dr. Tad Kostrubala in San Diego has written an excellent book called *The Joy of Running* that has been out for several years now and that deals with the mental changes rendered in patients who have participated in endurance running exercise. We are going to see many new and exciting developments in this area, for it offers us one of the newer horizons for research in the relationship of exercise to disease. Since mental depression is as common, if not more common, than the common cold in the United States, the many millions of people who are now jogging and running may have been drawn to this activity unconsciously by the fact that they have felt improvement in their mental status as a result. Indeed, this is one of the important factors in the popularity of jogging and running.

THE CHALLENGE TO THE PHYSICIAN

Now all of this brings us back to the role of the physician in exercise. In a day and age when the medical profession has suffered from poor public relations, we have an opportunity as physicians to once again regain the trust and respect of our patients through setting an example for them and giving them positive guidance in improving their health and the quality of their lives. I do not say that this is the only thing that can be done to improve our image with the American public, but it is one of the things that can be done easily and without the expenditure of any large amounts of money. I therefore would like to take this opportunity to humbly encourage you to set a positive example for your patients by taking up some form of endurance exercise. Remember you will not only be helping your patients but you will be helping yourself. I look forward to a future physician population in the United States that is trim, that looks its age, and that enjoys its leisure time and the quality of its life as much as can be expected in these tenuous times.

Index